684040946059

POKÉMON™ ADVENTURES

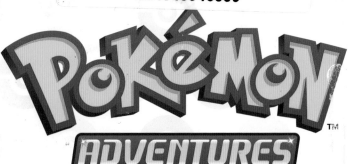

COLLECTOR'S EDITION

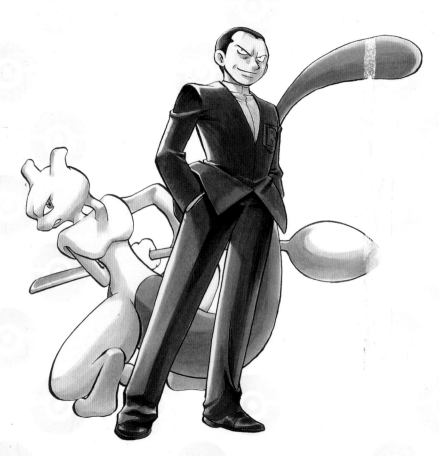

CONTENTS

ADVENTURE 288
Give It Your Best, Blastoise........................ 14

ADVENTURE 289
Surprised by Sneasel.................................. 36

ADVENTURE 290
A Well-Journeyed Jumpluff 58

ADVENTURE 291
Can Mewtwo Dish It Out with a Spoon? ... 72

ADVENTURE 292
Bested by Banette....................................... 86

ADVENTURE 293
Down-for-the-Count Deoxys...................... 101

ADVENTURE 294
Mewtwo and Mew Too 116

ADVENTURE 295
Double Down, Deoxys 131

ADVENTURE 296
It's Starting to Make Sense Now 148

ADVENTURE 297
Mewtwo Comes Through........................... 166

ADVENTURE 298
Start the Countdown, Starmie 182

ADVENTURE 299
Distant Relation Deoxys............................. 206

ADVENTURE 300
Right on Time, Rhydon 218

ADVENTURE 301
Storming the Forretress.............................. 236

ADVENTURE 302
Phew for Mew.. 254

EMERALD

ADVENTURE 303
Never Spritz a Knotty Sudowoodo 274

ADVENTURE 304
Swanky Showdown with Swalot................. 286

ADVENTURE 305
Interesting Interactions
Involving Illumise... 308

ADVENTURE 306
Pinsir Me, I Must Be Dreaming................... 330

ADVENTURE 307
Gotcha Where I Wantcha, Glalie 352

ADVENTURE 308
As Luck Would Have It, Kirlia..................... 374

ADVENTURE 309
Moving Past Milotic...................................... 398

ADVENTURE 310
Just My Luck…Shuckle 418

ADVENTURE 311
A Dustup with Dusclops 440

ADVENTURE 312
Chipping Away at Regirock 462

ADVENTURE 313
You Need to Chill Out, Regice..................... 484

ADVENTURE 314
A Sketchy Smattering of Smeargle............. 506

ADVENTURE 315
Skirting Around Surskit, Part 1 527

ADVENTURE 316
Skirting Around Surskit, Part 2 544

ADVENTURE 317
Sneaky like Shedinja 562

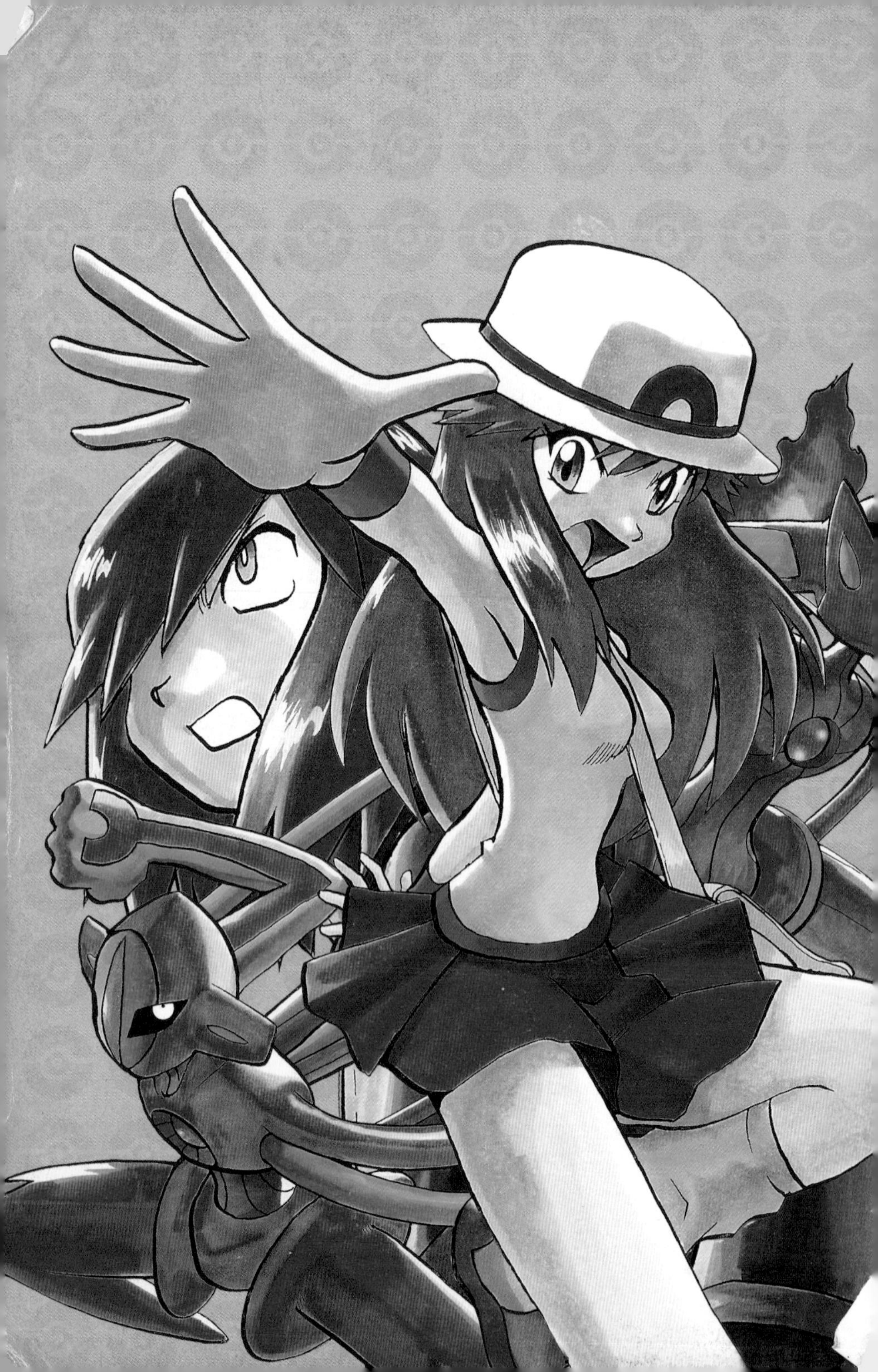

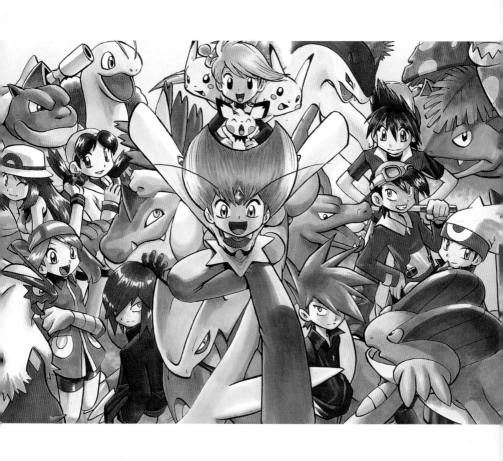

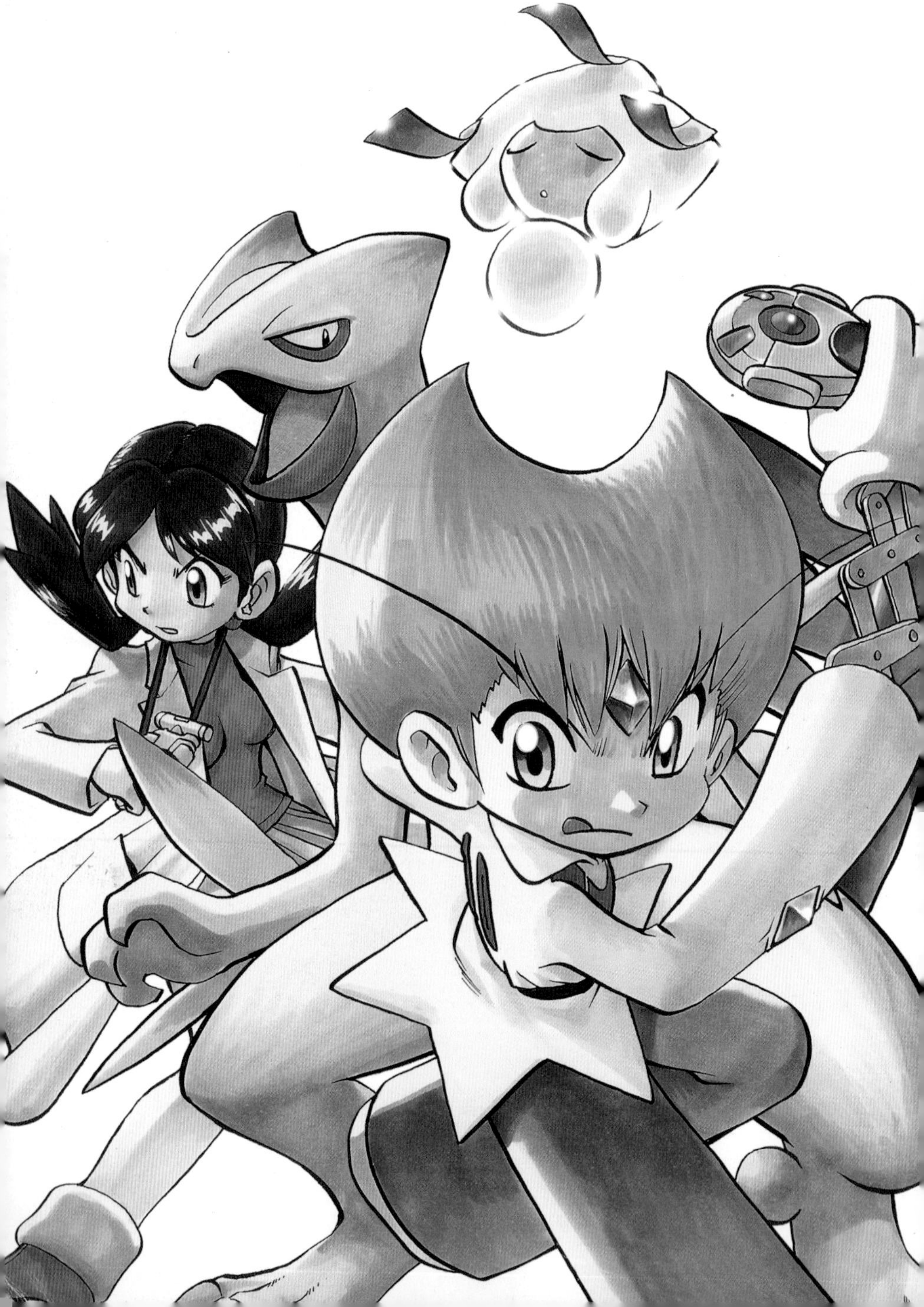

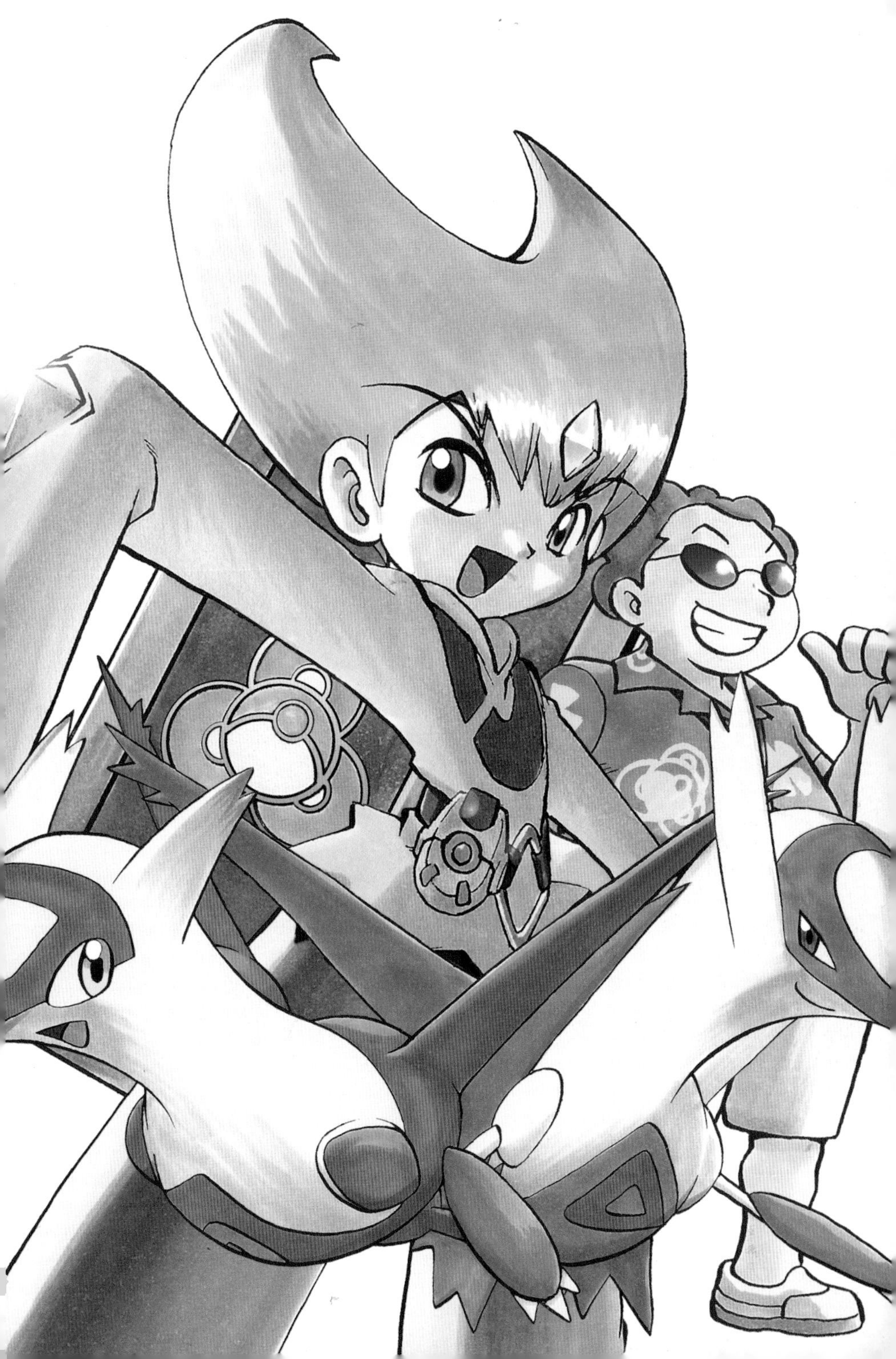

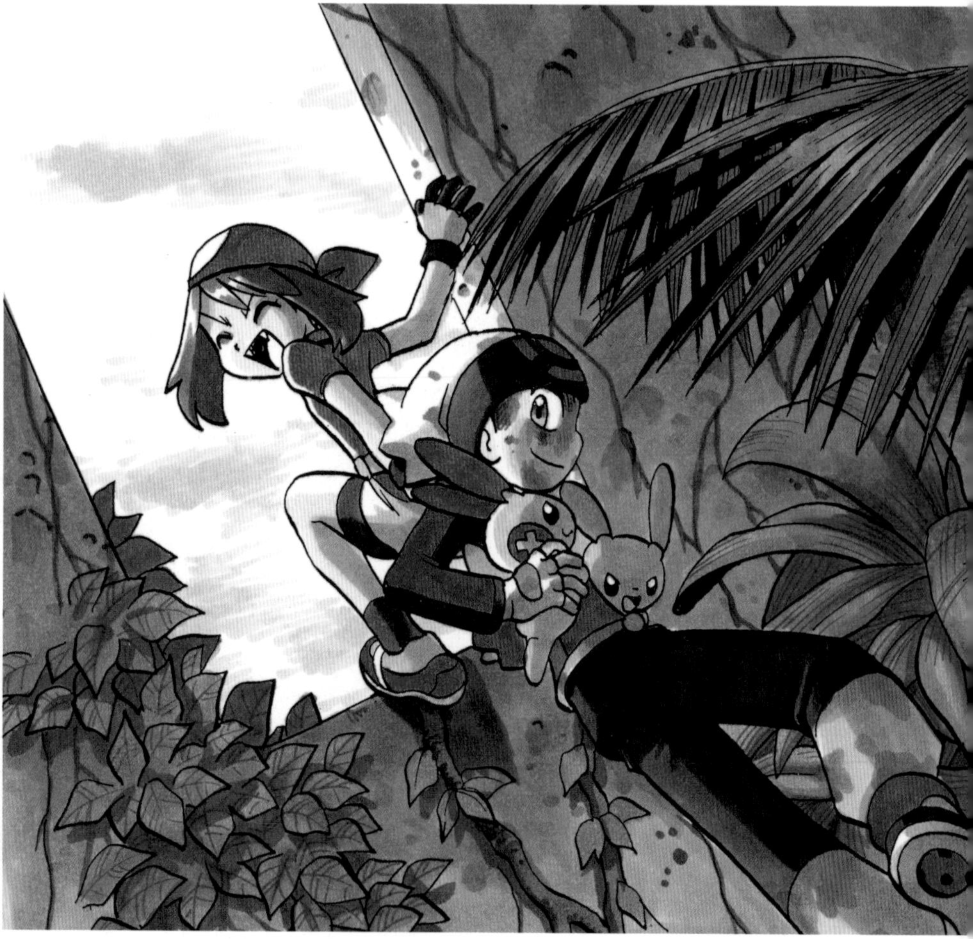

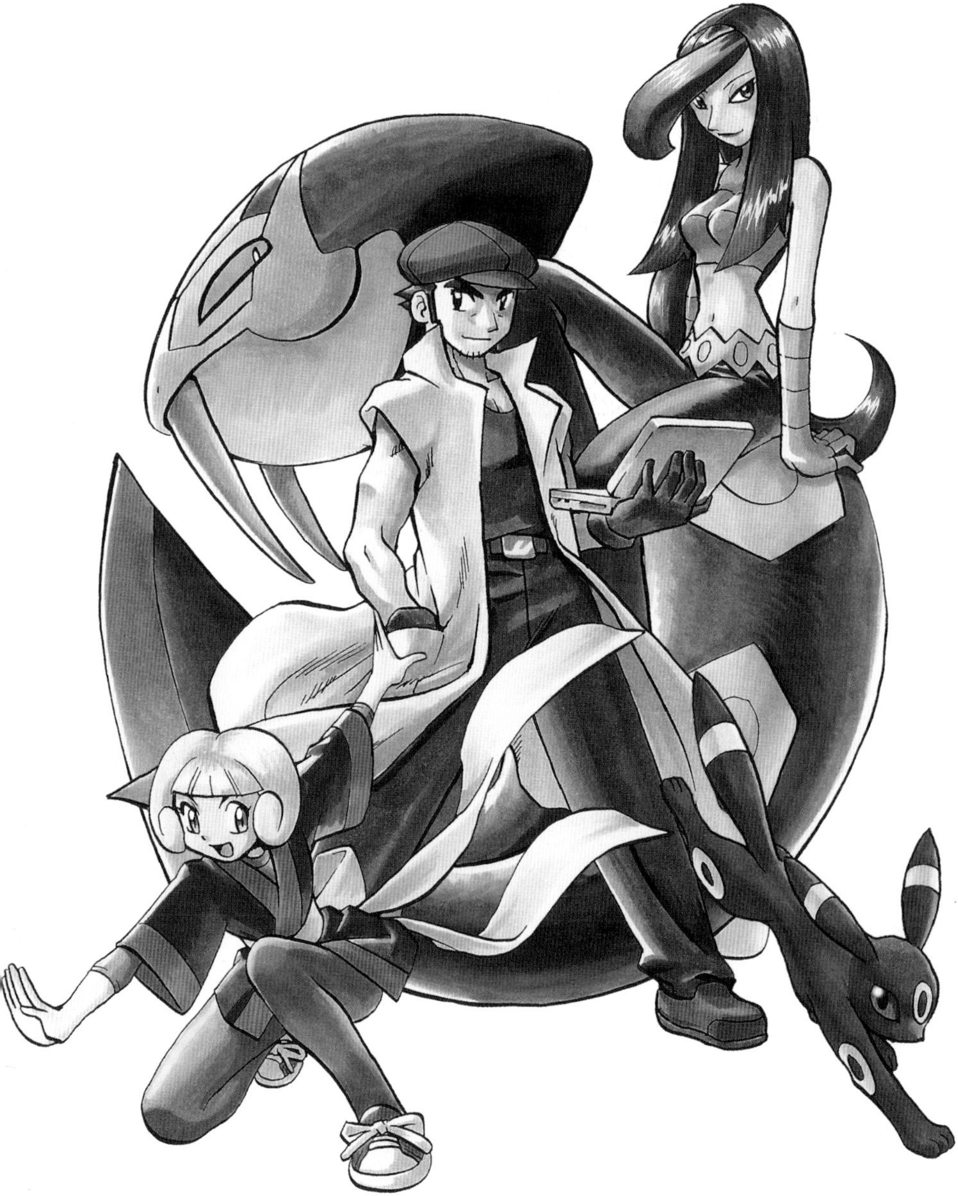

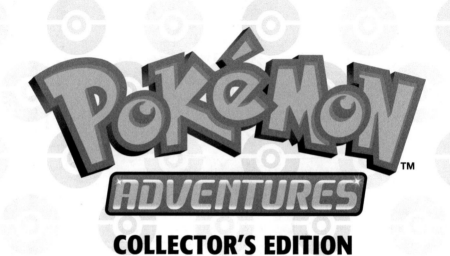

COLLECTOR'S EDITION

09

Story by **HIDENORI KUSAKA** Art by **SATOSHI YAMAMOTO**

SPECIAL OBJECT

The Pokédex holders and their stories

Kanto region

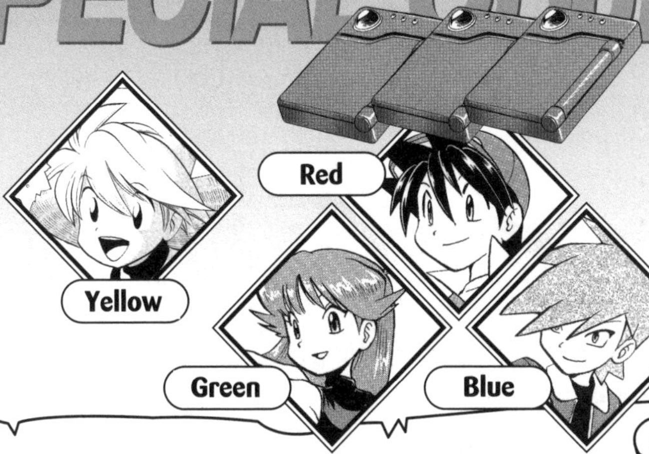
Red
Yellow
Green
Blue

1st Chapter

Red, a young boy from Pallet Town, receives a Pokédex from Professor Oak and heads out on a Pokémon training journey. Along the way, he meets two other Trainers, Blue, who becomes his rival, and Green. Red fights evil Team Rocket with his new friends and then becomes Champion of the Pokémon League.

2nd Chapter

Two years later, Red suddenly disappears and Yellow, a mysterious new Trainer, appears at Professor Oak's laboratory in search of him.

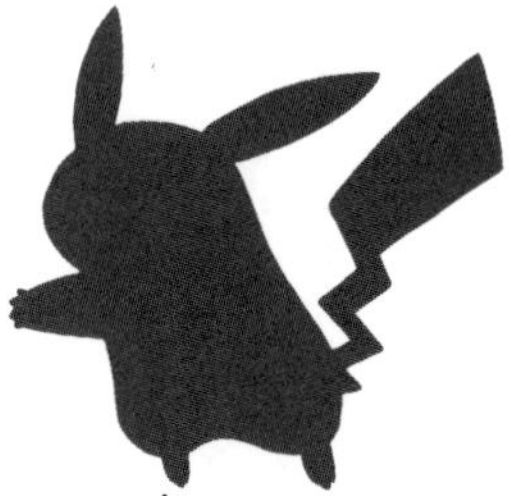

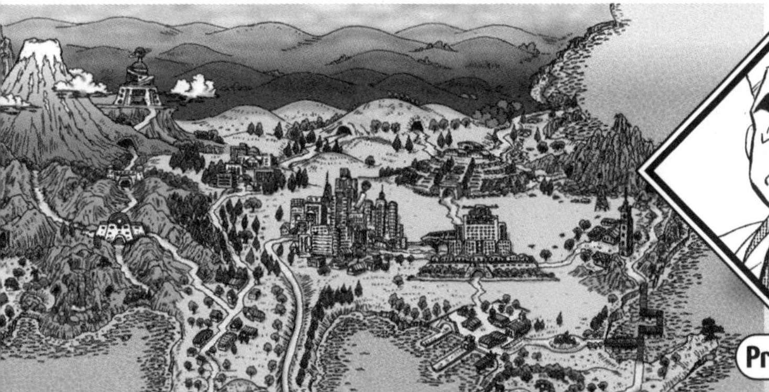

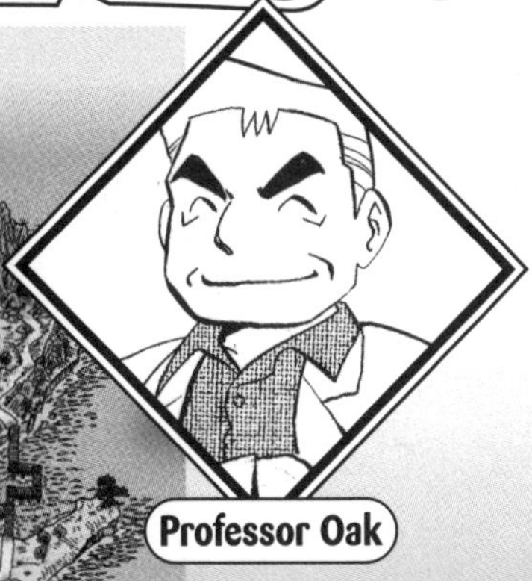
Professor Oak

Johto region

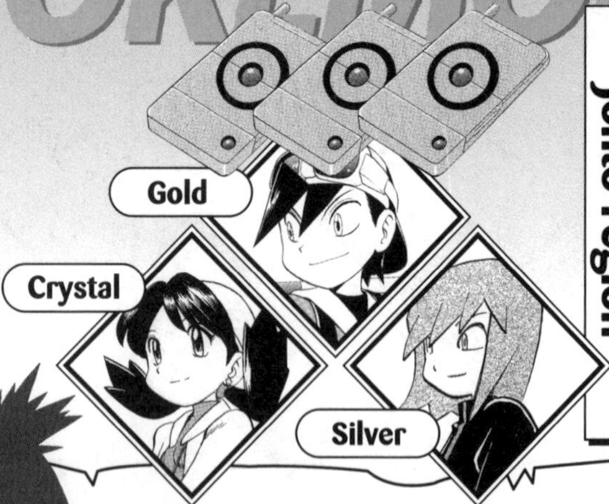

Gold
Crystal
Silver

Standing in Yellow's way is the Kanto Elite Four, led by Lance. In a major battle at Cerise Island, Yellow manages to stymie the group's evil ambitions.

3rd Chapter

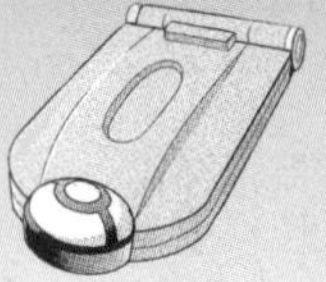

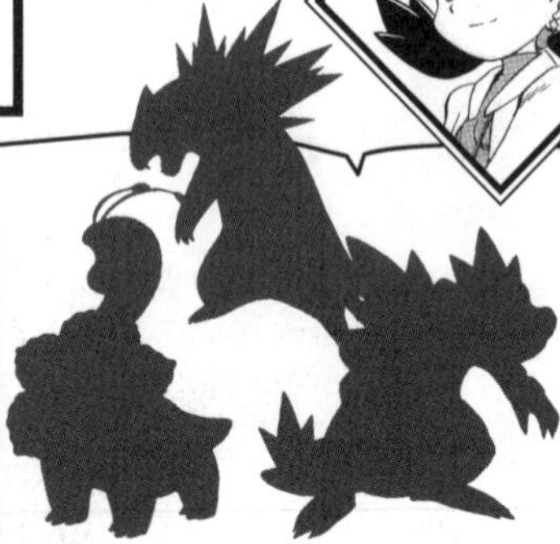

A year later, Gold, a boy living in New Bark Town in a house full of Pokémon, sets out on a journey in pursuit of Silver, a Trainer who stole a Totodile from Professor Elm's laboratory. The two don't get along at first, but eventually they become partners fighting side by side. During their journey, they meet Crystal, the Trainer who Professor Elm entrusts with the completion of his Pokédex. Together, the trio succeed in shattering the evil scheme of the Mask of Ice, a villian who leads what remians of Team Rocket.

Hoenn region

4th Chapter

Pokémon Trainer Ruby has a passion for Pokémon Contests. He runs away from home right after his family moves to Littleroot Town. He meets a wild girl named Sapphire and they pledge to compete with each other in an 80-day challenge to...

Professor Elm

Professor Birch

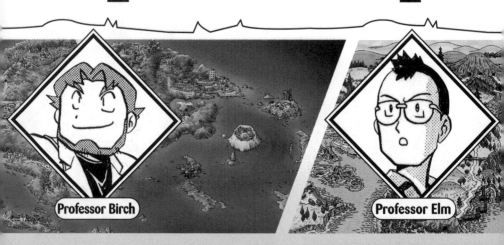

SPECIAL OBJECT

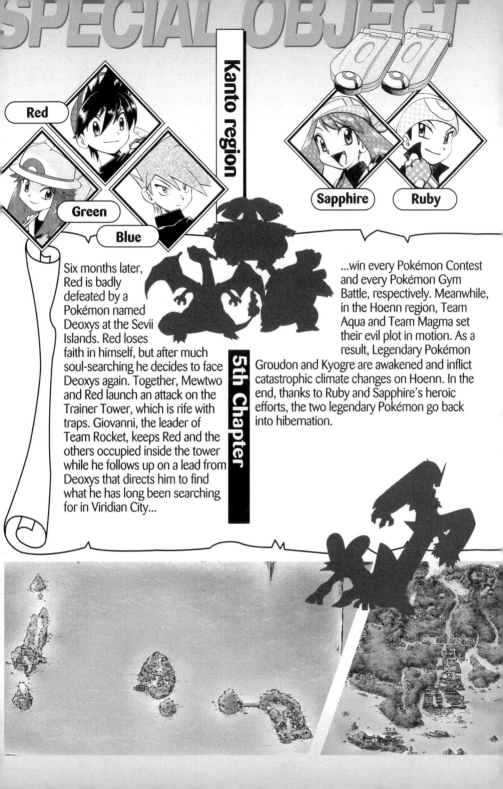

Kanto region

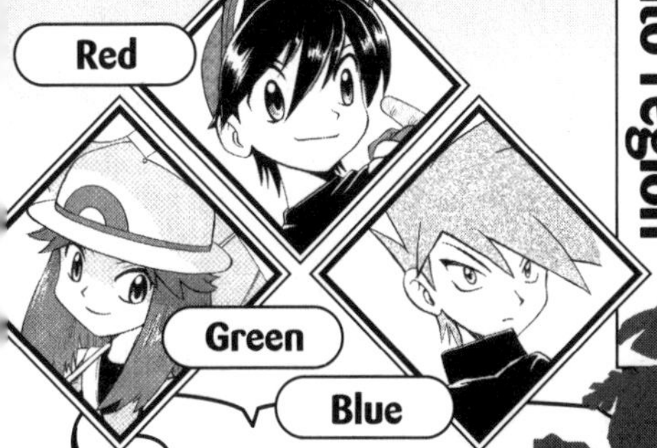
Red
Green
Blue

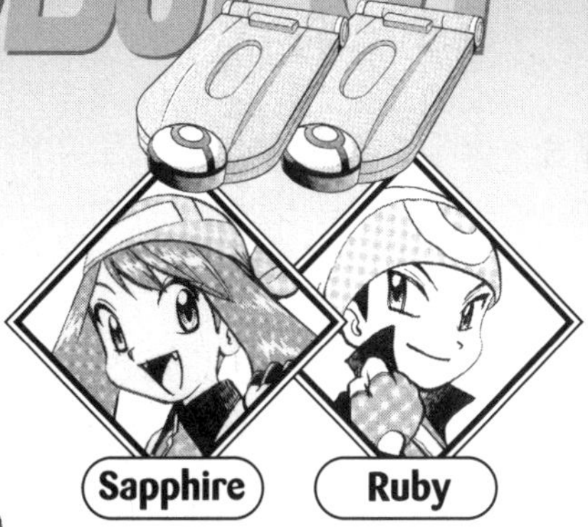
Sapphire
Ruby

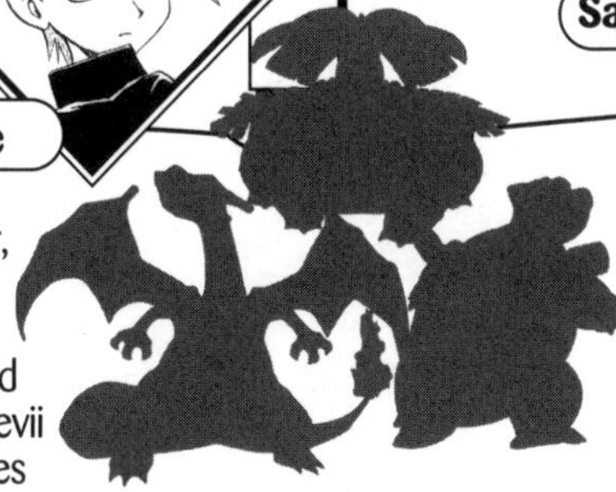

5th Chapter

Six months later, Red is badly defeated by a Pokémon named Deoxys at the Sevii Islands. Red loses faith in himself, but after much soul-searching he decides to face Deoxys again. Together, Mewtwo and Red launch an attack on the Trainer Tower, which is rife with traps. Giovanni, the leader of Team Rocket, keeps Red and the others occupied inside the tower while he follows up on a lead from Deoxys that directs him to find what he has long been searching for in Viridian City...

...win every Pokémon Contest and every Pokémon Gym Battle, respectively. Meanwhile, in the Hoenn region, Team Aqua and Team Magma set their evil plot in motion. As a result, Legendary Pokémon Groudon and Kyogre are awakened and inflict catastrophic climate changes on Hoenn. In the end, thanks to Ruby and Sapphire's heroic efforts, the two legendary Pokémon go back into hibernation.

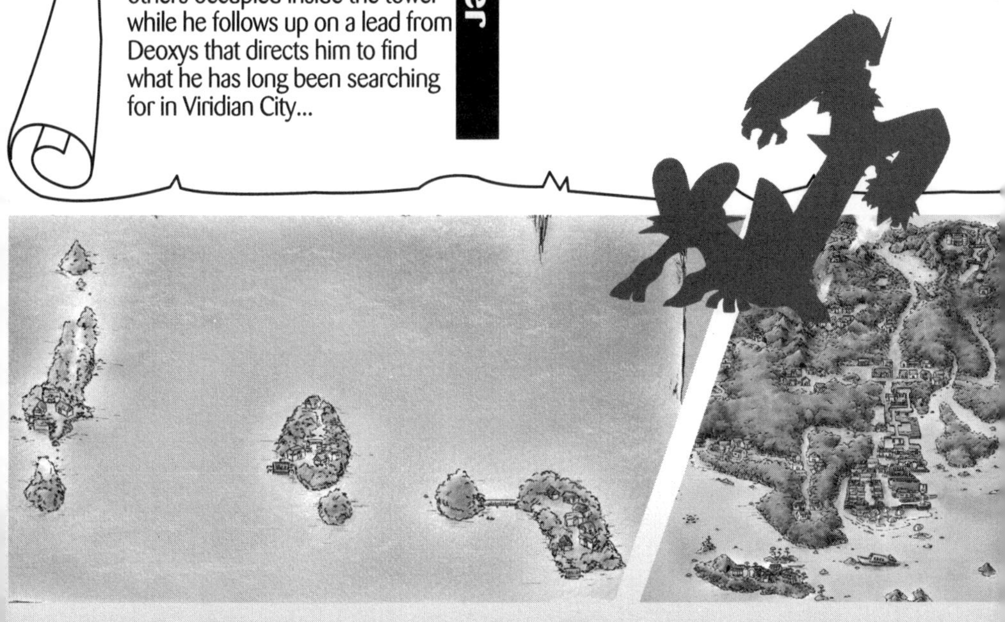

Message from
Hidenori Kusaka

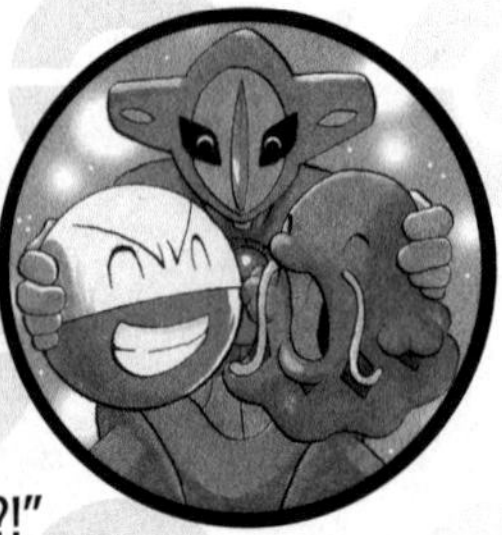

Deoxys is the main character of the fifth arc. I still remember the surprise I felt the first time I saw it. It had such a unique design that I kept asking myself, "What kind of Pokémon is that?!" I later learned about its Attack and Defense Formes and that it originated in outer space—which made it all the more intriguing! The FireRed & LeafGreen story arc has been running for 38 months, but even after all that time, I feel like Deoxys hasn't run out of surprises for us yet!

—2007

Message from
Satoshi Yamamoto

The fifth arc is finally reaching its climax. The dots are starting to connect... The characters and Pokémon are intertwined by the strings of fate! Volume 25 will have one of the most dramatic stories in the *Pokémon Adventures* series. I hope you enjoy it!

—2007

● Adventure 288 ●
Give It Your Best, Blastoise

Pokémon™ Adventures FireRed & LeafGreen
The Fifth Chapter

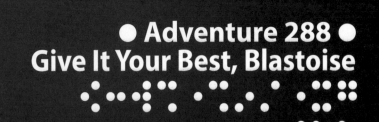

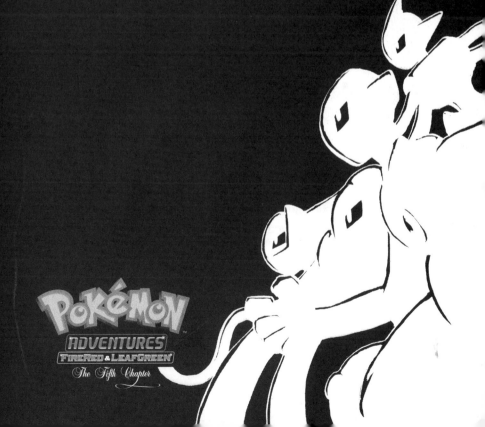

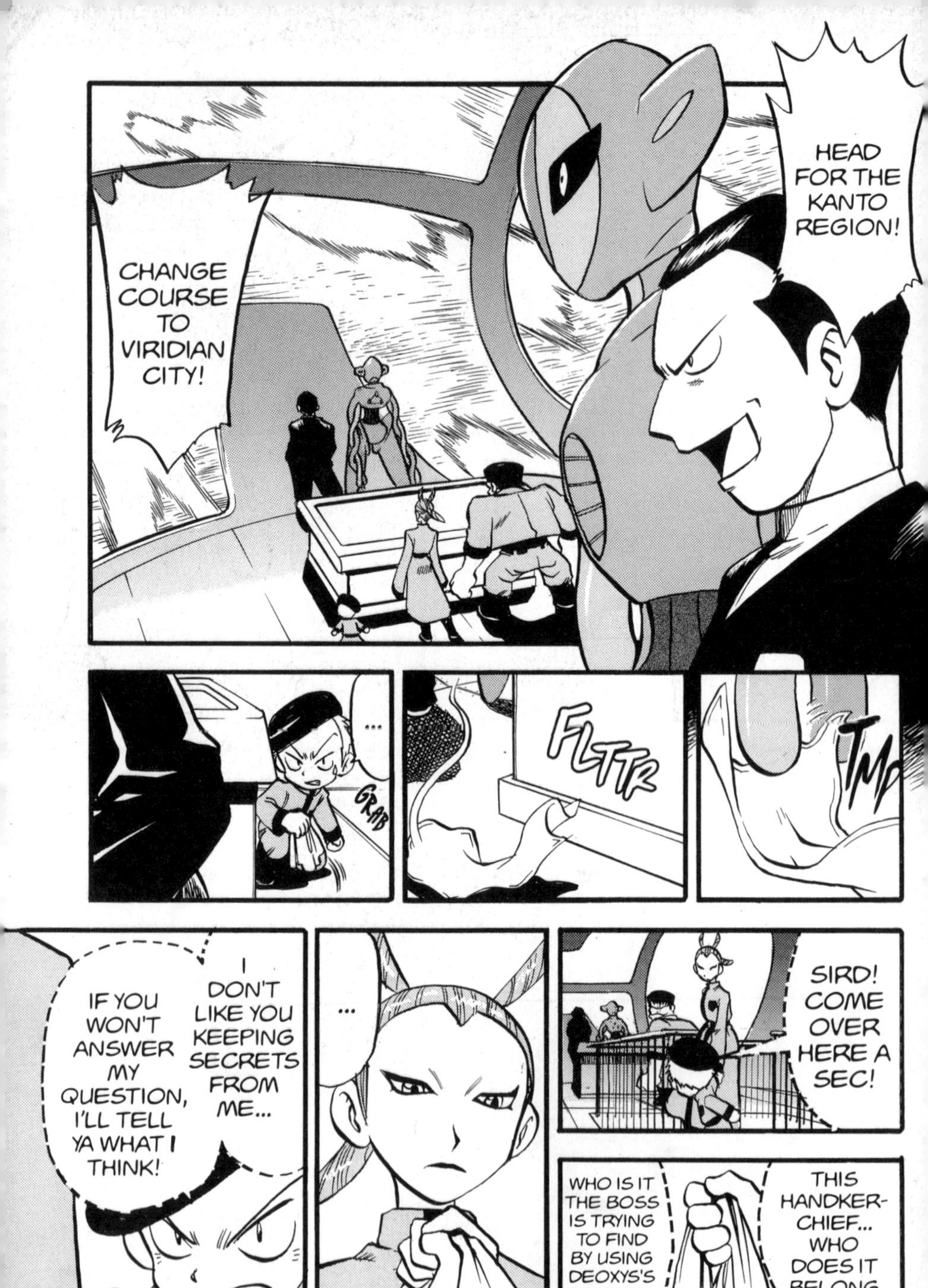
HEAD FOR THE KANTO REGION!
CHANGE COURSE TO VIRIDIAN CITY!
TMP
FLTTR
...
GRAB
SIRD! COME OVER HERE A SEC!
THIS HANDKER-CHIEF... WHO DOES IT BELONG TO?
WHO IS IT THE BOSS IS TRYING TO FIND BY USING DEOXYS'S POWERS, ANYWAY?
...
I DON'T LIKE YOU KEEPING SECRETS FROM ME...
IF YOU WON'T ANSWER MY QUESTION, I'LL TELL YA WHAT I THINK!

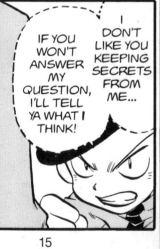

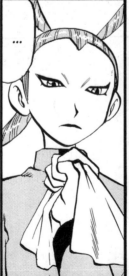

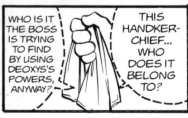

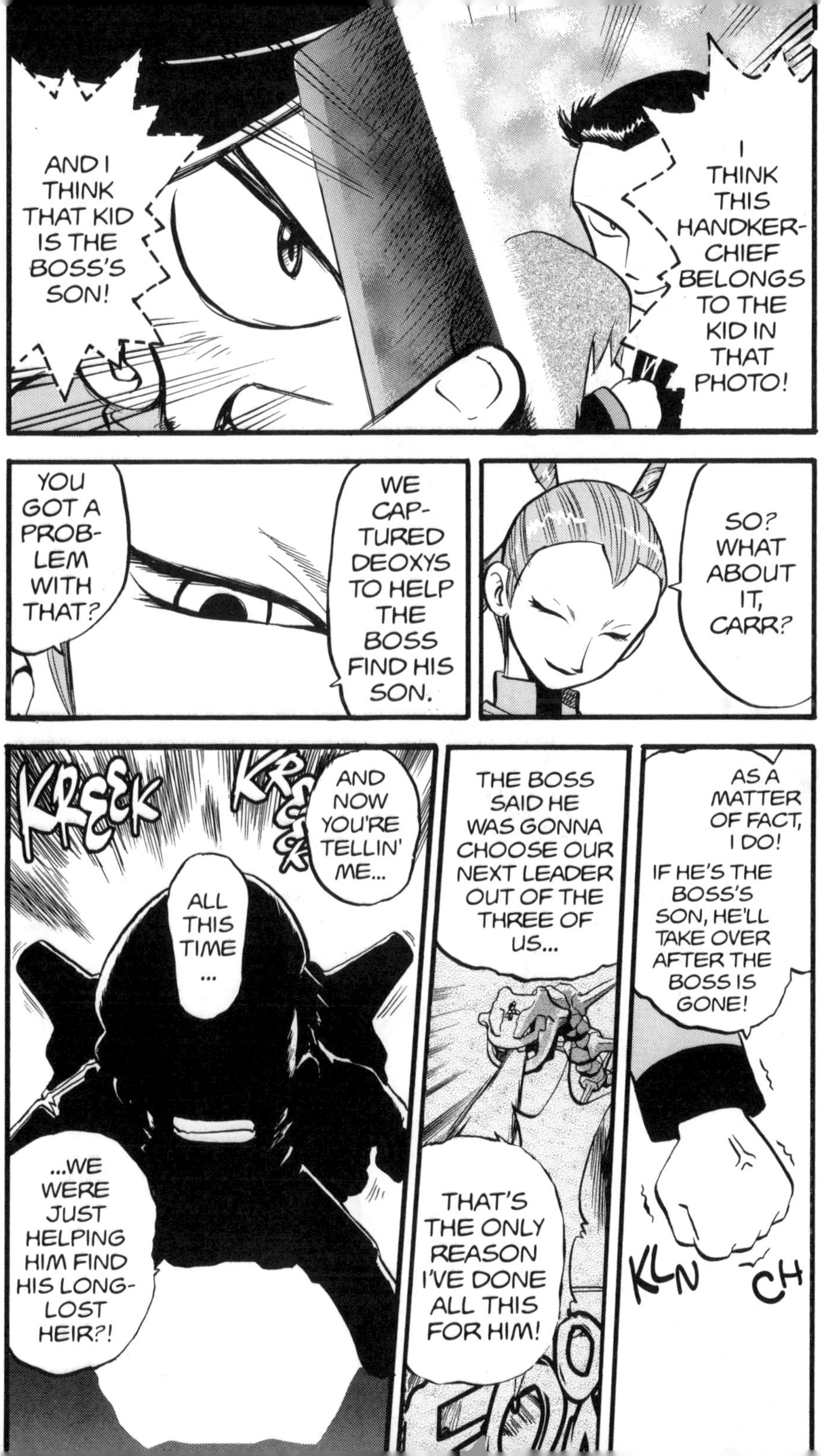
I THINK THIS HANDKERCHIEF BELONGS TO THE KID IN THAT PHOTO!
AND I THINK THAT KID IS THE BOSS'S SON!
SO? WHAT ABOUT IT, CARR?
WE CAPTURED DEOXYS TO HELP THE BOSS FIND HIS SON.
YOU GOT A PROBLEM WITH THAT?
AS A MATTER OF FACT, I DO!
IF HE'S THE BOSS'S SON, HE'LL TAKE OVER AFTER THE BOSS IS GONE!
KLNCH
THE BOSS SAID HE WAS GONNA CHOOSE OUR NEXT LEADER OUT OF THE THREE OF US...
THAT'S THE ONLY REASON I'VE DONE ALL THIS FOR HIM!
KREEK
AND NOW YOU'RE TELLIN' ME...
ALL THIS TIME...
...WE WERE JUST HELPING HIM FIND HIS LONG-LOST HEIR?!

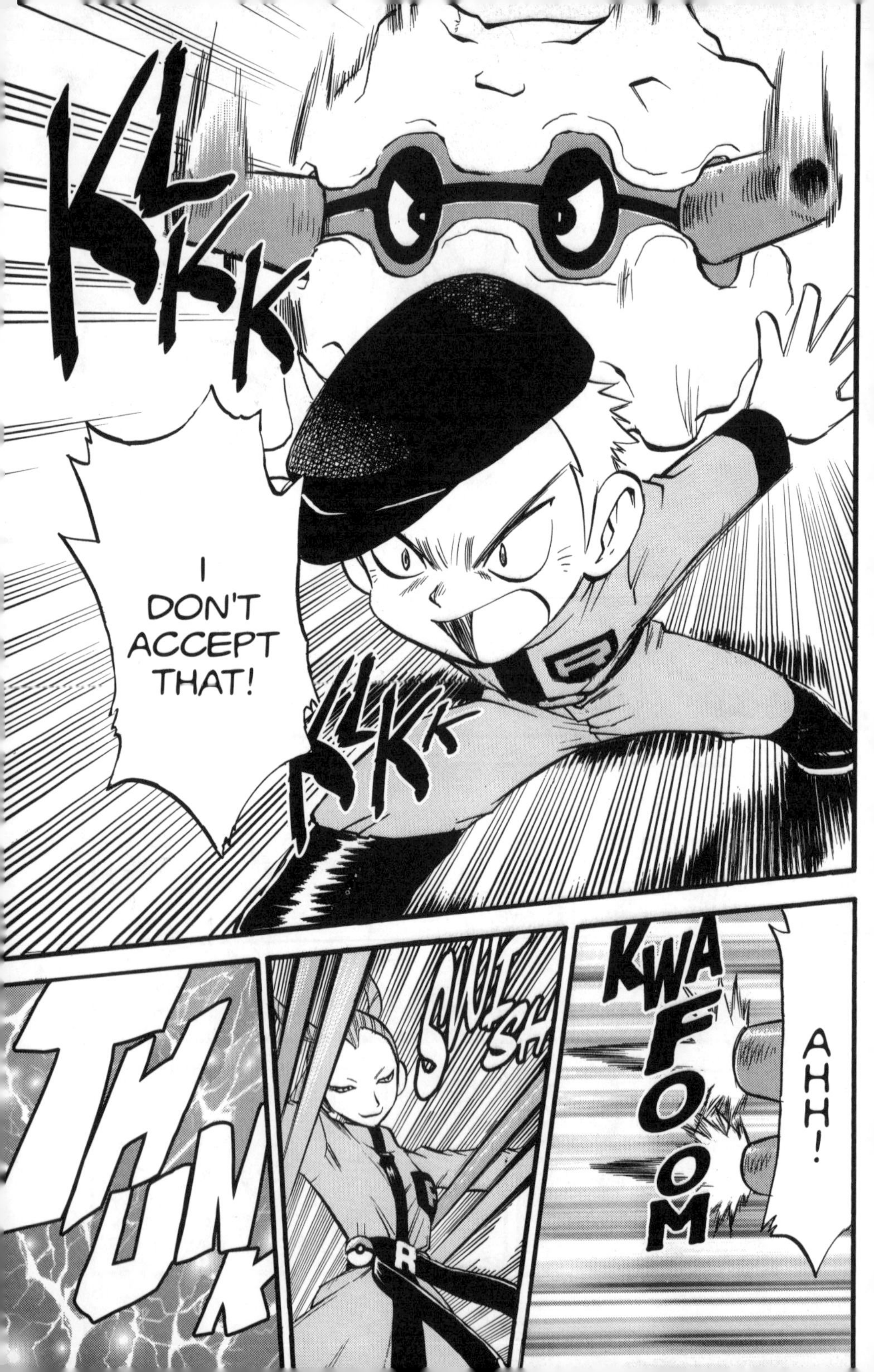
I DON'T ACCEPT THAT!
AHH!
KWAFOOM

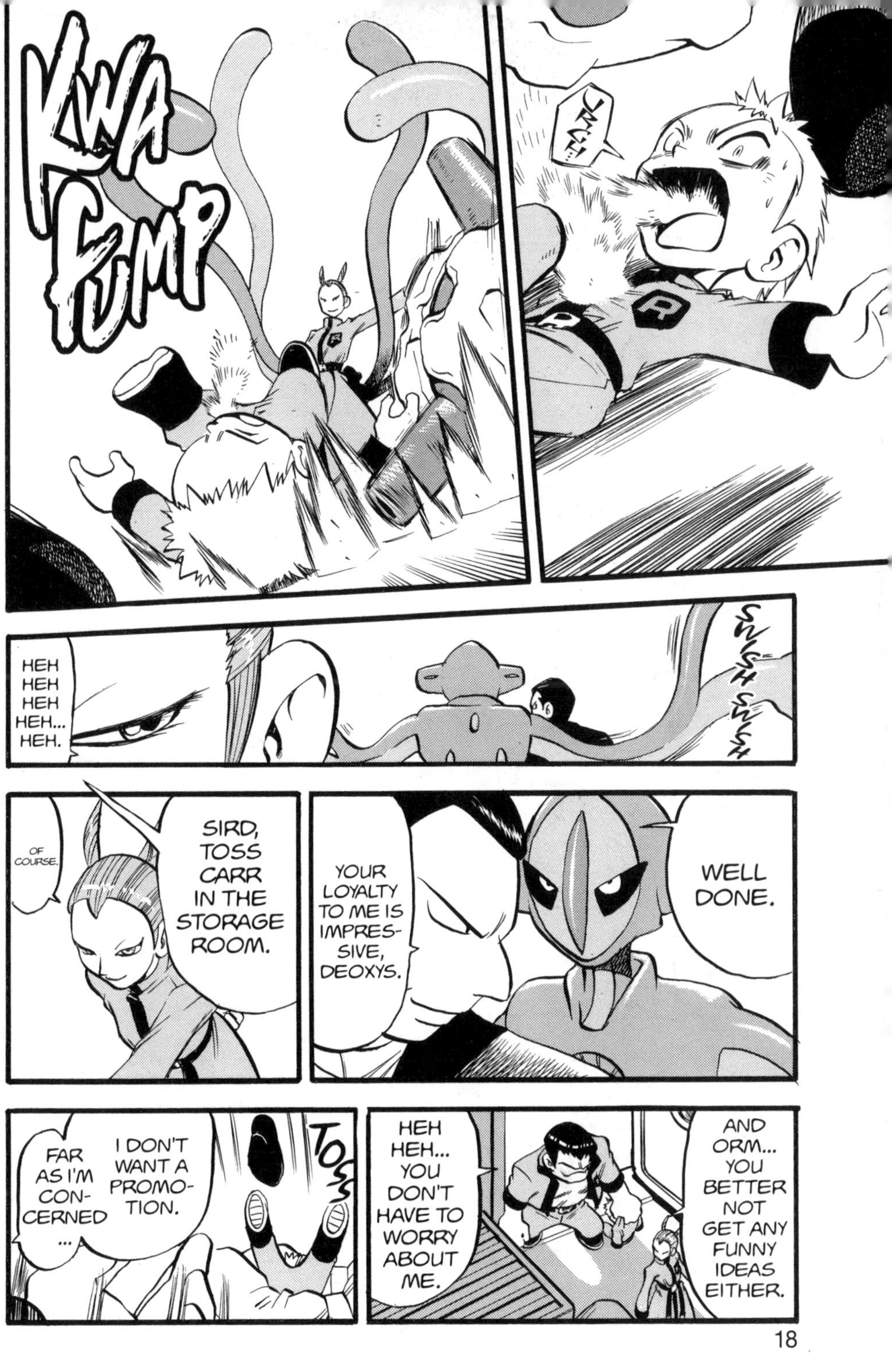
URGH...
KWA FUMP
SWISH SWISH
HEH HEH HEH HEH... HEH.
WELL DONE.
YOUR LOYALTY TO ME IS IMPRESSIVE, DEOXYS.
SIRD, TOSS CARR IN THE STORAGE ROOM.
OF COURSE.
AND ORM... YOU BETTER NOT GET ANY FUNNY IDEAS EITHER.
HEH HEH... YOU DON'T HAVE TO WORRY ABOUT ME.
TOSS
I DON'T WANT A PROMOTION.
FAR AS I'M CONCERNED...

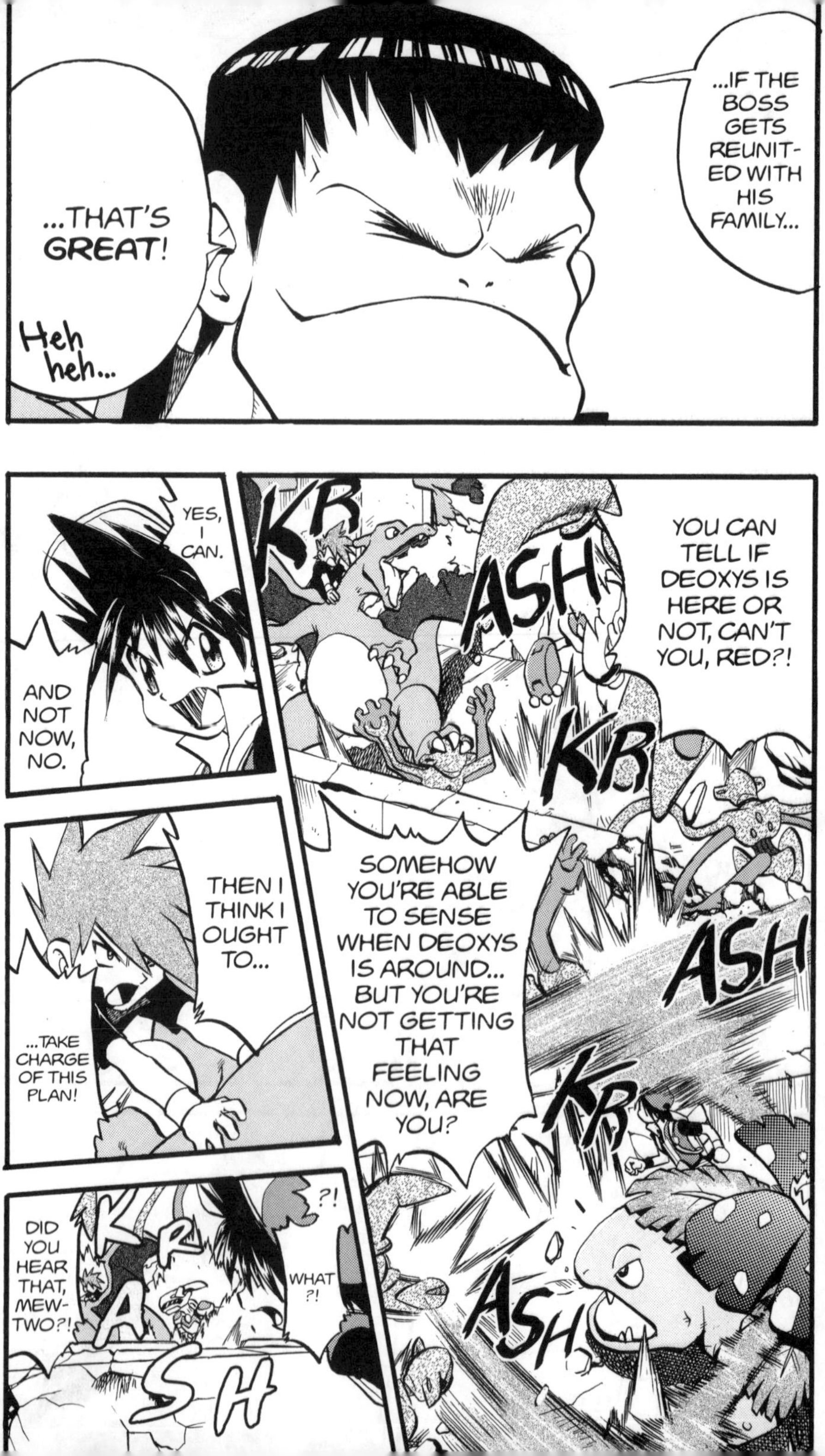

...IF THE BOSS GETS REUNIT-ED WITH HIS FAMILY...
...THAT'S GREAT!
Heh heh...
YOU CAN TELL IF DEOXYS IS HERE OR NOT, CAN'T YOU, RED?!
KRASH
SOMEHOW YOU'RE ABLE TO SENSE WHEN DEOXYS IS AROUND... BUT YOU'RE NOT GETTING THAT FEELING NOW, ARE YOU?
KRASH
KRASH
YES, I CAN.
AND NOT NOW, NO.
THEN I THINK I OUGHT TO...
...TAKE CHARGE OF THIS PLAN!
?!
WHAT ?!
DID YOU HEAR THAT, MEW-TWO?!
KRASH

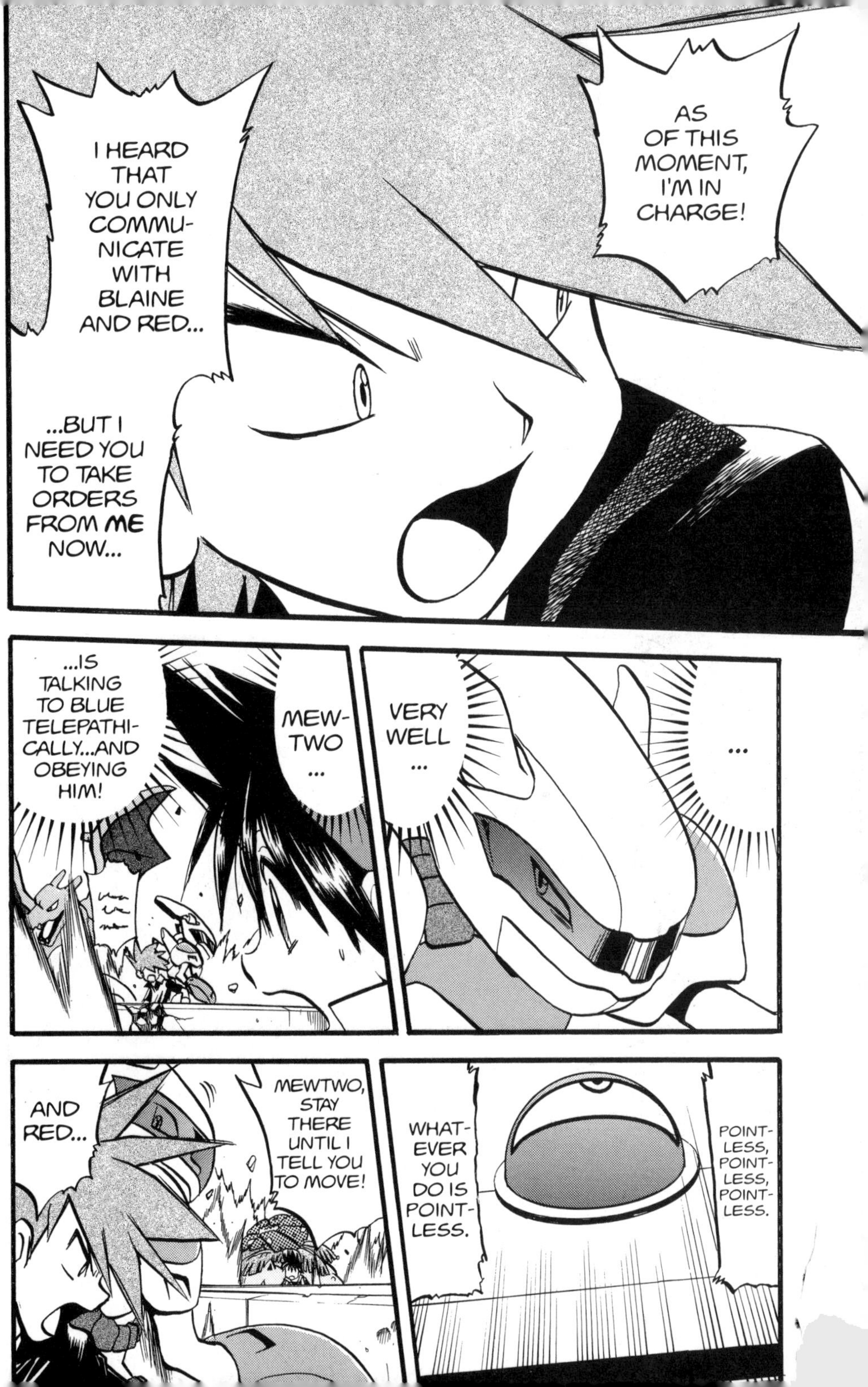
AS OF THIS MOMENT, I'M IN CHARGE!
I HEARD THAT YOU ONLY COMMUNI-NICATE WITH BLAINE AND RED...
...BUT I NEED YOU TO TAKE ORDERS FROM ME NOW...
...
VERY WELL ...
MEW-TWO ...
...IS TALKING TO BLUE TELEPATHI-CALLY...AND OBEYING HIM!
POINT-LESS, POINT-LESS, POINT-LESS.
WHAT-EVER YOU DO IS POINT-LESS.
MEWTWO, STAY THERE UNTIL I TELL YOU TO MOVE!
AND RED...

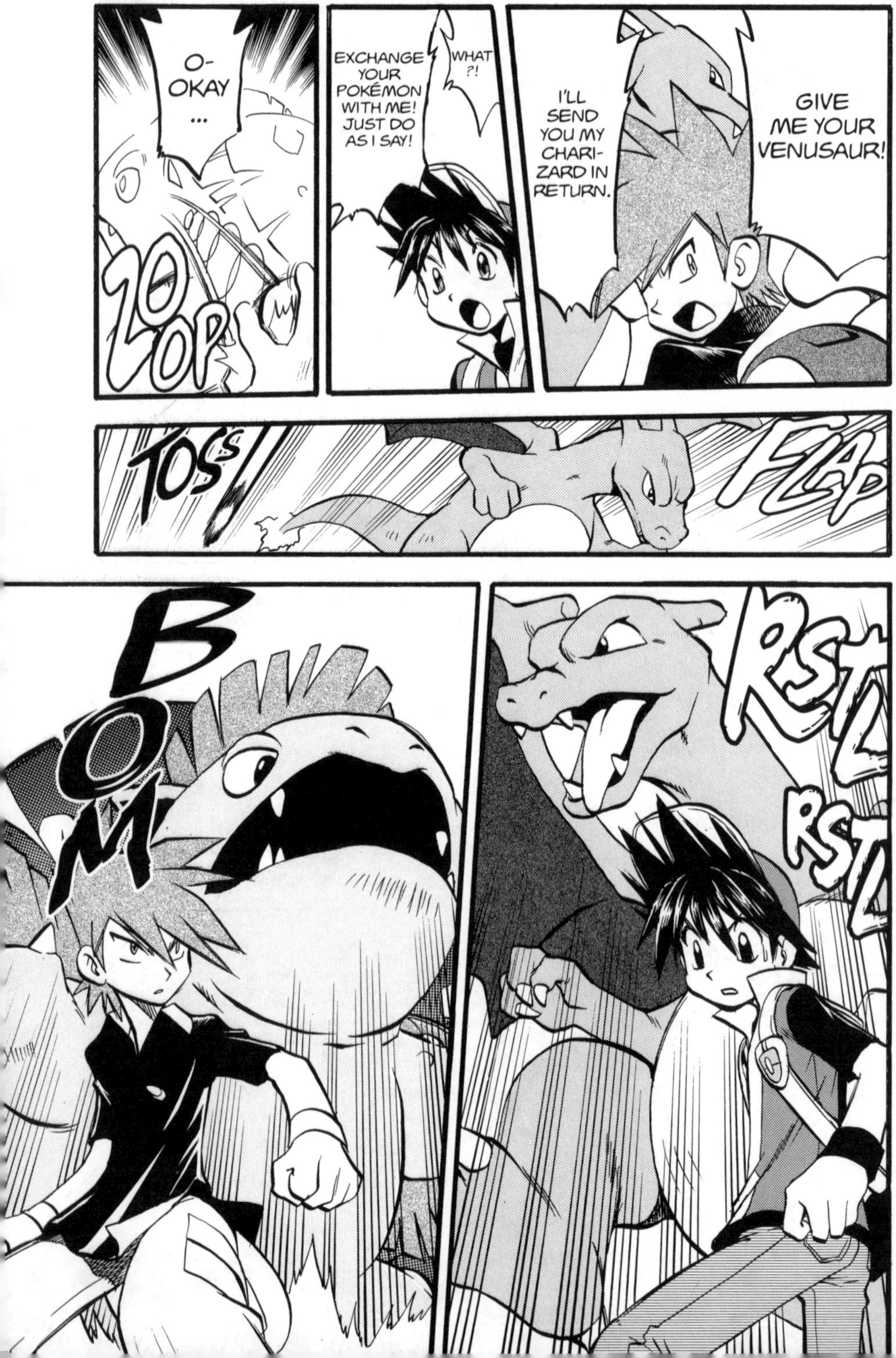
GIVE ME YOUR VENUSAUR!
I'LL SEND YOU MY CHARI-ZARD IN RETURN.
WHAT ?!
EXCHANGE YOUR POKÉMON WITH ME! JUST DO AS I SAY!
O-OKAY ...
ZOOP
FLAP
TOSS
RSTL
RSTL
BOOM

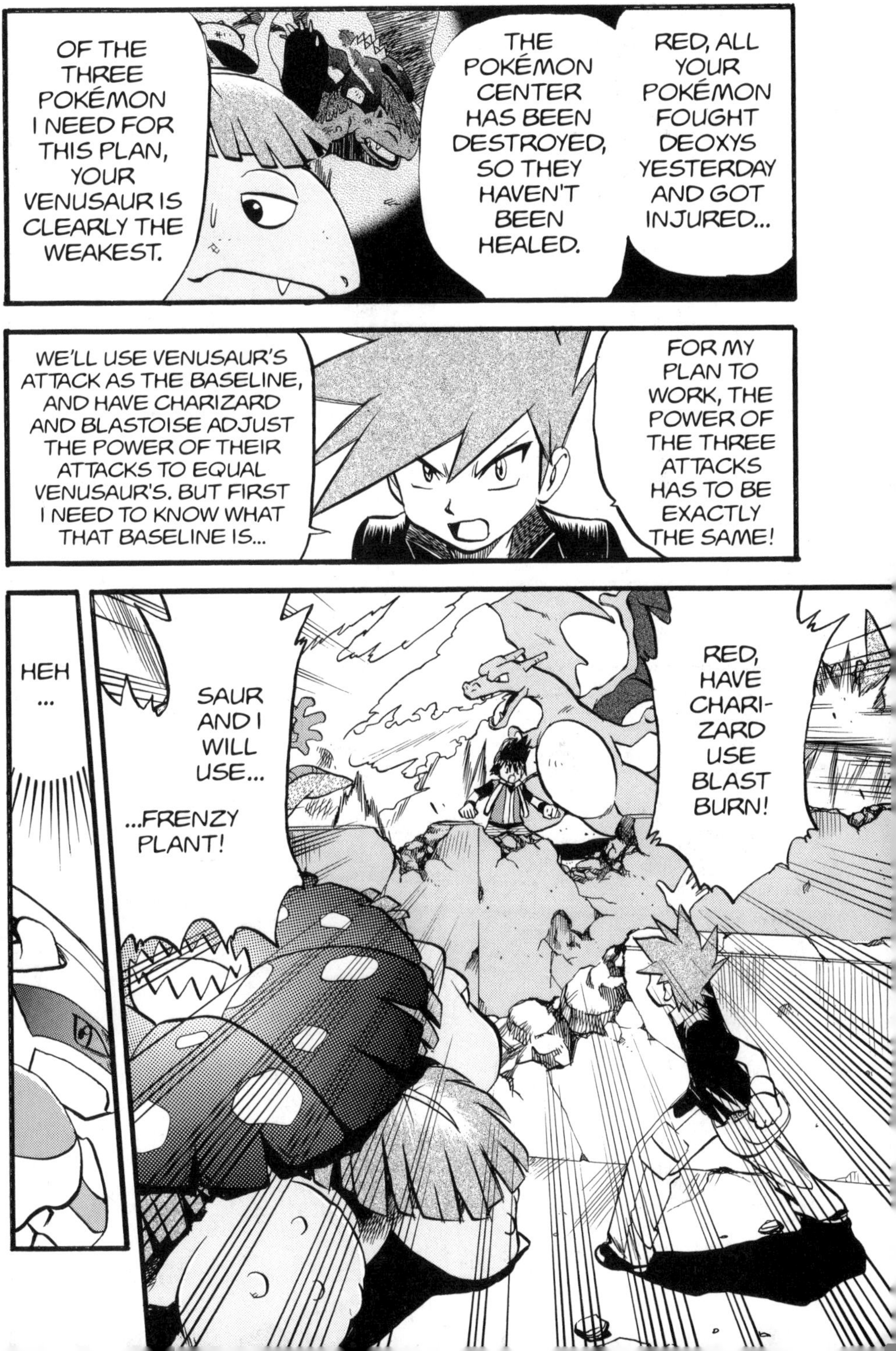
RED, ALL YOUR POKÉMON FOUGHT DEOXYS YESTERDAY AND GOT INJURED...
THE POKÉMON CENTER HAS BEEN DESTROYED, SO THEY HAVEN'T BEEN HEALED.
OF THE THREE POKÉMON I NEED FOR THIS PLAN, YOUR VENUSAUR IS CLEARLY THE WEAKEST.
FOR MY PLAN TO WORK, THE POWER OF THE THREE ATTACKS HAS TO BE EXACTLY THE SAME!
WE'LL USE VENUSAUR'S ATTACK AS THE BASELINE, AND HAVE CHARIZARD AND BLASTOISE ADJUST THE POWER OF THEIR ATTACKS TO EQUAL VENUSAUR'S. BUT FIRST I NEED TO KNOW WHAT THAT BASELINE IS...
RED, HAVE CHARI-ZARD USE BLAST BURN!
SAUR AND I WILL USE...
...FRENZY PLANT!
HEH ...

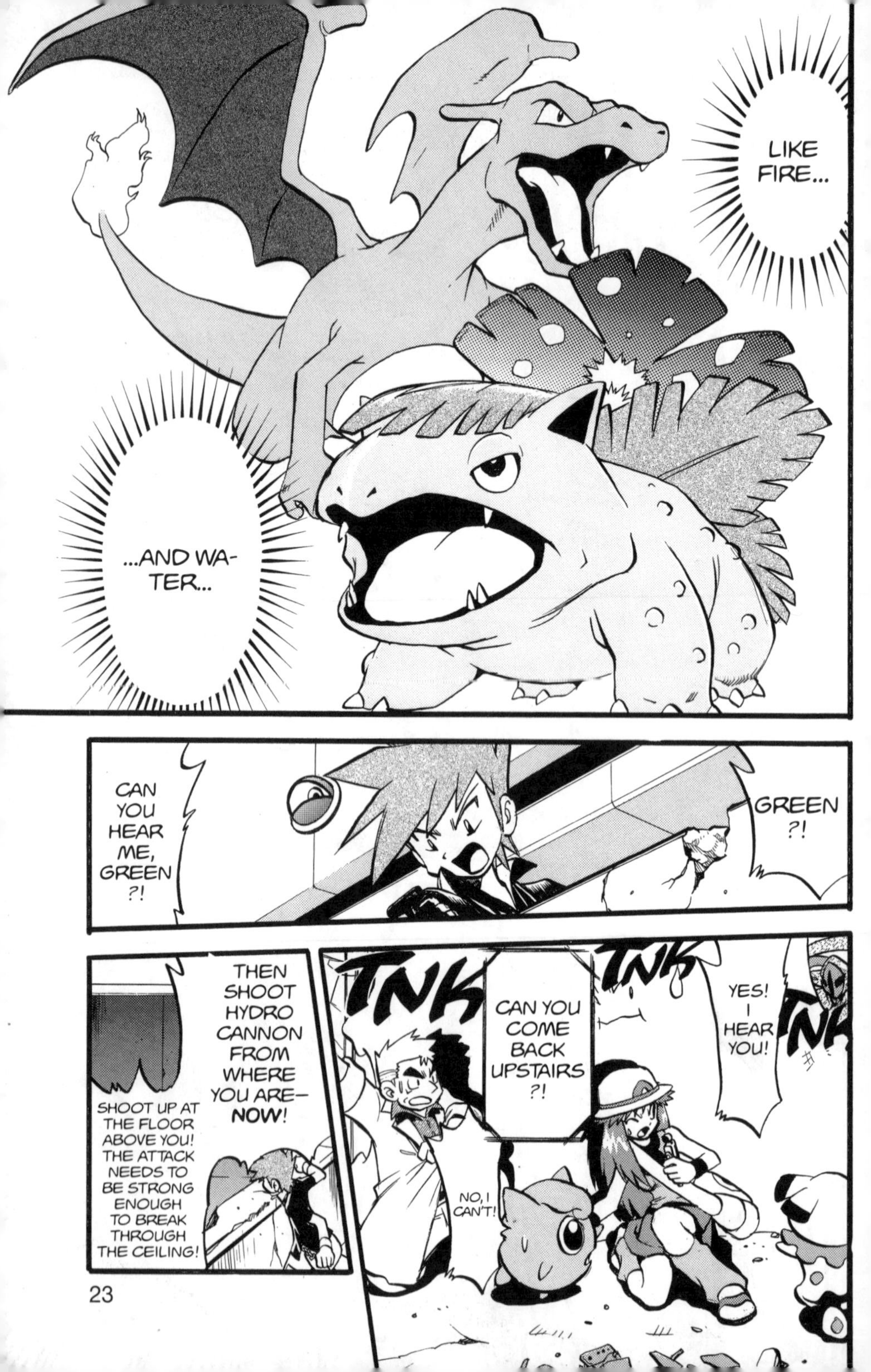
LIKE FIRE...
...AND WA-TER...
GREEN ?!
CAN YOU HEAR ME, GREEN ?!
TNK
TNK
TNK
YES! I HEAR YOU!
CAN YOU COME BACK UPSTAIRS ?!
NO, I CAN'T!
THEN SHOOT HYDRO CANNON FROM WHERE YOU ARE— **NOW**!
SHOOT UP AT THE FLOOR ABOVE YOU! THE ATTACK NEEDS TO BE STRONG ENOUGH TO BREAK THROUGH THE CEILING!

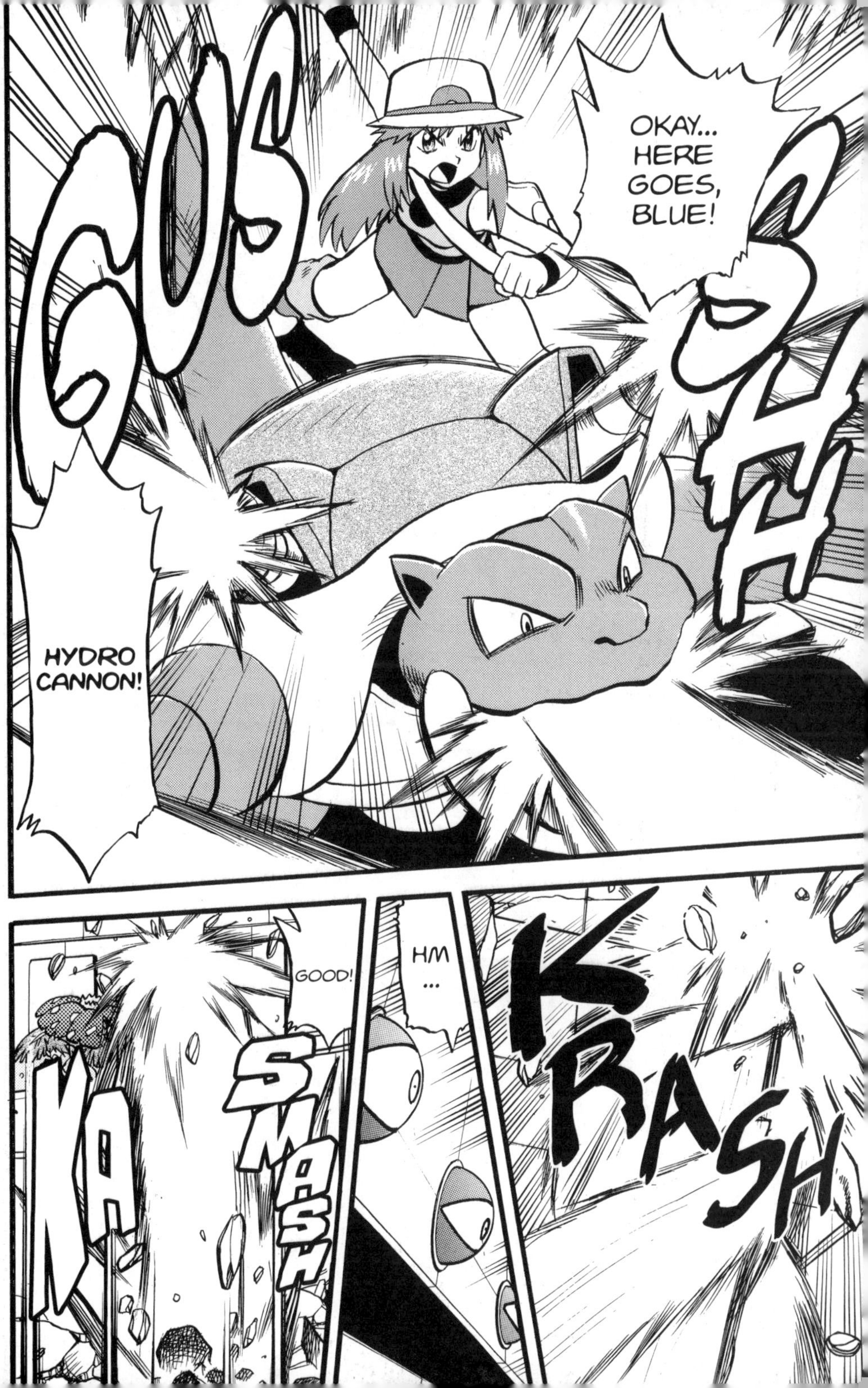
OKAY... HERE GOES, BLUE!
HYDRO CANNON!
KRASH
HM ...
GOOD!
SMASH

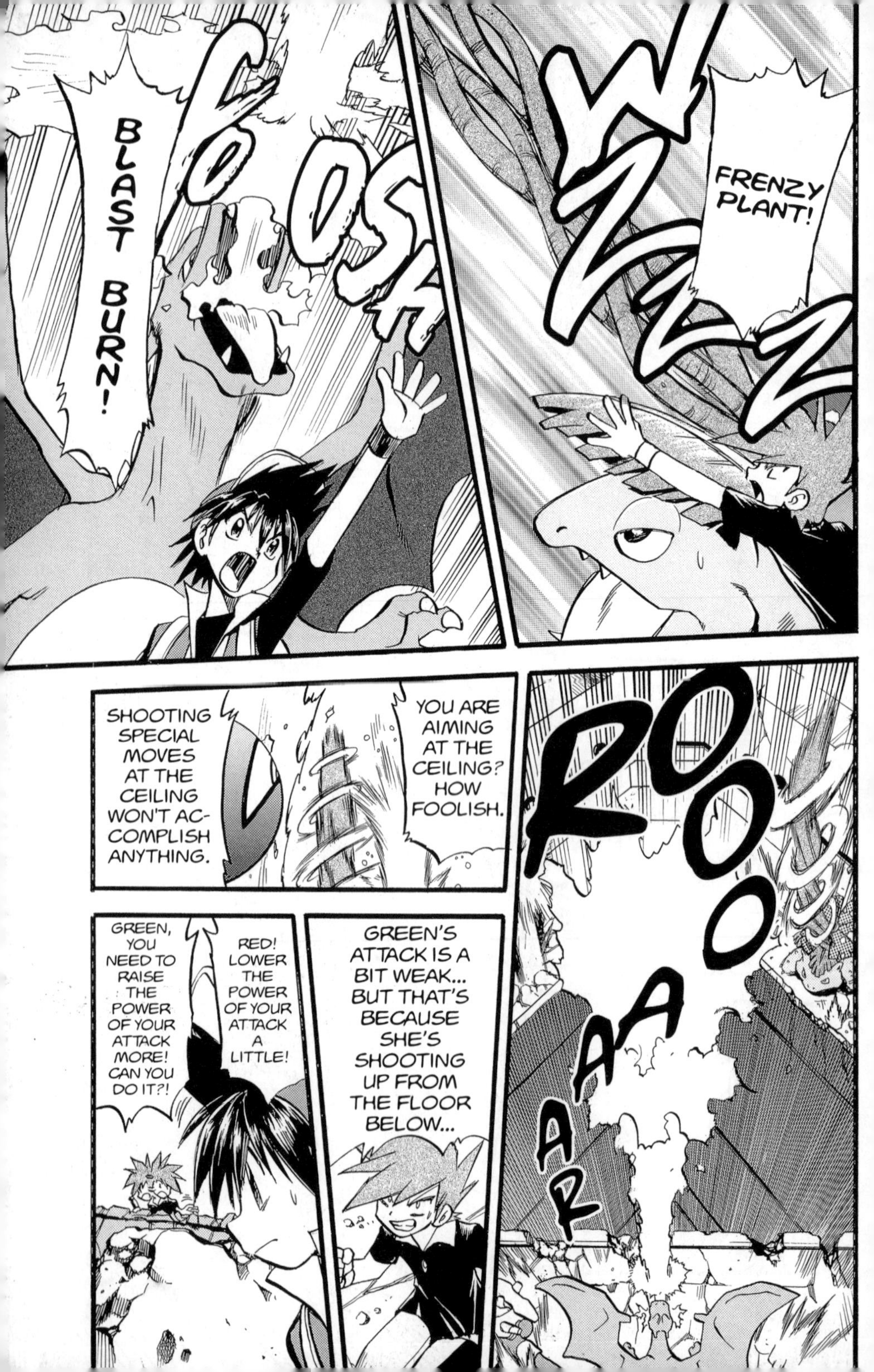
FRENZY PLANT!
BLAST BURN!
ROOOAAAR
YOU ARE AIMING AT THE CEILING? HOW FOOLISH.
SHOOTING SPECIAL MOVES AT THE CEILING WON'T ACCOMPLISH ANYTHING.
GREEN'S ATTACK IS A BIT WEAK... BUT THAT'S BECAUSE SHE'S SHOOTING UP FROM THE FLOOR BELOW...
RED! LOWER THE POWER OF YOUR ATTACK A LITTLE!
GREEN, YOU NEED TO RAISE THE POWER OF YOUR ATTACK MORE! CAN YOU DO IT?!

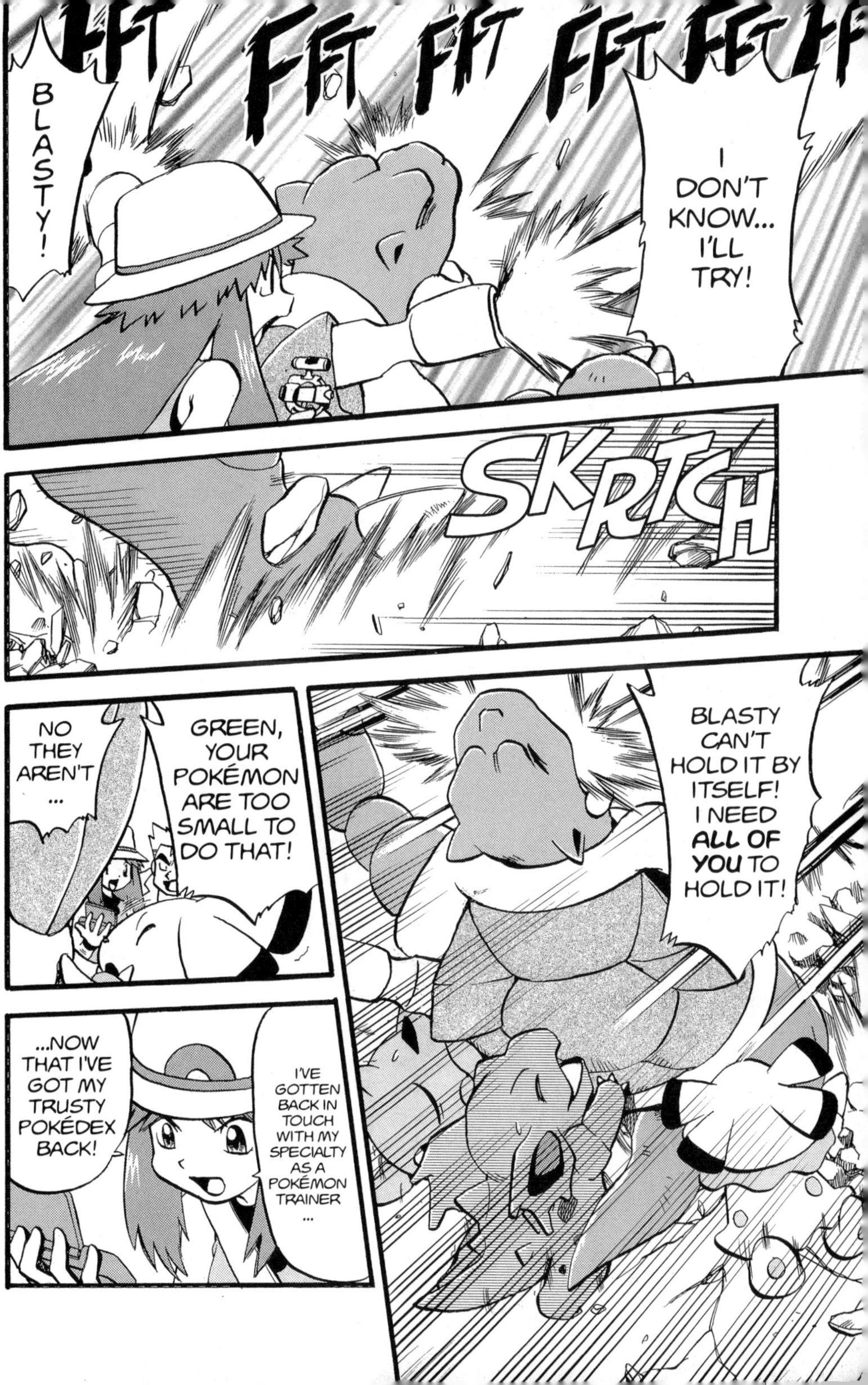
FFT FFT FFT FFT FFT FFT
I DON'T KNOW... I'LL TRY!
BLASTY!
SKRTCH
BLASTY CAN'T HOLD IT BY ITSELF! I NEED **ALL OF YOU** TO HOLD IT!
GREEN, YOUR POKÉMON ARE TOO SMALL TO DO THAT!
NO THEY AREN'T ...
I'VE GOTTEN BACK IN TOUCH WITH MY SPECIALTY AS A POKÉMON TRAINER ...
...NOW THAT I'VE GOT MY TRUSTY POKÉDEX BACK!

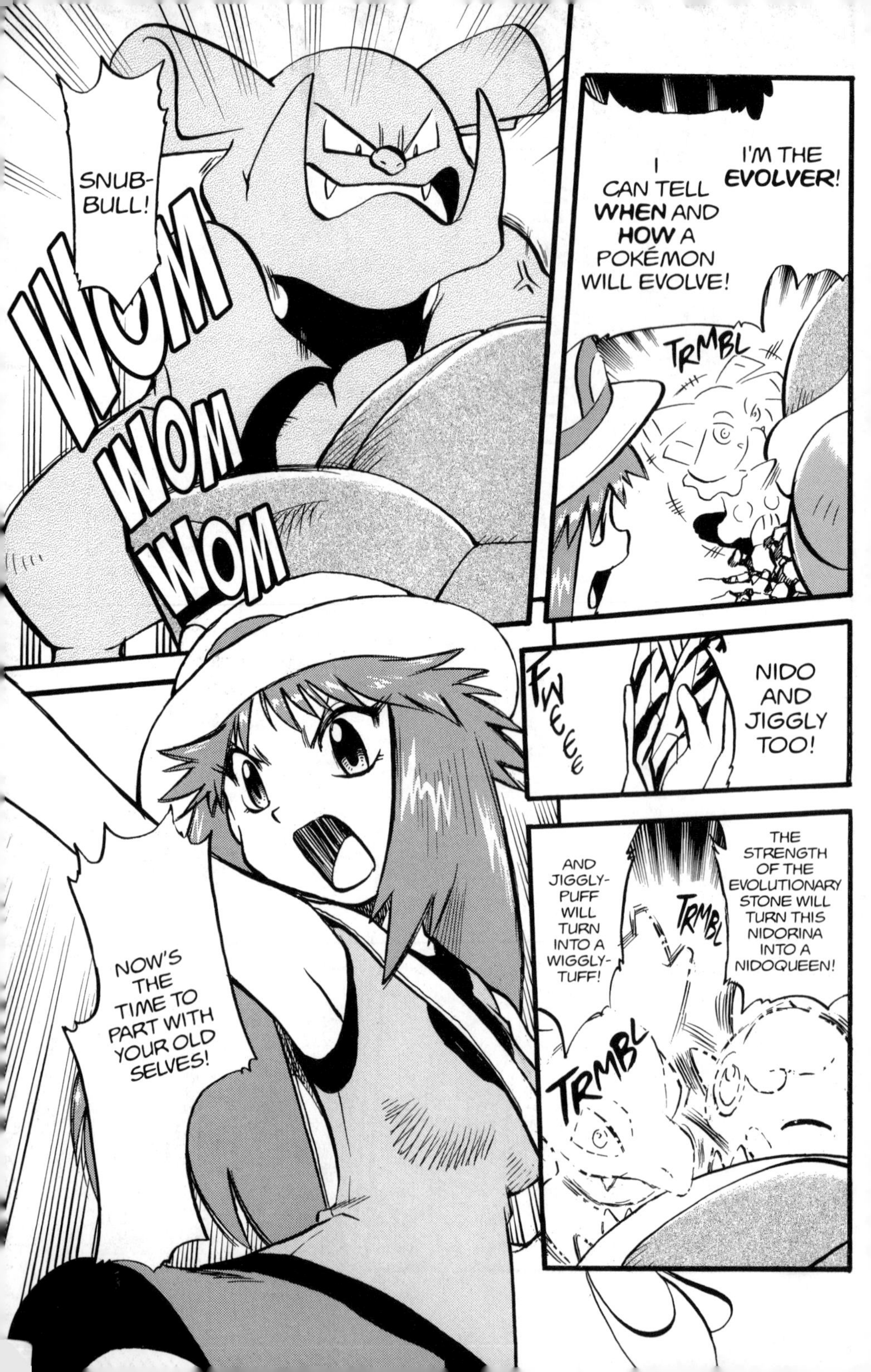
I'M THE EVOLVER!
I CAN TELL WHEN AND HOW A POKÉMON WILL EVOLVE!
TRMBL
SNUB-BULL!
WOM WOM WOM WOM
NIDO AND JIGGLY TOO!
FWEEEE
THE STRENGTH OF THE EVOLUTIONARY STONE WILL TURN THIS NIDORINA INTO A NIDOQUEEN!
AND JIGGLY-PUFF WILL TURN INTO A WIGGLY-TUFF!
TRMBL
TRMBL
NOW'S THE TIME TO PART WITH YOUR OLD SELVES!

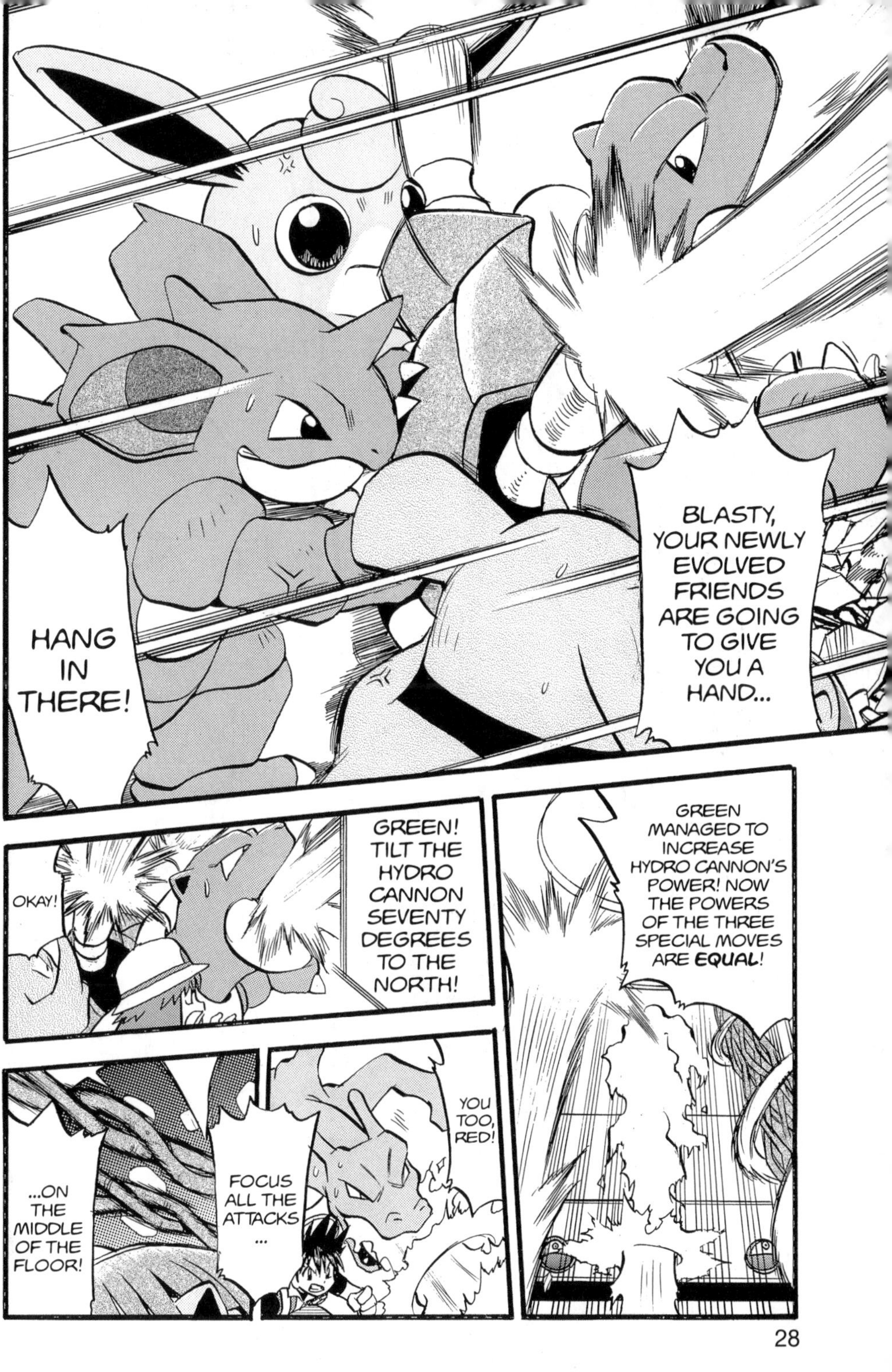

BLASTY, YOUR NEWLY EVOLVED FRIENDS ARE GOING TO GIVE YOU A HAND...
HANG IN THERE!
GREEN MANAGED TO INCREASE HYDRO CANNON'S POWER! NOW THE POWERS OF THE THREE SPECIAL MOVES ARE **EQUAL**!
GREEN! TILT THE HYDRO CANNON SEVENTY DEGREES TO THE NORTH!
OKAY!
YOU TOO, RED!
FOCUS ALL THE ATTACKS ...
...ON THE MIDDLE OF THE FLOOR!

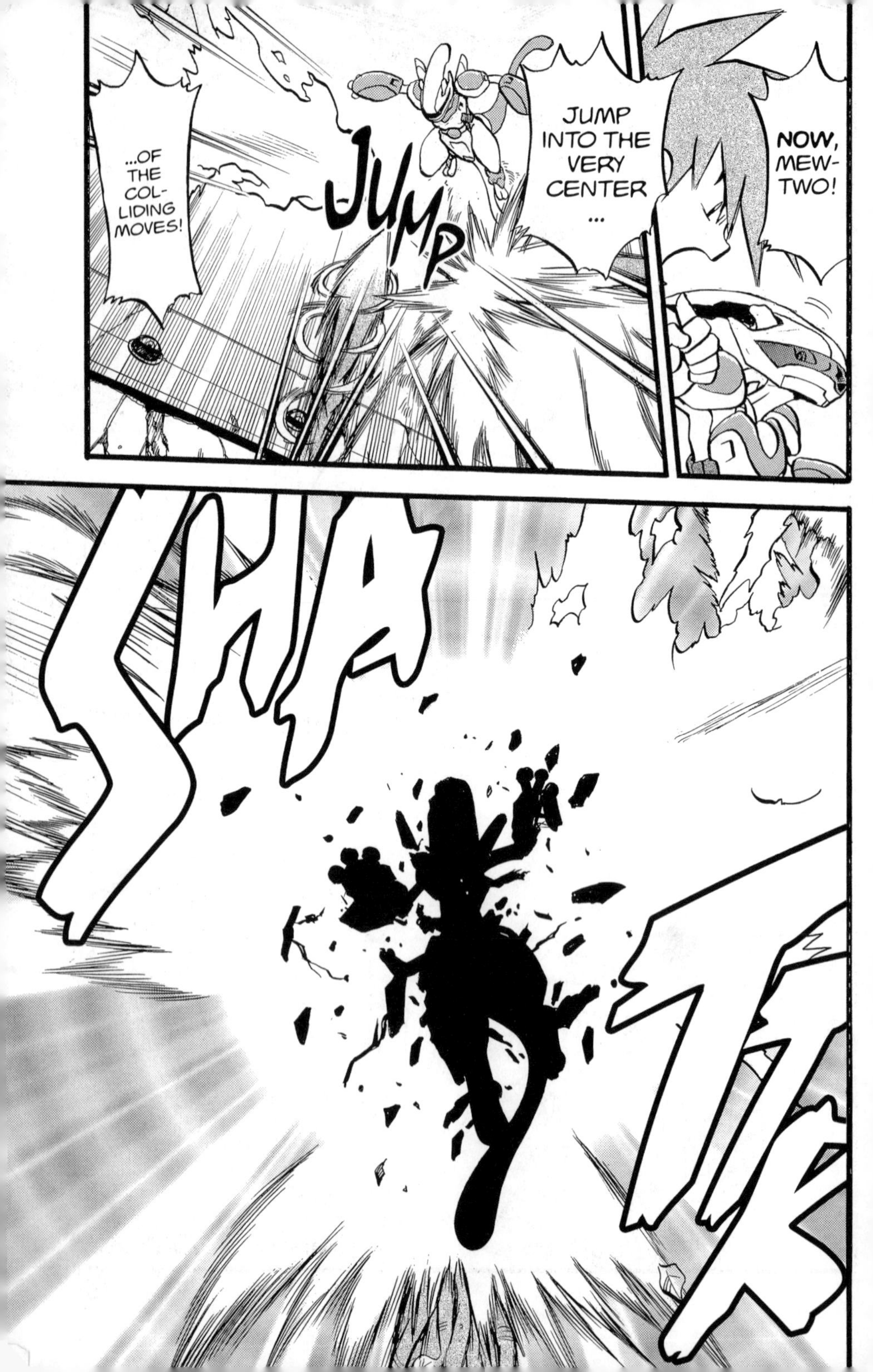
NOW, MEW-TWO!
JUMP INTO THE VERY CENTER ...
...OF THE COL-LIDING MOVES!
JUMP
SHA

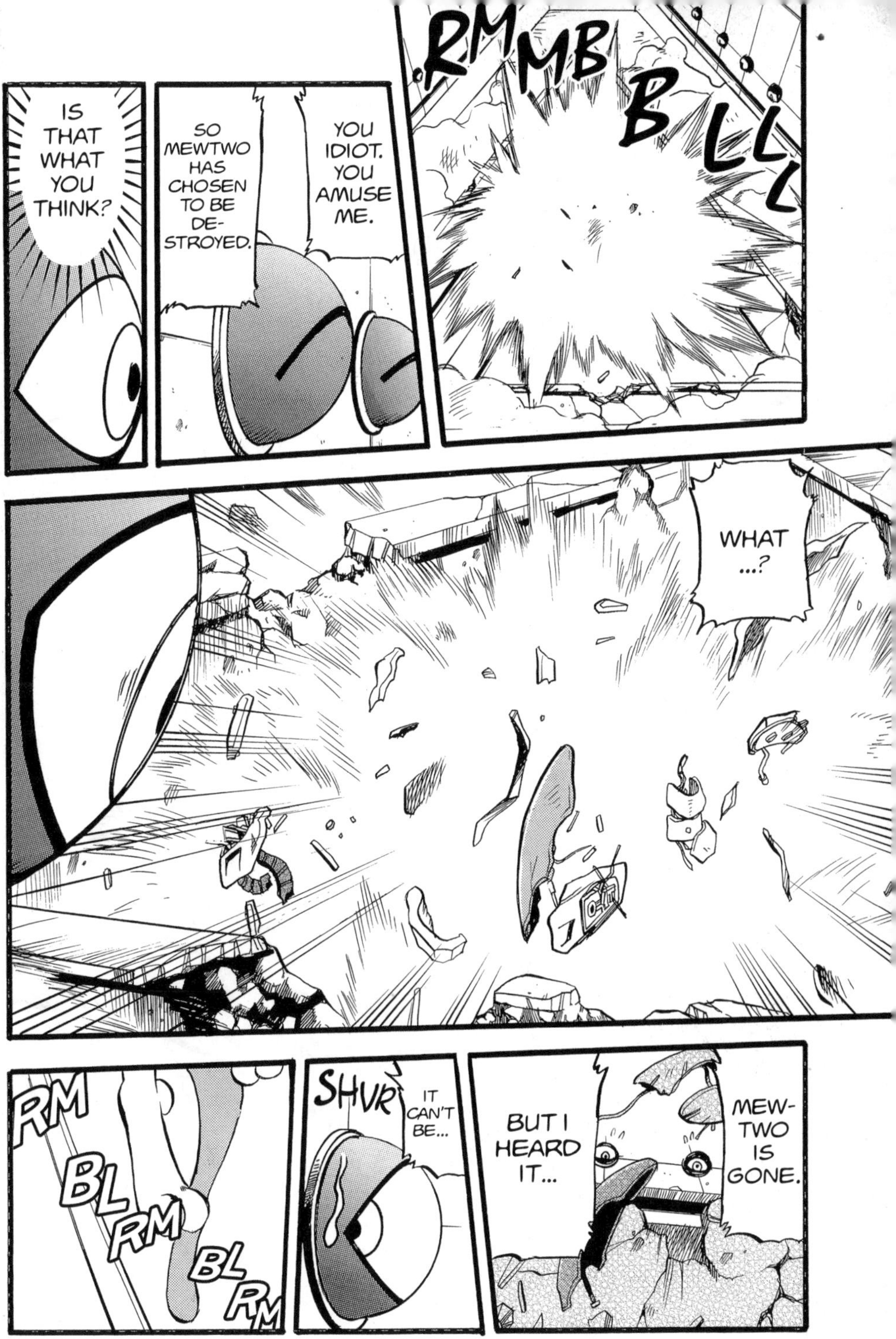
RMMB
BLLL
YOU IDIOT. YOU AMUSE ME.
SO MEWTWO HAS CHOSEN TO BE DE-STROYED.
IS THAT WHAT YOU THINK?
WHAT ...?
MEW-TWO IS GONE.
BUT I HEARD IT...
IT CAN'T BE...
SHVR
RM
BL
RM
BL
RM

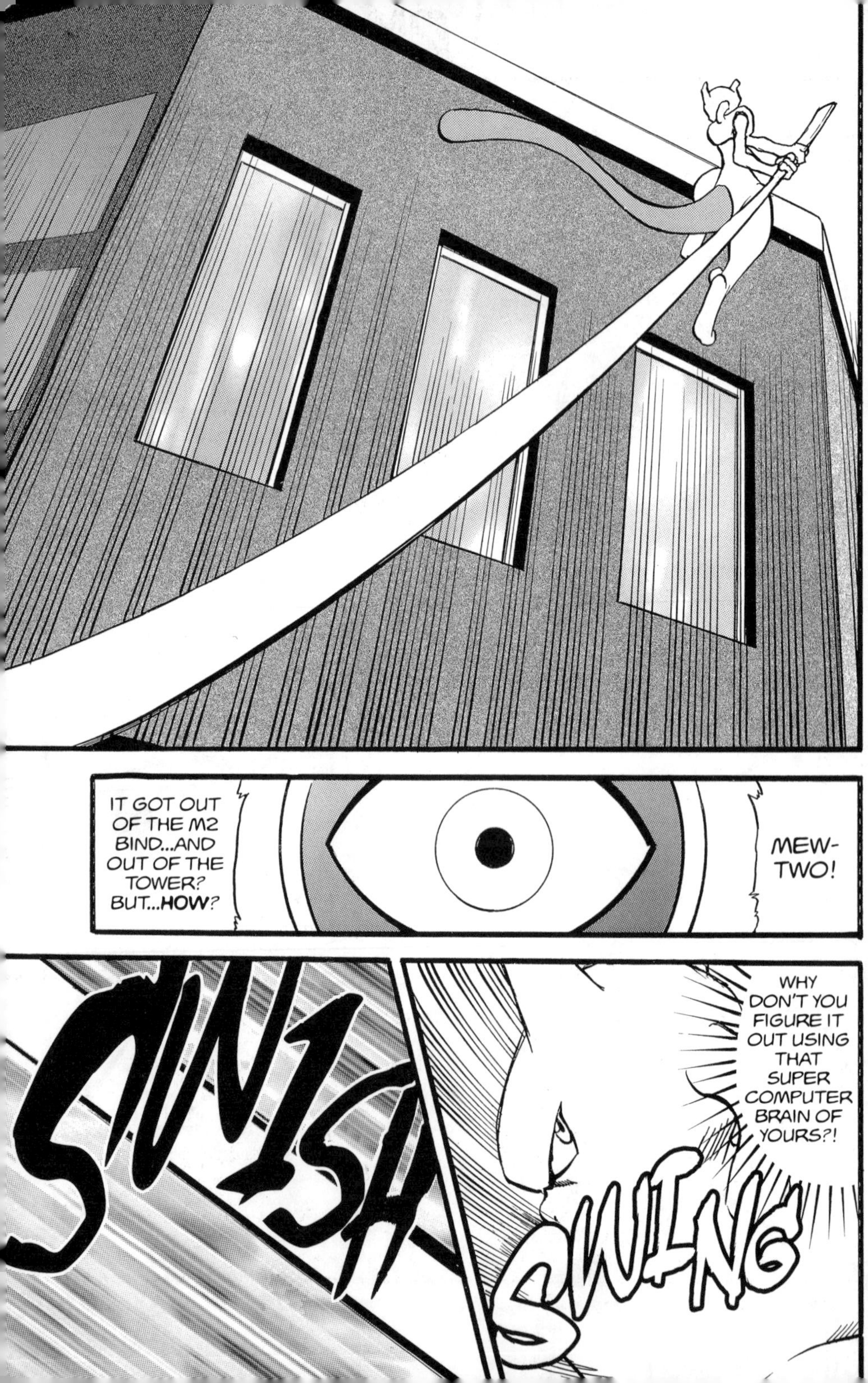
MEW-TWO!
IT GOT OUT OF THE M2 BIND...AND OUT OF THE TOWER? BUT...**HOW**?
WHY DON'T YOU FIGURE IT OUT USING THAT SUPER COMPUTER BRAIN OF YOURS?!
SWING
SWISH

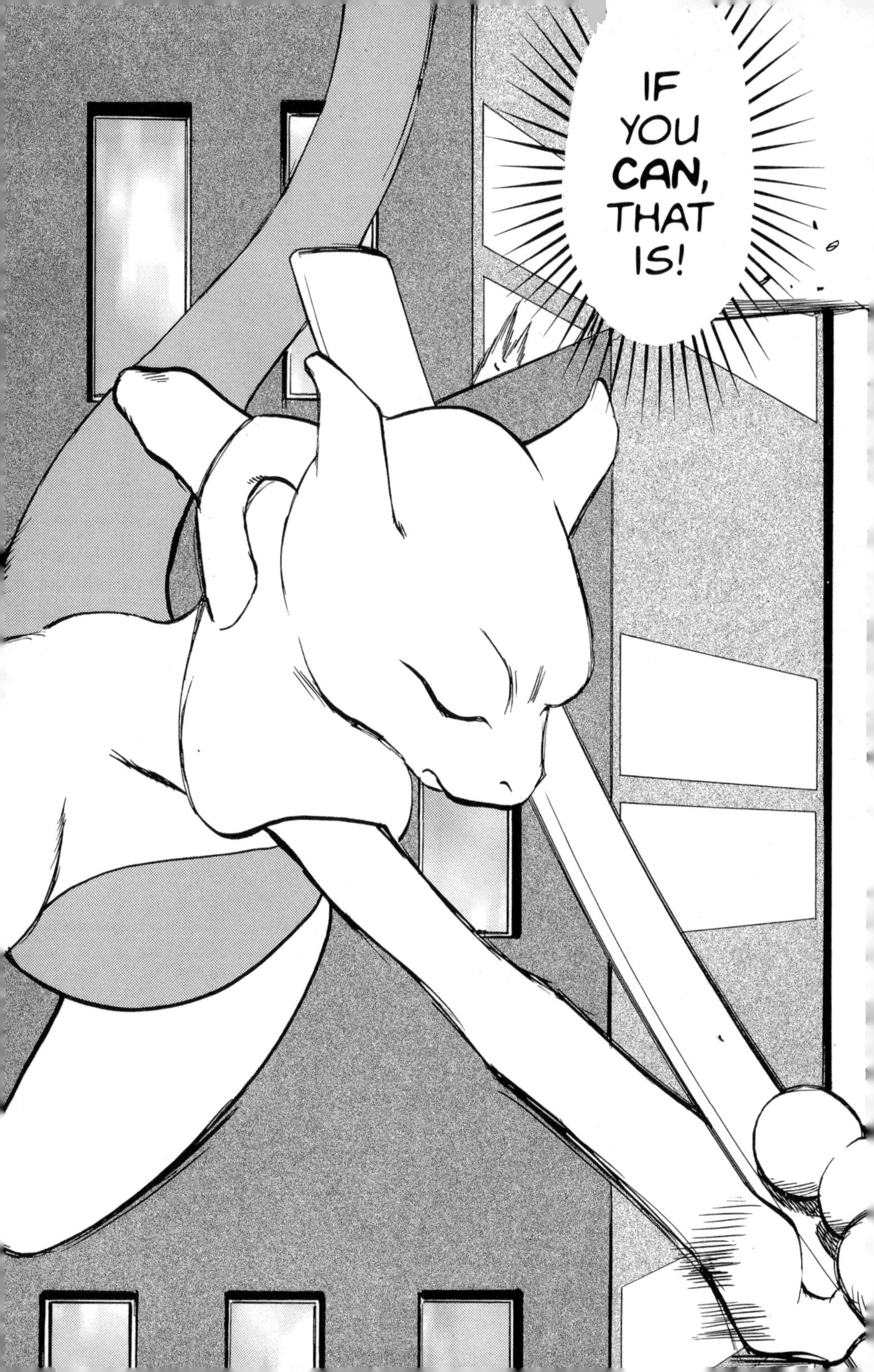
IF YOU CAN, THAT IS!

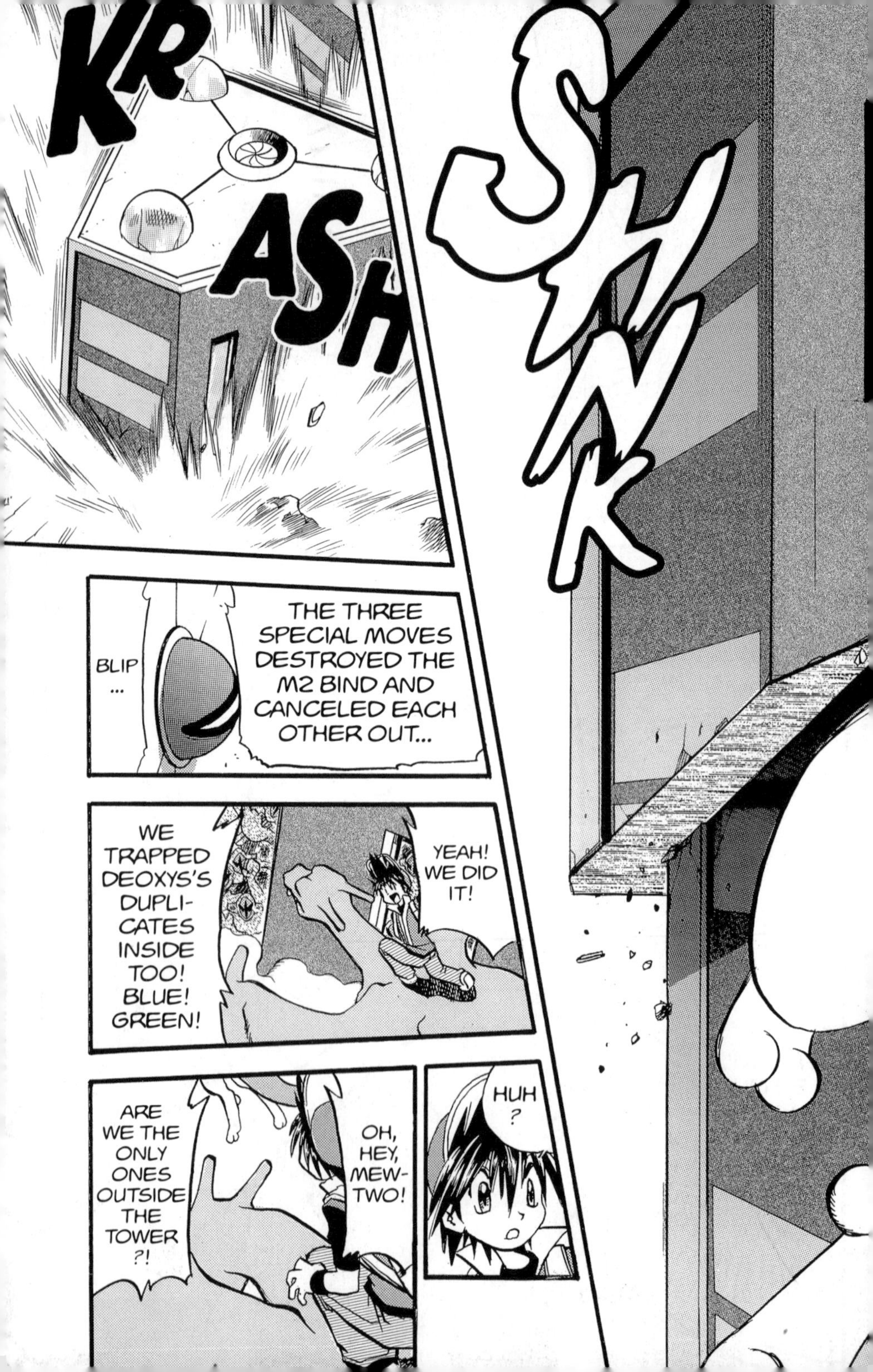
SHINK
KRASH
THE THREE SPECIAL MOVES DESTROYED THE M2 BIND AND CANCELED EACH OTHER OUT...
BLIP ...
YEAH! WE DID IT!
WE TRAPPED DEOXYS'S DUPLI-CATES INSIDE TOO! BLUE! GREEN!
HUH?
OH, HEY, MEW-TWO!
ARE WE THE ONLY ONES OUTSIDE THE TOWER?!

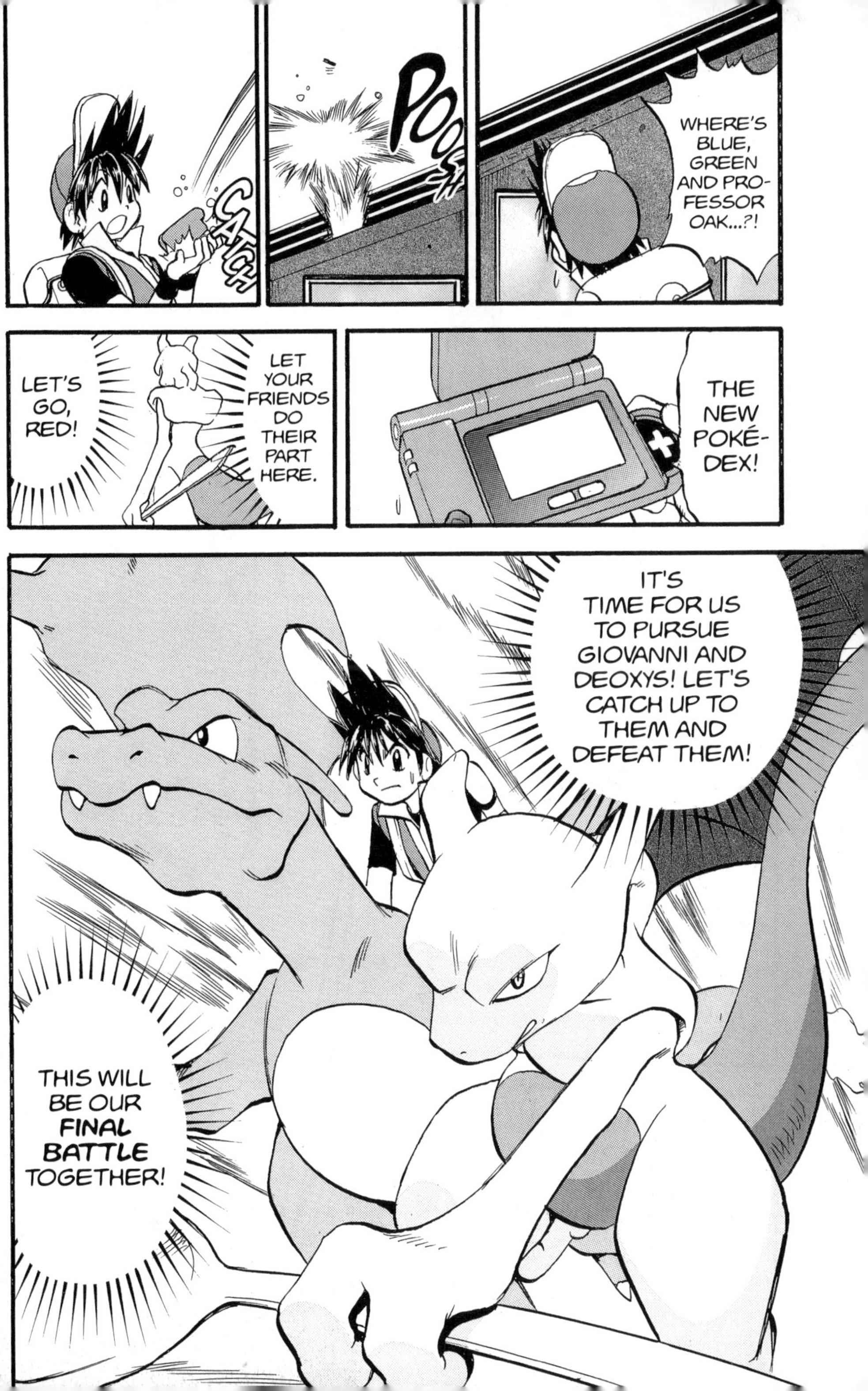
WHERE'S BLUE, GREEN AND PRO-FESSOR OAK...?!
POOF
CATCH
THE NEW POKÉ-DEX!
LET YOUR FRIENDS DO THEIR PART HERE.
LET'S GO, RED!
IT'S TIME FOR US TO PURSUE GIOVANNI AND DEOXYS! LET'S CATCH UP TO THEM AND DEFEAT THEM!
THIS WILL BE OUR **FINAL BATTLE** TOGETHER!

PROFESSOR OAK

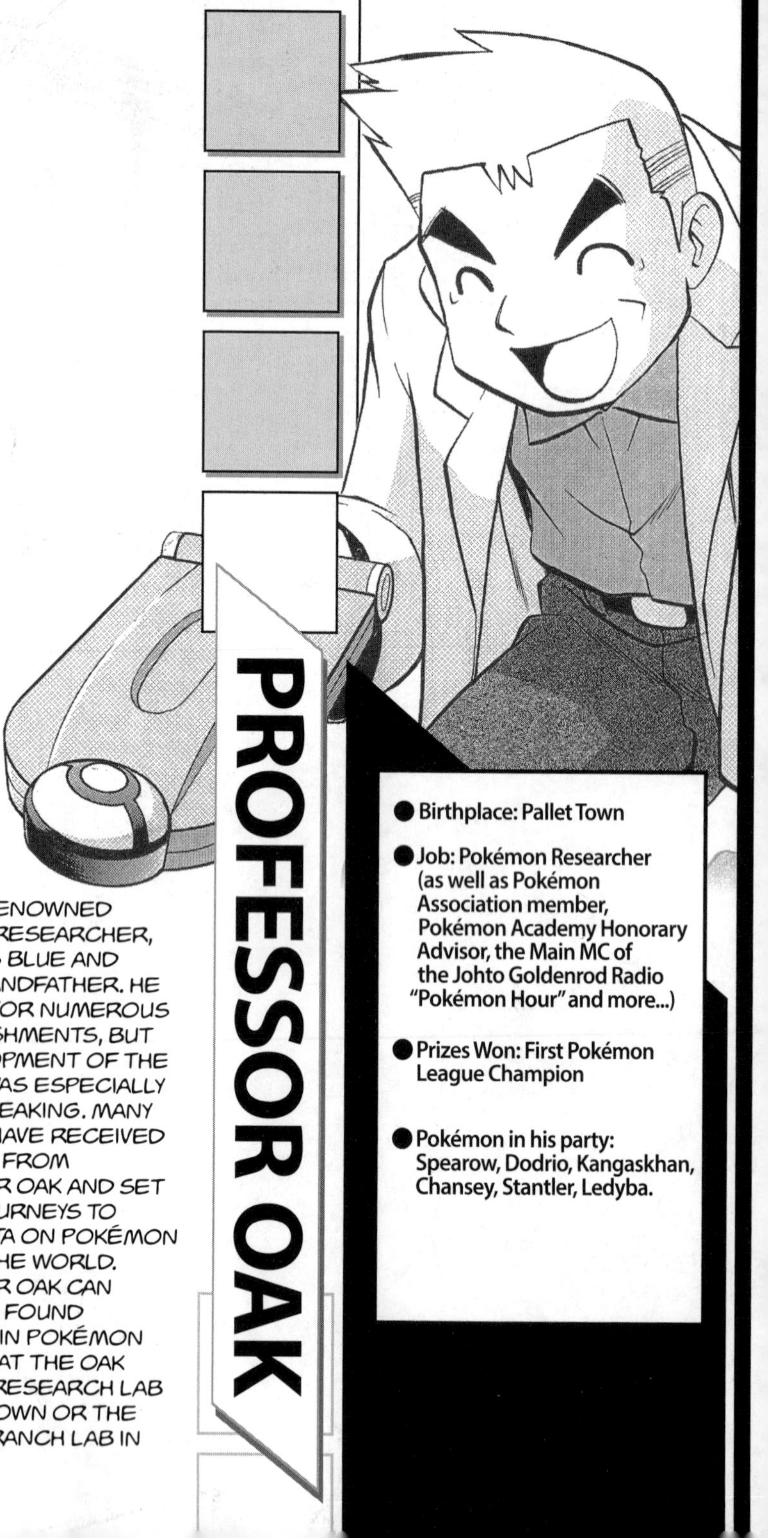

A WORLD RENOWNED POKÉMON RESEARCHER, AS WELL AS BLUE AND DAISY'S GRANDFATHER. HE IS KNOWN FOR NUMEROUS ACCOMPLISHMENTS, BUT HIS DEVELOPMENT OF THE POKÉDEX WAS ESPECIALLY GROUNDBREAKING. MANY CHILDREN HAVE RECEIVED A POKÉDEX FROM PROFESSOR OAK AND SET OUT ON JOURNEYS TO GATHER DATA ON POKÉMON ALL OVER THE WORLD. PROFESSOR OAK CAN USUALLY BE FOUND IMMERSED IN POKÉMON RESEARCH AT THE OAK POKÉMON RESEARCH LAB IN PALLET TOWN OR THE SECOND BRANCH LAB IN JOHTO.

- Birthplace: Pallet Town
- Job: Pokémon Researcher (as well as Pokémon Association member, Pokémon Academy Honorary Advisor, the Main MC of the Johto Goldenrod Radio "Pokémon Hour" and more...)
- Prizes Won: First Pokémon League Champion
- Pokémon in his party: Spearow, Dodrio, Kangaskhan, Chansey, Stantler, Ledyba.

● Adventure 289 ●
Surprised by Sneasel

Pokémon Adventures
FireRed & LeafGreen
The Fifth Chapter

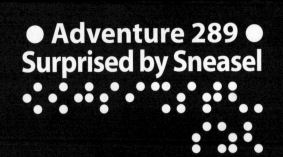

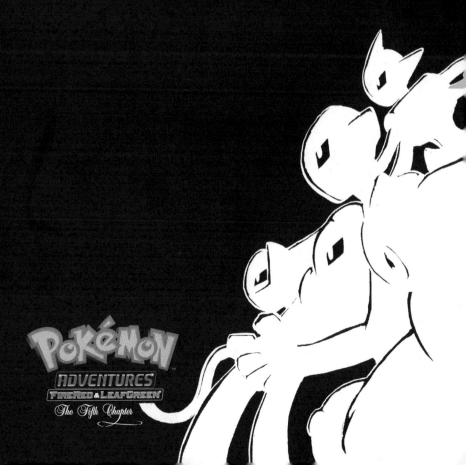

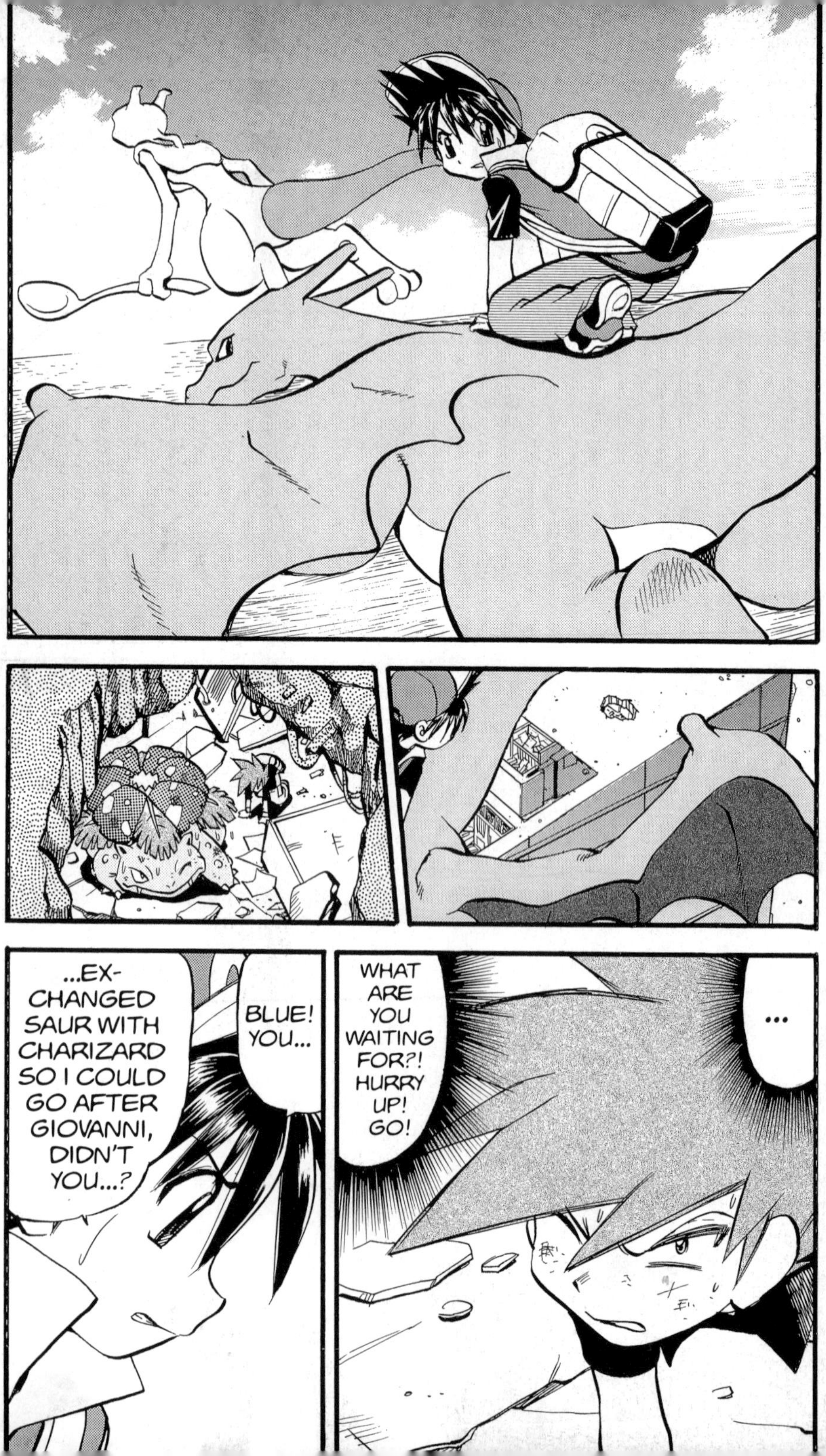
...
WHAT ARE YOU WAITING FOR?! HURRY UP! GO!
BLUE! YOU...
...EX-CHANGED SAUR WITH CHARIZARD SO I COULD GO AFTER GIOVANNI, DIDN'T YOU...?

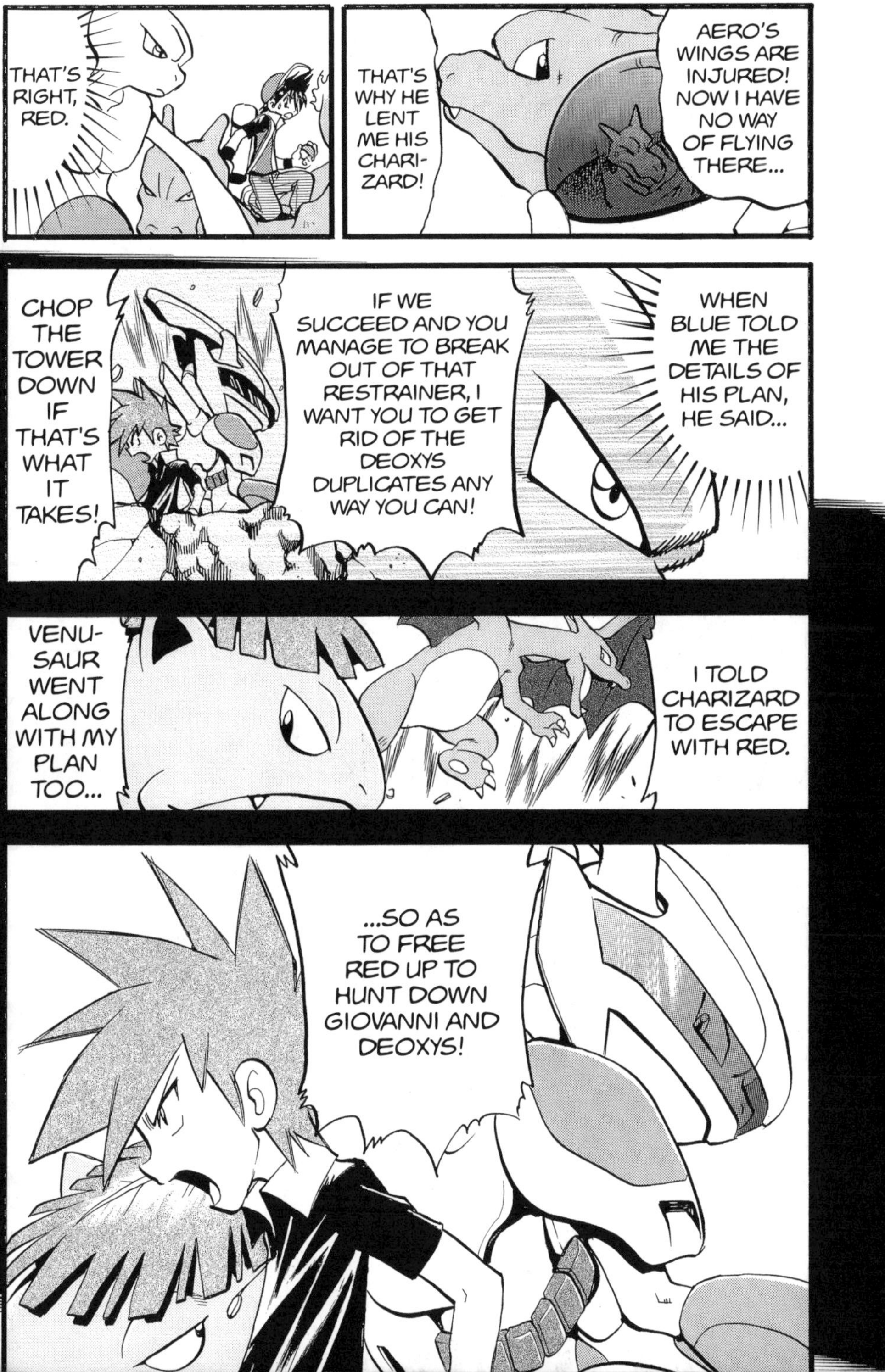
AERO'S WINGS ARE INJURED! NOW I HAVE NO WAY OF FLYING THERE...
THAT'S WHY HE LENT ME HIS CHARI-ZARD!
THAT'S RIGHT, RED.
WHEN BLUE TOLD ME THE DETAILS OF HIS PLAN, HE SAID...
IF WE SUCCEED AND YOU MANAGE TO BREAK OUT OF THAT RESTRAINER, I WANT YOU TO GET RID OF THE DEOXYS DUPLICATES ANY WAY YOU CAN!
CHOP THE TOWER DOWN IF THAT'S WHAT IT TAKES!
I TOLD CHARIZARD TO ESCAPE WITH RED.
VENU-SAUR WENT ALONG WITH MY PLAN TOO...
...SO AS TO FREE RED UP TO HUNT DOWN GIOVANNI AND DEOXYS!

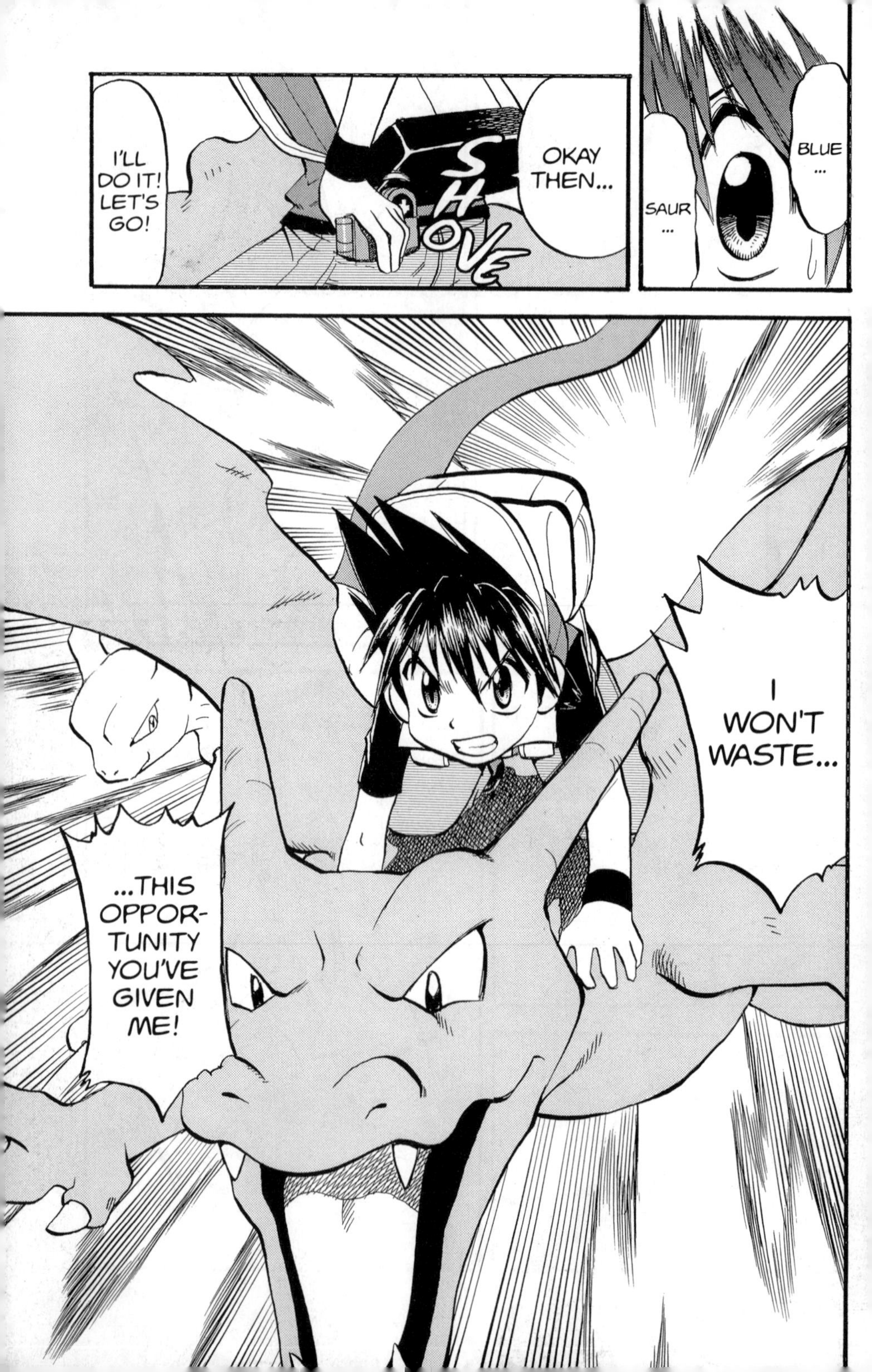
BLUE ...
SAUR ...
OKAY THEN...
SHOVE
I'LL DO IT! LET'S GO!
I WON'T WASTE...
...THIS OPPOR-TUNITY YOU'VE GIVEN ME!

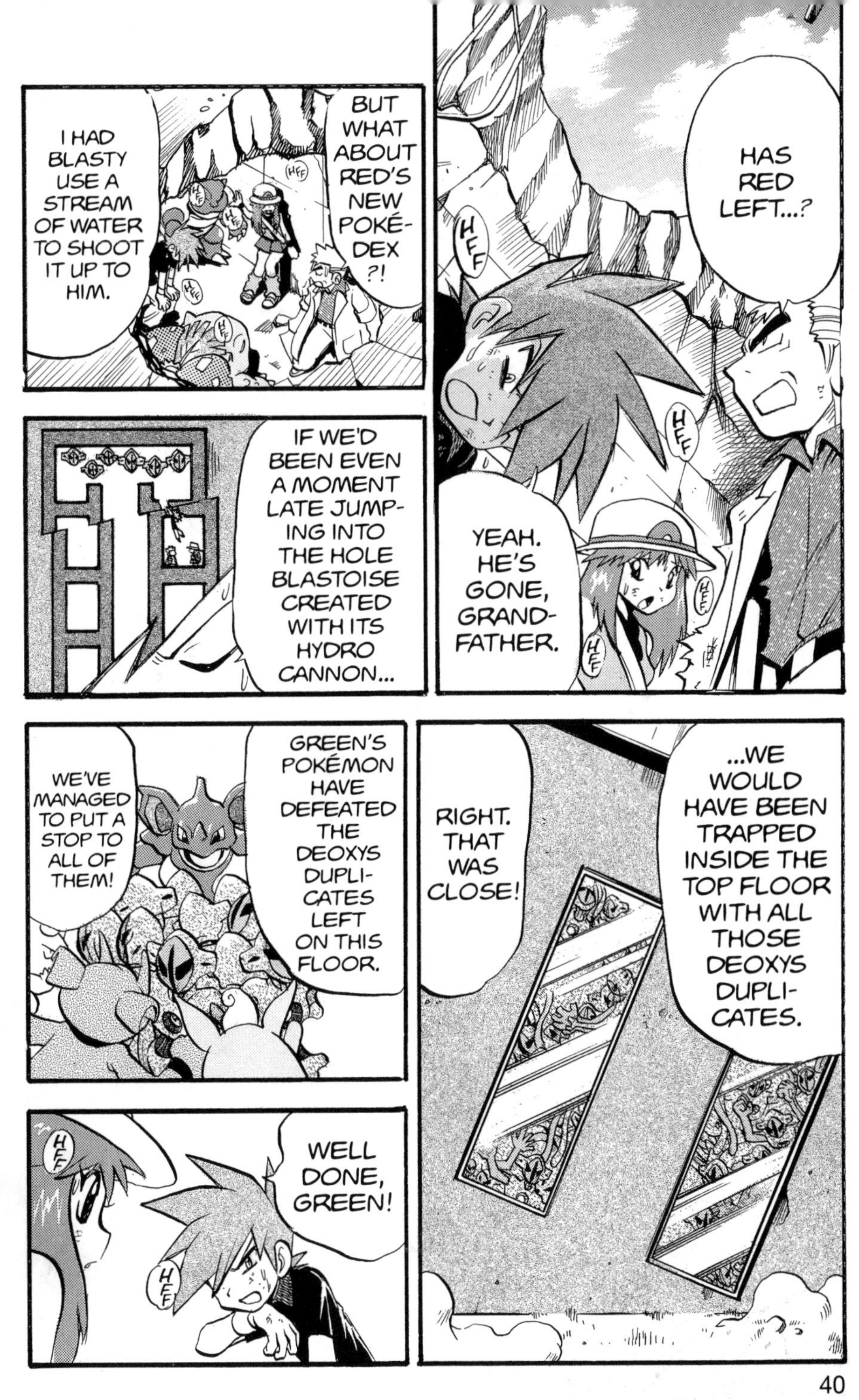
HAS RED LEFT...?
HFF
HFF
YEAH. HE'S GONE, GRANDFATHER.
HFF
HFF
BUT WHAT ABOUT RED'S NEW POKÉ-DEX?!
I HAD BLASTY USE A STREAM OF WATER TO SHOOT IT UP TO HIM.
HFF
HFF
HFF
HFF
IF WE'D BEEN EVEN A MOMENT LATE JUMP-ING INTO THE HOLE BLASTOISE CREATED WITH ITS HYDRO CANNON...
...WE WOULD HAVE BEEN TRAPPED INSIDE THE TOP FLOOR WITH ALL THOSE DEOXYS DUPLI-CATES.
RIGHT. THAT WAS CLOSE!
GREEN'S POKÉMON HAVE DEFEATED THE DEOXYS DUPLI-CATES LEFT ON THIS FLOOR.
WE'VE MANAGED TO PUT A STOP TO ALL OF THEM!
WELL DONE, GREEN!
HFF
HFF

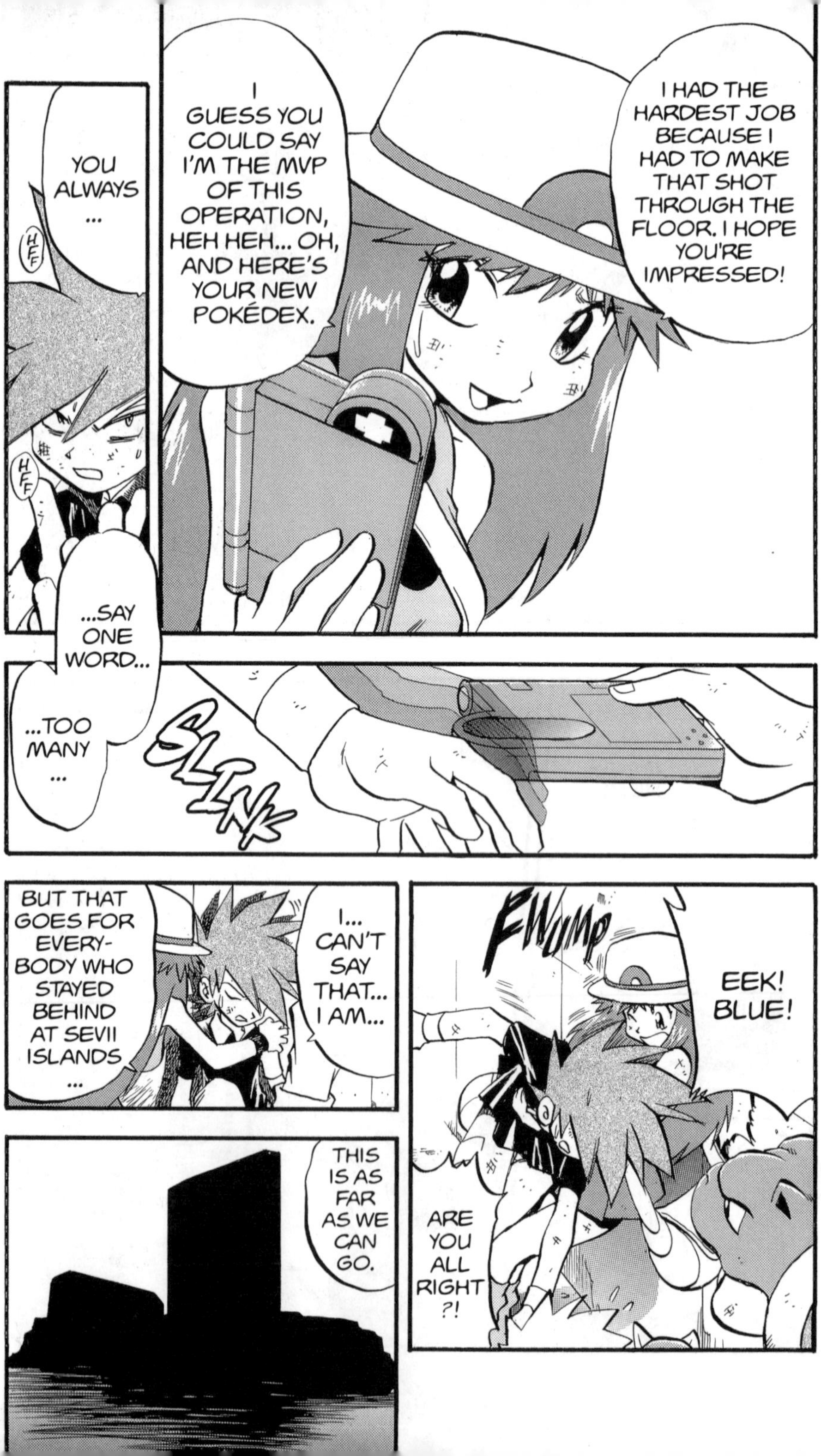
I HAD THE HARDEST JOB BECAUSE I HAD TO MAKE THAT SHOT THROUGH THE FLOOR. I HOPE YOU'RE IMPRESSED!
I GUESS YOU COULD SAY I'M THE MVP OF THIS OPERATION, HEH HEH... OH, AND HERE'S YOUR NEW POKÉDEX.
YOU ALWAYS ...
HFF
HFF
...SAY ONE WORD...
...TOO MANY ...
SLINK
FWUMP
EEK! BLUE!
ARE YOU ALL RIGHT ?!
I... CAN'T SAY THAT... I AM...
BUT THAT GOES FOR EVERY-BODY WHO STAYED BEHIND AT SEVII ISLANDS ...
THIS IS AS FAR AS WE CAN GO.

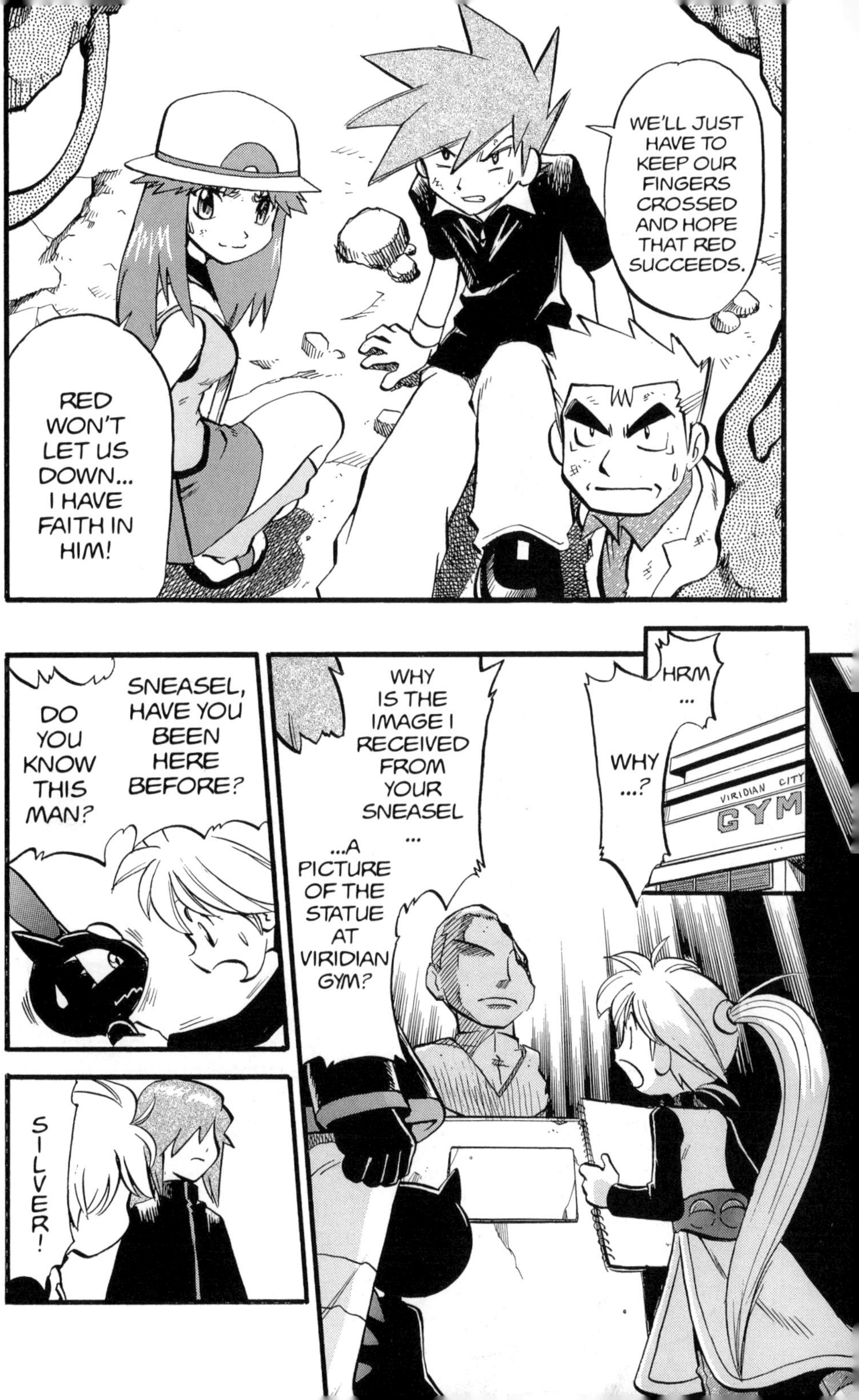
WE'LL JUST HAVE TO KEEP OUR FINGERS CROSSED AND HOPE THAT RED SUCCEEDS.
RED WON'T LET US DOWN... I HAVE FAITH IN HIM!
HRM ...
WHY ...?
VIRIDIAN CITY GYM
WHY IS THE IMAGE I RECEIVED FROM YOUR SNEASEL ...
...A PICTURE OF THE STATUE AT VIRIDIAN GYM?
SNEASEL, HAVE YOU BEEN HERE BEFORE?
DO YOU KNOW THIS MAN?
SILVER!

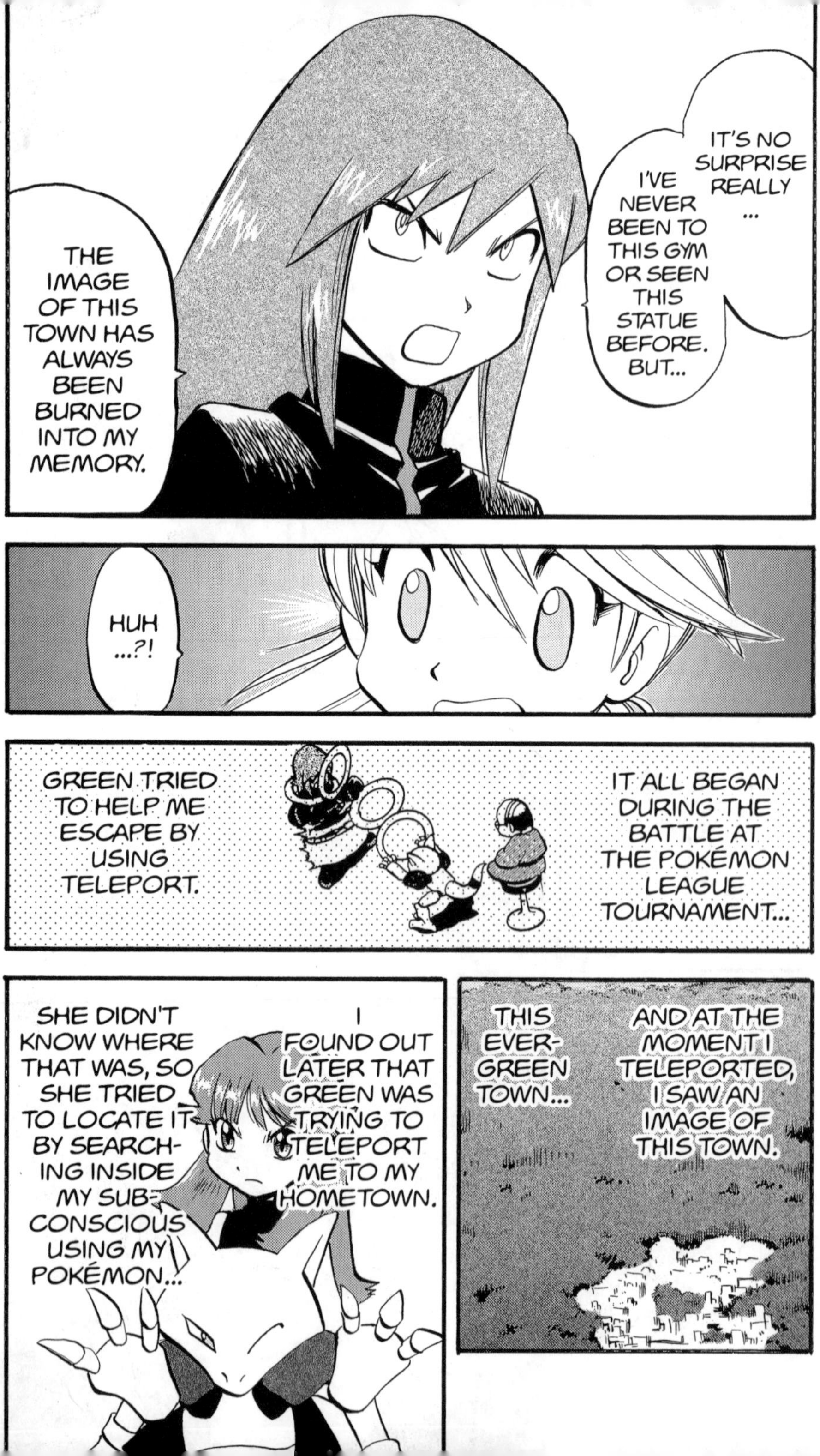
IT'S NO SURPRISE REALLY ...
I'VE NEVER BEEN TO THIS GYM OR SEEN THIS STATUE BEFORE. BUT...
THE IMAGE OF THIS TOWN HAS ALWAYS BEEN BURNED INTO MY MEMORY.
HUH ...?!
IT ALL BEGAN DURING THE BATTLE AT THE POKÉMON LEAGUE TOURNAMENT...
GREEN TRIED TO HELP ME ESCAPE BY USING TELEPORT.
AND AT THE MOMENT I TELEPORTED, I SAW AN IMAGE OF THIS TOWN.
THIS EVER-GREEN TOWN...
I FOUND OUT LATER THAT GREEN WAS TRYING TO TELEPORT ME TO MY HOMETOWN.
SHE DIDN'T KNOW WHERE THAT WAS, SO SHE TRIED TO LOCATE IT BY SEARCH-ING INSIDE MY SUB-CONSCIOUS USING MY POKÉMON...

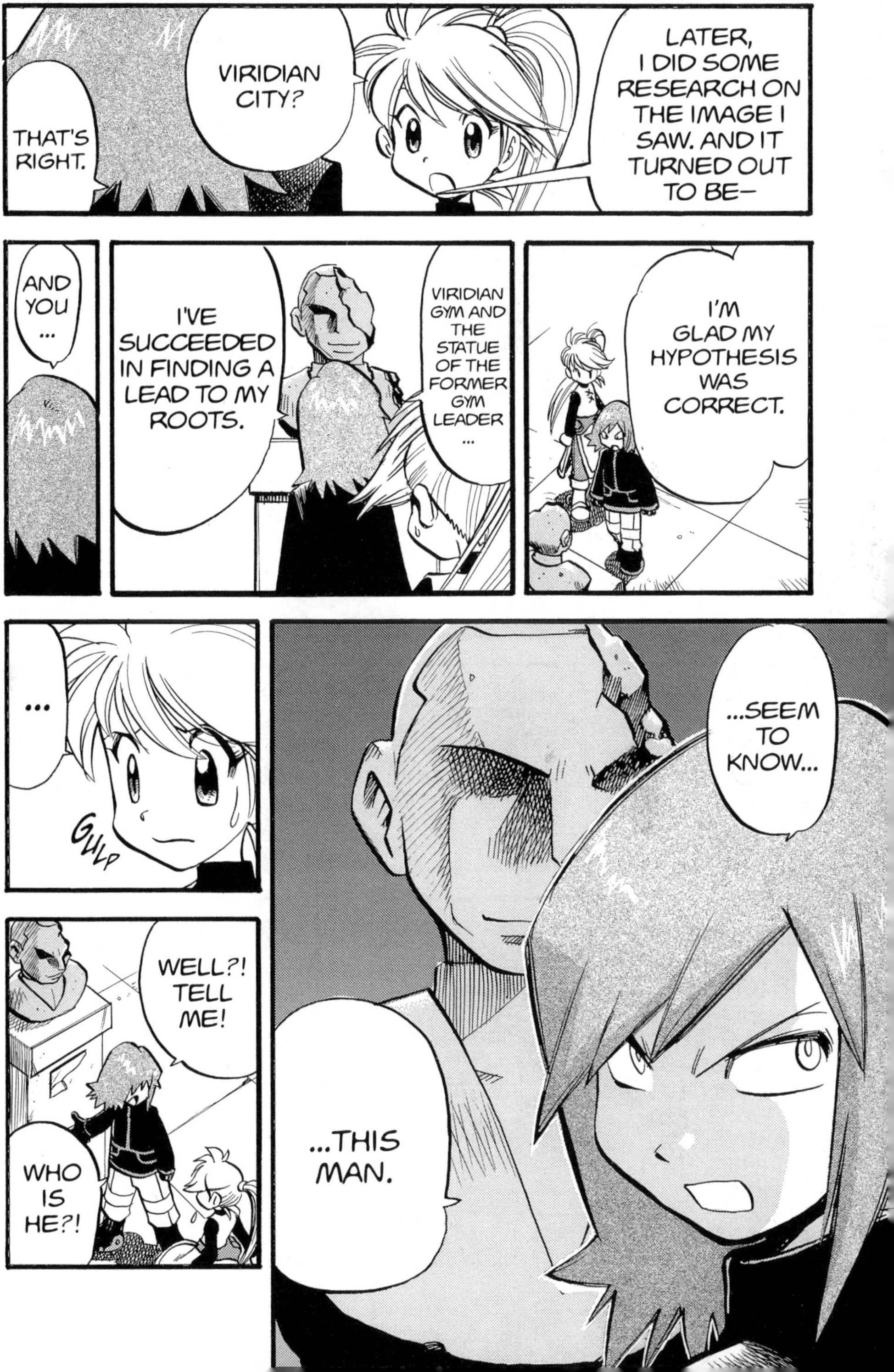
LATER, I DID SOME RESEARCH ON THE IMAGE I SAW. AND IT TURNED OUT TO BE—
VIRIDIAN CITY?
THAT'S RIGHT.
I'M GLAD MY HYPOTHESIS WAS CORRECT.
VIRIDIAN GYM AND THE STATUE OF THE FORMER GYM LEADER ...
I'VE SUCCEEDED IN FINDING A LEAD TO MY ROOTS.
AND YOU ...
...SEEM TO KNOW...
...THIS MAN.
...
GULP
WELL?! TELL ME!
WHO IS HE?!

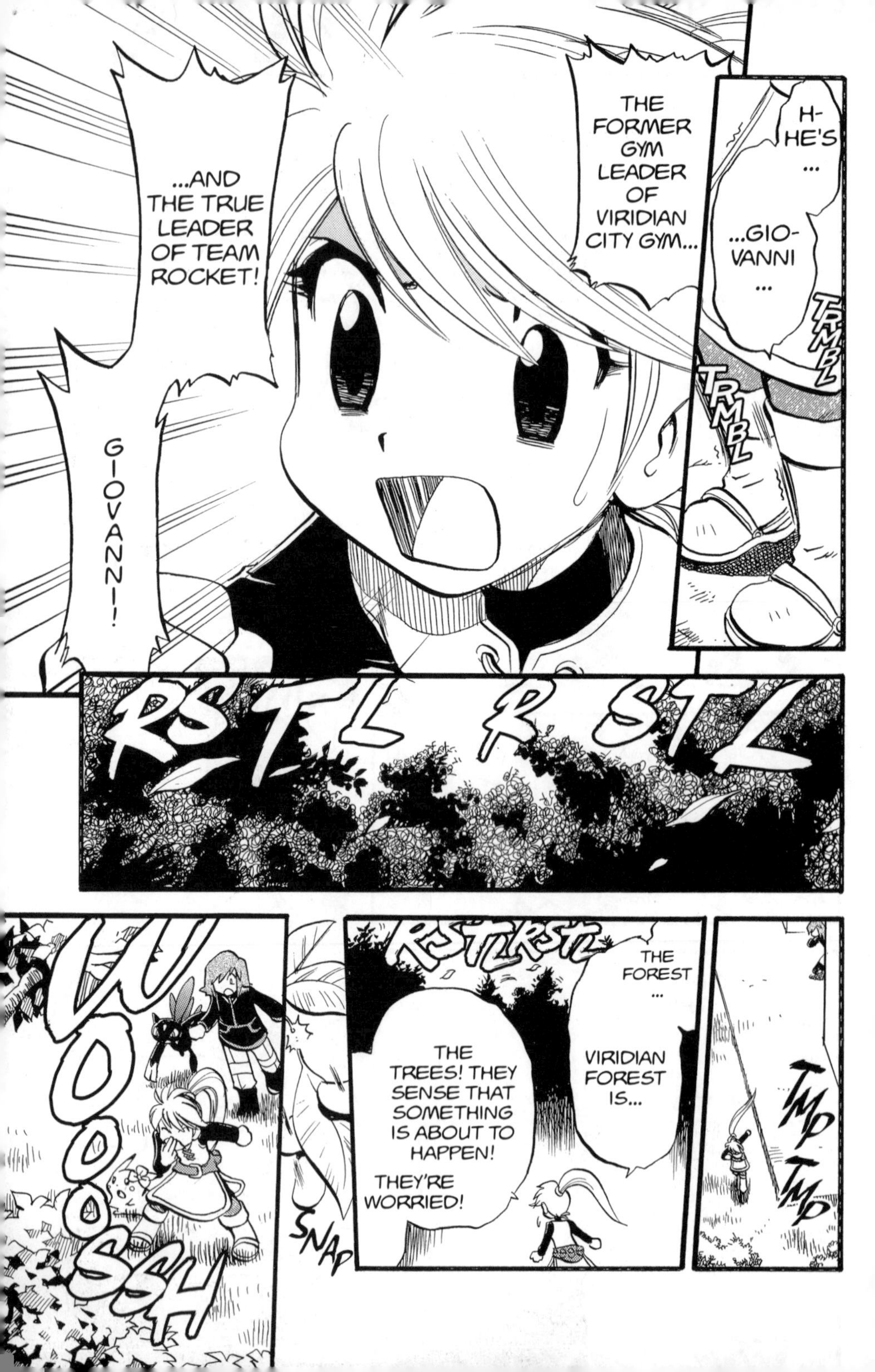
H-HE'S...
...GIO-VANNI...
TRMBL
TRMBL
THE FORMER GYM LEADER OF VIRIDIAN CITY GYM...
...AND THE TRUE LEADER OF TEAM ROCKET!
GIOVANNI!!
RSTL RSTL
TMP TMP
RSTLRSTL
THE FOREST...
VIRIDIAN FOREST IS...
THE TREES! THEY SENSE THAT SOMETHING IS ABOUT TO HAPPEN!
THEY'RE WORRIED!
SNAP
WOOOOSH

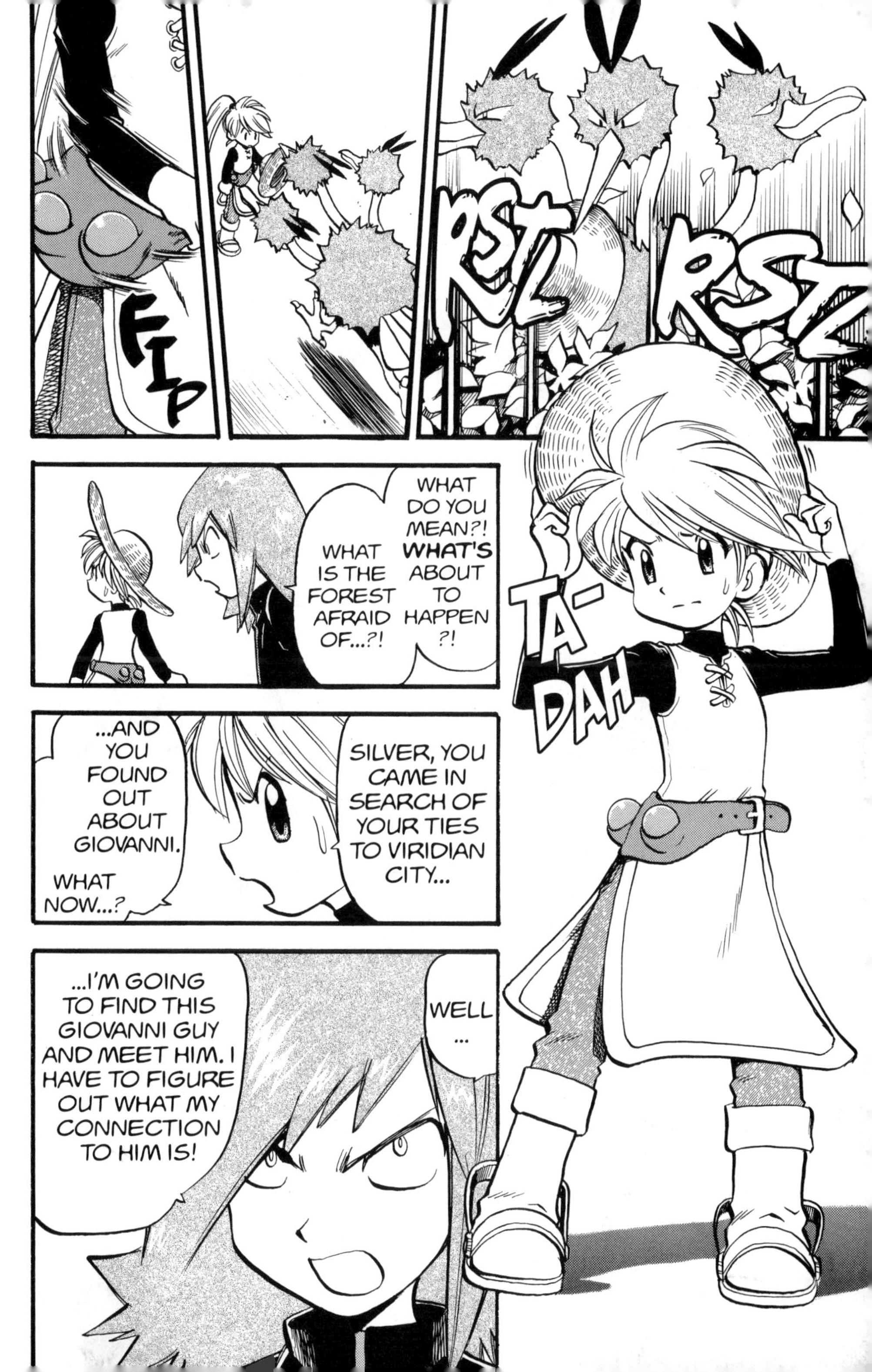
RSTL
RSTL
FLIP
TA-DAH
WHAT DO YOU MEAN?! WHAT'S ABOUT TO HAPPEN?!
WHAT IS THE FOREST AFRAID OF...?!
SILVER, YOU CAME IN SEARCH OF YOUR TIES TO VIRIDIAN CITY...
...AND YOU FOUND OUT ABOUT GIOVANNI.
WHAT NOW...?
WELL...
...I'M GOING TO FIND THIS GIOVANNI GUY AND MEET HIM. I HAVE TO FIGURE OUT WHAT MY CONNECTION TO HIM IS!

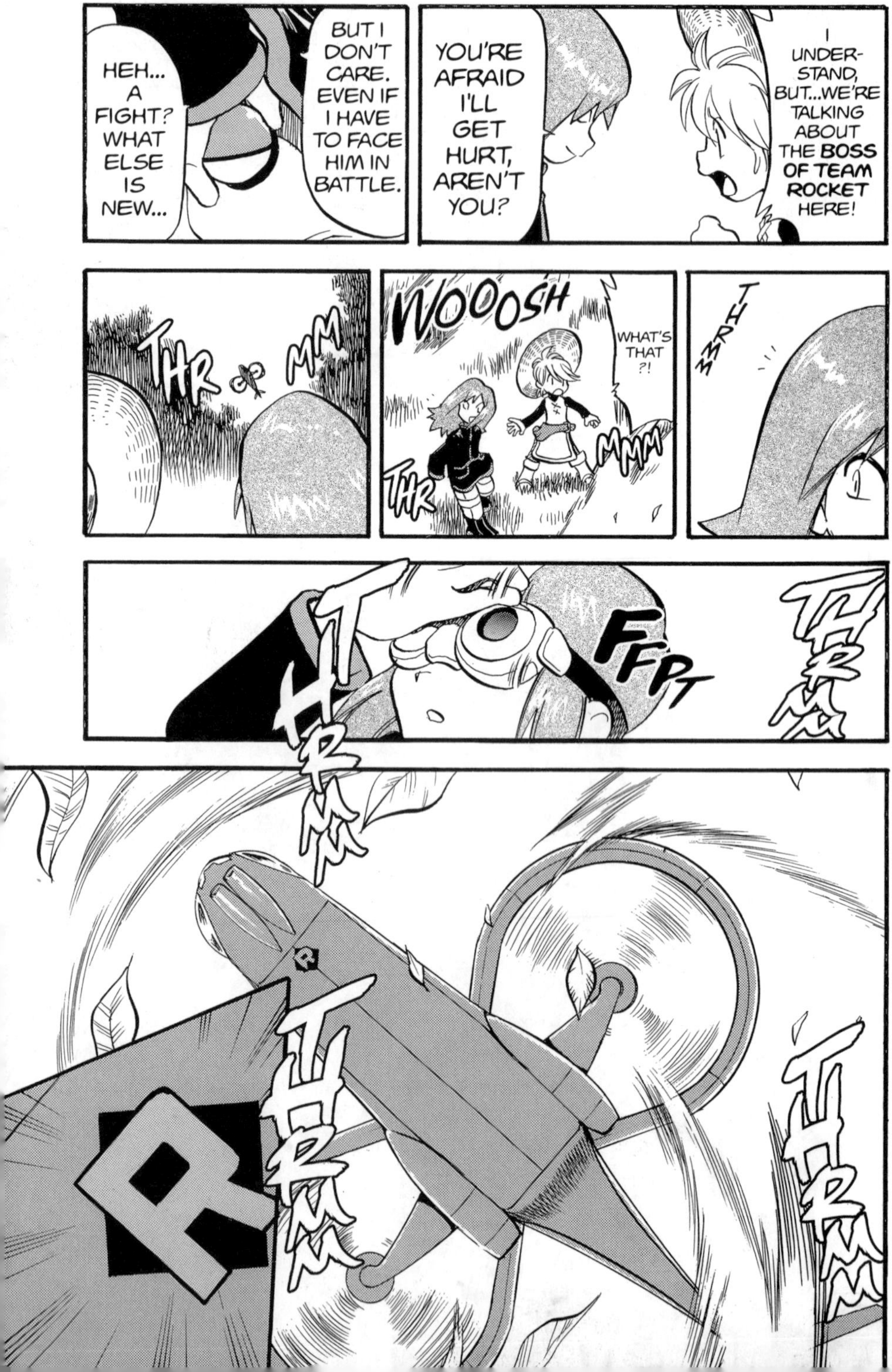

I UNDER-STAND, BUT...WE'RE TALKING ABOUT THE **BOSS OF TEAM ROCKET** HERE!
YOU'RE AFRAID I'LL GET HURT, AREN'T YOU?
BUT I DON'T CARE. EVEN IF I HAVE TO FACE HIM IN BATTLE.
HEH... A FIGHT? WHAT ELSE IS NEW...
THRMM
WOOOSH
WHAT'S THAT ?!
THR
MMM
THR
MM
THRMM
FFPT
THRMM
THRMM
THRMM

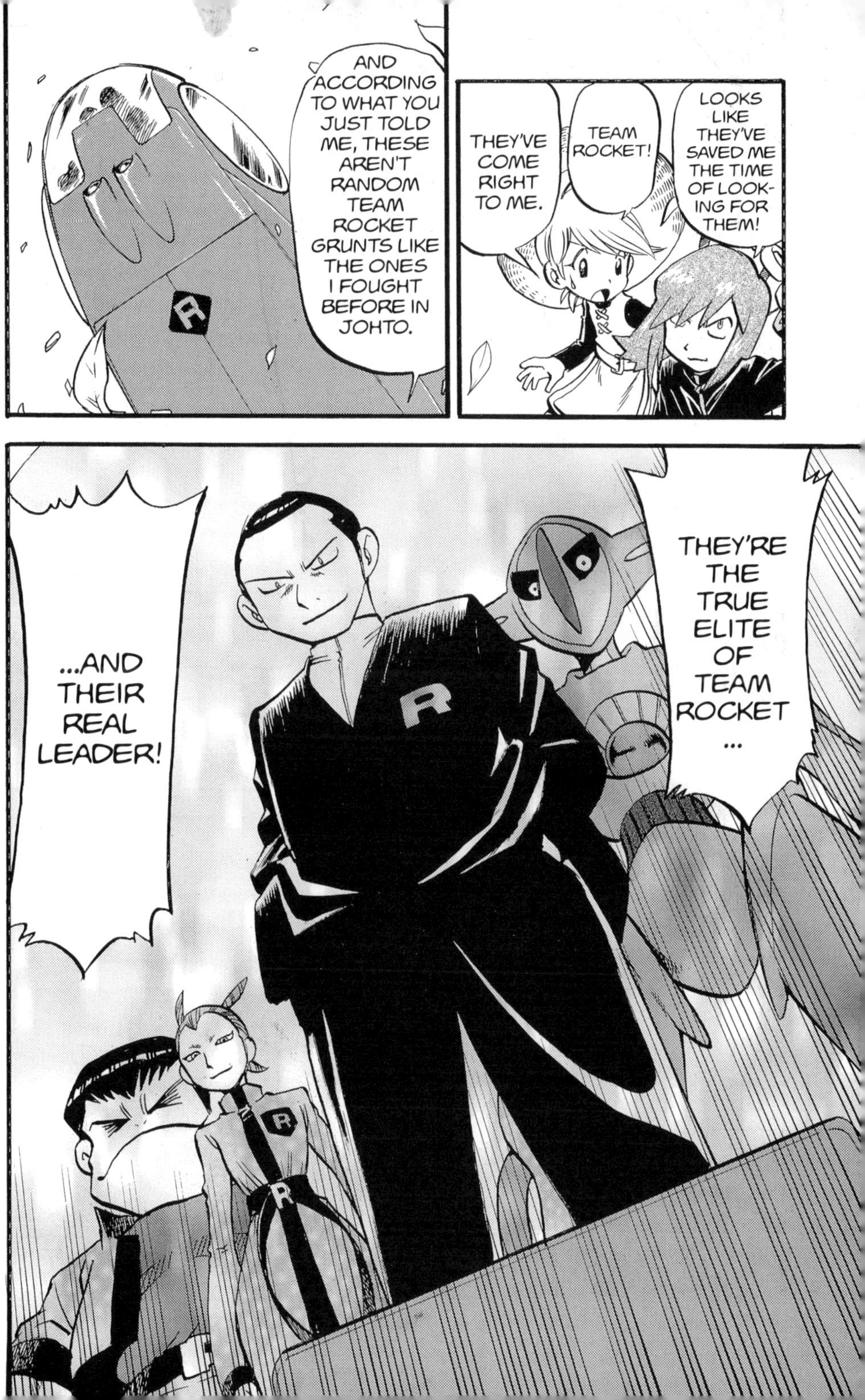
LOOKS LIKE THEY'VE SAVED ME THE TIME OF LOOK-ING FOR THEM!
TEAM ROCKET!
THEY'VE COME RIGHT TO ME.
AND ACCORDING TO WHAT YOU JUST TOLD ME, THESE AREN'T RANDOM TEAM ROCKET GRUNTS LIKE THE ONES I FOUGHT BEFORE IN JOHTO.
THEY'RE THE TRUE ELITE OF TEAM ROCKET ...
...AND THEIR REAL LEADER!

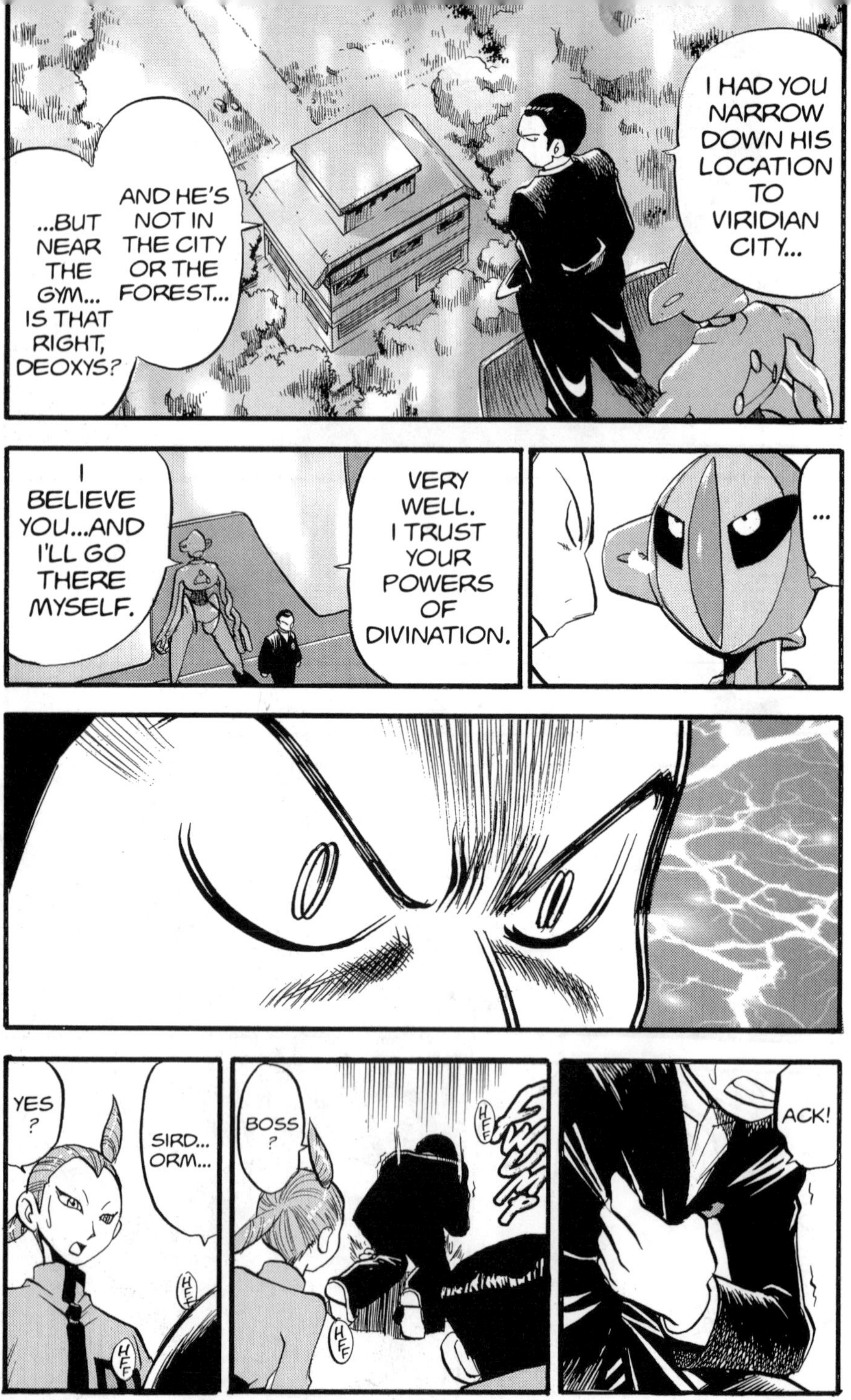
I HAD YOU NARROW DOWN HIS LOCATION TO VIRIDIAN CITY...
AND HE'S NOT IN THE CITY OR THE FOREST...
...BUT NEAR THE GYM... IS THAT RIGHT, DEOXYS?
...
VERY WELL. I TRUST YOUR POWERS OF DIVINATION.
I BELIEVE YOU...AND I'LL GO THERE MYSELF.
ACK!
HFF
BOSS?
HFF
SIRD... ORM...
YES?
HFF
HFF

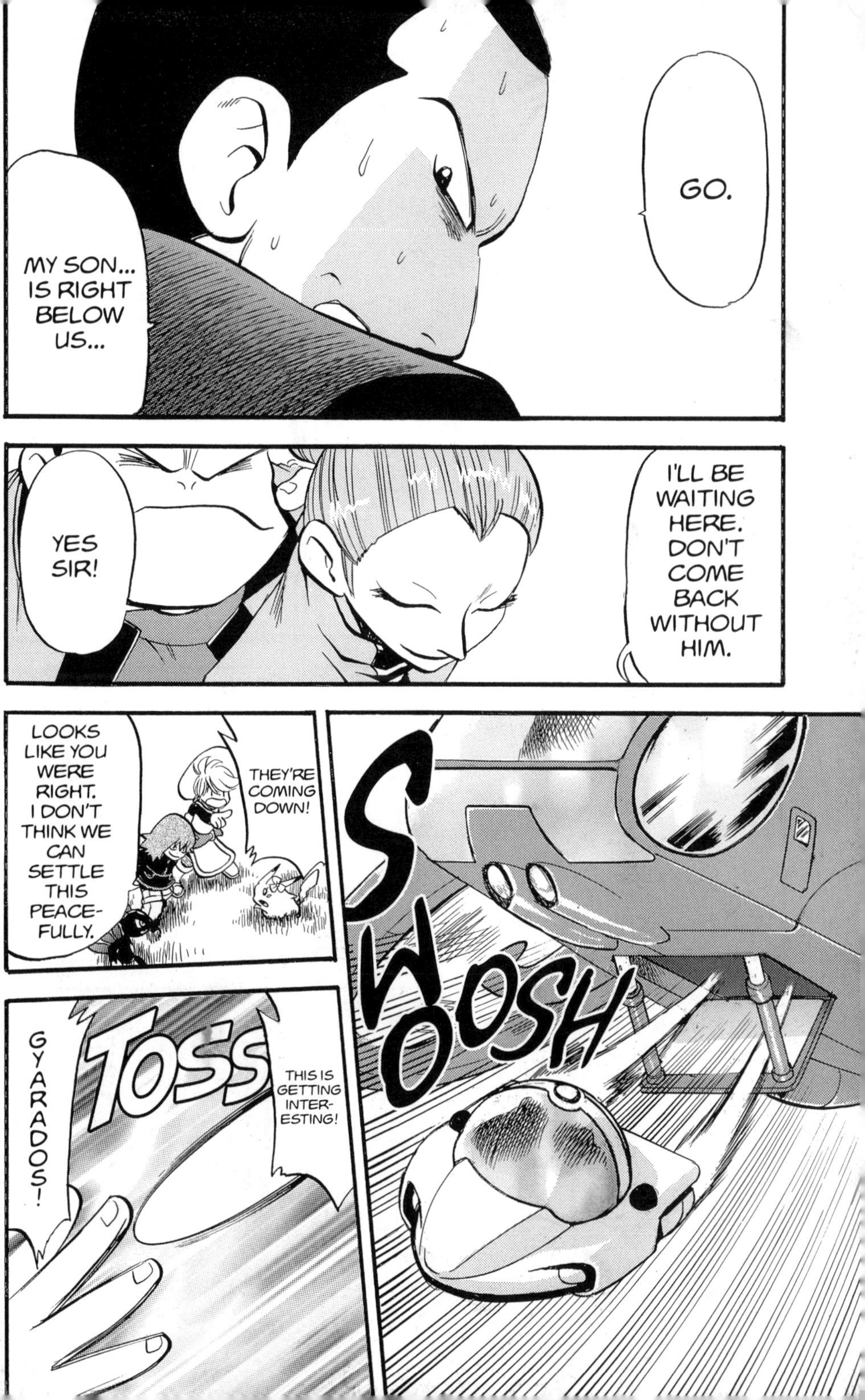
GO.
MY SON... IS RIGHT BELOW US...
I'LL BE WAITING HERE. DON'T COME BACK WITHOUT HIM.
YES SIR!
SWOOSH
THEY'RE COMING DOWN!
LOOKS LIKE YOU WERE RIGHT. I DON'T THINK WE CAN SETTLE THIS PEACE-FULLY.
TOSS
THIS IS GETTING INTER-ESTING!
GYARADOS!

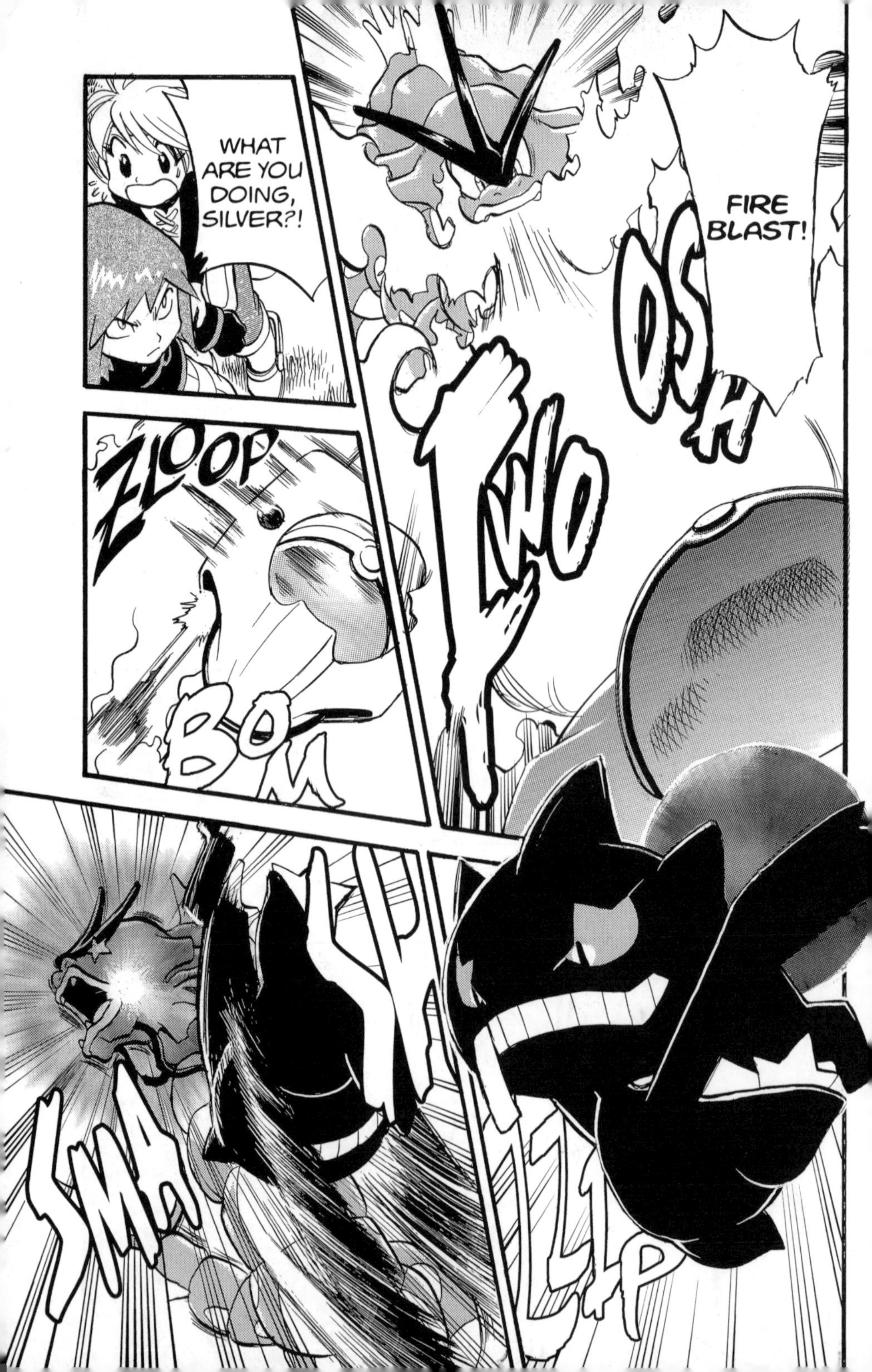
FIRE BLAST!
WHOOSH
WHAT ARE YOU DOING, SILVER?!
ZLOOP
BOOM

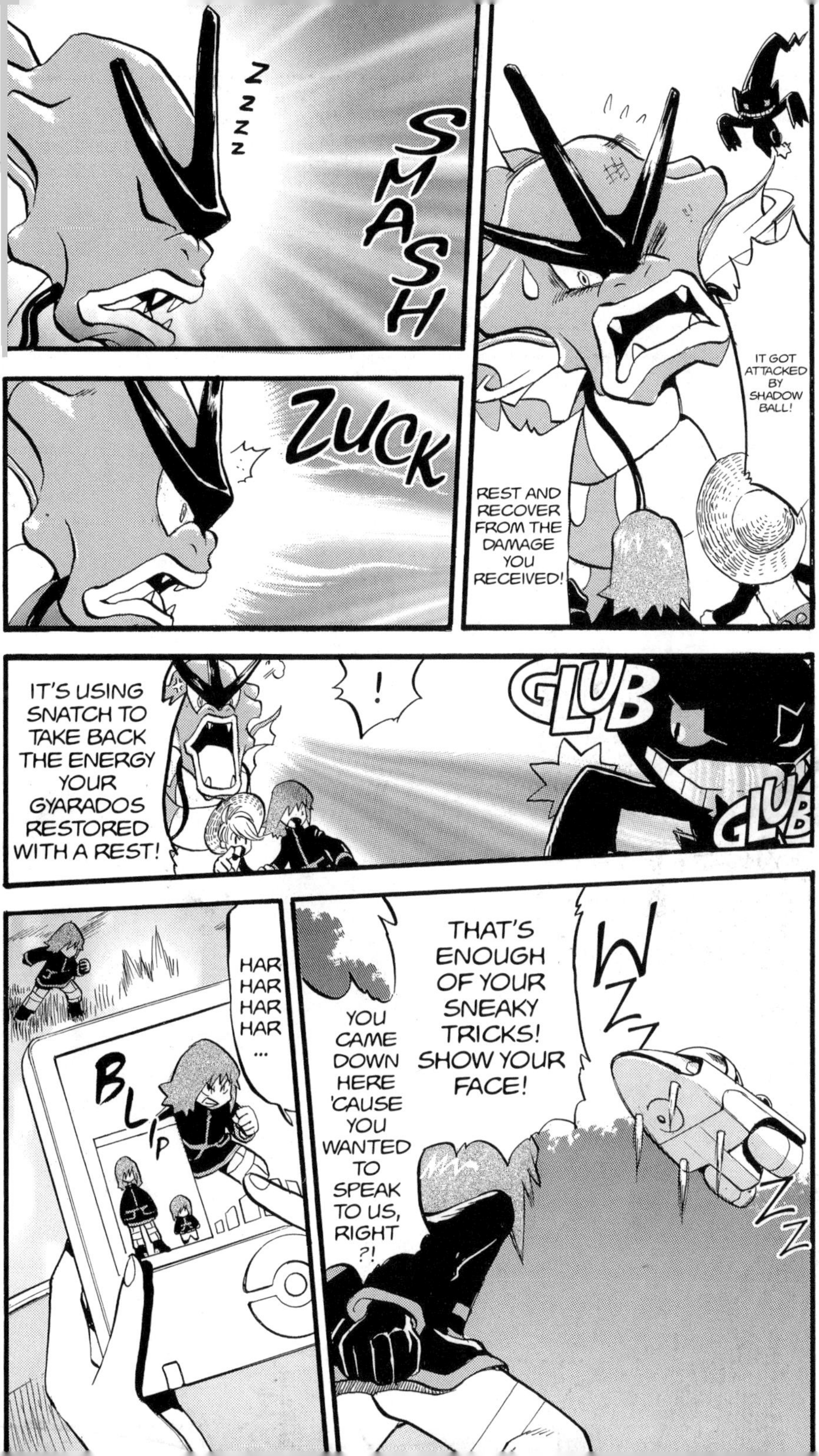
IT GOT ATTACKED BY SHADOW BALL!
REST AND RECOVER FROM THE DAMAGE YOU RECEIVED!
Z Z Z Z
SMASH
ZUCK
GLUB
GLUB
!
IT'S USING SNATCH TO TAKE BACK THE ENERGY YOUR GYARADOS RESTORED WITH A REST!
THAT'S ENOUGH OF YOUR SNEAKY TRICKS! SHOW YOUR FACE!
YOU CAME DOWN HERE 'CAUSE YOU WANTED TO SPEAK TO US, RIGHT?!
HAR HAR HAR HAR ...
BLIP

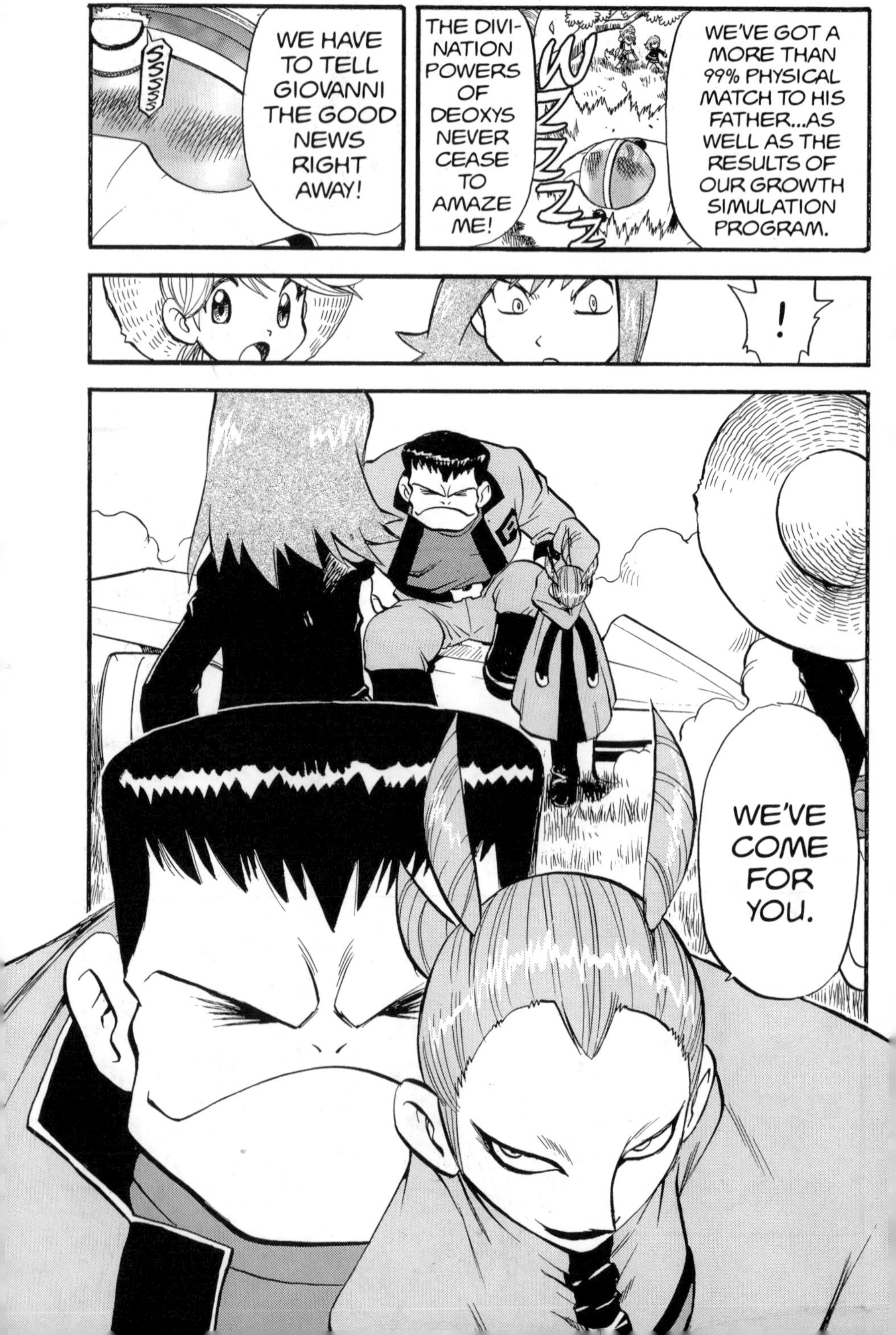
WE'VE GOT A MORE THAN 99% PHYSICAL MATCH TO HIS FATHER...AS WELL AS THE RESULTS OF OUR GROWTH SIMULATION PROGRAM.
WZZZZZ
THE DIVI-NATION POWERS OF DEOXYS NEVER CEASE TO AMAZE ME!
SSSSSS
WE HAVE TO TELL GIOVANNI THE GOOD NEWS RIGHT AWAY!
!
WE'VE COME FOR YOU.

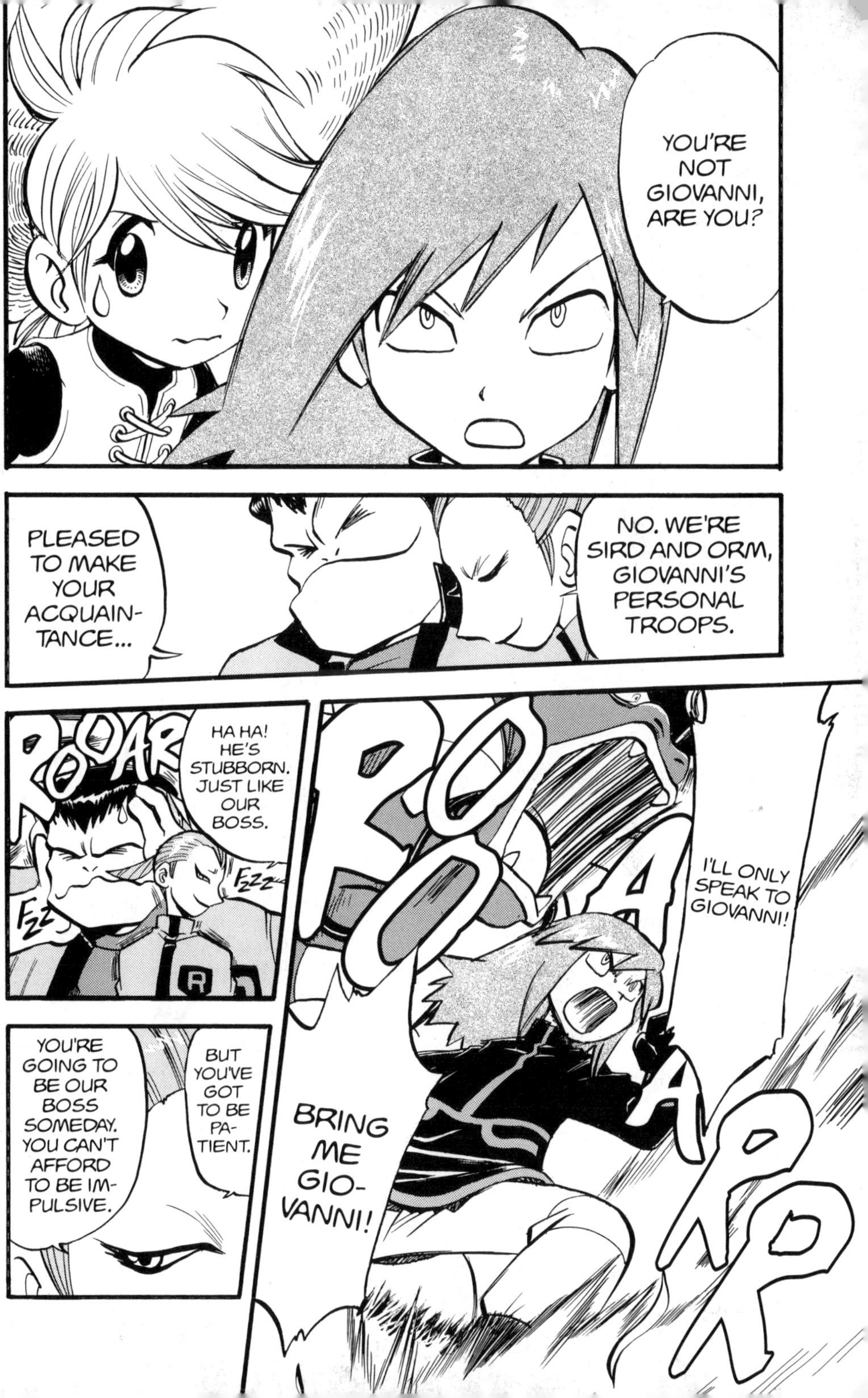
YOU'RE NOT GIOVANNI, ARE YOU?
NO. WE'RE SIRD AND ORM, GIOVANNI'S PERSONAL TROOPS.
PLEASED TO MAKE YOUR ACQUAINTANCE...
I'LL ONLY SPEAK TO GIOVANNI!
BRING ME GIO-VANNI!
ROOAR
HA HA! HE'S STUBBORN. JUST LIKE OUR BOSS.
FZZZ
FZZ
BUT YOU'VE GOT TO BE PA-TIENT.
YOU'RE GOING TO BE OUR BOSS SOMEDAY. YOU CAN'T AFFORD TO BE IM-PULSIVE.

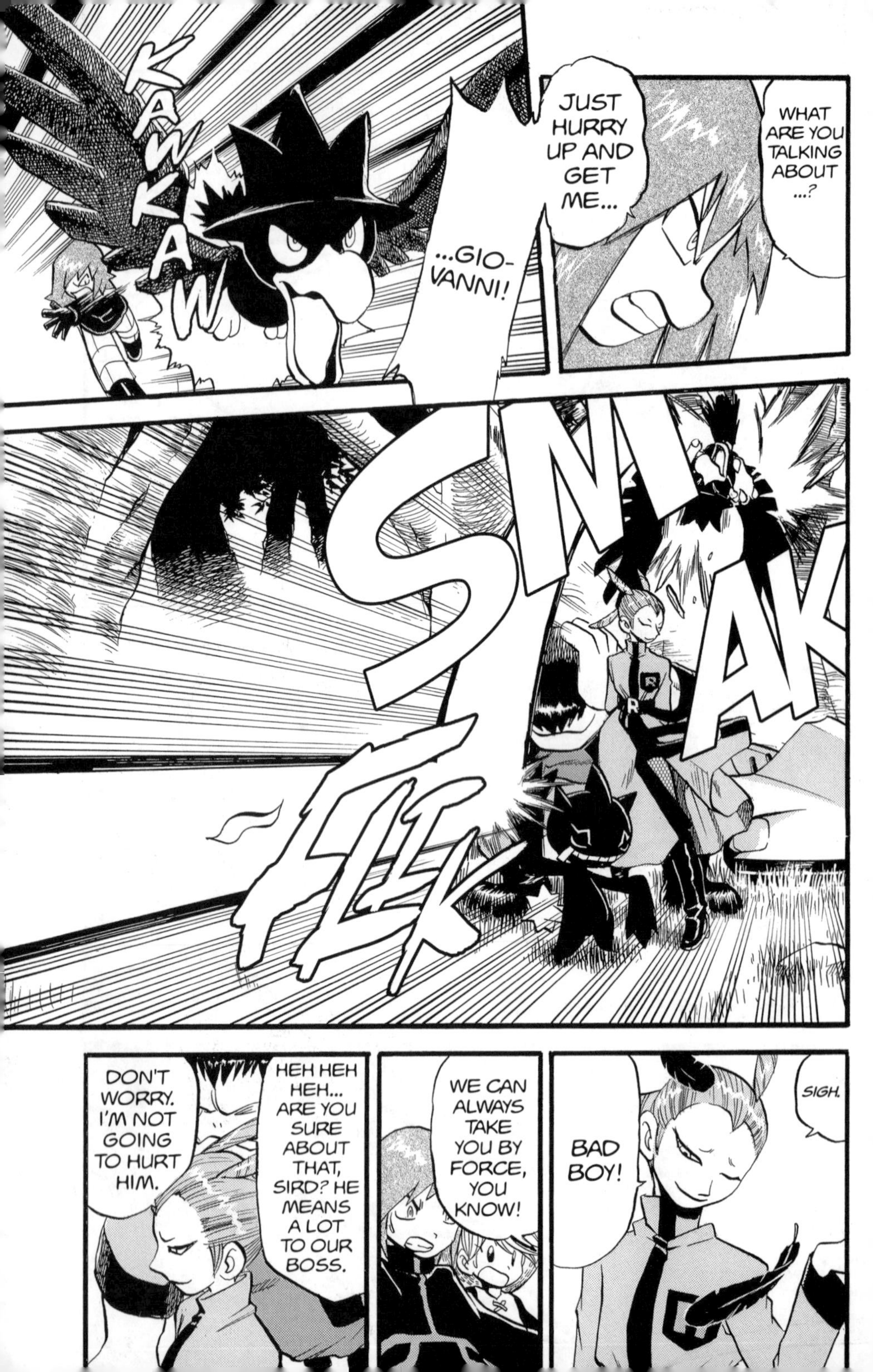
WHAT ARE YOU TALKING ABOUT ...?
JUST HURRY UP AND GET ME...
...GIO-VANNI!
KAW KAW
SMAK
FLIK
SIGH.
BAD BOY!
WE CAN ALWAYS TAKE YOU BY FORCE, YOU KNOW!
HEH HEH HEH... ARE YOU SURE ABOUT THAT, SIRD? HE MEANS A LOT TO OUR BOSS.
DON'T WORRY. I'M NOT GOING TO HURT HIM.

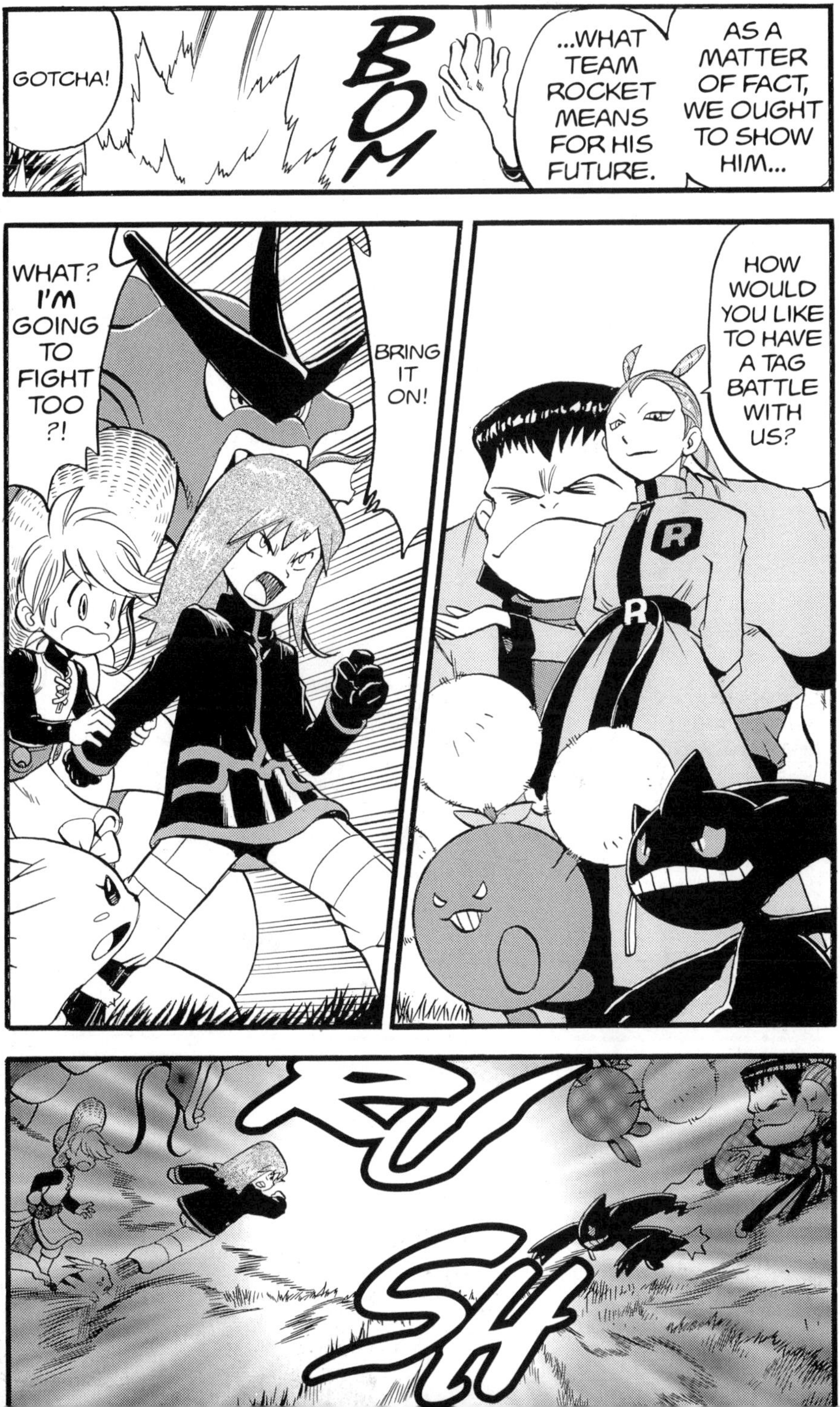
AS A MATTER OF FACT, WE OUGHT TO SHOW HIM...
...WHAT TEAM ROCKET MEANS FOR HIS FUTURE.
BOM
GOTCHA!
HOW WOULD YOU LIKE TO HAVE A TAG BATTLE WITH US?
BRING IT ON!
WHAT? **I'M** GOING TO FIGHT TOO?!
RUSH

C H A R A C T E R   P R O F I L E

LANETTE & BRIGETTE

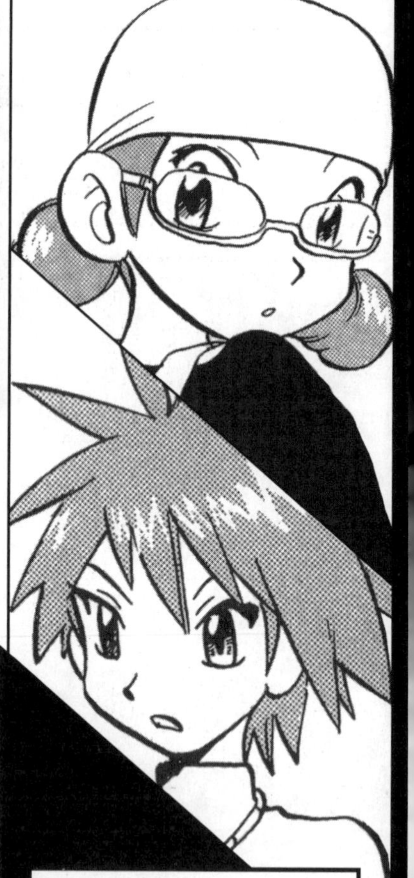

LANETTE & BRIGETTE

THESE TWO BRILLIANT SISTERS ARE IN CHARGE OF THE HOENN REGION POKÉMON TRANSPORTER SYSTEM. THEY ARE FRIENDS OF BILL AND CELIO, AND THE FOUR TECHNOLOGY DEVELOPERS OFTEN PROBLEM-SOLVE TOGETHER. BRIGETTE, THE OLDER SISTER, IS A LINEAR THINKER, WHILE LANETTE, THE RESTLESS YOUNGER SISTER, IS PRONE TO FLASHES OF INTUITION. THEY ARE POLAR OPPOSITES, BUT THEY COMPLEMENT WHAT THE OTHER LACKS. DURING THE SEVII ISLANDS INCIDENT, THEY AIDED BILL BY FIGURING OUT HOW A GEOGRAPHICAL LOCATION COULD INFLUENCE A POKÉMON'S FORM.

- Workplace: Route 114, Hoenn region

- Job: Pokémon Transporter System Developer (Lanette). Pokémon Storage Management (Brigette).

- Hobby: Finding bargains at the Lilycove Department Store (Lanette). Playing roulette at Mauville City (Brigette).

● Adventure 290 ●
A Well-Journeyed Jumpluff

Pokémon Adventures FireRed & LeafGreen The Fifth Chapter

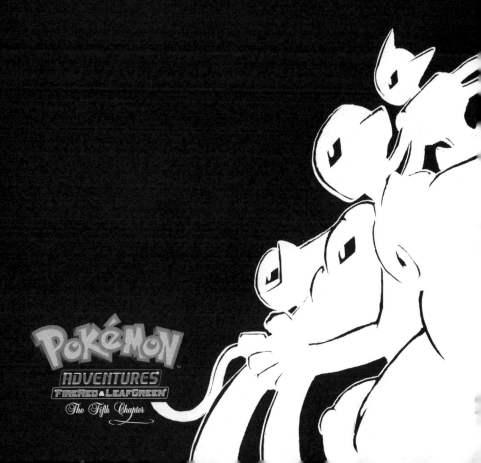

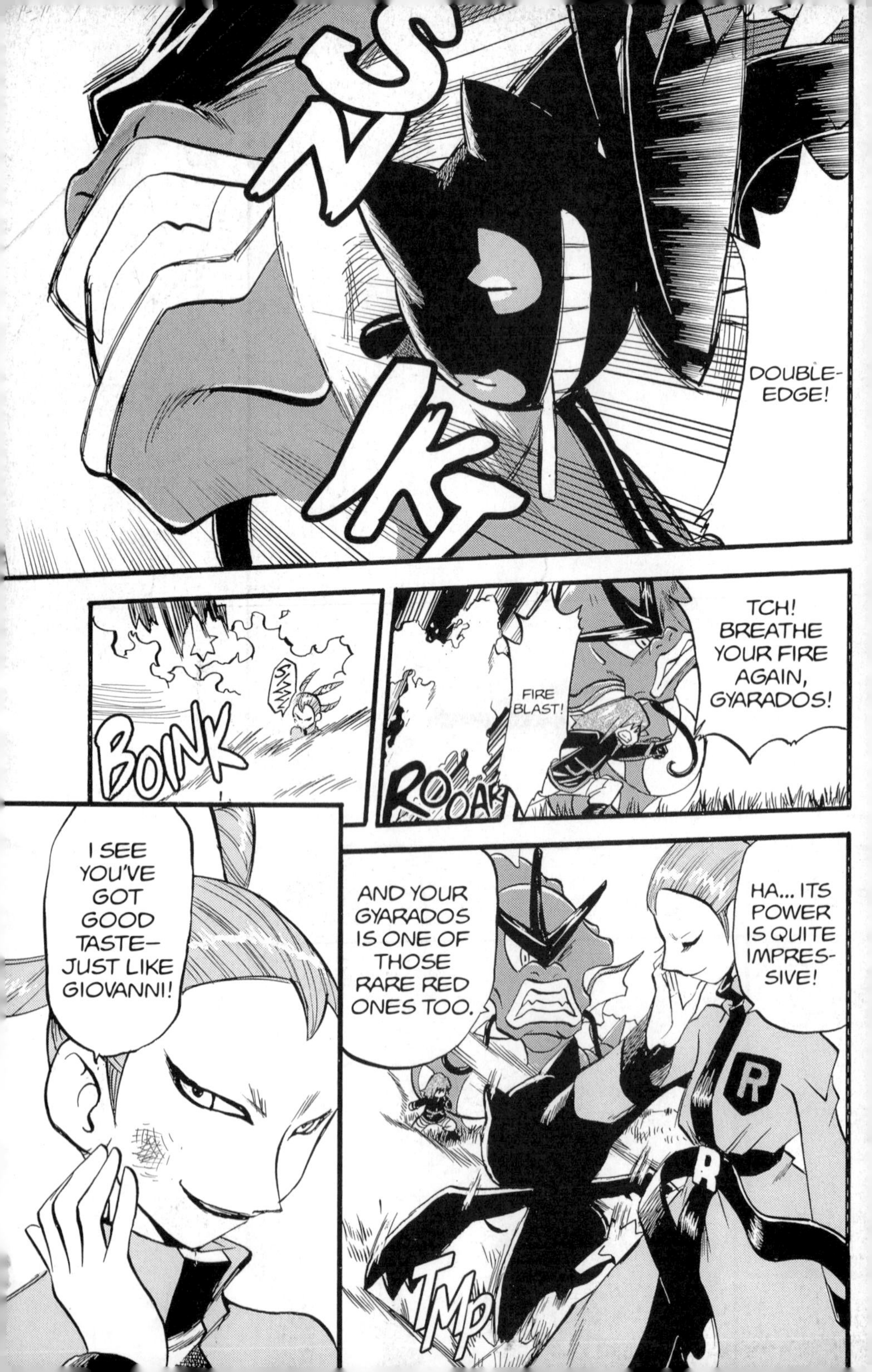
DOUBLE-EDGE!
TCH! BREATHE YOUR FIRE AGAIN, GYARADOS!
FIRE BLAST!
ROOAR
BOINK
HA... ITS POWER IS QUITE IMPRESSIVE!
AND YOUR GYARADOS IS ONE OF THOSE RARE RED ONES TOO.
TMP
I SEE YOU'VE GOT GOOD TASTE—JUST LIKE GIOVANNI!

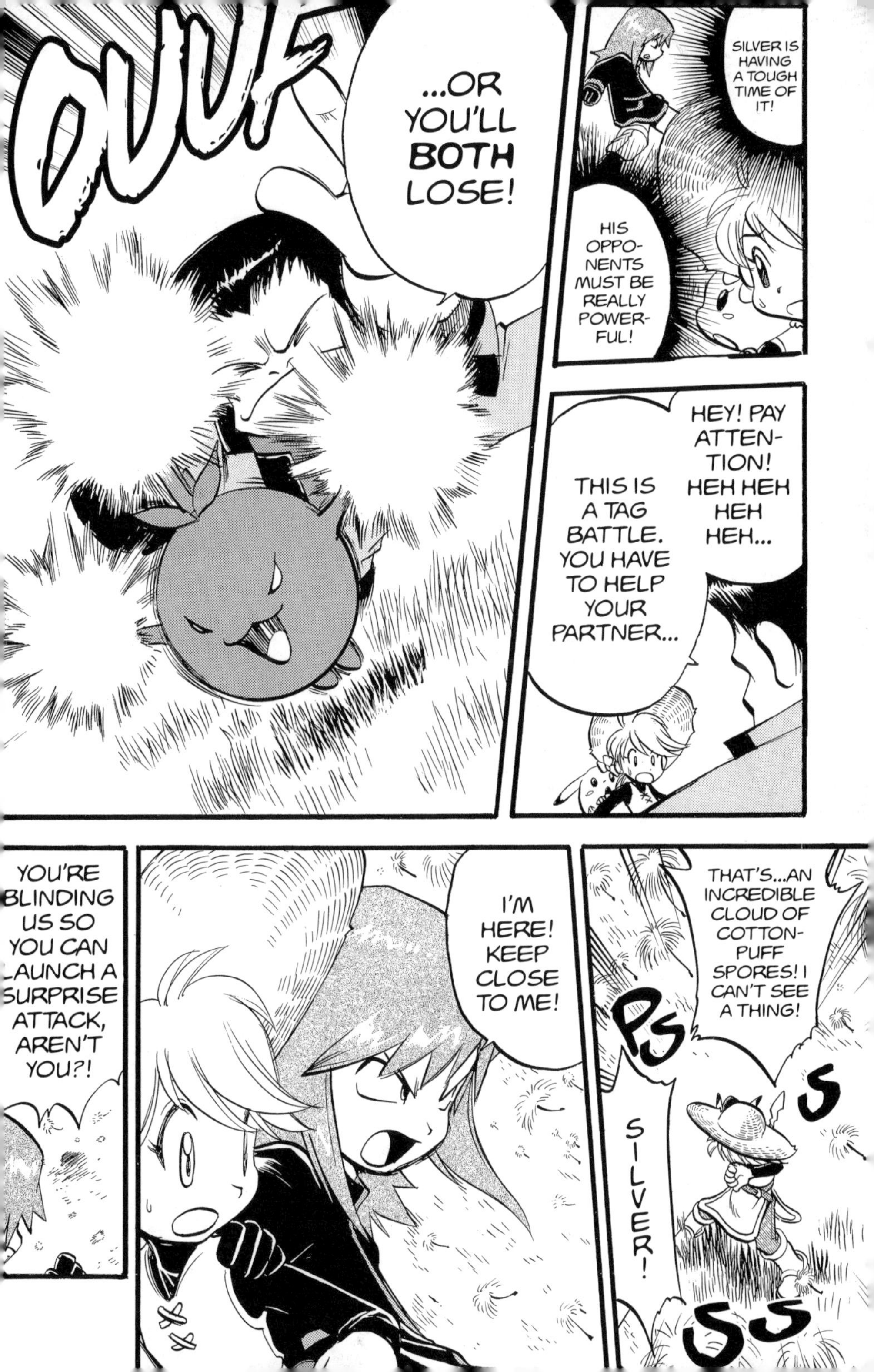
SILVER IS HAVING A TOUGH TIME OF IT!
HIS OPPONENTS MUST BE REALLY POWERFUL!
HEY! PAY ATTENTION! HEH HEH HEH HEH...
THIS IS A TAG BATTLE. YOU HAVE TO HELP YOUR PARTNER...
...OR YOU'LL BOTH LOSE!
OUUF
THAT'S...AN INCREDIBLE CLOUD OF COTTON-PUFF SPORES! I CAN'T SEE A THING!
PSS
S
SILVER!
SS
I'M HERE! KEEP CLOSE TO ME!
YOU'RE BLINDING US SO YOU CAN LAUNCH A SURPRISE ATTACK, AREN'T YOU?!

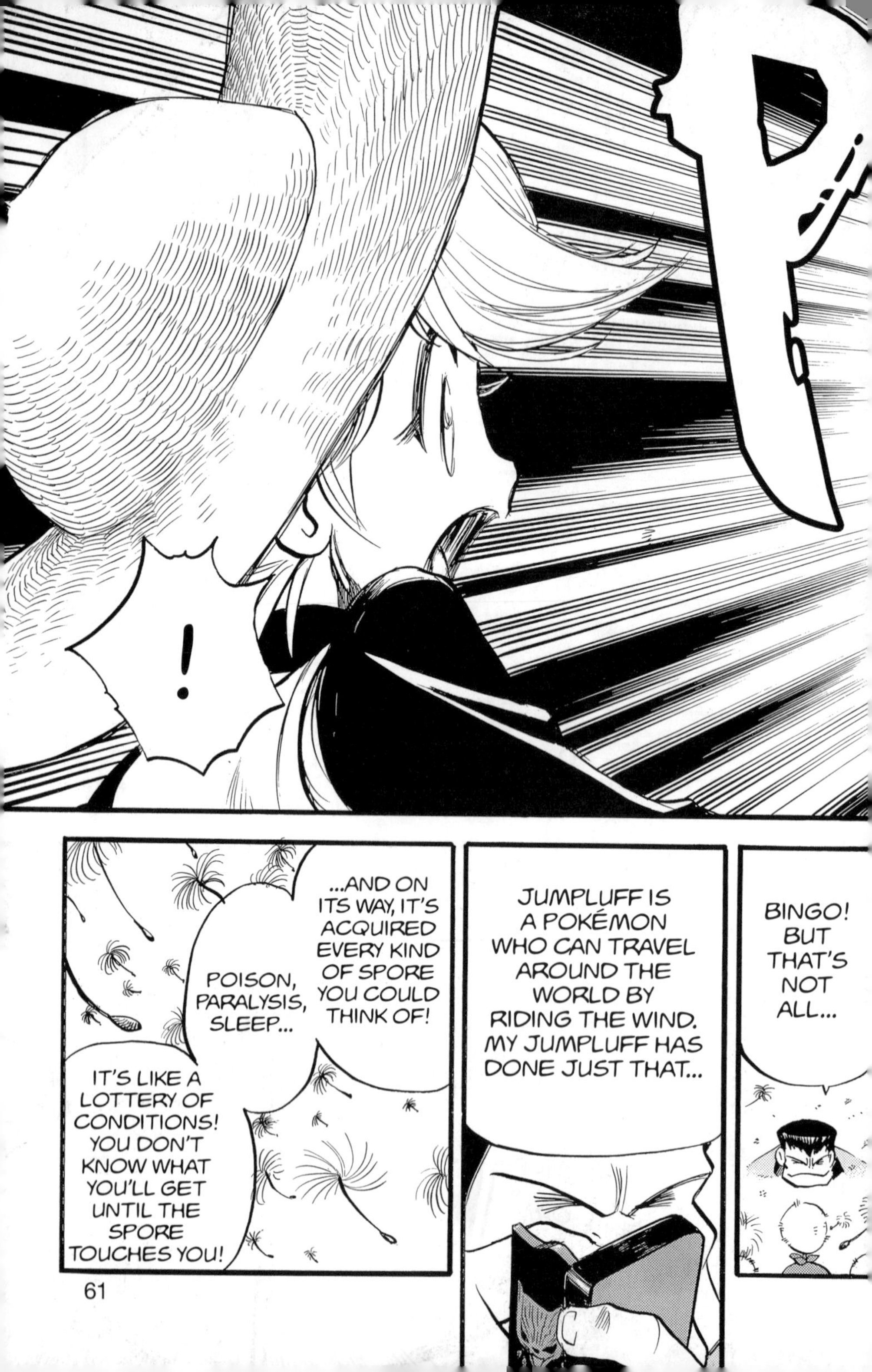
!
BINGO! BUT THAT'S NOT ALL...
JUMPLUFF IS A POKÉMON WHO CAN TRAVEL AROUND THE WORLD BY RIDING THE WIND. MY JUMPLUFF HAS DONE JUST THAT...
...AND ON ITS WAY, IT'S ACQUIRED EVERY KIND OF SPORE YOU COULD THINK OF!
POISON, PARALYSIS, SLEEP...
IT'S LIKE A LOTTERY OF CONDITIONS! YOU DON'T KNOW WHAT YOU'LL GET UNTIL THE SPORE TOUCHES YOU!

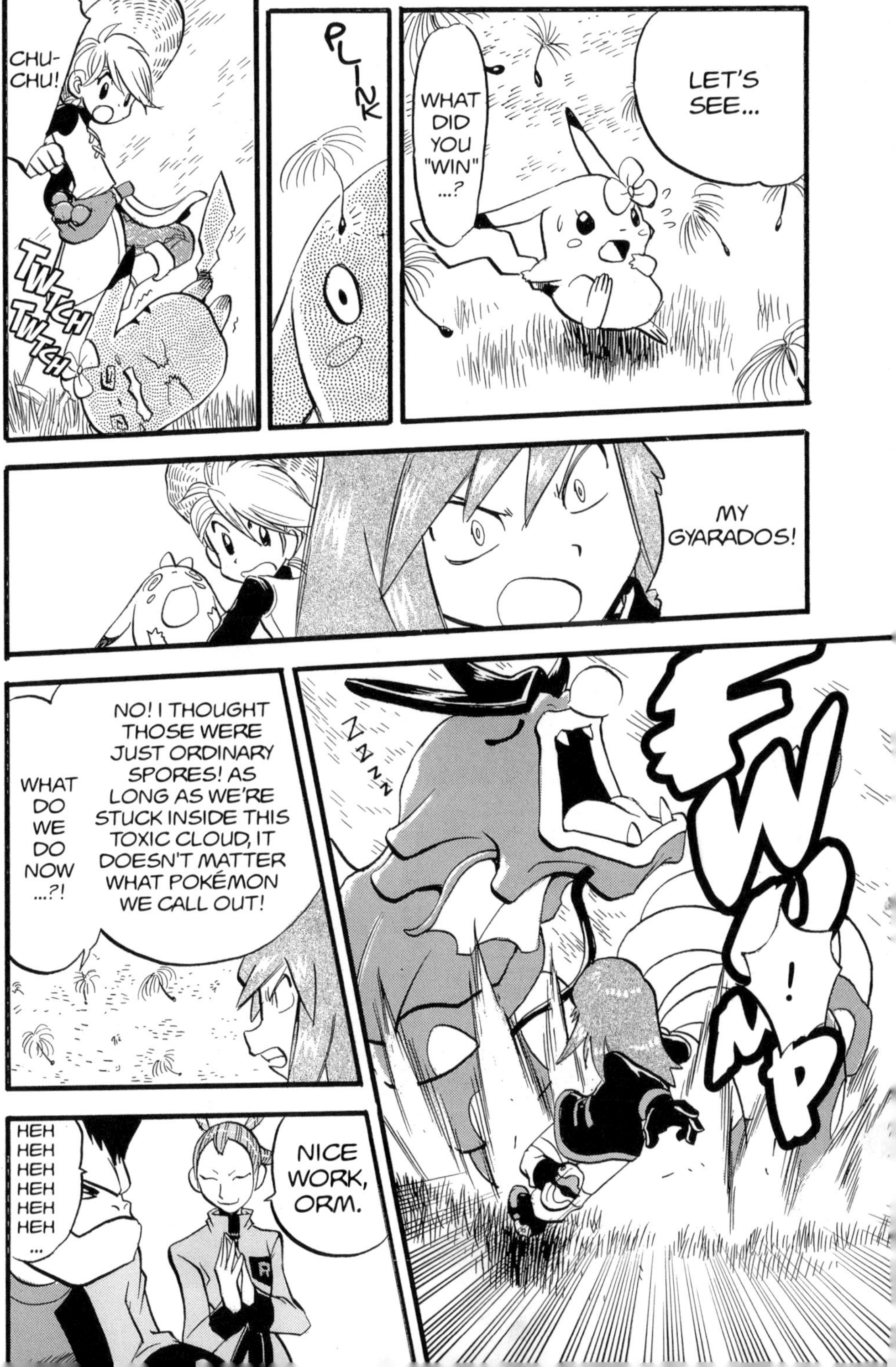

LET'S SEE...
WHAT DID YOU "WIN" ...?
PLINK
CHU-CHU!
TWITCH TWITCH
MY GYARADOS!
FWUMP!
NO! I THOUGHT THOSE WERE JUST ORDINARY SPORES! AS LONG AS WE'RE STUCK INSIDE THIS TOXIC CLOUD, IT DOESN'T MATTER WHAT POKÉMON WE CALL OUT!
WHAT DO WE DO NOW ...?!
NICE WORK, ORM.
HEH HEH HEH HEH HEH HEH ...

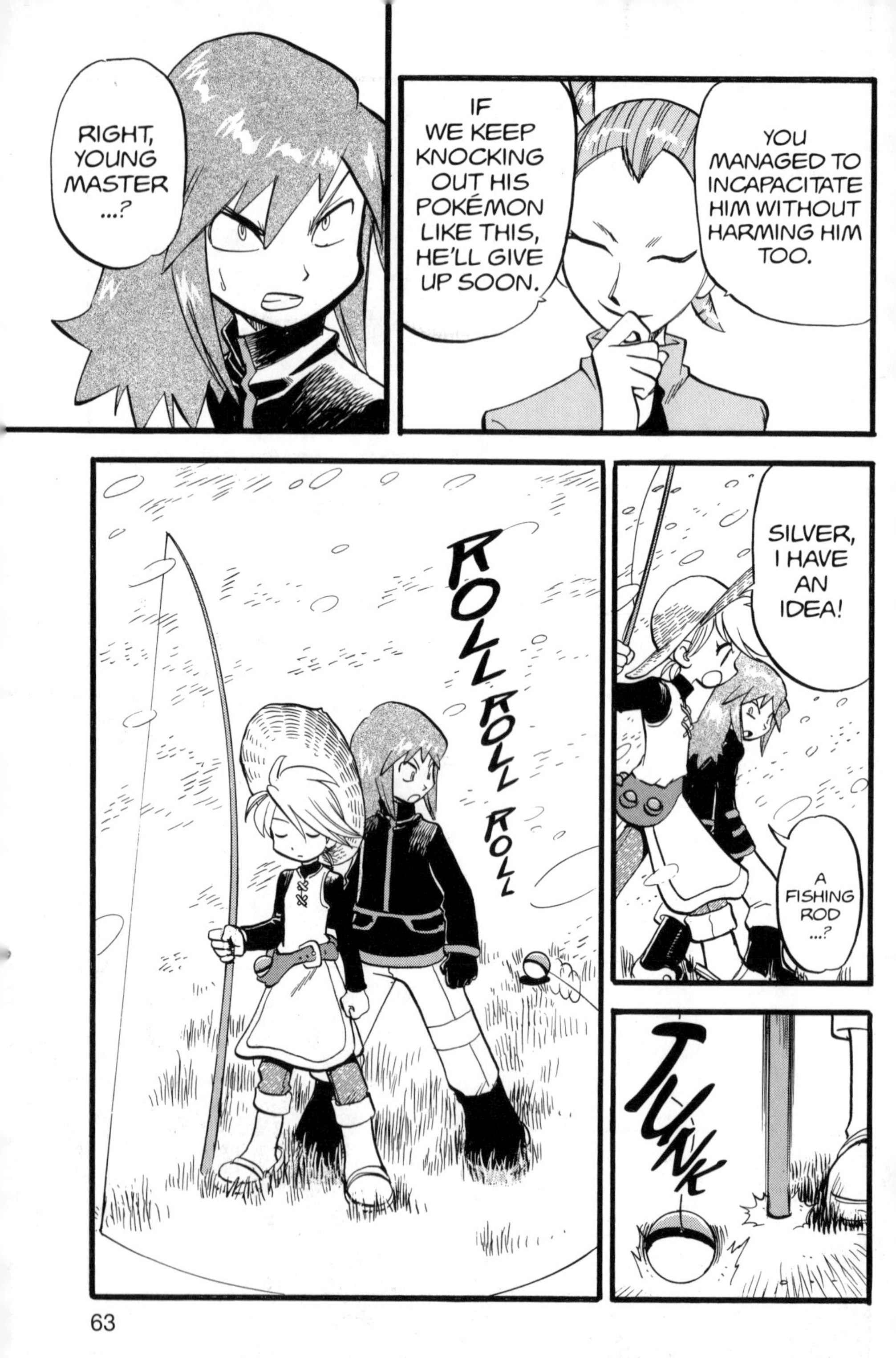
YOU MANAGED TO INCAPACITATE HIM WITHOUT HARMING HIM TOO.
IF WE KEEP KNOCKING OUT HIS POKÉMON LIKE THIS, HE'LL GIVE UP SOON.
RIGHT, YOUNG MASTER ...?
SILVER, I HAVE AN IDEA!
A FISHING ROD ...?
TUNK
ROLL ROLL ROLL ROLL

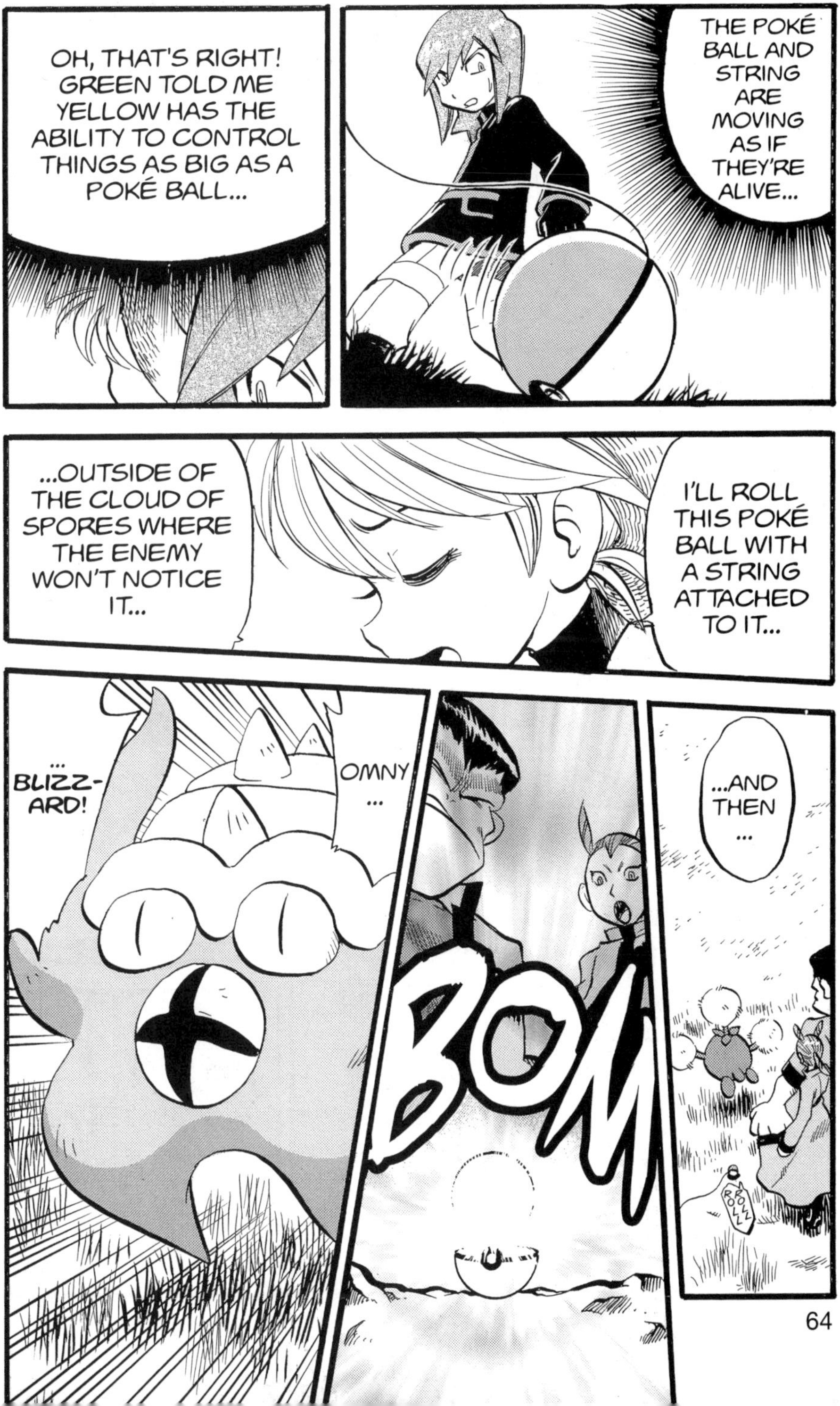
THE POKÉ BALL AND STRING ARE MOVING AS IF THEY'RE ALIVE...
OH, THAT'S RIGHT! GREEN TOLD ME YELLOW HAS THE ABILITY TO CONTROL THINGS AS BIG AS A POKÉ BALL...
I'LL ROLL THIS POKÉ BALL WITH A STRING ATTACHED TO IT...
...OUTSIDE OF THE CLOUD OF SPORES WHERE THE ENEMY WON'T NOTICE IT...
...AND THEN ...
ROLL ROLL
OMNY ...
BOM
... BLIZZ-ARD!

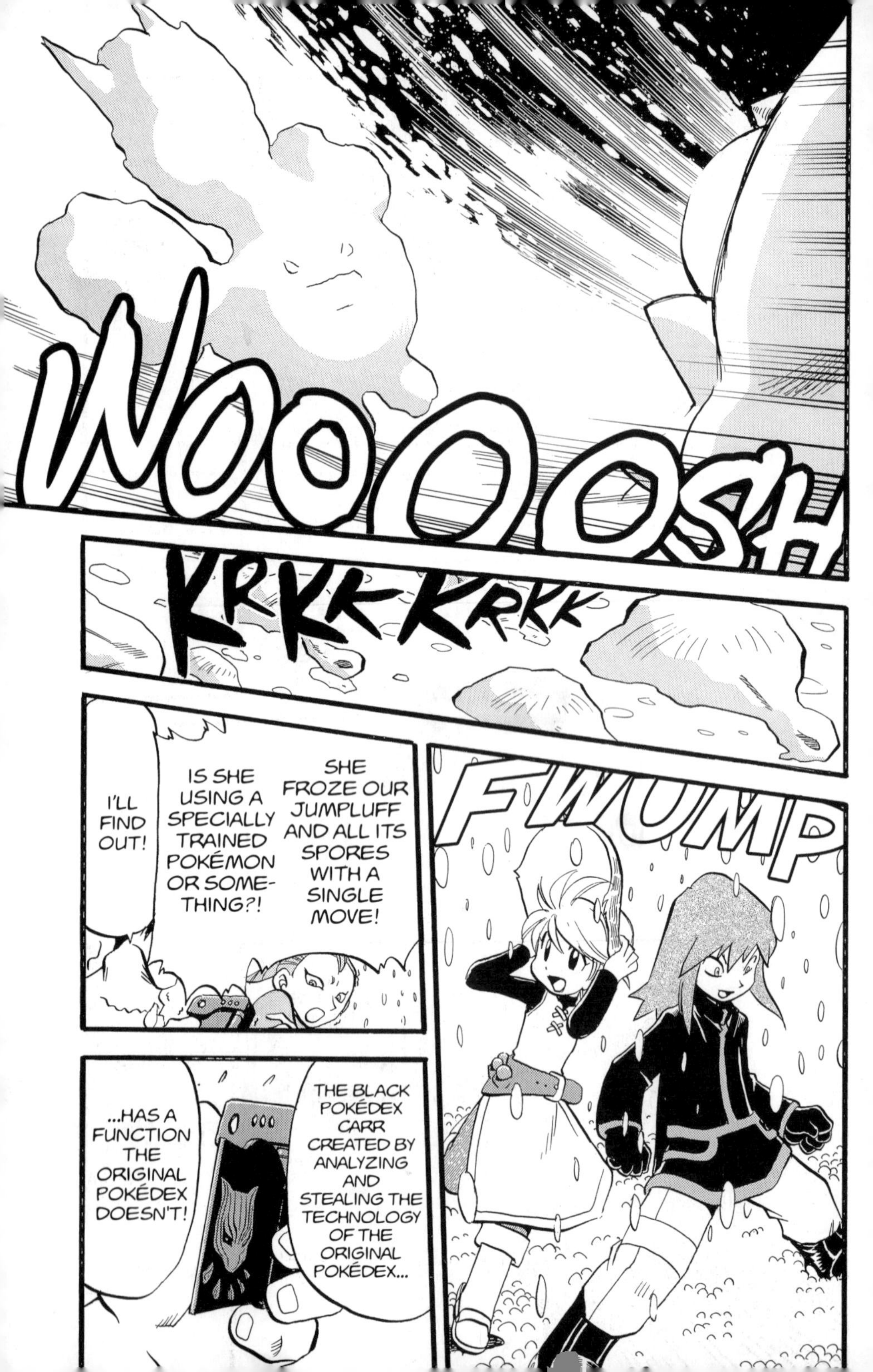
WOOOOSH
KRKKKRKK
FWUMP
SHE FROZE OUR JUMPLUFF AND ALL ITS SPORES WITH A SINGLE MOVE!
IS SHE USING A SPECIALLY TRAINED POKÉMON OR SOME-THING?!
I'LL FIND OUT!
THE BLACK POKÉDEX CARR CREATED BY ANALYZING AND STEALING THE TECHNOLOGY OF THE ORIGINAL POKÉDEX...
...HAS A FUNCTION THE ORIGINAL POKÉDEX DOESN'T!

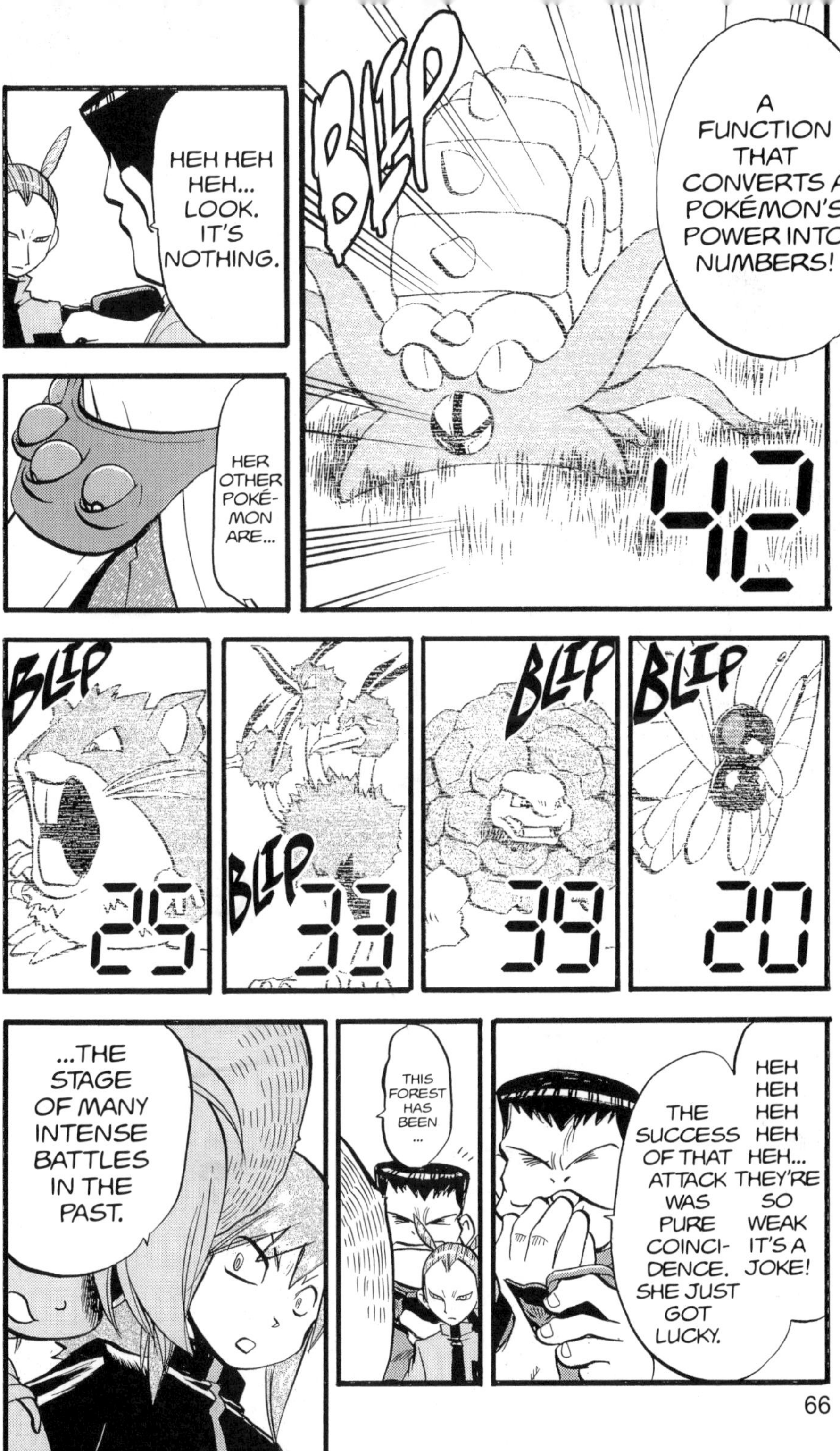
BLIP
A FUNCTION THAT CONVERTS A POKÉMON'S POWER INTO NUMBERS!
42
HEH HEH HEH... LOOK. IT'S NOTHING.
HER OTHER POKÉ-MON ARE...
BLIP
20
BLIP
39
BLIP
33
BLIP
25
HEH HEH HEH HEH HEH... THEY'RE SO WEAK IT'S A JOKE!
THE SUCCESS OF THAT ATTACK WAS PURE COINCI-DENCE. SHE JUST GOT LUCKY.
THIS FOREST HAS BEEN ...
...THE STAGE OF MANY INTENSE BATTLES IN THE PAST.

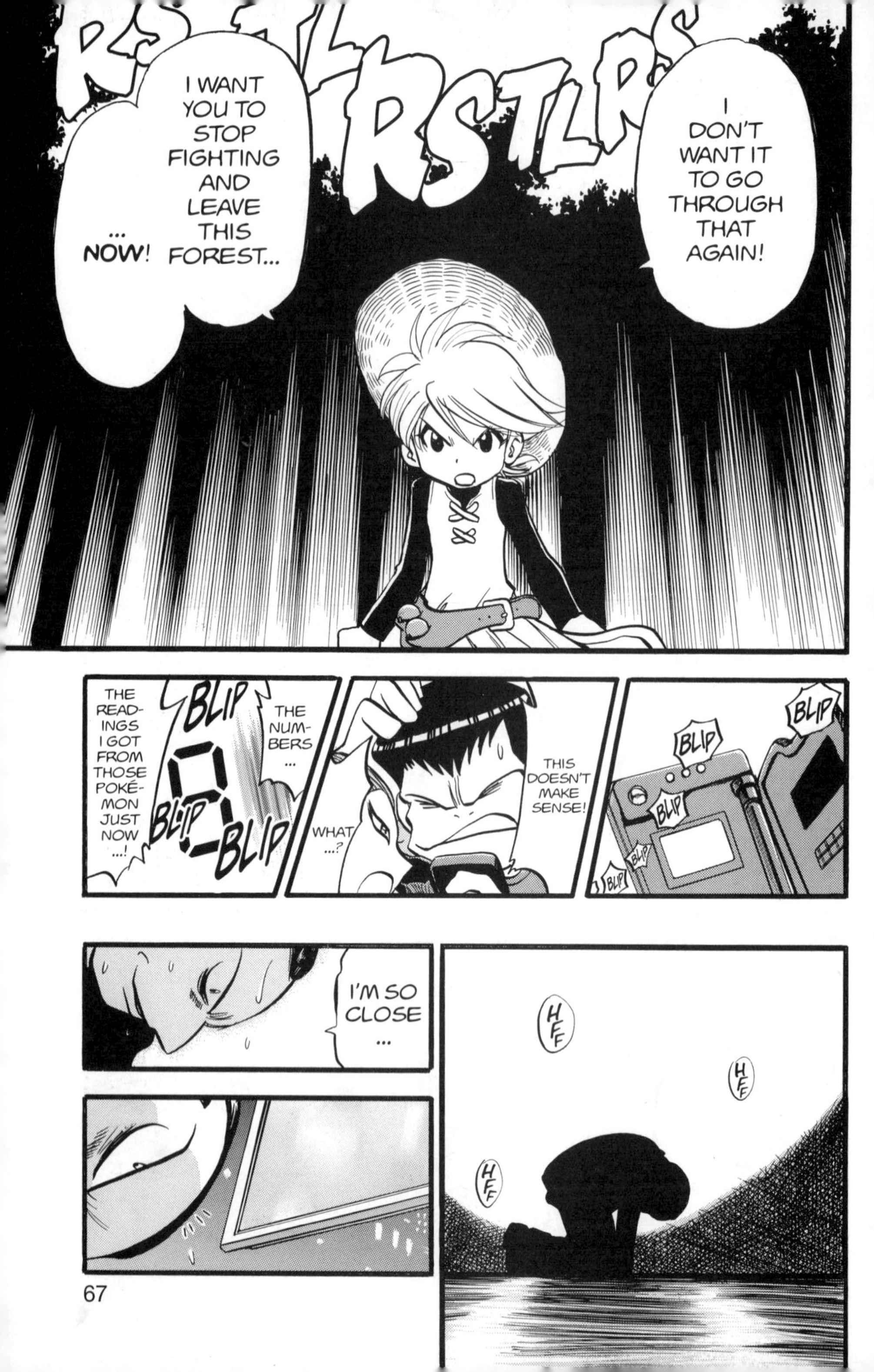
RSTLRS
I DON'T WANT IT TO GO THROUGH THAT AGAIN!
I WANT YOU TO STOP FIGHTING AND LEAVE THIS FOREST...
...NOW!
BLIP
BLIP
BLIP
BLIP
BLIP
BLIP
THIS DOESN'T MAKE SENSE!
WHAT...?
THE NUMBERS...
BLIP
BLIP
BLIP
THE READINGS I GOT FROM THOSE POKÉMON JUST NOW...!
HFF
HFF
HFF
I'M SO CLOSE...

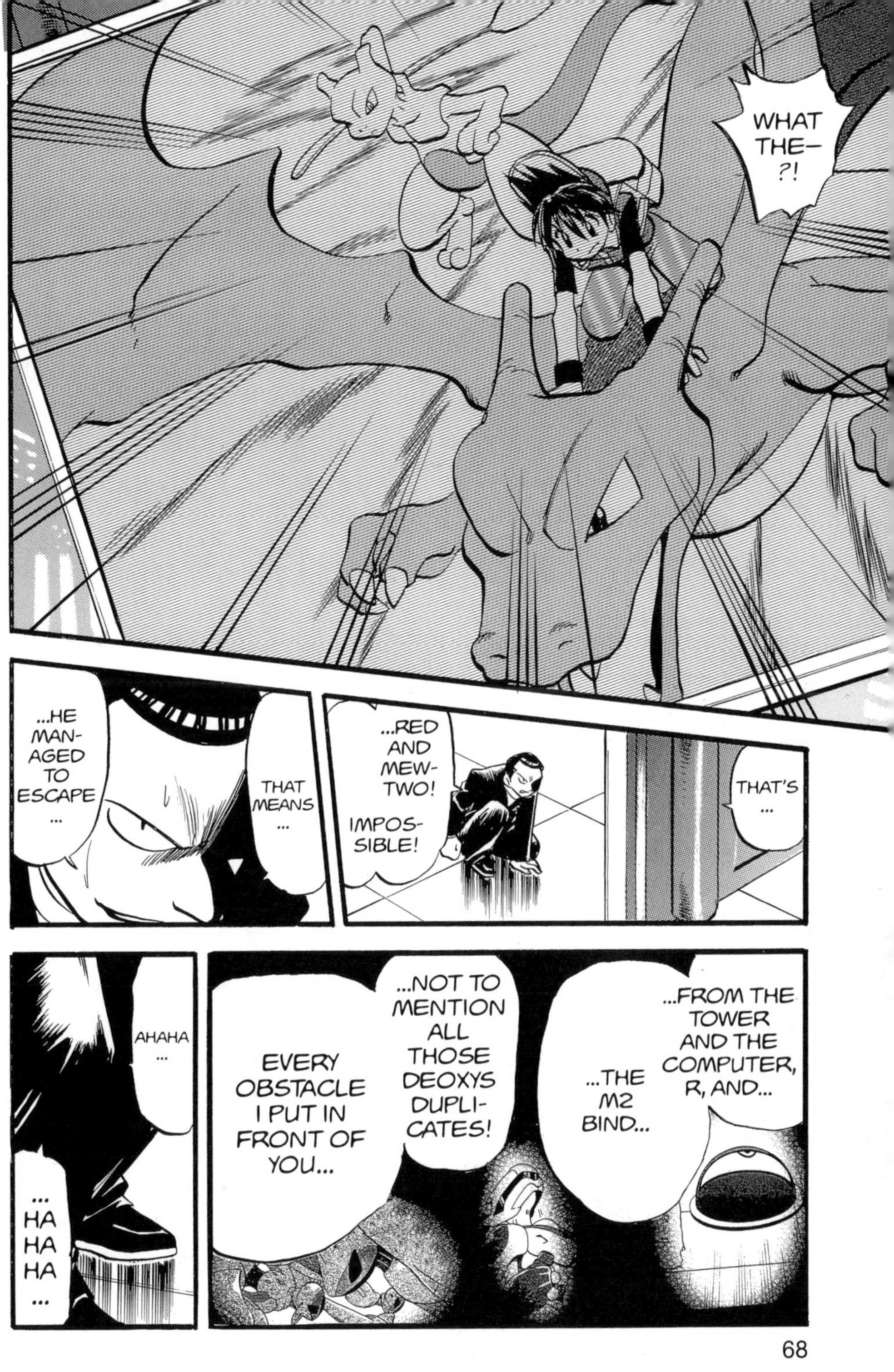
WHAT THE—?!
THAT'S ...
...RED AND MEW-TWO!
IMPOS-SIBLE!
THAT MEANS ...
...HE MAN-AGED TO ESCAPE ...
...FROM THE TOWER AND THE COMPUTER, R, AND...
...THE M2 BIND...
...NOT TO MENTION ALL THOSE DEOXYS DUPLI-CATES!
EVERY OBSTACLE I PUT IN FRONT OF YOU...
AHAHA ...
... HA HA HA ...

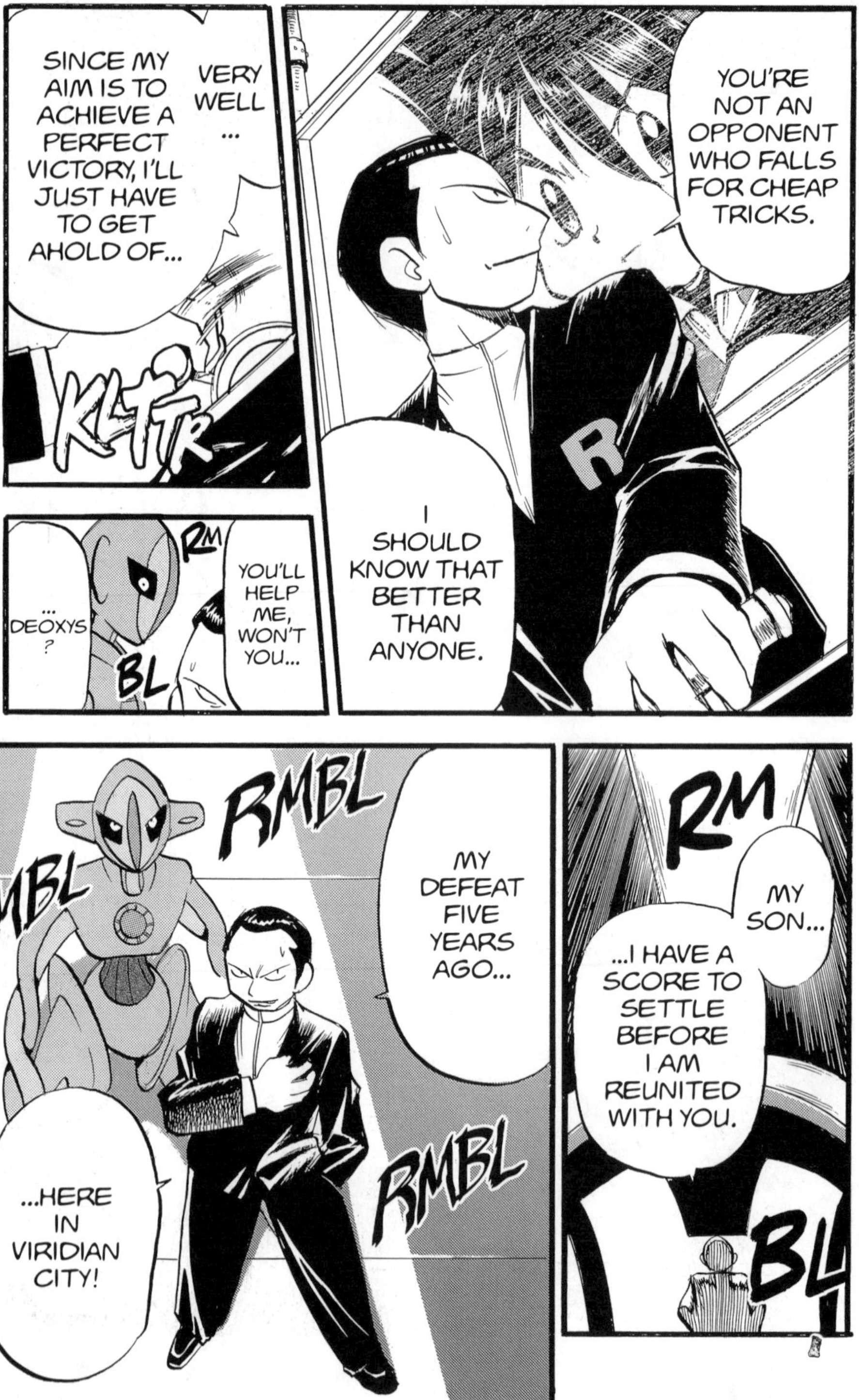
YOU'RE NOT AN OPPONENT WHO FALLS FOR CHEAP TRICKS.
I SHOULD KNOW THAT BETTER THAN ANYONE.
VERY WELL...
SINCE MY AIM IS TO ACHIEVE A PERFECT VICTORY, I'LL JUST HAVE TO GET AHOLD OF...
KLTTR
YOU'LL HELP ME, WON'T YOU...
RM
BL
...DEOXYS?
RM
MY SON...
...I HAVE A SCORE TO SETTLE BEFORE I AM REUNITED WITH YOU.
BL
RMBL
MY DEFEAT FIVE YEARS AGO...
RMBL
...HERE IN VIRIDIAN CITY!
RMBL

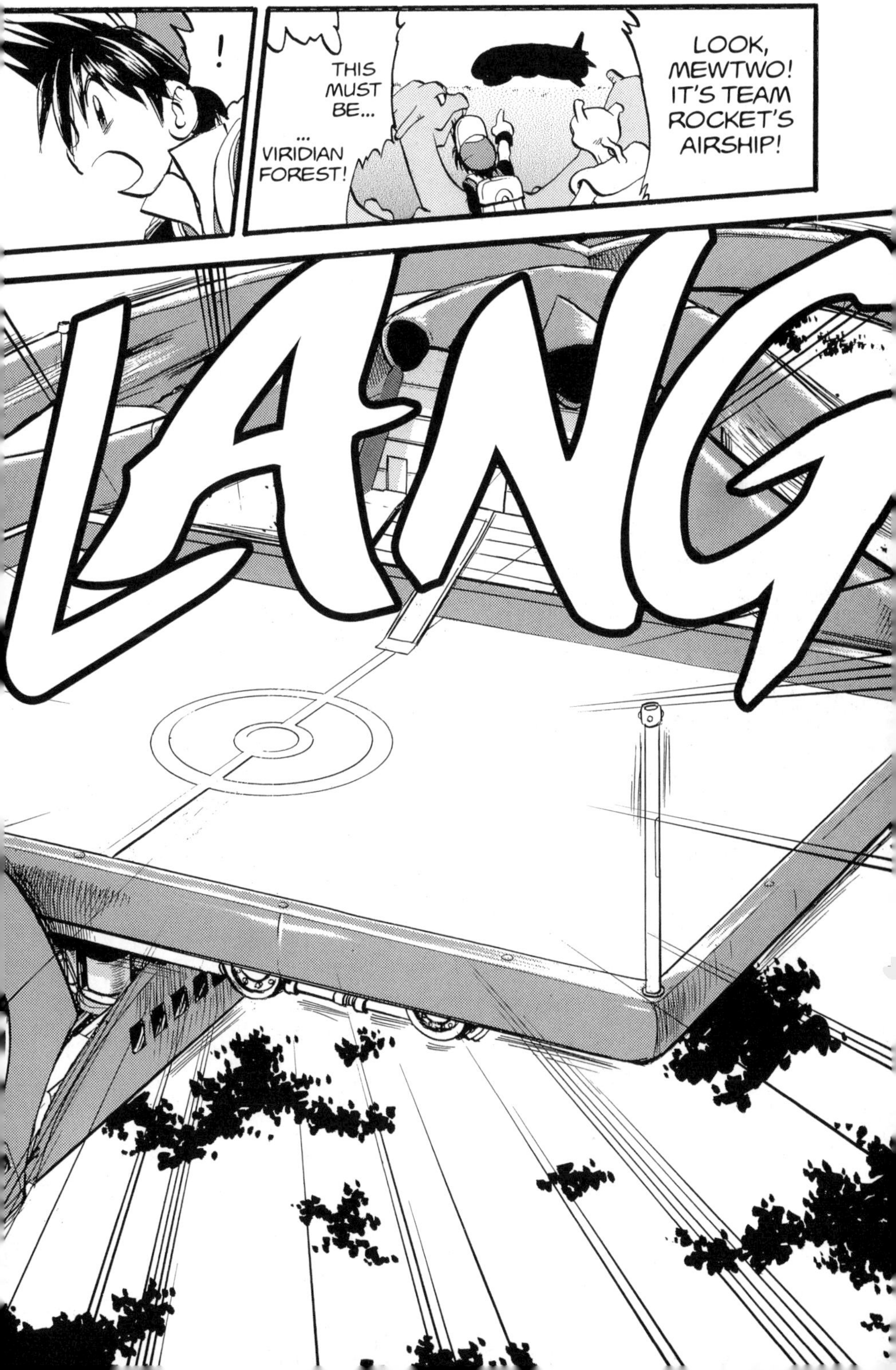
LOOK, MEWTWO! IT'S TEAM ROCKET'S AIRSHIP!
THIS MUST BE...
...VIRIDIAN FOREST!
!
LANG

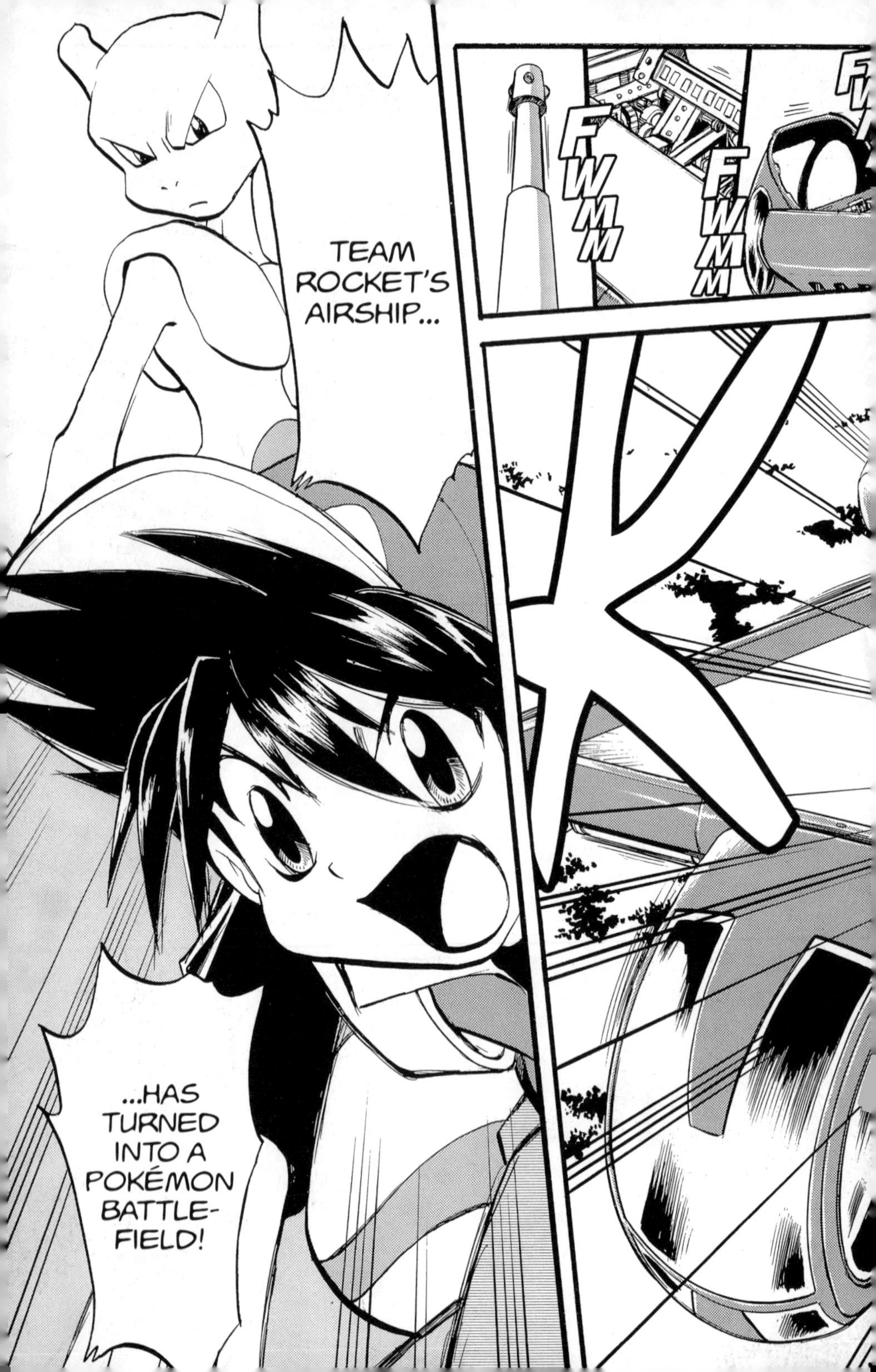
FWMM
FWMM
TEAM ROCKET'S AIRSHIP...
...HAS TURNED INTO A POKÉMON BATTLE-FIELD!

● Adventure 291 ●
Can Mewtwo Dish It Out with a Spoon?

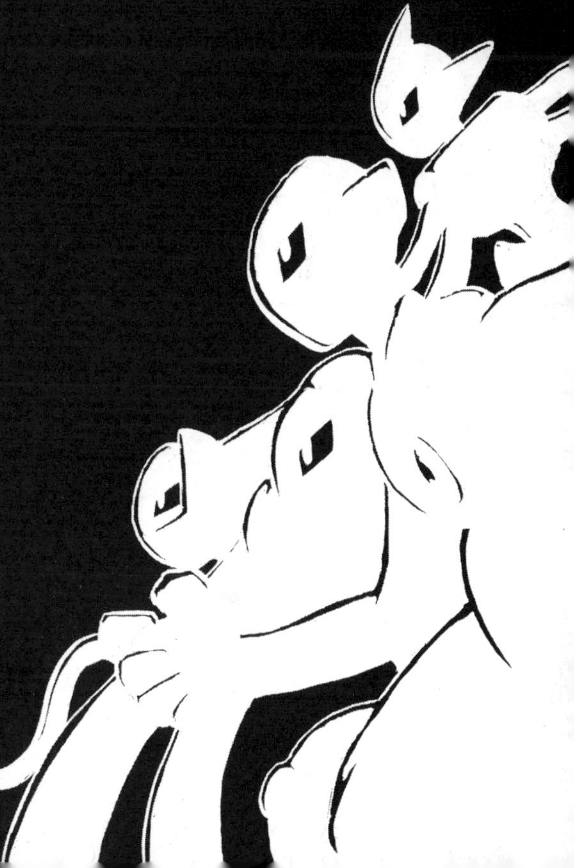

Pokémon Adventures
FireRed & LeafGreen
The Fifth Chapter

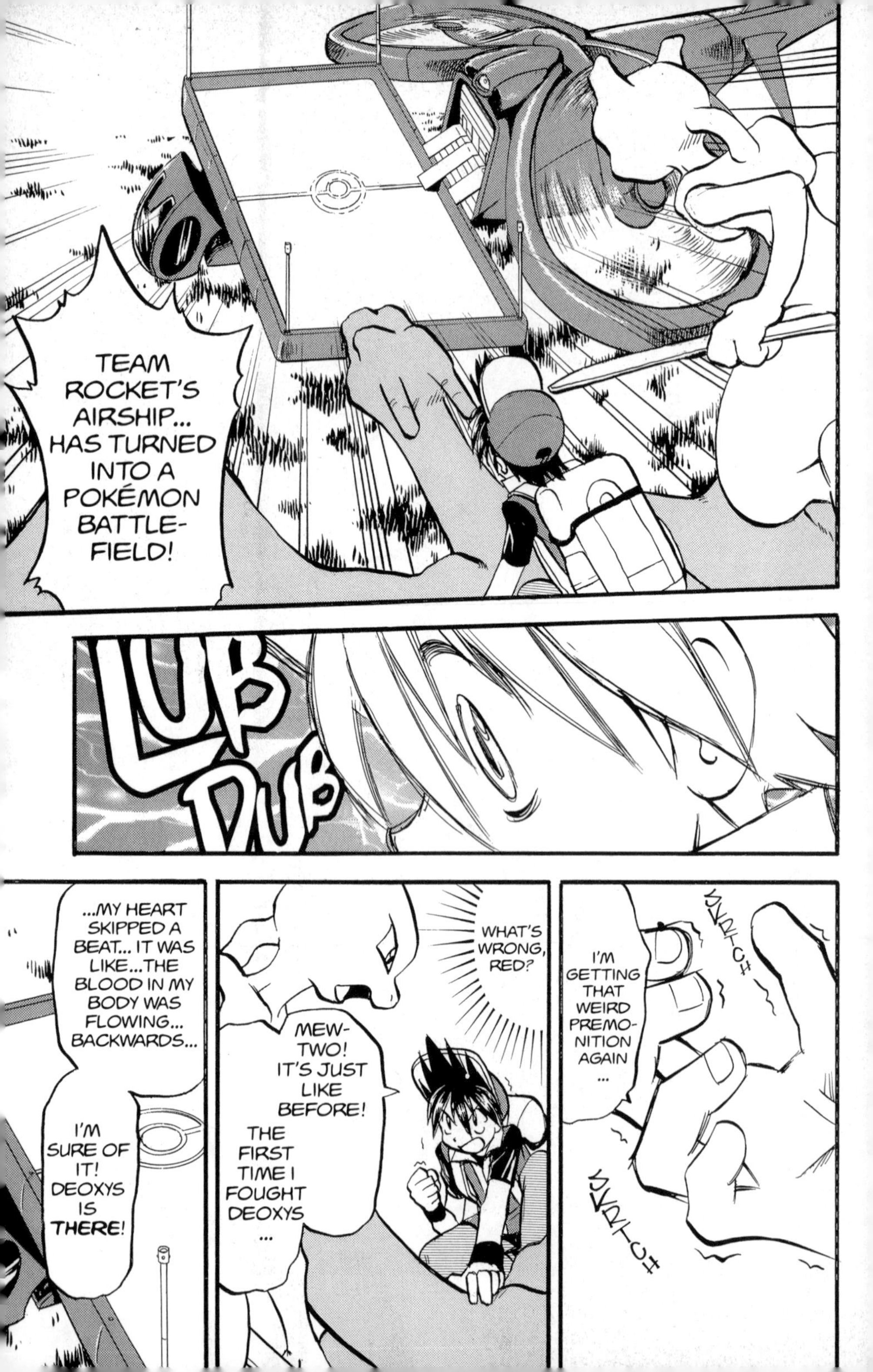
TEAM ROCKET'S AIRSHIP... HAS TURNED INTO A POKÉMON BATTLE-FIELD!
LUB
DUB
I'M GETTING THAT WEIRD PREMO-NITION AGAIN ...
SVRTCH
SVRTCH
WHAT'S WRONG, RED?
MEW-TWO! IT'S JUST LIKE BEFORE!
THE FIRST TIME I FOUGHT DEOXYS ...
...MY HEART SKIPPED A BEAT... IT WAS LIKE...THE BLOOD IN MY BODY WAS FLOWING... BACKWARDS...
I'M SURE OF IT! DEOXYS IS **THERE**!

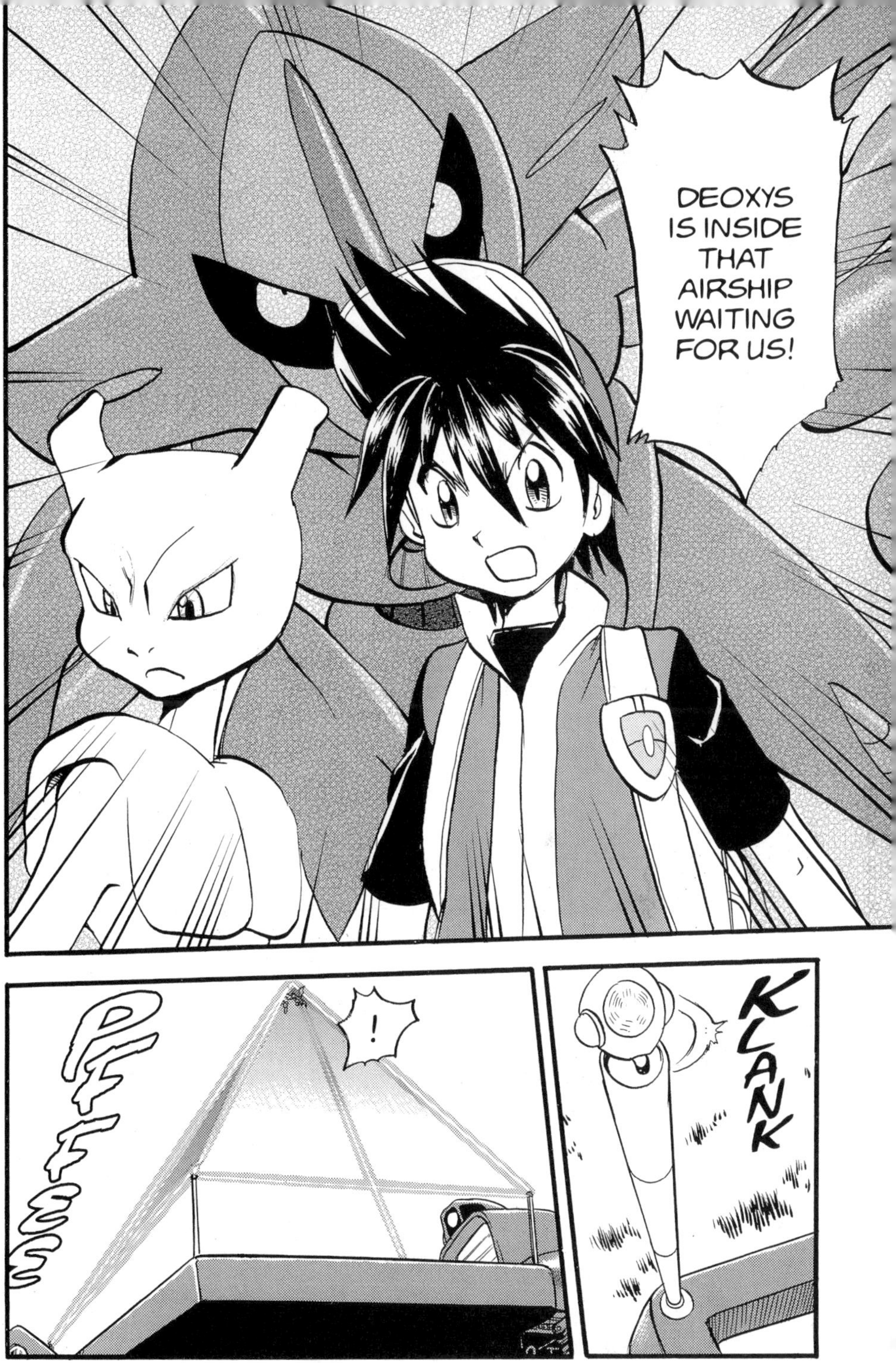
DEOXYS IS INSIDE THAT AIRSHIP WAITING FOR US!
K'LANK
!
PFFEE

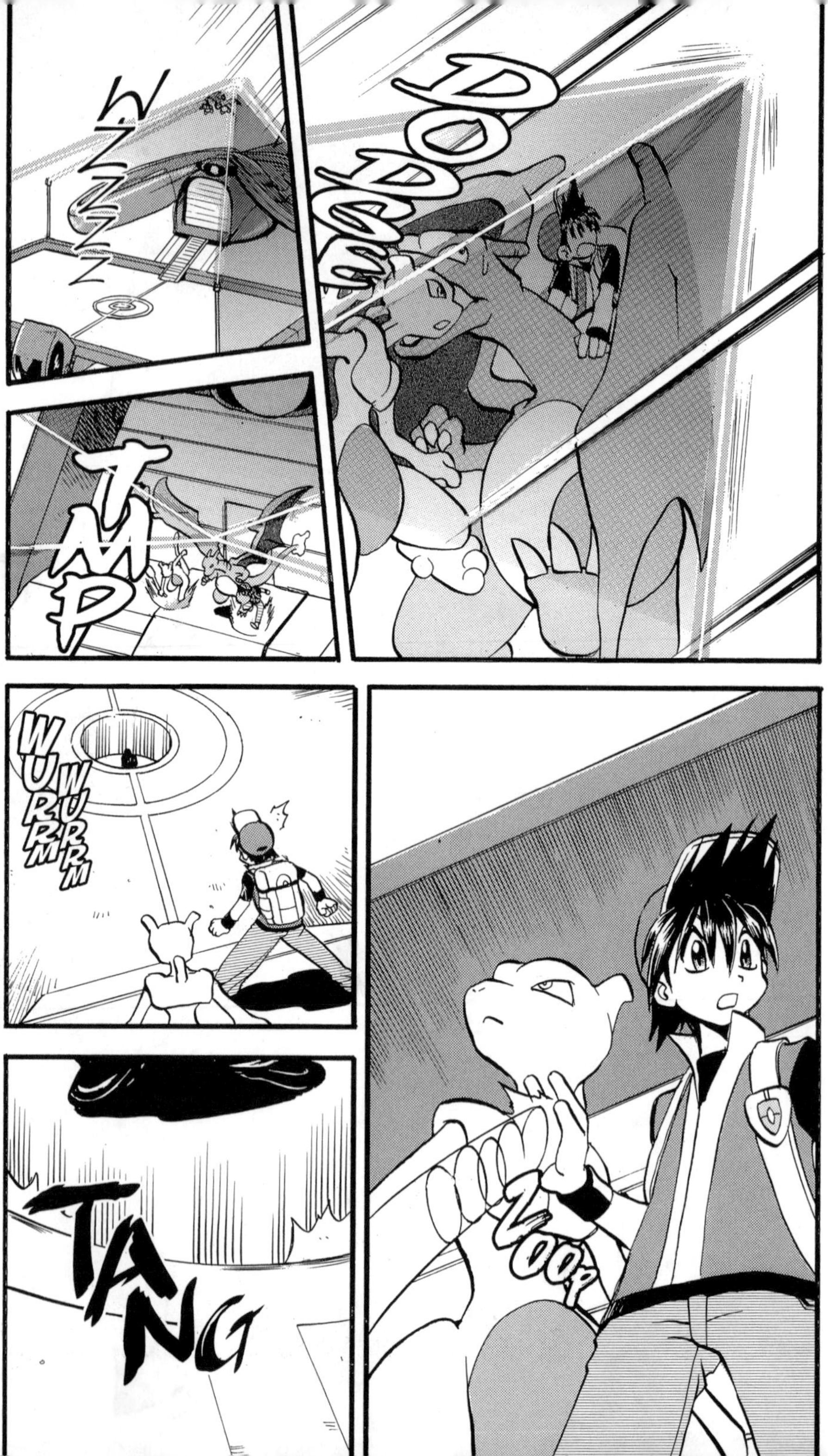
DODGE
WHZZZZ
TMP
ZOOP
WURRM WURRM
TANG

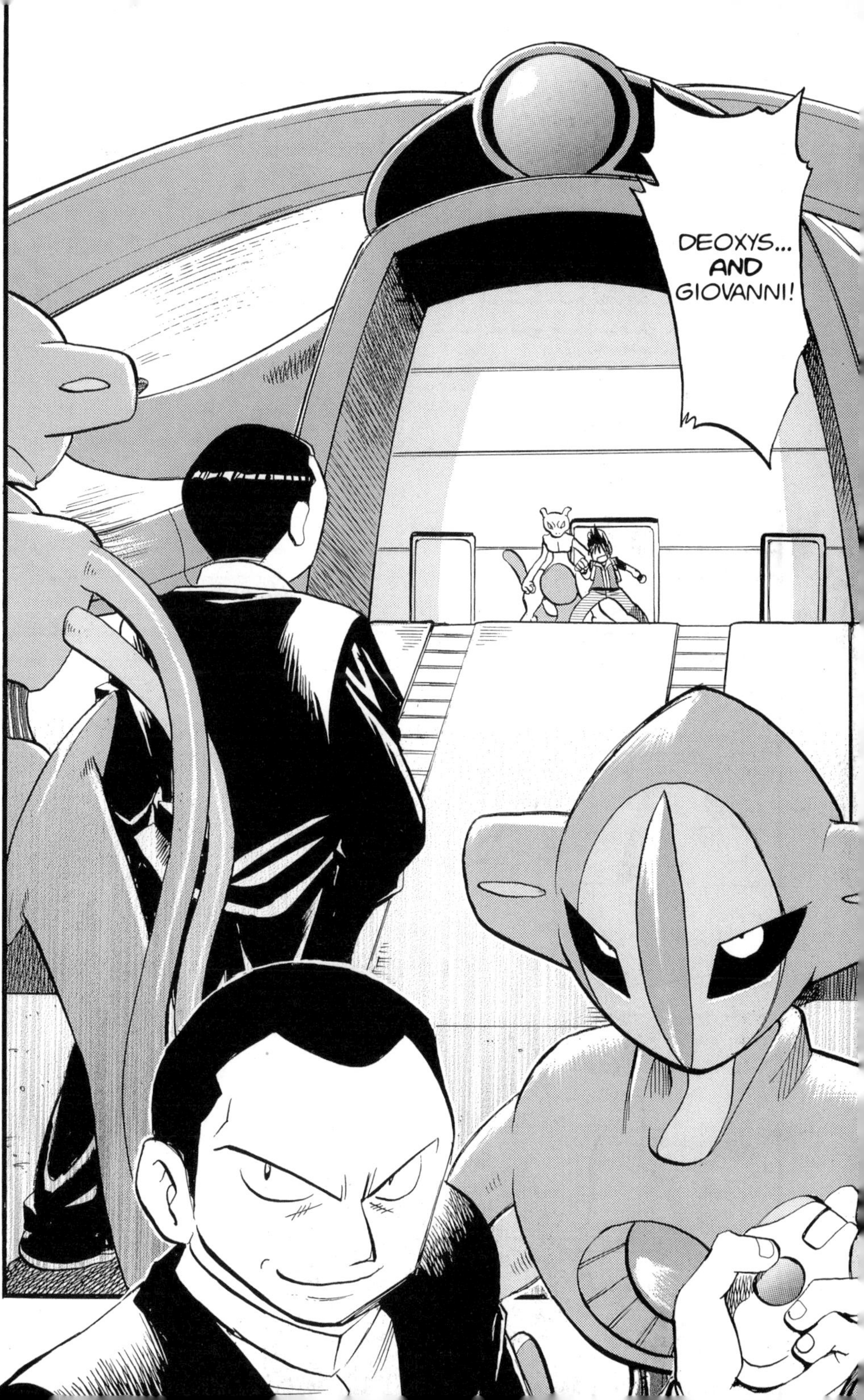
DEOXYS... **AND** GIOVANNI!

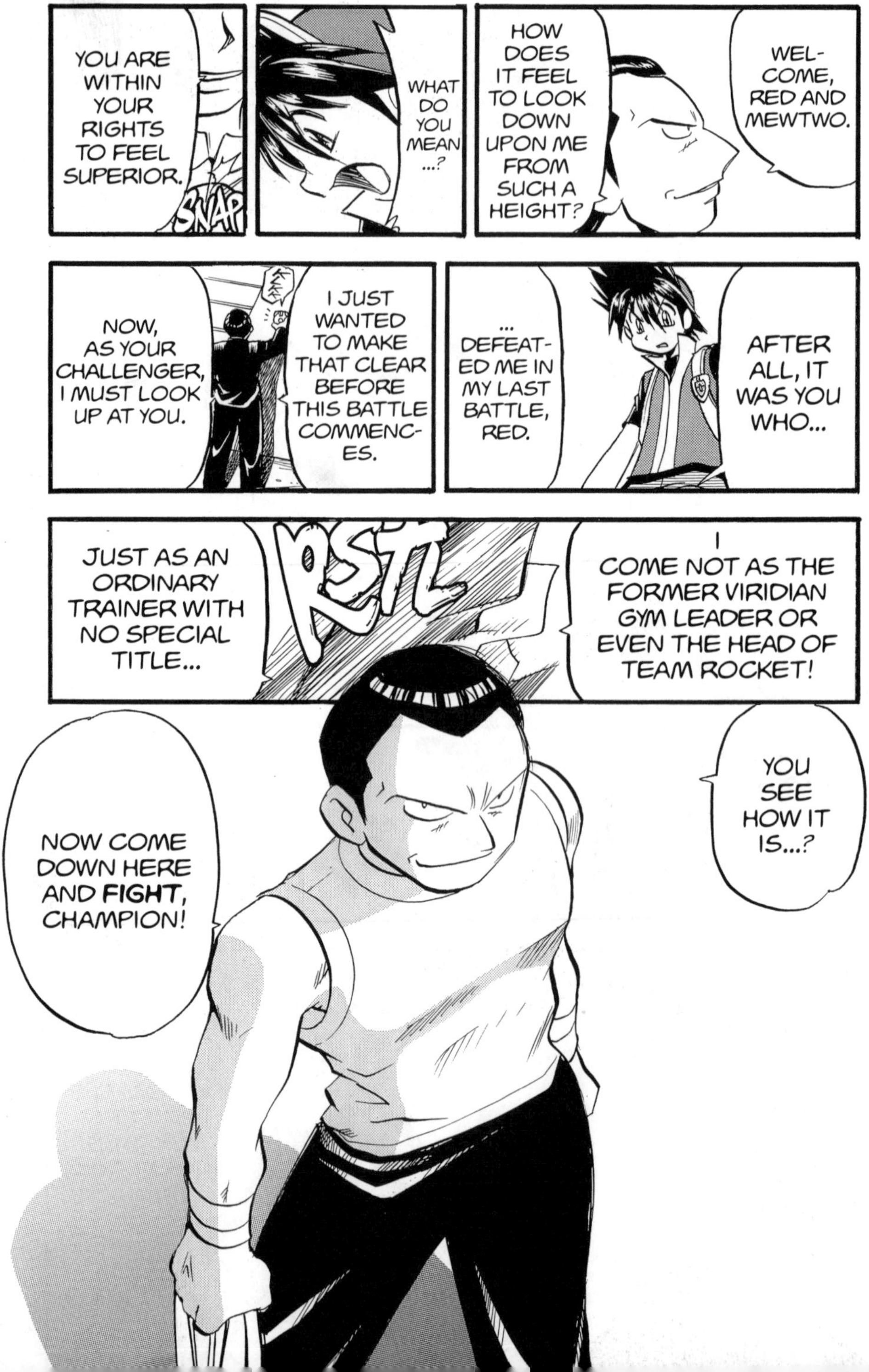
WEL-COME, RED AND MEWTWO.
HOW DOES IT FEEL TO LOOK DOWN UPON ME FROM SUCH A HEIGHT?
WHAT DO YOU MEAN ...?
YOU ARE WITHIN YOUR RIGHTS TO FEEL SUPERIOR.
SNAP
AFTER ALL, IT WAS YOU WHO...
... DEFEAT-ED ME IN MY LAST BATTLE, RED.
I JUST WANTED TO MAKE THAT CLEAR BEFORE THIS BATTLE COMMENC-ES.
NOW, AS YOUR CHALLENGER, I MUST LOOK UP AT YOU.
I COME NOT AS THE FORMER VIRIDIAN GYM LEADER OR EVEN THE HEAD OF TEAM ROCKET!
RSTL
JUST AS AN ORDINARY TRAINER WITH NO SPECIAL TITLE...
YOU SEE HOW IT IS...?
NOW COME DOWN HERE AND **FIGHT**, CHAMPION!

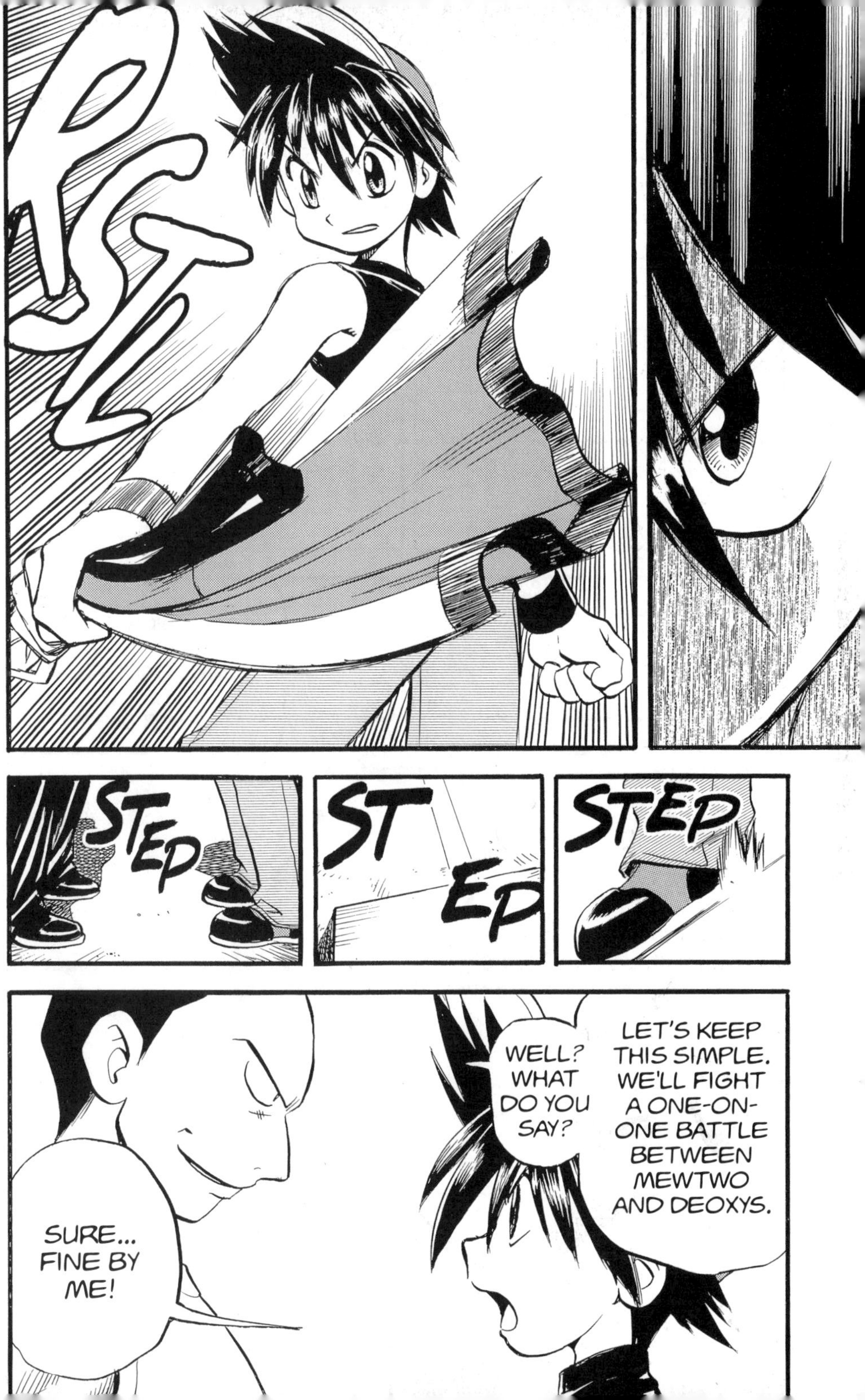
STEP
ST EP
STEP
LET'S KEEP THIS SIMPLE. WE'LL FIGHT A ONE-ON-ONE BATTLE BETWEEN MEWTWO AND DEOXYS.
WELL? WHAT DO YOU SAY?
SURE... FINE BY ME!

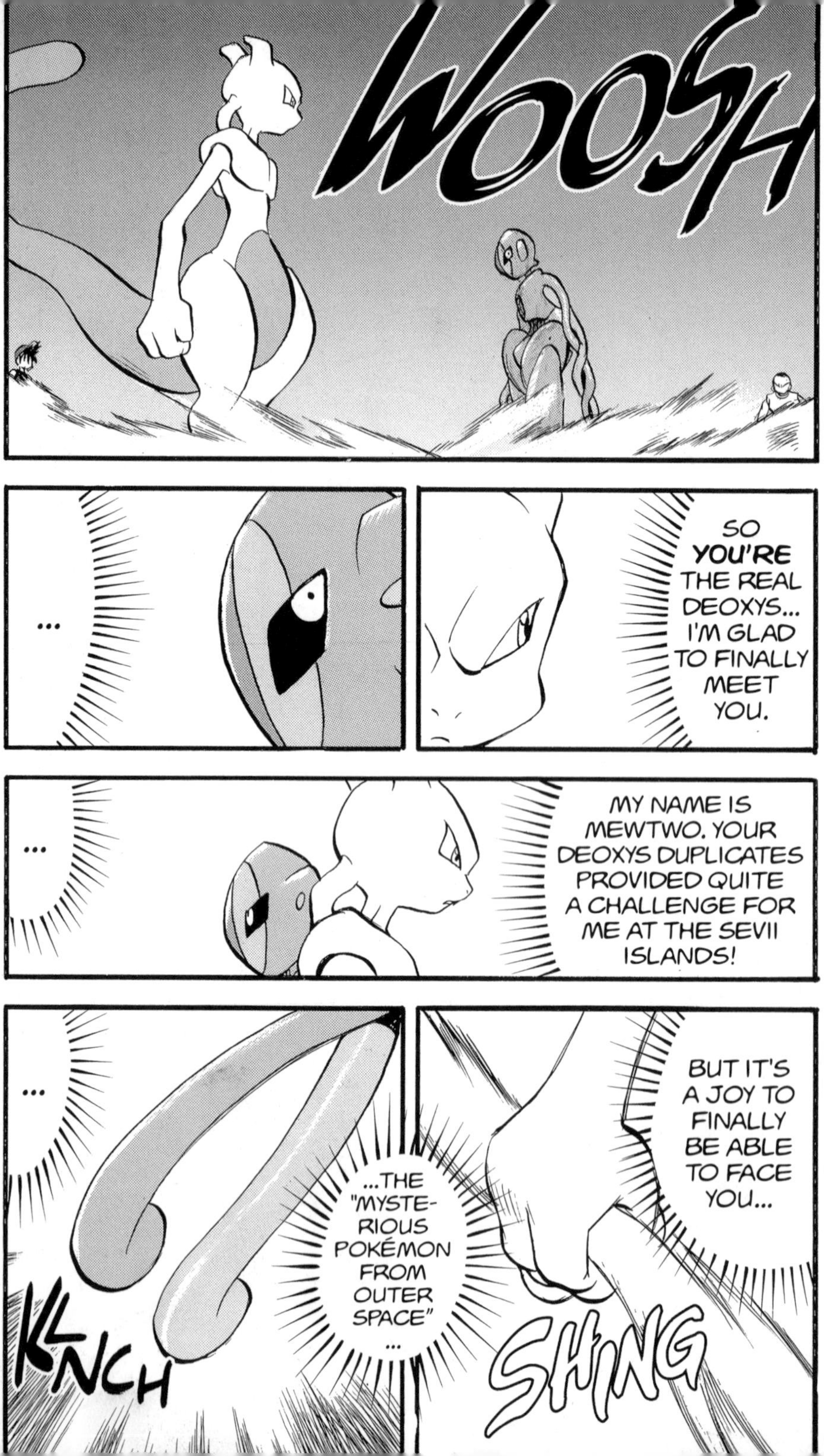
WOOSH
SO YOU'RE THE REAL DEOXYS... I'M GLAD TO FINALLY MEET YOU.
...
MY NAME IS MEWTWO. YOUR DEOXYS DUPLICATES PROVIDED QUITE A CHALLENGE FOR ME AT THE SEVII ISLANDS!
...
BUT IT'S A JOY TO FINALLY BE ABLE TO FACE YOU...
...THE "MYSTE-RIOUS POKÉMON FROM OUTER SPACE"...
SHING
...
KLNCH

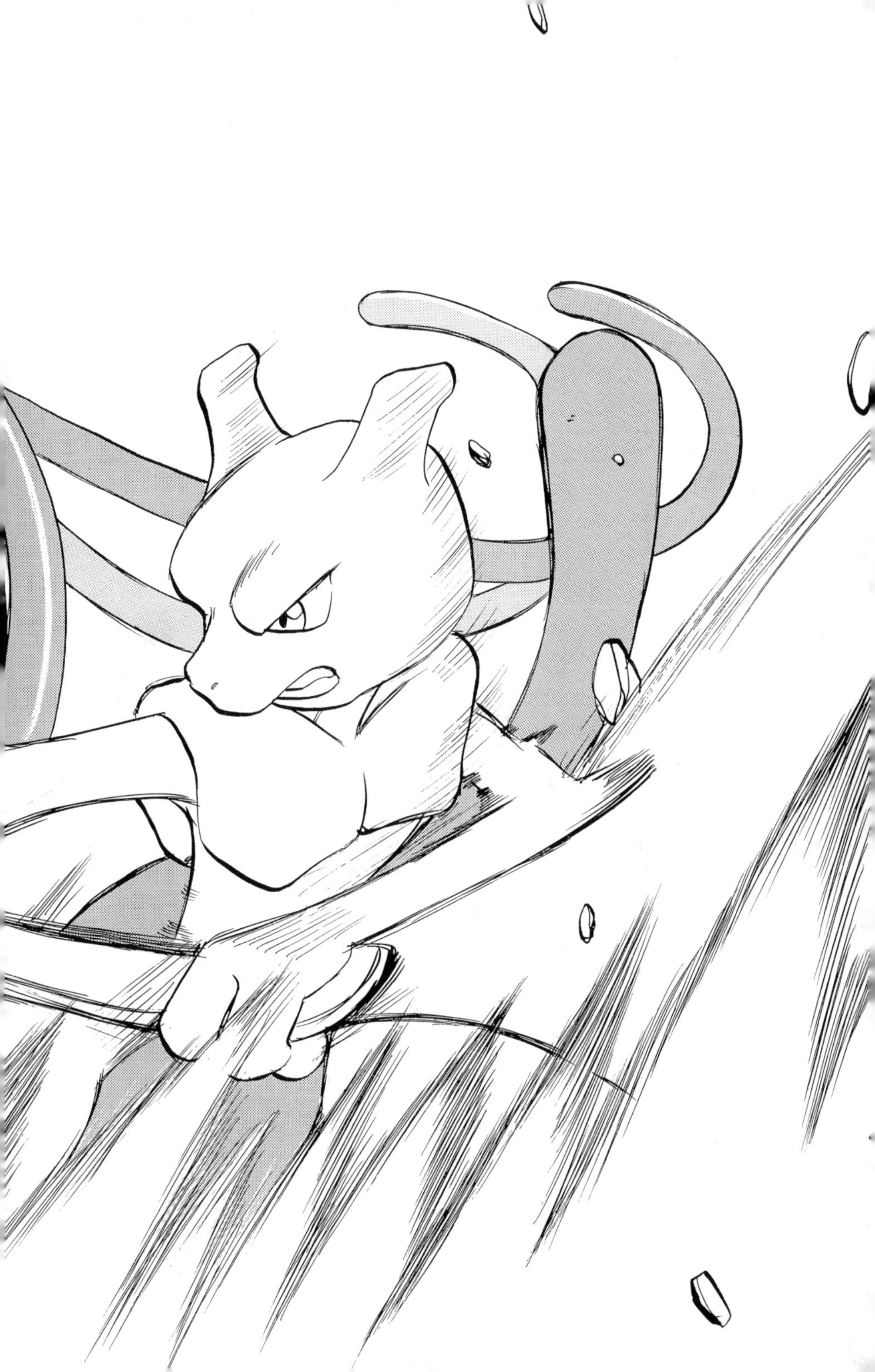

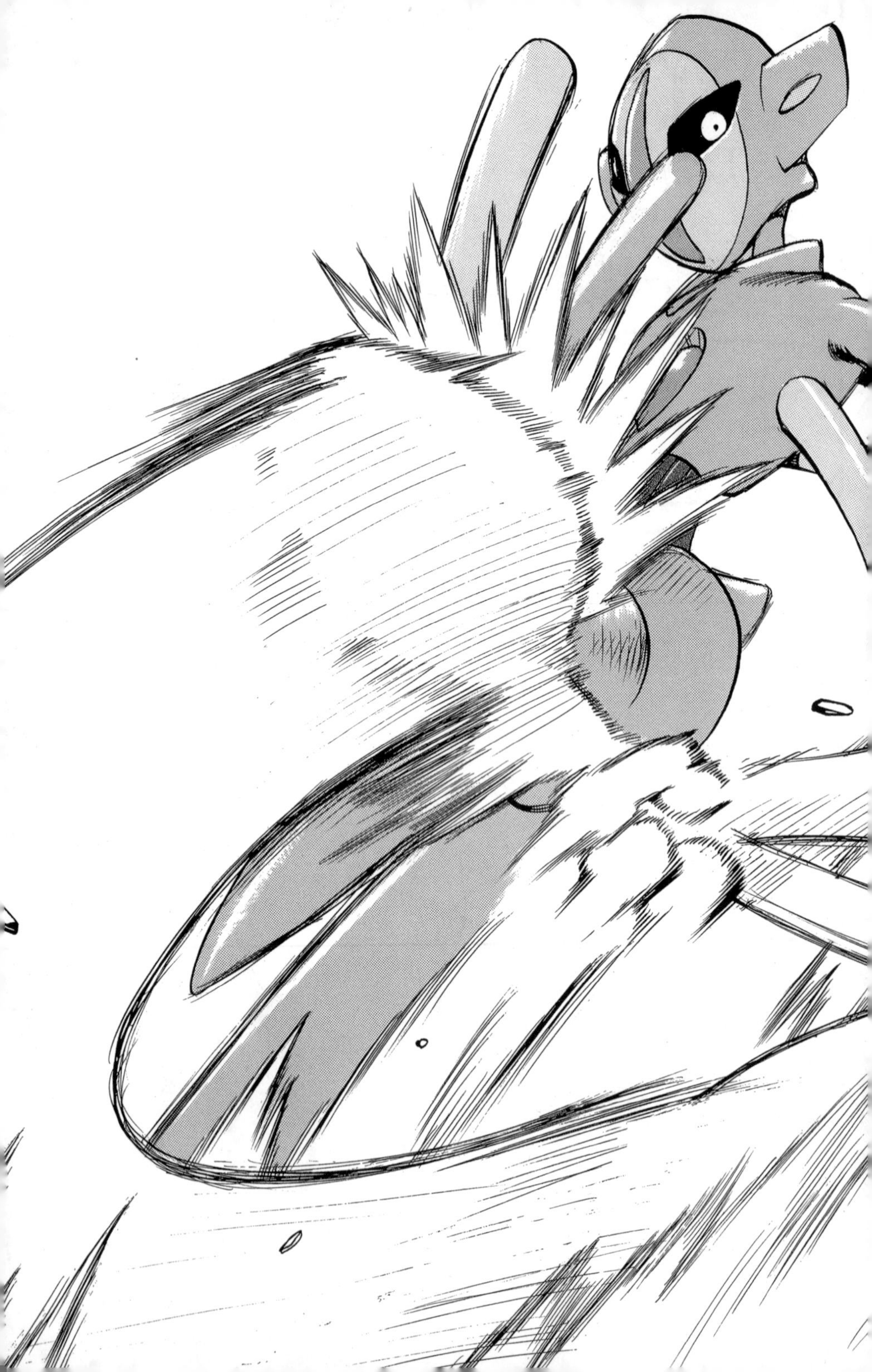

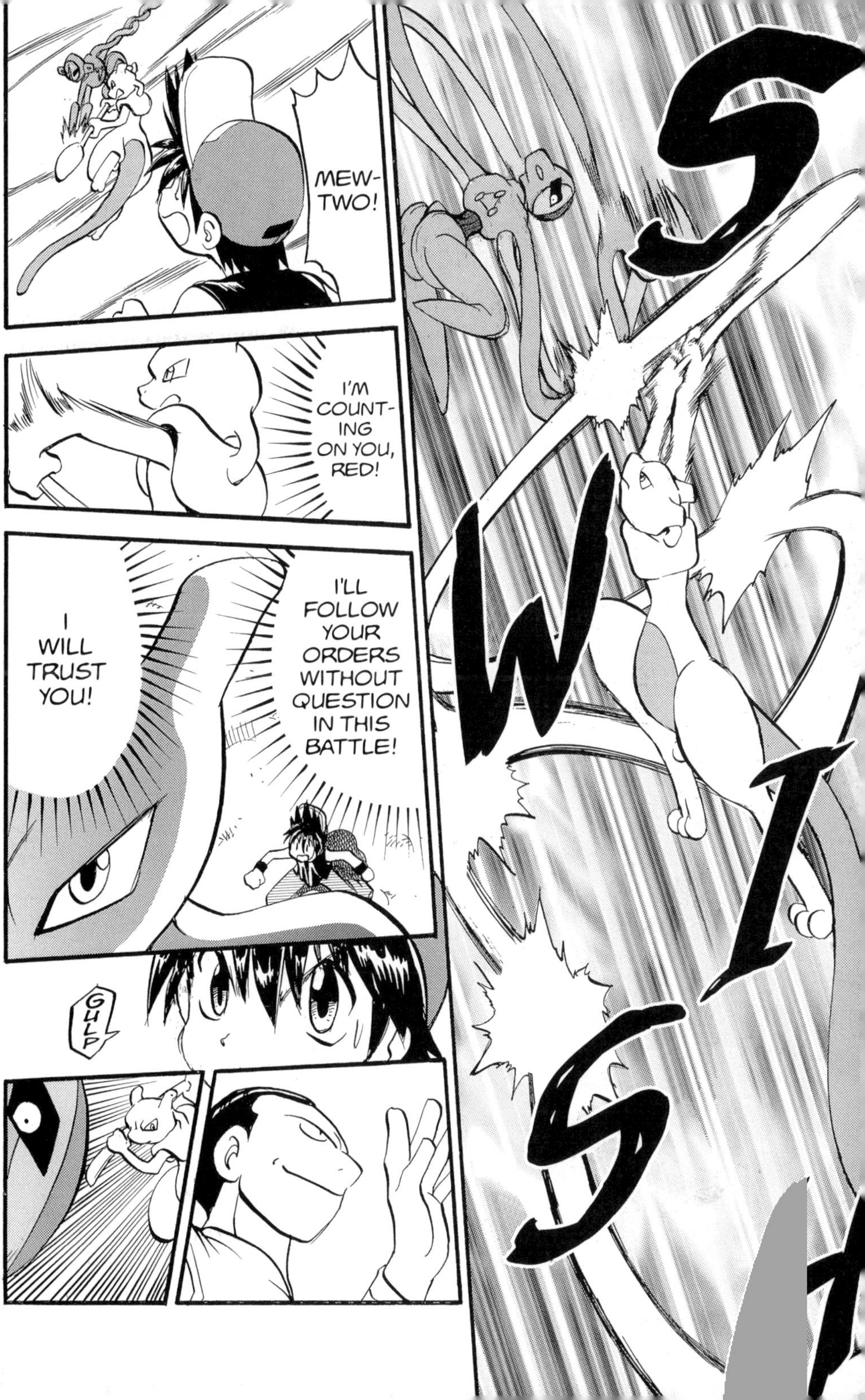
SWISS
MEW-TWO!
I'M COUNTING ON YOU, RED!
I'LL FOLLOW YOUR ORDERS WITHOUT QUESTION IN THIS BATTLE!
I WILL TRUST YOU!
GULP

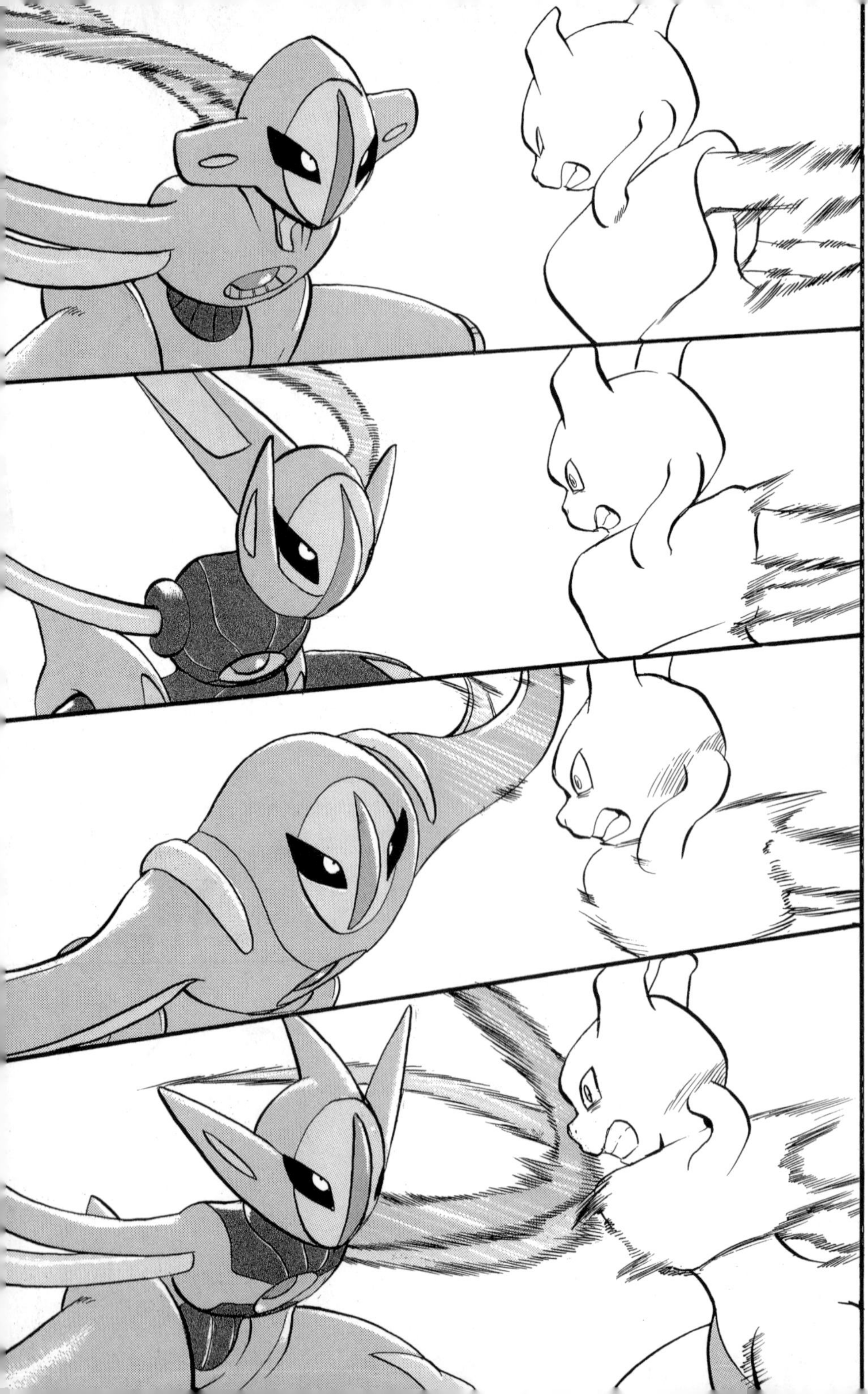

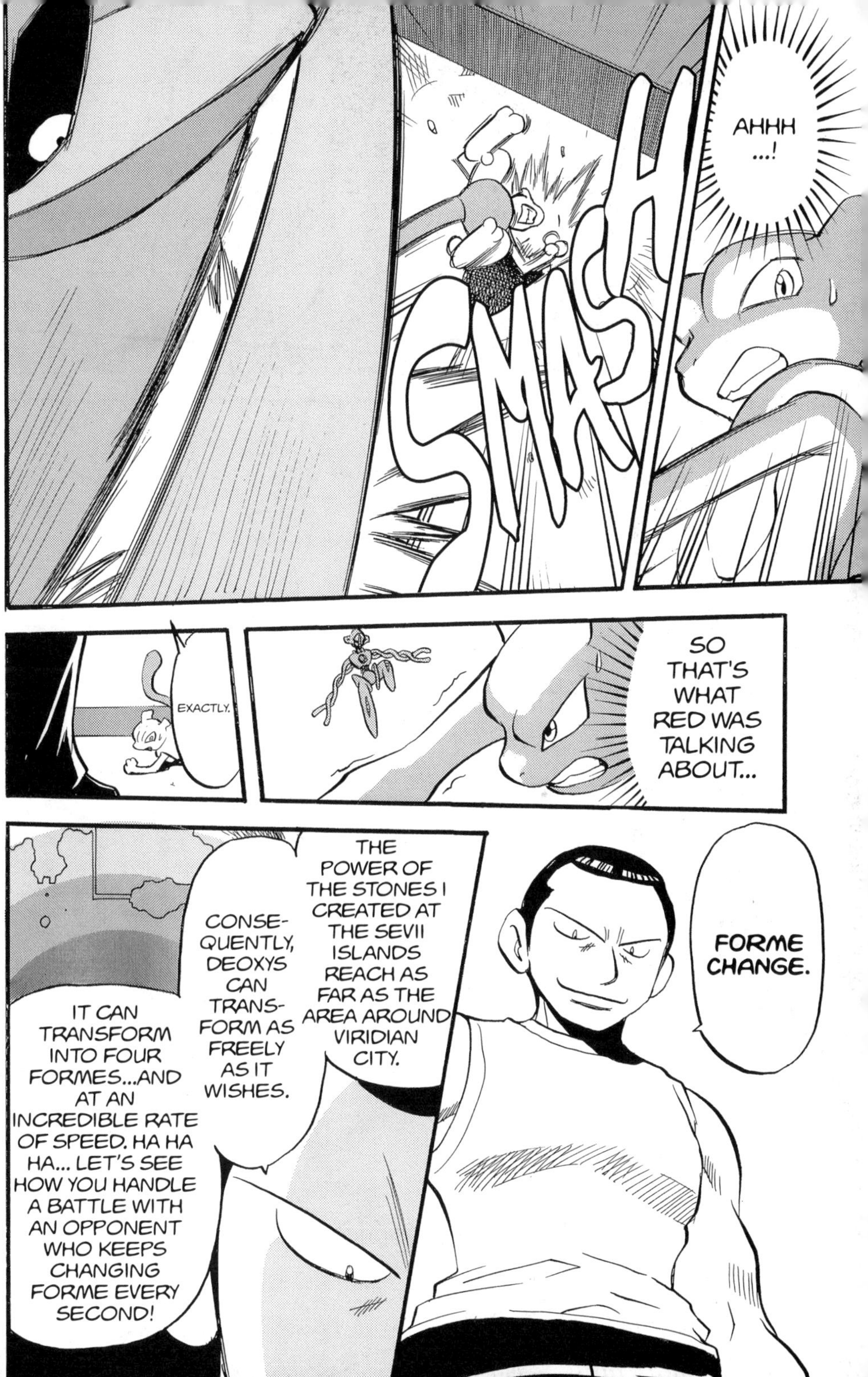
AHHH ...!
SMASH
SO THAT'S WHAT RED WAS TALKING ABOUT...
EXACTLY.
FORME CHANGE.
THE POWER OF THE STONES I CREATED AT THE SEVII ISLANDS REACH AS FAR AS THE AREA AROUND VIRIDIAN CITY.
CONSE-QUENTLY, DEOXYS CAN TRANS-FORM AS FREELY AS IT WISHES.
IT CAN TRANSFORM INTO FOUR FORMES...AND AT AN INCREDIBLE RATE OF SPEED. HA HA HA... LET'S SEE HOW YOU HANDLE A BATTLE WITH AN OPPONENT WHO KEEPS CHANGING FORME EVERY SECOND!

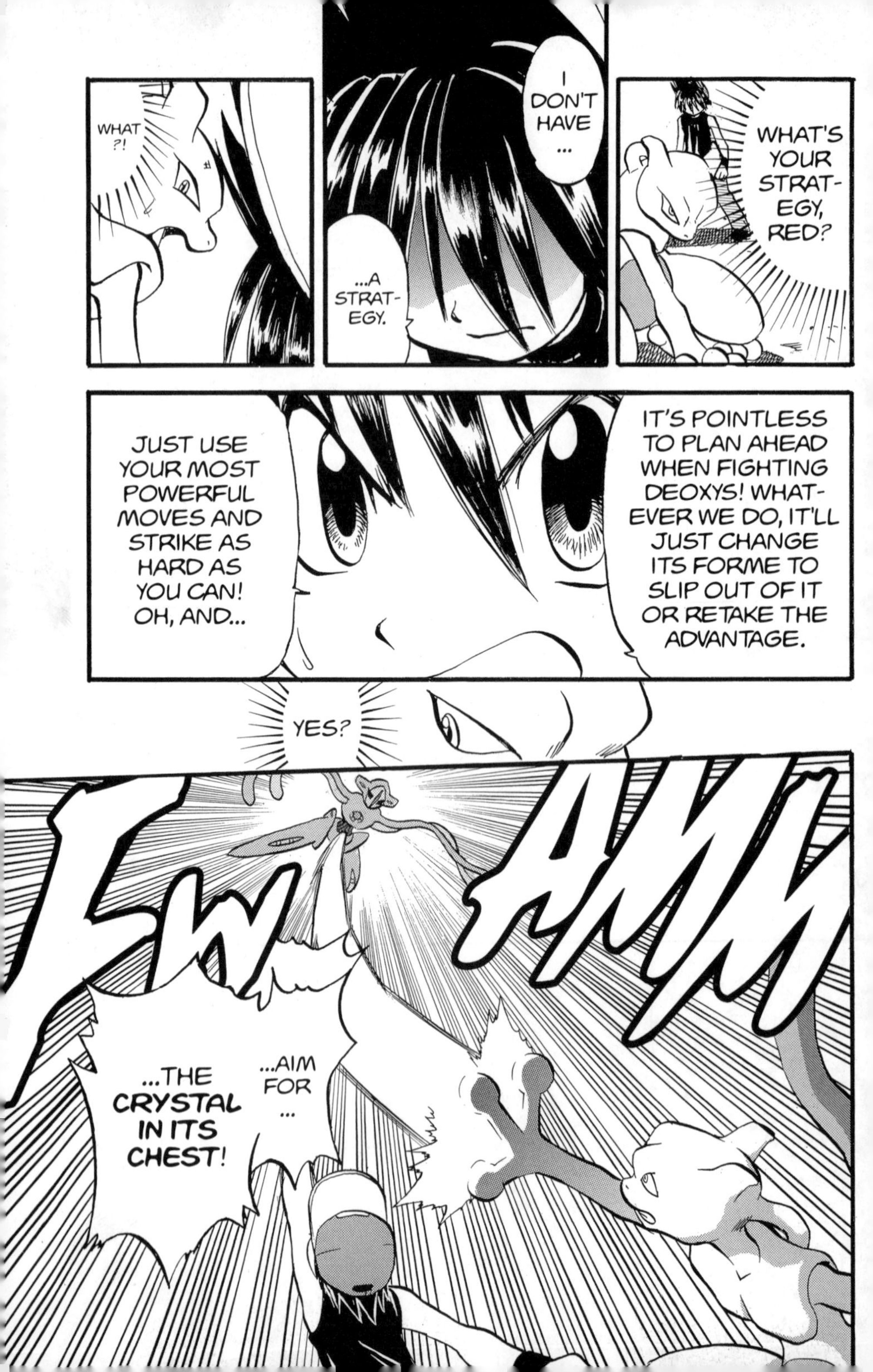
WHAT'S YOUR STRAT-EGY, RED?
I DON'T HAVE ...
...A STRAT-EGY.
WHAT ?!
IT'S POINTLESS TO PLAN AHEAD WHEN FIGHTING DEOXYS! WHAT-EVER WE DO, IT'LL JUST CHANGE ITS FORME TO SLIP OUT OF IT OR RETAKE THE ADVANTAGE.
JUST USE YOUR MOST POWERFUL MOVES AND STRIKE AS HARD AS YOU CAN! OH, AND...
YES?
...AIM FOR ...
...THE **CRYSTAL IN ITS CHEST**!

● Adventure 292 ●
Bested by Banette

Pokémon™ Adventures FireRed & LeafGreen

The Fifth Chapter

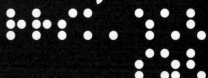

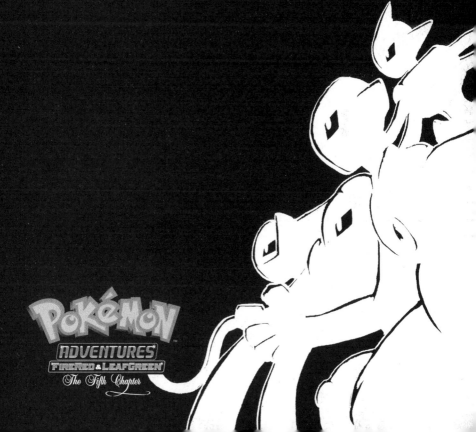

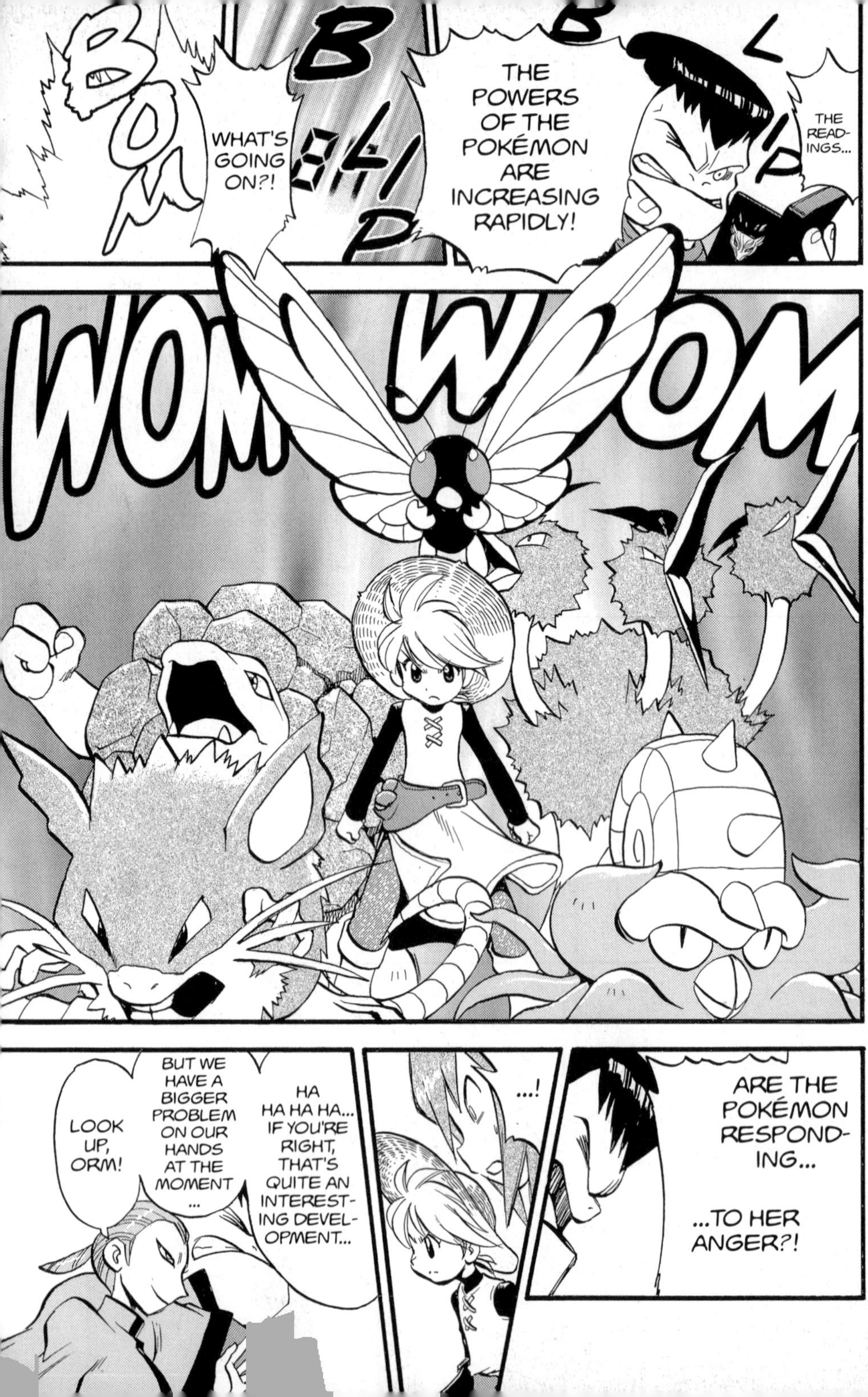
BLIP
THE READINGS...
THE POWERS OF THE POKÉMON ARE INCREASING RAPIDLY!
841
BLIP
WHAT'S GOING ON?!
BOOM
WOM
WOOM
ARE THE POKÉMON RESPONDING...
...TO HER ANGER?!
...!
HA HA HA HA... IF YOU'RE RIGHT, THAT'S QUITE AN INTERESTING DEVELOPMENT...
BUT WE HAVE A BIGGER PROBLEM ON OUR HANDS AT THE MOMENT...
LOOK UP, ORM!

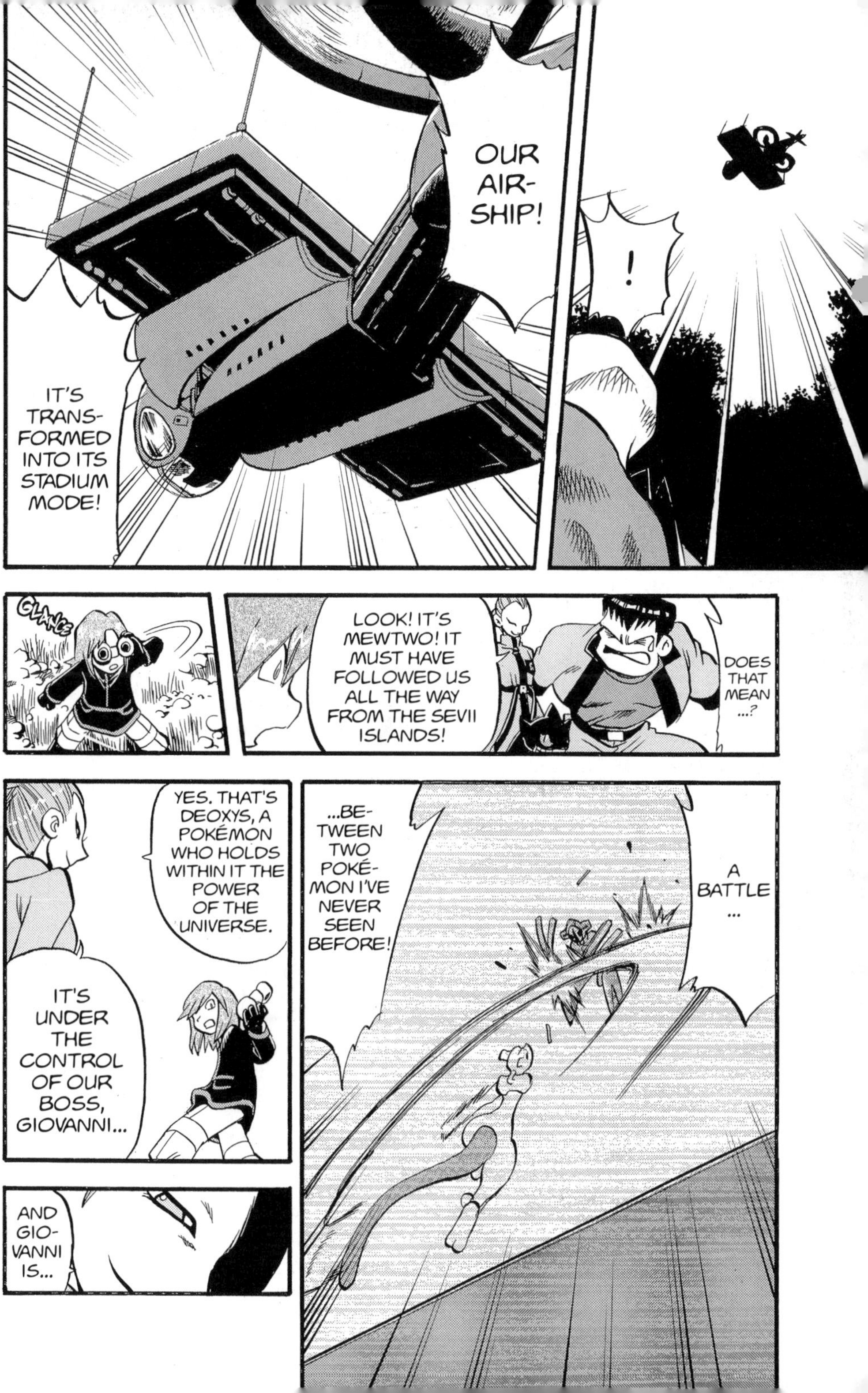
!
OUR AIR-SHIP!
IT'S TRANS-FORMED INTO ITS STADIUM MODE!
LOOK! IT'S MEWTWO! IT MUST HAVE FOLLOWED US ALL THE WAY FROM THE SEVII ISLANDS!
DOES THAT MEAN ...?
GLANCE
A BATTLE ...
...BE-TWEEN TWO POKÉ-MON I'VE NEVER SEEN BEFORE!
YES. THAT'S DEOXYS, A POKÉMON WHO HOLDS WITHIN IT THE POWER OF THE UNIVERSE.
IT'S UNDER THE CONTROL OF OUR BOSS, GIOVANNI...
AND GIO-VANNI IS...

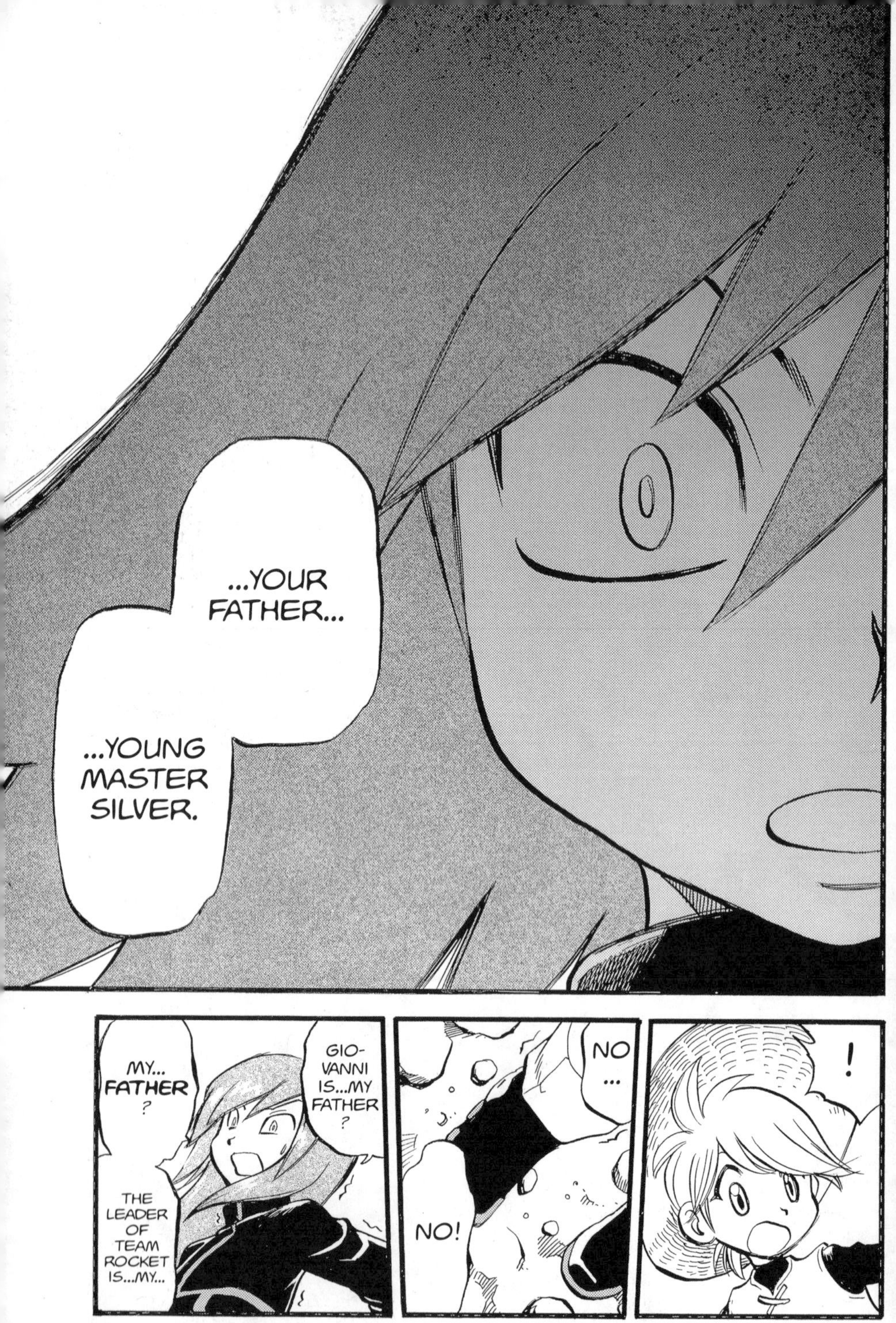
...YOUR FATHER...
...YOUNG MASTER SILVER.
!
NO ...
NO!
GIO-VANNI IS...MY FATHER?
MY... **FATHER**?
THE LEADER OF TEAM ROCKET IS...MY...

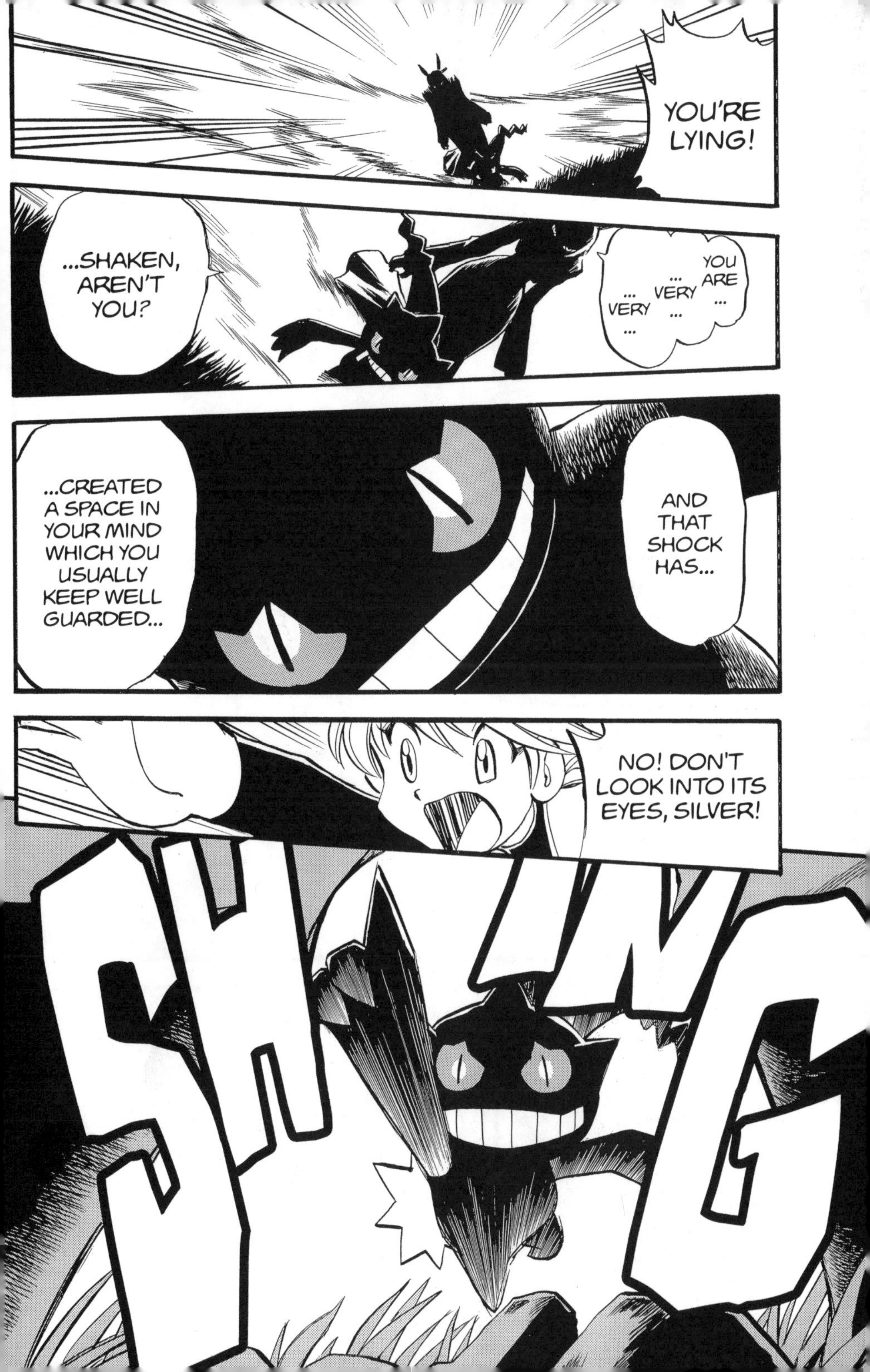
YOU'RE LYING!
YOU ARE ... ... VERY ... ... VERY ...
...SHAKEN, AREN'T YOU?
AND THAT SHOCK HAS...
...CREATED A SPACE IN YOUR MIND WHICH YOU USUALLY KEEP WELL GUARDED...
NO! DON'T LOOK INTO ITS EYES, SILVER!
SHING

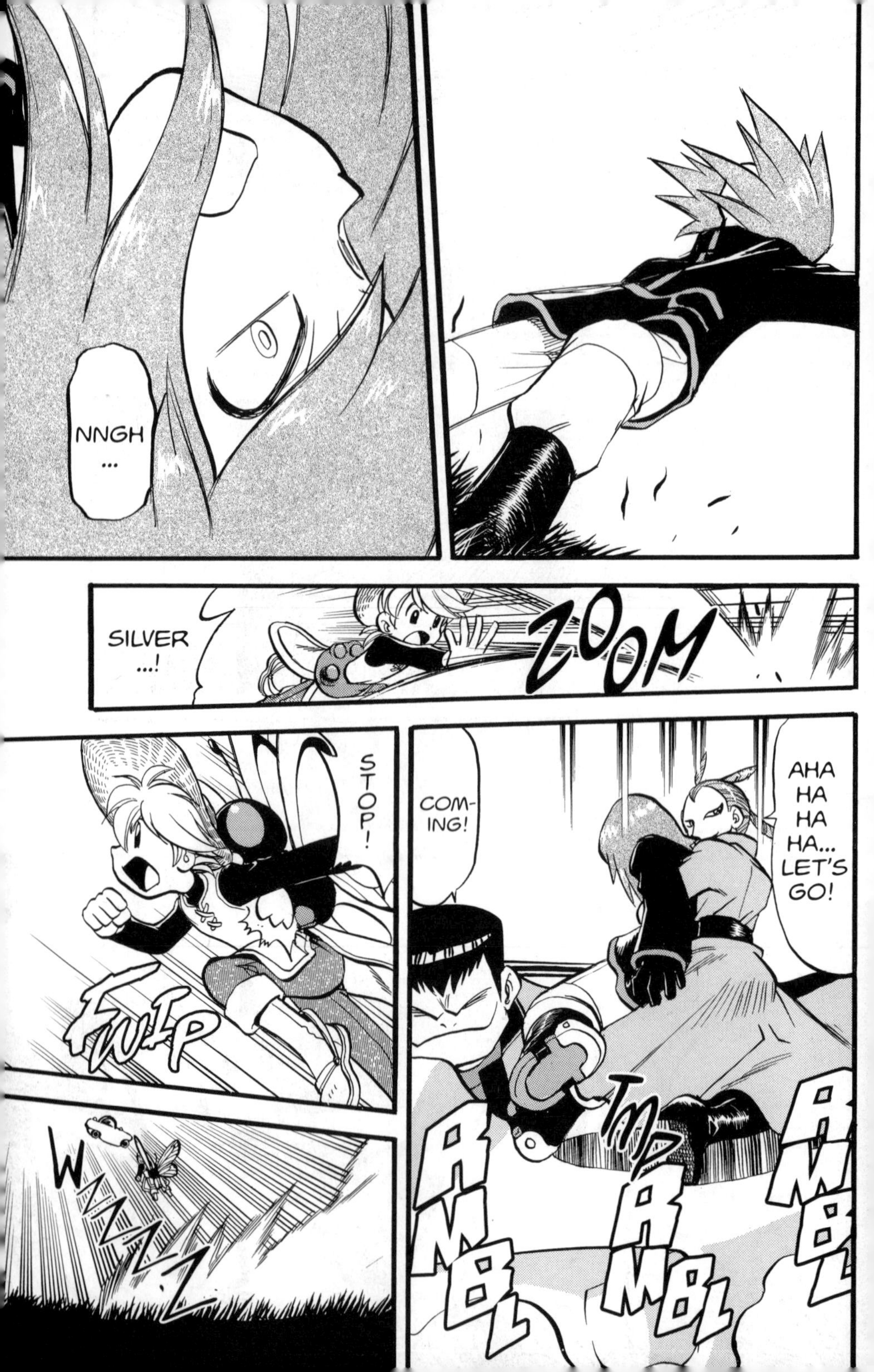
NNGH ...
SILVER ...!
ZOOM
AHA HA HA HA... LET'S GO!
COM-ING!
RMBL
TMP
RMBL
RMBL
STOP!
FWIP
WZZZZZ

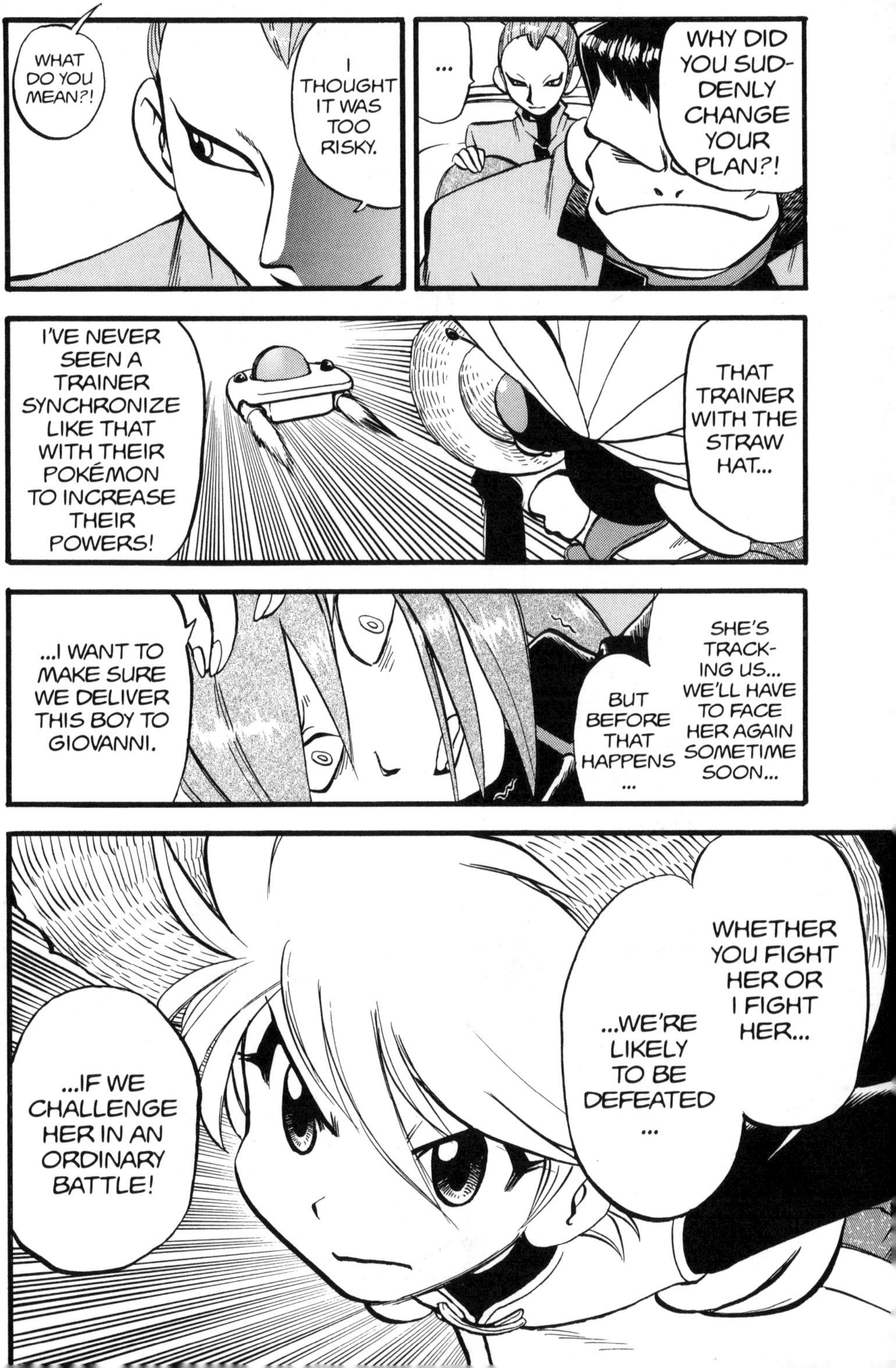
WHY DID YOU SUDDENLY CHANGE YOUR PLAN?!
...
I THOUGHT IT WAS TOO RISKY.
WHAT DO YOU MEAN?!
THAT TRAINER WITH THE STRAW HAT...
I'VE NEVER SEEN A TRAINER SYNCHRONIZE LIKE THAT WITH THEIR POKÉMON TO INCREASE THEIR POWERS!
SHE'S TRACKING US... WE'LL HAVE TO FACE HER AGAIN SOMETIME SOON...
BUT BEFORE THAT HAPPENS ...
...I WANT TO MAKE SURE WE DELIVER THIS BOY TO GIOVANNI.
WHETHER YOU FIGHT HER OR I FIGHT HER...
...WE'RE LIKELY TO BE DEFEATED ...
...IF WE CHALLENGE HER IN AN ORDINARY BATTLE!

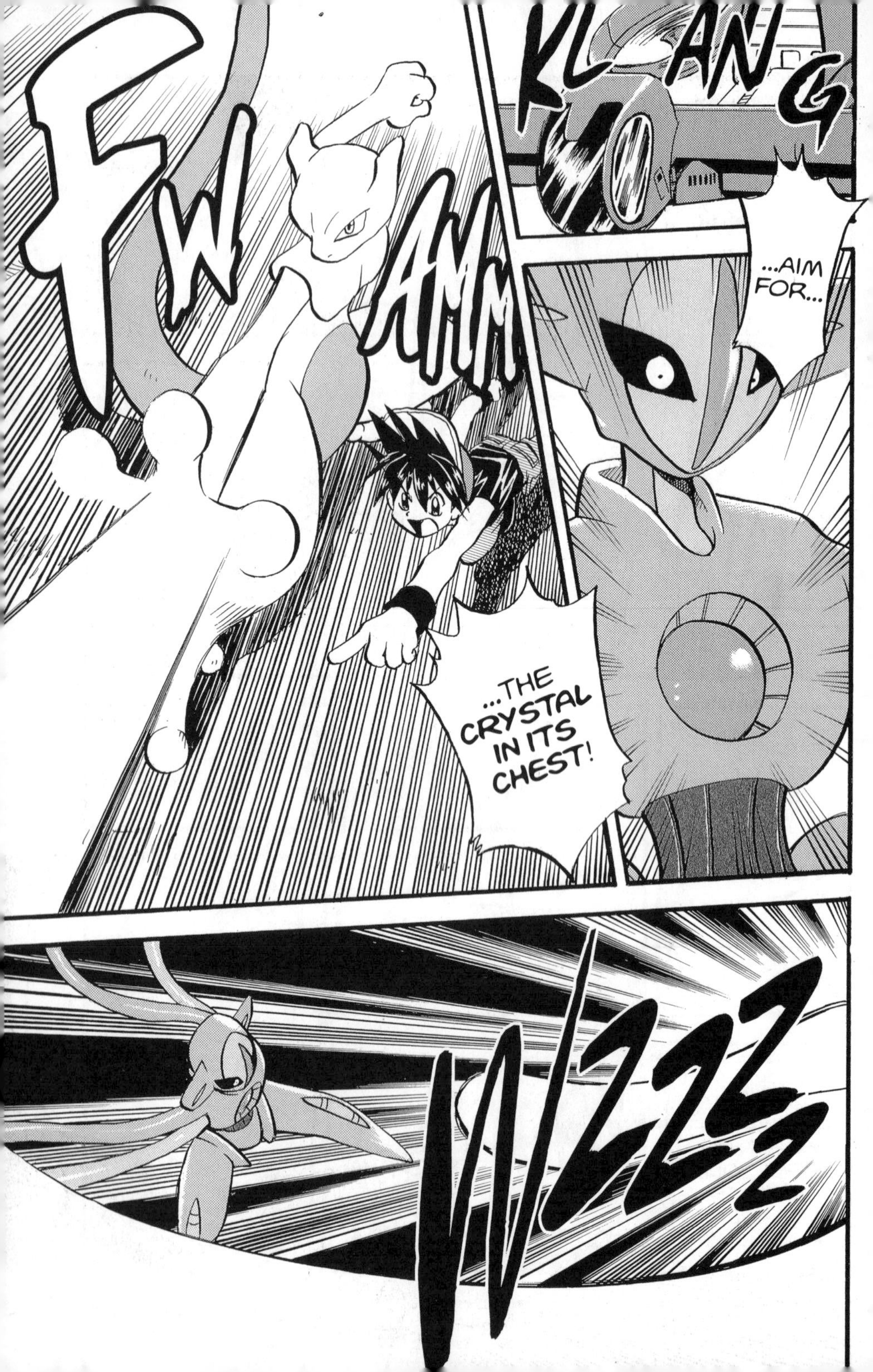
KLANG
...AIM FOR...
FWAMM
...THE CRYSTAL IN ITS CHEST!
WZZZZ

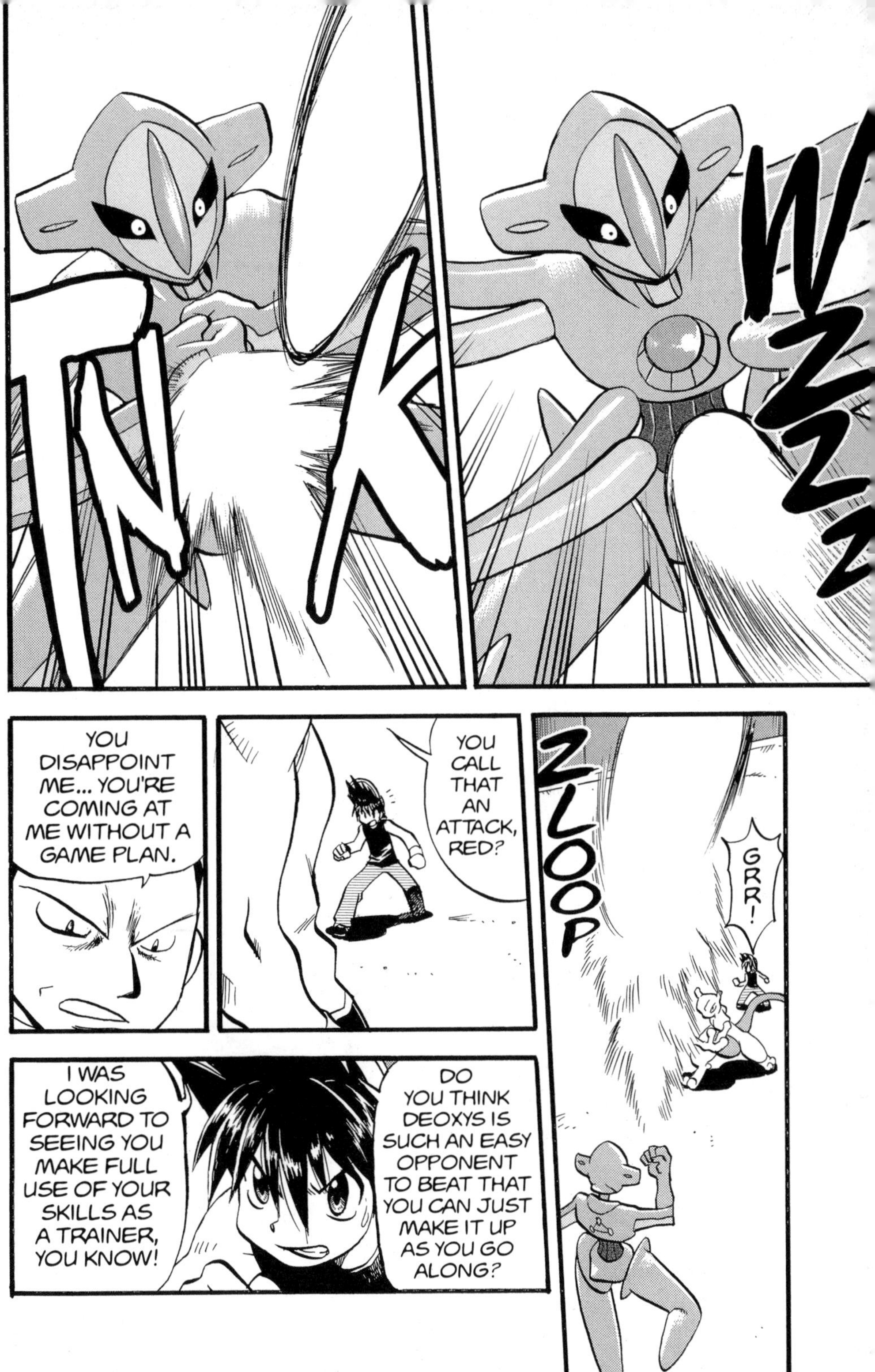
WZZZ
TNK
ZLOOP
GRR!
YOU CALL THAT AN ATTACK, RED?
YOU DISAPPOINT ME... YOU'RE COMING AT ME WITHOUT A GAME PLAN.
DO YOU THINK DEOXYS IS SUCH AN EASY OPPONENT TO BEAT THAT YOU CAN JUST MAKE IT UP AS YOU GO ALONG?
I WAS LOOKING FORWARD TO SEEING YOU MAKE FULL USE OF YOUR SKILLS AS A TRAINER, YOU KNOW!

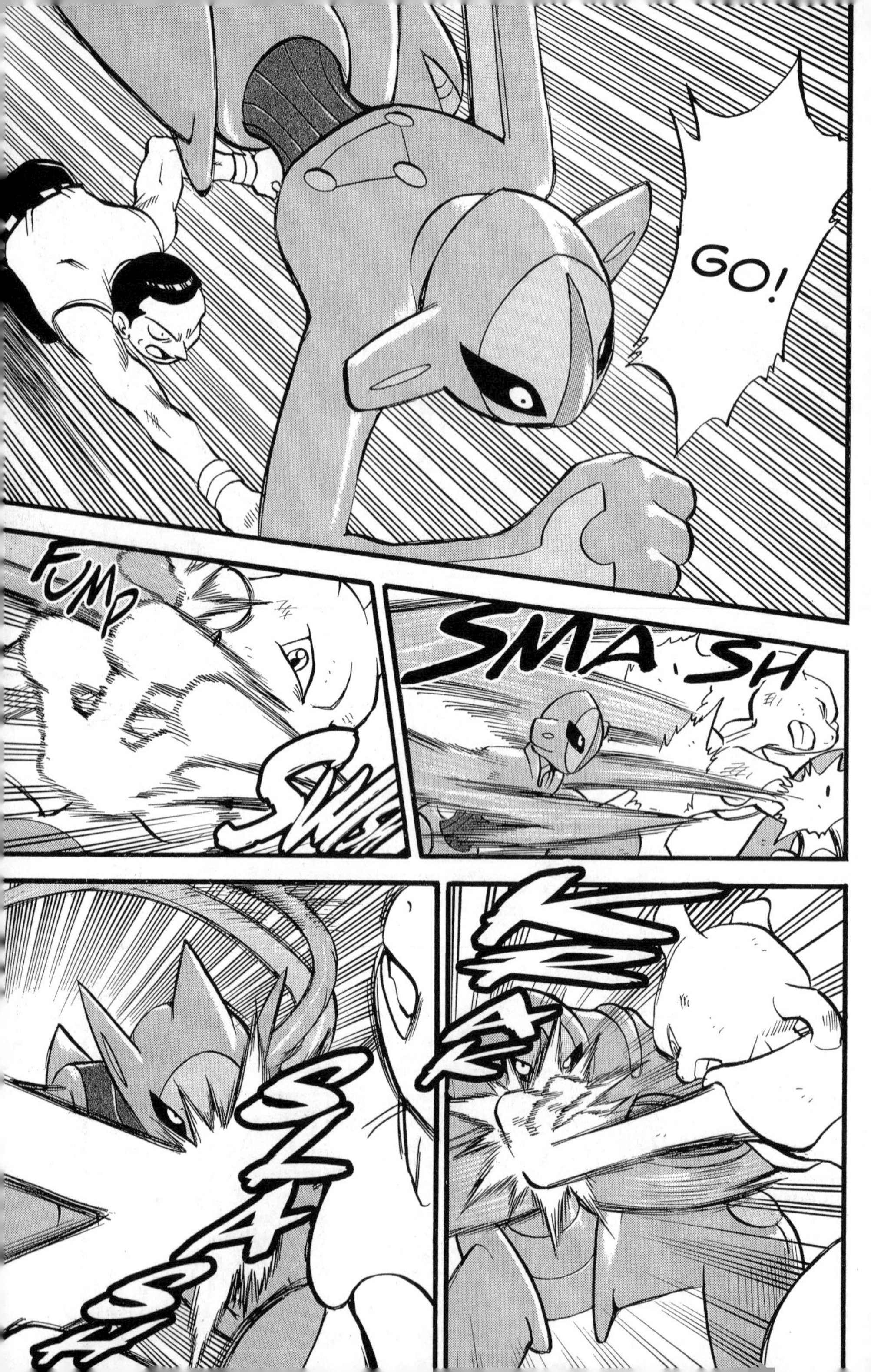
GO!
SMASH
FUMP

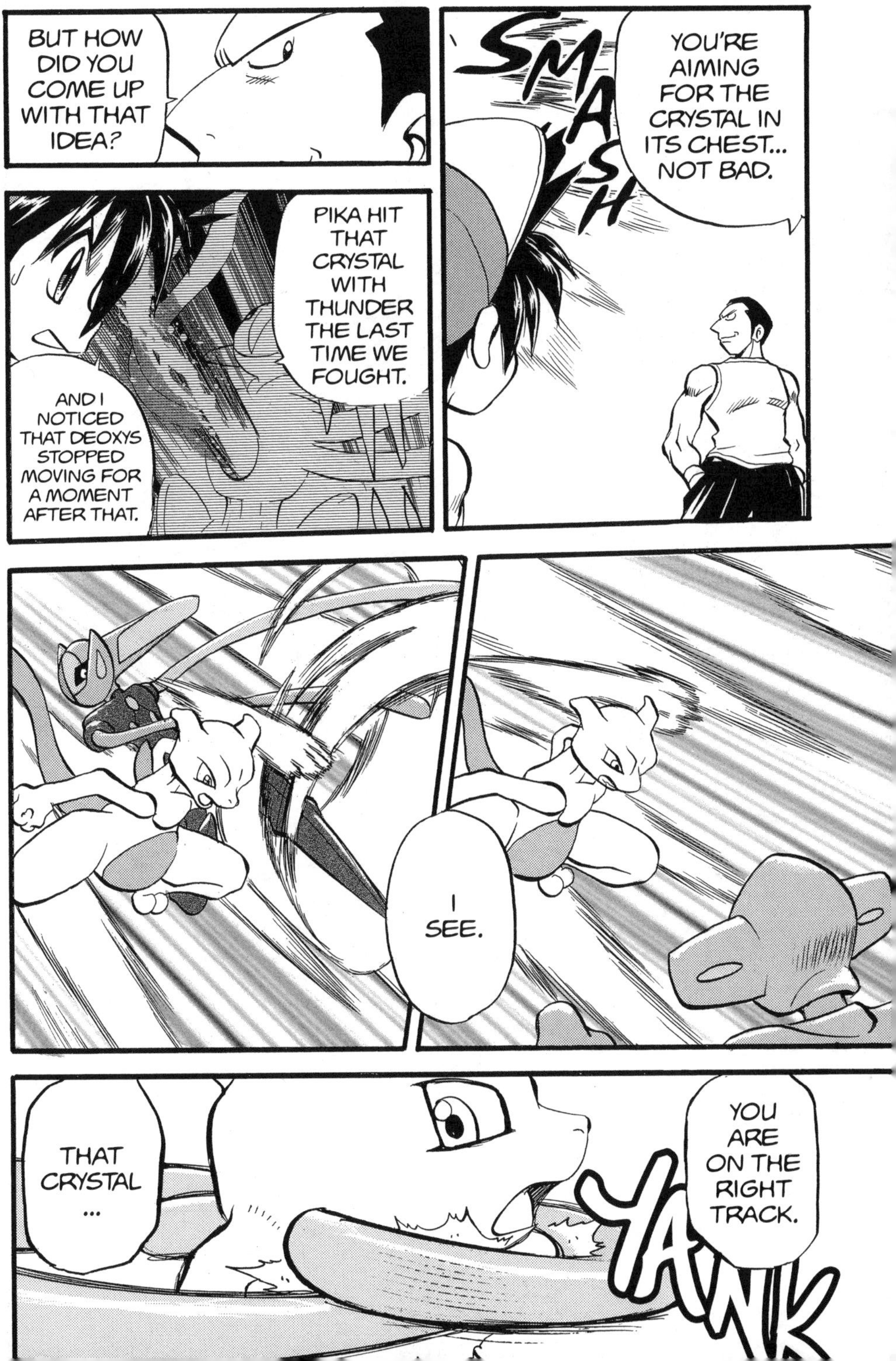
SMASH
YOU'RE AIMING FOR THE CRYSTAL IN ITS CHEST... NOT BAD.
BUT HOW DID YOU COME UP WITH THAT IDEA?
PIKA HIT THAT CRYSTAL WITH THUNDER THE LAST TIME WE FOUGHT.
AND I NOTICED THAT DEOXYS STOPPED MOVING FOR A MOMENT AFTER THAT.
I SEE.
YOU ARE ON THE RIGHT TRACK.
YANK
THAT CRYSTAL ...

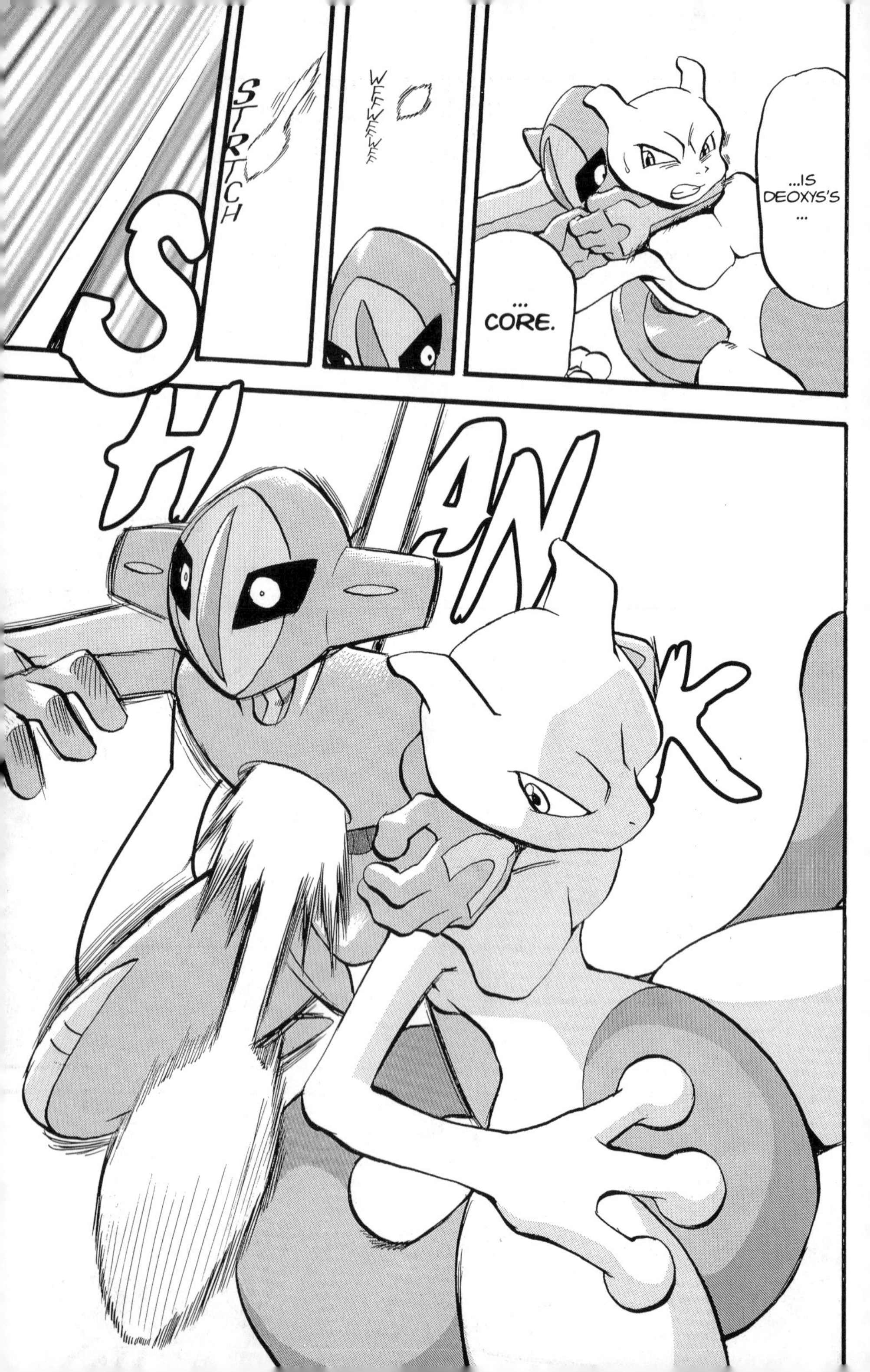
...IS DEOXYS'S ...
... CORE.
WFFWFFWFF
STIRTCH
SHANK

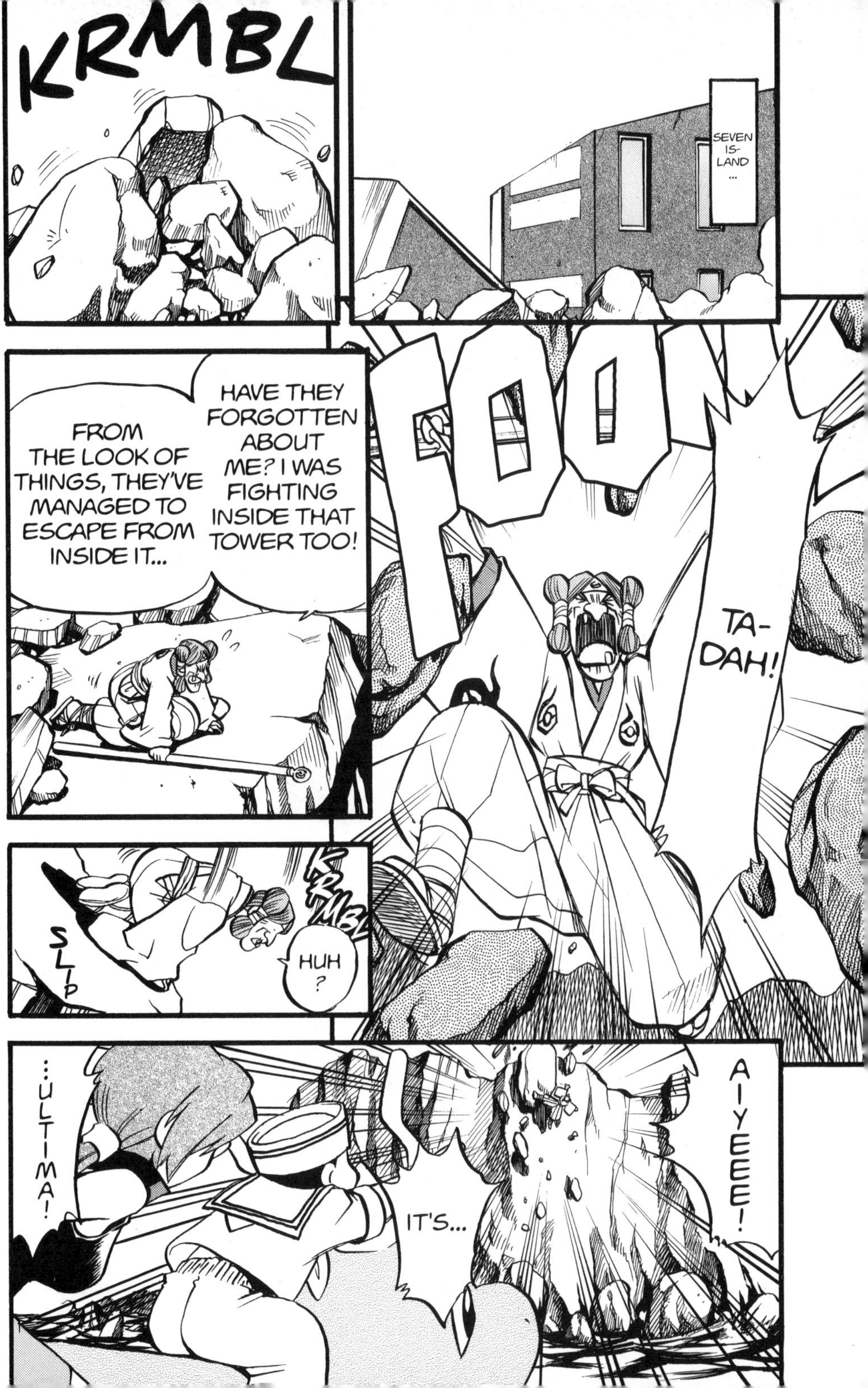
SEVEN IS- LAND ...
KRMBL
FOOM
TA- DAH!
HAVE THEY FORGOTTEN ABOUT ME? I WAS FIGHTING INSIDE THAT TOWER TOO!
FROM THE LOOK OF THINGS, THEY'VE MANAGED TO ESCAPE FROM INSIDE IT...
KRMBL
HUH ?
SLIP
AIYEEEE!
IT'S...
...ULTIMA!

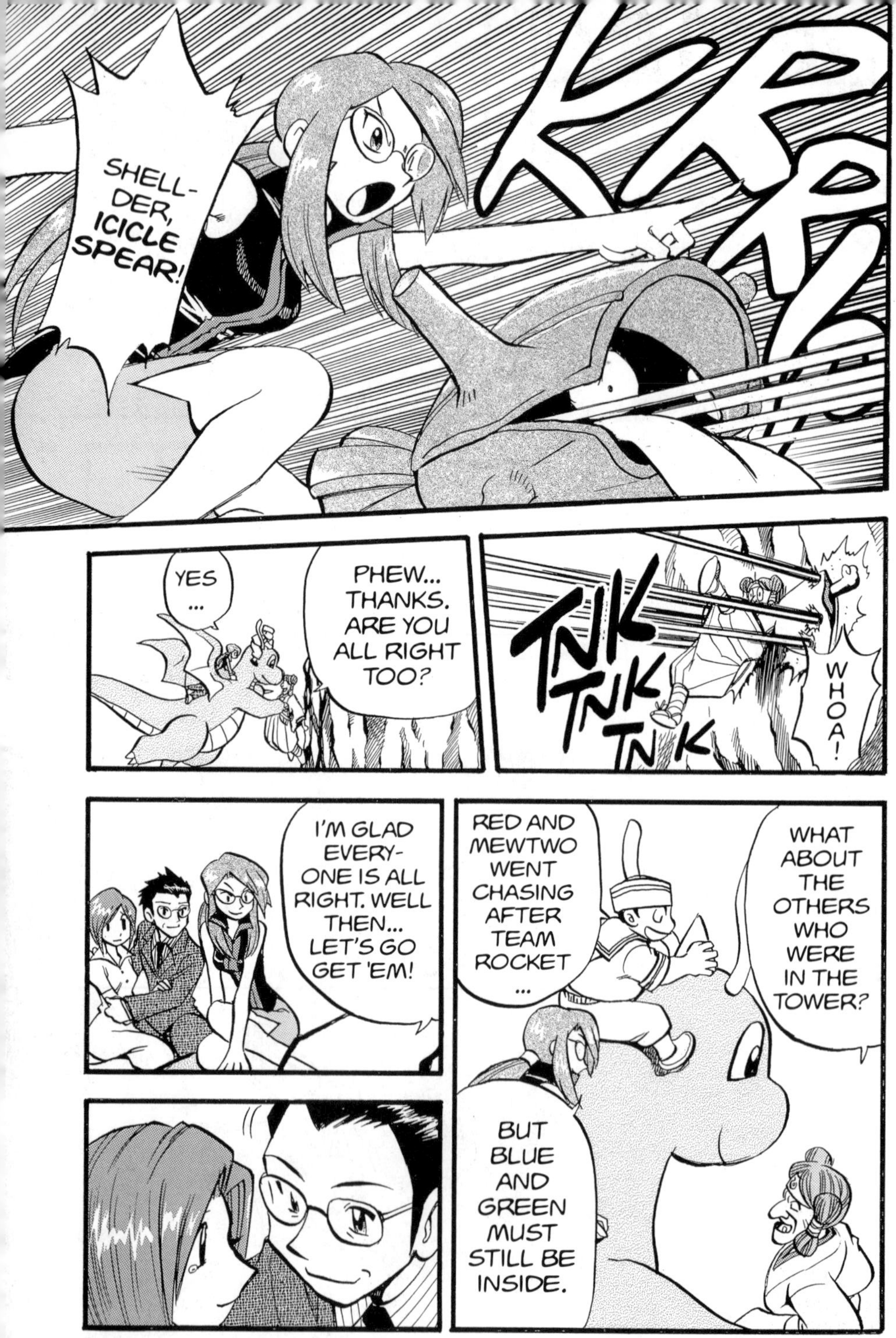
SHELL-DER, ICICLE SPEAR!
TNK TNK TNK
WHOA!
PHEW... THANKS. ARE YOU ALL RIGHT TOO?
YES ...
WHAT ABOUT THE OTHERS WHO WERE IN THE TOWER?
RED AND MEWTWO WENT CHASING AFTER TEAM ROCKET ...
BUT BLUE AND GREEN MUST STILL BE INSIDE.
I'M GLAD EVERY-ONE IS ALL RIGHT. WELL THEN... LET'S GO GET 'EM!

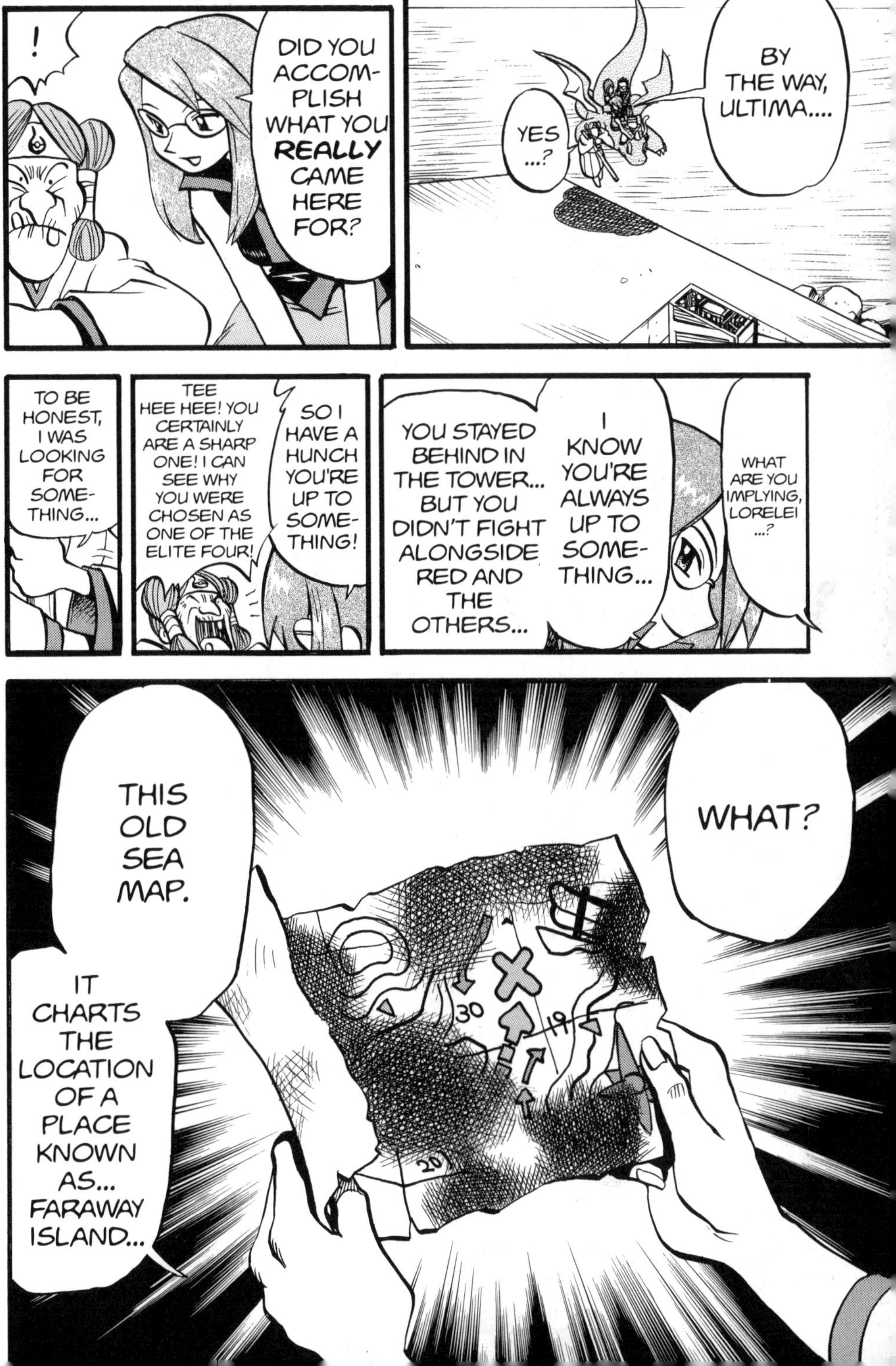
BY THE WAY, ULTIMA....
YES ...?
!
DID YOU ACCOMPLISH WHAT YOU **REALLY** CAME HERE FOR?
WHAT ARE YOU IMPLYING, LORELEI ...?
I KNOW YOU'RE ALWAYS UP TO SOMETHING...
YOU STAYED BEHIND IN THE TOWER... BUT YOU DIDN'T FIGHT ALONGSIDE RED AND THE OTHERS...
SO I HAVE A HUNCH YOU'RE UP TO SOMETHING!
TEE HEE HEE! YOU CERTAINLY ARE A SHARP ONE! I CAN SEE WHY YOU WERE CHOSEN AS ONE OF THE ELITE FOUR!
TO BE HONEST, I WAS LOOKING FOR SOMETHING...
WHAT?
THIS OLD SEA MAP.
30
19
20
IT CHARTS THE LOCATION OF A PLACE KNOWN AS... FARAWAY ISLAND...

● Adventure 293 ●
Down-for-the-Count Deoxys

Pokémon Adventures
FireRed & LeafGreen
The Fifth Chapter

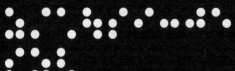

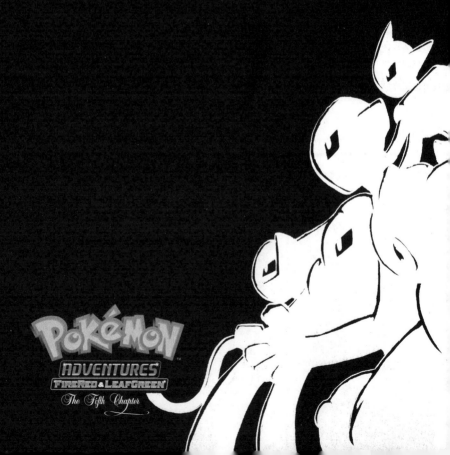

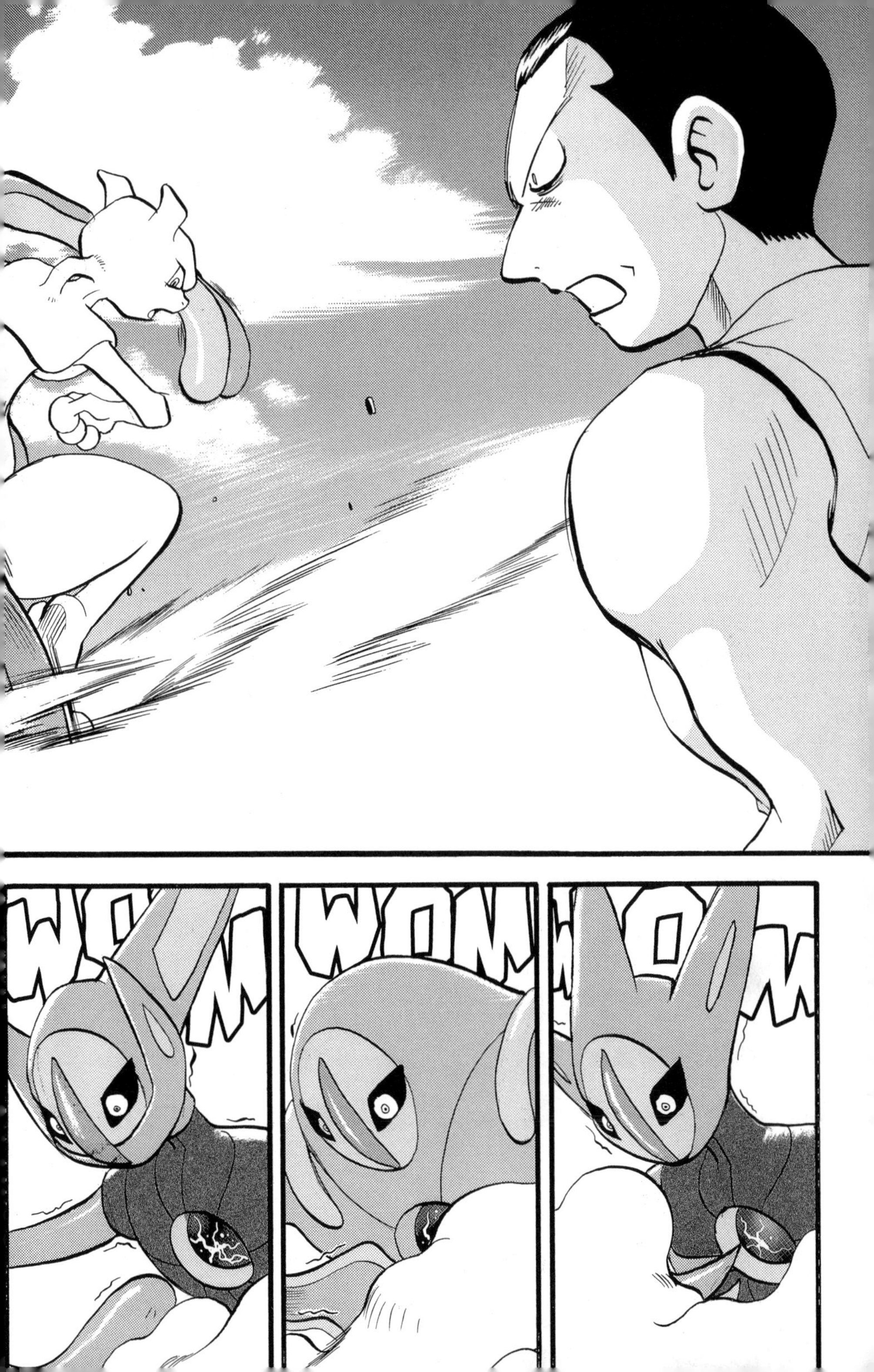
WOM
WOM
WOM

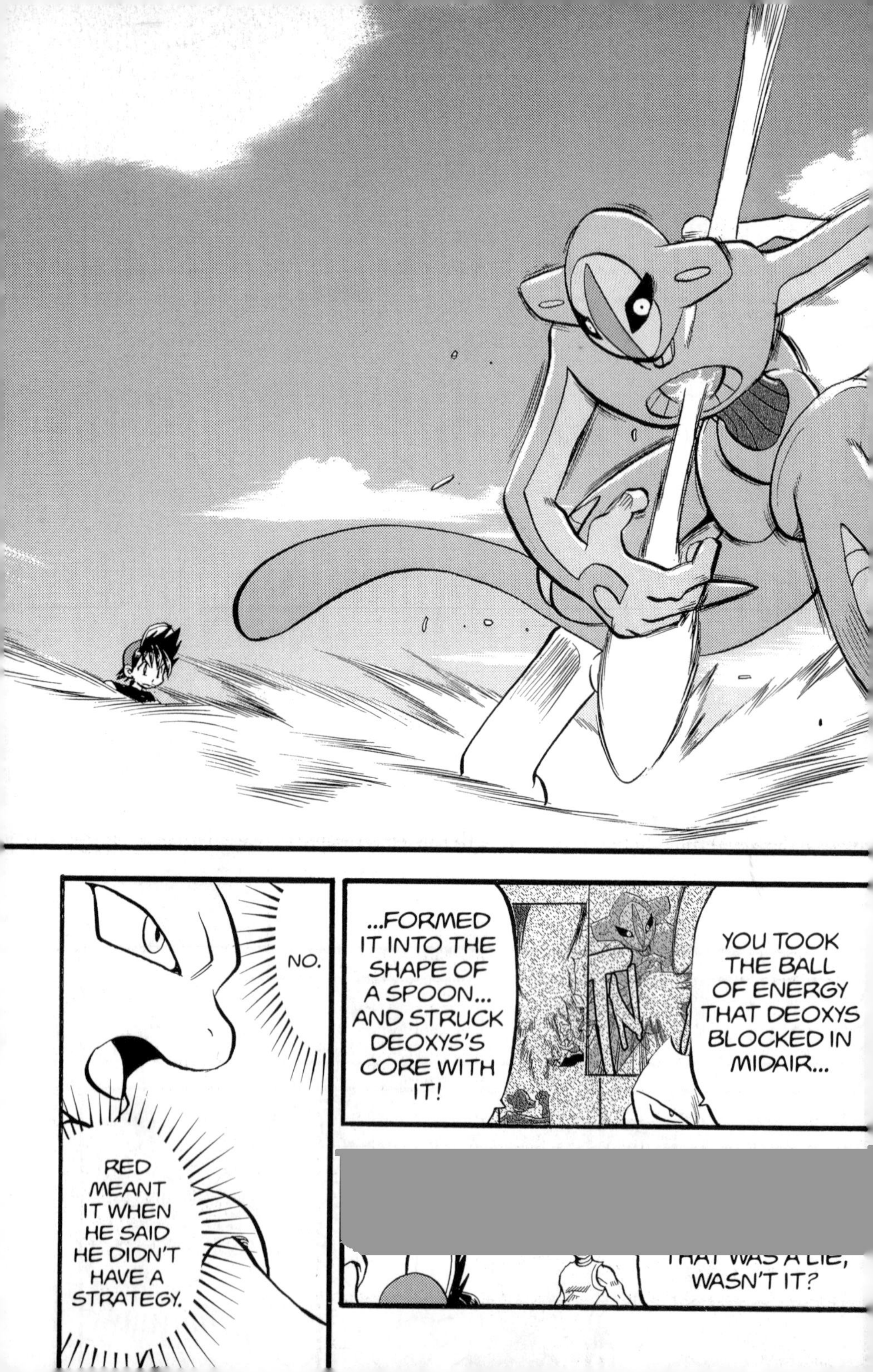
YOU TOOK THE BALL OF ENERGY THAT DEOXYS BLOCKED IN MIDAIR...
...FORMED IT INTO THE SHAPE OF A SPOON... AND STRUCK DEOXYS'S CORE WITH IT!
THAT WAS A LIE, WASN'T IT?
NO.
RED MEANT IT WHEN HE SAID HE DIDN'T HAVE A STRATEGY.

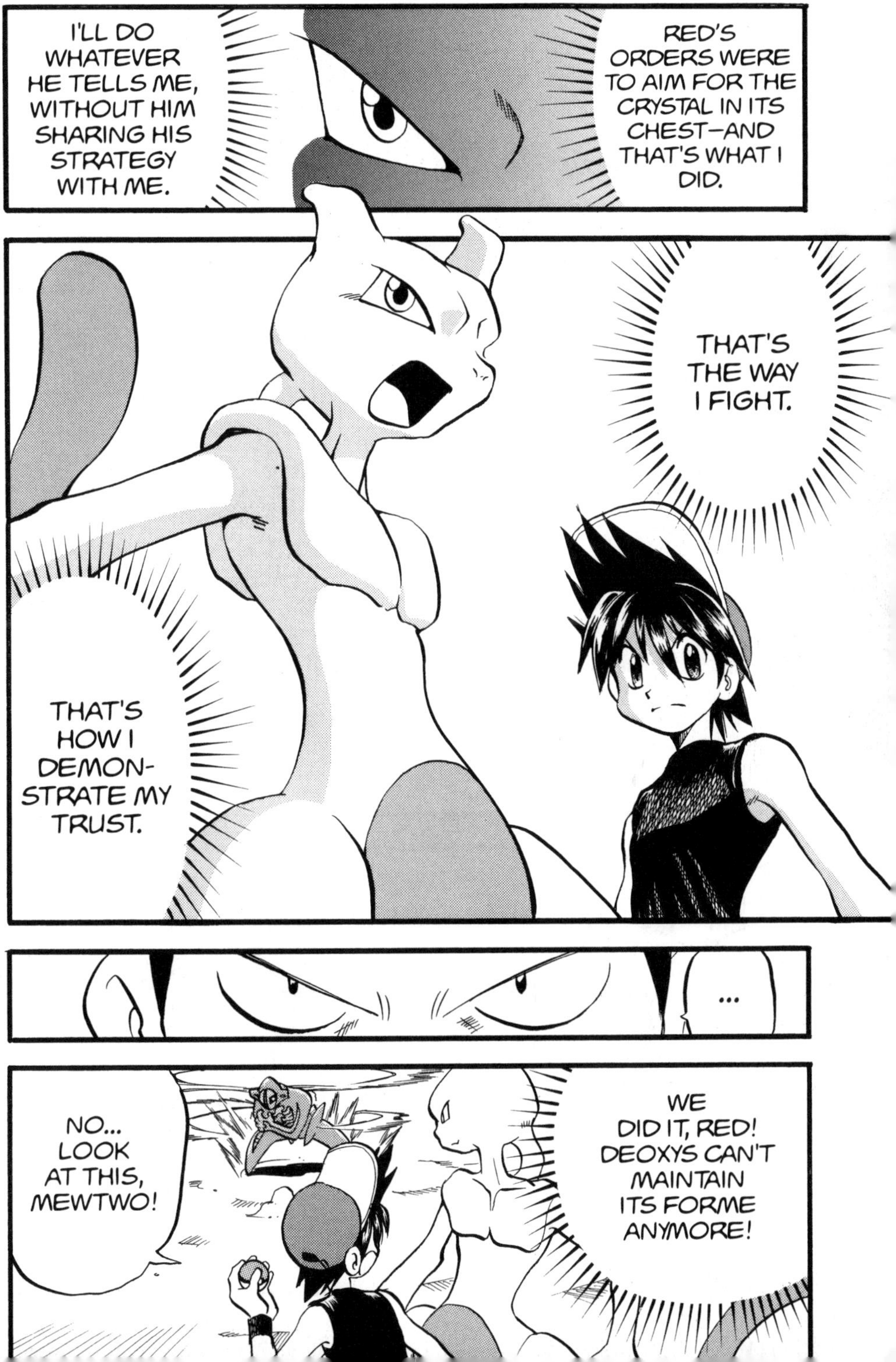
RED'S ORDERS WERE TO AIM FOR THE CRYSTAL IN ITS CHEST—AND THAT'S WHAT I DID.
I'LL DO WHATEVER HE TELLS ME, WITHOUT HIM SHARING HIS STRATEGY WITH ME.
THAT'S THE WAY I FIGHT.
THAT'S HOW I DEMON-STRATE MY TRUST.
...
WE DID IT, RED! DEOXYS CAN'T MAINTAIN ITS FORME ANYMORE!
NO... LOOK AT THIS, MEWTWO!

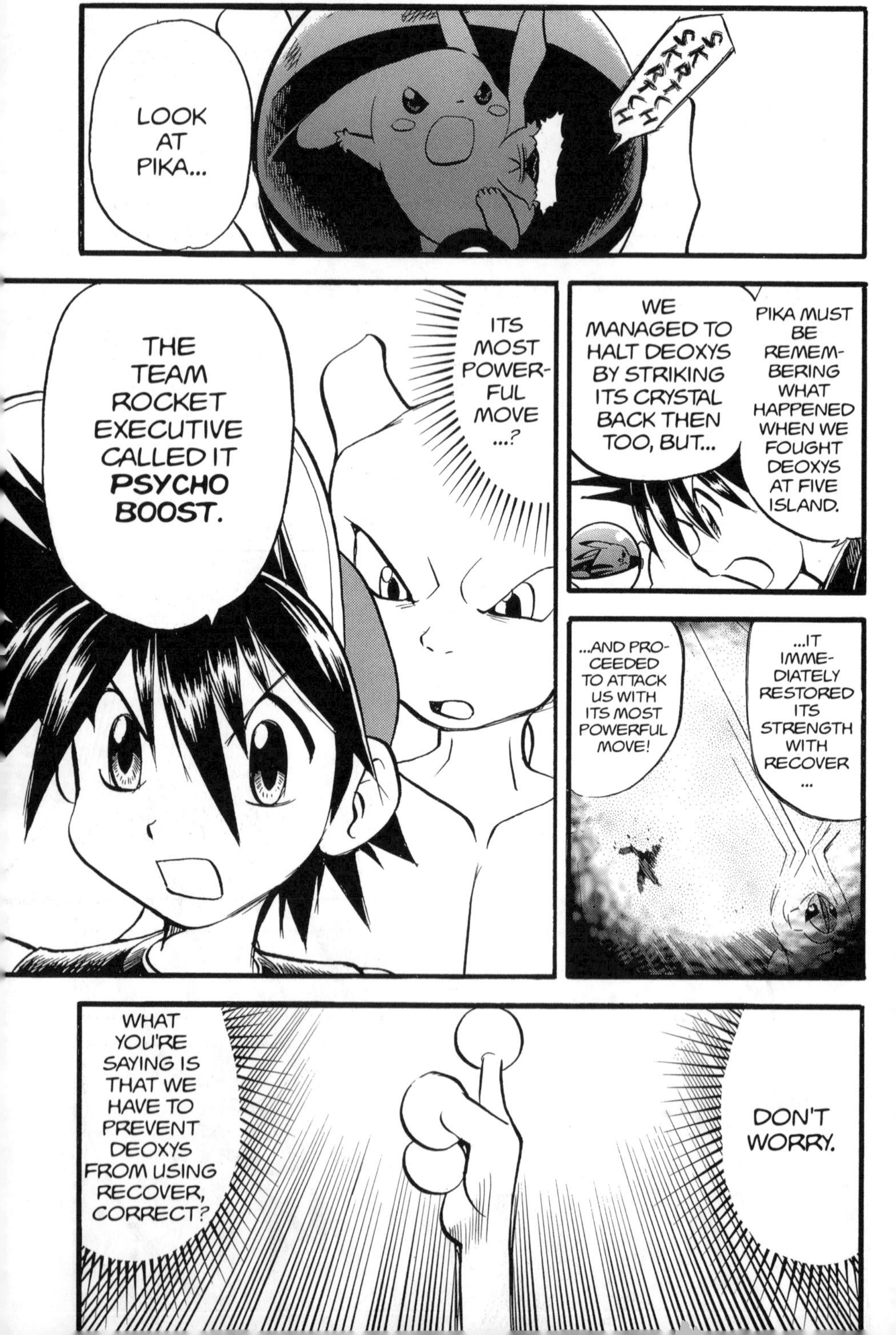
SKRTCH SKRTCH
LOOK AT PIKA...
PIKA MUST BE REMEMBERING WHAT HAPPENED WHEN WE FOUGHT DEOXYS AT FIVE ISLAND.
WE MANAGED TO HALT DEOXYS BY STRIKING ITS CRYSTAL BACK THEN TOO, BUT...
...IT IMMEDIATELY RESTORED ITS STRENGTH WITH RECOVER...
...AND PROCEEDED TO ATTACK US WITH ITS MOST POWERFUL MOVE!
ITS MOST POWERFUL MOVE...?
THE TEAM ROCKET EXECUTIVE CALLED IT **PSYCHO BOOST**.
DON'T WORRY.
WHAT YOU'RE SAYING IS THAT WE HAVE TO PREVENT DEOXYS FROM USING RECOVER, CORRECT?

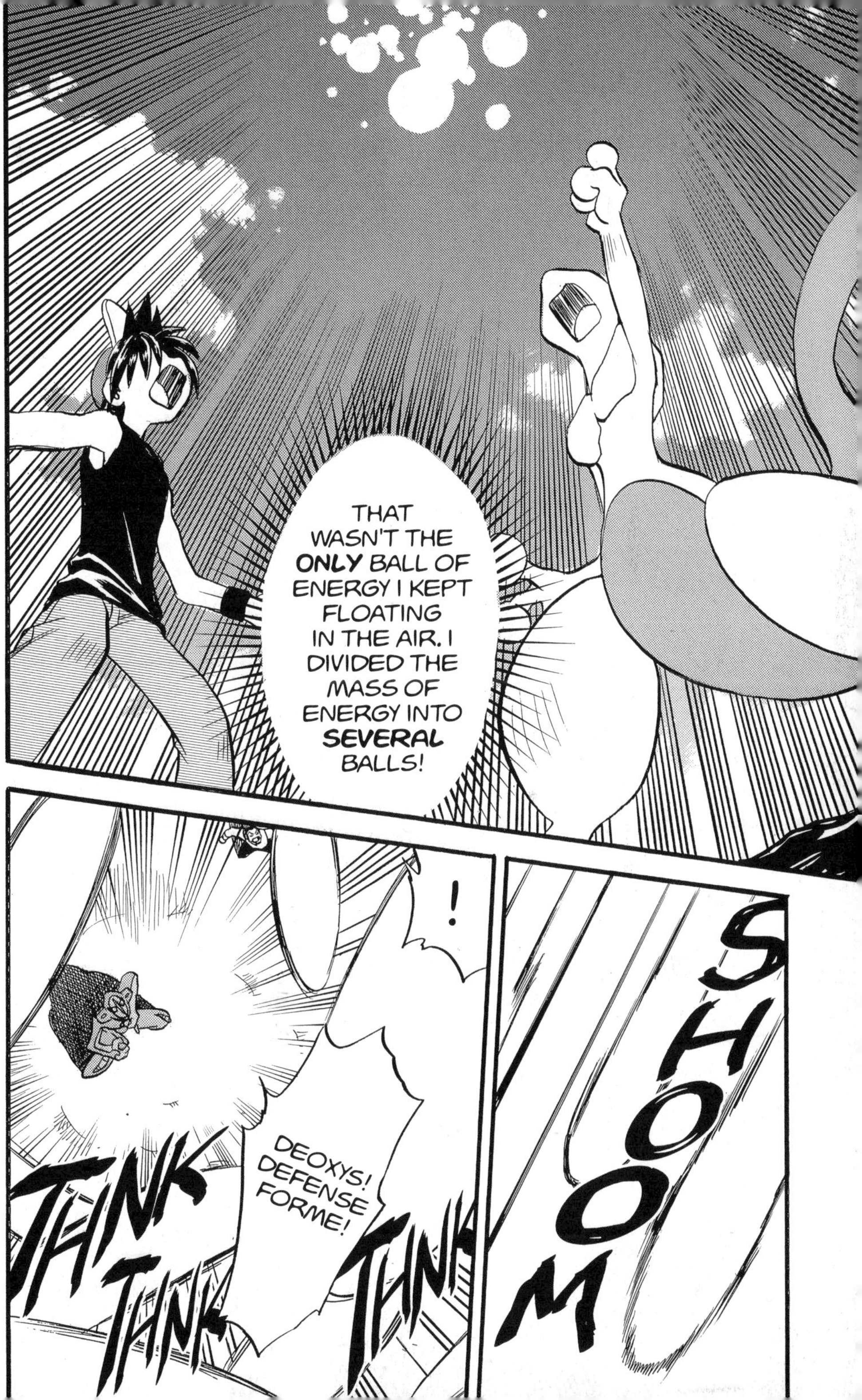
THAT WASN'T THE **ONLY** BALL OF ENERGY I KEPT FLOATING IN THE AIR. I DIVIDED THE MASS OF ENERGY INTO **SEVERAL** BALLS!
SHOOOM
!
DEOXYS! DEFENSE FORME!
THNK
THNK
THNK
THNK

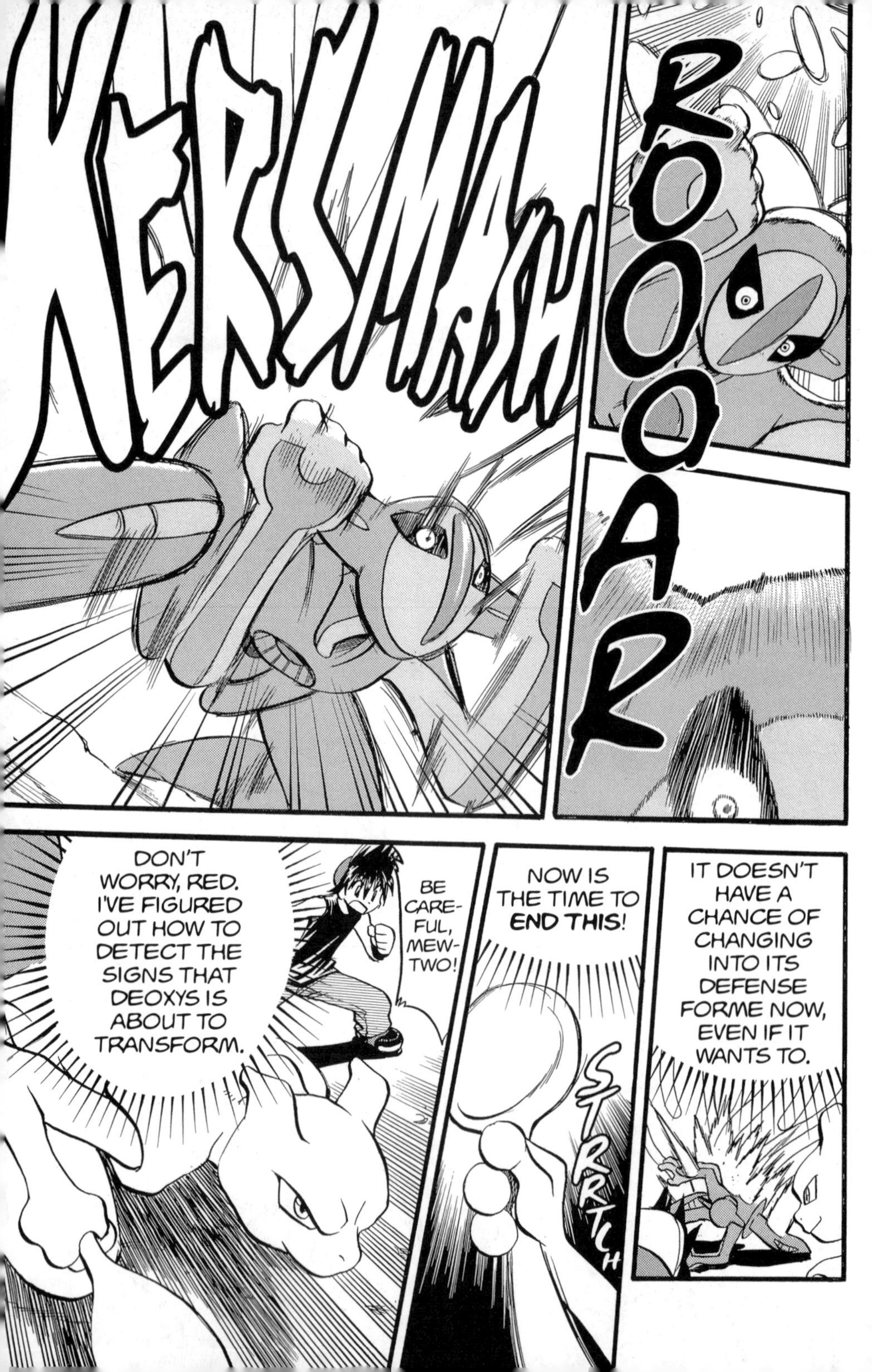
ROOOOAR
KERSMASH
IT DOESN'T HAVE A CHANCE OF CHANGING INTO ITS DEFENSE FORME NOW, EVEN IF IT WANTS TO.
NOW IS THE TIME TO **END THIS**!
STRRRTCH
BE CARE-FUL, MEW-TWO!
DON'T WORRY, RED. I'VE FIGURED OUT HOW TO DETECT THE SIGNS THAT DEOXYS IS ABOUT TO TRANSFORM.

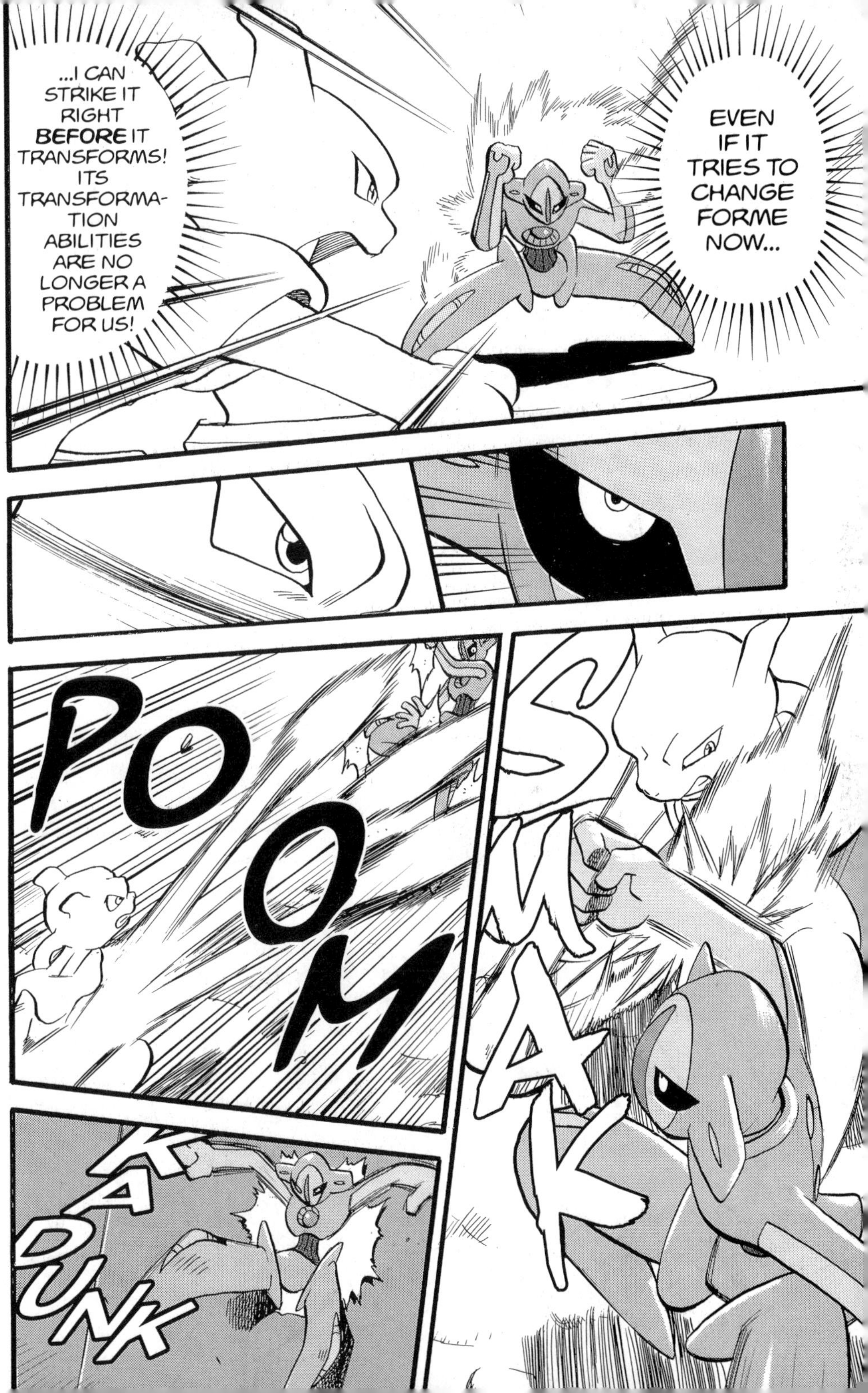
EVEN IF IT TRIES TO CHANGE FORME NOW...
...I CAN STRIKE IT RIGHT **BEFORE** IT TRANSFORMS! ITS TRANSFORMATION ABILITIES ARE NO LONGER A PROBLEM FOR US!
SMACK
POOM
KADUNK

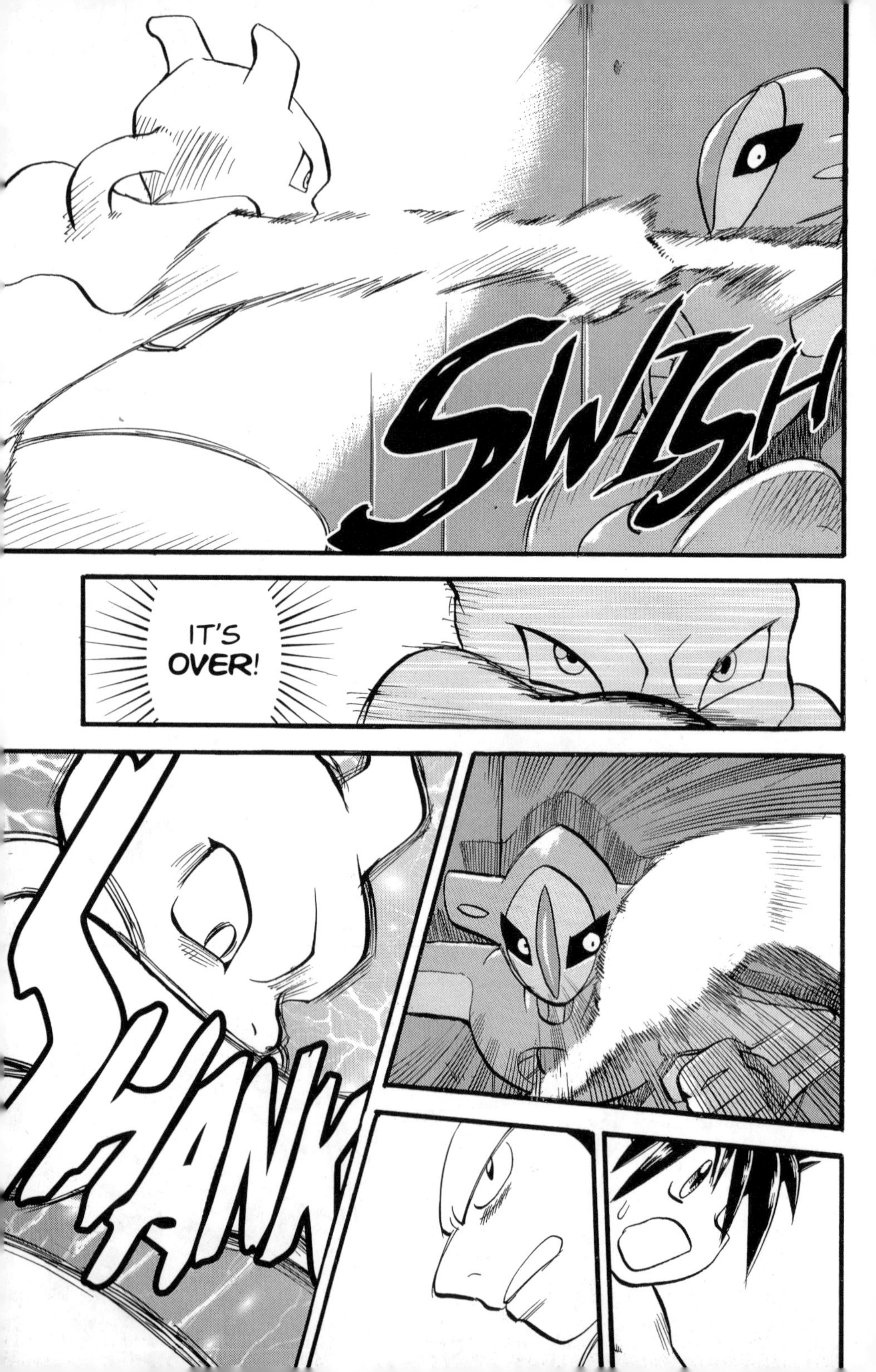
SWISH
IT'S OVER!

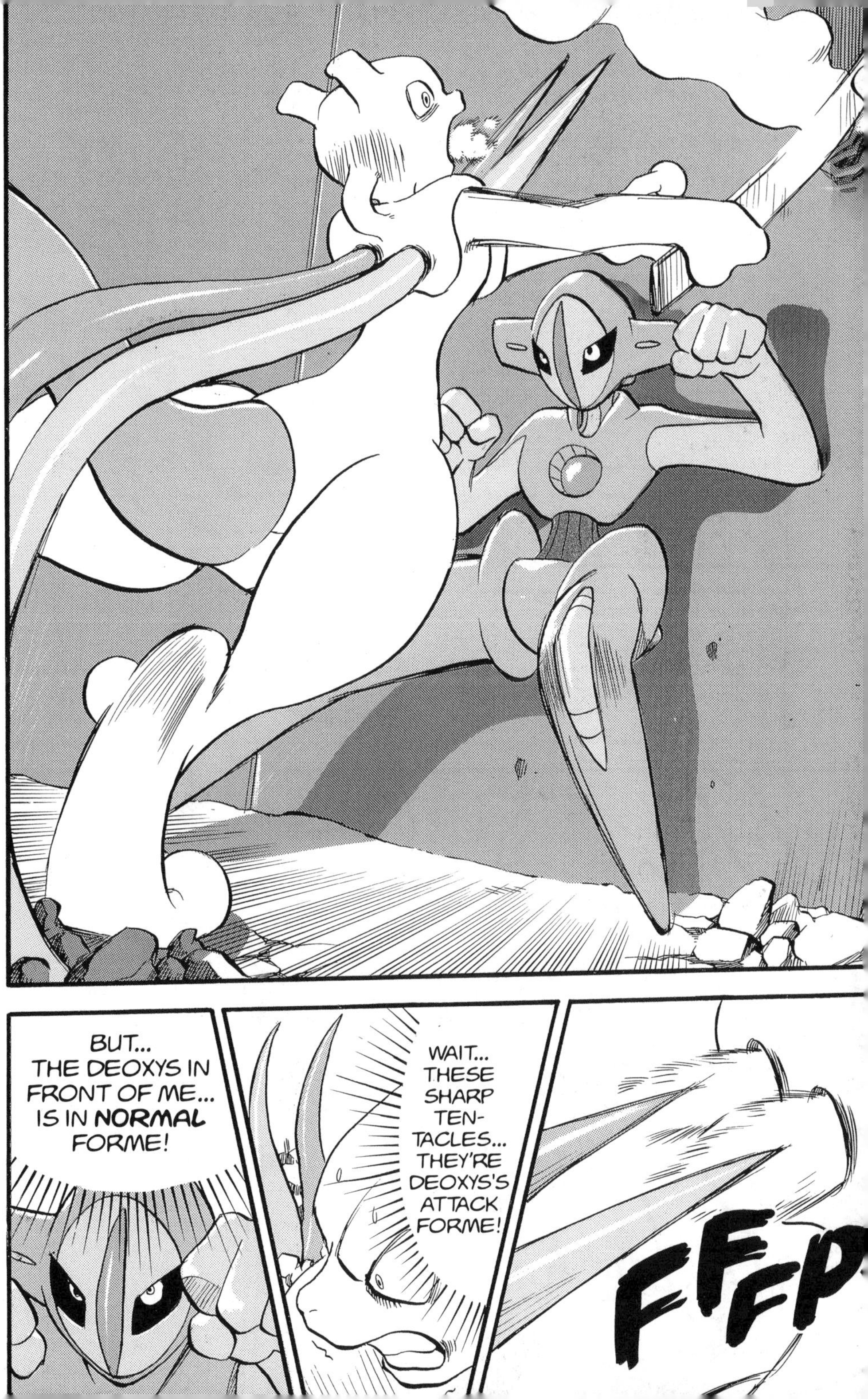
FFFP
WAIT... THESE SHARP TEN-TACLES... THEY'RE DEOXYS'S ATTACK FORME!
BUT... THE DEOXYS IN FRONT OF ME... IS IN **NORMAL** FORME!

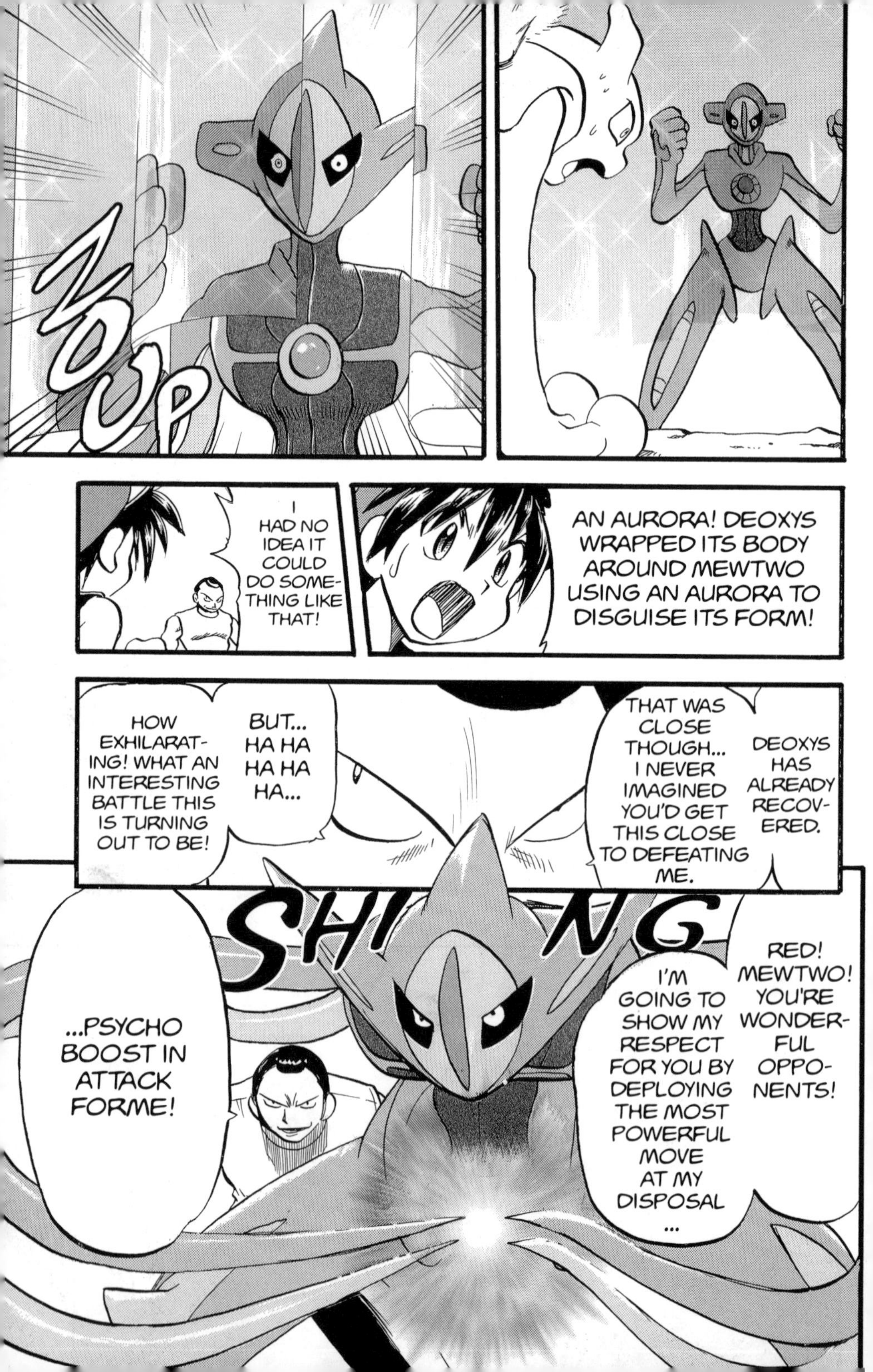
ZOOP
AN AURORA! DEOXYS WRAPPED ITS BODY AROUND MEWTWO USING AN AURORA TO DISGUISE ITS FORM!
I HAD NO IDEA IT COULD DO SOMETHING LIKE THAT!
DEOXYS HAS ALREADY RECOVERED.
THAT WAS CLOSE THOUGH... I NEVER IMAGINED YOU'D GET THIS CLOSE TO DEFEATING ME.
BUT... HA HA HA HA HA...
HOW EXHILARATING! WHAT AN INTERESTING BATTLE THIS IS TURNING OUT TO BE!
SHI NG
RED! MEWTWO! YOU'RE WONDERFUL OPPONENTS!
I'M GOING TO SHOW MY RESPECT FOR YOU BY DEPLOYING THE MOST POWERFUL MOVE AT MY DISPOSAL...
...PSYCHO BOOST IN ATTACK FORME!

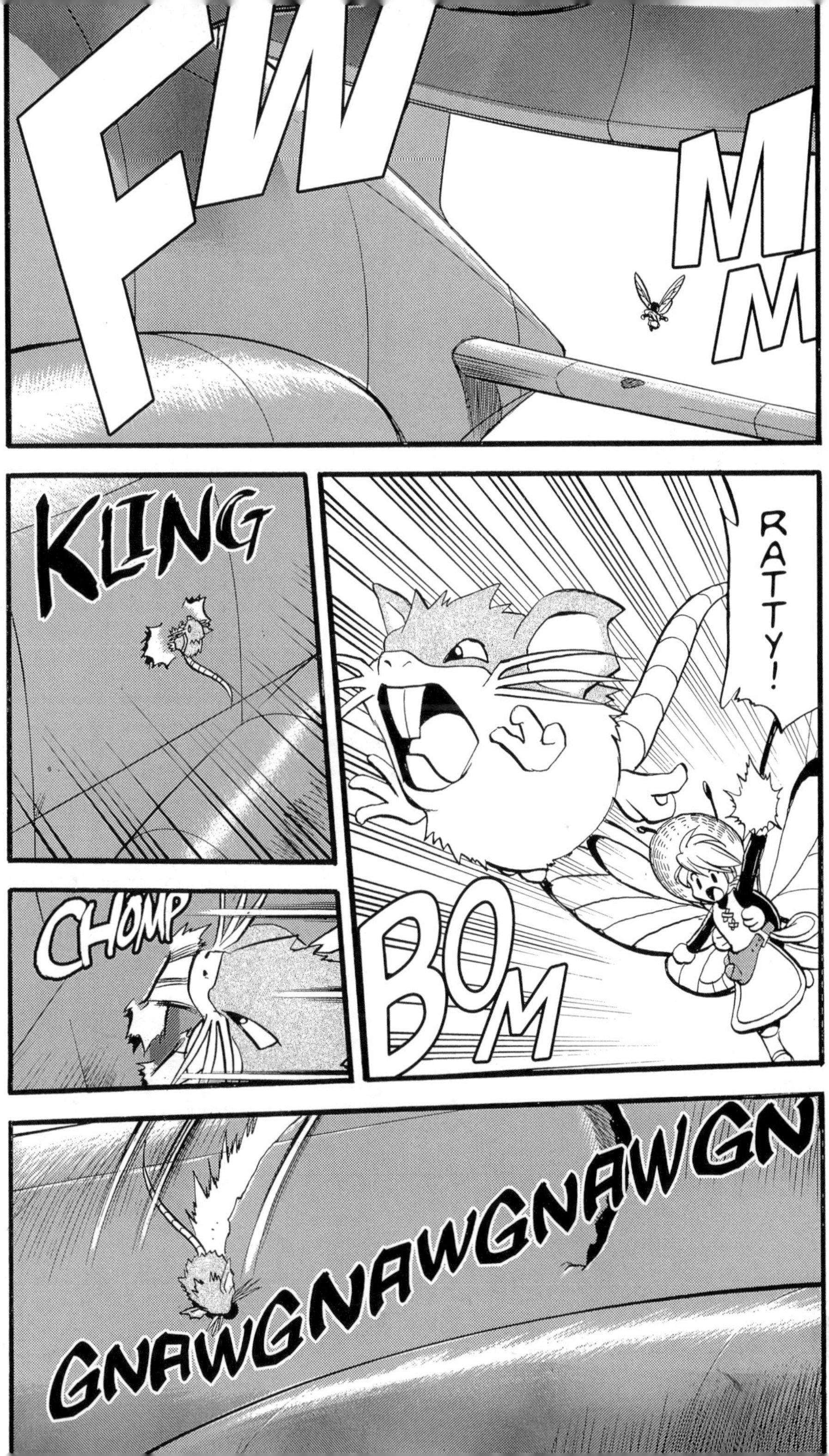
FW
M M
RATTY!
BOM
KLING
CHOMP
GNAWGNAWGNAWGN

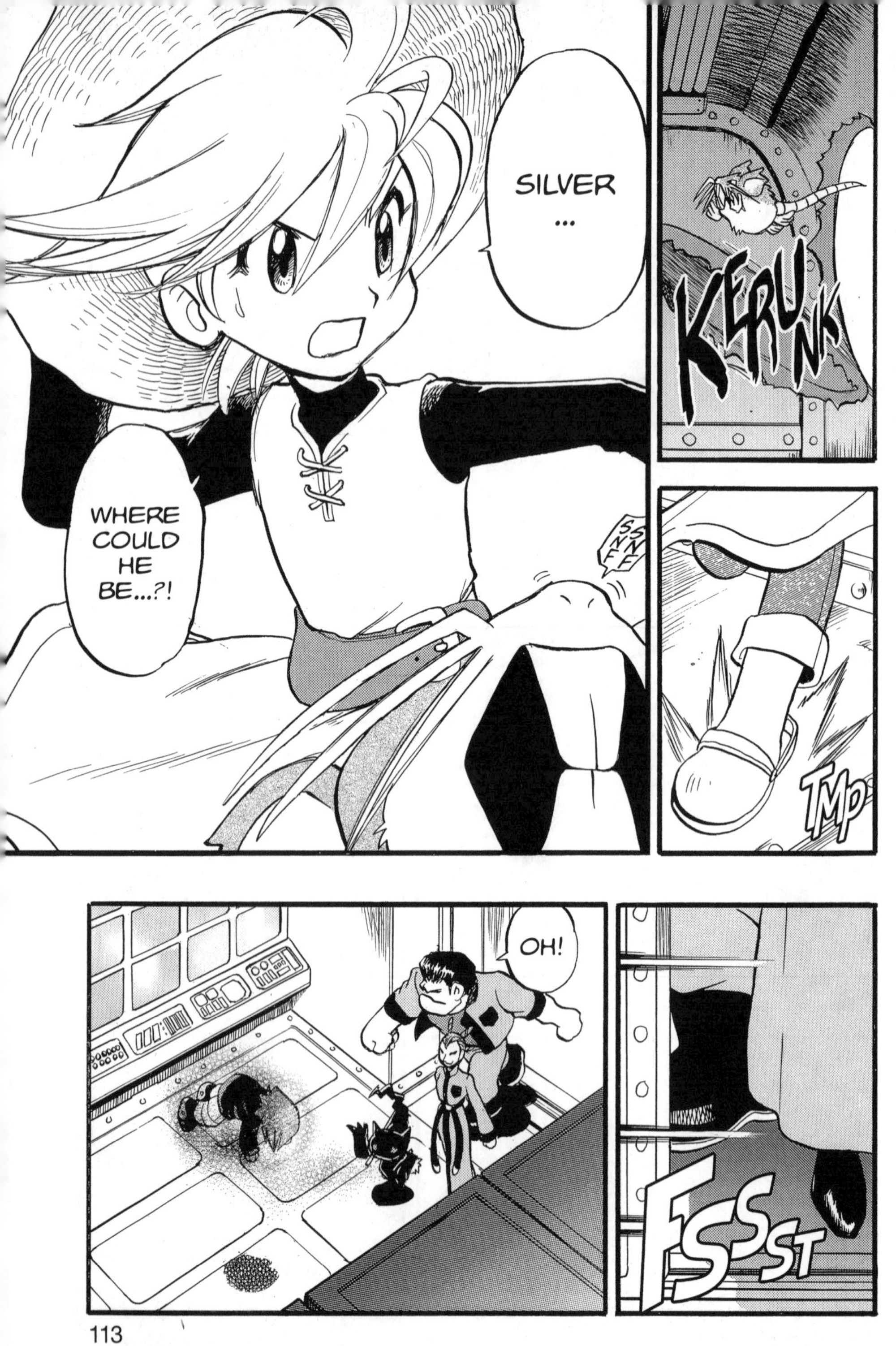
KERUNK
TMP
SILVER ...
WHERE COULD HE BE...?!
SNFF SNFF
FSSST
OH!

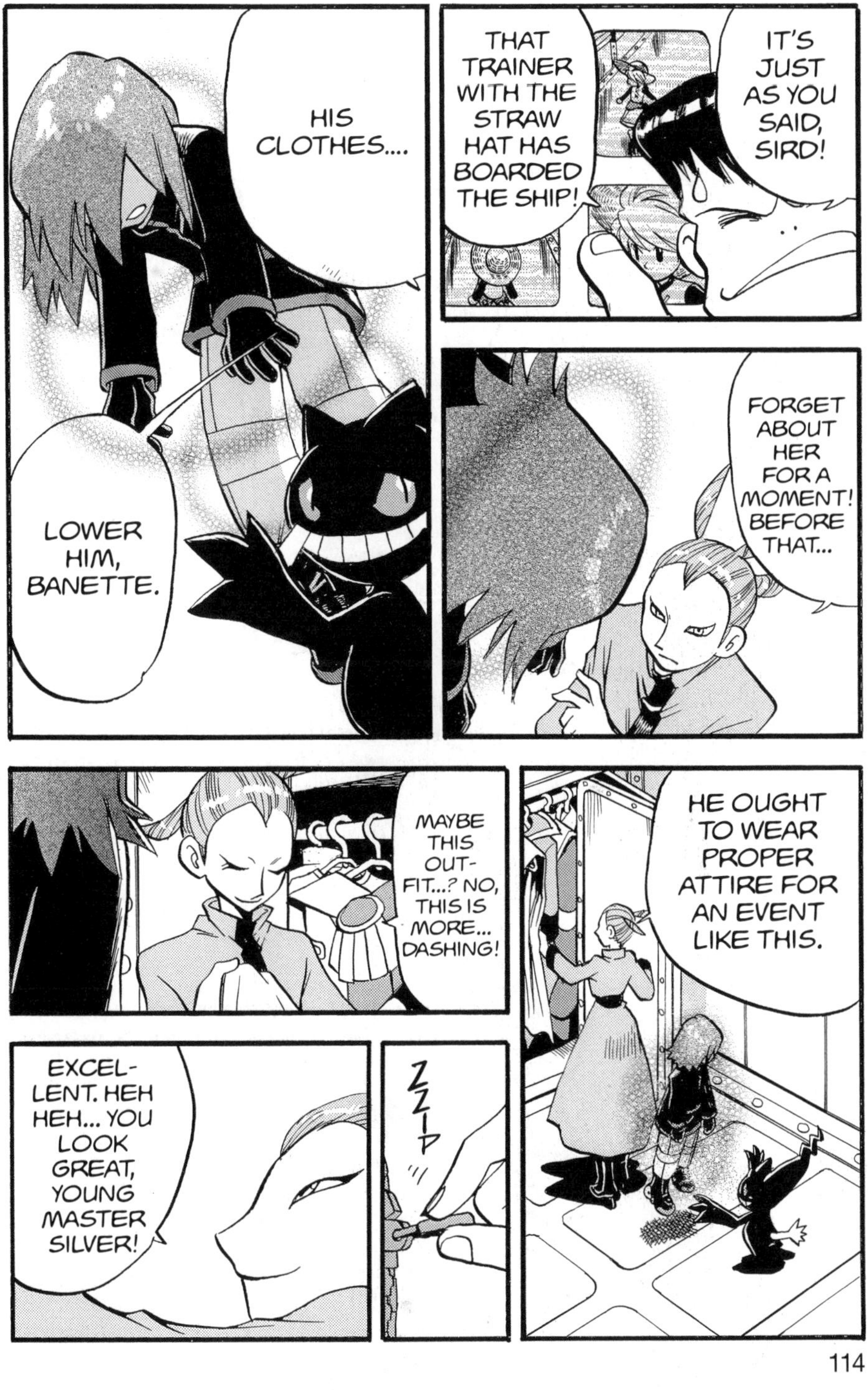

IT'S JUST AS YOU SAID, SIRD!
THAT TRAINER WITH THE STRAW HAT HAS BOARDED THE SHIP!
FORGET ABOUT HER FOR A MOMENT! BEFORE THAT...
HIS CLOTHES....
LOWER HIM, BANETTE.
HE OUGHT TO WEAR PROPER ATTIRE FOR AN EVENT LIKE THIS.
MAYBE THIS OUT-FIT...? NO, THIS IS MORE... DASHING!
ZZIP
EXCEL-LENT. HEH HEH... YOU LOOK GREAT, YOUNG MASTER SILVER!

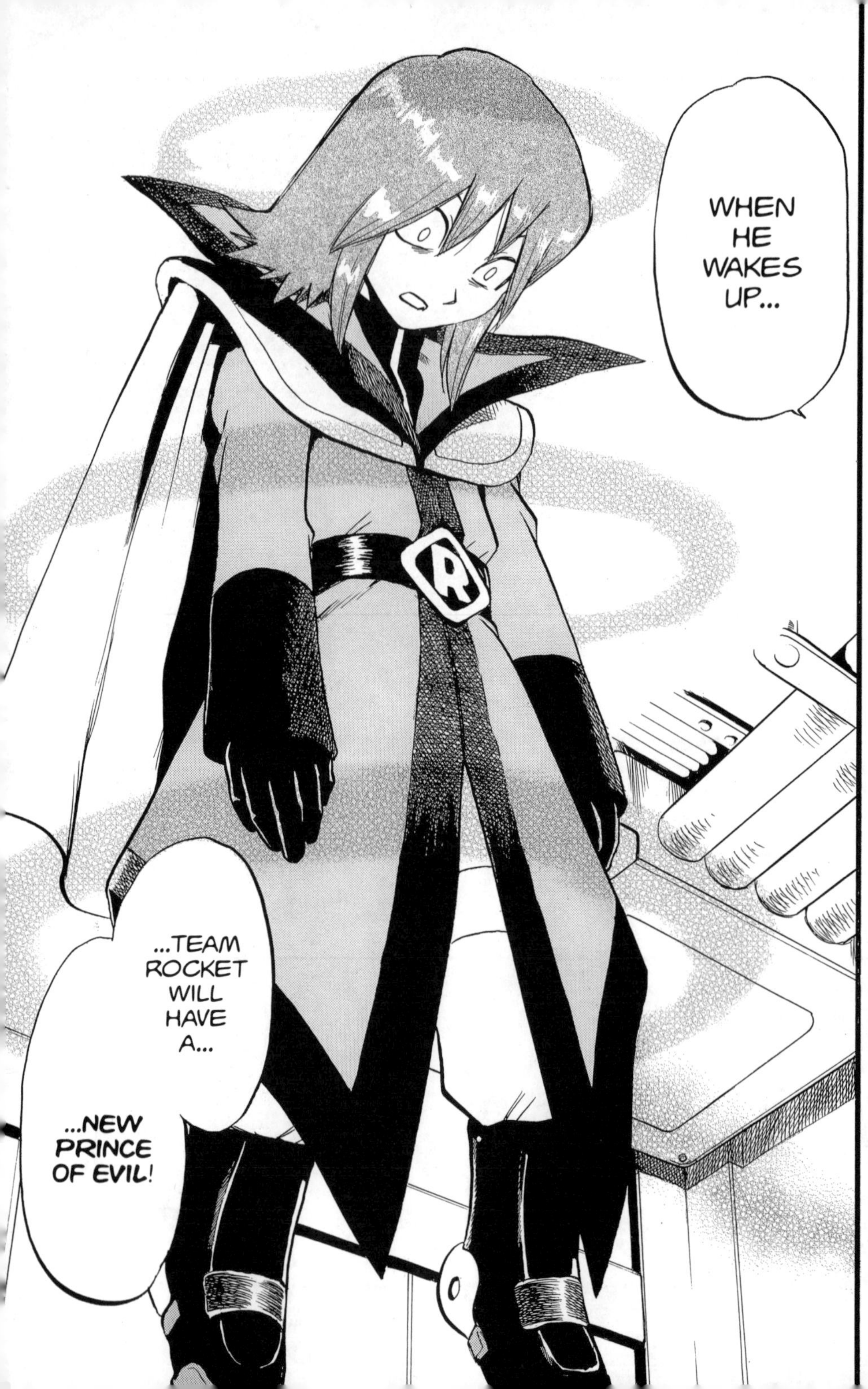
WHEN HE WAKES UP...
...TEAM ROCKET WILL HAVE A...
...NEW PRINCE OF EVIL!

● Adventure 294 ●
Mewtwo and Mew Too

Pokémon Adventures
FireRed & LeafGreen
The Fifth Chapter

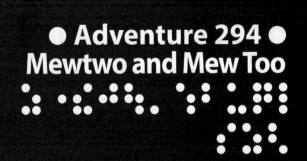

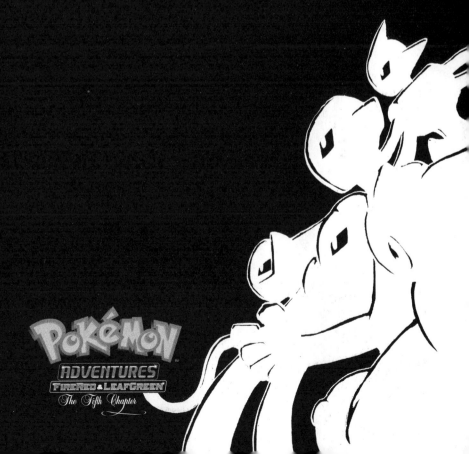

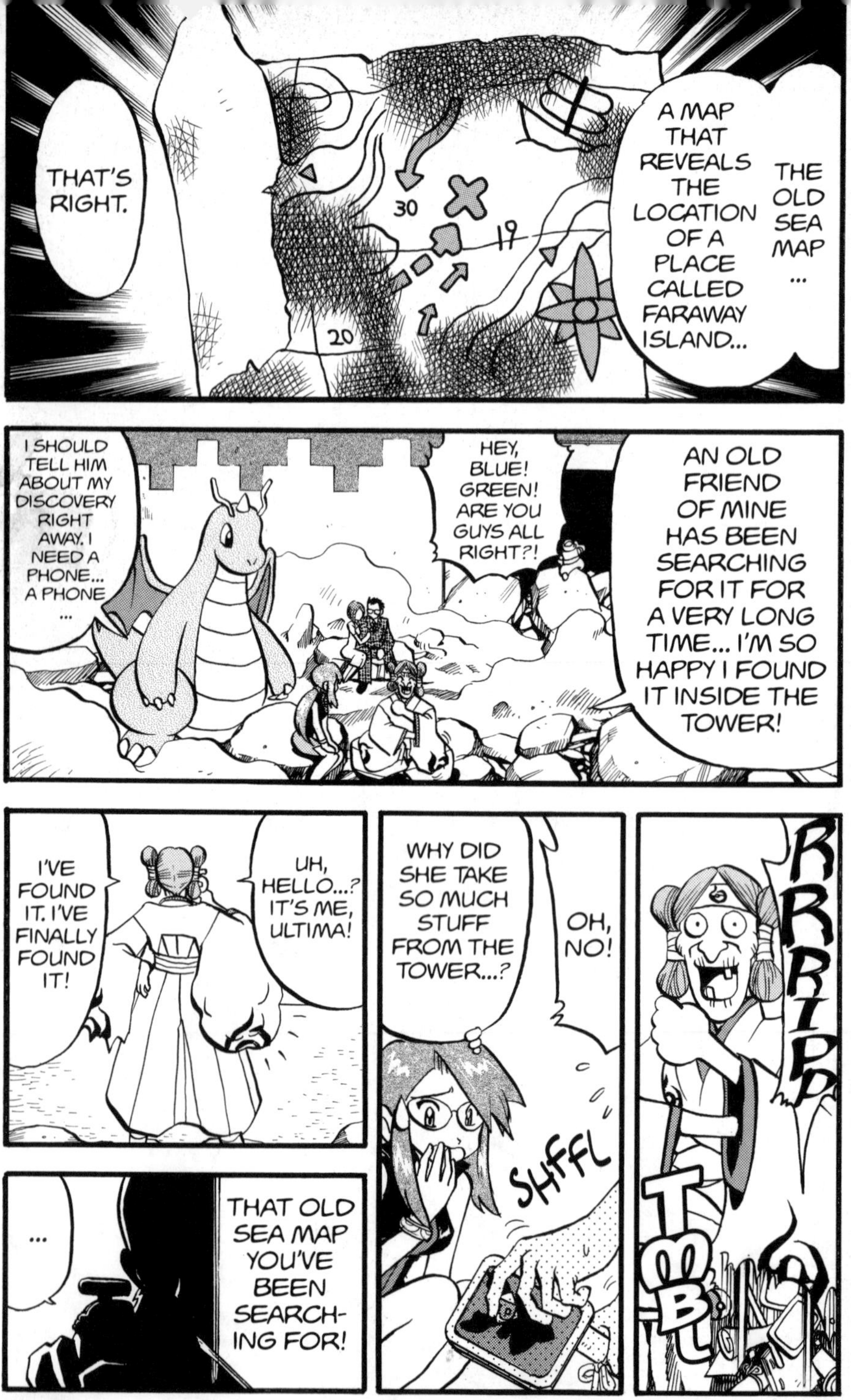
THE OLD SEA MAP ...
A MAP THAT REVEALS THE LOCATION OF A PLACE CALLED FARAWAY ISLAND...
30
19
20
THAT'S RIGHT.
AN OLD FRIEND OF MINE HAS BEEN SEARCHING FOR IT FOR A VERY LONG TIME... I'M SO HAPPY I FOUND IT INSIDE THE TOWER!
HEY, BLUE! GREEN! ARE YOU GUYS ALL RIGHT?!
I SHOULD TELL HIM ABOUT MY DISCOVERY RIGHT AWAY. I NEED A PHONE... A PHONE ...
RRRIPP
TMBL
OH, NO!
WHY DID SHE TAKE SO MUCH STUFF FROM THE TOWER...?
SHFFL
UH, HELLO...? IT'S ME, ULTIMA!
I'VE FOUND IT. I'VE FINALLY FOUND IT!
THAT OLD SEA MAP YOU'VE BEEN SEARCH-ING FOR!
...

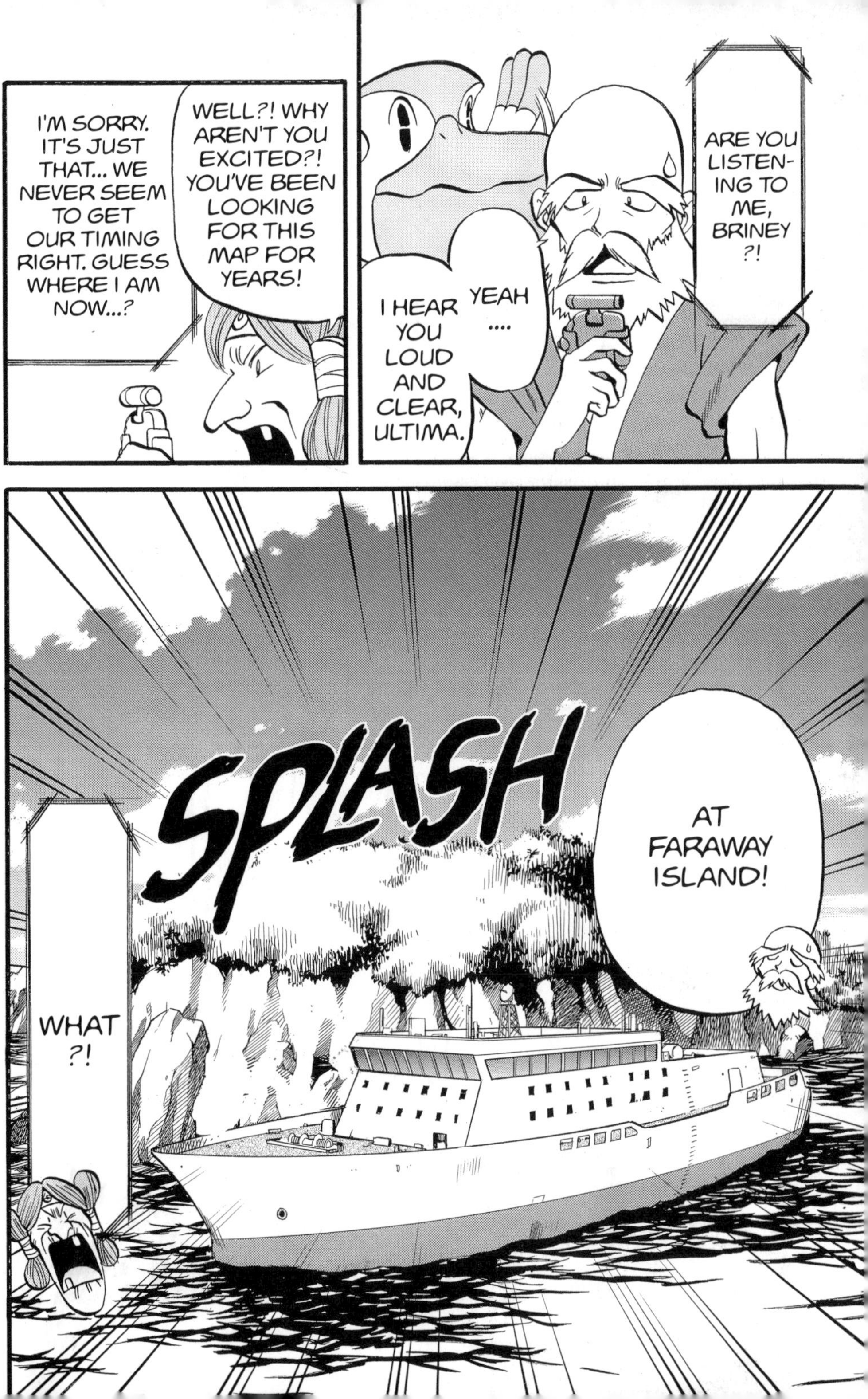
ARE YOU LISTENING TO ME, BRINEY?!
YEAH ....
I HEAR YOU LOUD AND CLEAR, ULTIMA.
WELL?! WHY AREN'T YOU EXCITED?! YOU'VE BEEN LOOKING FOR THIS MAP FOR YEARS!
I'M SORRY. IT'S JUST THAT... WE NEVER SEEM TO GET OUR TIMING RIGHT. GUESS WHERE I AM NOW...?
SPLASH
AT FARAWAY ISLAND!
WHAT?!

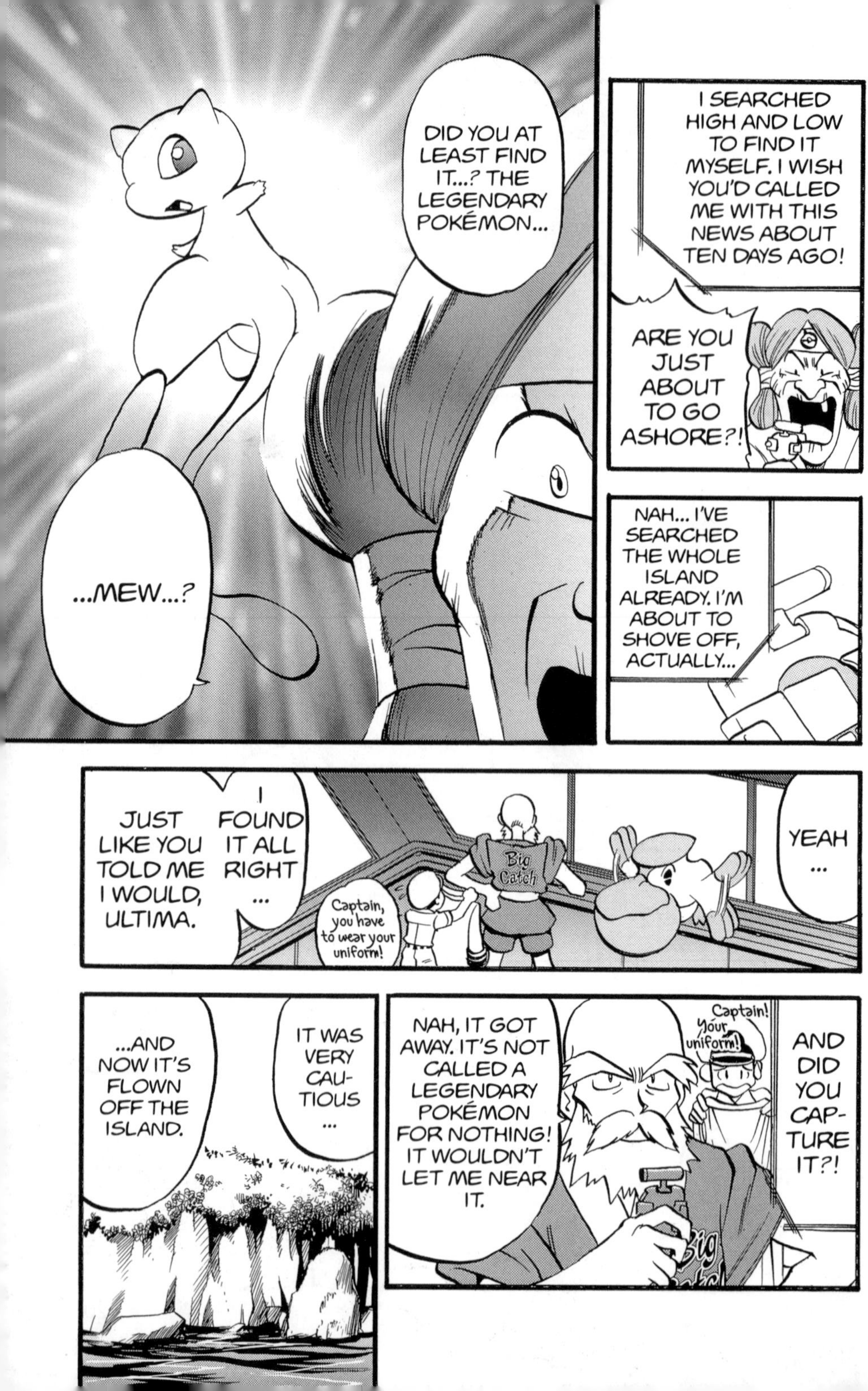
I SEARCHED HIGH AND LOW TO FIND IT MYSELF. I WISH YOU'D CALLED ME WITH THIS NEWS ABOUT TEN DAYS AGO!
ARE YOU JUST ABOUT TO GO ASHORE?!
NAH... I'VE SEARCHED THE WHOLE ISLAND ALREADY. I'M ABOUT TO SHOVE OFF, ACTUALLY...
DID YOU AT LEAST FIND IT...? THE LEGENDARY POKÉMON...
...MEW...?
YEAH ...
I FOUND IT ALL RIGHT ...
JUST LIKE YOU TOLD ME I WOULD, ULTIMA.
Big Catch
Captain, you have to wear your uniform!
AND DID YOU CAP-TURE IT?!
Captain! Your uniform!
NAH, IT GOT AWAY. IT'S NOT CALLED A LEGENDARY POKÉMON FOR NOTHING! IT WOULDN'T LET ME NEAR IT.
IT WAS VERY CAU-TIOUS ...
...AND NOW IT'S FLOWN OFF THE ISLAND.

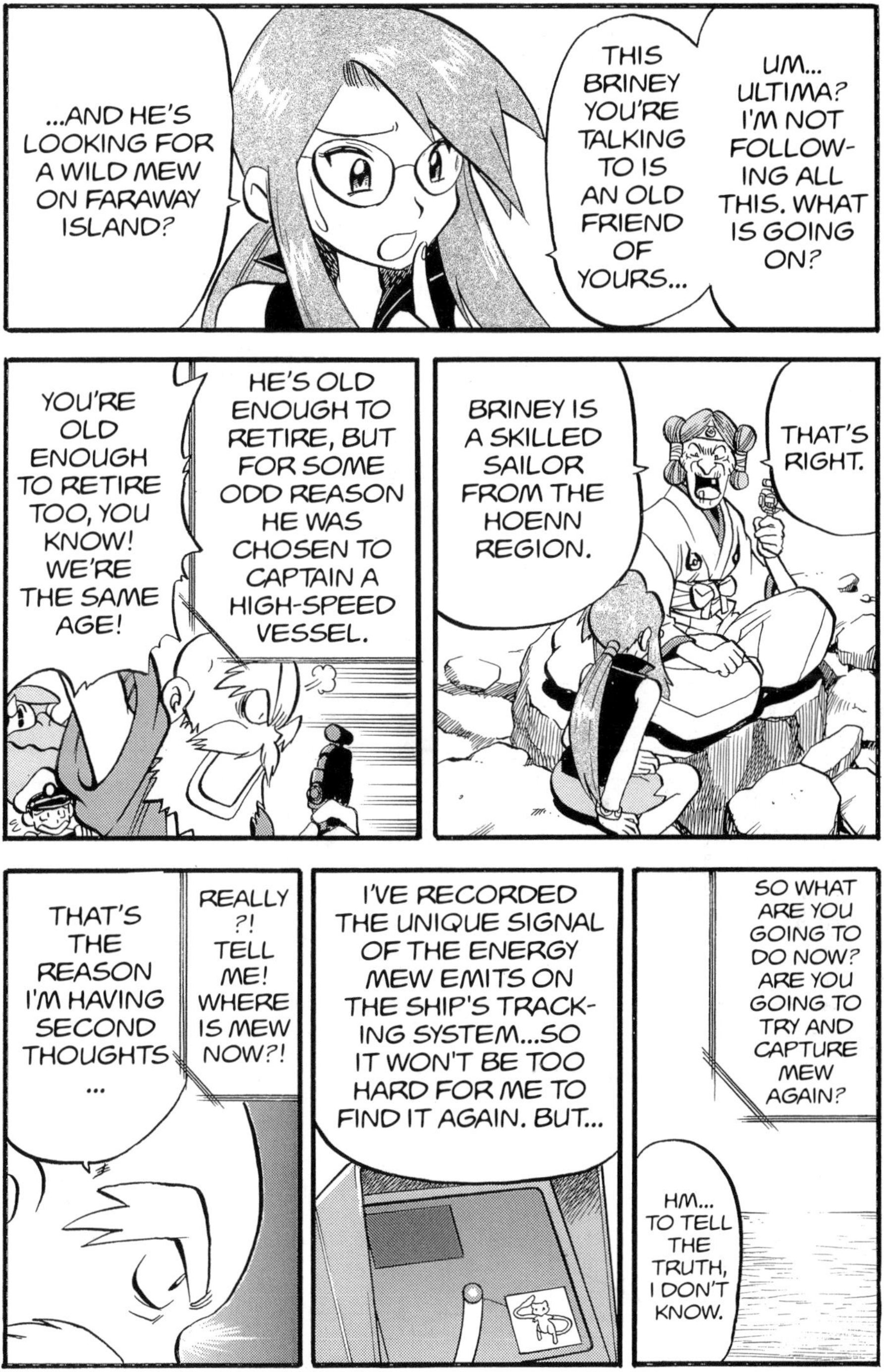
UM... ULTIMA? I'M NOT FOLLOW-ING ALL THIS. WHAT IS GOING ON?
THIS BRINEY YOU'RE TALKING TO IS AN OLD FRIEND OF YOURS...
...AND HE'S LOOKING FOR A WILD MEW ON FARAWAY ISLAND?
THAT'S RIGHT.
BRINEY IS A SKILLED SAILOR FROM THE HOENN REGION.
HE'S OLD ENOUGH TO RETIRE, BUT FOR SOME ODD REASON HE WAS CHOSEN TO CAPTAIN A HIGH-SPEED VESSEL.
YOU'RE OLD ENOUGH TO RETIRE TOO, YOU KNOW! WE'RE THE SAME AGE!
SO WHAT ARE YOU GOING TO DO NOW? ARE YOU GOING TO TRY AND CAPTURE MEW AGAIN?
HM... TO TELL THE TRUTH, I DON'T KNOW.
I'VE RECORDED THE UNIQUE SIGNAL OF THE ENERGY MEW EMITS ON THE SHIP'S TRACK-ING SYSTEM...SO IT WON'T BE TOO HARD FOR ME TO FIND IT AGAIN. BUT...
REALLY ?! TELL ME! WHERE IS MEW NOW?!
THAT'S THE REASON I'M HAVING SECOND THOUGHTS ...

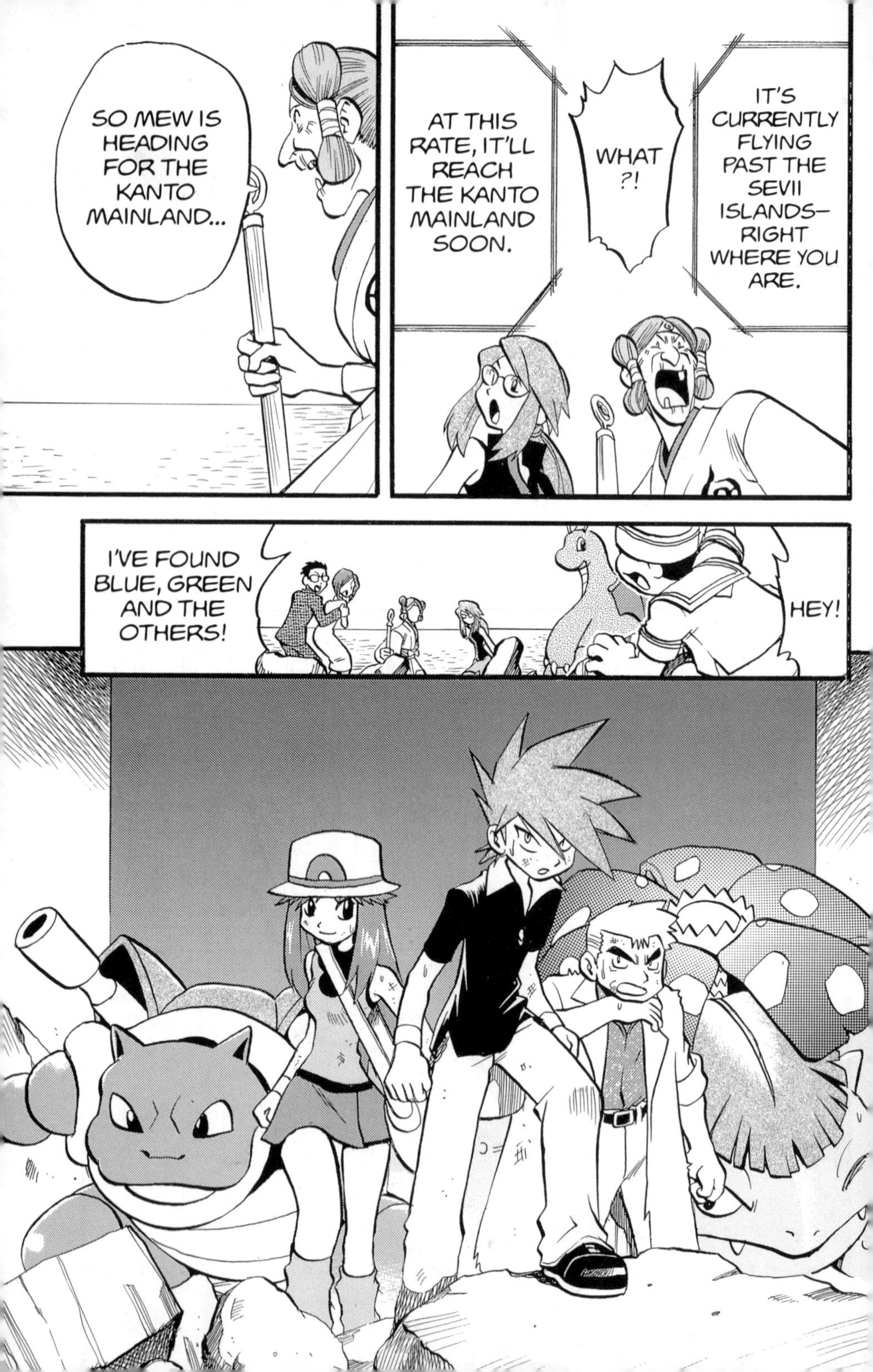
IT'S CURRENTLY FLYING PAST THE SEVII ISLANDS—RIGHT WHERE YOU ARE.
WHAT?!
AT THIS RATE, IT'LL REACH THE KANTO MAINLAND SOON.
SO MEW IS HEADING FOR THE KANTO MAINLAND...
HEY!
I'VE FOUND BLUE, GREEN AND THE OTHERS!

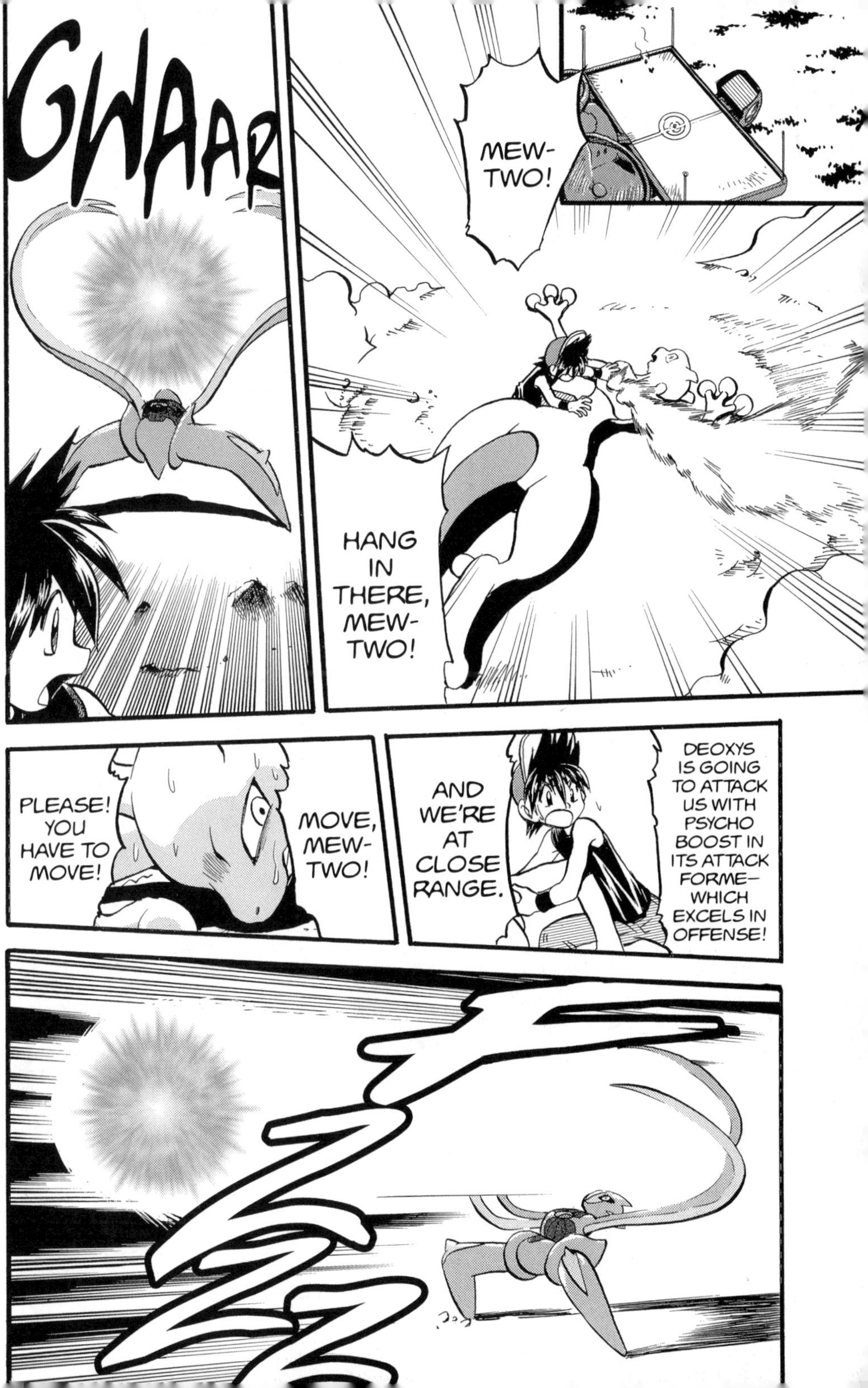
MEW-TWO!
HANG IN THERE, MEW-TWO!
GWAAR
DEOXYS IS GOING TO ATTACK US WITH PSYCHO BOOST IN ITS ATTACK FORME—WHICH EXCELS IN OFFENSE!
AND WE'RE AT CLOSE RANGE.
MOVE, MEW-TWO!
PLEASE! YOU HAVE TO MOVE!

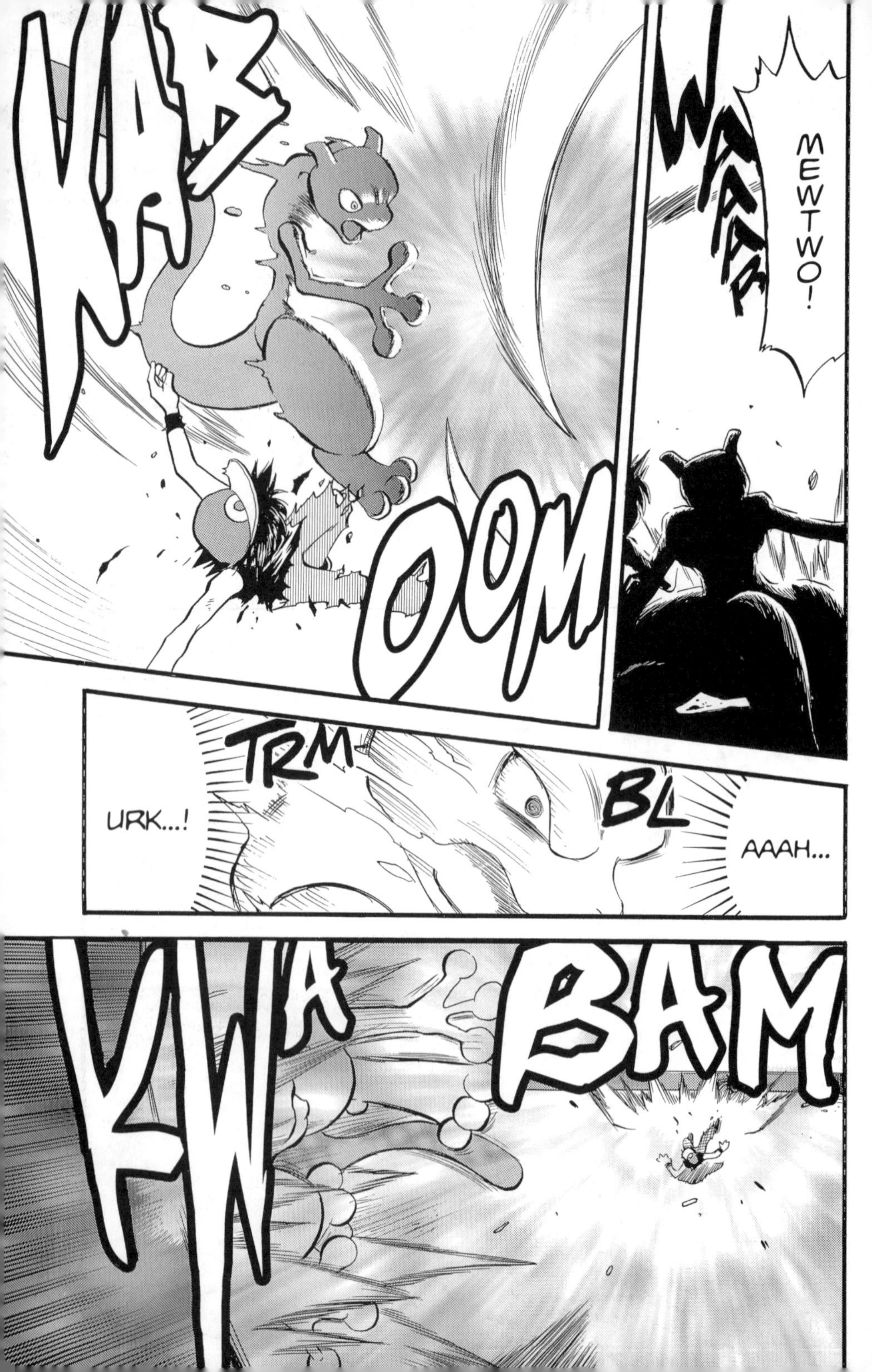
MEWTWO!
WAAAR
KAB
OOM
AAAH...
TRM
BL
URK...!
KWA
BAM

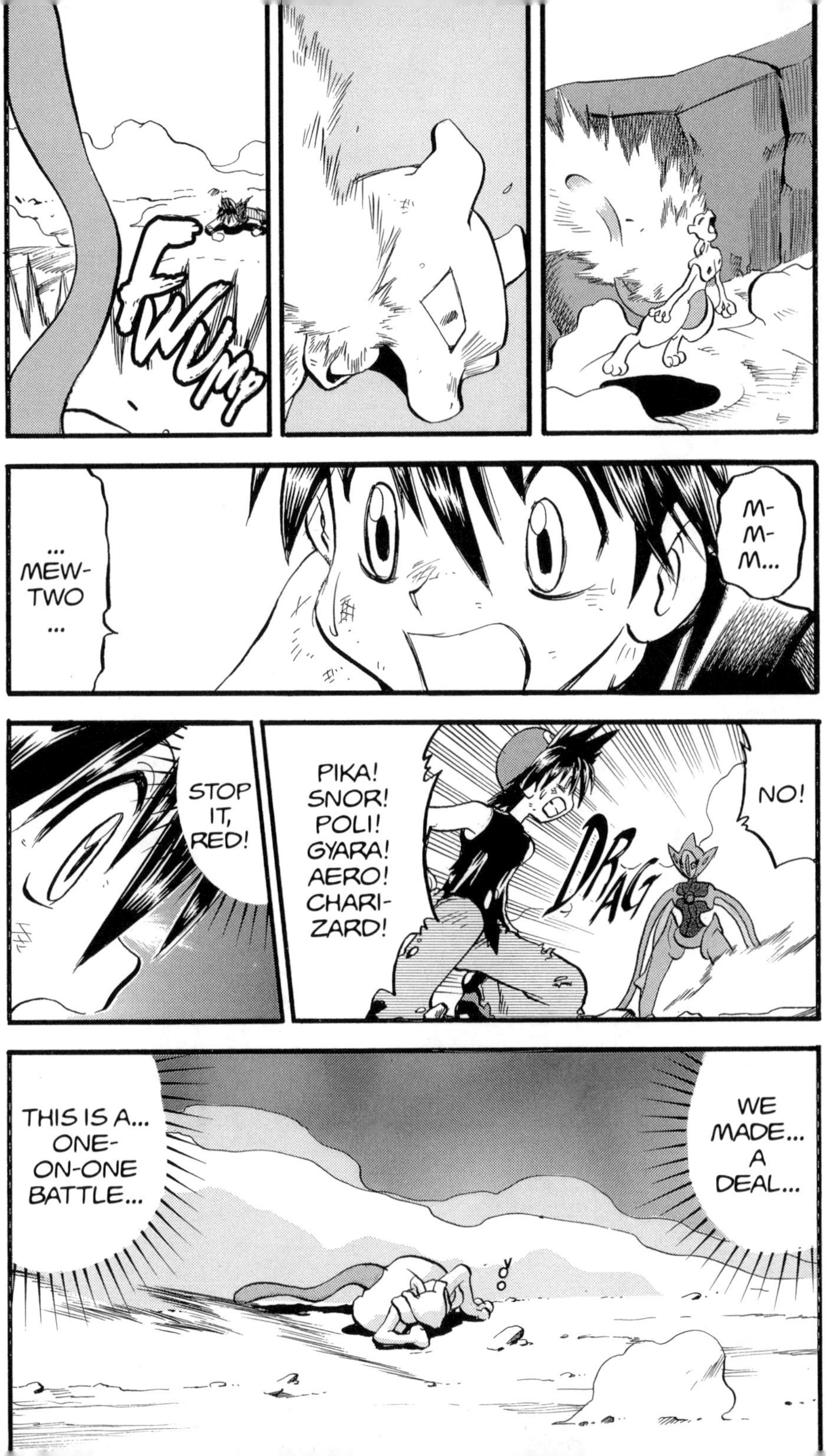
FWUMP
M-M-M...
...MEW-TWO...
NO!
PIKA! SNOR! POLI! GYARA! AERO! CHARIZARD!
DRAG
STOP IT, RED!
WE MADE... A DEAL...
THIS IS A... ONE-ON-ONE BATTLE...

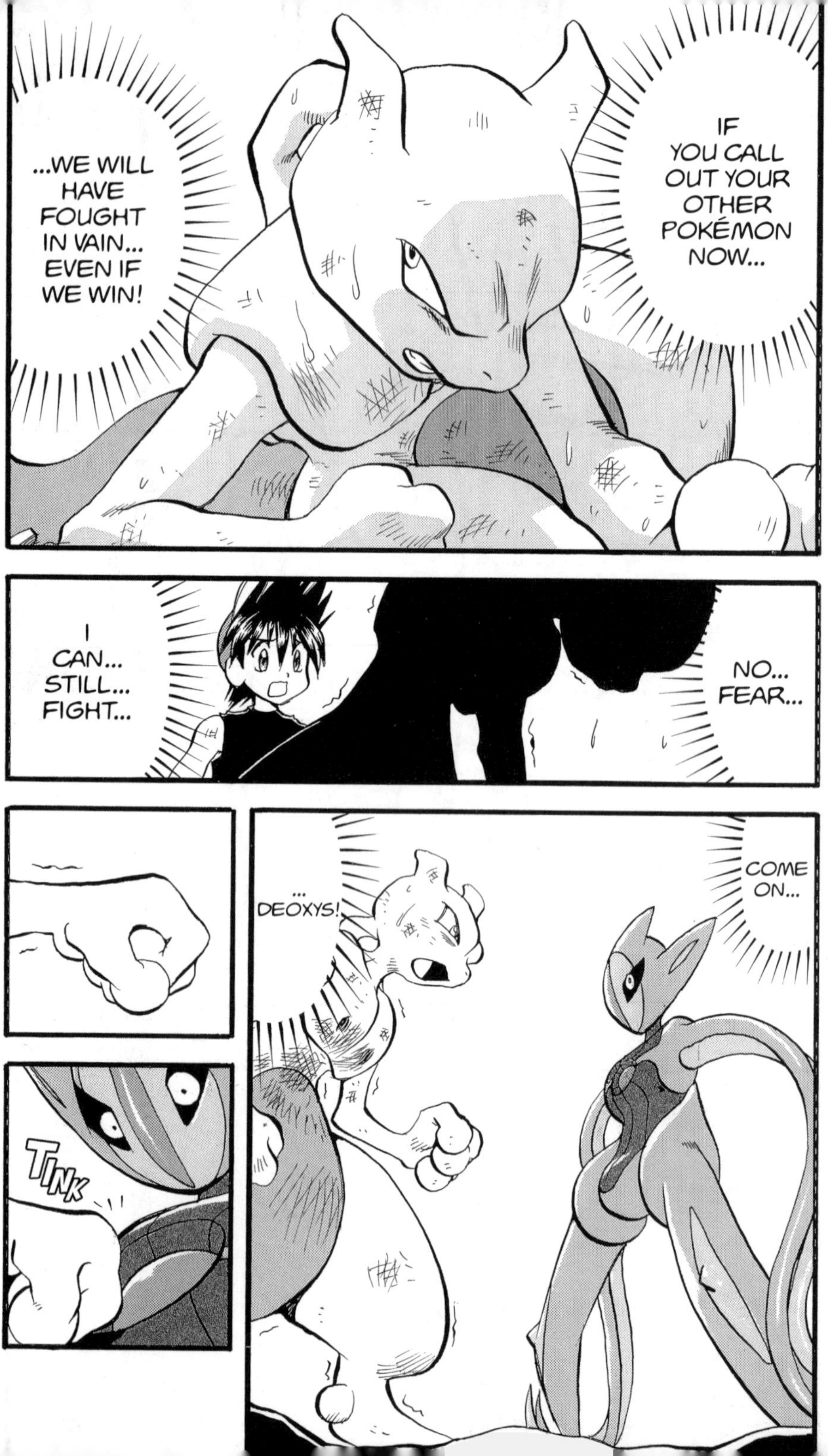
IF YOU CALL OUT YOUR OTHER POKÉMON NOW...
...WE WILL HAVE FOUGHT IN VAIN... EVEN IF WE WIN!
NO... FEAR...
I CAN... STILL... FIGHT...
COME ON...
... DEOXYS!
TINK

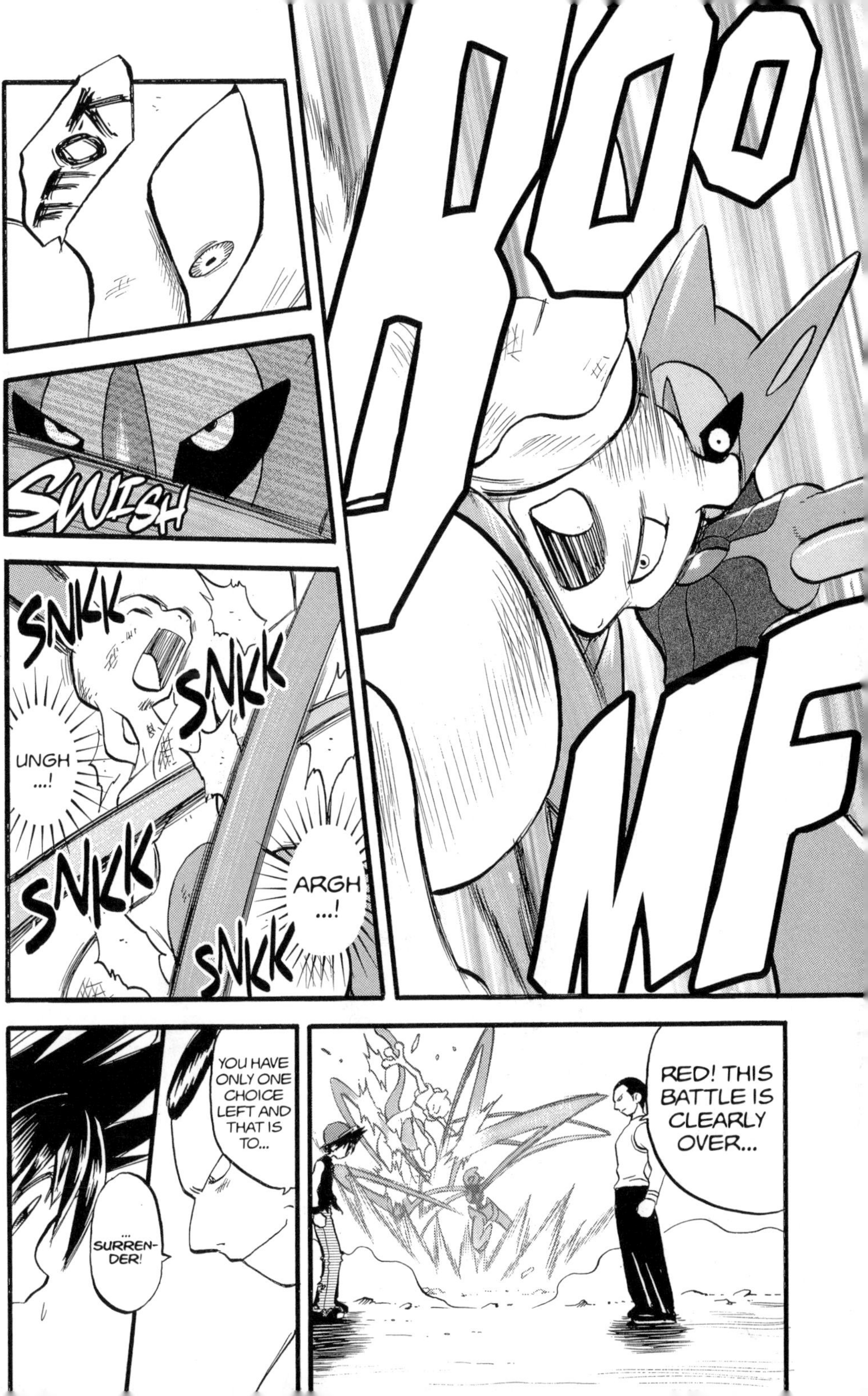
SWISH
SNKK
SNKK
UNGH ...!
ARGH ...!
SNKK
SNKK
RED! THIS BATTLE IS CLEARLY OVER...
YOU HAVE ONLY ONE CHOICE LEFT AND THAT IS TO...
...SURRENDER!

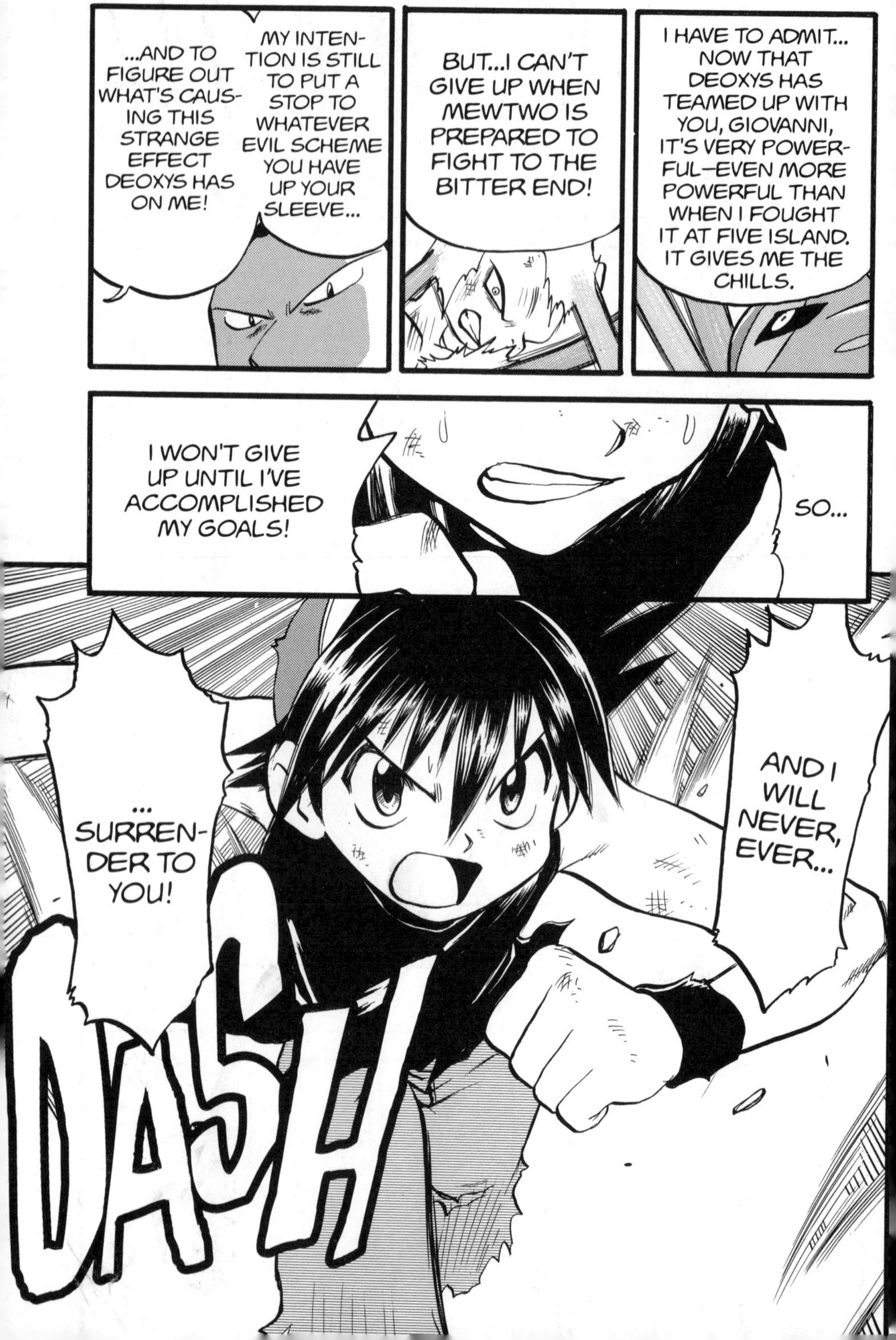
I HAVE TO ADMIT... NOW THAT DEOXYS HAS TEAMED UP WITH YOU, GIOVANNI, IT'S VERY POWERFUL—EVEN MORE POWERFUL THAN WHEN I FOUGHT IT AT FIVE ISLAND. IT GIVES ME THE CHILLS.
BUT...I CAN'T GIVE UP WHEN MEWTWO IS PREPARED TO FIGHT TO THE BITTER END!
MY INTENTION IS STILL TO PUT A STOP TO WHATEVER EVIL SCHEME YOU HAVE UP YOUR SLEEVE...
...AND TO FIGURE OUT WHAT'S CAUSING THIS STRANGE EFFECT DEOXYS HAS ON ME!
SO...
I WON'T GIVE UP UNTIL I'VE ACCOMPLISHED MY GOALS!
AND I WILL NEVER, EVER...
... SURRENDER TO YOU!
DASH

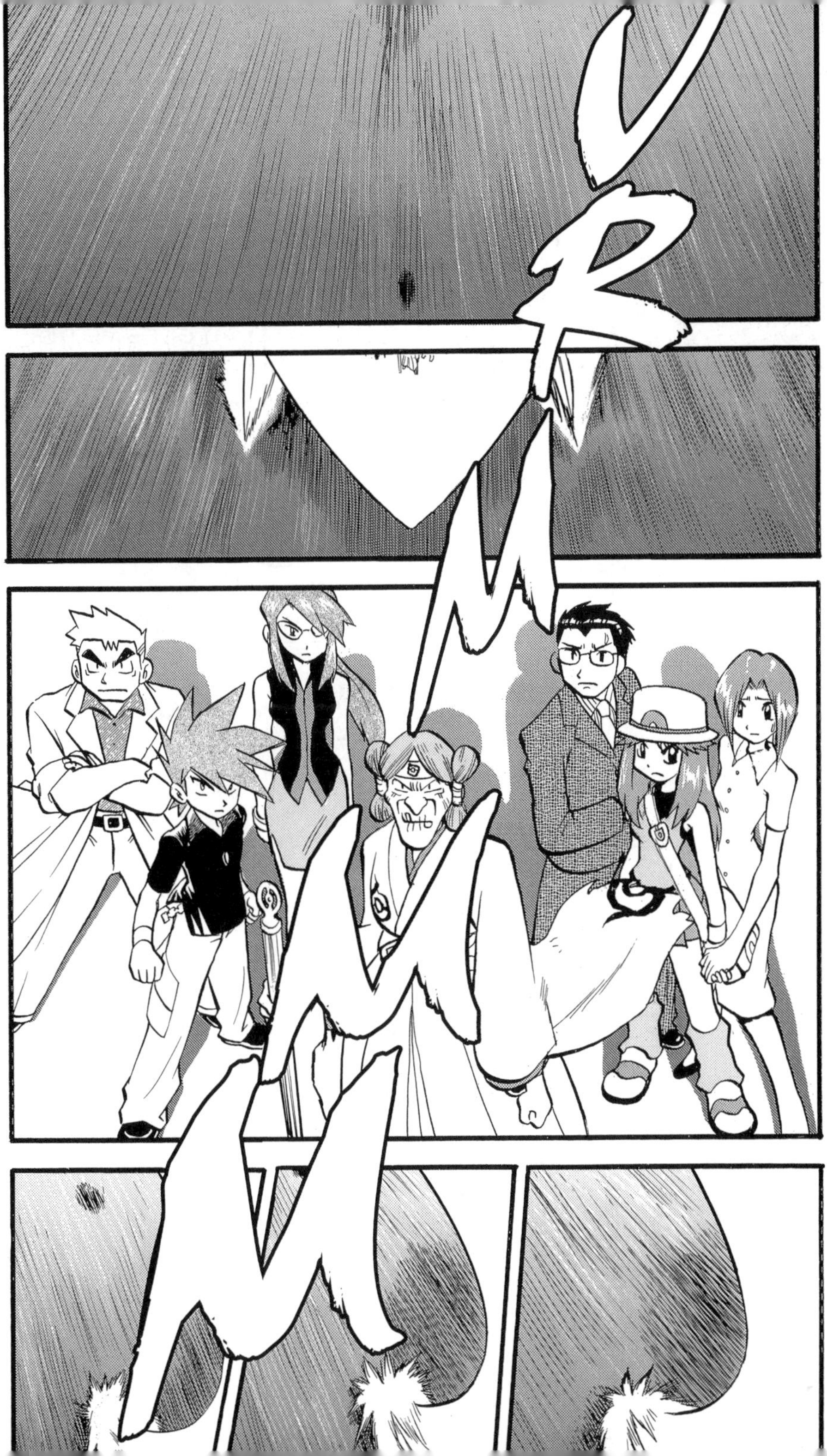
VRMMM

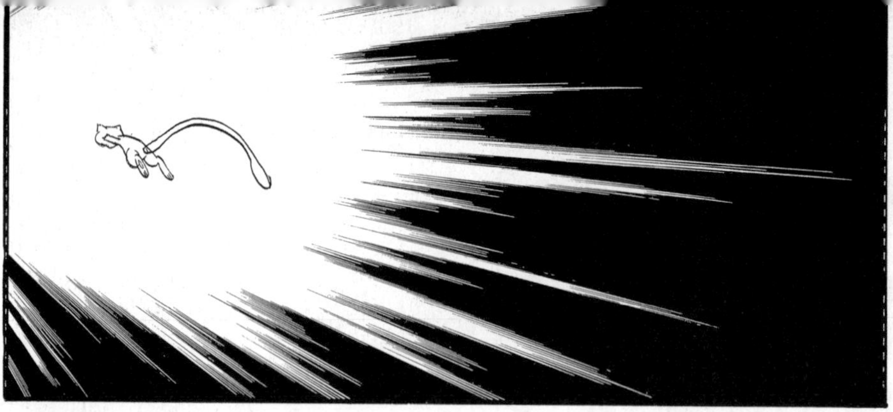
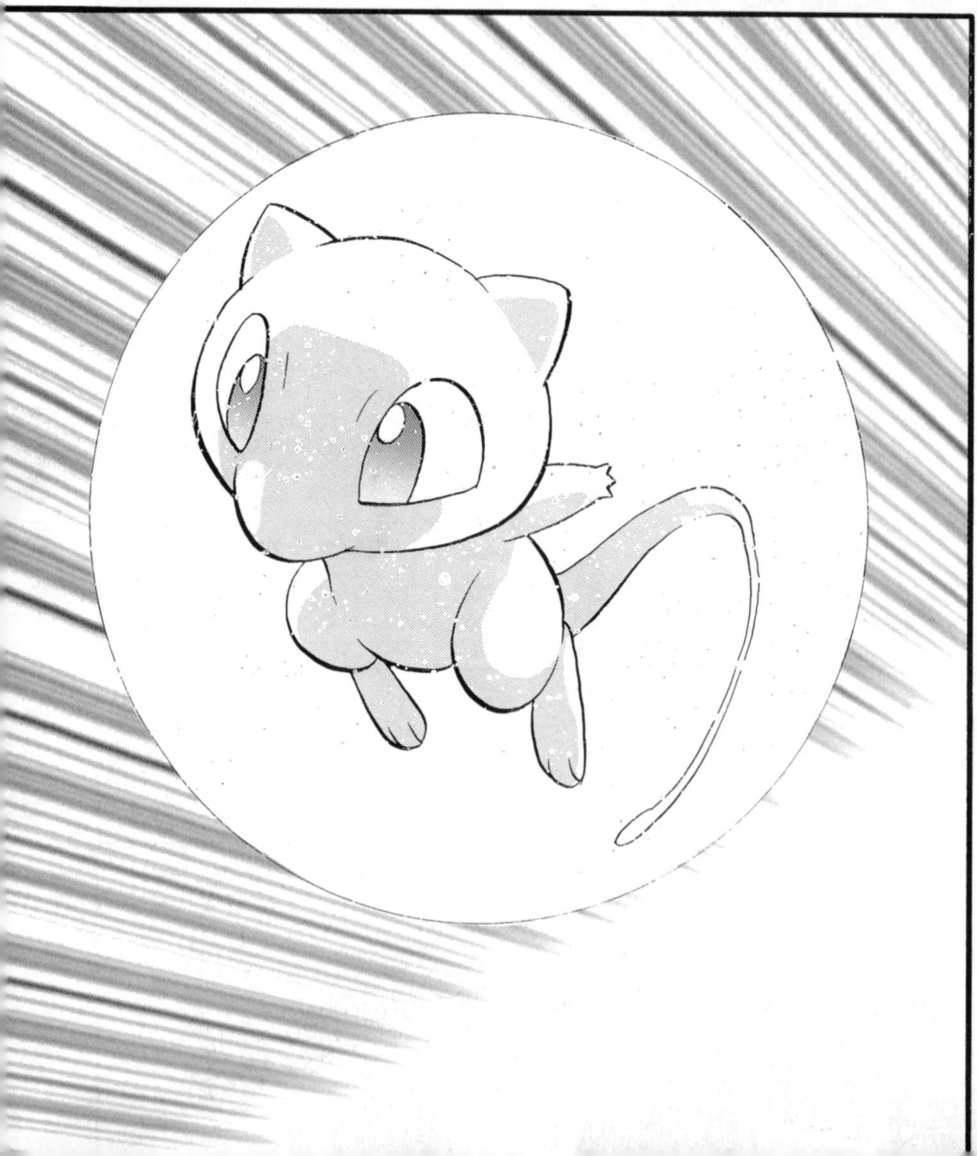

Character Profile Yellow

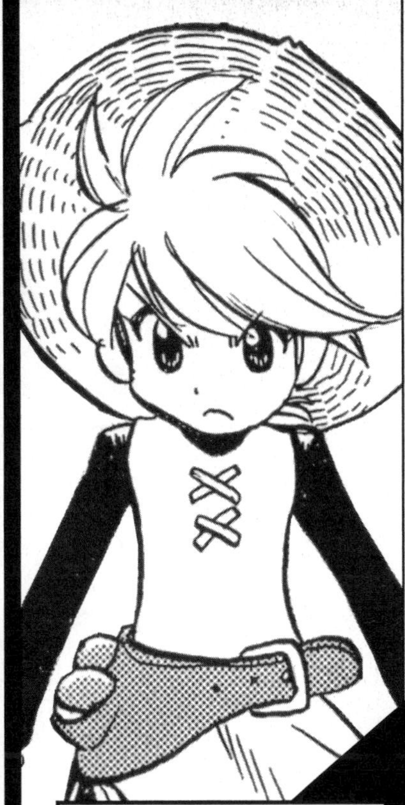

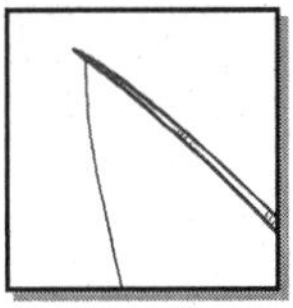

YELLOW

- Birthplace: Viridian City
- Birthday: March 3
- Blood Type: A
- Age: 14 Years Old (as of the 5th Arc)
- Hobby: Drawing, Fishing
- Family members: Uncle Wilton the fisherman

IT IS SAID THAT EVERY TEN YEARS A GIRL IS BORN WHO IS IMBUED WITH PSYCHIC POWERS FROM THE VIRIDIAN FOREST. YELLOW HAS THE ABILITY TO READ THE MINDS OF POKÉMON AND TO HEAL THEIR WOUNDS. HER FULL NAME IS "AMARILLO DEL BOSQUE VERDE." SHE USED TO LIVE AN ORDINARY LIFE IN VIRIDIAN CITY, BUT HER LIFE CHANGED DRASTICALLY AFTER SHE MET RED. WHEN RED WENT MISSING DURING HIS CHALLENGE AGAINST THE KANTO ELITE FOUR, YELLOW SET OUT WITH RED'S POKÉMON PIKA ON A JOURNEY TO FIND HIM. FOR SOME REASON, SHE CHOSE TO HIDE HER IDENTITY AS A GIRL.

YELLOW IS CURRENTLY TRYING TO RESCUE SILVER, WHO WAS KIDNAPPED BY THE THREE BEASTS OF TEAM ROCKET AND IS NOW ABOARD THEIR AIRSHIP. HOW WILL HER UNIQUE POWERS BE OF USE...?

● Adventure 295 ●
Double Down, Deoxys

Pokémon Adventures
FireRed & LeafGreen
The Fifth Chapter

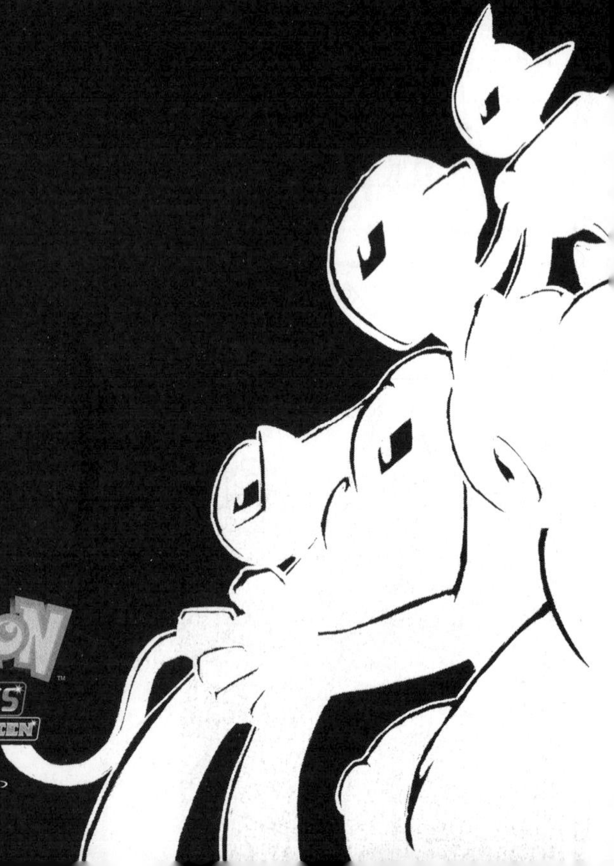

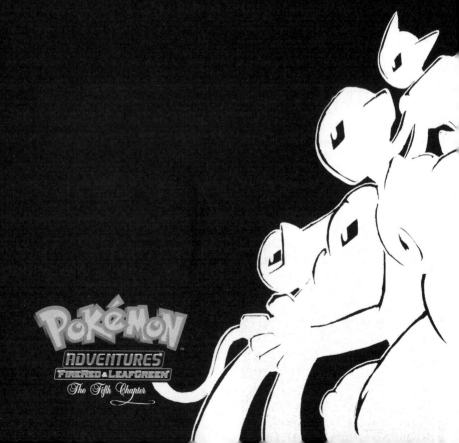

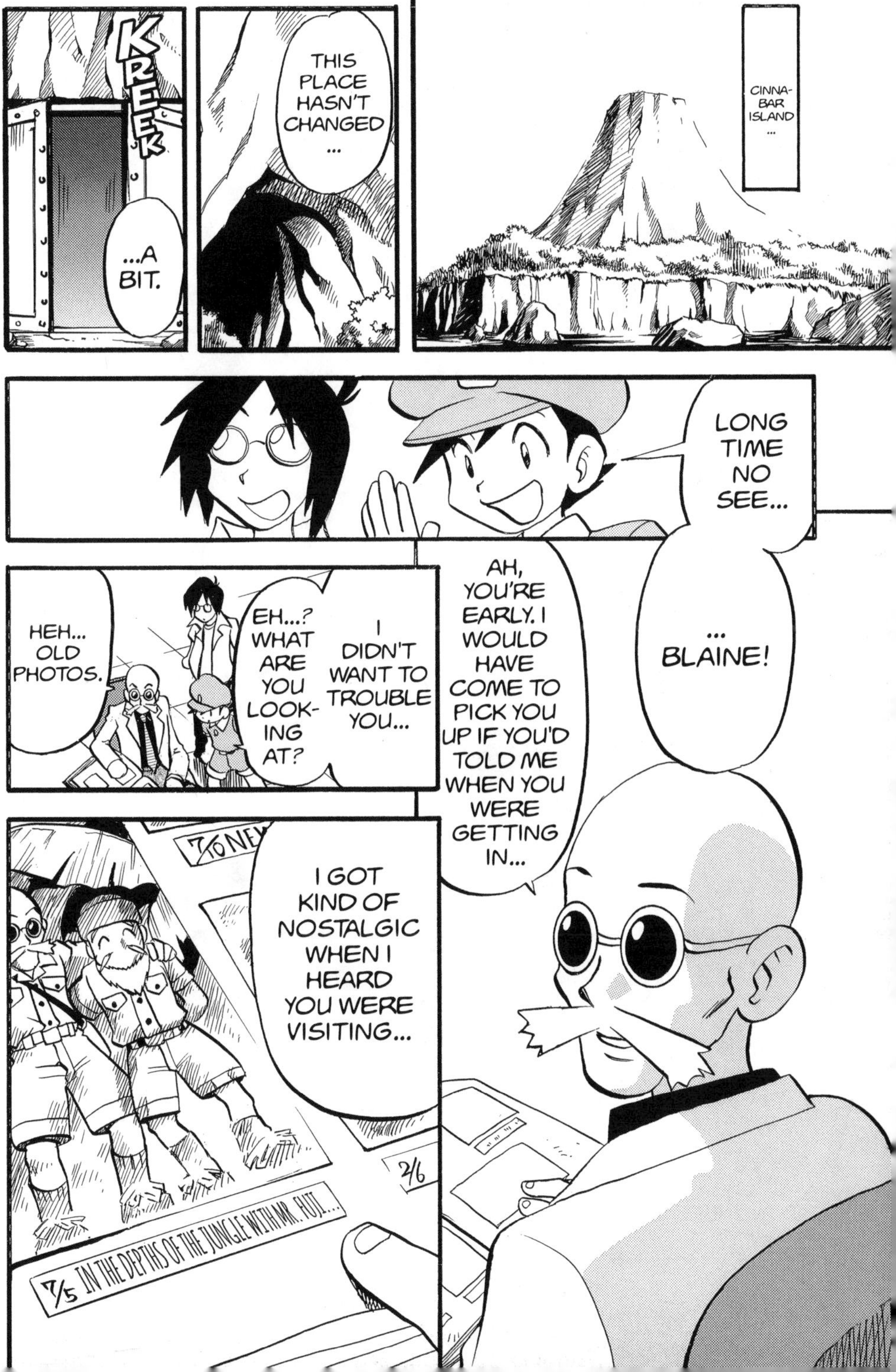
CINNA-BAR ISLAND ...
THIS PLACE HASN'T CHANGED ...
KREEK
...A BIT.
LONG TIME NO SEE...
... BLAINE!
AH, YOU'RE EARLY. I WOULD HAVE COME TO PICK YOU UP IF YOU'D TOLD ME WHEN YOU WERE GETTING IN...
I DIDN'T WANT TO TROUBLE YOU...
EH...? WHAT ARE YOU LOOKING AT?
HEH... OLD PHOTOS.
I GOT KIND OF NOSTALGIC WHEN I HEARD YOU WERE VISITING...
2/6
7/5 IN THE DEPTHS OF THE JUNGLE WITH MR. FUJI...

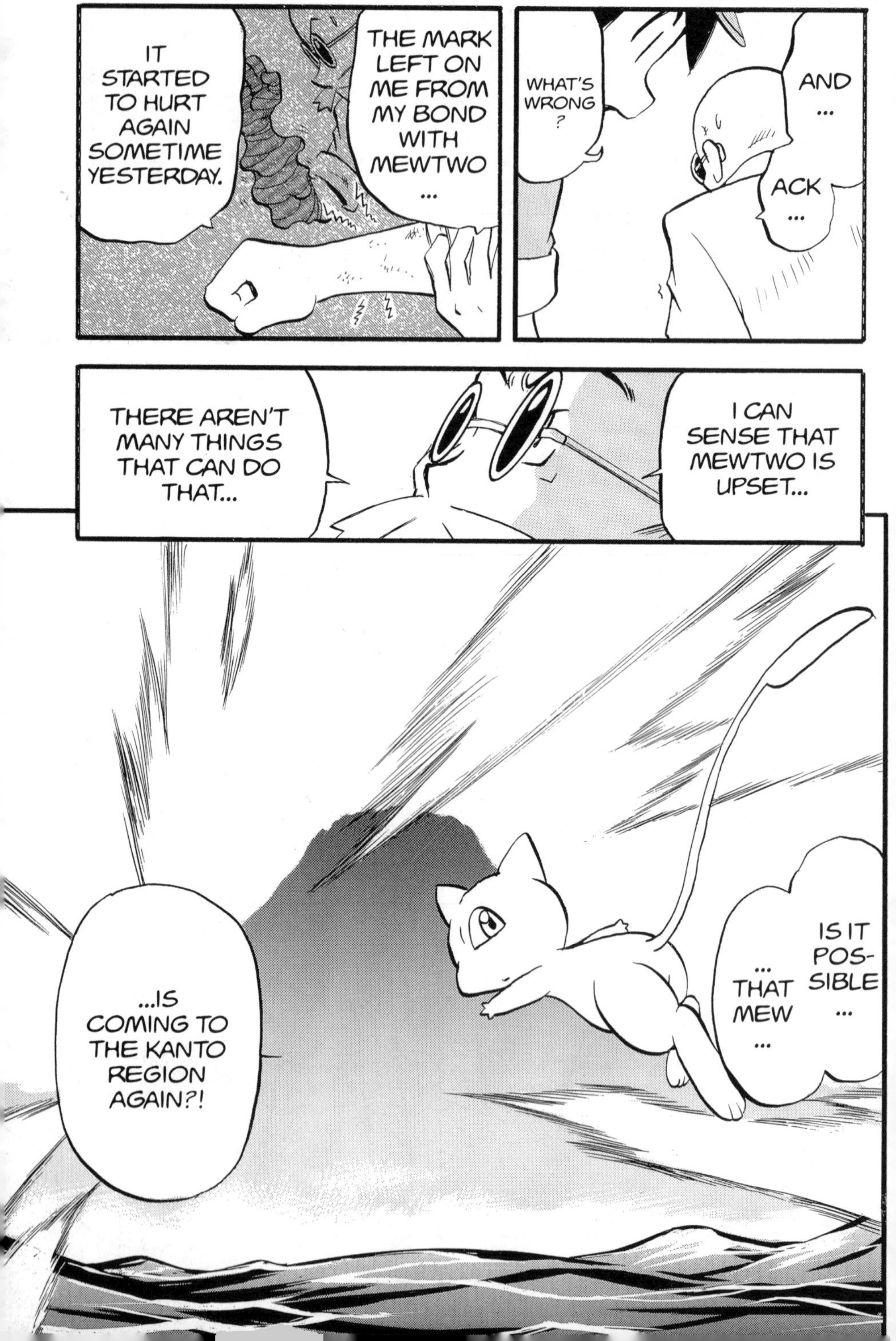
AND ...
WHAT'S WRONG?
ACK ...
THE MARK LEFT ON ME FROM MY BOND WITH MEWTWO ...
IT STARTED TO HURT AGAIN SOMETIME YESTERDAY.
I CAN SENSE THAT MEWTWO IS UPSET...
THERE AREN'T MANY THINGS THAT CAN DO THAT...
IS IT POSSIBLE ...
... THAT MEW ...
...IS COMING TO THE KANTO REGION AGAIN?!

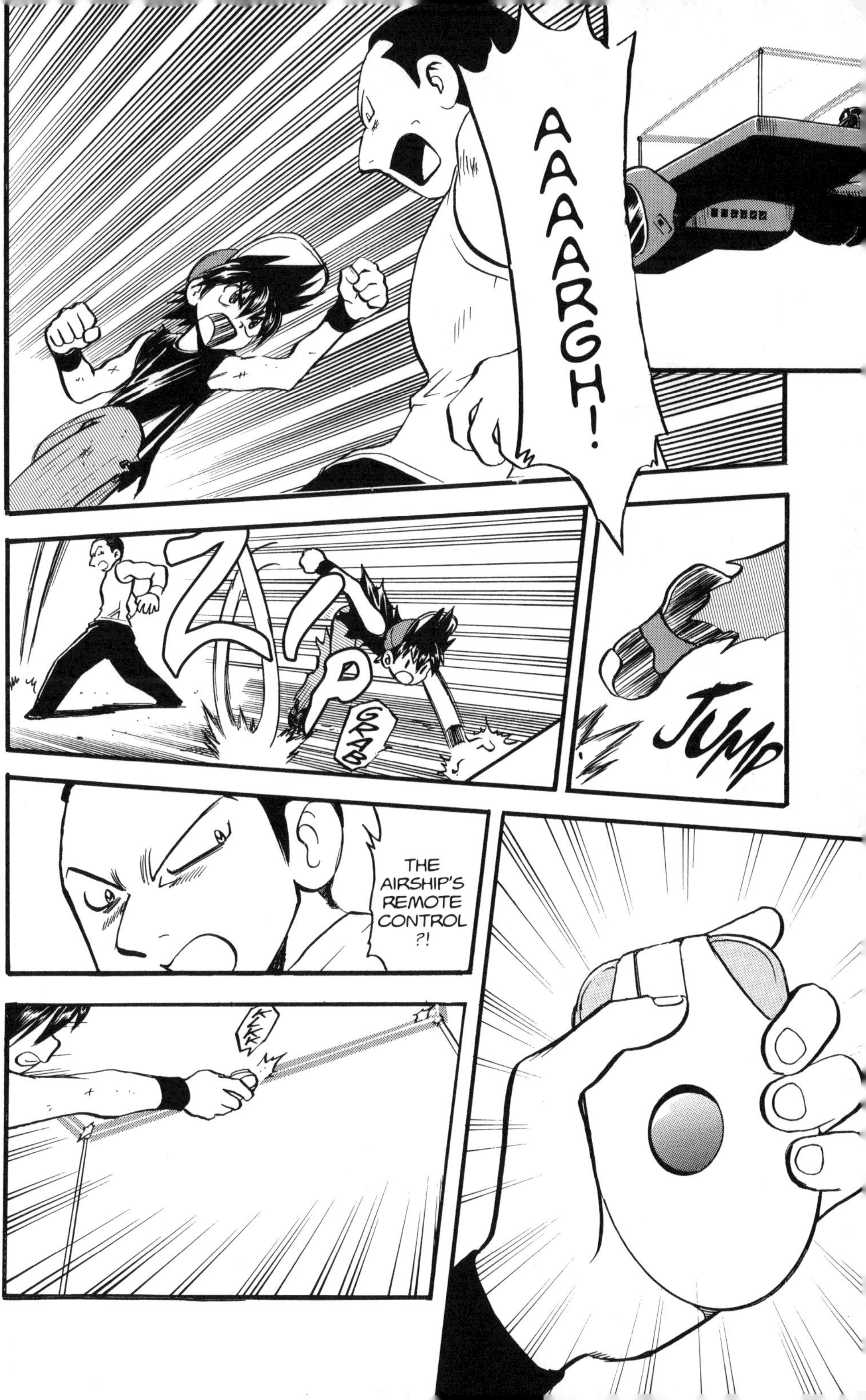
AAAARGH!
JUMP
ZAP
GRAB
THE AIRSHIP'S REMOTE CONTROL ?!

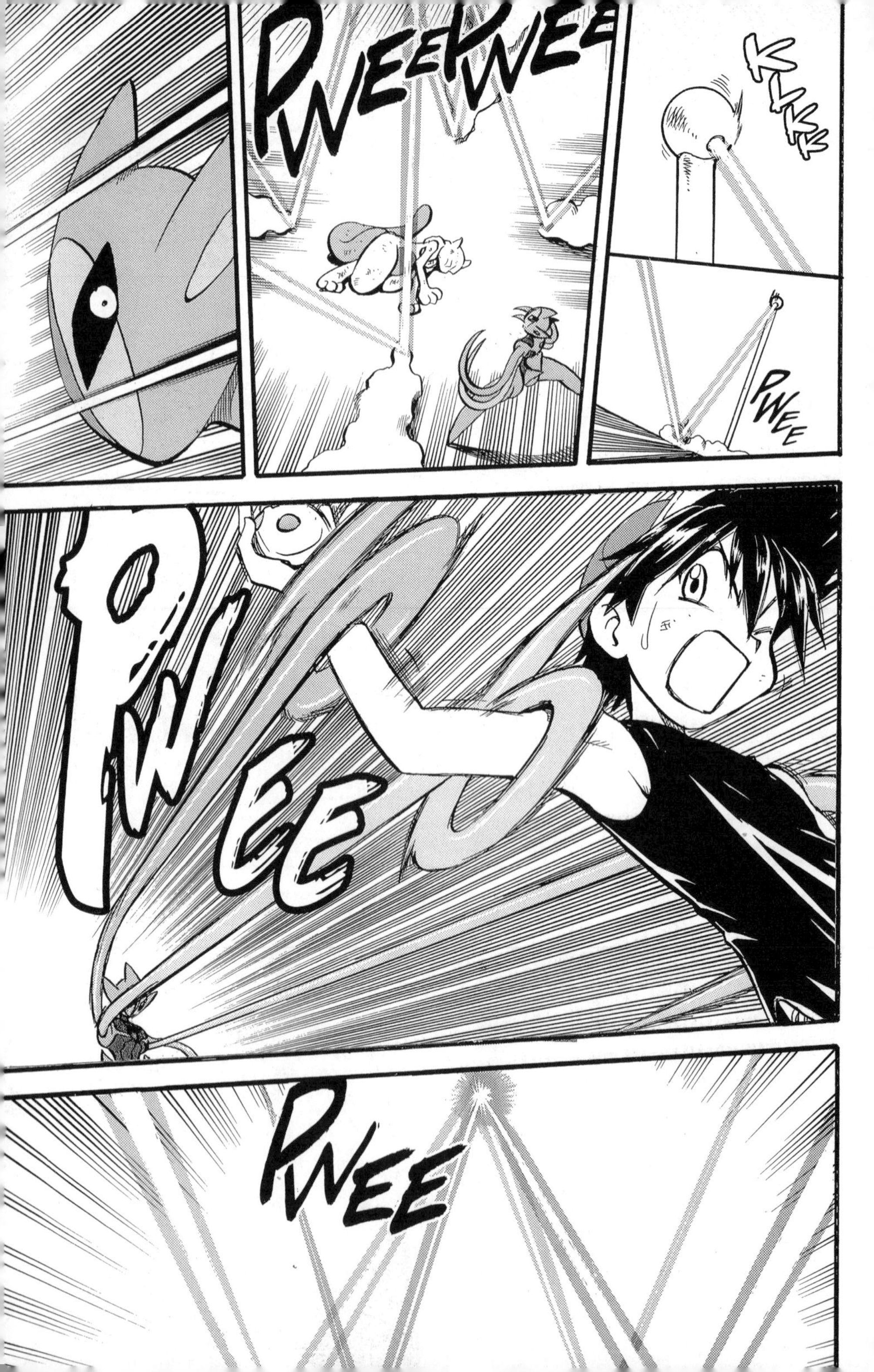
KLKK
PWEE
PWEEPWEE
PWEE
PWEE

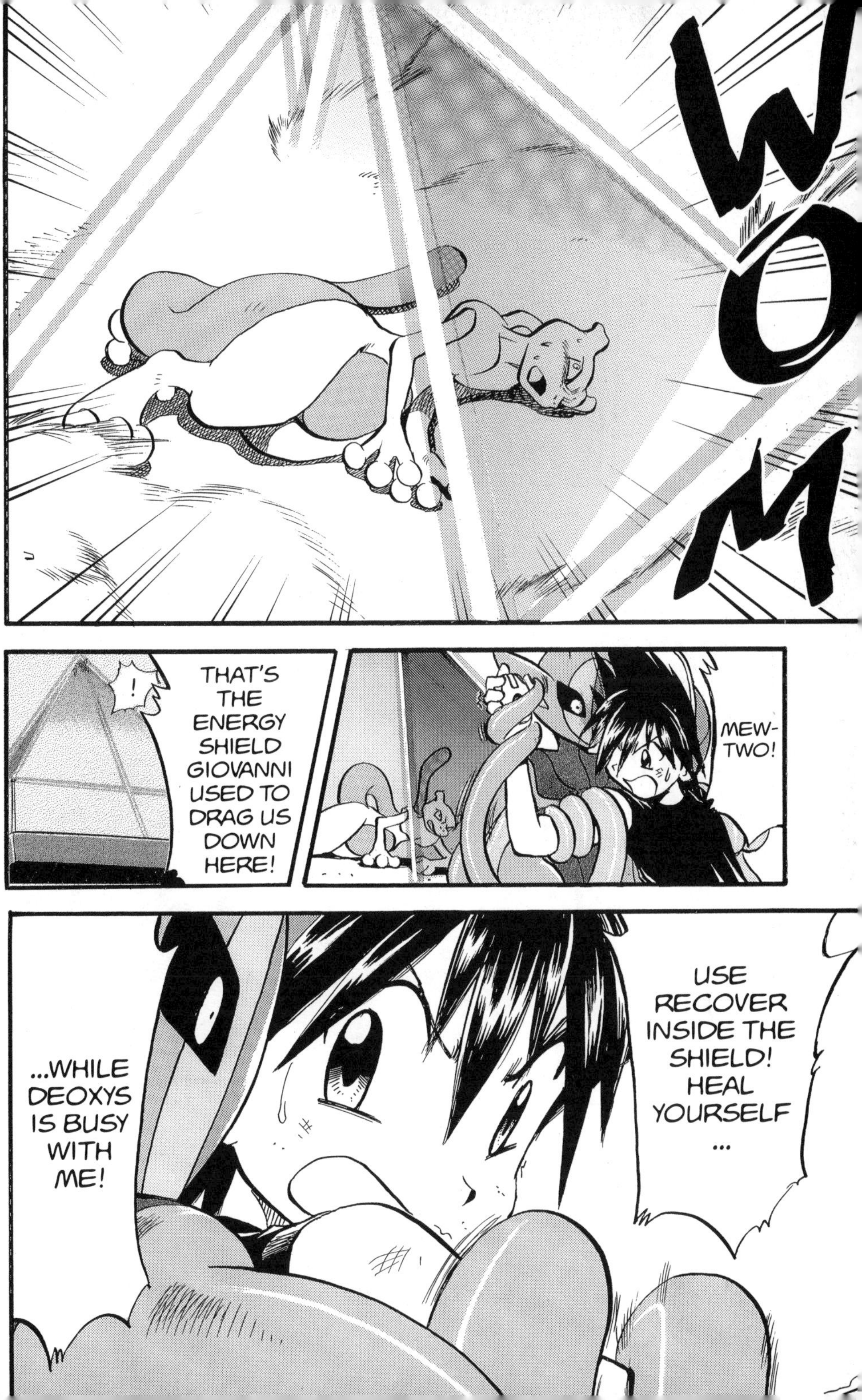
WOOM
MEW-TWO!
!
THAT'S THE ENERGY SHIELD GIOVANNI USED TO DRAG US DOWN HERE!
USE RECOVER INSIDE THE SHIELD! HEAL YOURSELF...
...WHILE DEOXYS IS BUSY WITH ME!

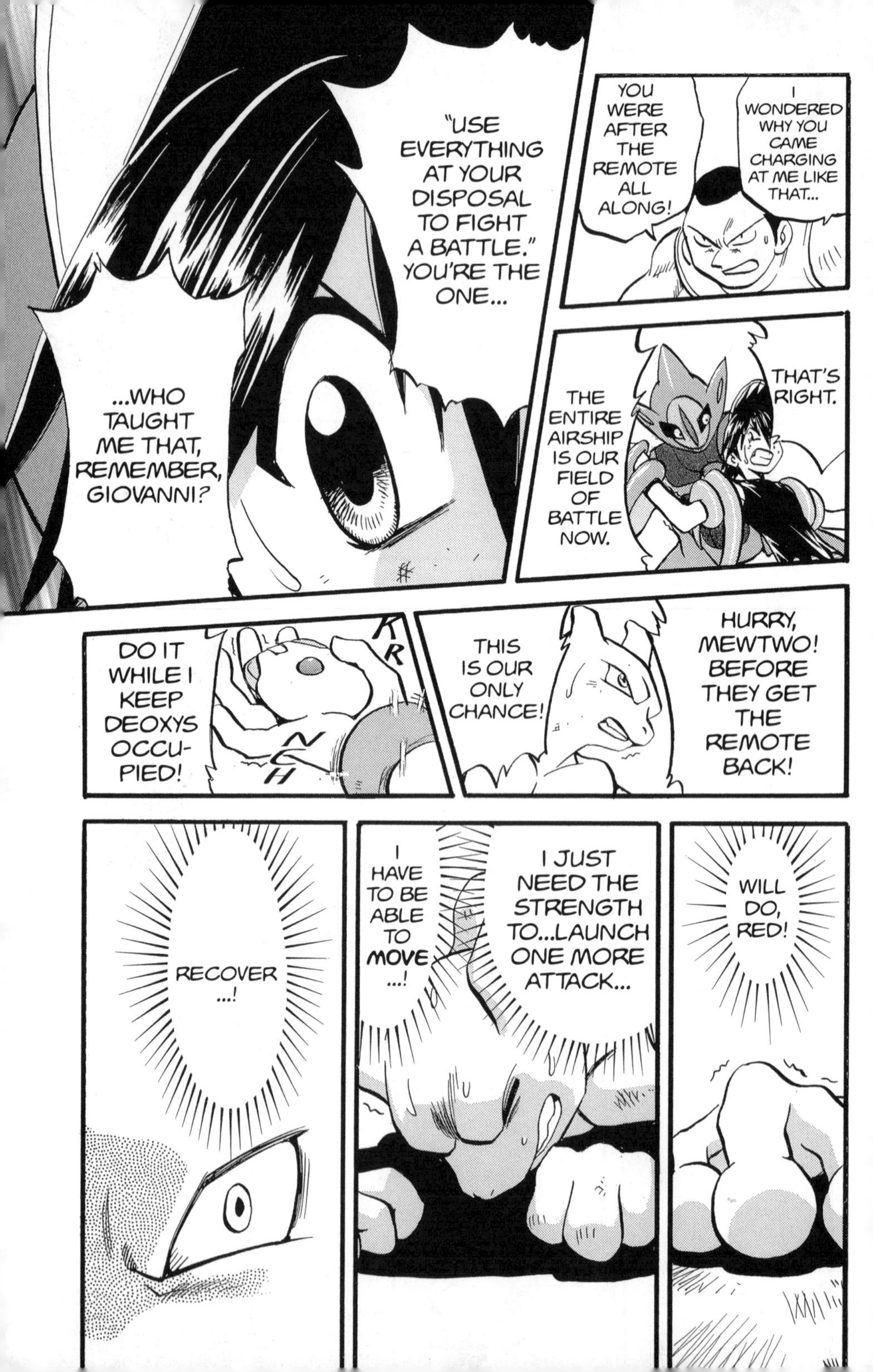
I WONDERED WHY YOU CAME CHARGING AT ME LIKE THAT...
YOU WERE AFTER THE REMOTE ALL ALONG!
THAT'S RIGHT.
THE ENTIRE AIRSHIP IS OUR FIELD OF BATTLE NOW.
"USE EVERYTHING AT YOUR DISPOSAL TO FIGHT A BATTLE." YOU'RE THE ONE...
...WHO TAUGHT ME THAT, REMEMBER, GIOVANNI?
HURRY, MEWTWO! BEFORE THEY GET THE REMOTE BACK!
THIS IS OUR ONLY CHANCE!
DO IT WHILE I KEEP DEOXYS OCCUPIED!
KRRNCH
WILL DO, RED!
I JUST NEED THE STRENGTH TO...LAUNCH ONE MORE ATTACK...
I HAVE TO BE ABLE TO **MOVE**...!
RECOVER...!

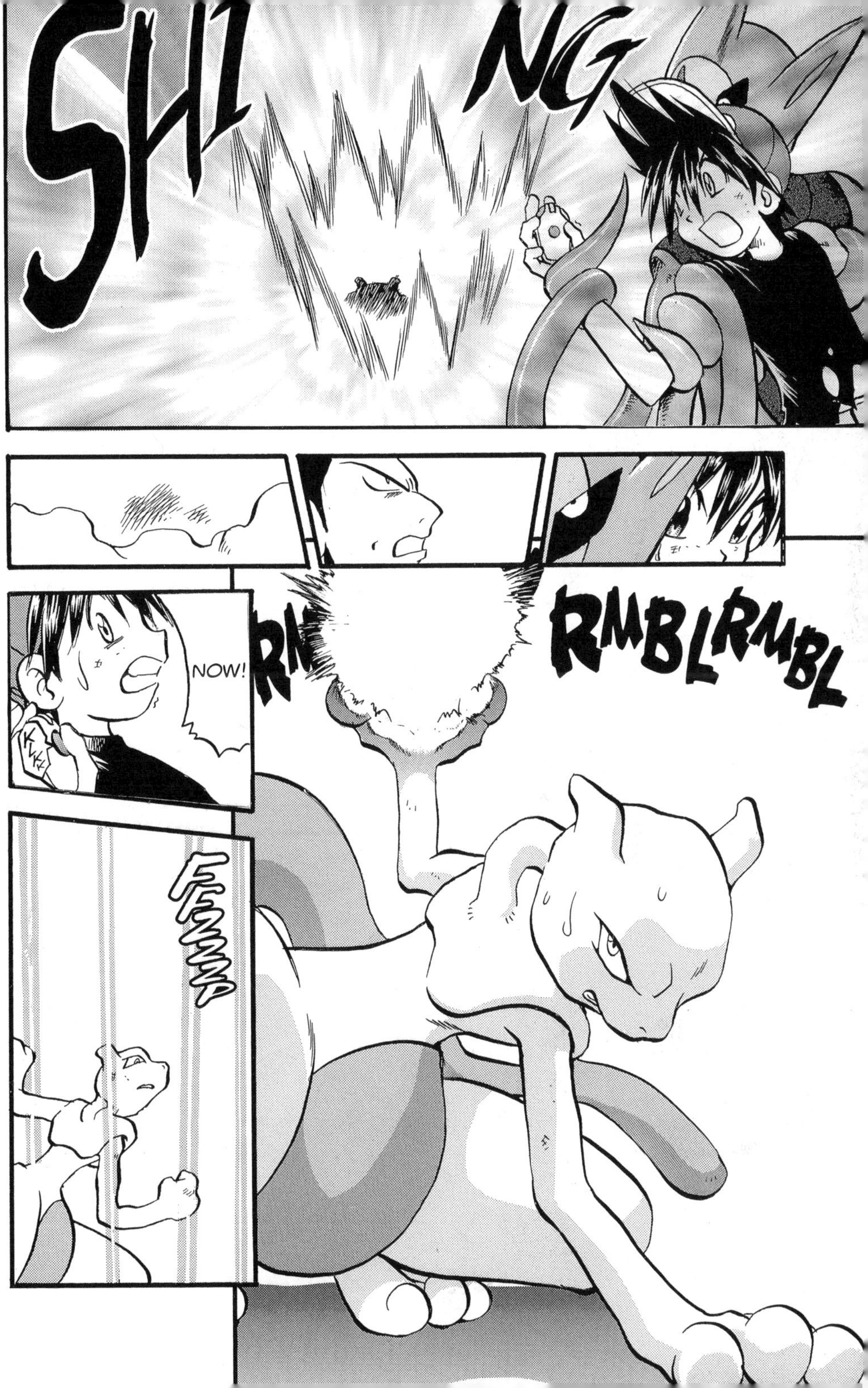
SHI NG
RMBLRMBL
NOW!

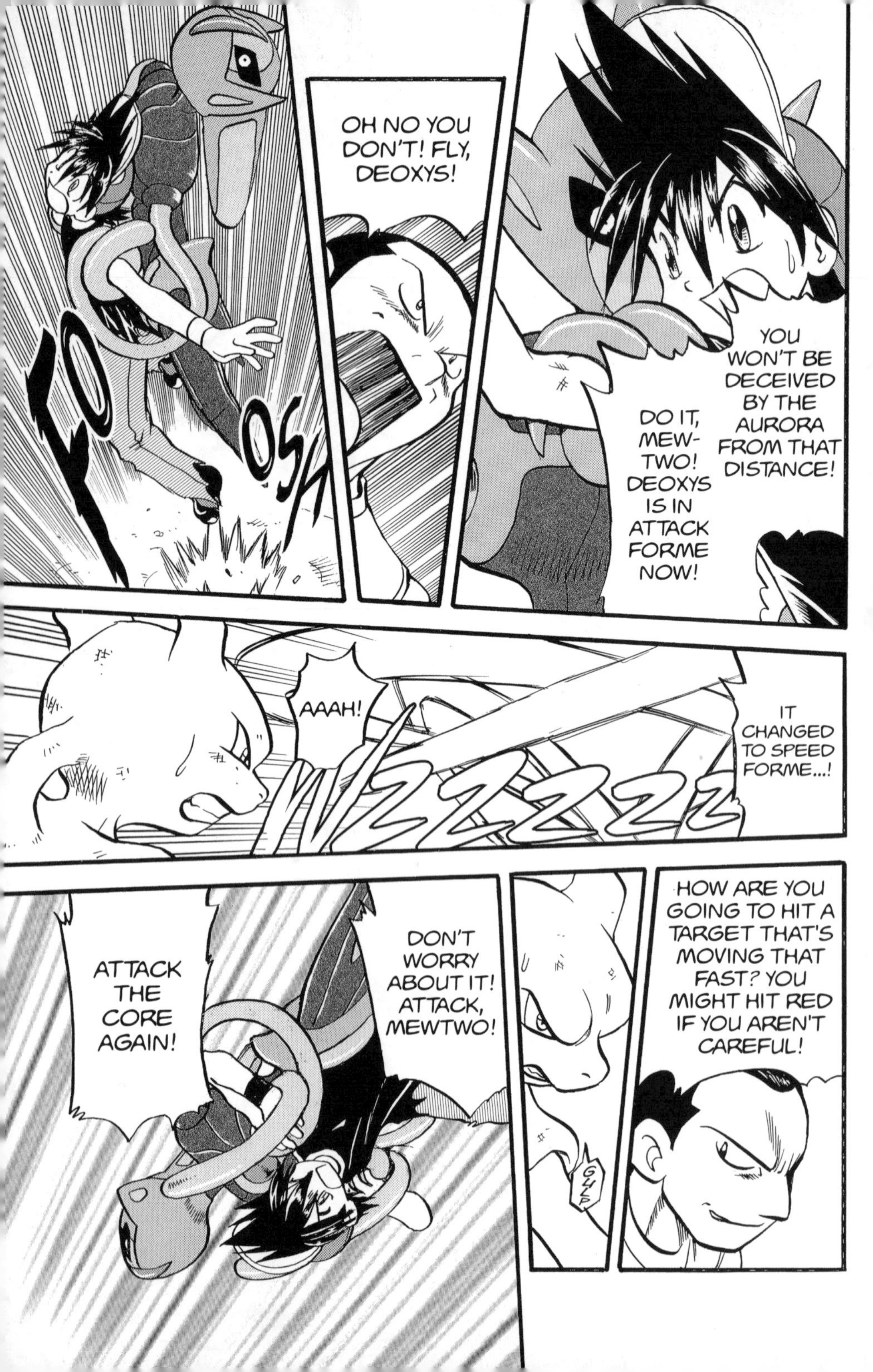
YOU WON'T BE DECEIVED BY THE AURORA FROM THAT DISTANCE!
DO IT, MEW-TWO! DEOXYS IS IN ATTACK FORME NOW!
OH NO YOU DON'T! FLY, DEOXYS!
FOOSH
IT CHANGED TO SPEED FORME...!
AAAH!
WZZZZZ
HOW ARE YOU GOING TO HIT A TARGET THAT'S MOVING THAT FAST? YOU MIGHT HIT RED IF YOU AREN'T CAREFUL!
GULP
DON'T WORRY ABOUT IT! ATTACK, MEWTWO!
ATTACK THE CORE AGAIN!

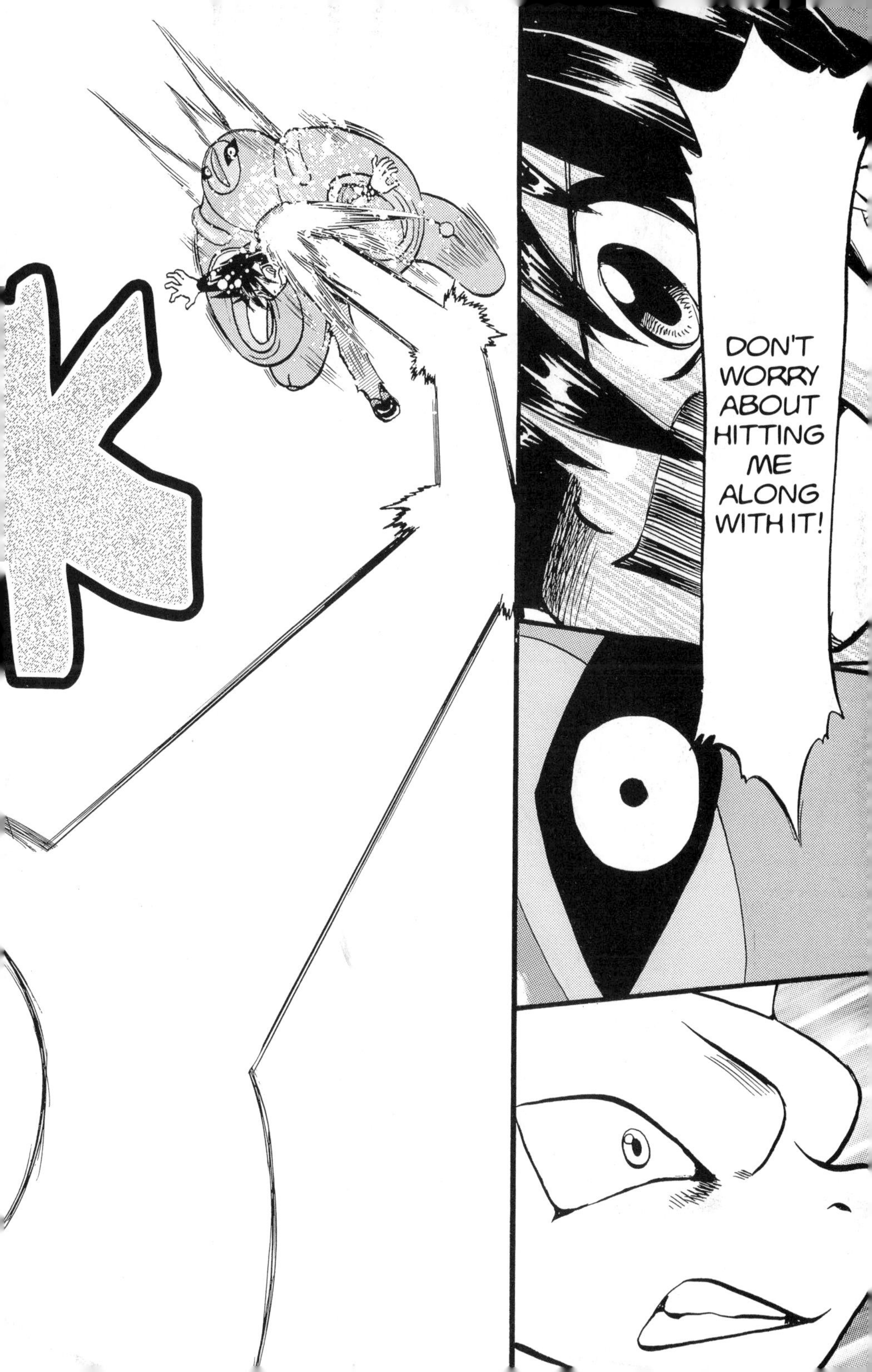
DON'T WORRY ABOUT HITTING ME ALONG WITH IT!

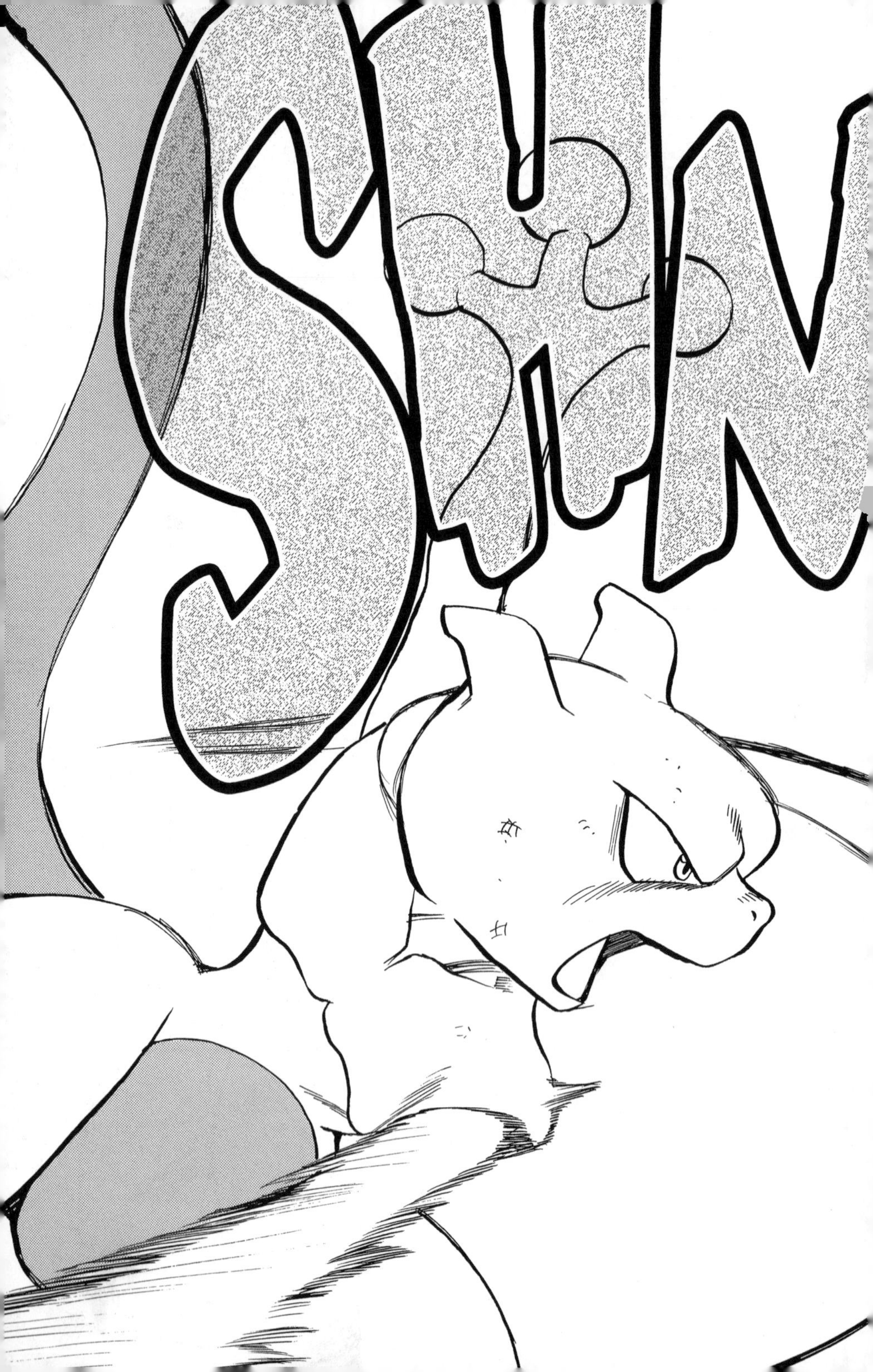
SHUN

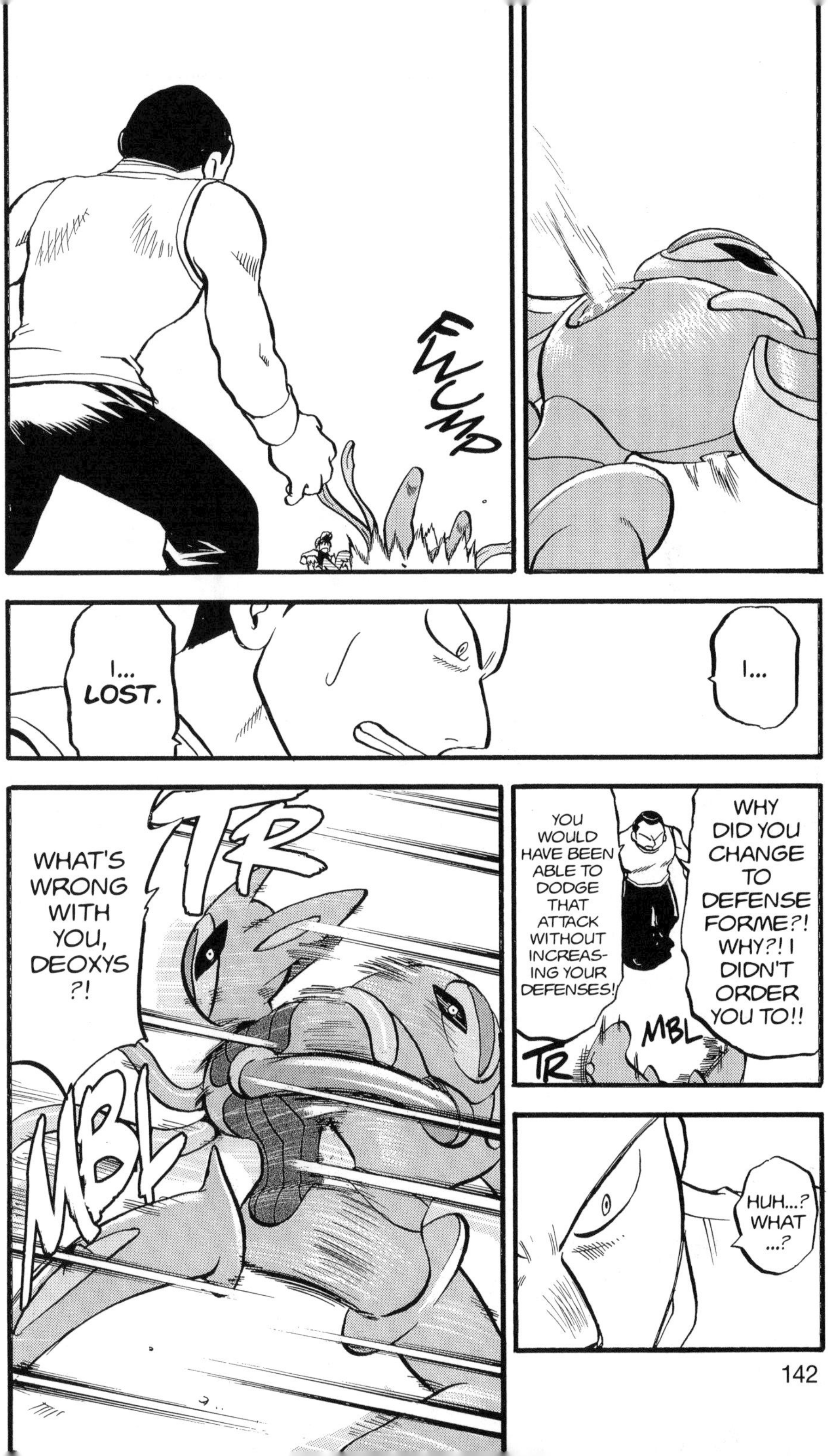
FWUMP
I...
I... LOST.
WHY DID YOU CHANGE TO DEFENSE FORME?! WHY?! I DIDN'T ORDER YOU TO!!
YOU WOULD HAVE BEEN ABLE TO DODGE THAT ATTACK WITHOUT INCREASING YOUR DEFENSES!
MBL
TR
HUH...? WHAT ...?
TR
WHAT'S WRONG WITH YOU, DEOXYS ?!
MBL

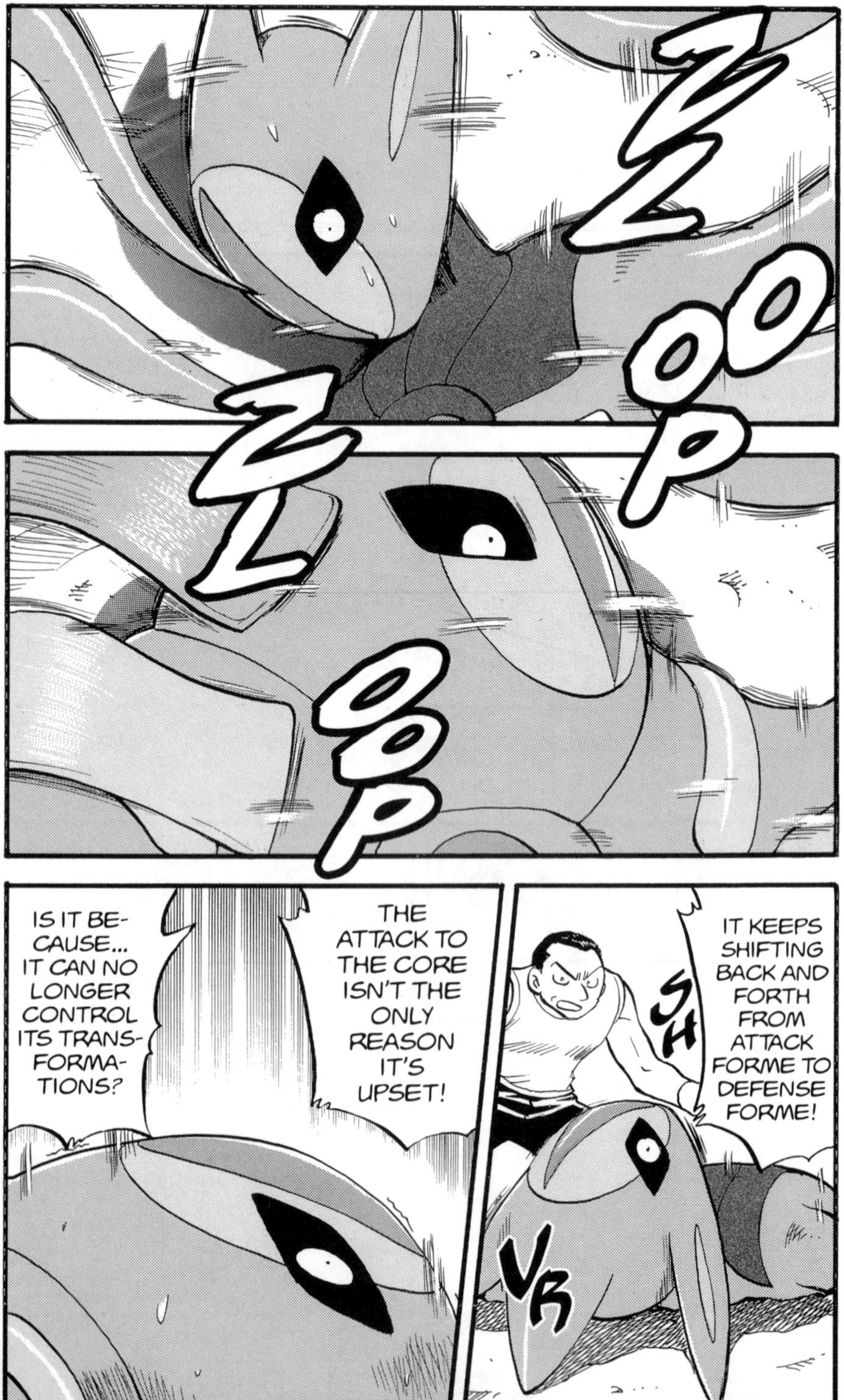
ZOOP
ZOOP
SH
IT KEEPS SHIFTING BACK AND FORTH FROM ATTACK FORME TO DEFENSE FORME!
VR
THE ATTACK TO THE CORE ISN'T THE ONLY REASON IT'S UPSET!
IS IT BE-CAUSE... IT CAN NO LONGER CONTROL ITS TRANS-FORMA-TIONS?

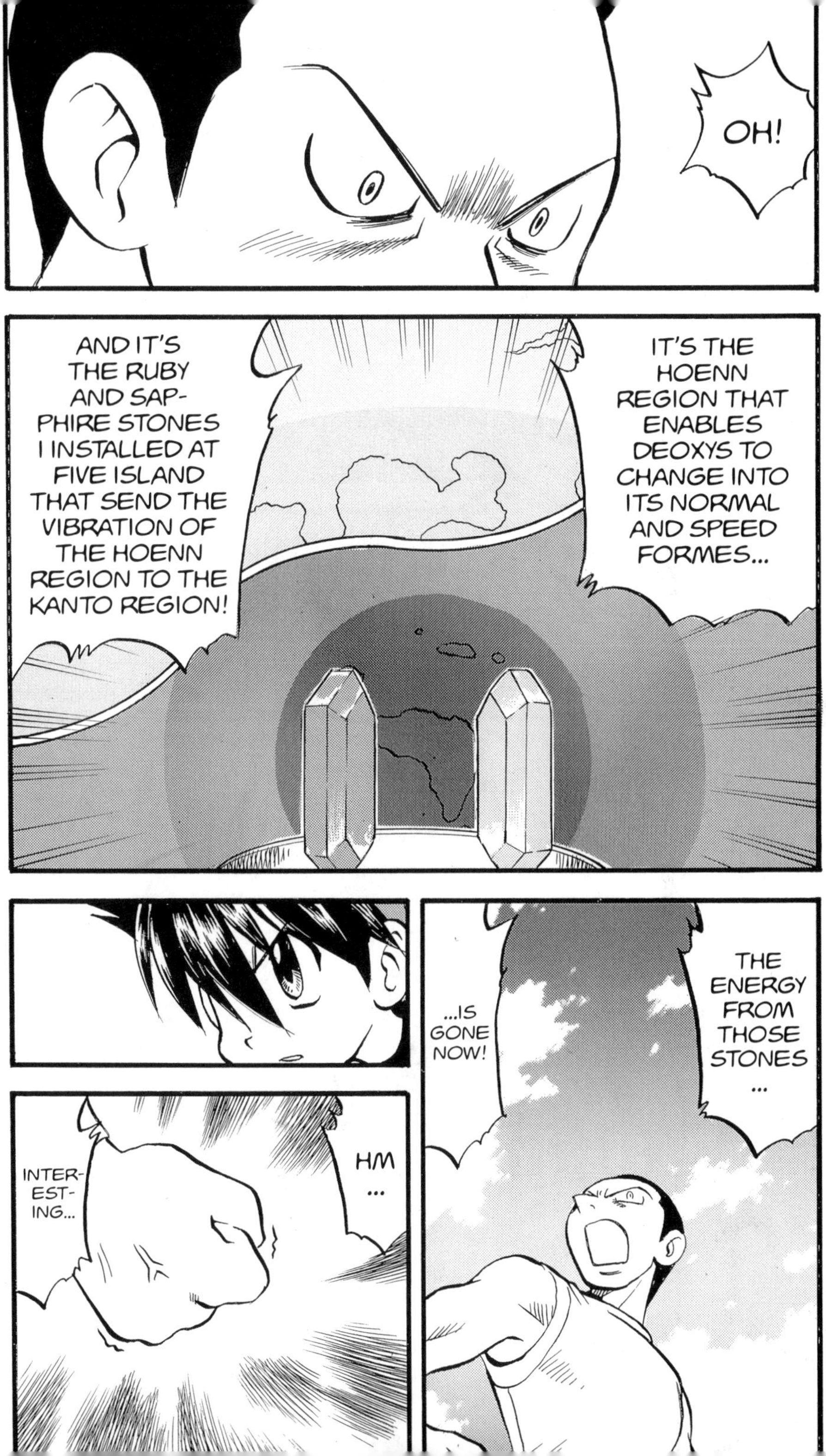
OH!
IT'S THE HOENN REGION THAT ENABLES DEOXYS TO CHANGE INTO ITS NORMAL AND SPEED FORMES...
AND IT'S THE RUBY AND SAP-PHIRE STONES I INSTALLED AT FIVE ISLAND THAT SEND THE VIBRATION OF THE HOENN REGION TO THE KANTO REGION!
THE ENERGY FROM THOSE STONES ...
...IS GONE NOW!
HM ...
INTER-EST-ING...

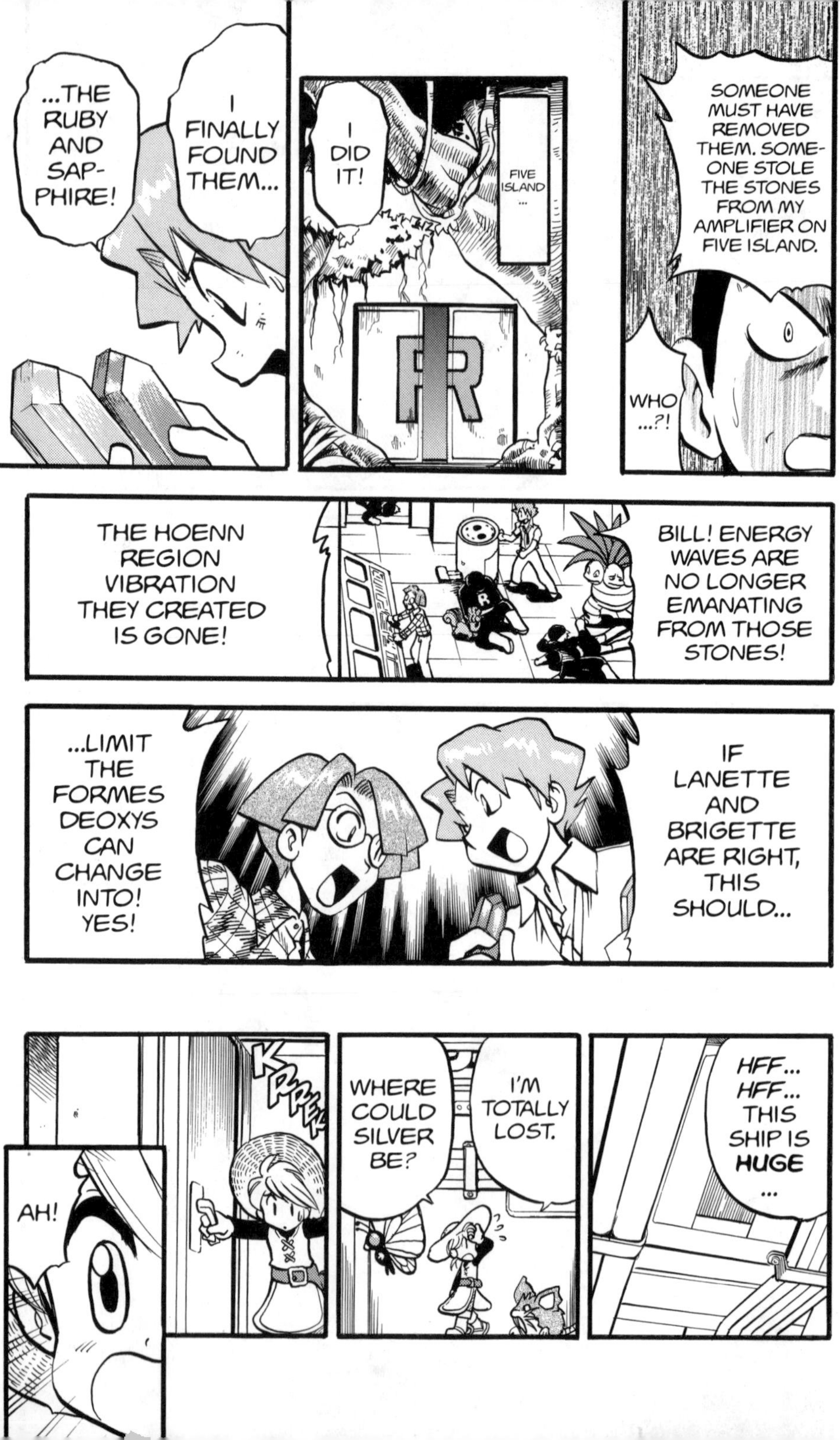
SOMEONE MUST HAVE REMOVED THEM. SOMEONE STOLE THE STONES FROM MY AMPLIFIER ON FIVE ISLAND.
WHO ...?!
FIVE ISLAND ...
I DID IT!
I FINALLY FOUND THEM...
...THE RUBY AND SAPPHIRE!
BILL! ENERGY WAVES ARE NO LONGER EMANATING FROM THOSE STONES!
THE HOENN REGION VIBRATION THEY CREATED IS GONE!
IF LANETTE AND BRIGETTE ARE RIGHT, THIS SHOULD...
...LIMIT THE FORMES DEOXYS CAN CHANGE INTO! YES!
HFF... HFF... THIS SHIP IS **HUGE** ...
I'M TOTALLY LOST.
WHERE COULD SILVER BE?
KPPREEK
AH!

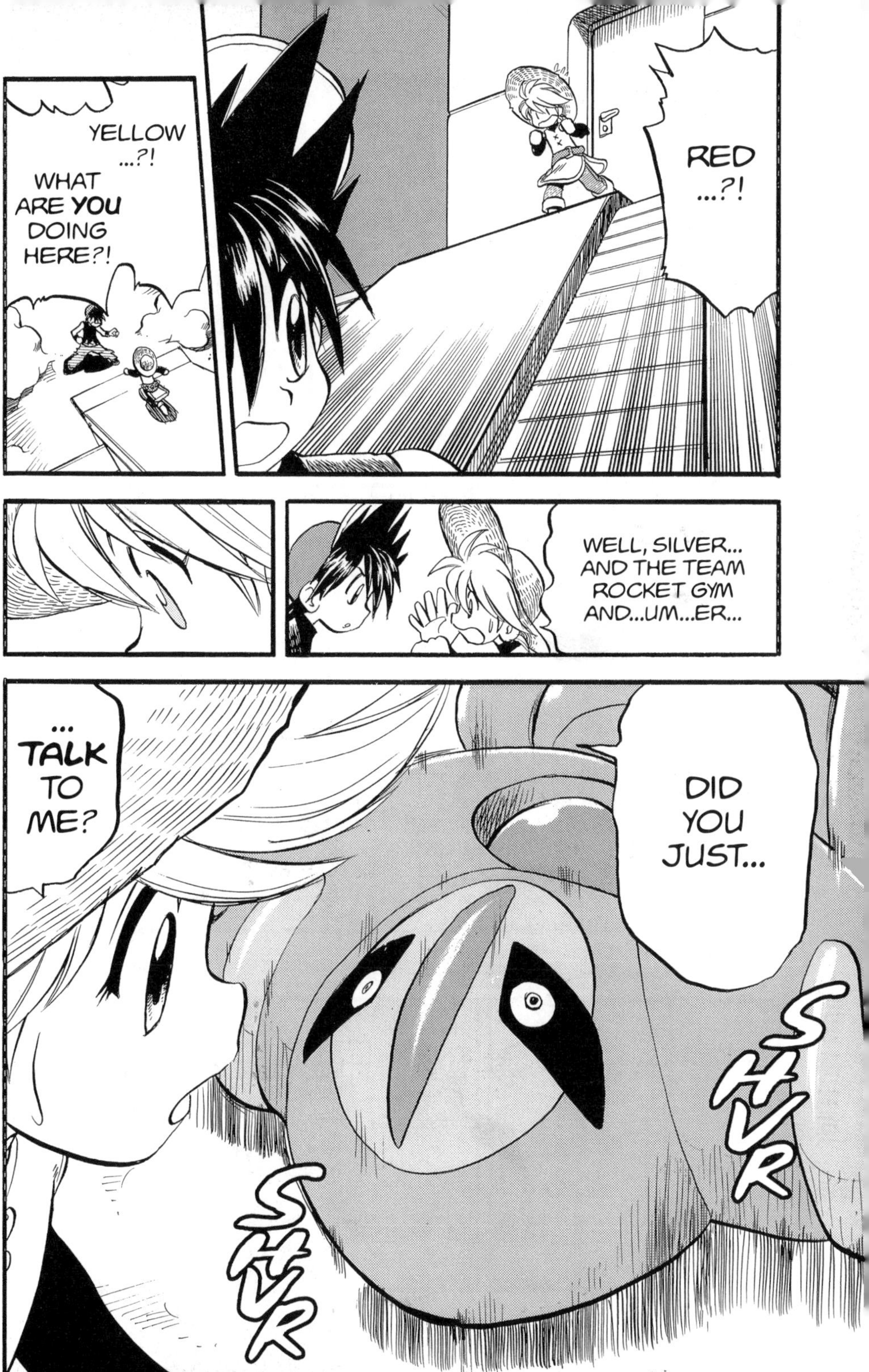
RED ...?!
YELLOW ...?! WHAT ARE **YOU** DOING HERE?!
WELL, SILVER... AND THE TEAM ROCKET GYM AND...UM...ER...
DID YOU JUST...
... **TALK** TO ME?
SHVR
SHVR

THE POKÉMON ON TEAM YELLOW 1

Chuchu/Pikachu ♀

Electric

LV. ?? (As of Adventure 295)

Ability: Static

Mild Nature

Yellow saved Chuchu when she found it injured in the Viridian Forest.

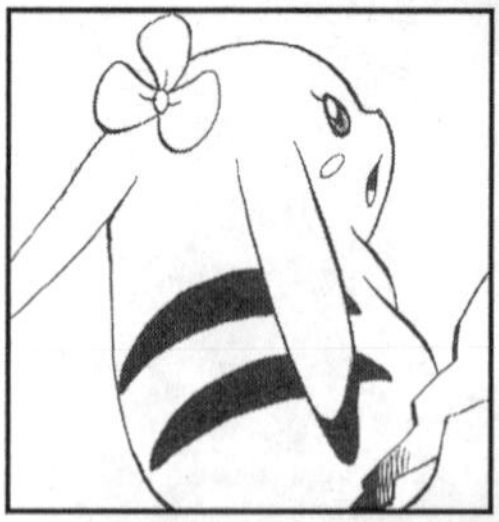

Ratty/Raticate ♂

Normal

LV. ?? (As of Adventure 295)

Ability: Guts

Hardy Nature

Yellow captured Ratty with the help of Red. Its sharp teeth can even bite through hardened steel.

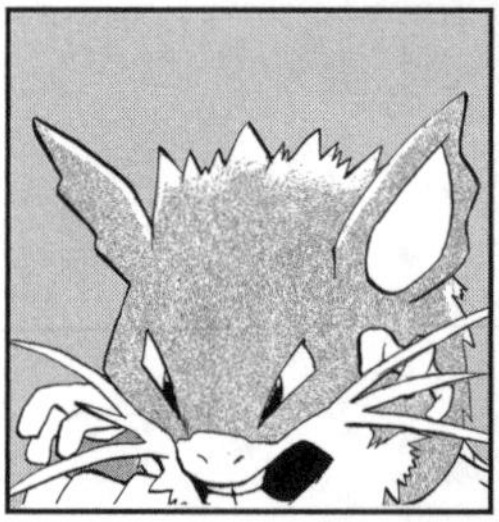

Dody/Dodrio ♂

Normal
Flying

LV. ?? (As of Adventure 295)

Ability: Early Bird

Hasty Nature

Yellow received Dody from her uncle. It can carry Yellow on its back for miles running at top speed with its powerful legs.

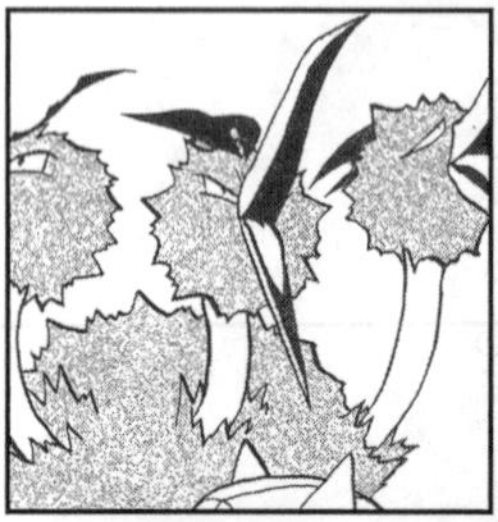

● Adventure 296 ●
It's Starting to Make Sense Now

Pokémon Adventures
FireRed & LeafGreen
The Fifth Chapter

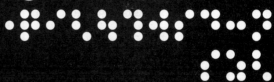

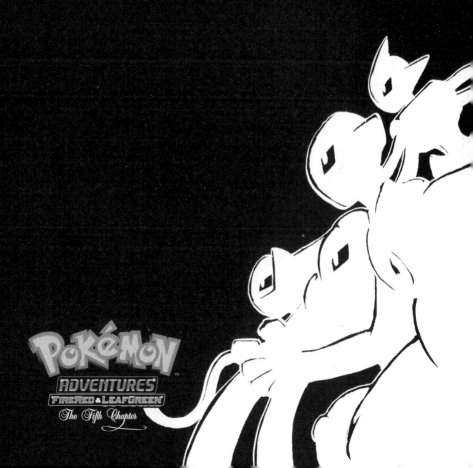

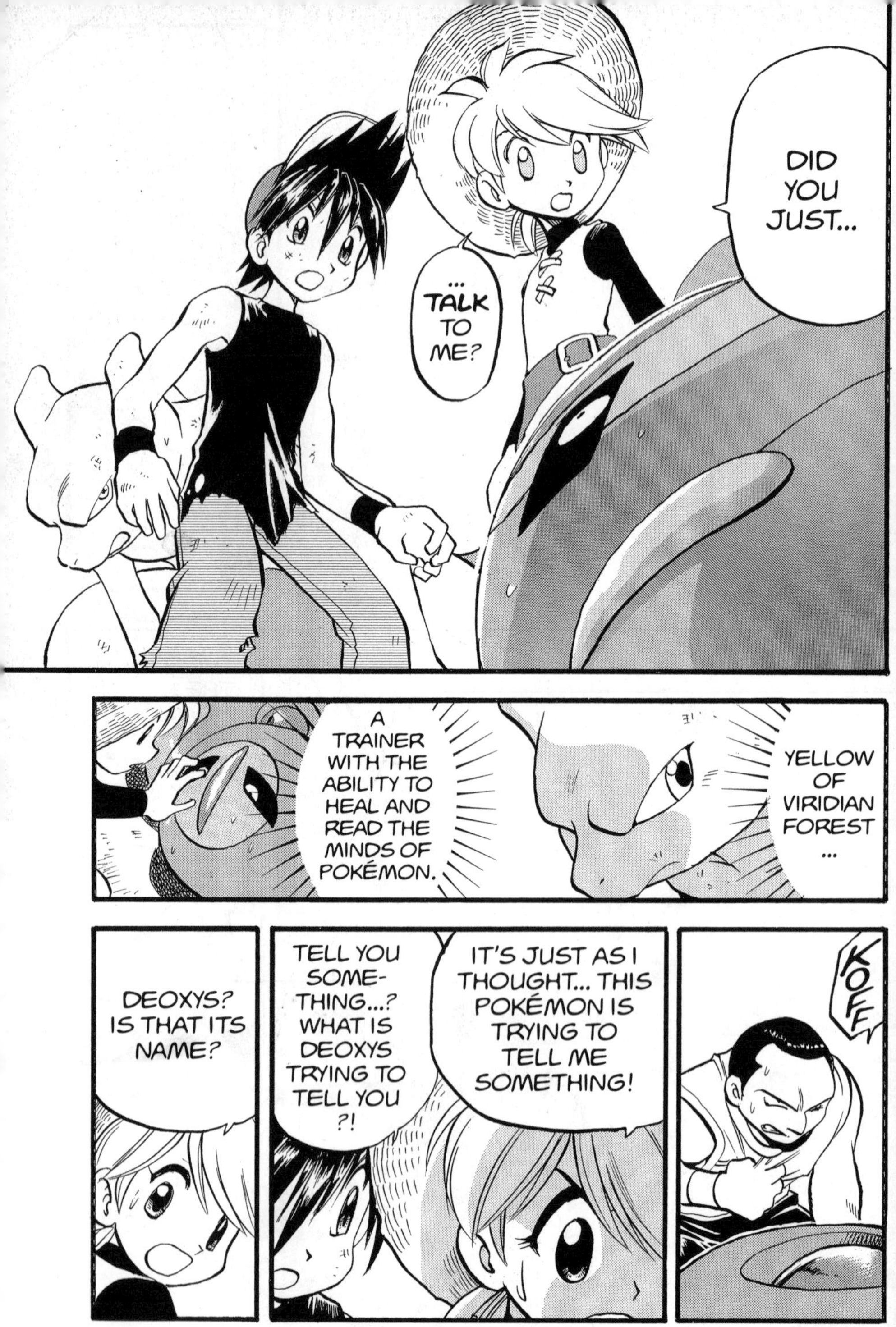
DID YOU JUST...
...TALK TO ME?
YELLOW OF VIRIDIAN FOREST ...
A TRAINER WITH THE ABILITY TO HEAL AND READ THE MINDS OF POKÉMON.
KOFF
IT'S JUST AS I THOUGHT... THIS POKÉMON IS TRYING TO TELL ME SOMETHING!
TELL YOU SOMETHING...? WHAT IS DEOXYS TRYING TO TELL YOU ?!
DEOXYS? IS THAT ITS NAME?

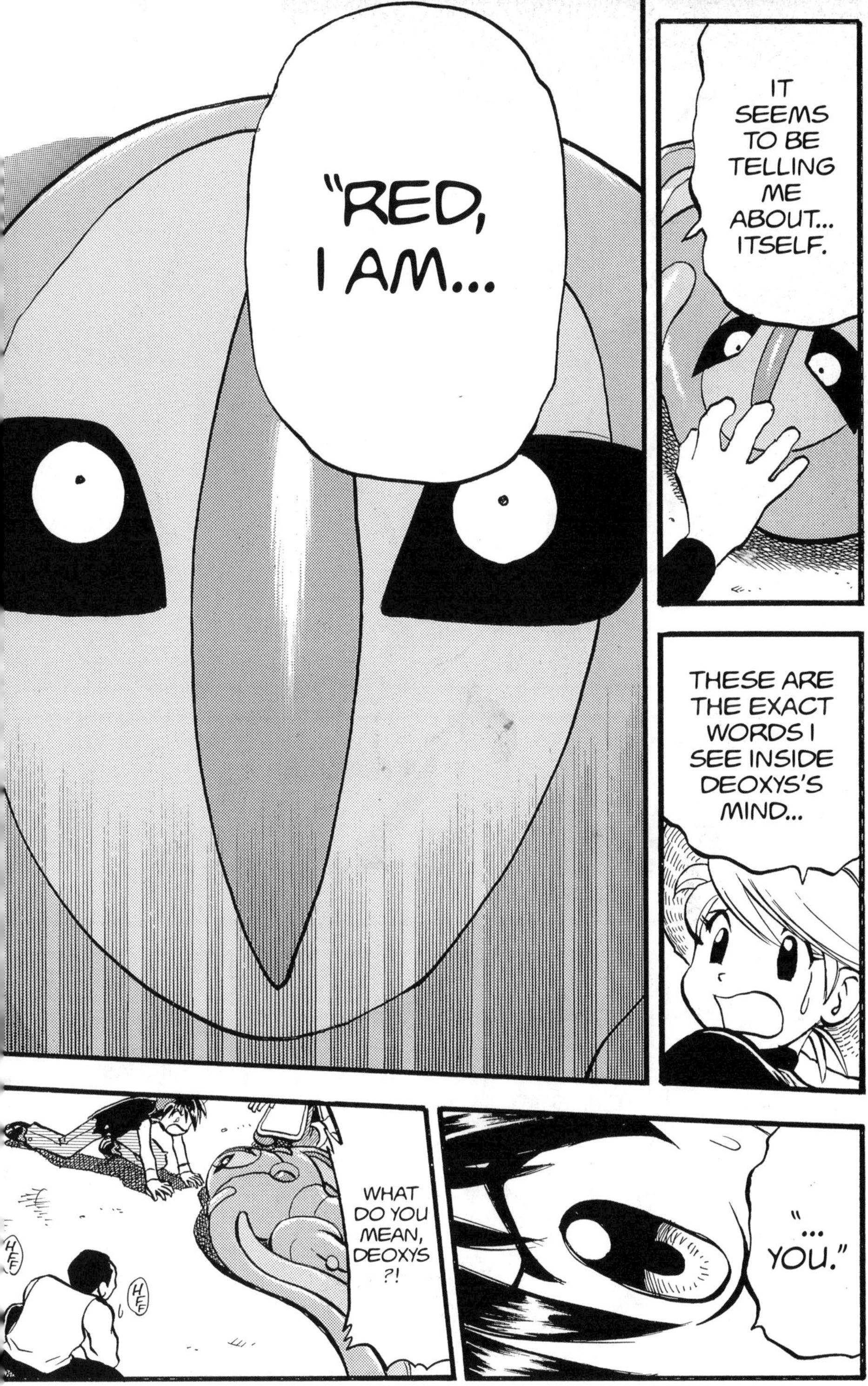
IT SEEMS TO BE TELLING ME ABOUT... ITSELF.
THESE ARE THE EXACT WORDS I SEE INSIDE DEOXYS'S MIND...
"RED, I AM...
"... YOU."
WHAT DO YOU MEAN, DEOXYS ?!
HFF
HFF

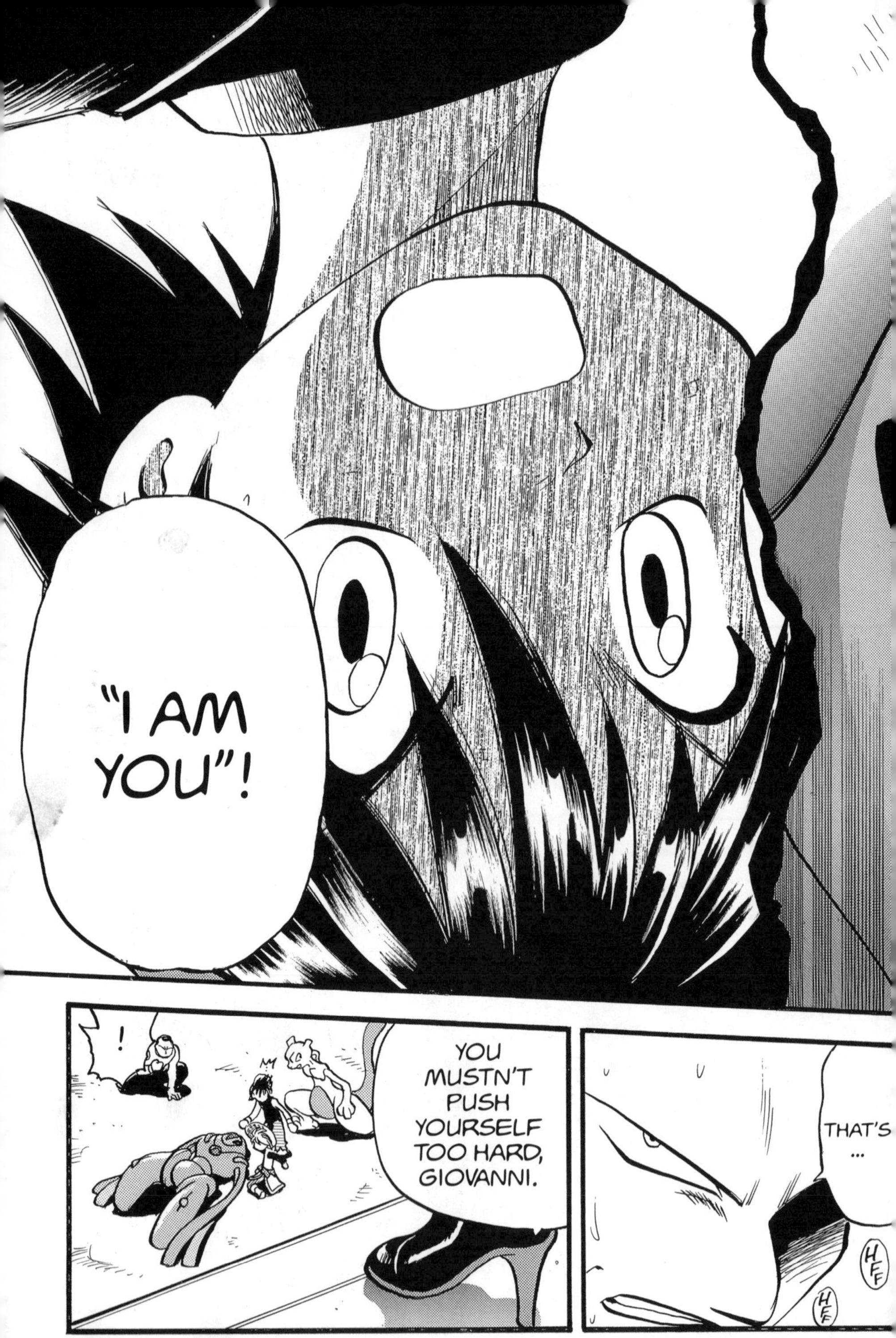
"I AM YOU"!
THAT'S ...
HFF
HFF
YOU MUSTN'T PUSH YOURSELF TOO HARD, GIOVANNI.
!

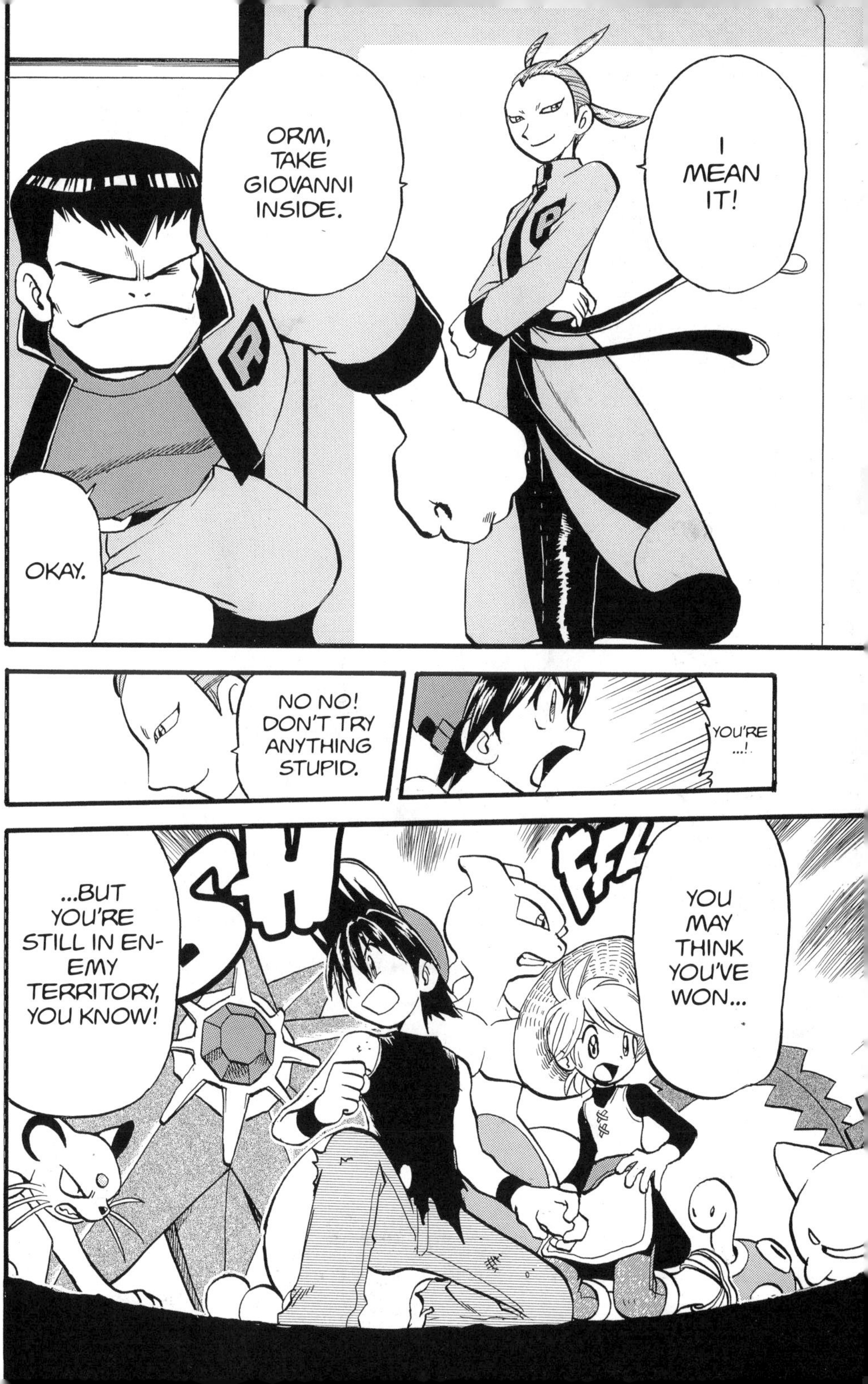
I MEAN IT!
ORM, TAKE GIOVANNI INSIDE.
OKAY.
YOU'RE ...!
NO NO! DON'T TRY ANYTHING STUPID.
YOU MAY THINK YOU'VE WON...
...BUT YOU'RE STILL IN EN-EMY TERRITORY, YOU KNOW!

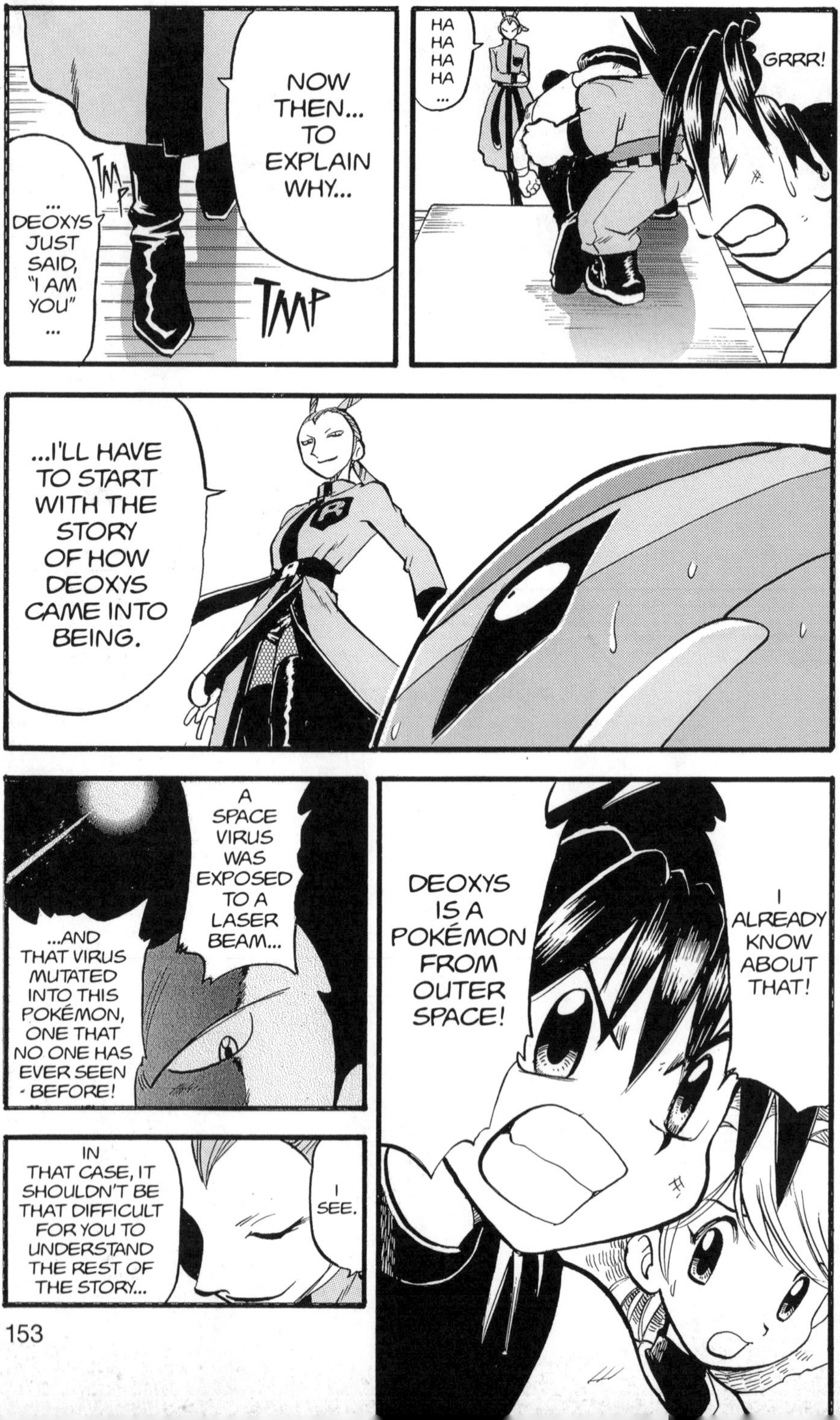
GRRR!
HA HA HA HA ...
NOW THEN... TO EXPLAIN WHY...
... DEOXYS JUST SAID, "I AM YOU" ...
TMP
TMP
...I'LL HAVE TO START WITH THE STORY OF HOW DEOXYS CAME INTO BEING.
I ALREADY KNOW ABOUT THAT!
DEOXYS IS A POKÉMON FROM OUTER SPACE!
A SPACE VIRUS WAS EXPOSED TO A LASER BEAM...
...AND THAT VIRUS MUTATED INTO THIS POKÉMON, ONE THAT NO ONE HAS EVER SEEN BEFORE!
I SEE.
IN THAT CASE, IT SHOULDN'T BE THAT DIFFICULT FOR YOU TO UNDERSTAND THE REST OF THE STORY...

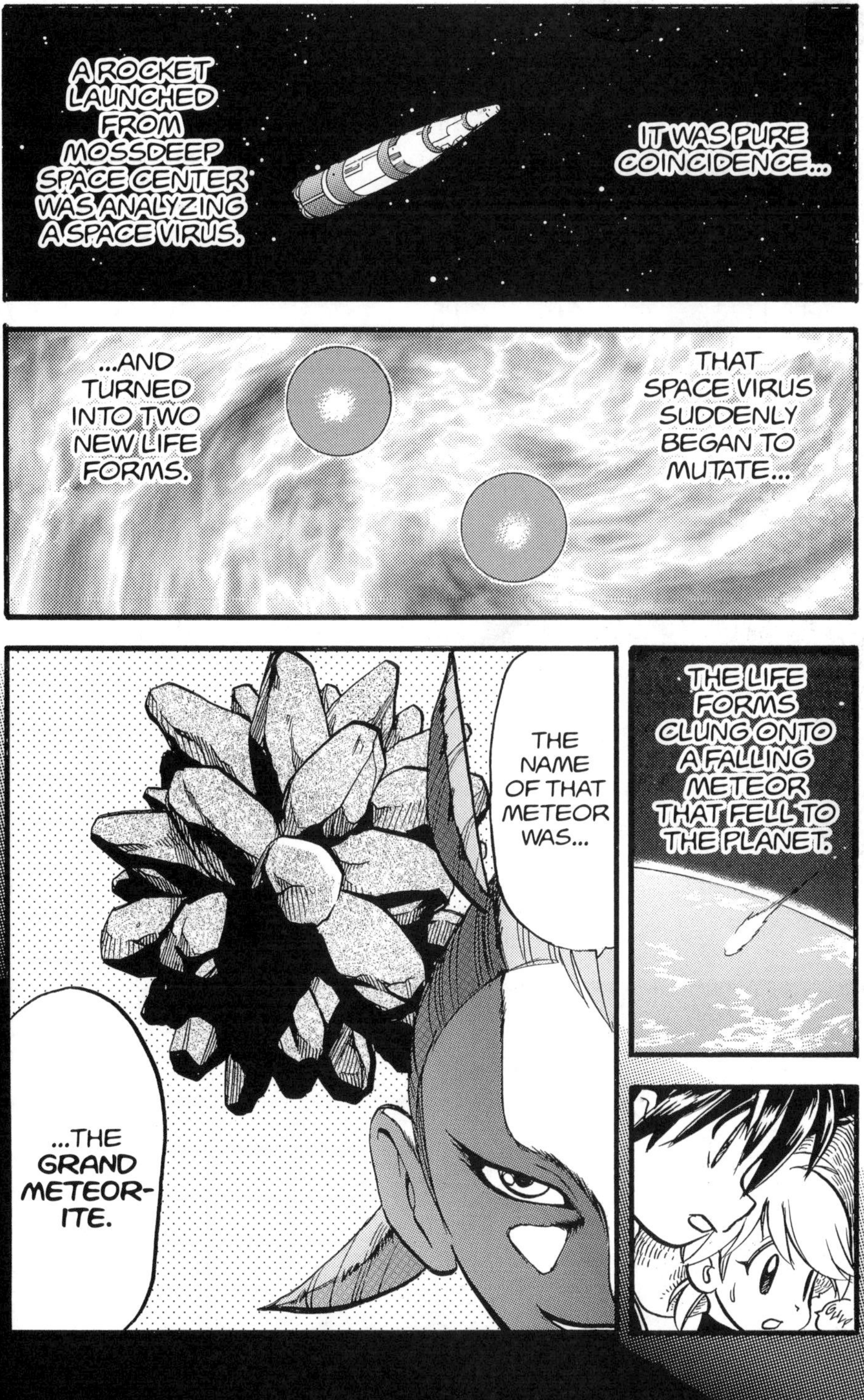
IT WAS PURE COINCIDENCE...
A ROCKET LAUNCHED FROM MOSSDEEP SPACE CENTER WAS ANALYZING A SPACE VIRUS.
THAT SPACE VIRUS SUDDENLY BEGAN TO MUTATE...
...AND TURNED INTO TWO NEW LIFE FORMS.
THE LIFE FORMS CLUNG ONTO A FALLING METEOR THAT FELL TO THE PLANET.
THE NAME OF THAT METEOR WAS...
...THE GRAND METEOR-ITE.

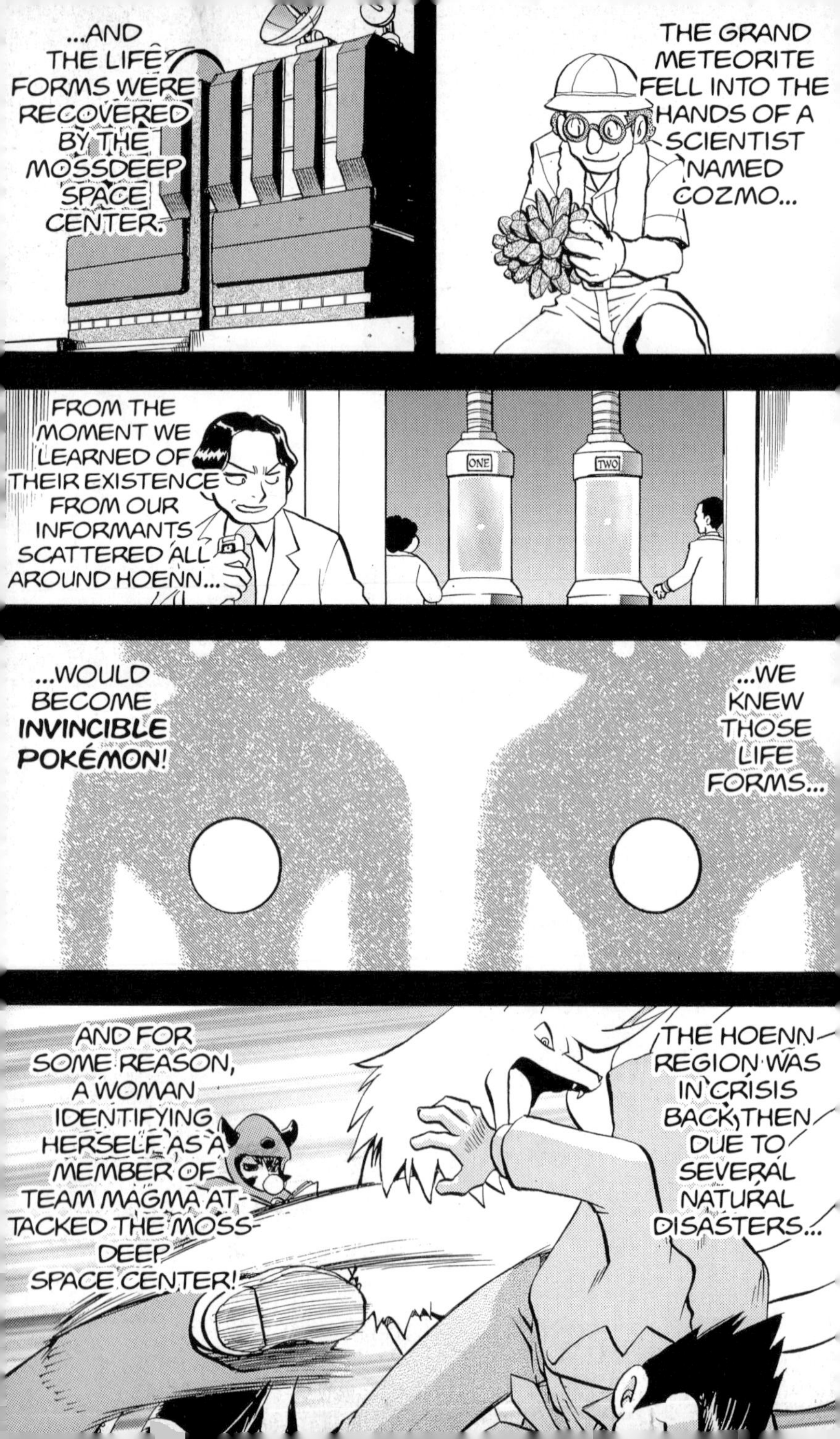
THE GRAND METEORITE FELL INTO THE HANDS OF A SCIENTIST NAMED COZMO...
...AND THE LIFE FORMS WERE RECOVERED BY THE MOSSDEEP SPACE CENTER.
ONE
TWO
FROM THE MOMENT WE LEARNED OF THEIR EXISTENCE FROM OUR INFORMANTS SCATTERED ALL AROUND HOENN...
...WE KNEW THOSE LIFE FORMS...
...WOULD BECOME **INVINCIBLE POKÉMON**!
THE HOENN REGION WAS IN CRISIS BACK THEN DUE TO SEVERAL NATURAL DISASTERS...
AND FOR SOME REASON, A WOMAN IDENTIFYING HERSELF AS A MEMBER OF TEAM MAGMA AT-TACKED THE MOSS-DEEP SPACE CENTER!

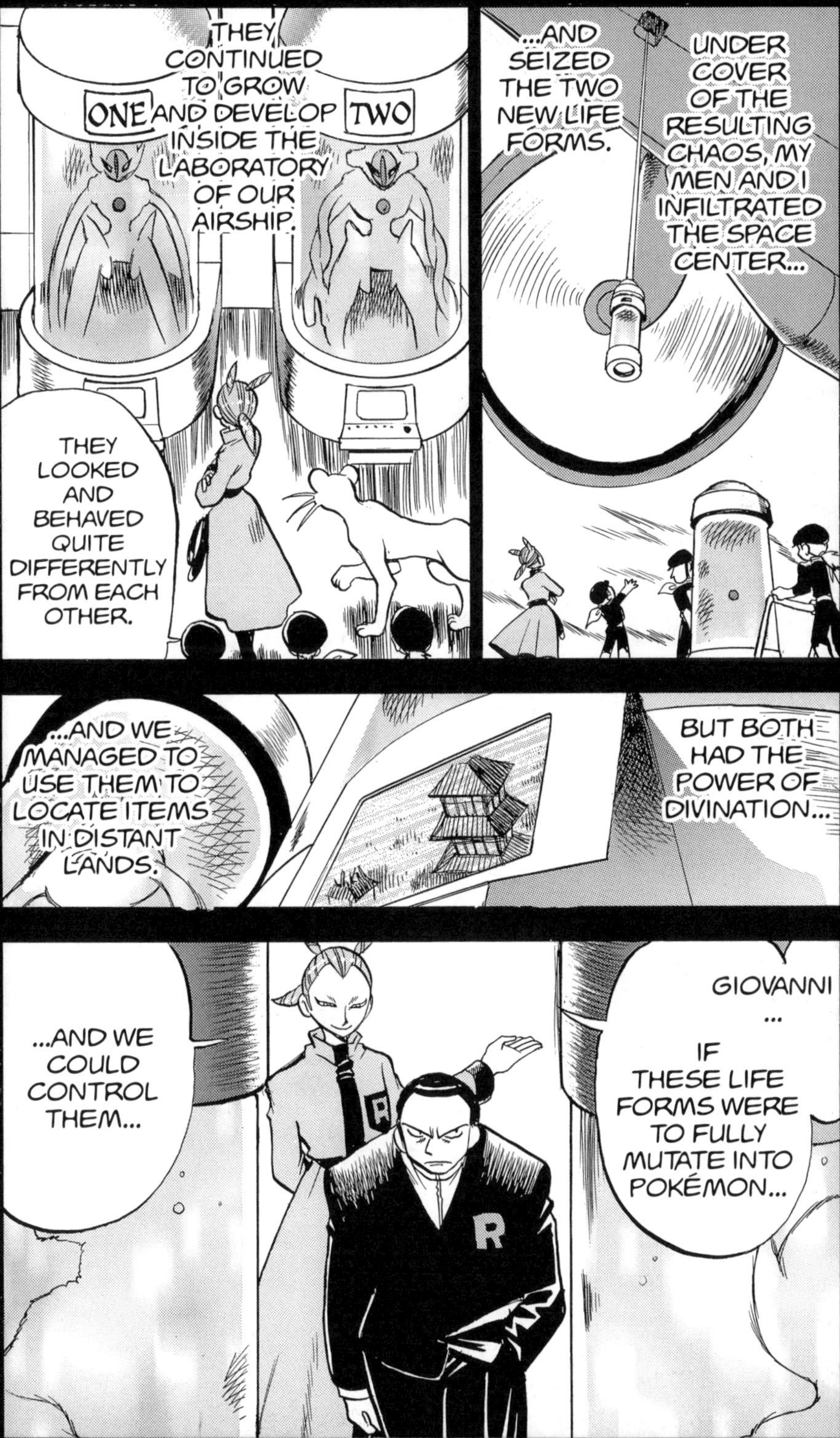
UNDER COVER OF THE RESULTING CHAOS, MY MEN AND I INFILTRATED THE SPACE CENTER...
...AND SEIZED THE TWO NEW LIFE FORMS.
THEY CONTINUED TO GROW AND DEVELOP INSIDE THE LABORATORY OF OUR AIRSHIP.
TWO
ONE
THEY LOOKED AND BEHAVED QUITE DIFFERENTLY FROM EACH OTHER.
BUT BOTH HAD THE POWER OF DIVINATION...
...AND WE MANAGED TO USE THEM TO LOCATE ITEMS IN DISTANT LANDS.
GIOVANNI ... IF THESE LIFE FORMS WERE TO FULLY MUTATE INTO POKÉMON...
...AND WE COULD CONTROL THEM...

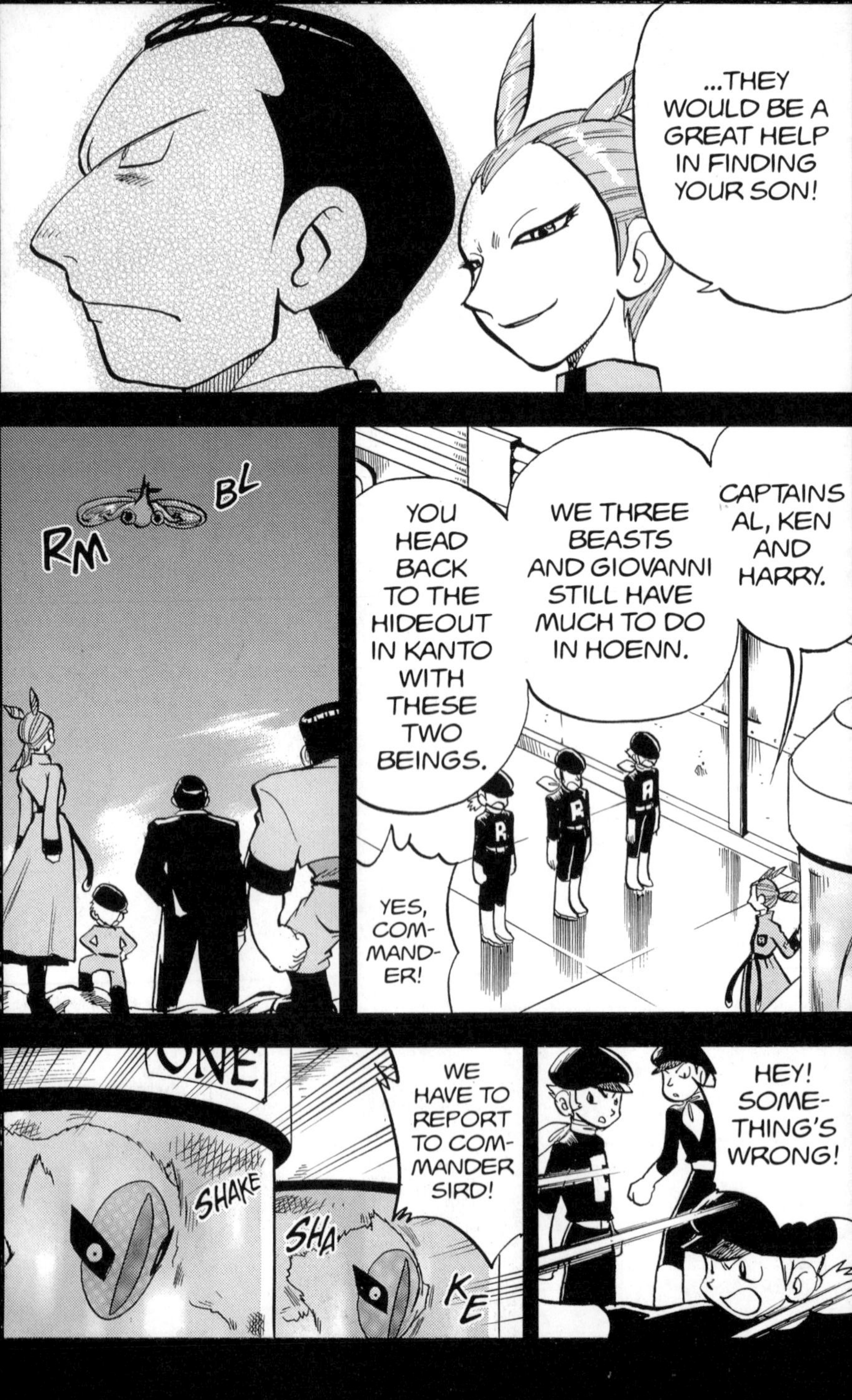
...THEY WOULD BE A GREAT HELP IN FINDING YOUR SON!
CAPTAINS AL, KEN AND HARRY.
WE THREE BEASTS AND GIOVANNI STILL HAVE MUCH TO DO IN HOENN.
YOU HEAD BACK TO THE HIDEOUT IN KANTO WITH THESE TWO BEINGS.
YES, COM-MAND-ER!
BL
RM
HEY! SOME-THING'S WRONG!
WE HAVE TO REPORT TO COM-MANDER SIRD!
SHAKE
SHA
KE

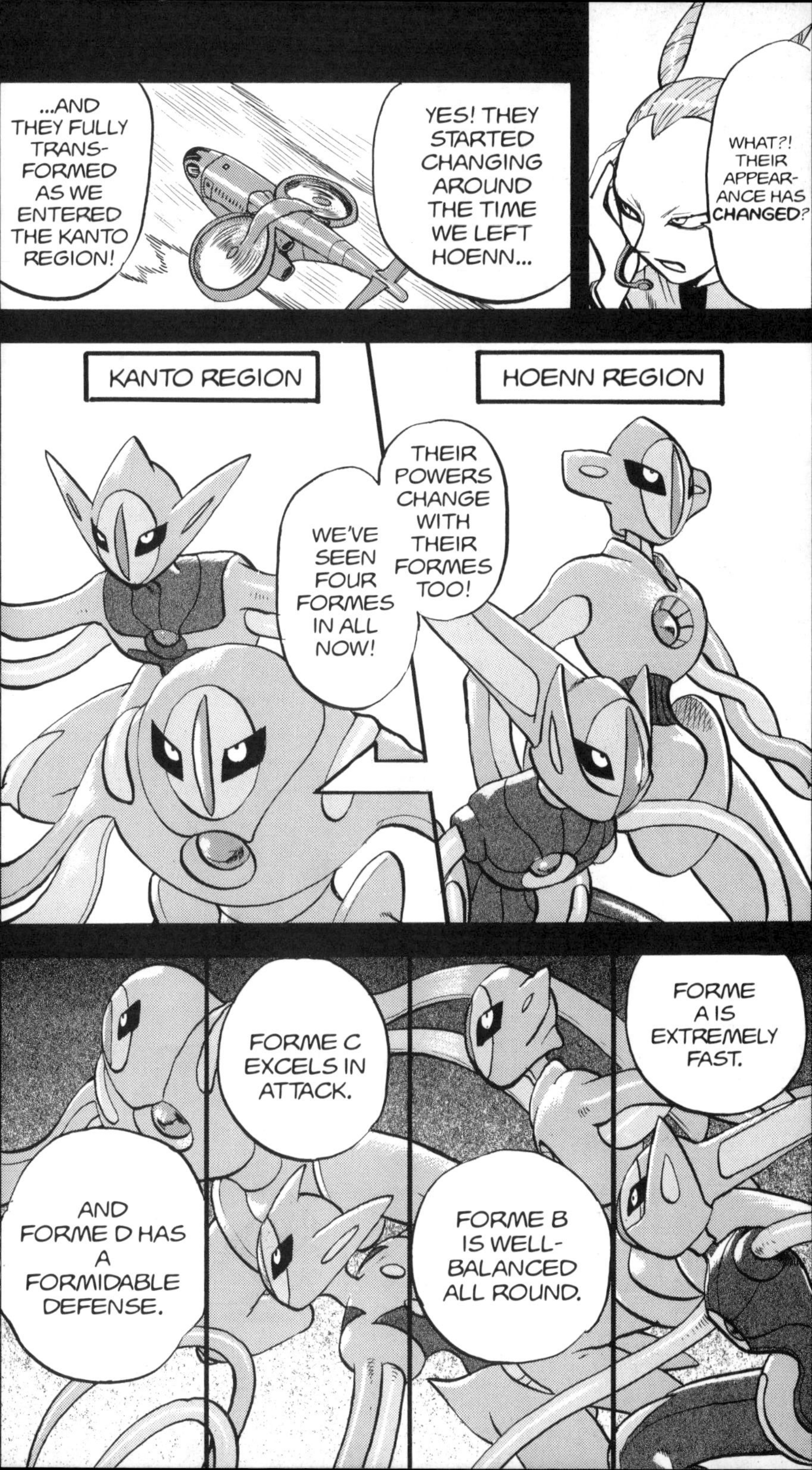
WHAT?! THEIR APPEARANCE HAS **CHANGED**?
YES! THEY STARTED CHANGING AROUND THE TIME WE LEFT HOENN...
...AND THEY FULLY TRANSFORMED AS WE ENTERED THE KANTO REGION!
HOENN REGION
KANTO REGION
THEIR POWERS CHANGE WITH THEIR FORMES TOO!
WE'VE SEEN FOUR FORMES IN ALL NOW!
FORME A IS EXTREMELY FAST.
FORME B IS WELL-BALANCED ALL ROUND.
FORME C EXCELS IN ATTACK.
AND FORME D HAS A FORMIDABLE DEFENSE.

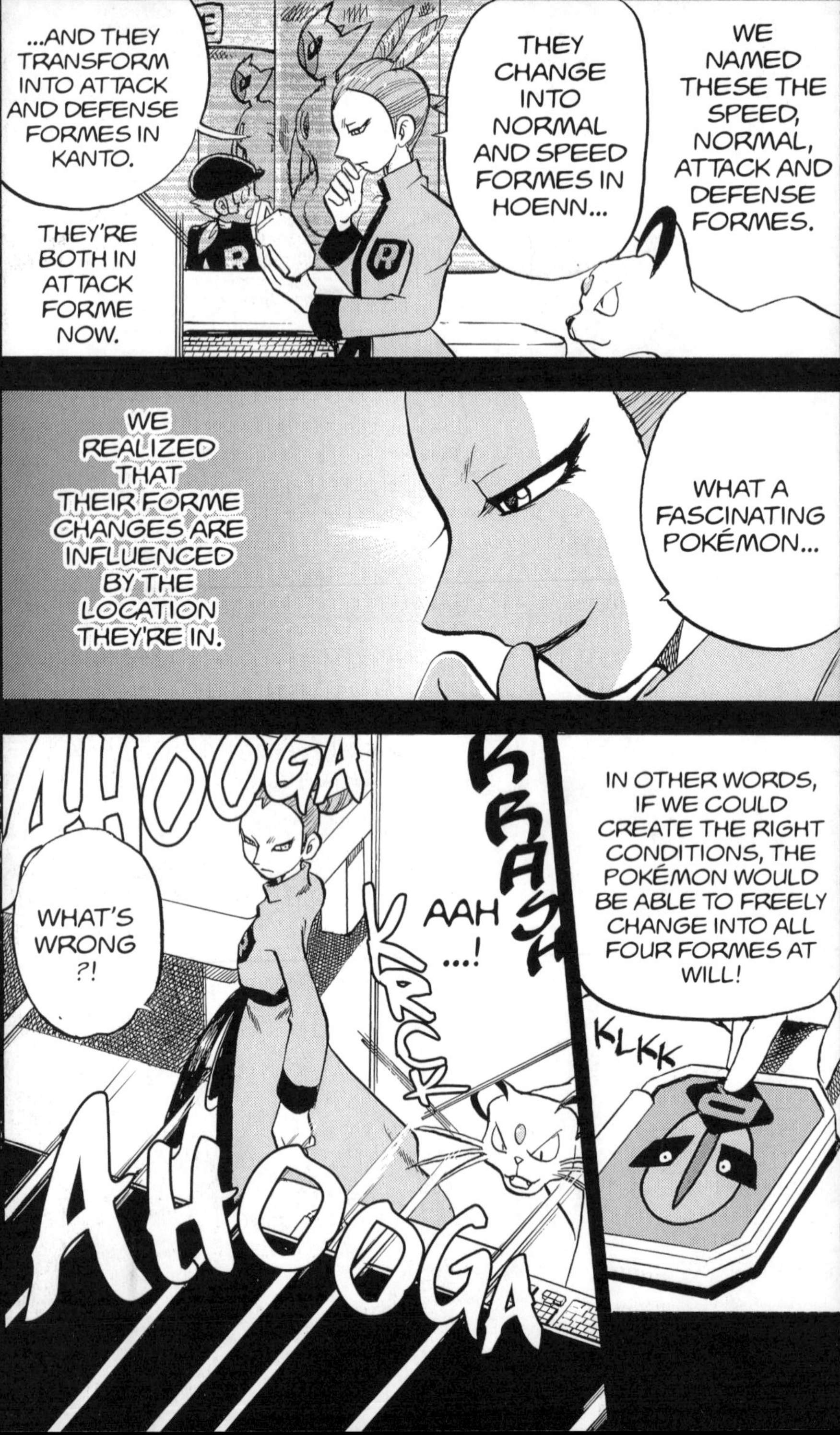
WE NAMED THESE THE SPEED, NORMAL, ATTACK AND DEFENSE FORMES.
THEY CHANGE INTO NORMAL AND SPEED FORMES IN HOENN...
...AND THEY TRANSFORM INTO ATTACK AND DEFENSE FORMES IN KANTO.
THEY'RE BOTH IN ATTACK FORME NOW.
WHAT A FASCINATING POKÉMON...
WE REALIZED THAT THEIR FORME CHANGES ARE INFLUENCED BY THE LOCATION THEY'RE IN.
IN OTHER WORDS, IF WE COULD CREATE THE RIGHT CONDITIONS, THE POKÉMON WOULD BE ABLE TO FREELY CHANGE INTO ALL FOUR FORMES AT WILL!
KLKK
AHOOGA
KRASH
AAH ...!
KRCK
WHAT'S WRONG ?!
AHOOGA

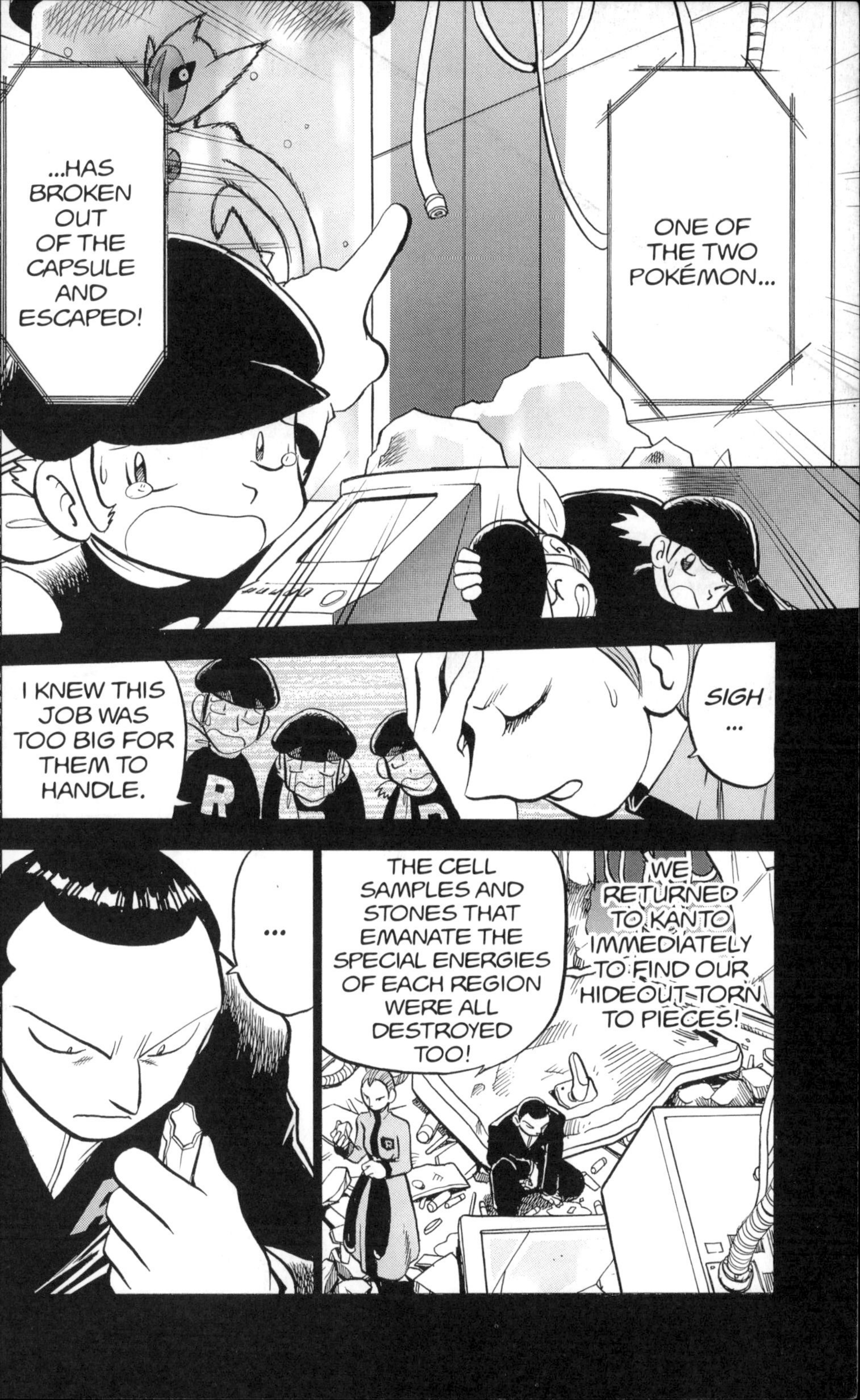
ONE OF THE TWO POKÉMON...
...HAS BROKEN OUT OF THE CAPSULE AND ESCAPED!
SIGH ...
I KNEW THIS JOB WAS TOO BIG FOR THEM TO HANDLE.
WE RETURNED TO KANTO IMMEDIATELY TO FIND OUR HIDEOUT TORN TO PIECES!
THE CELL SAMPLES AND STONES THAT EMANATE THE SPECIAL ENERGIES OF EACH REGION WERE ALL DESTROYED TOO!
...

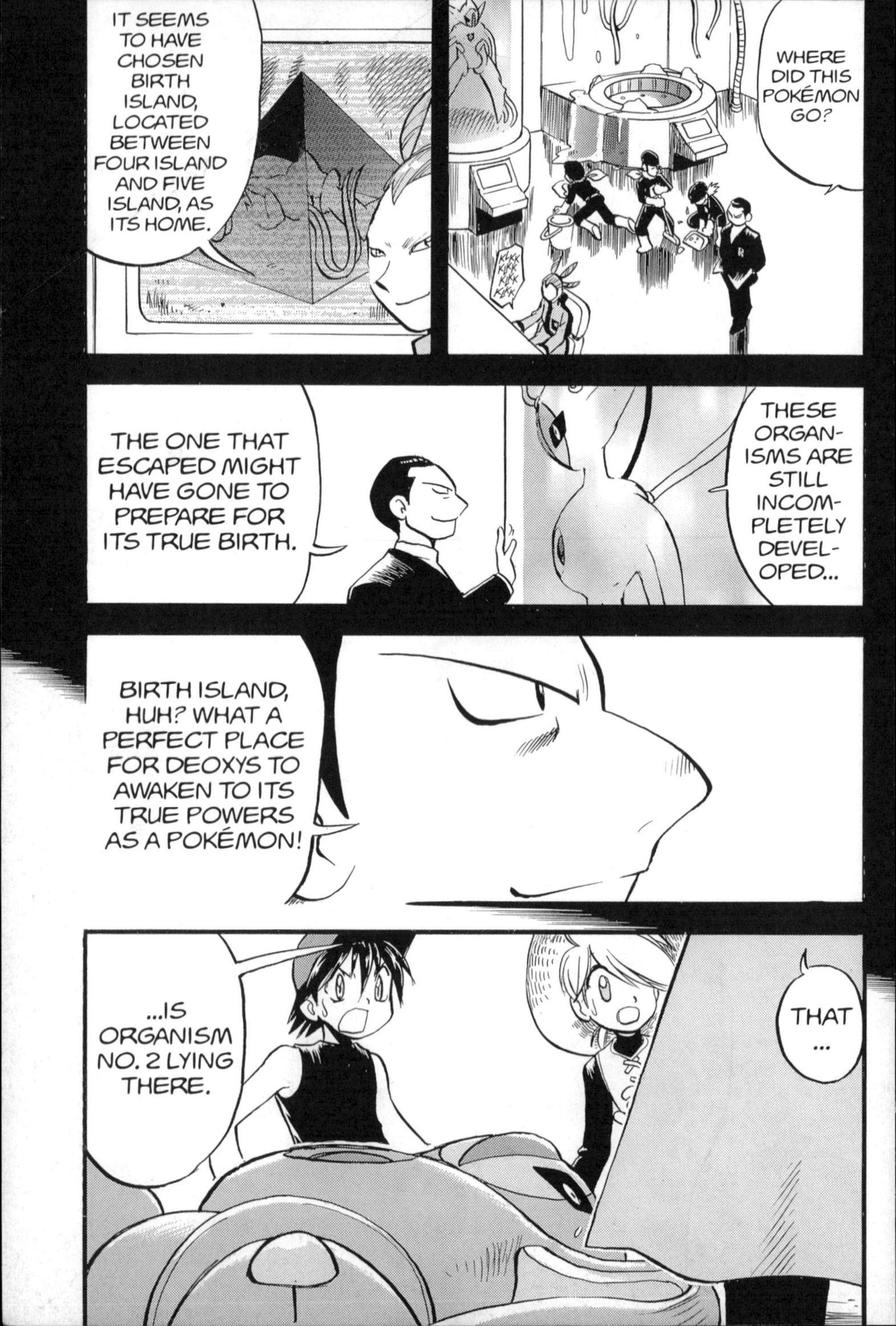
WHERE DID THIS POKÉMON GO?
IT SEEMS TO HAVE CHOSEN BIRTH ISLAND, LOCATED BETWEEN FOUR ISLAND AND FIVE ISLAND, AS ITS HOME.
THESE ORGANISMS ARE STILL INCOMPLETELY DEVELOPED...
THE ONE THAT ESCAPED MIGHT HAVE GONE TO PREPARE FOR ITS TRUE BIRTH.
BIRTH ISLAND, HUH? WHAT A PERFECT PLACE FOR DEOXYS TO AWAKEN TO ITS TRUE POWERS AS A POKÉMON!
THAT...
...IS ORGANISM NO. 2 LYING THERE.

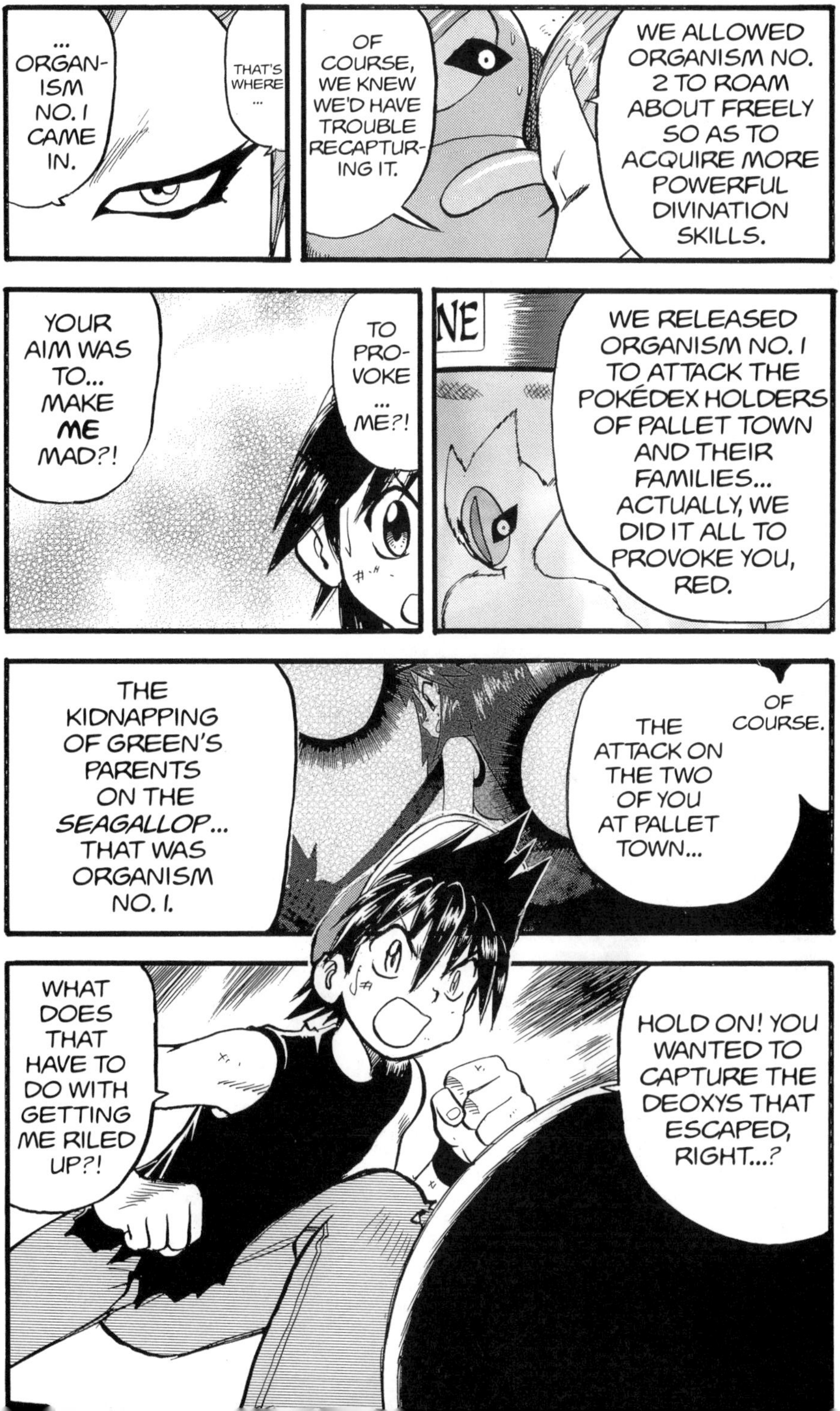
WE ALLOWED ORGANISM NO. 2 TO ROAM ABOUT FREELY SO AS TO ACQUIRE MORE POWERFUL DIVINATION SKILLS.
OF COURSE, WE KNEW WE'D HAVE TROUBLE RECAPTURING IT.
THAT'S WHERE ...
... ORGANISM NO. 1 CAME IN.
WE RELEASED ORGANISM NO. 1 TO ATTACK THE POKÉDEX HOLDERS OF PALLET TOWN AND THEIR FAMILIES... ACTUALLY, WE DID IT ALL TO PROVOKE YOU, RED.
TO PROVOKE ... ME?!
YOUR AIM WAS TO... MAKE **ME** MAD?!
OF COURSE.
THE ATTACK ON THE TWO OF YOU AT PALLET TOWN...
THE KIDNAPPING OF GREEN'S PARENTS ON THE *SEAGALLOP*... THAT WAS ORGANISM NO. 1.
HOLD ON! YOU WANTED TO CAPTURE THE DEOXYS THAT ESCAPED, RIGHT...?
WHAT DOES THAT HAVE TO DO WITH GETTING ME RILED UP?!

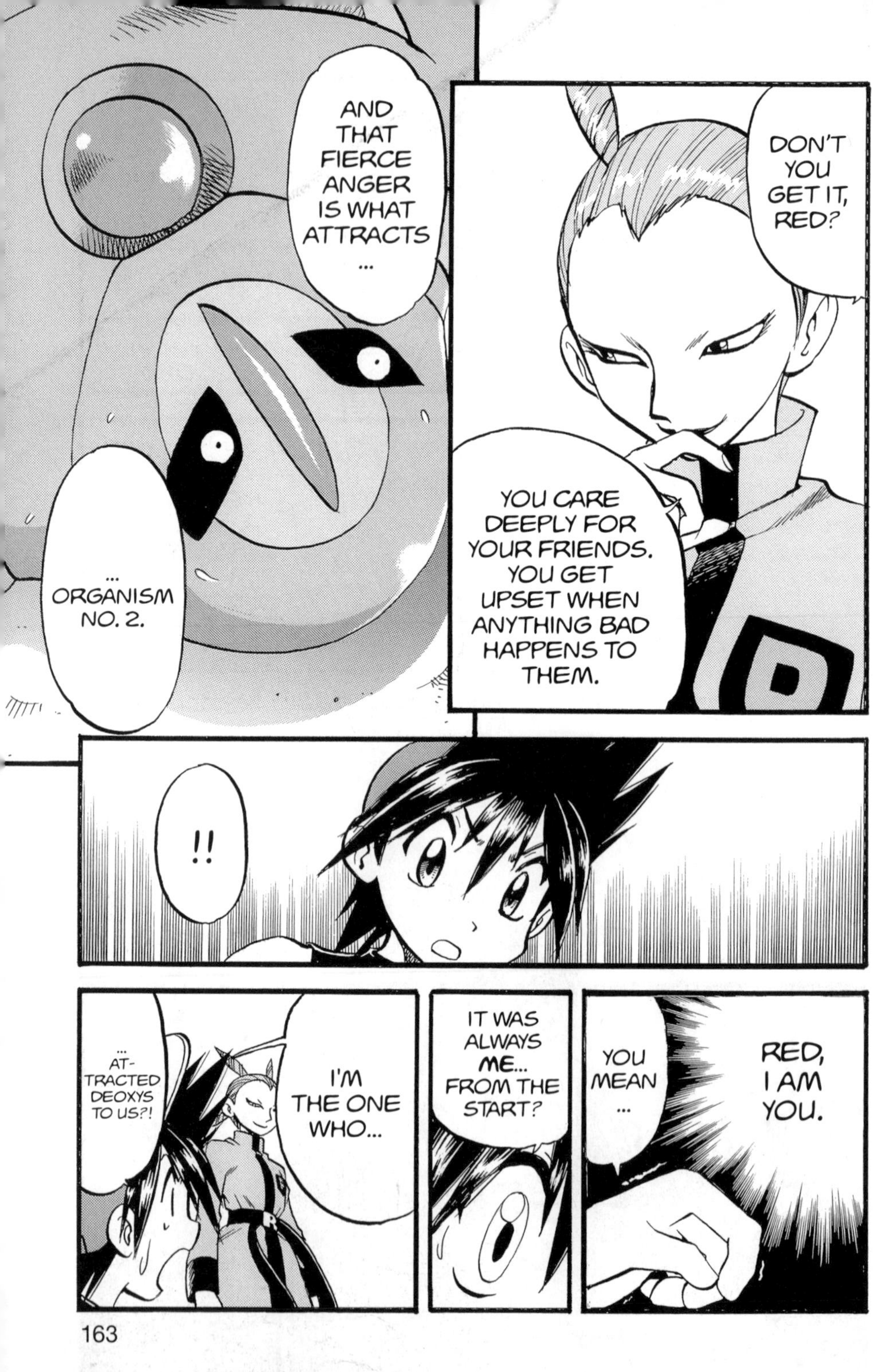
DON'T YOU GET IT, RED?
YOU CARE DEEPLY FOR YOUR FRIENDS. YOU GET UPSET WHEN ANYTHING BAD HAPPENS TO THEM.
AND THAT FIERCE ANGER IS WHAT ATTRACTS ...
... ORGANISM NO. 2.
!!
RED, I AM YOU.
YOU MEAN ...
IT WAS ALWAYS ME... FROM THE START?
I'M THE ONE WHO...
... AT-TRACTED DEOXYS TO US?!

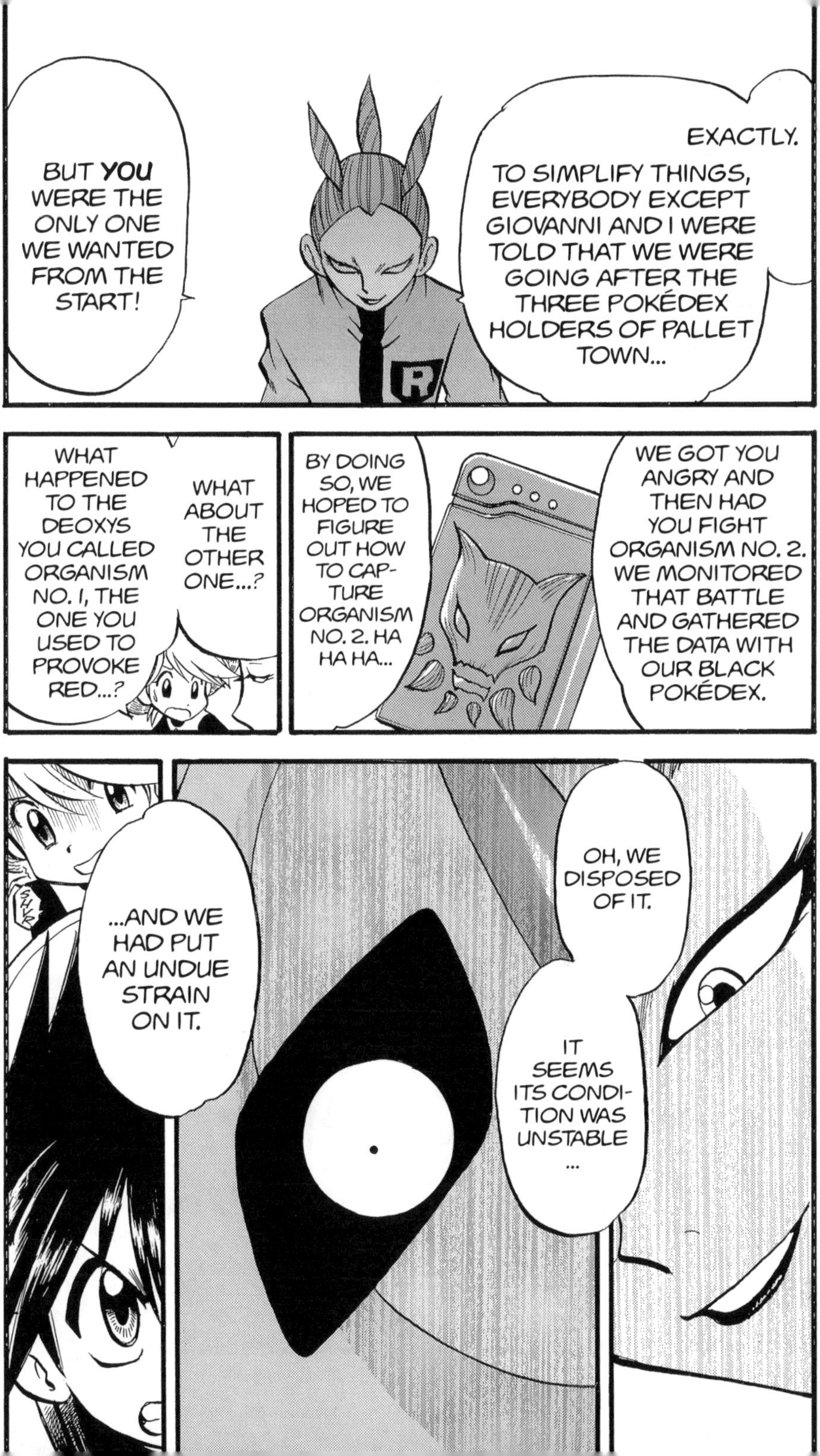
EXACTLY.
TO SIMPLIFY THINGS, EVERYBODY EXCEPT GIOVANNI AND I WERE TOLD THAT WE WERE GOING AFTER THE THREE POKÉDEX HOLDERS OF PALLET TOWN...
BUT **YOU** WERE THE ONLY ONE WE WANTED FROM THE START!
WE GOT YOU ANGRY AND THEN HAD YOU FIGHT ORGANISM NO. 2. WE MONITORED THAT BATTLE AND GATHERED THE DATA WITH OUR BLACK POKÉDEX.
BY DOING SO, WE HOPED TO FIGURE OUT HOW TO CAPTURE ORGANISM NO. 2. HA HA HA...
WHAT ABOUT THE OTHER ONE...?
WHAT HAPPENED TO THE DEOXYS YOU CALLED ORGANISM NO. 1, THE ONE YOU USED TO PROVOKE RED...?
OH, WE DISPOSED OF IT.
IT SEEMS ITS CONDITION WAS UNSTABLE ...
...AND WE HAD PUT AN UNDUE STRAIN ON IT.

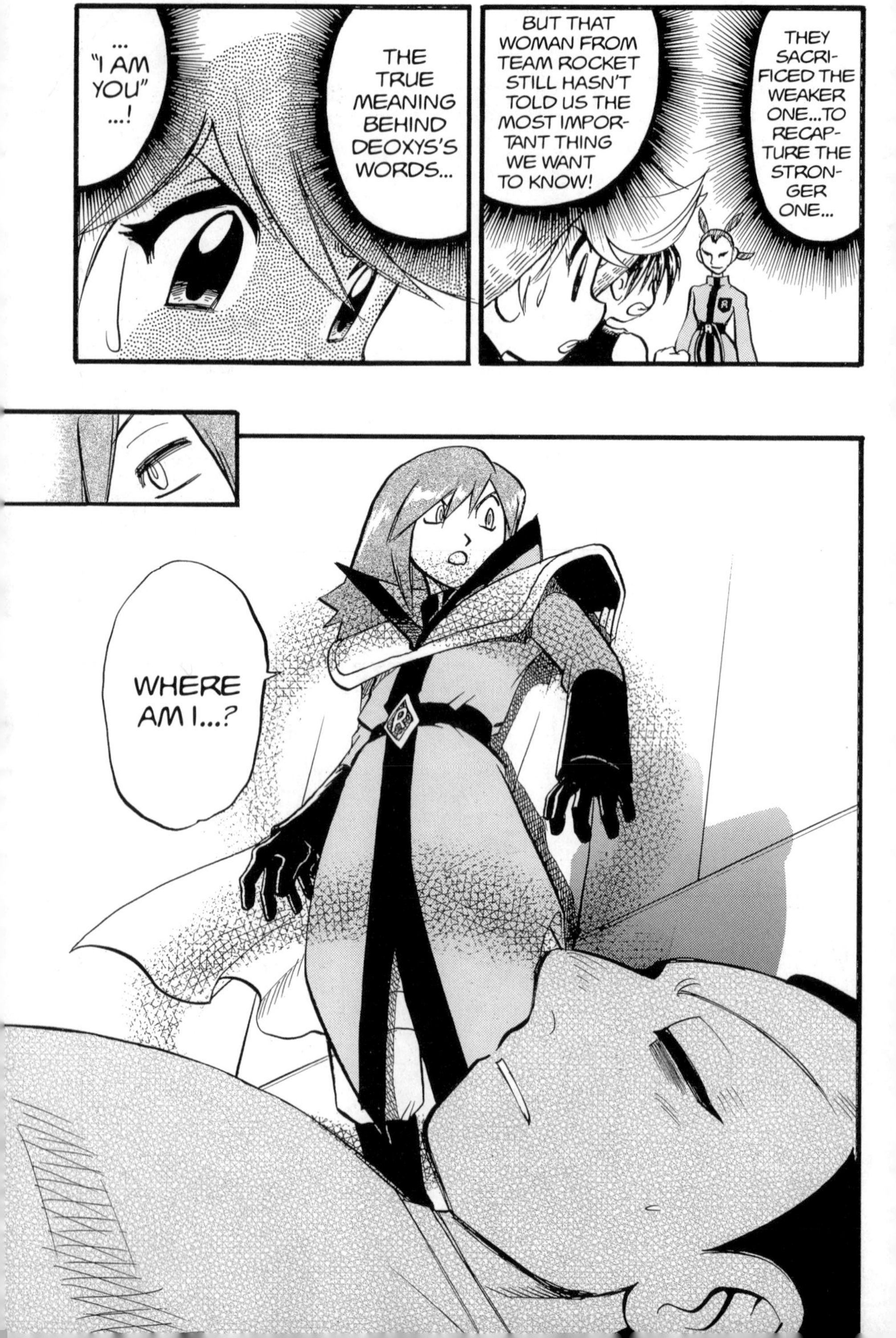
THEY SACRIFICED THE WEAKER ONE...TO RECAPTURE THE STRONGER ONE...
BUT THAT WOMAN FROM TEAM ROCKET STILL HASN'T TOLD US THE MOST IMPORTANT THING WE WANT TO KNOW!
THE TRUE MEANING BEHIND DEOXYS'S WORDS...
... "I AM YOU" ...!
WHERE AM I...?

Adventure 297
Mewtwo Comes Through

Pokémon Adventures
FireRed & LeafGreen
The Fifth Chapter

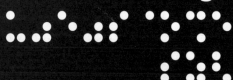

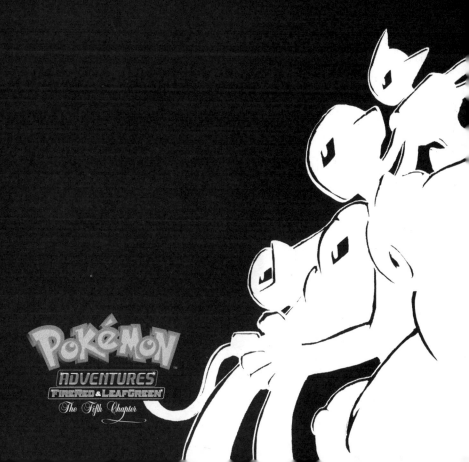

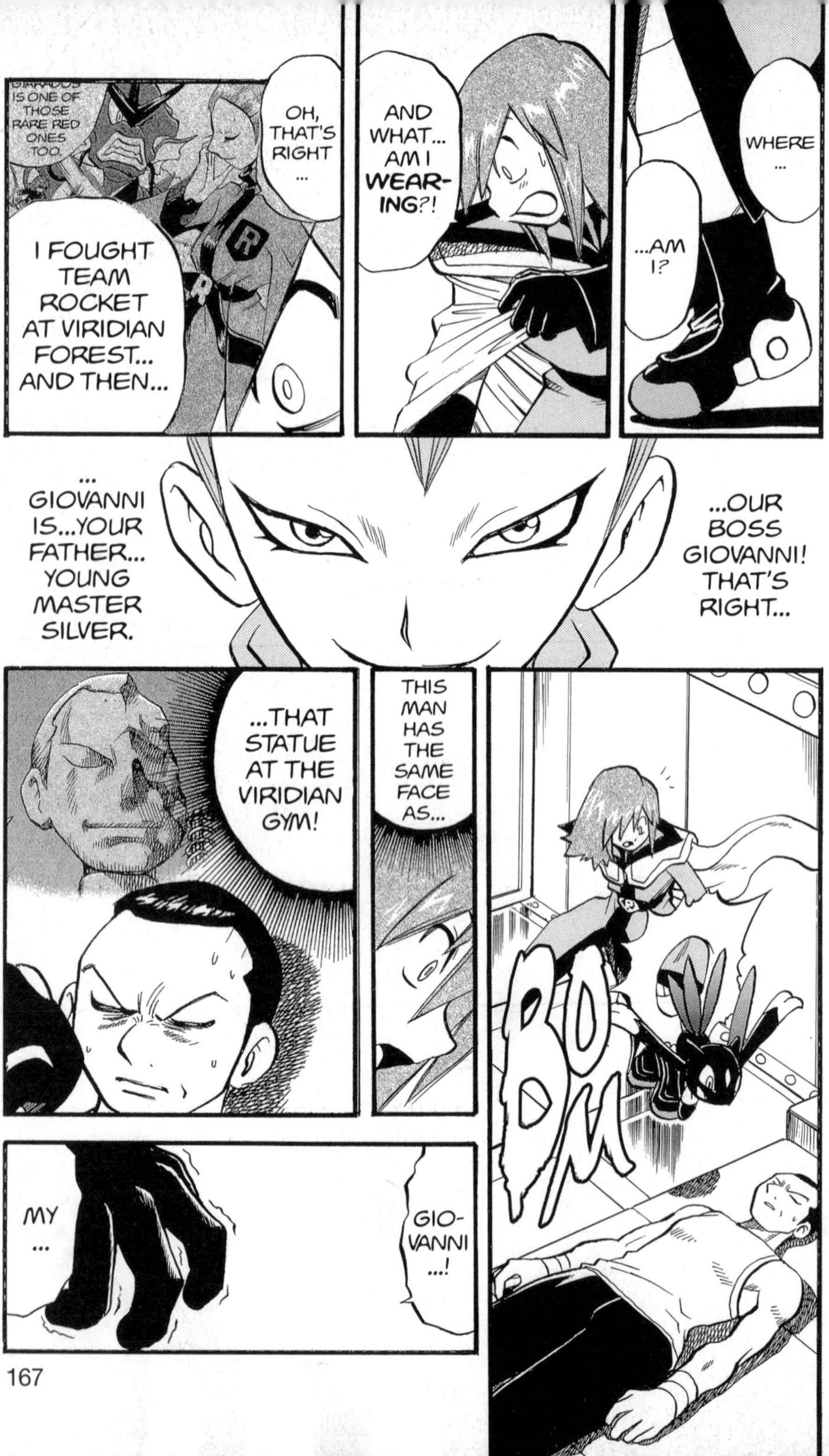
WHERE ...
...AM I?
AND WHAT... AM I WEARING?!
OH, THAT'S RIGHT ...
GYARADOS IS ONE OF THOSE RARE RED ONES TOO.
I FOUGHT TEAM ROCKET AT VIRIDIAN FOREST... AND THEN...
...OUR BOSS GIOVANNI! THAT'S RIGHT...
... GIOVANNI IS...YOUR FATHER... YOUNG MASTER SILVER.
BOOM
THIS MAN HAS THE SAME FACE AS...
...THAT STATUE AT THE VIRIDIAN GYM!
GIO-VANNI ...!
MY ...

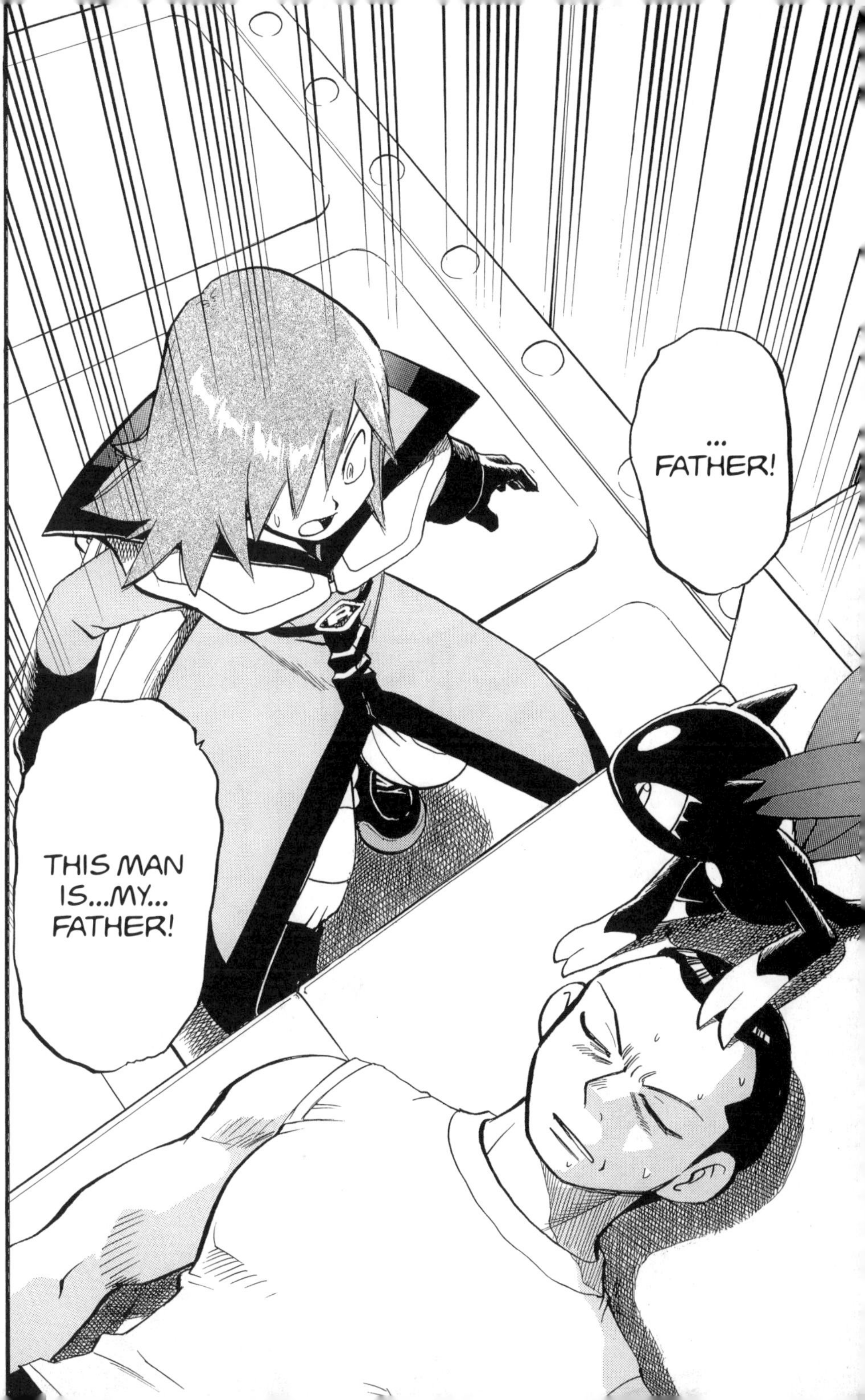
... FATHER!
THIS MAN IS...MY... FATHER!

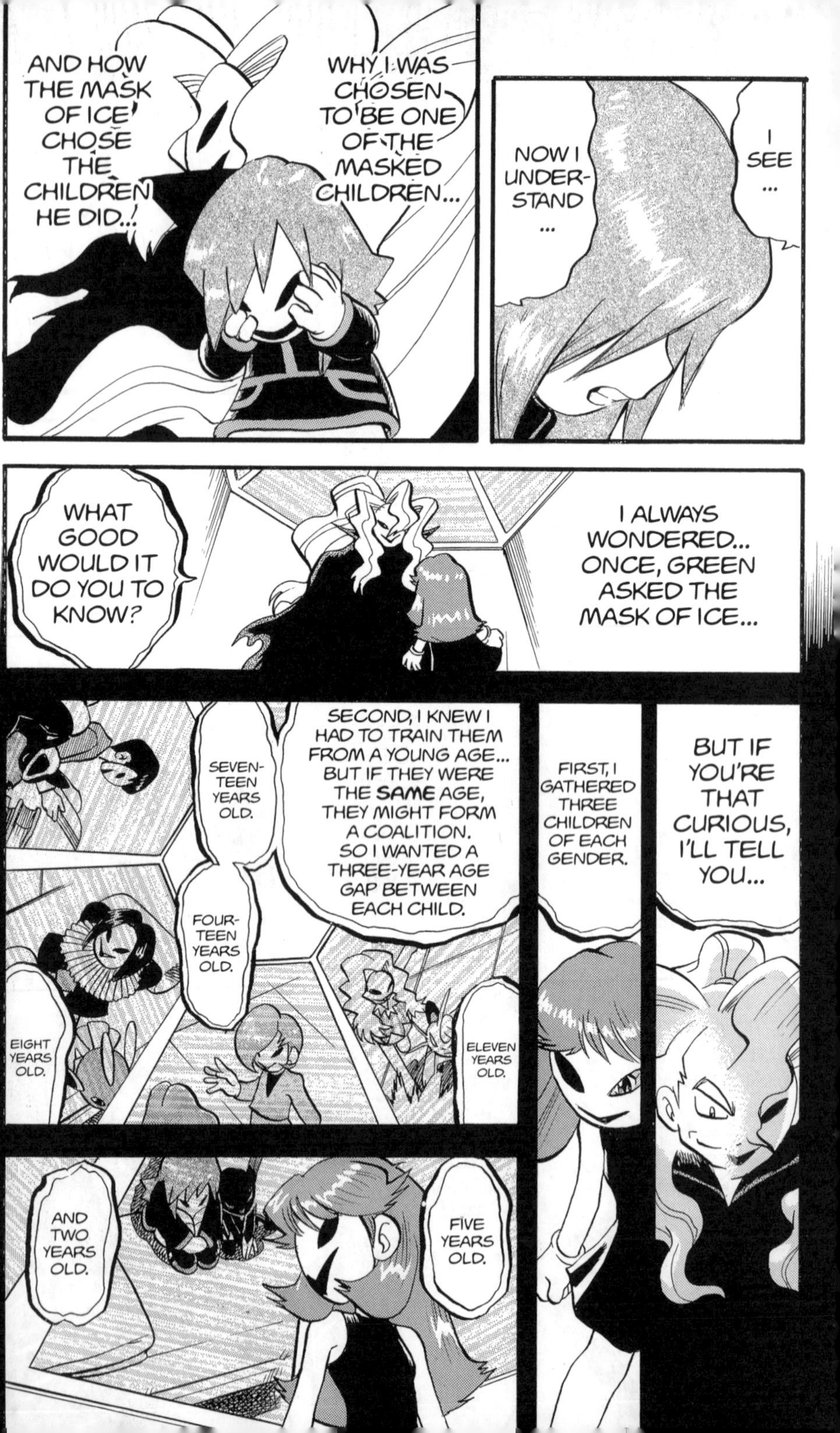
I SEE...
NOW I UNDERSTAND...
WHY I WAS CHOSEN TO BE ONE OF THE MASKED CHILDREN...
AND HOW THE MASK OF ICE CHOSE THE CHILDREN HE DID...!
I ALWAYS WONDERED... ONCE, GREEN ASKED THE MASK OF ICE...
WHAT GOOD WOULD IT DO YOU TO KNOW?
BUT IF YOU'RE THAT CURIOUS, I'LL TELL YOU...
FIRST, I GATHERED THREE CHILDREN OF EACH GENDER.
SECOND, I KNEW I HAD TO TRAIN THEM FROM A YOUNG AGE... BUT IF THEY WERE THE **SAME** AGE, THEY MIGHT FORM A COALITION. SO I WANTED A THREE-YEAR AGE GAP BETWEEN EACH CHILD.
SEVENTEEN YEARS OLD.
FOURTEEN YEARS OLD.
ELEVEN YEARS OLD.
EIGHT YEARS OLD.
FIVE YEARS OLD.
AND TWO YEARS OLD.

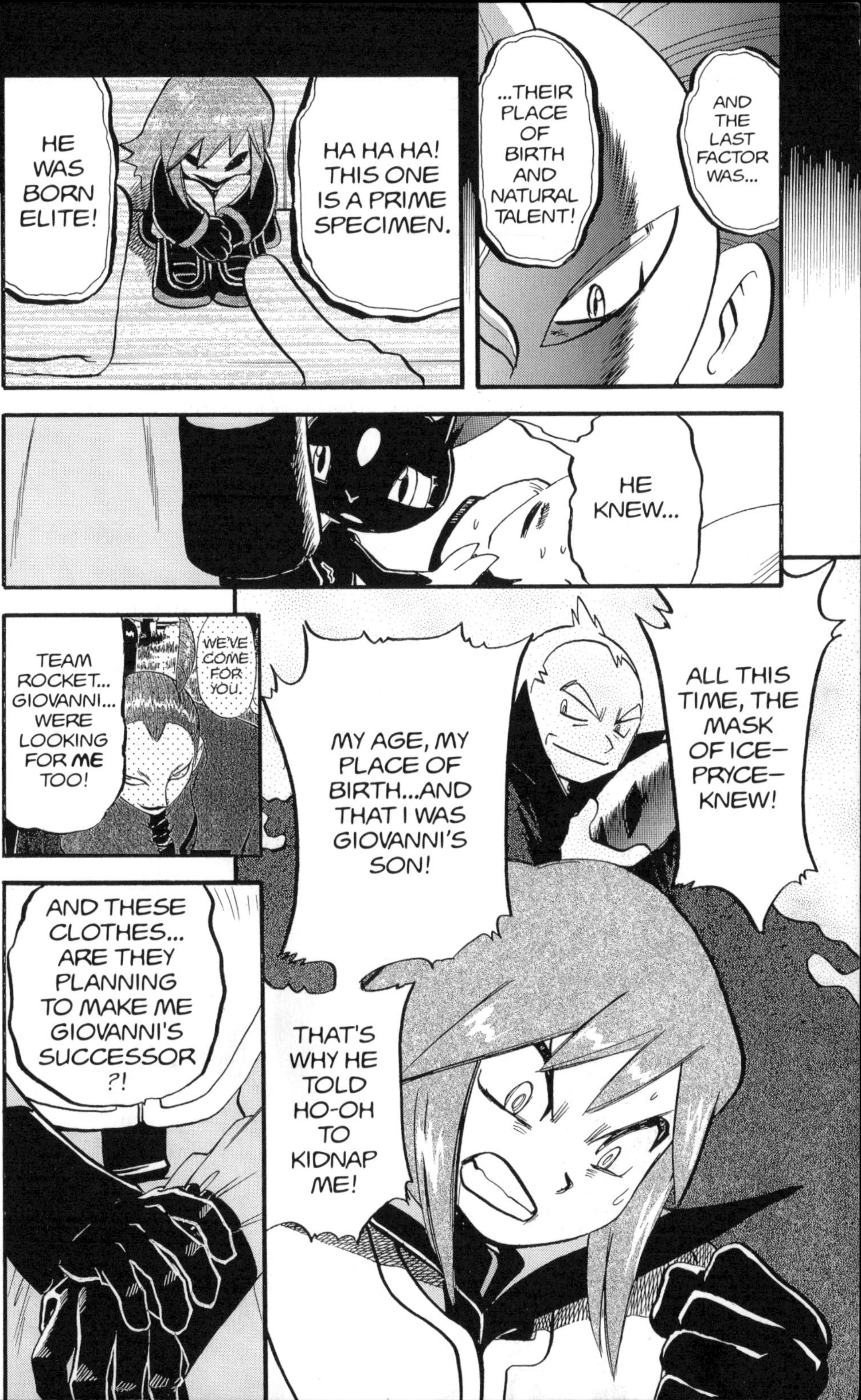
AND THE LAST FACTOR WAS...
...THEIR PLACE OF BIRTH AND NATURAL TALENT!
HA HA HA! THIS ONE IS A PRIME SPECIMEN.
HE WAS BORN ELITE!
HE KNEW...
ALL THIS TIME, THE MASK OF ICE—PRYCE—KNEW!
MY AGE, MY PLACE OF BIRTH...AND THAT I WAS GIOVANNI'S SON!
THAT'S WHY HE TOLD HO-OH TO KIDNAP ME!
WE'VE COME FOR YOU.
TEAM ROCKET... GIOVANNI... WERE LOOKING FOR ME TOO!
AND THESE CLOTHES... ARE THEY PLANNING TO MAKE ME GIOVANNI'S SUCCESSOR?!

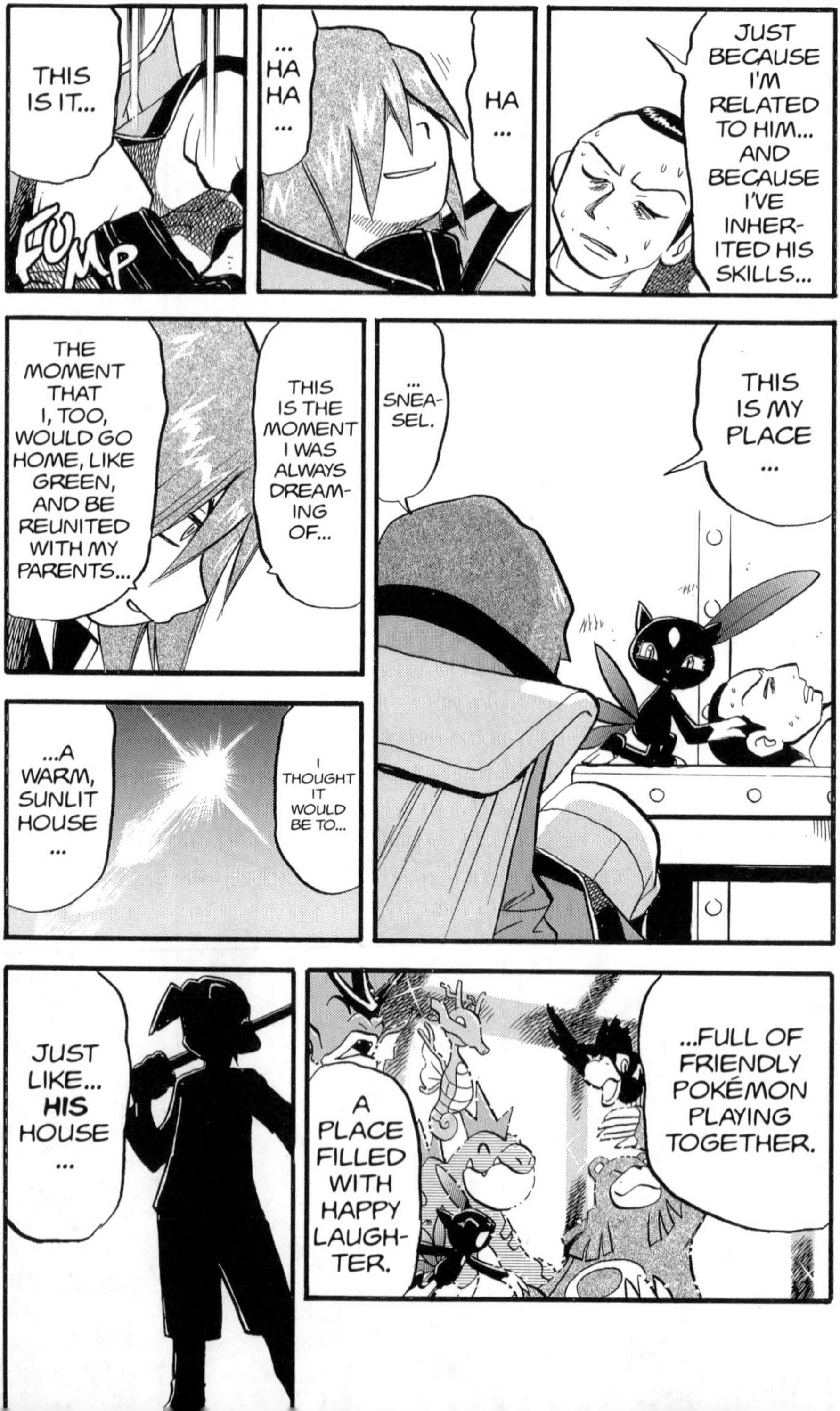
JUST BECAUSE I'M RELATED TO HIM... AND BECAUSE I'VE INHERITED HIS SKILLS...
HA...
...HA HA...
THIS IS IT...
FUMP
THIS IS MY PLACE...
...SNEASEL.
THIS IS THE MOMENT I WAS ALWAYS DREAMING OF...
THE MOMENT THAT I, TOO, WOULD GO HOME, LIKE GREEN, AND BE REUNITED WITH MY PARENTS...
I THOUGHT IT WOULD BE TO...
...A WARM, SUNLIT HOUSE...
...FULL OF FRIENDLY POKÉMON PLAYING TOGETHER.
A PLACE FILLED WITH HAPPY LAUGHTER.
JUST LIKE... **HIS** HOUSE...

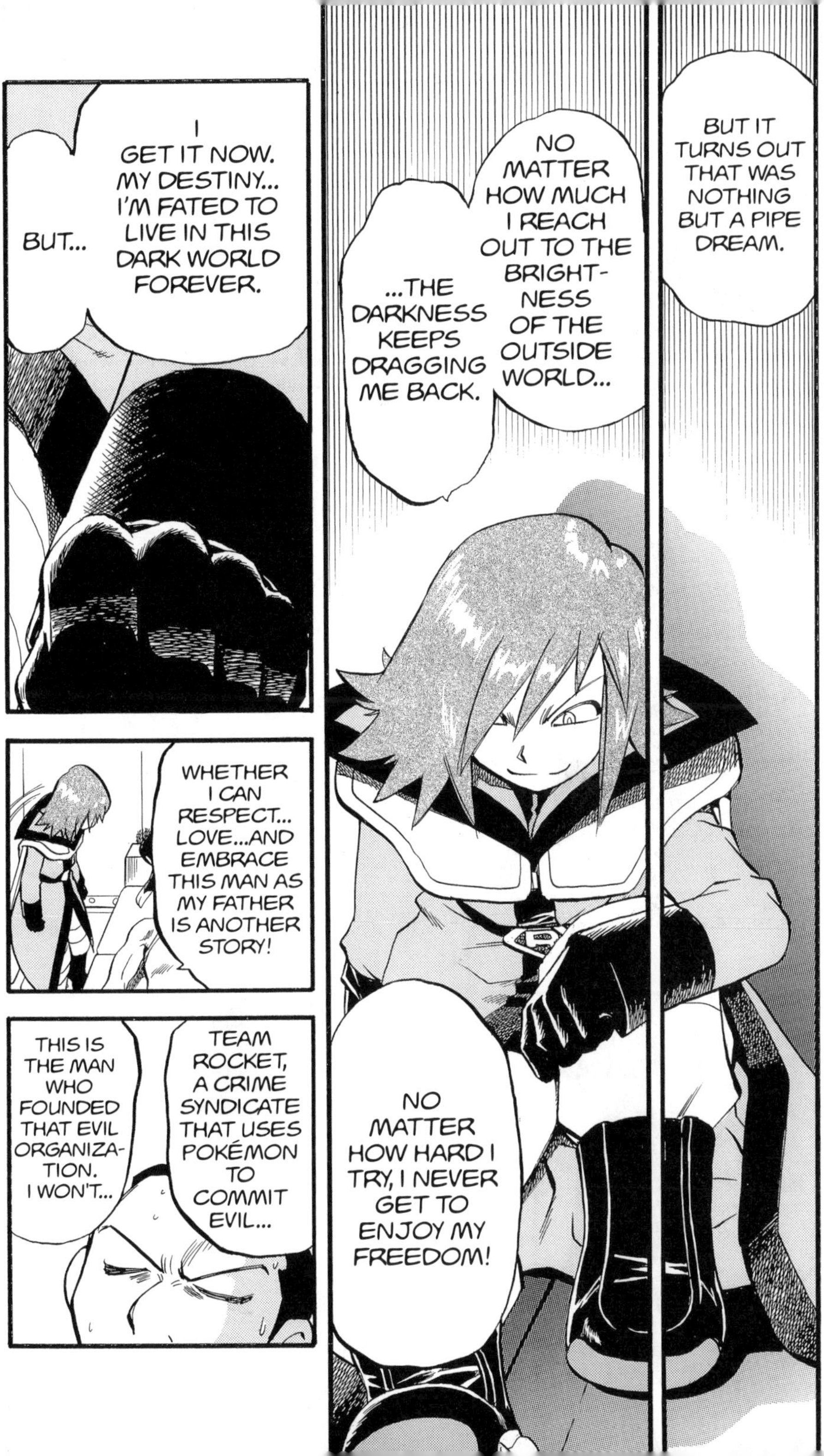
BUT IT TURNS OUT THAT WAS NOTHING BUT A PIPE DREAM.
NO MATTER HOW MUCH I REACH OUT TO THE BRIGHT-NESS OF THE OUTSIDE WORLD...
...THE DARKNESS KEEPS DRAGGING ME BACK.
NO MATTER HOW HARD I TRY, I NEVER GET TO ENJOY MY FREEDOM!
I GET IT NOW. MY DESTINY... I'M FATED TO LIVE IN THIS DARK WORLD FOREVER.
BUT...
WHETHER I CAN RESPECT... LOVE...AND EMBRACE THIS MAN AS MY FATHER IS ANOTHER STORY!
TEAM ROCKET, A CRIME SYNDICATE THAT USES POKÉMON TO COMMIT EVIL...
THIS IS THE MAN WHO FOUNDED THAT EVIL ORGANIZA-TION. I WON'T...

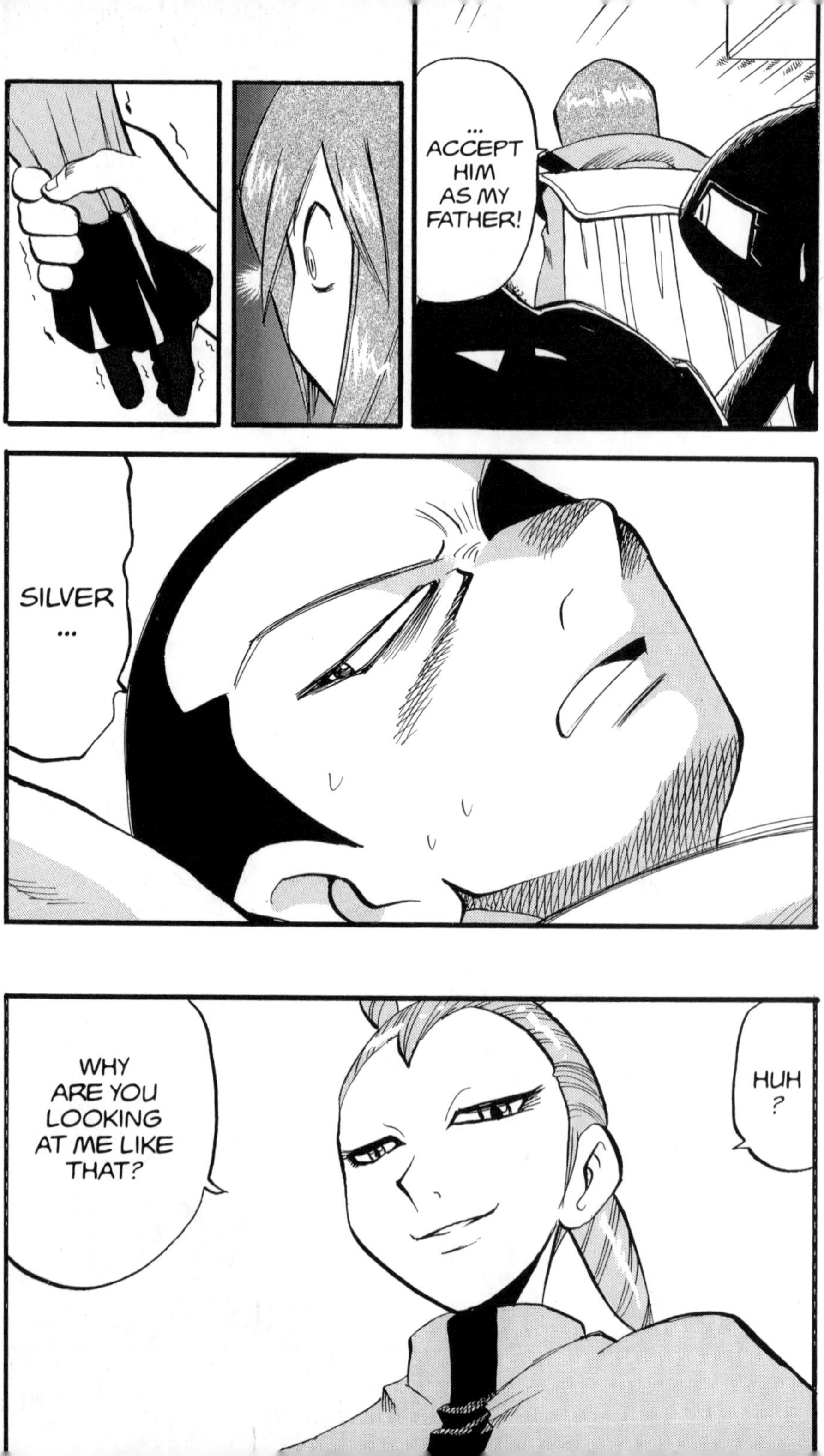
... ACCEPT HIM AS MY FATHER!
SILVER ...
HUH?
WHY ARE YOU LOOKING AT ME LIKE THAT?

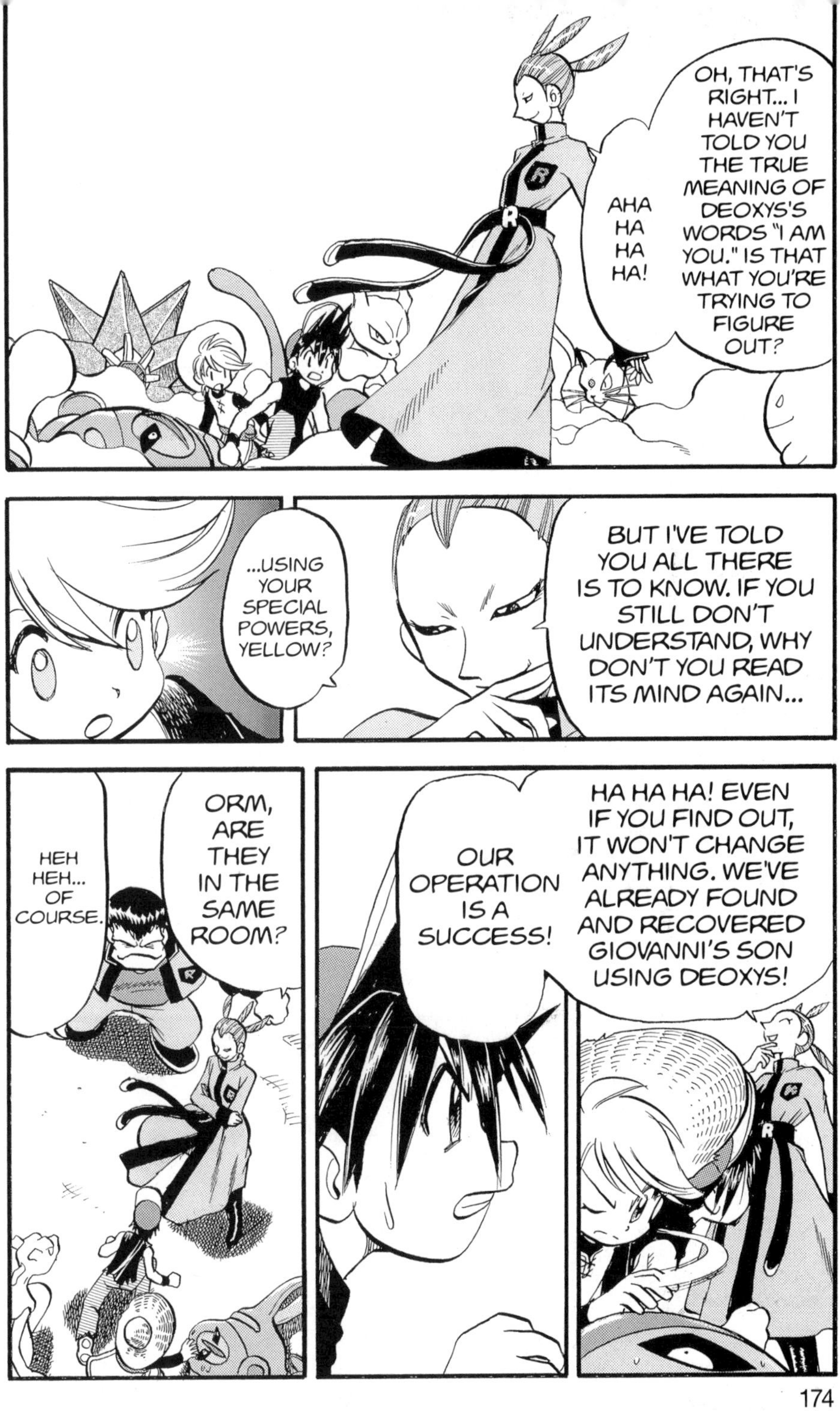
OH, THAT'S RIGHT... I HAVEN'T TOLD YOU THE TRUE MEANING OF DEOXYS'S WORDS "I AM YOU." IS THAT WHAT YOU'RE TRYING TO FIGURE OUT?
AHA HA HA HA!
BUT I'VE TOLD YOU ALL THERE IS TO KNOW. IF YOU STILL DON'T UNDERSTAND, WHY DON'T YOU READ ITS MIND AGAIN...
...USING YOUR SPECIAL POWERS, YELLOW?
HA HA HA! EVEN IF YOU FIND OUT, IT WON'T CHANGE ANYTHING. WE'VE ALREADY FOUND AND RECOVERED GIOVANNI'S SON USING DEOXYS!
OUR OPERATION IS A SUCCESS!
ORM, ARE THEY IN THE SAME ROOM?
HEH HEH... OF COURSE.

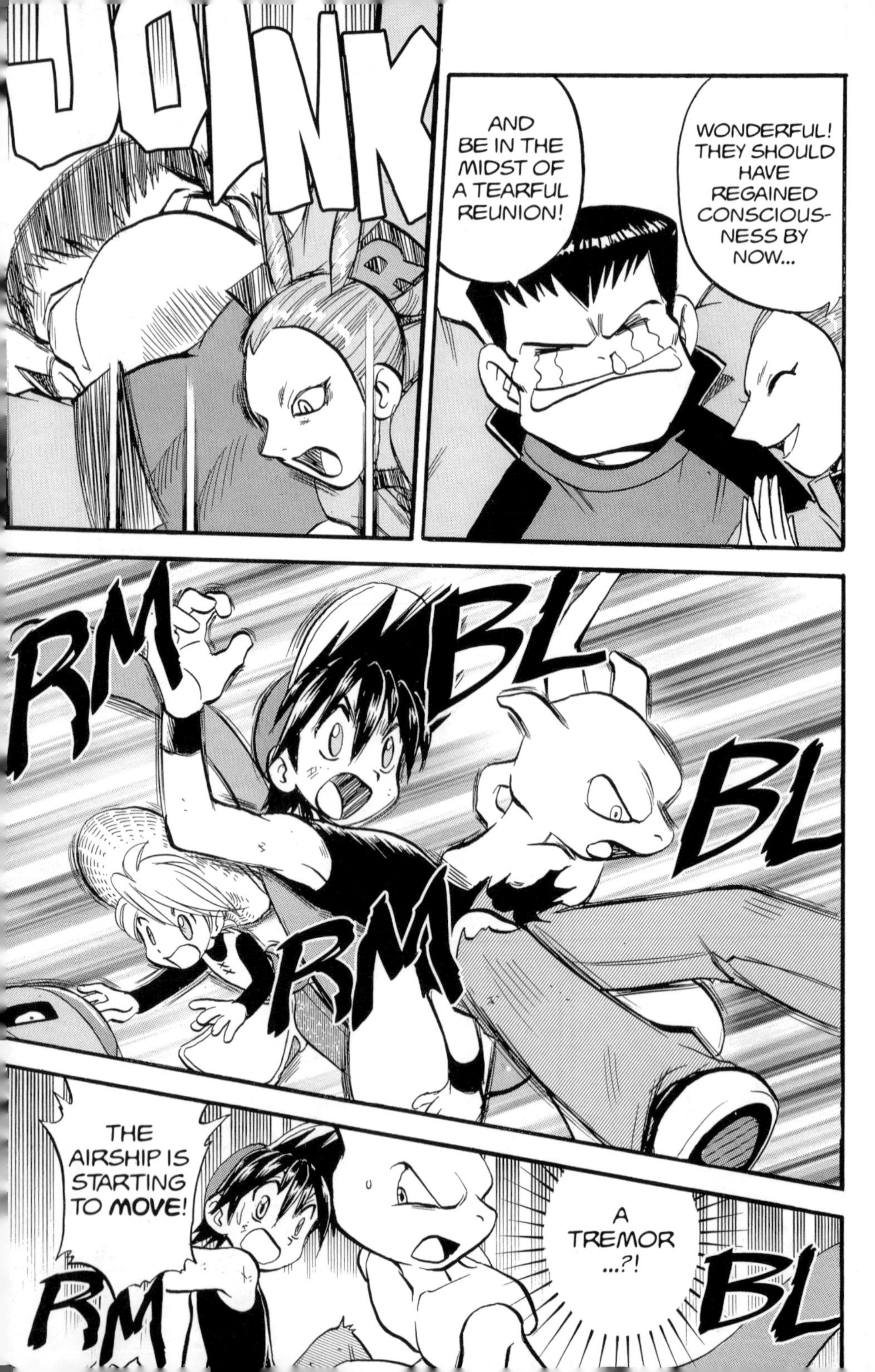
WONDERFUL! THEY SHOULD HAVE REGAINED CONSCIOUSNESS BY NOW...
AND BE IN THE MIDST OF A TEARFUL REUNION!
JOINK
RMBL
BL
RM
A TREMOR ...?!
THE AIRSHIP IS STARTING TO **MOVE**!
BL
RM

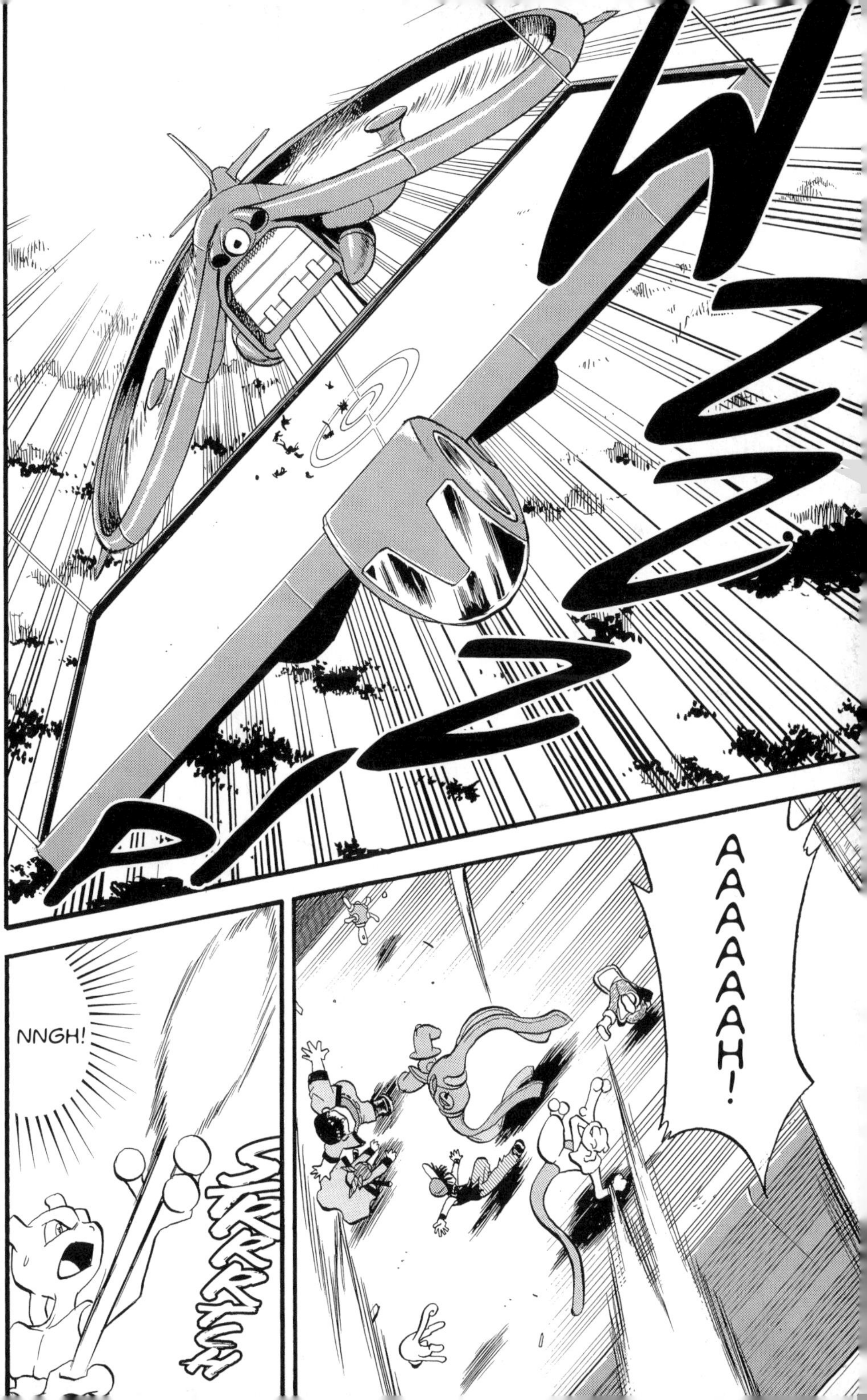
AAAAAAAH!
NNGH!

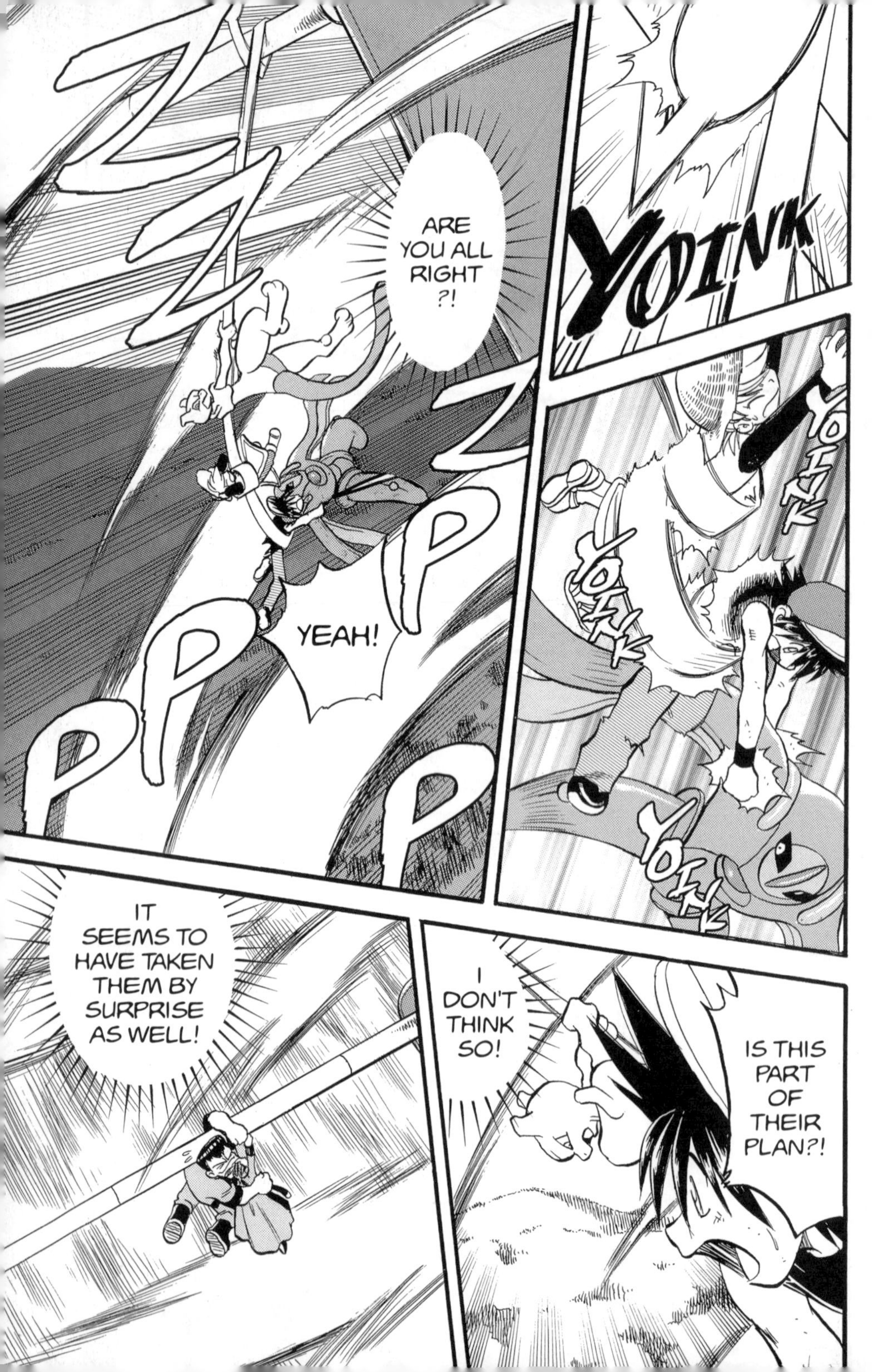

YOINK
YOINK
YOINK
YOINK
ZZZZ
ARE YOU ALL RIGHT?!
YEAH!
PPPP
IS THIS PART OF THEIR PLAN?!
I DON'T THINK SO!
IT SEEMS TO HAVE TAKEN THEM BY SURPRISE AS WELL!

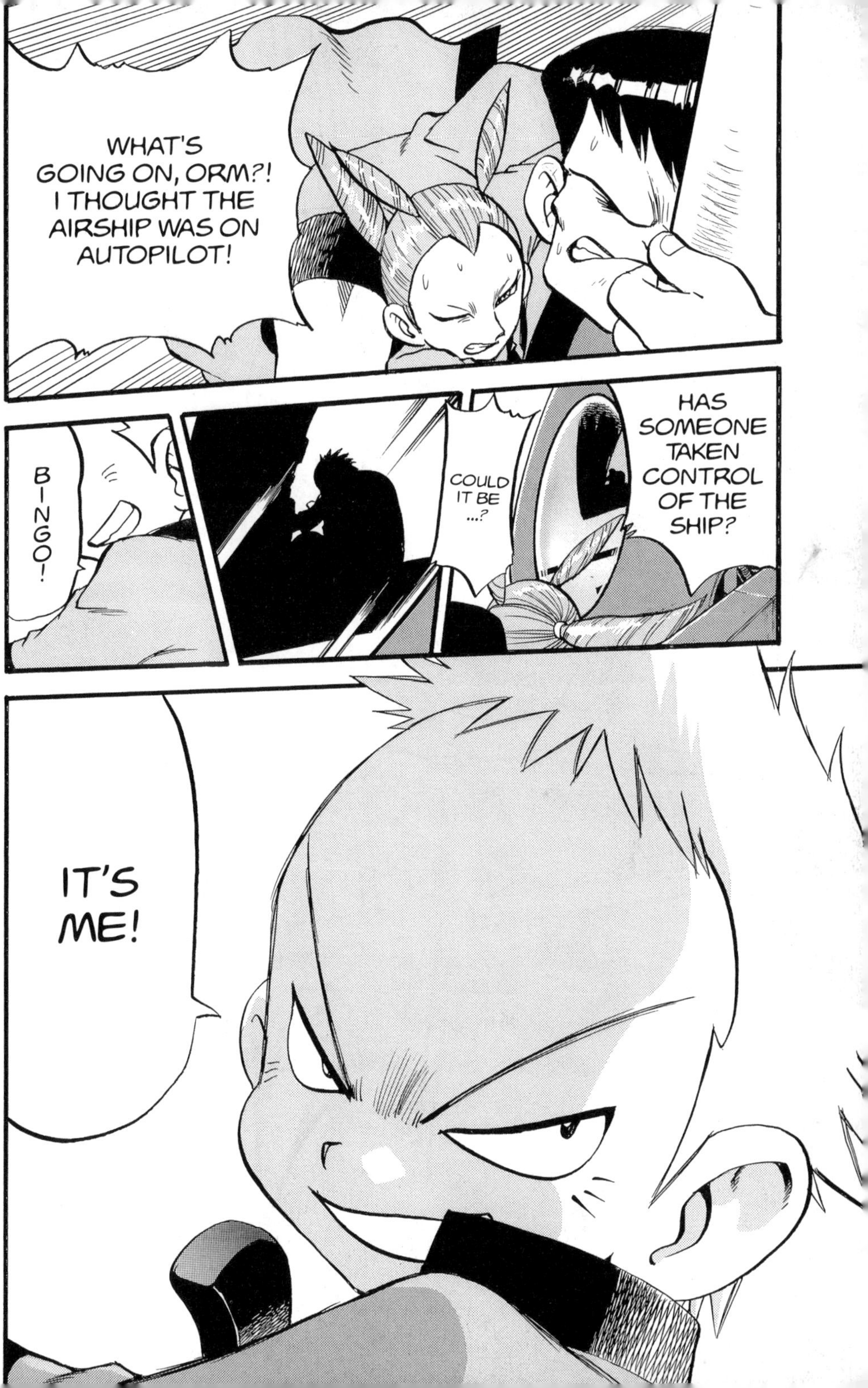
WHAT'S GOING ON, ORM?! I THOUGHT THE AIRSHIP WAS ON AUTOPILOT!
HAS SOMEONE TAKEN CONTROL OF THE SHIP?
COULD IT BE ...?
BINGO!
IT'S ME!

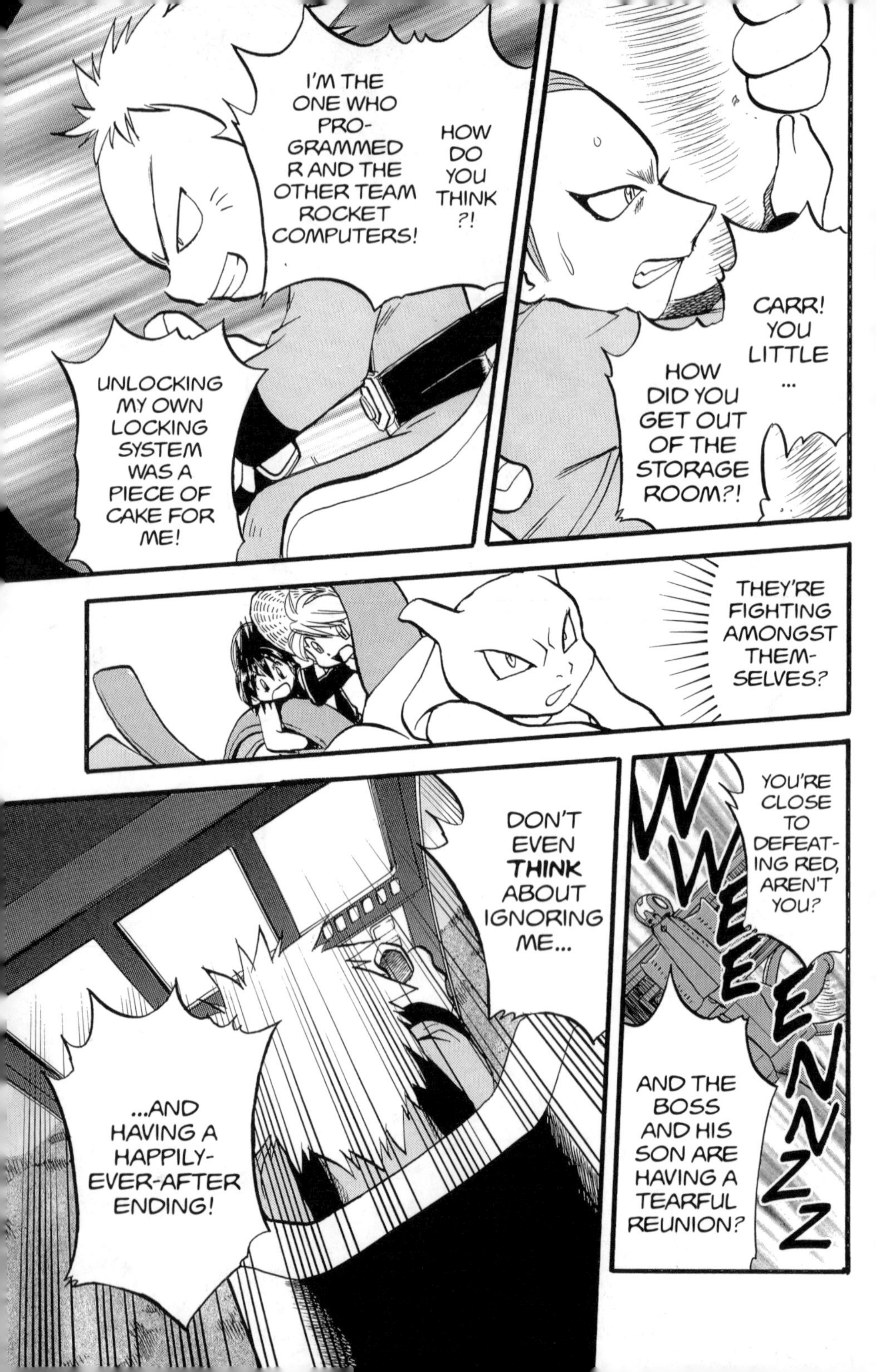
CARR! YOU LITTLE ...
HOW DID YOU GET OUT OF THE STORAGE ROOM?!
HOW DO YOU THINK ?!
I'M THE ONE WHO PRO-GRAMMED R AND THE OTHER TEAM ROCKET COMPUTERS!
UNLOCKING MY OWN LOCKING SYSTEM WAS A PIECE OF CAKE FOR ME!
THEY'RE FIGHTING AMONGST THEM-SELVES?
YOU'RE CLOSE TO DEFEAT-ING RED, AREN'T YOU?
WWEEEENNZZ
AND THE BOSS AND HIS SON ARE HAVING A TEARFUL REUNION?
DON'T EVEN **THINK** ABOUT IGNORING ME...
...AND HAVING A HAPPILY-EVER-AFTER ENDING!

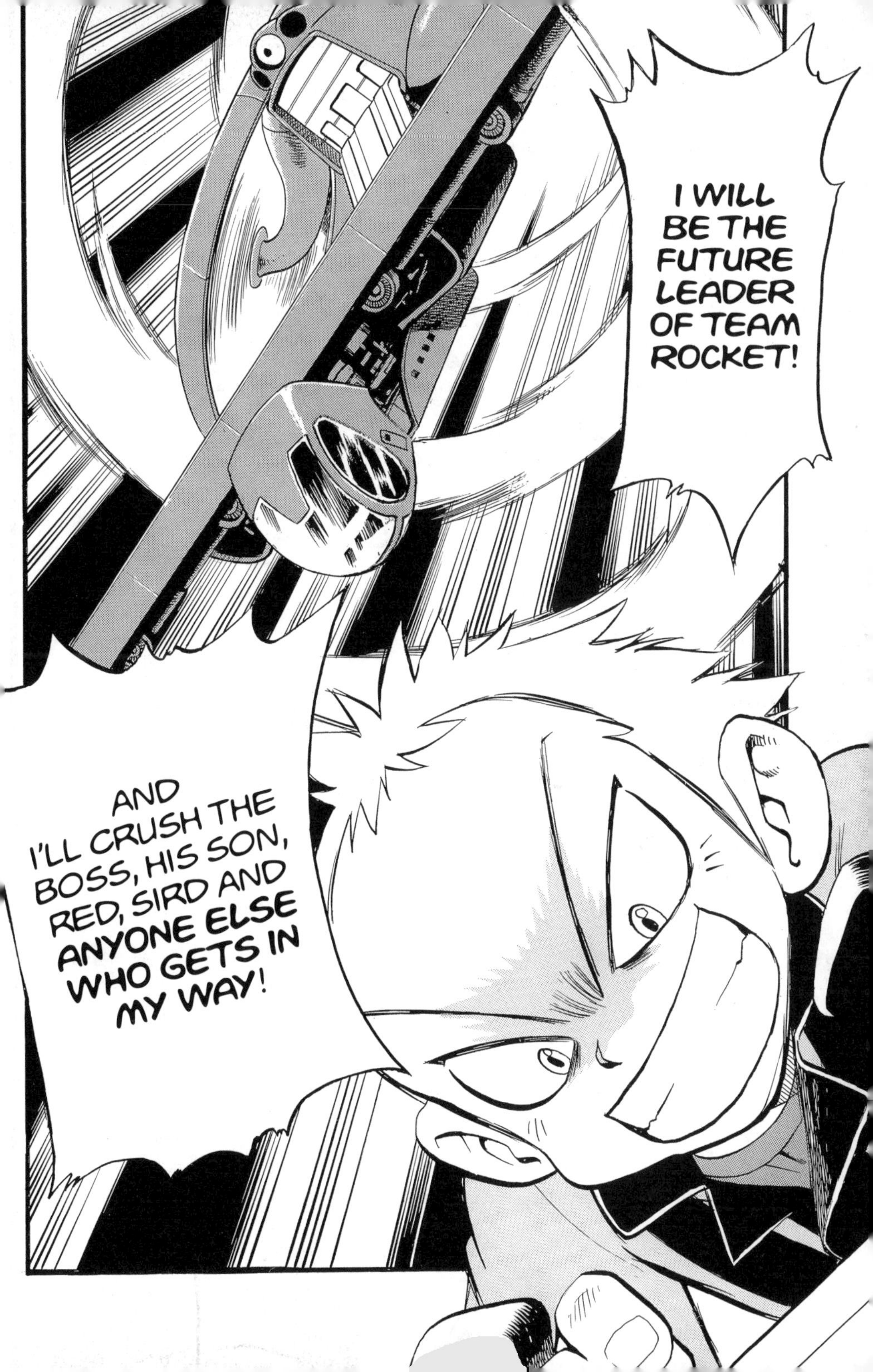
I WILL BE THE FUTURE LEADER OF TEAM ROCKET!
AND I'LL CRUSH THE BOSS, HIS SON, RED, SIRD AND ANYONE ELSE WHO GETS IN MY WAY!

Omny/Omastar ♂

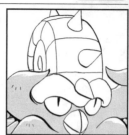

Rock
Water

◄LV. ?? (As of Adventure 297)
◄Ability: Swift Swim
◄Docile Nature

The Omanyte Yellow received from Misty evolved into an Omastar at Cerise Island and was a big help in the battle against the Kanto Elite Four.

Gravvy/Golem ♂

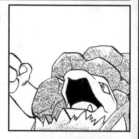

Rock
Ground

◄LV. ?? (As of Adventure 297)
◄Ability: Sturdy
◄Quirky Nature

Brock gave Gravvy to Yellow in Celadon City. It uses powerful moves like Take Down.

Kitty/Butterfree ♂

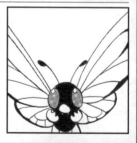

Bug
Flying

◄LV. ?? (As of Adventure 297)
◄Ability: Compound Eyes
◄Brave Nature

Yellow saved Kitty when it was a Caterpie and it evolved into a Butterfree. Kitty holds onto Yellow's back to carry her through the air.

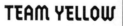

TEAM YELLOW 2

POKÉMON STATS

TEAM YELLOW

THE POKÉMON ON TEAM YELLOW 2

● Adventure 298 ●
Start the Countdown, Starmie

Pokémon Adventures FireRed & LeafGreen The Fifth Chapter

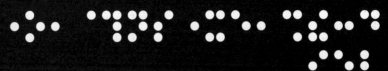

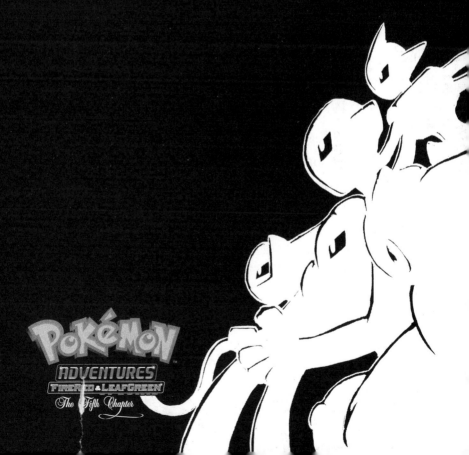

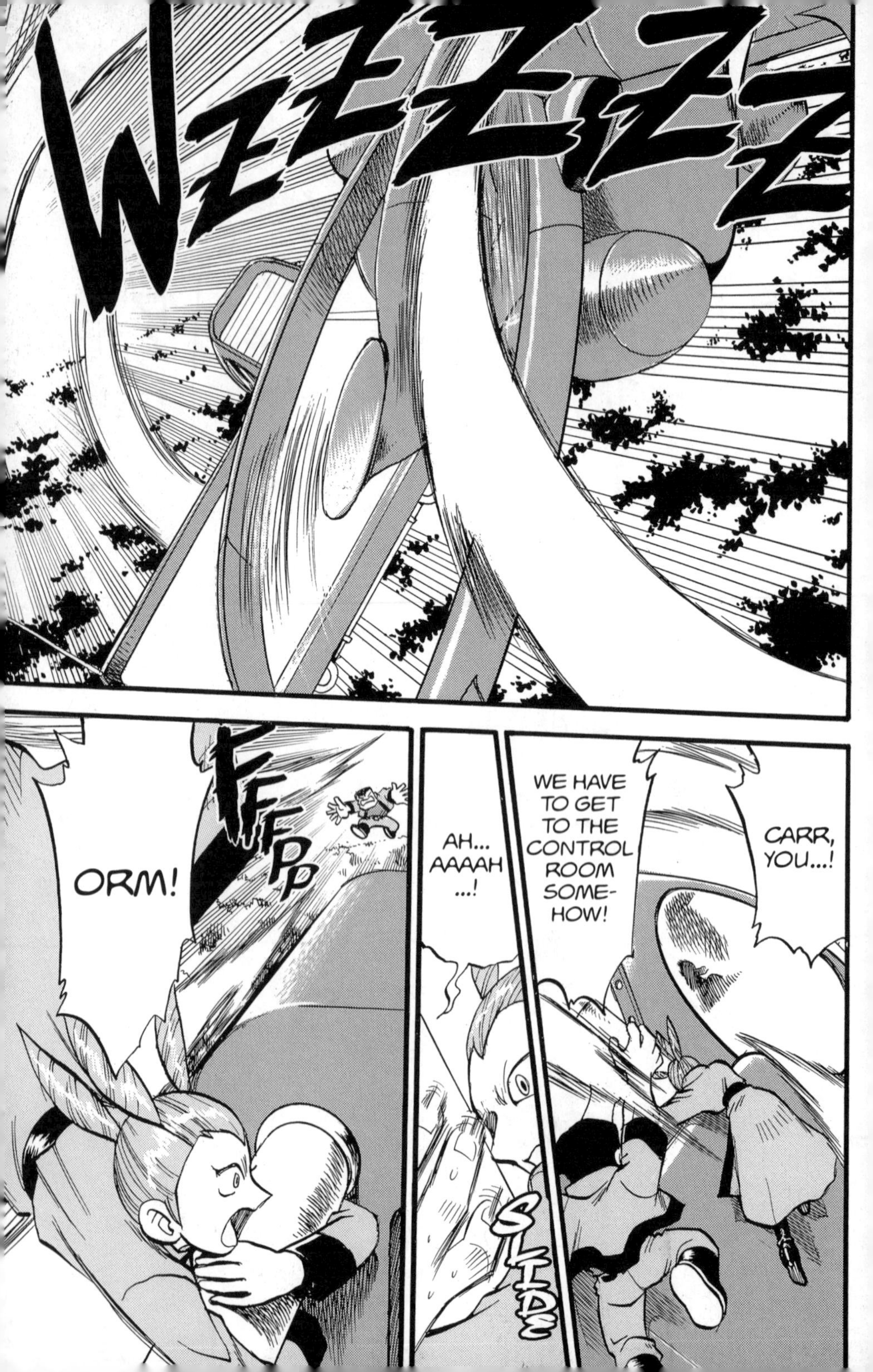
CARR, YOU...!
WE HAVE TO GET TO THE CONTROL ROOM SOMEHOW!
AH... AAAAH ...!
SLIDE
FFFPP
ORM!

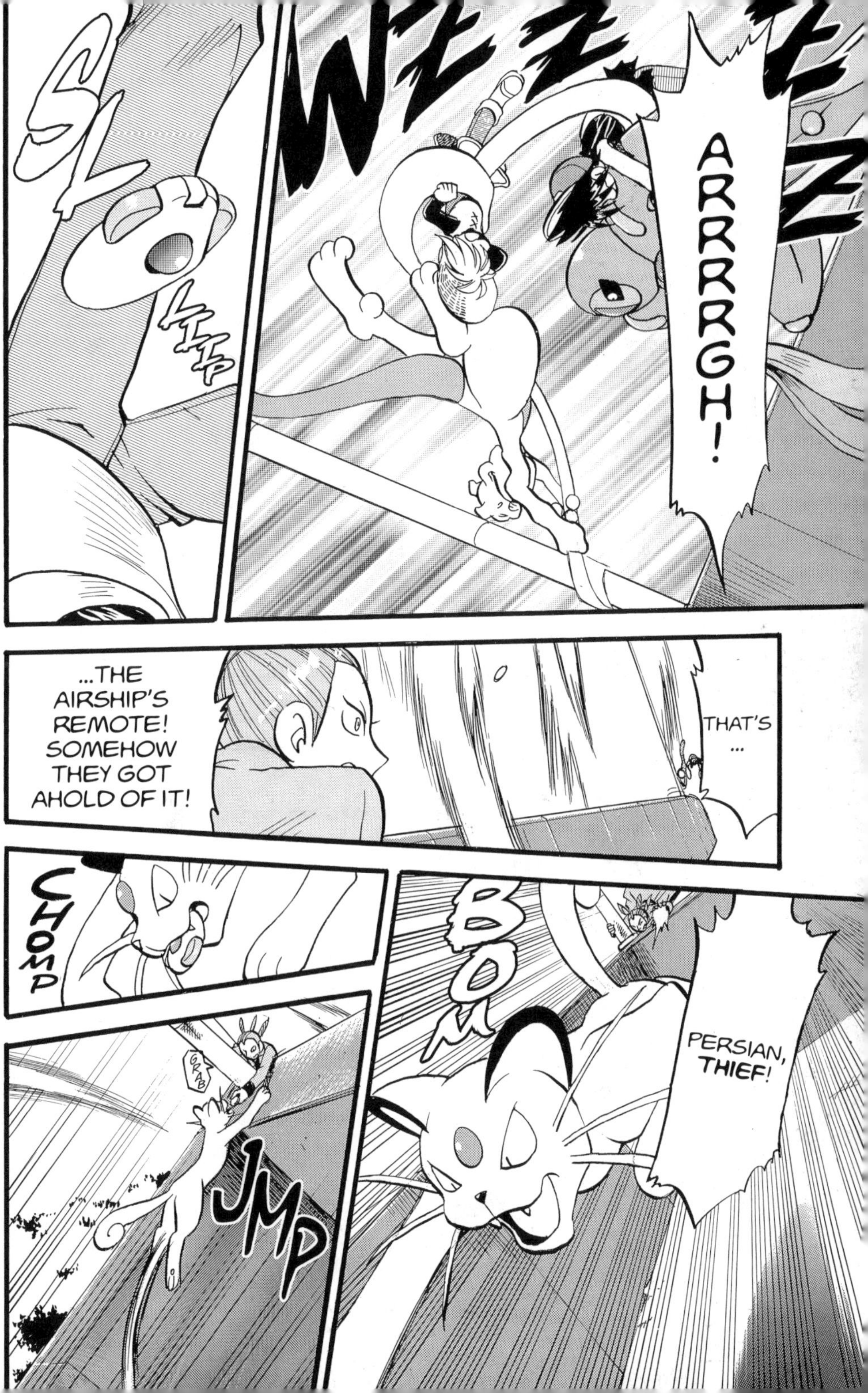
ARRRRGH!
WHZZZZ
SLIIIP
THAT'S...
...THE AIRSHIP'S REMOTE! SOMEHOW THEY GOT AHOLD OF IT!
BOM
PERSIAN, THIEF!
CHOMP
GRAB
JMP

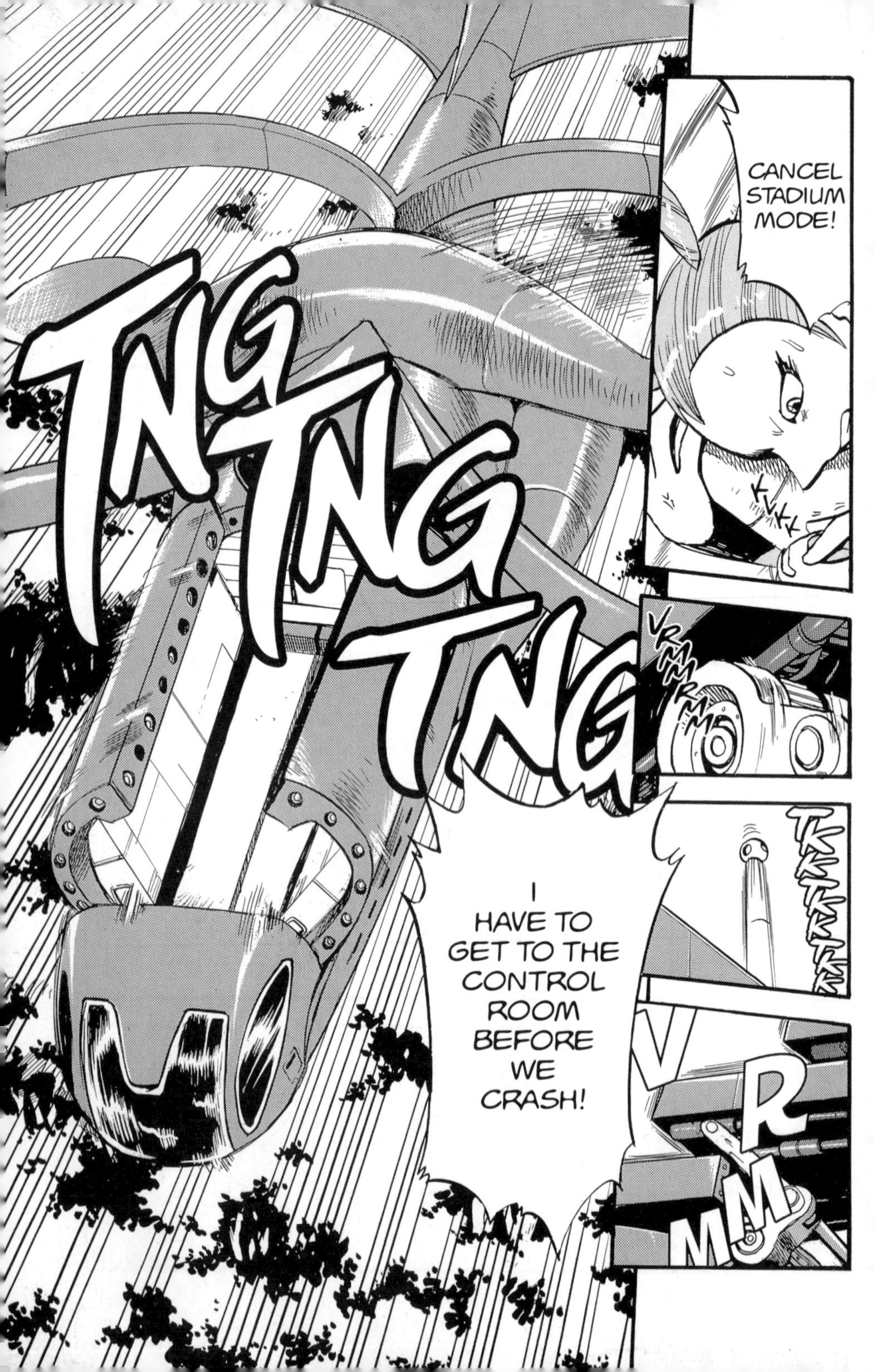
CANCEL STADIUM MODE!
VRMMM
TNG TNG TNG
I HAVE TO GET TO THE CONTROL ROOM BEFORE WE CRASH!

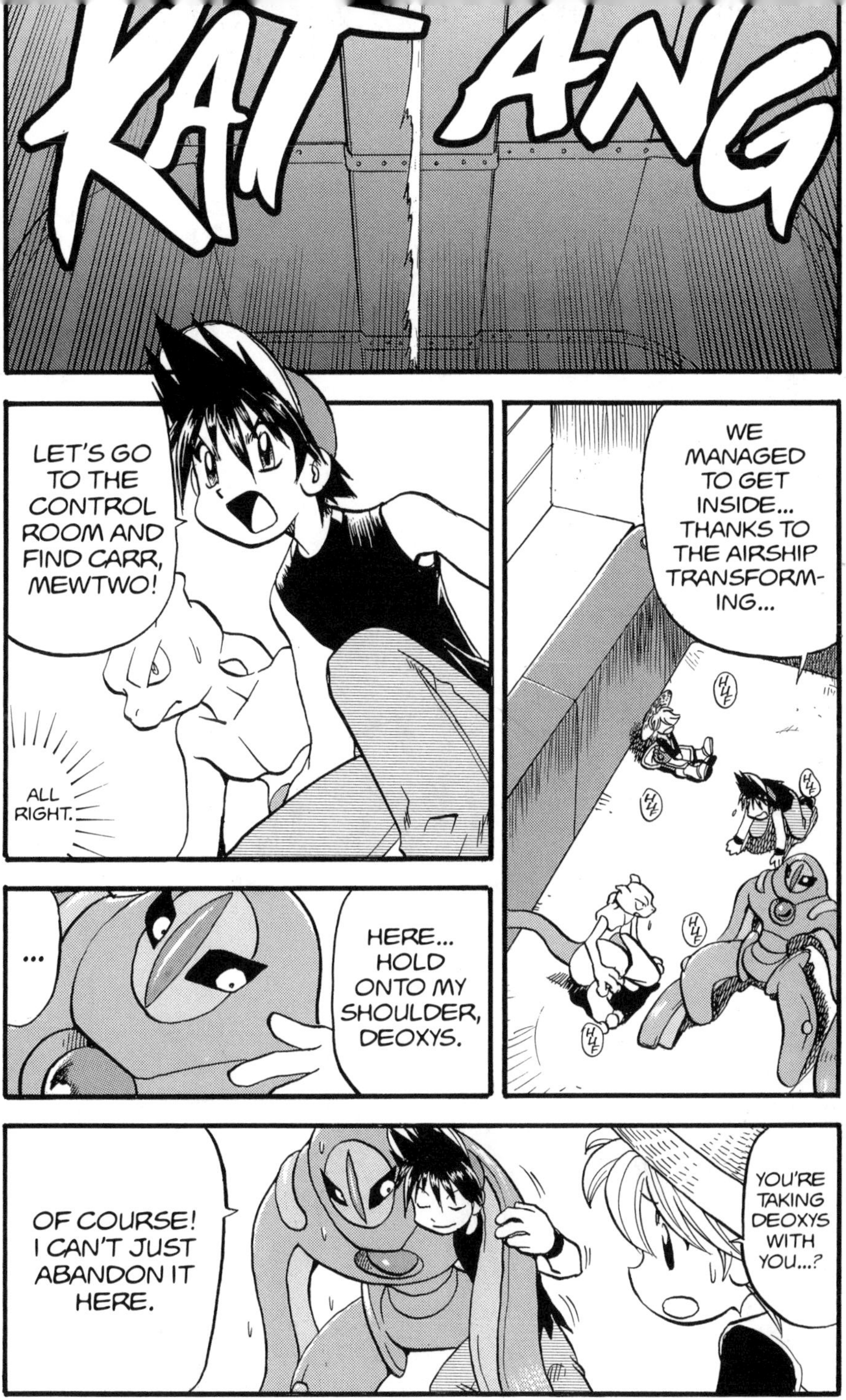
KAT ANG
WE MANAGED TO GET INSIDE... THANKS TO THE AIRSHIP TRANSFORM-ING...
HUF
HUF
HUF
HUF
HUF
LET'S GO TO THE CONTROL ROOM AND FIND CARR, MEWTWO!
ALL RIGHT.
HERE... HOLD ONTO MY SHOULDER, DEOXYS.
...
YOU'RE TAKING DEOXYS WITH YOU...?
OF COURSE! I CAN'T JUST ABANDON IT HERE.

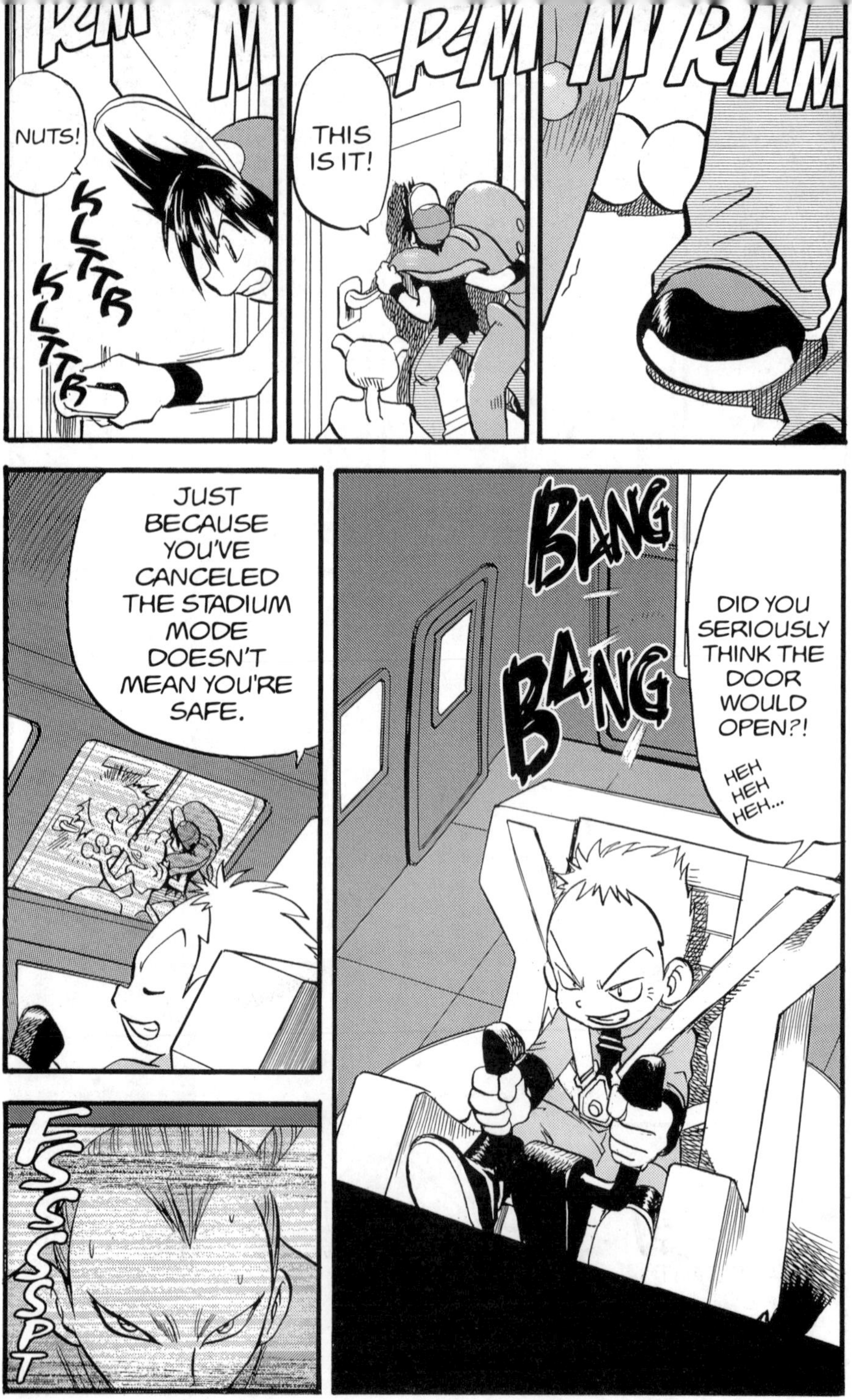
M RMM
RM
THIS IS IT!
RM M
NUTS!
KLTTR KLTTR
BANG BANG
DID YOU SERIOUSLY THINK THE DOOR WOULD OPEN?!
HEH HEH HEH...
JUST BECAUSE YOU'VE CANCELED THE STADIUM MODE DOESN'T MEAN YOU'RE SAFE.
FSSSPT

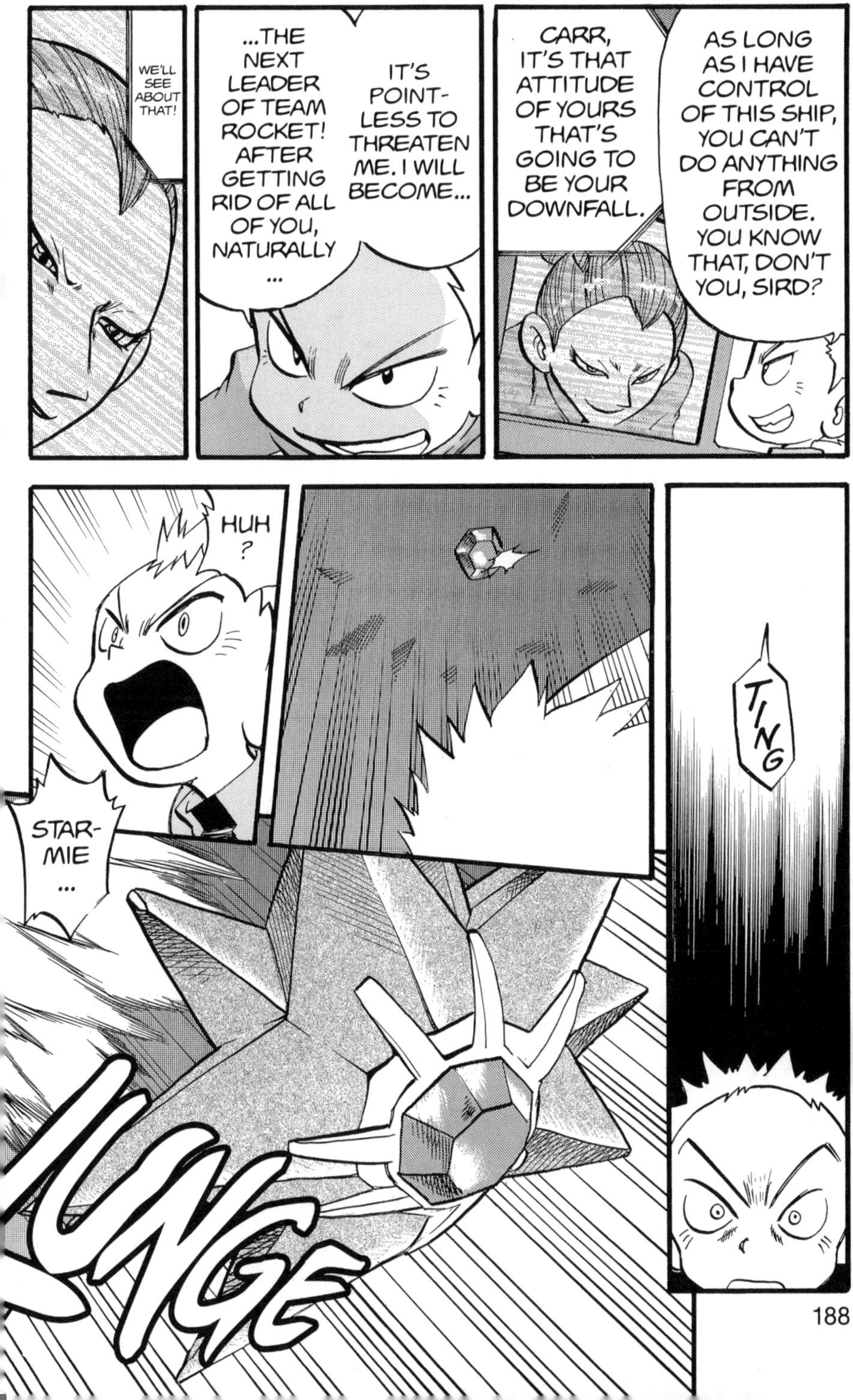
AS LONG AS I HAVE CONTROL OF THIS SHIP, YOU CAN'T DO ANYTHING FROM OUTSIDE. YOU KNOW THAT, DON'T YOU, SIRD?
CARR, IT'S THAT ATTITUDE OF YOURS THAT'S GOING TO BE YOUR DOWNFALL.
IT'S POINT-LESS TO THREATEN ME. I WILL BECOME...
...THE NEXT LEADER OF TEAM ROCKET! AFTER GETTING RID OF ALL OF YOU, NATURALLY ...
WE'LL SEE ABOUT THAT!
TING
HUH ?
STAR-MIE ...
UNGE

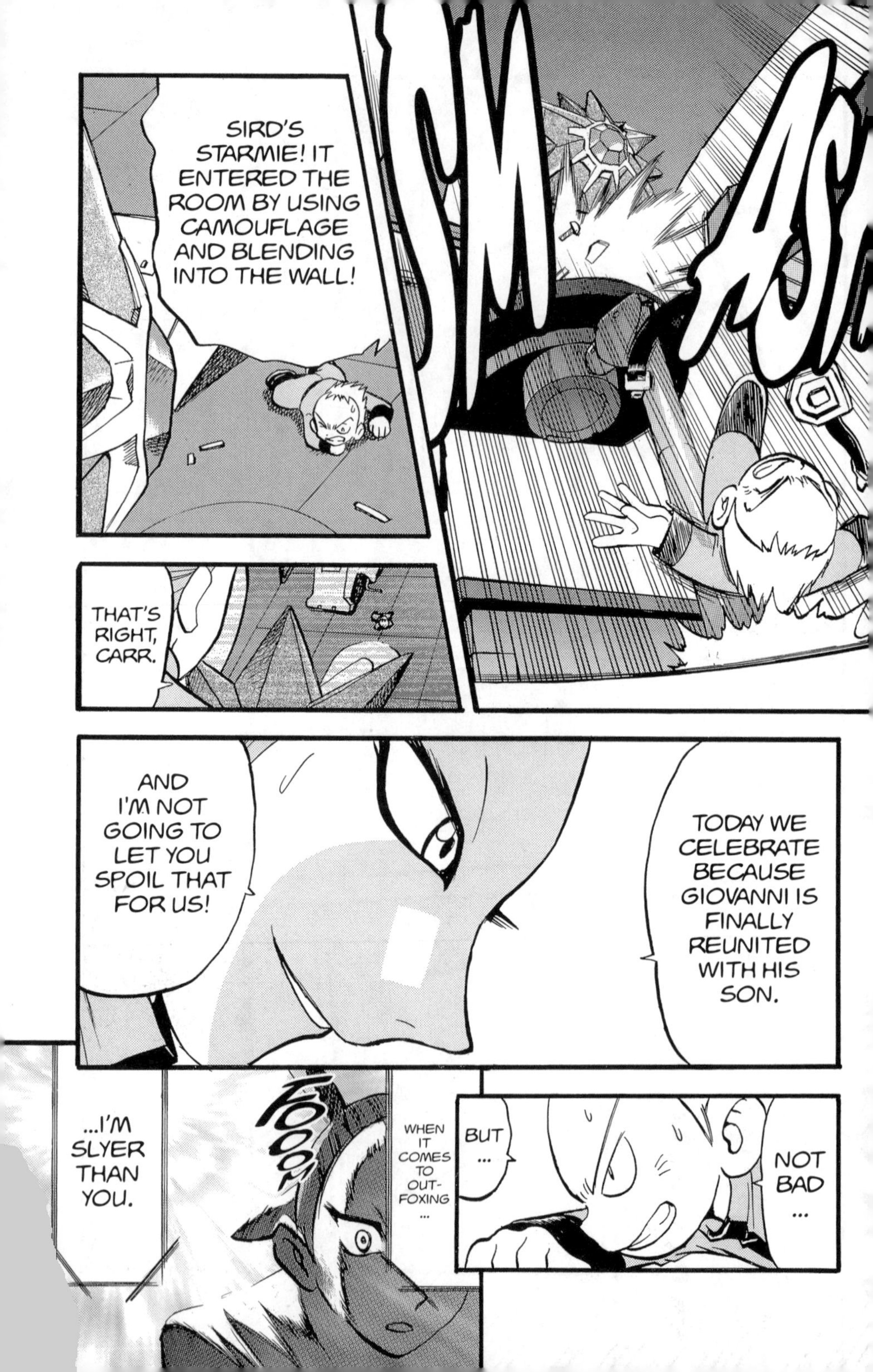
SM
AS
SIRD'S STARMIE! IT ENTERED THE ROOM BY USING CAMOUFLAGE AND BLENDING INTO THE WALL!
THAT'S RIGHT, CARR.
TODAY WE CELEBRATE BECAUSE GIOVANNI IS FINALLY REUNITED WITH HIS SON.
AND I'M NOT GOING TO LET YOU SPOIL THAT FOR US!
NOT BAD ...
BUT ...
WHEN IT COMES TO OUT-FOXING ...
...I'M SLYER THAN YOU.

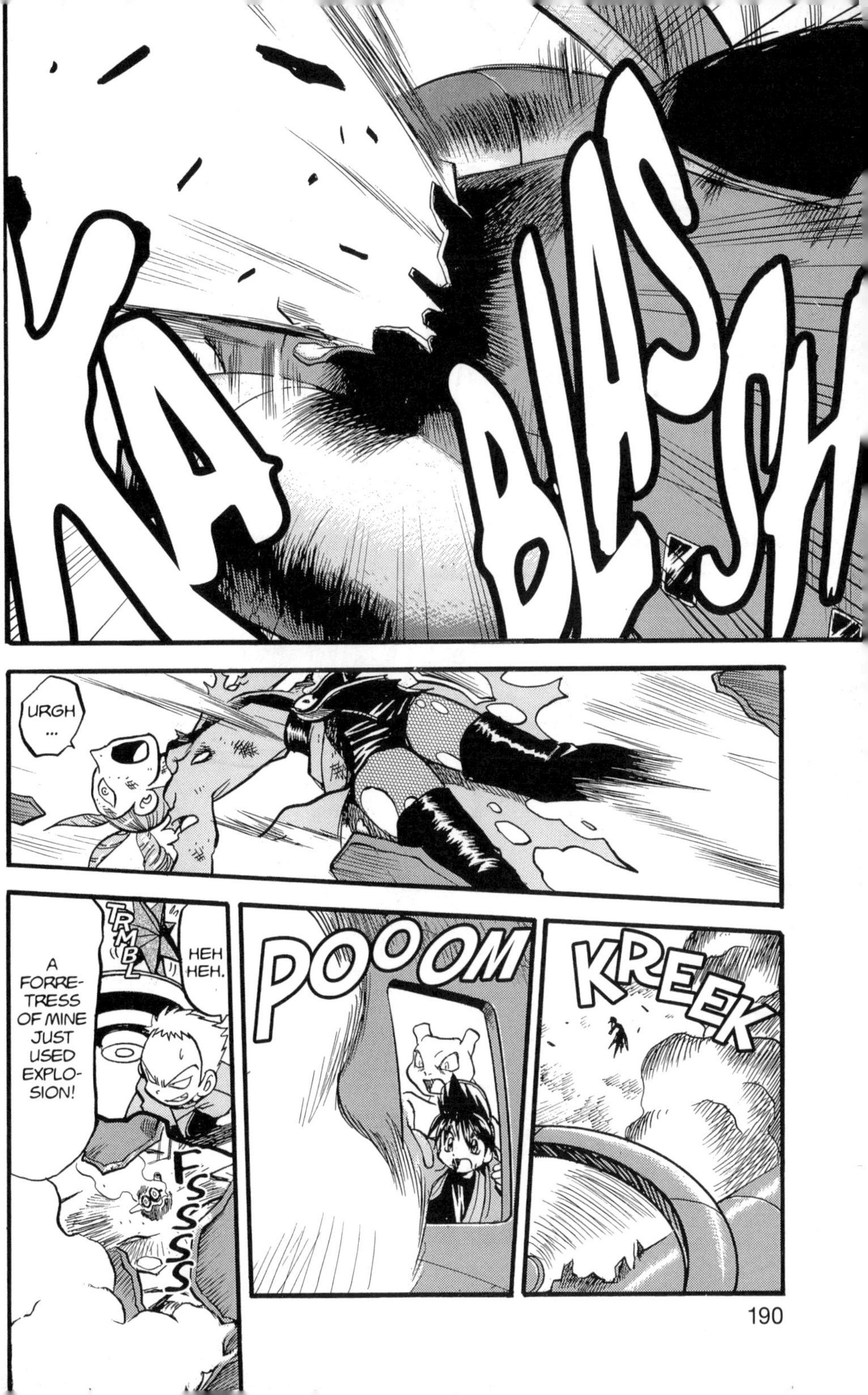
KABLASH
URGH ...
KREEK
POOOOM
TRMBL
HEH HEH.
A FORRETRESS OF MINE JUST USED EXPLOSION!
FSSSSS

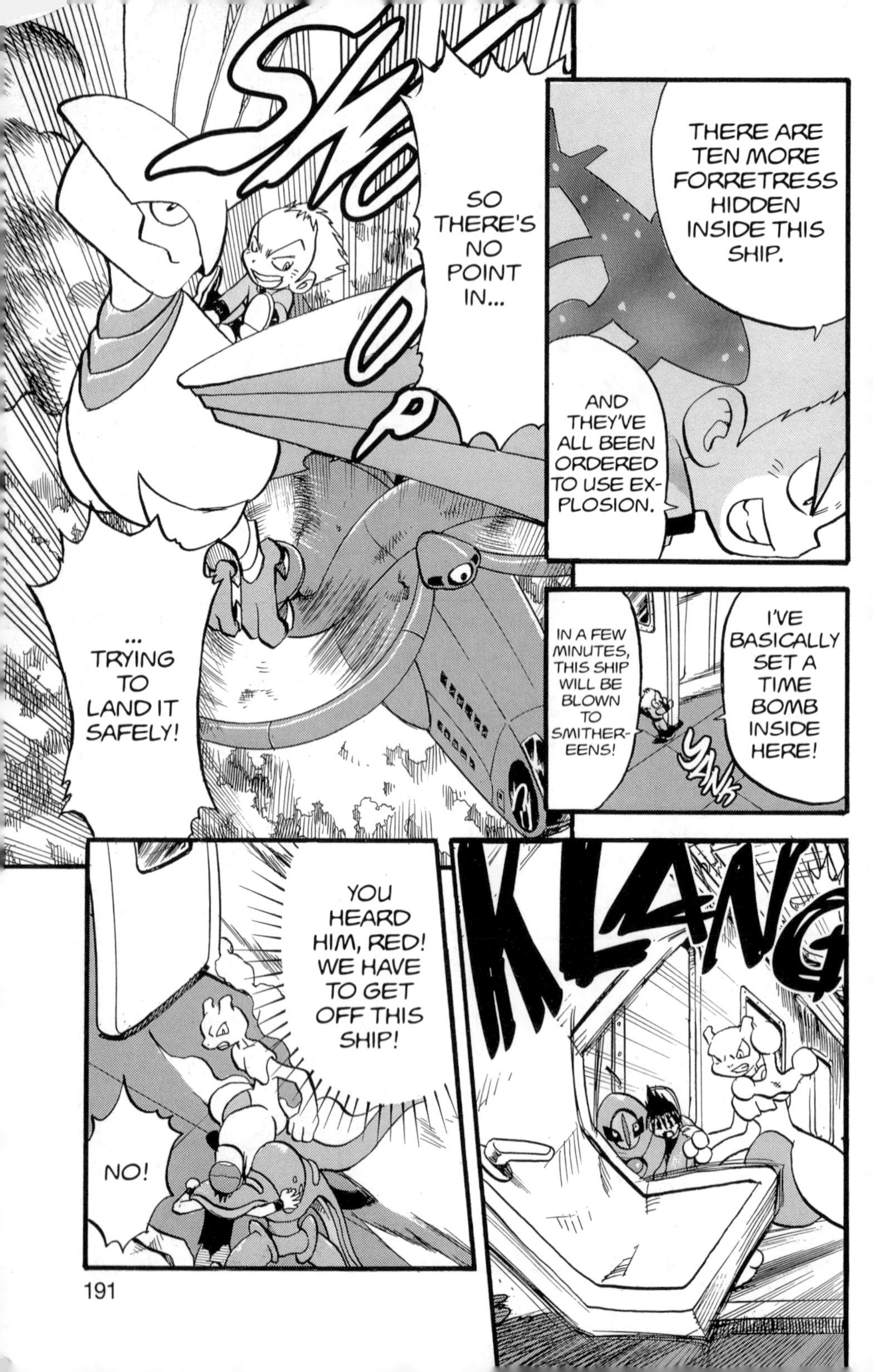
THERE ARE TEN MORE FORRETRESS HIDDEN INSIDE THIS SHIP.
AND THEY'VE ALL BEEN ORDERED TO USE EX-PLOSION.
I'VE BASICALLY SET A TIME BOMB INSIDE HERE!
IN A FEW MINUTES, THIS SHIP WILL BE BLOWN TO SMITHER-EENS!
YANK
SHOOP
SO THERE'S NO POINT IN...
... TRYING TO LAND IT SAFELY!
KLANG
YOU HEARD HIM, RED! WE HAVE TO GET OFF THIS SHIP!
NO!

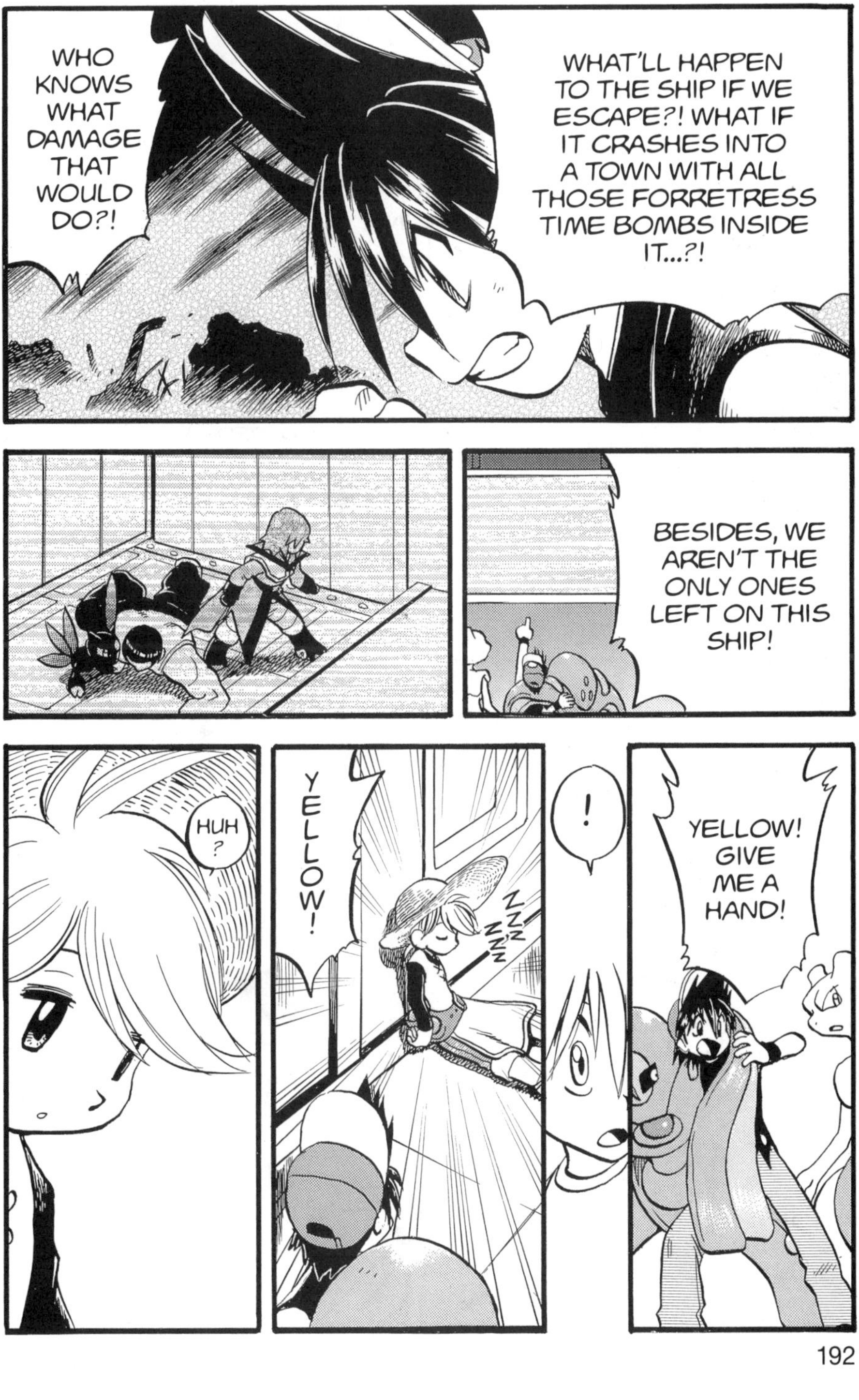

WHAT'LL HAPPEN TO THE SHIP IF WE ESCAPE?! WHAT IF IT CRASHES INTO A TOWN WITH ALL THOSE FORRETRESS TIME BOMBS INSIDE IT...?!
WHO KNOWS WHAT DAMAGE THAT WOULD DO?!
BESIDES, WE AREN'T THE ONLY ONES LEFT ON THIS SHIP!
YELLOW! GIVE ME A HAND!
!
ZZZ ZZZ
YELLOW!
HUH?

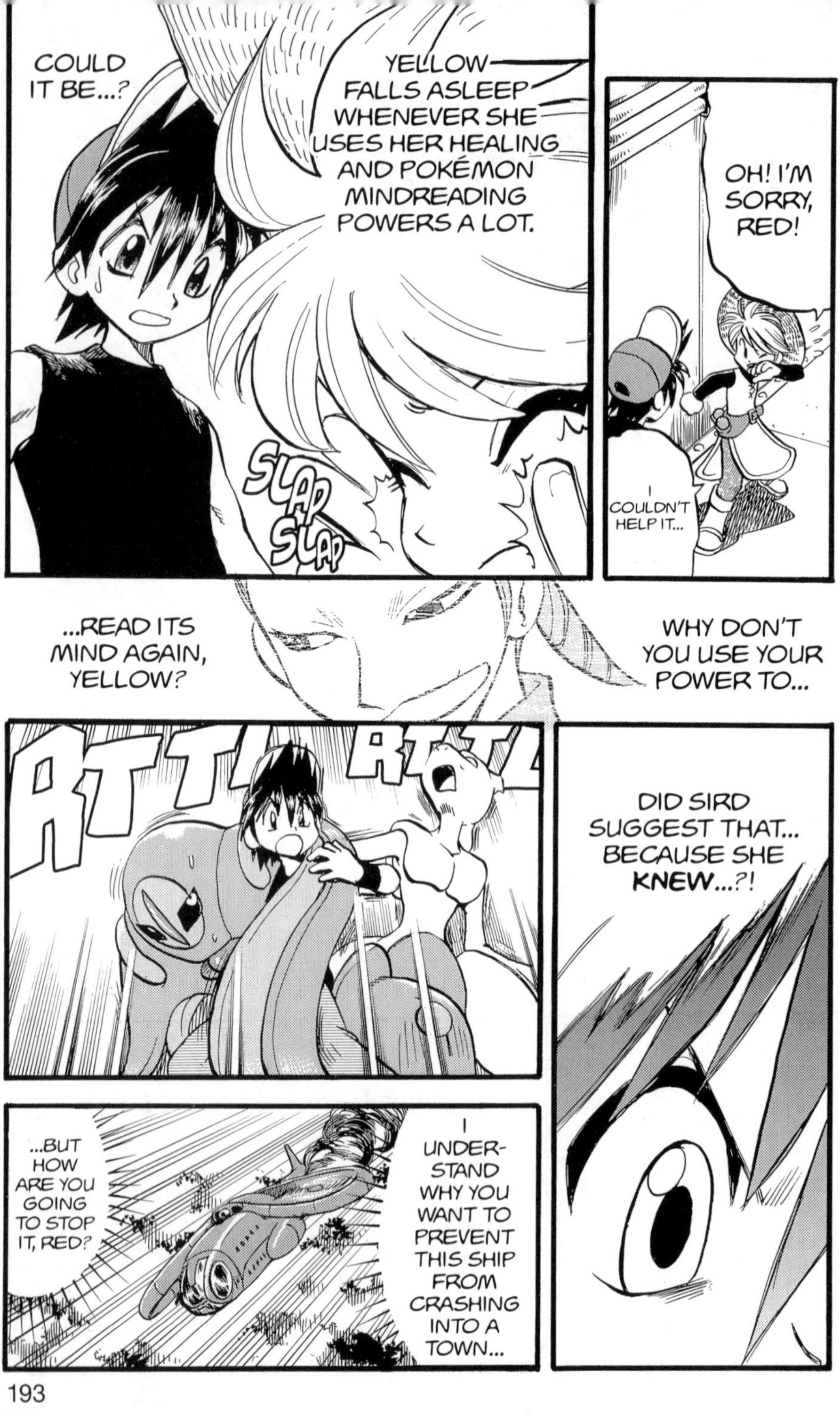
OH! I'M SORRY, RED!
I COULDN'T HELP IT...
YELLOW FALLS ASLEEP WHENEVER SHE USES HER HEALING AND POKÉMON MINDREADING POWERS A LOT.
COULD IT BE...?
SLAP SLAP
WHY DON'T YOU USE YOUR POWER TO...
...READ ITS MIND AGAIN, YELLOW?
DID SIRD SUGGEST THAT... BECAUSE SHE **KNEW**...?!
I UNDERSTAND WHY YOU WANT TO PREVENT THIS SHIP FROM CRASHING INTO A TOWN...
...BUT HOW ARE YOU GOING TO STOP IT, RED?

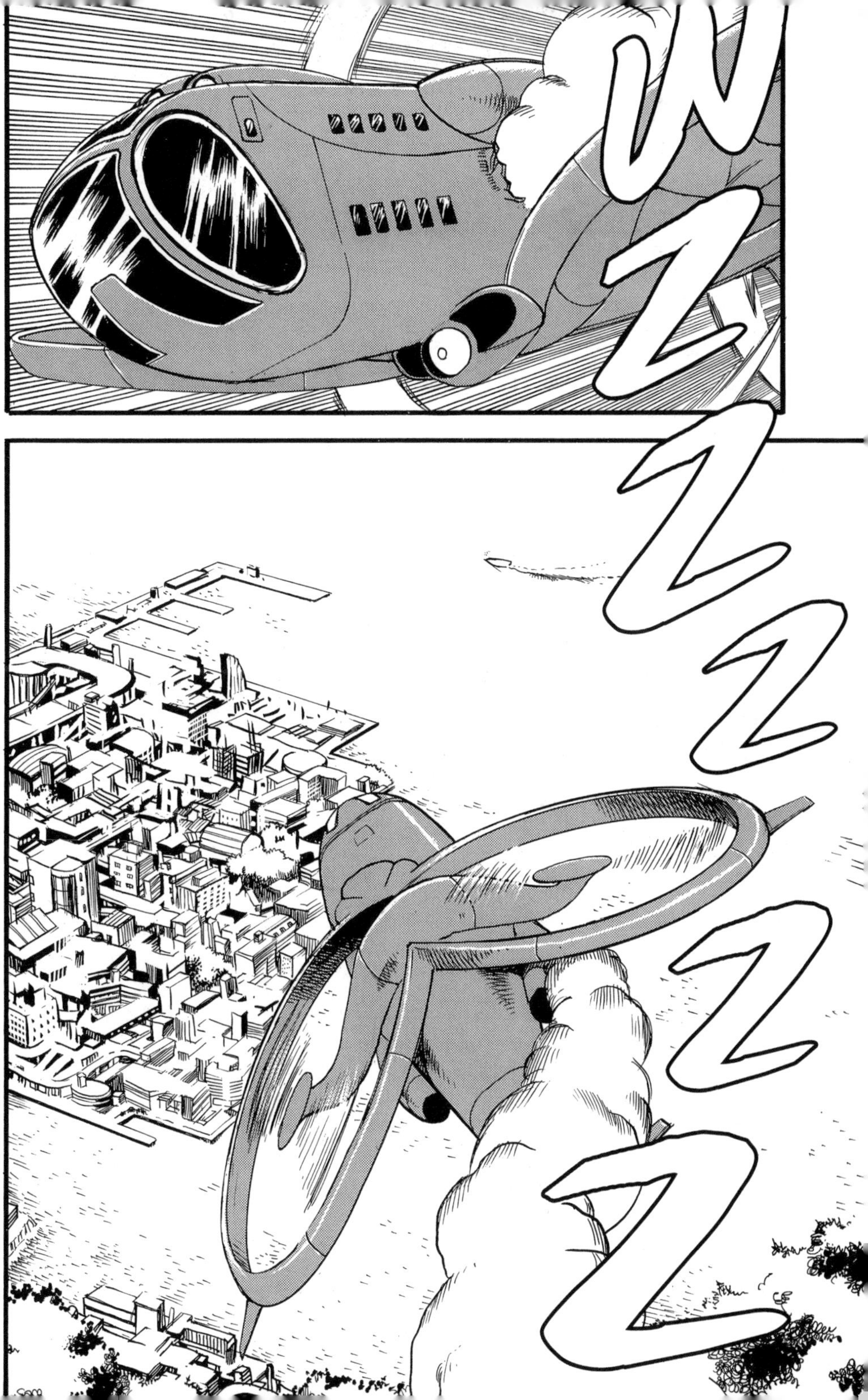

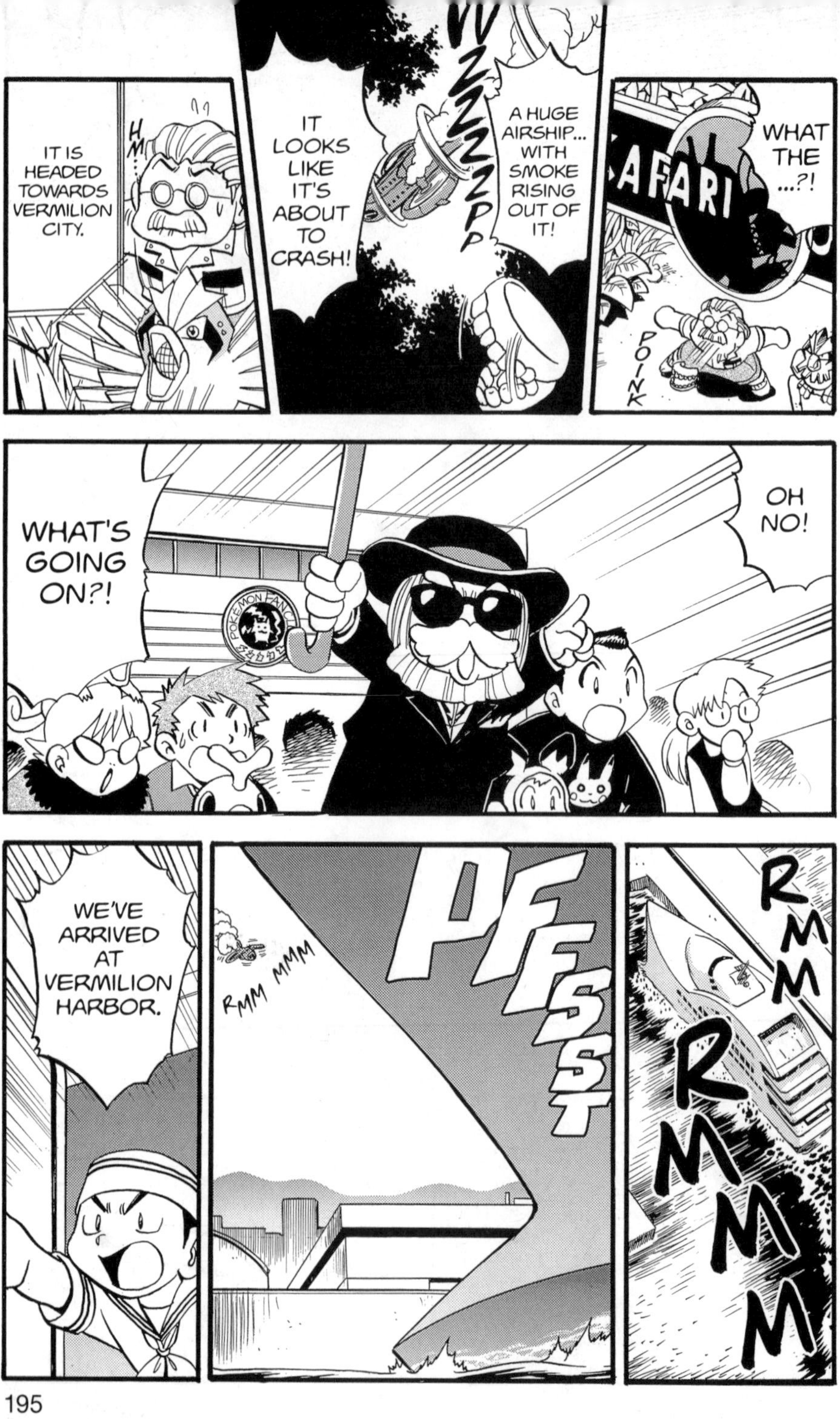
WHAT THE ...?!
POINK
A HUGE AIRSHIP... WITH SMOKE RISING OUT OF IT!
VVZZZZZPP
IT LOOKS LIKE IT'S ABOUT TO CRASH!
HM...
IT IS HEADED TOWARDS VERMILION CITY.
OH NO!
WHAT'S GOING ON?!
RMM RMMMM
PFFST
RMM MMM
WE'VE ARRIVED AT VERMILION HARBOR.

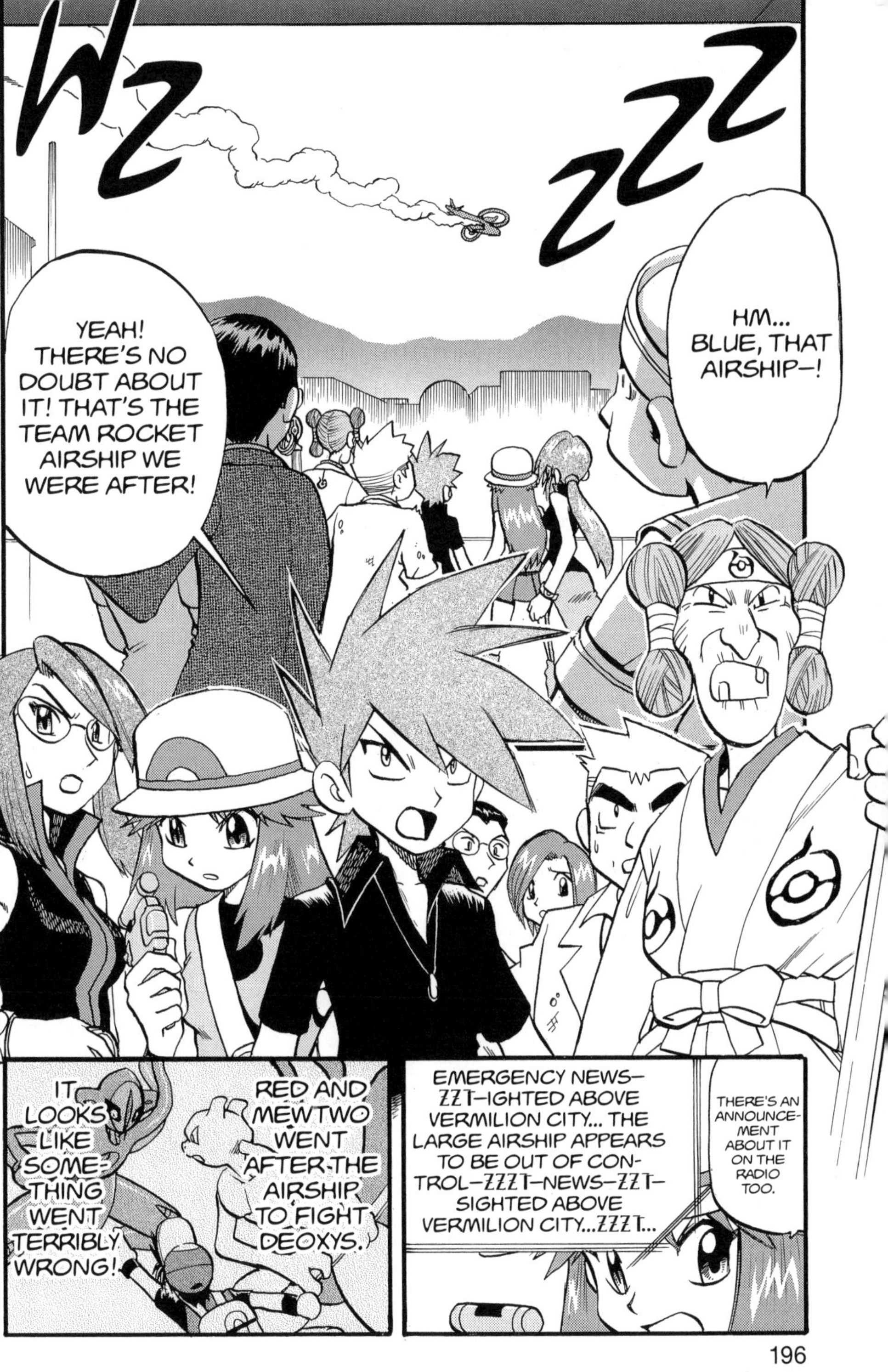
WZZZZ
HM... BLUE, THAT AIRSHIP—!
YEAH! THERE'S NO DOUBT ABOUT IT! THAT'S THE TEAM ROCKET AIRSHIP WE WERE AFTER!
THERE'S AN ANNOUNCEMENT ABOUT IT ON THE RADIO TOO.
EMERGENCY NEWS— ZZT—IGHTED ABOVE VERMILION CITY... THE LARGE AIRSHIP APPEARS TO BE OUT OF CONTROL—ZZZT—NEWS—ZZT— SIGHTED ABOVE VERMILION CITY...ZZZT...
RED AND MEWTWO WENT AFTER THE AIRSHIP TO FIGHT DEOXYS.
IT LOOKS LIKE SOMETHING WENT TERRIBLY WRONG!

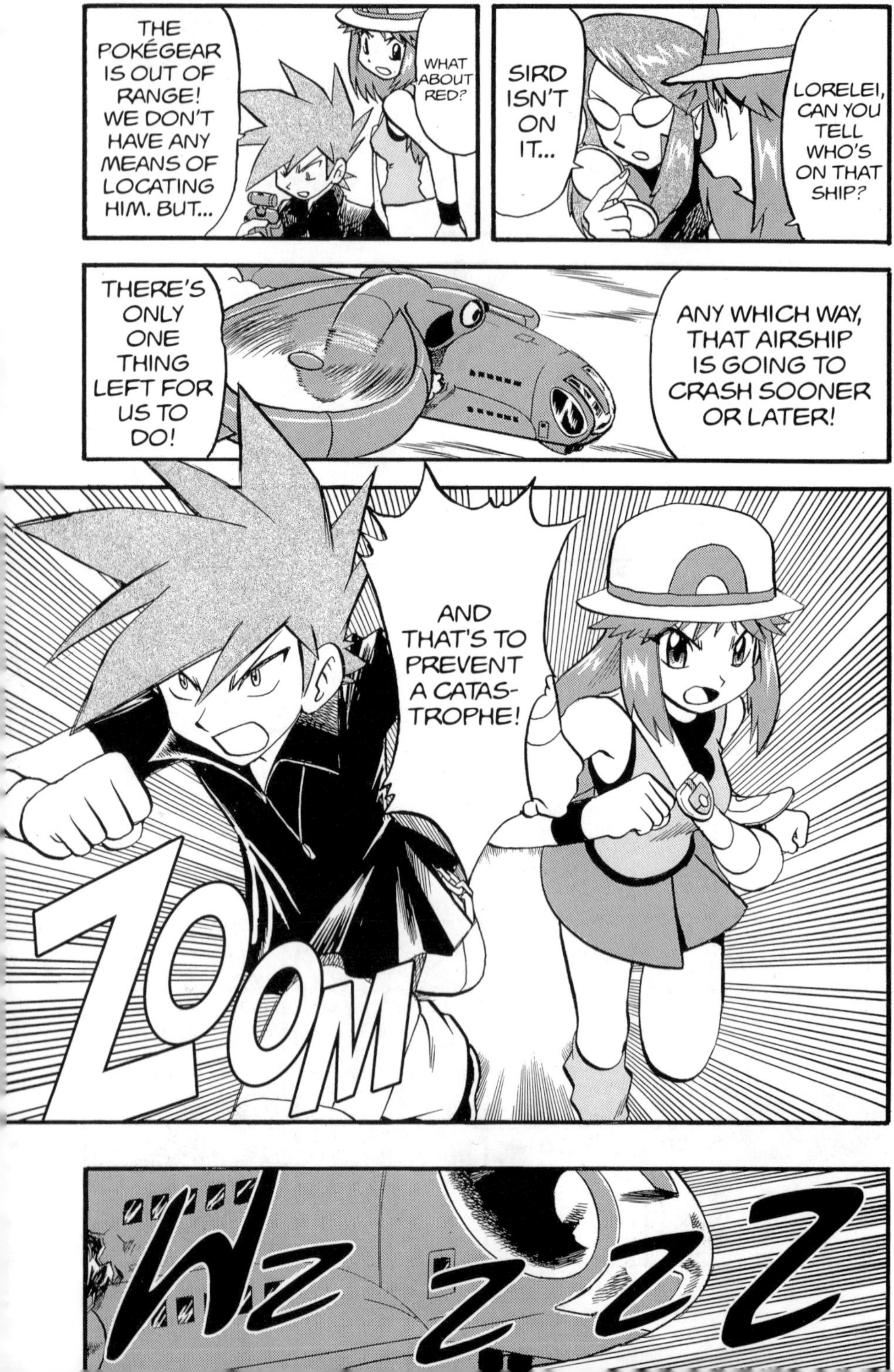
LORELEI, CAN YOU TELL WHO'S ON THAT SHIP?
SIRD ISN'T ON IT...
WHAT ABOUT RED?
THE POKÉGEAR IS OUT OF RANGE! WE DON'T HAVE ANY MEANS OF LOCATING HIM. BUT...
ANY WHICH WAY, THAT AIRSHIP IS GOING TO CRASH SOONER OR LATER!
THERE'S ONLY ONE THING LEFT FOR US TO DO!
AND THAT'S TO PREVENT A CATAS-TROPHE!
ZOOM
WZZZZ

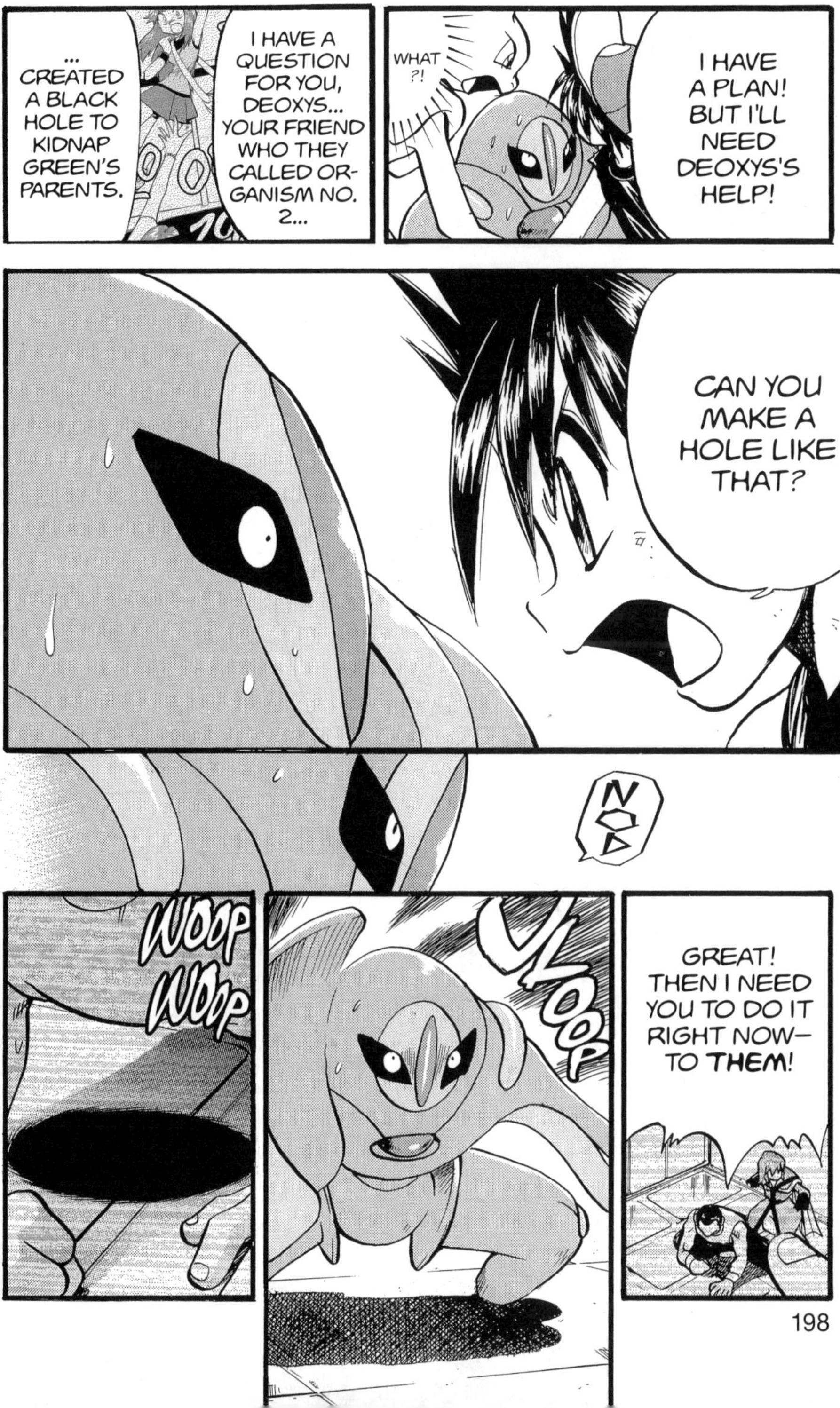
I HAVE A PLAN! BUT I'LL NEED DEOXYS'S HELP!
WHAT?!
I HAVE A QUESTION FOR YOU, DEOXYS... YOUR FRIEND WHO THEY CALLED ORGANISM NO. 2...
...CREATED A BLACK HOLE TO KIDNAP GREEN'S PARENTS.
CAN YOU MAKE A HOLE LIKE THAT?
NOD
GREAT! THEN I NEED YOU TO DO IT RIGHT NOW—TO **THEM**!
VLOOP
WOOP WOOP

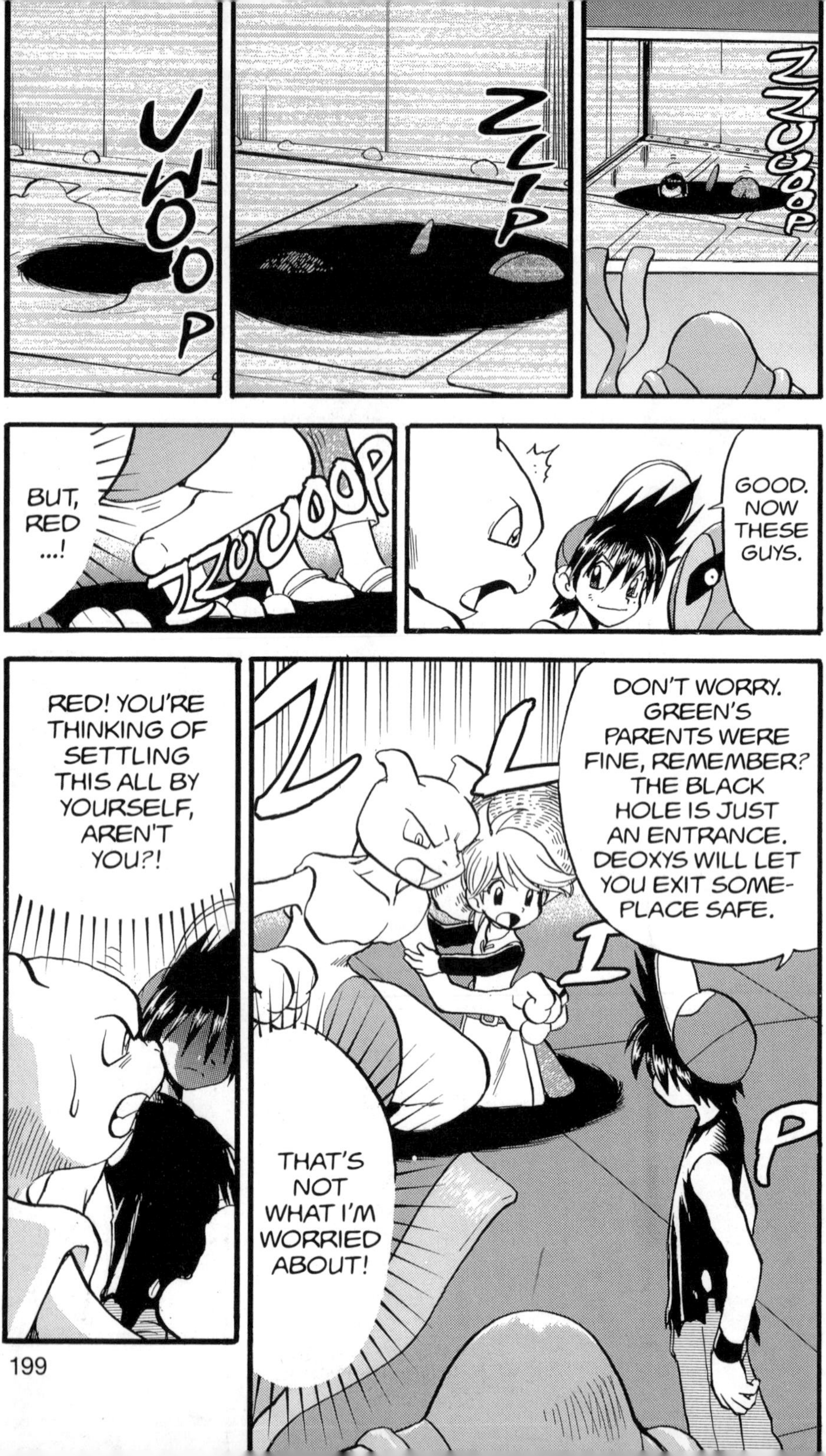
ZZUOOOP
ZLIP
WHOOP
GOOD. NOW THESE GUYS.
BUT, RED ...!
ZZUOOOP
DON'T WORRY. GREEN'S PARENTS WERE FINE, REMEMBER? THE BLACK HOLE IS JUST AN ENTRANCE. DEOXYS WILL LET YOU EXIT SOME-PLACE SAFE.
ZLIP
THAT'S NOT WHAT I'M WORRIED ABOUT!
RED! YOU'RE THINKING OF SETTLING THIS ALL BY YOURSELF, AREN'T YOU?!

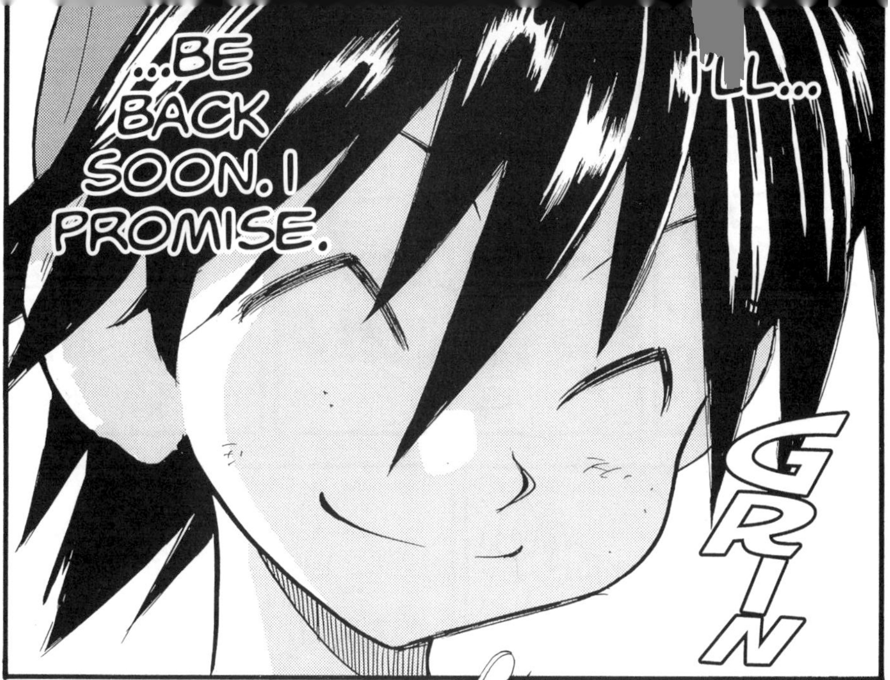
I'LL...
...BE BACK SOON. I PROMISE.
GRIN

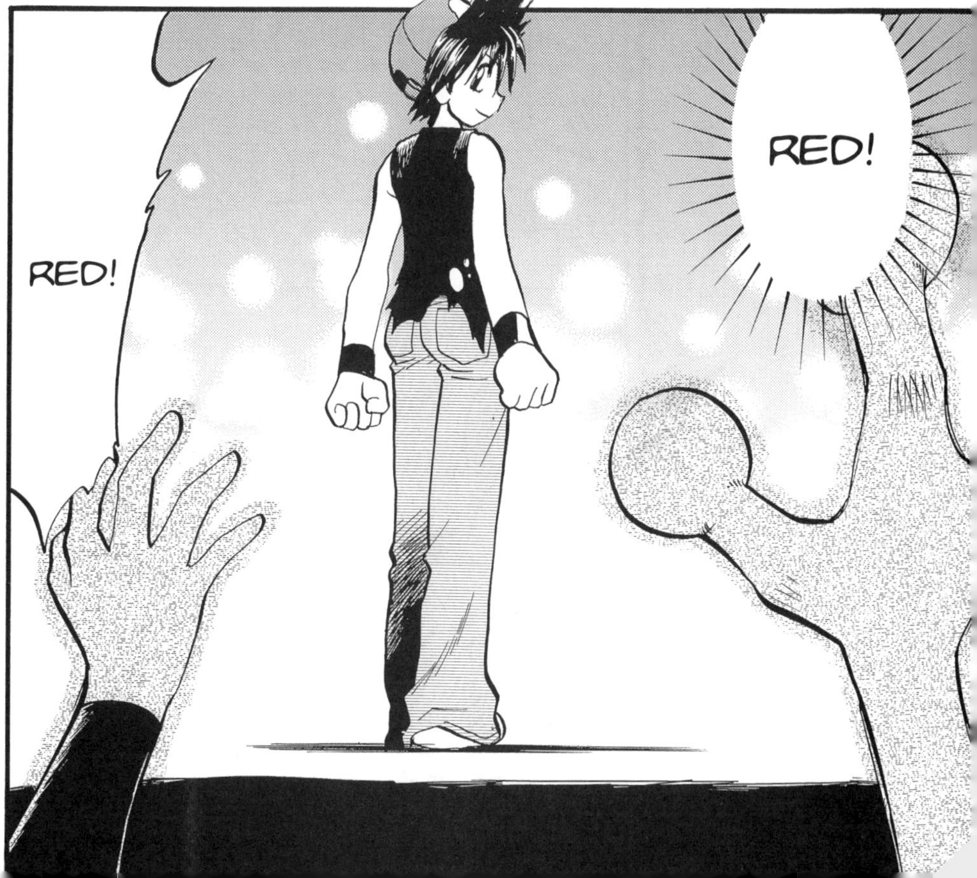
RED!
RED!

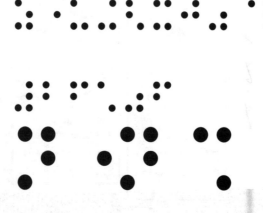

DEOXYS

SPECIAL FEATURE: DNA POKÉMON.

DEOXYS IS A POKÉMON WITH SEVERAL MYSTERIOUS POWERS. THIS IS THE DATA GATHERED ON DEOXYS IN THE MIDST OF THE PRECEDING FIERCE BATTLE, REVEALING THE FORMIDABLE POWER OF THE ENERGIES OF THE UNIVERSE.

THE SECRET BEHIND ITS ORIGIN FINALLY REVEALED!

DEOXYS'S ROOTS LIE IN A SPACE VIRUS. IT CAME DOWN TO EARTH ON A METEOR.

A ROCKET LAUNCHED FROM THE MOSSDEEP SPACE CENTER CAME ACROSS A VIRUS IN OUTER SPACE AND BEGAN TO CONDUCT EXPERIMENTS ON IT. DURING THE EXPERIMENTS, THE VIRUS WAS EXPOSED TO A LASER BEAM, WHICH CAUSED IT TO MUTATE. THE VIRUS HAS NOW TURNED INTO A NEW ORGANISM...

1 ORIGIN

THIS NEW ORGANISM TRAVELED TO OUR HEROES' WORLD BY CLINGING ONTO THE GRAND METEOR. BOTH WERE RECOVERED BY THE MOSSDEEP SPACE CENTER AND KEPT THERE.

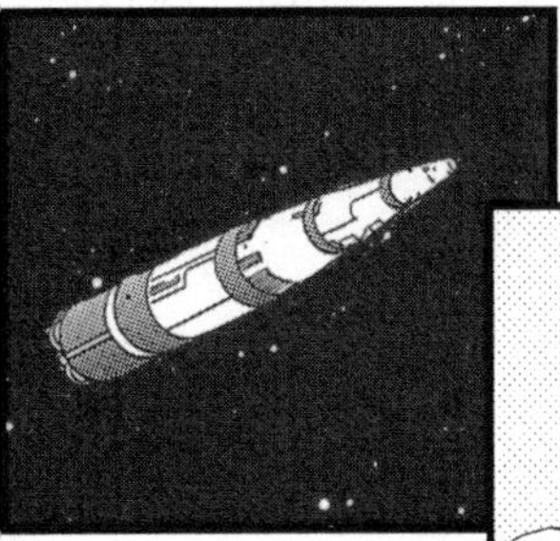

▲ THE ROCKET THAT DISCOVERED THE VIRUS AND EXPOSED IT TO THE LASER.

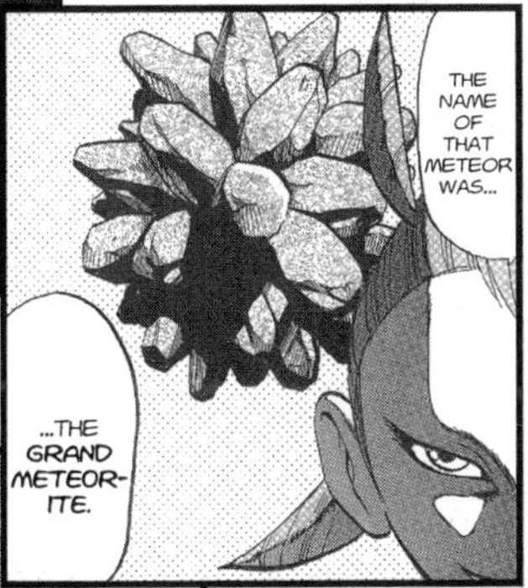
THE NAME OF THAT METEOR WAS...
...THE GRAND METEORITE.

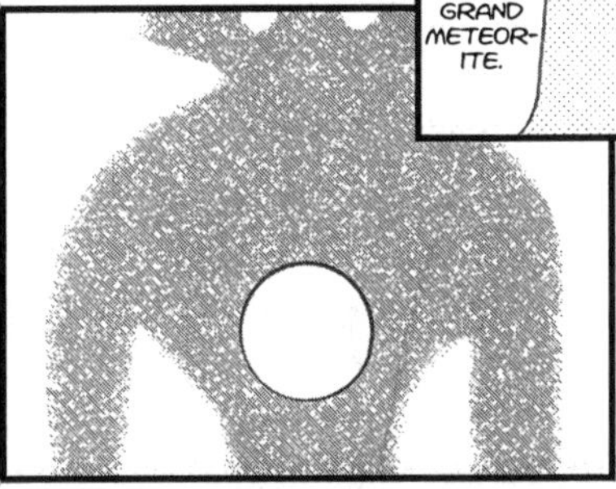

◀▲PROFESSOR COZMO GOT AHOLD OF THE GRAND METEOR. MEANWHILE, THE VIRUS BEGAN TO GROW LIMBS AROUND ITS CORE.

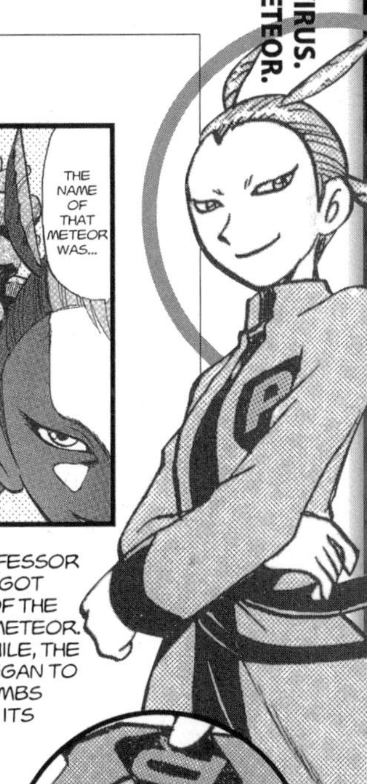

●TWO NEW ORGANISMS ARE SPAWNED.

▼ THE TWO ORGANISMS ARE STILL INCOMPLETELY FORMED AND ARE NOW HOUSED INSIDE TEAM ROCKET'S AIRSHIP.

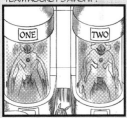

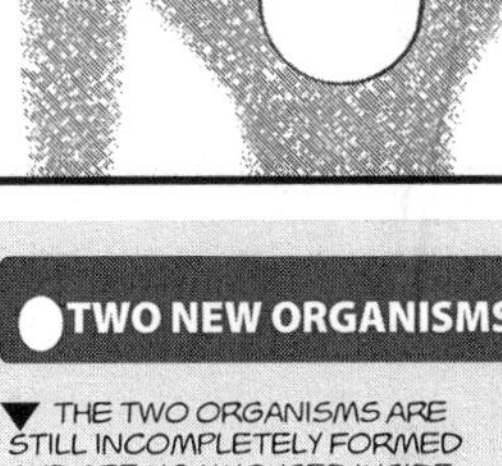
ONE
TWO

THESE TWO ORGANISMS WERE HOUSED AT THE SPACE CENTER. THEY WERE STOLEN BY TEAM ROCKET AND NAMED ORGANISM NO. 1 AND ORGANISM NO. 2. NO. 2 ESCAPED.

DEOXYS FILE

THIS IS TEAM ROCKET'S REPORT CONTAINING THE FULL DETAILS OF THEIR "OPERATION-D," A STUDY OF DEOXYS.

THREE BEASTS: SIRD

SIRD IS IN CHARGE OF THE RESEARCH ON DEOXYS. SHE HAS DIVULGED SOME OF ITS SECRETS.

2 FORMES

IT HAS BEEN REVEALED THAT DEOXYS IS ABLE TO ALTER ITS SHAPE INTO SEVERAL DIFFERENT FORMES. ITS POWERS CHANGE SIGNIFICANTLY DEPENDING ON ITS FORME.

ATTACK FORME: ATTACK TYPE

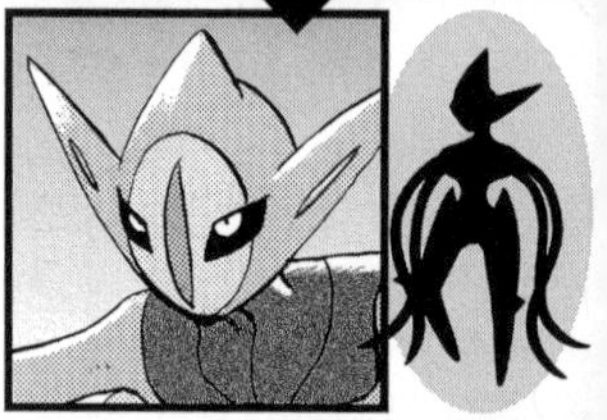

DEFENSE FORME: DEFENSE TYPE

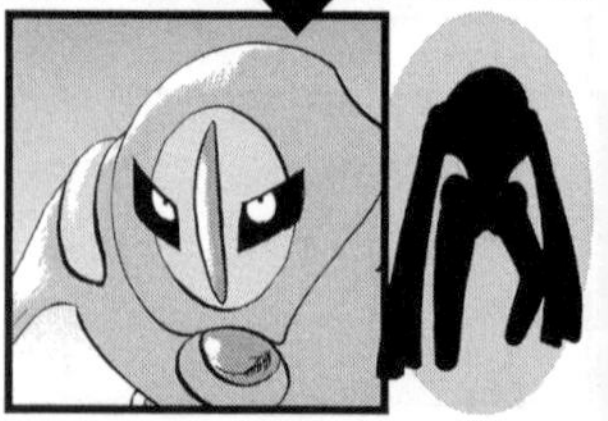

SPEED FORME: SPEED TYPE

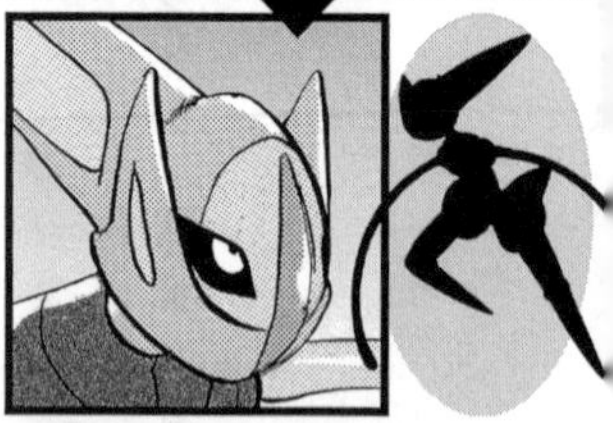

NORMAL FORME: BALANCED TYPE

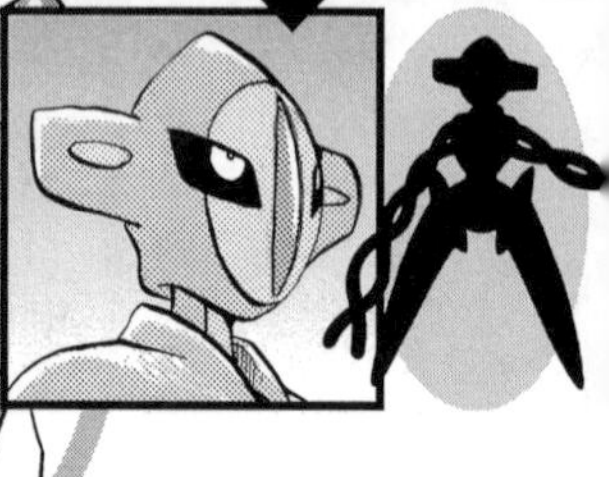

3 CHANGE

WE'VE ALSO DISCOVERED THAT THE CHANGE IN FORME IS TRIGGERED BY THE ORGANISM'S LOCATION. THAT'S WHY DEOXYS BEGAN TO TRANSFORM DURING ITS JOURNEY.

HOENN REGION

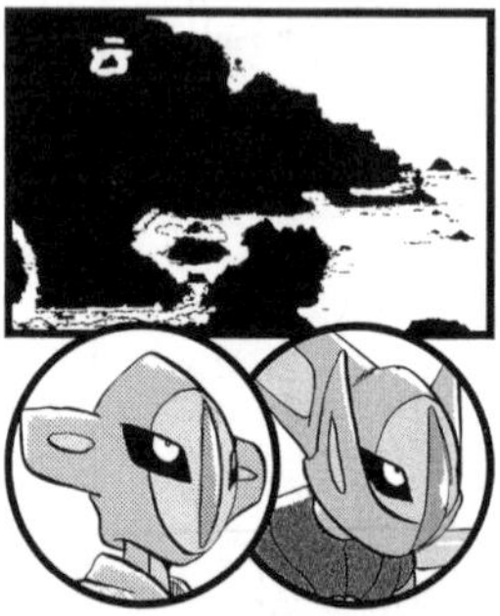

KANTO REGION

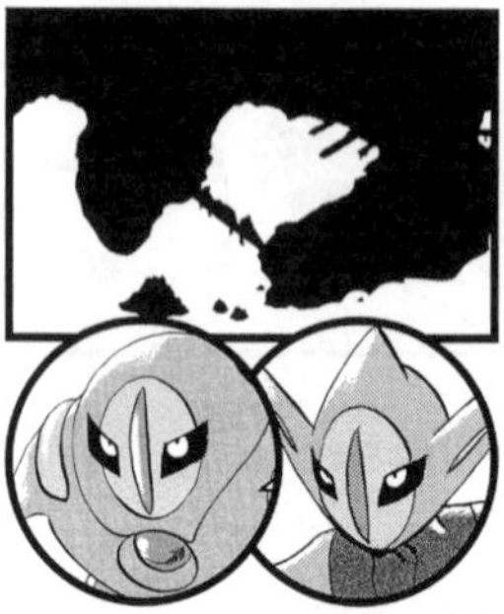

▲THE KANTO AND HOENN REGIONS TRIGGER DIFFERENT FORMES. WHAT WILL HAPPEN WHEN DEOXYS REACHES THE OTHER REGIONS...?

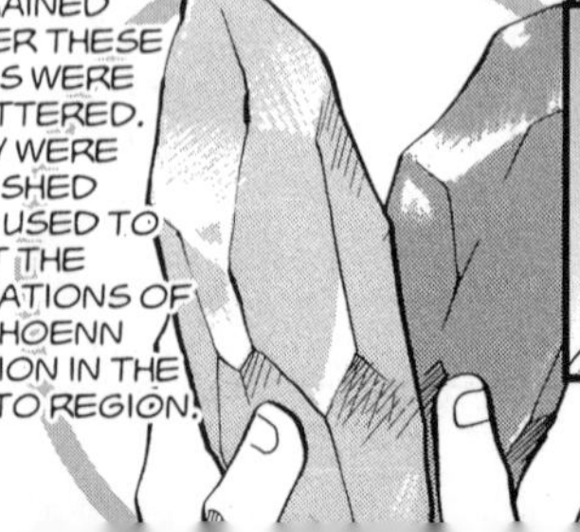

THESE ▶ ARE THE RAW STONES THAT REMAINED AFTER THESE ORBS WERE SHATTERED. THEY WERE POLISHED AND USED TO EMIT THE VIBRATIONS OF THE HOENN REGION IN THE KANTO REGION.

4 RECAPTURE

TEAM ROCKET'S SCHEME REVOLVED AROUND ORGANISM NO. 2. GIOVANNI TOOK THE OPPORTUNITY TO RECAPTURE IT WHILE DEOXYS WAS HEALING.

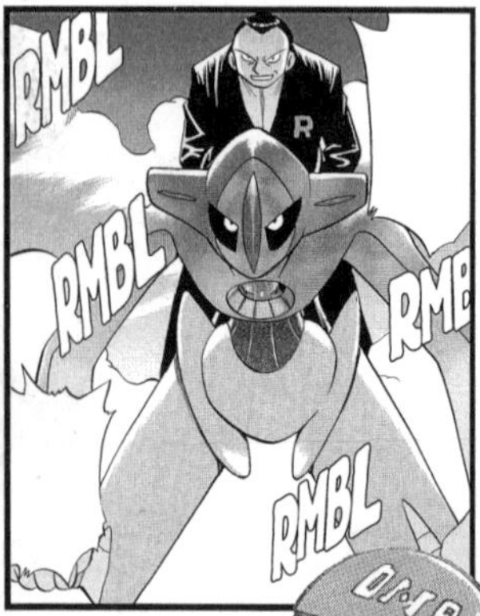
RMBL
RMBL
RMBL
RMBL

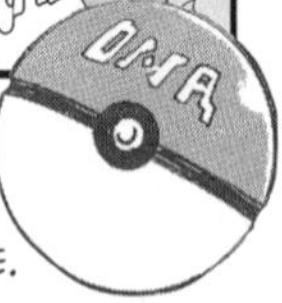

▲▶THE SPECIAL POKÉ BALL TEAM ROCKET USED FOR THE CAPTURE.

WHERE IS BIRTH ISLAND?

IT'S A SMALL PIECE OF LAND LOCATED TO THE SOUTH OF SIX ISLAND. THIS IS THE SPOT DEOXYS ORGANISM NO. 2 CHOSE FOR ITS HOME AFTER ITS ESCAPE.

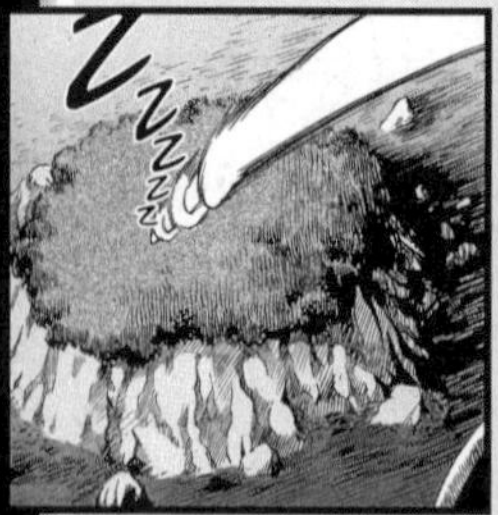

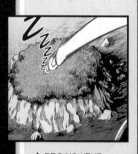

▲DEOXYS WENT STRAIGHT BACK TO THIS ISLAND AFTER ITS BATTLE AGAINST RED.

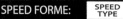

5 CAPABILITIES

AS THE DNA POKÉMON FROM OUTER SPACE, DEOXYS HAS MANY UNIQUE AND POWERFUL CAPABILITIES.

DIVINATION

DEOXYS CAN FIND THE OWNER OF AN OBJECT BY SIMPLY TOUCHING IT.

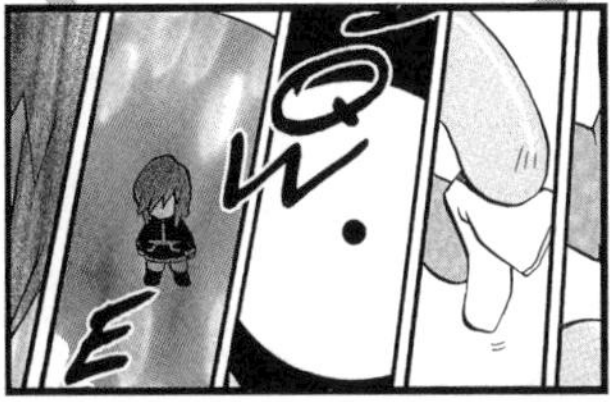

▲ DEOXYS QUICKLY DISCOVERED SILVER'S WHEREABOUTS.

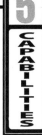

FIST

DEOXYS USES ITS FISTS AND TENTACLES IN ITS NORMAL FORME, AN ALL-AROUND FORME THAT CAN HANDLE ANY TYPE OF BATTLE.

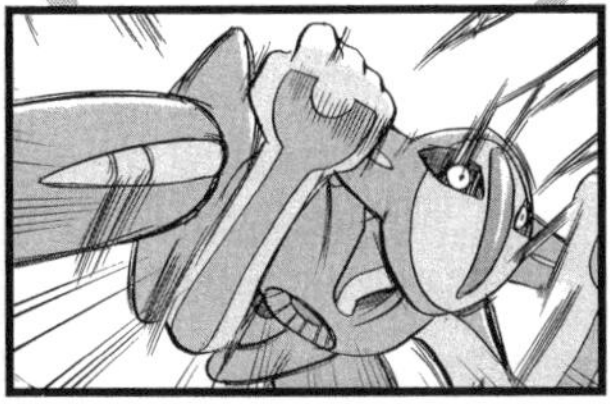

▲ IT USES ITS FISTS FOR CLOSE COMBAT.

MOST POWERFUL MOVE: PSYCHO BOOST

A POWERFUL MOVE WHICH ONLY DEOXYS CAN USE. RED'S TEAM WAS DEFEATED WITH JUST THIS MOVE!

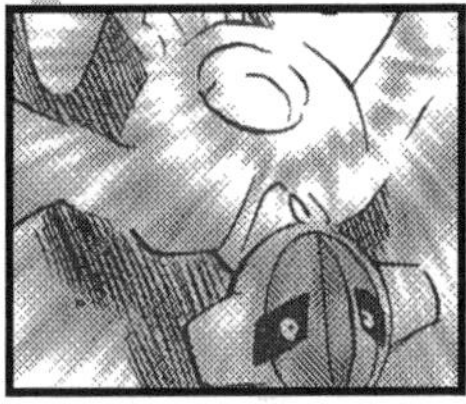

▲ AN AWESOME MOVE. POWER: 140.

BLACK HOLE

DEOXYS CAN CREATE A BLACK HOLE THAT CONNECTS TO A MYSTERIOUS VOID TO CAPTURE ITS OPPONENT. THE BLACK HOLE CAN APPEAR ANYWHERE.

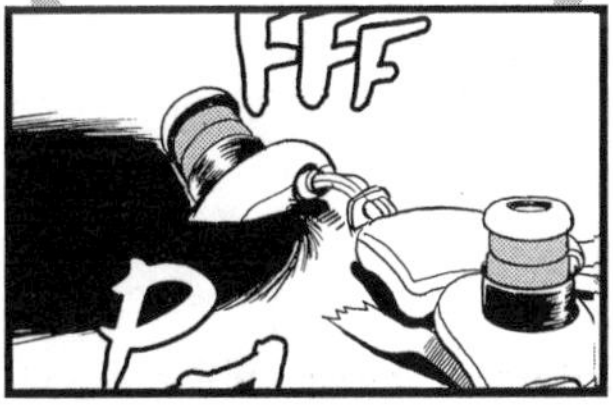
FFF

▲ IT WAS ABSORBED INTO THE DARKNESS.

DUPLICATES

DEOXYS CAN CREATE NUMEROUS DUPLICATES AND CONTROL THEM FROM A DISTANCE. EACH ONE ISN'T VERY STRONG BY ITSELF, BUT THEY CAN OVERWHELM THEIR OPPONENT BY FORCE OF NUMBERS.

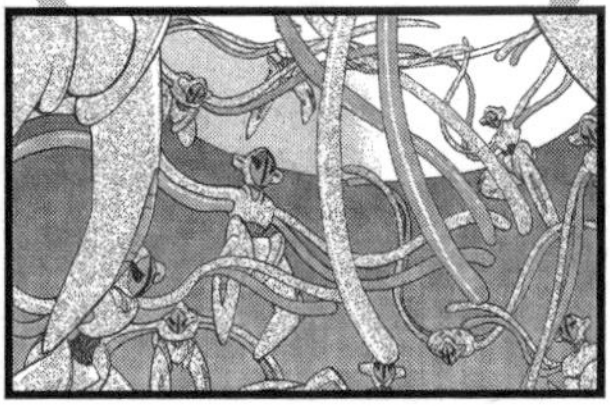

▲ INNUMERABLE DUPLICATES STAND IN OUR HEROES' WAY.

DELTA SHIELD

THIS TRIANGULAR SHIELD INCREASES DEOXYS'S POWER AND PROTECTS IT FROM ATTACKS. IT CAN BE USED WHILE MOVING. DEOXYS OFTEN RAISES THIS SHIELD TO PROVIDE AN OPPORTUNITY TO RESTORE ITS STRENGTH.

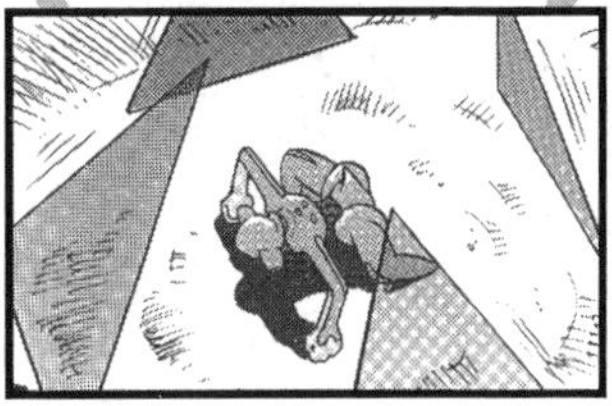

▲ AKA "THE MOVING SHIELD."

DECEPTION

DEOXYS CREATES AN AURORA IN FRONT OF ITS BODY TO DISGUISE ITS ACTUAL FORME. A HIGHLY ADVANCED TACTIC WHICH IS ESPECIALLY USEFUL WHEN BATTLING TRAINERS WHO ARE GOOD AT STRATEGIZING AGAINST DIFFERENT POKÉMON TYPES.

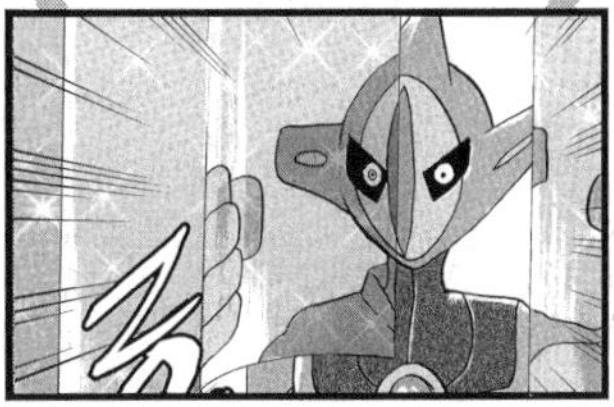

▲ THIS IS ACTUALLY ATTACK FORME, NOT NORMAL FORME.

● WHAT WILL BECOME OF DEOXYS...?

DEOXYS HAS BEEN DEFEATED AND HAS LOST ITS ABILITY TO CHANGE INTO FOUR DIFFERENT FORMES. NEVERTHELESS, MANY VILLAINS WISH TO HARNESS ITS UNIQUE POWERS. DEOXYS APPEARS TO BE IN GREAT DANGER!

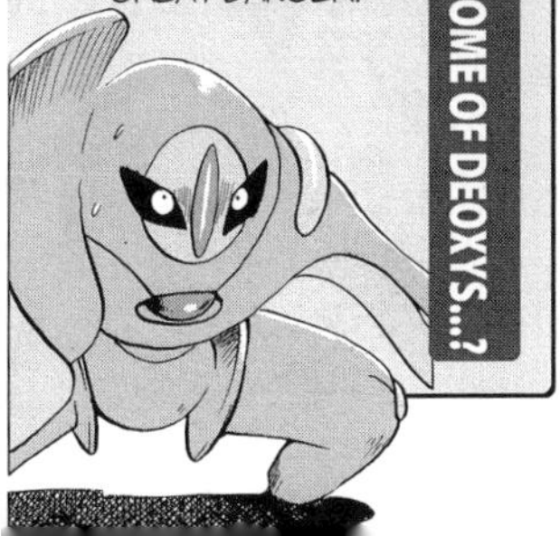

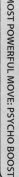

THE FIFTH CHAPTER TRAVEL ROUTES

THE DEOXYS INCIDENT BEGAN AT VERMILION CITY AND SPREAD THROUGHOUT THE SEVII ISLANDS. LET'S TRACK IT OVER THE MAP!

FROM VERMILION CITY

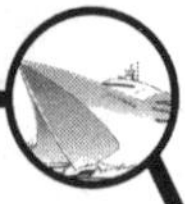

ONE ISLAND — GREEN IS ATTACKED BY DEOXYS (ORGANISM NO. 1) ON THE SHIP AND HOSPITALIZED AT ONE ISLAND.

TWO ISLAND — OUR HEROES TRAIN WITH ULTIMA, LEARNING HER SPECIAL MOVES.

THREE ISLAND — DEOXYS (ORGANISM NO. 2) APPEARS.

FOUR ISLAND — THE THREE BEASTS SHOW UP IN LORELEI'S HOMETOWN.

TEAM ROCKET LAUNCHES AN ALL-OUT ATTACK. RED AND THE OTHERS SPLIT UP AND HEAD TO THE THREE ISLANDS TO FACE THEM.

FIVE ISLAND — ●RED VERSUS CARR○

SIX ISLAND — ○BLUE VERSUS ORM●

SEVEN ISLAND — ●LORELEI VERSUS SIRD○

GIOVANNI CAPTURES DEOXYS (ORGANISM NO. 2) WHEN IT RETURNS TO BIRTH ISLAND TO REGAIN ITS STRENGTH.

SEVEN ISLAND — A REMATCH AT THE TRAINER TOWER.

GIOVANNI TRAVELS TO VIRIDIAN CITY.

TWO ISLAND
THREE ISLAND
ONE ISLAND
FIVE ISLAND
FOUR ISLAND
SEVEN ISLAND
SIX ISLAND
BIRTH ISLAND

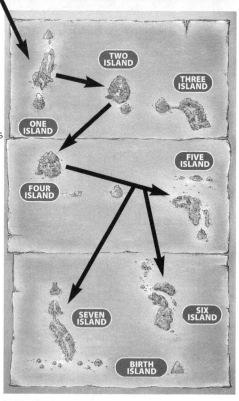

VIRIDIAN CITY

RED FACES GIOVANNI IN THE SKY. MEANWHILE, DOWN ON THE GROUND, SILVER AND YELLOW ARE REUNITED.

CARR REBELS, LEAVING THE TEAM ROCKET AIRSHIP OUT OF CONTROL AND ON A CRASH COURSE TOWARDS VERMILION CITY...

VERMILION CITY
VIRIDIAN CITY

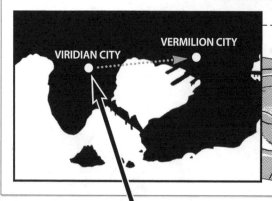

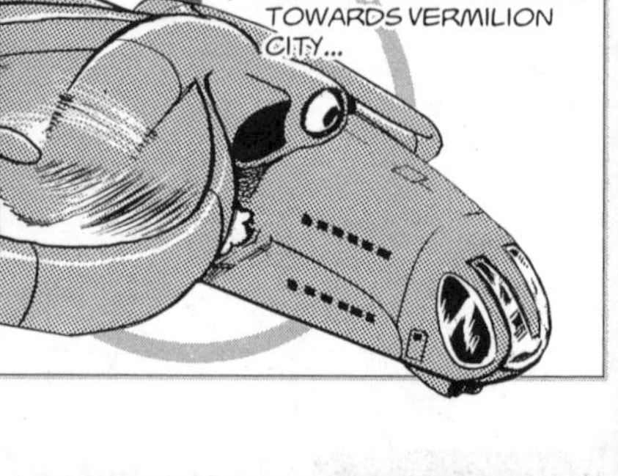

● Adventure 299 ●
Distant Relation Deoxys

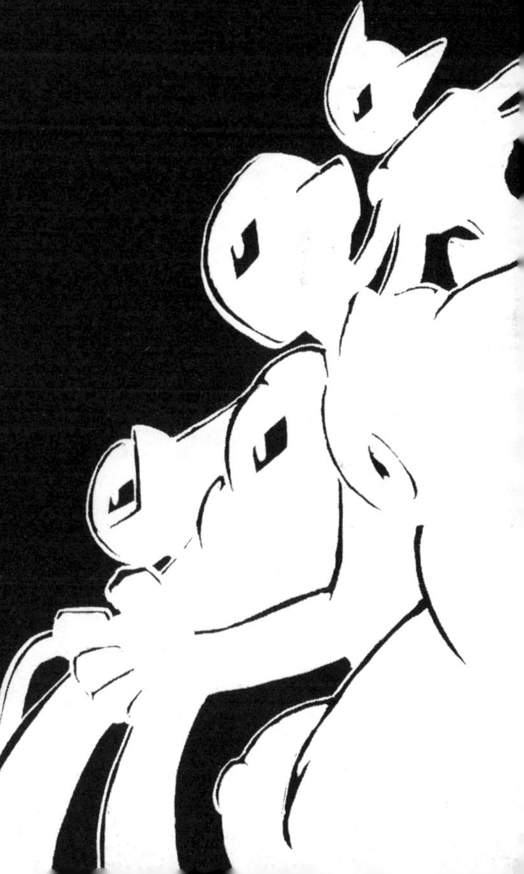

Pokémon Adventures
FireRed & LeafGreen
The Fifth Chapter

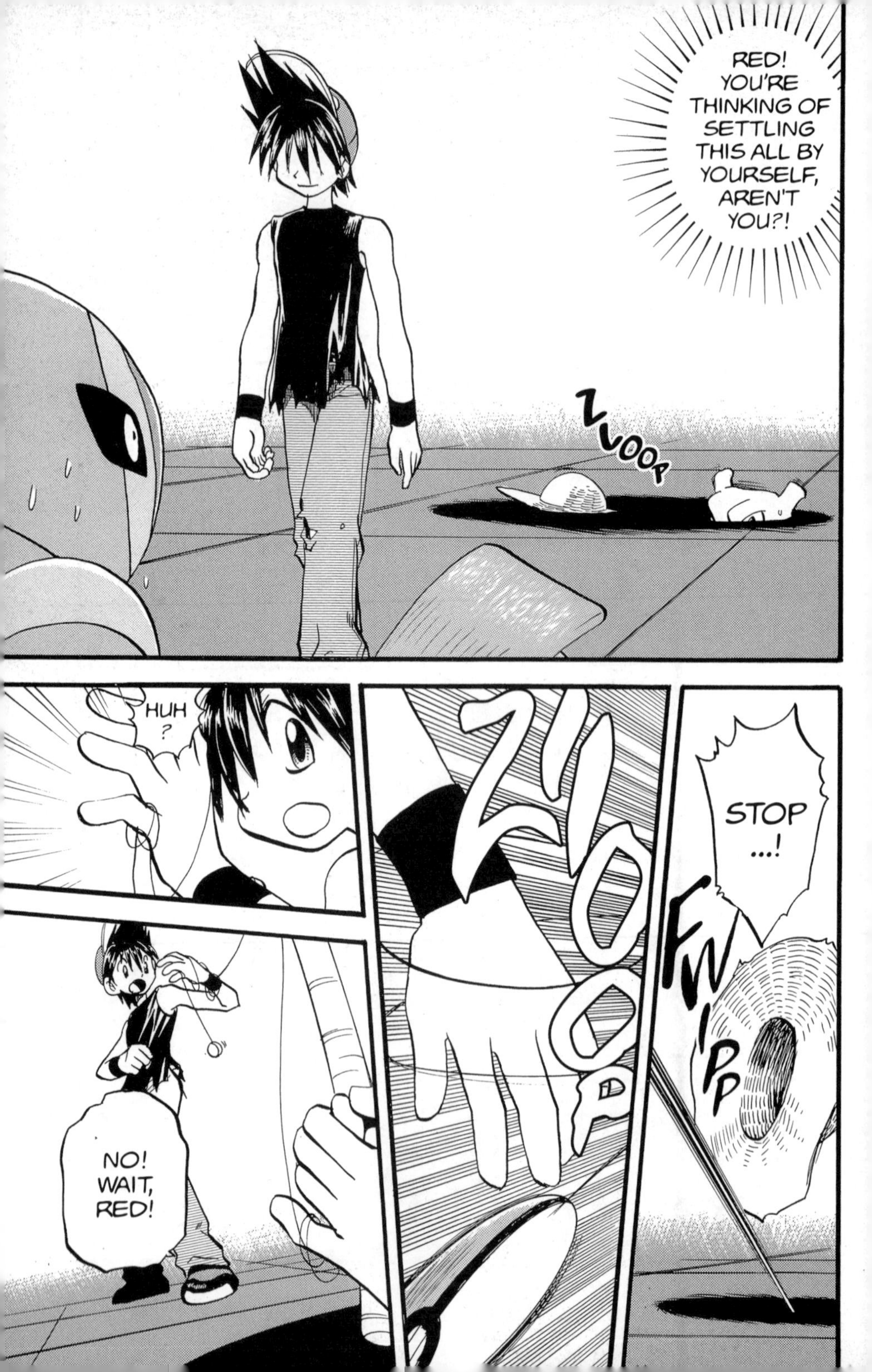
RED! YOU'RE THINKING OF SETTLING THIS ALL BY YOURSELF, AREN'T YOU?!
ZVOOP
STOP ...!
FWIPP
ZVOOP
HUH ?
NO! WAIT, RED!

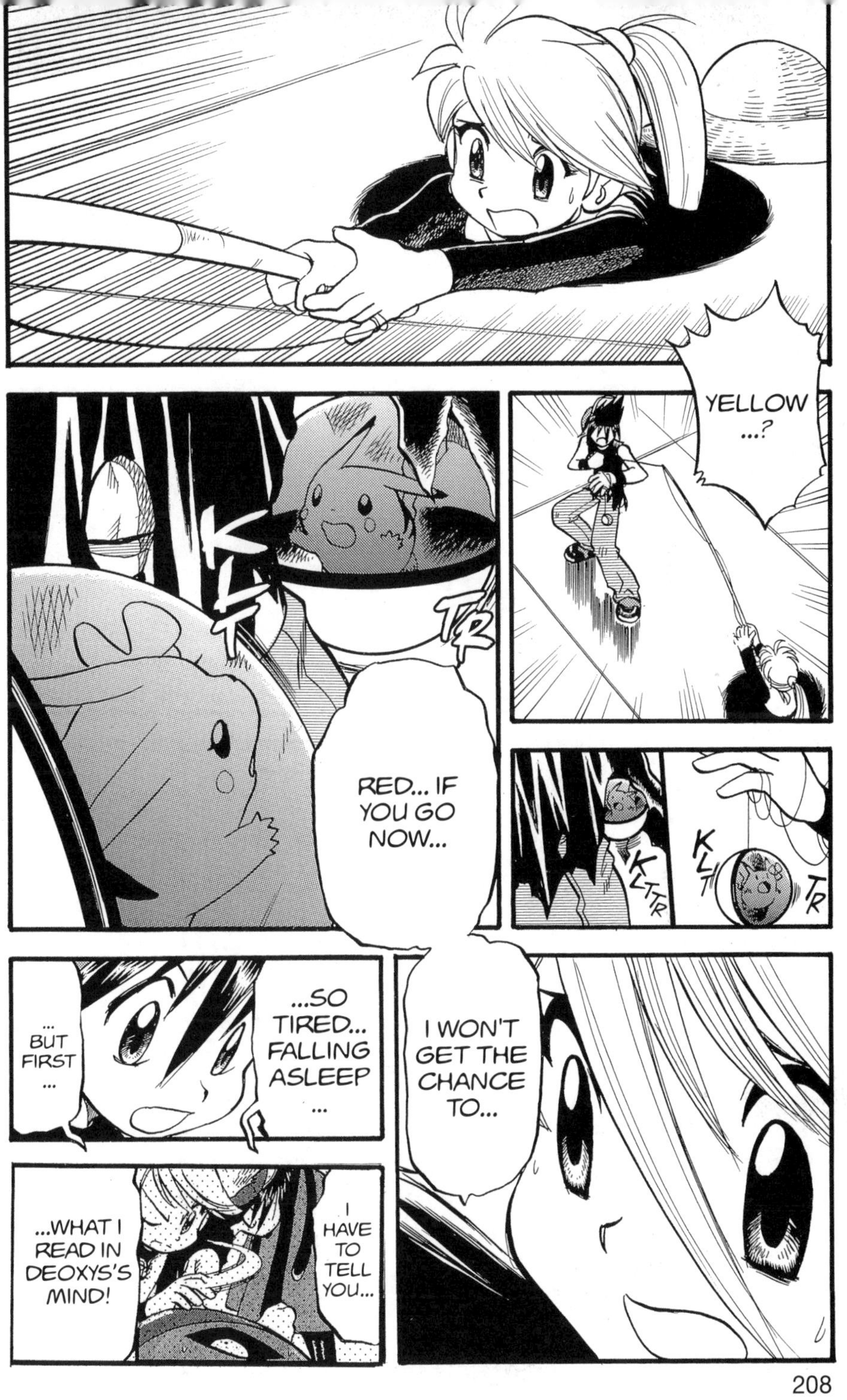
YELLOW ...?
KLTTR
KLT
TR
RED... IF YOU GO NOW...
KLLT
TR
I WON'T GET THE CHANCE TO...
...SO TIRED... FALLING ASLEEP ...
... BUT FIRST ...
I HAVE TO TELL YOU...
...WHAT I READ IN DEOXYS'S MIND!

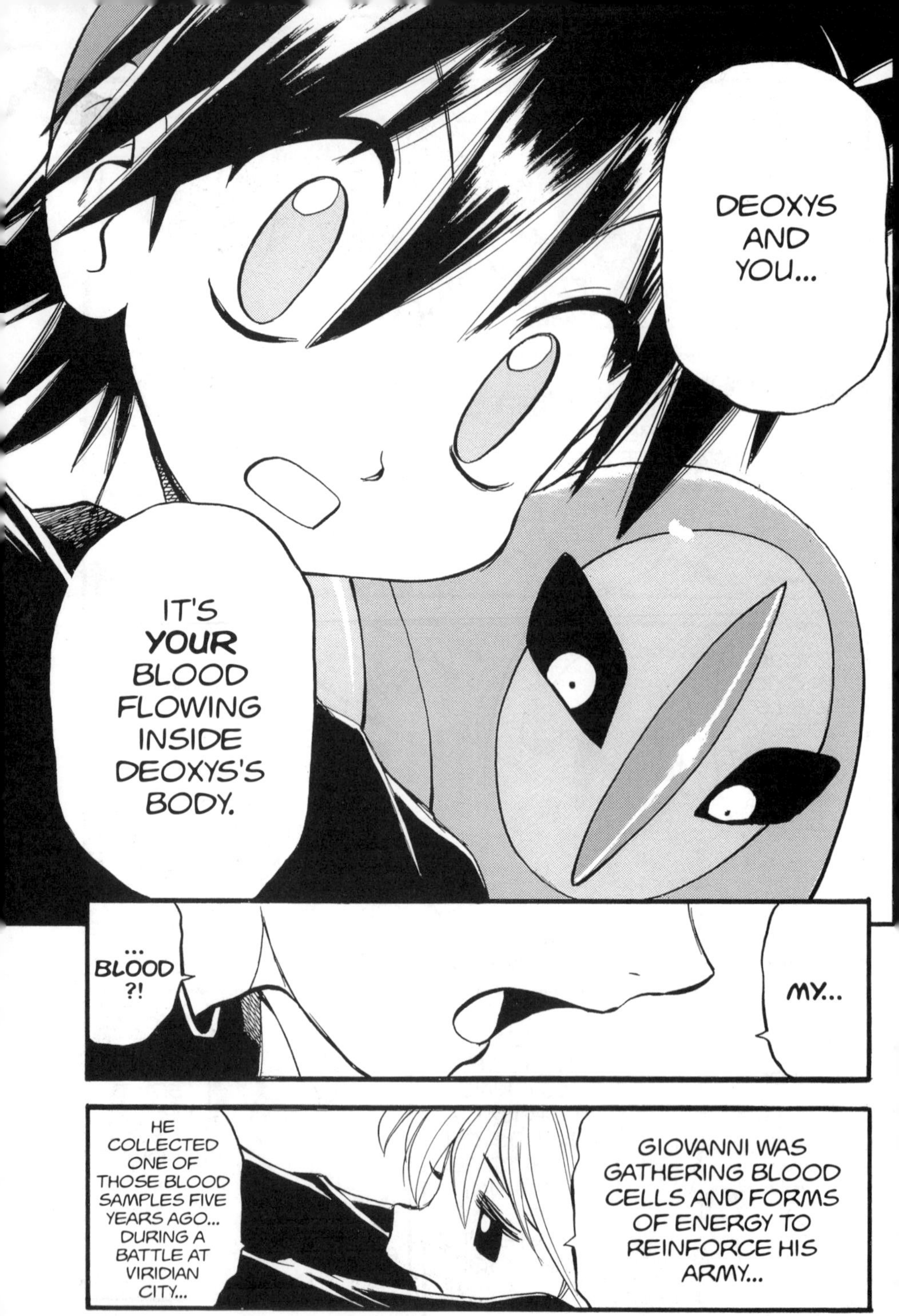
DEOXYS AND YOU...
IT'S **YOUR** BLOOD FLOWING INSIDE DEOXYS'S BODY.
MY...
... BLOOD ?!
GIOVANNI WAS GATHERING BLOOD CELLS AND FORMS OF ENERGY TO REINFORCE HIS ARMY...
HE COLLECTED ONE OF THOSE BLOOD SAMPLES FIVE YEARS AGO... DURING A BATTLE AT VIRIDIAN CITY...

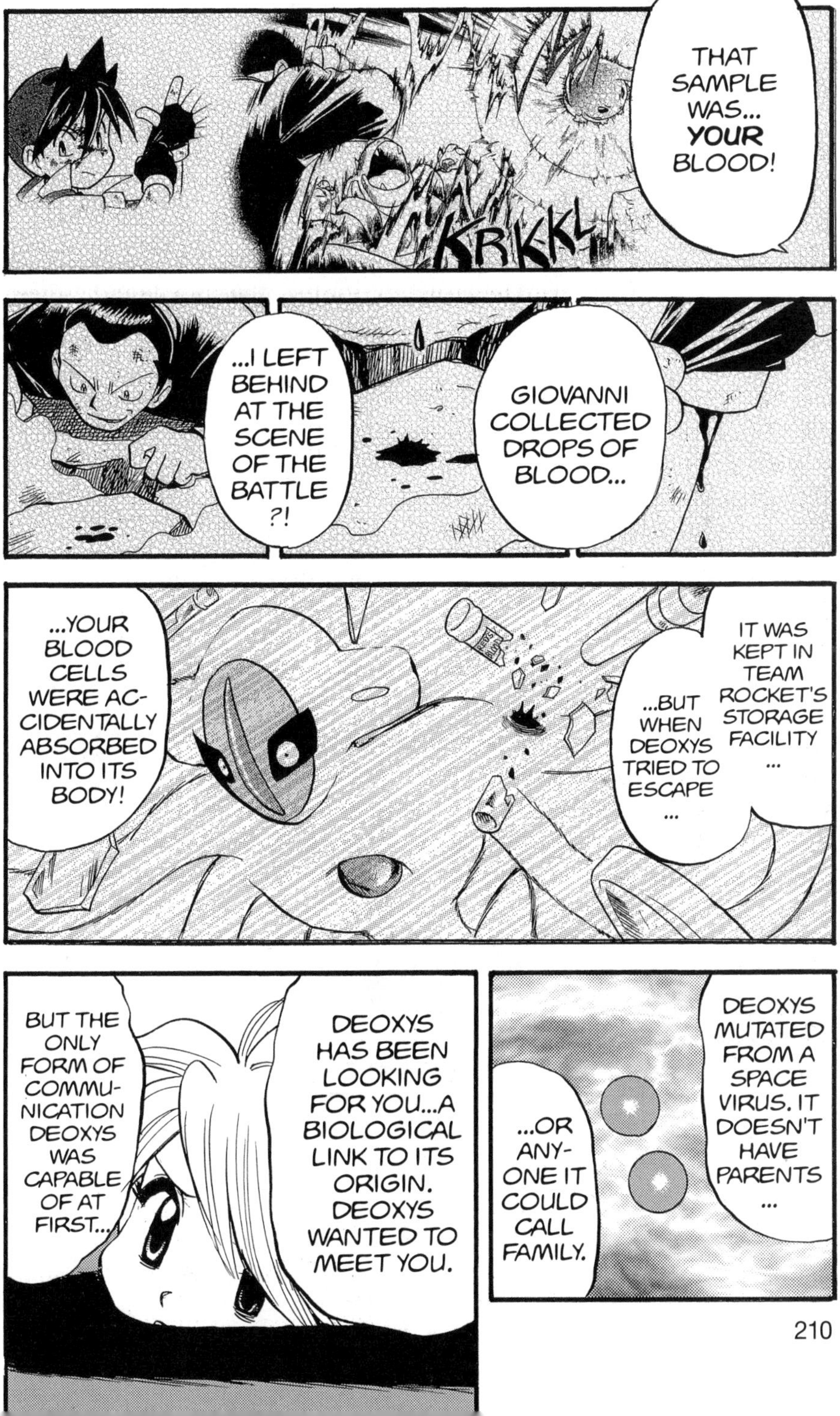
THAT SAMPLE WAS... **YOUR** BLOOD!
KRKKL
GIOVANNI COLLECTED DROPS OF BLOOD...
...I LEFT BEHIND AT THE SCENE OF THE BATTLE?!
IT WAS KEPT IN TEAM ROCKET'S STORAGE FACILITY...
...BUT WHEN DEOXYS TRIED TO ESCAPE...
...YOUR BLOOD CELLS WERE ACCIDENTALLY ABSORBED INTO ITS BODY!
DEOXYS MUTATED FROM A SPACE VIRUS. IT DOESN'T HAVE PARENTS...
...OR ANYONE IT COULD CALL FAMILY.
DEOXYS HAS BEEN LOOKING FOR YOU...A BIOLOGICAL LINK TO ITS ORIGIN. DEOXYS WANTED TO MEET YOU.
BUT THE ONLY FORM OF COMMUNICATION DEOXYS WAS CAPABLE OF AT FIRST...

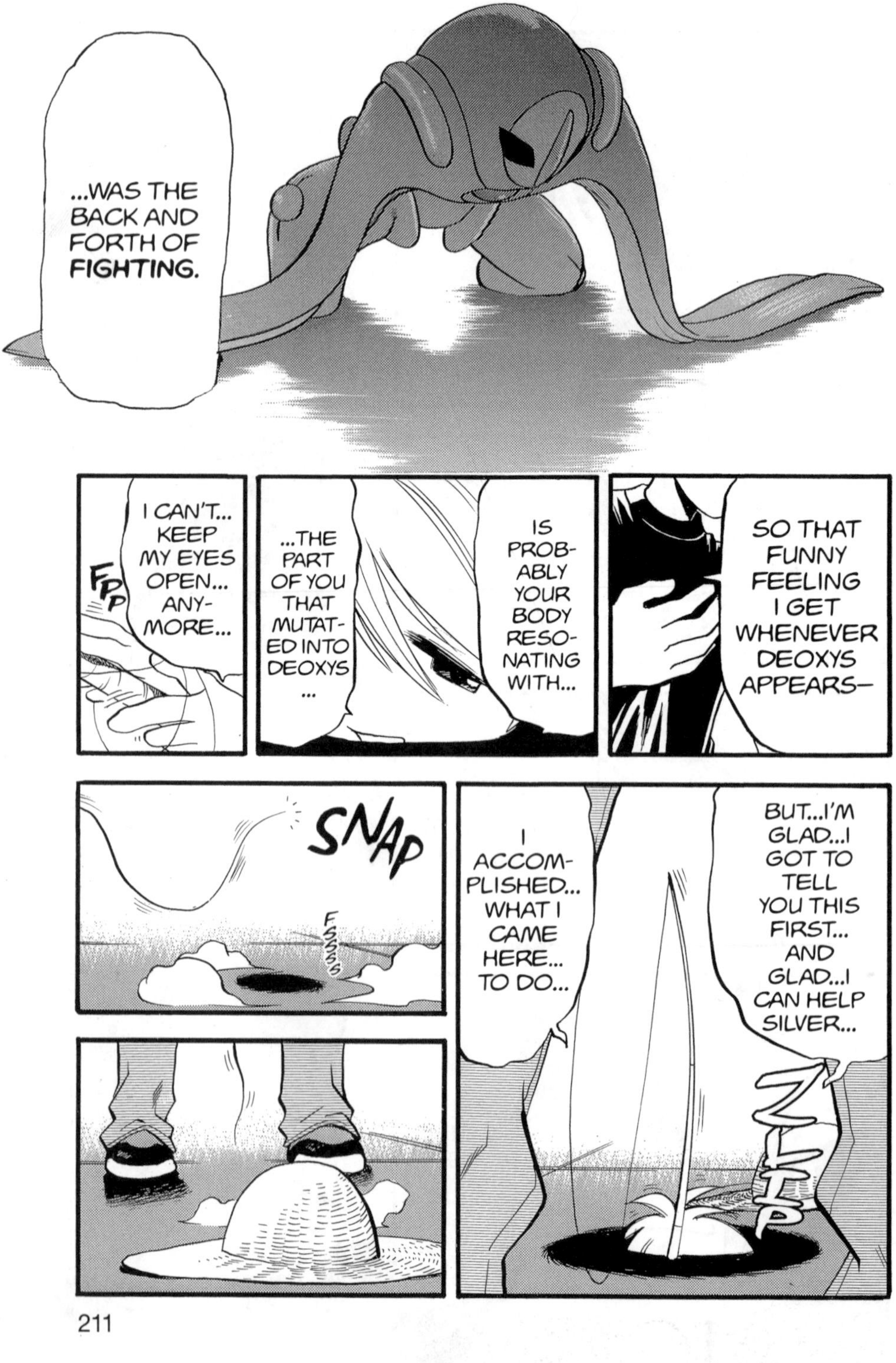
...WAS THE BACK AND FORTH OF FIGHTING.
SO THAT FUNNY FEELING I GET WHENEVER DEOXYS APPEARS—
IS PROBABLY YOUR BODY RESONATING WITH...
...THE PART OF YOU THAT MUTATED INTO DEOXYS...
FPP
I CAN'T... KEEP MY EYES OPEN... ANYMORE...
BUT...I'M GLAD...I GOT TO TELL YOU THIS FIRST... AND GLAD...I CAN HELP SILVER...
I ACCOMPLISHED... WHAT I CAME HERE... TO DO...
ZLIP
SNAP
FSSSS

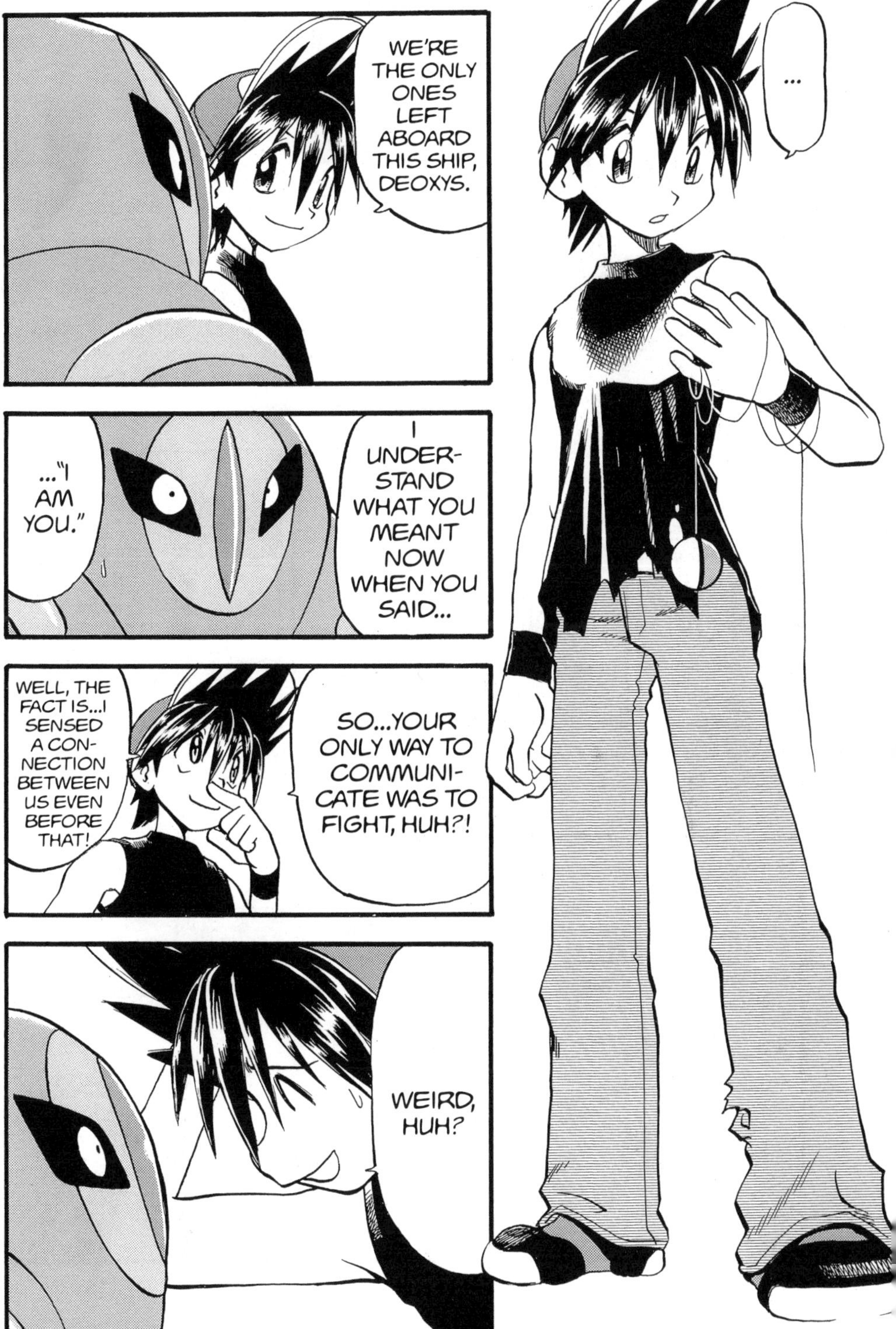
...
WE'RE THE ONLY ONES LEFT ABOARD THIS SHIP, DEOXYS.
I UNDERSTAND WHAT YOU MEANT NOW WHEN YOU SAID...
..."I AM YOU."
SO...YOUR ONLY WAY TO COMMUNICATE WAS TO FIGHT, HUH?!
WELL, THE FACT IS...I SENSED A CONNECTION BETWEEN US EVEN BEFORE THAT!
WEIRD, HUH?

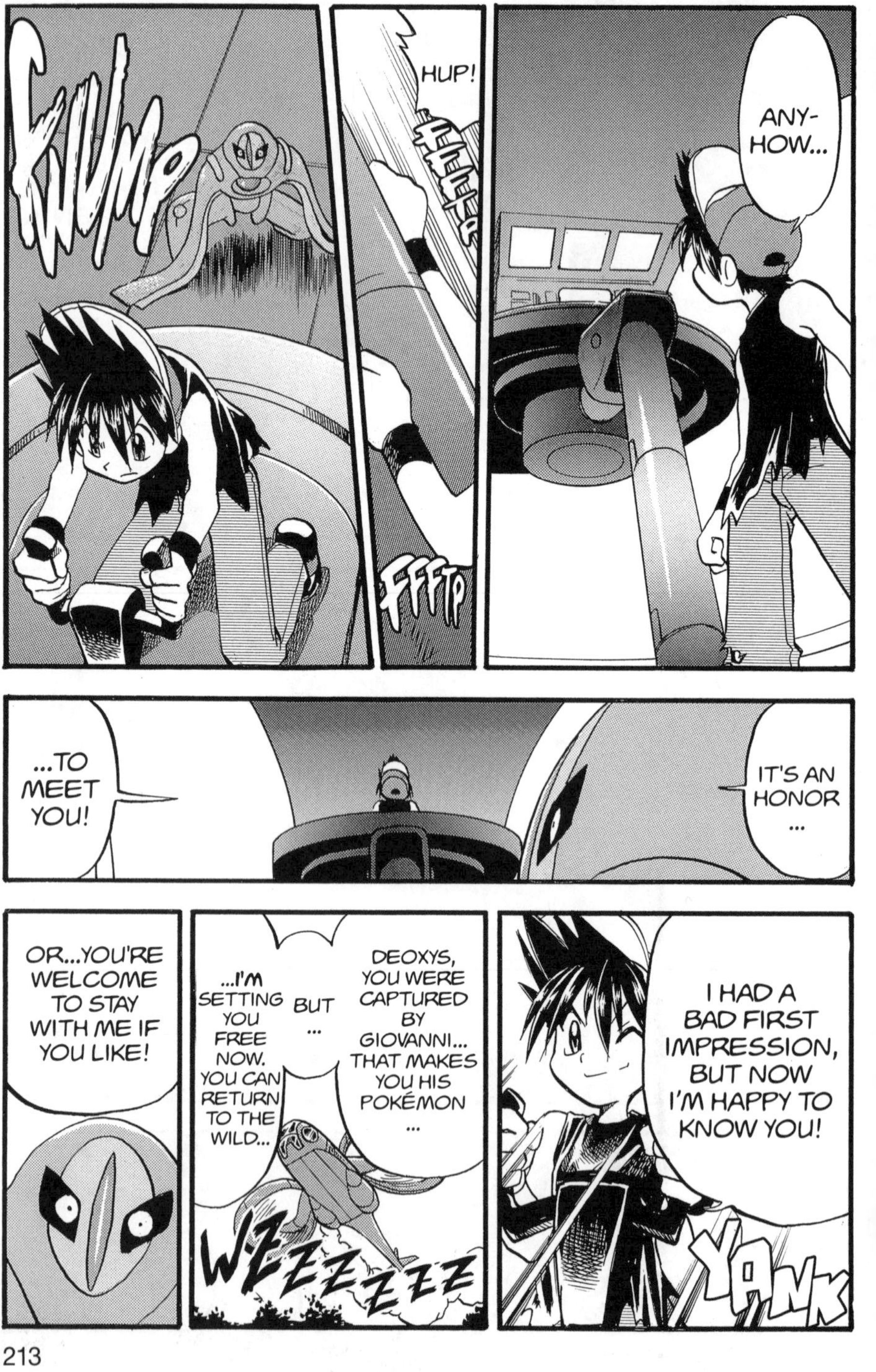
ANY-HOW...
HUP!
FFFFTP
FFFTP
FWUMP
IT'S AN HONOR ...
...TO MEET YOU!
I HAD A BAD FIRST IMPRESSION, BUT NOW I'M HAPPY TO KNOW YOU!
YANK
DEOXYS, YOU WERE CAPTURED BY GIOVANNI... THAT MAKES YOU HIS POKÉMON ...
BUT ...
...I'M SETTING YOU FREE NOW. YOU CAN RETURN TO THE WILD...
WZZZZZZZZ
OR...YOU'RE WELCOME TO STAY WITH ME IF YOU LIKE!

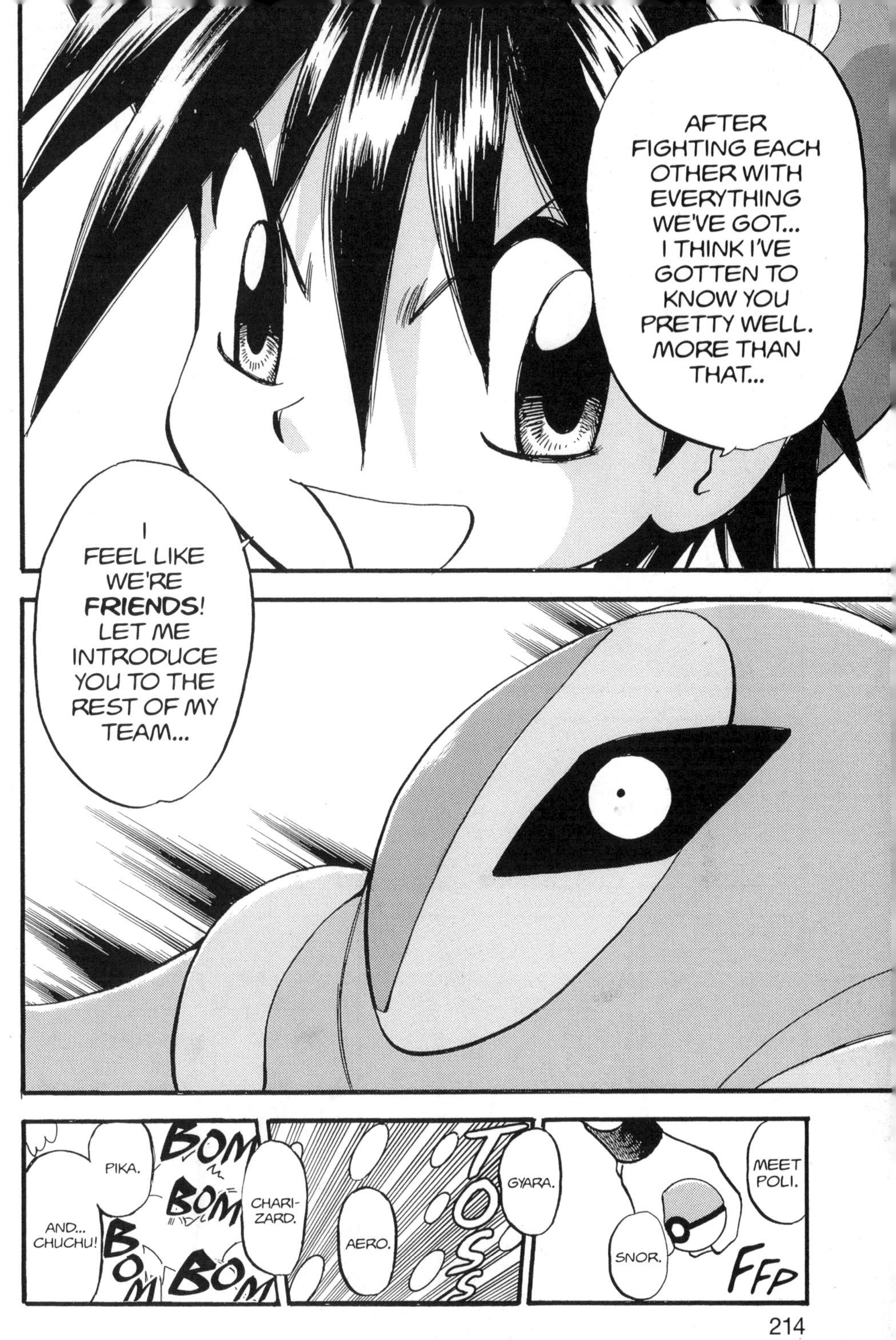
AFTER FIGHTING EACH OTHER WITH EVERYTHING WE'VE GOT... I THINK I'VE GOTTEN TO KNOW YOU PRETTY WELL. MORE THAN THAT...
I FEEL LIKE WE'RE **FRIENDS**! LET ME INTRODUCE YOU TO THE REST OF MY TEAM...
MEET POLI.
SNOR.
FFP
GYARA.
TOSS
CHARI-ZARD.
AERO.
BOM
PIKA.
BOM
AND... CHUCHU!
BOM
BOM

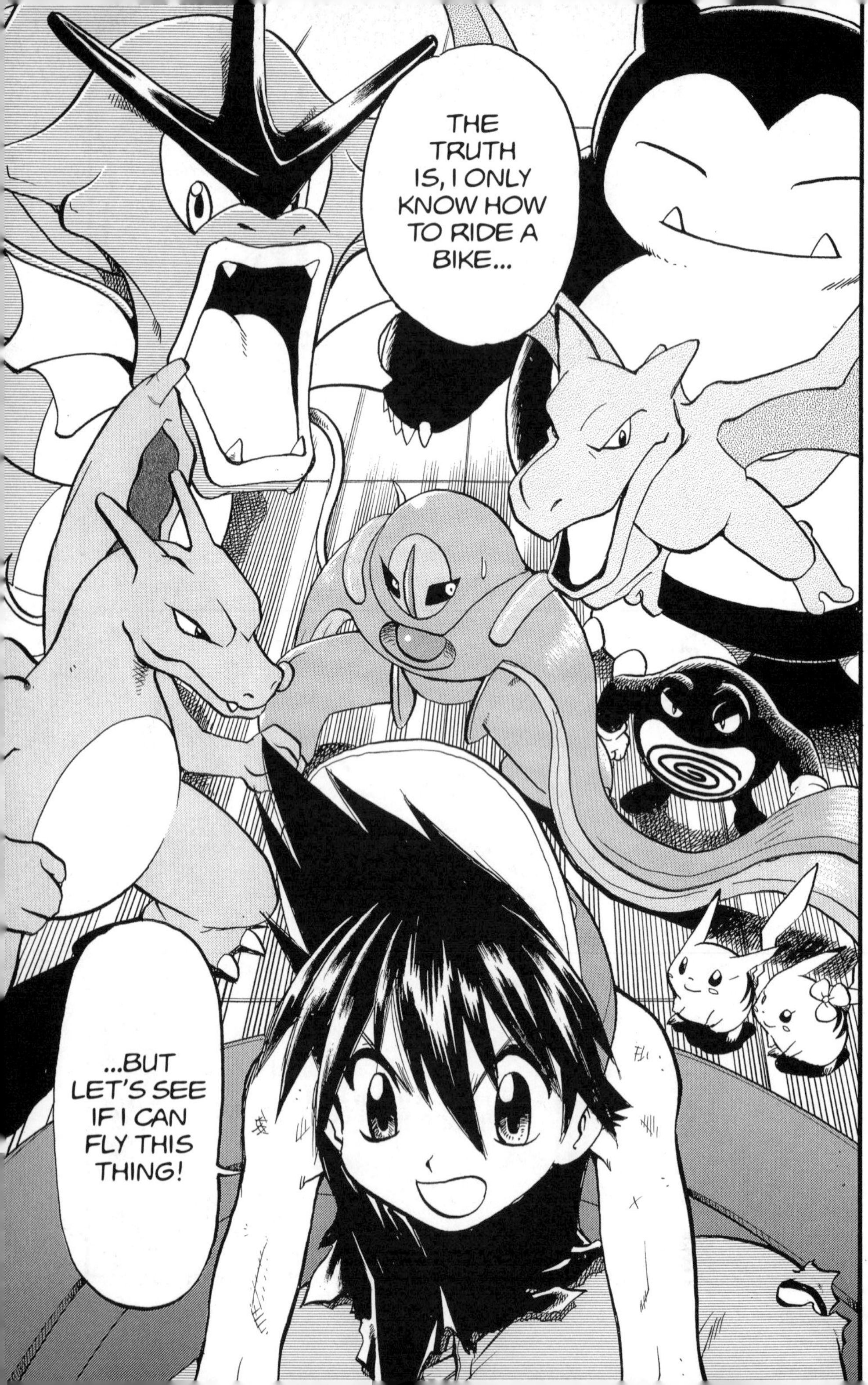
THE TRUTH IS, I ONLY KNOW HOW TO RIDE A BIKE...
...BUT LET'S SEE IF I CAN FLY THIS THING!

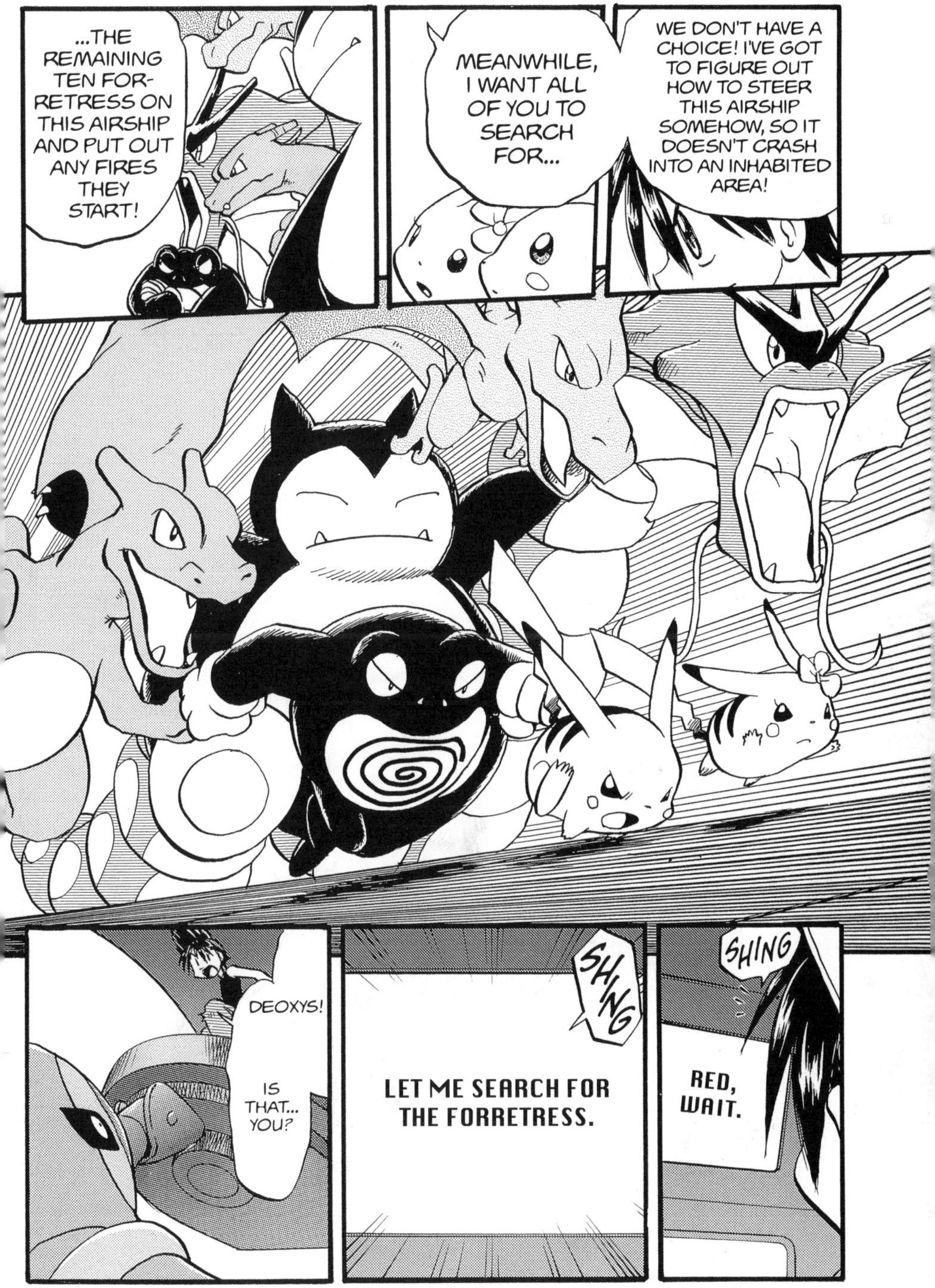
WE DON'T HAVE A CHOICE! I'VE GOT TO FIGURE OUT HOW TO STEER THIS AIRSHIP SOMEHOW, SO IT DOESN'T CRASH INTO AN INHABITED AREA!
MEANWHILE, I WANT ALL OF YOU TO SEARCH FOR...
...THE REMAINING TEN FOR-RETRESS ON THIS AIRSHIP AND PUT OUT ANY FIRES THEY START!
SHING
RED, WAIT.
SHING
LET ME SEARCH FOR THE FORRETRESS.
DEOXYS!
IS THAT... YOU?

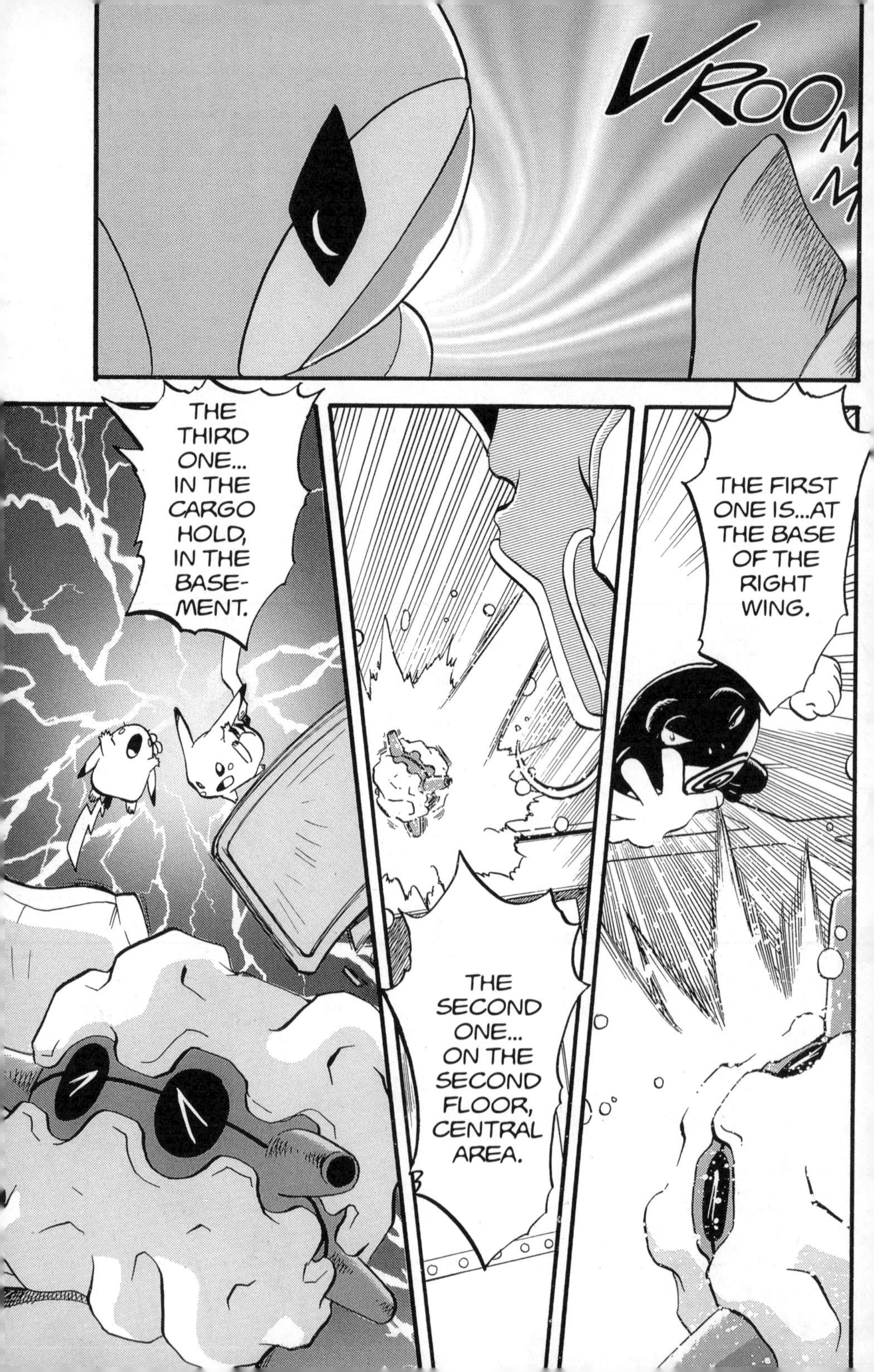
VROOMM
THE FIRST ONE IS...AT THE BASE OF THE RIGHT WING.
THE SECOND ONE... ON THE SECOND FLOOR, CENTRAL AREA.
THE THIRD ONE... IN THE CARGO HOLD, IN THE BASEMENT.

● Adventure 300 ●
Right on Time, Rhydon

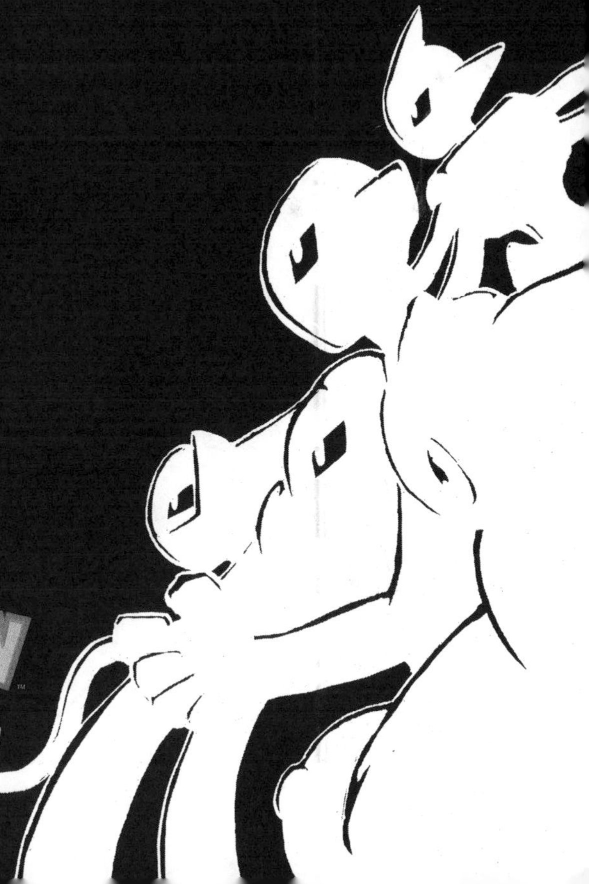

Pokémon Adventures FireRed & LeafGreen The Fifth Chapter

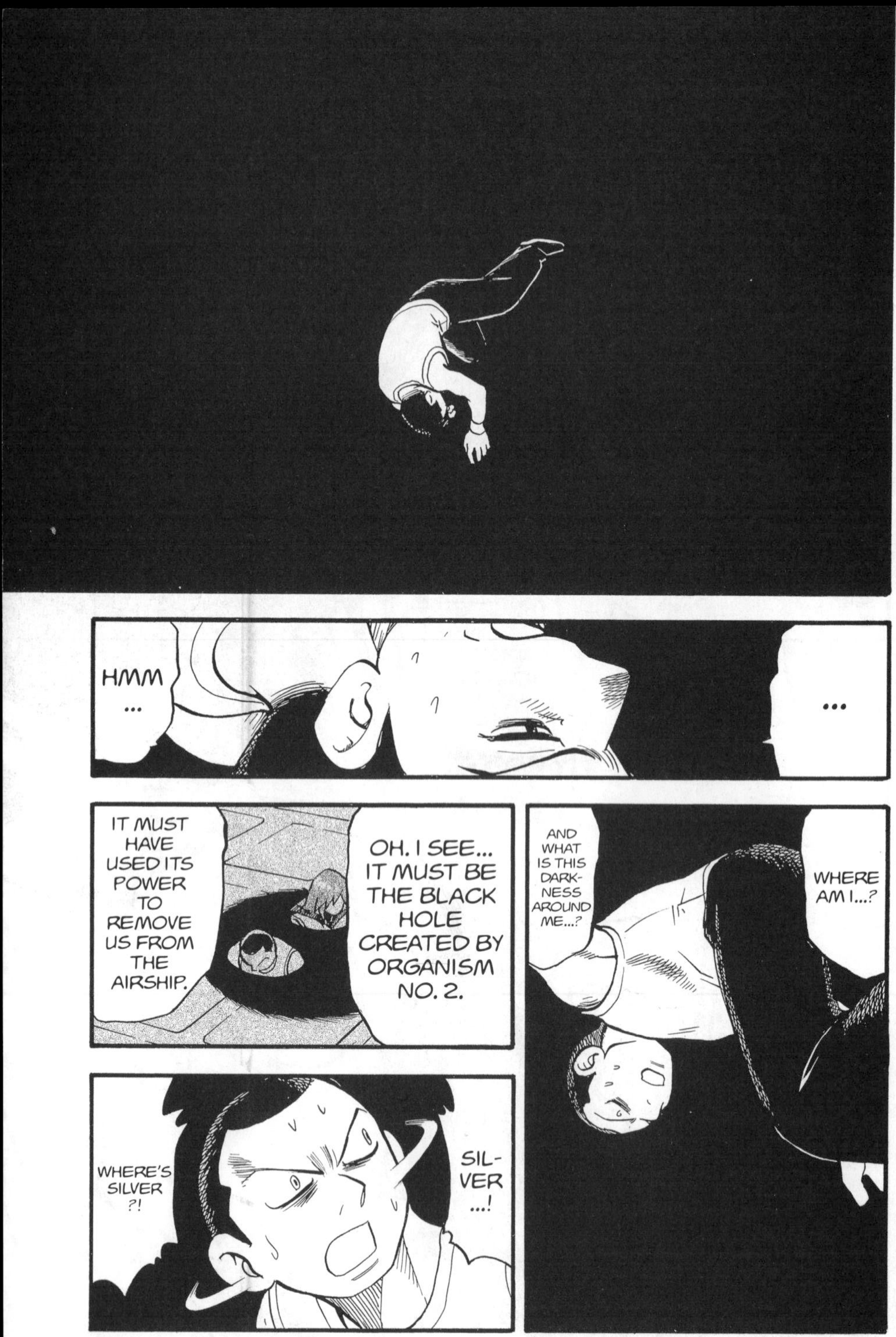
...
HMM ...
WHERE AM I...?
AND WHAT IS THIS DARKNESS AROUND ME...?
OH. I SEE... IT MUST BE THE BLACK HOLE CREATED BY ORGANISM NO. 2.
IT MUST HAVE USED ITS POWER TO REMOVE US FROM THE AIRSHIP.
SILVER ...!
WHERE'S SILVER ?!

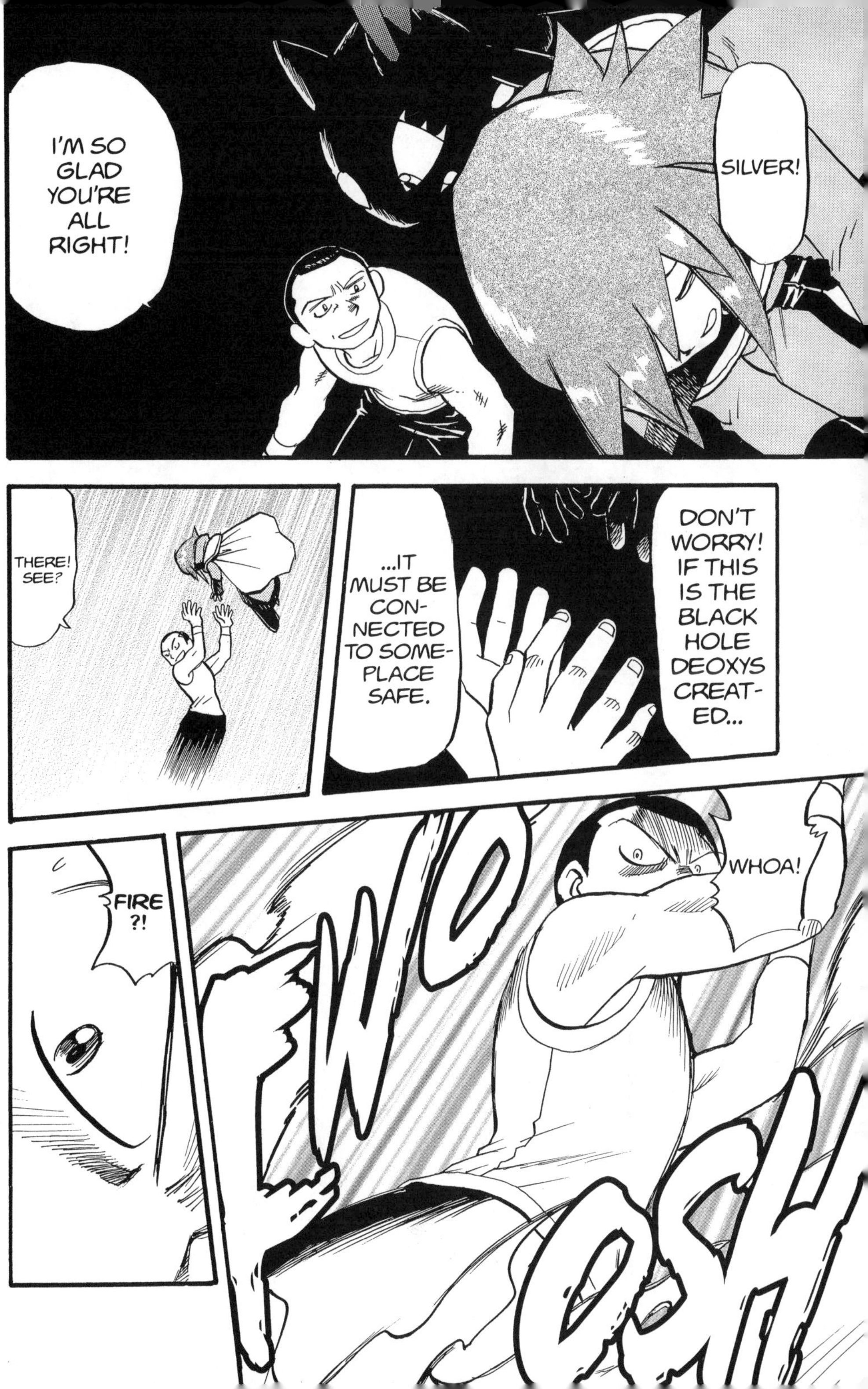
SILVER!
I'M SO GLAD YOU'RE ALL RIGHT!
DON'T WORRY! IF THIS IS THE BLACK HOLE DEOXYS CREAT-ED...
...IT MUST BE CON-NECTED TO SOME-PLACE SAFE.
THERE! SEE?
WHOA!
WOOSH
FIRE ?!

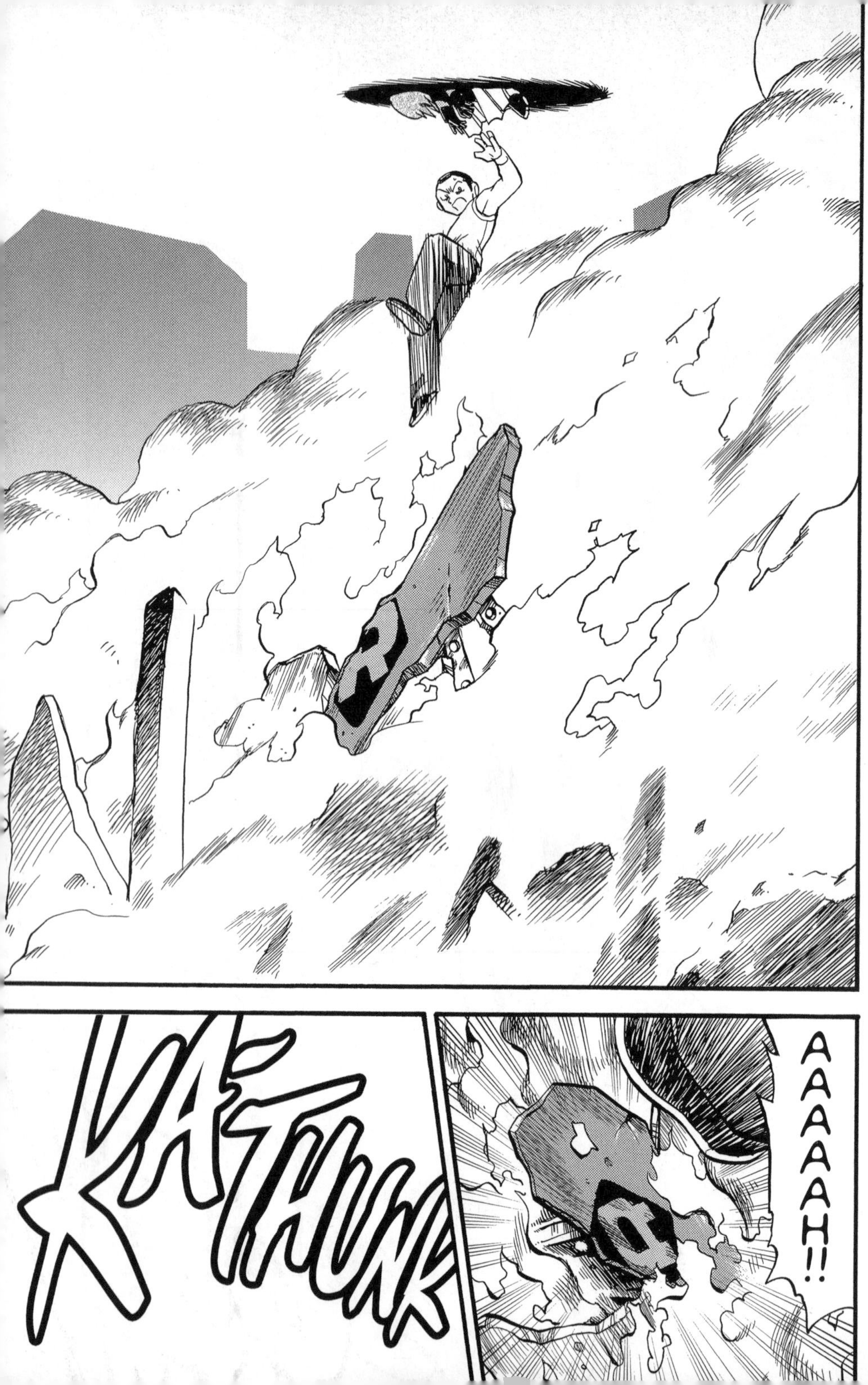
AAAAAH!!
KA-THUNK

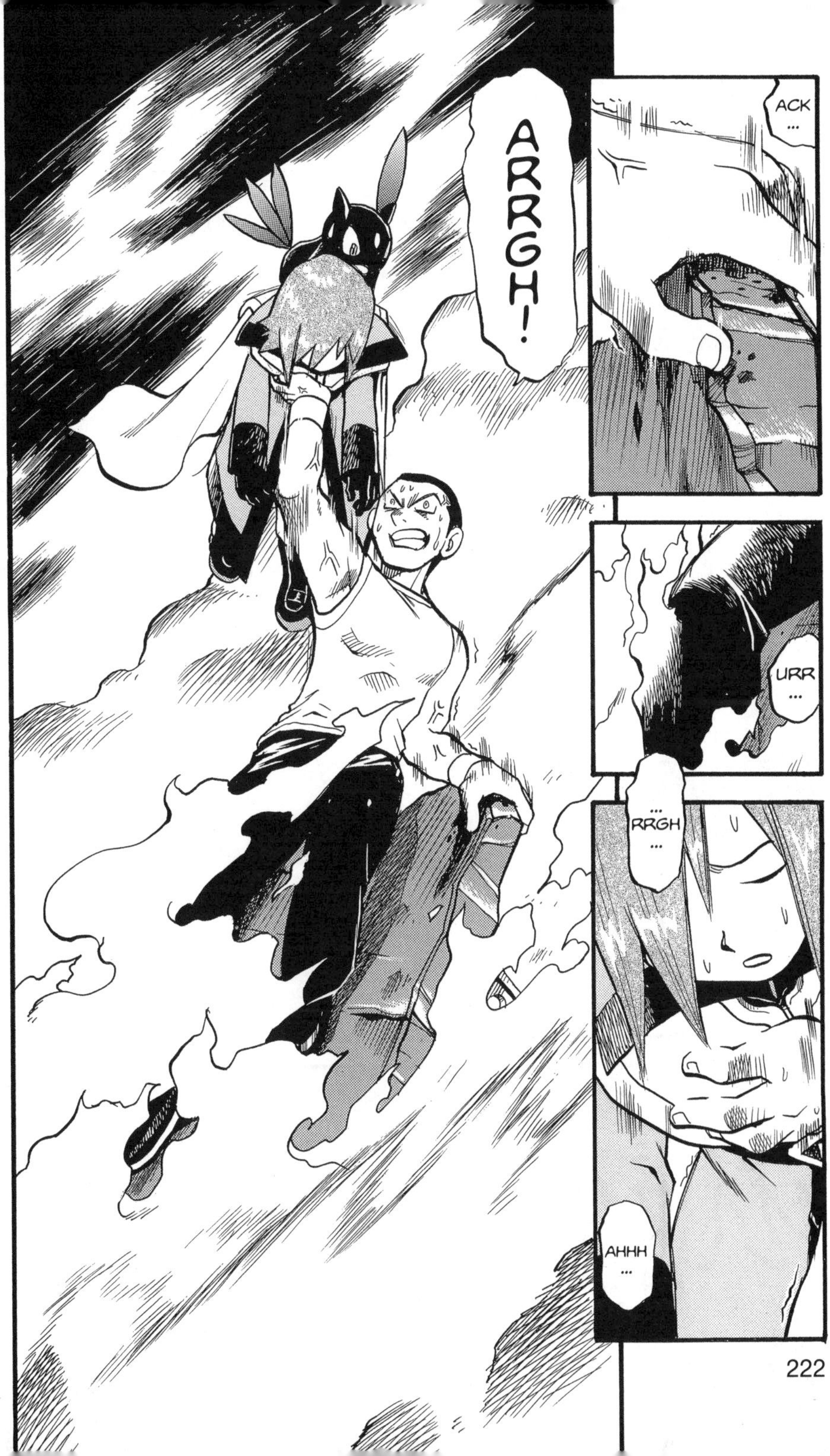
ACK...
URR...
...RRGH...
AHHH...
ARRGH!

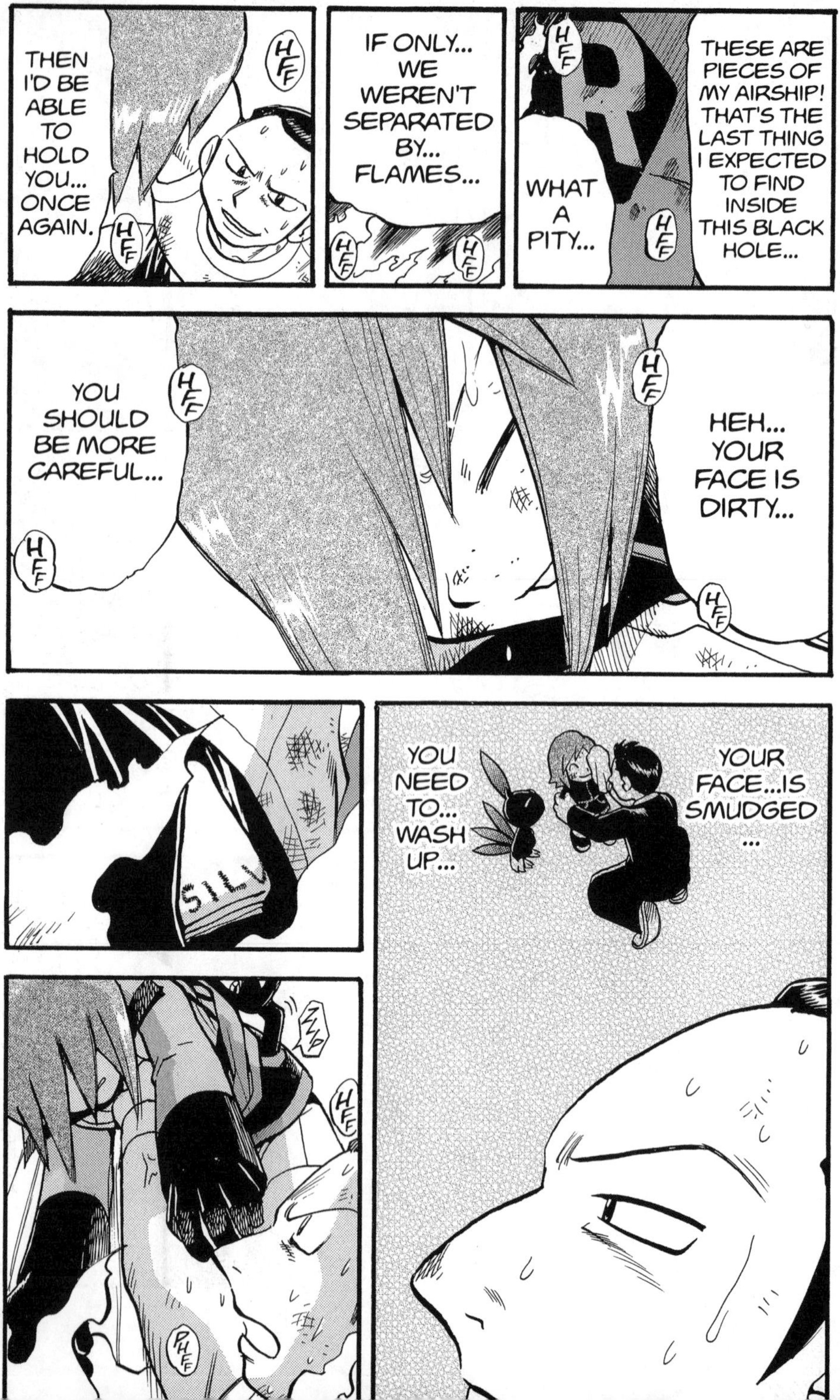
HFF
THESE ARE PIECES OF MY AIRSHIP! THAT'S THE LAST THING I EXPECTED TO FIND INSIDE THIS BLACK HOLE...
HFF
WHAT A PITY...
IF ONLY... WE WEREN'T SEPARATED BY... FLAMES...
HFF
HFF
HFF
THEN I'D BE ABLE TO HOLD YOU... ONCE AGAIN.
HFF
HFF
HEH... YOUR FACE IS DIRTY...
HFF
HFF
YOU SHOULD BE MORE CAREFUL...
HFF
YOUR FACE...IS SMUDGED ...
YOU NEED TO... WASH UP...
HFF
PHFF

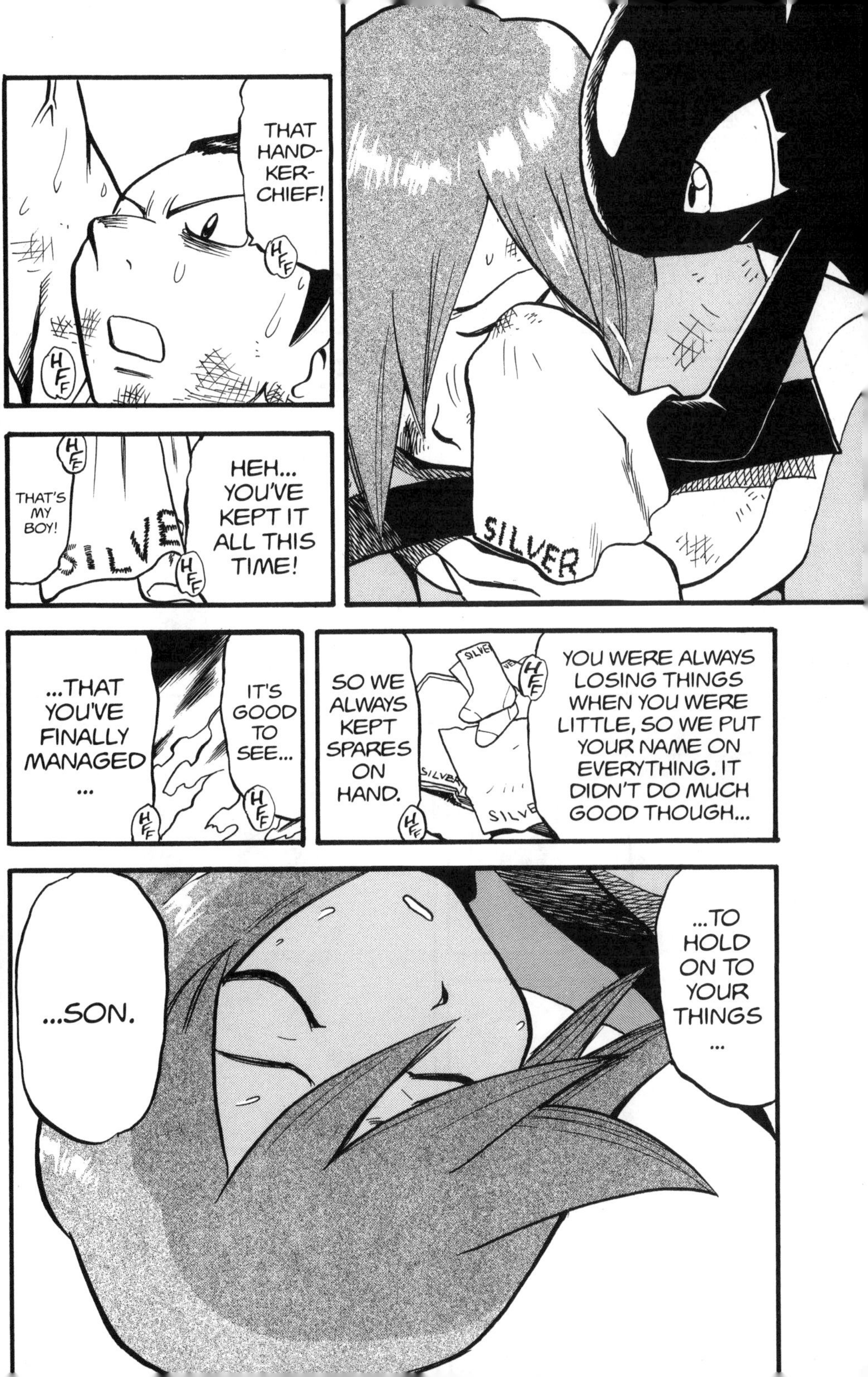
SILVER
THAT HAND-KER-CHIEF!
HFF
HFF
HEH... YOU'VE KEPT IT ALL THIS TIME!
SILVE
HFF
THAT'S MY BOY!
HFF
YOU WERE ALWAYS LOSING THINGS WHEN YOU WERE LITTLE, SO WE PUT YOUR NAME ON EVERYTHING. IT DIDN'T DO MUCH GOOD THOUGH...
HFF
SO WE ALWAYS KEPT SPARES ON HAND.
HFF
IT'S GOOD TO SEE...
HFF
...THAT YOU'VE FINALLY MANAGED ...
HFF
...TO HOLD ON TO YOUR THINGS ...
...SON.

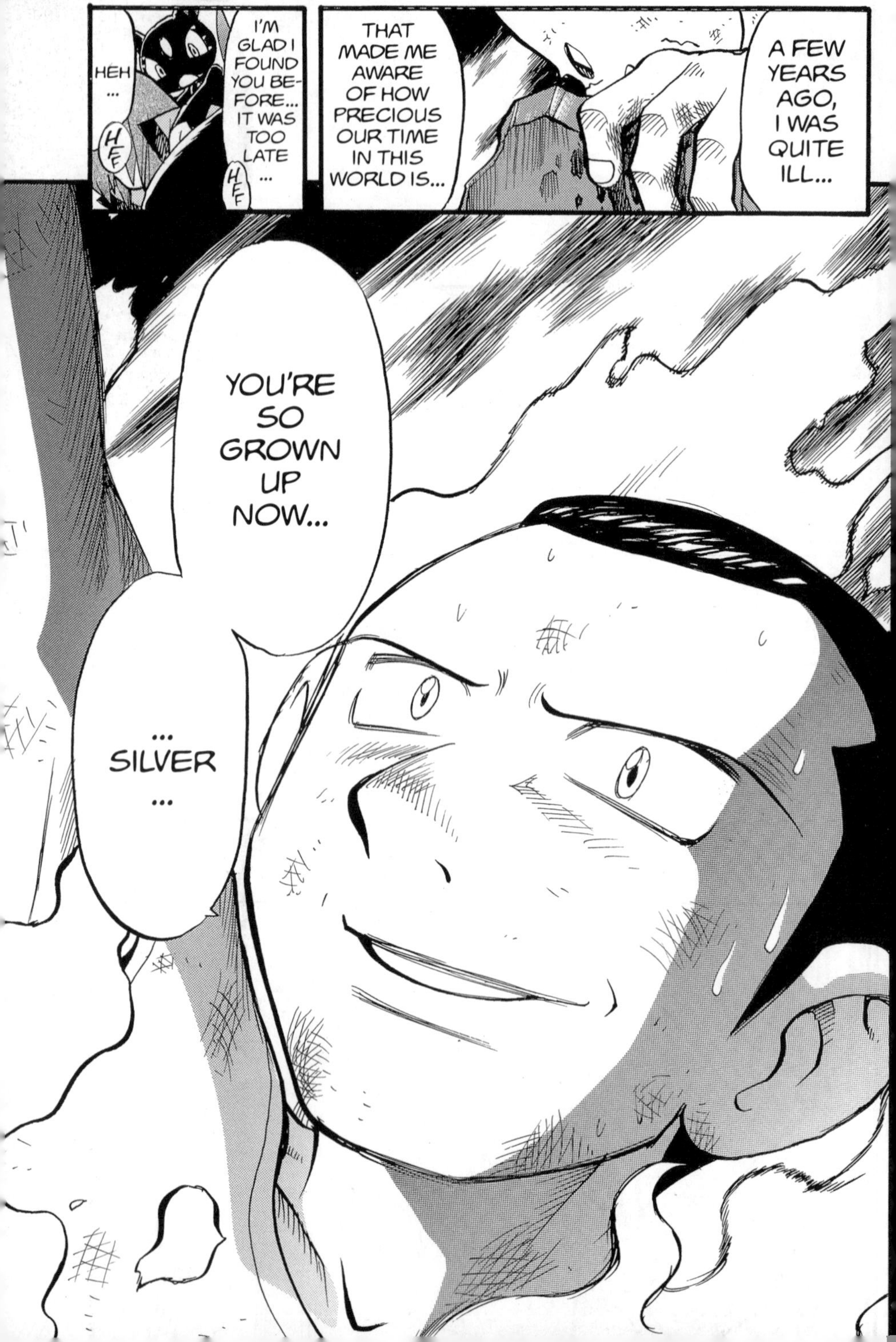
A FEW YEARS AGO, I WAS QUITE ILL...
THAT MADE ME AWARE OF HOW PRECIOUS OUR TIME IN THIS WORLD IS...
I'M GLAD I FOUND YOU BEFORE... IT WAS TOO LATE...
HFF
HEH...
HFF
YOU'RE SO GROWN UP NOW...
... SILVER ...

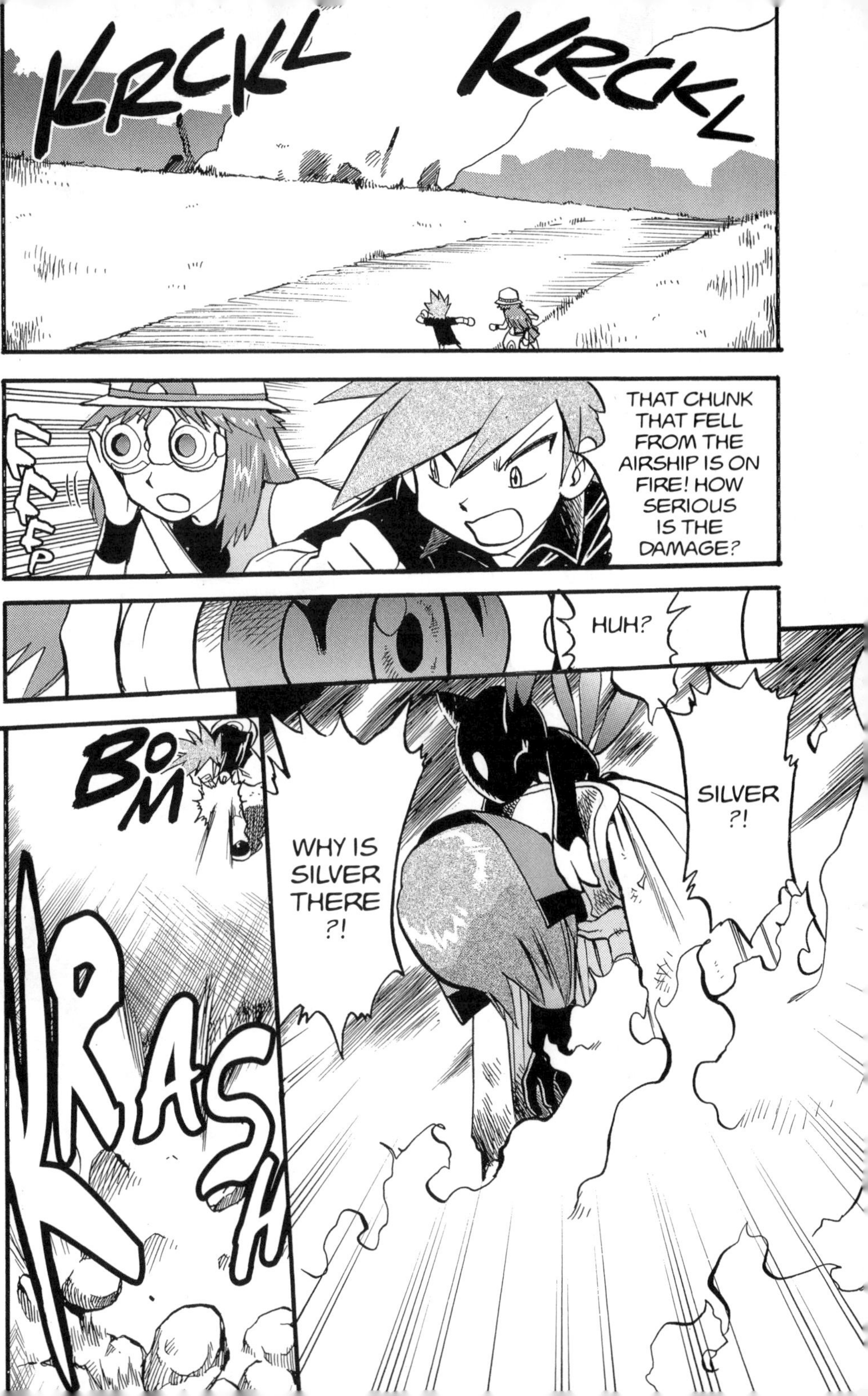
KRCKL
KRCKL
THAT CHUNK THAT FELL FROM THE AIRSHIP IS ON FIRE! HOW SERIOUS IS THE DAMAGE?
HUH?
SILVER ?!
WHY IS SILVER THERE ?!
KRASH

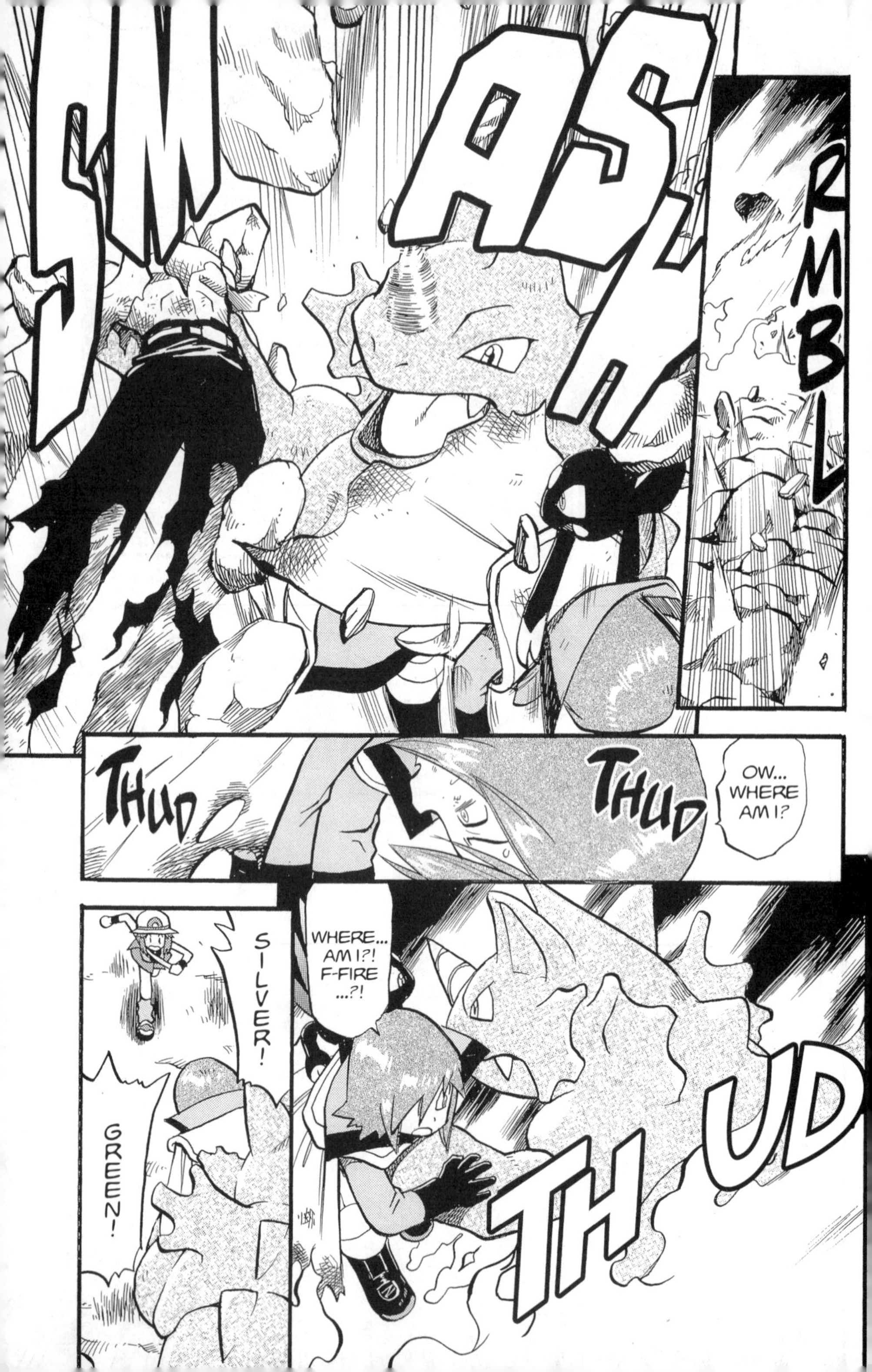
RMBL
SMASH
OW... WHERE AM I?
THUD
THUD
WHERE... AM I?! F-FIRE ...?!
THUD
SILVER!
GREEN!

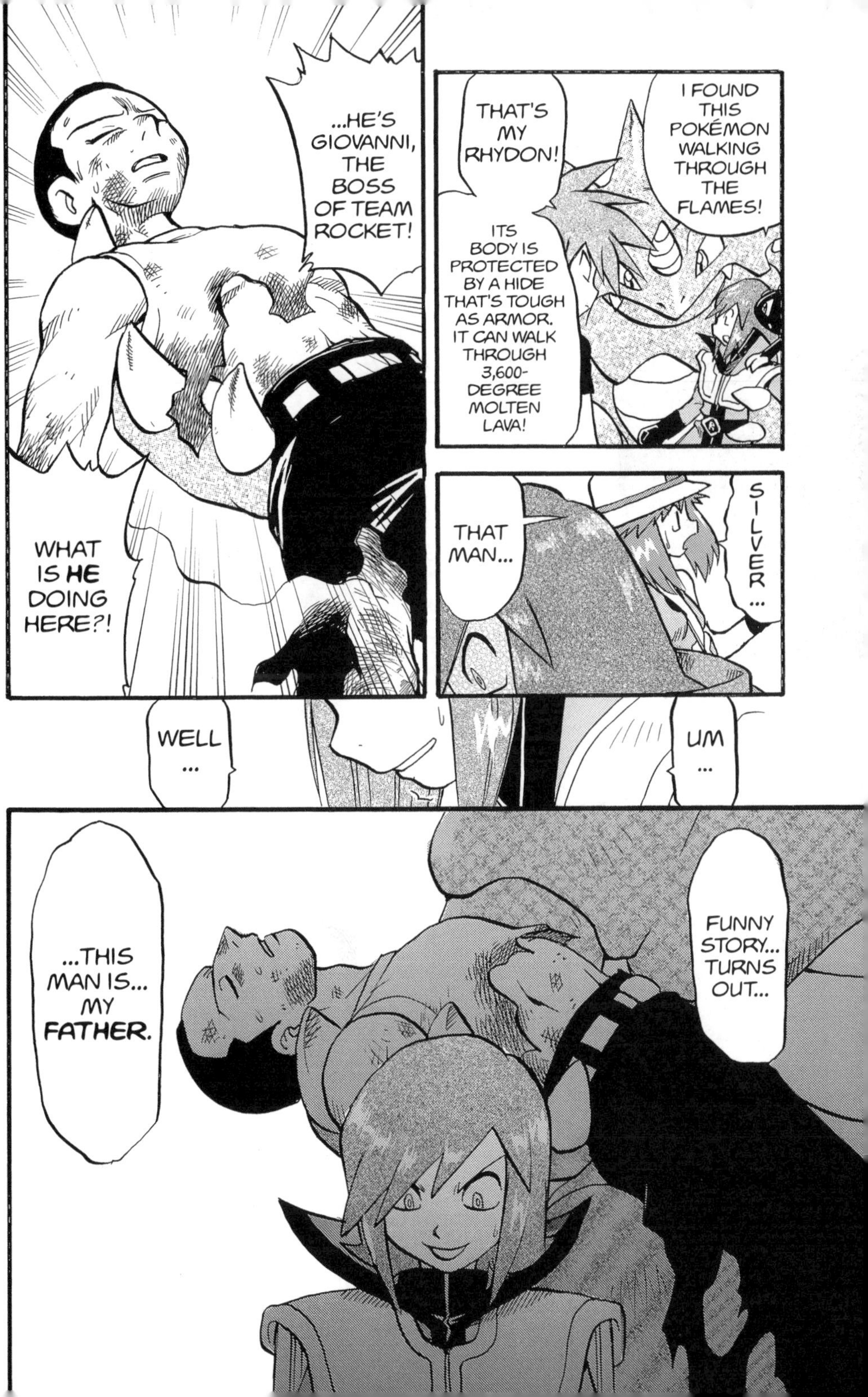
I FOUND THIS POKÉMON WALKING THROUGH THE FLAMES!
THAT'S MY RHYDON!
ITS BODY IS PROTECTED BY A HIDE THAT'S TOUGH AS ARMOR. IT CAN WALK THROUGH 3,600-DEGREE MOLTEN LAVA!
SILVER...
THAT MAN...
...HE'S GIOVANNI, THE BOSS OF TEAM ROCKET!
WHAT IS **HE** DOING HERE?!
UM...
WELL...
FUNNY STORY... TURNS OUT...
...THIS MAN IS... MY **FATHER.**

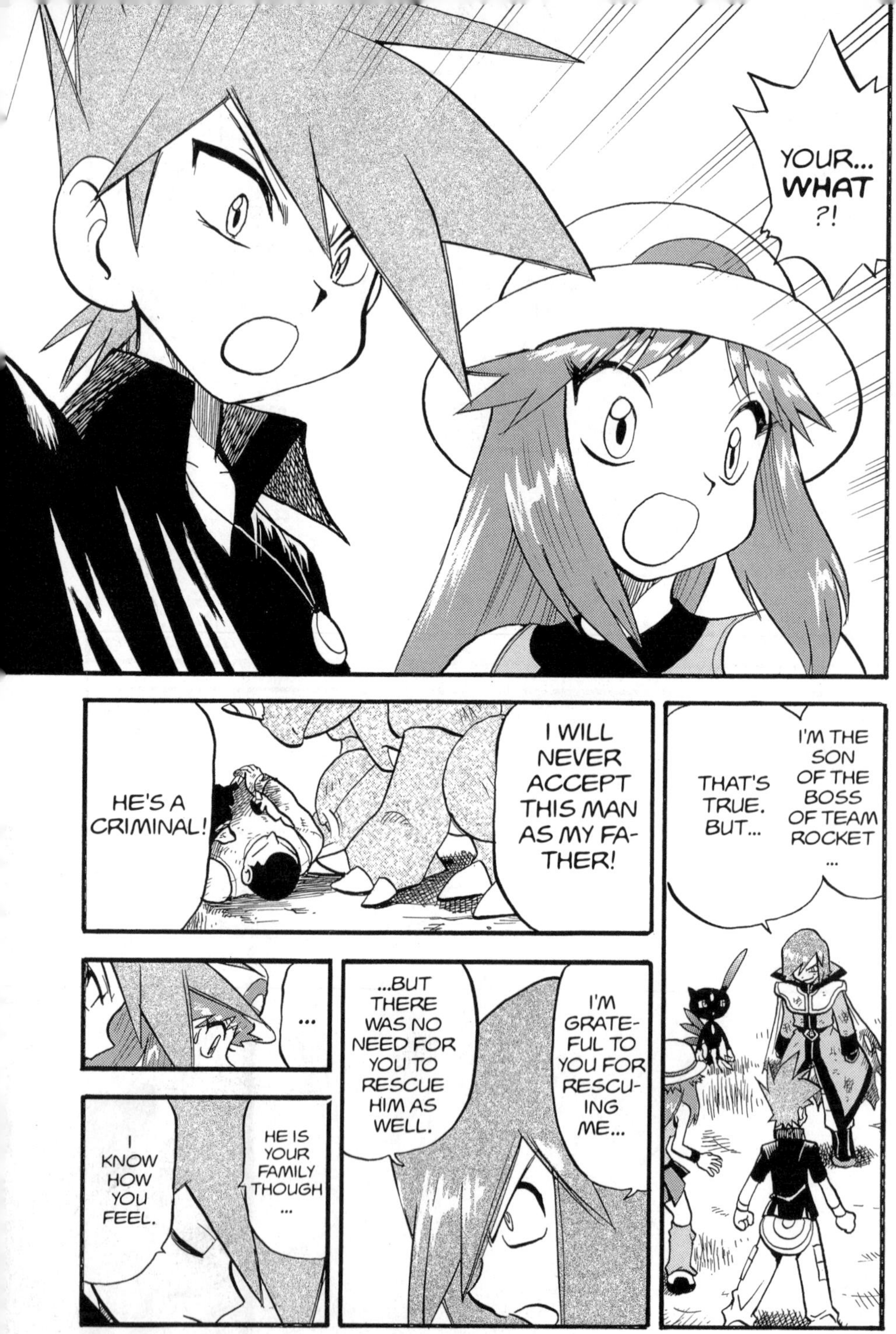

YOUR... WHAT ?!
I'M THE SON OF THE BOSS OF TEAM ROCKET ...
THAT'S TRUE. BUT...
I WILL NEVER ACCEPT THIS MAN AS MY FA-THER!
HE'S A CRIMINAL!
I'M GRATE-FUL TO YOU FOR RESCU-ING ME...
...BUT THERE WAS NO NEED FOR YOU TO RESCUE HIM AS WELL.
...
HE IS YOUR FAMILY THOUGH ...
I KNOW HOW YOU FEEL.

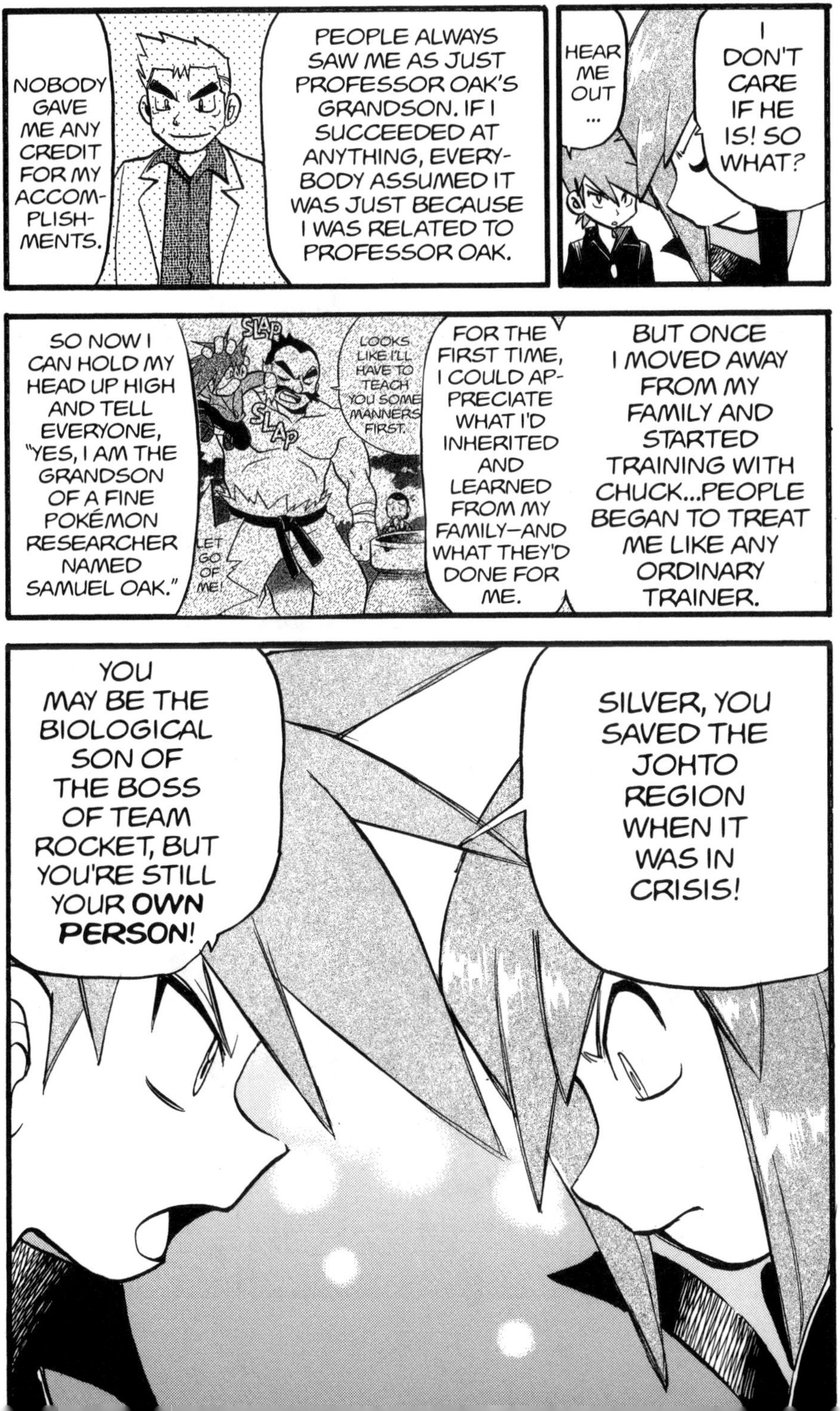
I DON'T CARE IF HE IS! SO WHAT?
HEAR ME OUT...
PEOPLE ALWAYS SAW ME AS JUST PROFESSOR OAK'S GRANDSON. IF I SUCCEEDED AT ANYTHING, EVERYBODY ASSUMED IT WAS JUST BECAUSE I WAS RELATED TO PROFESSOR OAK.
NOBODY GAVE ME ANY CREDIT FOR MY ACCOMPLISHMENTS.
BUT ONCE I MOVED AWAY FROM MY FAMILY AND STARTED TRAINING WITH CHUCK...PEOPLE BEGAN TO TREAT ME LIKE ANY ORDINARY TRAINER.
FOR THE FIRST TIME, I COULD APPRECIATE WHAT I'D INHERITED AND LEARNED FROM MY FAMILY—AND WHAT THEY'D DONE FOR ME.
LOOKS LIKE I'LL HAVE TO TEACH YOU SOME MANNERS FIRST.
SLAP
SLAP
LET GO OF ME!
SO NOW I CAN HOLD MY HEAD UP HIGH AND TELL EVERYONE, "YES, I AM THE GRANDSON OF A FINE POKÉMON RESEARCHER NAMED SAMUEL OAK."
SILVER, YOU SAVED THE JOHTO REGION WHEN IT WAS IN CRISIS!
YOU MAY BE THE BIOLOGICAL SON OF THE BOSS OF TEAM ROCKET, BUT YOU'RE STILL YOUR **OWN PERSON**!

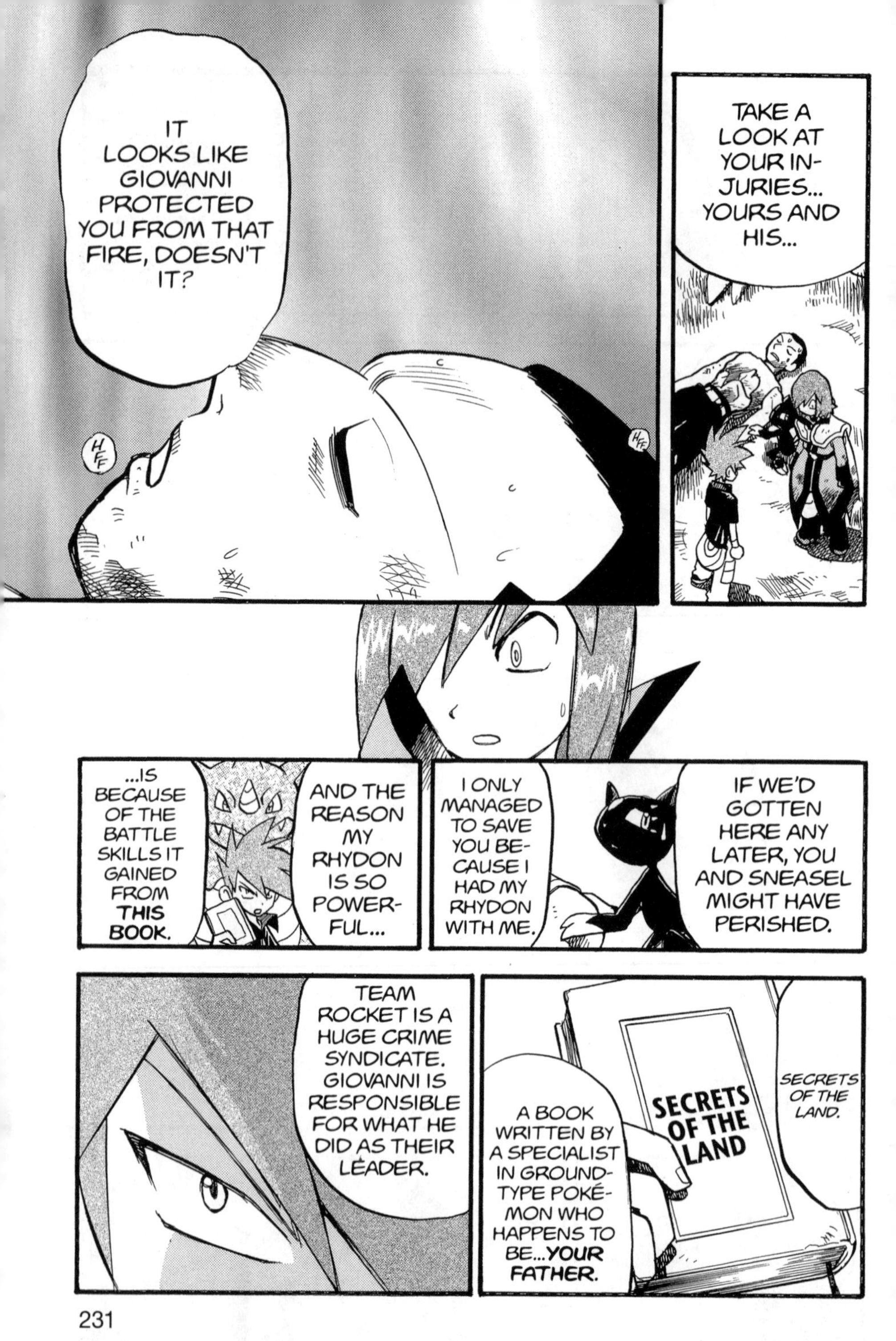
TAKE A LOOK AT YOUR INJURIES... YOURS AND HIS...
IT LOOKS LIKE GIOVANNI PROTECTED YOU FROM THAT FIRE, DOESN'T IT?
HFF
HFF
IF WE'D GOTTEN HERE ANY LATER, YOU AND SNEASEL MIGHT HAVE PERISHED.
I ONLY MANAGED TO SAVE YOU BECAUSE I HAD MY RHYDON WITH ME.
AND THE REASON MY RHYDON IS SO POWERFUL...
...IS BECAUSE OF THE BATTLE SKILLS IT GAINED FROM **THIS BOOK**.
SECRETS OF THE LAND.
SECRETS OF THE LAND
A BOOK WRITTEN BY A SPECIALIST IN GROUND-TYPE POKÉMON WHO HAPPENS TO BE... **YOUR FATHER**.
TEAM ROCKET IS A HUGE CRIME SYNDICATE. GIOVANNI IS RESPONSIBLE FOR WHAT HE DID AS THEIR LEADER.

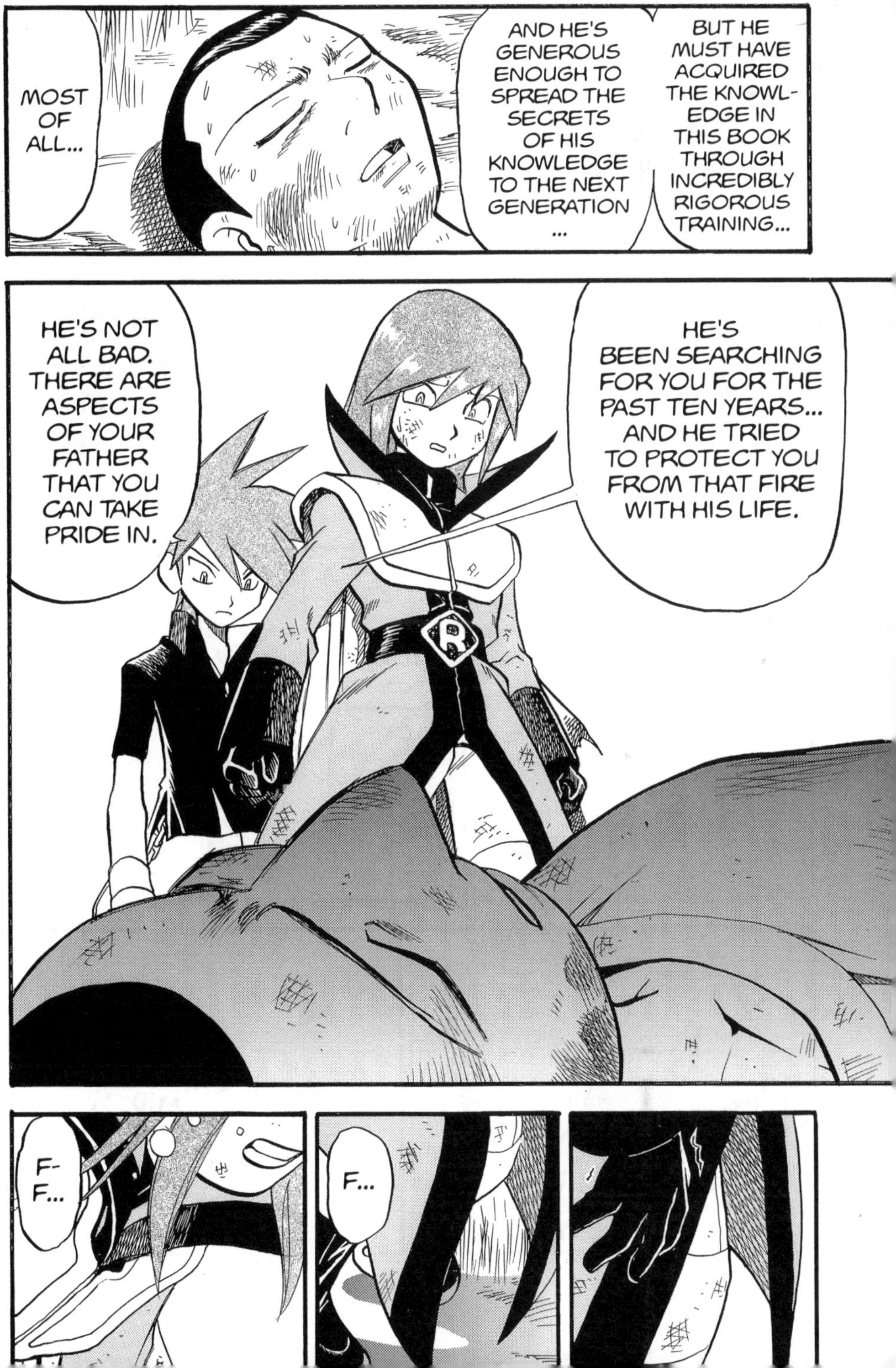
BUT HE MUST HAVE ACQUIRED THE KNOWLEDGE IN THIS BOOK THROUGH INCREDIBLY RIGOROUS TRAINING...
AND HE'S GENEROUS ENOUGH TO SPREAD THE SECRETS OF HIS KNOWLEDGE TO THE NEXT GENERATION ...
MOST OF ALL...
HE'S BEEN SEARCHING FOR YOU FOR THE PAST TEN YEARS... AND HE TRIED TO PROTECT YOU FROM THAT FIRE WITH HIS LIFE.
HE'S NOT ALL BAD. THERE ARE ASPECTS OF YOUR FATHER THAT YOU CAN TAKE PRIDE IN.
F...
F- F...

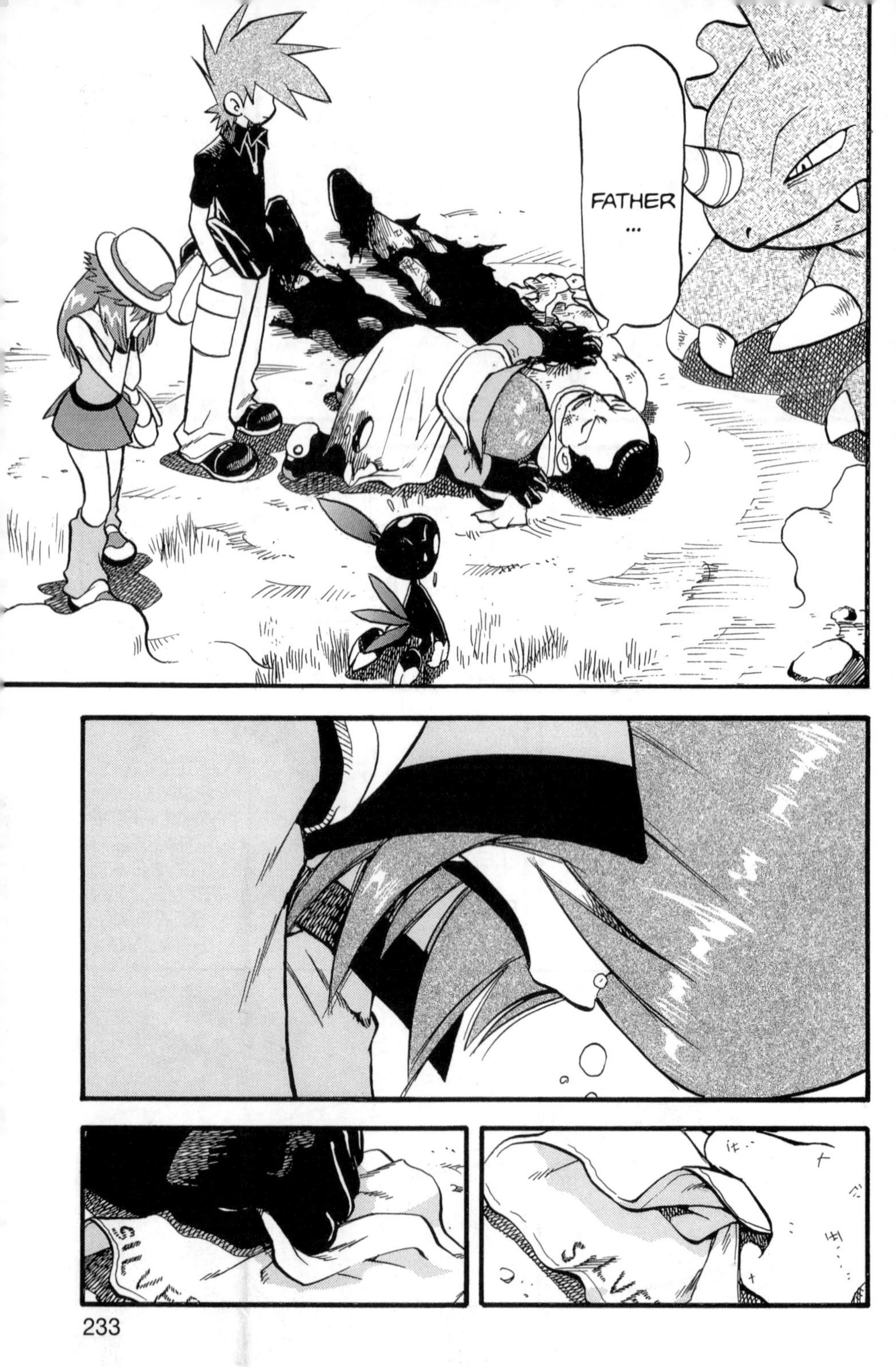
FATHER
...

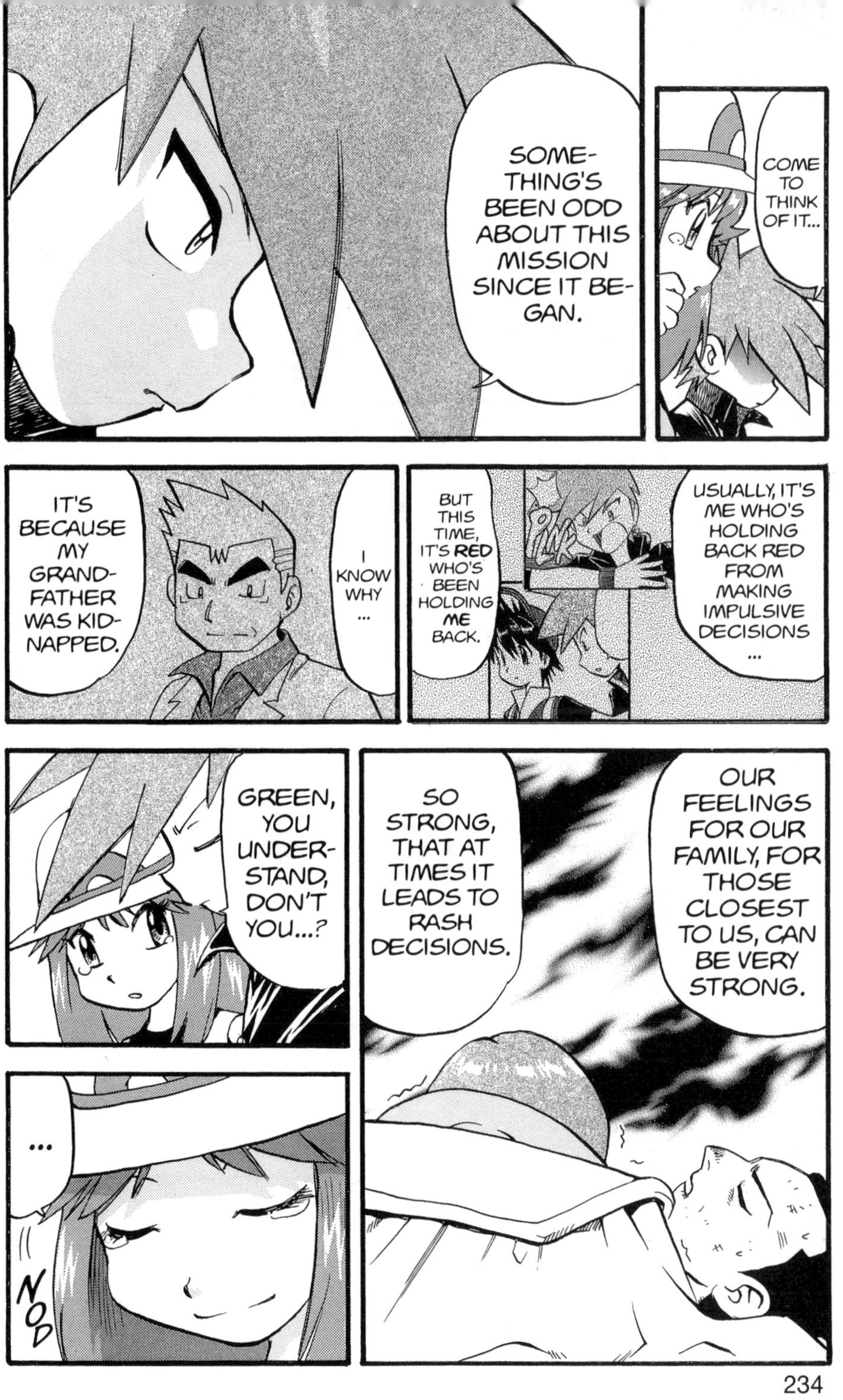
COME TO THINK OF IT...
SOMETHING'S BEEN ODD ABOUT THIS MISSION SINCE IT BEGAN.
USUALLY, IT'S ME WHO'S HOLDING BACK RED FROM MAKING IMPULSIVE DECISIONS...
BUT THIS TIME, IT'S RED WHO'S BEEN HOLDING ME BACK.
I KNOW WHY...
IT'S BECAUSE MY GRANDFATHER WAS KIDNAPPED.
OUR FEELINGS FOR OUR FAMILY, FOR THOSE CLOSEST TO US, CAN BE VERY STRONG.
SO STRONG, THAT AT TIMES IT LEADS TO RASH DECISIONS.
GREEN, YOU UNDERSTAND, DON'T YOU...?
...
NOD

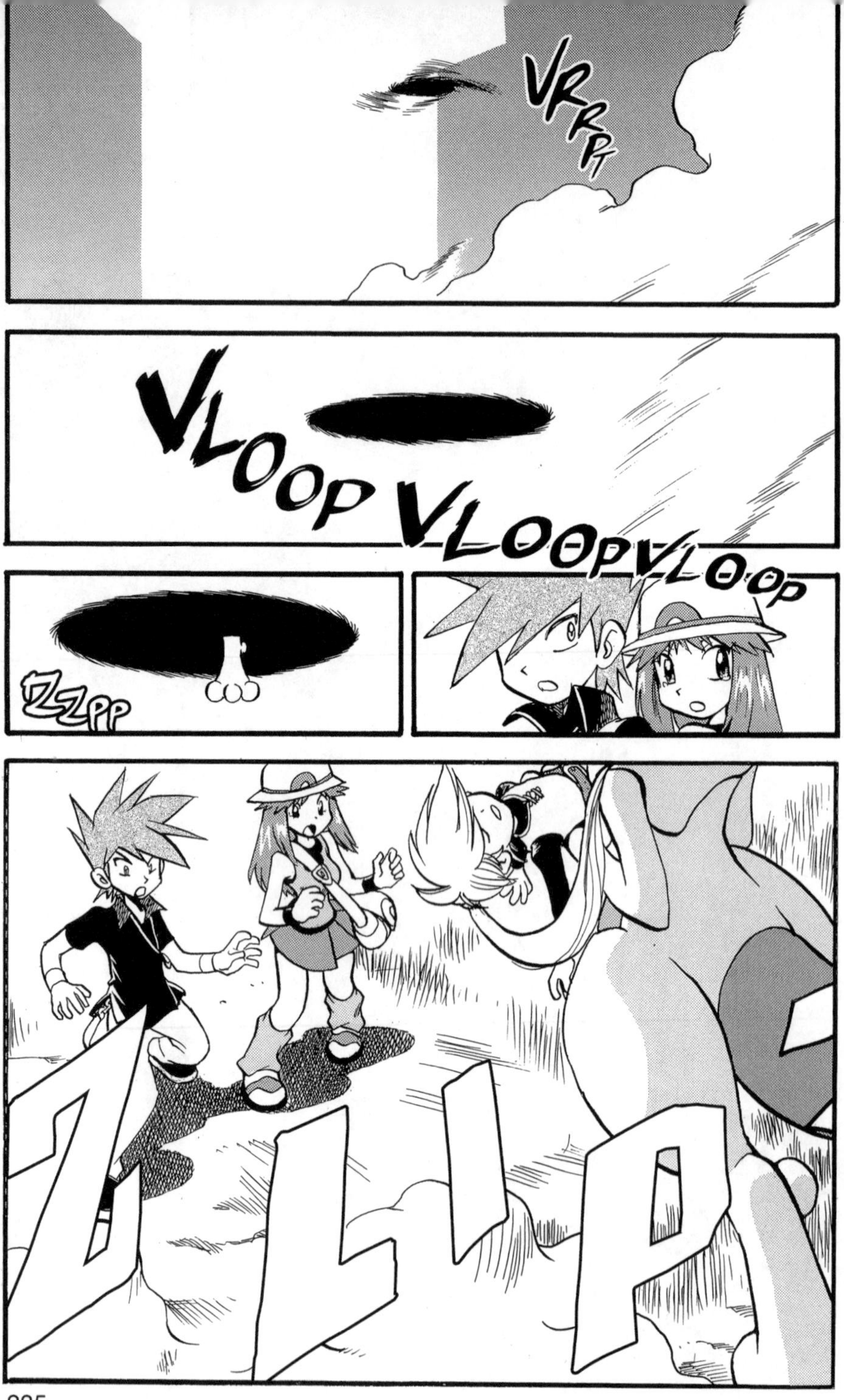
VRRPT
VLOOP VLOOP VLOOP
ZZPP
ZLIP

● Adventure 301 ●
Storming the Forretress

Pokémon™ Adventures
FireRed & LeafGreen
The Fifth Chapter

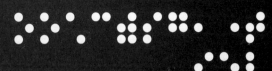

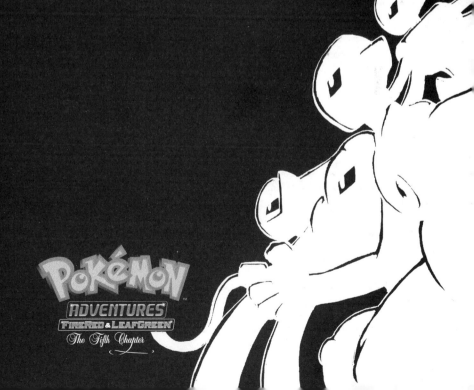

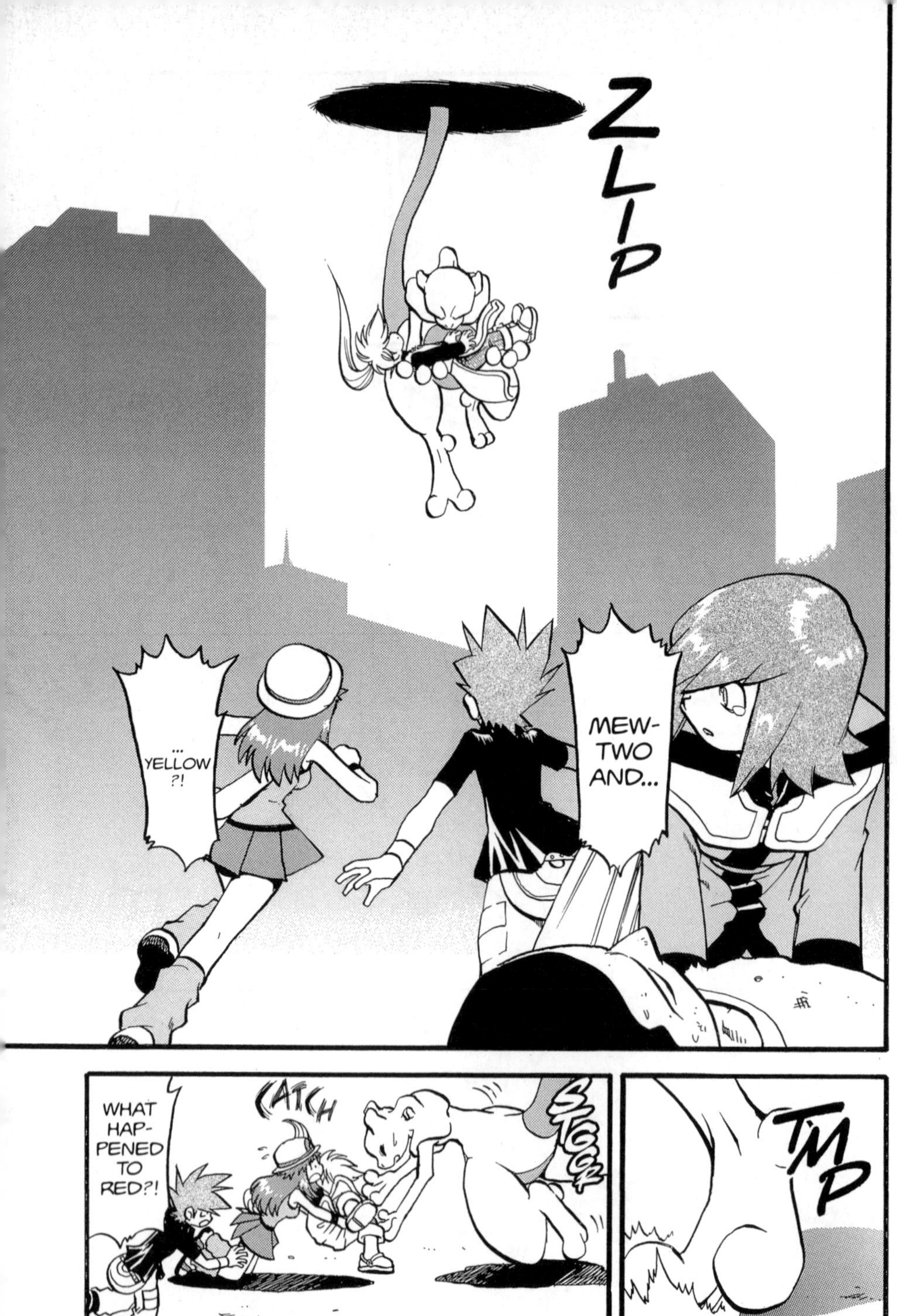
ZLIP
MEW-TWO AND...
...YELLOW?!
TMP
STGGR
CATCH
WHAT HAPPENED TO RED?!

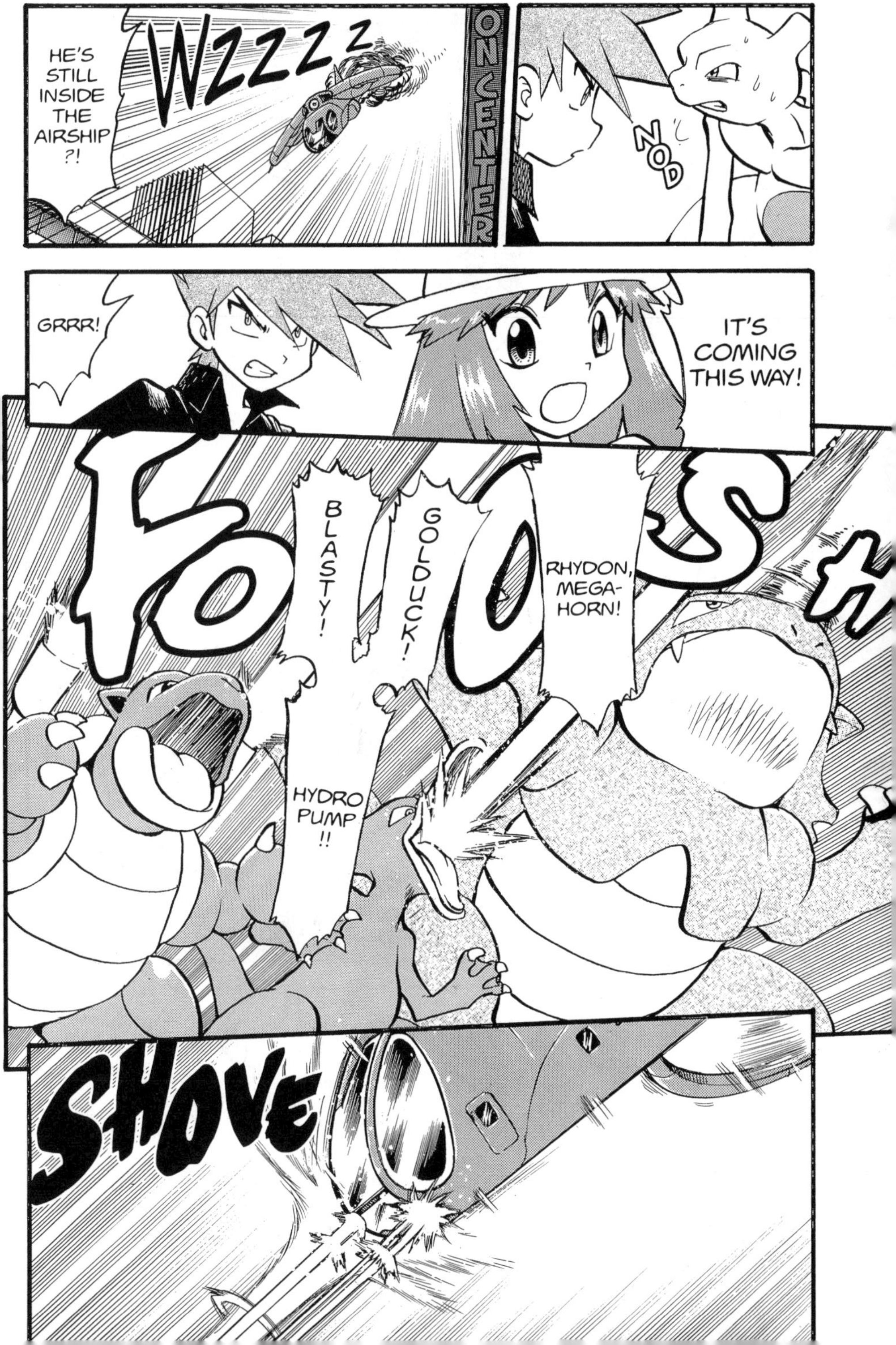
NOD
WZZZZ
HE'S STILL INSIDE THE AIRSHIP ?!
IT'S COMING THIS WAY!
GRRR!
RHYDON, MEGA-HORN!
GOLDUCK!
BLASTY!
HYDRO PUMP !!
SHOVE

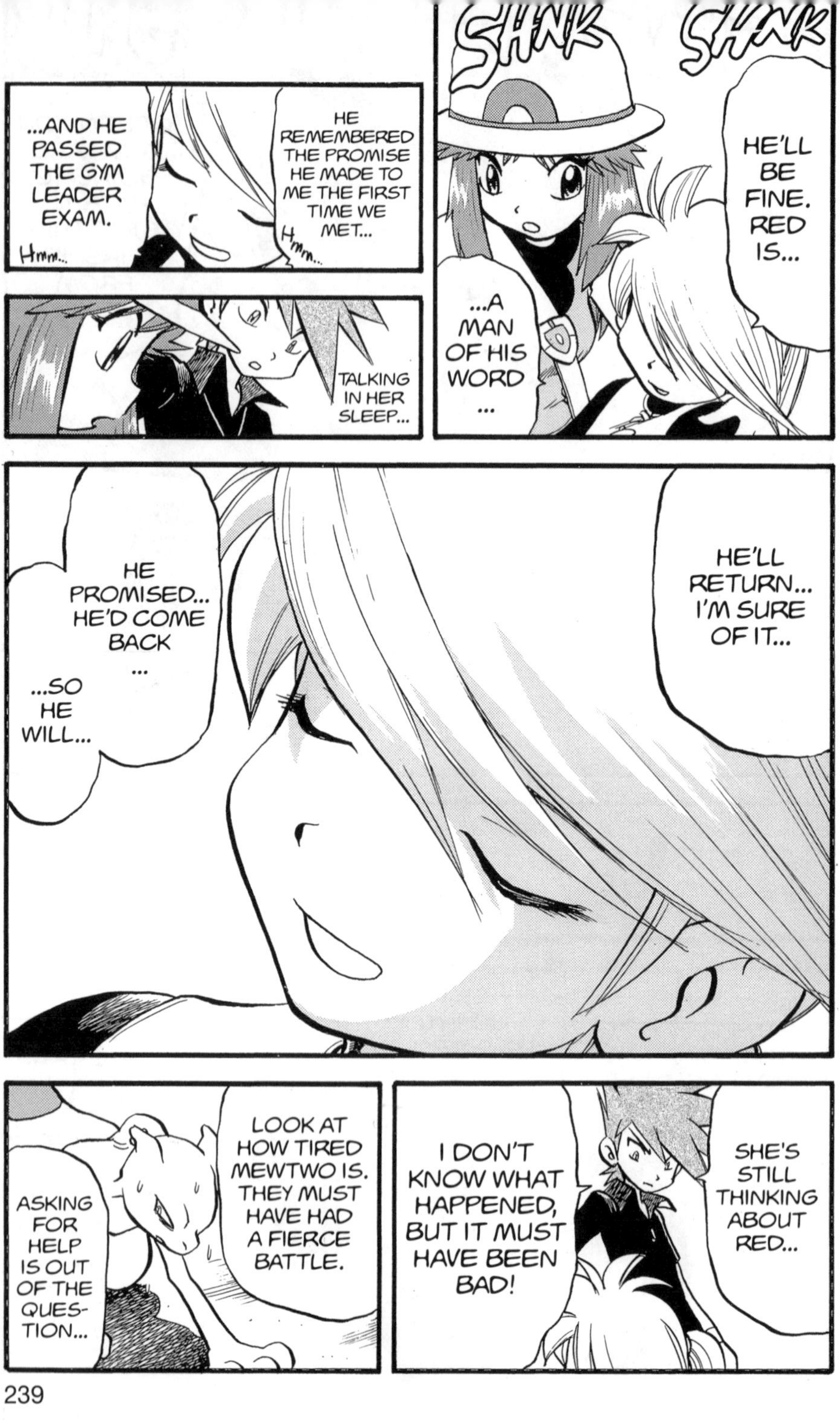
SHNK
SHNK
HE'LL BE FINE. RED IS...
...A MAN OF HIS WORD ...
HE REMEMBERED THE PROMISE HE MADE TO ME THE FIRST TIME WE MET...
Hmm...
...AND HE PASSED THE GYM LEADER EXAM.
Hmm...
TALKING IN HER SLEEP...
HE'LL RETURN... I'M SURE OF IT...
HE PROMISED... HE'D COME BACK ...
...SO HE WILL...
SHE'S STILL THINKING ABOUT RED...
I DON'T KNOW WHAT HAPPENED, BUT IT MUST HAVE BEEN BAD!
LOOK AT HOW TIRED MEWTWO IS. THEY MUST HAVE HAD A FIERCE BATTLE.
ASKING FOR HELP IS OUT OF THE QUES-TION...

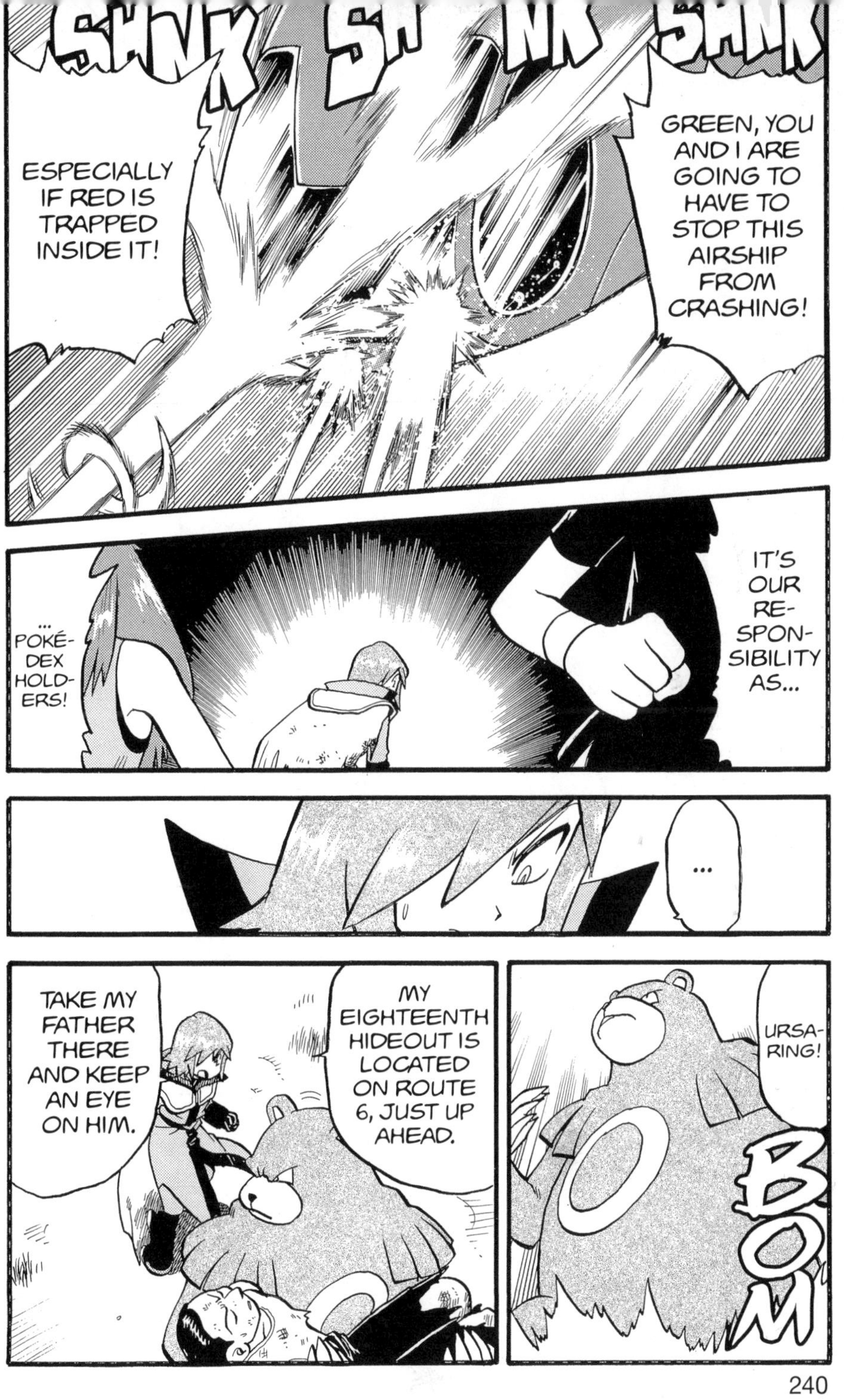
SHNK
SH NK
SHNK
GREEN, YOU AND I ARE GOING TO HAVE TO STOP THIS AIRSHIP FROM CRASHING!
ESPECIALLY IF RED IS TRAPPED INSIDE IT!
IT'S OUR RE-SPON-SIBILITY AS...
...POKÉ-DEX HOLD-ERS!
...
URSA-RING!
BOOM
MY EIGHTEENTH HIDEOUT IS LOCATED ON ROUTE 6, JUST UP AHEAD.
TAKE MY FATHER THERE AND KEEP AN EYE ON HIM.

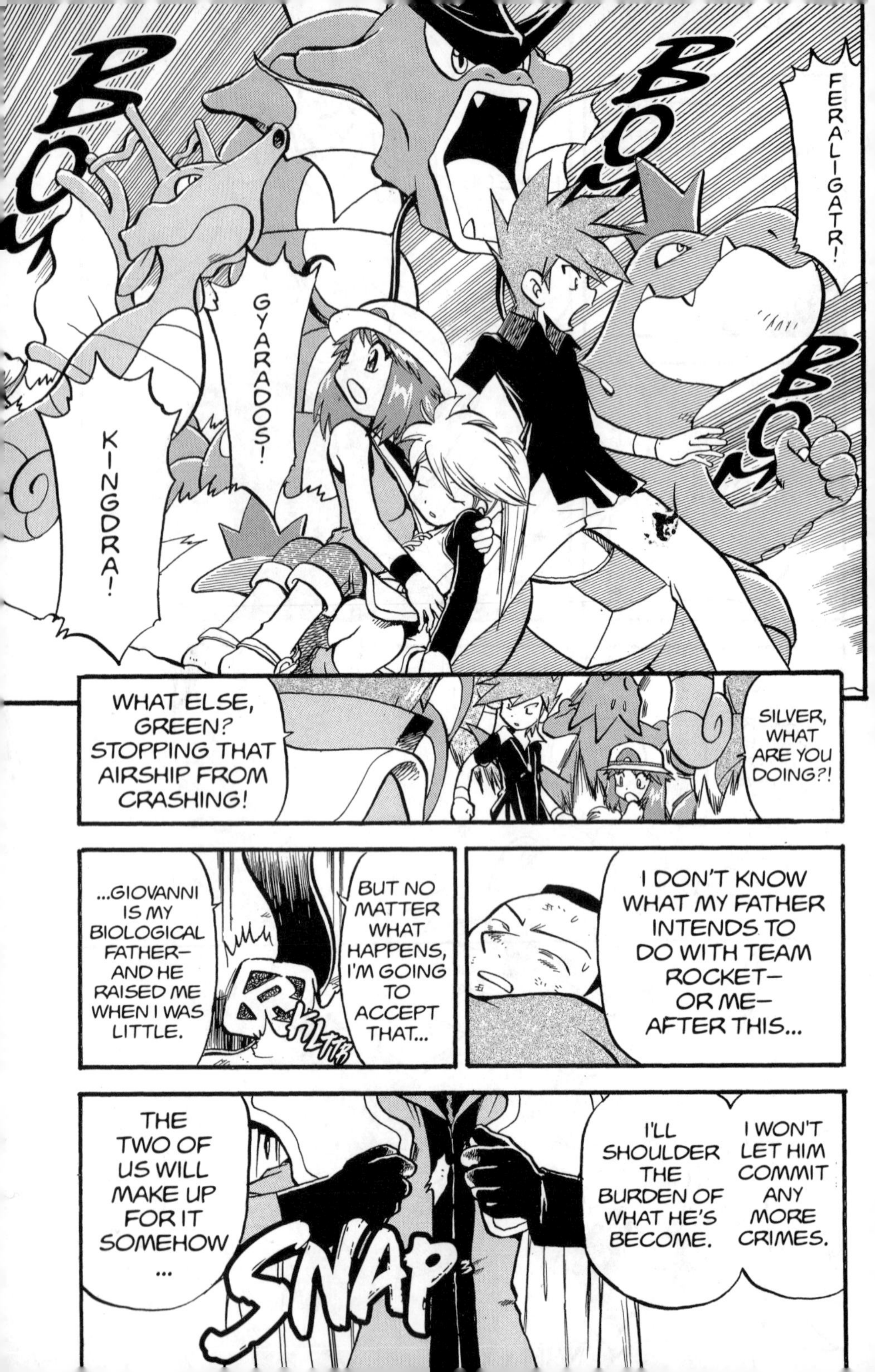
FERALIGATR!
BOOM
BOOM
GYARADOS!
BOOM
KINGDRA!
SILVER, WHAT ARE YOU DOING?!
WHAT ELSE, GREEN? STOPPING THAT AIRSHIP FROM CRASHING!
I DON'T KNOW WHAT MY FATHER INTENDS TO DO WITH TEAM ROCKET— OR ME— AFTER THIS...
BUT NO MATTER WHAT HAPPENS, I'M GOING TO ACCEPT THAT...
...GIOVANNI IS MY BIOLOGICAL FATHER— AND HE RAISED ME WHEN I WAS LITTLE.
KRKLTTR
I WON'T LET HIM COMMIT ANY MORE CRIMES.
I'LL SHOULDER THE BURDEN OF WHAT HE'S BECOME.
THE TWO OF US WILL MAKE UP FOR IT SOMEHOW ...
SNAP

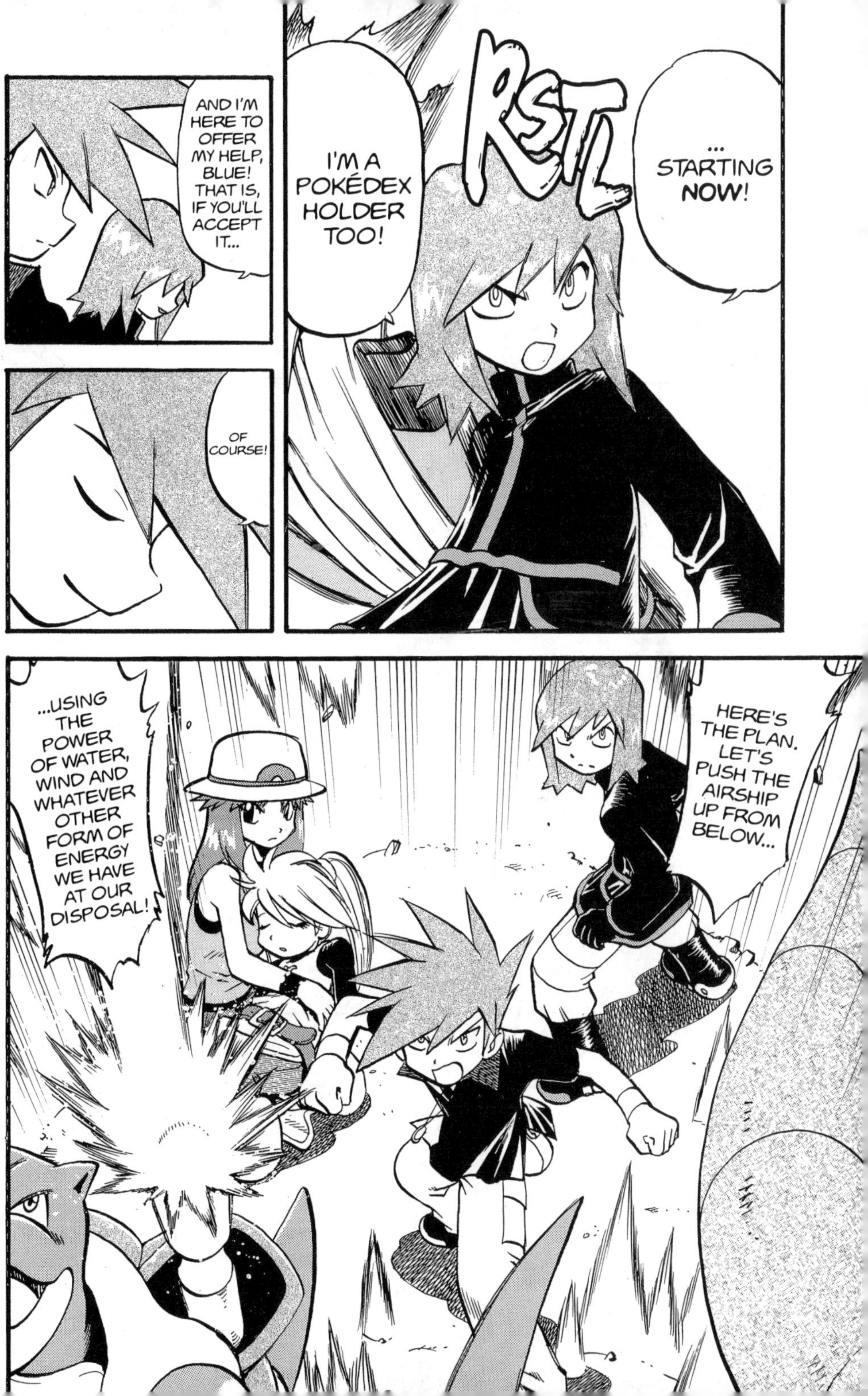
... STARTING NOW!
RSTL
I'M A POKÉDEX HOLDER TOO!
AND I'M HERE TO OFFER MY HELP, BLUE! THAT IS, IF YOU'LL ACCEPT IT...
OF COURSE!
HERE'S THE PLAN. LET'S PUSH THE AIRSHIP UP FROM BELOW...
...USING THE POWER OF WATER, WIND AND WHATEVER OTHER FORM OF ENERGY WE HAVE AT OUR DISPOSAL!

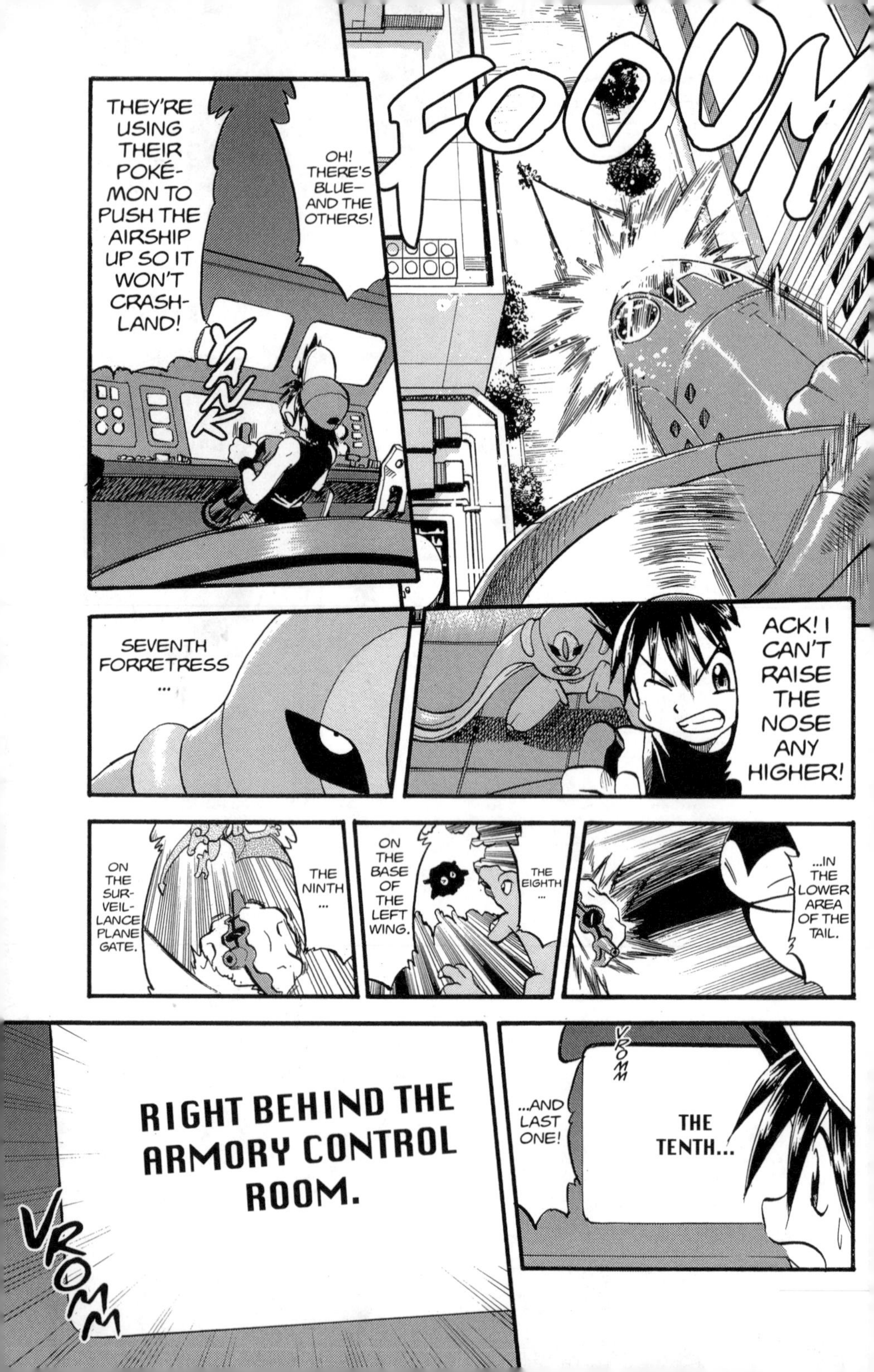
FOOOM
OH! THERE'S BLUE— AND THE OTHERS!
THEY'RE USING THEIR POKÉ-MON TO PUSH THE AIRSHIP UP SO IT WON'T CRASH-LAND!
YANK
ACK! I CAN'T RAISE THE NOSE ANY HIGHER!
SEVENTH FORRETRESS ...
...IN THE LOWER AREA OF THE TAIL.
THE EIGHTH ...
ON THE BASE OF THE LEFT WING.
THE NINTH ...
ON THE SUR-VEIL-LANCE PLANE GATE.
VROMM
THE TENTH...
...AND LAST ONE!
RIGHT BEHIND THE ARMORY CONTROL ROOM.
VROMM

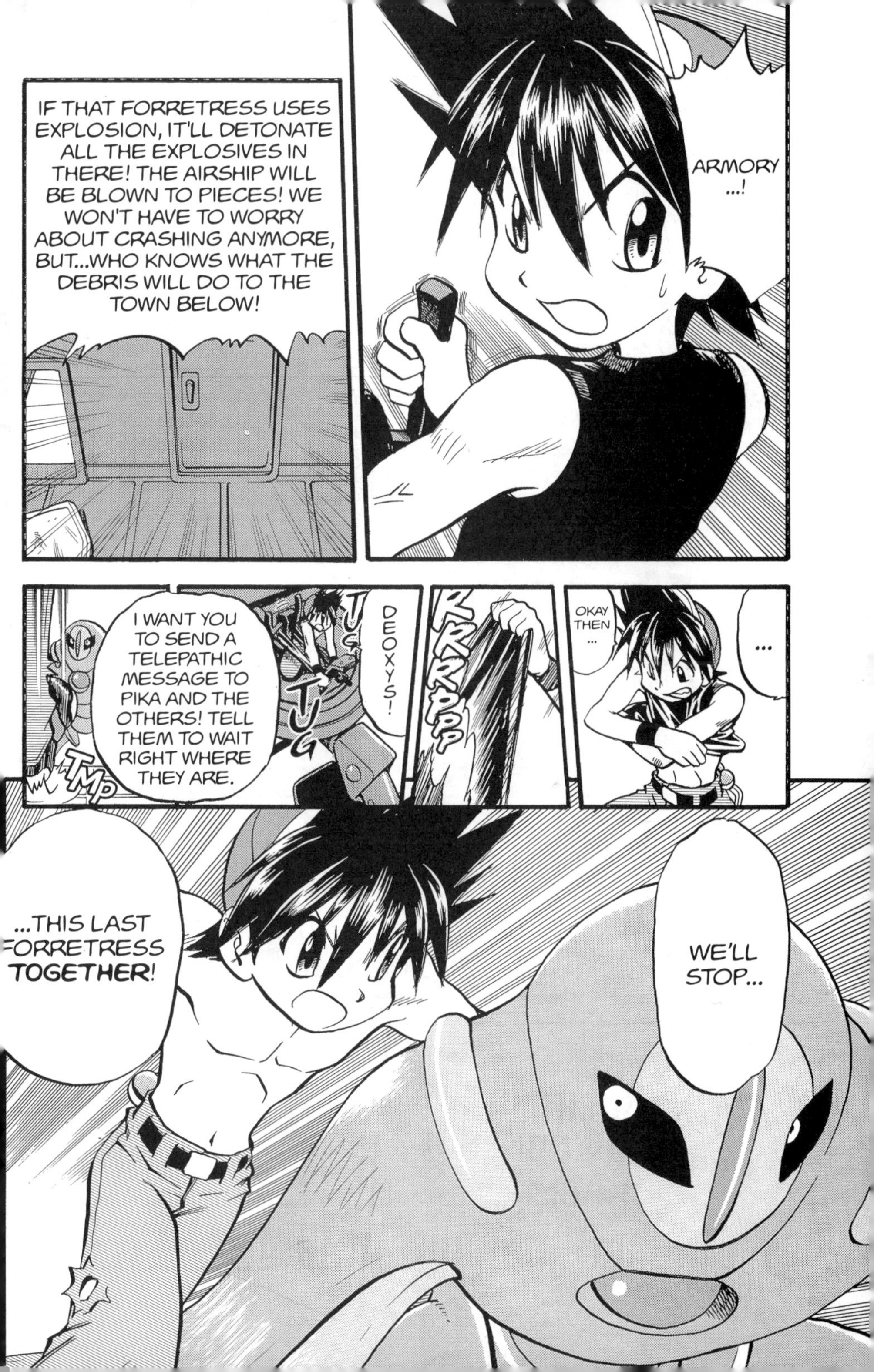
ARMORY ...!
IF THAT FORRETRESS USES EXPLOSION, IT'LL DETONATE ALL THE EXPLOSIVES IN THERE! THE AIRSHIP WILL BE BLOWN TO PIECES! WE WON'T HAVE TO WORRY ABOUT CRASHING ANYMORE, BUT...WHO KNOWS WHAT THE DEBRIS WILL DO TO THE TOWN BELOW!
...
OKAY THEN ...
DEOXYS!
TUG
TUG
I WANT YOU TO SEND A TELEPATHIC MESSAGE TO PIKA AND THE OTHERS! TELL THEM TO WAIT RIGHT WHERE THEY ARE.
TMP
WE'LL STOP...
...THIS LAST FORRETRESS TOGETHER!

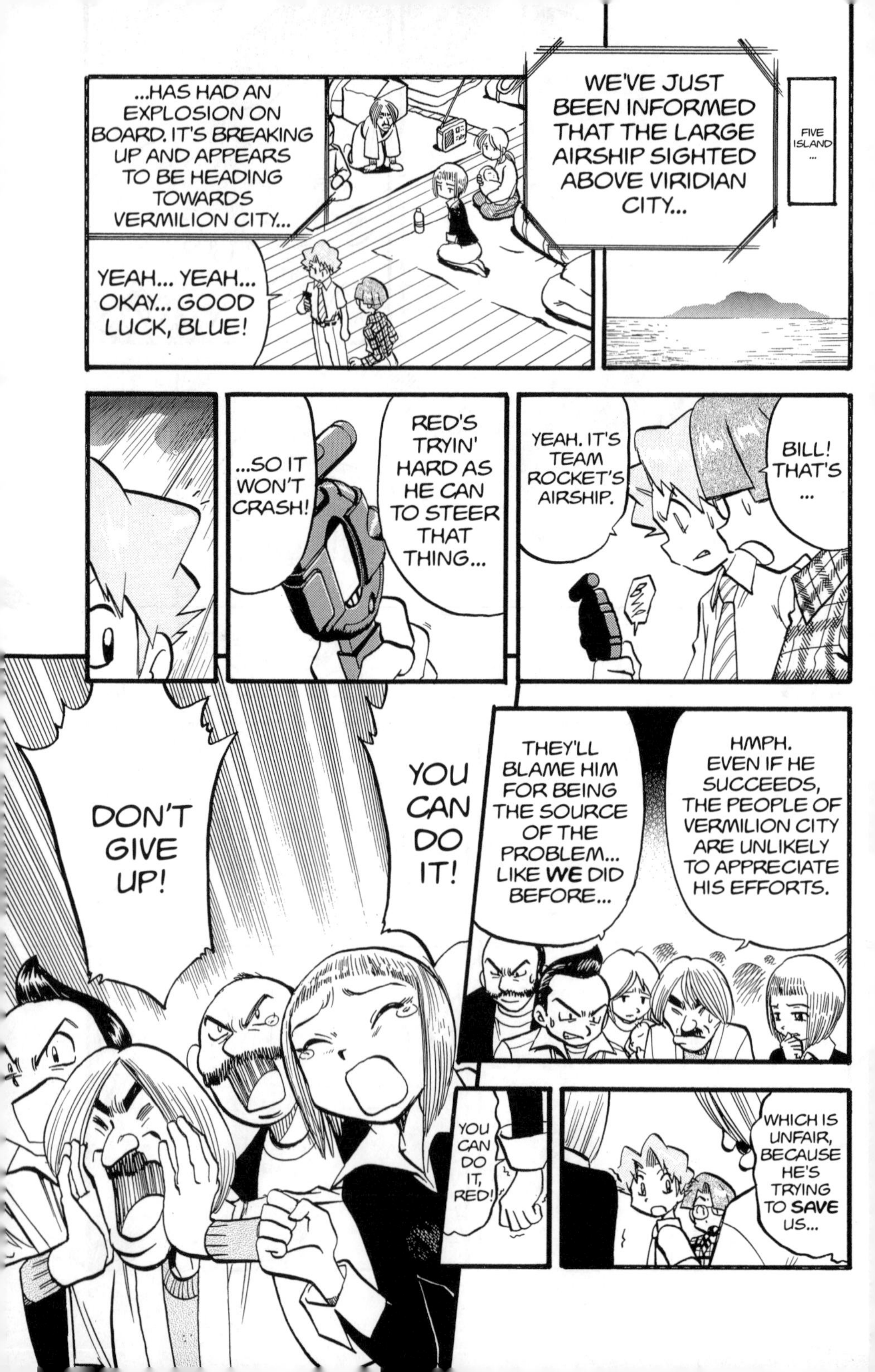
FIVE ISLAND ...
WE'VE JUST BEEN INFORMED THAT THE LARGE AIRSHIP SIGHTED ABOVE VIRIDIAN CITY...
...HAS HAD AN EXPLOSION ON BOARD. IT'S BREAKING UP AND APPEARS TO BE HEADING TOWARDS VERMILION CITY...
YEAH... YEAH... OKAY... GOOD LUCK, BLUE!
BILL! THAT'S ...
YEAH. IT'S TEAM ROCKET'S AIRSHIP.
RED'S TRYIN' HARD AS HE CAN TO STEER THAT THING...
...SO IT WON'T CRASH!
HMPH. EVEN IF HE SUCCEEDS, THE PEOPLE OF VERMILION CITY ARE UNLIKELY TO APPRECIATE HIS EFFORTS.
THEY'LL BLAME HIM FOR BEING THE SOURCE OF THE PROBLEM... LIKE **WE** DID BEFORE...
WHICH IS UNFAIR, BECAUSE HE'S TRYING TO **SAVE** US...
YOU CAN DO IT, RED!
YOU CAN DO IT!
DON'T GIVE UP!

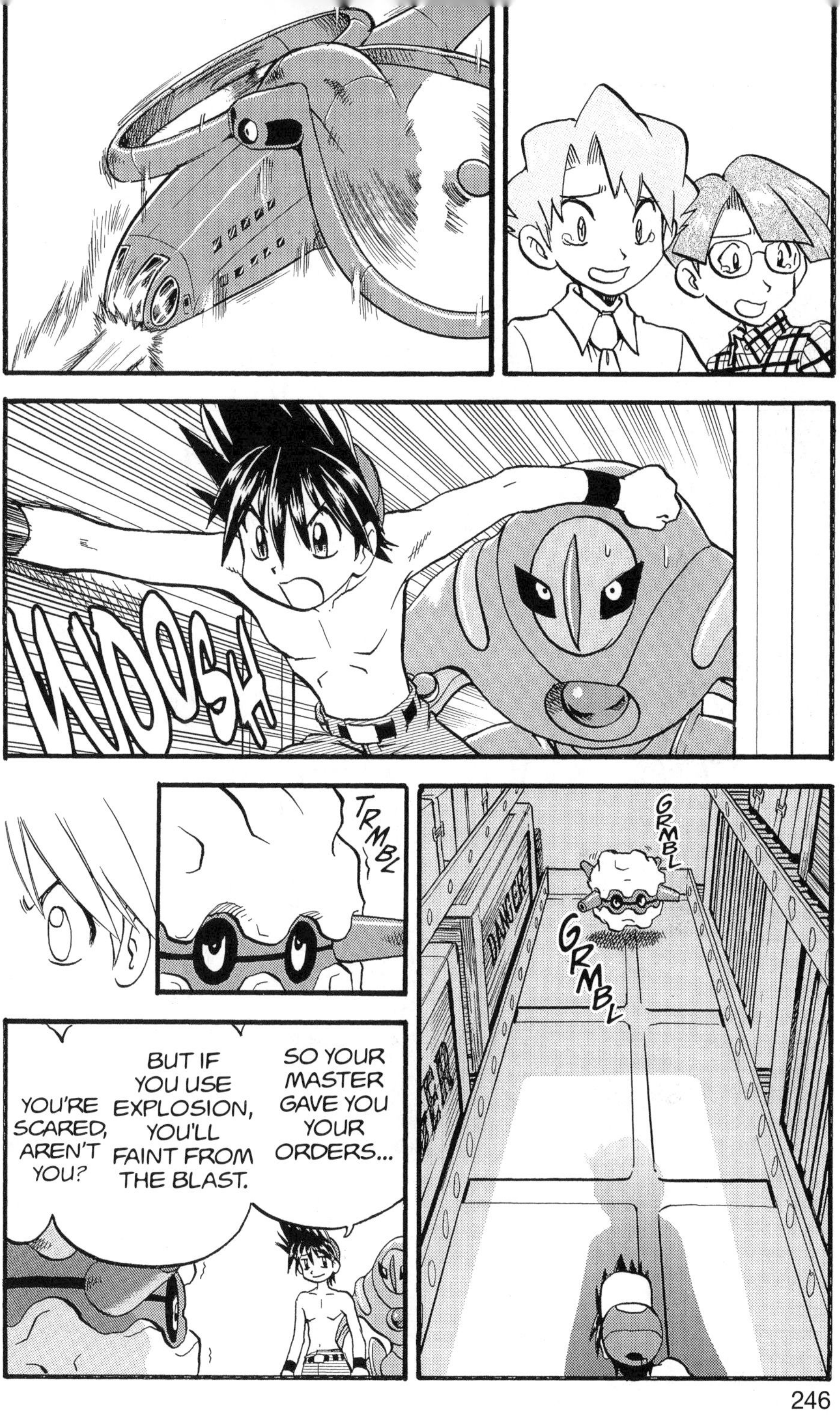
GRMBL
GRMBL
DANGER
TRMBL
SO YOUR MASTER GAVE YOU YOUR ORDERS...
BUT IF YOU USE EXPLOSION, YOU'LL FAINT FROM THE BLAST.
YOU'RE SCARED, AREN'T YOU?

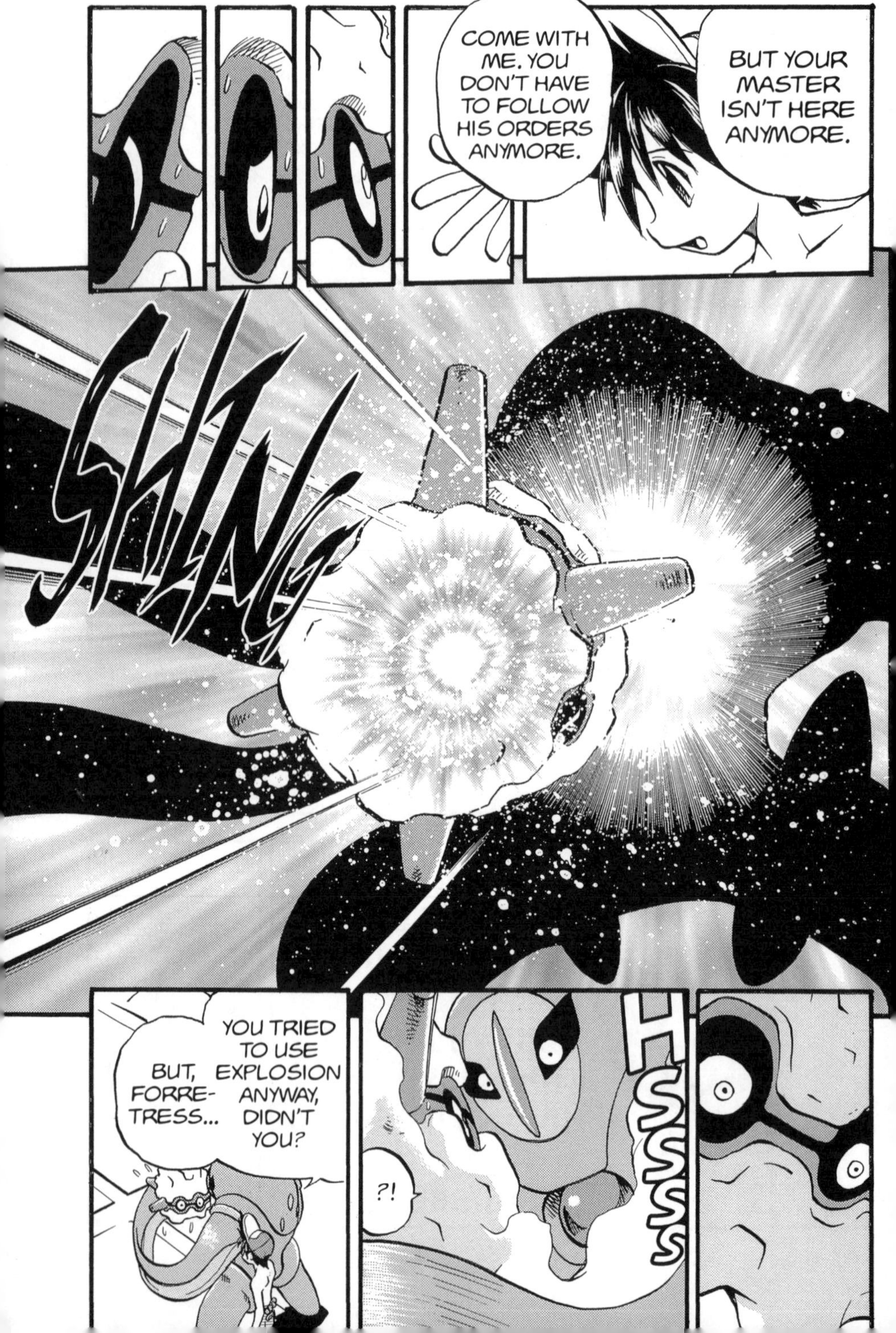
BUT YOUR MASTER ISN'T HERE ANYMORE.
COME WITH ME. YOU DON'T HAVE TO FOLLOW HIS ORDERS ANYMORE.
SHING
HSSSS
?!
BUT, FORRE-TRESS... YOU TRIED TO USE EXPLOSION ANYWAY, DIDN'T YOU?

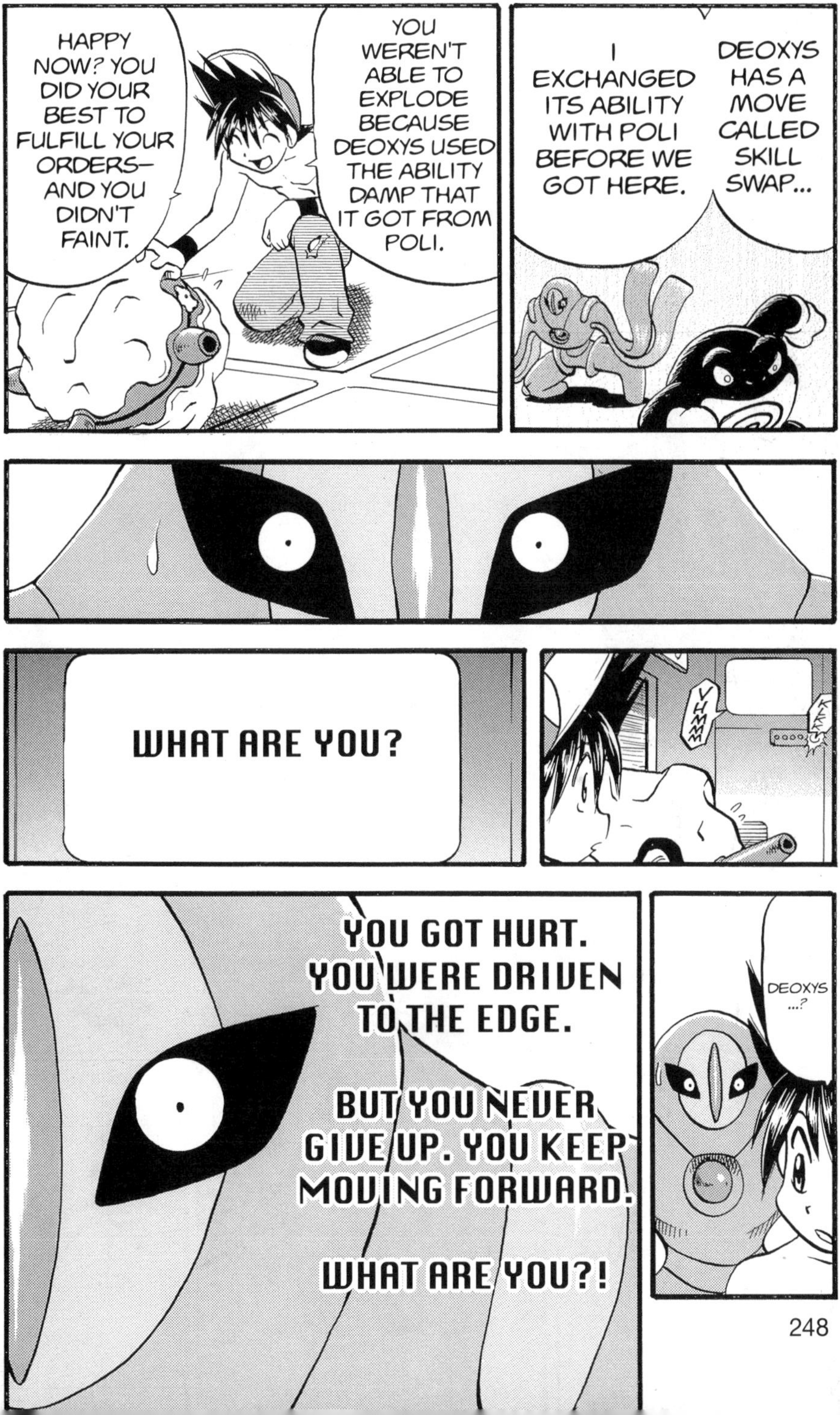
DEOXYS HAS A MOVE CALLED SKILL SWAP...
I EXCHANGED ITS ABILITY WITH POLI BEFORE WE GOT HERE.
YOU WEREN'T ABLE TO EXPLODE BECAUSE DEOXYS USED THE ABILITY DAMP THAT IT GOT FROM POLI.
HAPPY NOW? YOU DID YOUR BEST TO FULFILL YOUR ORDERS—AND YOU DIDN'T FAINT.
VHMMM
WHAT ARE YOU?
DEOXYS...?
YOU GOT HURT. YOU WERE DRIVEN TO THE EDGE.
BUT YOU NEVER GIVE UP. YOU KEEP MOVING FORWARD.
WHAT ARE YOU?!

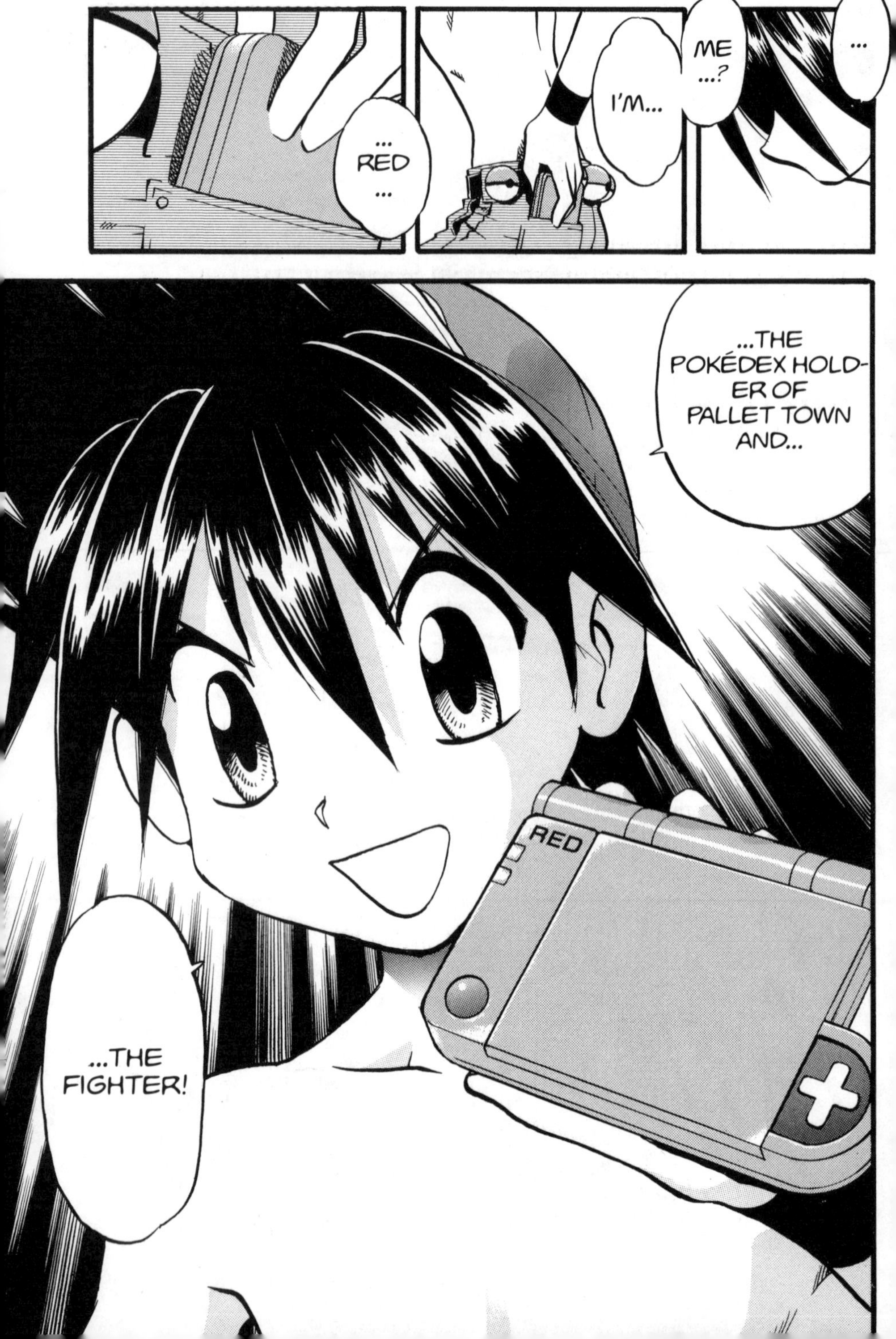
...
ME ...?
I'M...
... RED ...
...THE POKÉDEX HOLDER OF PALLET TOWN AND...
...THE FIGHTER!

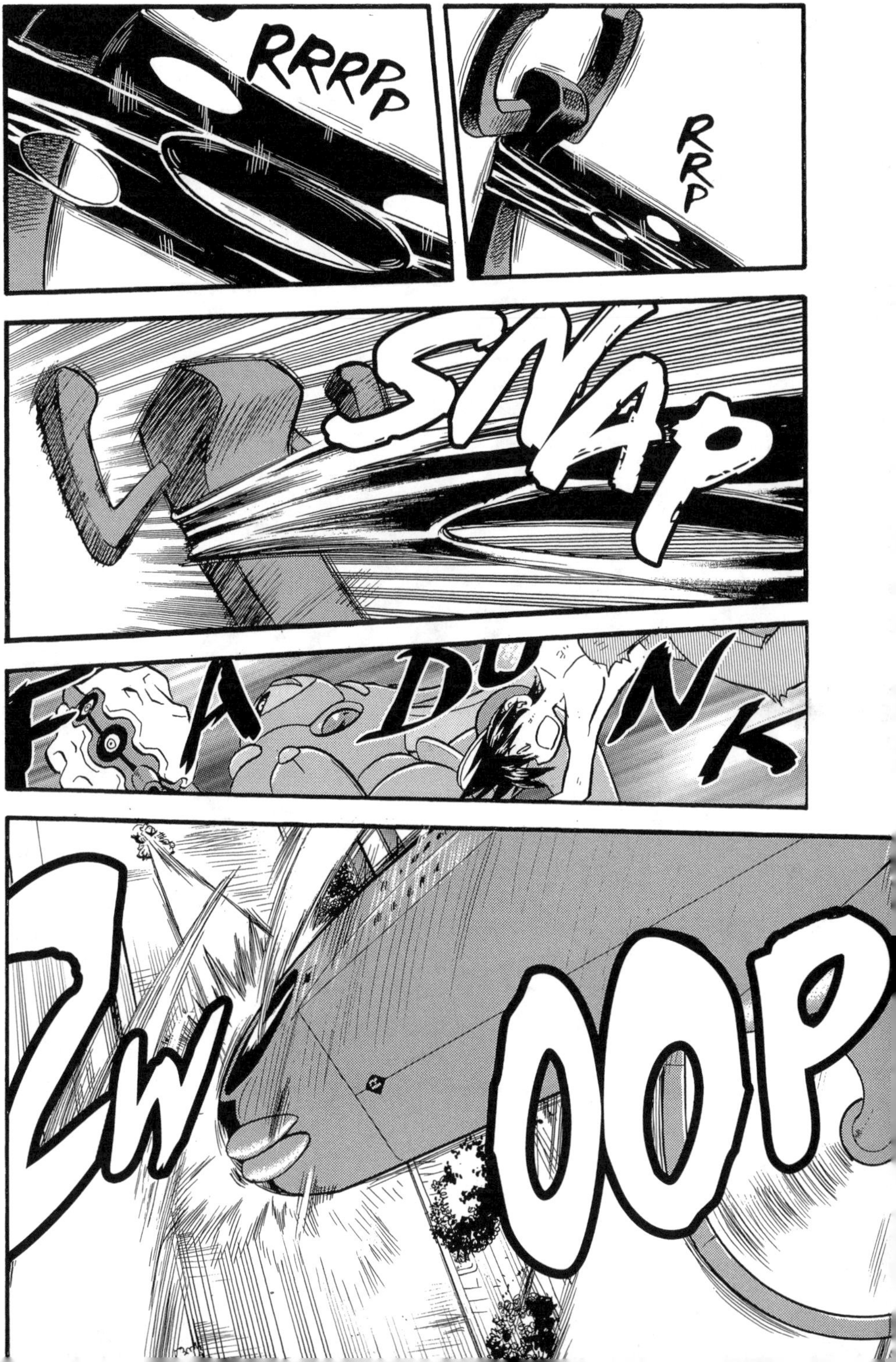
RRP
RRRPP
SNAP
FADUNK
ZWOOP

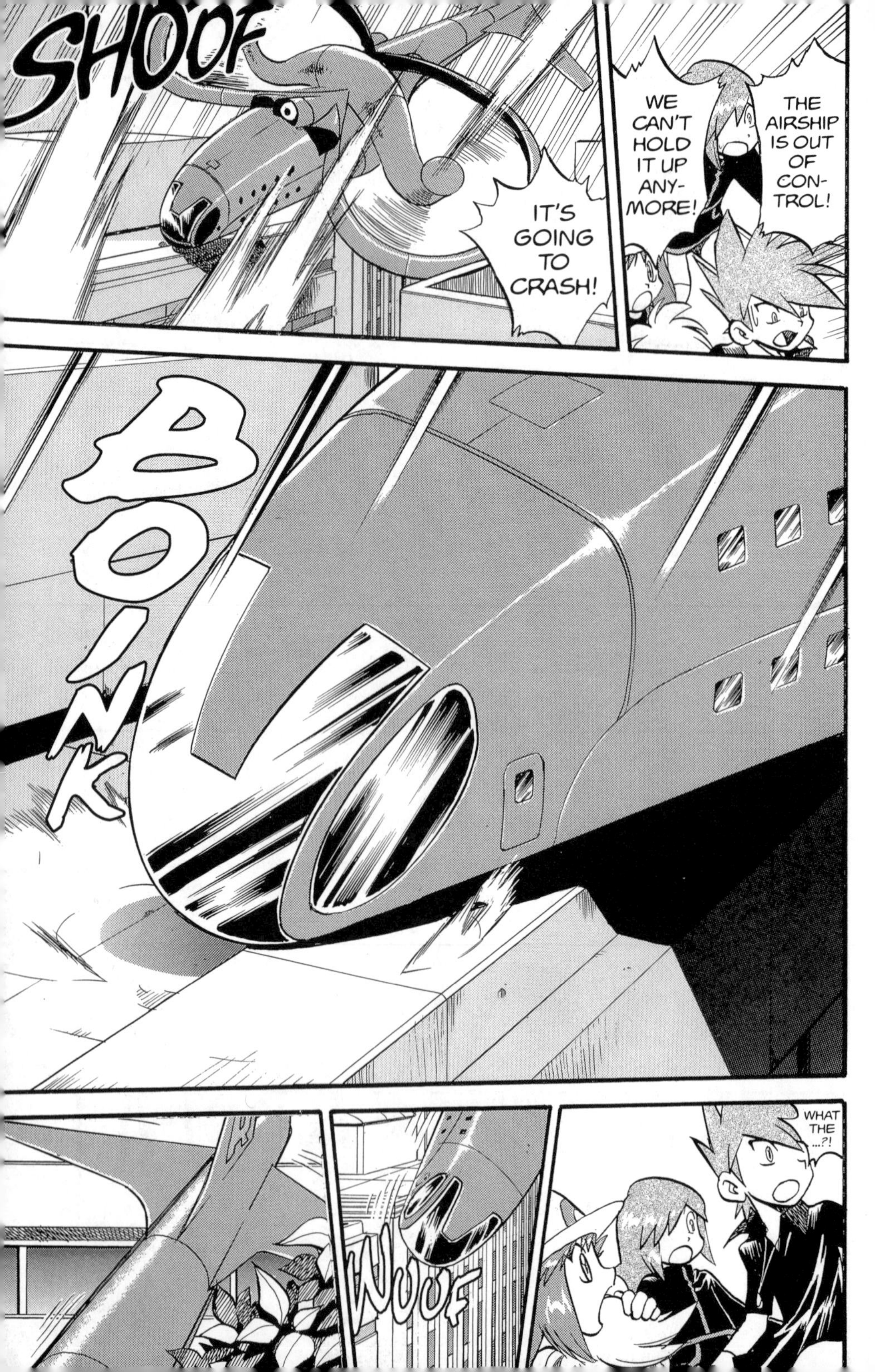
THE AIRSHIP IS OUT OF CON-TROL!
WE CAN'T HOLD IT UP ANY-MORE!
SHOOF
IT'S GOING TO CRASH!
BOINK
WHAT THE ...?!
WUUF

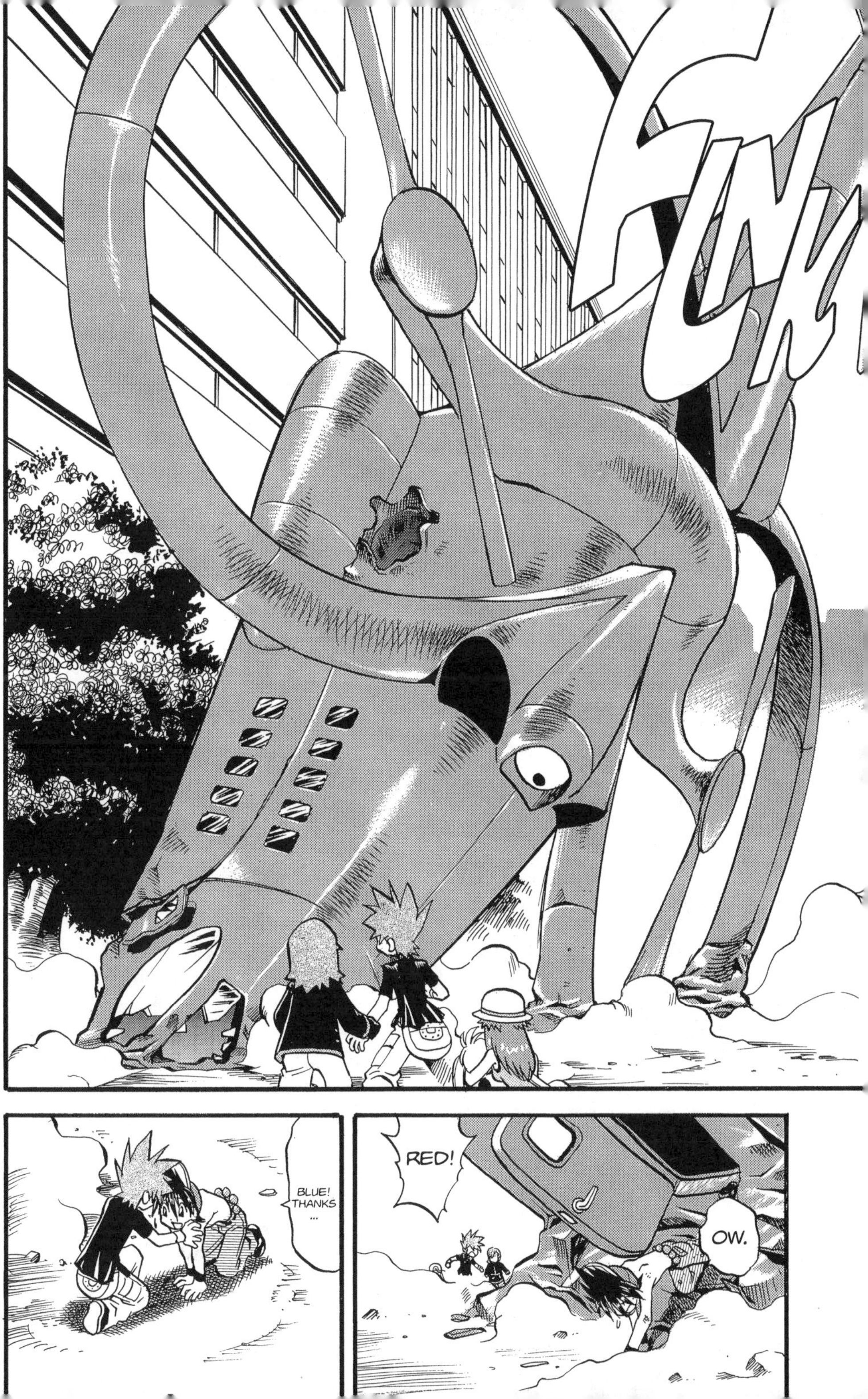
RED!
OW.
BLUE! THANKS ...

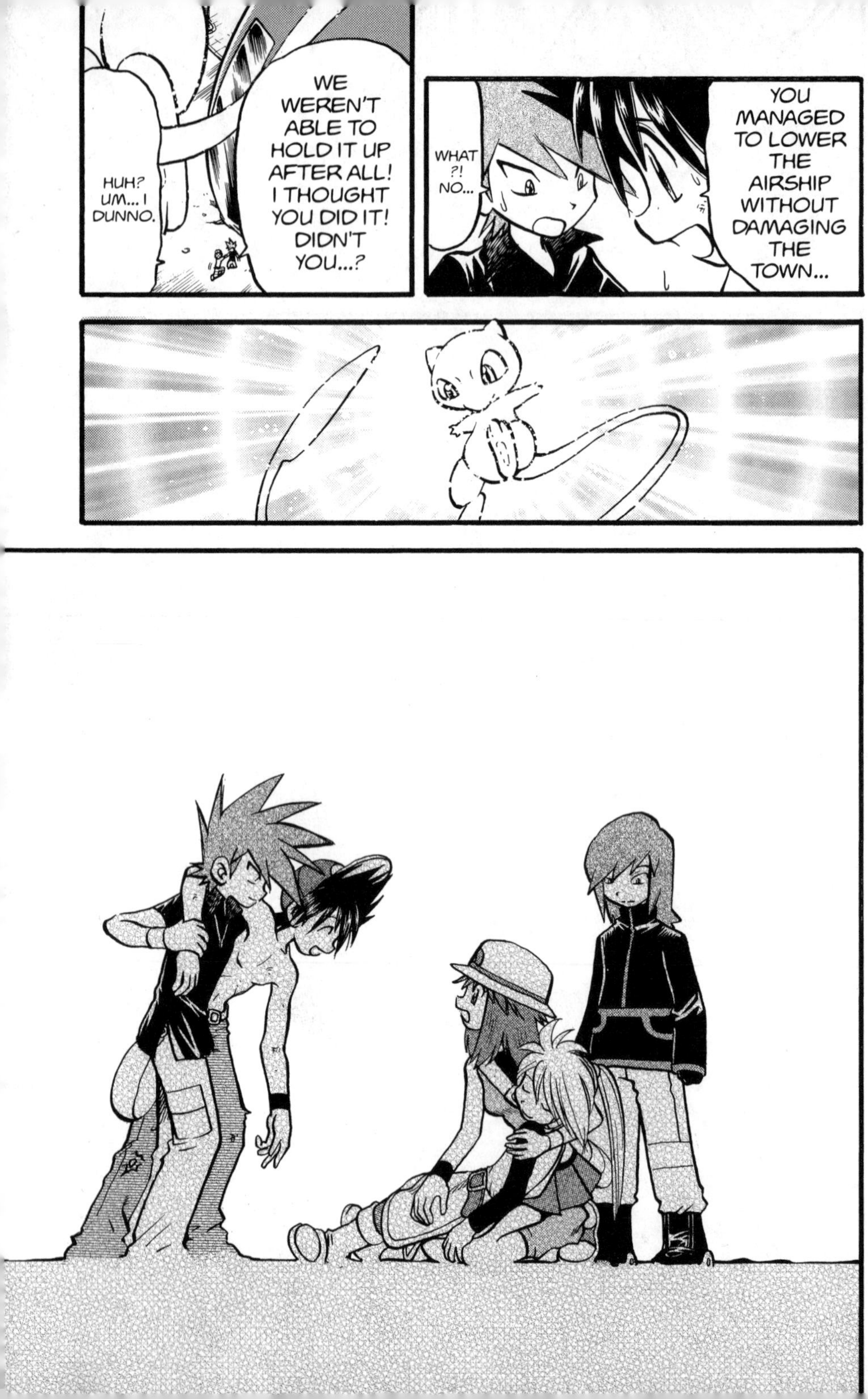
YOU MANAGED TO LOWER THE AIRSHIP WITHOUT DAMAGING THE TOWN...
WHAT?! NO...
WE WEREN'T ABLE TO HOLD IT UP AFTER ALL! I THOUGHT YOU DID IT! DIDN'T YOU...?
HUH? UM... I DUNNO.

● Adventure 302 ●
Phew for Mew

Pokémon Adventures FireRed & LeafGreen
The Fifth Chapter

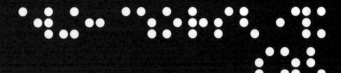

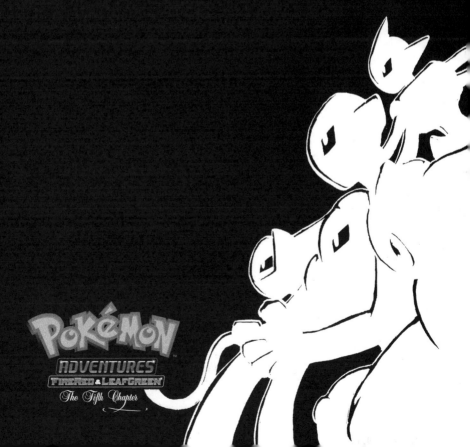

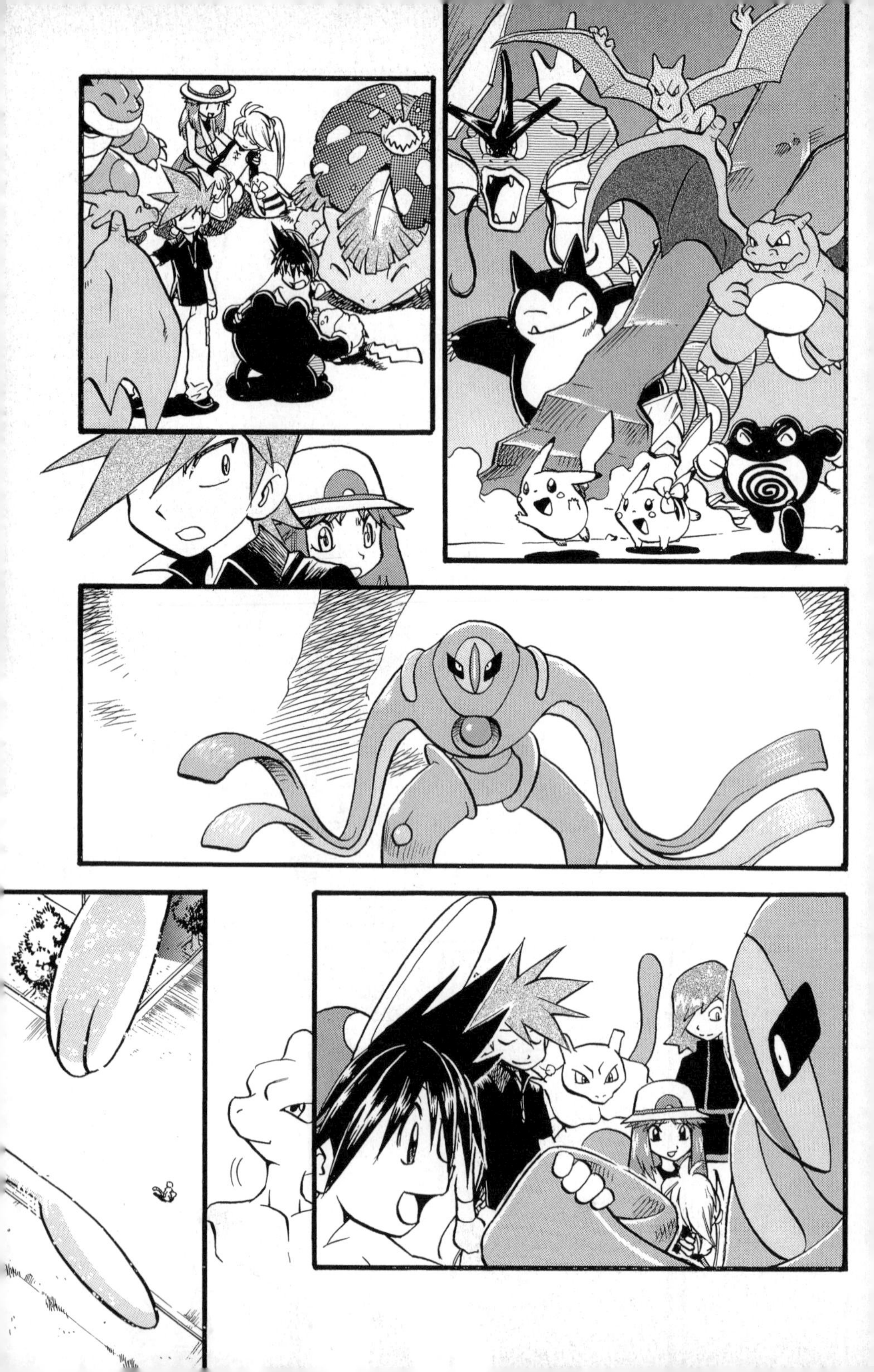

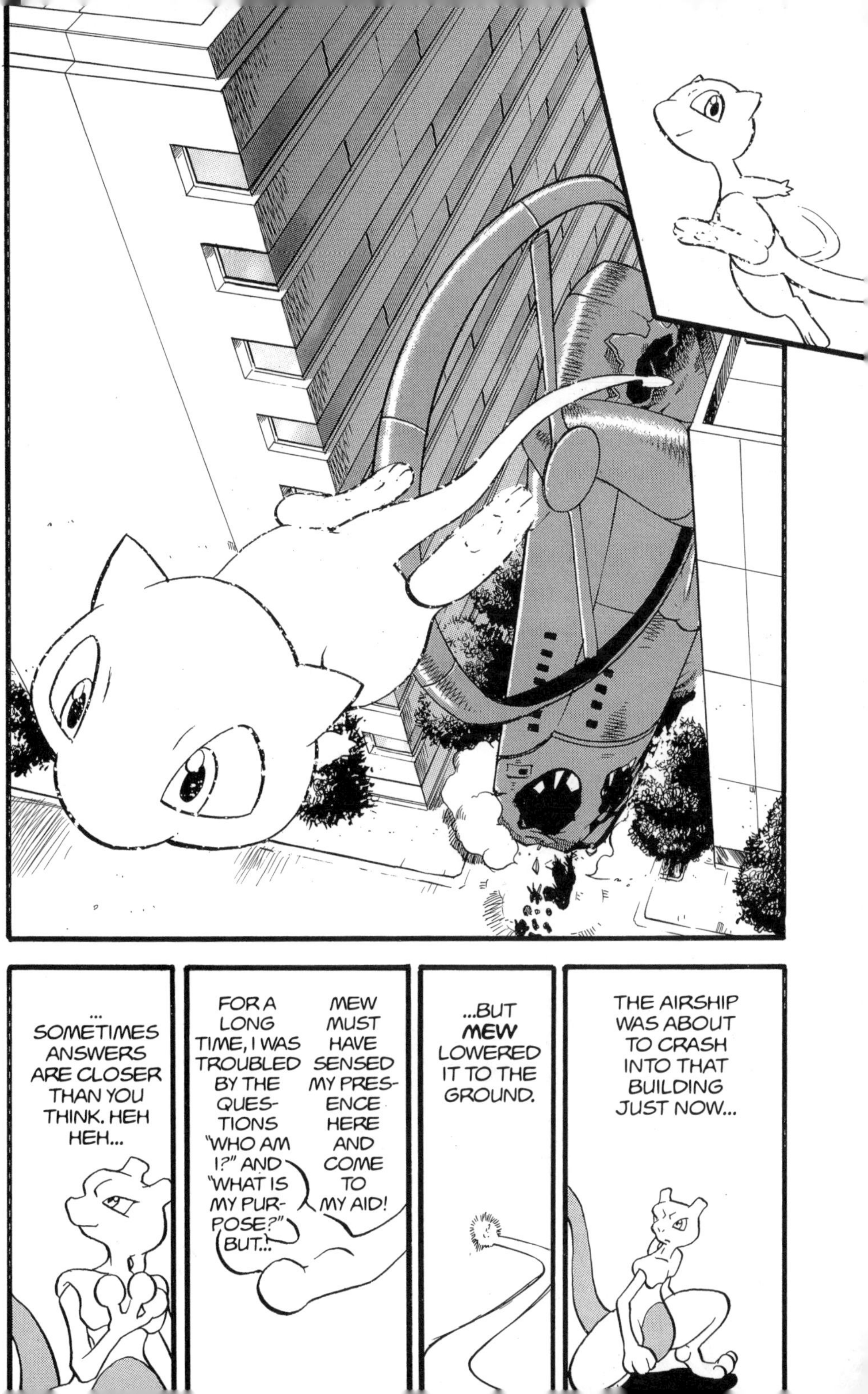
THE AIRSHIP WAS ABOUT TO CRASH INTO THAT BUILDING JUST NOW...
...BUT **MEW** LOWERED IT TO THE GROUND.
MEW MUST HAVE SENSED MY PRESENCE HERE AND COME TO MY AID!
FOR A LONG TIME, I WAS TROUBLED BY THE QUESTIONS "WHO AM I?" AND "WHAT IS MY PURPOSE?" BUT...
... SOMETIMES ANSWERS ARE CLOSER THAN YOU THINK. HEH HEH...

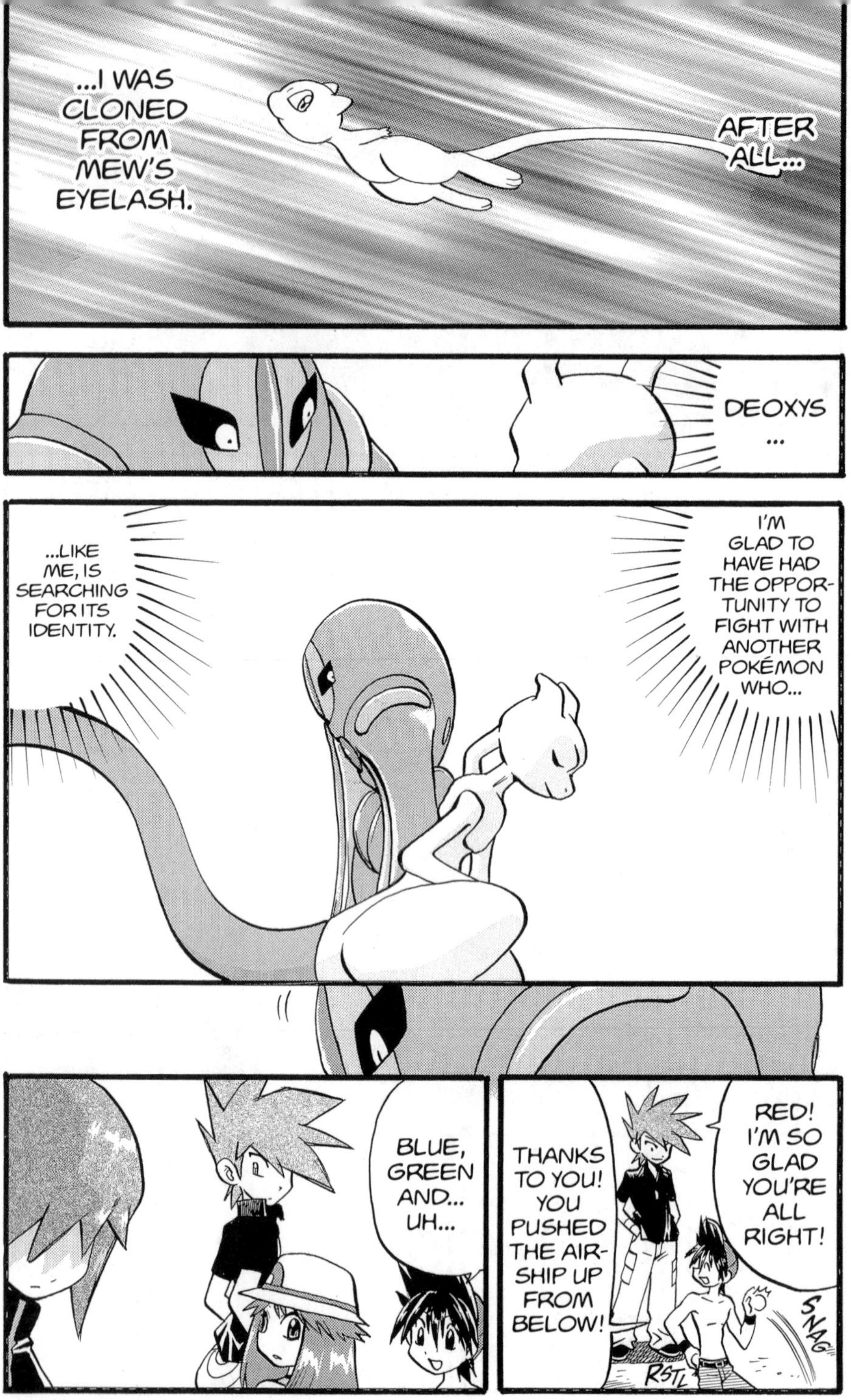
AFTER ALL...
...I WAS CLONED FROM MEW'S EYELASH.
DEOXYS ...
I'M GLAD TO HAVE HAD THE OPPOR-TUNITY TO FIGHT WITH ANOTHER POKÉMON WHO...
...LIKE ME, IS SEARCHING FOR ITS IDENTITY.
RED! I'M SO GLAD YOU'RE ALL RIGHT!
THANKS TO YOU! YOU PUSHED THE AIR-SHIP UP FROM BELOW!
SNAG
RSTL
BLUE, GREEN AND... UH...

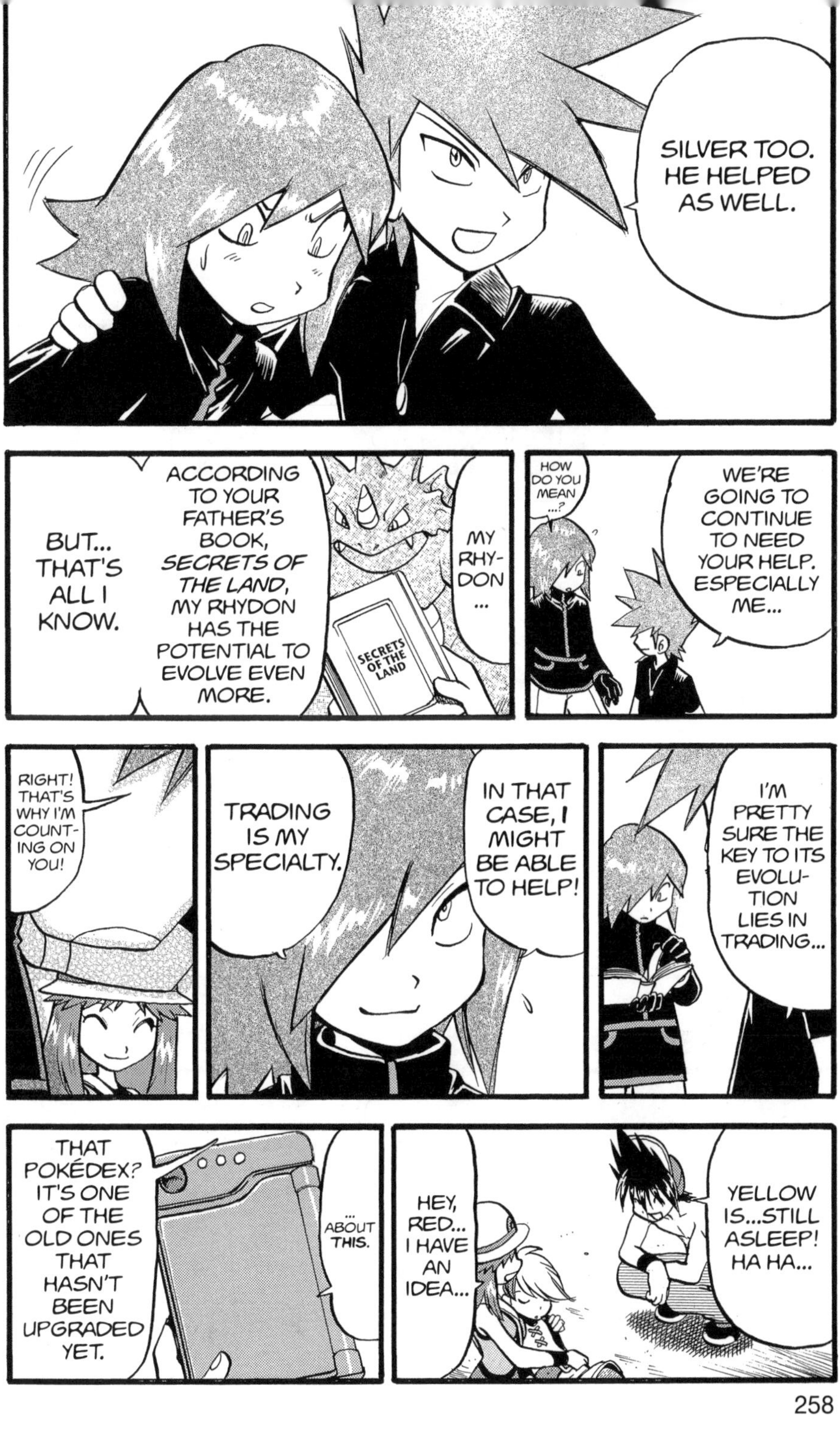
SILVER TOO. HE HELPED AS WELL.
WE'RE GOING TO CONTINUE TO NEED YOUR HELP. ESPECIALLY ME...
HOW DO YOU MEAN ...?
MY RHYDON ...
ACCORDING TO YOUR FATHER'S BOOK, *SECRETS OF THE LAND*, MY RHYDON HAS THE POTENTIAL TO EVOLVE EVEN MORE.
SECRETS OF THE LAND
BUT... THAT'S ALL I KNOW.
I'M PRETTY SURE THE KEY TO ITS EVOLUTION LIES IN TRADING...
IN THAT CASE, I MIGHT BE ABLE TO HELP!
TRADING IS MY SPECIALTY.
RIGHT! THAT'S WHY I'M COUNTING ON YOU!
YELLOW IS...STILL ASLEEP! HA HA...
HEY, RED... I HAVE AN IDEA...
...ABOUT **THIS.**
THAT POKÉDEX? IT'S ONE OF THE OLD ONES THAT HASN'T BEEN UPGRADED YET.

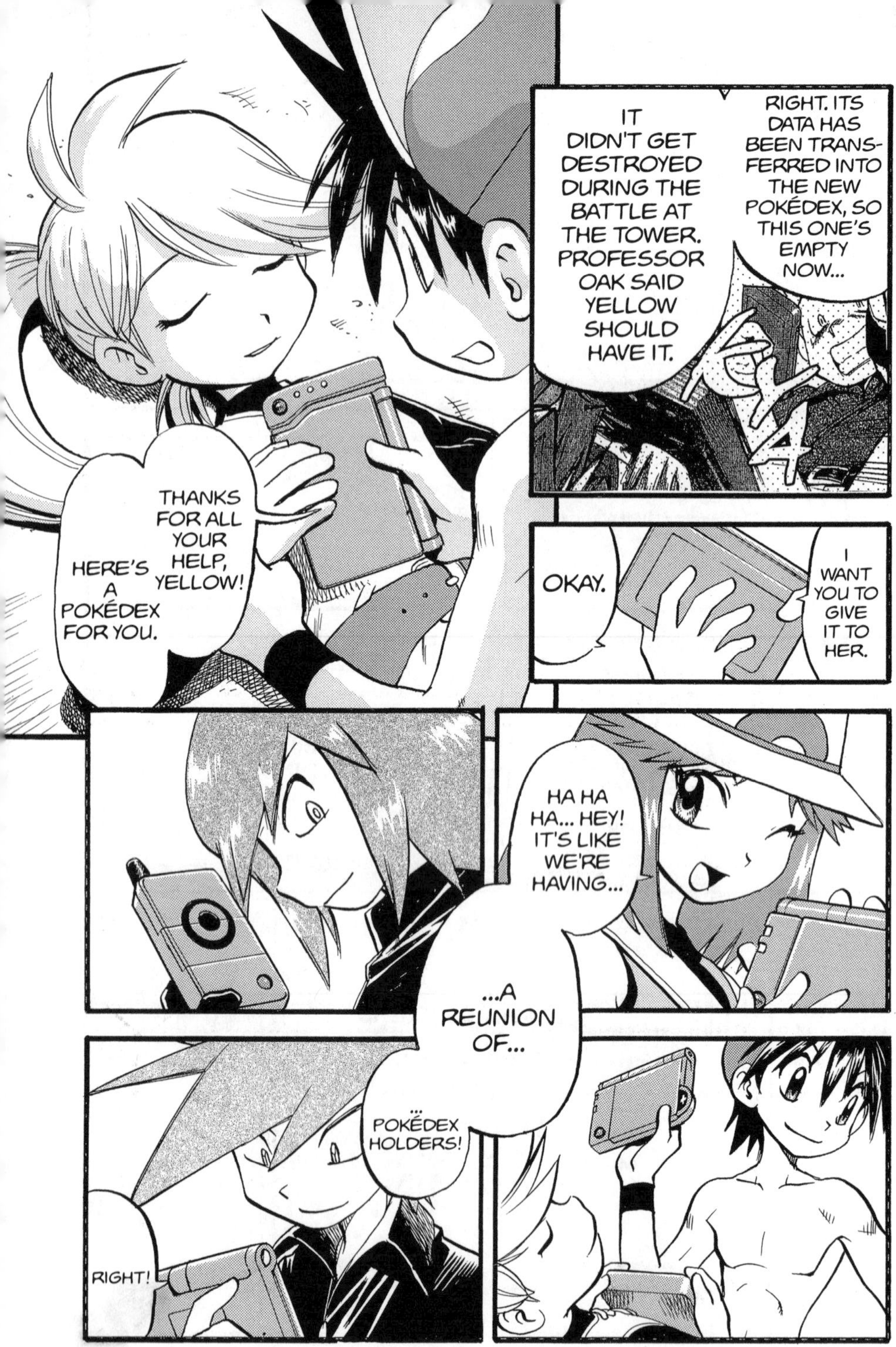
RIGHT. ITS DATA HAS BEEN TRANS-FERRED INTO THE NEW POKÉDEX, SO THIS ONE'S EMPTY NOW...
IT DIDN'T GET DESTROYED DURING THE BATTLE AT THE TOWER. PROFESSOR OAK SAID YELLOW SHOULD HAVE IT.
I WANT YOU TO GIVE IT TO HER.
OKAY.
THANKS FOR ALL YOUR HELP, YELLOW!
HERE'S A POKÉDEX FOR YOU.
HA HA HA... HEY! IT'S LIKE WE'RE HAVING...
...A REUNION OF...
... POKÉDEX HOLDERS!
RIGHT!

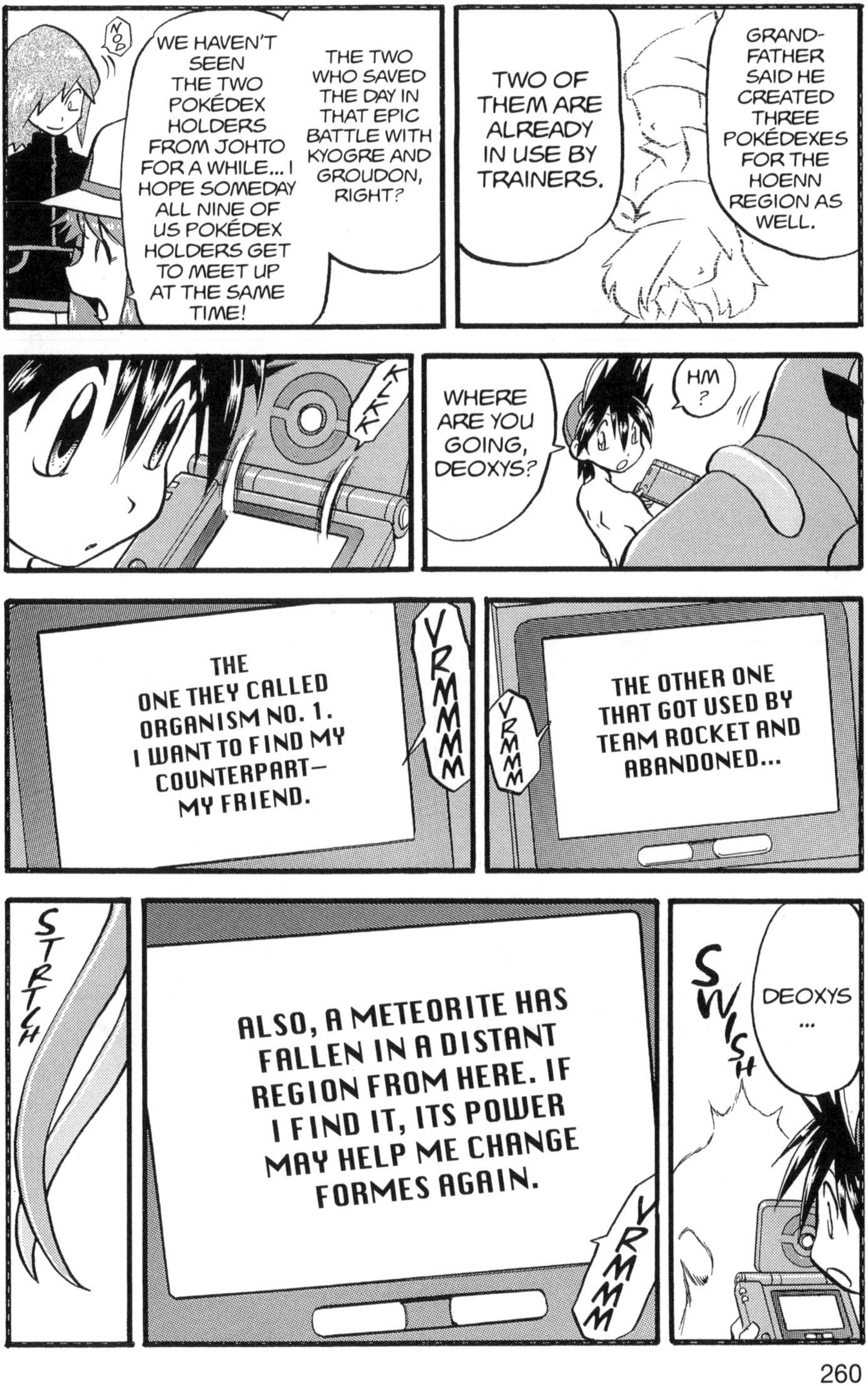
GRAND-FATHER SAID HE CREATED THREE POKÉDEXES FOR THE HOENN REGION AS WELL.
TWO OF THEM ARE ALREADY IN USE BY TRAINERS.
THE TWO WHO SAVED THE DAY IN THAT EPIC BATTLE WITH KYOGRE AND GROUDON, RIGHT?
NOD
WE HAVEN'T SEEN THE TWO POKÉDEX HOLDERS FROM JOHTO FOR A WHILE... I HOPE SOMEDAY ALL NINE OF US POKÉDEX HOLDERS GET TO MEET UP AT THE SAME TIME!
HM?
WHERE ARE YOU GOING, DEOXYS?
KLKK
THE OTHER ONE THAT GOT USED BY TEAM ROCKET AND ABANDONED...
VRMMM
VRMMMM
THE ONE THEY CALLED ORGANISM NO. 1. I WANT TO FIND MY COUNTERPART— MY FRIEND.
DEOXYS...
SWISH
VRMMMM
ALSO, A METEORITE HAS FALLEN IN A DISTANT REGION FROM HERE. IF I FIND IT, ITS POWER MAY HELP ME CHANGE FORMES AGAIN.
STRTCH

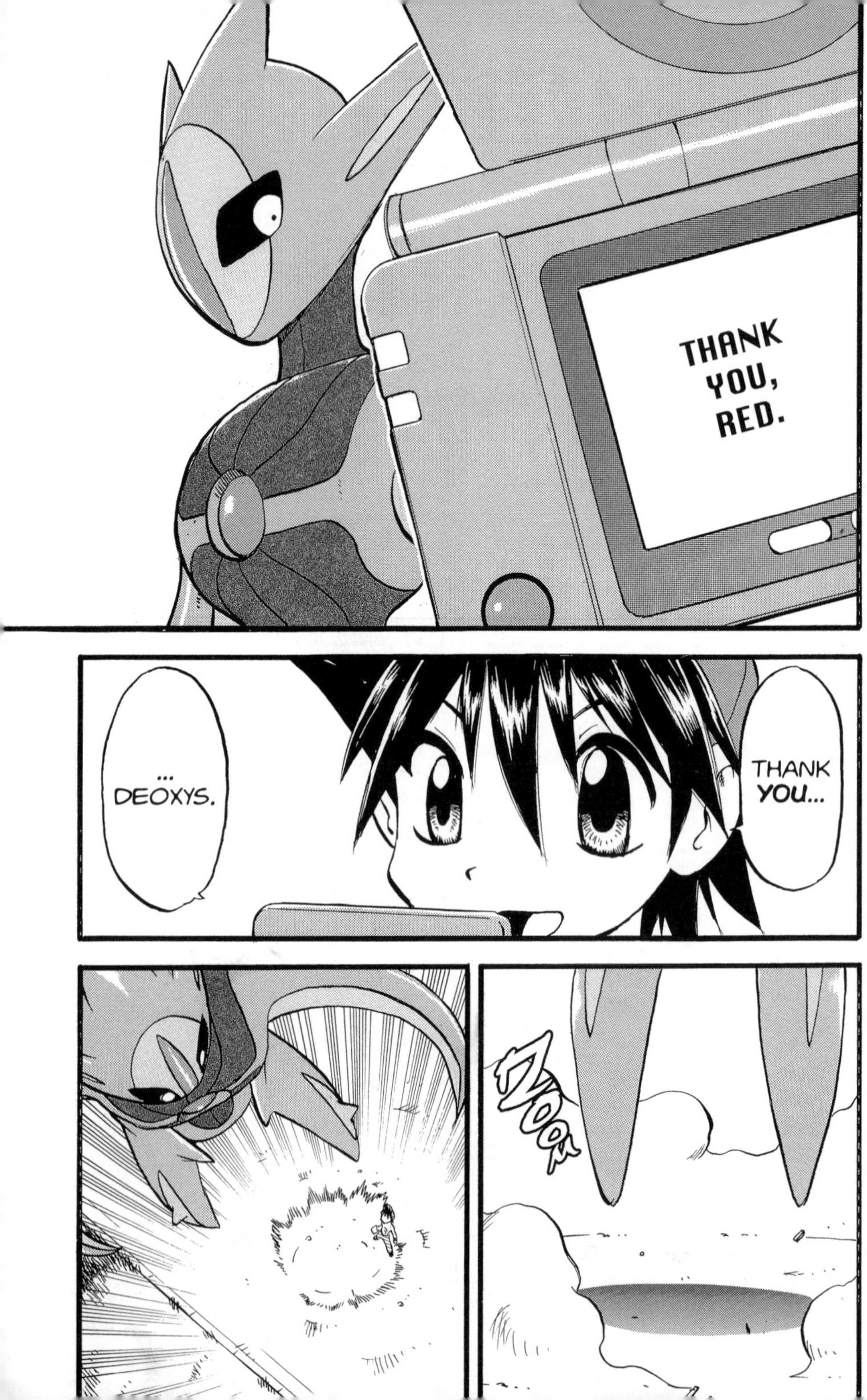
THANK YOU, RED.
THANK YOU...
...DEOXYS.
ZOOM

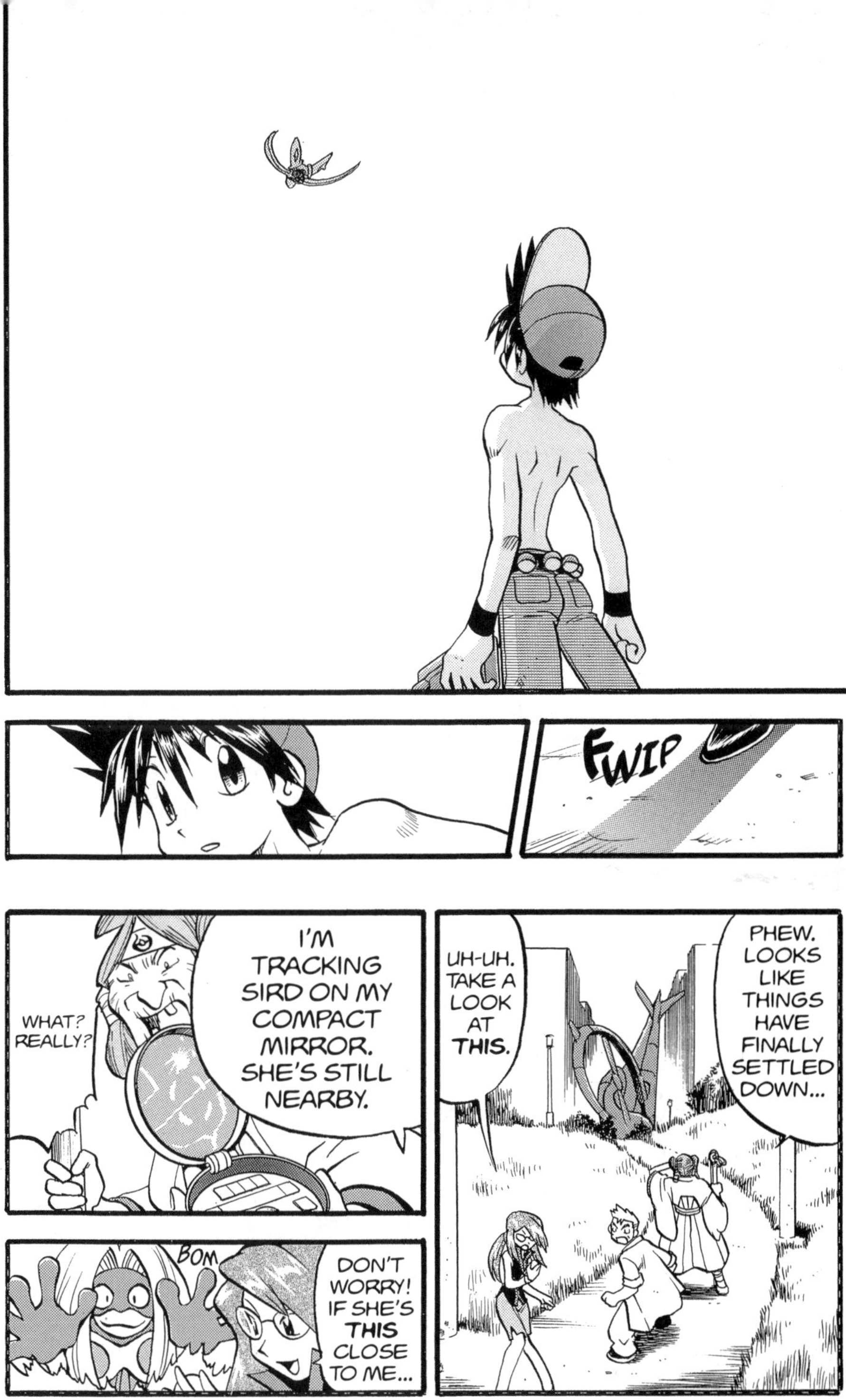
FWIP
PHEW. LOOKS LIKE THINGS HAVE FINALLY SETTLED DOWN...
UH-UH. TAKE A LOOK AT THIS.
I'M TRACKING SIRD ON MY COMPACT MIRROR. SHE'S STILL NEARBY.
WHAT? REALLY?
DON'T WORRY! IF SHE'S THIS CLOSE TO ME...
BOM

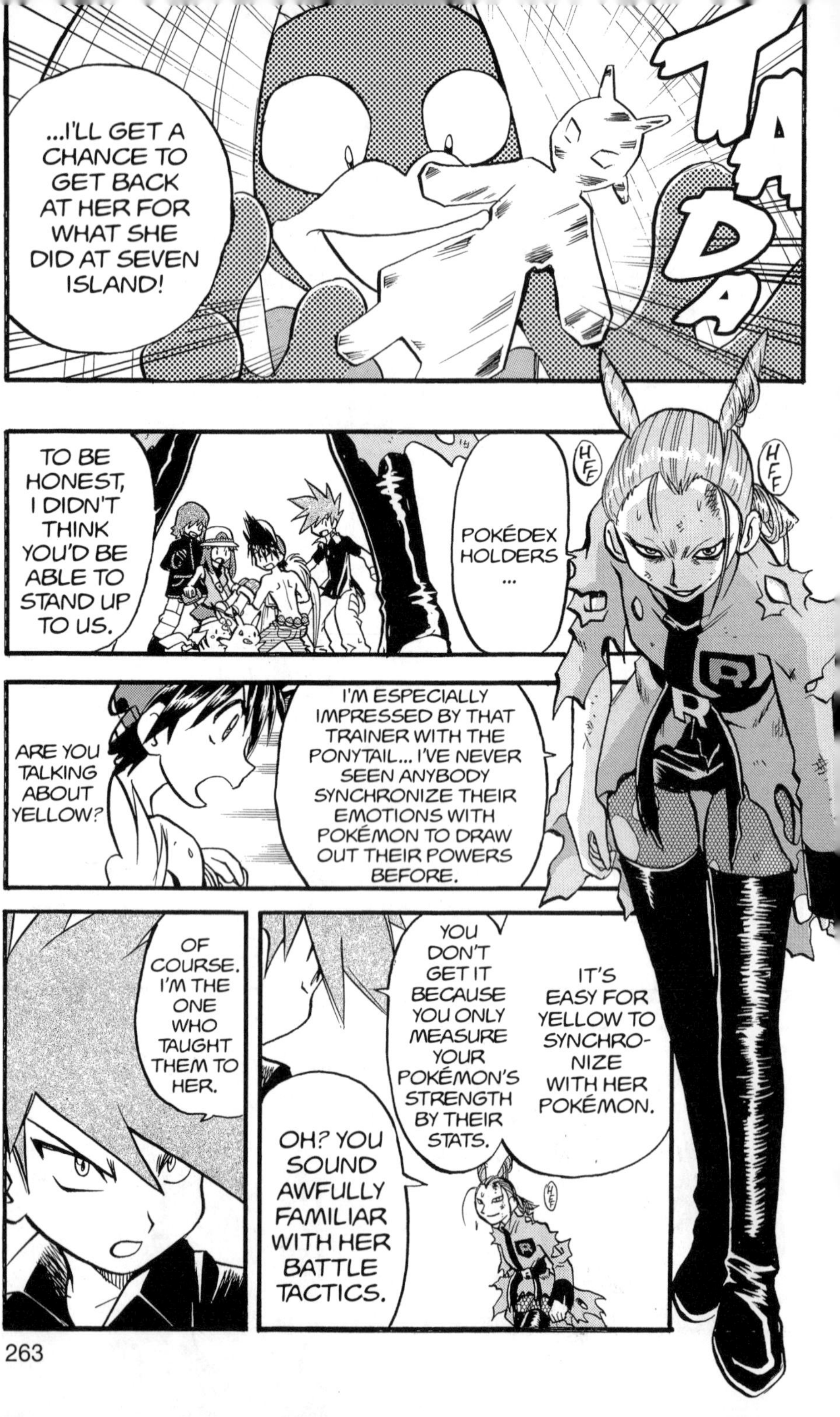
...I'LL GET A CHANCE TO GET BACK AT HER FOR WHAT SHE DID AT SEVEN ISLAND!
HFF
HFF
POKÉDEX HOLDERS ...
TO BE HONEST, I DIDN'T THINK YOU'D BE ABLE TO STAND UP TO US.
I'M ESPECIALLY IMPRESSED BY THAT TRAINER WITH THE PONYTAIL... I'VE NEVER SEEN ANYBODY SYNCHRONIZE THEIR EMOTIONS WITH POKÉMON TO DRAW OUT THEIR POWERS BEFORE.
ARE YOU TALKING ABOUT YELLOW?
YOU DON'T GET IT BECAUSE YOU ONLY MEASURE YOUR POKÉMON'S STRENGTH BY THEIR STATS.
IT'S EASY FOR YELLOW TO SYNCHRO-NIZE WITH HER POKÉMON.
HFF
OH? YOU SOUND AWFULLY FAMILIAR WITH HER BATTLE TACTICS.
OF COURSE. I'M THE ONE WHO TAUGHT THEM TO HER.

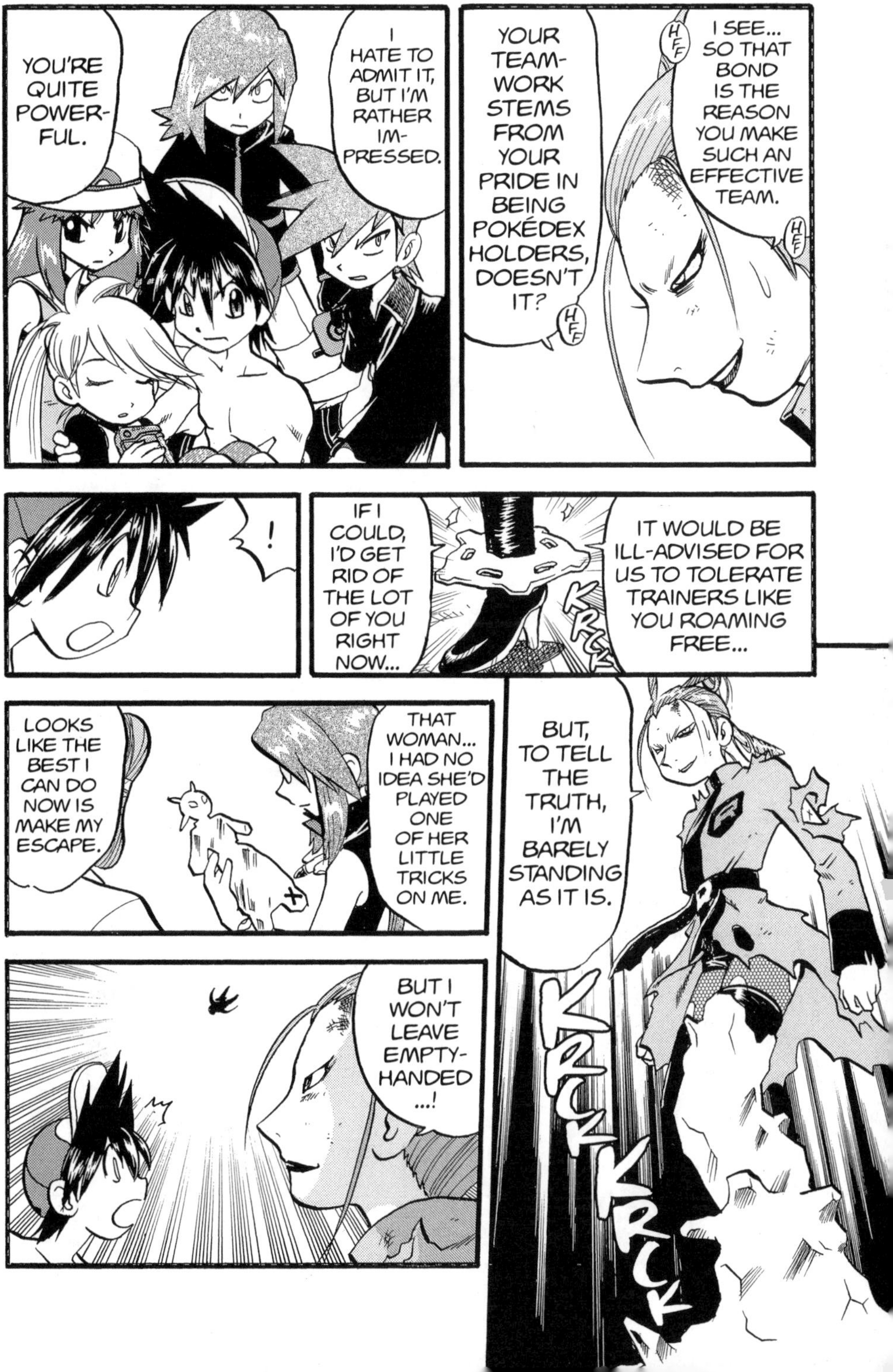
I SEE... SO THAT BOND IS THE REASON YOU MAKE SUCH AN EFFECTIVE TEAM.
HFF
HFF
YOUR TEAM-WORK STEMS FROM YOUR PRIDE IN BEING POKÉDEX HOLDERS, DOESN'T IT?
HFF
I HATE TO ADMIT IT, BUT I'M RATHER IM-PRESSED.
YOU'RE QUITE POWER-FUL.
IT WOULD BE ILL-ADVISED FOR US TO TOLERATE TRAINERS LIKE YOU ROAMING FREE...
IF I COULD, I'D GET RID OF THE LOT OF YOU RIGHT NOW...
KRCK
!
BUT, TO TELL THE TRUTH, I'M BARELY STANDING AS IT IS.
KRCK KRCK
THAT WOMAN... I HAD NO IDEA SHE'D PLAYED ONE OF HER LITTLE TRICKS ON ME.
LOOKS LIKE THE BEST I CAN DO NOW IS MAKE MY ESCAPE.
BUT I WON'T LEAVE EMPTY-HANDED ...!

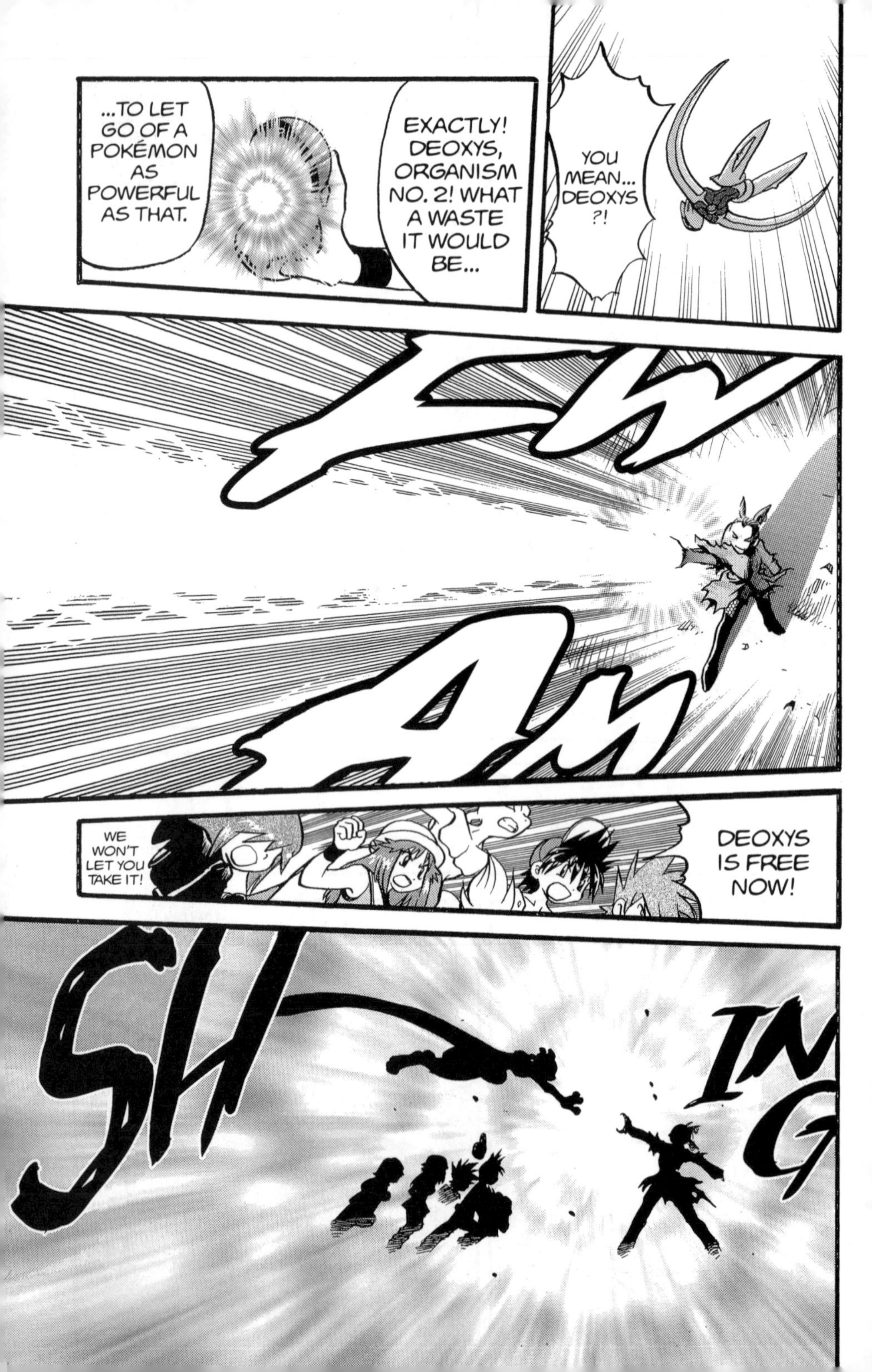
YOU MEAN... DEOXYS?!
EXACTLY! DEOXYS, ORGANISM NO. 2! WHAT A WASTE IT WOULD BE...
...TO LET GO OF A POKÉMON AS POWERFUL AS THAT.
DEOXYS IS FREE NOW!
WE WON'T LET YOU TAKE IT!

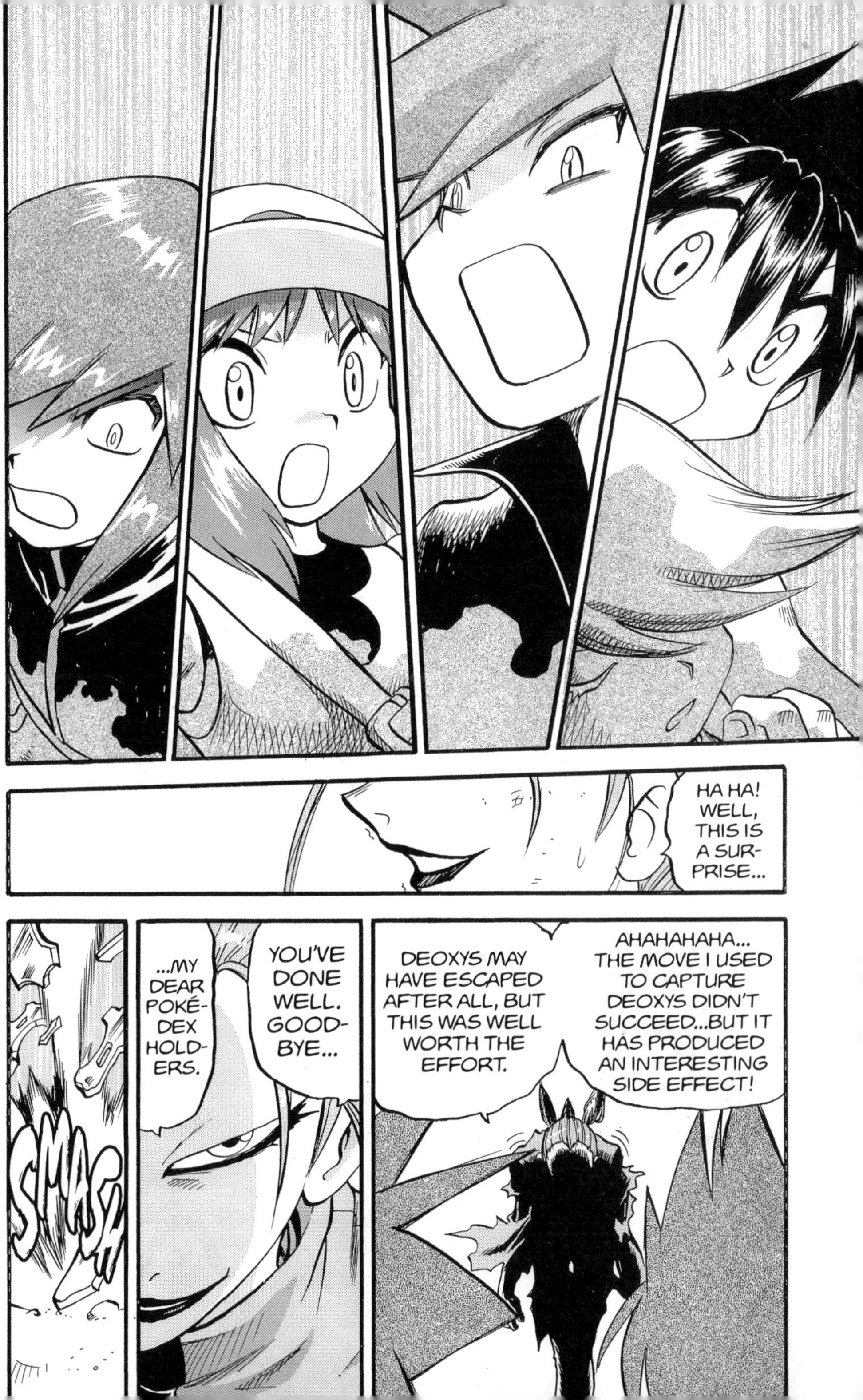
HA HA! WELL, THIS IS A SUR-PRISE...
AHAHAHAHA... THE MOVE I USED TO CAPTURE DEOXYS DIDN'T SUCCEED...BUT IT HAS PRODUCED AN INTERESTING SIDE EFFECT!
DEOXYS MAY HAVE ESCAPED AFTER ALL, BUT THIS WAS WELL WORTH THE EFFORT.
YOU'VE DONE WELL. GOOD-BYE...
...MY DEAR POKÉ-DEX HOLD-ERS.
SMASH

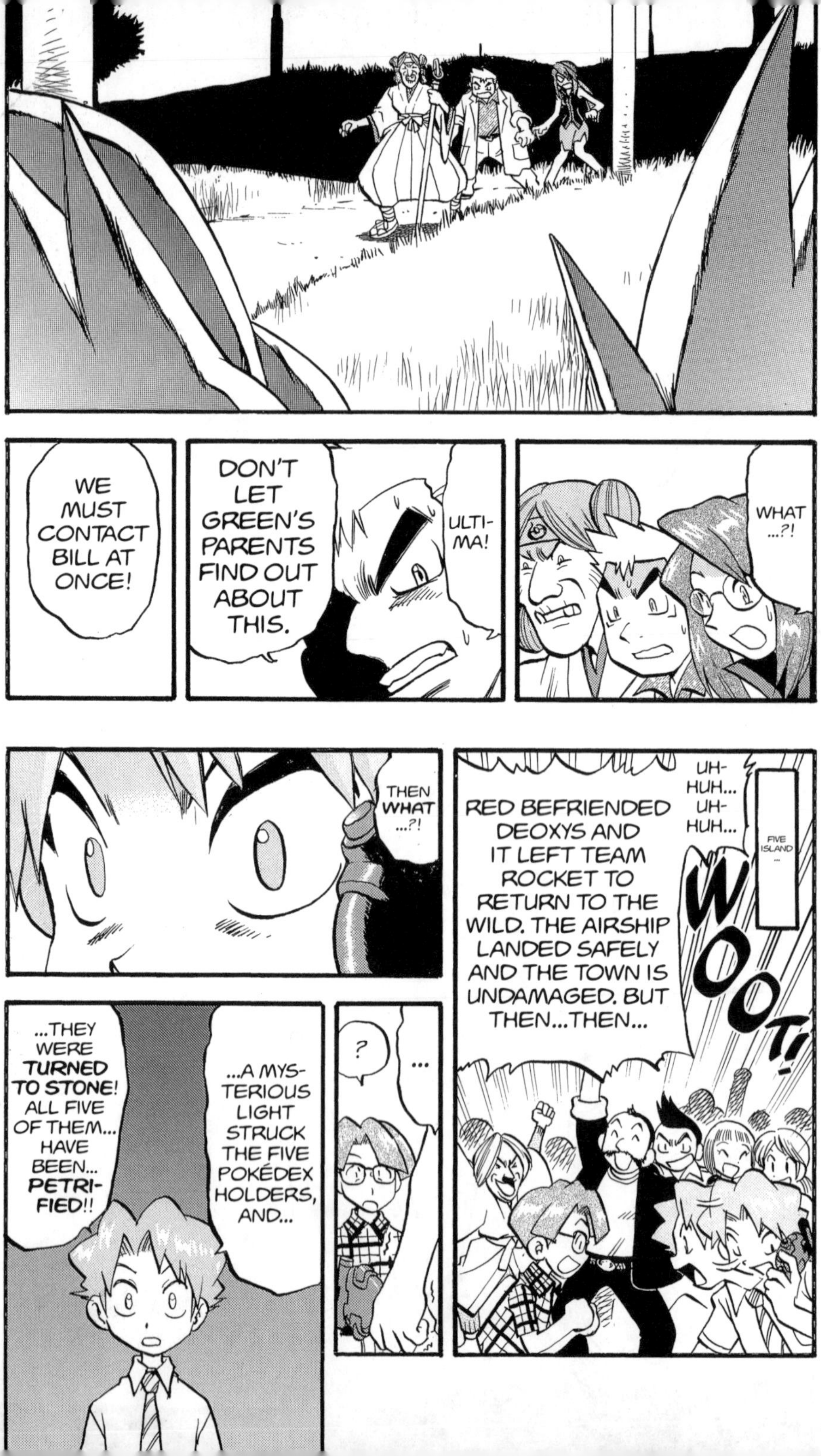
WHAT ...?!
ULTI-MA!
DON'T LET GREEN'S PARENTS FIND OUT ABOUT THIS.
WE MUST CONTACT BILL AT ONCE!
FIVE ISLAND ...
UH-HUH... UH-HUH...
RED BEFRIENDED DEOXYS AND IT LEFT TEAM ROCKET TO RETURN TO THE WILD. THE AIRSHIP LANDED SAFELY AND THE TOWN IS UNDAMAGED. BUT THEN...THEN...
WOOT!!
THEN WHAT ...?!
...
?
...A MYS-TERIOUS LIGHT STRUCK THE FIVE POKÉDEX HOLDERS, AND...
...THEY WERE TURNED TO STONE! ALL FIVE OF THEM... HAVE BEEN... PETRI-FIED!!

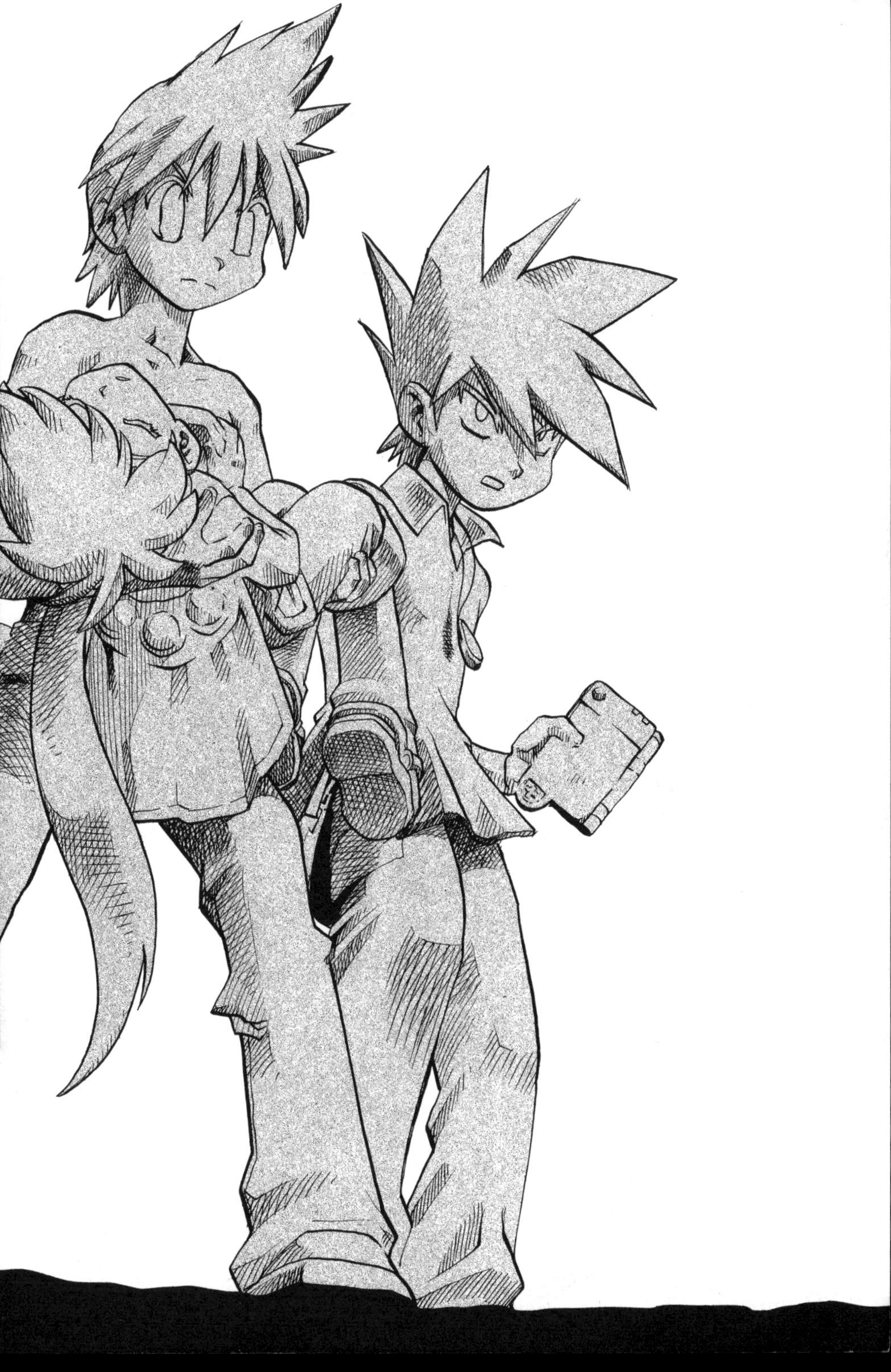

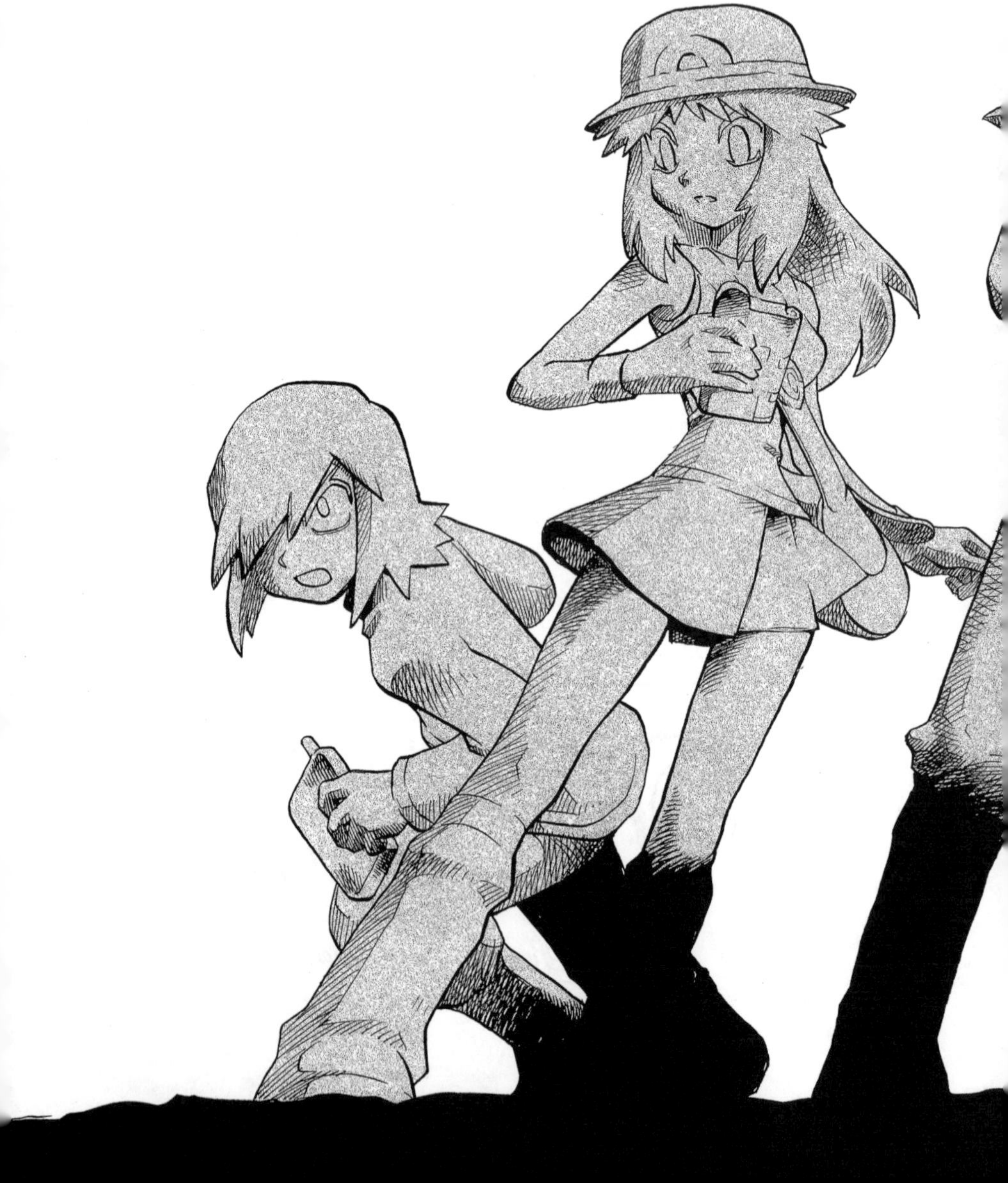

Fin The Fifth Chapter
FireRed & LeafGreen

Message from
Hidenori Kusaka

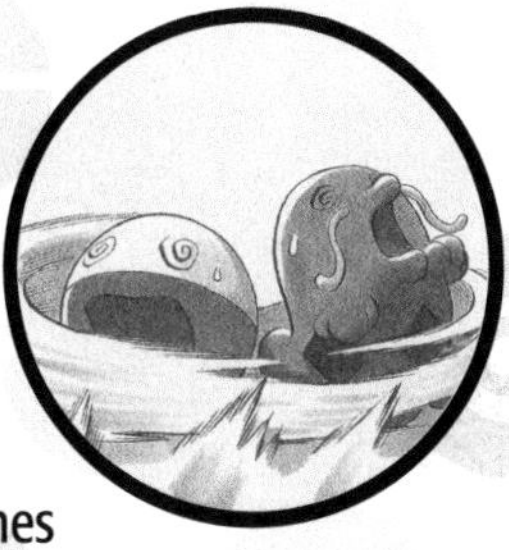

I've received the answers to a survey I placed in volume 23.* This survey was designed so I could get to know more about you, our readers. I asked how old you are and how many volumes of the *Pokémon Adventures* series you own. I like to analyze things, so I really enjoyed crunching the data from the survey–such as the range of readers' ages, who reads the series in serialized form in magazines as opposed to who reads it after it's compiled into graphic novels, etc. I'm working hard to use this data to improve the comic. I'd like to thank everyone who helped out by taking the survey!

*In the original Japanese edition.

–2007

Message from
Satoshi Yamamoto

The main concept behind the new battleground called the Battle Frontier is to show how fun and complex a Pokémon Battle can be. How will Emerald defeat the Frontier Brains, who fight using a variety of strategies, unlike Gym Leaders, who mostly strategize along the lines of the Pokémon's type?

–2007

Emerald

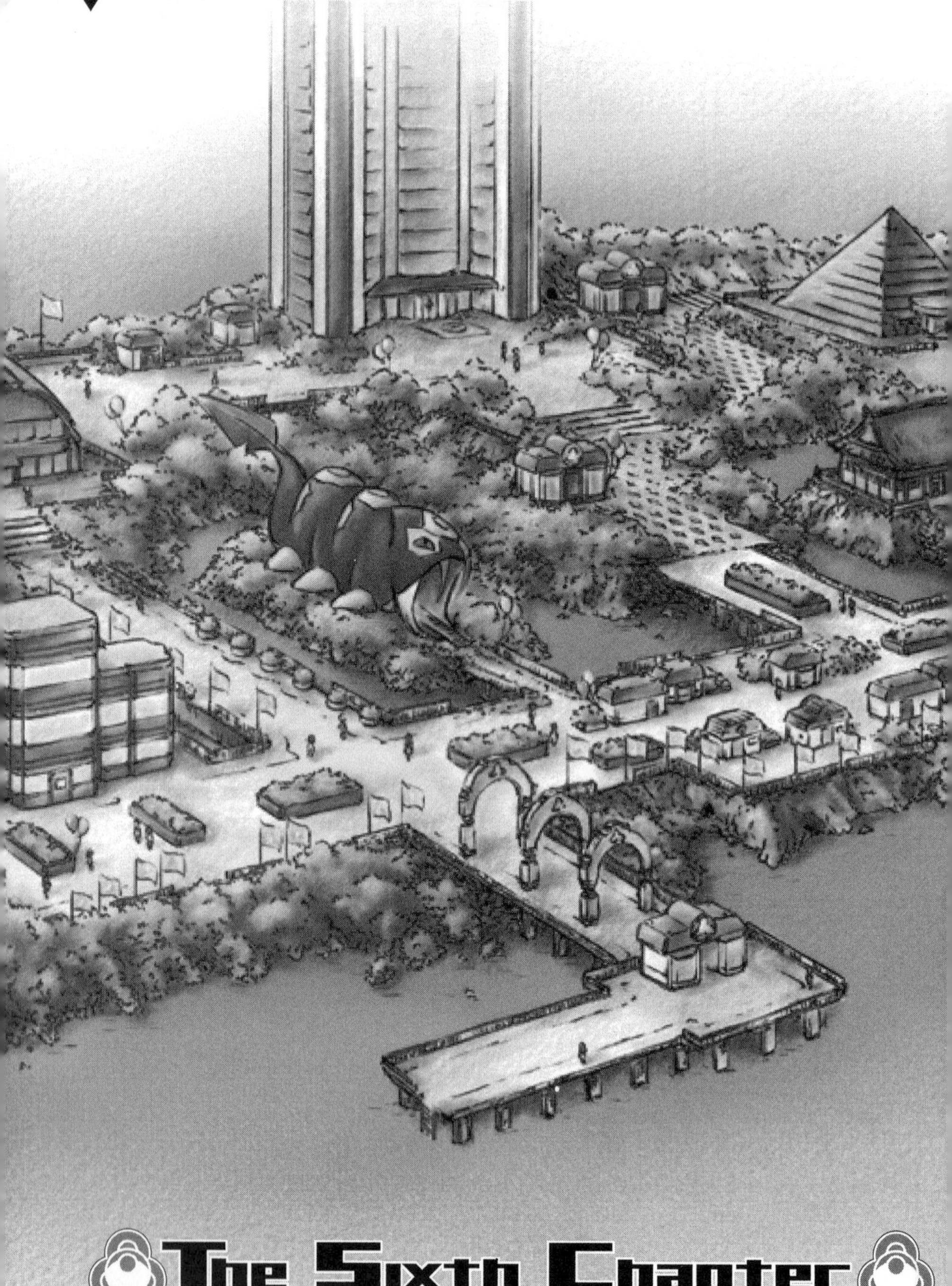

The Sixth Chapter

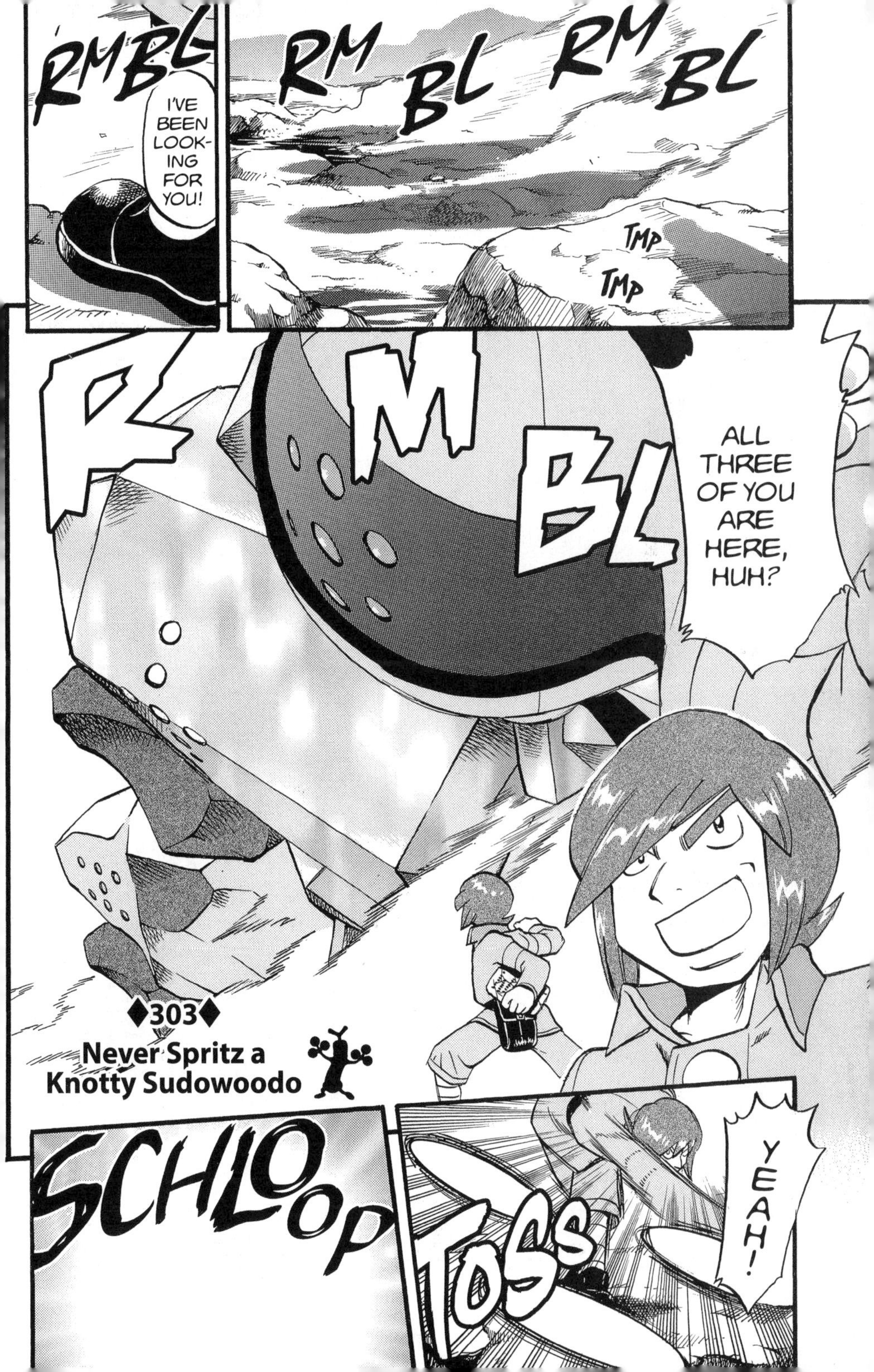
RM BL RM BL
TMP
TMP
RMBL
I'VE BEEN LOOKING FOR YOU!
RMBL
ALL THREE OF YOU ARE HERE, HUH?
◆303◆
Never Spritz a Knotty Sudowoodo
YEAH!
TOSS
SCHLOOP

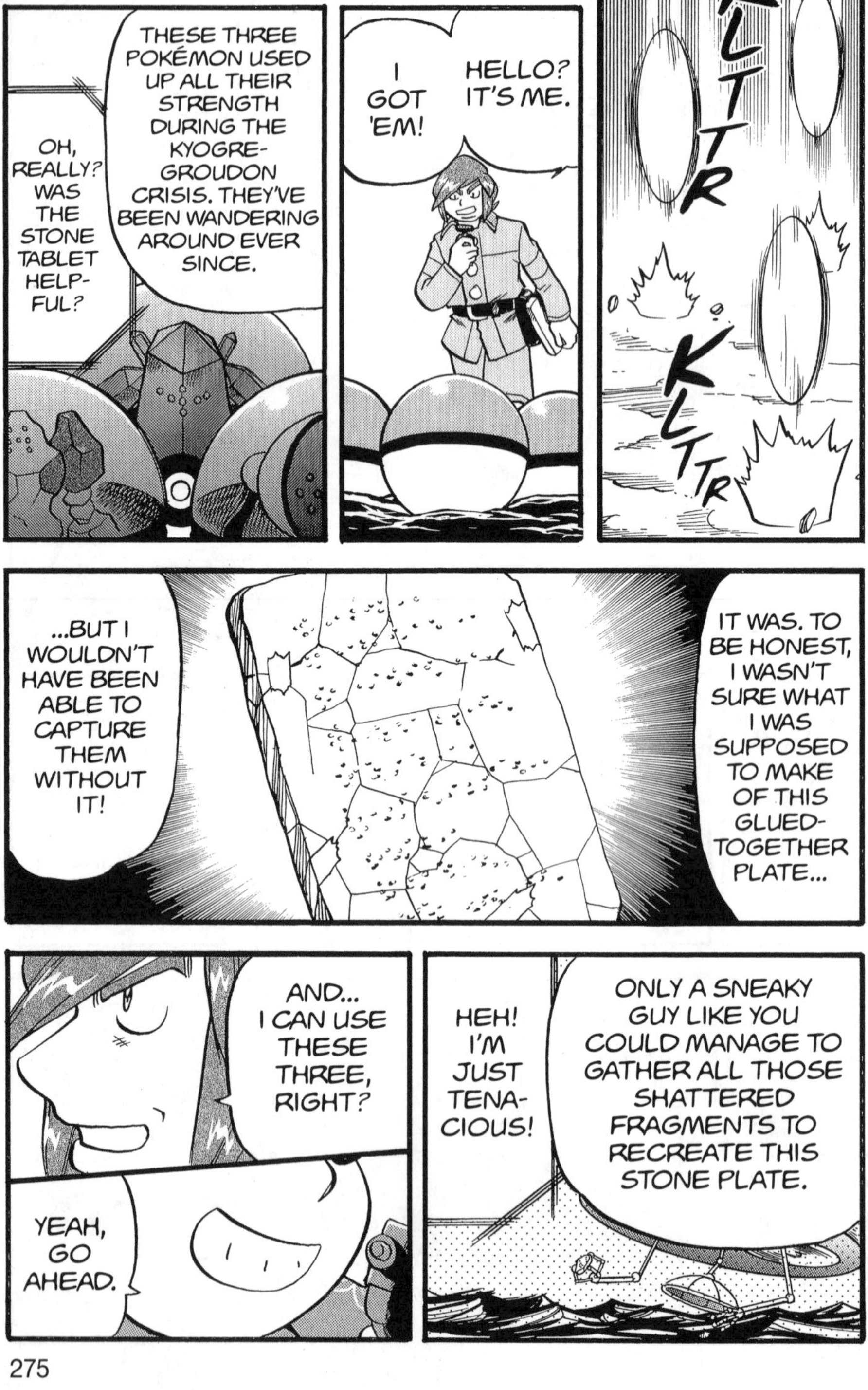
KLTTR
KLTTR
HELLO? IT'S ME.
I GOT 'EM!
THESE THREE POKÉMON USED UP ALL THEIR STRENGTH DURING THE KYOGRE-GROUDON CRISIS. THEY'VE BEEN WANDERING AROUND EVER SINCE.
OH, REALLY? WAS THE STONE TABLET HELPFUL?
IT WAS. TO BE HONEST, I WASN'T SURE WHAT I WAS SUPPOSED TO MAKE OF THIS GLUED-TOGETHER PLATE...
...BUT I WOULDN'T HAVE BEEN ABLE TO CAPTURE THEM WITHOUT IT!
ONLY A SNEAKY GUY LIKE YOU COULD MANAGE TO GATHER ALL THOSE SHATTERED FRAGMENTS TO RECREATE THIS STONE PLATE.
HEH! I'M JUST TENACIOUS!
AND... I CAN USE THESE THREE, RIGHT?
YEAH, GO AHEAD.

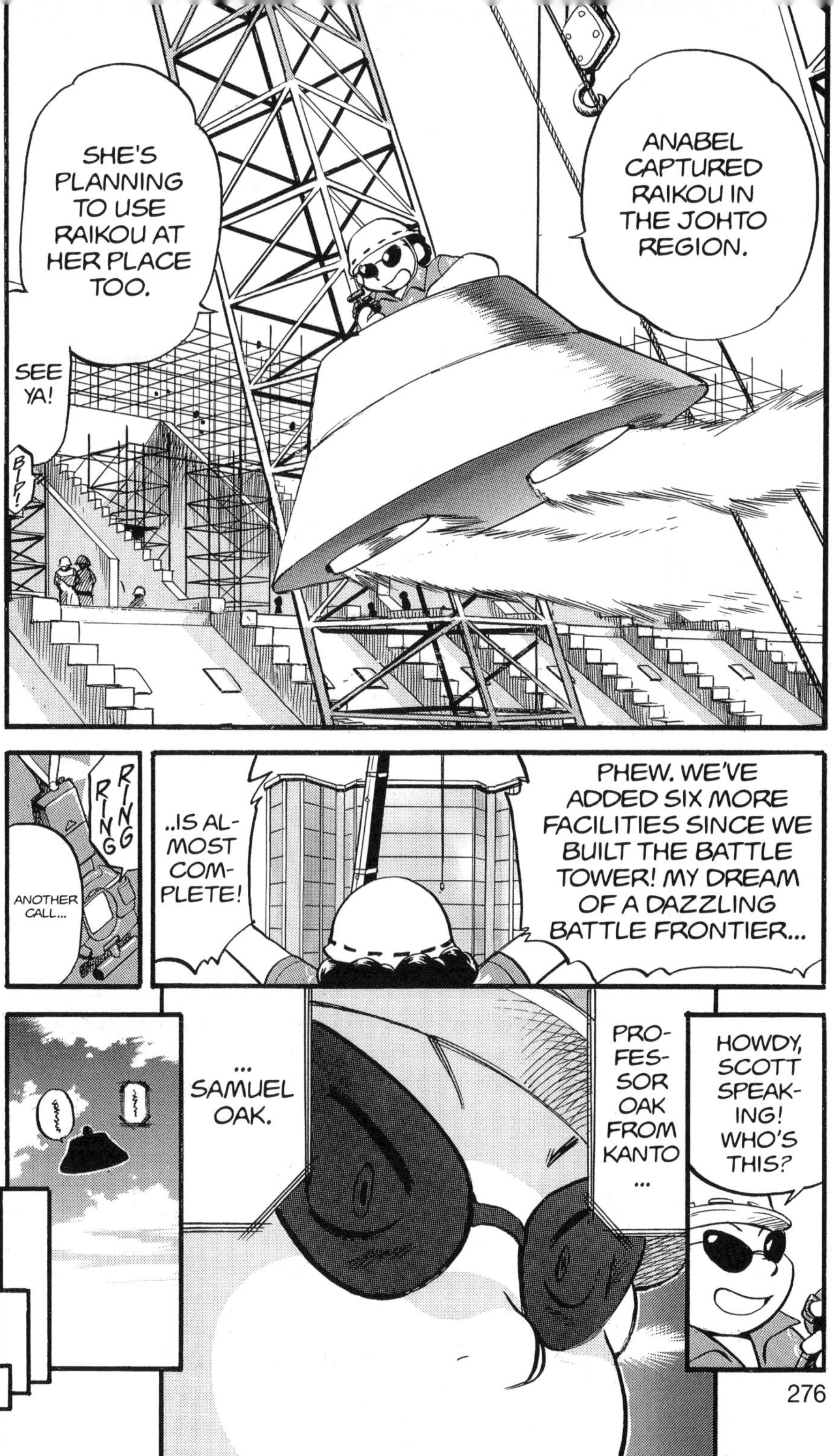
ANABEL CAPTURED RAIKOU IN THE JOHTO REGION.
SHE'S PLANNING TO USE RAIKOU AT HER PLACE TOO.
SEE YA!
BIP!
PHEW. WE'VE ADDED SIX MORE FACILITIES SINCE WE BUILT THE BATTLE TOWER! MY DREAM OF A DAZZLING BATTLE FRONTIER...
..IS AL-MOST COM-PLETE!
RING RING
ANOTHER CALL...
HOWDY, SCOTT SPEAK-ING! WHO'S THIS?
PRO-FES-SOR OAK FROM KANTO ...
... SAMUEL OAK.

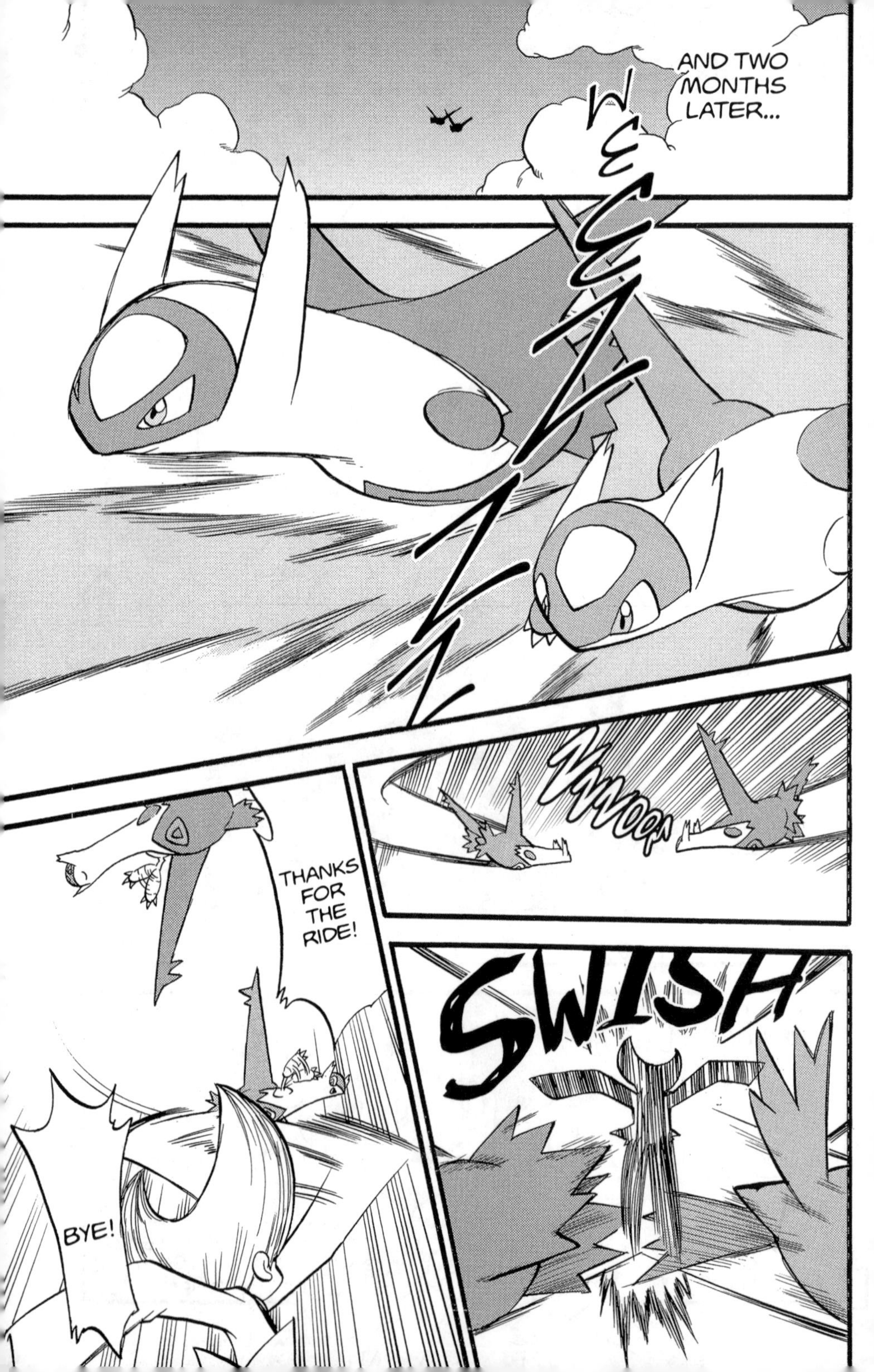
AND TWO MONTHS LATER...
SWISH
THANKS FOR THE RIDE!
BYE!

♦303♦

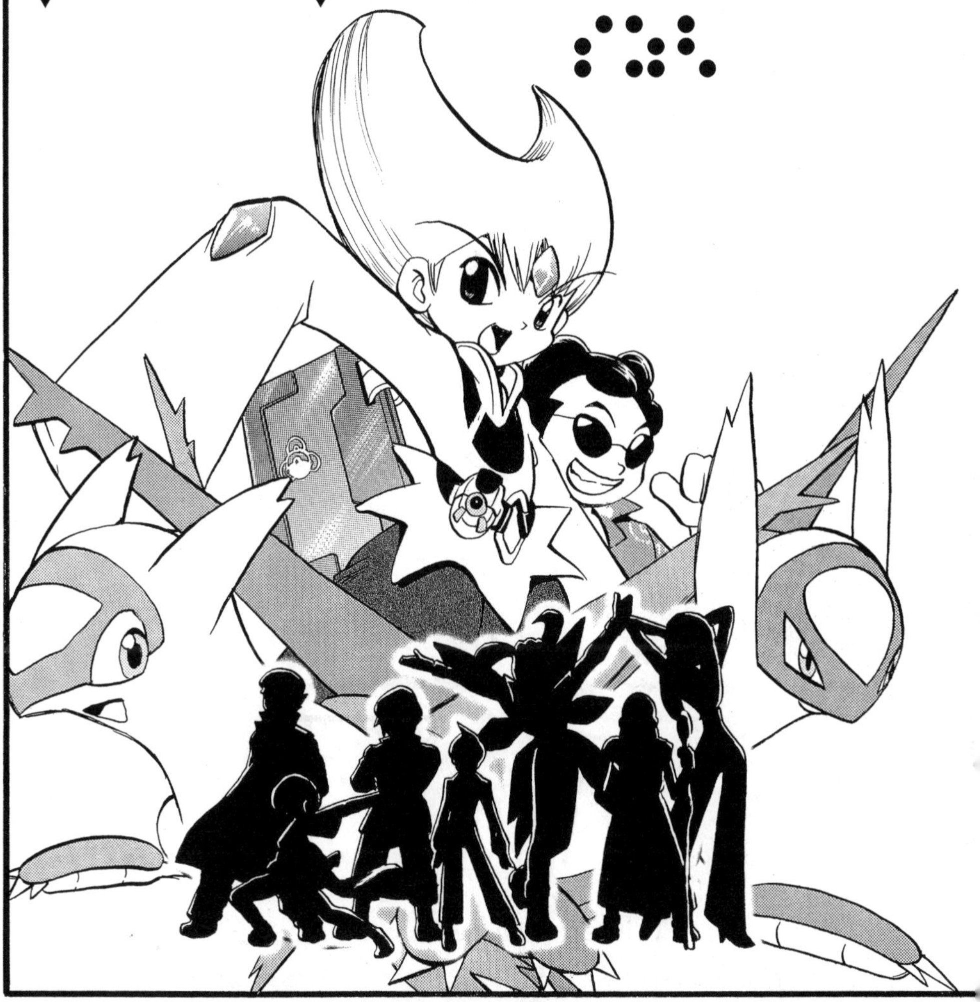

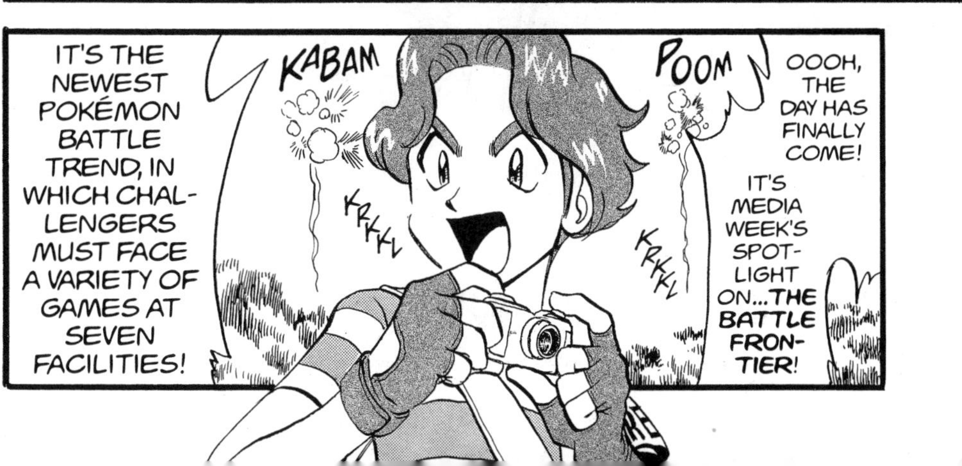
OOOH, THE DAY HAS FINALLY COME!
IT'S MEDIA WEEK'S SPOTLIGHT ON...THE BATTLE FRONTIER!
POOM
KRKKL
KABAM
KRKKL
IT'S THE NEWEST POKÉMON BATTLE TREND, IN WHICH CHALLENGERS MUST FACE A VARIETY OF GAMES AT SEVEN FACILITIES!

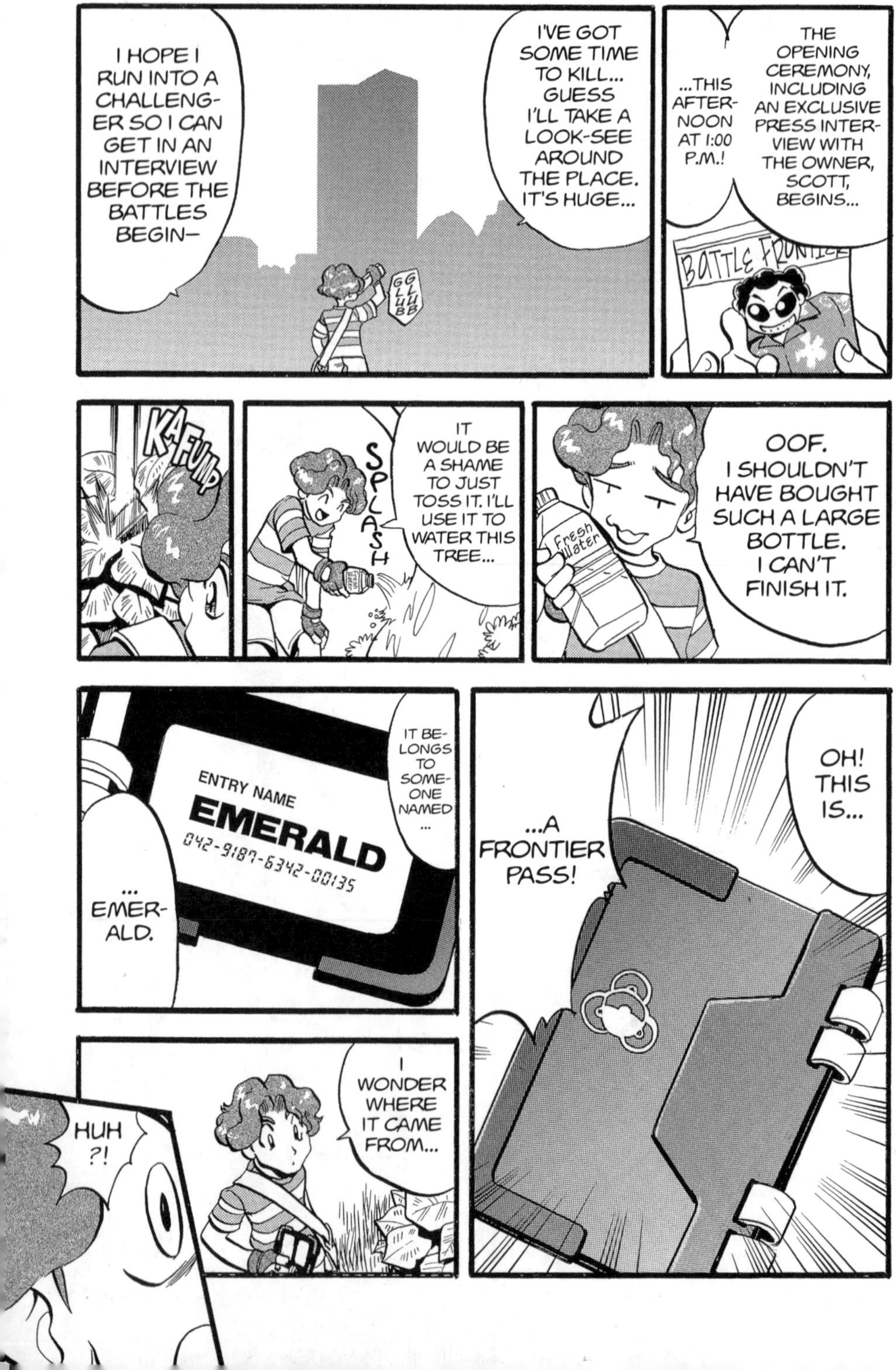
THE OPENING CEREMONY, INCLUDING AN EXCLUSIVE PRESS INTERVIEW WITH THE OWNER, SCOTT, BEGINS...
...THIS AFTERNOON AT 1:00 P.M.!
BATTLE FRONTIER
I'VE GOT SOME TIME TO KILL... GUESS I'LL TAKE A LOOK-SEE AROUND THE PLACE. IT'S HUGE...
I HOPE I RUN INTO A CHALLENGER SO I CAN GET IN AN INTERVIEW BEFORE THE BATTLES BEGIN—
GLUB GLUB
OOF. I SHOULDN'T HAVE BOUGHT SUCH A LARGE BOTTLE. I CAN'T FINISH IT.
Fresh Water
IT WOULD BE A SHAME TO JUST TOSS IT. I'LL USE IT TO WATER THIS TREE...
SPLASH
KAFUMP
OH! THIS IS...
...A FRONTIER PASS!
IT BELONGS TO SOMEONE NAMED...
ENTRY NAME
EMERALD
042-9187-6342-00135
...EMERALD.
I WONDER WHERE IT CAME FROM...
HUH?!

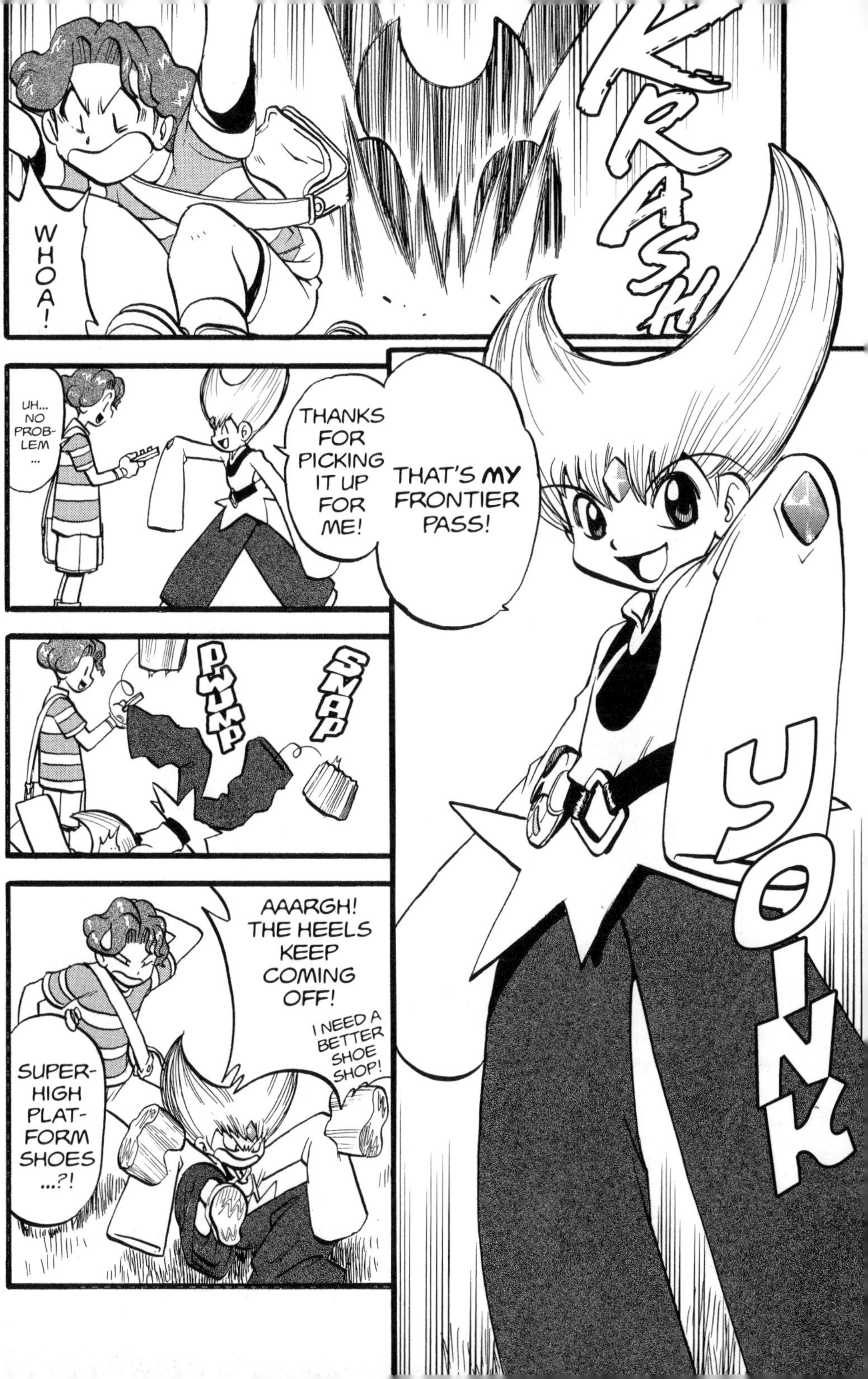
KRASH
WHOA!
THAT'S **MY** FRONTIER PASS!
YOINK
THANKS FOR PICKING IT UP FOR ME!
UH... NO PROBLEM...
SNAP
PWUMP
AAARGH! THE HEELS KEEP COMING OFF!
I NEED A BETTER SHOE SHOP!
SUPER-HIGH PLATFORM SHOES...?!

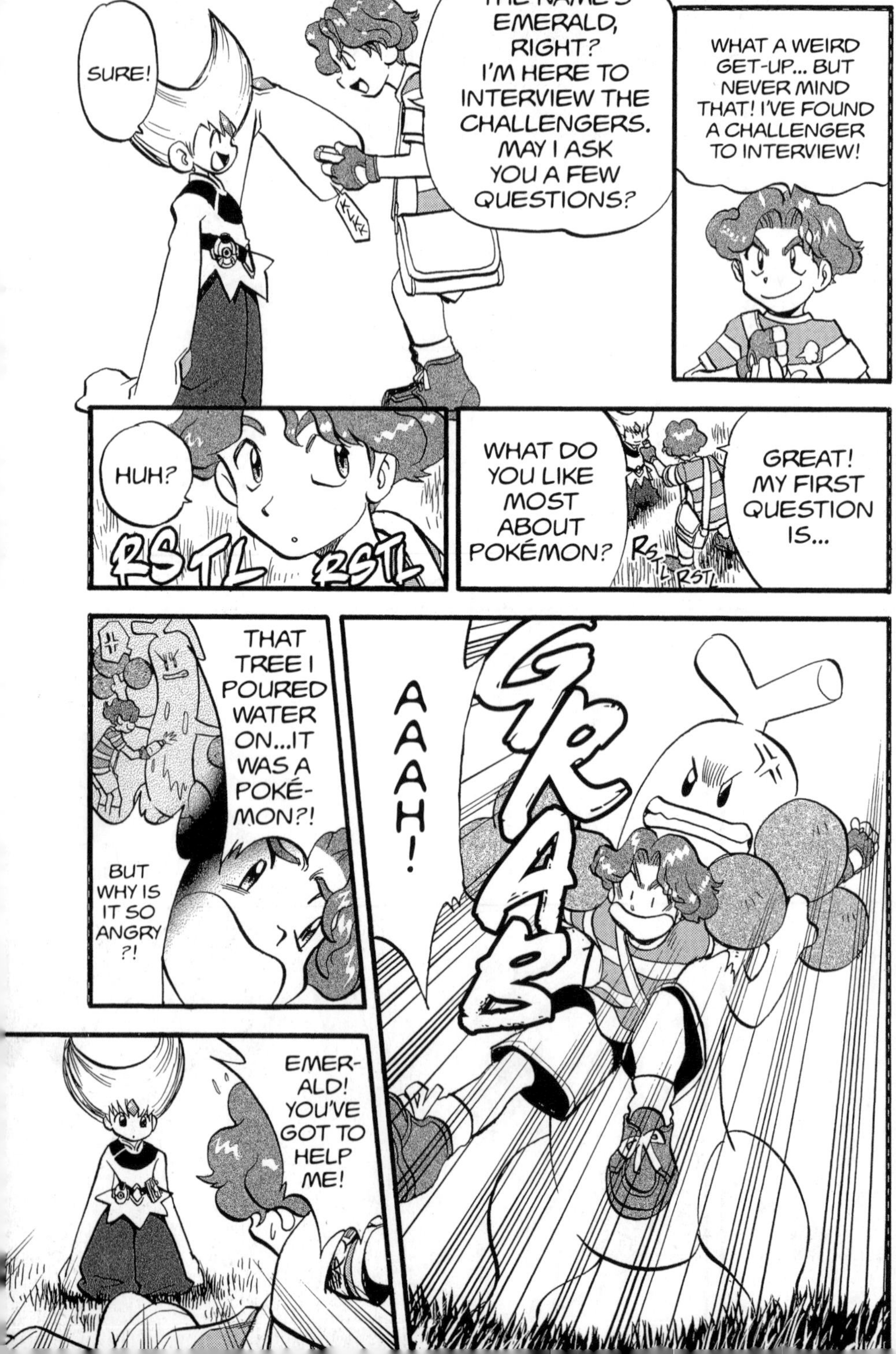
WHAT A WEIRD GET-UP... BUT NEVER MIND THAT! I'VE FOUND A CHALLENGER TO INTERVIEW!
THE NAME'S EMERALD, RIGHT? I'M HERE TO INTERVIEW THE CHALLENGERS. MAY I ASK YOU A FEW QUESTIONS?
SURE!
GREAT! MY FIRST QUESTION IS...
WHAT DO YOU LIKE MOST ABOUT POKÉMON?
RSTL RSTL
HUH?
RSTL RSTL
AAAAH!
THAT TREE I POURED WATER ON...IT WAS A POKÉMON?!
BUT WHY IS IT SO ANGRY?!
EMERALD! YOU'VE GOT TO HELP ME!

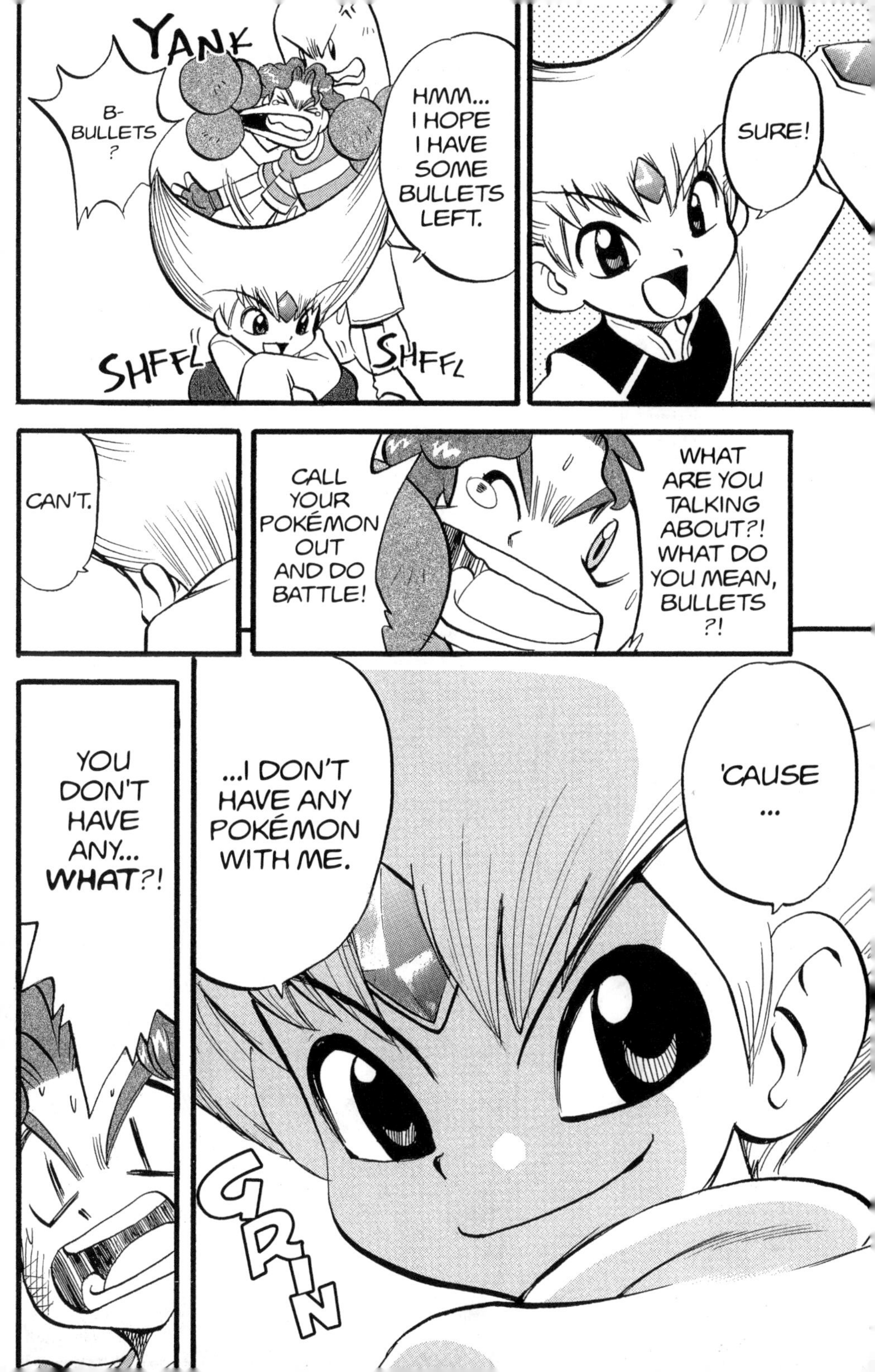
SURE!
HMM... I HOPE I HAVE SOME BULLETS LEFT.
YANK
B-BULLETS?
SHFFL
SHFFL
WHAT ARE YOU TALKING ABOUT?! WHAT DO YOU MEAN, BULLETS?!
CALL YOUR POKÉMON OUT AND DO BATTLE!
CAN'T.
'CAUSE...
...I DON'T HAVE ANY POKÉMON WITH ME.
GRIN
YOU DON'T HAVE ANY... WHAT?!

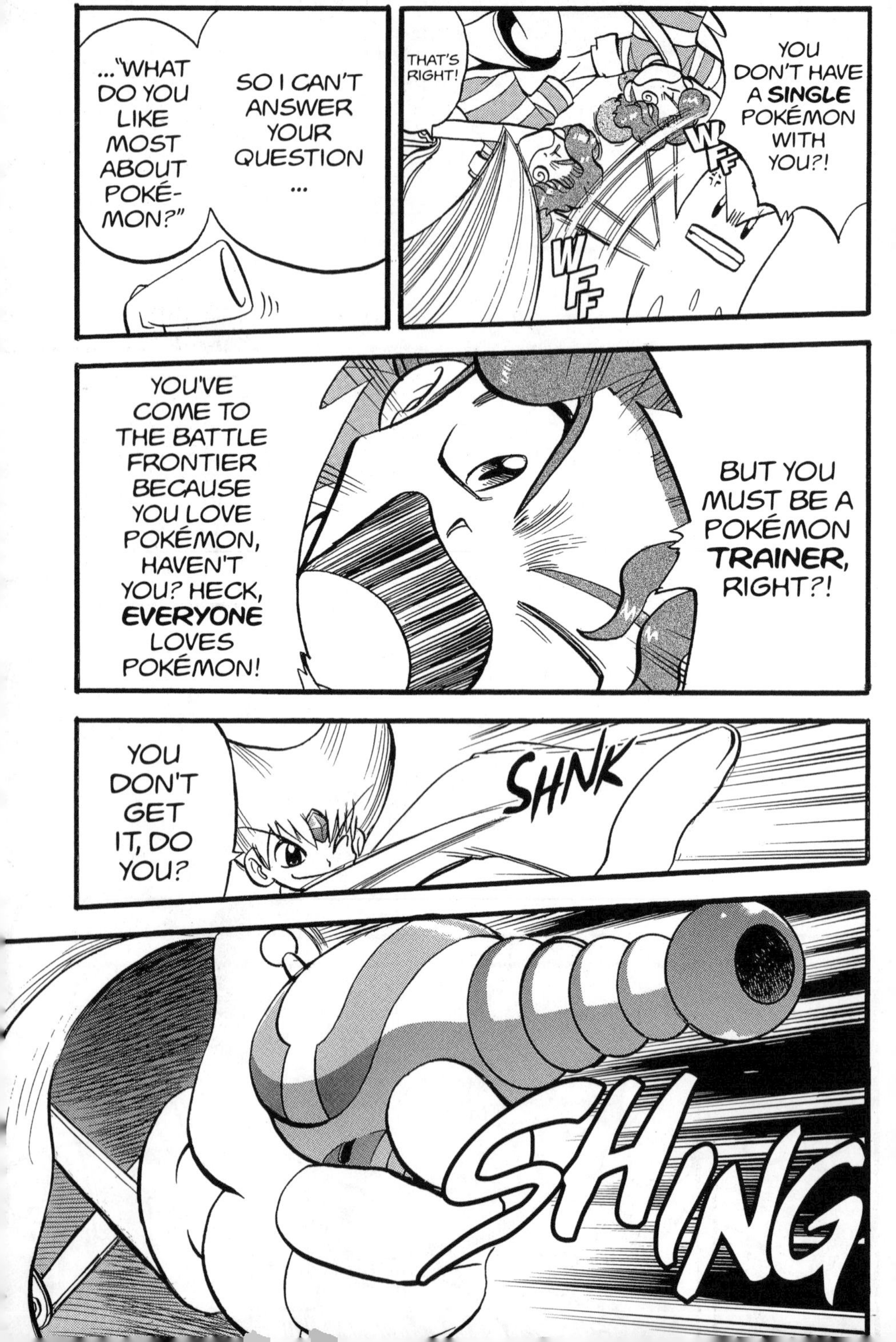
YOU DON'T HAVE A SINGLE POKÉMON WITH YOU?!
THAT'S RIGHT!
WFF
WFF
SO I CAN'T ANSWER YOUR QUESTION ...
..."WHAT DO YOU LIKE MOST ABOUT POKÉMON?"
BUT YOU MUST BE A POKÉMON TRAINER, RIGHT?!
YOU'VE COME TO THE BATTLE FRONTIER BECAUSE YOU LOVE POKÉMON, HAVEN'T YOU? HECK, EVERYONE LOVES POKÉMON!
SHNK
YOU DON'T GET IT, DO YOU?
SHING

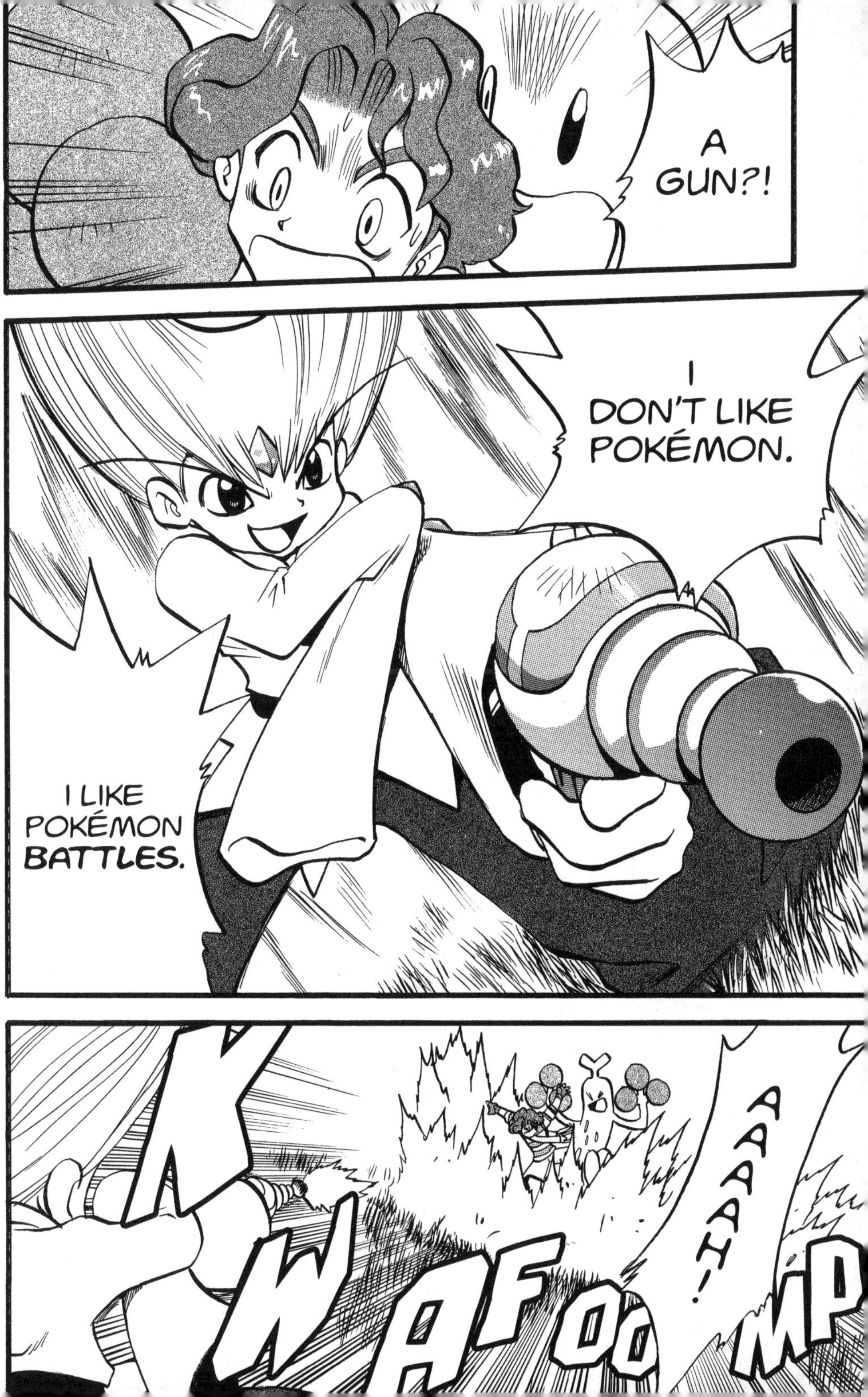
A GUN?!
I DON'T LIKE POKÉMON.
I LIKE POKÉMON BATTLES.
AAAAAH!!
WAFOOMP

TO THE PRESS...

Thank you so much for attending this press conference at the Battle Frontier today. I've spent a fortune creating this facility to offer Trainers the opportunity to participate in cutting-edge Pokémon Battles. We offer a variety of styles of battle at our facilities. Enjoy!

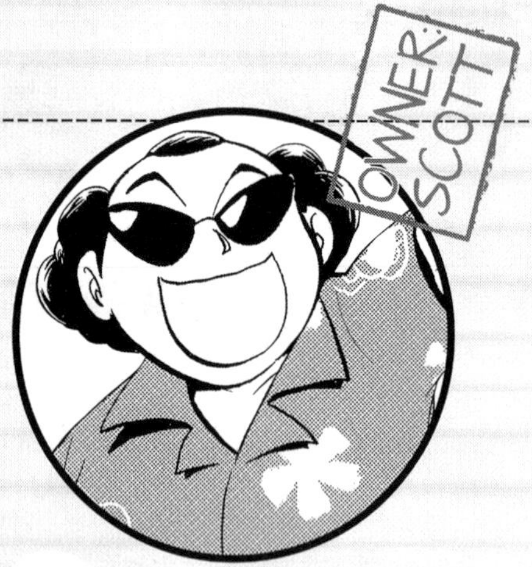

OWNER: SCOTT

PRE-OPENING EVENT FOR THE PRESS

The pre-opening Media Week starts tomorrow. The Battle Frontier will officially open to the public the following week.

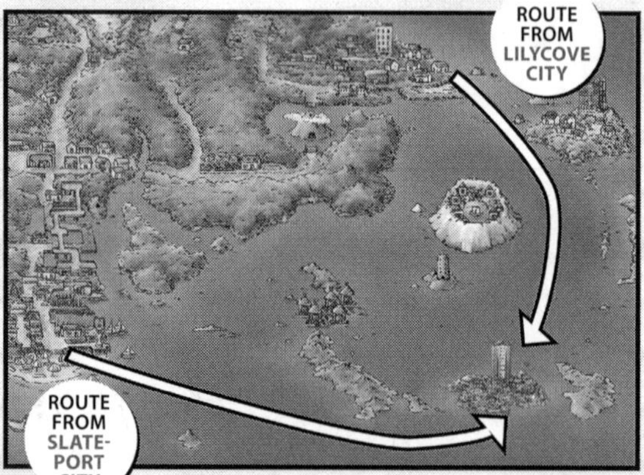

ROUTE FROM LILYCOVE CITY
ROUTE FROM SLATE-PORT CITY

LOCATION/ TRANSPORTATION

The Battle Frontier is located on an island in the Hoenn region, in between Pacifidlog Town and Ever Grande City. Enjoy a pleasant cruise there via ferry departing from Slateport City or Lilycove City.

◆ 304 ◆

Swanky Showdown with Swalot

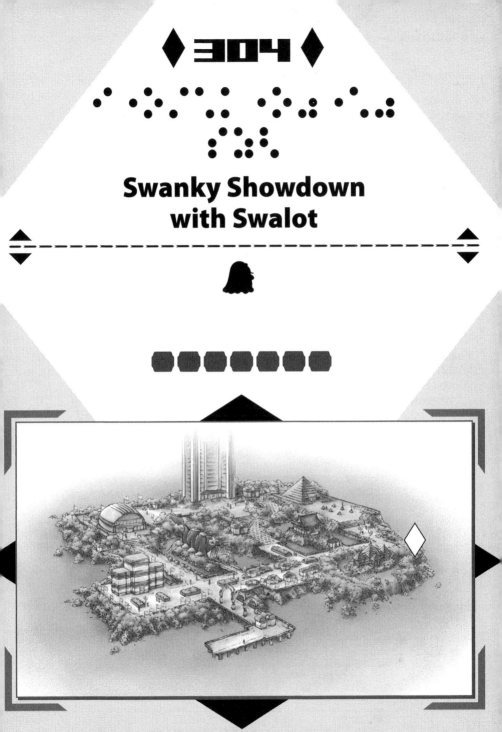

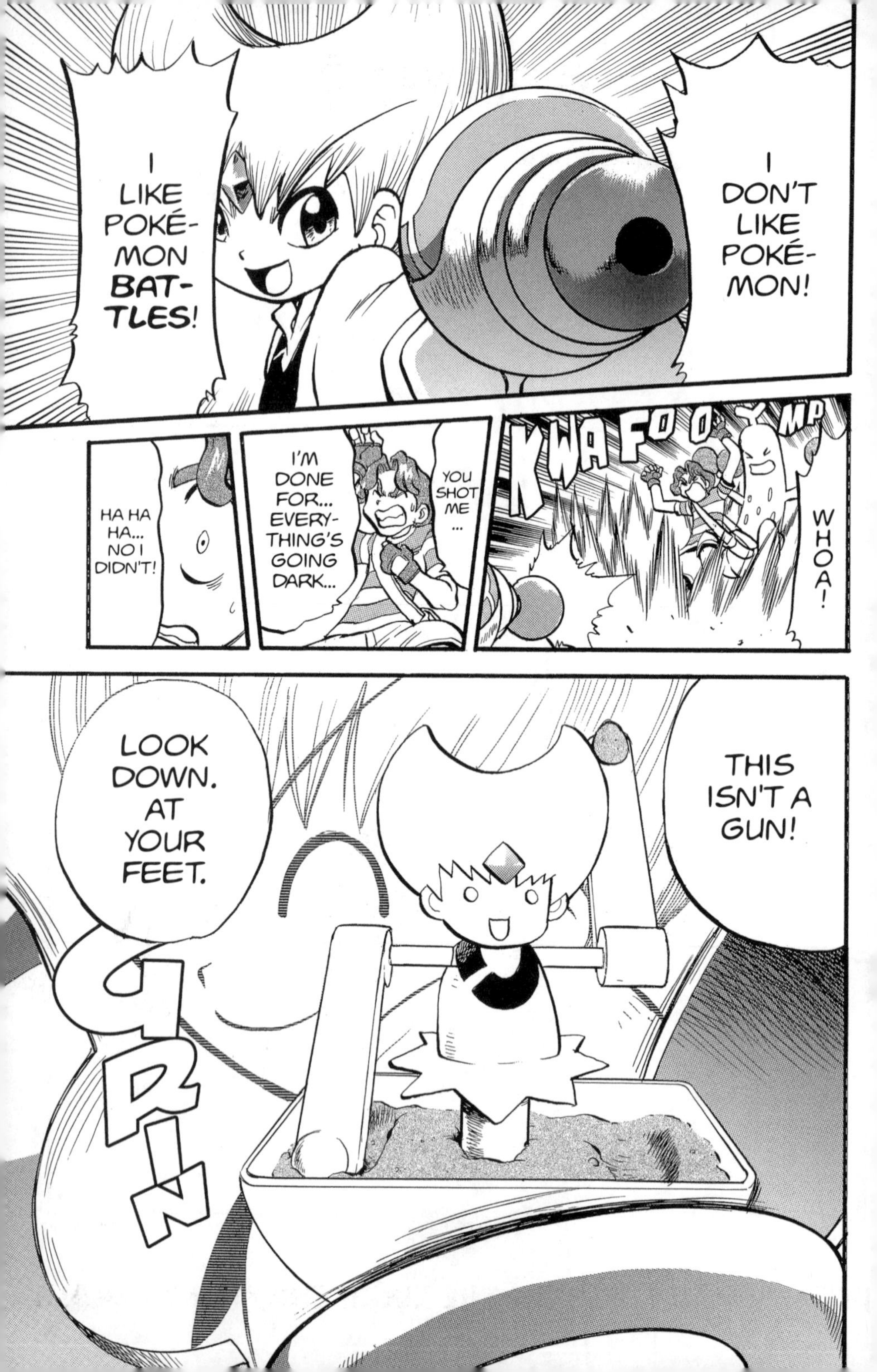
I DON'T LIKE POKÉMON!
I LIKE POKÉMON BATTLES!
KWAFOOMP
WHOA!
YOU SHOT ME...
I'M DONE FOR... EVERYTHING'S GOING DARK...
HA HA HA... NO I DIDN'T!
THIS ISN'T A GUN!
LOOK DOWN. AT YOUR FEET.
GRIN

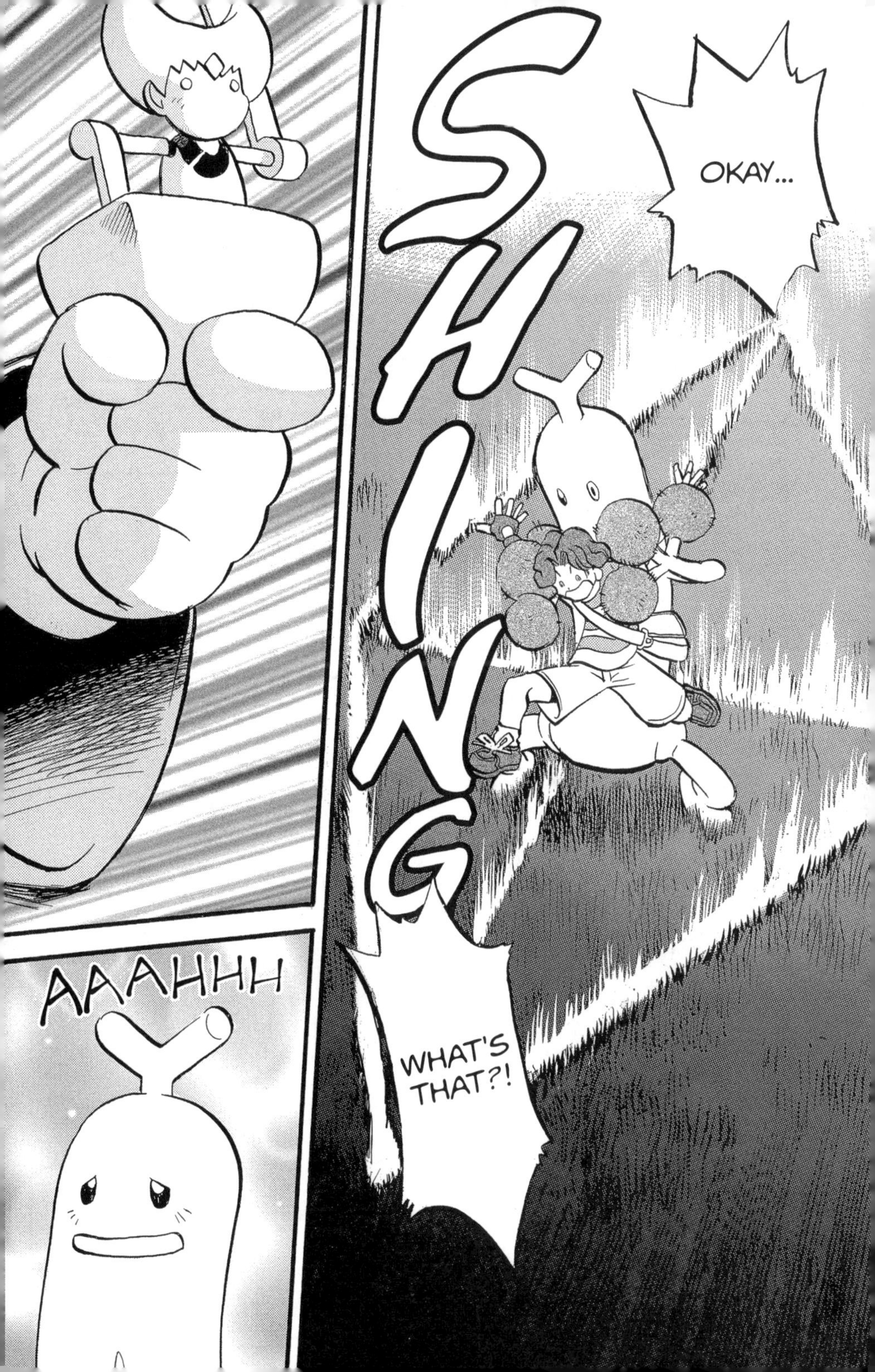
OKAY...
SHING
WHAT'S THAT?!
AAAHHH

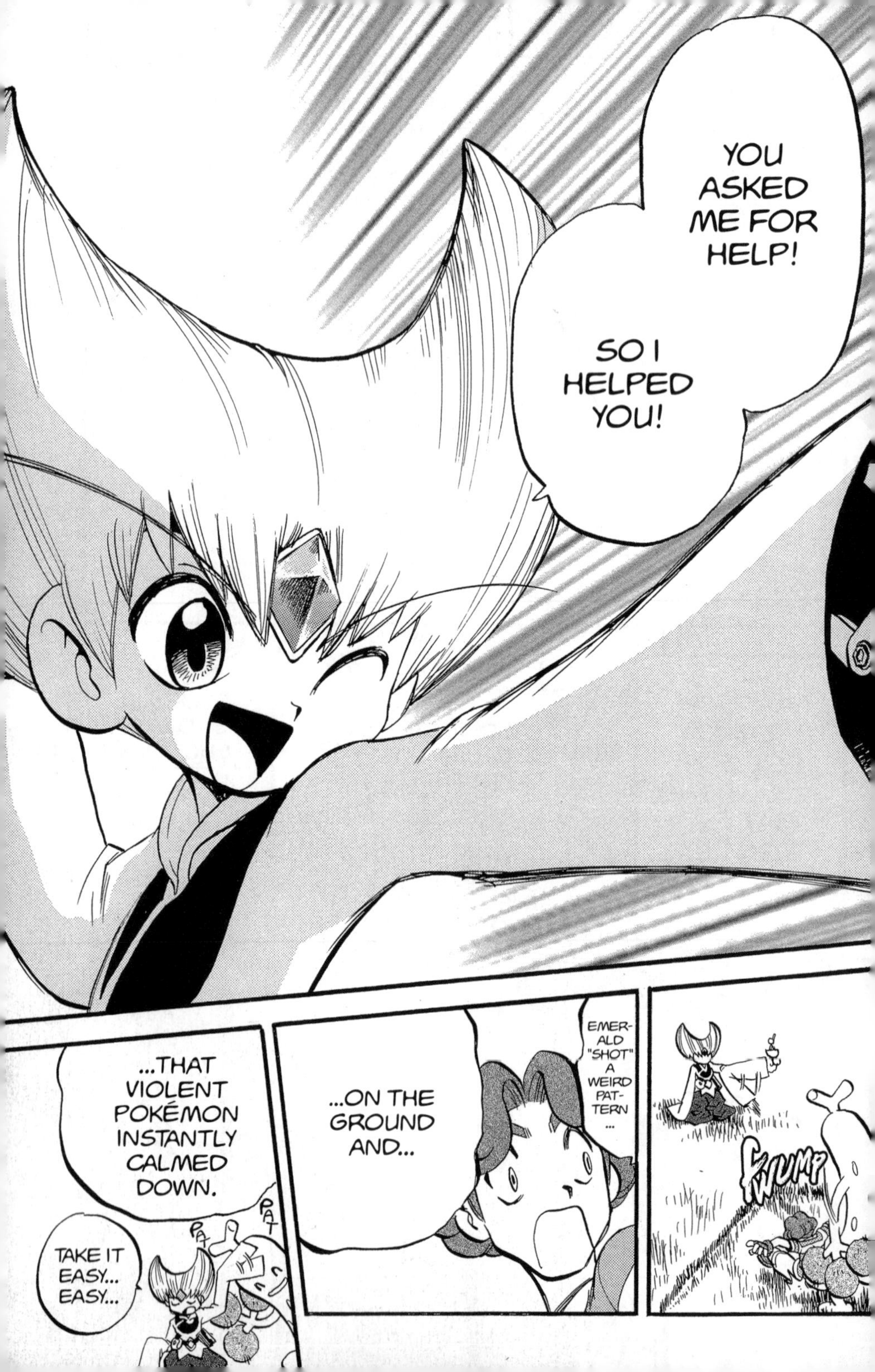
YOU ASKED ME FOR HELP!
SO I HELPED YOU!
FWUMP
EMER-ALD "SHOT" A WEIRD PAT-TERN ...
...ON THE GROUND AND...
...THAT VIOLENT POKÉMON INSTANTLY CALMED DOWN.
PAT PAT
TAKE IT EASY... EASY...

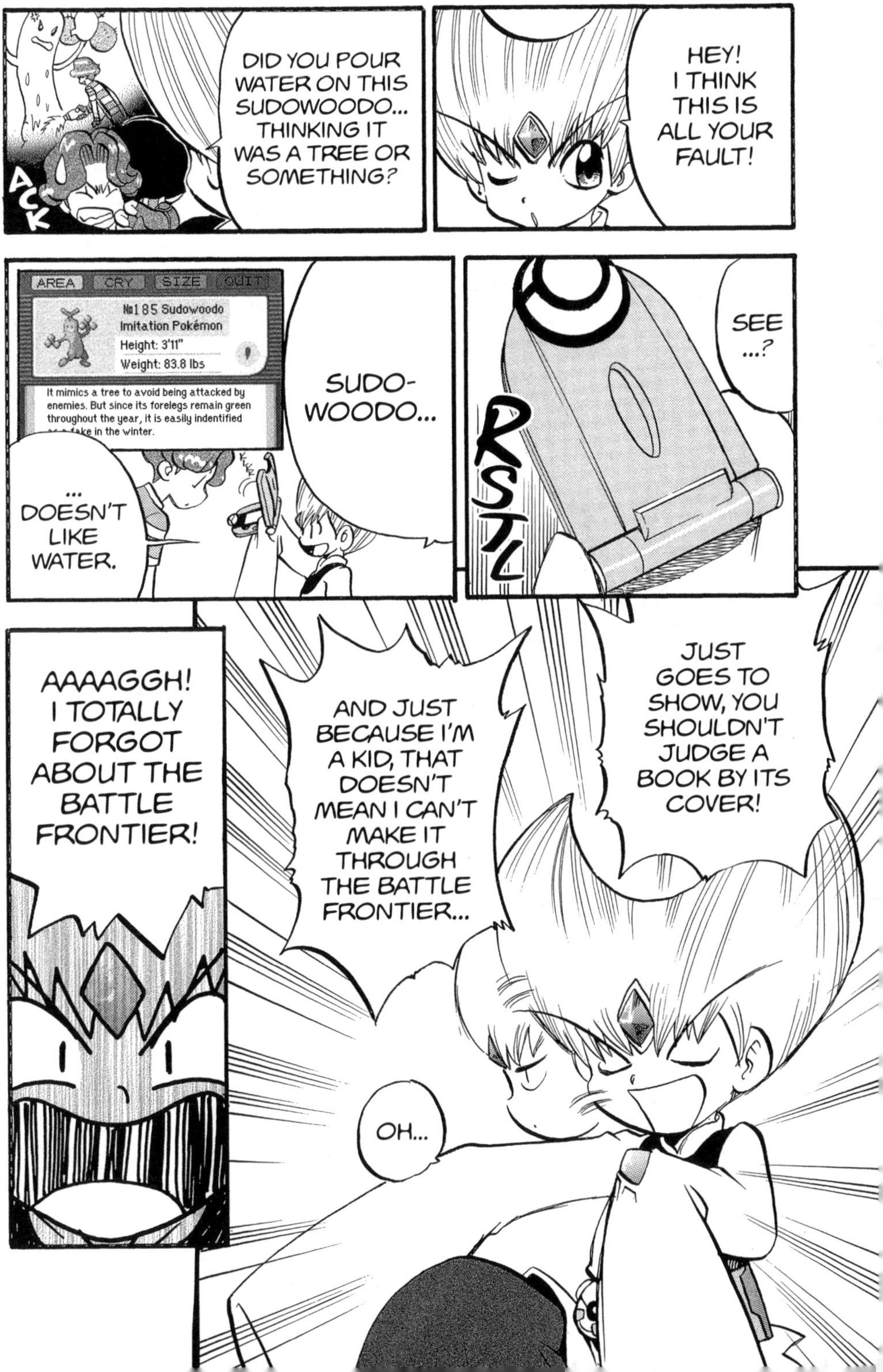
HEY! I THINK THIS IS ALL YOUR FAULT!
DID YOU POUR WATER ON THIS SUDOWOODO... THINKING IT WAS A TREE OR SOMETHING?
ACK
SEE ...?
RSTL
SUDO-WOODO...
AREA CRY SIZE QUIT
№185 Sudowoodo
Imitation Pokémon
Height: 3'11"
Weight: 83.8 lbs
It mimics a tree to avoid being attacked by enemies. But since its forelegs remain green throughout the year, it is easily indentified
fake in the winter.
... DOESN'T LIKE WATER.
JUST GOES TO SHOW, YOU SHOULDN'T JUDGE A BOOK BY ITS COVER!
AND JUST BECAUSE I'M A KID, THAT DOESN'T MEAN I CAN'T MAKE IT THROUGH THE BATTLE FRONTIER...
OH...
AAAAGGH! I TOTALLY FORGOT ABOUT THE BATTLE FRONTIER!

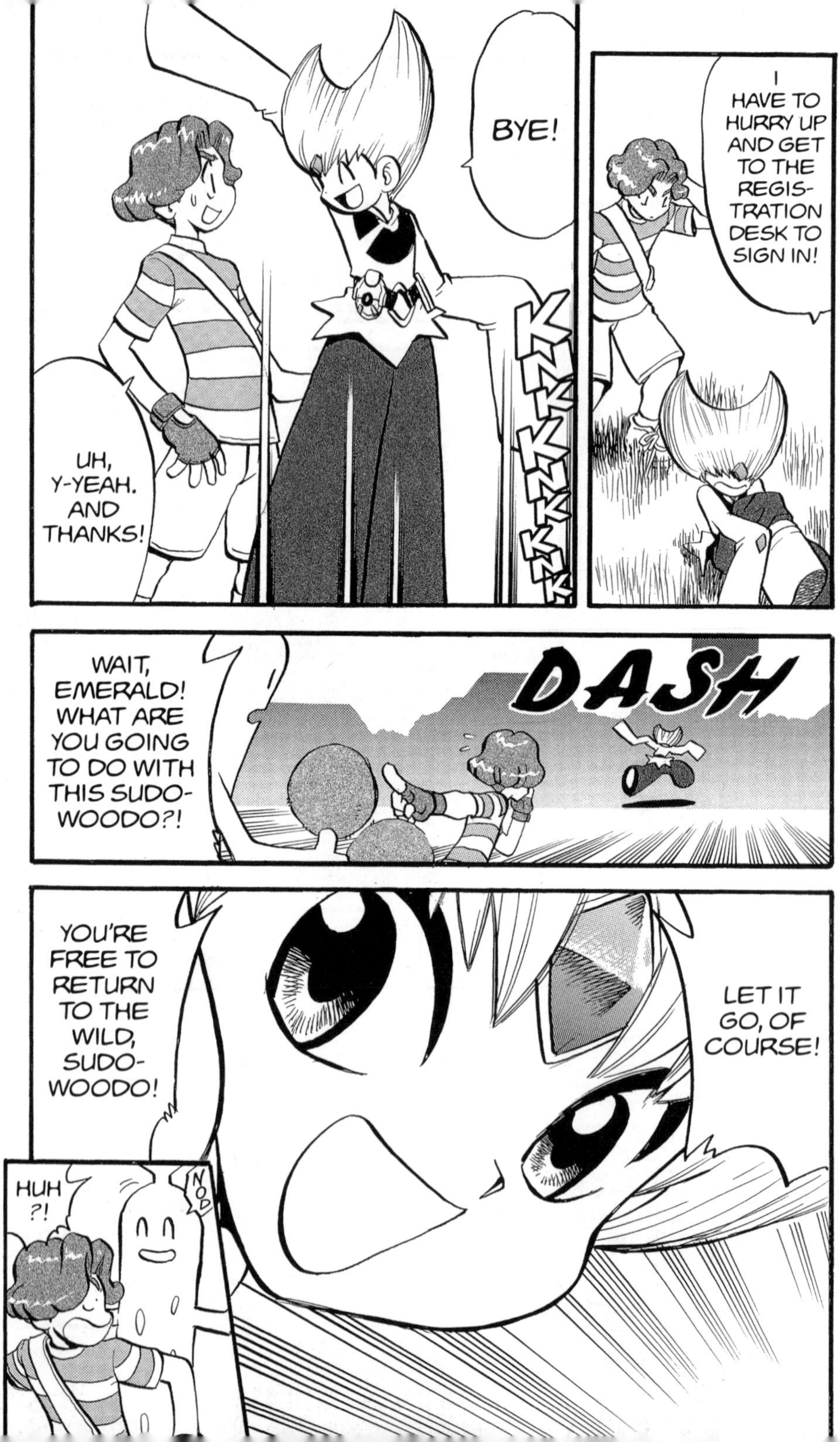
I HAVE TO HURRY UP AND GET TO THE REGIS-TRATION DESK TO SIGN IN!
BYE!
KNKKNKKNK
UH, Y-YEAH. AND THANKS!
DASH
WAIT, EMERALD! WHAT ARE YOU GOING TO DO WITH THIS SUDO-WOODO?!
LET IT GO, OF COURSE!
YOU'RE FREE TO RETURN TO THE WILD, SUDO-WOODO!
NOD
HUH?!

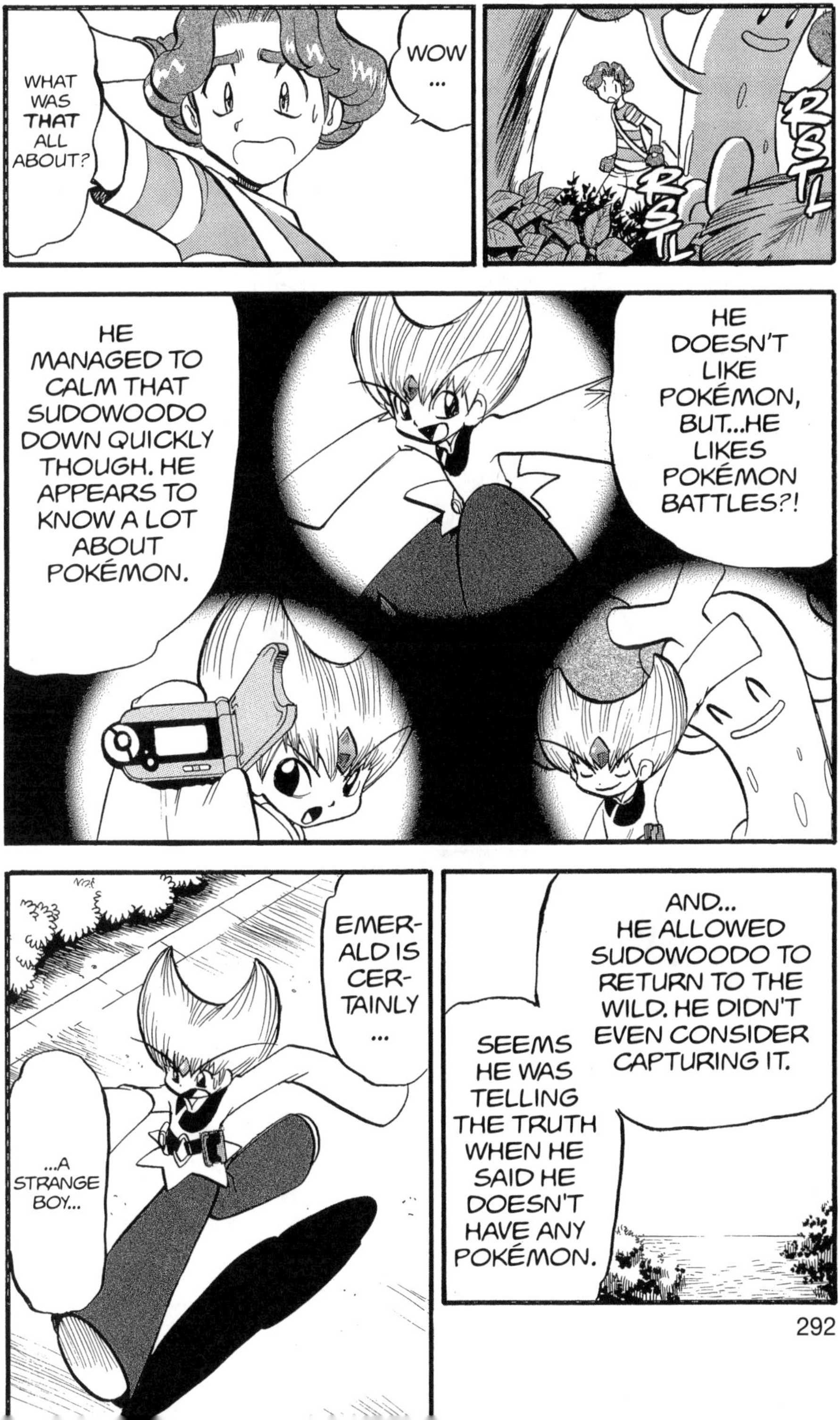
RSTL
RSTL
WOW...
WHAT WAS **THAT** ALL ABOUT?
HE DOESN'T LIKE POKÉMON, BUT...HE LIKES POKÉMON BATTLES?!
HE MANAGED TO CALM THAT SUDOWOODO DOWN QUICKLY THOUGH. HE APPEARS TO KNOW A LOT ABOUT POKÉMON.
AND... HE ALLOWED SUDOWOODO TO RETURN TO THE WILD. HE DIDN'T EVEN CONSIDER CAPTURING IT.
SEEMS HE WAS TELLING THE TRUTH WHEN HE SAID HE DOESN'T HAVE ANY POKÉMON.
EMER-ALD IS CER-TAINLY...
...A STRANGE BOY...

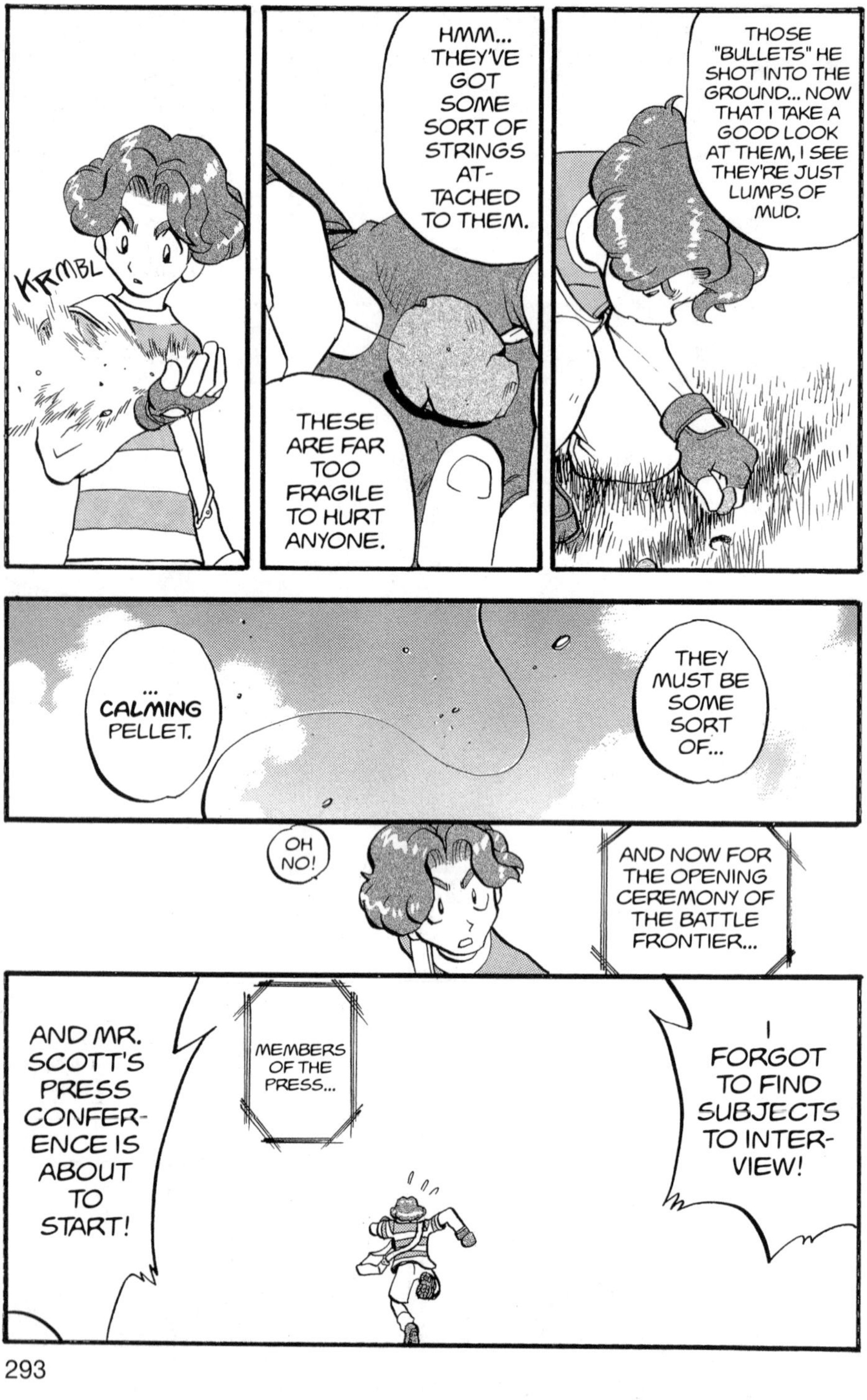
THOSE "BULLETS" HE SHOT INTO THE GROUND... NOW THAT I TAKE A GOOD LOOK AT THEM, I SEE THEY'RE JUST LUMPS OF MUD.
HMM... THEY'VE GOT SOME SORT OF STRINGS AT-TACHED TO THEM.
THESE ARE FAR TOO FRAGILE TO HURT ANYONE.
KRMBL
THEY MUST BE SOME SORT OF...
...CALMING PELLET.
AND NOW FOR THE OPENING CEREMONY OF THE BATTLE FRONTIER...
OH NO!
I FORGOT TO FIND SUBJECTS TO INTER-VIEW!
MEMBERS OF THE PRESS...
AND MR. SCOTT'S PRESS CONFER-ENCE IS ABOUT TO START!

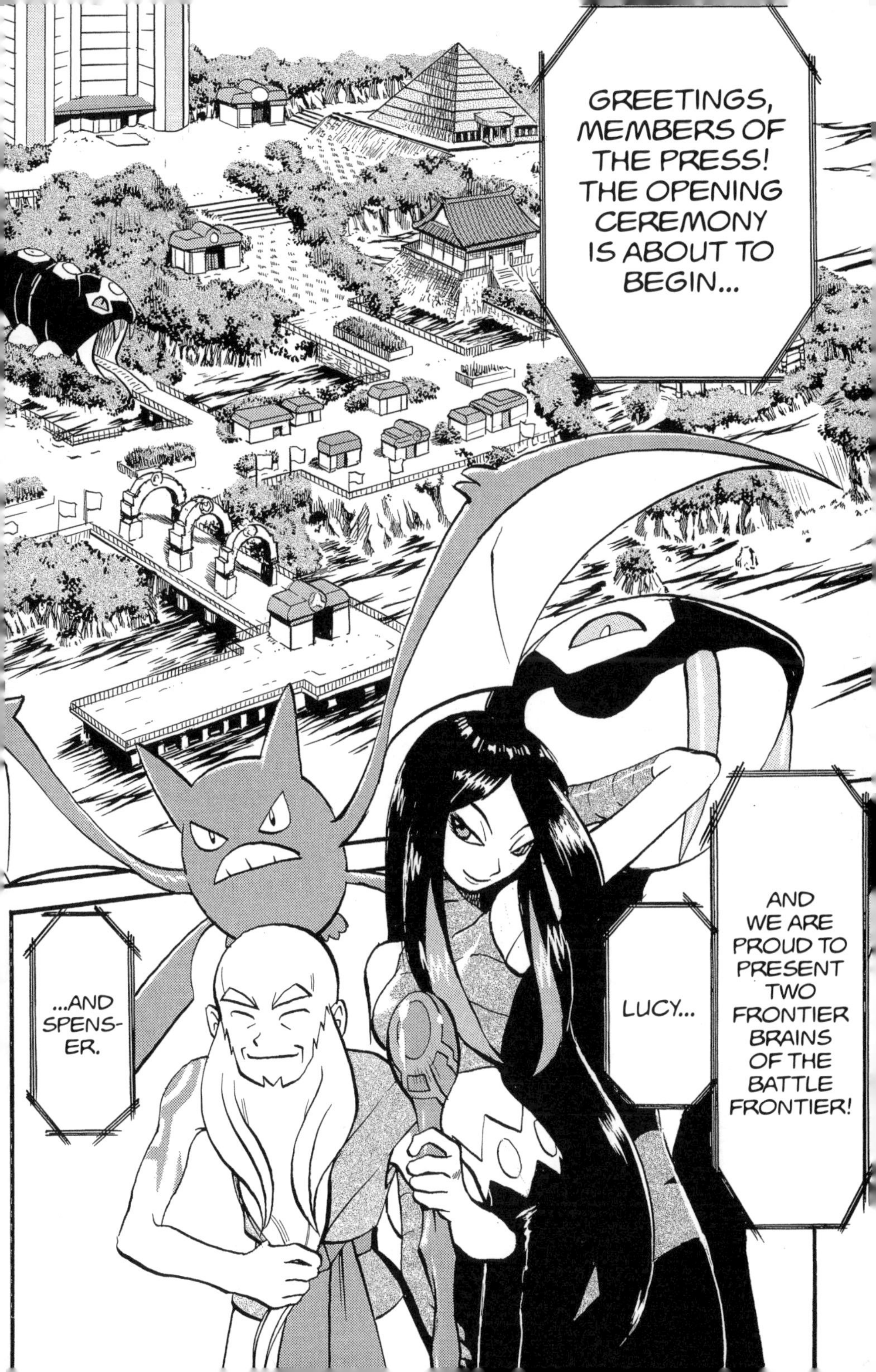
GREETINGS, MEMBERS OF THE PRESS! THE OPENING CEREMONY IS ABOUT TO BEGIN...
AND WE ARE PROUD TO PRESENT TWO FRONTIER BRAINS OF THE BATTLE FRONTIER!
LUCY...
...AND SPENS-ER.

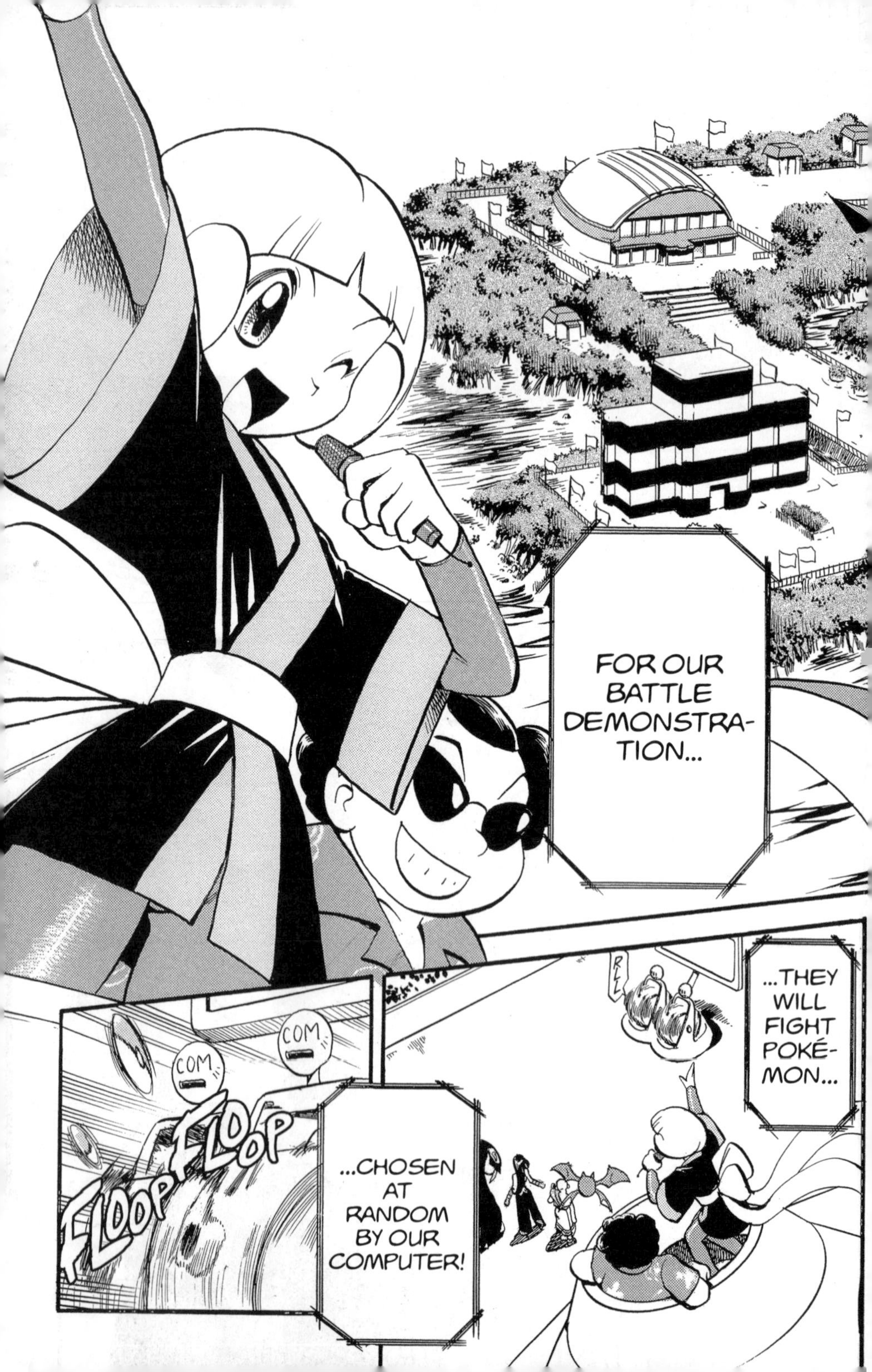
FOR OUR BATTLE DEMONSTRATION...
...THEY WILL FIGHT POKÉMON...
...CHOSEN AT RANDOM BY OUR COMPUTER!
COM
COM
FLOOP FLOOP

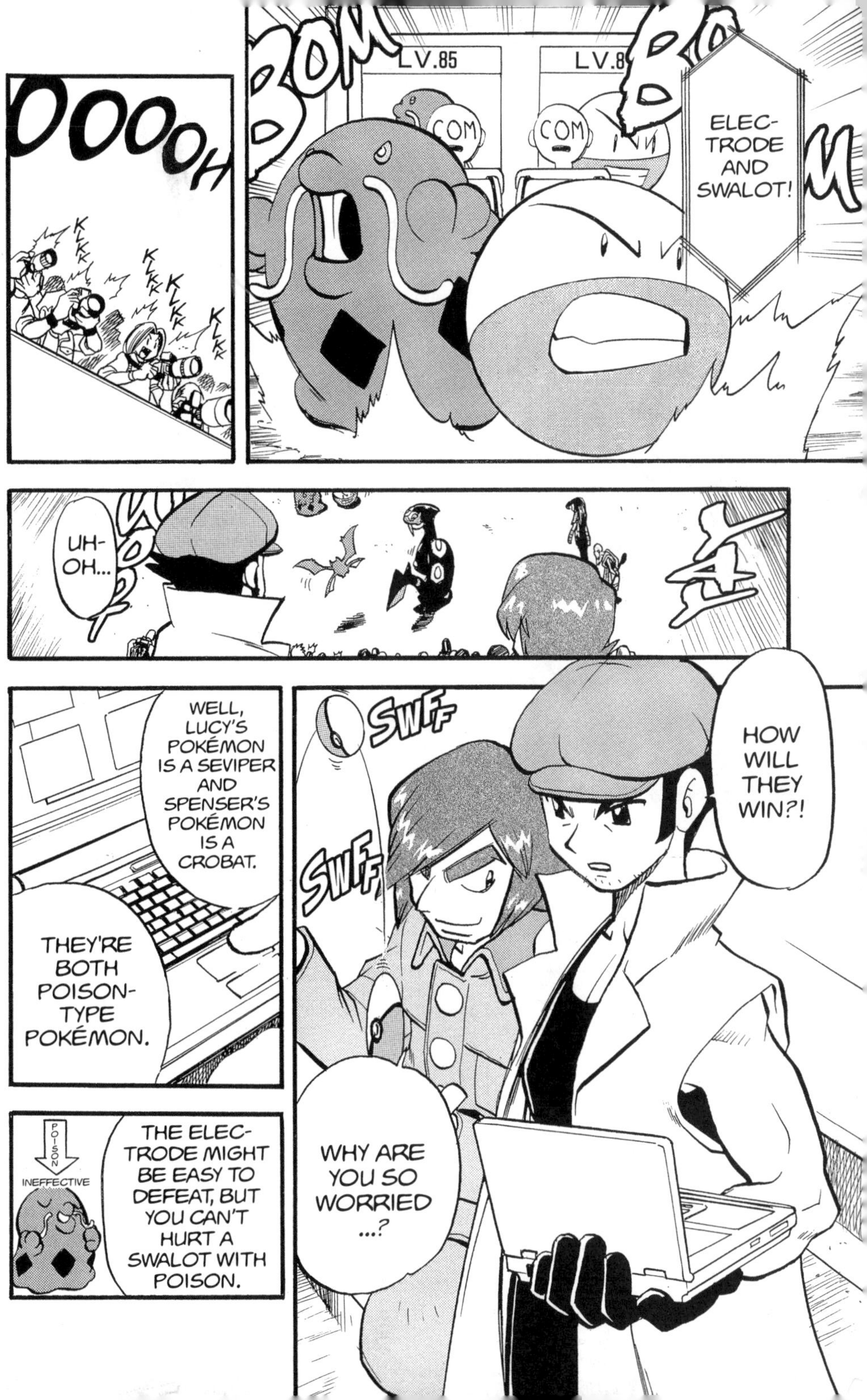
LV.85
LV.8
COM
COM
ELEC-TRODE AND SWALOT!
OOOOOH
KLKK
KLKK
KLKK
KLKK
UH-OH...
HOW WILL THEY WIN?!
WHY ARE YOU SO WORRIED ...?
WELL, LUCY'S POKÉMON IS A SEVIPER AND SPENSER'S POKÉMON IS A CROBAT.
THEY'RE BOTH POISON-TYPE POKÉMON.
THE ELEC-TRODE MIGHT BE EASY TO DEFEAT, BUT YOU CAN'T HURT A SWALOT WITH POISON.
POISON
INEFFECTIVE

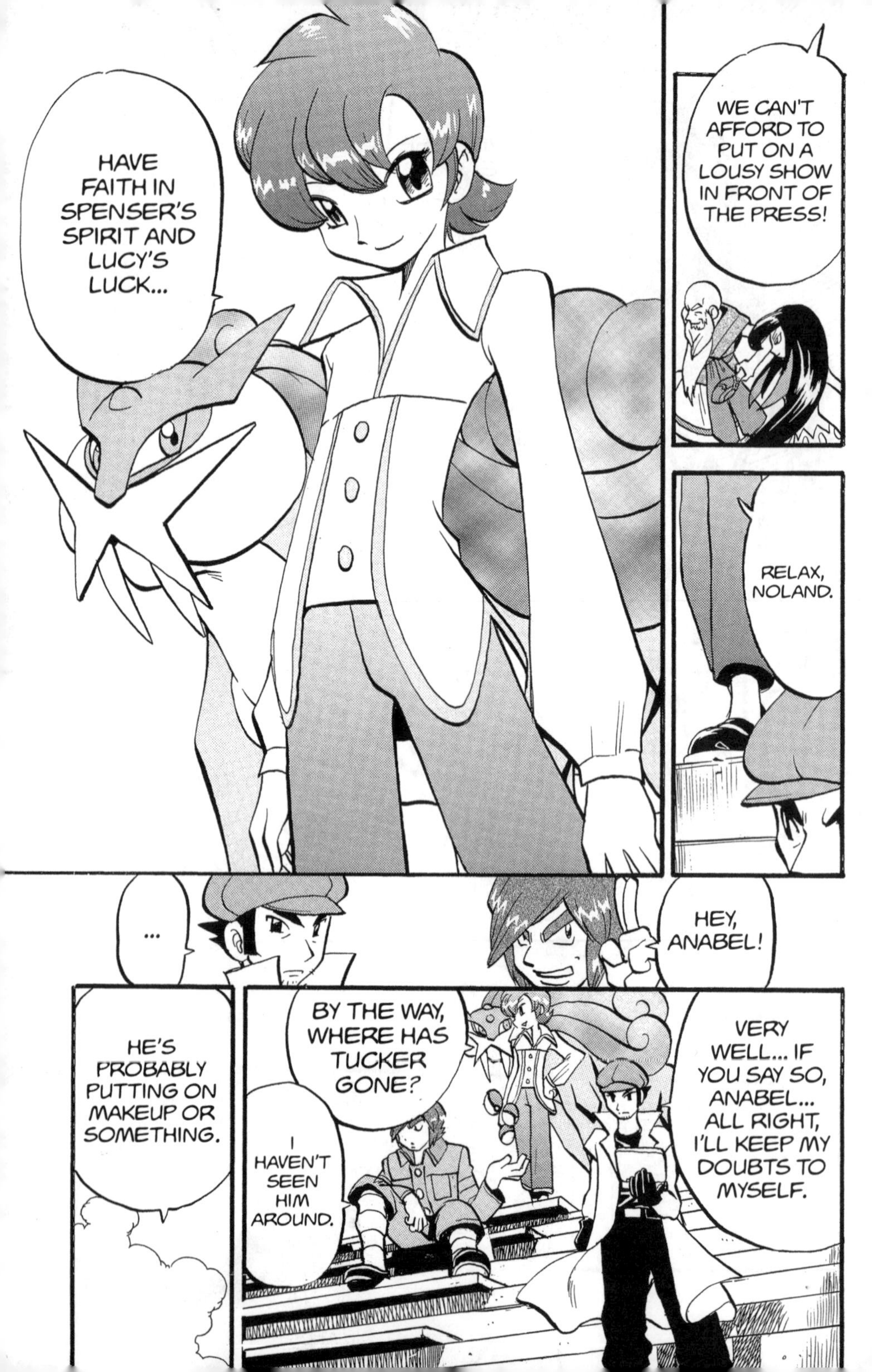
WE CAN'T AFFORD TO PUT ON A LOUSY SHOW IN FRONT OF THE PRESS!
RELAX, NOLAND.
HAVE FAITH IN SPENSER'S SPIRIT AND LUCY'S LUCK...
HEY, ANABEL!
...
VERY WELL... IF YOU SAY SO, ANABEL... ALL RIGHT, I'LL KEEP MY DOUBTS TO MYSELF.
BY THE WAY, WHERE HAS TUCKER GONE?
I HAVEN'T SEEN HIM AROUND.
HE'S PROBABLY PUTTING ON MAKEUP OR SOMETHING.

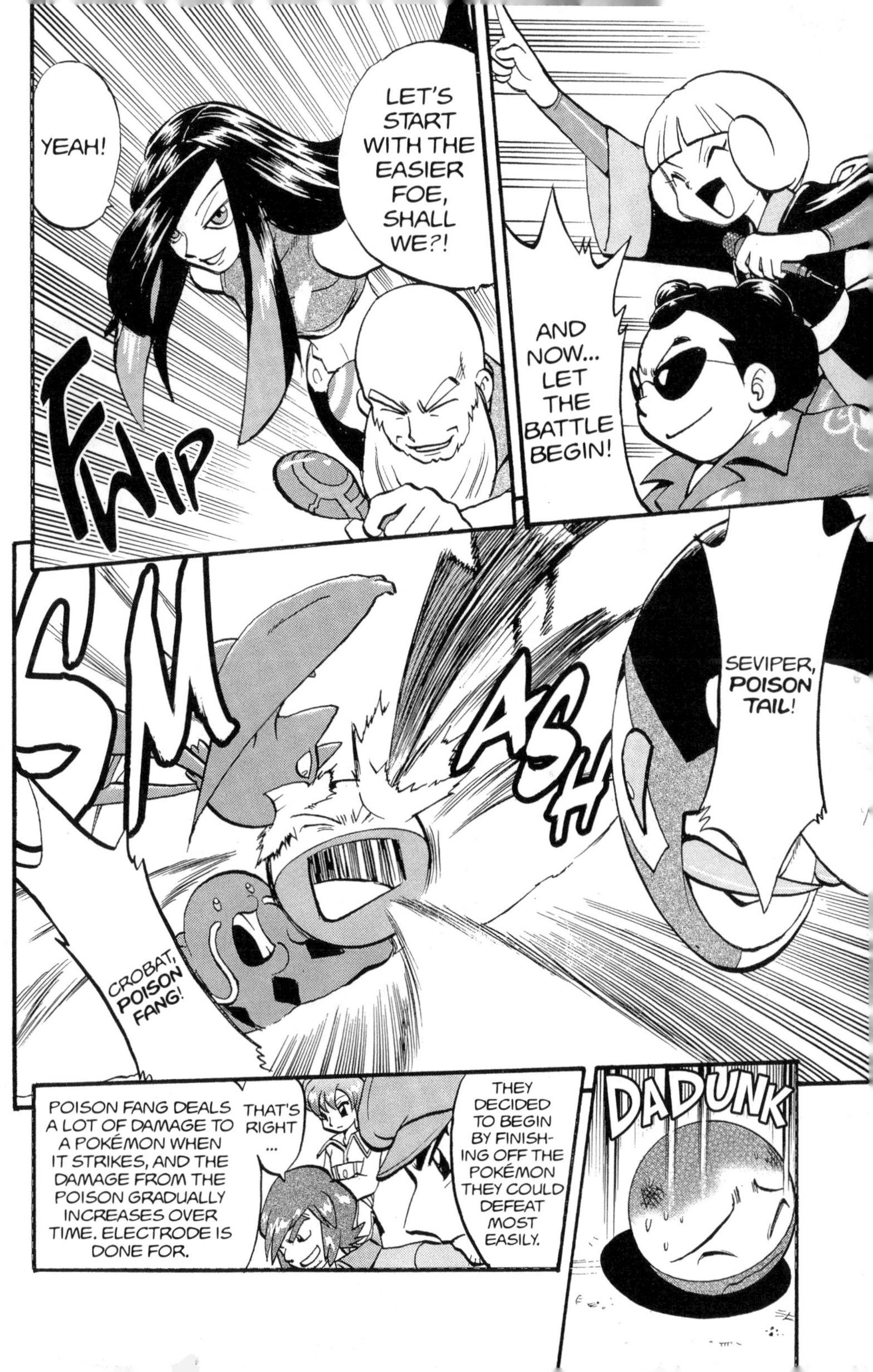
AND NOW... LET THE BATTLE BEGIN!
LET'S START WITH THE EASIER FOE, SHALL WE?!
YEAH!
FWIP
SEVIPER, POISON TAIL!
ASH
SM
CROBAT, POISON FANG!
DADUNK
THEY DECIDED TO BEGIN BY FINISHING OFF THE POKÉMON THEY COULD DEFEAT MOST EASILY.
THAT'S RIGHT ...
POISON FANG DEALS A LOT OF DAMAGE TO A POKÉMON WHEN IT STRIKES, AND THE DAMAGE FROM THE POISON GRADUALLY INCREASES OVER TIME. ELECTRODE IS DONE FOR.

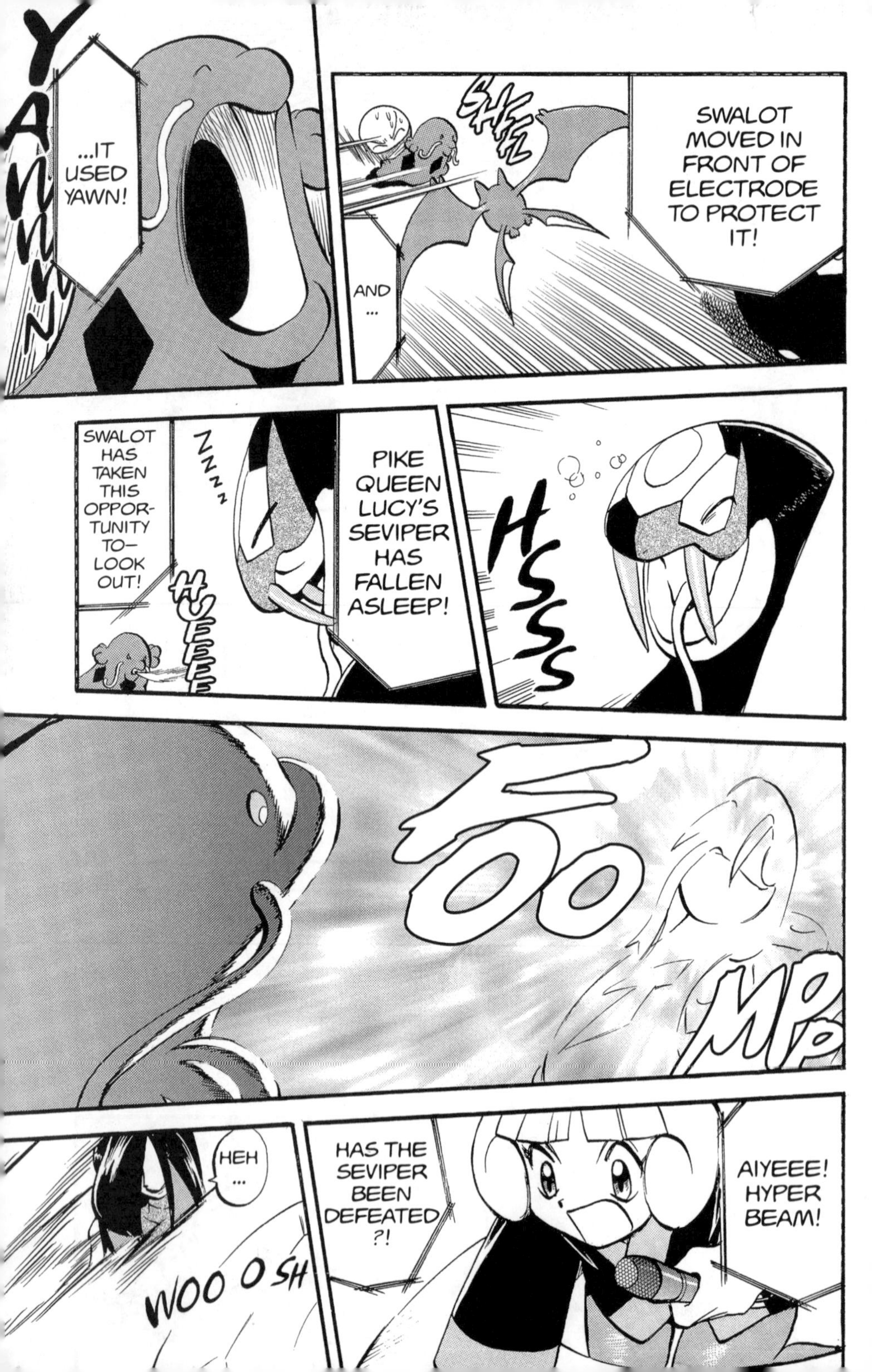

SWALOT MOVED IN FRONT OF ELECTRODE TO PROTECT IT!
SHEN
AND ...
YAWWWWN
...IT USED YAWN!
HSSS
PIKE QUEEN LUCY'S SEVIPER HAS FALLEN ASLEEP!
ZZZZ
SWALOT HAS TAKEN THIS OPPOR-TUNITY TO—LOOK OUT!
HUFFFF
FOOMP
AIYEEE! HYPER BEAM!
HAS THE SEVIPER BEEN DEFEATED ?!
HEH ...
WOO O SH

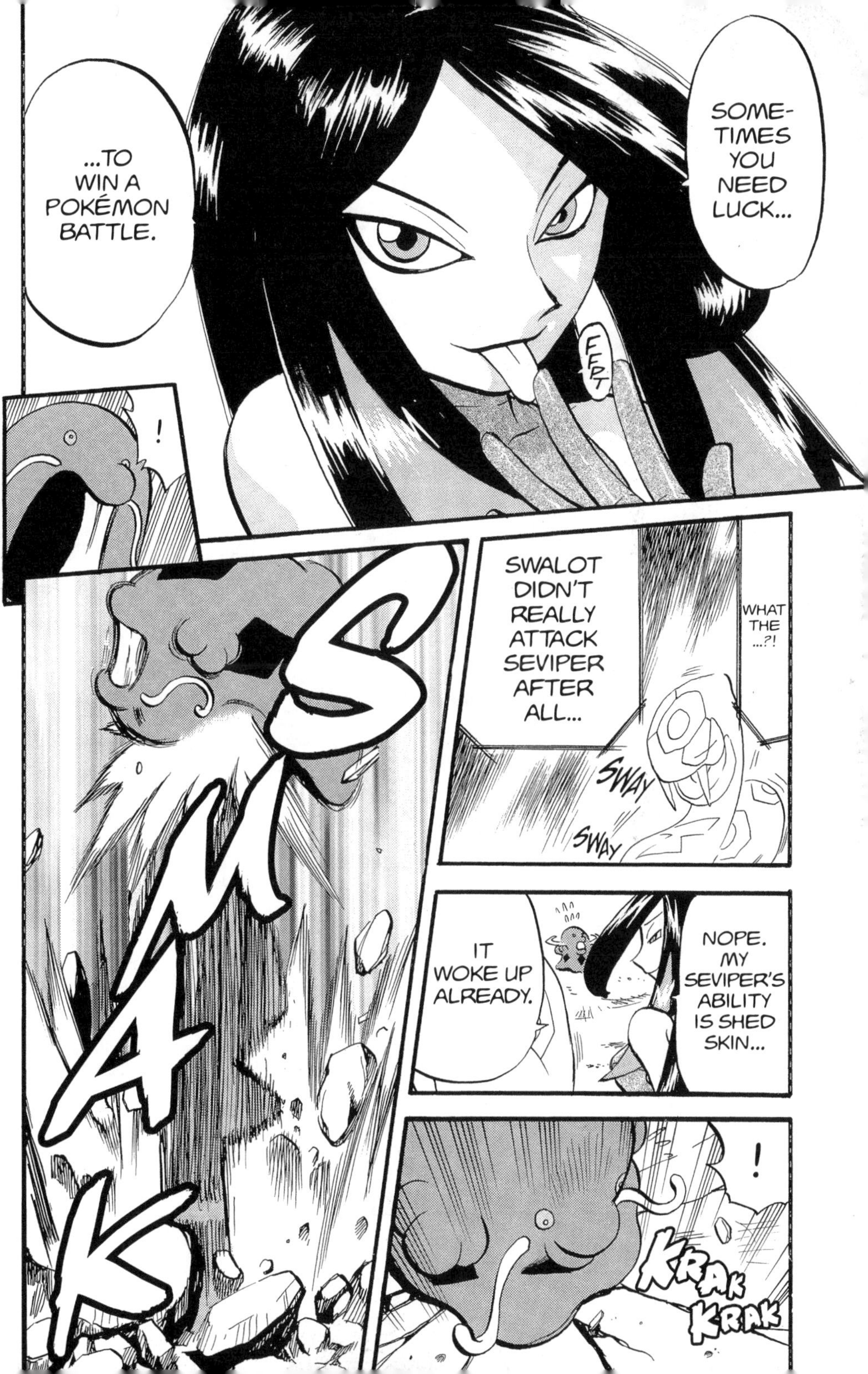
SOME-TIMES YOU NEED LUCK...
...TO WIN A POKÉMON BATTLE.
FFPT
!
WHAT THE ...?!
SWALOT DIDN'T REALLY ATTACK SEVIPER AFTER ALL...
SWAY
SWAY
NOPE. MY SEVIPER'S ABILITY IS SHED SKIN...
IT WOKE UP ALREADY.
!
KRAK KRAK
SMAK

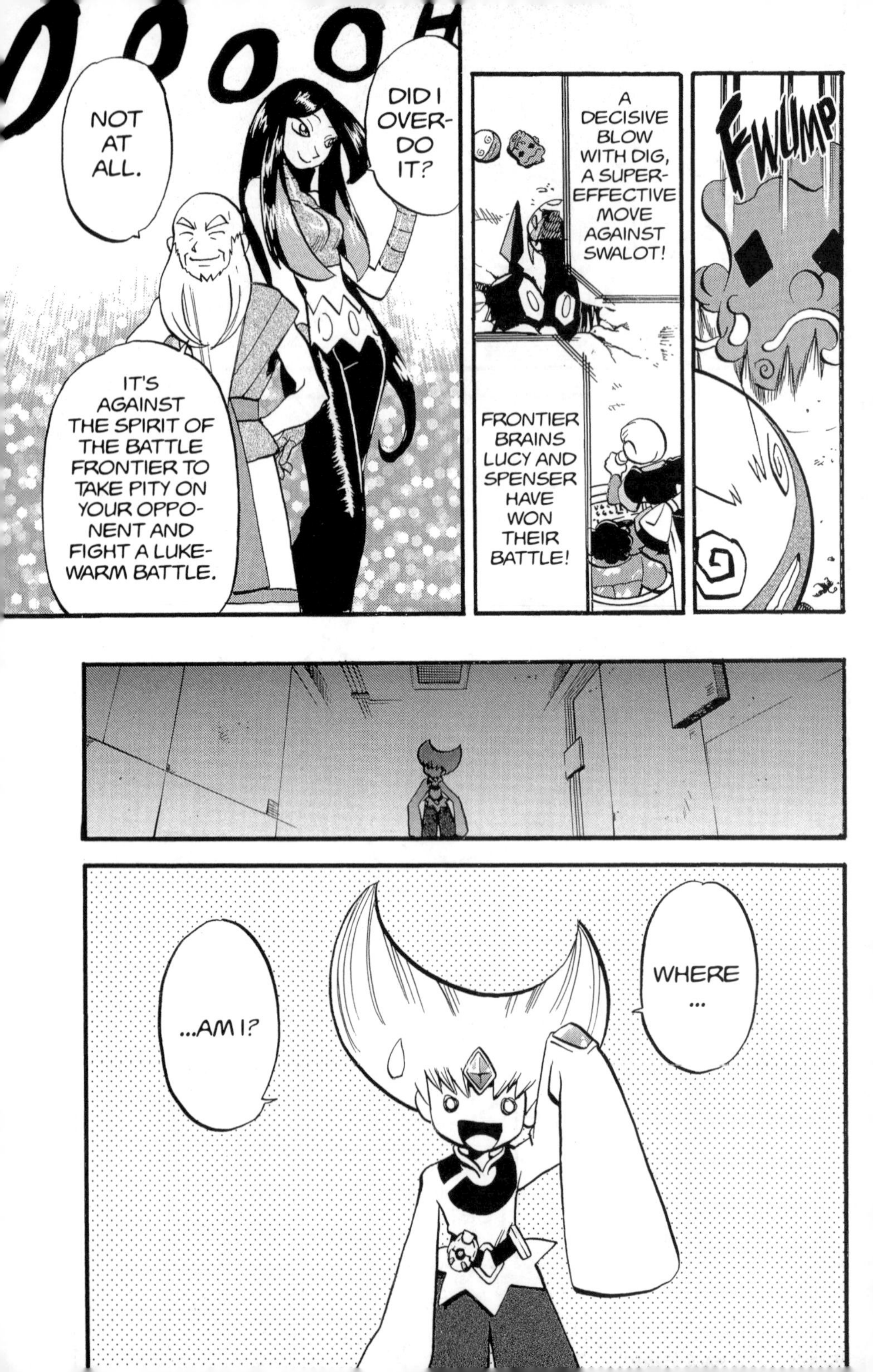
FWUMP
A DECISIVE BLOW WITH DIG, A SUPER-EFFECTIVE MOVE AGAINST SWALOT!
FRONTIER BRAINS LUCY AND SPENSER HAVE WON THEIR BATTLE!
OOOOH
DID I OVER-DO IT?
NOT AT ALL.
IT'S AGAINST THE SPIRIT OF THE BATTLE FRONTIER TO TAKE PITY ON YOUR OPPO-NENT AND FIGHT A LUKE-WARM BATTLE.
WHERE ...
...AM I?

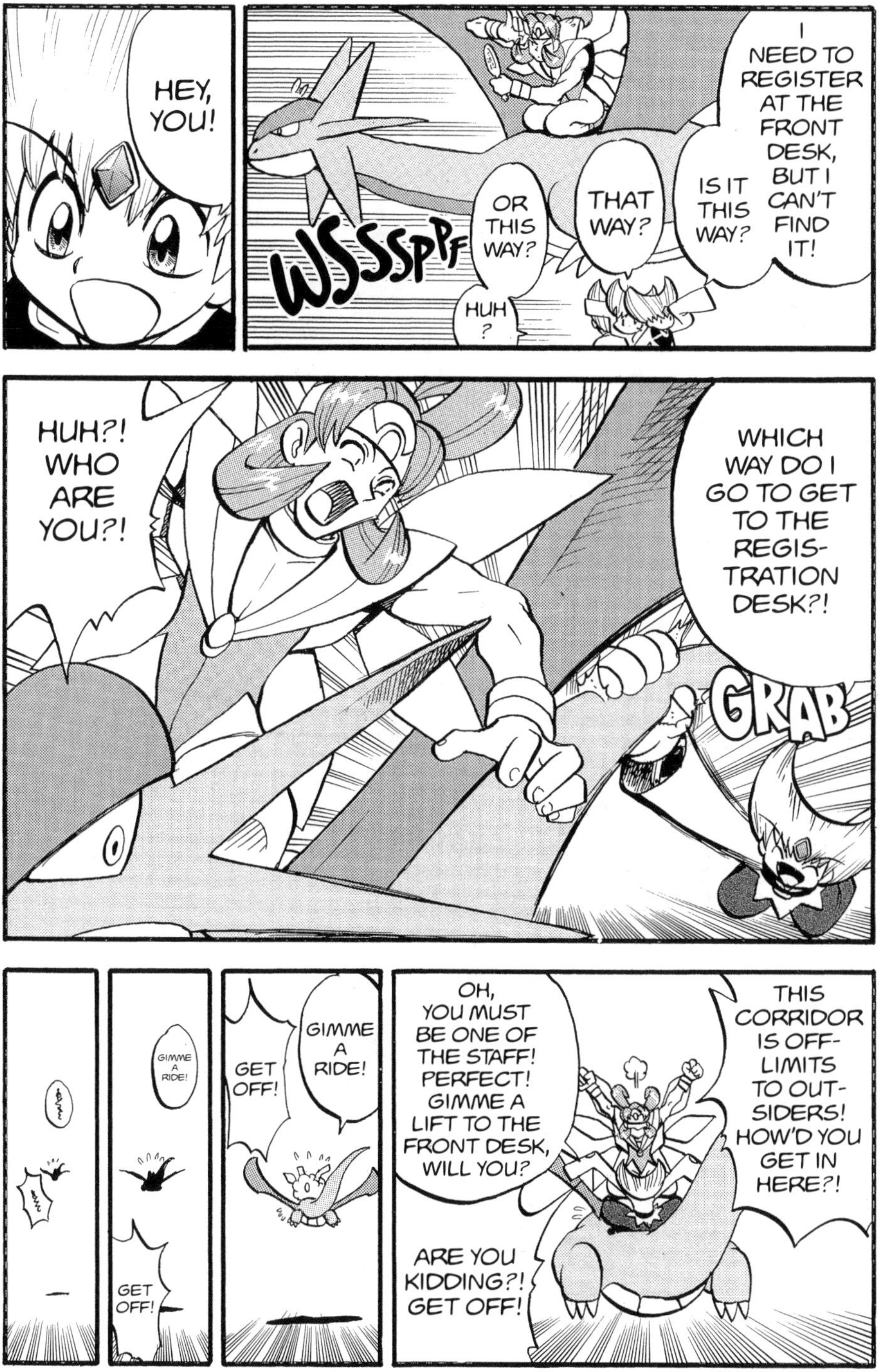
I NEED TO REGISTER AT THE FRONT DESK, BUT I CAN'T FIND IT!
IS IT THIS WAY?
THAT WAY?
OR THIS WAY?
WSSSPPF
HUH?
HEY, YOU!
WHICH WAY DO I GO TO GET TO THE REGIS-TRATION DESK?!
GRAB
HUH?! WHO ARE YOU?!
THIS CORRIDOR IS OFF-LIMITS TO OUT-SIDERS! HOW'D YOU GET IN HERE?!
OH, YOU MUST BE ONE OF THE STAFF! PERFECT! GIMME A LIFT TO THE FRONT DESK, WILL YOU?
ARE YOU KIDDING?! GET OFF!
GIMME A RIDE!
GET OFF!
GIMME A RIDE!
GET OFF!

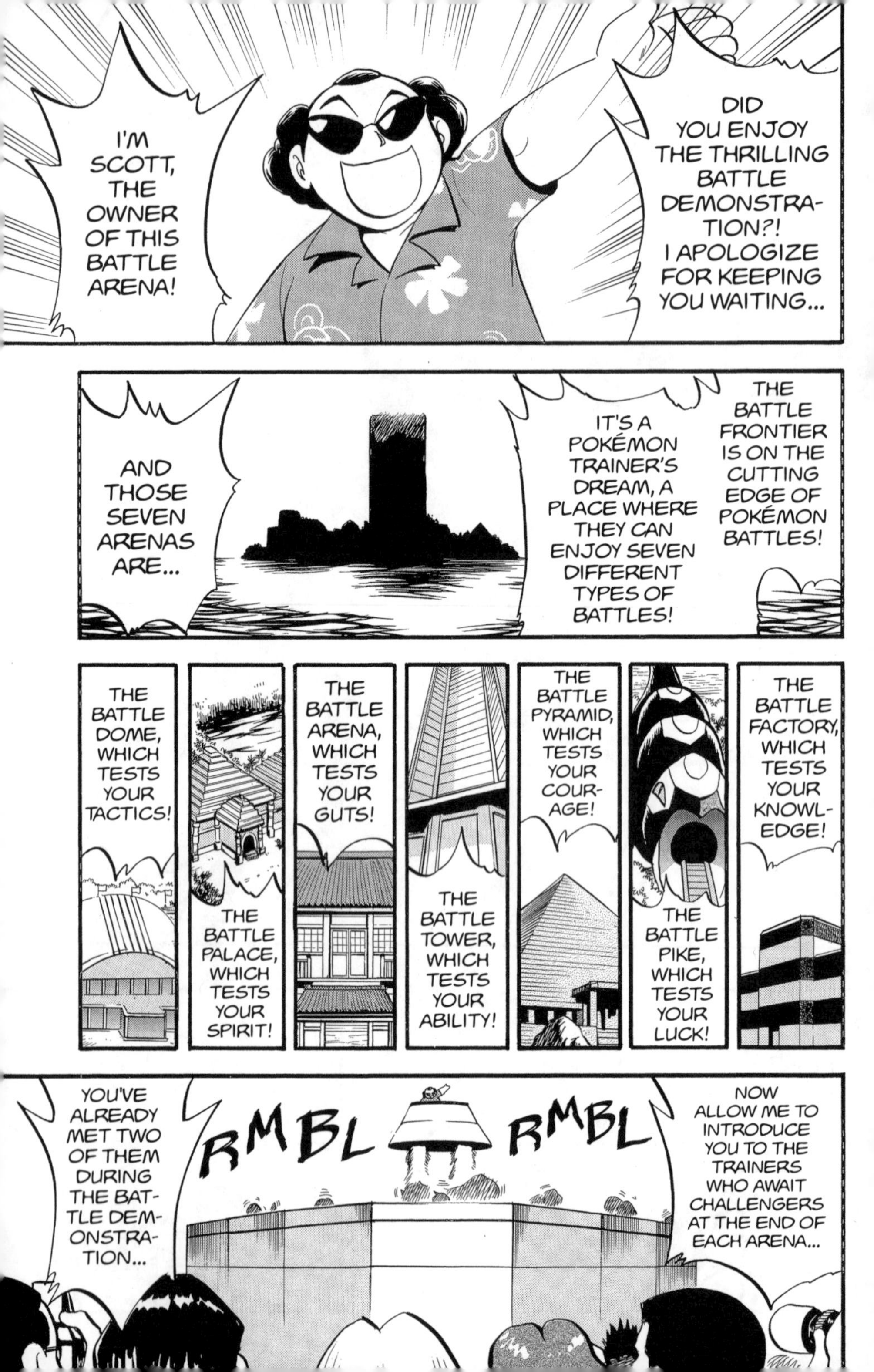
DID YOU ENJOY THE THRILLING BATTLE DEMONSTRATION?! I APOLOGIZE FOR KEEPING YOU WAITING...
I'M SCOTT, THE OWNER OF THIS BATTLE ARENA!
THE BATTLE FRONTIER IS ON THE CUTTING EDGE OF POKÉMON BATTLES!
IT'S A POKÉMON TRAINER'S DREAM, A PLACE WHERE THEY CAN ENJOY SEVEN DIFFERENT TYPES OF BATTLES!
AND THOSE SEVEN ARENAS ARE...
THE BATTLE FACTORY, WHICH TESTS YOUR KNOWLEDGE!
THE BATTLE PIKE, WHICH TESTS YOUR LUCK!
THE BATTLE PYRAMID, WHICH TESTS YOUR COURAGE!
THE BATTLE TOWER, WHICH TESTS YOUR ABILITY!
THE BATTLE ARENA, WHICH TESTS YOUR GUTS!
THE BATTLE PALACE, WHICH TESTS YOUR SPIRIT!
THE BATTLE DOME, WHICH TESTS YOUR TACTICS!
NOW ALLOW ME TO INTRODUCE YOU TO THE TRAINERS WHO AWAIT CHALLENGERS AT THE END OF EACH ARENA...
RMBL RMBL
YOU'VE ALREADY MET TWO OF THEM DURING THE BATTLE DEMONSTRATION...

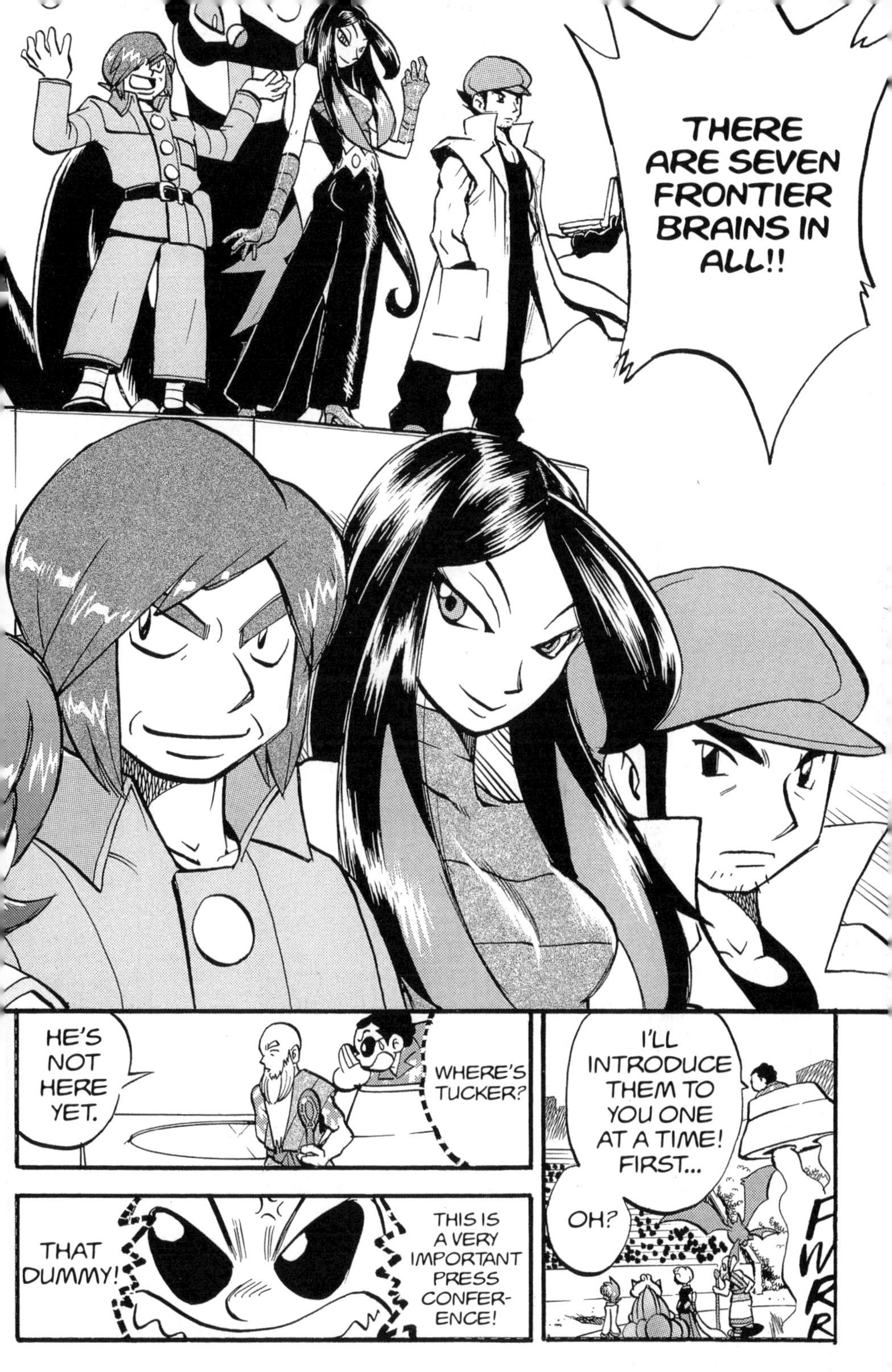
THERE ARE SEVEN FRONTIER BRAINS IN ALL!!
I'LL INTRODUCE THEM TO YOU ONE AT A TIME! FIRST...
OH?
FWRR
WHERE'S TUCKER?
HE'S NOT HERE YET.
THIS IS A VERY IMPORTANT PRESS CONFERENCE!
THAT DUMMY!

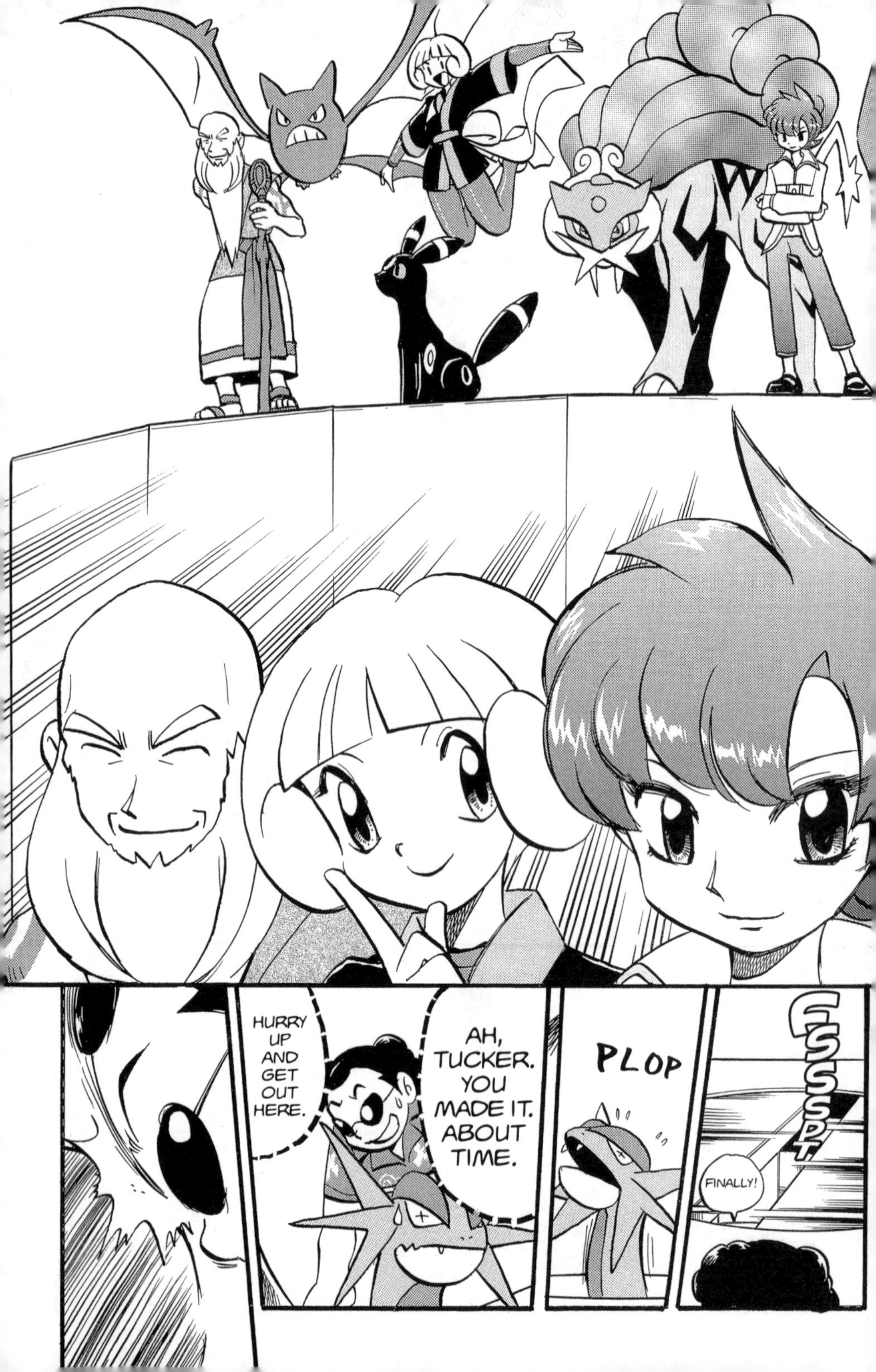
FSSSPT
FINALLY!
PLOP
AH, TUCKER. YOU MADE IT. ABOUT TIME.
HURRY UP AND GET OUT HERE.

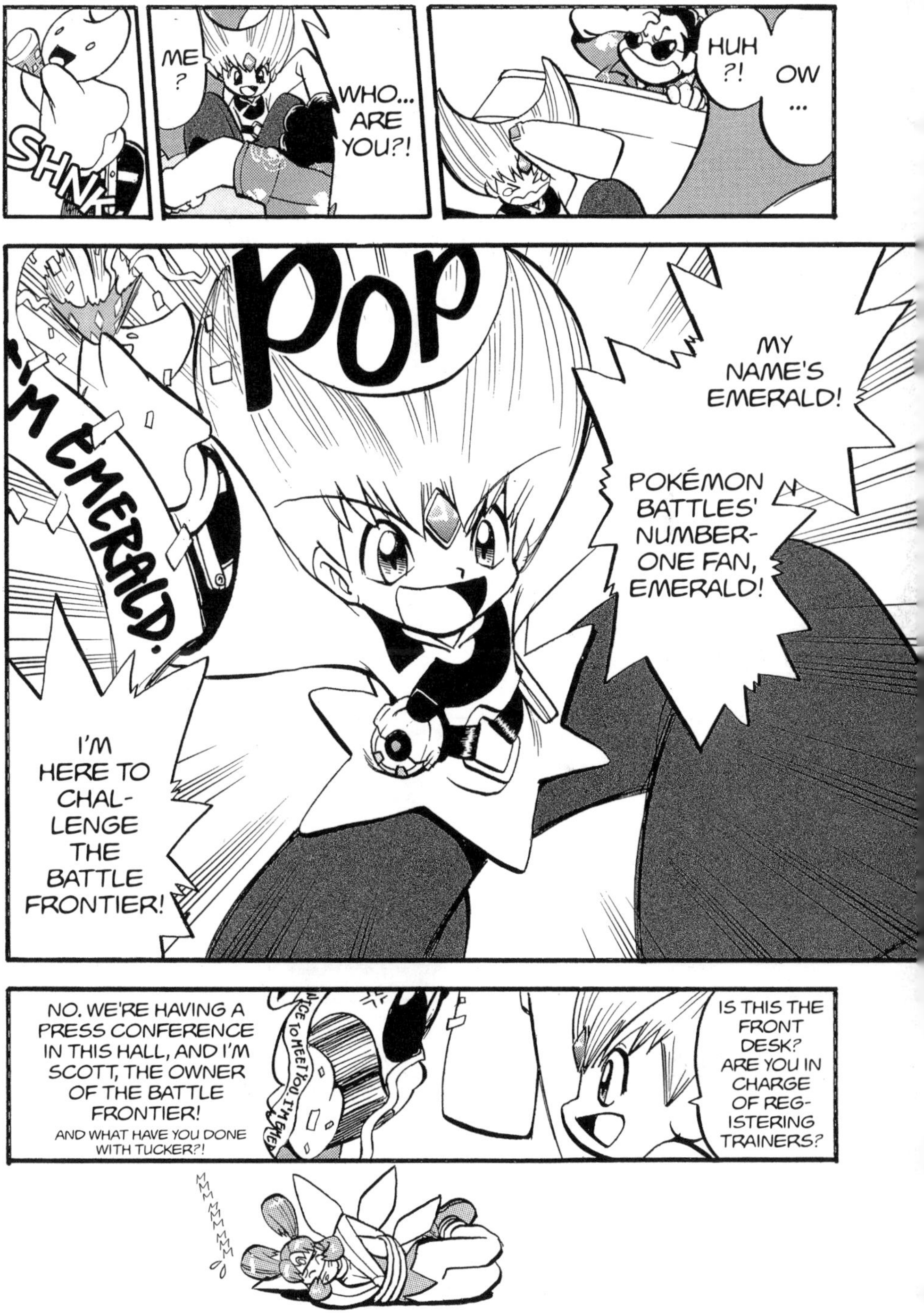
OW ...
HUH ?!
WHO... ARE YOU?!
ME ?
SHNK
POP
MY NAME'S EMERALD!
POKÉMON BATTLES' NUMBER-ONE FAN, EMERALD!
I'M EMERALD!
I'M HERE TO CHAL-LENGE THE BATTLE FRONTIER!
IS THIS THE FRONT DESK? ARE YOU IN CHARGE OF REG-ISTERING TRAINERS?
ICE TO MEET YOU. I'M
NO. WE'RE HAVING A PRESS CONFERENCE IN THIS HALL, AND I'M SCOTT, THE OWNER OF THE BATTLE FRONTIER!
AND WHAT HAVE YOU DONE WITH TUCKER?!
MMMMMMMM

DEAR MEMBERS OF THE PRESS...

Thank you so much for coming to my Battle Frontier today. Allow me to take this opportunity to explain the rules for Pokémon Battles here...

OWNER: SCOTT

LIMITED POKÉMON USAGE

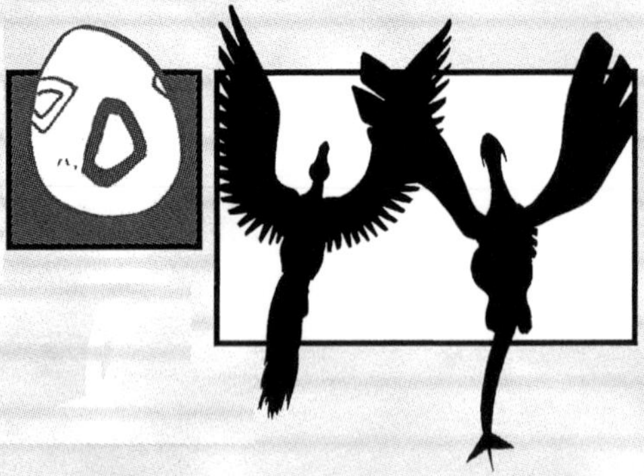

You may not enter two of the same Pokémon into a battle.

*Prior permission must be obtained to participate with an Egg or Legendary Pokémon.

*Your challenge might not be accepted.

*On the other hand, there is a possibility that our Frontier Brains will use **your** Pokémon in battle.

ITEM USAGE

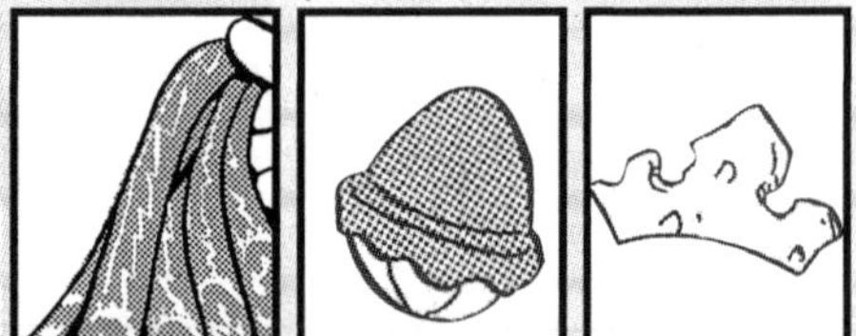

Apart from certain exceptions, Trainers are not allowed to use items during challenges. But Pokémon may hold an item before battle.

NUMBER OF MOVES PERMITTED

Each Pokémon is only allowed four moves during a battle. These moves must be registered before the battle. No other moves are permitted.

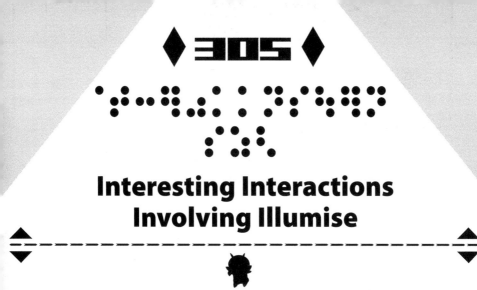

♦ 305 ♦

Interesting Interactions Involving Illumise

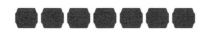

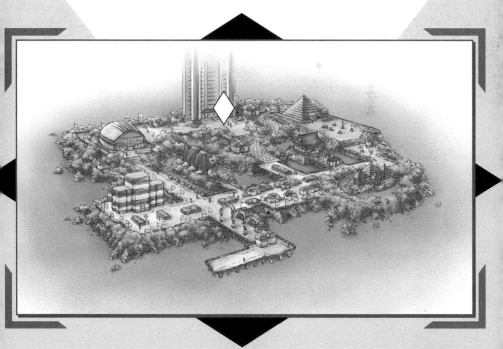

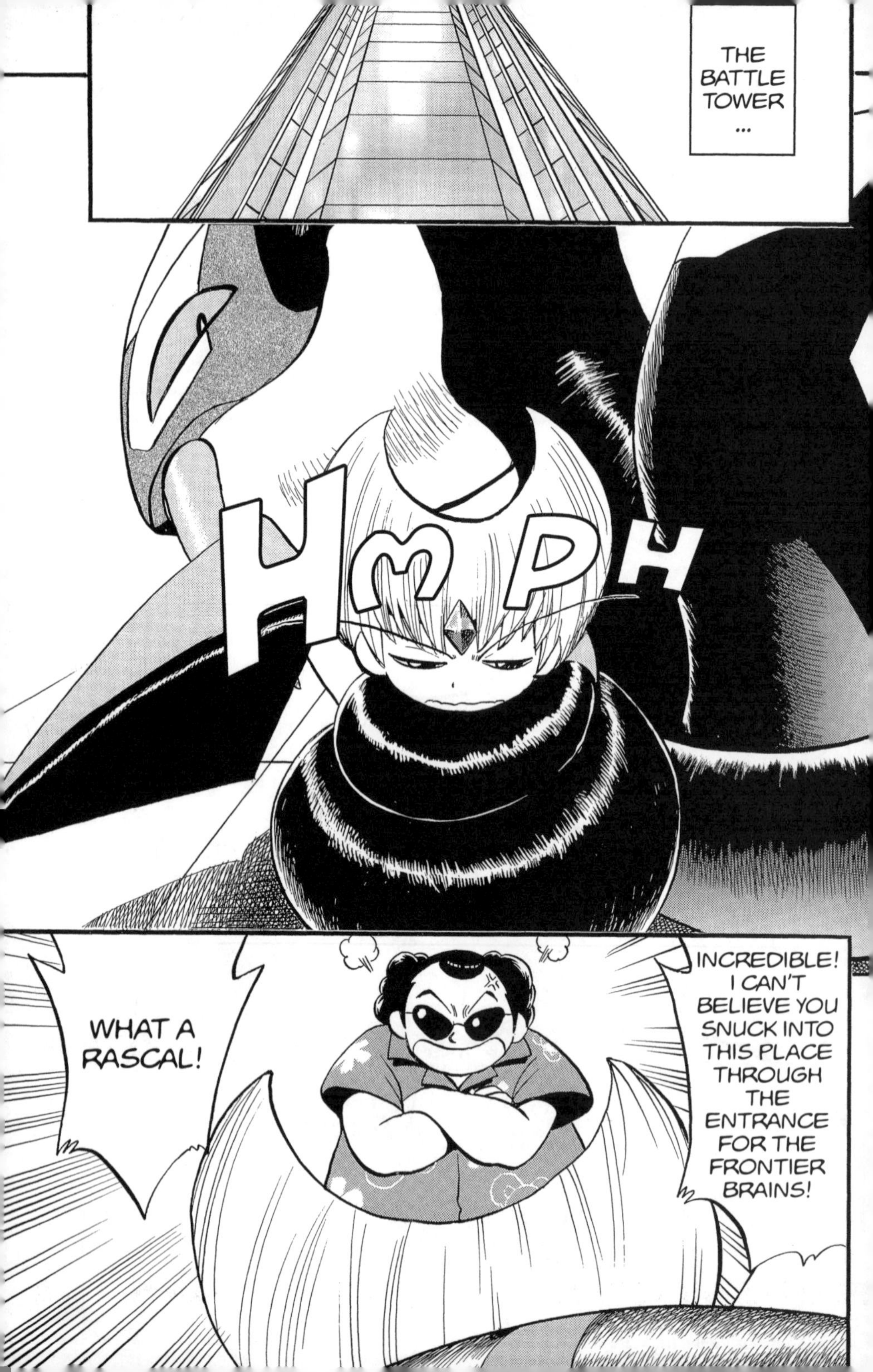
THE BATTLE TOWER ...
HMPH
INCREDIBLE! I CAN'T BELIEVE YOU SNUCK INTO THIS PLACE THROUGH THE ENTRANCE FOR THE FRONTIER BRAINS!
WHAT A RASCAL!

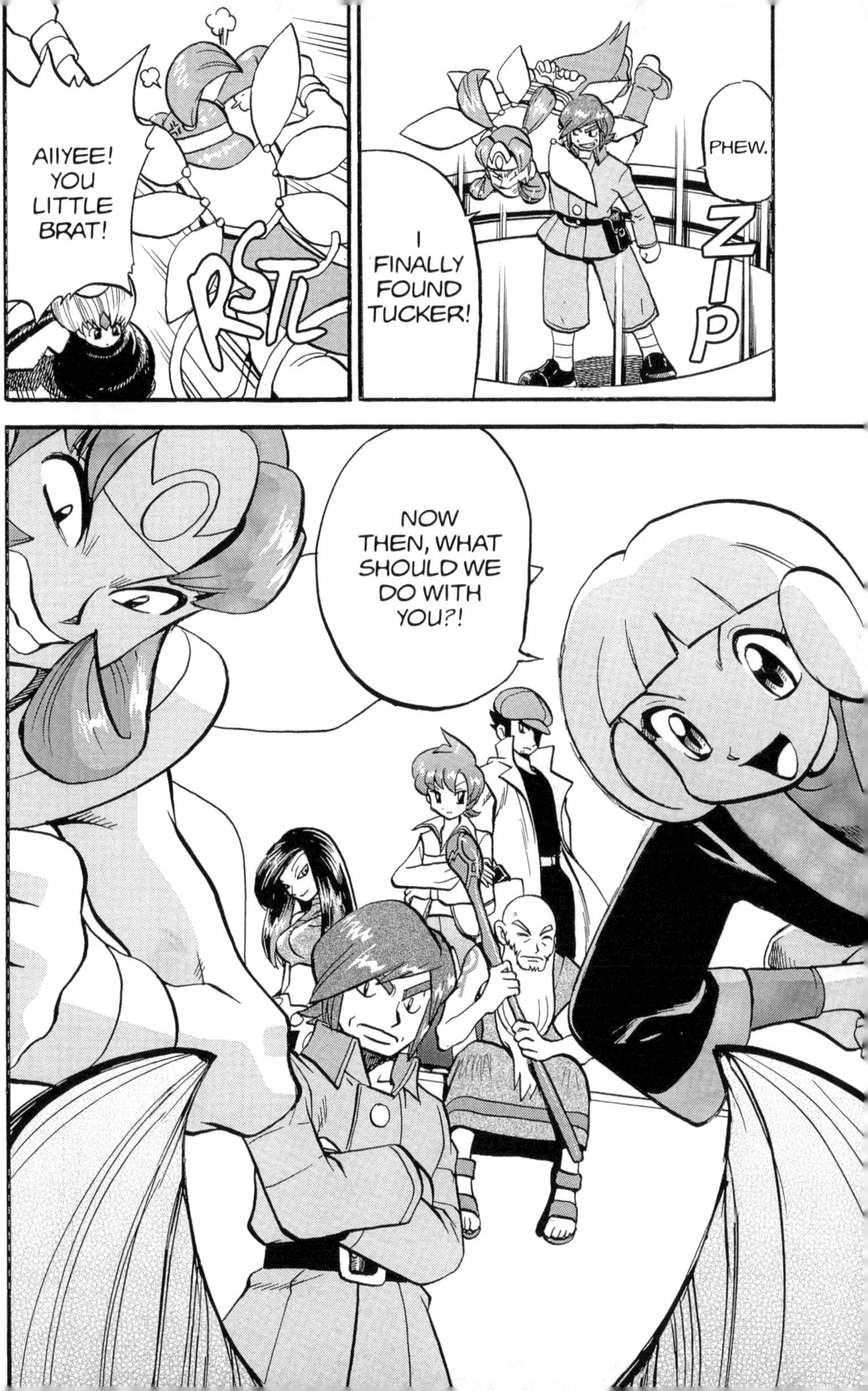
PHEW.
ZIP
I FINALLY FOUND TUCKER!
AIIYEE! YOU LITTLE BRAT!
RSTL
NOW THEN, WHAT SHOULD WE DO WITH YOU?!

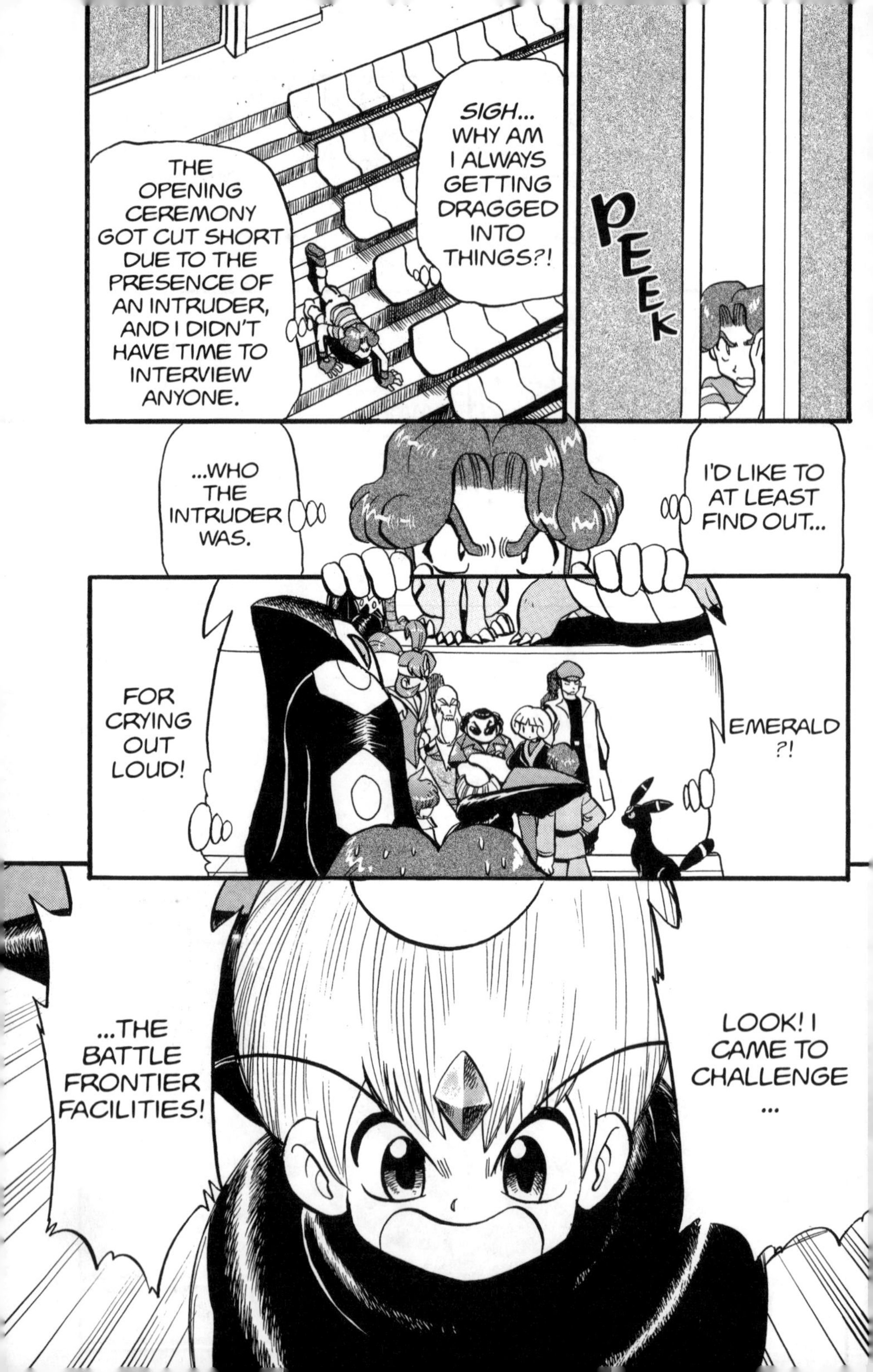
PEEK
SIGH... WHY AM I ALWAYS GETTING DRAGGED INTO THINGS?!
THE OPENING CEREMONY GOT CUT SHORT DUE TO THE PRESENCE OF AN INTRUDER, AND I DIDN'T HAVE TIME TO INTERVIEW ANYONE.
I'D LIKE TO AT LEAST FIND OUT...
...WHO THE INTRUDER WAS.
EMERALD?!
FOR CRYING OUT LOUD!
LOOK! I CAME TO CHALLENGE...
...THE BATTLE FRONTIER FACILITIES!

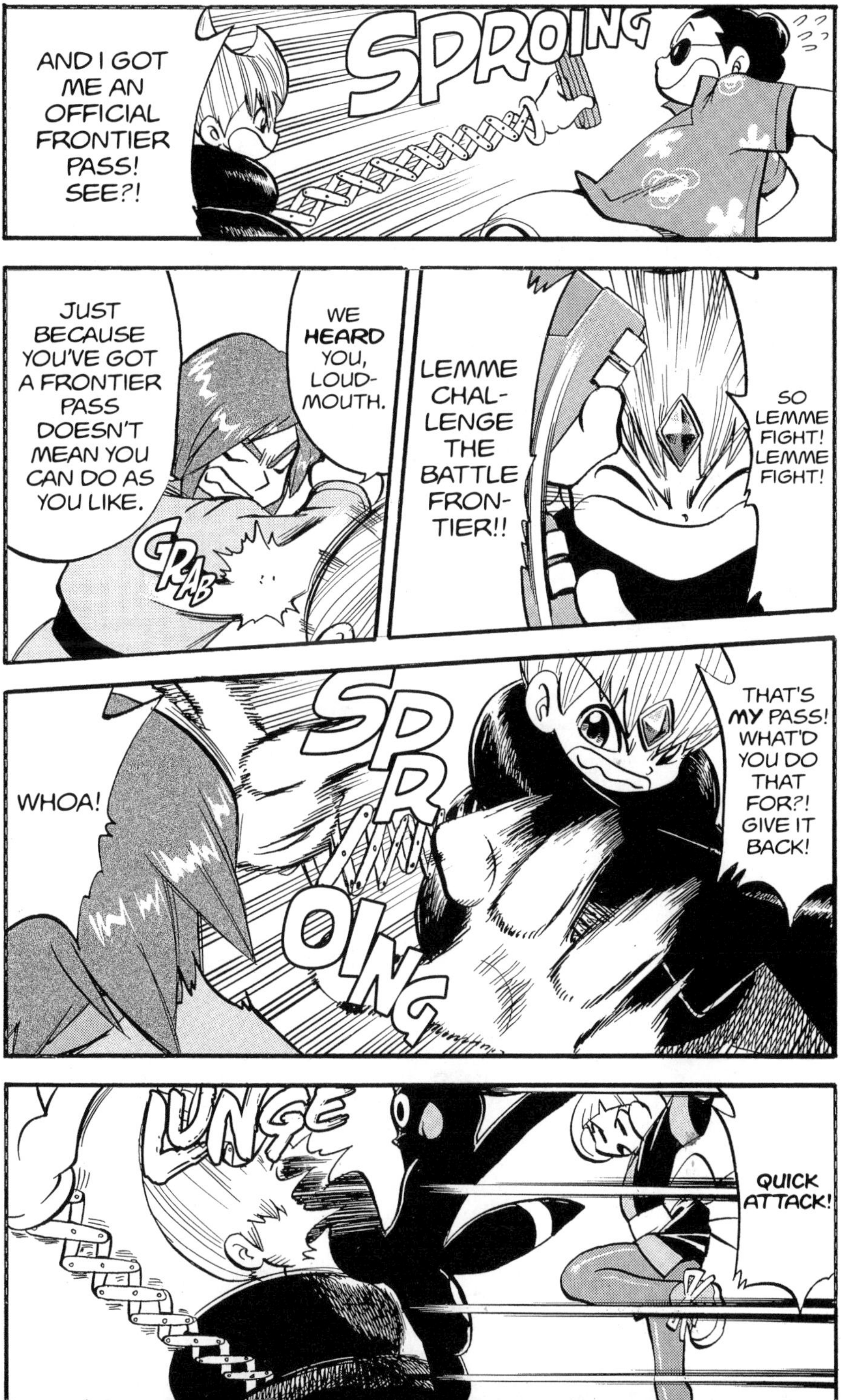
SPROING
AND I GOT ME AN OFFICIAL FRONTIER PASS! SEE?!
SO LEMME FIGHT! LEMME FIGHT!
LEMME CHALLENGE THE BATTLE FRONTIER!!
WE **HEARD** YOU, LOUDMOUTH.
JUST BECAUSE YOU'VE GOT A FRONTIER PASS DOESN'T MEAN YOU CAN DO AS YOU LIKE.
GRAB
THAT'S **MY** PASS! WHAT'D YOU DO THAT FOR?! GIVE IT BACK!
SPROING
WHOA!
QUICK ATTACK!
LUNGE

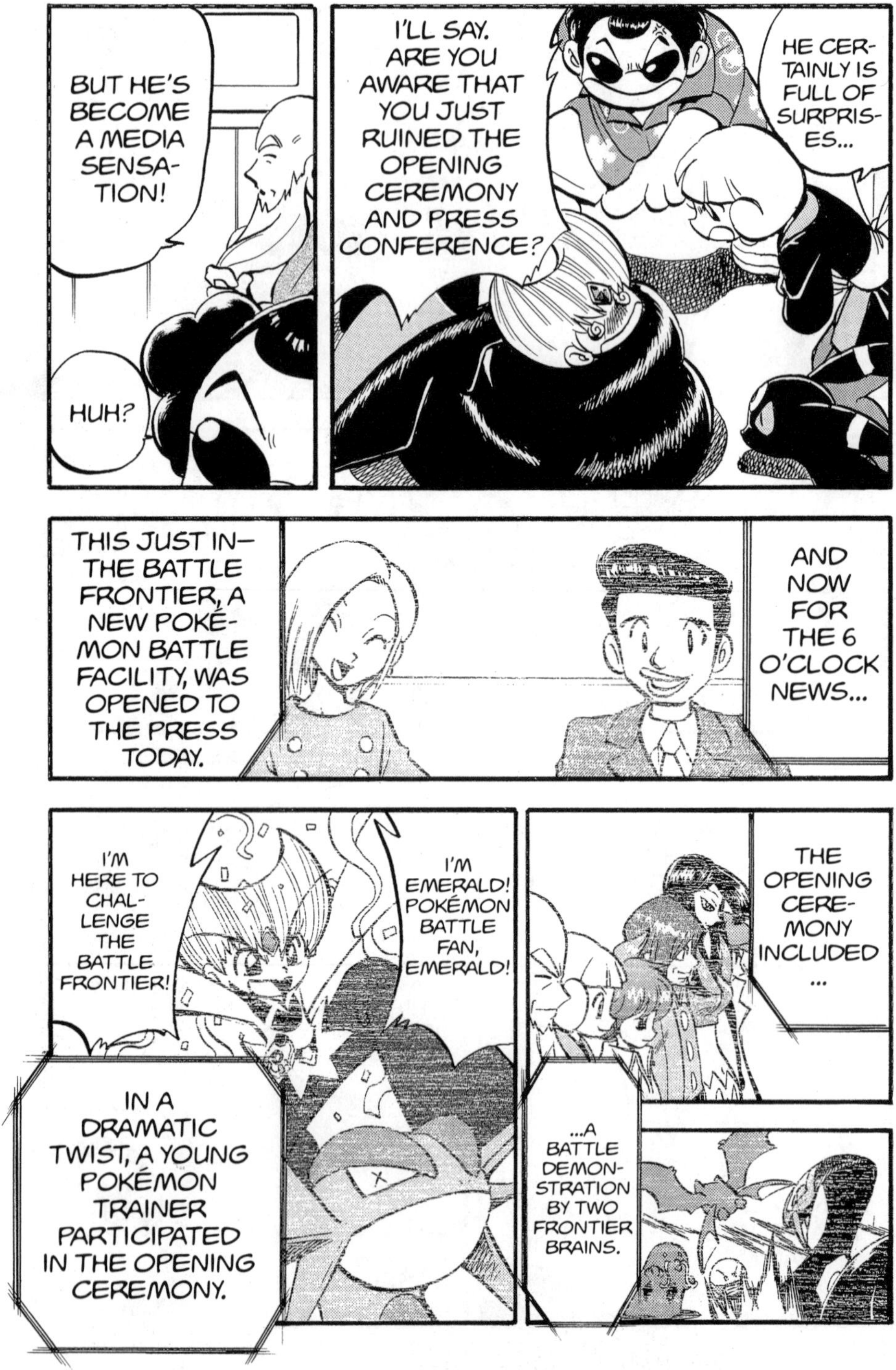
HE CER-TAINLY IS FULL OF SURPRIS-ES...
I'LL SAY. ARE YOU AWARE THAT YOU JUST RUINED THE OPENING CEREMONY AND PRESS CONFERENCE?
BUT HE'S BECOME A MEDIA SENSA-TION!
HUH?
AND NOW FOR THE 6 O'CLOCK NEWS...
THIS JUST IN—THE BATTLE FRONTIER, A NEW POKÉ-MON BATTLE FACILITY, WAS OPENED TO THE PRESS TODAY.
THE OPENING CERE-MONY INCLUDED ...
...A BATTLE DEMON-STRATION BY TWO FRONTIER BRAINS.
I'M EMERALD! POKÉMON BATTLE FAN, EMERALD!
I'M HERE TO CHAL-LENGE THE BATTLE FRONTIER!
IN A DRAMATIC TWIST, A YOUNG POKÉMON TRAINER PARTICIPATED IN THE OPENING CEREMONY.

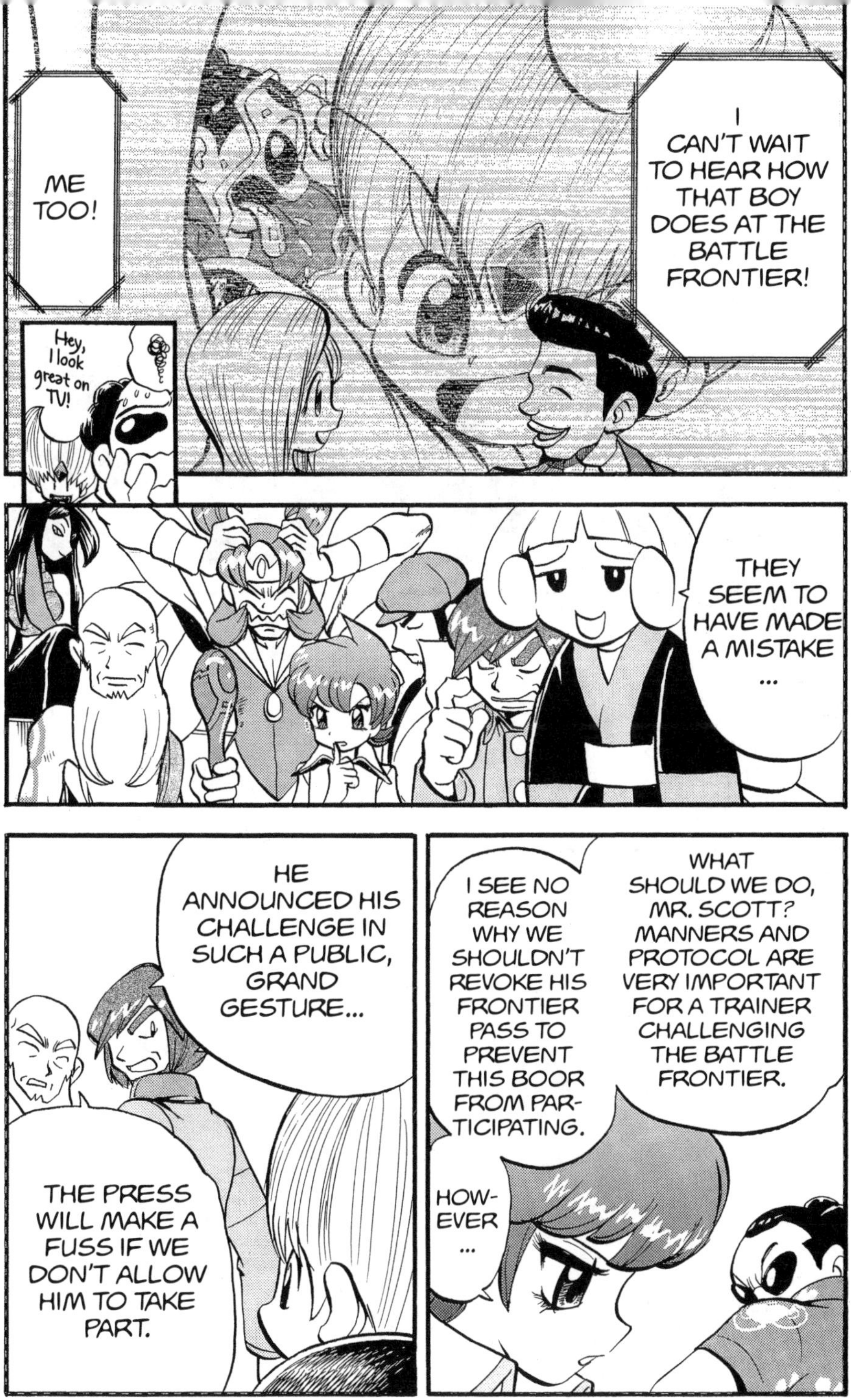
I CAN'T WAIT TO HEAR HOW THAT BOY DOES AT THE BATTLE FRONTIER!
ME TOO!
Hey, I look great on TV!
THEY SEEM TO HAVE MADE A MISTAKE ...
WHAT SHOULD WE DO, MR. SCOTT? MANNERS AND PROTOCOL ARE VERY IMPORTANT FOR A TRAINER CHALLENGING THE BATTLE FRONTIER.
I SEE NO REASON WHY WE SHOULDN'T REVOKE HIS FRONTIER PASS TO PREVENT THIS BOOR FROM PAR-TICIPATING.
HOW-EVER ...
HE ANNOUNCED HIS CHALLENGE IN SUCH A PUBLIC, GRAND GESTURE...
THE PRESS WILL MAKE A FUSS IF WE DON'T ALLOW HIM TO TAKE PART.

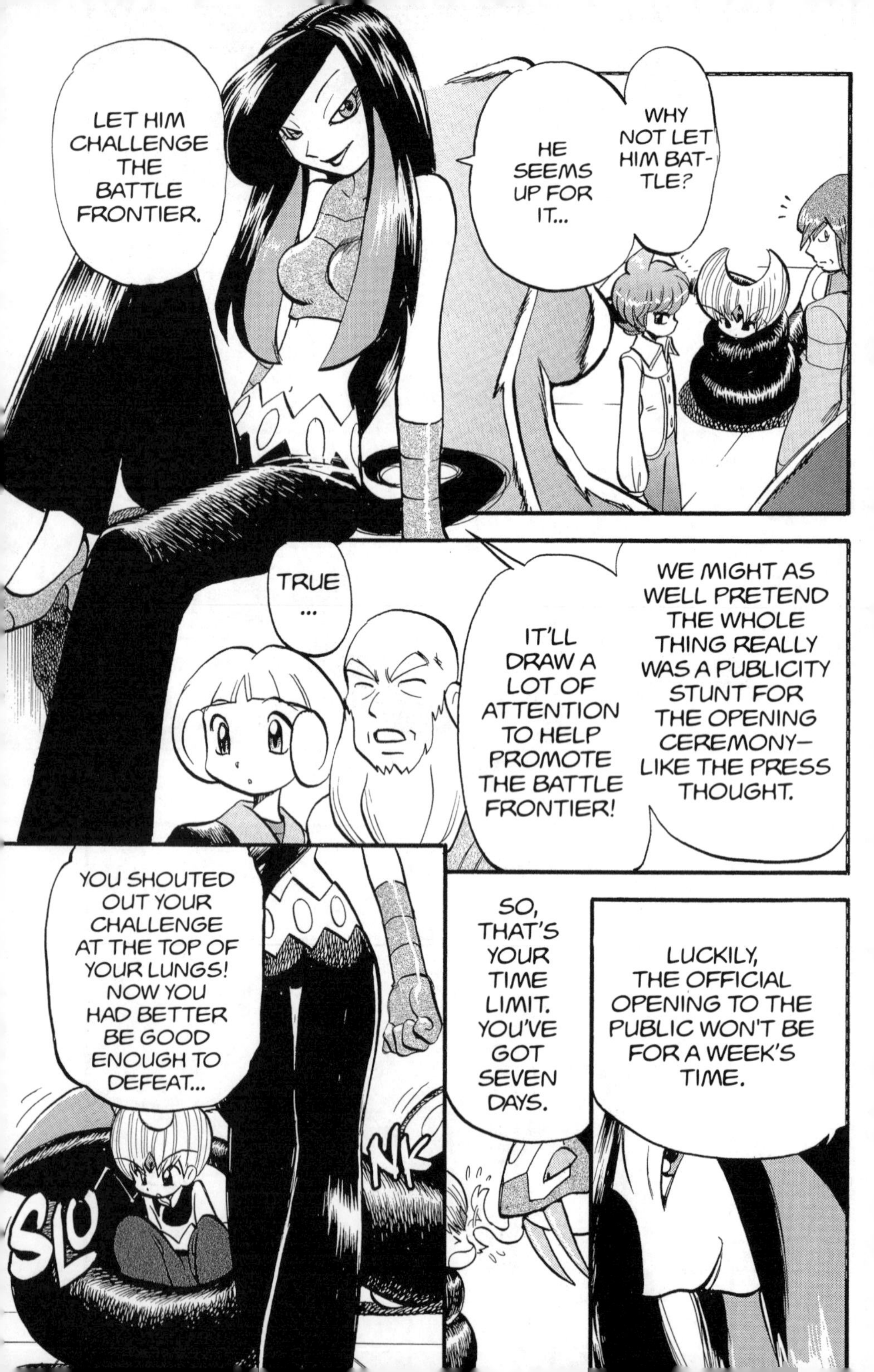
WHY NOT LET HIM BATTLE?
HE SEEMS UP FOR IT...
LET HIM CHALLENGE THE BATTLE FRONTIER.
WE MIGHT AS WELL PRETEND THE WHOLE THING REALLY WAS A PUBLICITY STUNT FOR THE OPENING CEREMONY—LIKE THE PRESS THOUGHT.
IT'LL DRAW A LOT OF ATTENTION TO HELP PROMOTE THE BATTLE FRONTIER!
TRUE ...
LUCKILY, THE OFFICIAL OPENING TO THE PUBLIC WON'T BE FOR A WEEK'S TIME.
SO, THAT'S YOUR TIME LIMIT. YOU'VE GOT SEVEN DAYS.
YOU SHOUTED OUT YOUR CHALLENGE AT THE TOP OF YOUR LUNGS! NOW YOU HAD BETTER BE GOOD ENOUGH TO DEFEAT...
SLU
NK

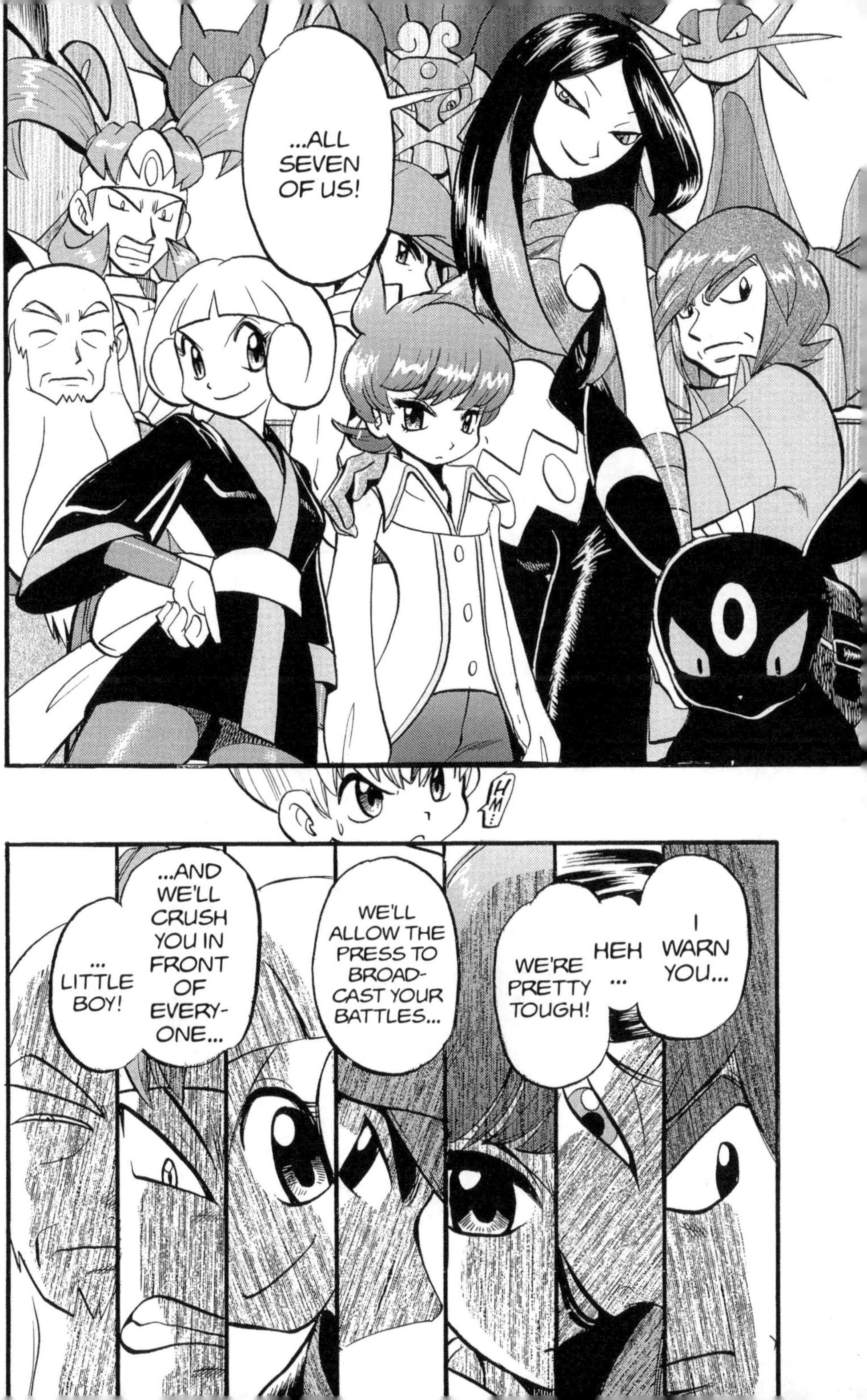
...ALL SEVEN OF US!
HM...
I WARN YOU...
HEH...
WE'RE PRETTY TOUGH!
WE'LL ALLOW THE PRESS TO BROADCAST YOUR BATTLES...
...AND WE'LL CRUSH YOU IN FRONT OF EVERYONE...
...LITTLE BOY!

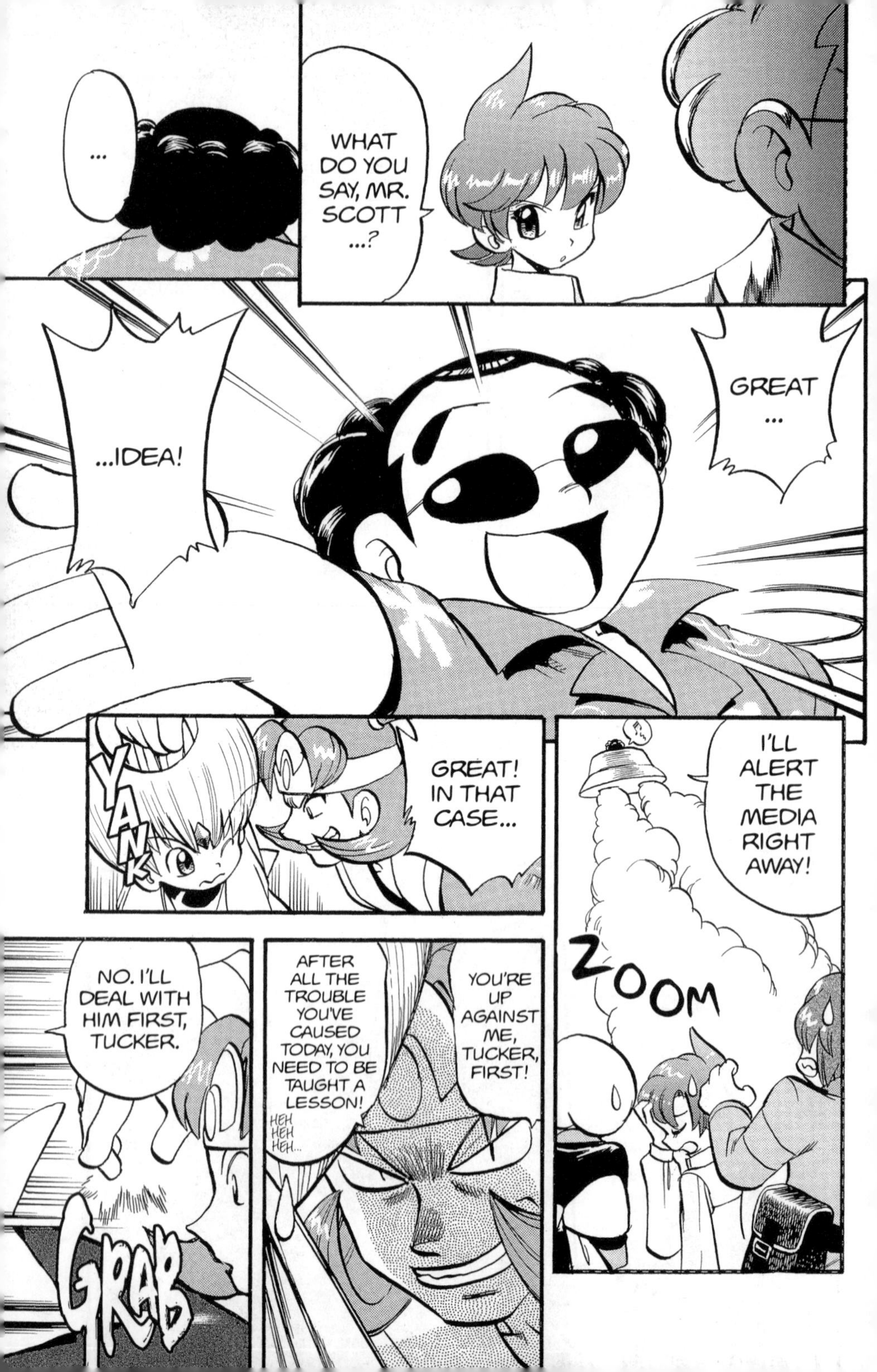
WHAT DO YOU SAY, MR. SCOTT ...?
...
GREAT ...
...IDEA!
I'LL ALERT THE MEDIA RIGHT AWAY!
ZOOM
GREAT! IN THAT CASE...
YANK
YOU'RE UP AGAINST ME, TUCKER, FIRST!
AFTER ALL THE TROUBLE YOU'VE CAUSED TODAY, YOU NEED TO BE TAUGHT A LESSON!
HEH HEH HEH...
NO. I'LL DEAL WITH HIM FIRST, TUCKER.
GRAB

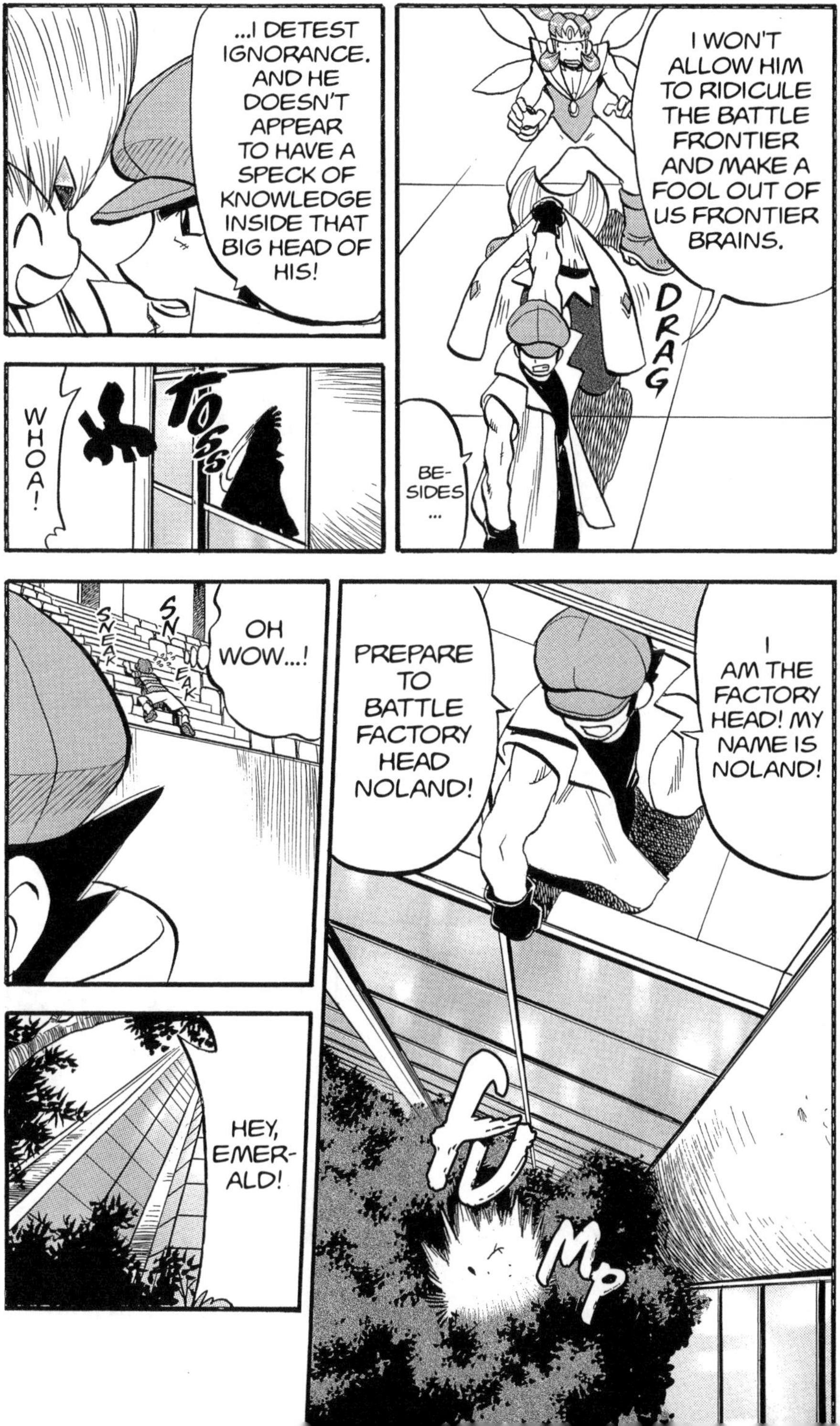
I WON'T ALLOW HIM TO RIDICULE THE BATTLE FRONTIER AND MAKE A FOOL OUT OF US FRONTIER BRAINS.
DRAG
BE-SIDES...
...I DETEST IGNORANCE. AND HE DOESN'T APPEAR TO HAVE A SPECK OF KNOWLEDGE INSIDE THAT BIG HEAD OF HIS!
TOSS
WHOA!
I AM THE FACTORY HEAD! MY NAME IS NOLAND!
PREPARE TO BATTLE FACTORY HEAD NOLAND!
OH WOW...!
SNEAK
SNEAK
HEY, EMER-ALD!

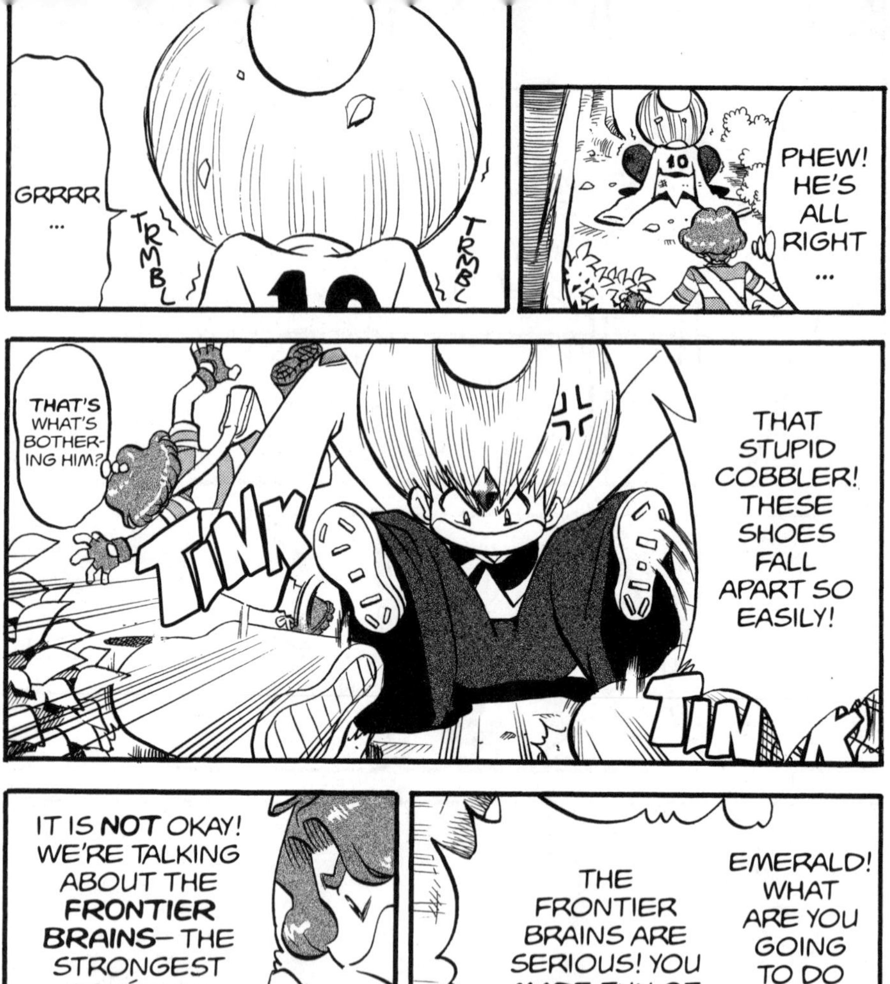
PHEW! HE'S ALL RIGHT ...
GRRRR ...
TRMBL
TRMBL
THAT STUPID COBBLER! THESE SHOES FALL APART SO EASILY!
THAT'S WHAT'S BOTHER-ING HIM?
TINK
TINK
EMERALD! WHAT ARE YOU GOING TO DO NOW?!
THE FRONTIER BRAINS ARE SERIOUS! YOU MADE FUN OF THEM, AND NOW THEY'RE MAD!
IT'S OKAY. DON'T WORRY ABOUT IT.
IT IS **NOT** OKAY! WE'RE TALKING ABOUT THE **FRONTIER BRAINS**— THE STRONGEST POKÉMON TRAINERS HERE!
THEY'RE ALL PRE-PARED TO FIGHT YOU WITH ALL THEIR MIGHT...
OW ...
ROLL
WILL YOU LISTEN TO ME ...?!

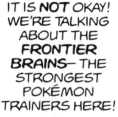

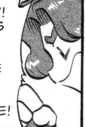

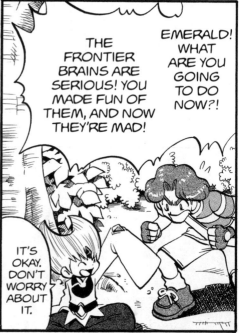

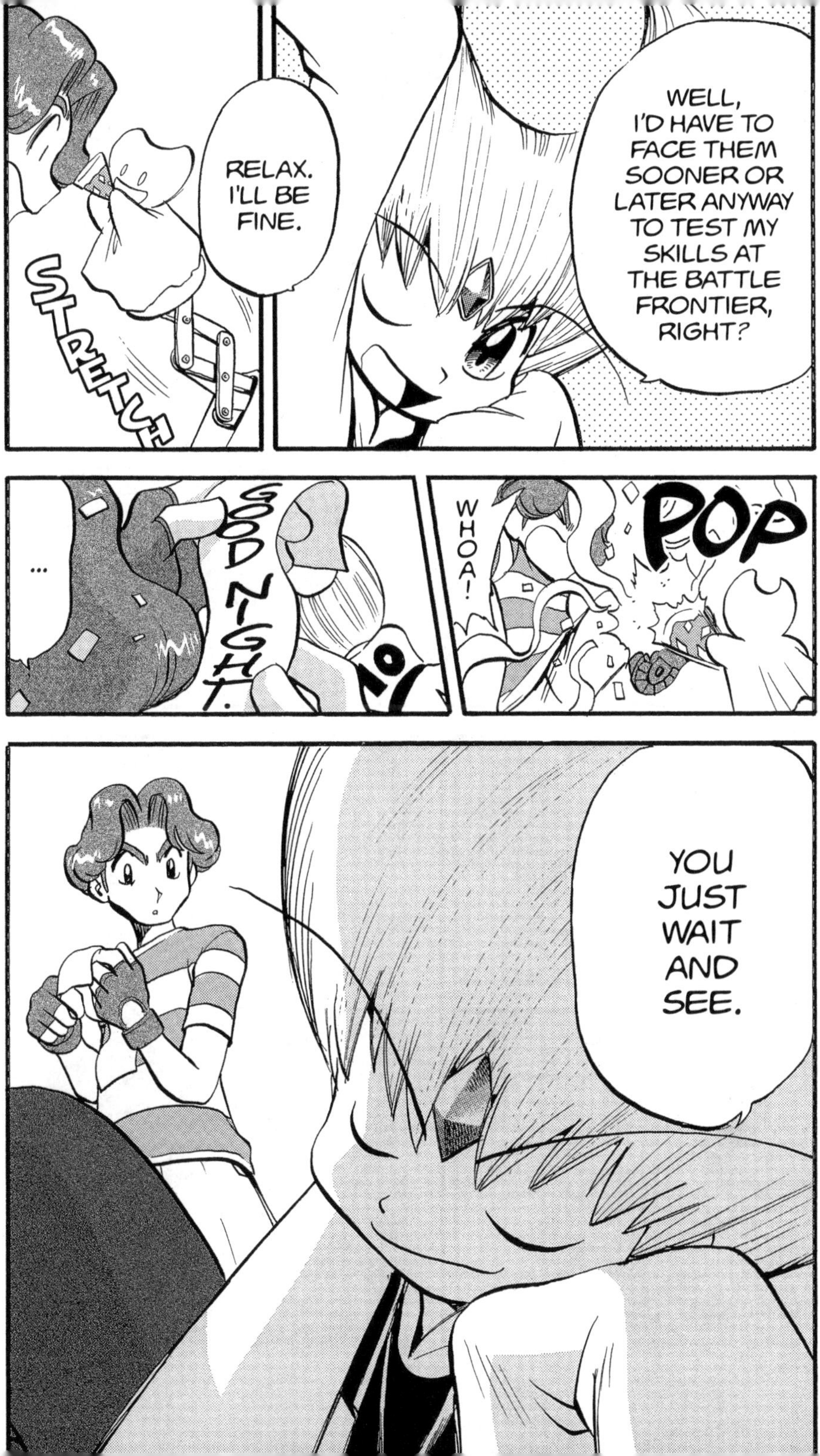
WELL, I'D HAVE TO FACE THEM SOONER OR LATER ANYWAY TO TEST MY SKILLS AT THE BATTLE FRONTIER, RIGHT?
RELAX. I'LL BE FINE.
STRETCH
POP
WHOA!
GOOD NIGHT.
...
YOU JUST WAIT AND SEE.

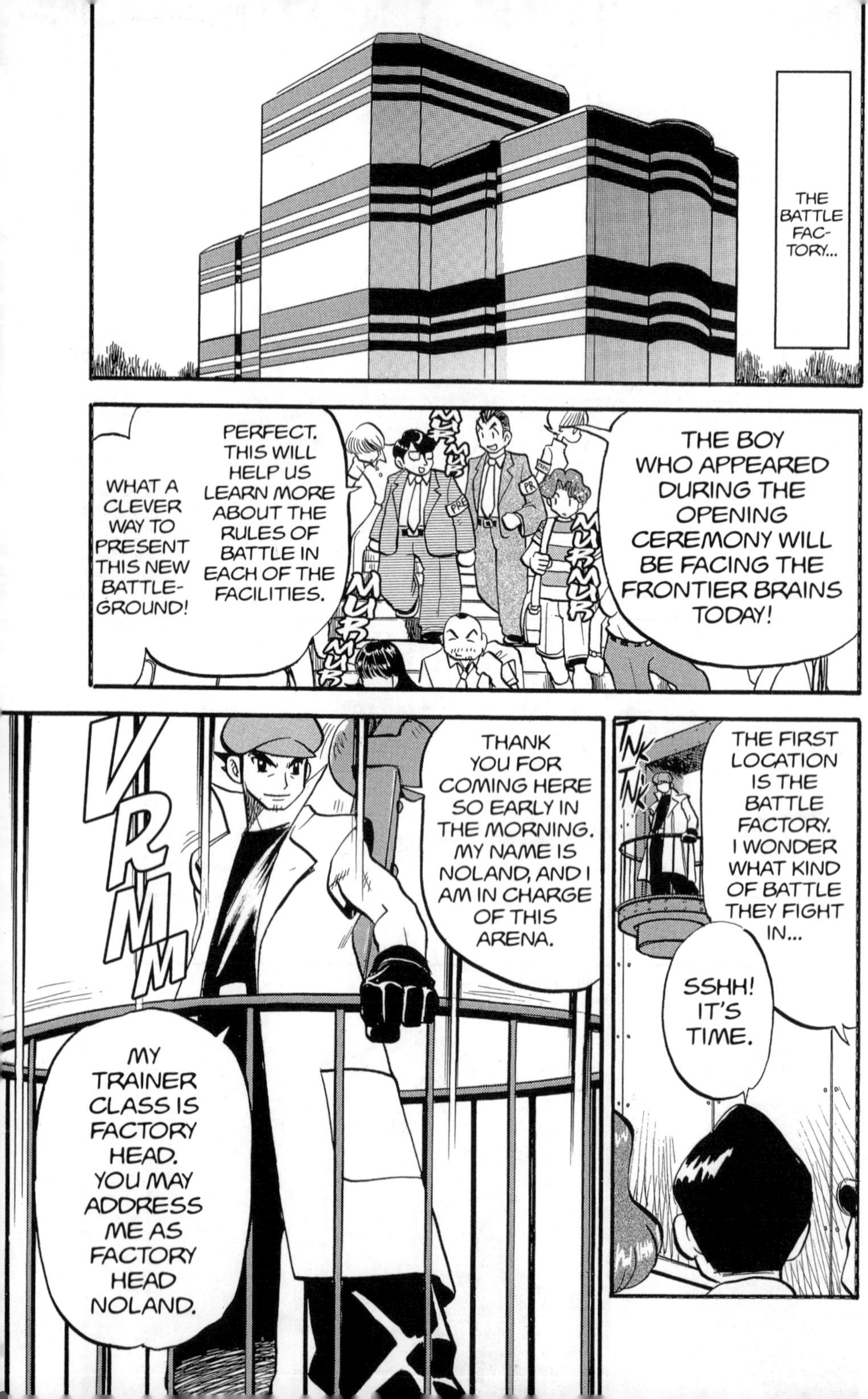
THE BATTLE FACTORY...
THE BOY WHO APPEARED DURING THE OPENING CEREMONY WILL BE FACING THE FRONTIER BRAINS TODAY!
MURMUR
MURMUR
PERFECT. THIS WILL HELP US LEARN MORE ABOUT THE RULES OF BATTLE IN EACH OF THE FACILITIES.
MURMUR
WHAT A CLEVER WAY TO PRESENT THIS NEW BATTLE-GROUND!
TNK
TNK
THE FIRST LOCATION IS THE BATTLE FACTORY. I WONDER WHAT KIND OF BATTLE THEY FIGHT IN...
SSHH! IT'S TIME.
VRMMM
THANK YOU FOR COMING HERE SO EARLY IN THE MORNING. MY NAME IS NOLAND, AND I AM IN CHARGE OF THIS ARENA.
MY TRAINER CLASS IS FACTORY HEAD. YOU MAY ADDRESS ME AS FACTORY HEAD NOLAND.

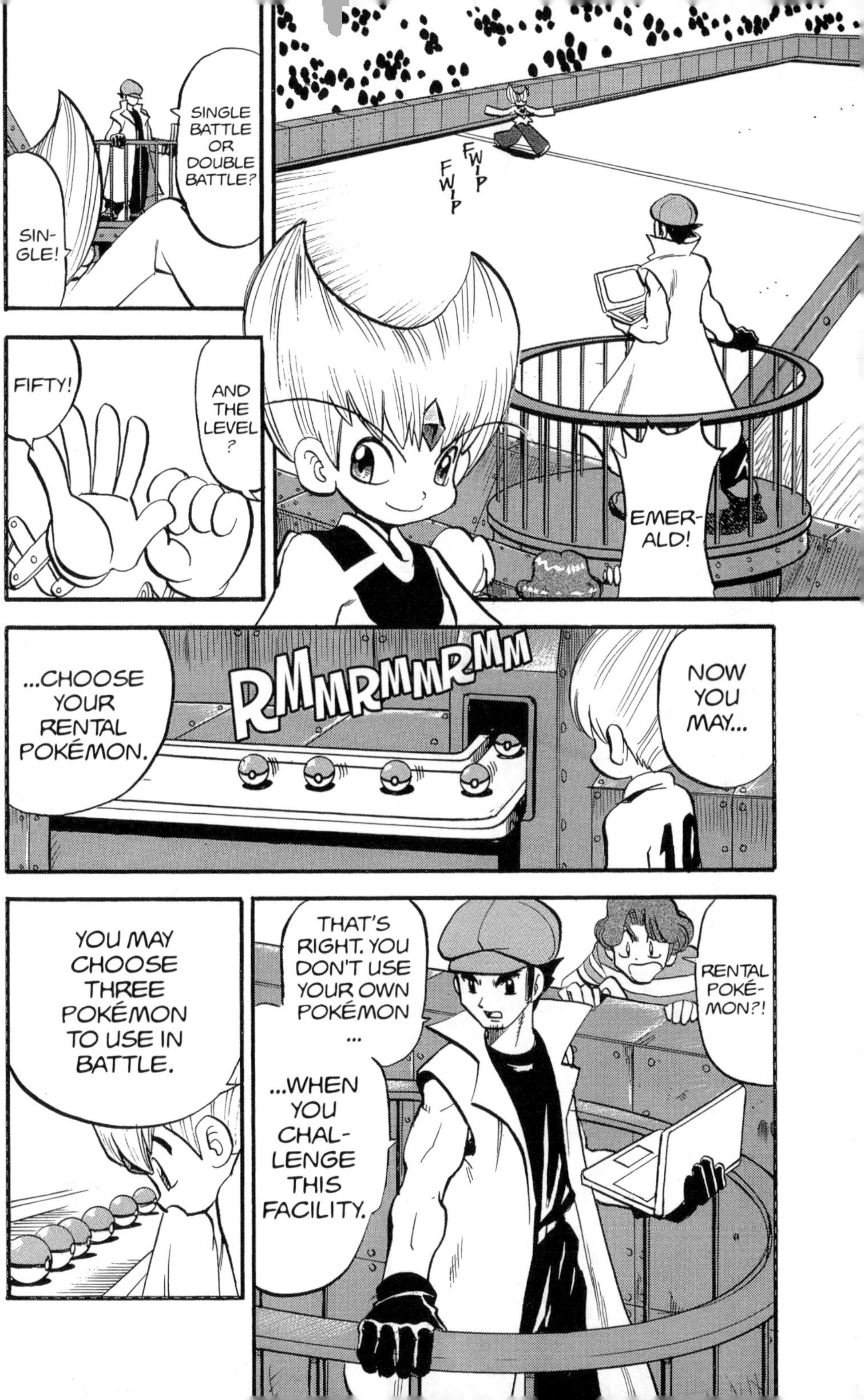
FWIP
FWIP
EMERALD!
SINGLE BATTLE OR DOUBLE BATTLE?
SINGLE!
AND THE LEVEL?
FIFTY!
NOW YOU MAY...
...CHOOSE YOUR RENTAL POKÉMON.
RMMRMMRMM
RENTAL POKÉMON?!
THAT'S RIGHT. YOU DON'T USE YOUR OWN POKÉMON...
...WHEN YOU CHALLENGE THIS FACILITY.
YOU MAY CHOOSE THREE POKÉMON TO USE IN BATTLE.

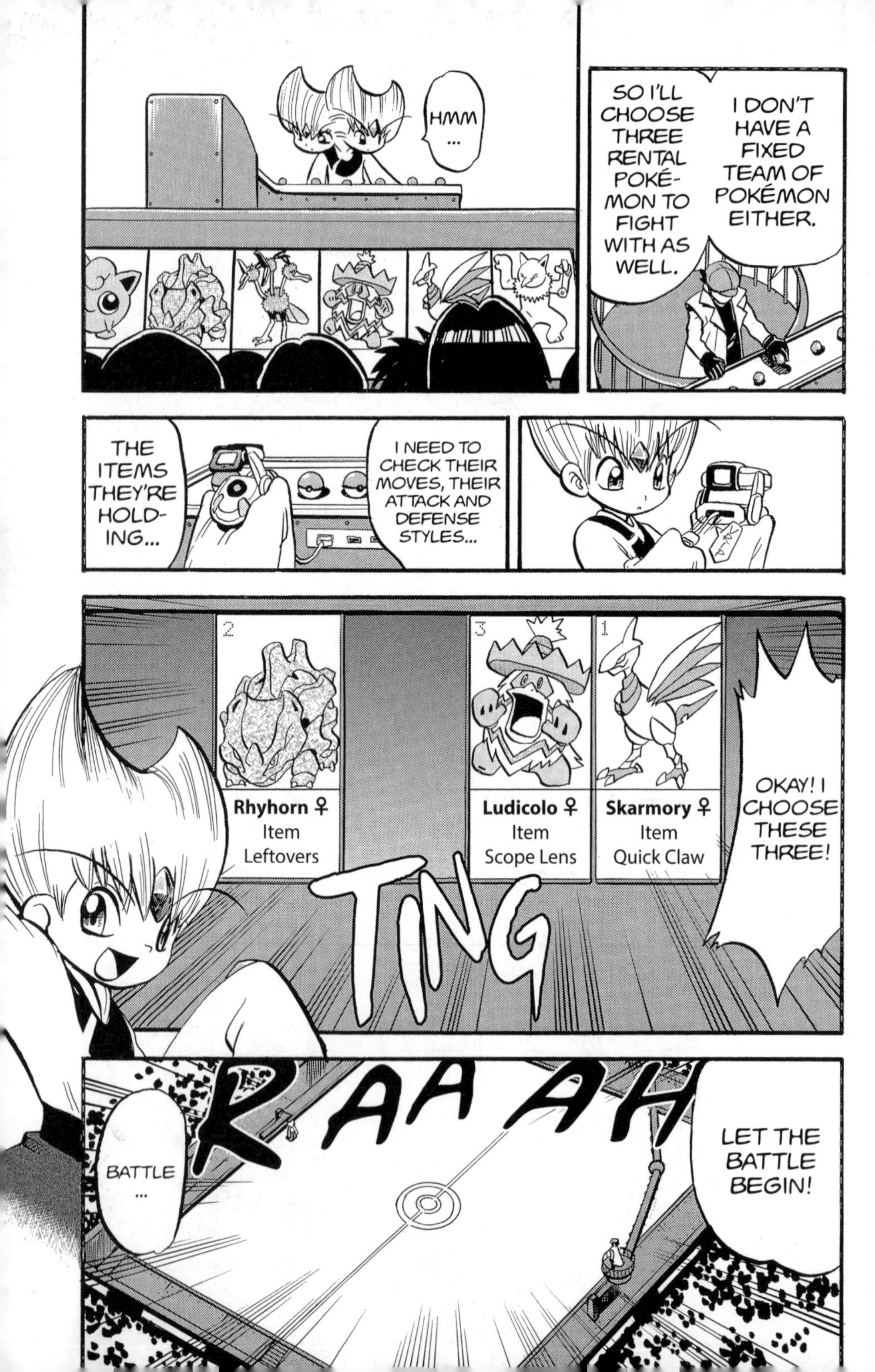
I DON'T HAVE A FIXED TEAM OF POKÉMON EITHER.
SO I'LL CHOOSE THREE RENTAL POKÉMON TO FIGHT WITH AS WELL.
HMM ...
I NEED TO CHECK THEIR MOVES, THEIR ATTACK AND DEFENSE STYLES...
THE ITEMS THEY'RE HOLDING...
OKAY! I CHOOSE THESE THREE!
1
Skarmory ♀
Item
Quick Claw
3
Ludicolo ♀
Item
Scope Lens
2
Rhyhorn ♀
Item
Leftovers
TING
RAAAH
LET THE BATTLE BEGIN!
BATTLE ...

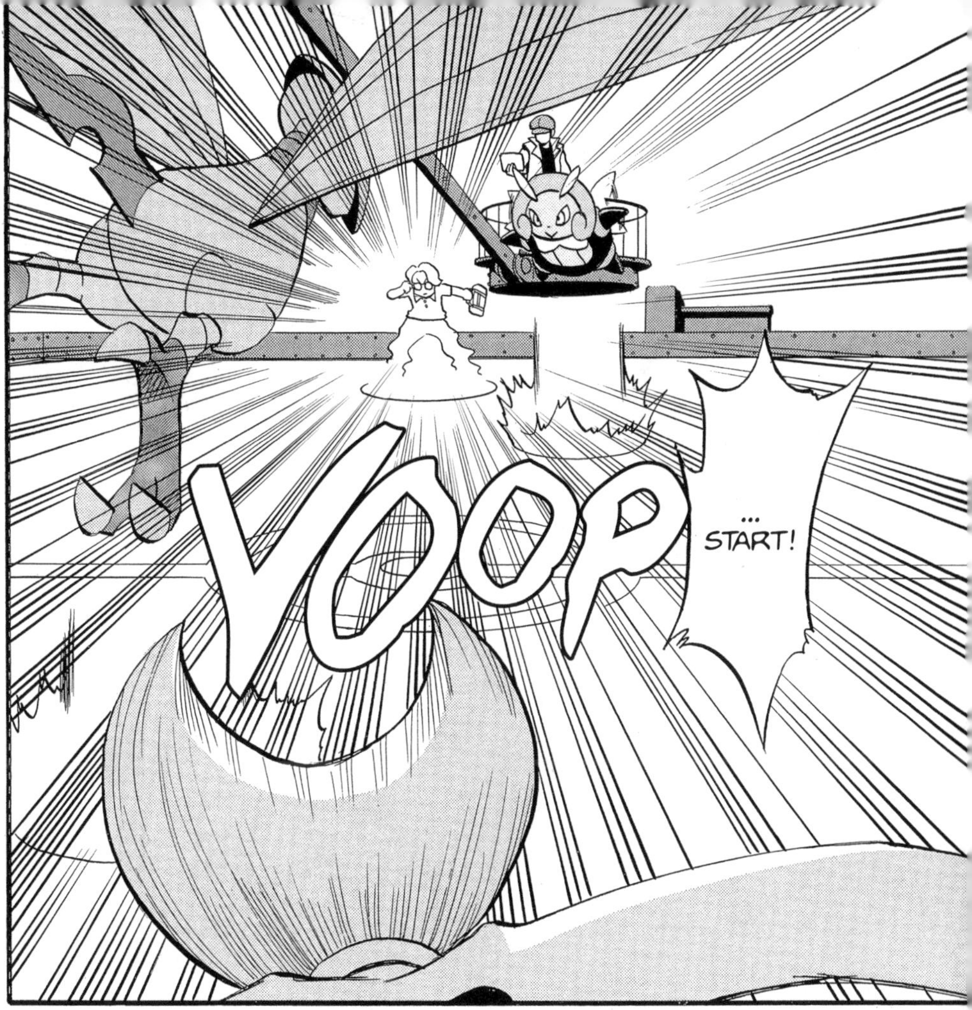
... START!
VOOP

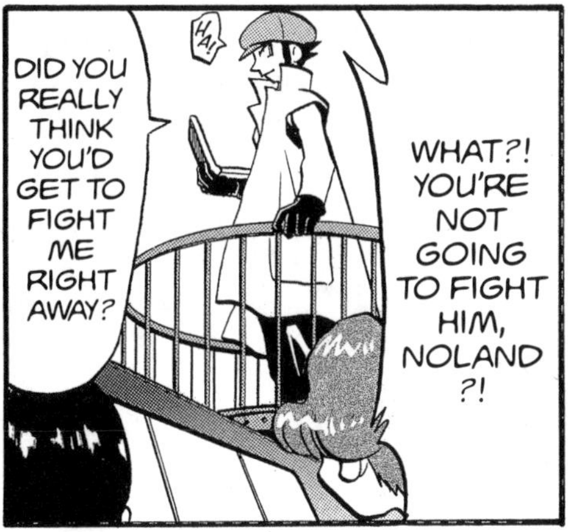
WHAT?! YOU'RE NOT GOING TO FIGHT HIM, NOLAND?!
HA!
DID YOU REALLY THINK YOU'D GET TO FIGHT ME RIGHT AWAY?

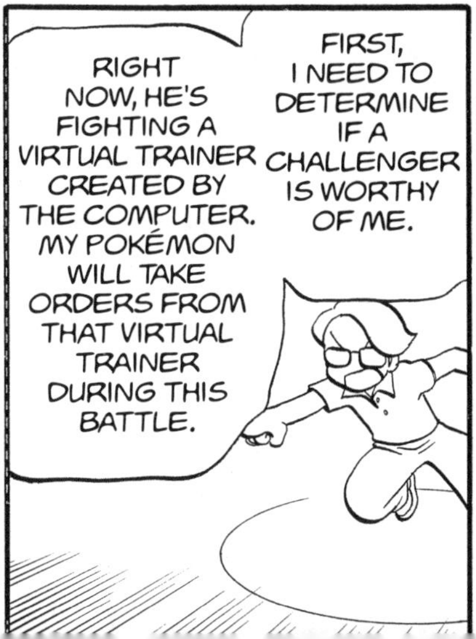
FIRST, I NEED TO DETERMINE IF A CHALLENGER IS WORTHY OF ME.
RIGHT NOW, HE'S FIGHTING A VIRTUAL TRAINER CREATED BY THE COMPUTER. MY POKÉMON WILL TAKE ORDERS FROM THAT VIRTUAL TRAINER DURING THIS BATTLE.

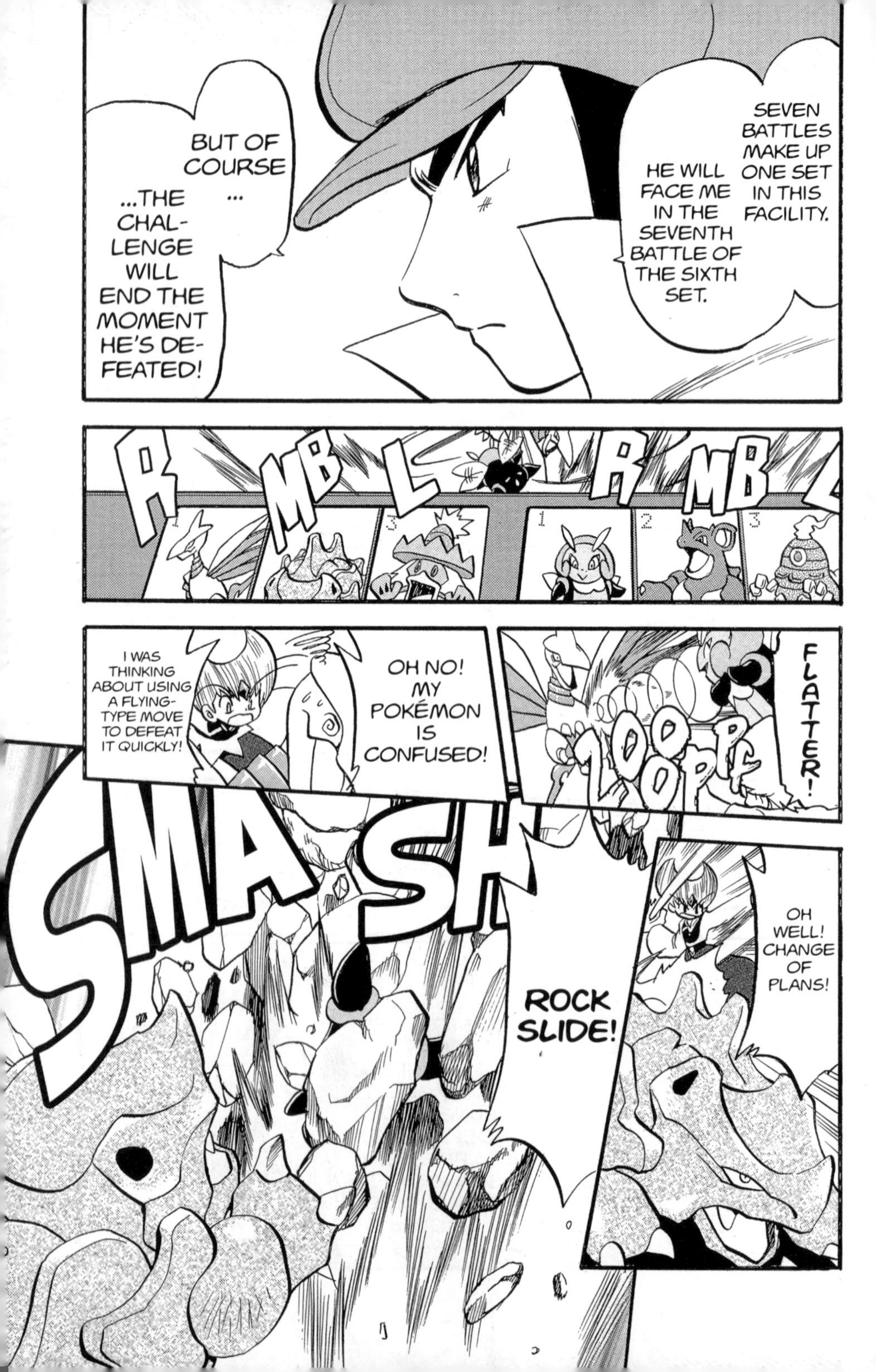
SEVEN BATTLES MAKE UP ONE SET IN THIS FACILITY.
HE WILL FACE ME IN THE SEVENTH BATTLE OF THE SIXTH SET.
BUT OF COURSE ...
...THE CHAL-LENGE WILL END THE MOMENT HE'S DE-FEATED!
R MB L R MB L
FLATTER!
ZOOP ZOOP
OH NO! MY POKÉMON IS CONFUSED!
I WAS THINKING ABOUT USING A FLYING-TYPE MOVE TO DEFEAT IT QUICKLY!
OH WELL! CHANGE OF PLANS!
ROCK SLIDE!
SMASH

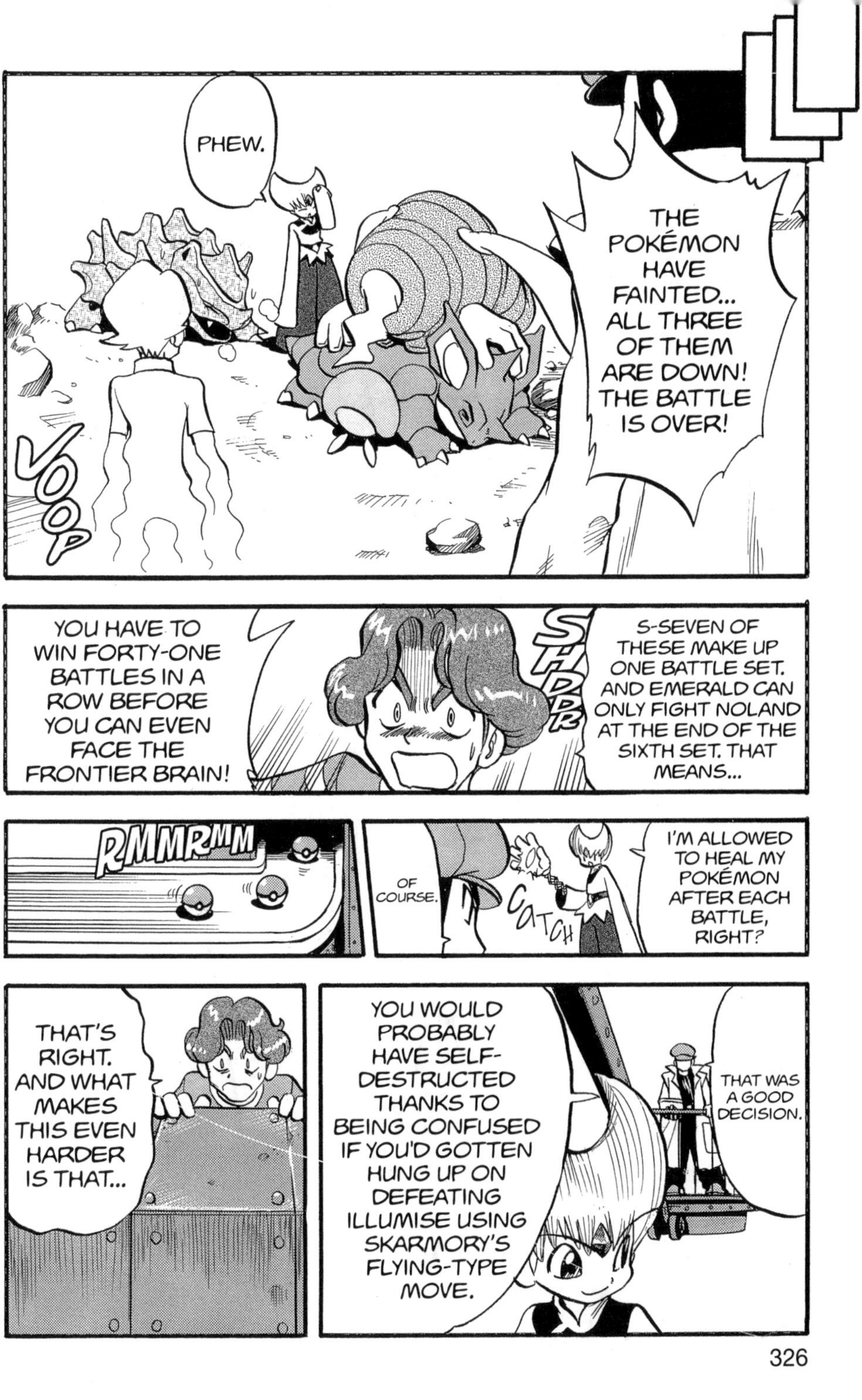
THE POKÉMON HAVE FAINTED... ALL THREE OF THEM ARE DOWN! THE BATTLE IS OVER!
PHEW.
VOOP
S-SEVEN OF THESE MAKE UP ONE BATTLE SET. AND EMERALD CAN ONLY FIGHT NOLAND AT THE END OF THE SIXTH SET. THAT MEANS...
SHDDR
YOU HAVE TO WIN FORTY-ONE BATTLES IN A ROW BEFORE YOU CAN EVEN FACE THE FRONTIER BRAIN!
I'M ALLOWED TO HEAL MY POKÉMON AFTER EACH BATTLE, RIGHT?
CATCH
OF COURSE.
RMMRMM
THAT WAS A GOOD DECISION.
YOU WOULD PROBABLY HAVE SELF-DESTRUCTED THANKS TO BEING CONFUSED IF YOU'D GOTTEN HUNG UP ON DEFEATING ILLUMISE USING SKARMORY'S FLYING-TYPE MOVE.
THAT'S RIGHT. AND WHAT MAKES THIS EVEN HARDER IS THAT...

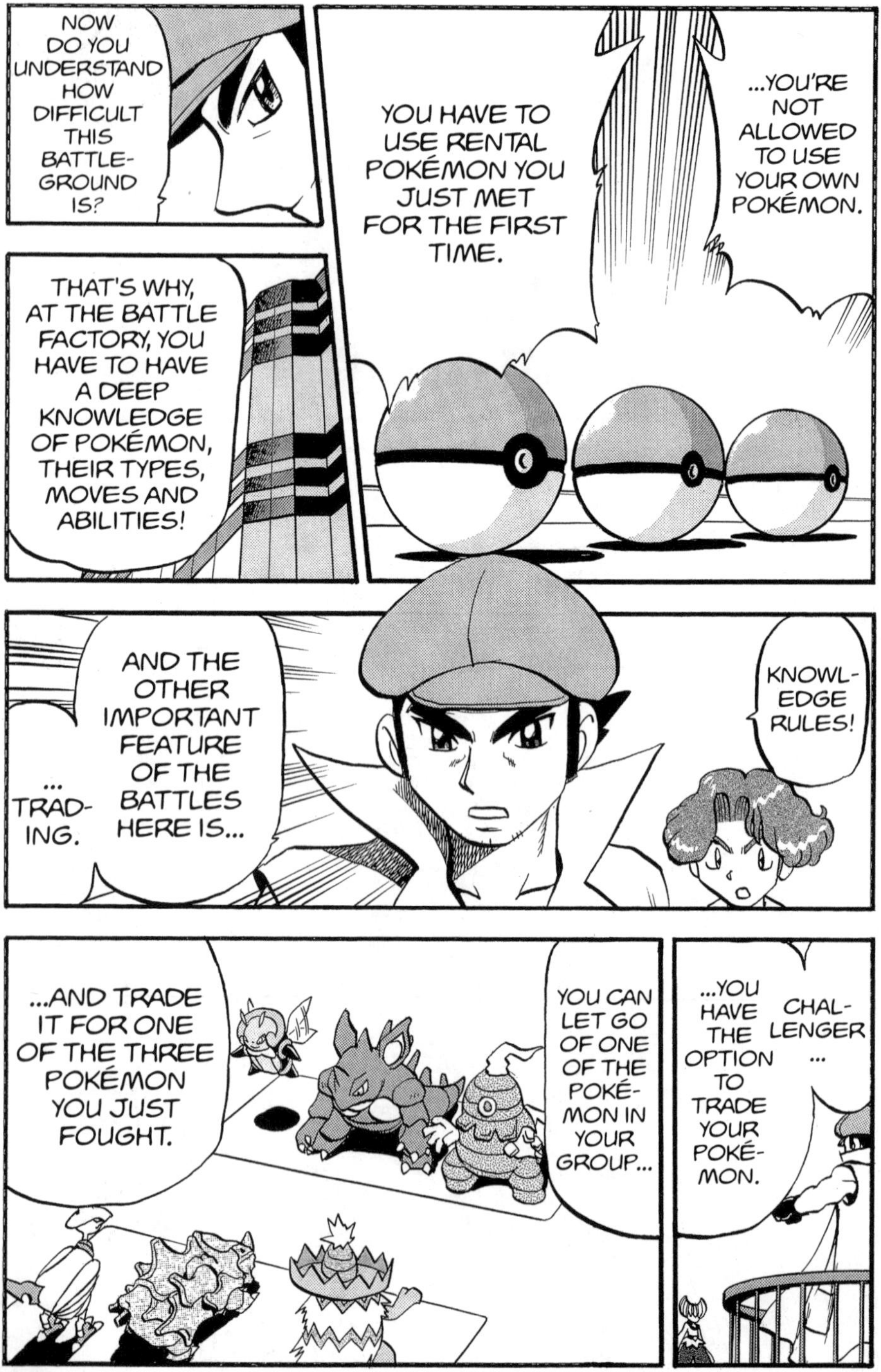
...YOU'RE NOT ALLOWED TO USE YOUR OWN POKÉMON.
YOU HAVE TO USE RENTAL POKÉMON YOU JUST MET FOR THE FIRST TIME.
NOW DO YOU UNDERSTAND HOW DIFFICULT THIS BATTLE-GROUND IS?
THAT'S WHY, AT THE BATTLE FACTORY, YOU HAVE TO HAVE A DEEP KNOWLEDGE OF POKÉMON, THEIR TYPES, MOVES AND ABILITIES!
KNOWL-EDGE RULES!
AND THE OTHER IMPORTANT FEATURE OF THE BATTLES HERE IS...
...TRAD-ING.
CHAL-LENGER...
...YOU HAVE THE OPTION TO TRADE YOUR POKÉ-MON.
YOU CAN LET GO OF ONE OF THE POKÉ-MON IN YOUR GROUP...
...AND TRADE IT FOR ONE OF THE THREE POKÉMON YOU JUST FOUGHT.

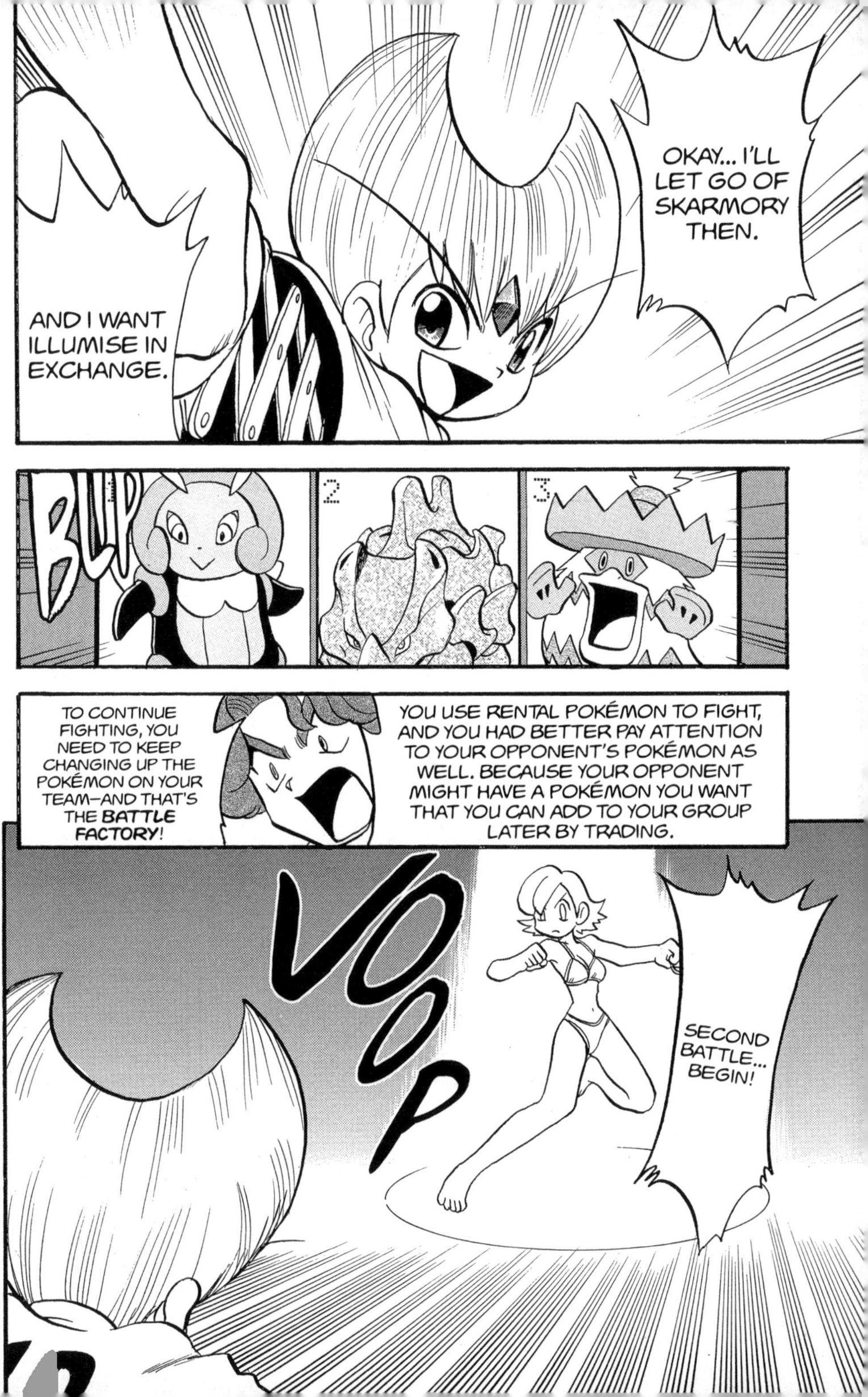
OKAY... I'LL LET GO OF SKARMORY THEN.
AND I WANT ILLUMISE IN EXCHANGE.
3
2
1
BLIP
YOU USE RENTAL POKÉMON TO FIGHT, AND YOU HAD BETTER PAY ATTENTION TO YOUR OPPONENT'S POKÉMON AS WELL. BECAUSE YOUR OPPONENT MIGHT HAVE A POKÉMON YOU WANT THAT YOU CAN ADD TO YOUR GROUP LATER BY TRADING.
TO CONTINUE FIGHTING, YOU NEED TO KEEP CHANGING UP THE POKÉMON ON YOUR TEAM—AND THAT'S THE **BATTLE FACTORY**!
SECOND BATTLE... BEGIN!
VOOP

DEAR MEMBERS OF THE PRESS...

Thank you for visiting my Battle Frontier today. Permit me to continue explaining the rules of this facility...

OWNER SCOTT

■ FOR CONVENIENCE, WE USE ■ NUMBERS TO REPRESENT A POKÉMON'S STRENGTH.

To ensure a fair battle, we represent the strengths of our Pokémon with numbers we call "levels." Challengers may use their PokéNav to check the level of their Pokémon before a battle.

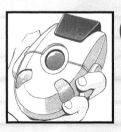

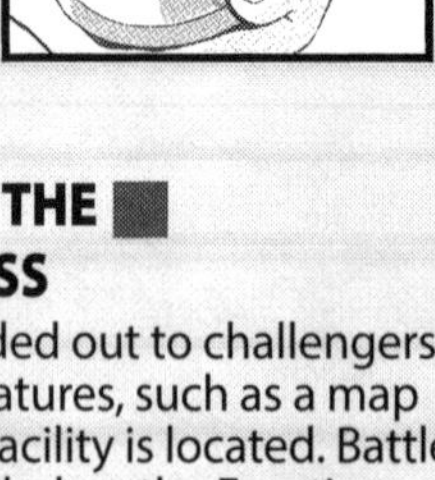

CHALLENGERS MAY CHOOSE BETWEEN LEVEL 50 AND OPEN LEVEL.

You may choose between two courses. In the "Level 50" course, the highest level for your Pokémon is 50. But the "Open Level" course has no Pokémon level limits.

■ FUNCTIONS OF THE ■ FRONTIER PASS

A Frontier Pass is handed out to challengers. This pass has many features, such as a map to check where each facility is located. Battle records are also recorded on the Frontier Pass. You may record any battle you wish and replay it later.

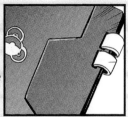

 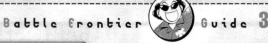

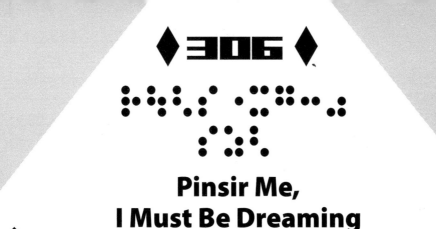

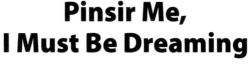

Pinsir Me,
I Must Be Dreaming

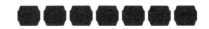

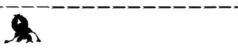

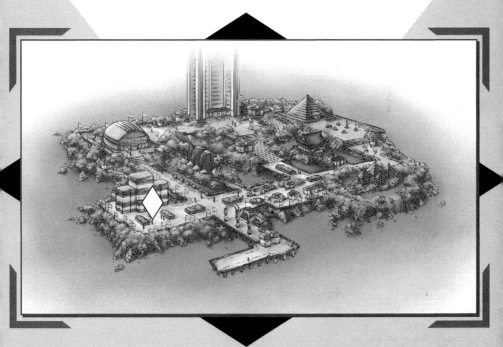

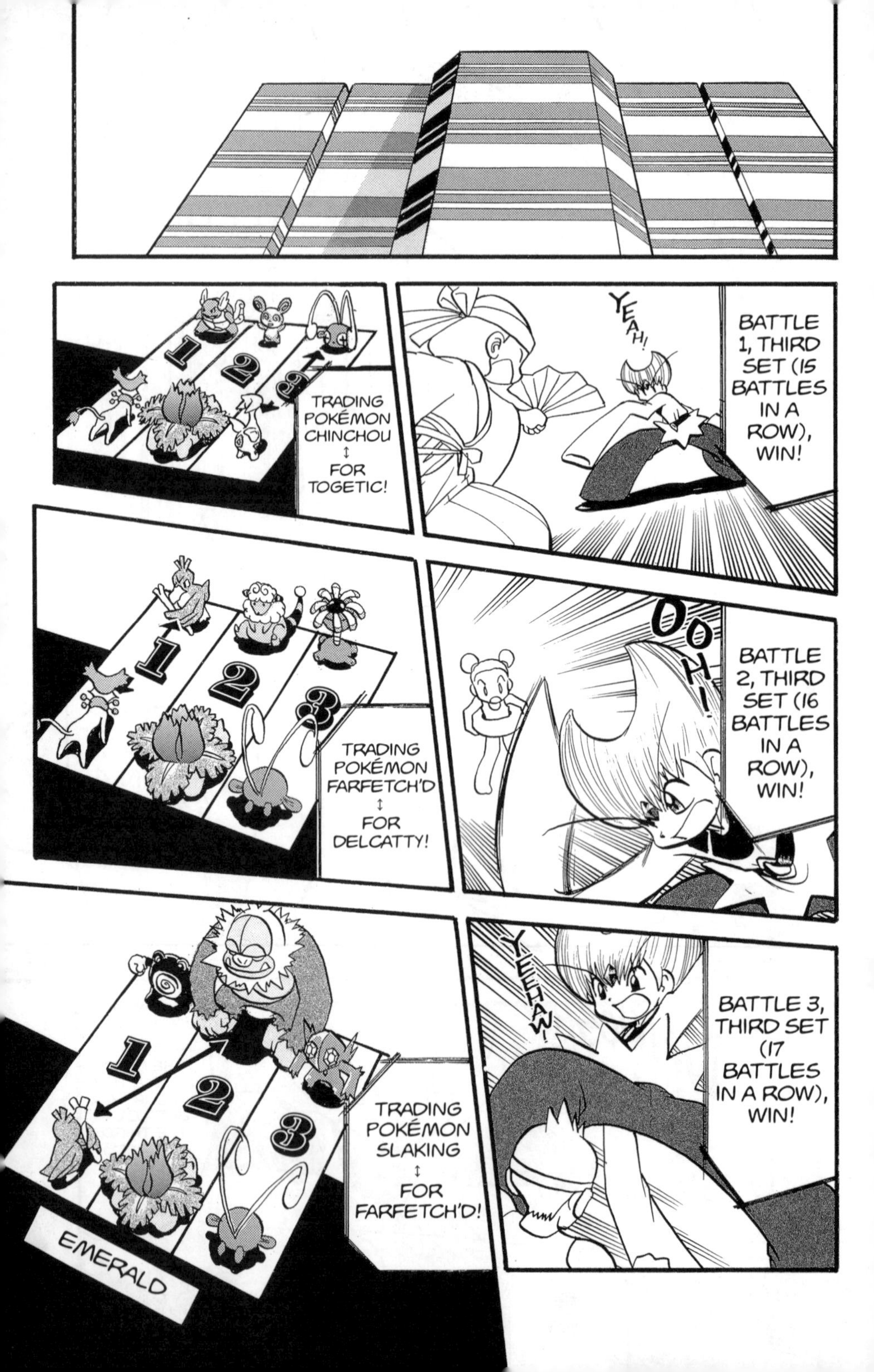
BATTLE 1, THIRD SET (15 BATTLES IN A ROW), WIN!
YEAH!
TRADING POKÉMON CHINCHOU ↕ FOR TOGETIC!
BATTLE 2, THIRD SET (16 BATTLES IN A ROW), WIN!
OOH!
TRADING POKÉMON FARFETCH'D ↕ FOR DELCATTY!
BATTLE 3, THIRD SET (17 BATTLES IN A ROW), WIN!
YEEHAW!
TRADING POKÉMON SLAKING ↕ FOR FARFETCH'D!
EMERALD

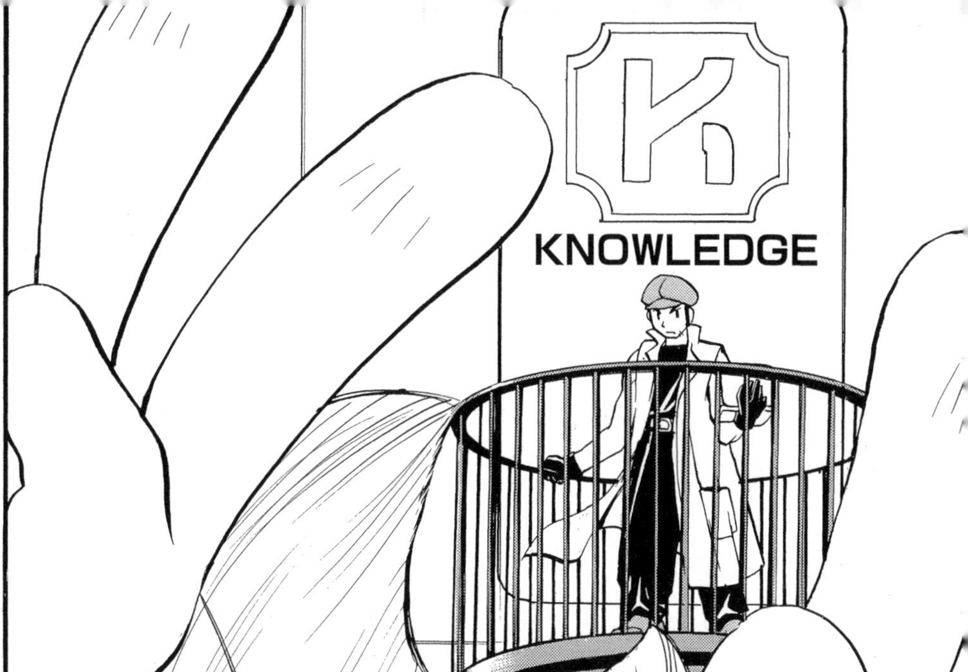
KNOWLEDGE
PHEW! THAT'S 17 WINS IN A ROW!

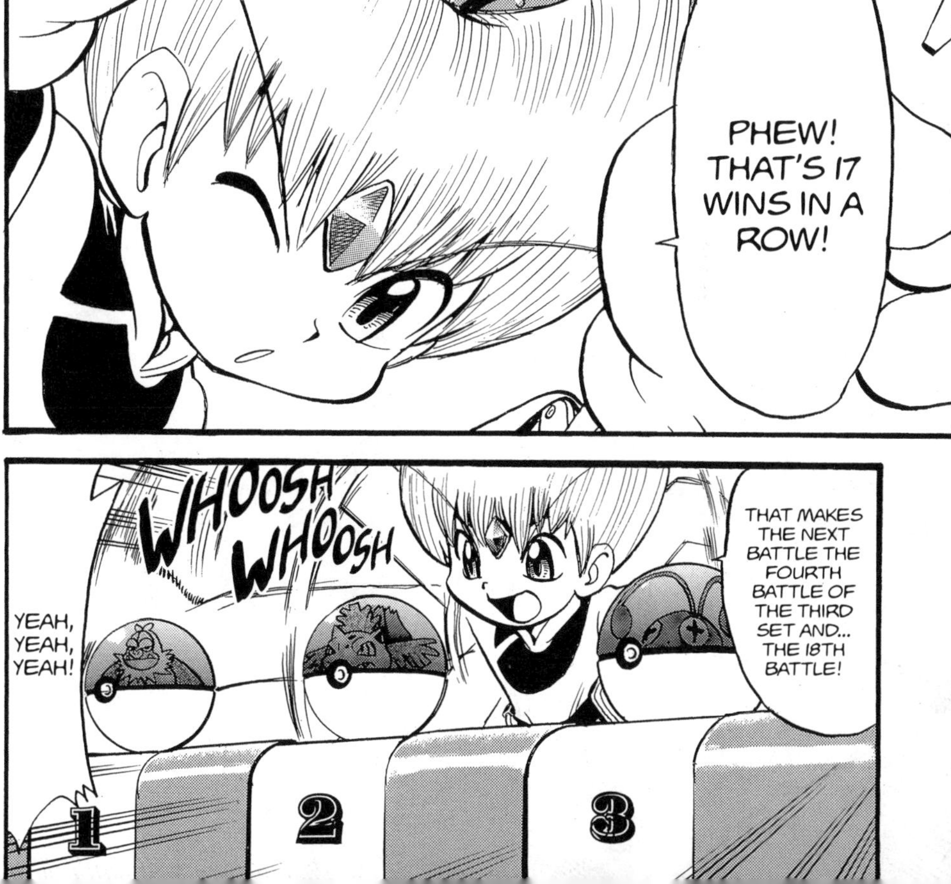
THAT MAKES THE NEXT BATTLE THE FOURTH BATTLE OF THE THIRD SET AND... THE 18TH BATTLE!
WHOOSH
WHOOSH
YEAH, YEAH, YEAH!
1
2
3

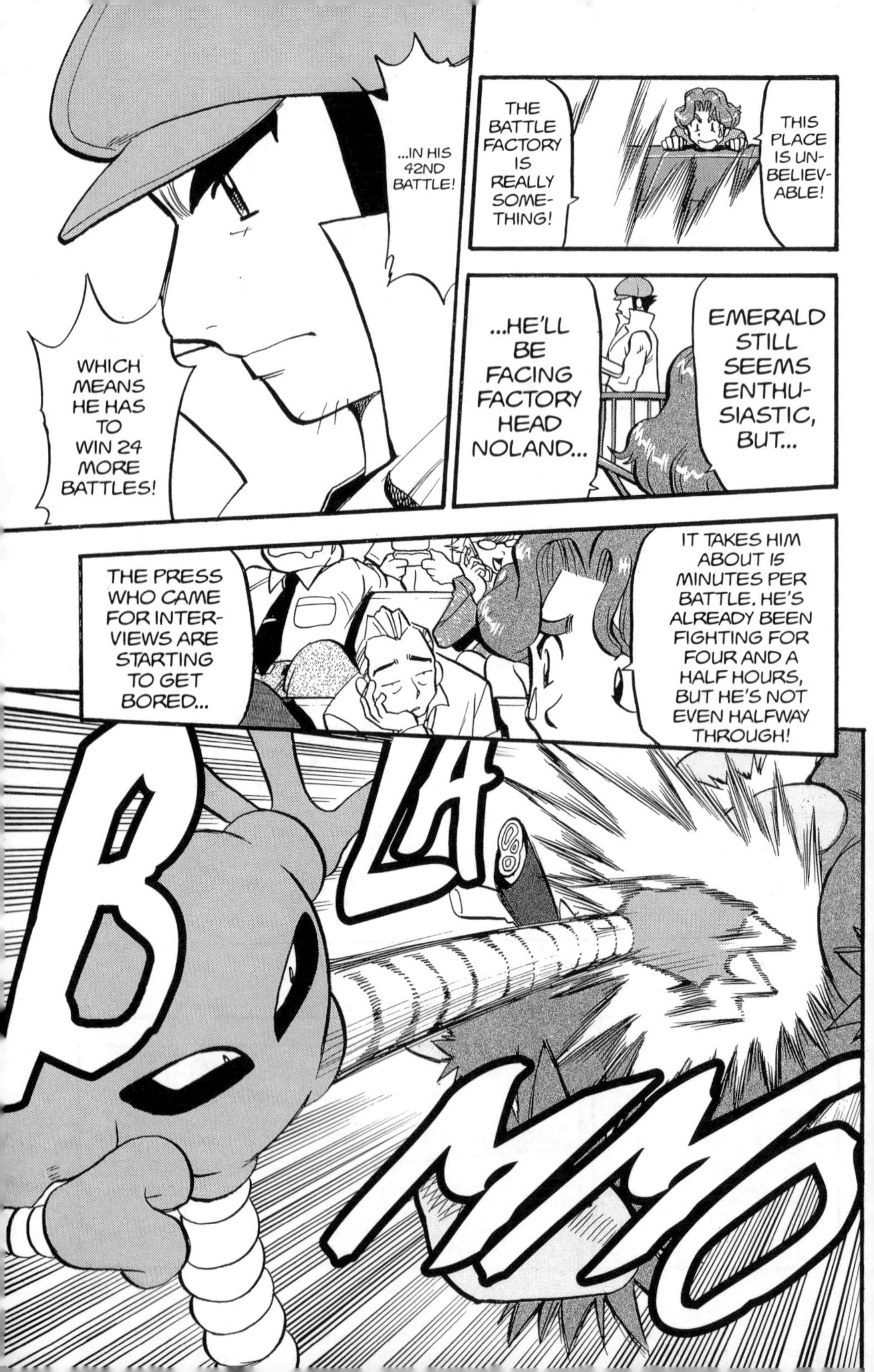
THIS PLACE IS UNBELIEVABLE!
THE BATTLE FACTORY IS REALLY SOMETHING!
EMERALD STILL SEEMS ENTHUSIASTIC, BUT...
...HE'LL BE FACING FACTORY HEAD NOLAND...
...IN HIS 42ND BATTLE!
WHICH MEANS HE HAS TO WIN 24 MORE BATTLES!
IT TAKES HIM ABOUT 15 MINUTES PER BATTLE. HE'S ALREADY BEEN FIGHTING FOR FOUR AND A HALF HOURS, BUT HE'S NOT EVEN HALFWAY THROUGH!
THE PRESS WHO CAME FOR INTERVIEWS ARE STARTING TO GET BORED...
BLAMMO

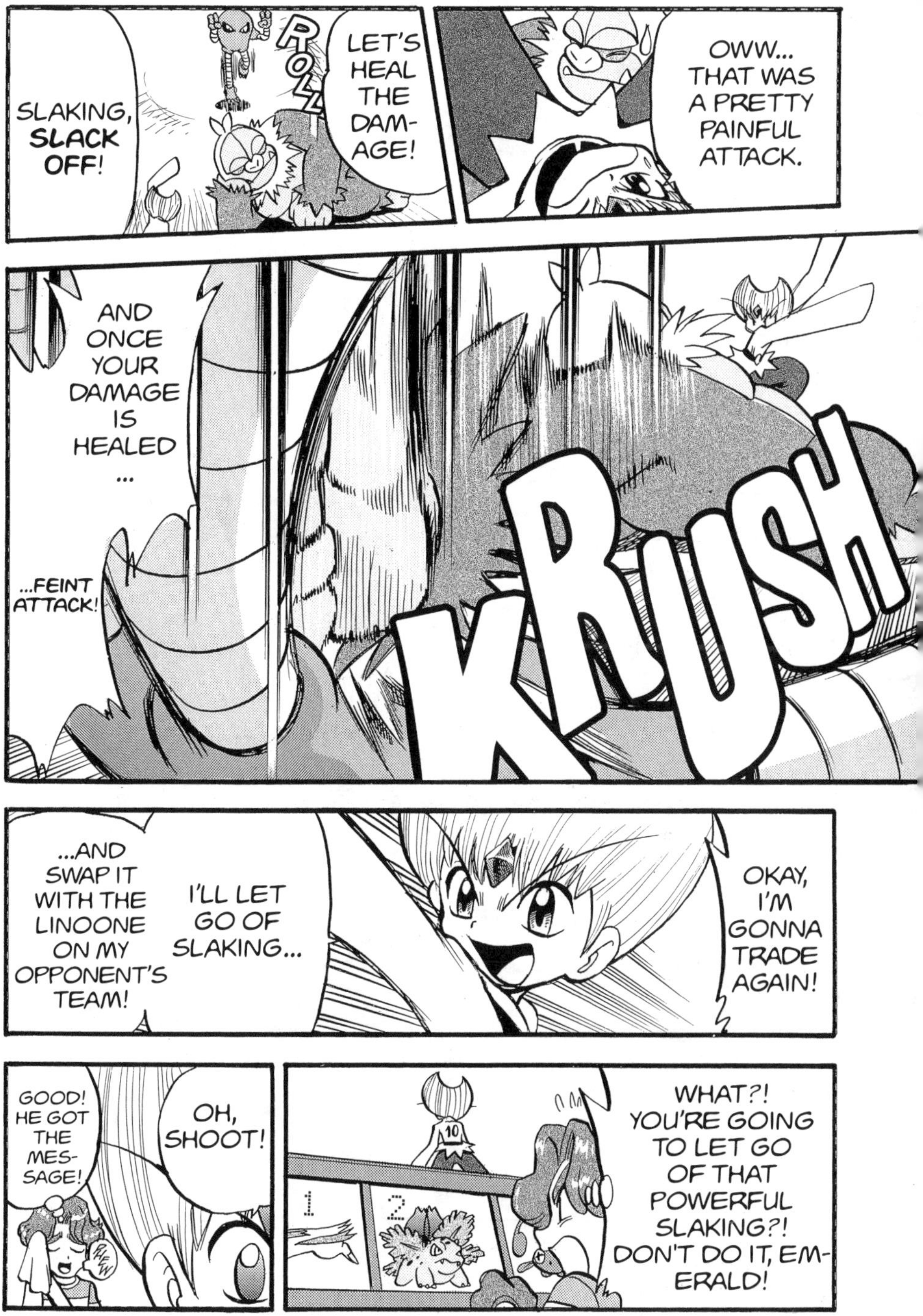
OWW... THAT WAS A PRETTY PAINFUL ATTACK.
LET'S HEAL THE DAM-AGE!
ROLL
SLAKING, **SLACK OFF**!
AND ONCE YOUR DAMAGE IS HEALED ...
...FEINT ATTACK!
KRUSH
OKAY, I'M GONNA TRADE AGAIN!
I'LL LET GO OF SLAKING...
...AND SWAP IT WITH THE LINOONE ON MY OPPONENT'S TEAM!
WHAT?! YOU'RE GOING TO LET GO OF THAT POWERFUL SLAKING?! DON'T DO IT, EM-ERALD!
10
1
2
OH, SHOOT!
GOOD! HE GOT THE MES-SAGE!
PHEW

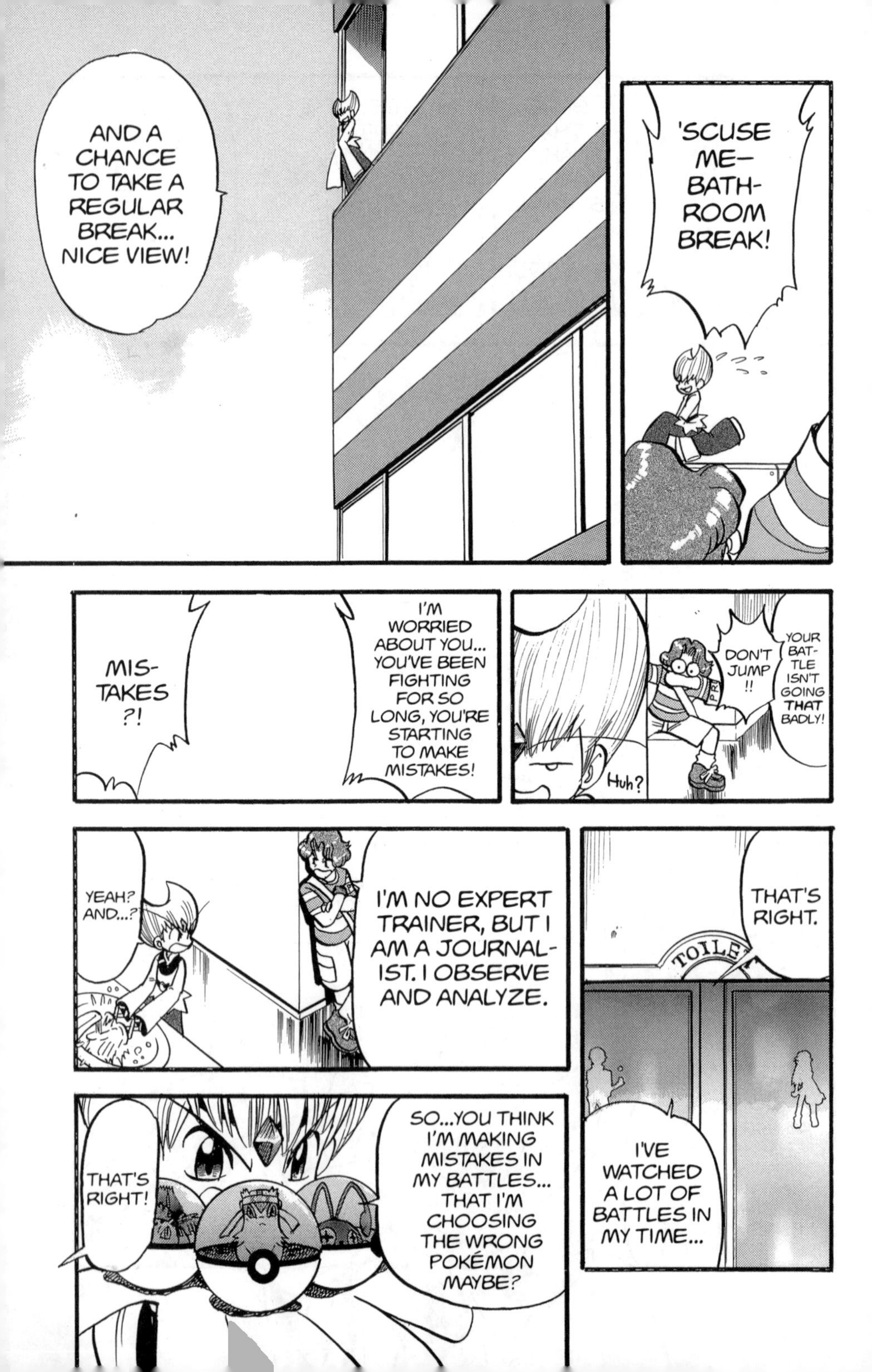
'SCUSE ME— BATH-ROOM BREAK!
AND A CHANCE TO TAKE A REGULAR BREAK... NICE VIEW!
YOUR BAT-TLE ISN'T GOING **THAT** BADLY!
DON'T JUMP!!
Huh?
I'M WORRIED ABOUT YOU... YOU'VE BEEN FIGHTING FOR SO LONG, YOU'RE STARTING TO MAKE MISTAKES!
MIS-TAKES?!
THAT'S RIGHT.
I'VE WATCHED A LOT OF BATTLES IN MY TIME...
I'M NO EXPERT TRAINER, BUT I AM A JOURNAL-IST. I OBSERVE AND ANALYZE.
YEAH? AND...?
SO...YOU THINK I'M MAKING MISTAKES IN MY BATTLES... THAT I'M CHOOSING THE WRONG POKÉMON MAYBE?
THAT'S RIGHT!

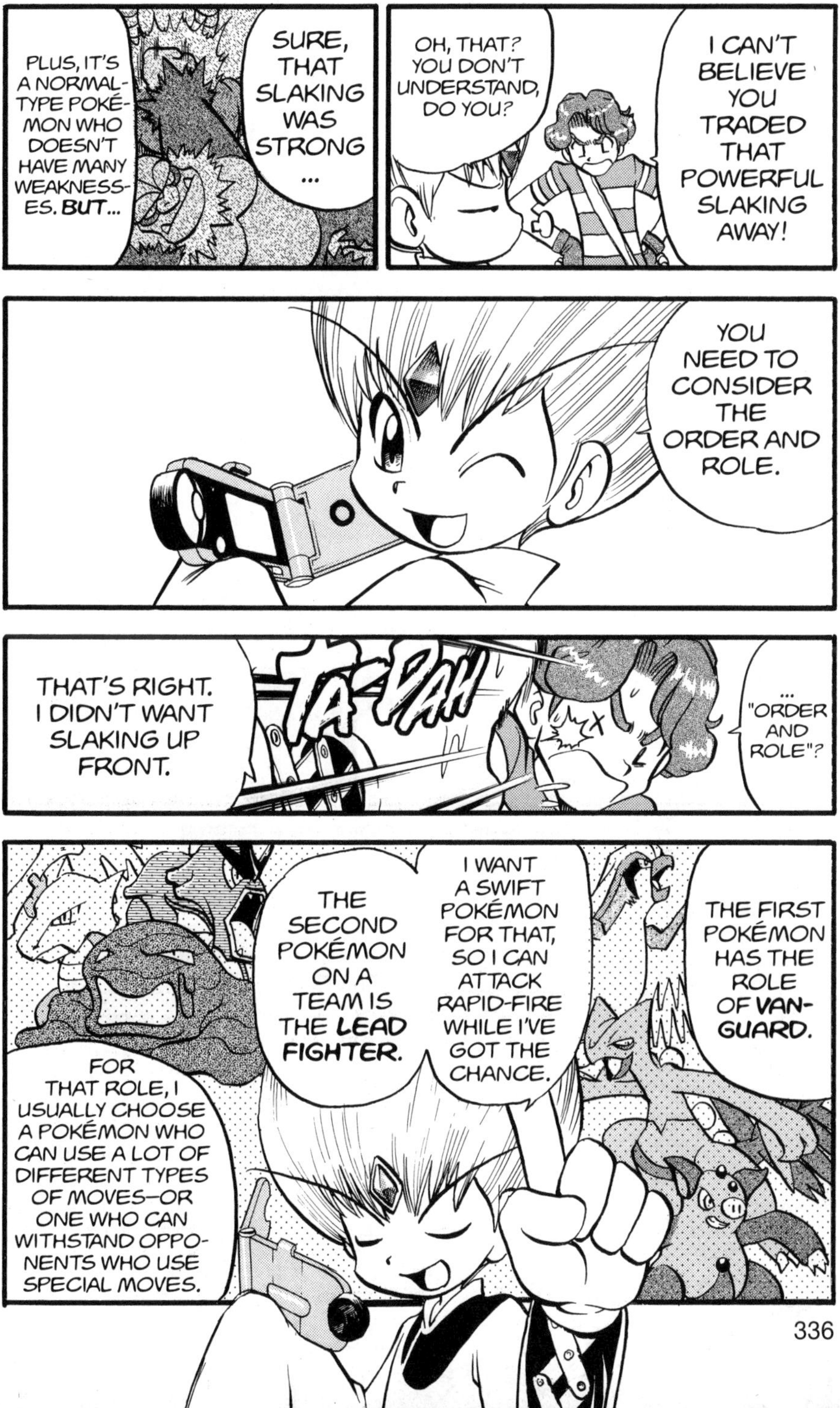
I CAN'T BELIEVE YOU TRADED THAT POWERFUL SLAKING AWAY!
OH, THAT? YOU DON'T UNDERSTAND, DO YOU?
SURE, THAT SLAKING WAS STRONG...
PLUS, IT'S A NORMAL-TYPE POKÉMON WHO DOESN'T HAVE MANY WEAKNESSES. **BUT...**
YOU NEED TO CONSIDER THE ORDER AND ROLE.
... "ORDER AND ROLE"?
TA-DAH
THAT'S RIGHT. I DIDN'T WANT SLAKING UP FRONT.
THE FIRST POKÉMON HAS THE ROLE OF **VANGUARD.**
I WANT A SWIFT POKÉMON FOR THAT, SO I CAN ATTACK RAPID-FIRE WHILE I'VE GOT THE CHANCE.
THE SECOND POKÉMON ON A TEAM IS THE **LEAD FIGHTER.**
FOR THAT ROLE, I USUALLY CHOOSE A POKÉMON WHO CAN USE A LOT OF DIFFERENT TYPES OF MOVES—OR ONE WHO CAN WITHSTAND OPPONENTS WHO USE SPECIAL MOVES.

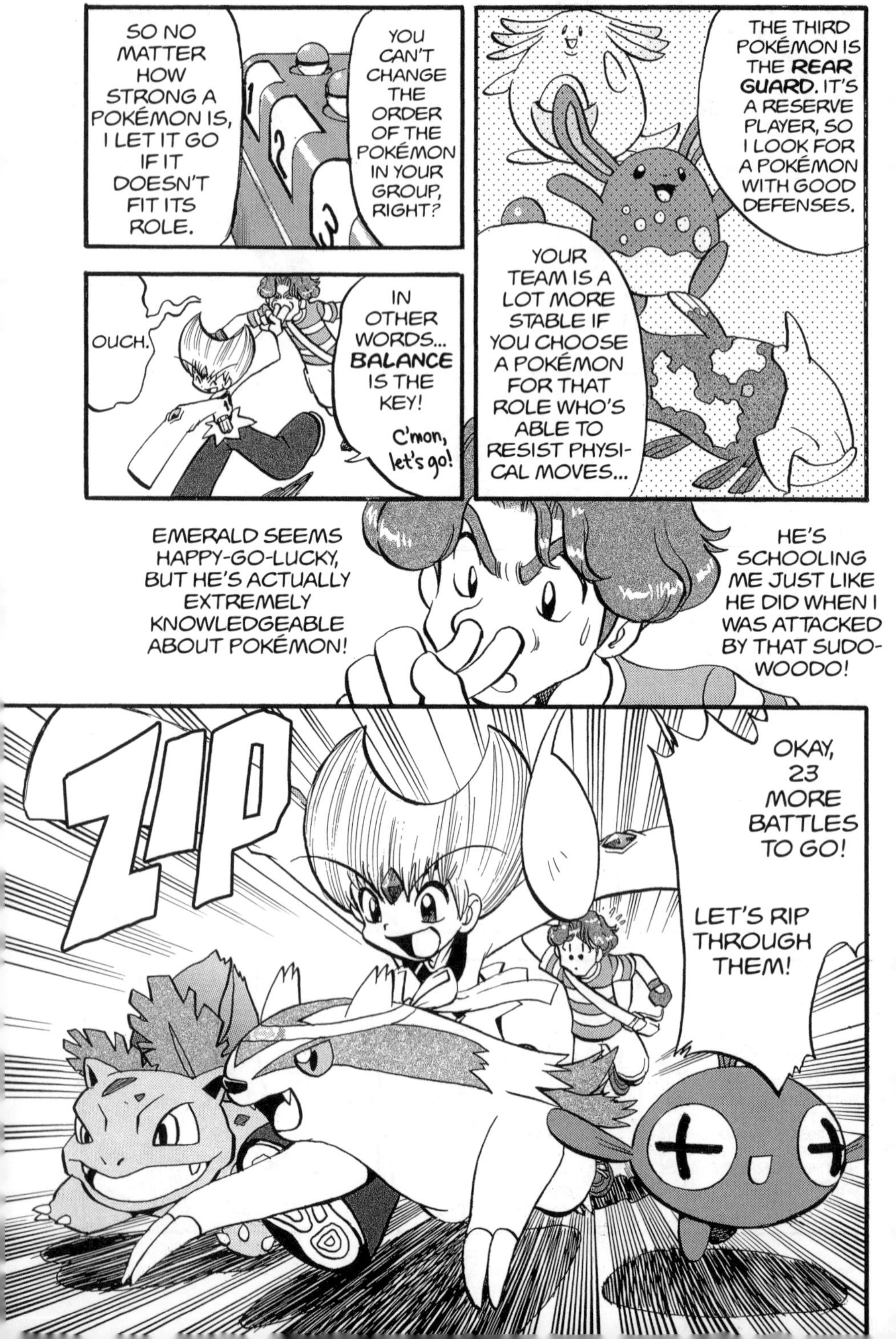

THE THIRD POKÉMON IS THE **REAR GUARD**. IT'S A RESERVE PLAYER, SO I LOOK FOR A POKÉMON WITH GOOD DEFENSES.
YOUR TEAM IS A LOT MORE STABLE IF YOU CHOOSE A POKÉMON FOR THAT ROLE WHO'S ABLE TO RESIST PHYSICAL MOVES...
YOU CAN'T CHANGE THE ORDER OF THE POKÉMON IN YOUR GROUP, RIGHT?
SO NO MATTER HOW STRONG A POKÉMON IS, I LET IT GO IF IT DOESN'T FIT ITS ROLE.
IN OTHER WORDS... **BALANCE** IS THE KEY!
C'mon, let's go!
OUCH.
HE'S SCHOOLING ME JUST LIKE HE DID WHEN I WAS ATTACKED BY THAT SUDOWOODO!
EMERALD SEEMS HAPPY-GO-LUCKY, BUT HE'S ACTUALLY EXTREMELY KNOWLEDGEABLE ABOUT POKÉMON!
OKAY, 23 MORE BATTLES TO GO!
LET'S RIP THROUGH THEM!
ZIP

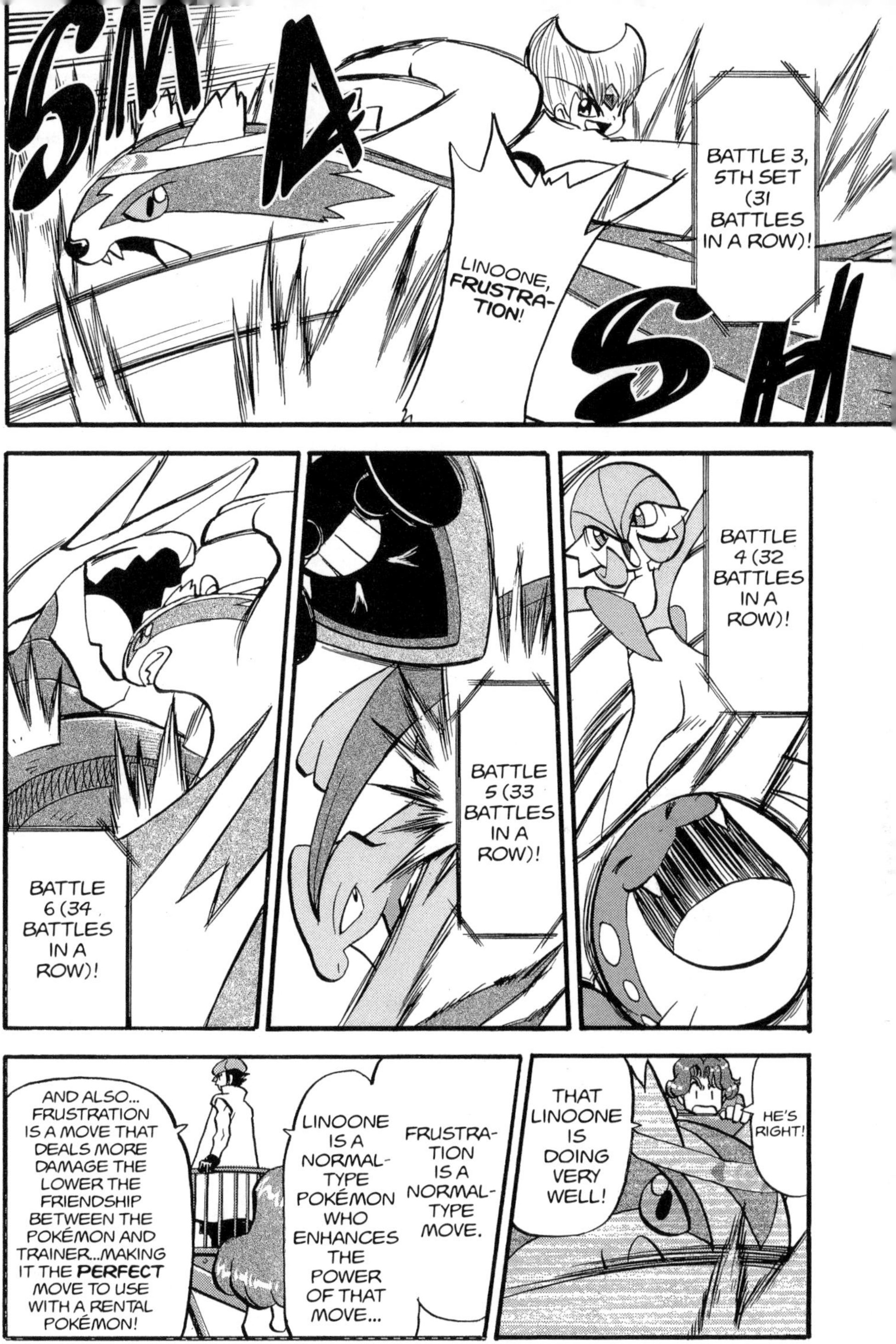
BATTLE 3, 5TH SET (31 BATTLES IN A ROW)!
LINOONE, **FRUSTRATION!**
SMASH
BATTLE 4 (32 BATTLES IN A ROW)!
BATTLE 5 (33 BATTLES IN A ROW)!
BATTLE 6 (34 BATTLES IN A ROW)!
HE'S RIGHT!
THAT LINOONE IS DOING VERY WELL!
FRUSTRATION IS A NORMAL-TYPE MOVE.
LINOONE IS A NORMAL-TYPE POKÉMON WHO ENHANCES THE POWER OF THAT MOVE...
AND ALSO... FRUSTRATION IS A MOVE THAT DEALS MORE DAMAGE THE LOWER THE FRIENDSHIP BETWEEN THE POKÉMON AND TRAINER...MAKING IT THE **PERFECT** MOVE TO USE WITH A RENTAL POKÉMON!

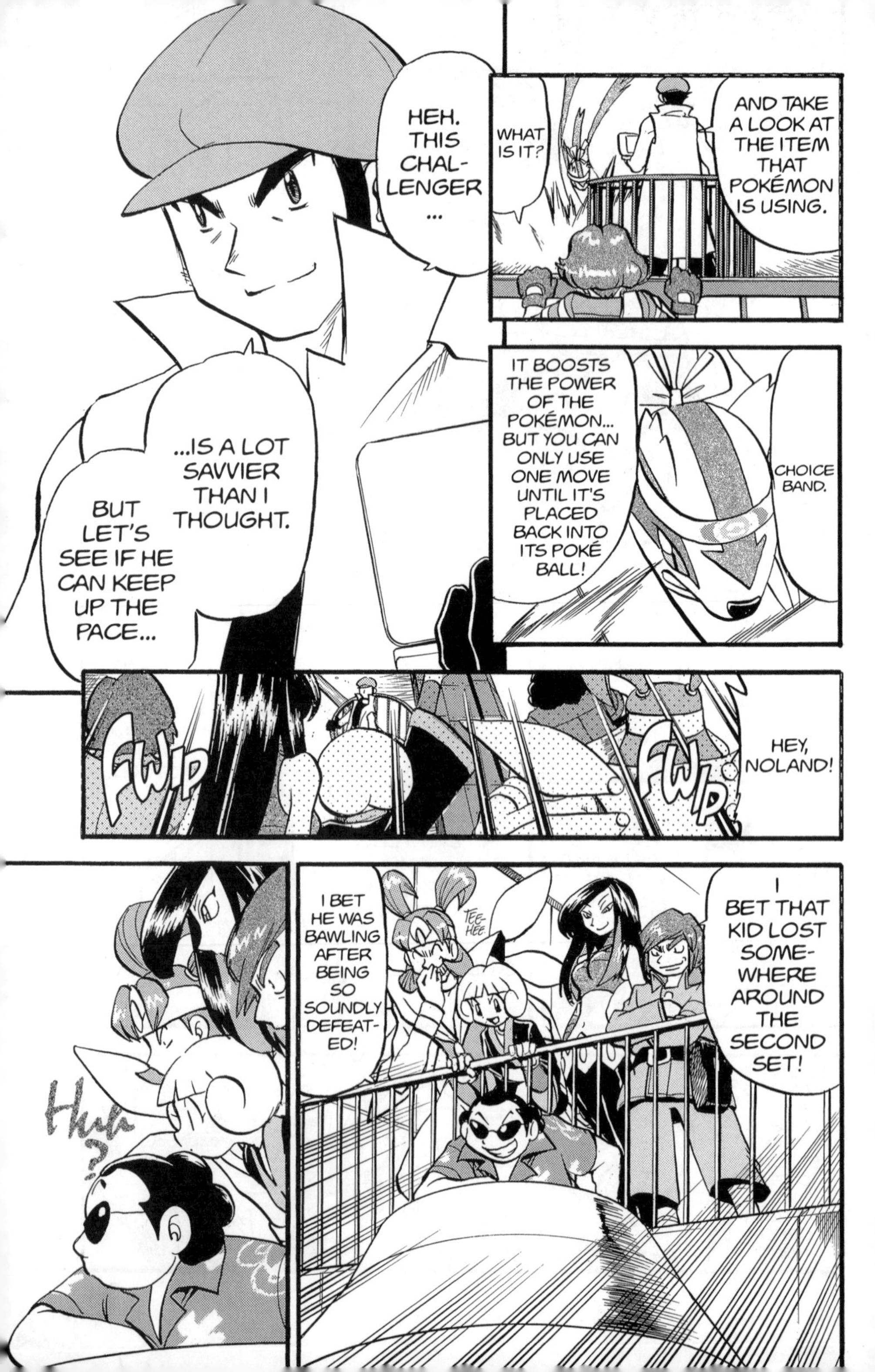
AND TAKE A LOOK AT THE ITEM THAT POKÉMON IS USING.
WHAT IS IT?
CHOICE BAND.
IT BOOSTS THE POWER OF THE POKÉMON... BUT YOU CAN ONLY USE ONE MOVE UNTIL IT'S PLACED BACK INTO ITS POKÉ BALL!
HEH. THIS CHALLENGER...
...IS A LOT SAVVIER THAN I THOUGHT.
BUT LET'S SEE IF HE CAN KEEP UP THE PACE...
HEY, NOLAND!
FWIP
FWIP
I BET THAT KID LOST SOMEWHERE AROUND THE SECOND SET!
TEE-HEE
I BET HE WAS BAWLING AFTER BEING SO SOUNDLY DEFEATED!
Huh?

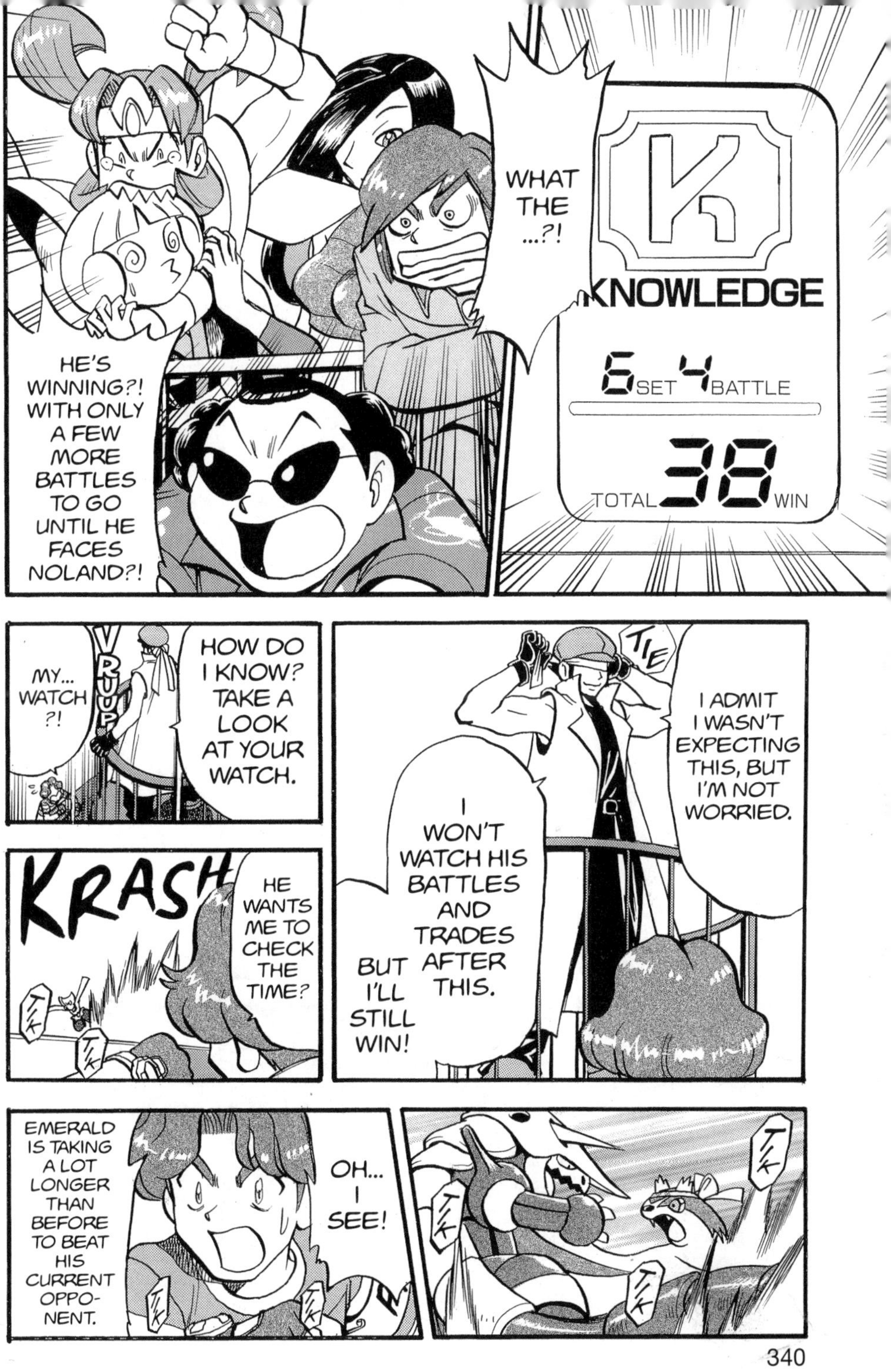
KNOWLEDGE
6 SET 4 BATTLE
TOTAL 38 WIN
WHAT THE ...?!
HE'S WINNING?! WITH ONLY A FEW MORE BATTLES TO GO UNTIL HE FACES NOLAND?!
TIE
I ADMIT I WASN'T EXPECTING THIS, BUT I'M NOT WORRIED.
I WON'T WATCH HIS BATTLES AND TRADES AFTER THIS.
BUT I'LL STILL WIN!
HOW DO I KNOW? TAKE A LOOK AT YOUR WATCH.
VRUUP
MY... WATCH?!
KRASH
HE WANTS ME TO CHECK THE TIME?
TIK
TIK
TIK
TIK
TIK
OH... I SEE!
EMERALD IS TAKING A LOT LONGER THAN BEFORE TO BEAT HIS CURRENT OPPO-NENT.
TIK
TIK

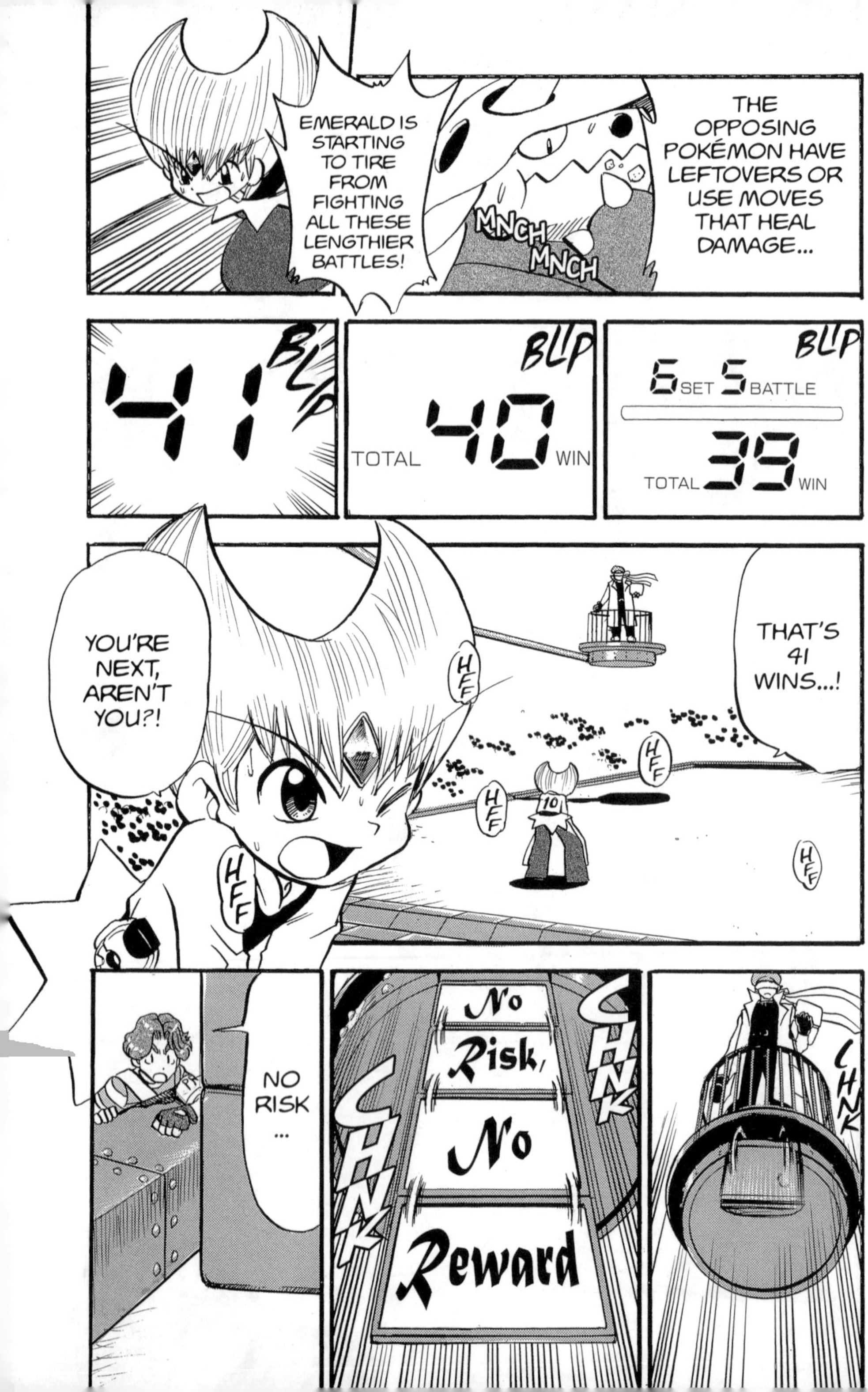
THE OPPOSING POKÉMON HAVE LEFTOVERS OR USE MOVES THAT HEAL DAMAGE...
MNCH MNCH
EMERALD IS STARTING TO TIRE FROM FIGHTING ALL THESE LENGTHIER BATTLES!
BLIP
6 SET 5 BATTLE
TOTAL 39 WIN
BLIP
TOTAL 40 WIN
BLIP
41
THAT'S 41 WINS...!
HFF
HFF
HFF
HFF
HFF
YOU'RE NEXT, AREN'T YOU?!
CHNK
CHNK
No Risk, No Reward
CHNK
NO RISK ...

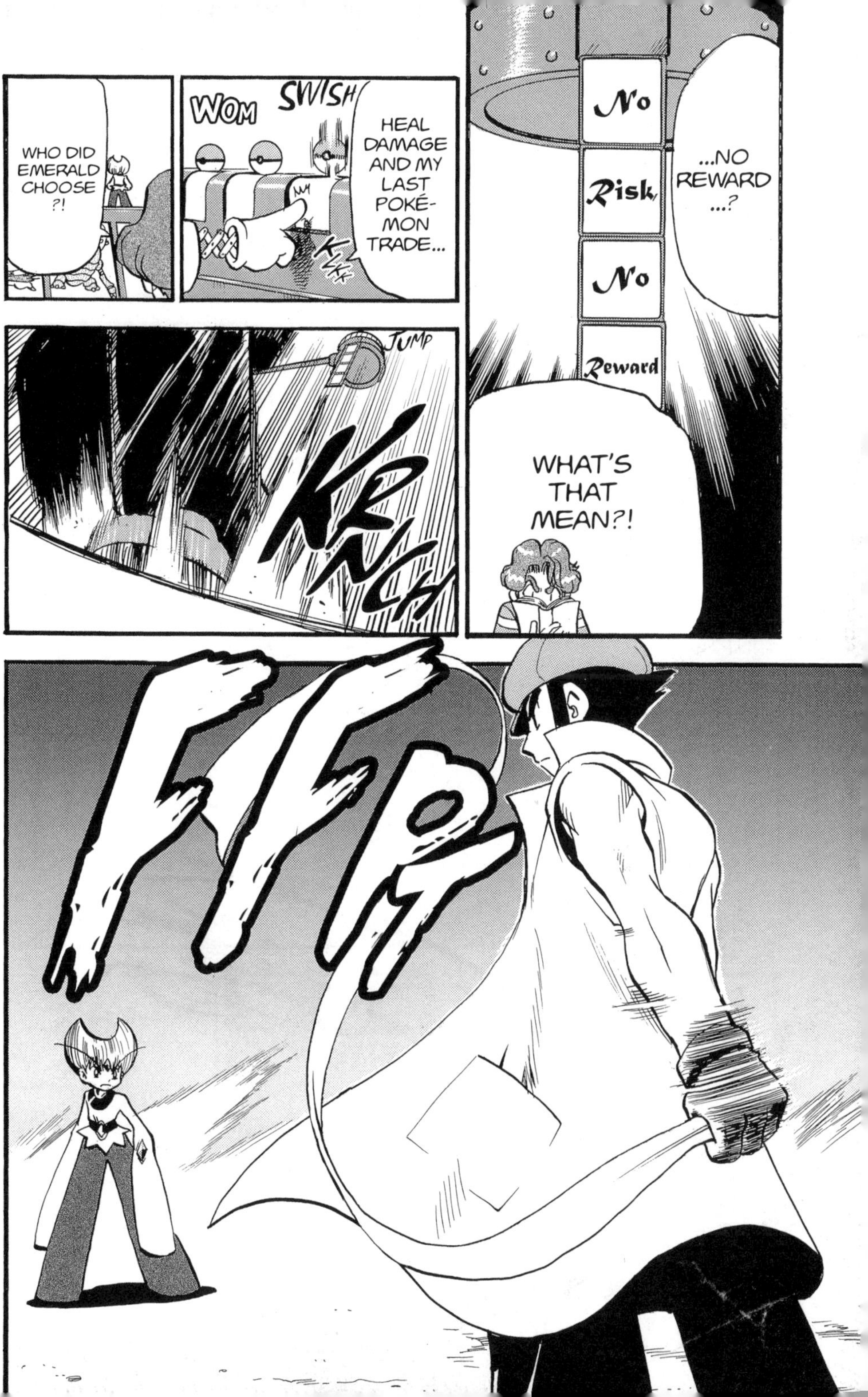
No Risk, No Reward
...NO REWARD ...?
WHAT'S THAT MEAN?!
WOM
SWISH
HEAL DAMAGE AND MY LAST POKÉ-MON TRADE...
KLKK
WHO DID EMERALD CHOOSE ?!
JUMP
KRNCH
FFP

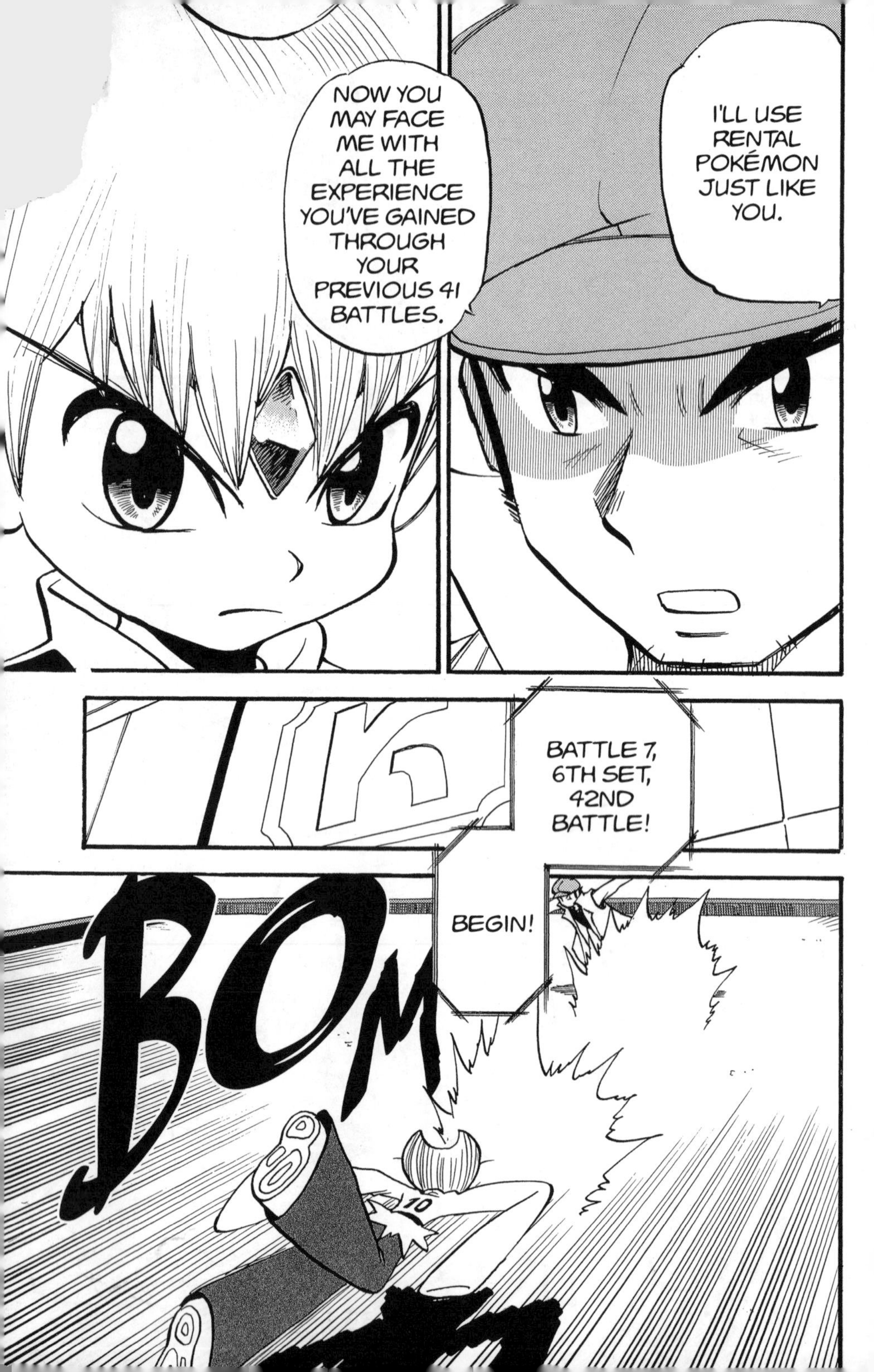
I'LL USE RENTAL POKÉMON JUST LIKE YOU.
NOW YOU MAY FACE ME WITH ALL THE EXPERIENCE YOU'VE GAINED THROUGH YOUR PREVIOUS 41 BATTLES.
BATTLE 7, 6TH SET, 42ND BATTLE!
BEGIN!
BOM

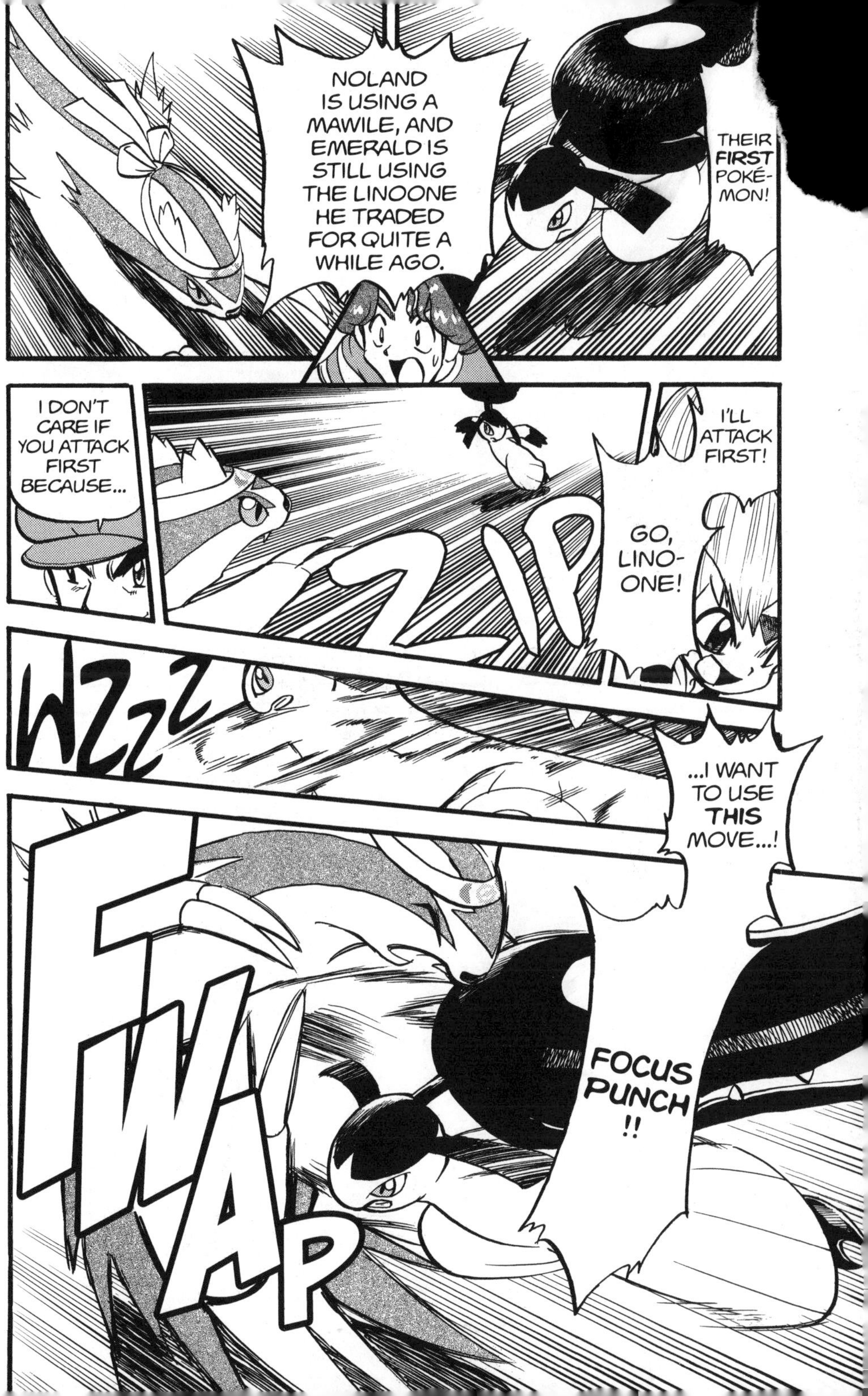
NOLAND IS USING A MAWILE, AND EMERALD IS STILL USING THE LINOONE HE TRADED FOR QUITE A WHILE AGO.
THEIR **FIRST** POKÉ-MON!
I'LL ATTACK FIRST!
GO, LINO-ONE!
ZIP
I DON'T CARE IF YOU ATTACK FIRST BECAUSE...
WZZZ
...I WANT TO USE **THIS** MOVE...!
FOCUS PUNCH !!
FWAP

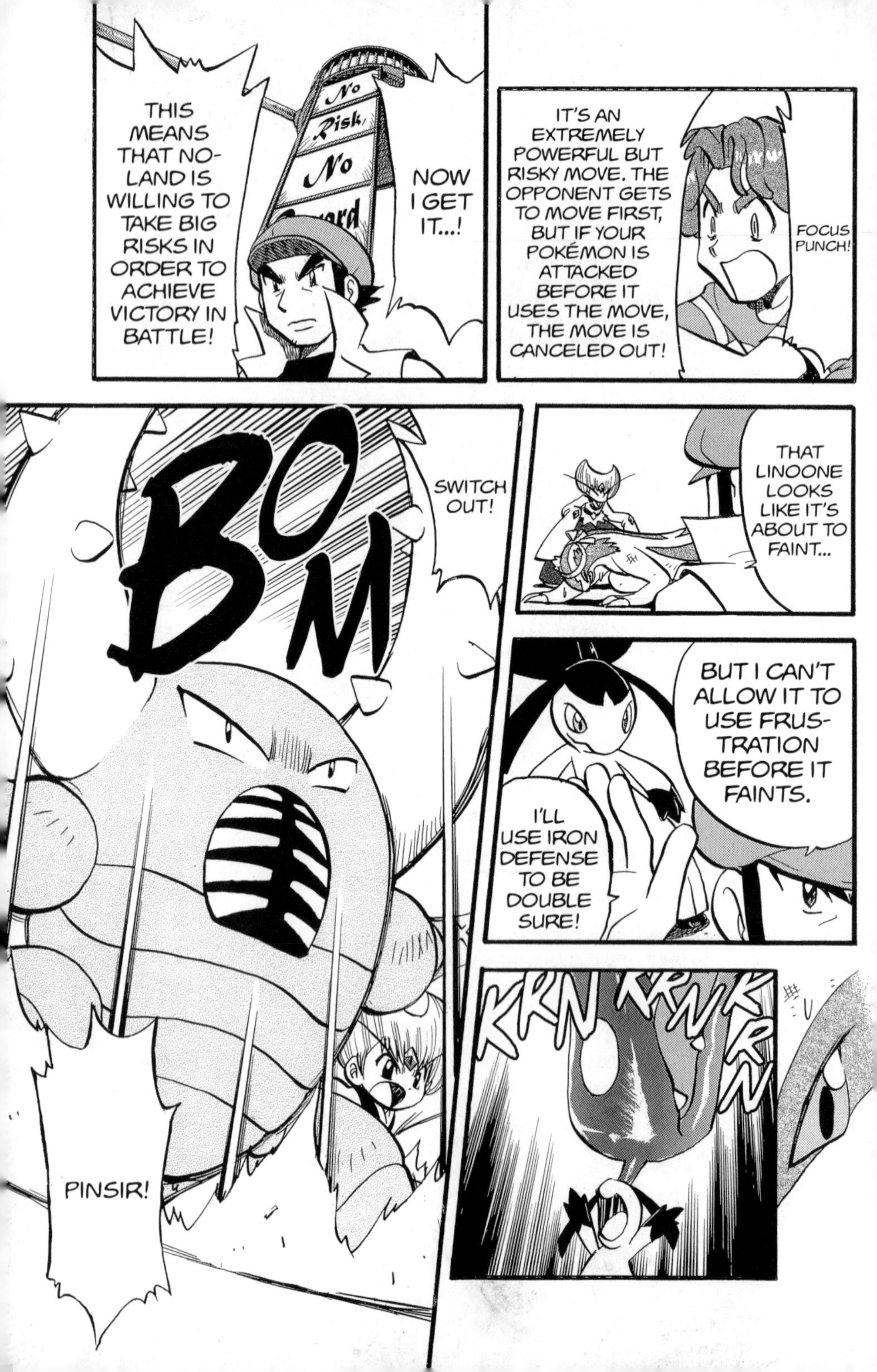
FOCUS PUNCH!
IT'S AN EXTREMELY POWERFUL BUT RISKY MOVE. THE OPPONENT GETS TO MOVE FIRST, BUT IF YOUR POKÉMON IS ATTACKED BEFORE IT USES THE MOVE, THE MOVE IS CANCELED OUT!
NOW I GET IT...!
No Risk, No Reward
THIS MEANS THAT NO-LAND IS WILLING TO TAKE BIG RISKS IN ORDER TO ACHIEVE VICTORY IN BATTLE!
THAT LINOONE LOOKS LIKE IT'S ABOUT TO FAINT...
BUT I CAN'T ALLOW IT TO USE FRUS-TRATION BEFORE IT FAINTS.
I'LL USE IRON DEFENSE TO BE DOUBLE SURE!
KRN KRN KRN
SWITCH OUT!
BOOM
PINSIR!

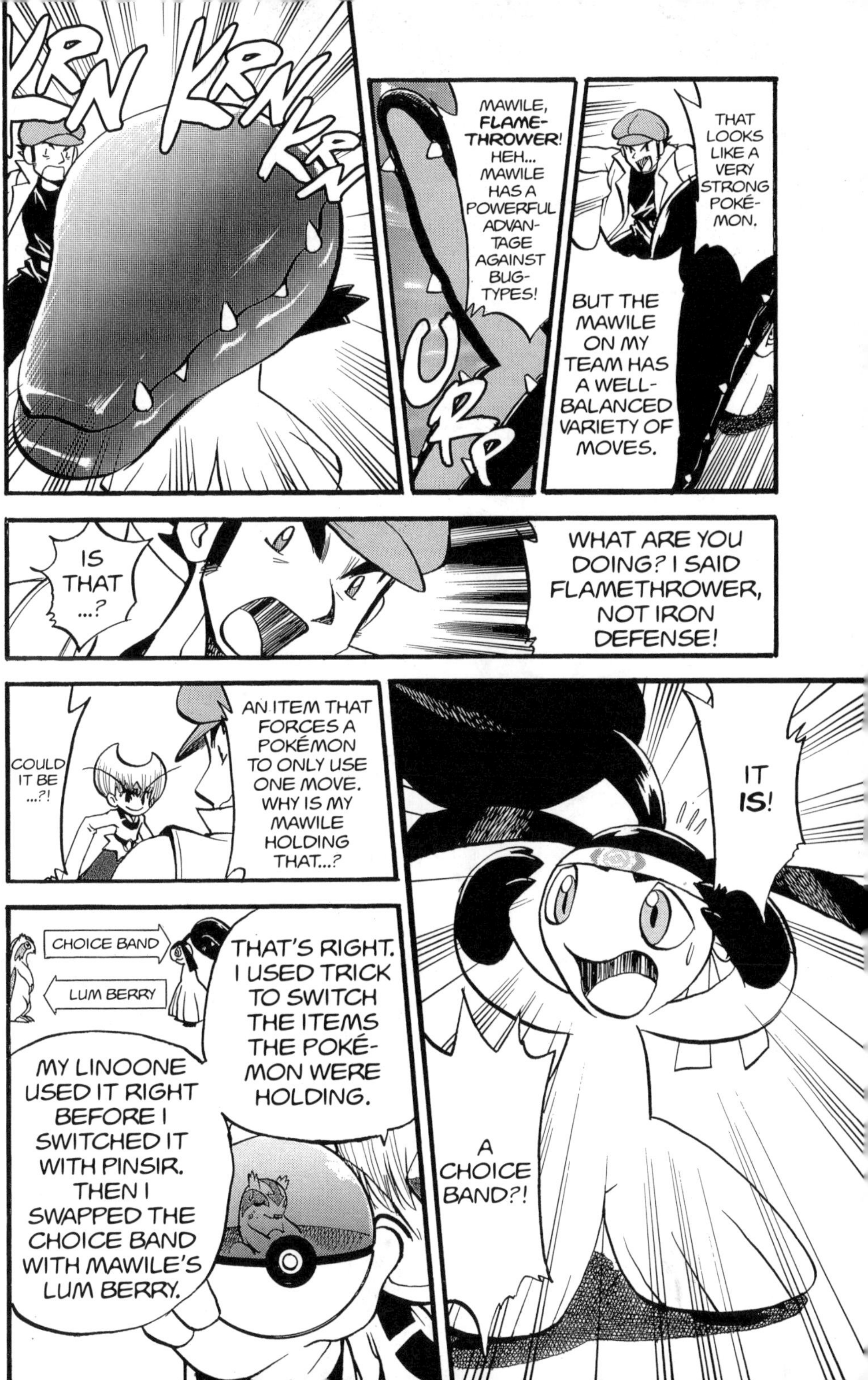
THAT LOOKS LIKE A VERY STRONG POKÉMON.
BUT THE MAWILE ON MY TEAM HAS A WELL-BALANCED VARIETY OF MOVES.
MAWILE, **FLAMETHROWER**! HEH... MAWILE HAS A POWERFUL ADVANTAGE AGAINST BUG-TYPES!
URP
KRN KRN KRN KRN
WHAT ARE YOU DOING? I SAID FLAMETHROWER, NOT IRON DEFENSE!
IS THAT ...?
IT **IS**!
A CHOICE BAND?!
AN ITEM THAT FORCES A POKÉMON TO ONLY USE ONE MOVE. WHY IS MY MAWILE HOLDING THAT...?
COULD IT BE ...?!
THAT'S RIGHT. I USED TRICK TO SWITCH THE ITEMS THE POKÉMON WERE HOLDING.
CHOICE BAND
LUM BERRY
MY LINOONE USED IT RIGHT BEFORE I SWITCHED IT WITH PINSIR. THEN I SWAPPED THE CHOICE BAND WITH MAWILE'S LUM BERRY.

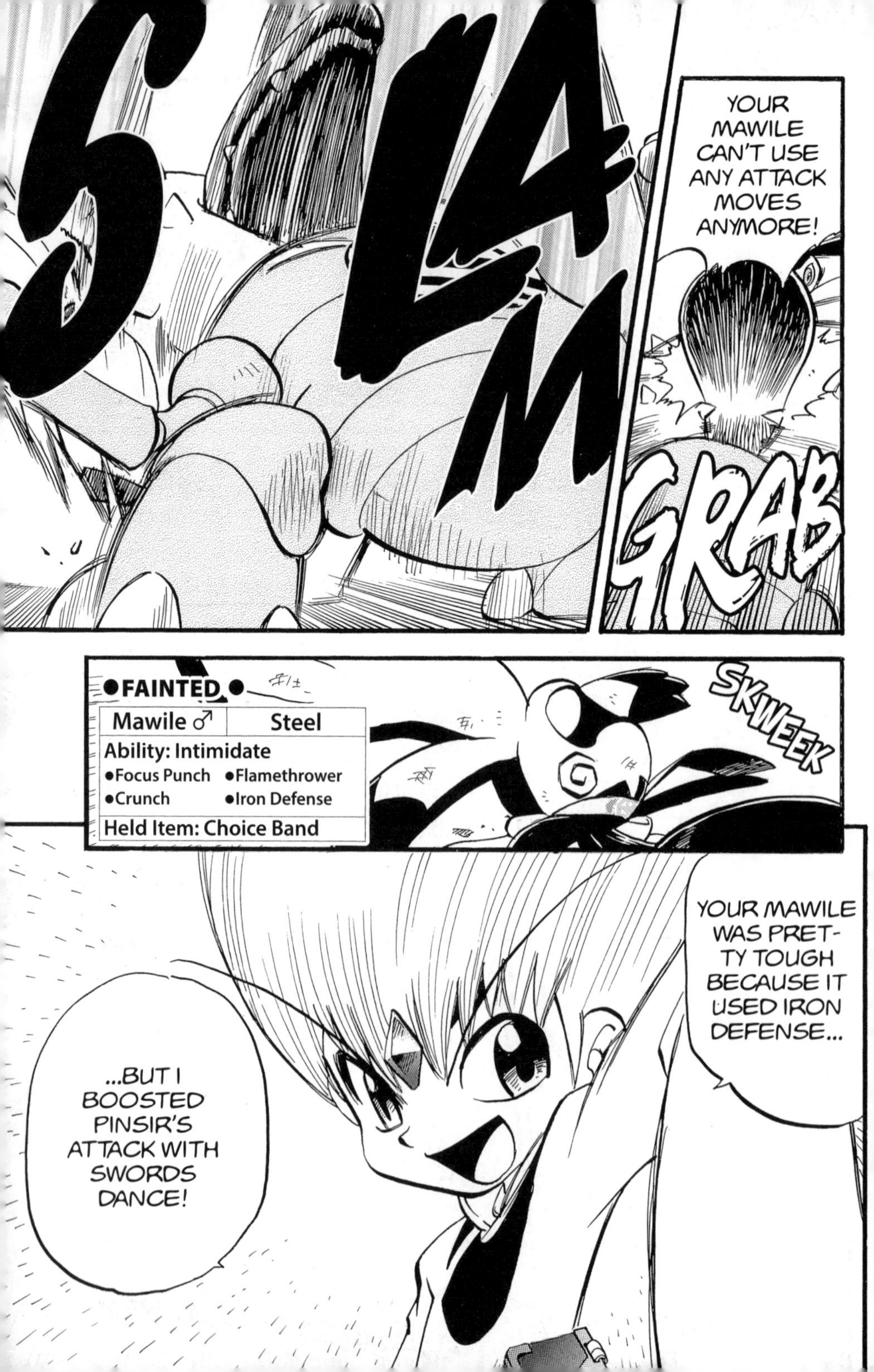
YOUR MAWILE CAN'T USE ANY ATTACK MOVES ANYMORE!
GRAB
SLAM
SKWEEK
FAINTED
Mawile ♂
Steel
Ability: Intimidate
●Focus Punch ●Flamethrower
●Crunch ●Iron Defense
Held Item: Choice Band
YOUR MAWILE WAS PRET-TY TOUGH BECAUSE IT USED IRON DEFENSE...
...BUT I BOOSTED PINSIR'S ATTACK WITH SWORDS DANCE!

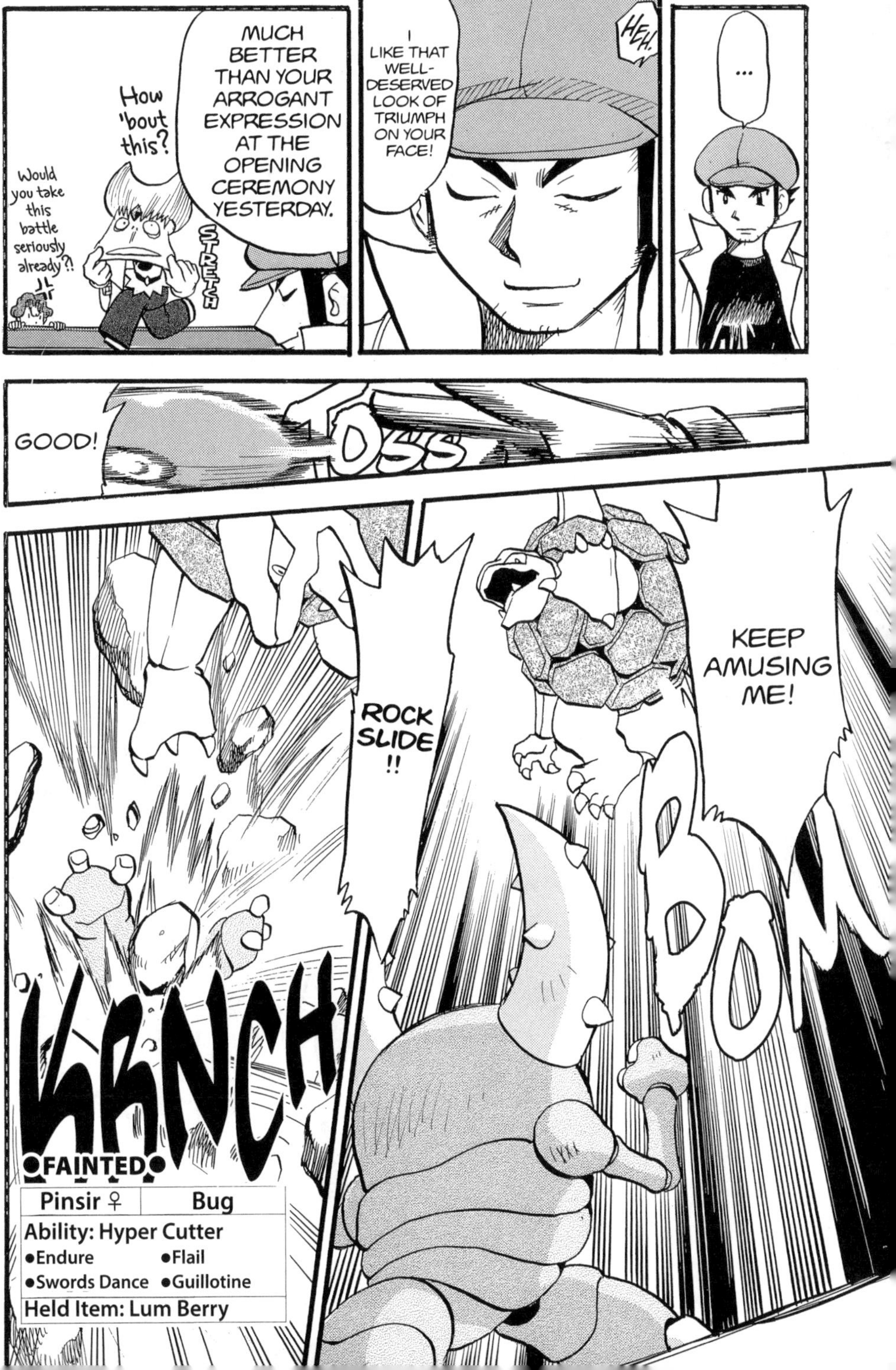
...
HEH!
I LIKE THAT WELL-DESERVED LOOK OF TRIUMPH ON YOUR FACE!
MUCH BETTER THAN YOUR ARROGANT EXPRESSION AT THE OPENING CEREMONY YESTERDAY.
How 'bout this?
STRETCH
Would you take this battle seriously already?!
TOSS
GOOD!
KEEP AMUSING ME!
BOM
ROCK SLIDE!!
KRNCH
FAINTED
Pinsir ♀ Bug
Ability: Hyper Cutter
●Endure ●Flail
●Swords Dance ●Guillotine
Held Item: Lum Berry

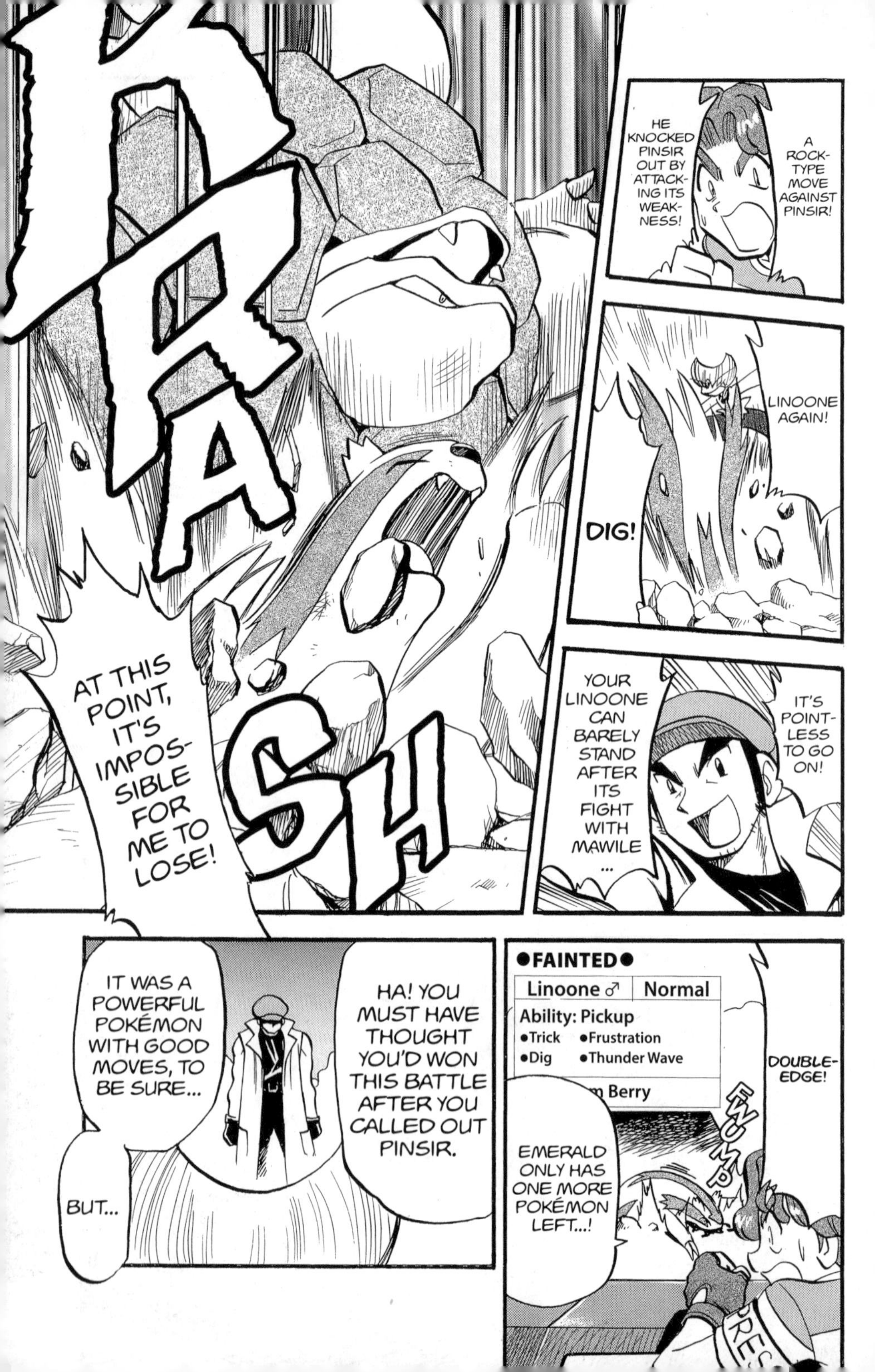
A ROCK-TYPE MOVE AGAINST PINSIR!
HE KNOCKED PINSIR OUT BY ATTACKING ITS WEAKNESS!
LINOONE AGAIN!
DIG!
IT'S POINTLESS TO GO ON!
YOUR LINOONE CAN BARELY STAND AFTER ITS FIGHT WITH MAWILE ...
KRASH
AT THIS POINT, IT'S IMPOSSIBLE FOR ME TO LOSE!
●FAINTED●
Linoone ♂ Normal
Ability: Pickup
●Trick ●Frustration
●Dig ●Thunder Wave
m Berry
DOUBLE-EDGE!
FWUMP
EMERALD ONLY HAS ONE MORE POKÉMON LEFT...!
HA! YOU MUST HAVE THOUGHT YOU'D WON THIS BATTLE AFTER YOU CALLED OUT PINSIR.
IT WAS A POWERFUL POKÉMON WITH GOOD MOVES, TO BE SURE...
BUT...

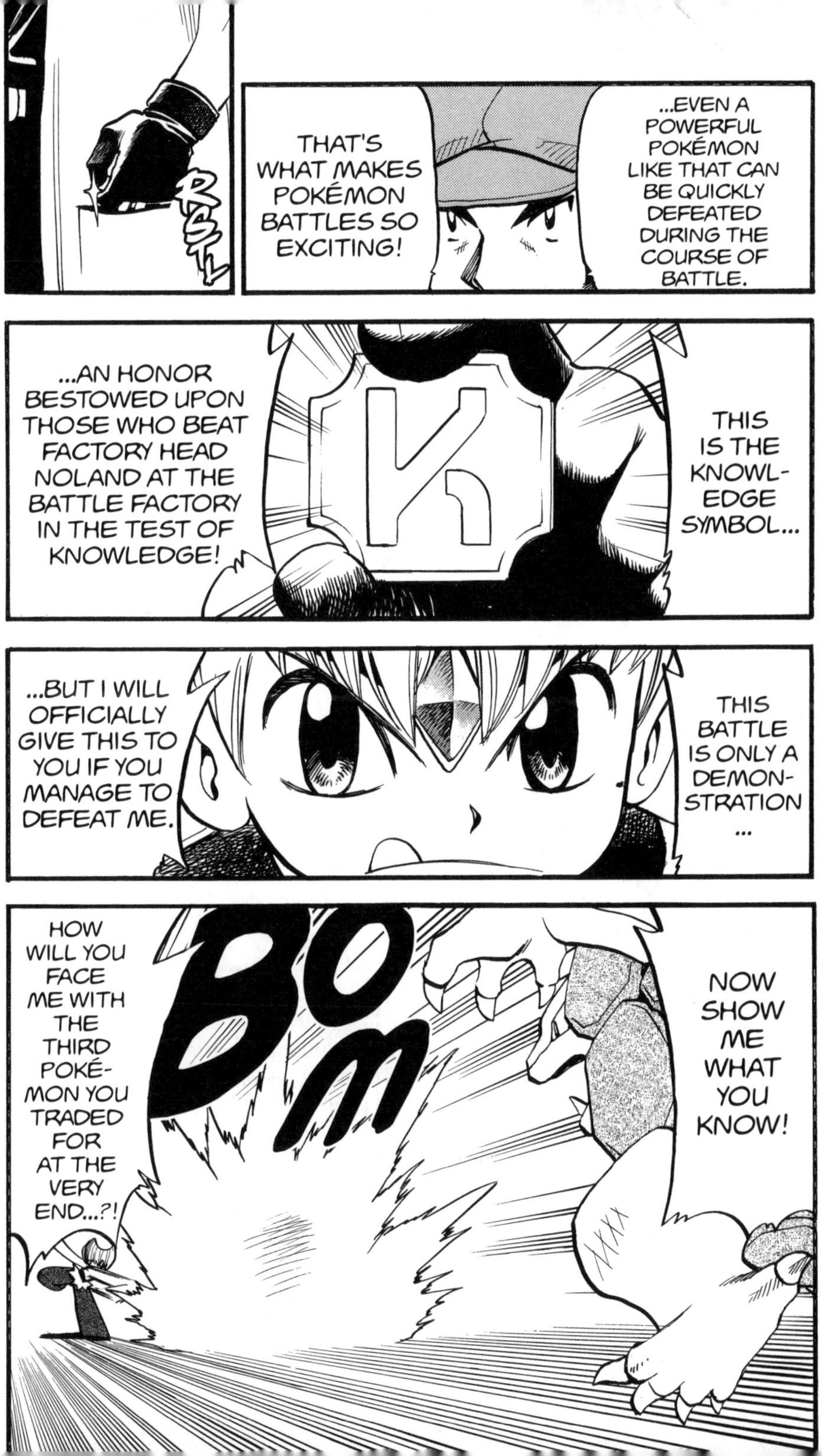
...EVEN A POWERFUL POKÉMON LIKE THAT CAN BE QUICKLY DEFEATED DURING THE COURSE OF BATTLE.
THAT'S WHAT MAKES POKÉMON BATTLES SO EXCITING!
RSTL
THIS IS THE KNOWLEDGE SYMBOL...
...AN HONOR BESTOWED UPON THOSE WHO BEAT FACTORY HEAD NOLAND AT THE BATTLE FACTORY IN THE TEST OF KNOWLEDGE!
THIS BATTLE IS ONLY A DEMONSTRATION...
...BUT I WILL OFFICIALLY GIVE THIS TO YOU IF YOU MANAGE TO DEFEAT ME.
NOW SHOW ME WHAT YOU KNOW!
BOM
HOW WILL YOU FACE ME WITH THE THIRD POKÉMON YOU TRADED FOR AT THE VERY END...?!

DEAR MEMBERS OF THE PRESS...

Thank you for visiting my Battle Frontier today. Permit me to continue explaining the rules of this facility...

OWNER: SCOTT

■ IN CASE OF A DOUBLE KNOCKOUT ■

The result is a tie, and a rematch will be arranged if the battle is between two regular Trainers. If the battle was against a Frontier Brain, the Brain is the winner.

■ BATTLE POINTS ■

The accumulation of Battle Points corresponds with your results at each facility. Collected Battle Points may be exchanged for items at the Battle Point Exchange Service Corner.

FACILITY RULES
BATTLE FACTORY

Battle-type	Number of Pokémon	Type of Symbol	Wins needed to attain the Symbol
Single	3 Pokémon	Knowledge	7 Battles × 6 Sets = 42 Consecutive Wins
Double	3 Pokémon	Knowledge	7 Battles × 6 Sets = 42 Consecutive Wins

Battle Factory battles are fought using rental Pokémon. The challenger chooses three out of six randomly selected Pokémon. If the challenger wins, they have the option of exchanging one of their Pokémon for one of their opponent's Pokémon. The newly acquired Pokémon takes the same position in the group as the one that was traded away.

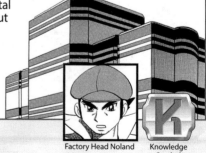

Factory Head Noland   Knowledge Symbol

◆ヨ07◆

Gotcha Where
I Wantcha, Glalie

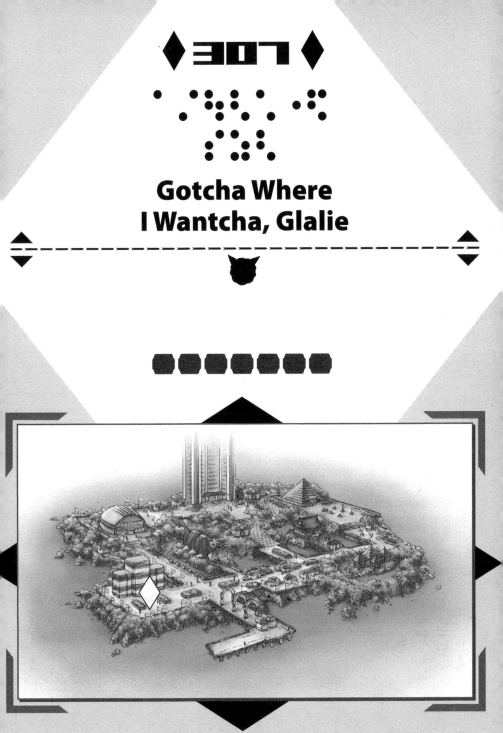

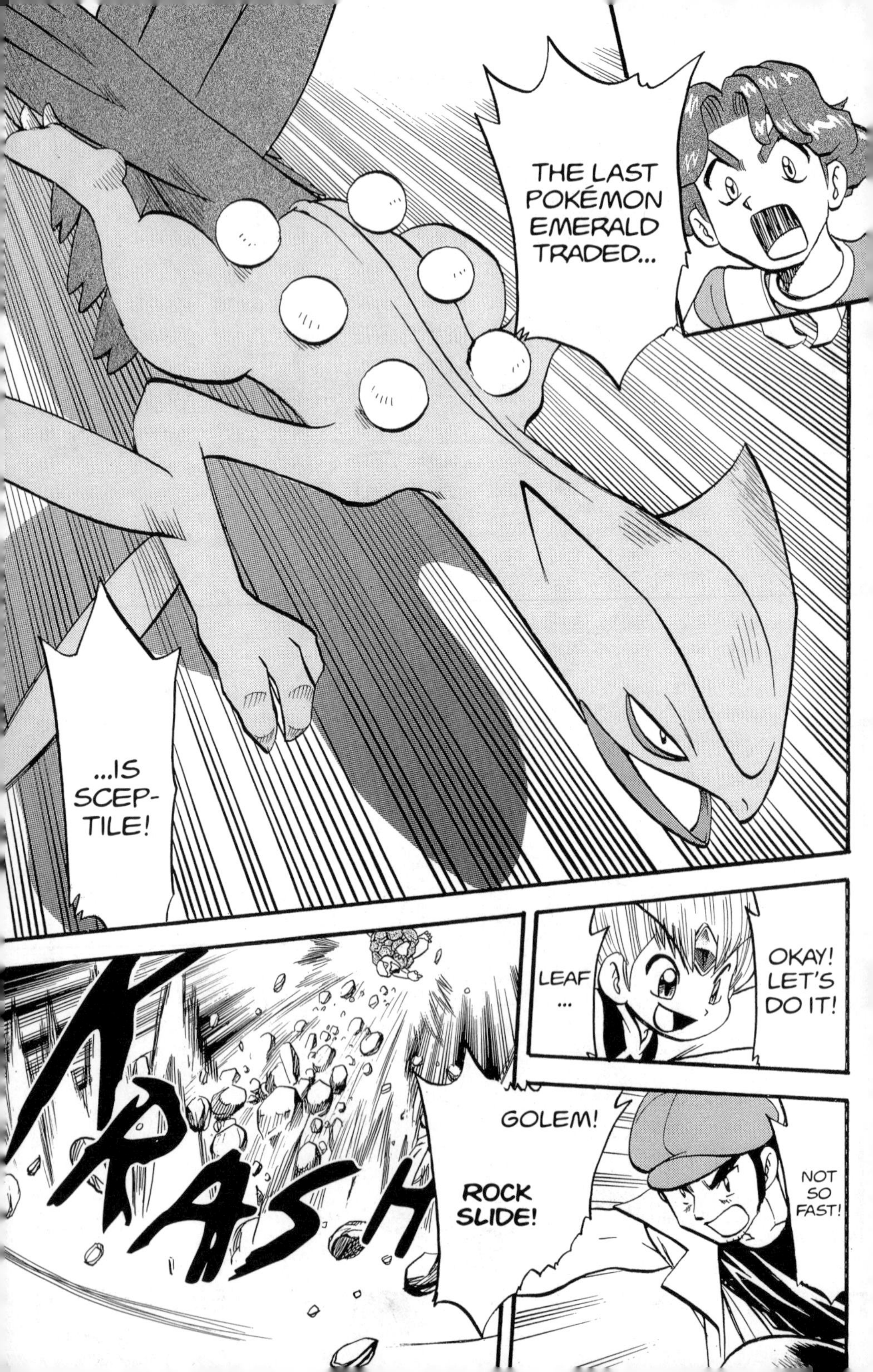
THE LAST POKÉMON EMERALD TRADED...
...IS SCEP-TILE!
OKAY! LET'S DO IT!
LEAF ...
NOT SO FAST!
GOLEM!
ROCK SLIDE!
KRASH

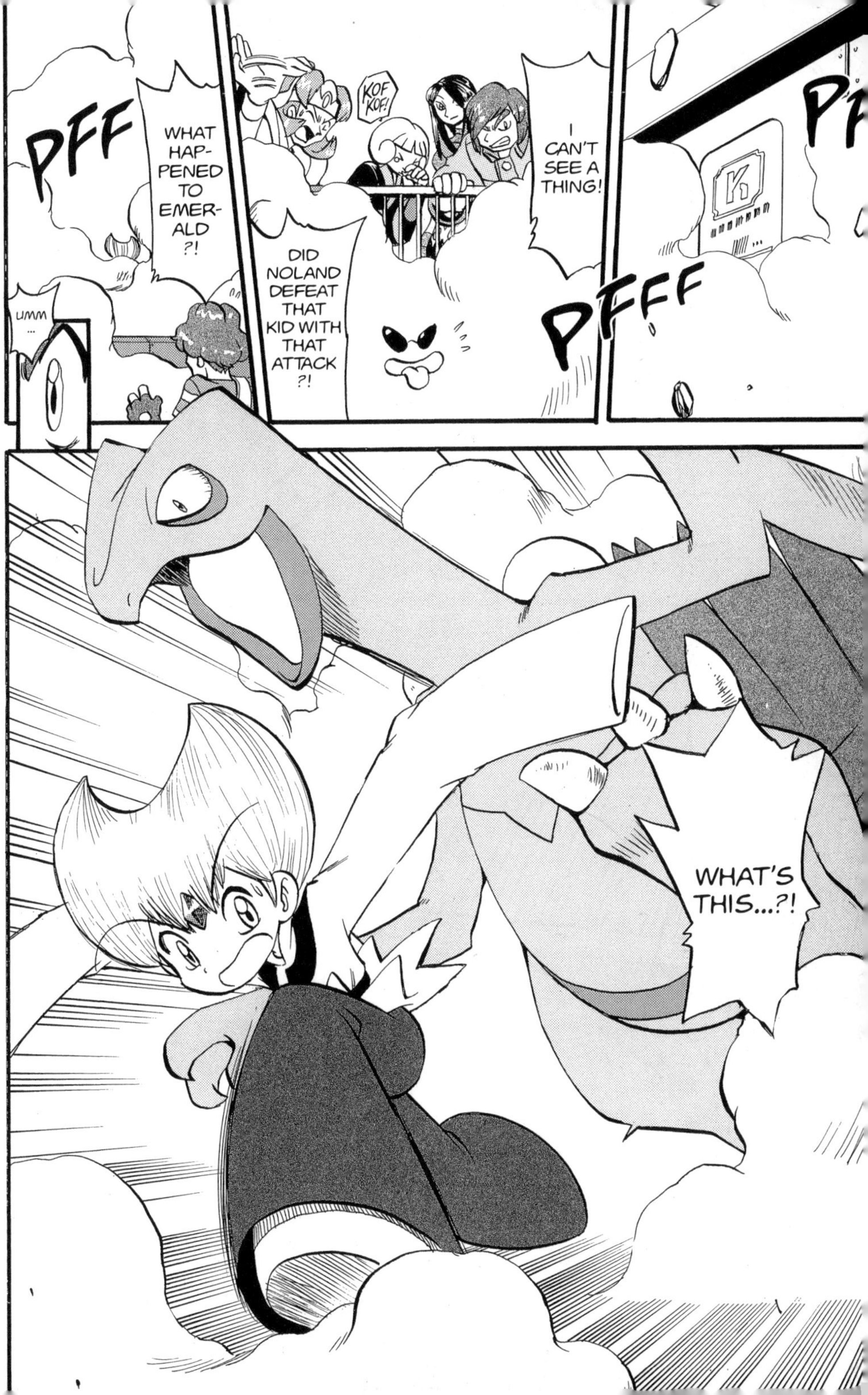
PFFF
I CAN'T SEE A THING!
KOF KOF!
DID NOLAND DEFEAT THAT KID WITH THAT ATTACK ?!
WHAT HAP-PENED TO EMER-ALD ?!
PFF
UMM ...
WHAT'S THIS...?!

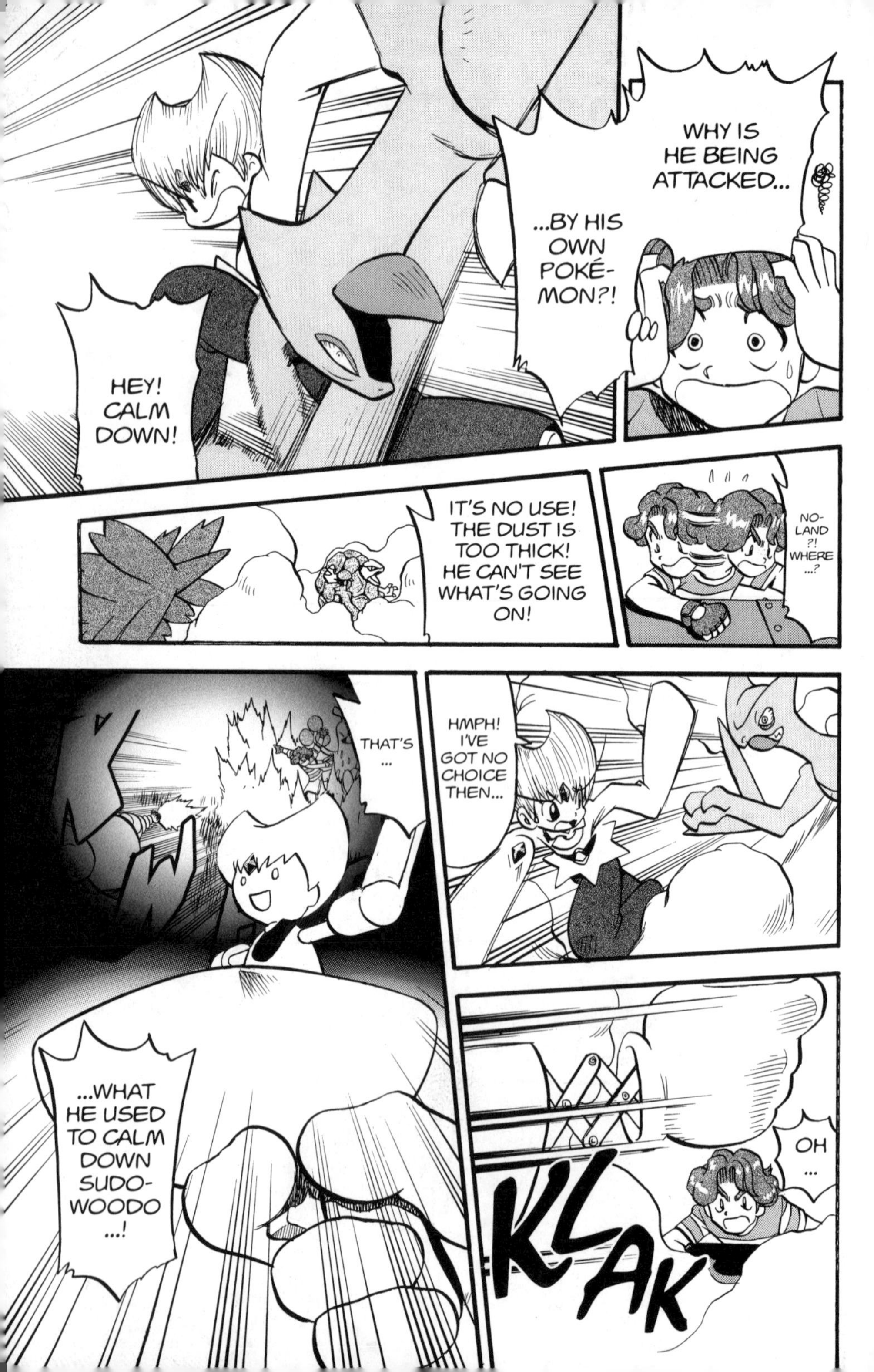
WHY IS HE BEING ATTACKED...
...BY HIS OWN POKÉ-MON?!
HEY! CALM DOWN!
NO-LAND ?! WHERE ...?
IT'S NO USE! THE DUST IS TOO THICK! HE CAN'T SEE WHAT'S GOING ON!
HMPH! I'VE GOT NO CHOICE THEN...
OH ...
KLAK
THAT'S ...
...WHAT HE USED TO CALM DOWN SUDO-WOODO ...!

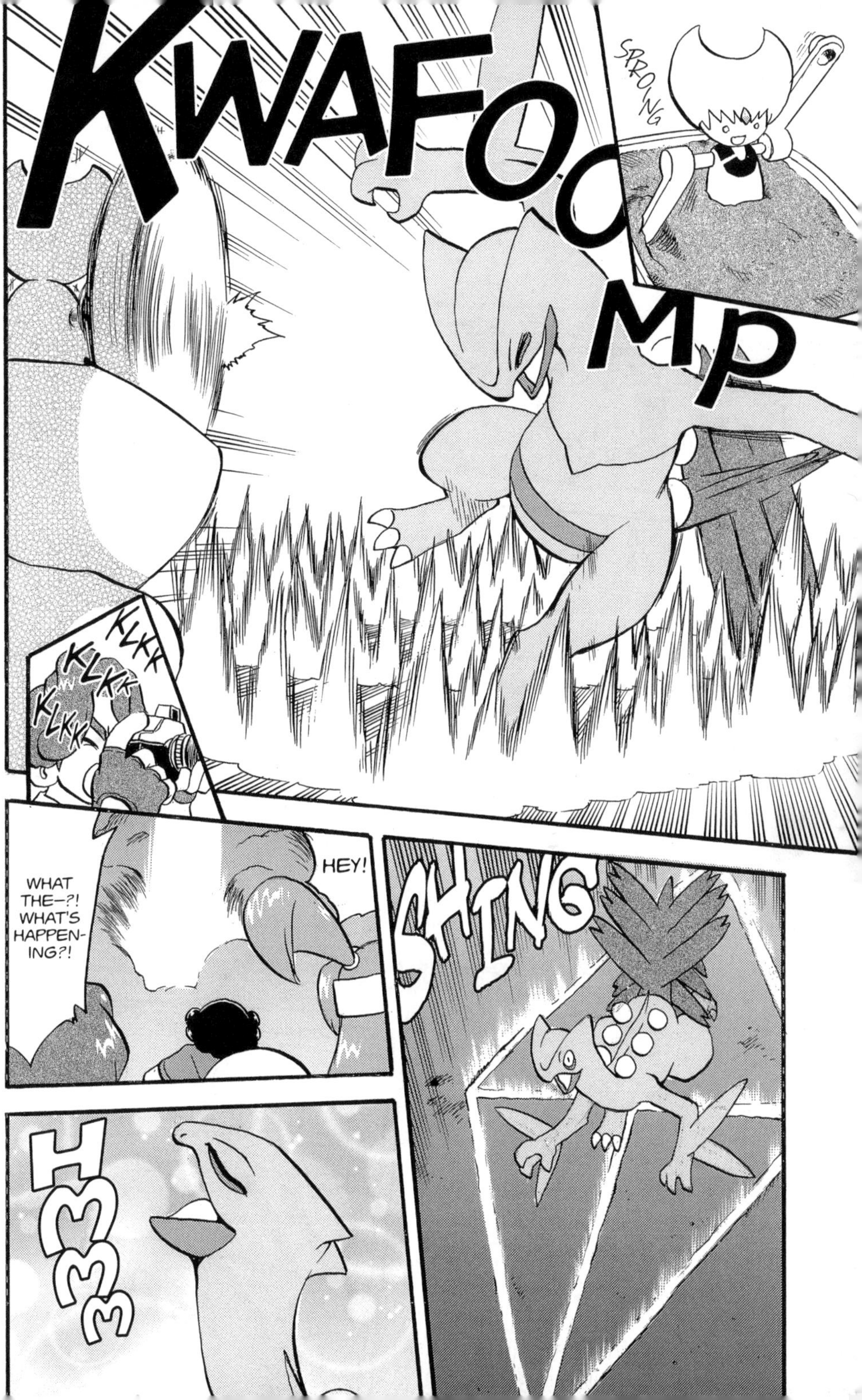
SPROING
KWAFOOMP
KLKK
KLKK
KLKK
SHING
HEY!
WHAT THE–?! WHAT'S HAPPENING?!
HMMM

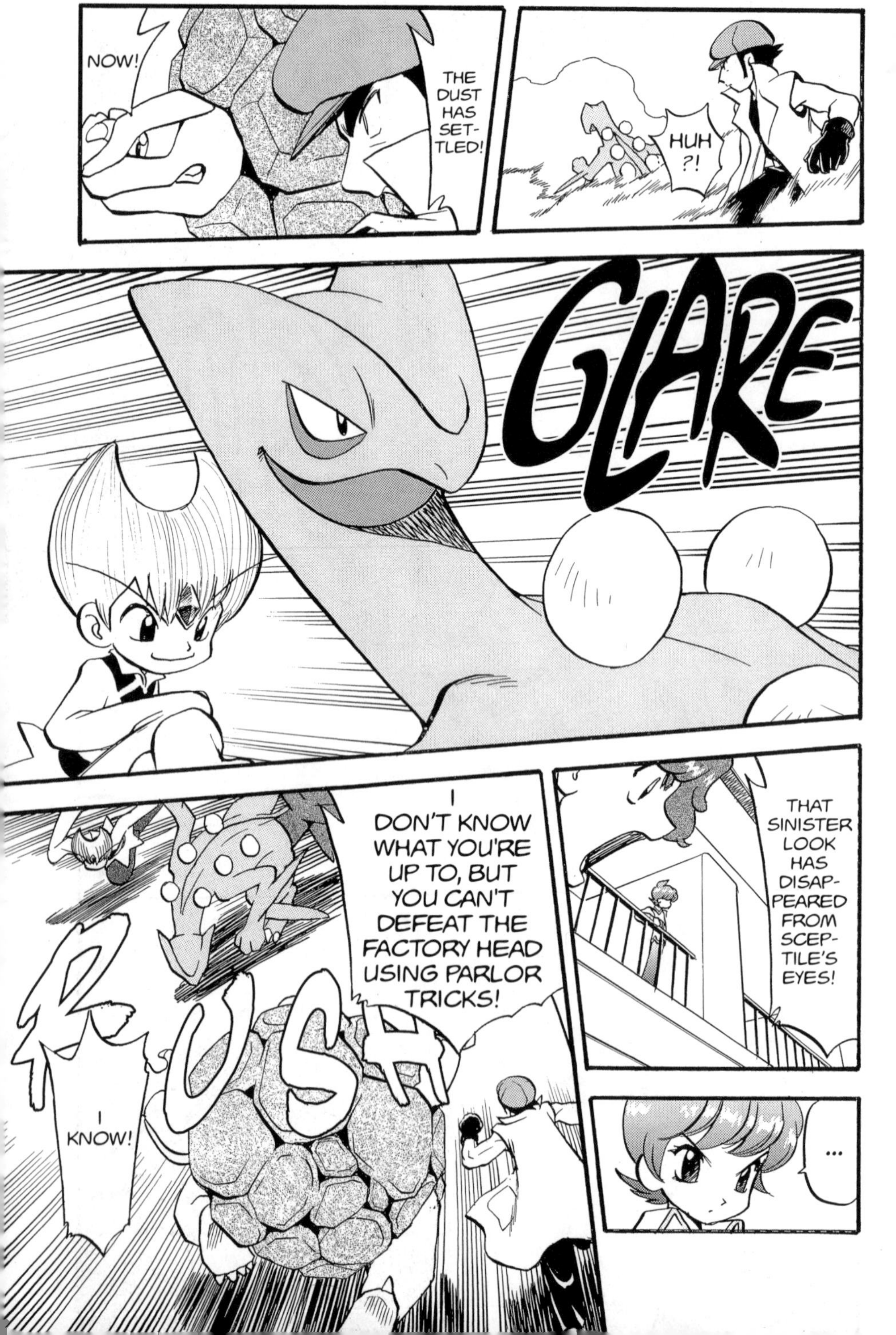
HUH ?!
THE DUST HAS SETTLED!
NOW!
GLARE
THAT SINISTER LOOK HAS DISAPPEARED FROM SCEPTILE'S EYES!
...
I DON'T KNOW WHAT YOU'RE UP TO, BUT YOU CAN'T DEFEAT THE FACTORY HEAD USING PARLOR TRICKS!
RUSH
I KNOW!

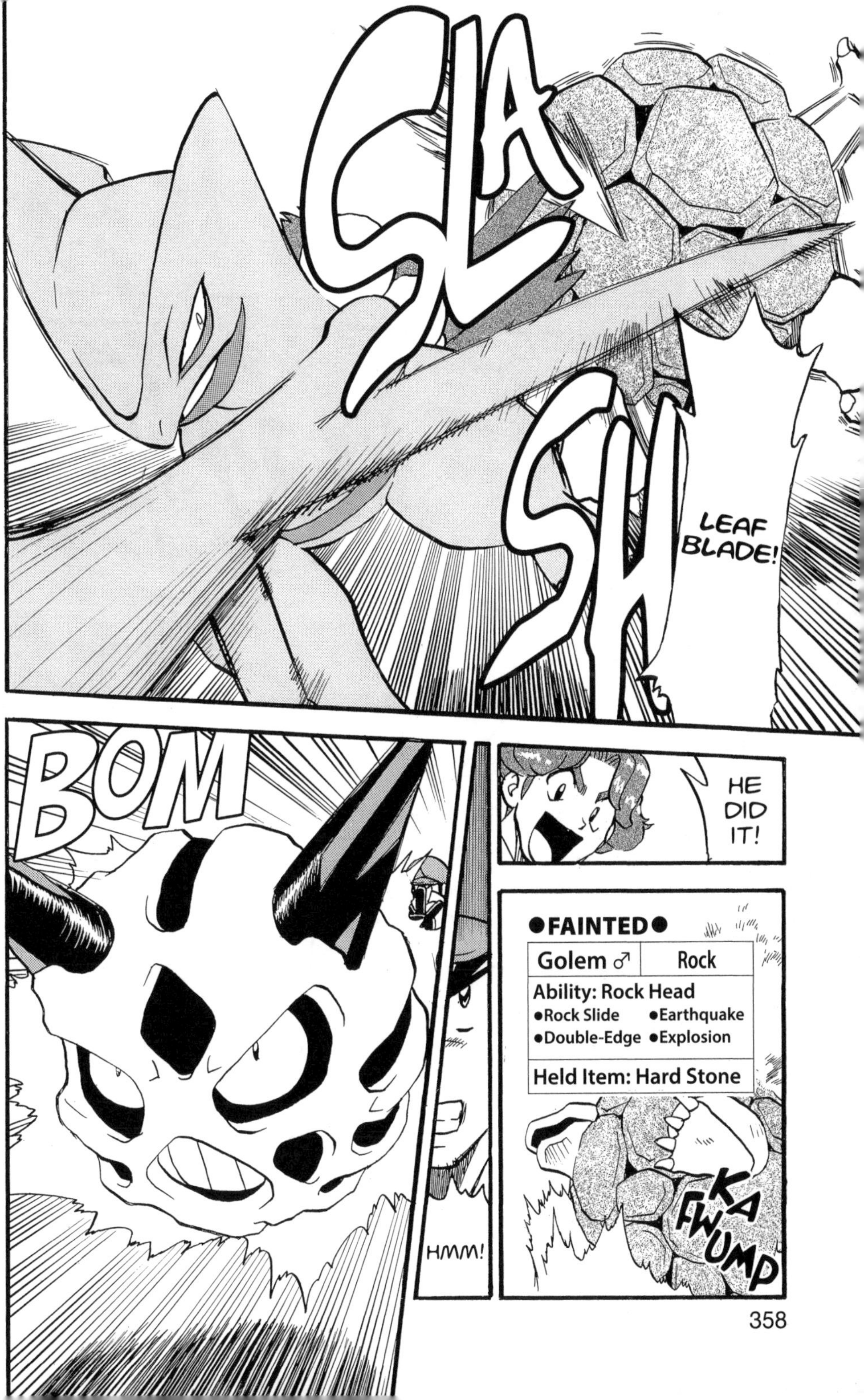
SLASH
LEAF BLADE!
HE DID IT!
●FAINTED●
Golem ♂ | Rock
Ability: Rock Head
●Rock Slide ●Earthquake
●Double-Edge ●Explosion
Held Item: Hard Stone
KA FWUMP
HMM!
BOM

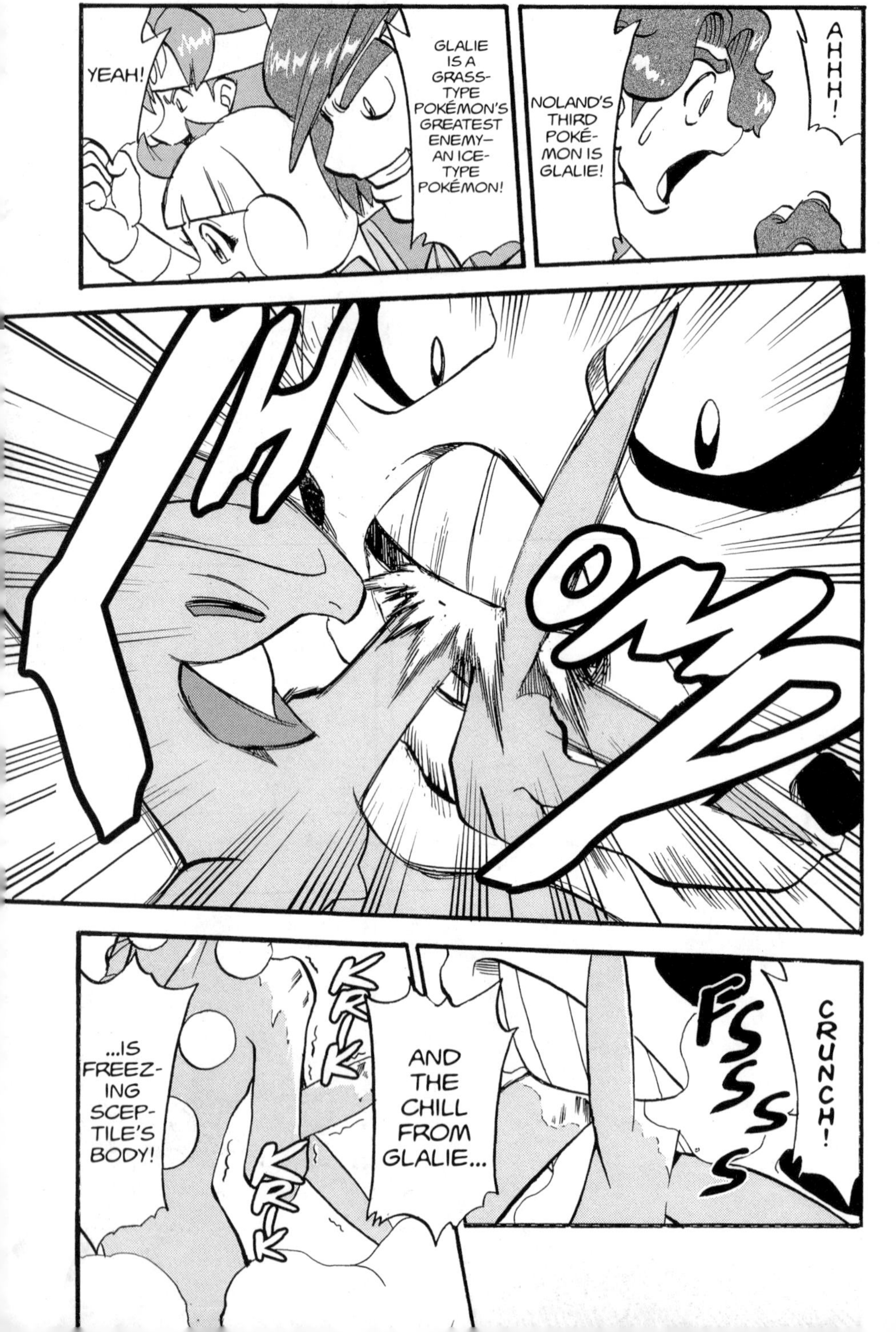
AHHH!
NOLAND'S THIRD POKÉMON IS GLALIE!
GLALIE IS A GRASS-TYPE POKÉMON'S GREATEST ENEMY—AN ICE-TYPE POKÉMON!
YEAH!
WHOMP
CRUNCH!
FSSSSS
AND THE CHILL FROM GLALIE...
...IS FREEZING SCEPTILE'S BODY!

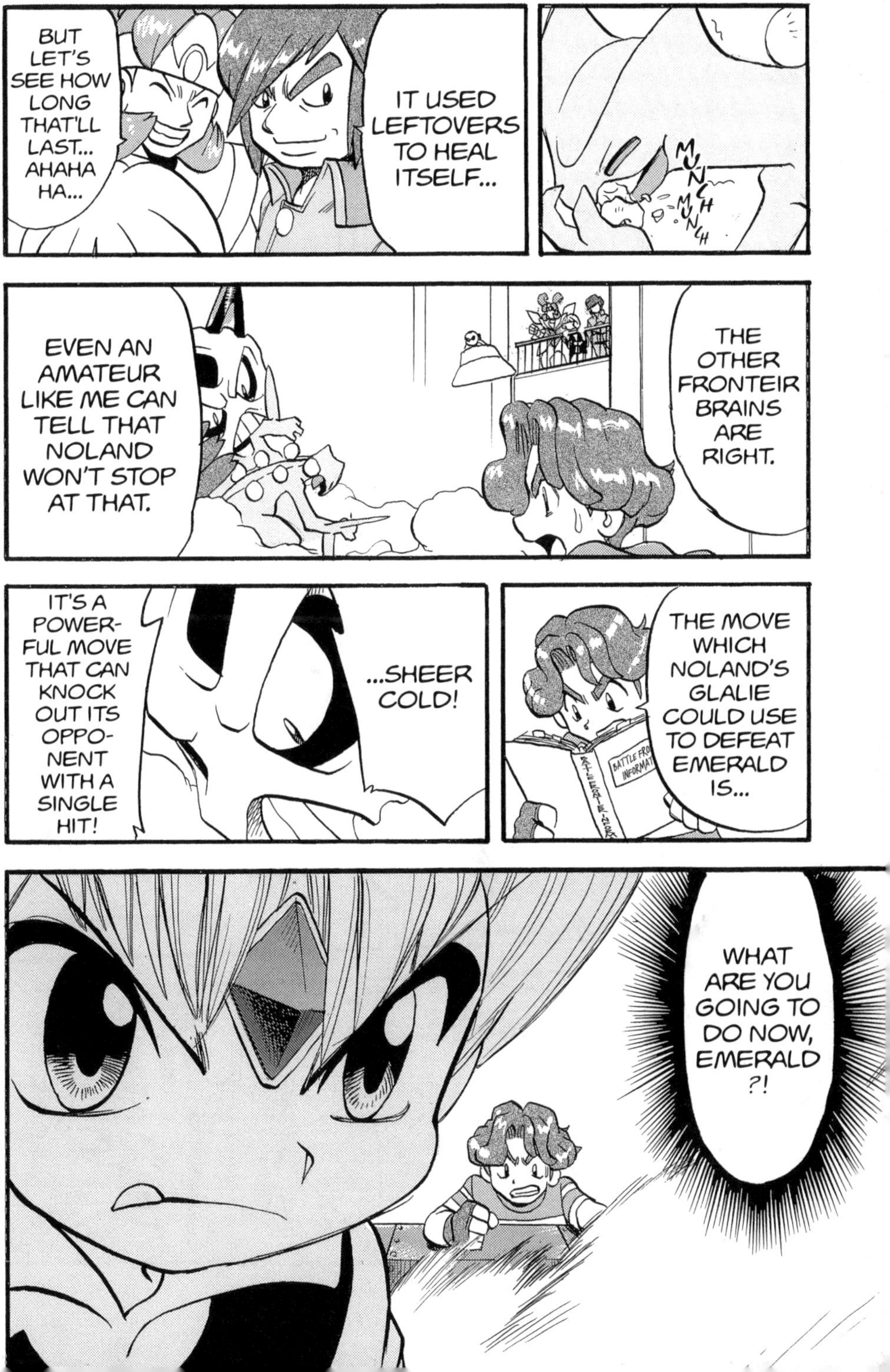
MUNCH
MUNCH
IT USED LEFTOVERS TO HEAL ITSELF...
BUT LET'S SEE HOW LONG THAT'LL LAST... AHAHA HA...
THE OTHER FRONTEIR BRAINS ARE RIGHT.
EVEN AN AMATEUR LIKE ME CAN TELL THAT NOLAND WON'T STOP AT THAT.
THE MOVE WHICH NOLAND'S GLALIE COULD USE TO DEFEAT EMERALD IS...
...SHEER COLD!
IT'S A POWER-FUL MOVE THAT CAN KNOCK OUT ITS OPPO-NENT WITH A SINGLE HIT!
WHAT ARE YOU GOING TO DO NOW, EMERALD?!

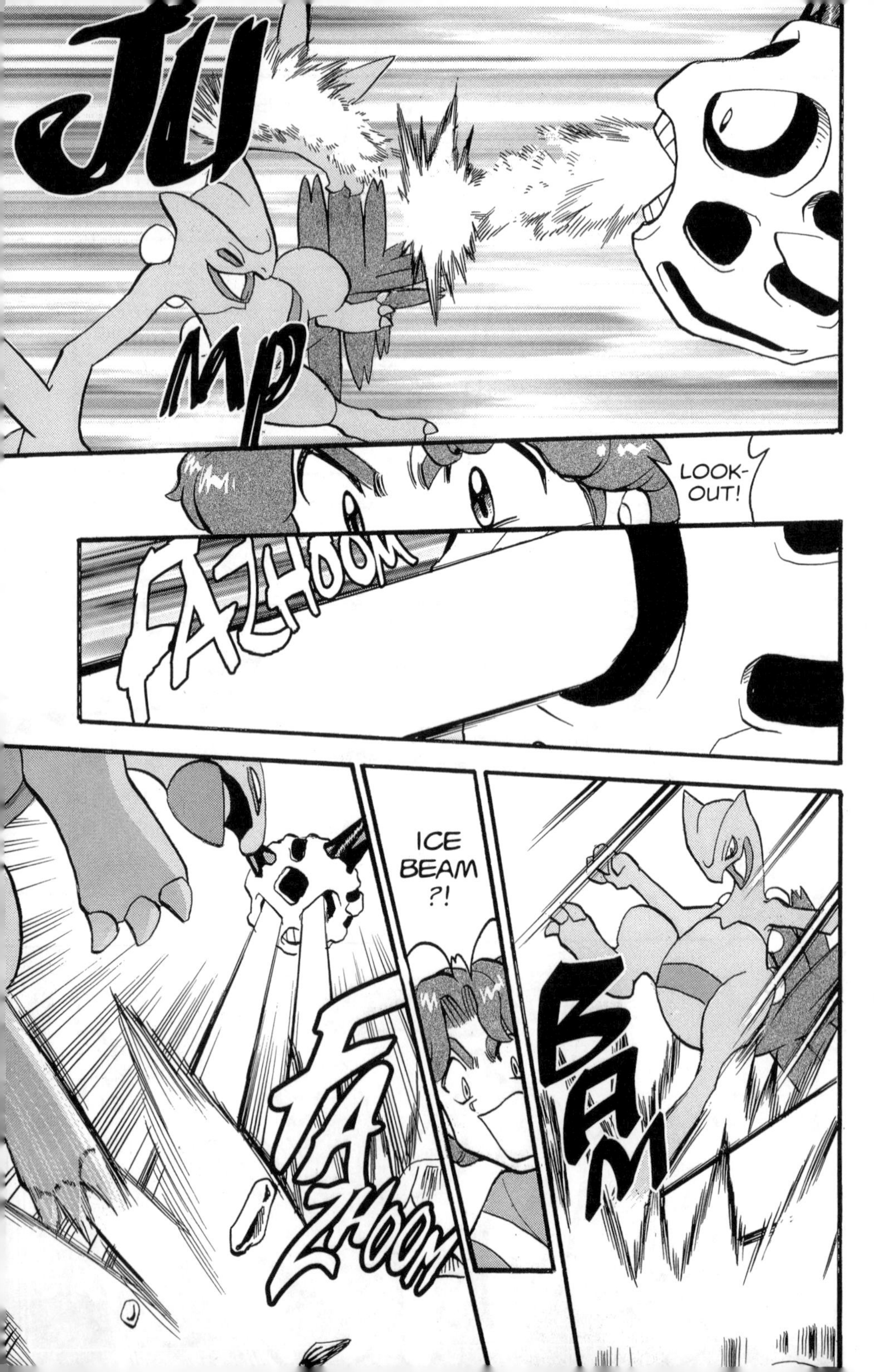
JUMP
LOOK-OUT!
FAZHOOM
BAM
ICE BEAM?!
FAZHOOM

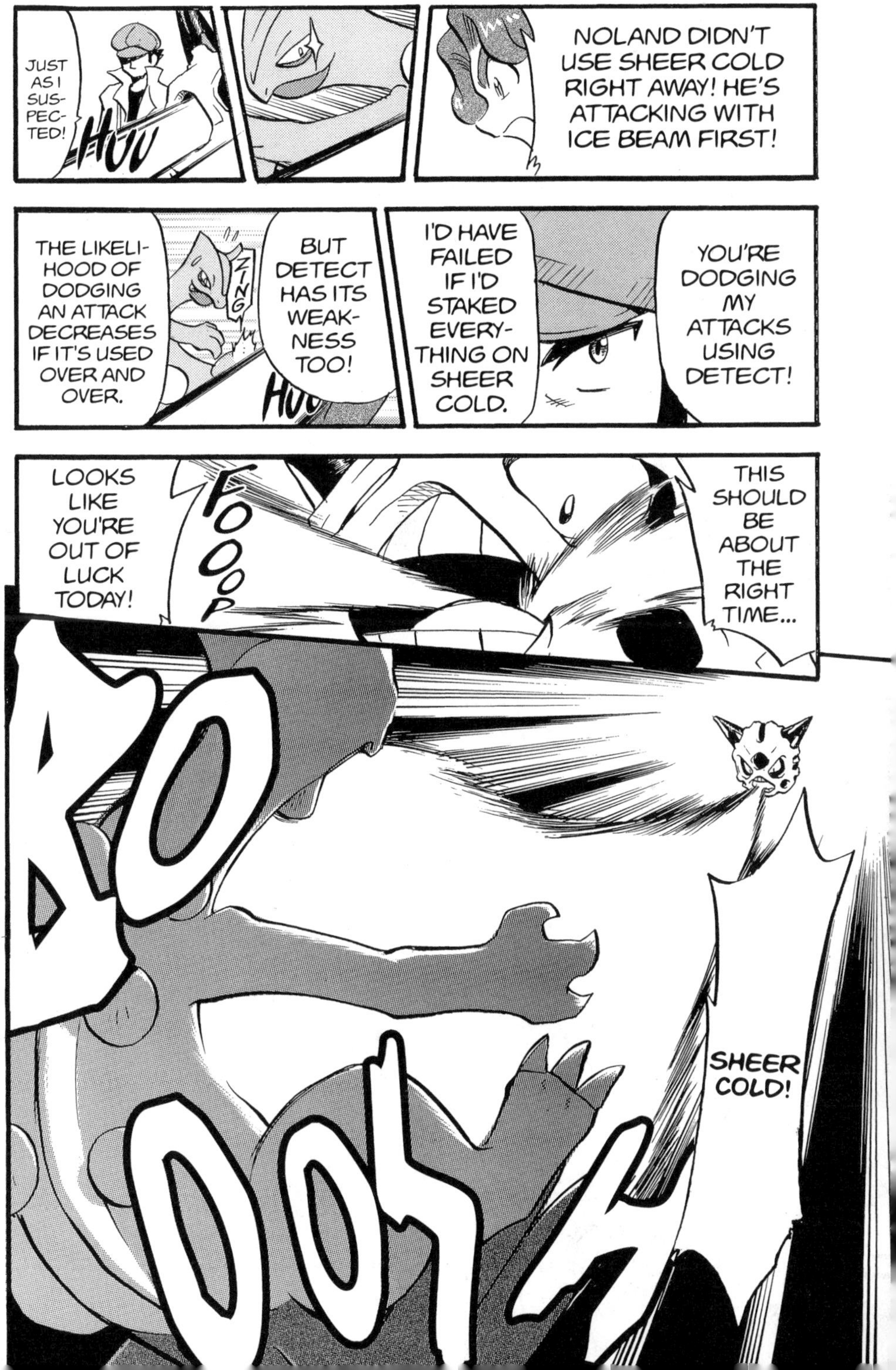
NOLAND DIDN'T USE SHEER COLD RIGHT AWAY! HE'S ATTACKING WITH ICE BEAM FIRST!
JUST AS I SUS-PEC-TED!
YOU'RE DODGING MY ATTACKS USING DETECT!
I'D HAVE FAILED IF I'D STAKED EVERY-THING ON SHEER COLD.
BUT DETECT HAS ITS WEAK-NESS TOO!
THE LIKELI-HOOD OF DODGING AN ATTACK DECREASES IF IT'S USED OVER AND OVER.
ZING
THIS SHOULD BE ABOUT THE RIGHT TIME...
LOOKS LIKE YOU'RE OUT OF LUCK TODAY!
FOOOP
SHEER COLD!
BOOOSH

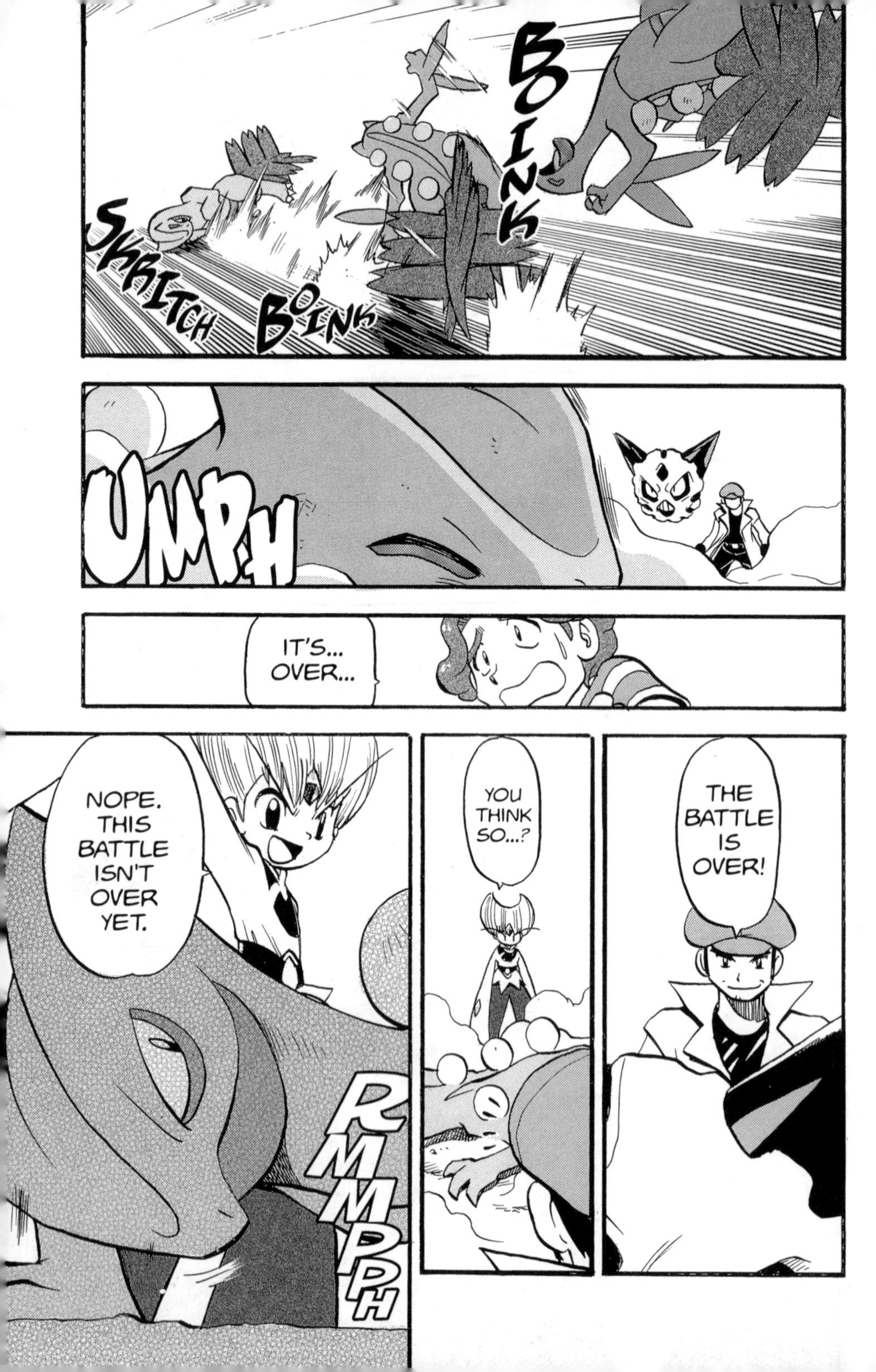
BOINK
BOINK
SKRITCH
UMPH
IT'S... OVER...
THE BATTLE IS OVER!
YOU THINK SO...?
NOPE. THIS BATTLE ISN'T OVER YET.
RMMMPH

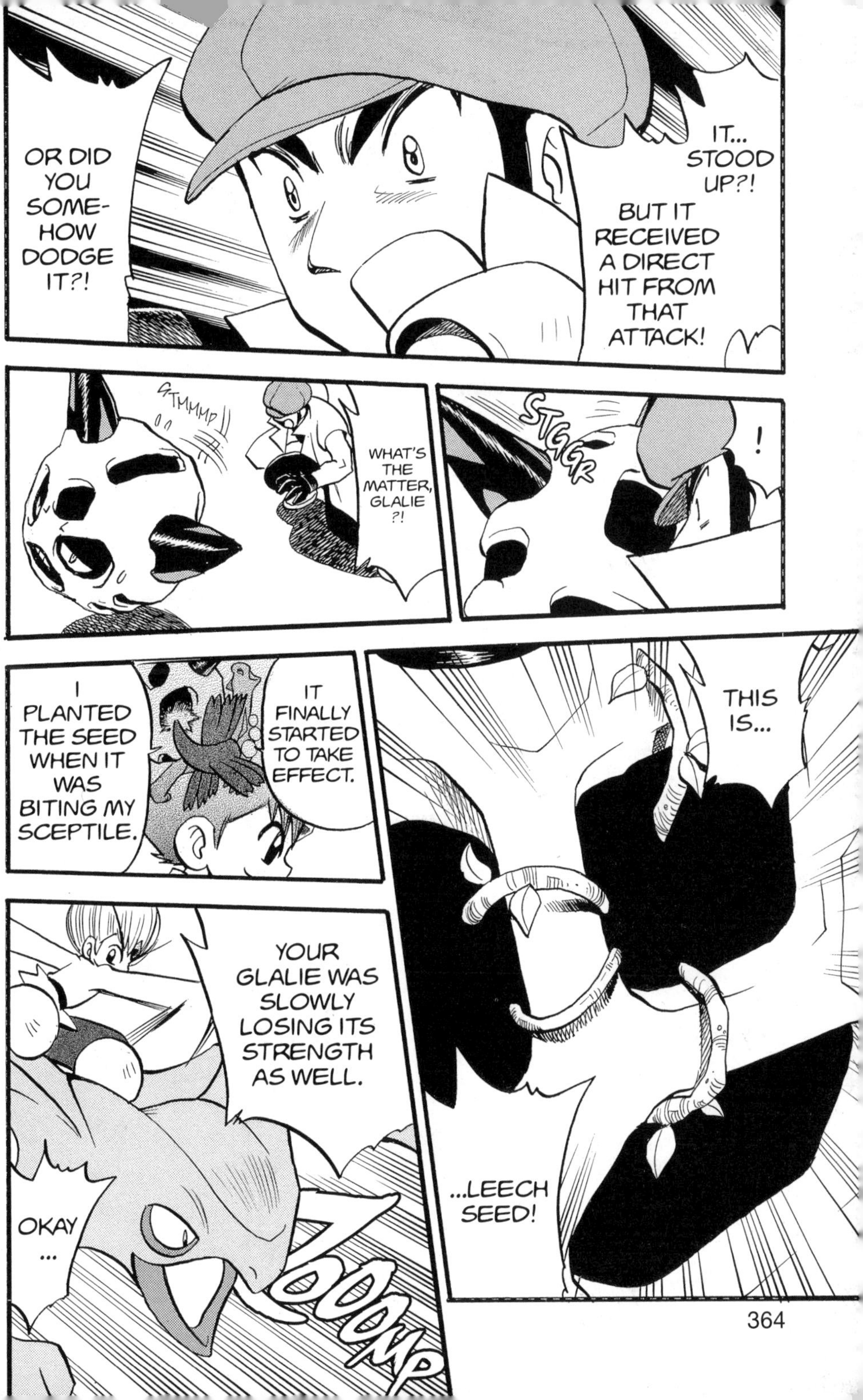
IT... STOOD UP?!
BUT IT RECEIVED A DIRECT HIT FROM THAT ATTACK!
OR DID YOU SOME-HOW DODGE IT?!
STGGR
!
STMMMP
WHAT'S THE MATTER, GLALIE?!
THIS IS...
...LEECH SEED!
IT FINALLY STARTED TO TAKE EFFECT.
I PLANTED THE SEED WHEN IT WAS BITING MY SCEPTILE.
YOUR GLALIE WAS SLOWLY LOSING ITS STRENGTH AS WELL.
OKAY ...
ZOOOMP

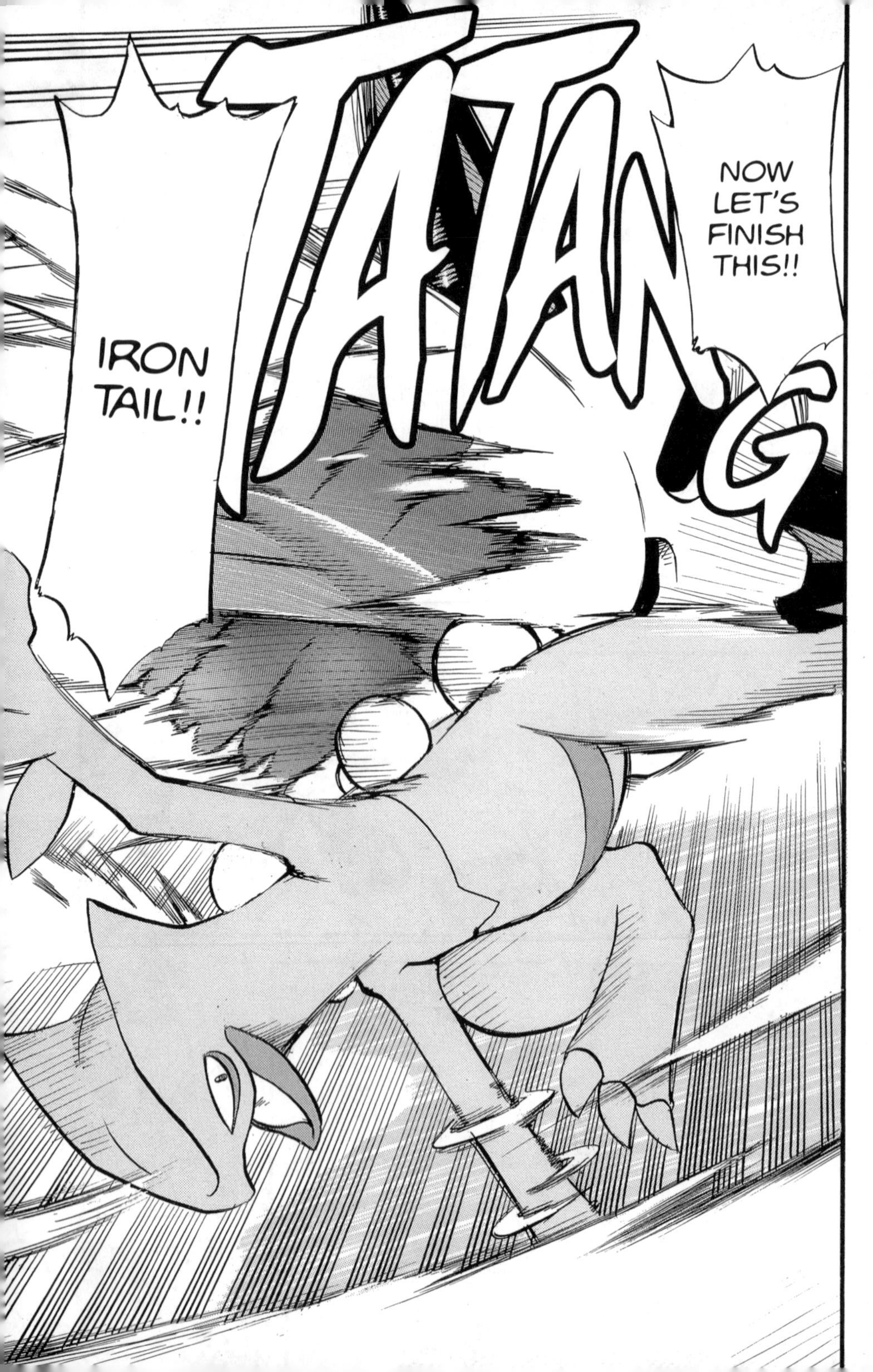
NOW LET'S FINISH THIS!!
TATANG
IRON TAIL!!

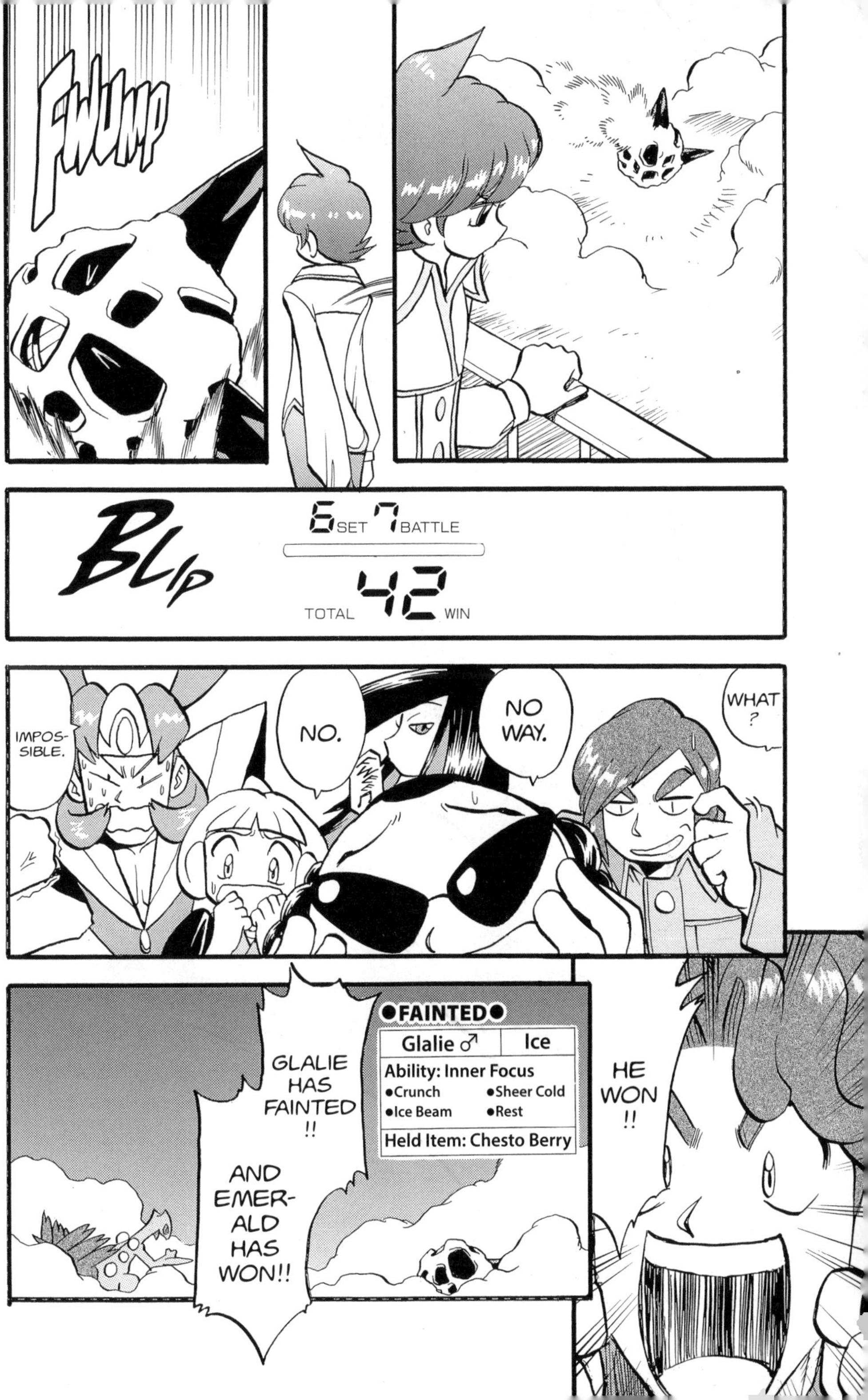
FWUMP
BLIP
6 SET 7 BATTLE
TOTAL 42 WIN
WHAT?
NO WAY.
NO.
IMPOSSIBLE.
HE WON!!
GLALIE HAS FAINTED!!
AND EMERALD HAS WON!!
●FAINTED●
Glalie ♂ | Ice
Ability: Inner Focus
●Crunch ●Sheer Cold
●Ice Beam ●Rest
Held Item: Chesto Berry

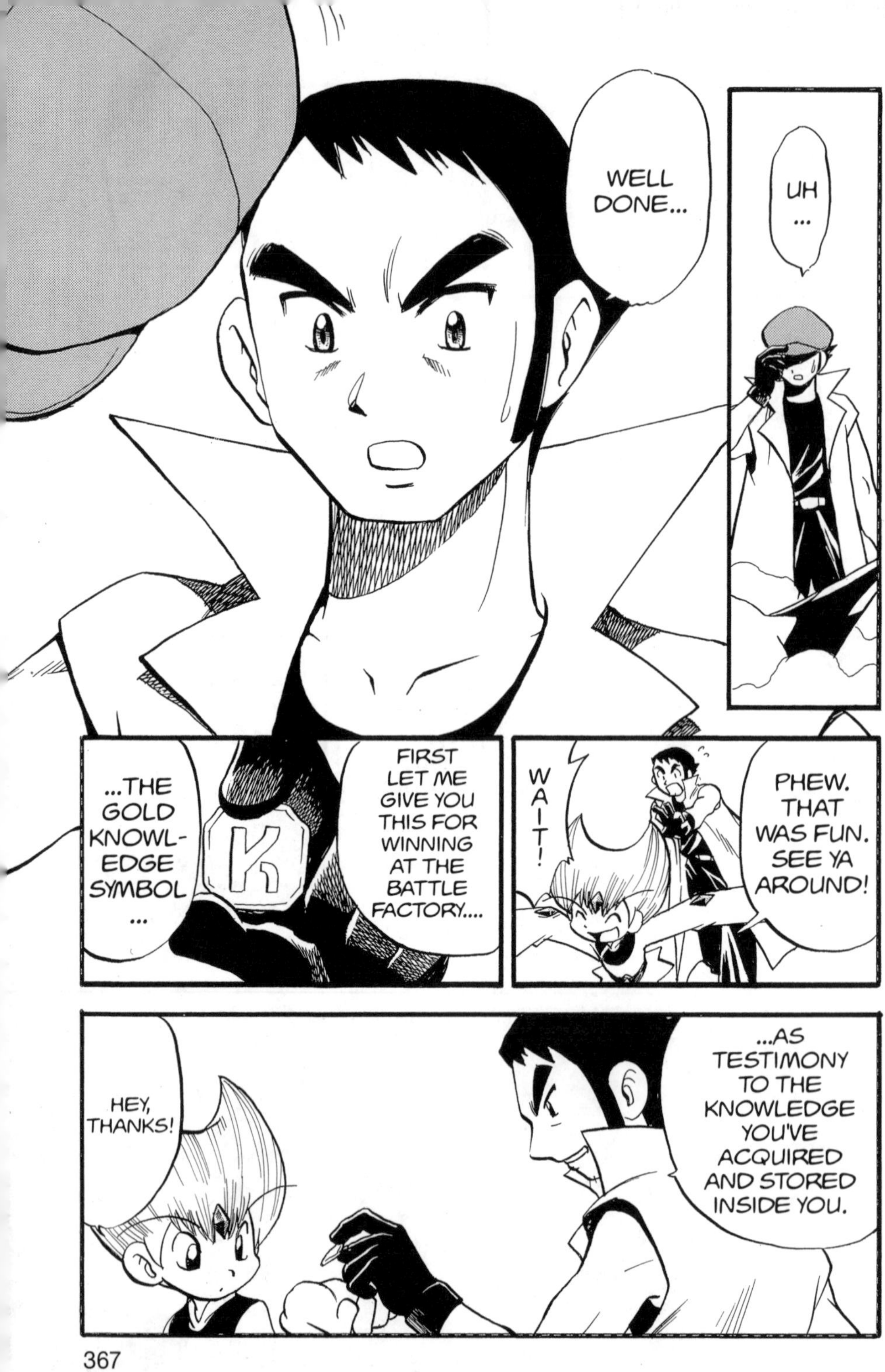
UH ...
WELL DONE...
PHEW. THAT WAS FUN. SEE YA AROUND!
WAIT!
FIRST LET ME GIVE YOU THIS FOR WINNING AT THE BATTLE FACTORY....
...THE GOLD KNOWL-EDGE SYMBOL ...
...AS TESTIMONY TO THE KNOWLEDGE YOU'VE ACQUIRED AND STORED INSIDE YOU.
HEY, THANKS!

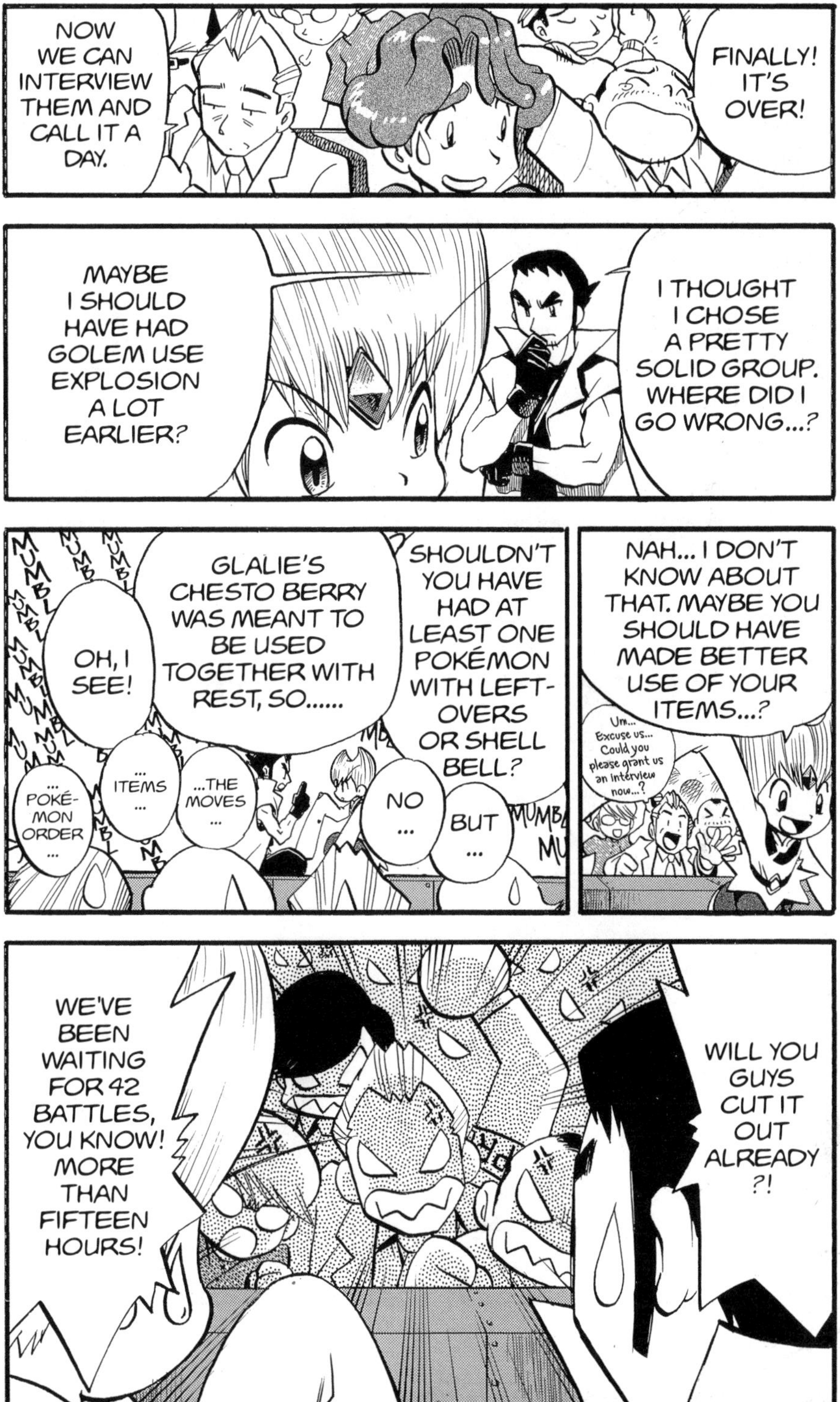
FINALLY! IT'S OVER!
NOW WE CAN INTERVIEW THEM AND CALL IT A DAY.
I THOUGHT I CHOSE A PRETTY SOLID GROUP. WHERE DID I GO WRONG...?
MAYBE I SHOULD HAVE HAD GOLEM USE EXPLOSION A LOT EARLIER?
NAH... I DON'T KNOW ABOUT THAT. MAYBE YOU SHOULD HAVE MADE BETTER USE OF YOUR ITEMS...?
Um... Excuse us... Could you please grant us an interview now...?
SHOULDN'T YOU HAVE HAD AT LEAST ONE POKÉMON WITH LEFT-OVERS OR SHELL BELL?
GLALIE'S CHESTO BERRY WAS MEANT TO BE USED TOGETHER WITH REST, SO......
OH, I SEE!
BUT ...
NO ...
...THE MOVES ...
... ITEMS ...
... POKÉ-MON ORDER ...
MUMBLE MUMBLE MUMBLE
WILL YOU GUYS CUT IT OUT ALREADY ?!
WE'VE BEEN WAITING FOR 42 BATTLES, YOU KNOW! MORE THAN FIFTEEN HOURS!

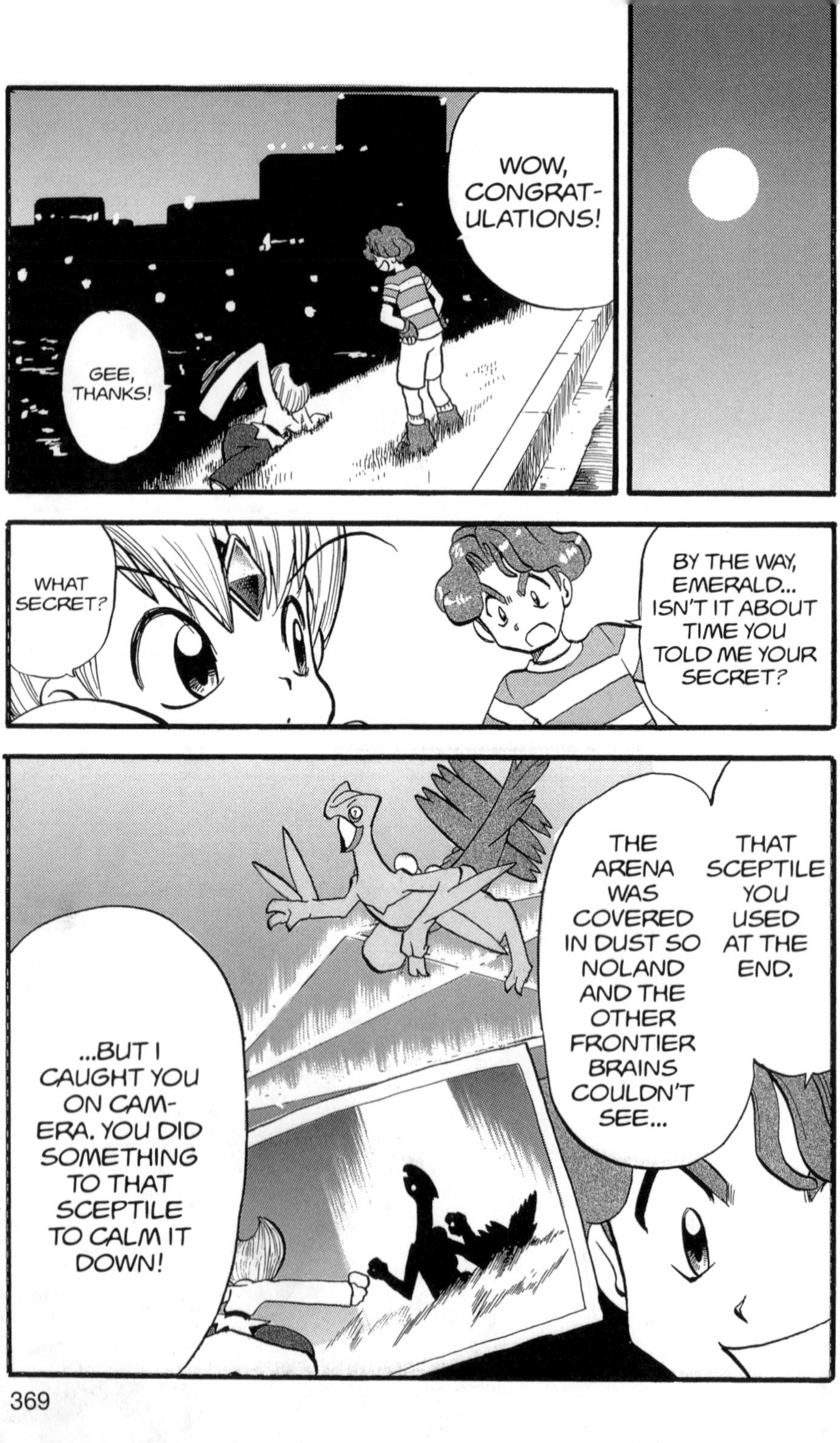
WOW, CONGRAT-ULATIONS!
GEE, THANKS!
BY THE WAY, EMERALD... ISN'T IT ABOUT TIME YOU TOLD ME YOUR SECRET?
WHAT SECRET?
THAT SCEPTILE YOU USED AT THE END.
THE ARENA WAS COVERED IN DUST SO NOLAND AND THE OTHER FRONTIER BRAINS COULDN'T SEE...
...BUT I CAUGHT YOU ON CAM-ERA. YOU DID SOMETHING TO THAT SCEPTILE TO CALM IT DOWN!

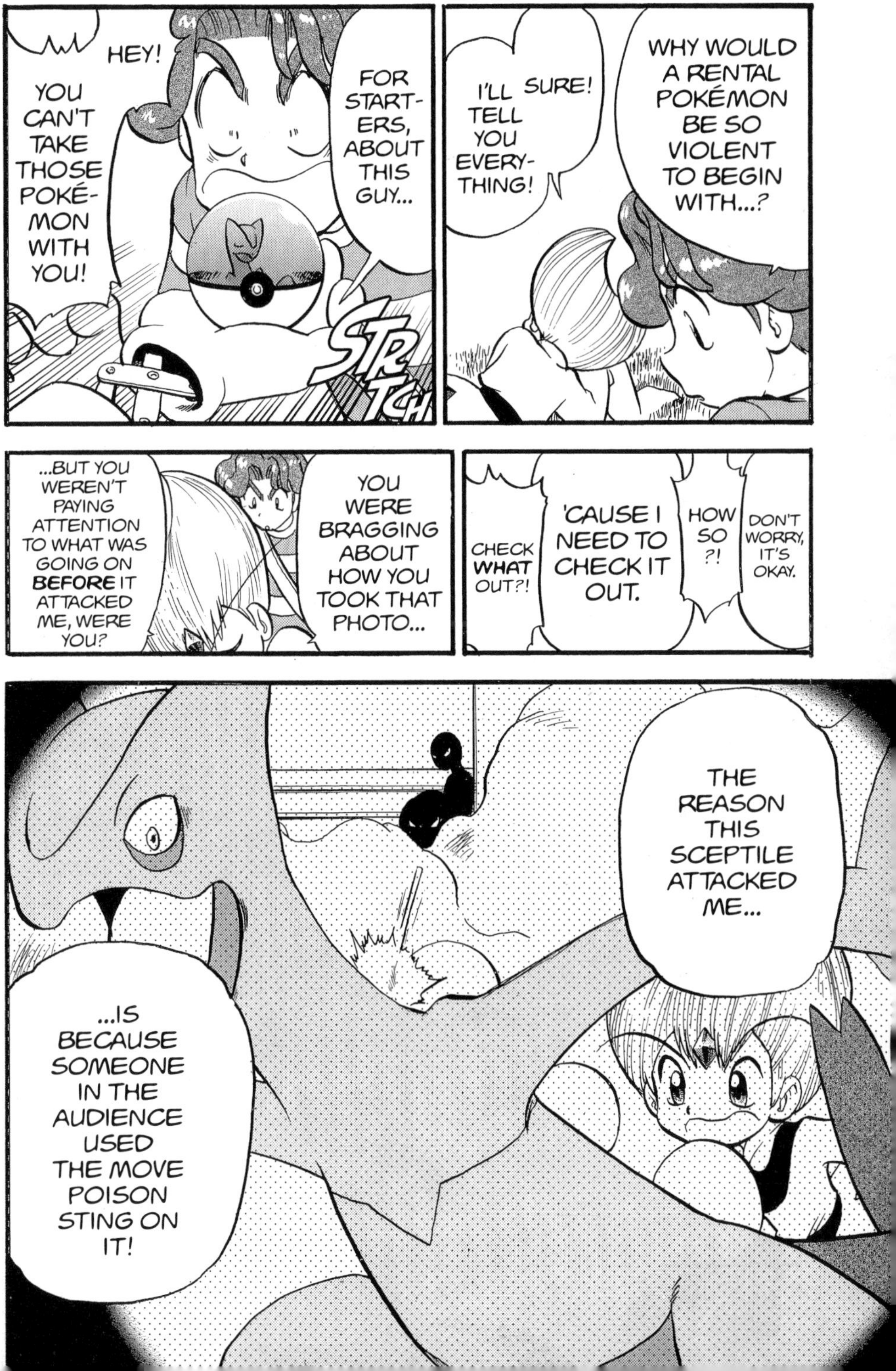
WHY WOULD A RENTAL POKÉMON BE SO VIOLENT TO BEGIN WITH...?
SURE!
I'LL TELL YOU EVERYTHING!
FOR STARTERS, ABOUT THIS GUY...
HEY!
YOU CAN'T TAKE THOSE POKÉMON WITH YOU!
STRTCH
DON'T WORRY, IT'S OKAY.
HOW SO?!
'CAUSE I NEED TO CHECK IT OUT.
CHECK WHAT OUT?!
YOU WERE BRAGGING ABOUT HOW YOU TOOK THAT PHOTO...
...BUT YOU WEREN'T PAYING ATTENTION TO WHAT WAS GOING ON BEFORE IT ATTACKED ME, WERE YOU?
THE REASON THIS SCEPTILE ATTACKED ME...
...IS BECAUSE SOMEONE IN THE AUDIENCE USED THE MOVE POISON STING ON IT!

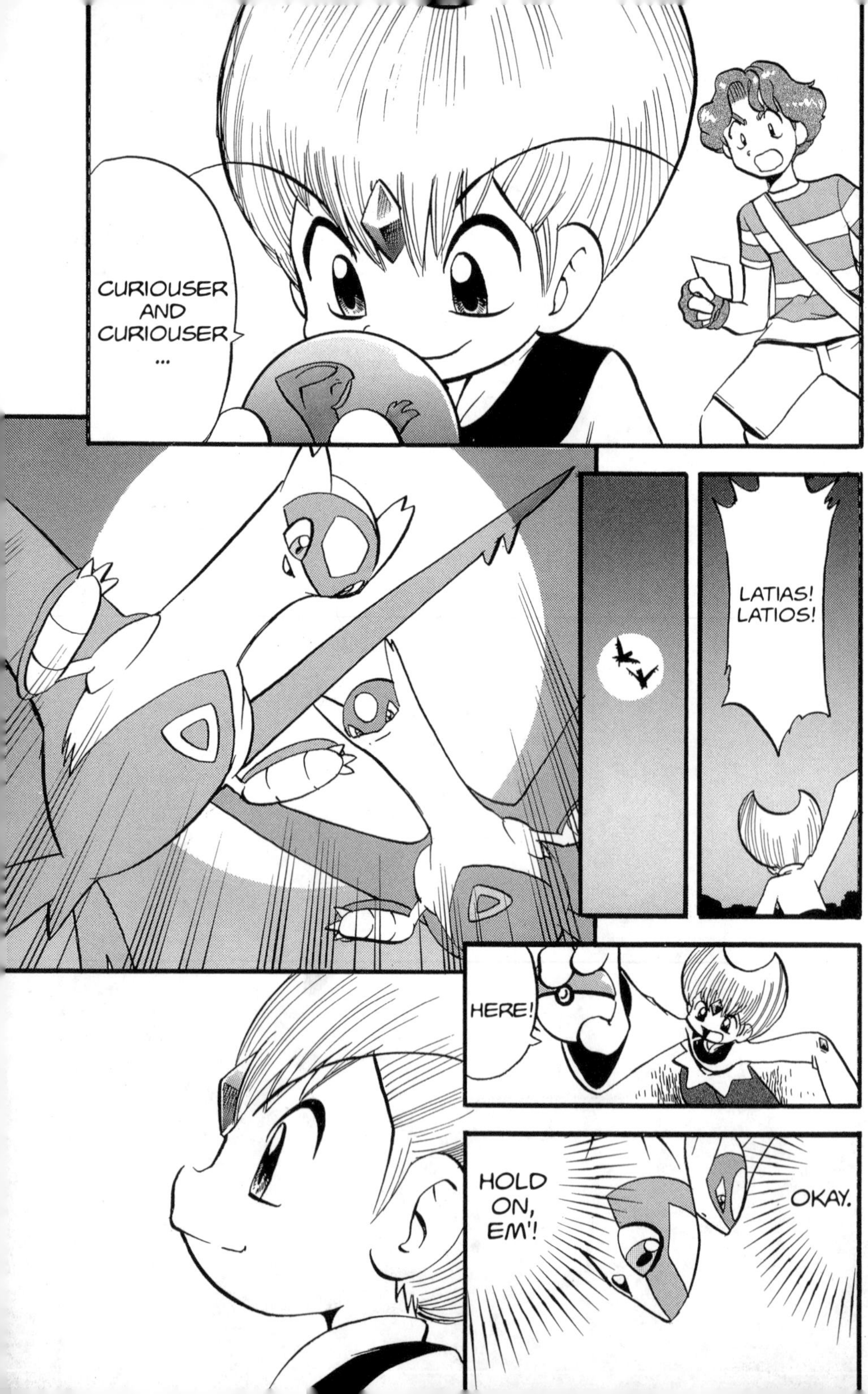
CURIOUSER AND CURIOUSER ...
LATIAS! LATIOS!
HERE!
HOLD ON, EM'!
OKAY.

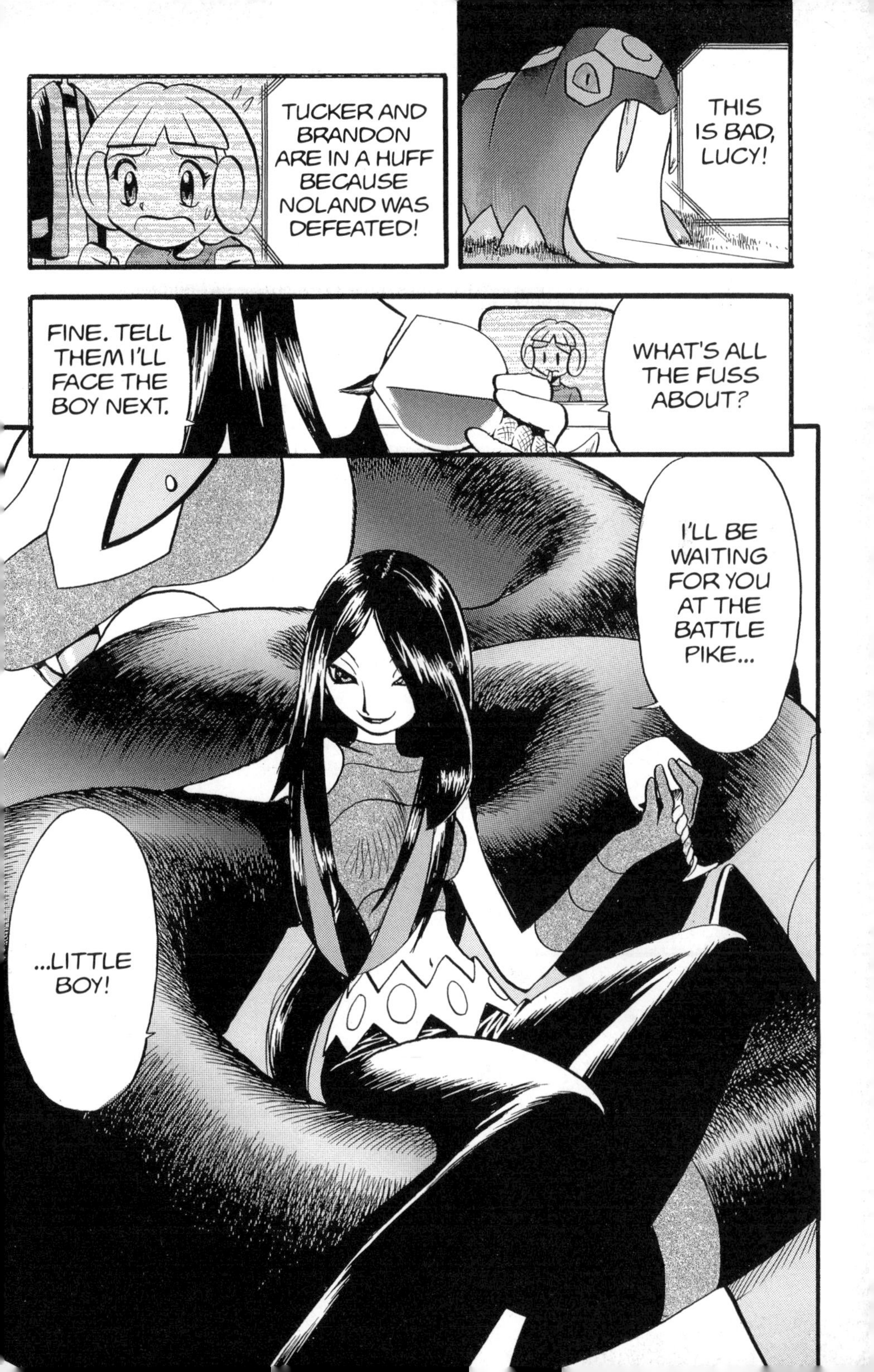
THIS IS BAD, LUCY!
TUCKER AND BRANDON ARE IN A HUFF BECAUSE NOLAND WAS DEFEATED!
WHAT'S ALL THE FUSS ABOUT?
FINE. TELL THEM I'LL FACE THE BOY NEXT.
I'LL BE WAITING FOR YOU AT THE BATTLE PIKE...
...LITTLE BOY!

DEAR MEMBERS OF THE PRESS...

Thank you for visiting the Battle Frontier today. Permit me to continue explaining the rules of this facility...

OWNER: SCOTT

FACILITY RULES
BATTLE PIKE

Battle-type	Number of Pokémon	Type of Symbol	Wins needed to attain the Symbol
•Single •Double •Wild Pokémon	3 Pokémon	Luck	14 Rooms × 10 Sets = 140 Rooms

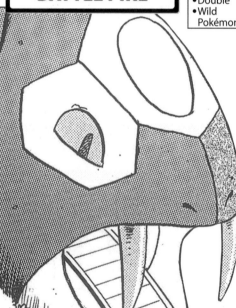

At this facility, you choose between three routes to travel until you reach the room at the very end. Eight possible events will occur inside each room. What you will encounter is determined at random.

A healing event, which heals the challenger's Pokémon, is included among the eight events.

There is also a Double Battle Event, but this will not occur if the challenger does not have two or more Pokémon capable of fighting.

Pike Queen Lucy

Luck Symbol

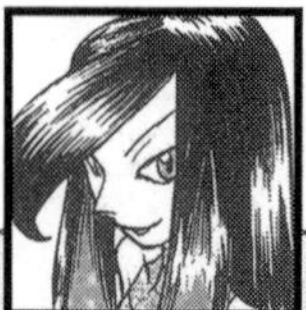

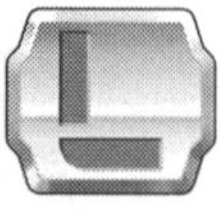

◆ 308 ◆

As Luck Would Have It, Kirlia

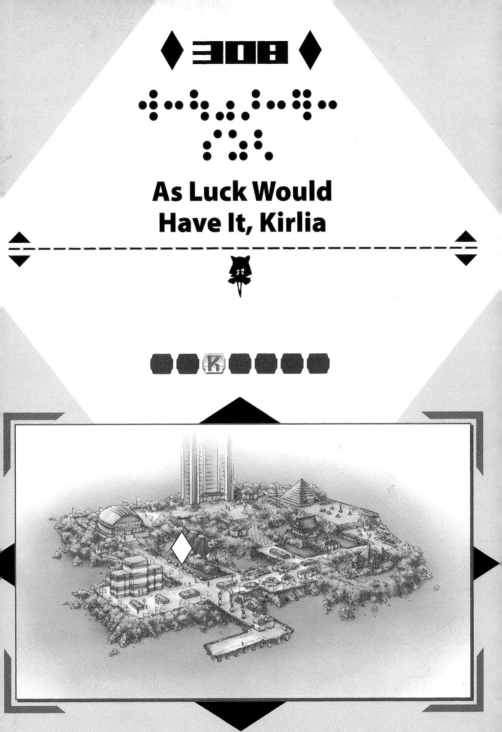

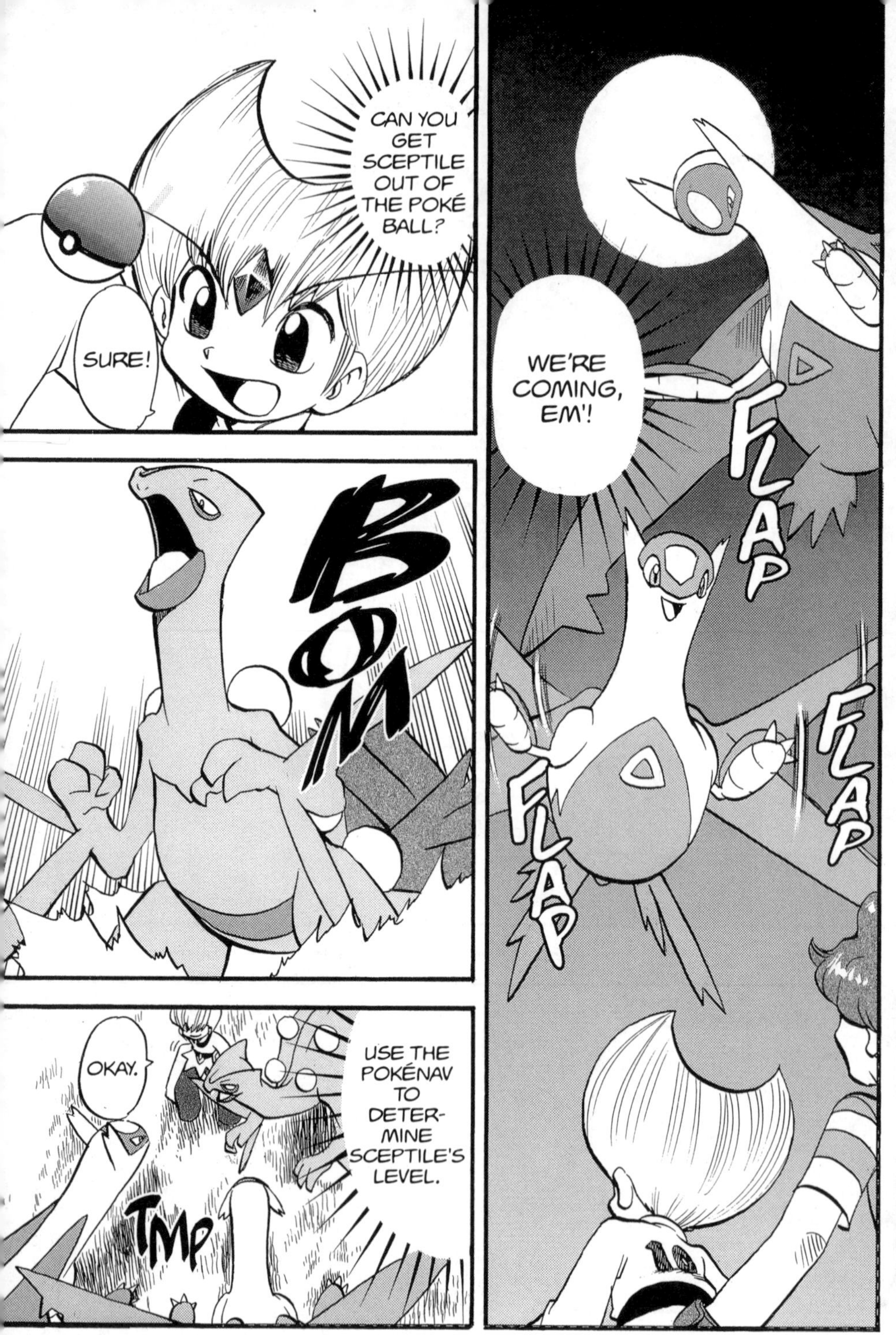
WE'RE COMING, EM'!
FLAP
FLAP
FLAP
CAN YOU GET SCEPTILE OUT OF THE POKÉ BALL?
SURE!
BOOM
USE THE POKÉNAV TO DETER-MINE SCEPTILE'S LEVEL.
OKAY.
TMP

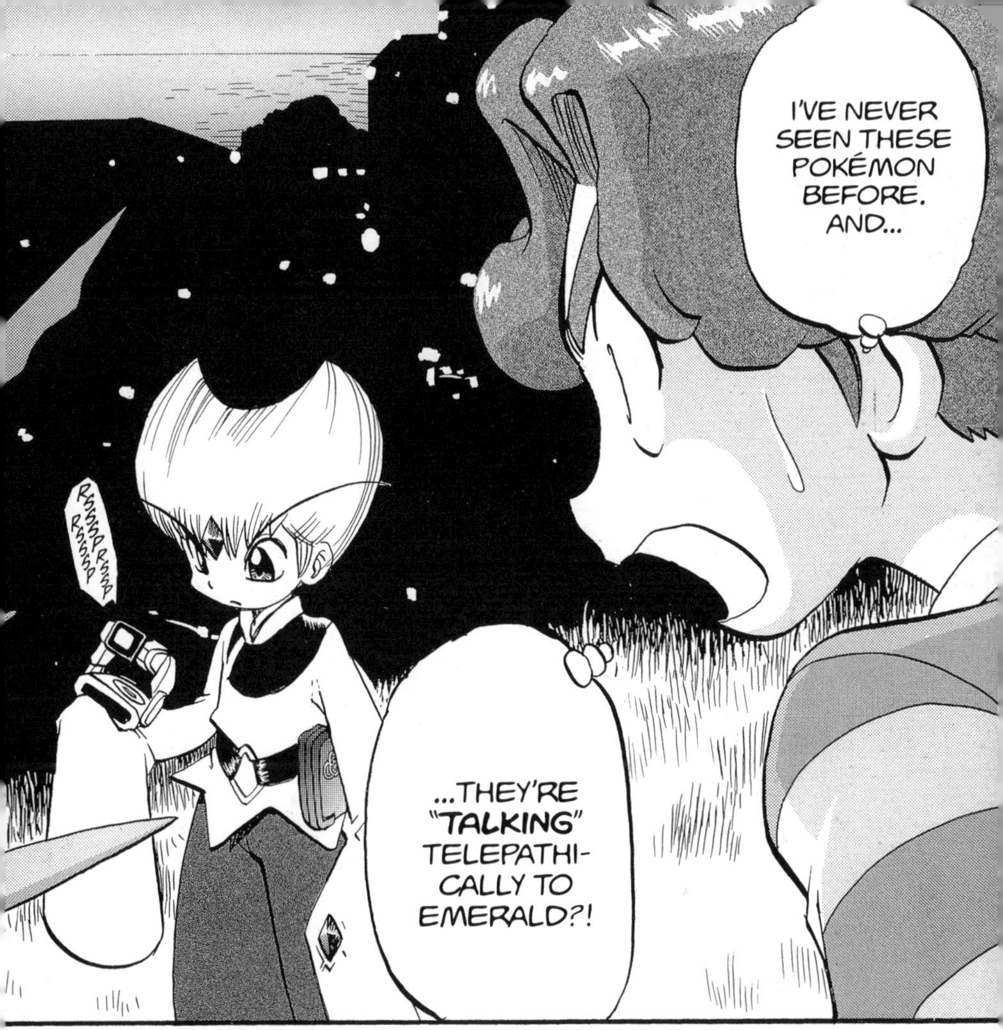
I'VE NEVER SEEN THESE POKÉMON BEFORE. AND...
...THEY'RE "**TALKING**" TELEPATHI-CALLY TO EMERALD?!

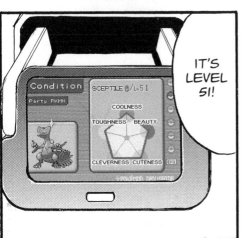

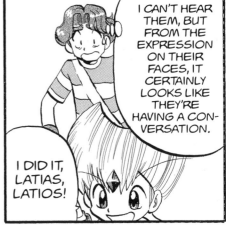

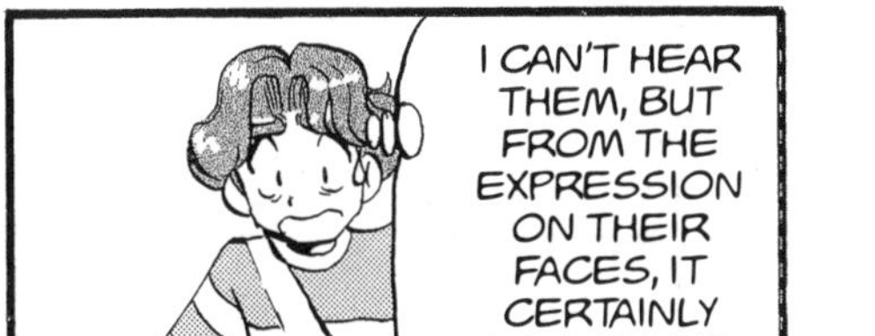
I CAN'T HEAR THEM, BUT FROM THE EXPRESSION ON THEIR FACES, IT CERTAINLY LOOKS LIKE THEY'RE HAVING A CON-VERSATION.
I DID IT, LATIAS, LATIOS!

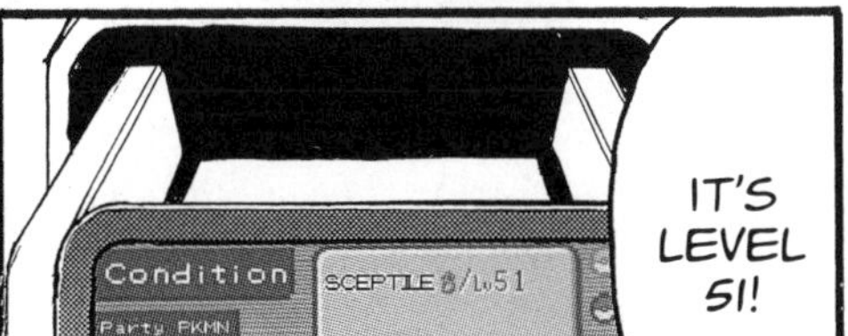
IT'S LEVEL 51!
Condition
Party PKMN
SCEPTILE ♂/Lv51
COOLNESS
TOUGHNESS
BEAUTY
CLEVERNESS
CUTENESS

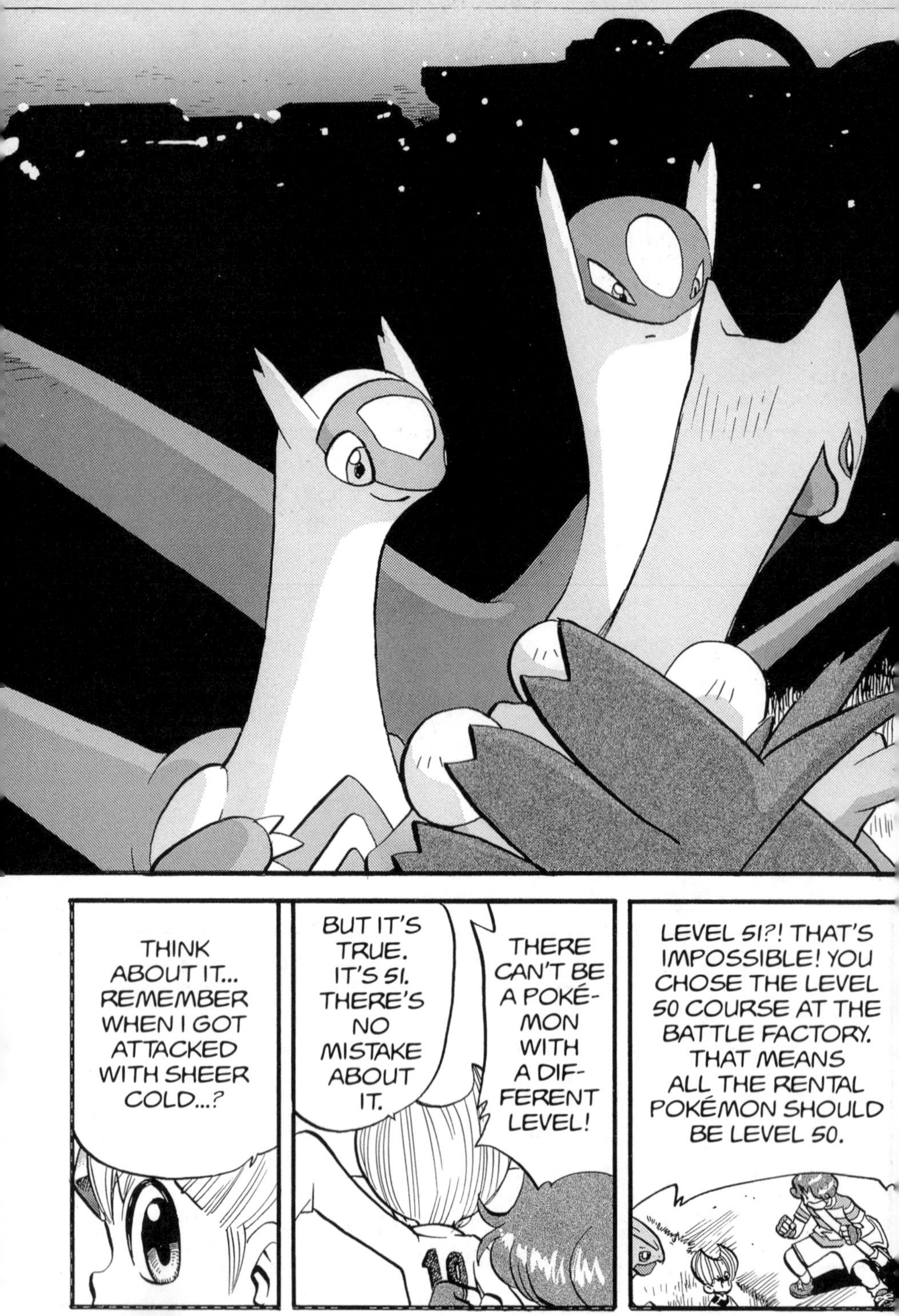
LEVEL 51?! THAT'S IMPOSSIBLE! YOU CHOSE THE LEVEL 50 COURSE AT THE BATTLE FACTORY. THAT MEANS ALL THE RENTAL POKÉMON SHOULD BE LEVEL 50.
THERE CAN'T BE A POKÉ-MON WITH A DIF-FERENT LEVEL!
BUT IT'S TRUE. IT'S 51. THERE'S NO MISTAKE ABOUT IT.
THINK ABOUT IT... REMEMBER WHEN I GOT ATTACKED WITH SHEER COLD...?

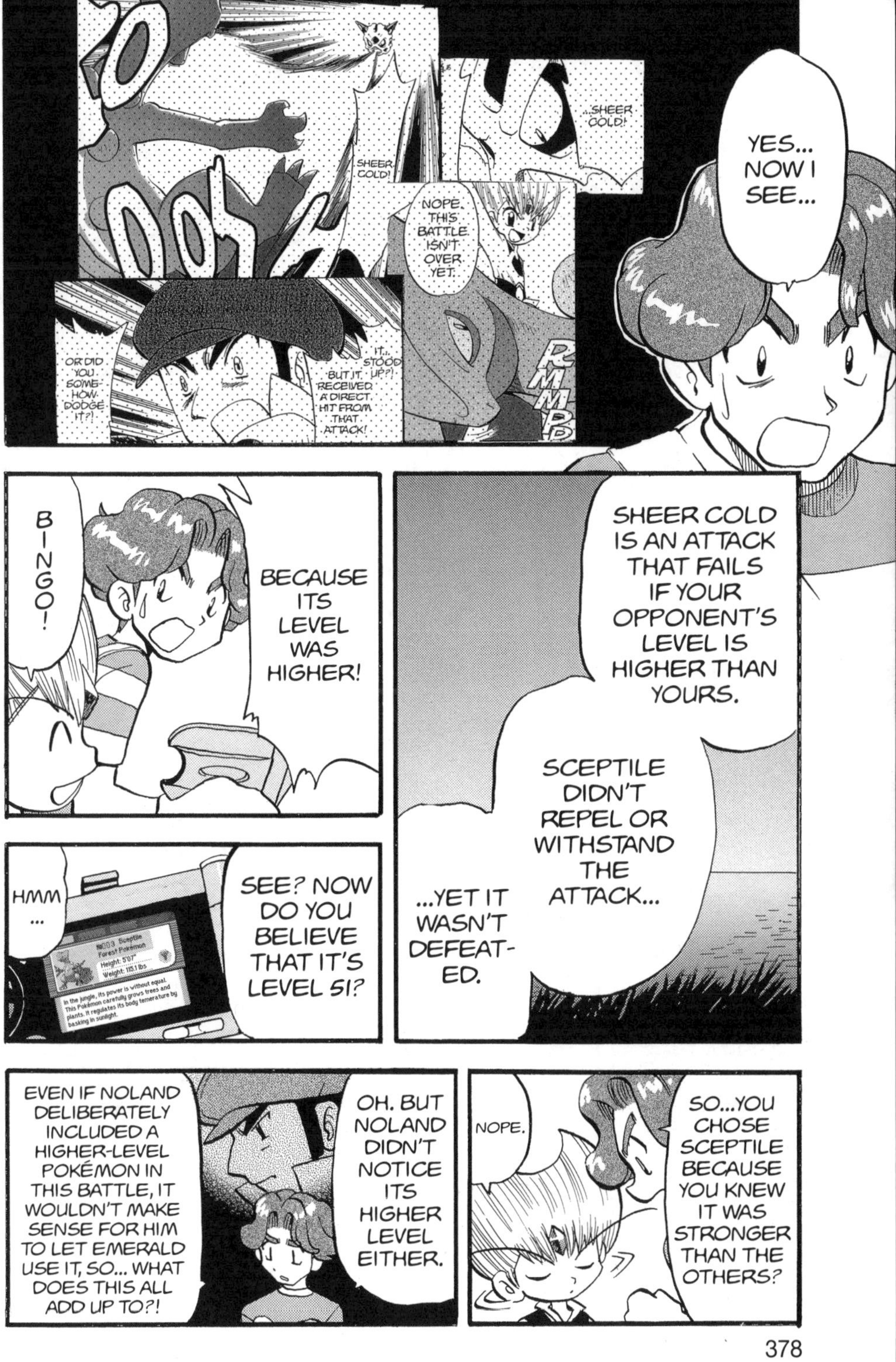

...SHEER COLD!
SHEER COLD!
NOPE. THIS BATTLE ISN'T OVER YET.
RMMPD
IT... STOOD UP?! BUT IT RECEIVED A DIRECT HIT FROM THAT ATTACK!
OR DID YOU SOMEHOW DODGE IT?!
YES... NOW I SEE...
SHEER COLD IS AN ATTACK THAT FAILS IF YOUR OPPONENT'S LEVEL IS HIGHER THAN YOURS.
SCEPTILE DIDN'T REPEL OR WITHSTAND THE ATTACK...
...YET IT WASN'T DEFEATED.
BECAUSE ITS LEVEL WAS HIGHER!
BINGO!
SEE? NOW DO YOU BELIEVE THAT IT'S LEVEL 51?
HMM...
Sceptile
Forest Pokémon
Height: 5'07"
Weight: 115.1 lbs
In the jungle, its power is without equal. This Pokémon carefully grows trees and plants. It regulates its body temerature by basking in sunlight.
SO...YOU CHOSE SCEPTILE BECAUSE YOU KNEW IT WAS STRONGER THAN THE OTHERS?
NOPE.
OH. BUT NOLAND DIDN'T NOTICE ITS HIGHER LEVEL EITHER.
EVEN IF NOLAND DELIBERATELY INCLUDED A HIGHER-LEVEL POKÉMON IN THIS BATTLE, IT WOULDN'T MAKE SENSE FOR HIM TO LET EMERALD USE IT, SO... WHAT DOES THIS ALL ADD UP TO?!

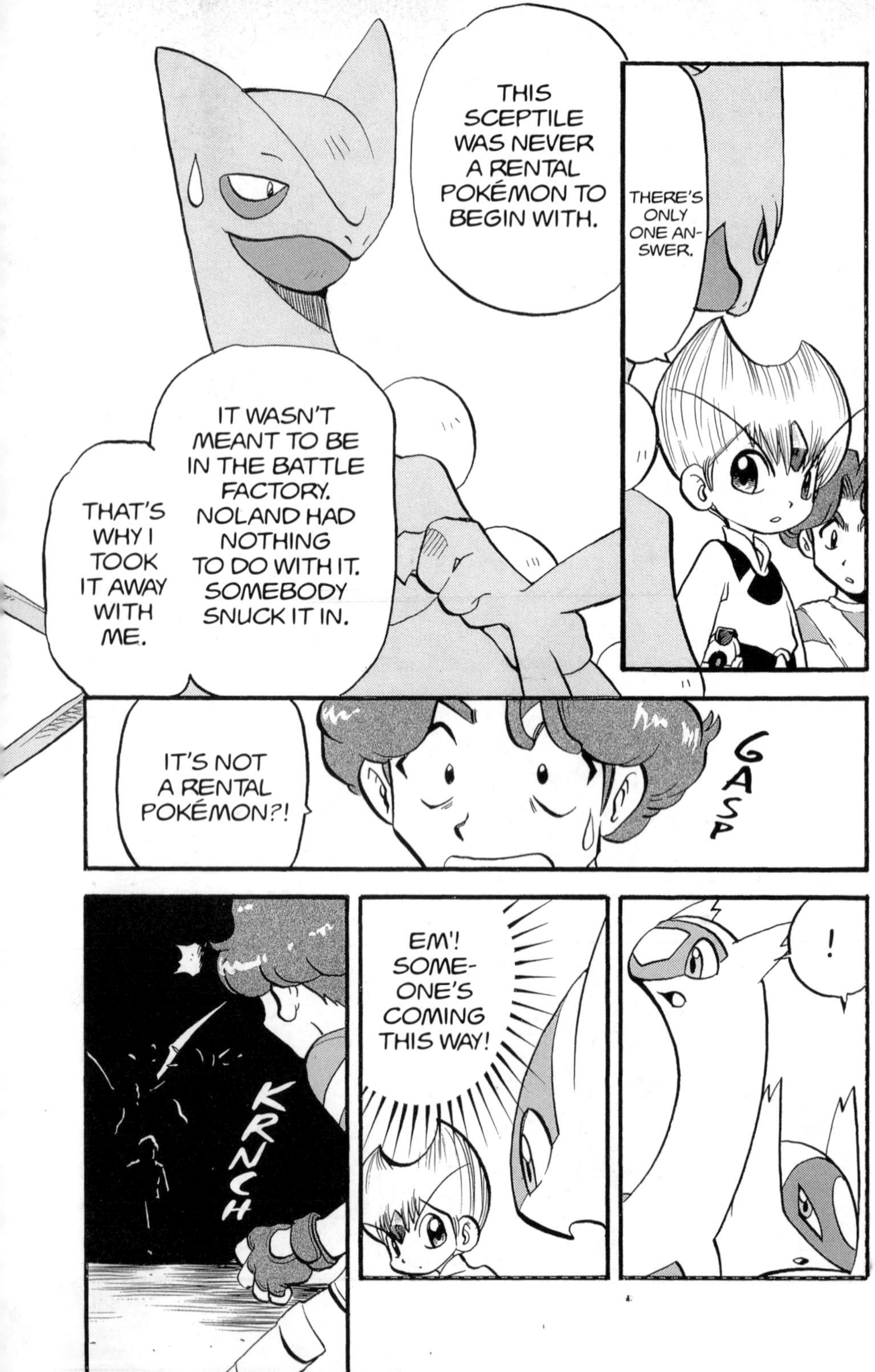
THERE'S ONLY ONE ANSWER.
THIS SCEPTILE WAS NEVER A RENTAL POKÉMON TO BEGIN WITH.
IT WASN'T MEANT TO BE IN THE BATTLE FACTORY. NOLAND HAD NOTHING TO DO WITH IT. SOMEBODY SNUCK IT IN.
THAT'S WHY I TOOK IT AWAY WITH ME.
GASP
IT'S NOT A RENTAL POKÉMON?!
!
EM'! SOMEONE'S COMING THIS WAY!
KRNCH

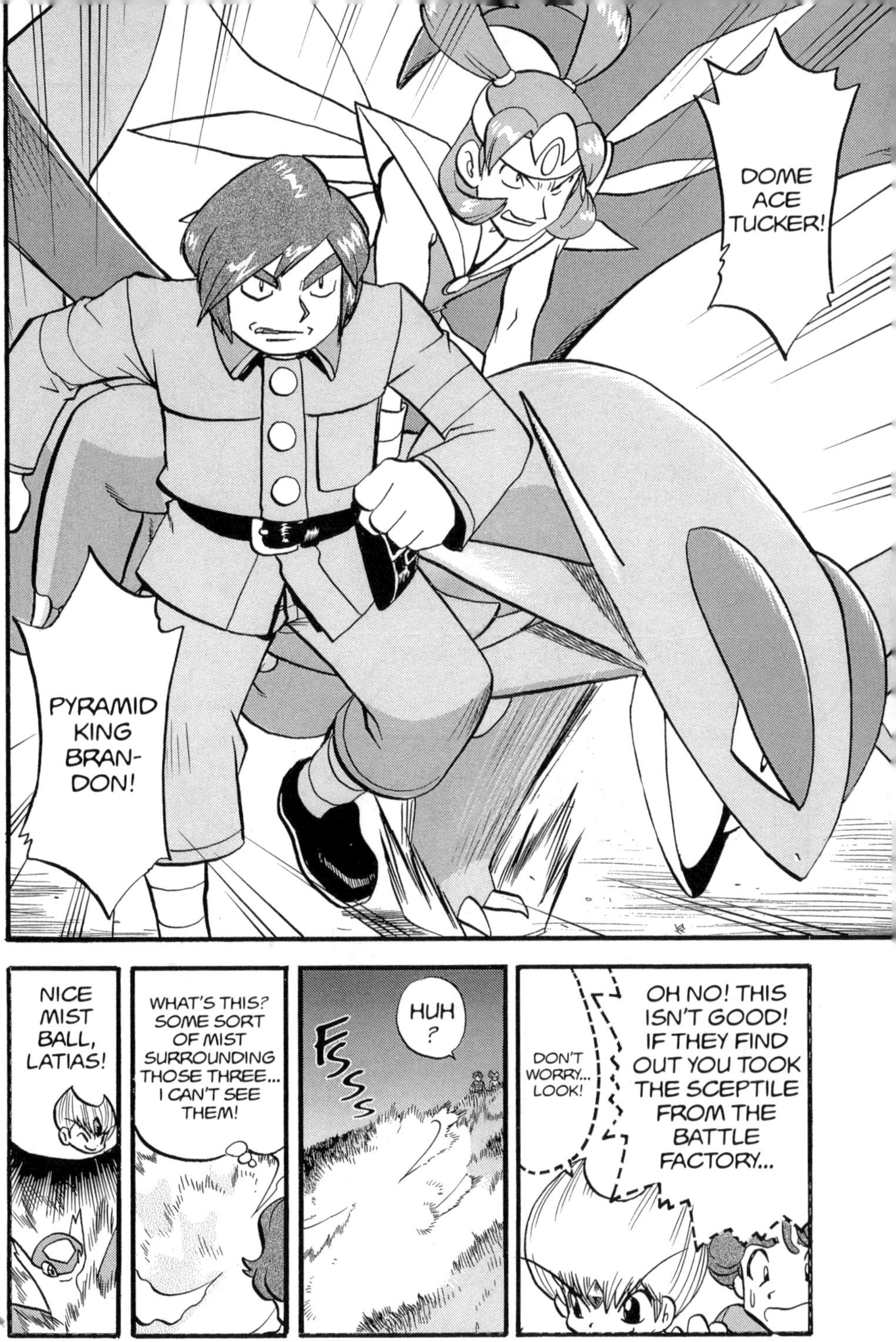
DOME ACE TUCKER!
PYRAMID KING BRAN-DON!
OH NO! THIS ISN'T GOOD! IF THEY FIND OUT YOU TOOK THE SCEPTILE FROM THE BATTLE FACTORY...
DON'T WORRY... LOOK!
HUH?
FSSS
WHAT'S THIS? SOME SORT OF MIST SURROUNDING THOSE THREE... I CAN'T SEE THEM!
NICE MIST BALL, LATIAS!

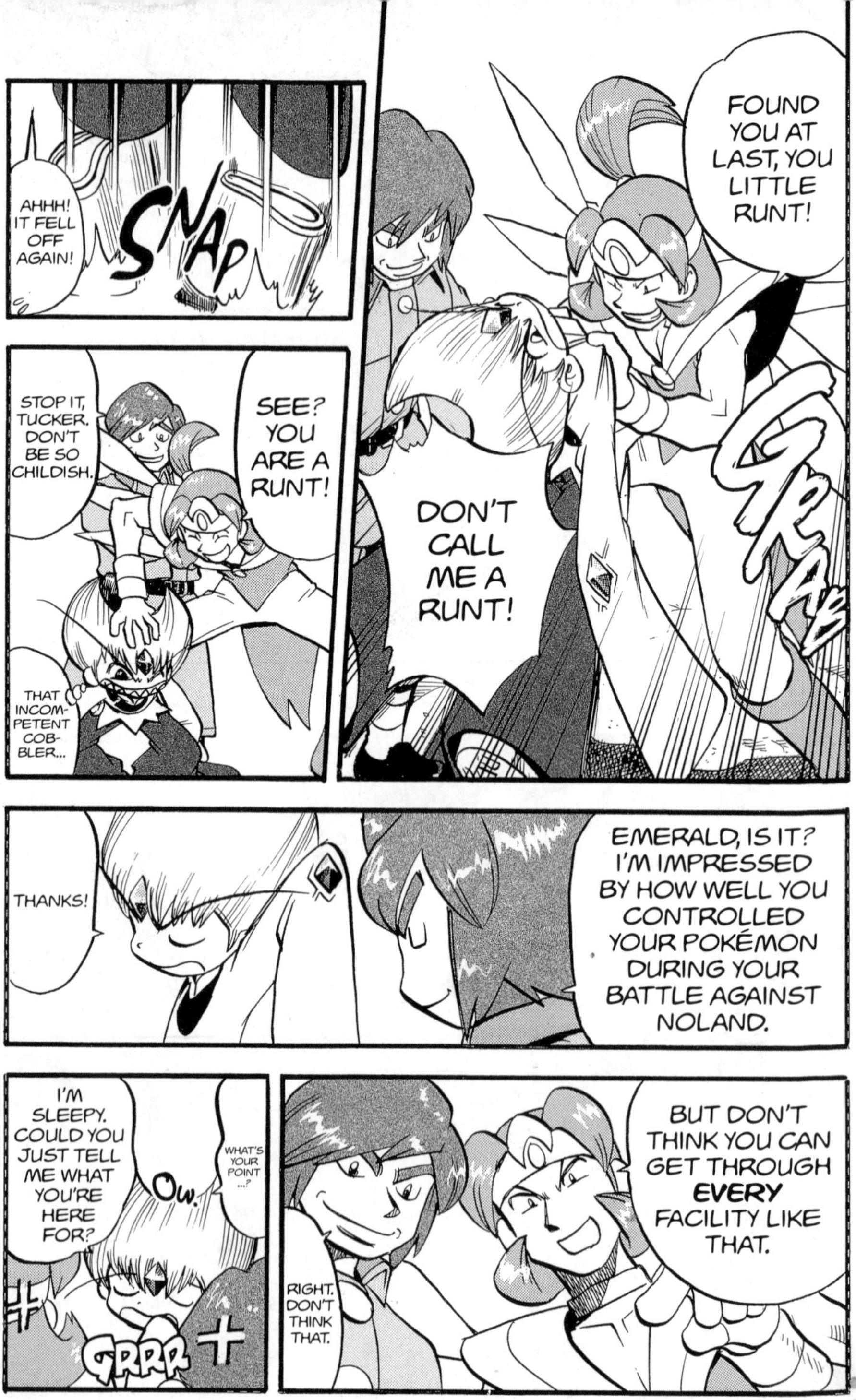
FOUND YOU AT LAST, YOU LITTLE RUNT!
GRAB
DON'T CALL ME A RUNT!
SNAP
AHHH! IT FELL OFF AGAIN!
SEE? YOU ARE A RUNT!
STOP IT, TUCKER. DON'T BE SO CHILDISH.
THAT INCOMPETENT COBBLER...
EMERALD, IS IT? I'M IMPRESSED BY HOW WELL YOU CONTROLLED YOUR POKÉMON DURING YOUR BATTLE AGAINST NOLAND.
THANKS!
BUT DON'T THINK YOU CAN GET THROUGH **EVERY** FACILITY LIKE THAT.
RIGHT. DON'T THINK THAT.
WHAT'S YOUR POINT ...?
OW.
I'M SLEEPY. COULD YOU JUST TELL ME WHAT YOU'RE HERE FOR?
GRRR

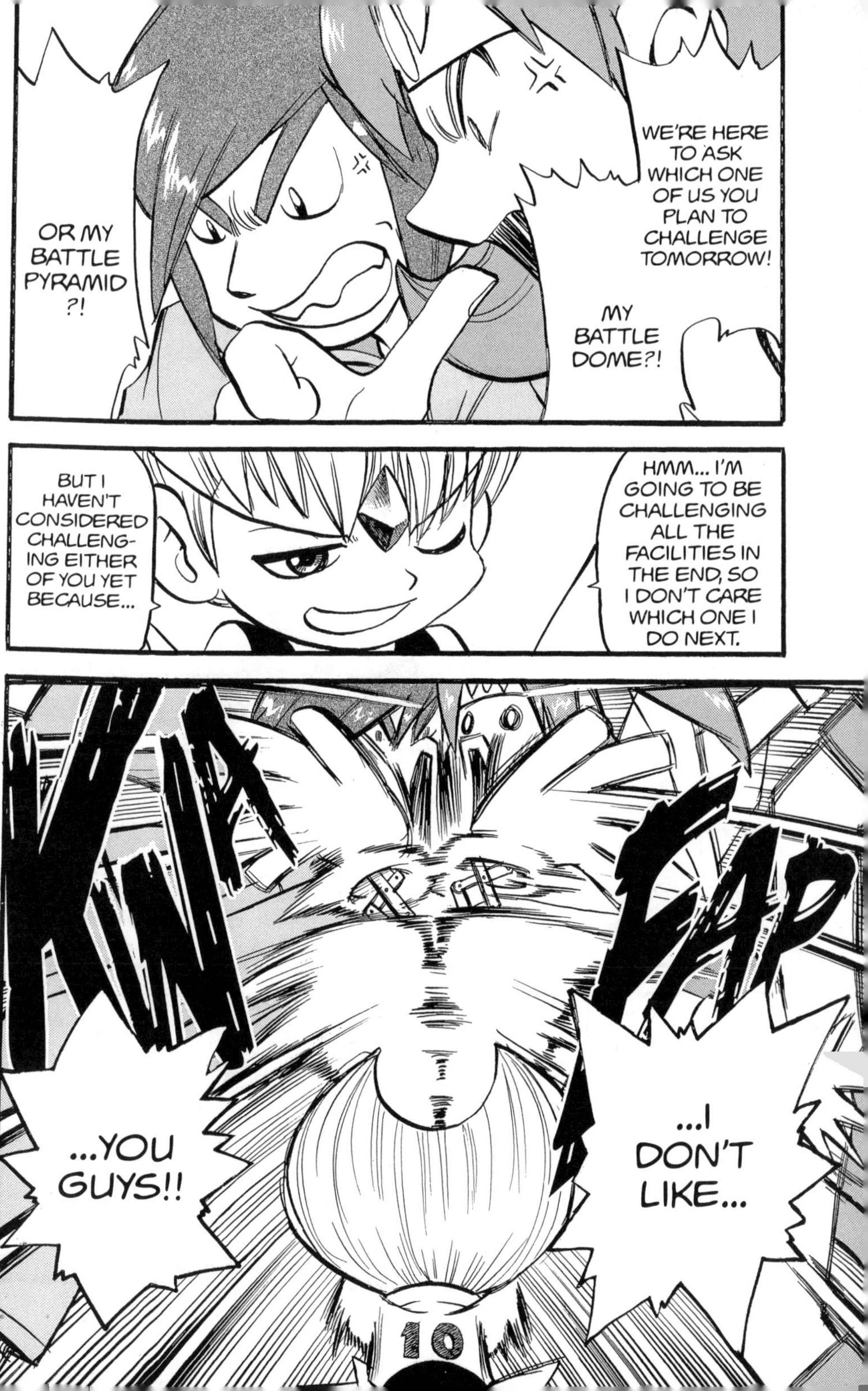
WE'RE HERE TO ASK WHICH ONE OF US YOU PLAN TO CHALLENGE TOMORROW!
MY BATTLE DOME?!
OR MY BATTLE PYRAMID?!
HMM... I'M GOING TO BE CHALLENGING ALL THE FACILITIES IN THE END, SO I DON'T CARE WHICH ONE I DO NEXT.
BUT I HAVEN'T CONSIDERED CHALLENG-ING EITHER OF YOU YET BECAUSE...
...I DON'T LIKE...
...YOU GUYS!!

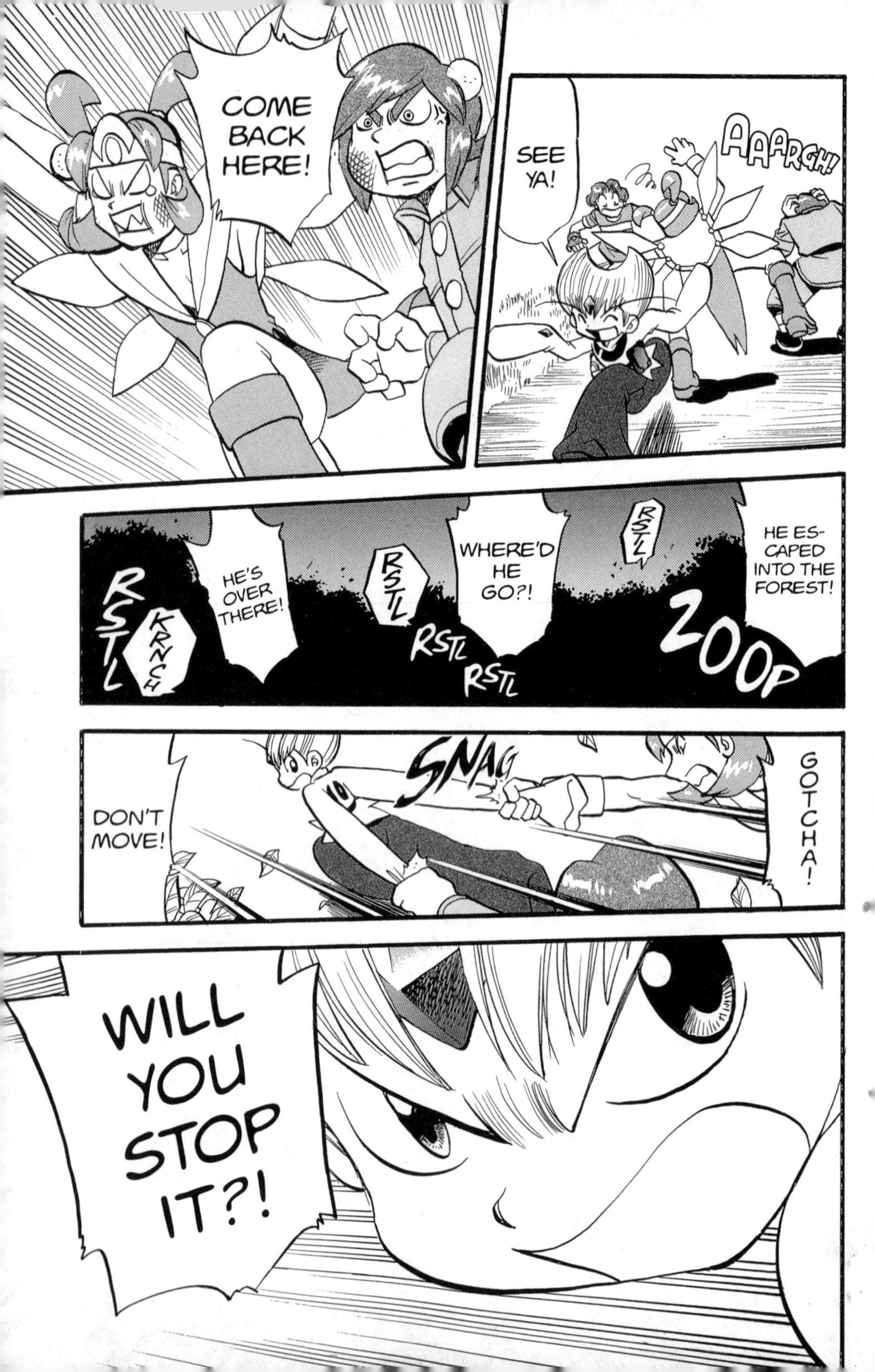
AAARGH!
SEE YA!
COME BACK HERE!
HE ES- CAPED INTO THE FOREST!
ZOOP
RSTL
WHERE'D HE GO?!
RSTL
RSTL
RSTL
HE'S OVER THERE!
KRNCH
RSTL
GOTCHA!
SNAG
DON'T MOVE!
WILL YOU STOP IT?!

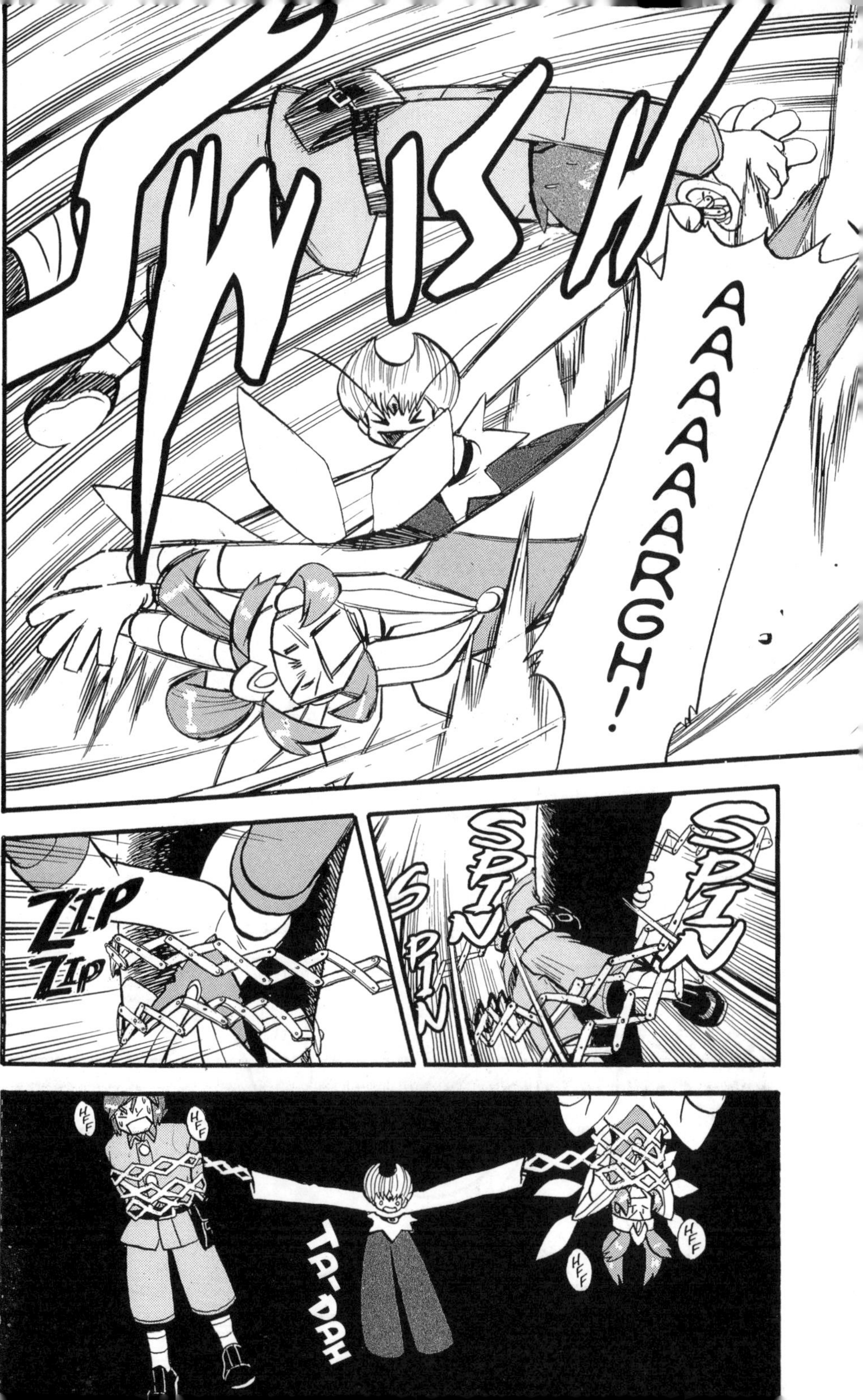
SWISH
AAAAAAARGH!
SPIN
SPIN
SPIN
ZIP
ZIP
HFF
HFF
HFF
HFF
TA-DAH

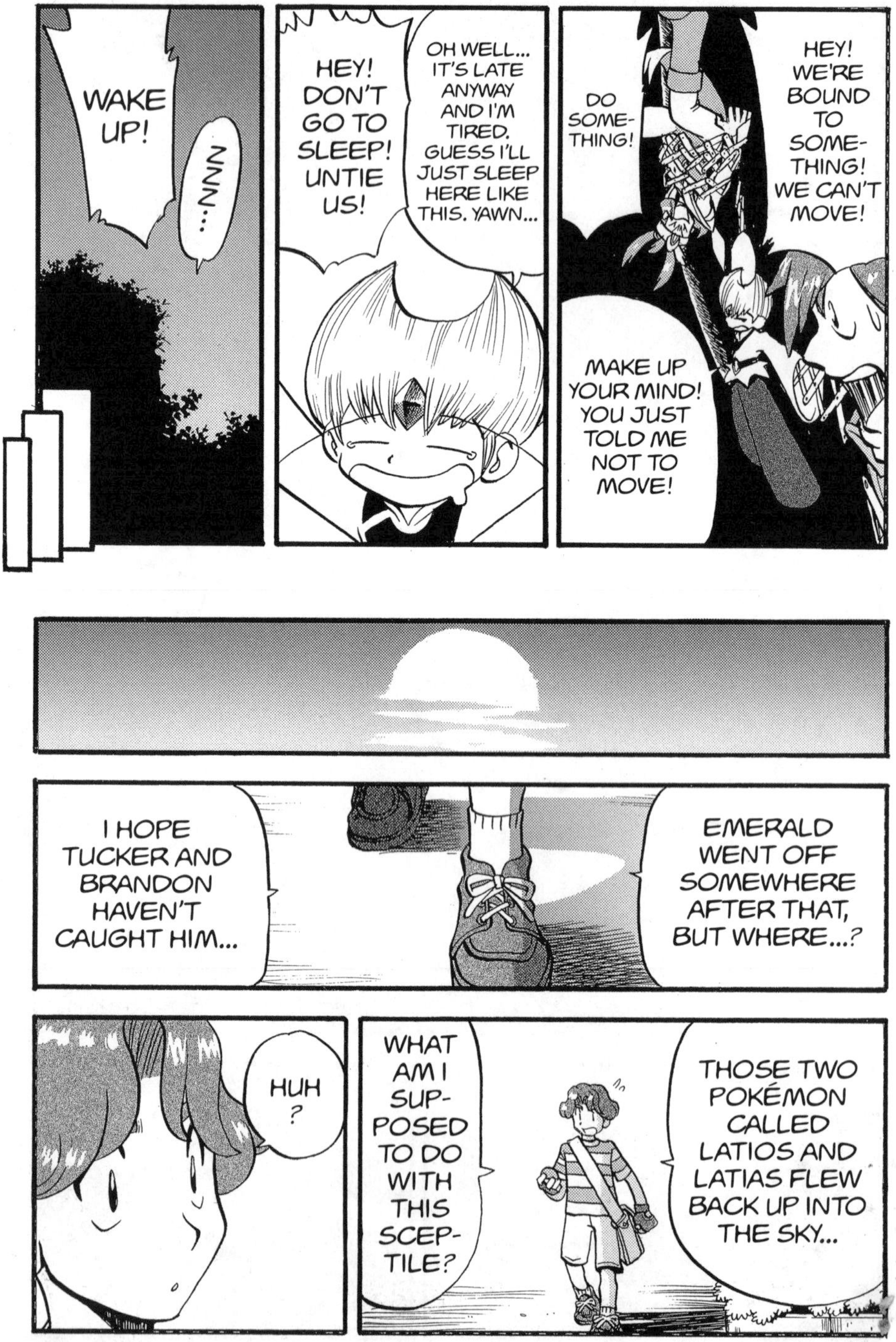
HEY! WE'RE BOUND TO SOME-THING! WE CAN'T MOVE!
DO SOME-THING!
MAKE UP YOUR MIND! YOU JUST TOLD ME NOT TO MOVE!
OH WELL... IT'S LATE ANYWAY AND I'M TIRED. GUESS I'LL JUST SLEEP HERE LIKE THIS. YAWN...
HEY! DON'T GO TO SLEEP! UNTIE US!
WAKE UP!
ZZZ...
EMERALD WENT OFF SOMEWHERE AFTER THAT, BUT WHERE...?
I HOPE TUCKER AND BRANDON HAVEN'T CAUGHT HIM...
THOSE TWO POKÉMON CALLED LATIOS AND LATIAS FLEW BACK UP INTO THE SKY...
WHAT AM I SUP-POSED TO DO WITH THIS SCEP-TILE?
HUH?

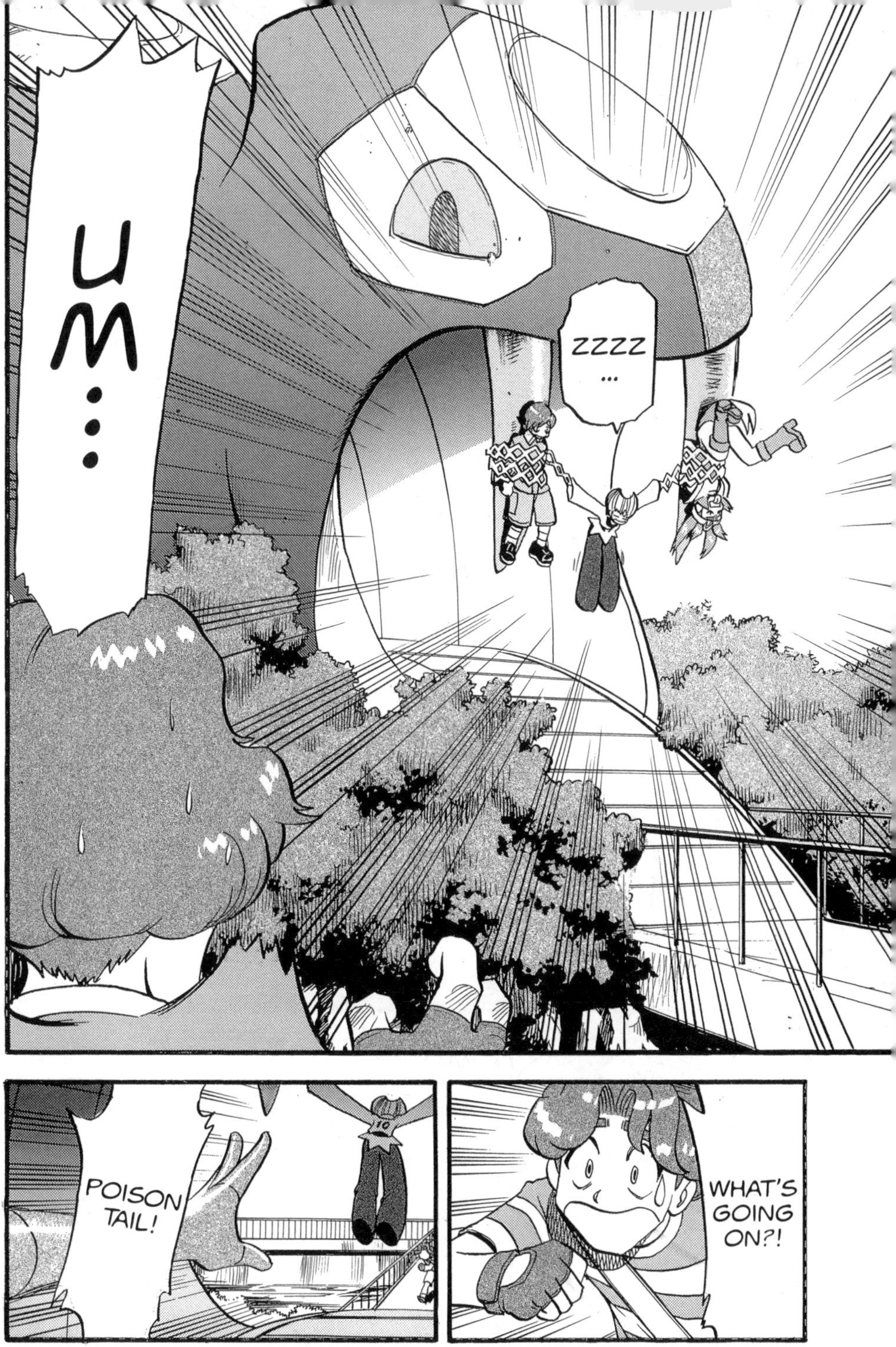
ZZZZ...
UM...
WHAT'S GOING ON?!
POISON TAIL!

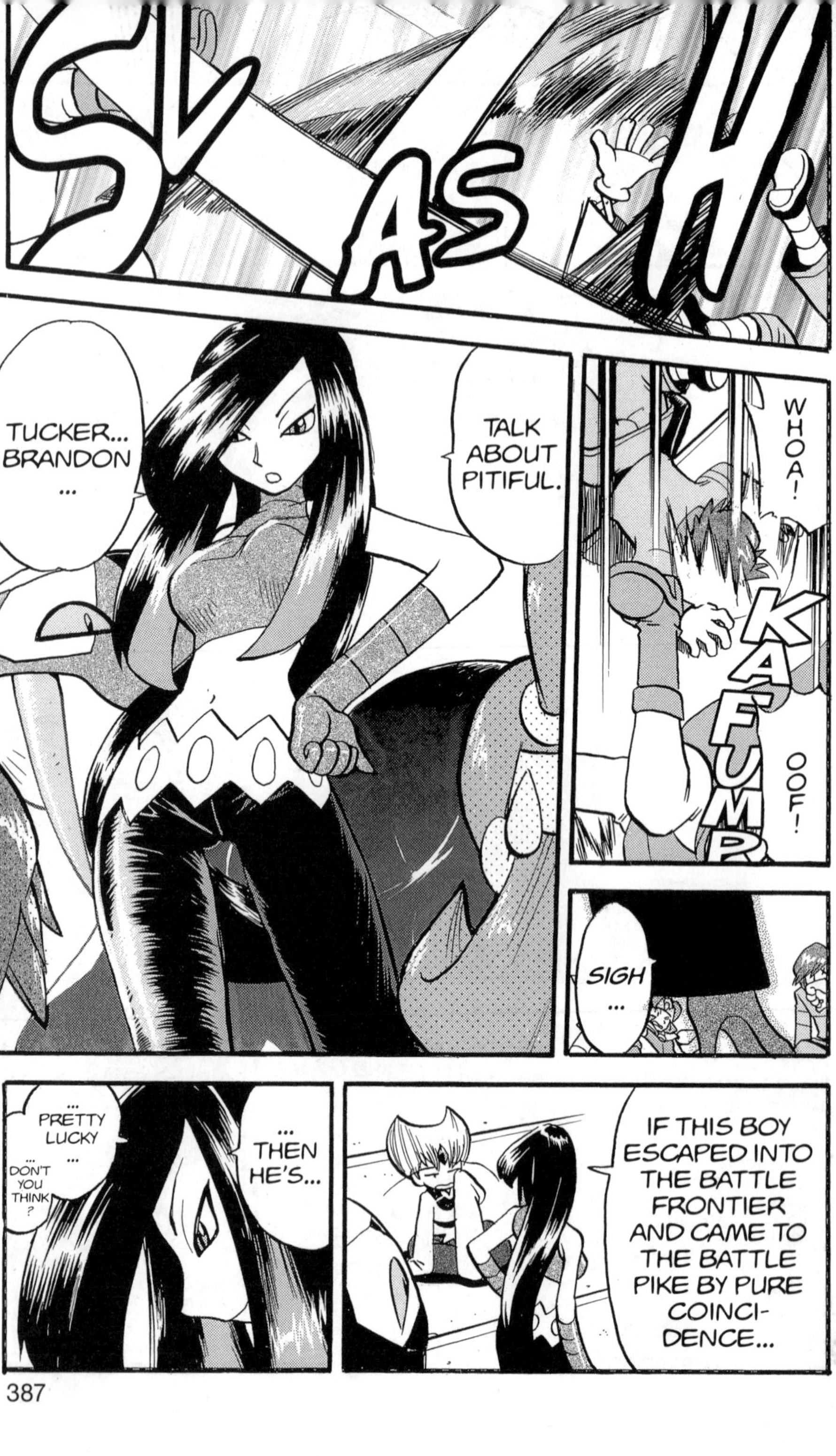
SLASH
WHOA!
KAFUMP
OOF!
SIGH...
TALK ABOUT PITIFUL.
TUCKER... BRANDON ...
IF THIS BOY ESCAPED INTO THE BATTLE FRONTIER AND CAME TO THE BATTLE PIKE BY PURE COINCI- DENCE...
... THEN HE'S...
... PRETTY LUCKY ...
... DON'T YOU THINK?

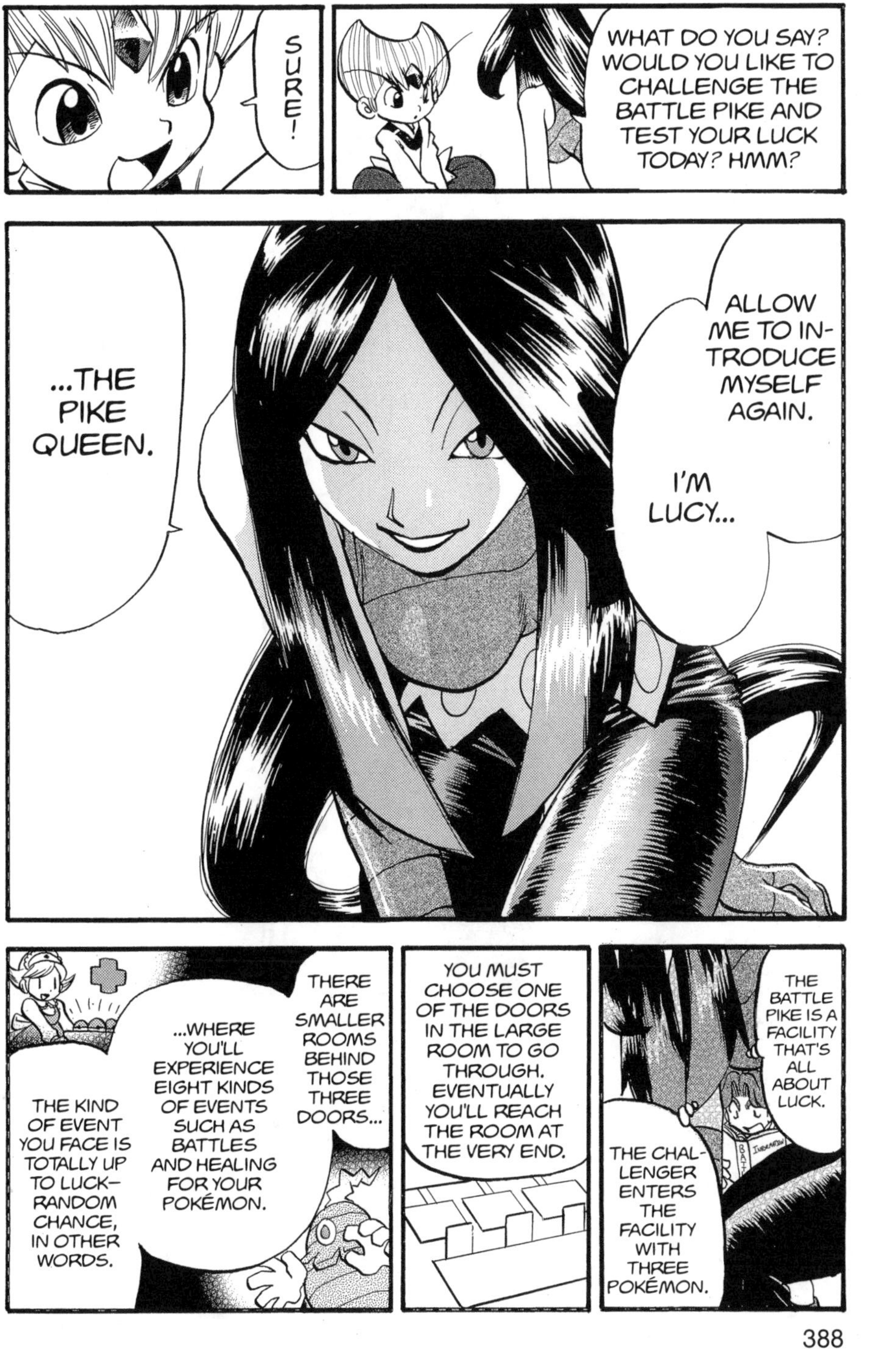
WHAT DO YOU SAY? WOULD YOU LIKE TO CHALLENGE THE BATTLE PIKE AND TEST YOUR LUCK TODAY? HMM?
SURE!
ALLOW ME TO INTRODUCE MYSELF AGAIN.
I'M LUCY...
...THE PIKE QUEEN.
THE BATTLE PIKE IS A FACILITY THAT'S ALL ABOUT LUCK.
THE CHALLENGER ENTERS THE FACILITY WITH THREE POKÉMON.
YOU MUST CHOOSE ONE OF THE DOORS IN THE LARGE ROOM TO GO THROUGH. EVENTUALLY YOU'LL REACH THE ROOM AT THE VERY END.
THERE ARE SMALLER ROOMS BEHIND THOSE THREE DOORS...
...WHERE YOU'LL EXPERIENCE EIGHT KINDS OF EVENTS SUCH AS BATTLES AND HEALING FOR YOUR POKÉMON.
THE KIND OF EVENT YOU FACE IS TOTALLY UP TO LUCK—RANDOM CHANCE, IN OTHER WORDS.

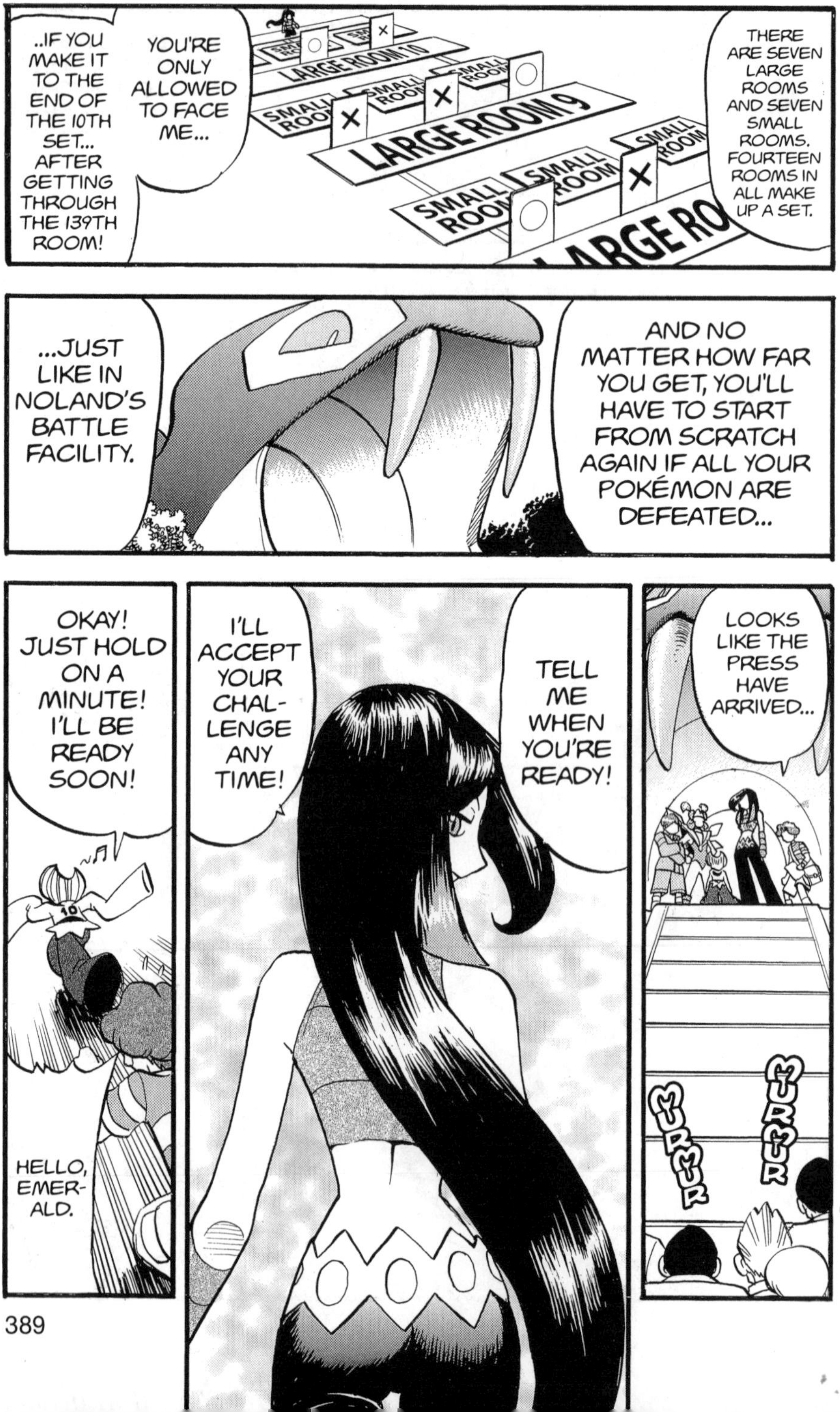
THERE ARE SEVEN LARGE ROOMS AND SEVEN SMALL ROOMS. FOURTEEN ROOMS IN ALL MAKE UP A SET.
LARGE ROOM 10
LARGE ROOM 9
SMALL ROOM
YOU'RE ONLY ALLOWED TO FACE ME...
..IF YOU MAKE IT TO THE END OF THE 10TH SET... AFTER GETTING THROUGH THE 139TH ROOM!
AND NO MATTER HOW FAR YOU GET, YOU'LL HAVE TO START FROM SCRATCH AGAIN IF ALL YOUR POKÉMON ARE DEFEATED...
...JUST LIKE IN NOLAND'S BATTLE FACILITY.
LOOKS LIKE THE PRESS HAVE ARRIVED...
MURMUR
MURMUR
TELL ME WHEN YOU'RE READY!
I'LL ACCEPT YOUR CHALLENGE ANY TIME!
OKAY! JUST HOLD ON A MINUTE! I'LL BE READY SOON!
HELLO, EMERALD.

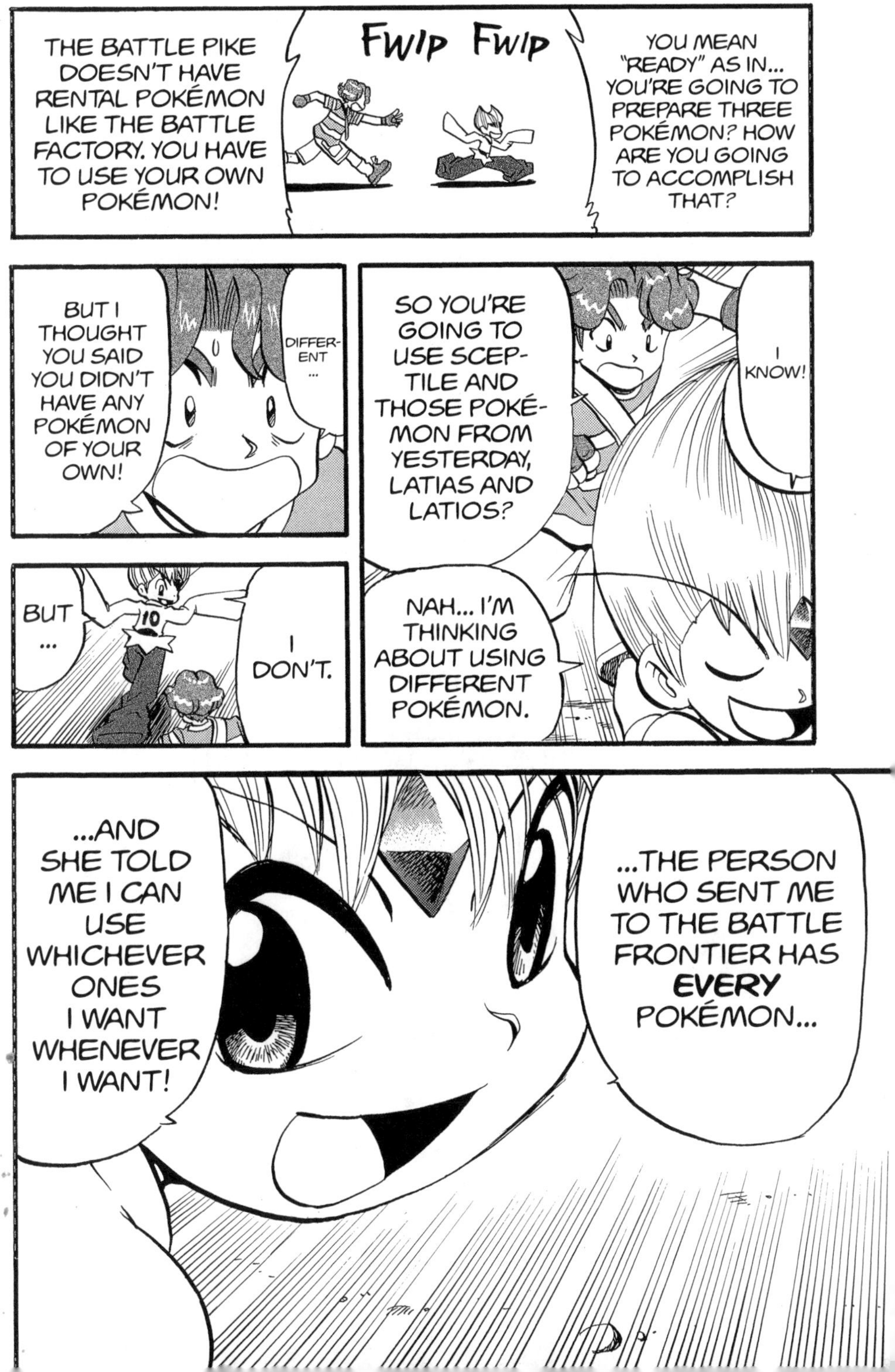
YOU MEAN "READY" AS IN... YOU'RE GOING TO PREPARE THREE POKÉMON? HOW ARE YOU GOING TO ACCOMPLISH THAT?
FWIP FWIP
THE BATTLE PIKE DOESN'T HAVE RENTAL POKÉMON LIKE THE BATTLE FACTORY. YOU HAVE TO USE YOUR OWN POKÉMON!
I KNOW!
SO YOU'RE GOING TO USE SCEPTILE AND THOSE POKÉMON FROM YESTERDAY, LATIAS AND LATIOS?
NAH... I'M THINKING ABOUT USING DIFFERENT POKÉMON.
DIFFERENT...
BUT I THOUGHT YOU SAID YOU DIDN'T HAVE ANY POKÉMON OF YOUR OWN!
I DON'T.
BUT...
...THE PERSON WHO SENT ME TO THE BATTLE FRONTIER HAS **EVERY** POKÉMON...
...AND SHE TOLD ME I CAN USE WHICHEVER ONES I WANT WHENEVER I WANT!

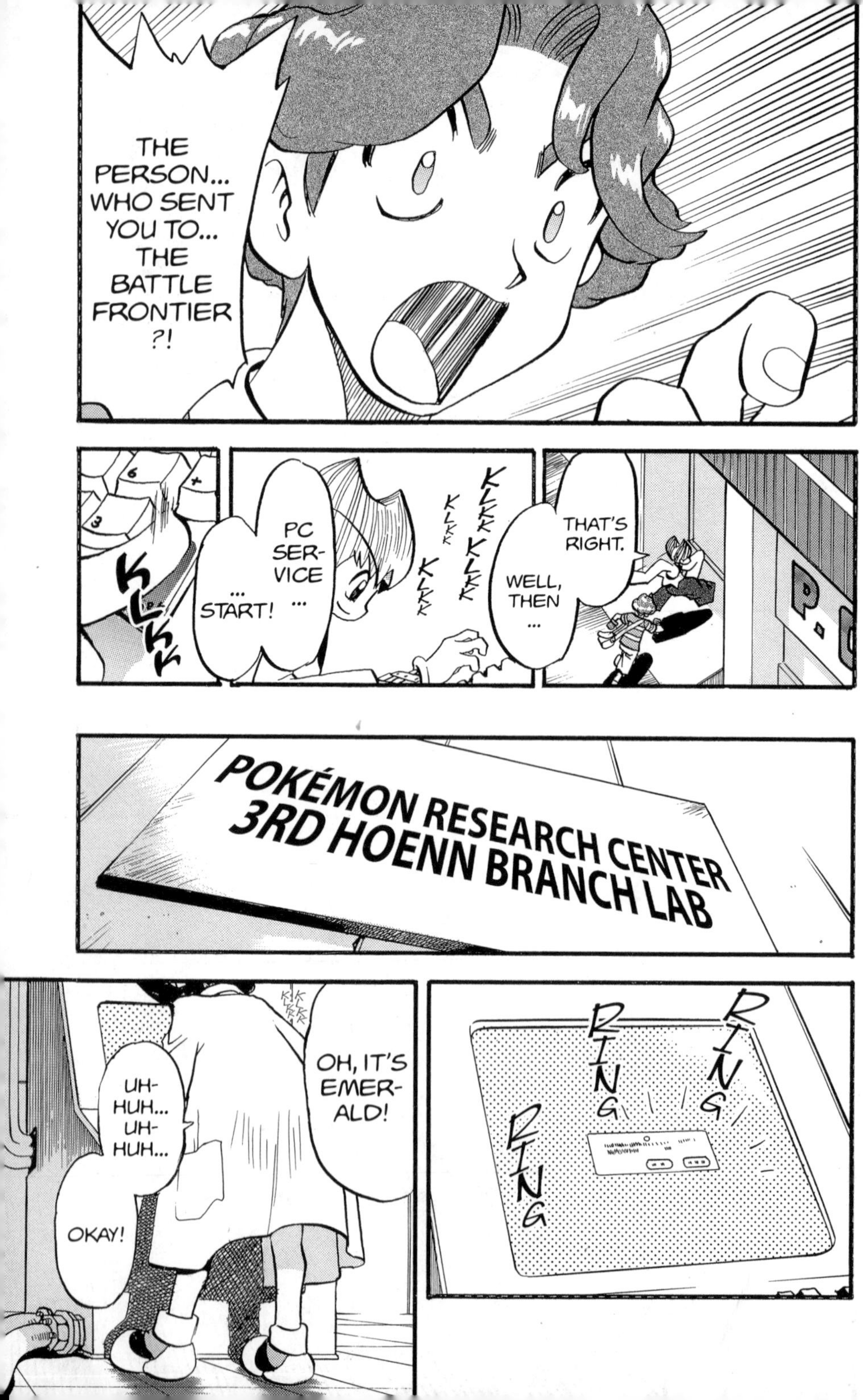
THE PERSON... WHO SENT YOU TO... THE BATTLE FRONTIER ?!
THAT'S RIGHT.
WELL, THEN ...
KLKK KLKK KLKK
KLKK KLKK
PC SERVICE ...
... START!
KLKK
POKÉMON RESEARCH CENTER
3RD HOENN BRANCH LAB
RING RING RING
KLKK KLKK
OH, IT'S EMERALD!
UH-HUH... UH-HUH...
OKAY!

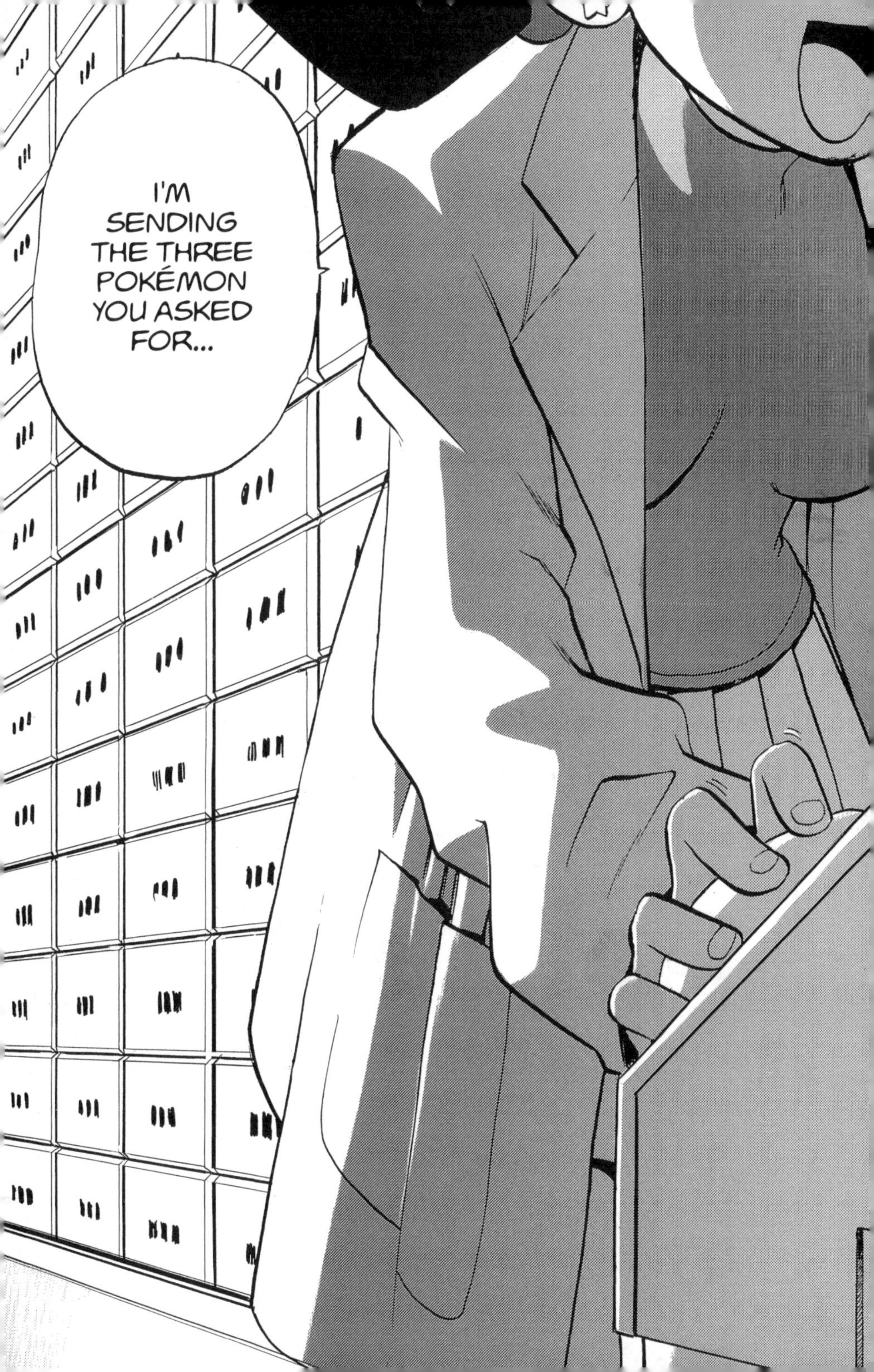
I'M SENDING THE THREE POKÉMON YOU ASKED FOR...

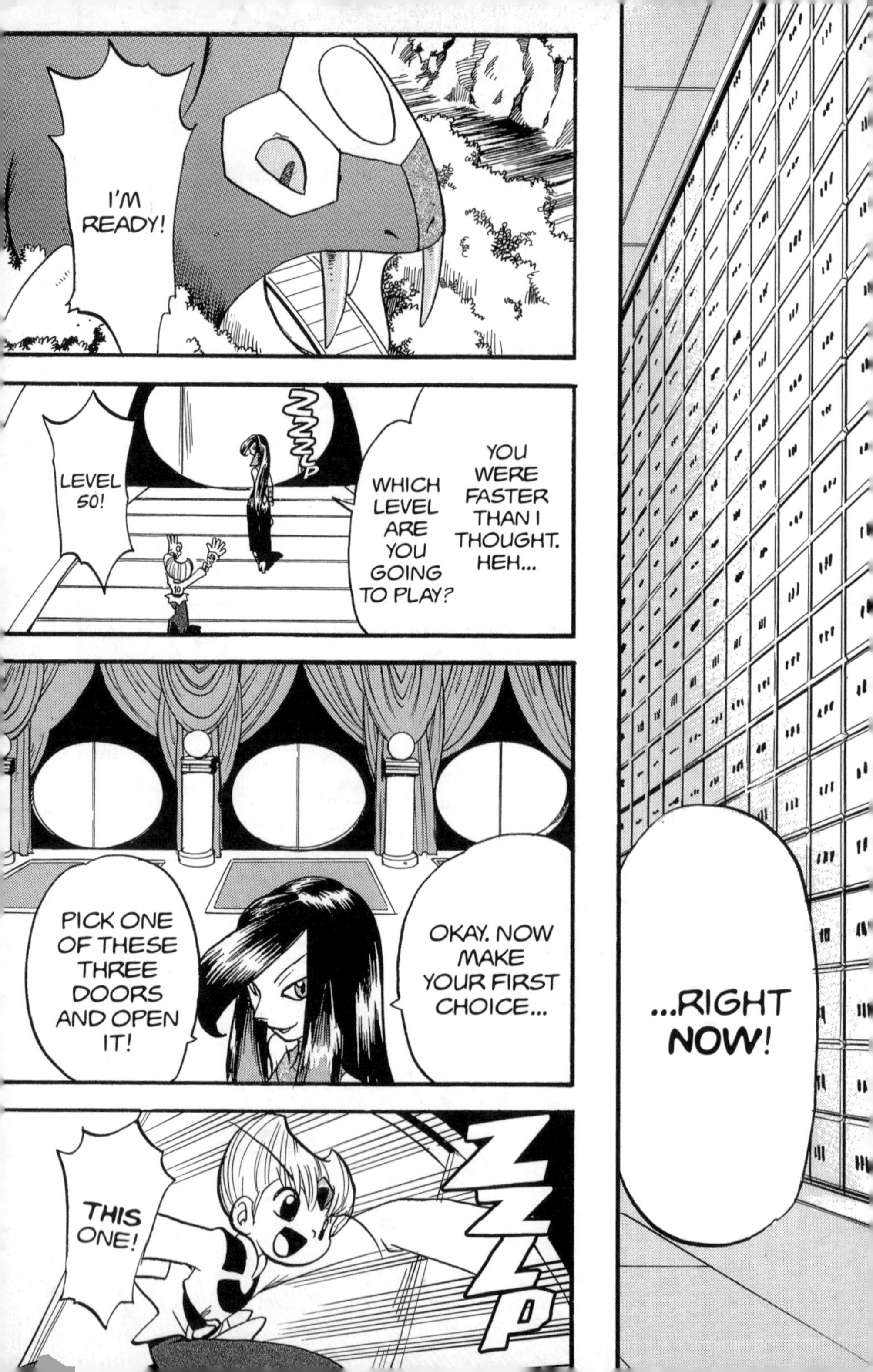
...RIGHT NOW!
I'M READY!
YOU WERE FASTER THAN I THOUGHT. HEH...
WHICH LEVEL ARE YOU GOING TO PLAY?
ZZZZP
LEVEL 50!
OKAY. NOW MAKE YOUR FIRST CHOICE...
PICK ONE OF THESE THREE DOORS AND OPEN IT!
ZZZP
THIS ONE!

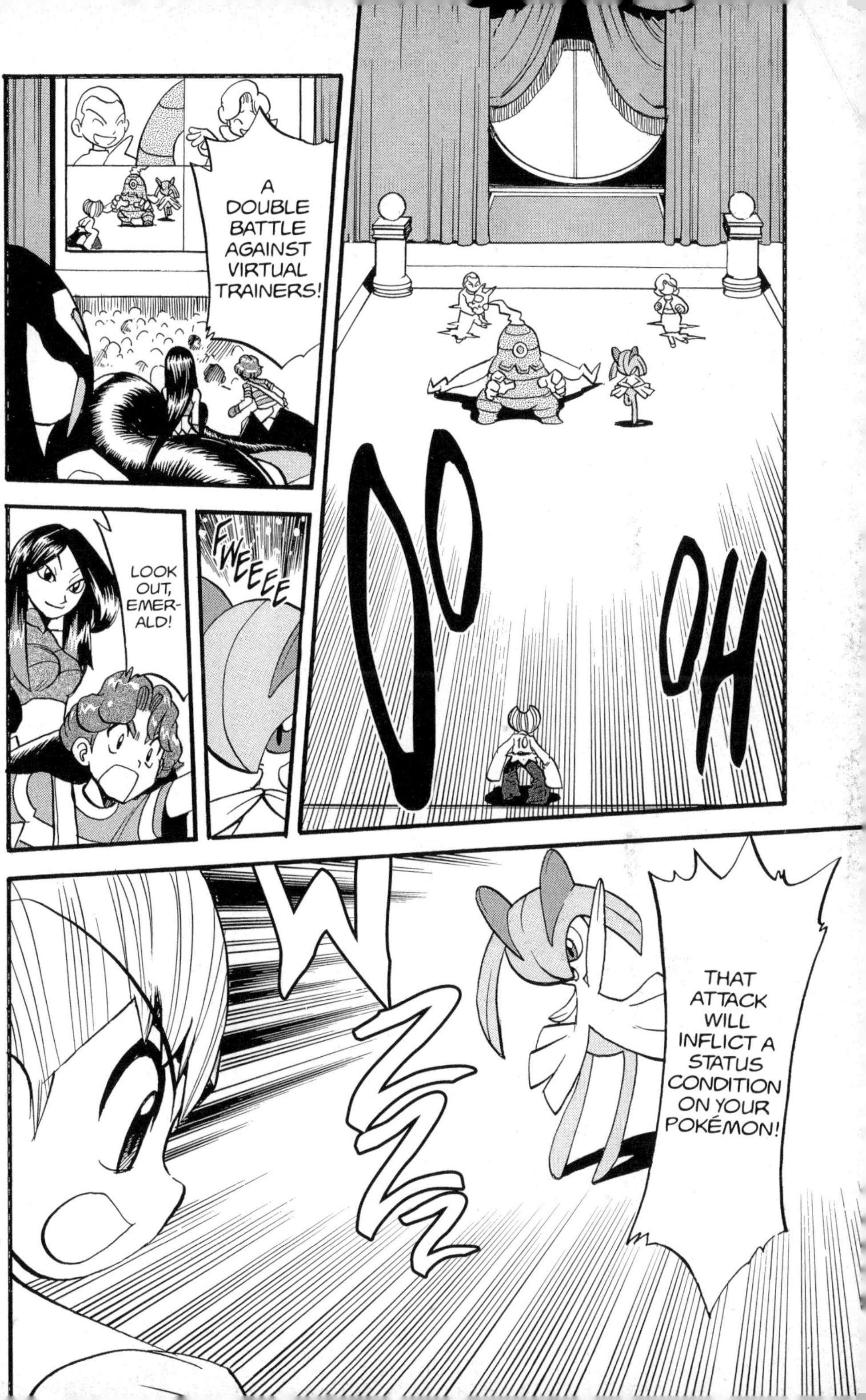
DOOH
A DOUBLE BATTLE AGAINST VIRTUAL TRAINERS!
FWEEEE
LOOK OUT, EMERALD!
THAT ATTACK WILL INFLICT A STATUS CONDITION ON YOUR POKÉMON!

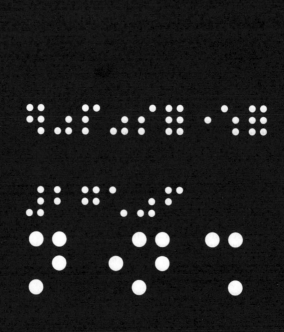

Message from
Hidenori Kusaka

Volume 27 of *Pokémon Adventures* was originally published ten years after the first volume of the series came out in Japan! I hardly ever think too much about what's happened in the past with it, but...this realization really affected me. Fans seemed to have an even stronger desire to celebrate, and I received many letters saying, "Congratulations on your tenth anniversary!" I was and continue to be so grateful...

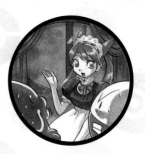

—2007

Message from
Satoshi Yamamoto

The challenges of the Battle Pike and the Battle Pyramid, the slightly klutzy but skilled Frontier Brains, a mysterious stranger, Emerald's secret mission, the Pokémon Latias's support of Emerald... Volume 27 is filled with all sorts of great adventures. I love all the adventures in this volume, and I've been reading them over and over again myself. I hope you enjoy them too!

—2007

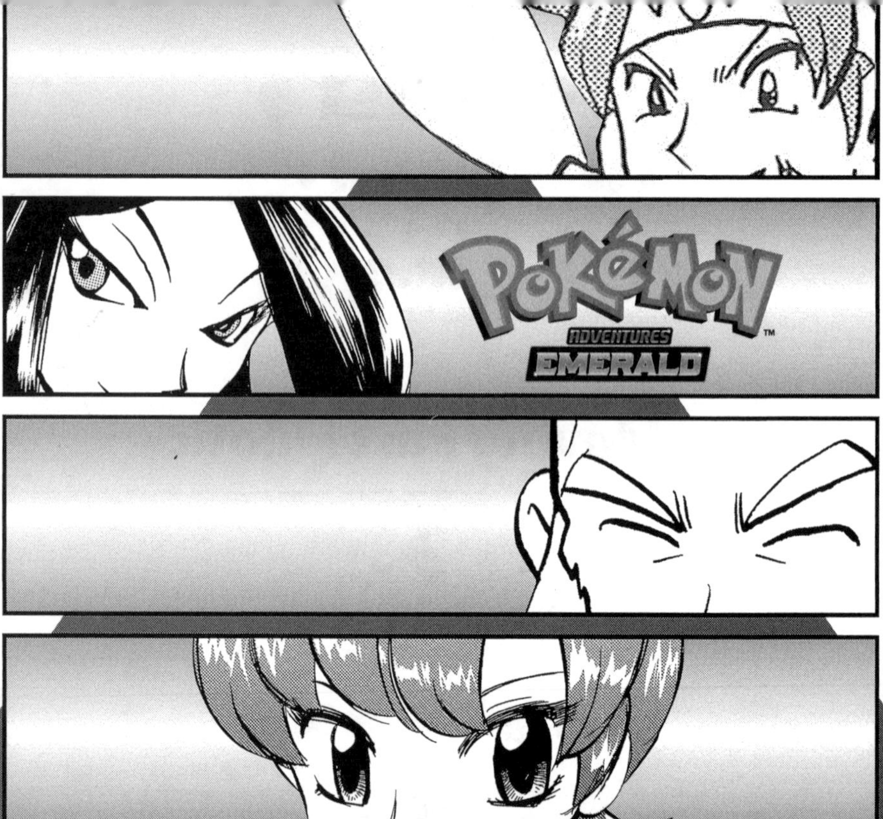
POKÉMON
ADVENTURES
EMERALD

Story by
Hidenori Kusaka

Art by
Satoshi Yamamoto

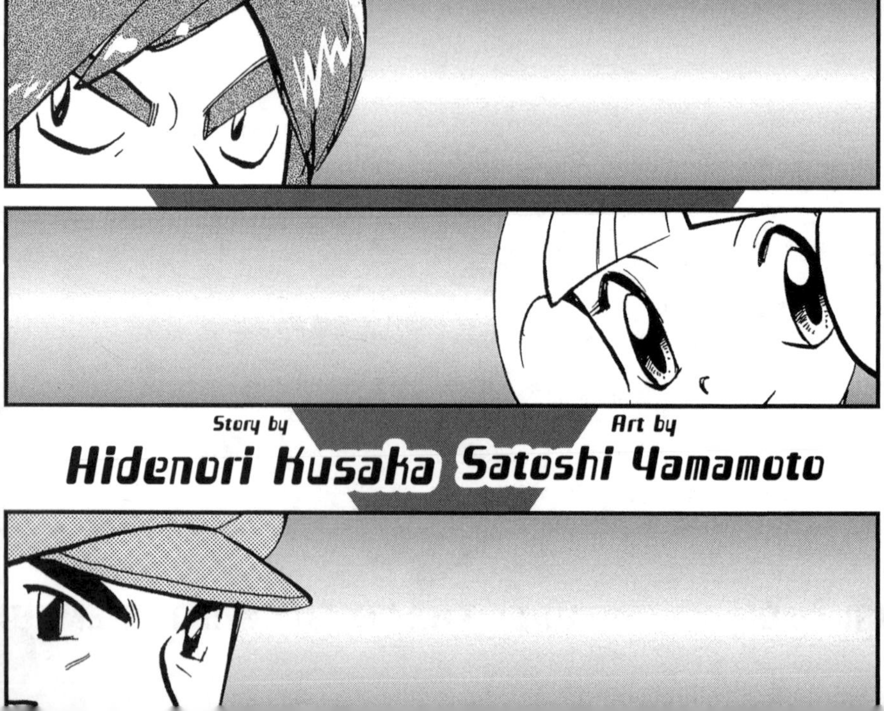

309

Moving Past Milotic

POKÉMON ADVENTURES•THE SIXTH CHAPTER•EMERALD

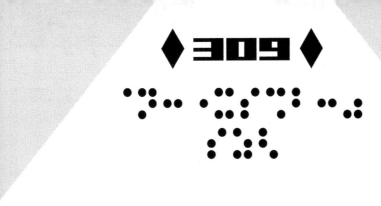

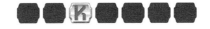

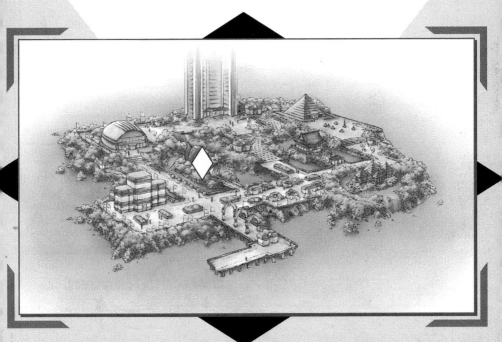

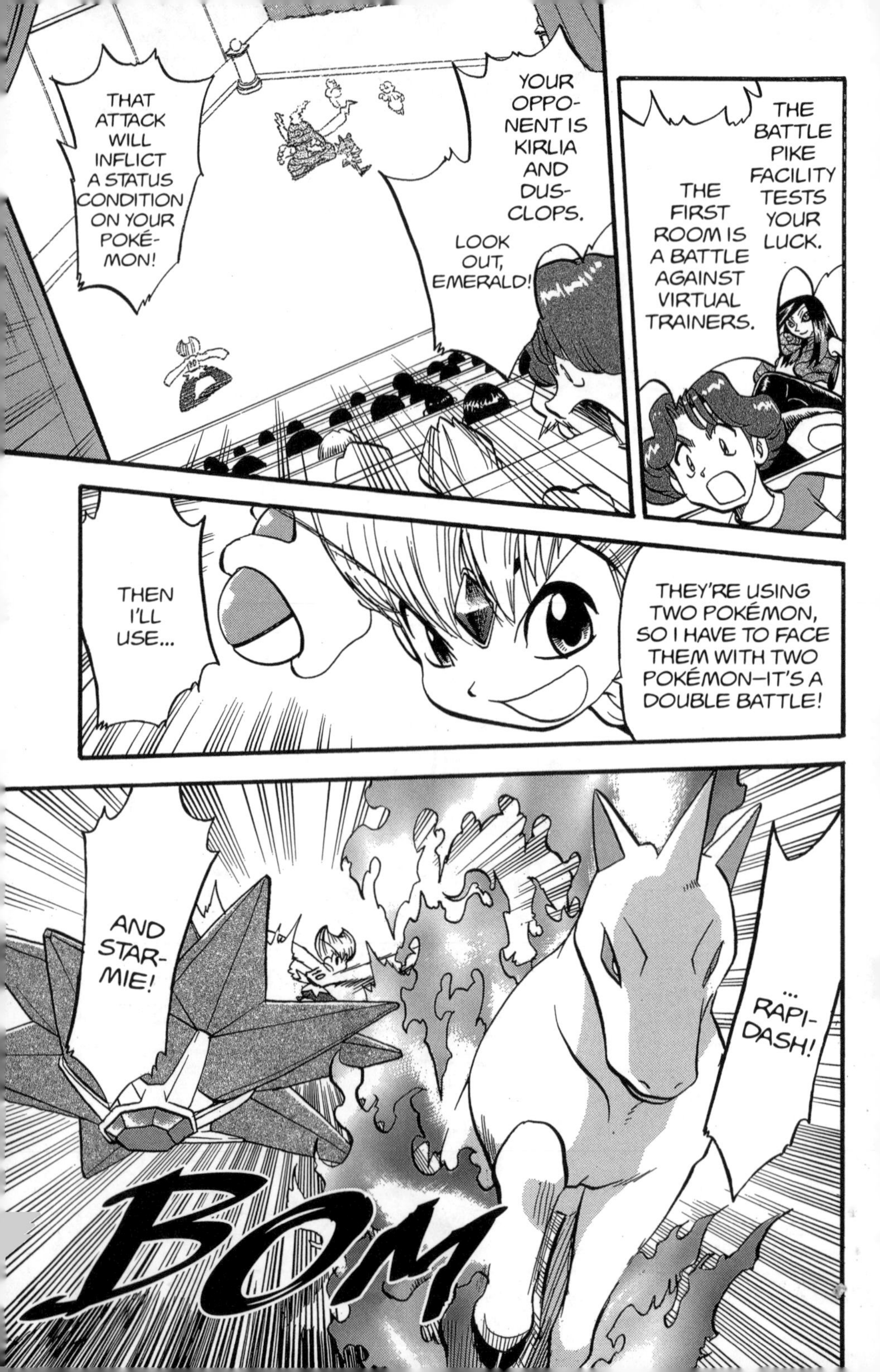
THE BATTLE PIKE FACILITY TESTS YOUR LUCK.
THE FIRST ROOM IS A BATTLE AGAINST VIRTUAL TRAINERS.
YOUR OPPO-NENT IS KIRLIA AND DUS-CLOPS.
LOOK OUT, EMERALD!
THAT ATTACK WILL INFLICT A STATUS CONDITION ON YOUR POKÉ-MON!
THEY'RE USING TWO POKÉMON, SO I HAVE TO FACE THEM WITH TWO POKÉMON—IT'S A DOUBLE BATTLE!
THEN I'LL USE...
...RAPI-DASH!
AND STAR-MIE!
BOM

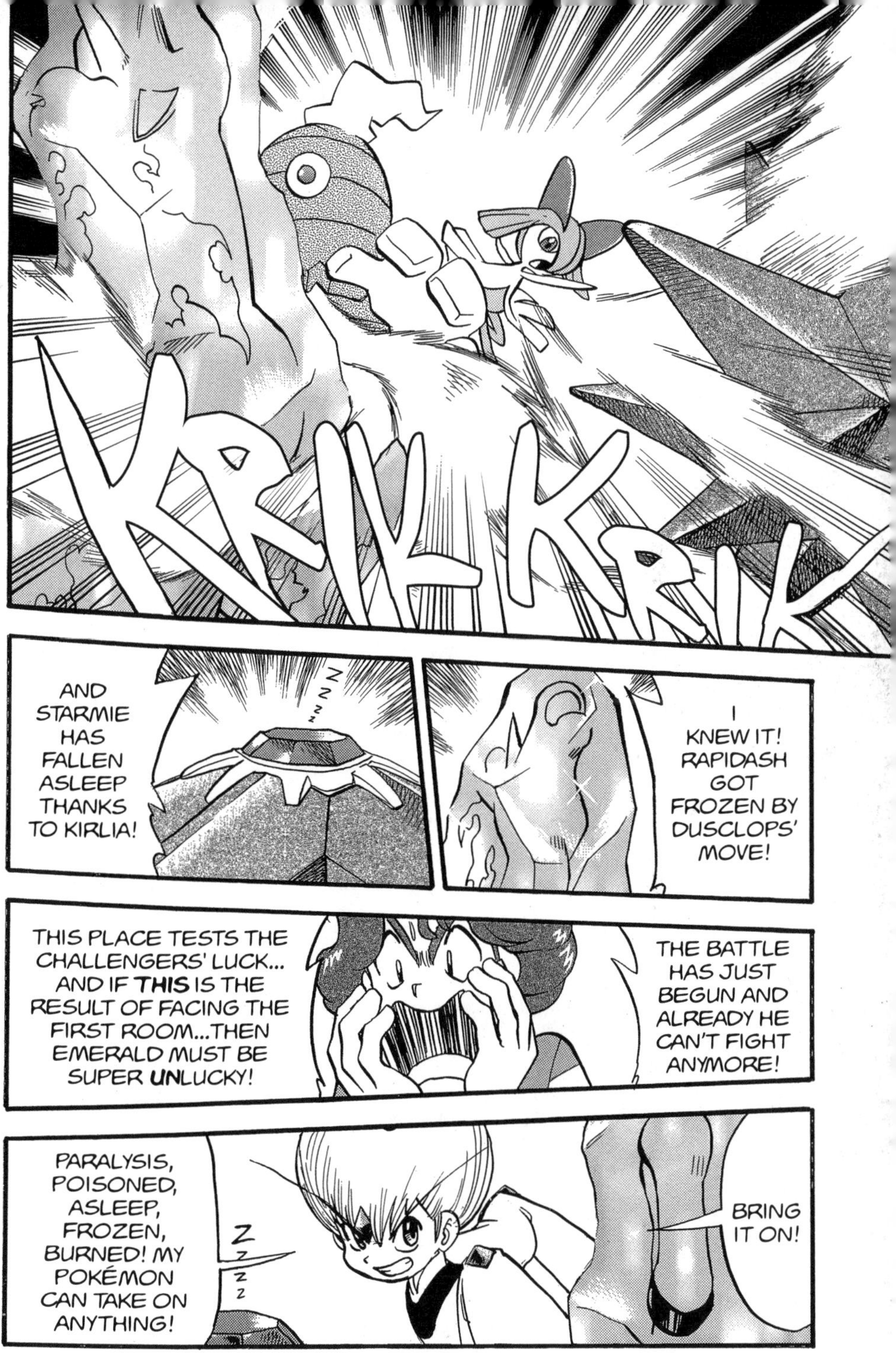
KRIK KRIK
I KNEW IT! RAPIDASH GOT FROZEN BY DUSCLOPS' MOVE!
ZZZZ
AND STARMIE HAS FALLEN ASLEEP THANKS TO KIRLIA!
THE BATTLE HAS JUST BEGUN AND ALREADY HE CAN'T FIGHT ANYMORE!
THIS PLACE TESTS THE CHALLENGERS' LUCK... AND IF **THIS** IS THE RESULT OF FACING THE FIRST ROOM...THEN EMERALD MUST BE SUPER **UN**LUCKY!
BRING IT ON!
ZZZ
PARALYSIS, POISONED, ASLEEP, FROZEN, BURNED! MY POKÉMON CAN TAKE ON ANYTHING!

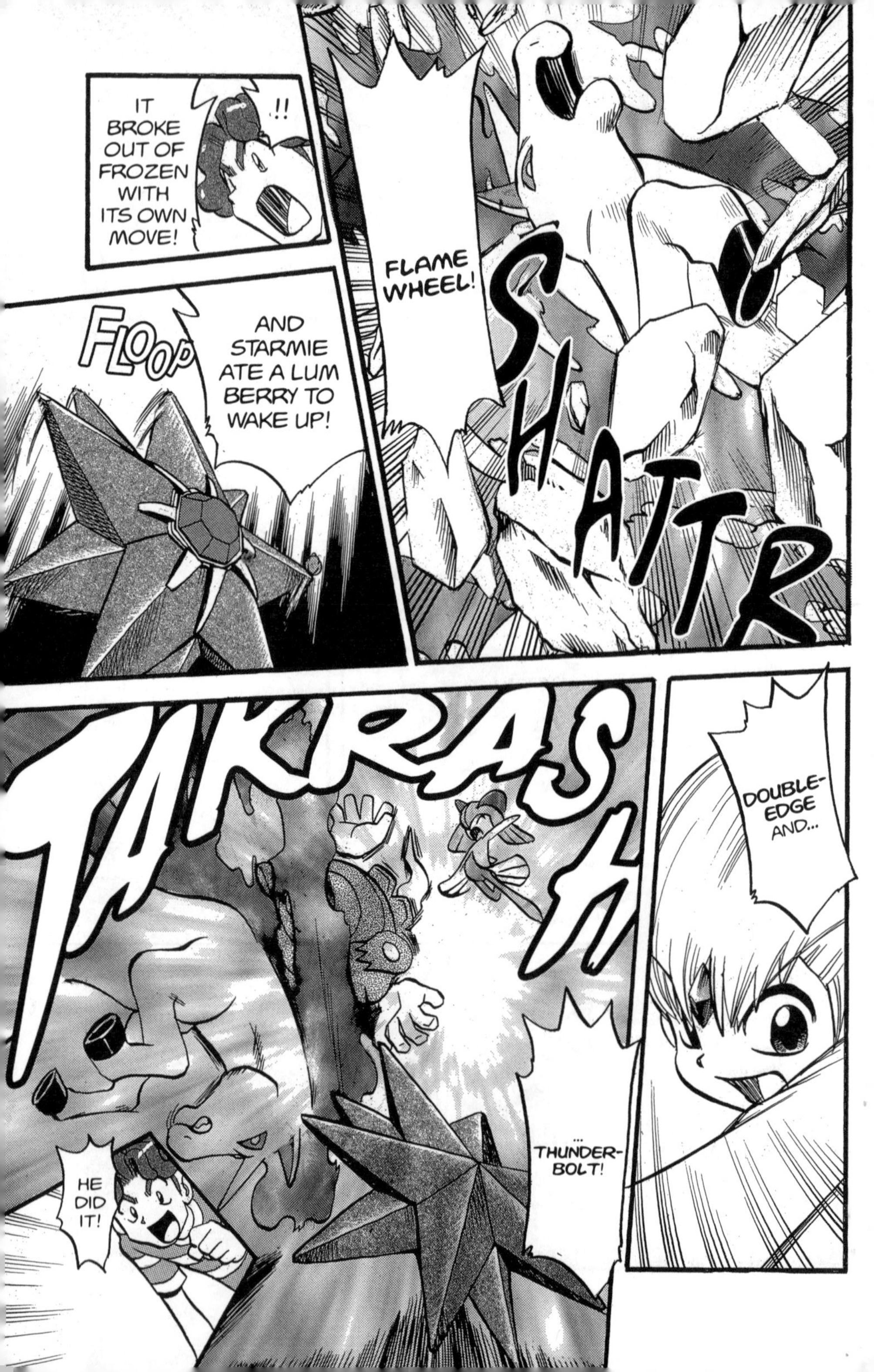
FLAME WHEEL!
SHATTR
IT BROKE OUT OF FROZEN WITH ITS OWN MOVE!
!!
FLOOP
AND STARMIE ATE A LUM BERRY TO WAKE UP!
DOUBLE-EDGE AND...
KRASH
...THUNDER-BOLT!
HE DID IT!

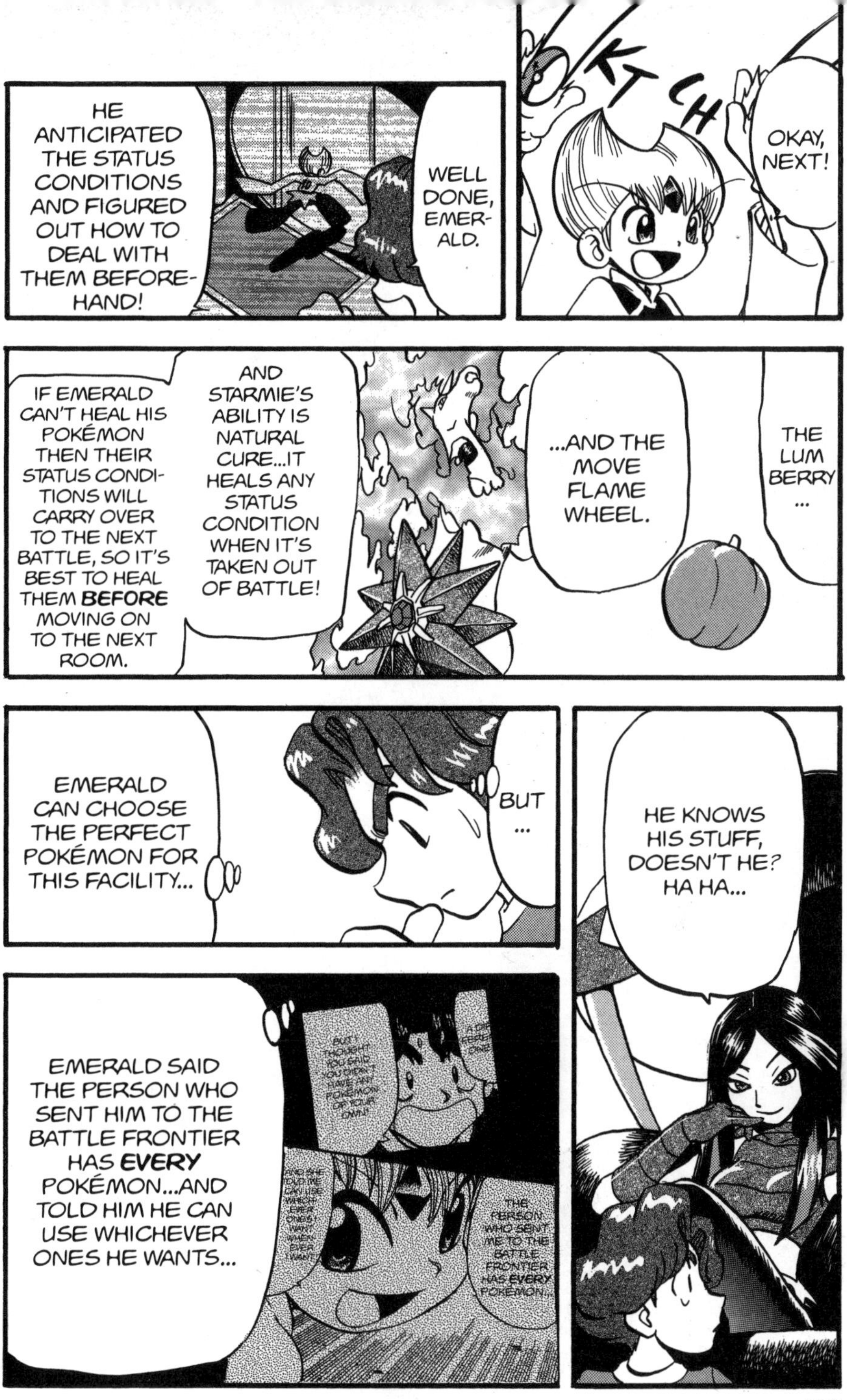
KTCH
OKAY, NEXT!
WELL DONE, EMERALD.
HE ANTICIPATED THE STATUS CONDITIONS AND FIGURED OUT HOW TO DEAL WITH THEM BEFOREHAND!
THE LUM BERRY...
...AND THE MOVE FLAME WHEEL.
AND STARMIE'S ABILITY IS NATURAL CURE...IT HEALS ANY STATUS CONDITION WHEN IT'S TAKEN OUT OF BATTLE!
IF EMERALD CAN'T HEAL HIS POKÉMON THEN THEIR STATUS CONDITIONS WILL CARRY OVER TO THE NEXT BATTLE, SO IT'S BEST TO HEAL THEM **BEFORE** MOVING ON TO THE NEXT ROOM.
HE KNOWS HIS STUFF, DOESN'T HE? HA HA...
BUT...
EMERALD CAN CHOOSE THE PERFECT POKÉMON FOR THIS FACILITY...
EMERALD SAID THE PERSON WHO SENT HIM TO THE BATTLE FRONTIER HAS **EVERY** POKÉMON...AND TOLD HIM HE CAN USE WHICHEVER ONES HE WANTS...
A DIFFERENT ONE
BUT I THOUGHT YOU SAID YOU DIDN'T HAVE ANY POKÉMON OF YOUR OWN!
THE PERSON WHO SENT ME TO THE BATTLE FRONTIER HAS **EVERY** POKÉMON...
AND SHE TOLD ME I CAN USE WHICHEVER ONES I WANT WHENEVER I WANT.

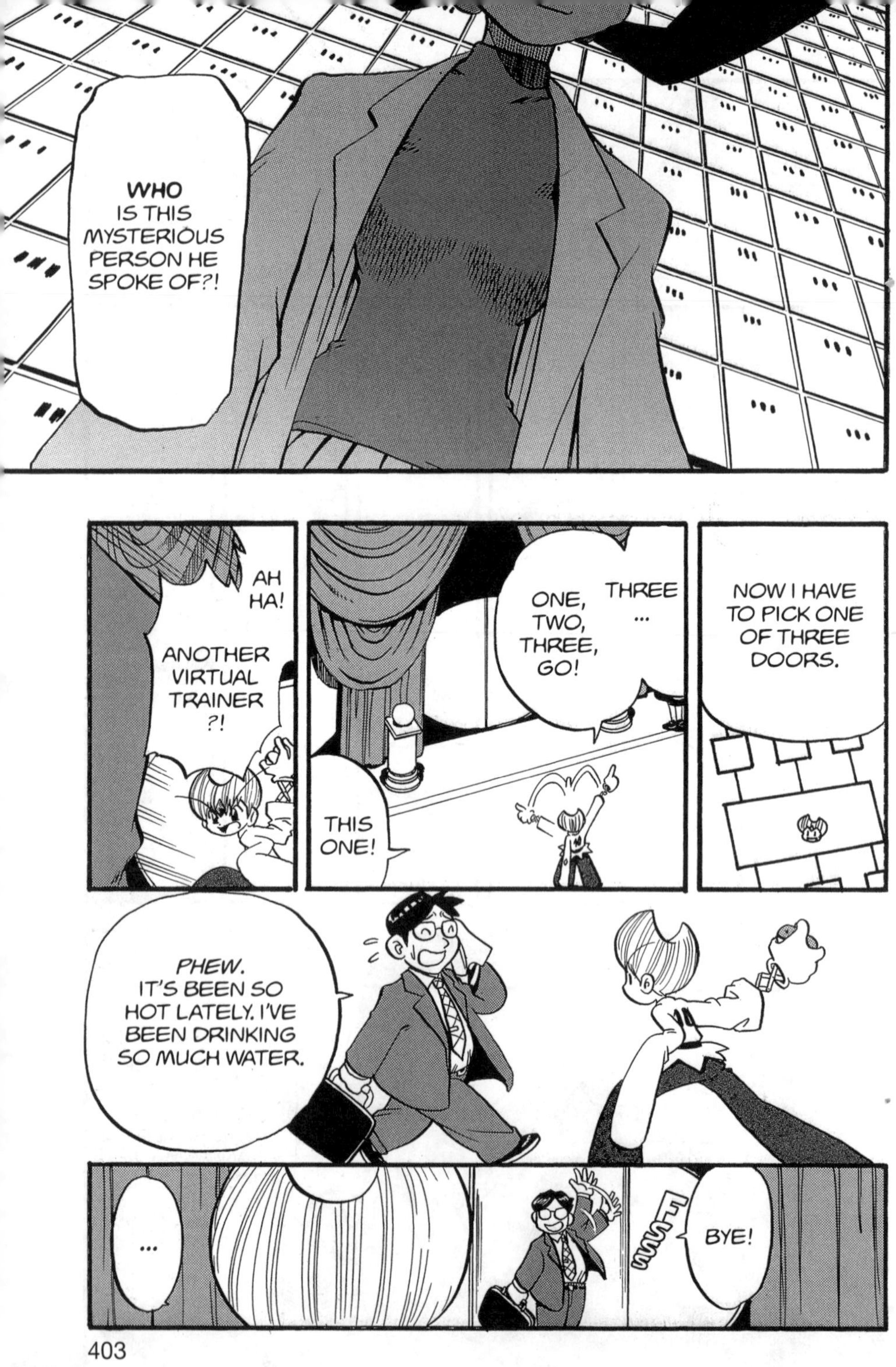
WHO IS THIS MYSTERIOUS PERSON HE SPOKE OF?!
NOW I HAVE TO PICK ONE OF THREE DOORS.
ONE, TWO, THREE, GO!
THREE ...
THIS ONE!
AH HA!
ANOTHER VIRTUAL TRAINER ?!
PHEW. IT'S BEEN SO HOT LATELY. I'VE BEEN DRINKING SO MUCH WATER.
BYE!
...

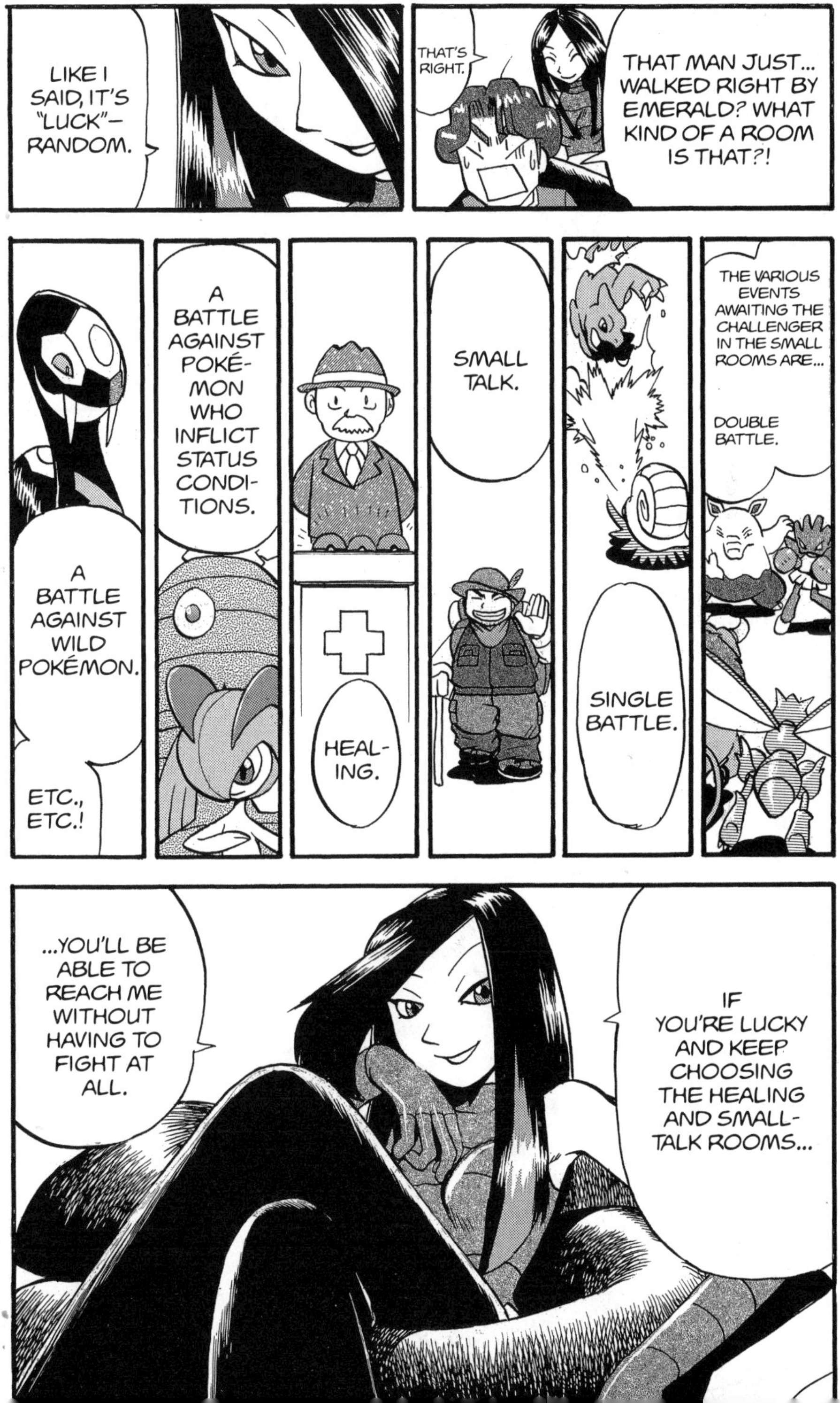
THAT MAN JUST... WALKED RIGHT BY EMERALD? WHAT KIND OF A ROOM IS THAT?!
THAT'S RIGHT.
LIKE I SAID, IT'S "LUCK"—RANDOM.
THE VARIOUS EVENTS AWAITING THE CHALLENGER IN THE SMALL ROOMS ARE...
DOUBLE BATTLE.
SINGLE BATTLE.
SMALL TALK.
HEALING.
A BATTLE AGAINST POKÉMON WHO INFLICT STATUS CONDITIONS.
A BATTLE AGAINST WILD POKÉMON.
ETC., ETC.!
IF YOU'RE LUCKY AND KEEP CHOOSING THE HEALING AND SMALL-TALK ROOMS...
...YOU'LL BE ABLE TO REACH ME WITHOUT HAVING TO FIGHT AT ALL.

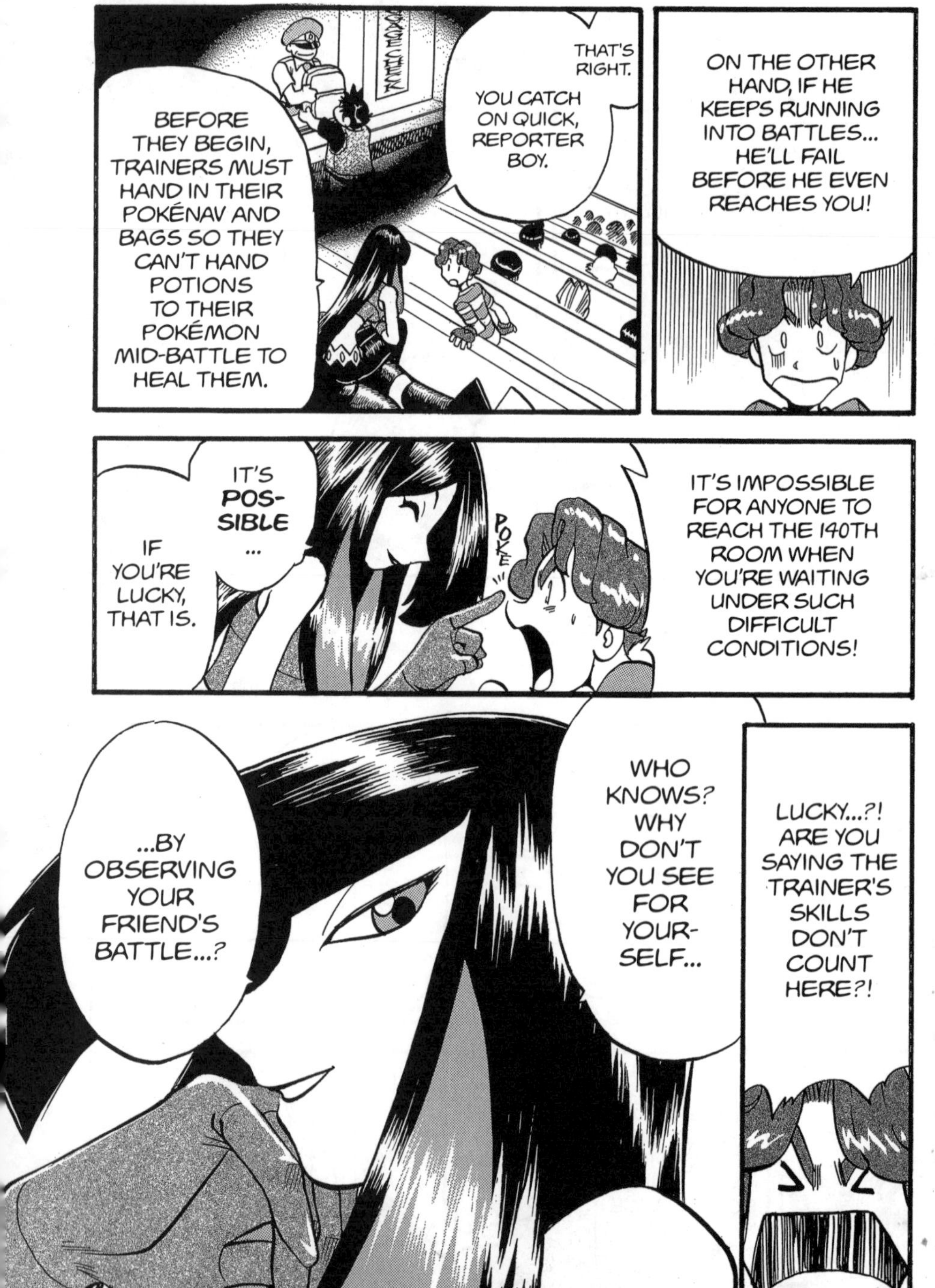
ON THE OTHER HAND, IF HE KEEPS RUNNING INTO BATTLES... HE'LL FAIL BEFORE HE EVEN REACHES YOU!
THAT'S RIGHT.
YOU CATCH ON QUICK, REPORTER BOY.
BEFORE THEY BEGIN, TRAINERS MUST HAND IN THEIR POKÉNAV AND BAGS SO THEY CAN'T HAND POTIONS TO THEIR POKÉMON MID-BATTLE TO HEAL THEM.
IT'S IMPOSSIBLE FOR ANYONE TO REACH THE 140TH ROOM WHEN YOU'RE WAITING UNDER SUCH DIFFICULT CONDITIONS!
POKE
IT'S **POSSIBLE**...
IF YOU'RE LUCKY, THAT IS.
LUCKY...?! ARE YOU SAYING THE TRAINER'S SKILLS DON'T COUNT HERE?!
WHO KNOWS? WHY DON'T YOU SEE FOR YOURSELF...
...BY OBSERVING YOUR FRIEND'S BATTLE...?

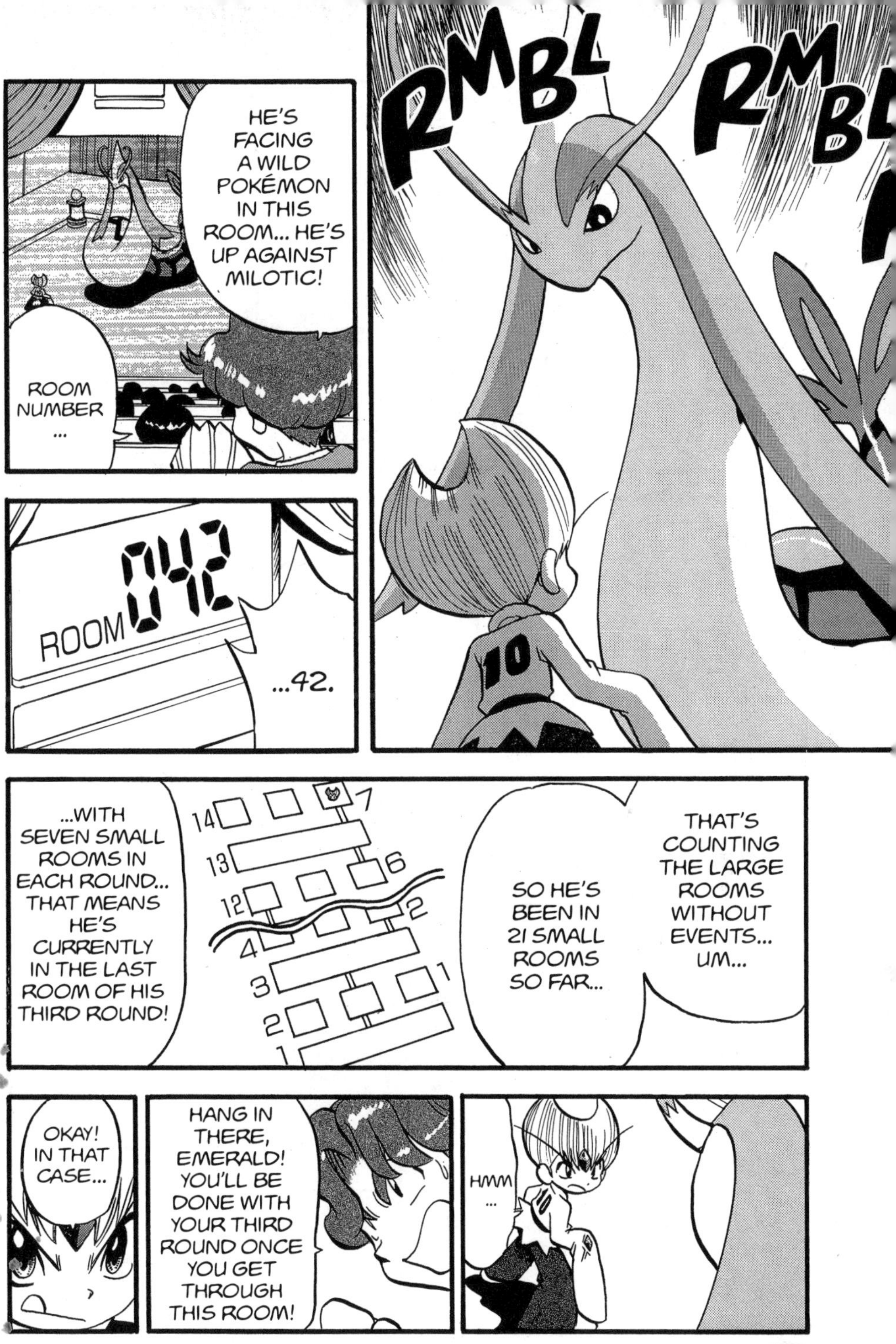
RMBL RMBL
HE'S FACING A WILD POKÉMON IN THIS ROOM... HE'S UP AGAINST MILOTIC!
ROOM NUMBER ...
ROOM 042
...42.
THAT'S COUNTING THE LARGE ROOMS WITHOUT EVENTS... UM...
SO HE'S BEEN IN 21 SMALL ROOMS SO FAR...
...WITH SEVEN SMALL ROOMS IN EACH ROUND... THAT MEANS HE'S CURRENTLY IN THE LAST ROOM OF HIS THIRD ROUND!
HMM ...
HANG IN THERE, EMERALD! YOU'LL BE DONE WITH YOUR THIRD ROUND ONCE YOU GET THROUGH THIS ROOM!
OKAY! IN THAT CASE...

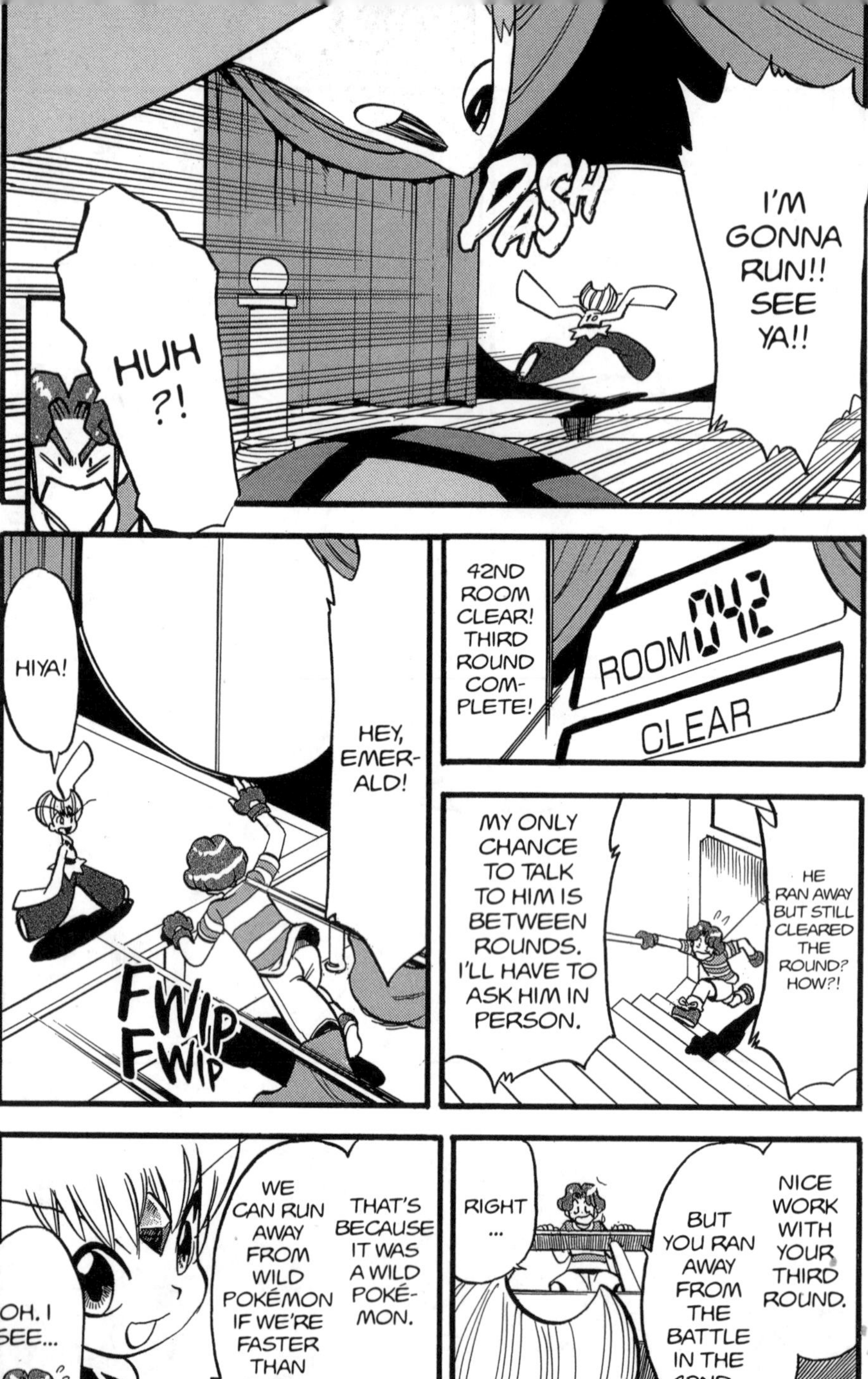
I'M GONNA RUN!! SEE YA!!
DASH
HUH ?!
ROOM 042
CLEAR
42ND ROOM CLEAR! THIRD ROUND COM-PLETE!
HE RAN AWAY BUT STILL CLEARED THE ROUND? HOW?!
MY ONLY CHANCE TO TALK TO HIM IS BETWEEN ROUNDS. I'LL HAVE TO ASK HIM IN PERSON.
HEY, EMER-ALD!
HIYA!
FWIP FWIP
NICE WORK WITH YOUR THIRD ROUND.
BUT YOU RAN AWAY FROM THE BATTLE IN THE 42ND...
RIGHT ...
THAT'S BECAUSE IT WAS A WILD POKÉ-MON.
WE CAN RUN AWAY FROM WILD POKÉMON IF WE'RE FASTER THAN THEM, RIGHT?
OH. I SEE...

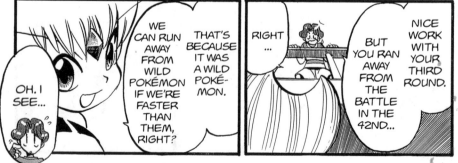

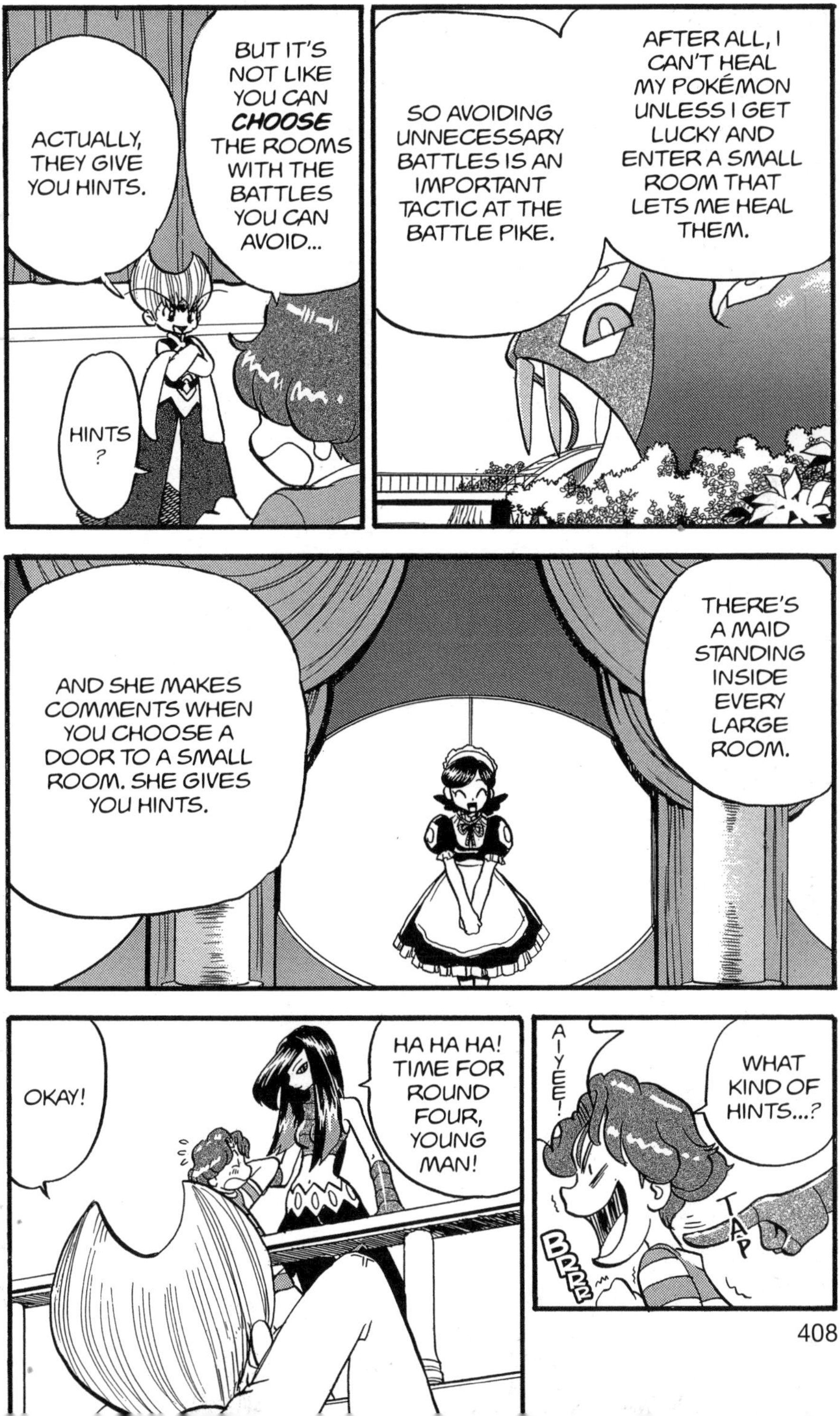
AFTER ALL, I CAN'T HEAL MY POKÉMON UNLESS I GET LUCKY AND ENTER A SMALL ROOM THAT LETS ME HEAL THEM.
SO AVOIDING UNNECESSARY BATTLES IS AN IMPORTANT TACTIC AT THE BATTLE PIKE.
BUT IT'S NOT LIKE YOU CAN ***CHOOSE*** THE ROOMS WITH THE BATTLES YOU CAN AVOID...
ACTUALLY, THEY GIVE YOU HINTS.
HINTS ?
THERE'S A MAID STANDING INSIDE EVERY LARGE ROOM.
AND SHE MAKES COMMENTS WHEN YOU CHOOSE A DOOR TO A SMALL ROOM. SHE GIVES YOU HINTS.
AIYEEE!
WHAT KIND OF HINTS...?
TAP
BRRR
HA HA HA! TIME FOR ROUND FOUR, YOUNG MAN!
OKAY!

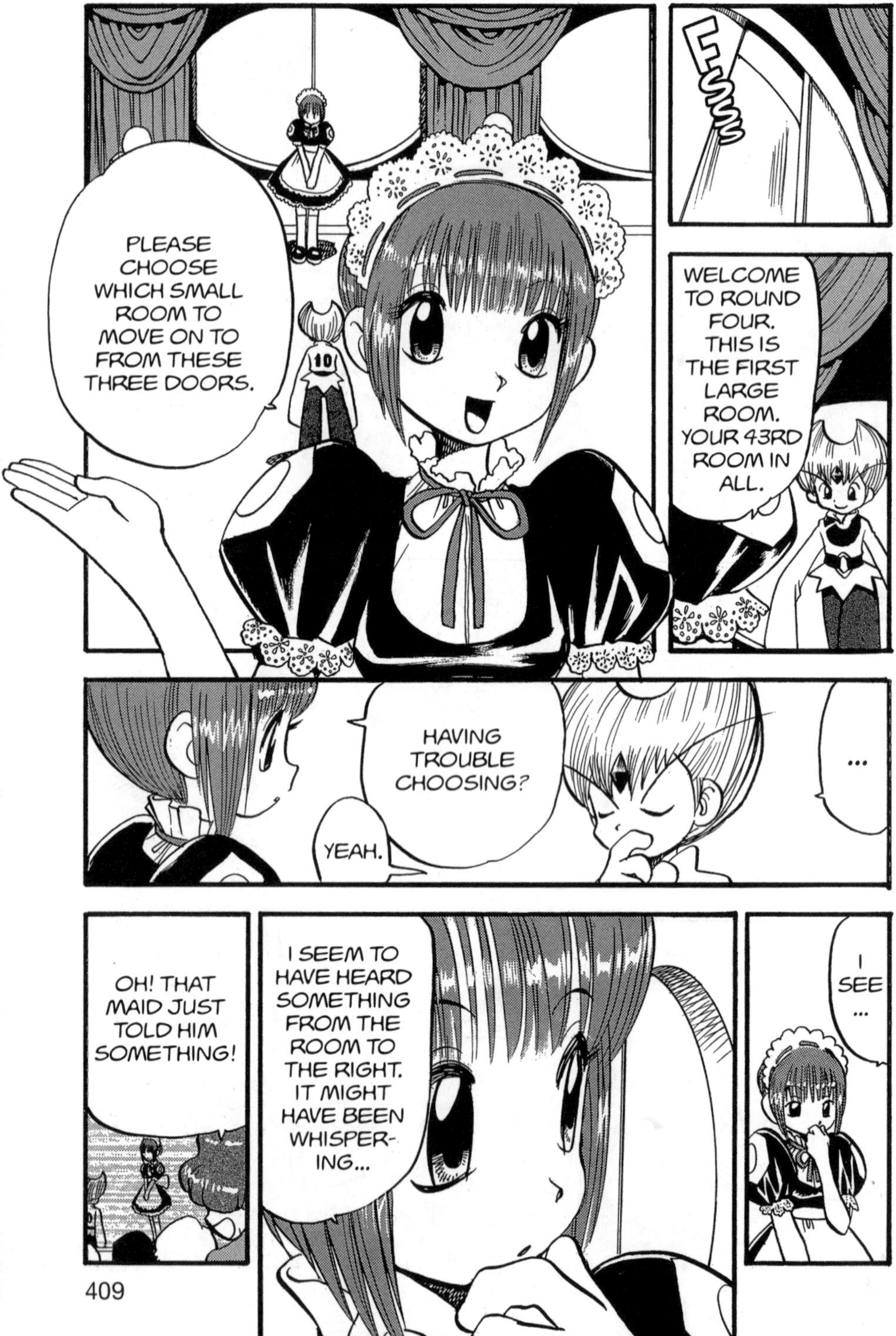
FSSS
WELCOME TO ROUND FOUR. THIS IS THE FIRST LARGE ROOM. YOUR 43RD ROOM IN ALL.
PLEASE CHOOSE WHICH SMALL ROOM TO MOVE ON TO FROM THESE THREE DOORS.
...
HAVING TROUBLE CHOOSING?
YEAH.
I SEE...
I SEEM TO HAVE HEARD SOMETHING FROM THE ROOM TO THE RIGHT. IT MIGHT HAVE BEEN WHISPER-ING...
OH! THAT MAID JUST TOLD HIM SOMETHING!

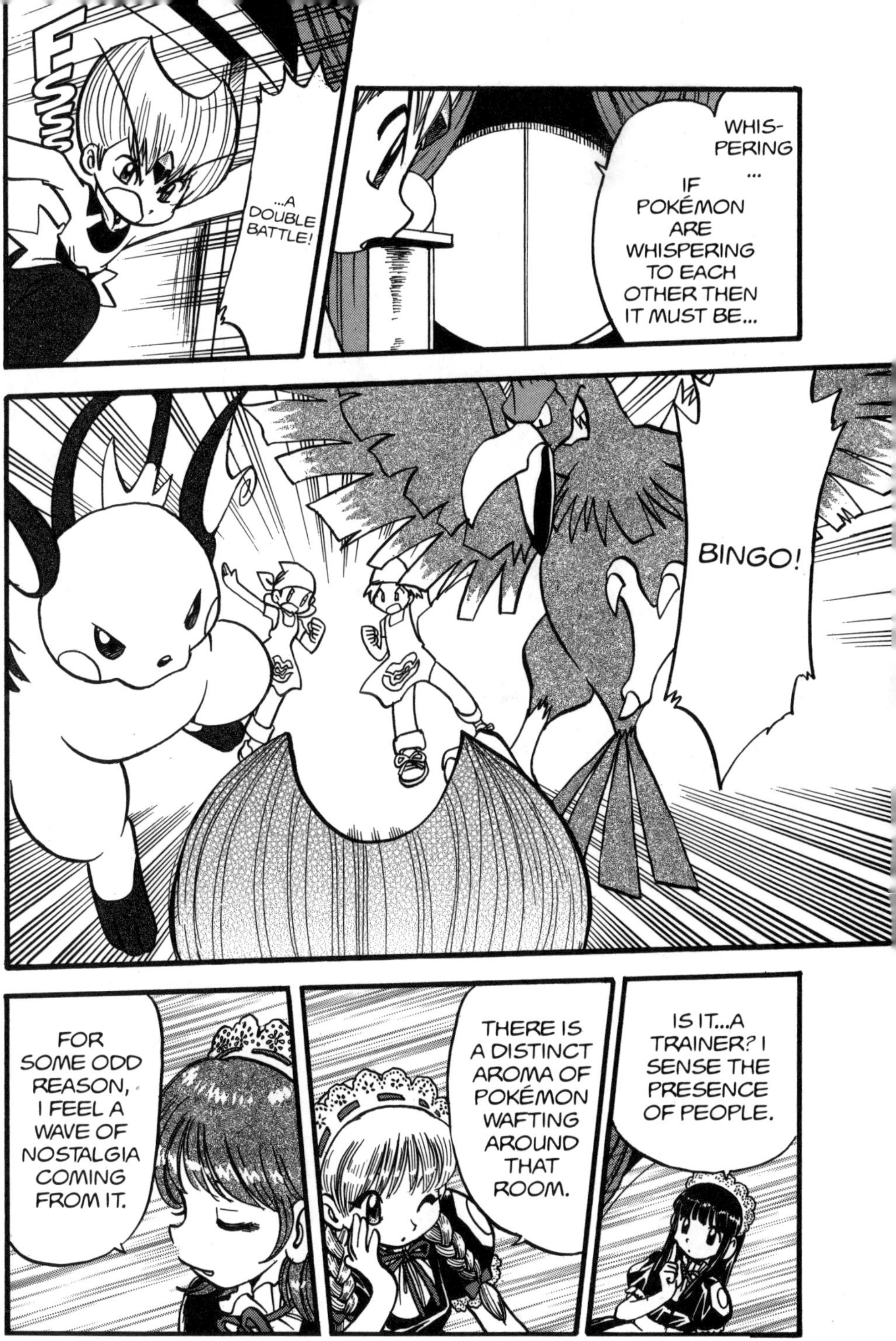
WHIS-PERING ...
IF POKÉMON ARE WHISPERING TO EACH OTHER THEN IT MUST BE...
FSSS
...A DOUBLE BATTLE!
BINGO!
IS IT...A TRAINER? I SENSE THE PRESENCE OF PEOPLE.
THERE IS A DISTINCT AROMA OF POKÉMON WAFTING AROUND THAT ROOM.
FOR SOME ODD REASON, I FEEL A WAVE OF NOSTALGIA COMING FROM IT.

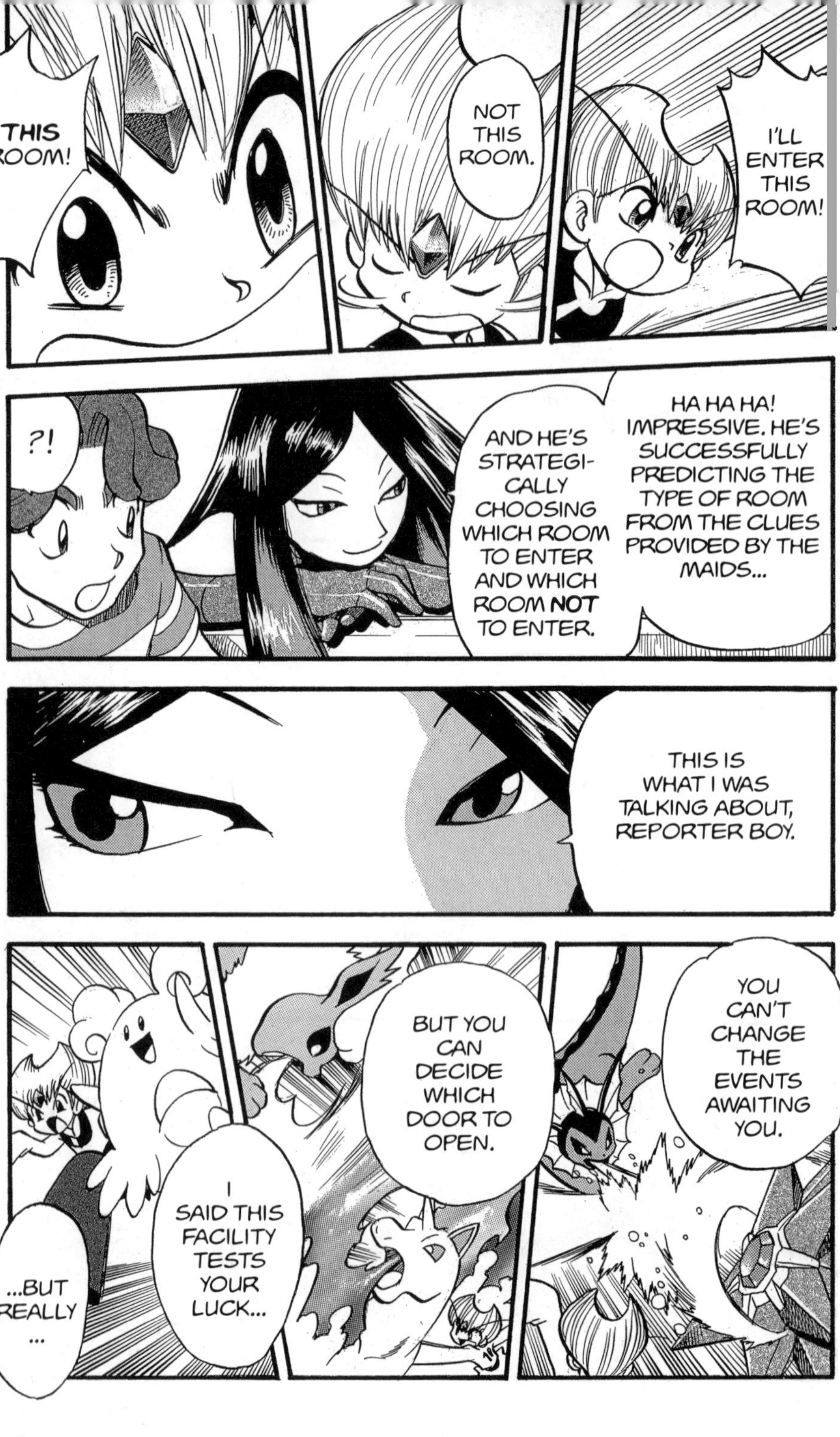
I'LL ENTER THIS ROOM!
NOT THIS ROOM.
THIS ROOM!
HA HA HA! IMPRESSIVE. HE'S SUCCESSFULLY PREDICTING THE TYPE OF ROOM FROM THE CLUES PROVIDED BY THE MAIDS...
AND HE'S STRATEGI-CALLY CHOOSING WHICH ROOM TO ENTER AND WHICH ROOM **NOT** TO ENTER.
?!
THIS IS WHAT I WAS TALKING ABOUT, REPORTER BOY.
YOU CAN'T CHANGE THE EVENTS AWAITING YOU.
BUT YOU CAN DECIDE WHICH DOOR TO OPEN.
I SAID THIS FACILITY TESTS YOUR LUCK...
...BUT REALLY ...

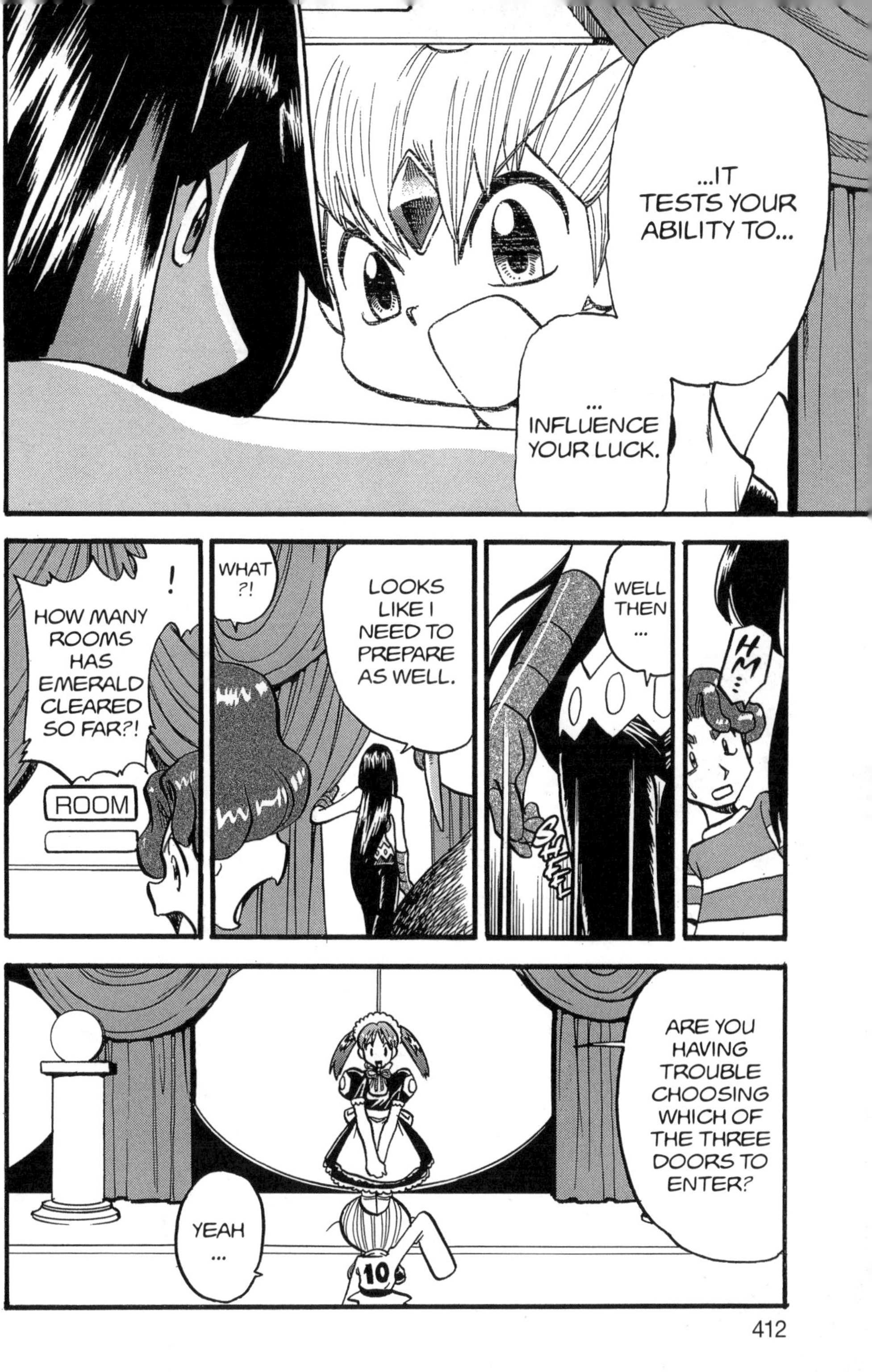
...IT TESTS YOUR ABILITY TO...
... INFLUENCE YOUR LUCK.
HM...
WELL THEN ...
LOOKS LIKE I NEED TO PREPARE AS WELL.
WHAT ?!
!
HOW MANY ROOMS HAS EMERALD CLEARED SO FAR?!
ROOM
ARE YOU HAVING TROUBLE CHOOSING WHICH OF THE THREE DOORS TO ENTER?
YEAH ...
10

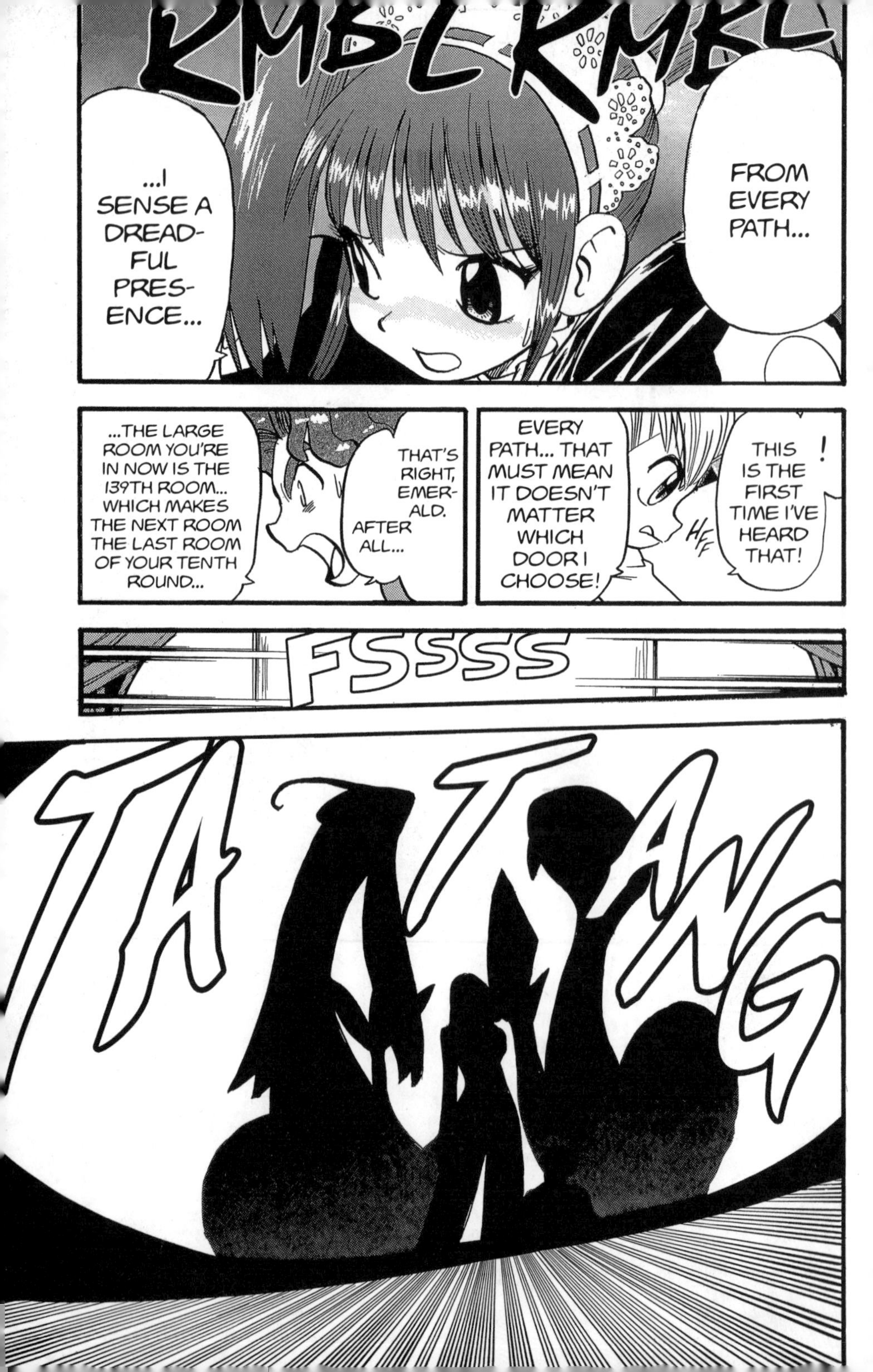
RMBL RMBL
FROM EVERY PATH...
...I SENSE A DREADFUL PRESENCE...
THIS IS THE FIRST TIME I'VE HEARD THAT!
!
HFF
EVERY PATH... THAT MUST MEAN IT DOESN'T MATTER WHICH DOOR I CHOOSE!
THAT'S RIGHT, EMERALD.
AFTER ALL...
...THE LARGE ROOM YOU'RE IN NOW IS THE 139TH ROOM... WHICH MAKES THE NEXT ROOM THE LAST ROOM OF YOUR TENTH ROUND...
FSSSS
TA TANG

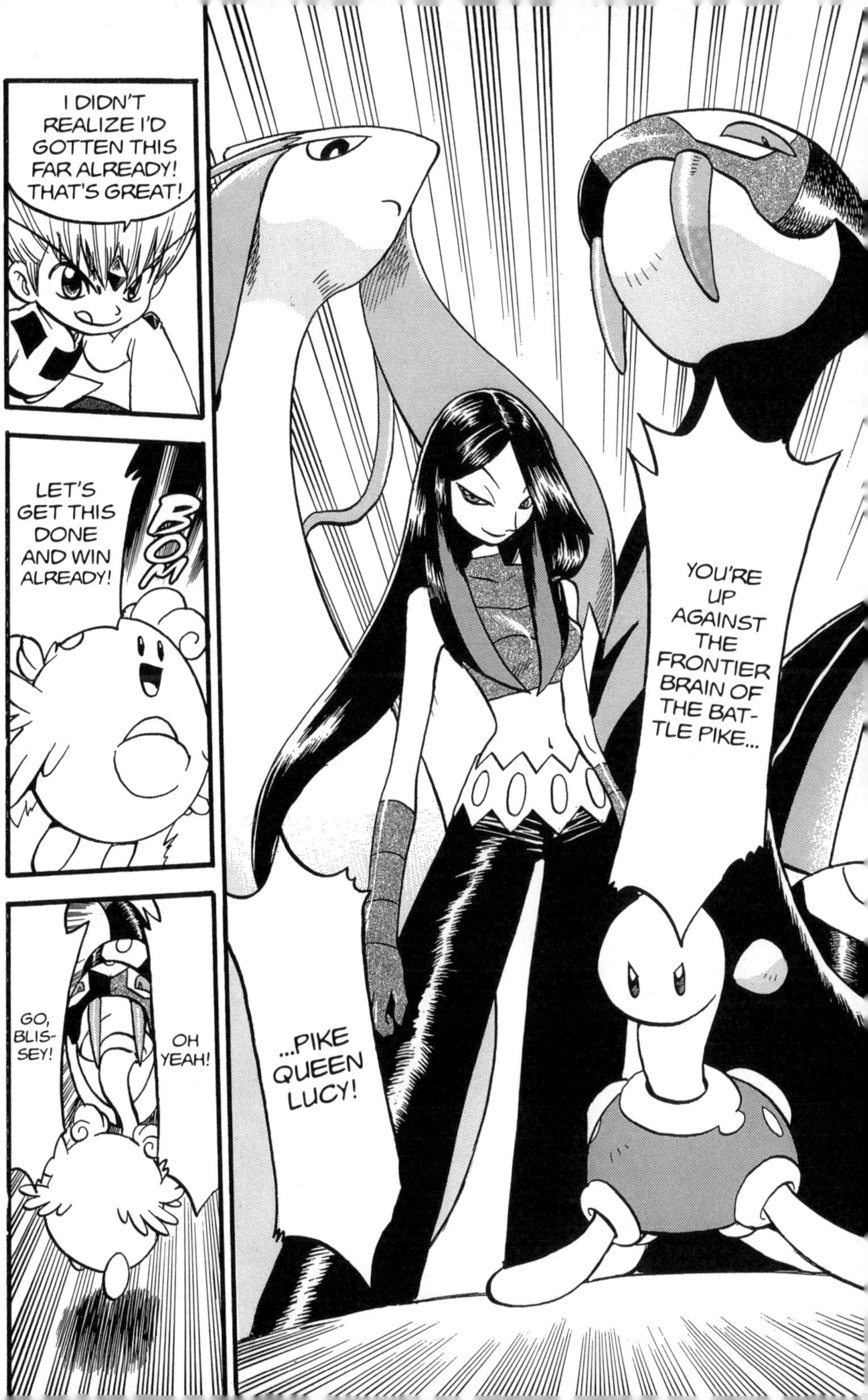
YOU'RE UP AGAINST THE FRONTIER BRAIN OF THE BAT-TLE PIKE...
...PIKE QUEEN LUCY!
I DIDN'T REALIZE I'D GOTTEN THIS FAR ALREADY! THAT'S GREAT!
LET'S GET THIS DONE AND WIN ALREADY!
BOM
OH YEAH!
GO, BLIS-SEY!

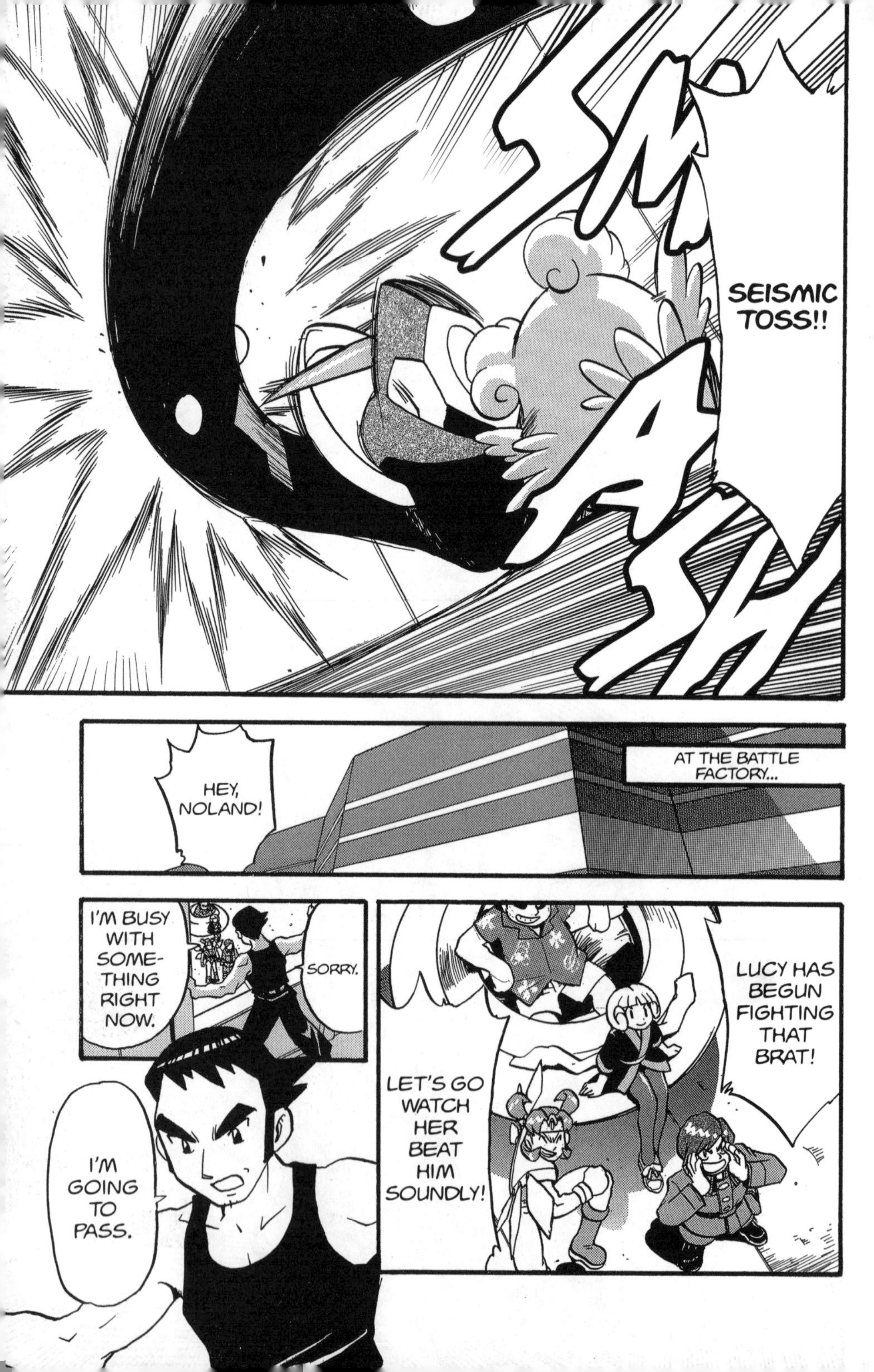
SMASH
SEISMIC TOSS!!
AT THE BATTLE FACTORY...
HEY, NOLAND!
LUCY HAS BEGUN FIGHTING THAT BRAT!
LET'S GO WATCH HER BEAT HIM SOUNDLY!
SORRY.
I'M BUSY WITH SOME-THING RIGHT NOW.
I'M GOING TO PASS.

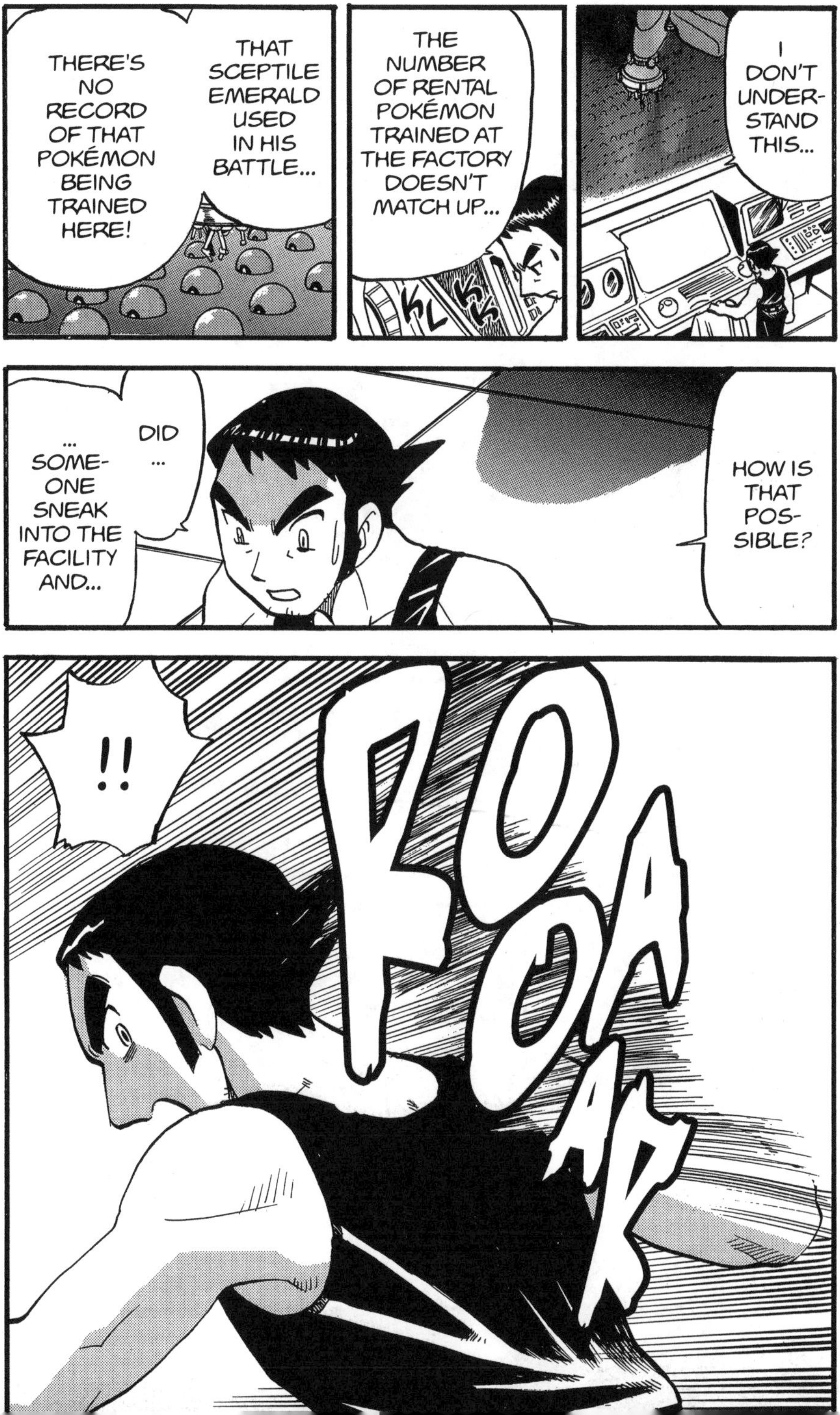
I DON'T UNDER-STAND THIS...
THE NUMBER OF RENTAL POKÉMON TRAINED AT THE FACTORY DOESN'T MATCH UP...
THAT SCEPTILE EMERALD USED IN HIS BATTLE...
THERE'S NO RECORD OF THAT POKÉMON BEING TRAINED HERE!
HOW IS THAT POS-SIBLE?
DID ...
... SOME-ONE SNEAK INTO THE FACILITY AND...
ROOAAR
!!

DEAR MEMBERS OF THE PRESS...

Thank you for visiting the Battle Frontier today. Permit me to continue explaining the rules of this facility...

OWNER: SCOTT

FACILITY RULES

BATTLE PIKE 2

There are eight encounters you may experience inside the small rooms in the Battle Pike. I will describe them here.

■ SMALL ROOM ENCOUNTERS (8 TYPES) ■

① Single Battle Room
A Single Battle against a Trainer with three Pokémon.

② Double Battle Room
A Double Battle against two Trainers who each have one Pokémon.

③ Tough Opponent Room
A Single Battle against a skilled Trainer with three Pokémon. If you win, your Pokémon will be fully healed.

④ Wild Pokémon Room
You will face wild Pokémon like Seviper, Milotic and Dusclops who have moves that inflict status conditions.

⑤ Status Condition Room
Kirlia or Dusclops will attack your Pokémon with Poison, Paralysis, Asleep, Burned or Frozen.

⑥ Small Talk Room
A Trainer inside this room will make random small talk about topics unrelated to Pokémon battles. You may ignore the small talk and move on.

⑦ Healing Room (1 to 2 Pokémon)
Someone from our facility will randomly heal one or two of your Pokémon.

⑧ Healing Room (All Pokémon)
Our facility staff will heal all three of your Pokémon.

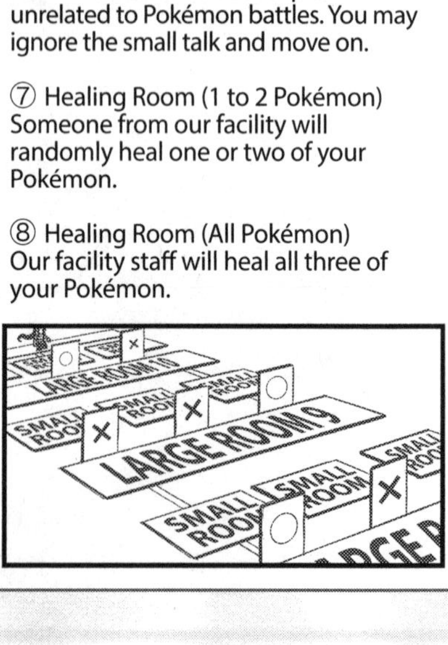
LARGE ROOM 10
SMALL ROOM
LARGE ROOM 9
SMALL ROOM
SMALL ROOM

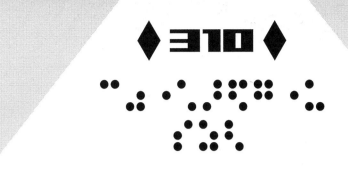

♦ 310 ♦

Just My Luck...Shuckle

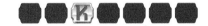

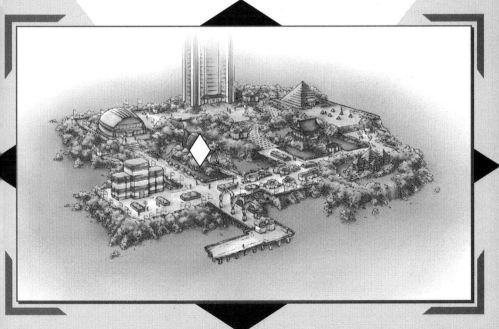

POKÉMON ADVENTURES·THE SIXTH CHAPTER·EMERALD

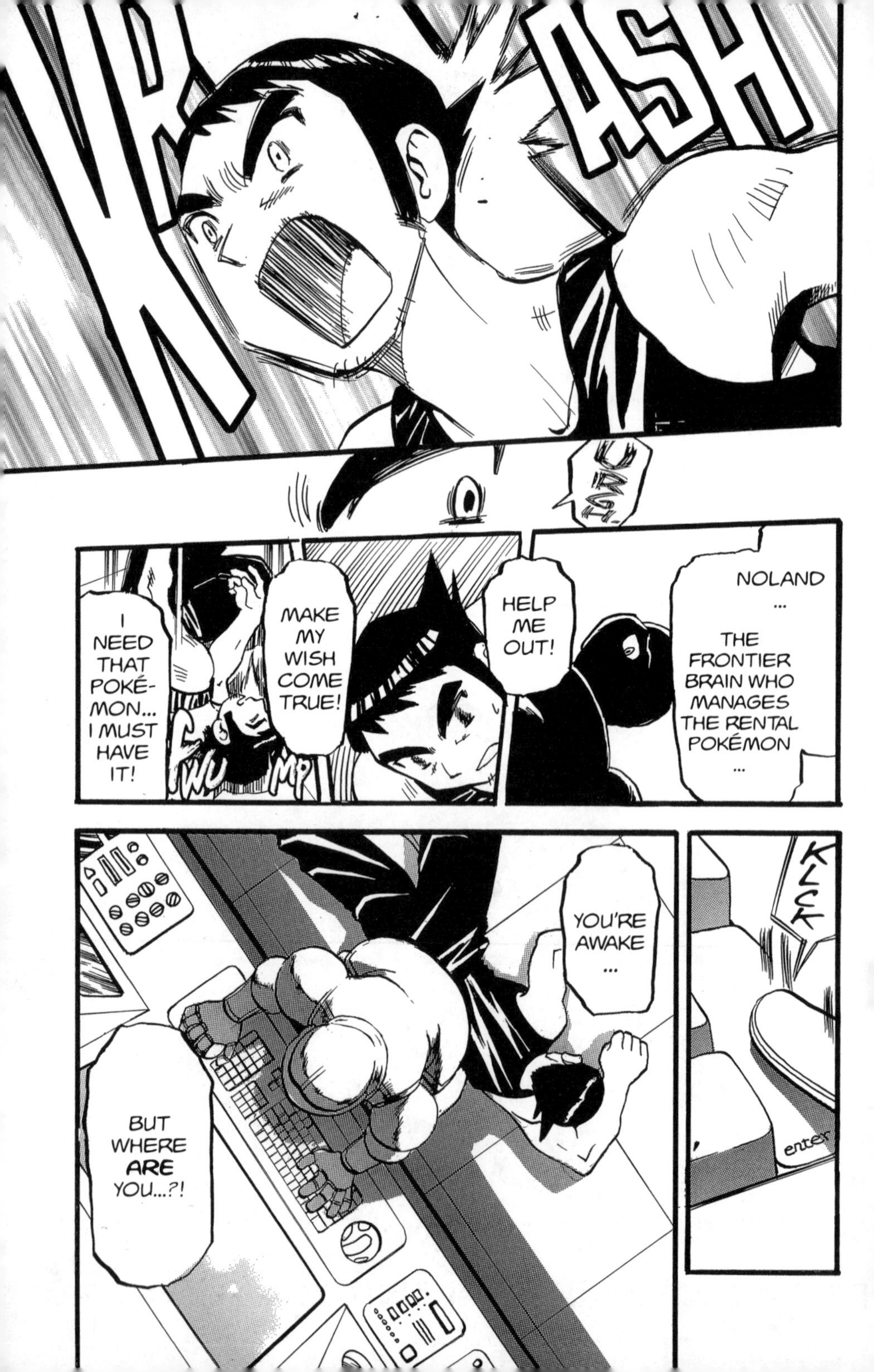
KRASH
URGH!
NOLAND ... THE FRONTIER BRAIN WHO MANAGES THE RENTAL POKÉMON ...
HELP ME OUT!
MAKE MY WISH COME TRUE!
I NEED THAT POKÉMON... I MUST HAVE IT!
FWUMP
KLCK
enter
YOU'RE AWAKE ...
BUT WHERE **ARE** YOU...?!

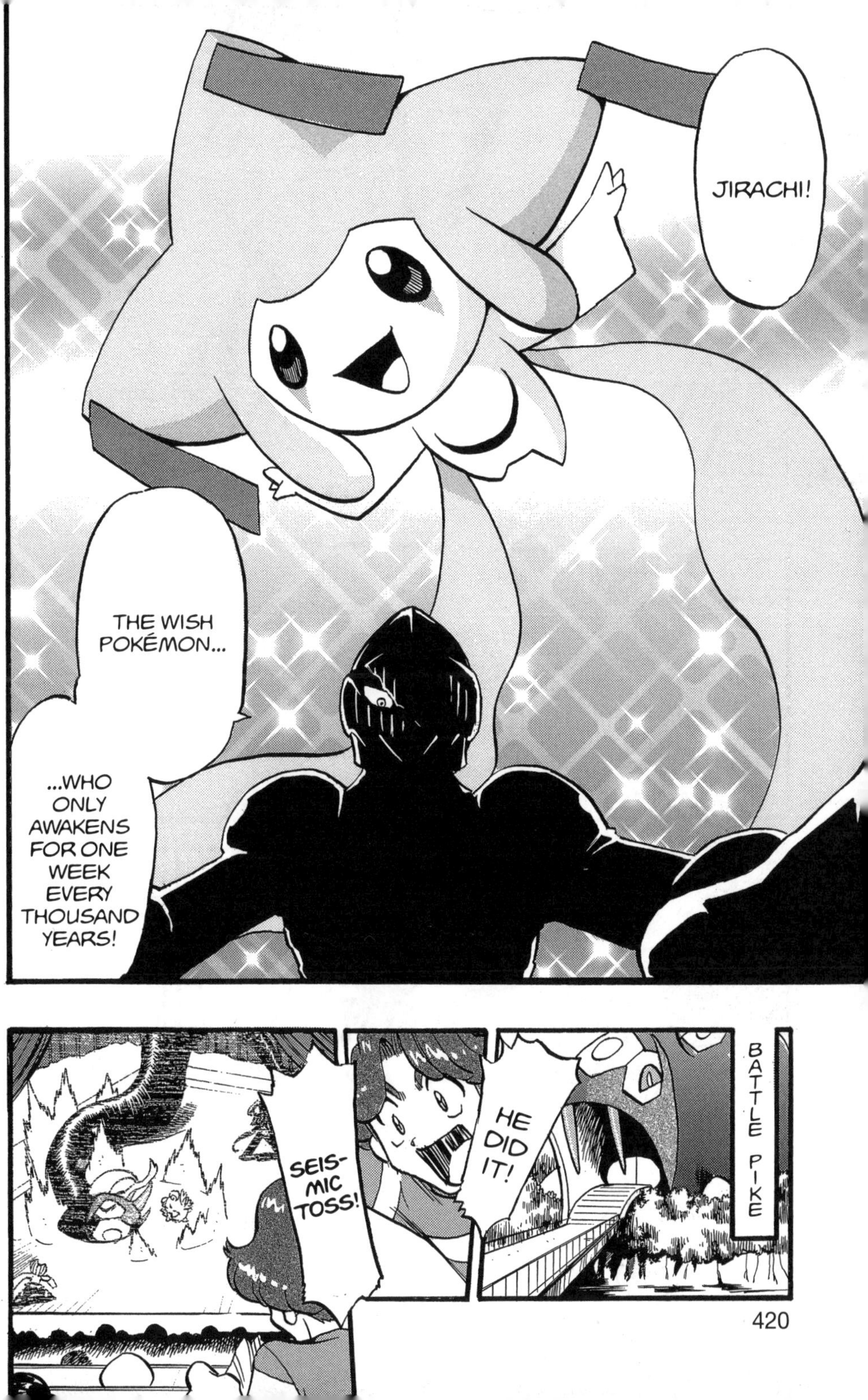
JIRACHI!
THE WISH POKÉMON...
...WHO ONLY AWAKENS FOR ONE WEEK EVERY THOUSAND YEARS!
BATTLE PIKE
HE DID IT!
SEIS-MIC TOSS!

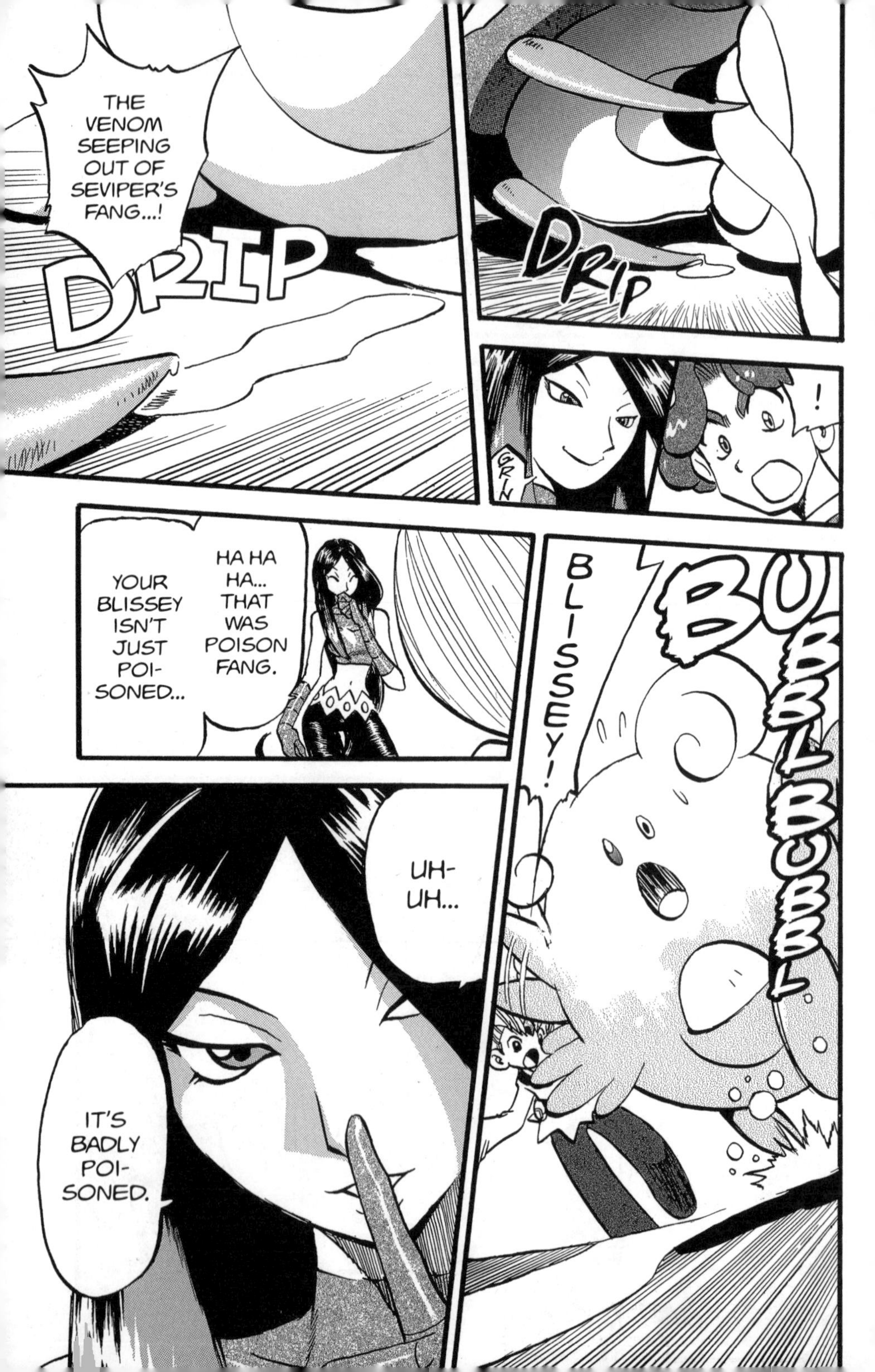
DRIP
THE VENOM SEEPING OUT OF SEVIPER'S FANG...!
DRIP
!
GRIN
BLISSEY!
BUBBLBUBBL
HA HA HA... THAT WAS POISON FANG.
YOUR BLISSEY ISN'T JUST POI-SONED...
UH-UH...
IT'S BADLY POI-SONED.

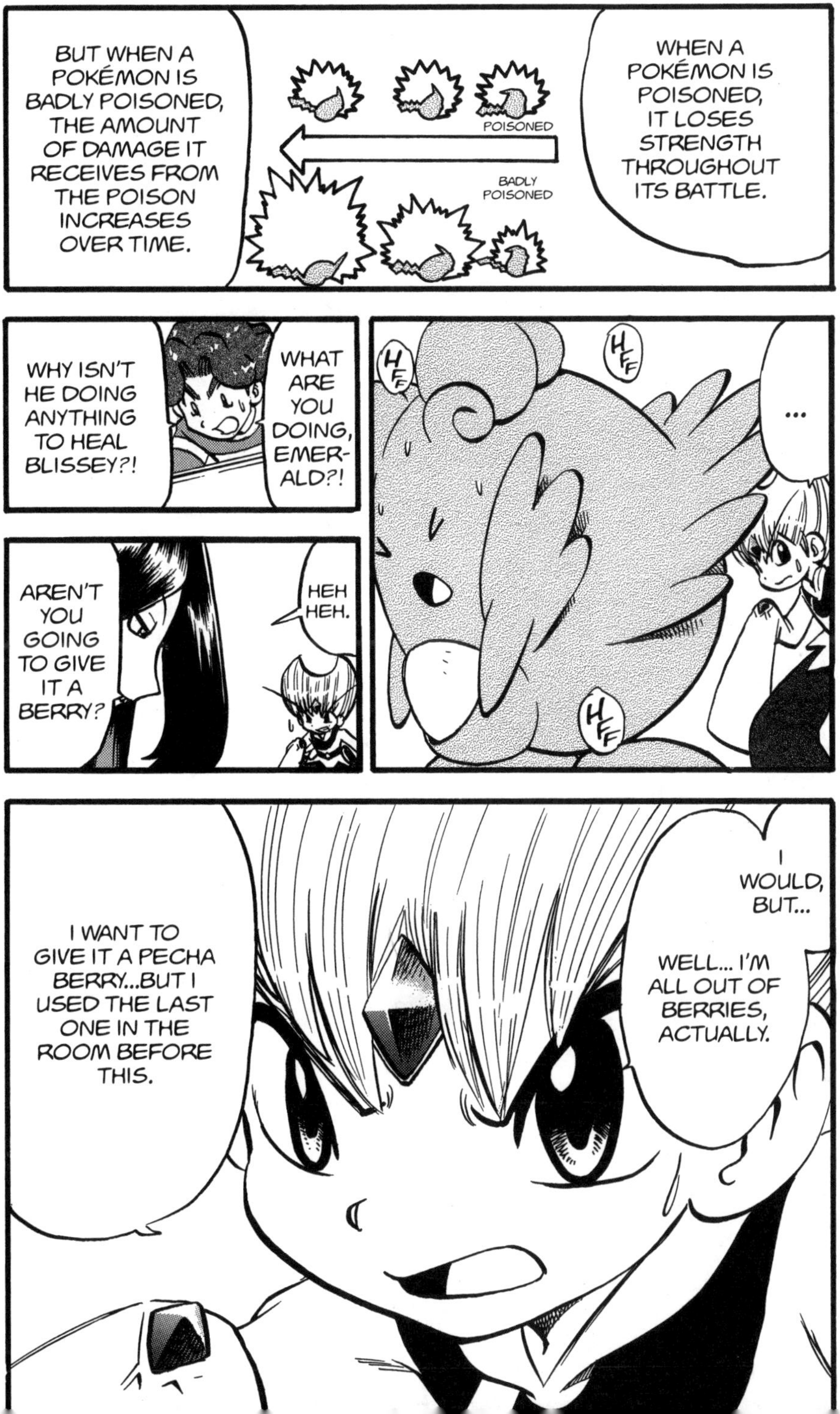
WHEN A POKÉMON IS POISONED, IT LOSES STRENGTH THROUGHOUT ITS BATTLE.
POISONED
BADLY POISONED
BUT WHEN A POKÉMON IS BADLY POISONED, THE AMOUNT OF DAMAGE IT RECEIVES FROM THE POISON INCREASES OVER TIME.
...
HFF
HFF
HFF
WHAT ARE YOU DOING, EMERALD?!
WHY ISN'T HE DOING ANYTHING TO HEAL BLISSEY?!
HEH HEH.
AREN'T YOU GOING TO GIVE IT A BERRY?
I WOULD, BUT...
WELL... I'M ALL OUT OF BERRIES, ACTUALLY.
I WANT TO GIVE IT A PECHA BERRY...BUT I USED THE LAST ONE IN THE ROOM BEFORE THIS.

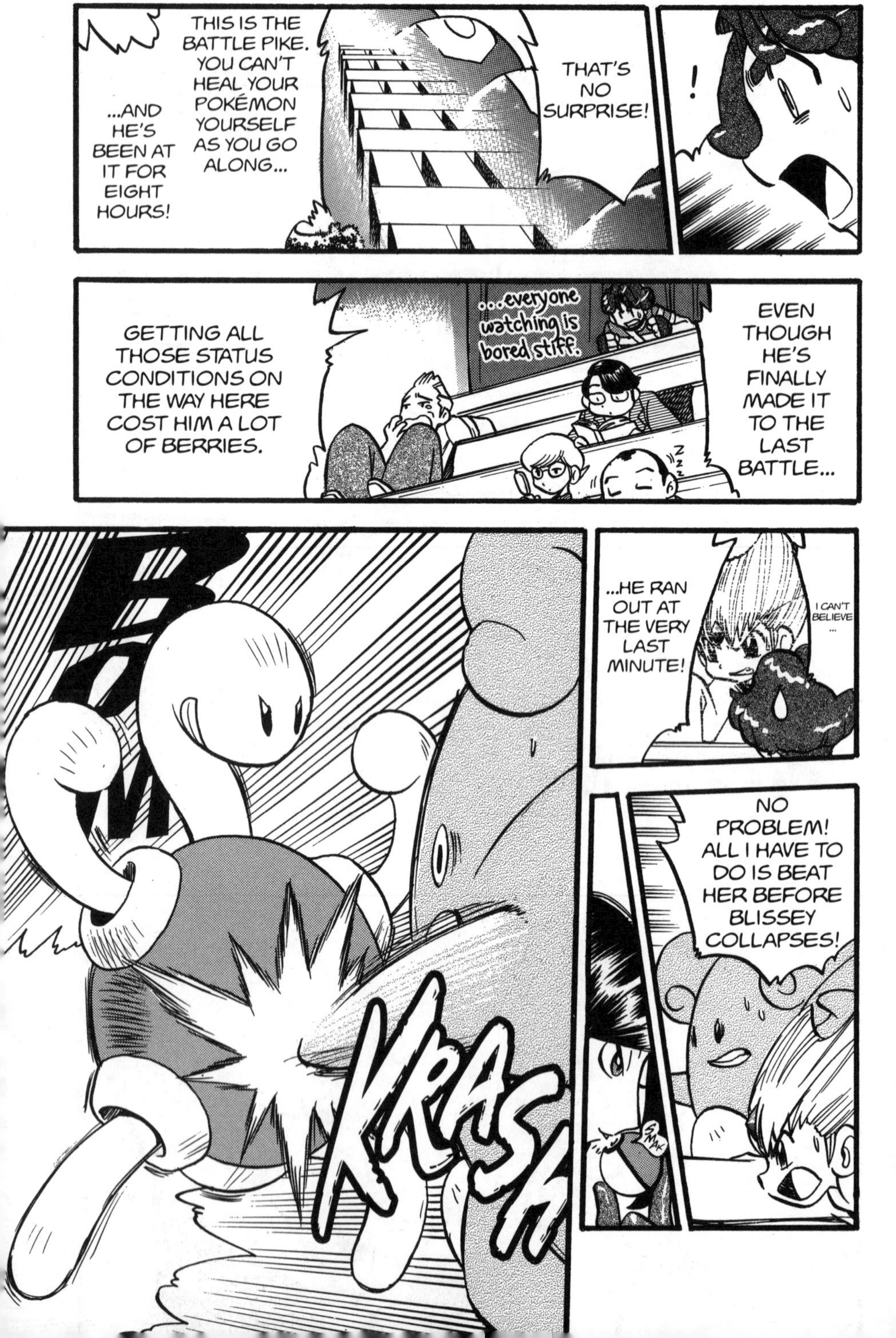
!
THAT'S NO SURPRISE!
THIS IS THE BATTLE PIKE. YOU CAN'T HEAL YOUR POKÉMON YOURSELF AS YOU GO ALONG...
...AND HE'S BEEN AT IT FOR EIGHT HOURS!
EVEN THOUGH HE'S FINALLY MADE IT TO THE LAST BATTLE...
...everyone watching is bored stiff.
ZZZ
GETTING ALL THOSE STATUS CONDITIONS ON THE WAY HERE COST HIM A LOT OF BERRIES.
I CAN'T BELIEVE...
...HE RAN OUT AT THE VERY LAST MINUTE!
NO PROBLEM! ALL I HAVE TO DO IS BEAT HER BEFORE BLISSEY COLLAPSES!
SMAK
KRASH

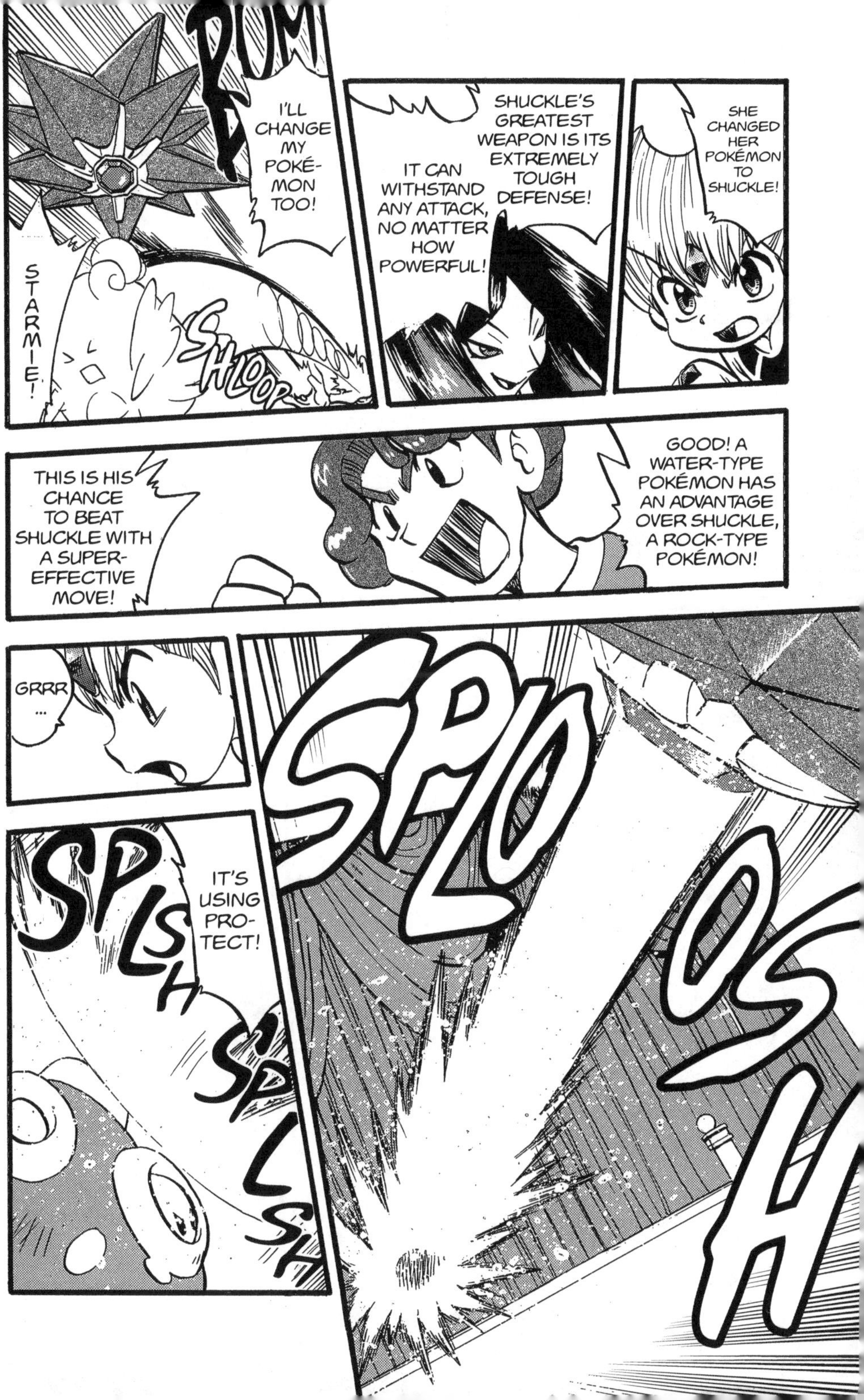
SHE CHANGED HER POKÉMON TO SHUCKLE!
SHUCKLE'S GREATEST WEAPON IS ITS EXTREMELY TOUGH DEFENSE!
IT CAN WITHSTAND ANY ATTACK, NO MATTER HOW POWERFUL!
I'LL CHANGE MY POKÉ-MON TOO!
STARMIE!
SHLOOP
GOOD! A WATER-TYPE POKÉMON HAS AN ADVANTAGE OVER SHUCKLE, A ROCK-TYPE POKÉMON!
THIS IS HIS CHANCE TO BEAT SHUCKLE WITH A SUPER-EFFECTIVE MOVE!
SPLOOSH
GRRR...
IT'S USING PRO-TECT!
SPLSH
SPLSH

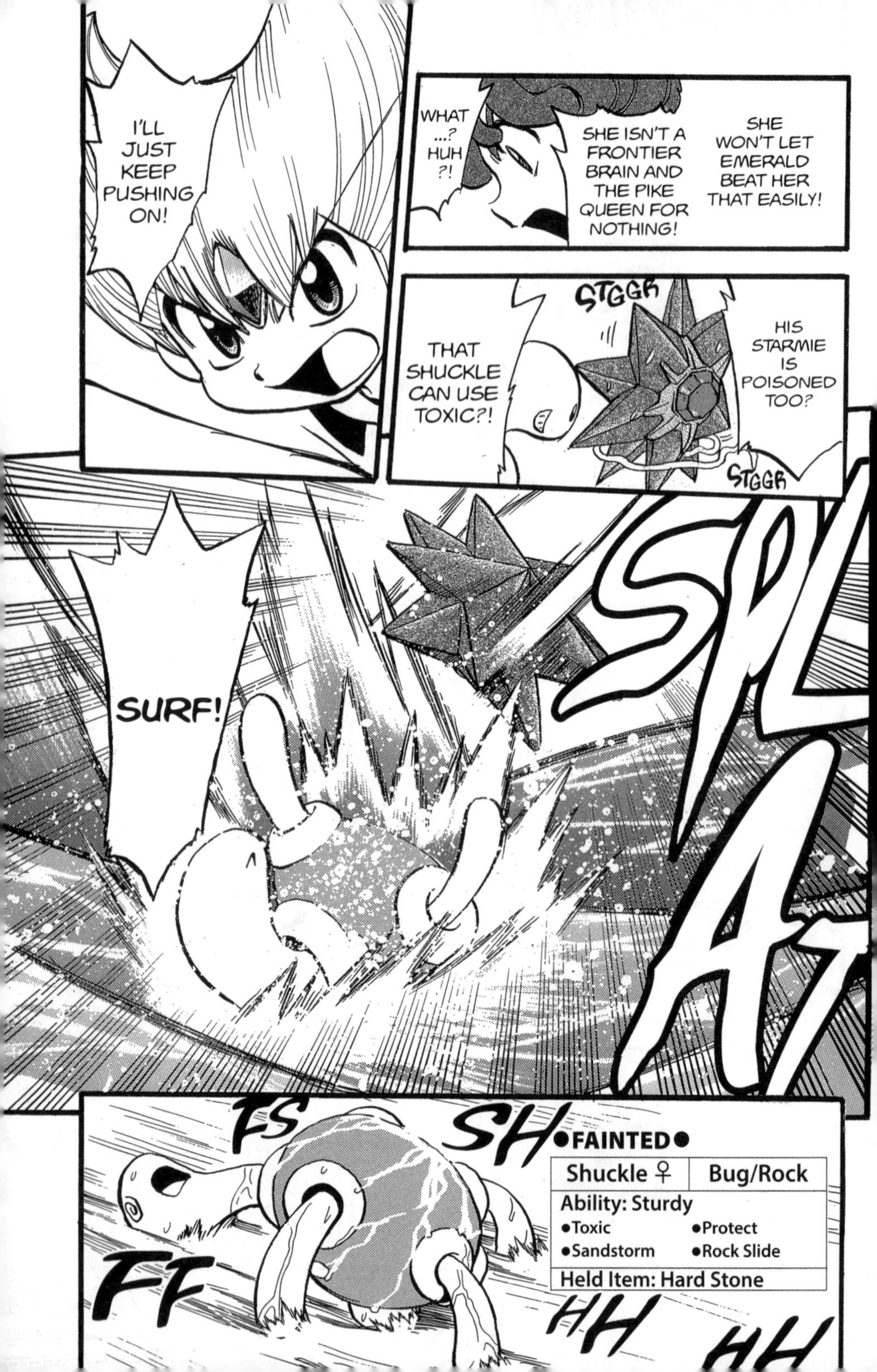
SHE WON'T LET EMERALD BEAT HER THAT EASILY!
SHE ISN'T A FRONTIER BRAIN AND THE PIKE QUEEN FOR NOTHING!
WHAT ...? HUH ?!
STGGR
HIS STARMIE IS POISONED TOO?
THAT SHUCKLE CAN USE TOXIC?!
STGGR
I'LL JUST KEEP PUSHING ON!
SPLAT
SURF!
FSSH
●FAINTED●
Shuckle ♀ | Bug/Rock
Ability: Sturdy
●Toxic ●Protect
●Sandstorm ●Rock Slide
Held Item: Hard Stone
FFHHHH

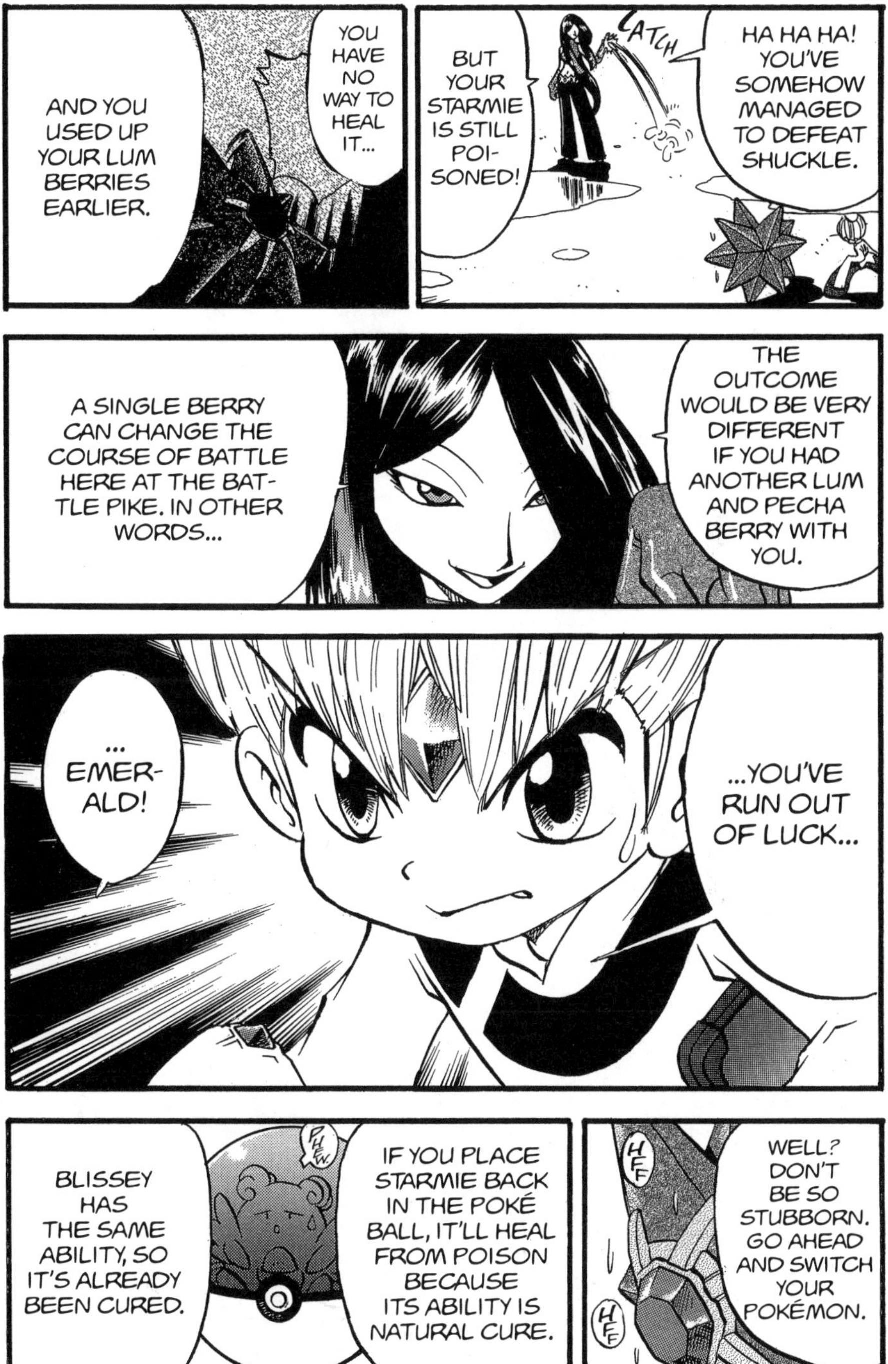
CATCH
HA HA HA! YOU'VE SOMEHOW MANAGED TO DEFEAT SHUCKLE.
BUT YOUR STARMIE IS STILL POI-SONED!
YOU HAVE NO WAY TO HEAL IT...
AND YOU USED UP YOUR LUM BERRIES EARLIER.
THE OUTCOME WOULD BE VERY DIFFERENT IF YOU HAD ANOTHER LUM AND PECHA BERRY WITH YOU.
A SINGLE BERRY CAN CHANGE THE COURSE OF BATTLE HERE AT THE BAT-TLE PIKE. IN OTHER WORDS...
...YOU'VE RUN OUT OF LUCK...
... EMER-ALD!
HFF
HFF
WELL? DON'T BE SO STUBBORN. GO AHEAD AND SWITCH YOUR POKÉMON.
PHEW
IF YOU PLACE STARMIE BACK IN THE POKÉ BALL, IT'LL HEAL FROM POISON BECAUSE ITS ABILITY IS NATURAL CURE.
BLISSEY HAS THE SAME ABILITY, SO IT'S ALREADY BEEN CURED.

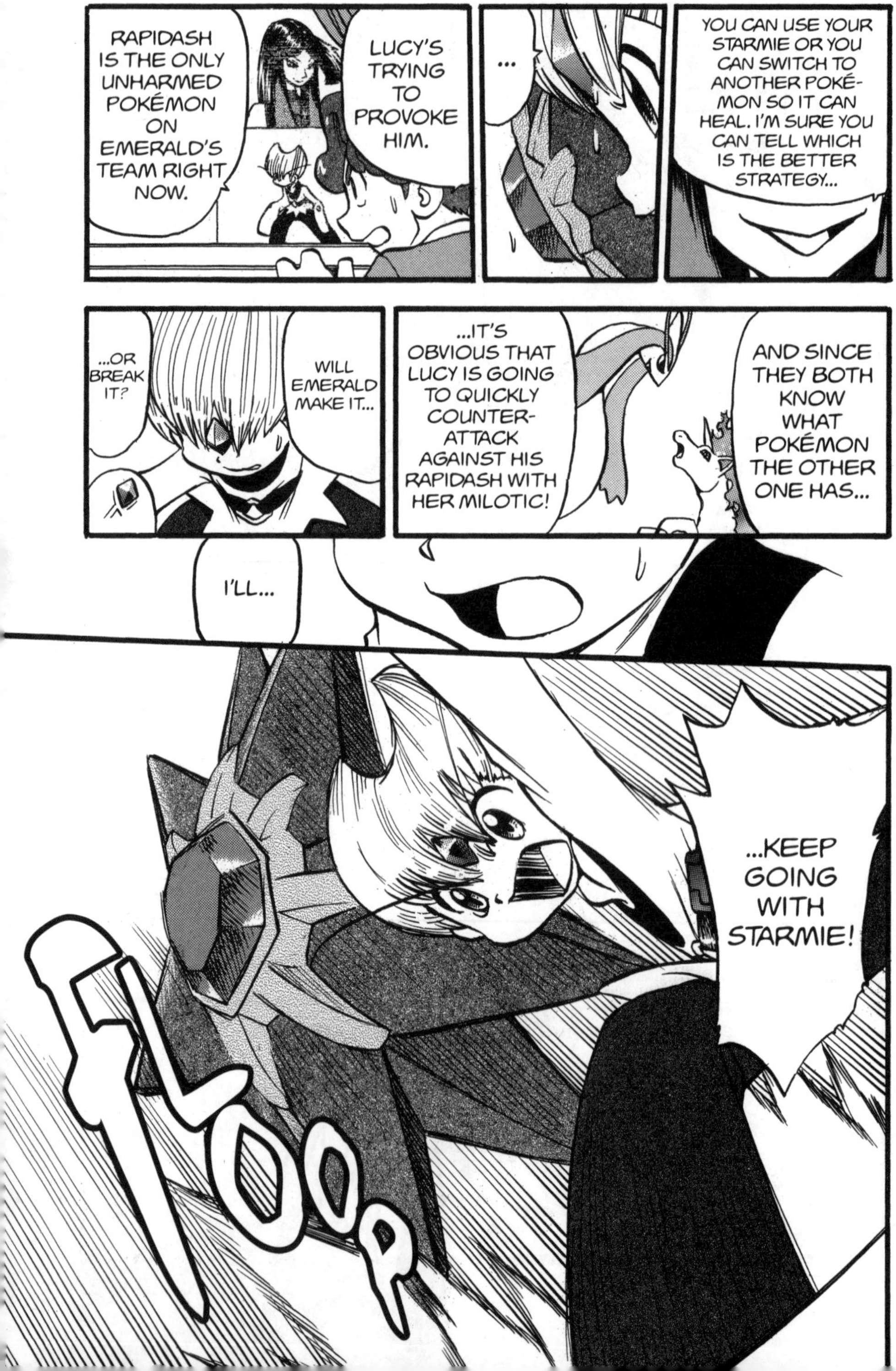
YOU CAN USE YOUR STARMIE OR YOU CAN SWITCH TO ANOTHER POKÉ-MON SO IT CAN HEAL. I'M SURE YOU CAN TELL WHICH IS THE BETTER STRATEGY...
...
LUCY'S TRYING TO PROVOKE HIM.
RAPIDASH IS THE ONLY UNHARMED POKÉMON ON EMERALD'S TEAM RIGHT NOW.
AND SINCE THEY BOTH KNOW WHAT POKÉMON THE OTHER ONE HAS...
...IT'S OBVIOUS THAT LUCY IS GOING TO QUICKLY COUNTER-ATTACK AGAINST HIS RAPIDASH WITH HER MILOTIC!
WILL EMERALD MAKE IT...
...OR BREAK IT?
I'LL...
...KEEP GOING WITH STARMIE!
FOOP

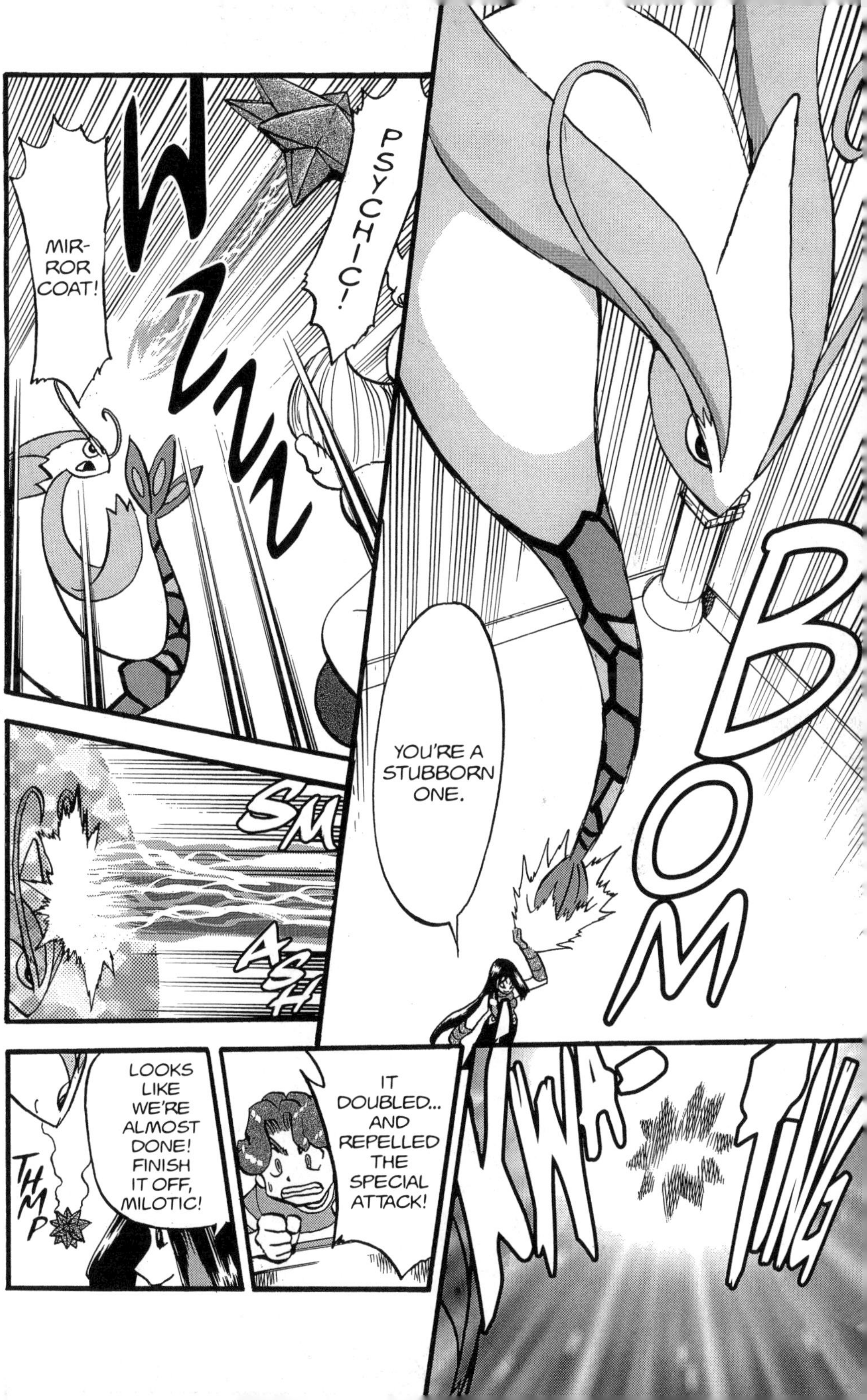

YOU'RE A STUBBORN ONE.
BOOM
PSYCHIC!
WHNNN
MIR-ROR COAT!
SM
ASH
IT DOUBLED... AND REPELLED THE SPECIAL ATTACK!
LOOKS LIKE WE'RE ALMOST DONE! FINISH IT OFF, MILOTIC!
THMP

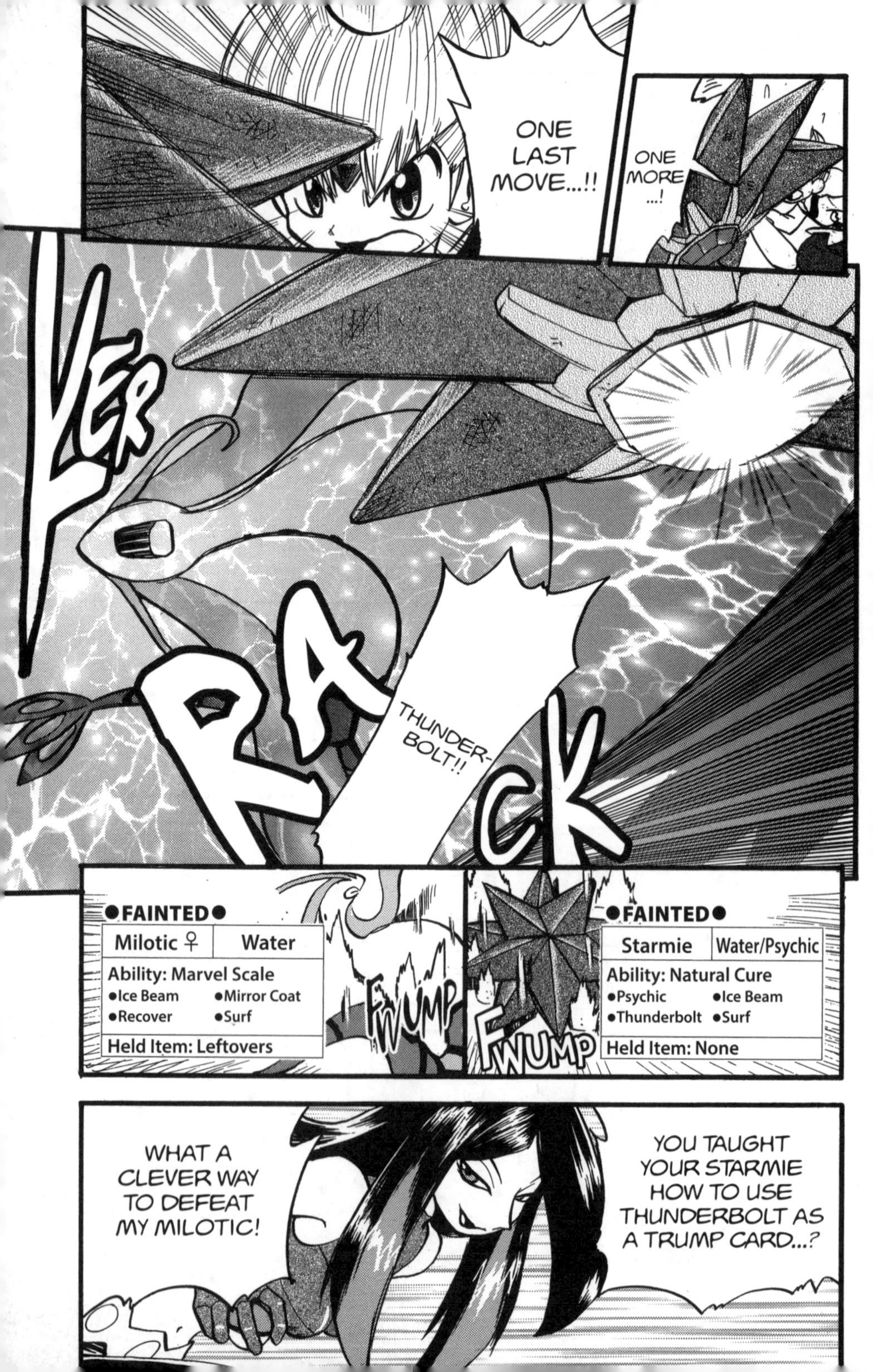
ONE MORE ...!
ONE LAST MOVE...!!
KERRACK
THUNDER-BOLT!!
●FAINTED●
Starmie | Water/Psychic
Ability: Natural Cure
●Psychic ●Ice Beam
●Thunderbolt ●Surf
Held Item: None
FWUMP
●FAINTED●
Milotic ♀ | Water
Ability: Marvel Scale
●Ice Beam ●Mirror Coat
●Recover ●Surf
Held Item: Leftovers
FWUMP
YOU TAUGHT YOUR STARMIE HOW TO USE THUNDERBOLT AS A TRUMP CARD...?
WHAT A CLEVER WAY TO DEFEAT MY MILOTIC!

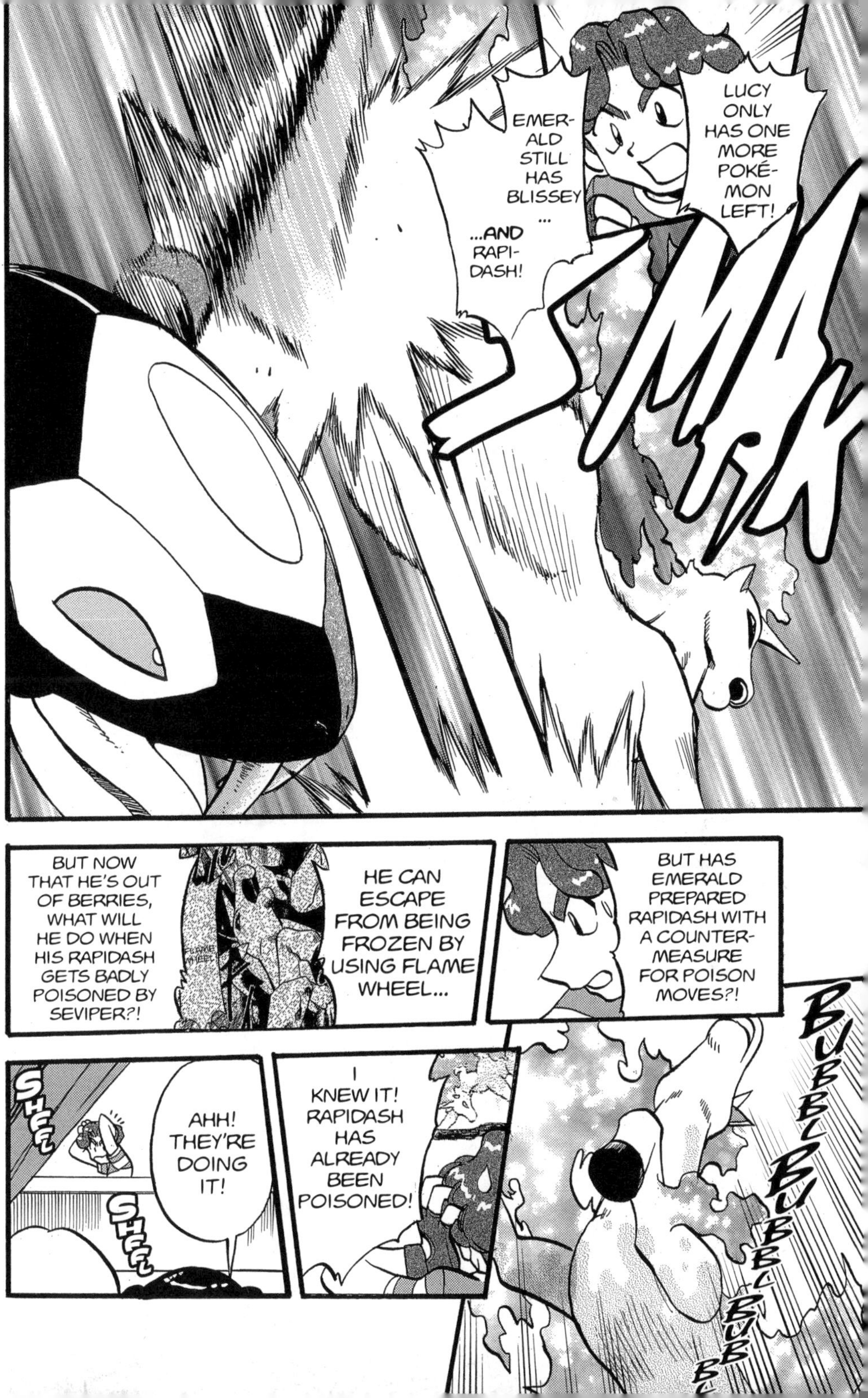
LUCY ONLY HAS ONE MORE POKÉMON LEFT!
EMERALD STILL HAS BLISSEY ...
...AND RAPIDASH!
BUT HAS EMERALD PREPARED RAPIDASH WITH A COUNTER-MEASURE FOR POISON MOVES?!
HE CAN ESCAPE FROM BEING FROZEN BY USING FLAME WHEEL...
BUT NOW THAT HE'S OUT OF BERRIES, WHAT WILL HE DO WHEN HIS RAPIDASH GETS BADLY POISONED BY SEVIPER?!
BUBBL BUBBL BUBBL BUBB
I KNEW IT! RAPIDASH HAS ALREADY BEEN POISONED!
AHH! THEY'RE DOING IT!
SHFFL
SHFFL

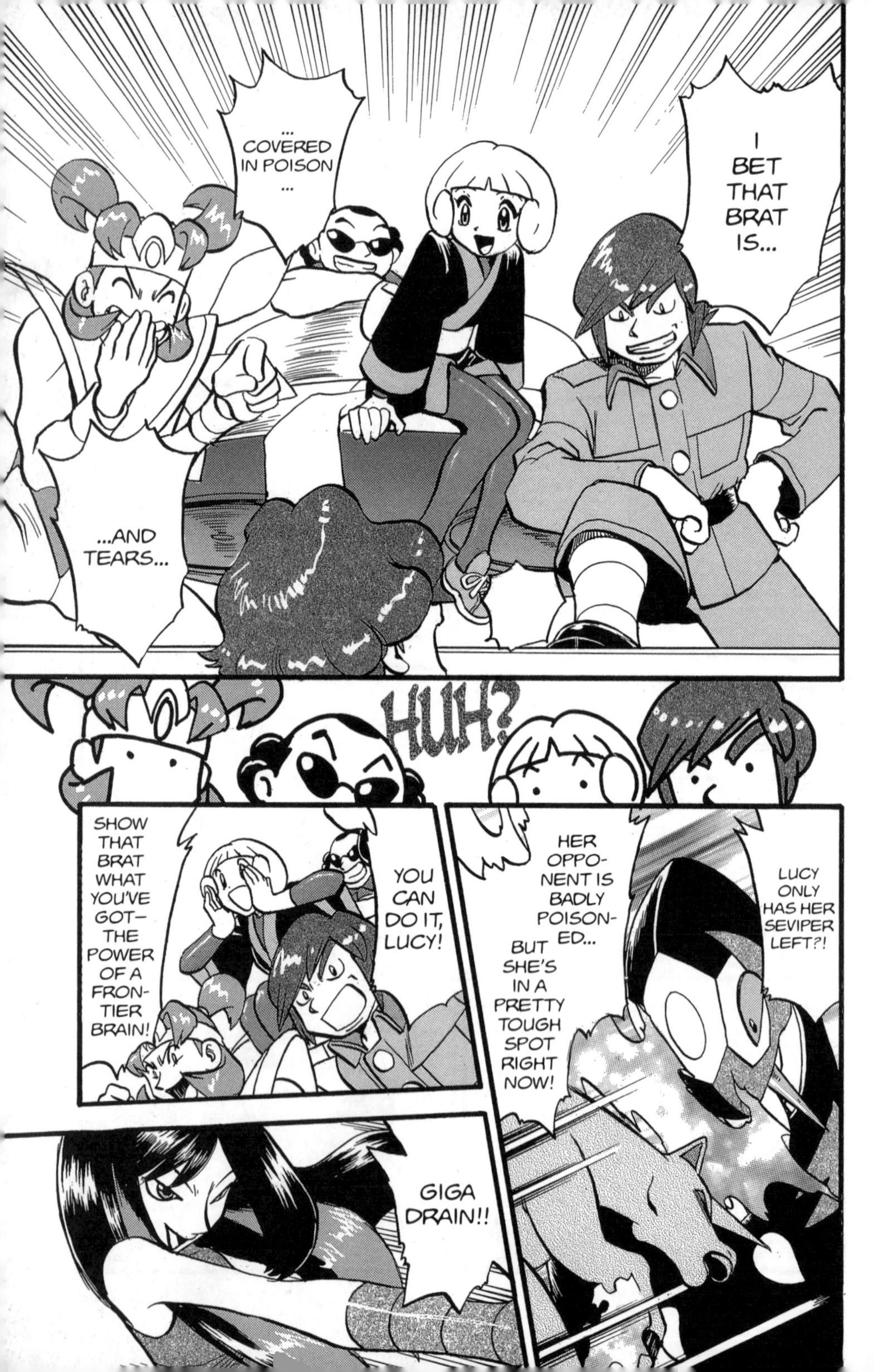
I BET THAT BRAT IS...
... COVERED IN POISON ...
...AND TEARS...
HUH?
LUCY ONLY HAS HER SEVIPER LEFT?!
HER OPPONENT IS BADLY POISONED...
BUT SHE'S IN A PRETTY TOUGH SPOT RIGHT NOW!
YOU CAN DO IT, LUCY!
SHOW THAT BRAT WHAT YOU'VE GOT— THE POWER OF A FRONTIER BRAIN!
GIGA DRAIN!!

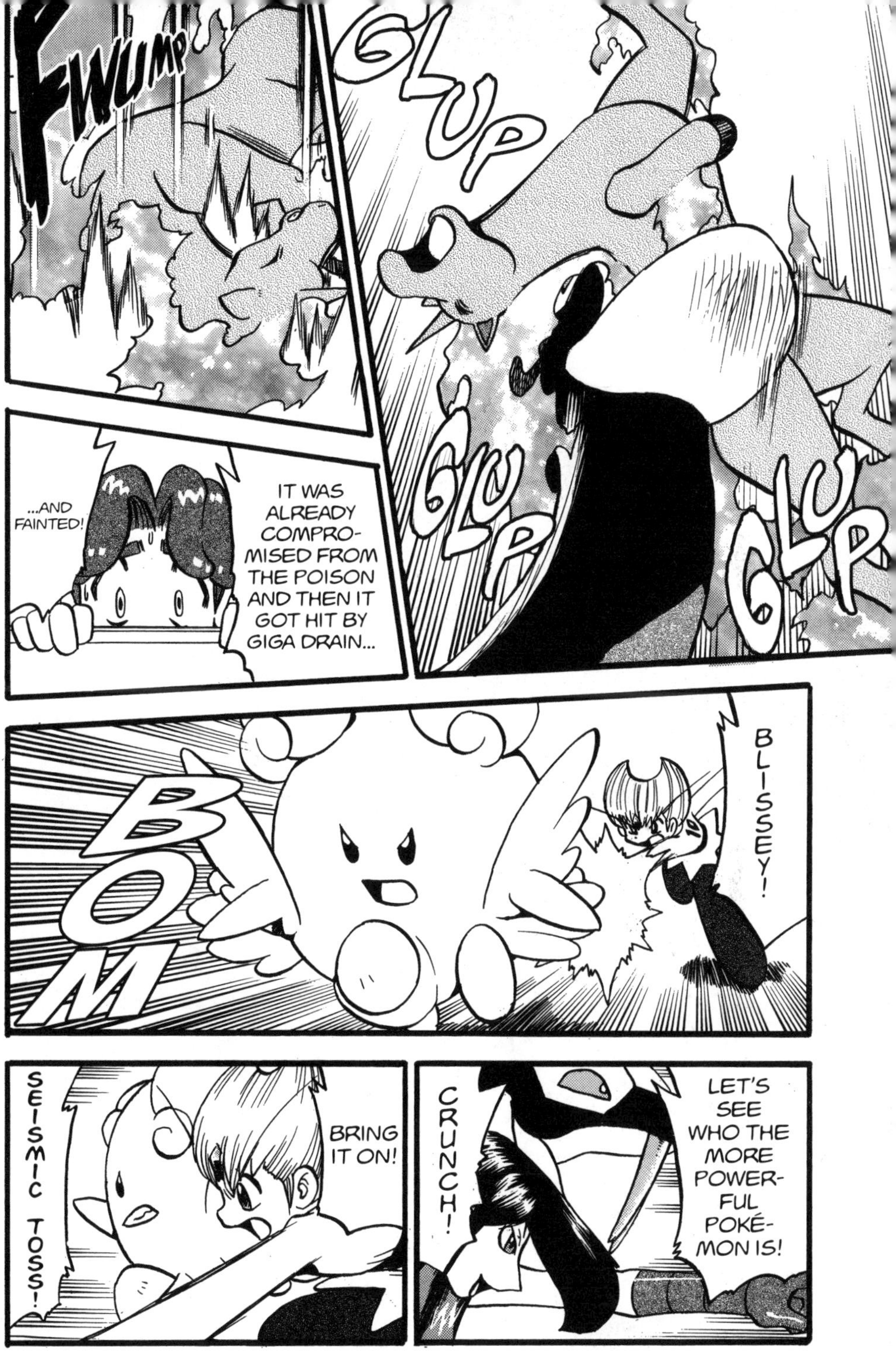
GLUP
GLUP
GLUP
FWUMP
IT WAS ALREADY COMPROMISED FROM THE POISON AND THEN IT GOT HIT BY GIGA DRAIN...
...AND FAINTED!
BLISSEY!
BOM
LET'S SEE WHO THE MORE POWERFUL POKÉMON IS!
CRUNCH!
BRING IT ON!
SEISMIC TOSS!

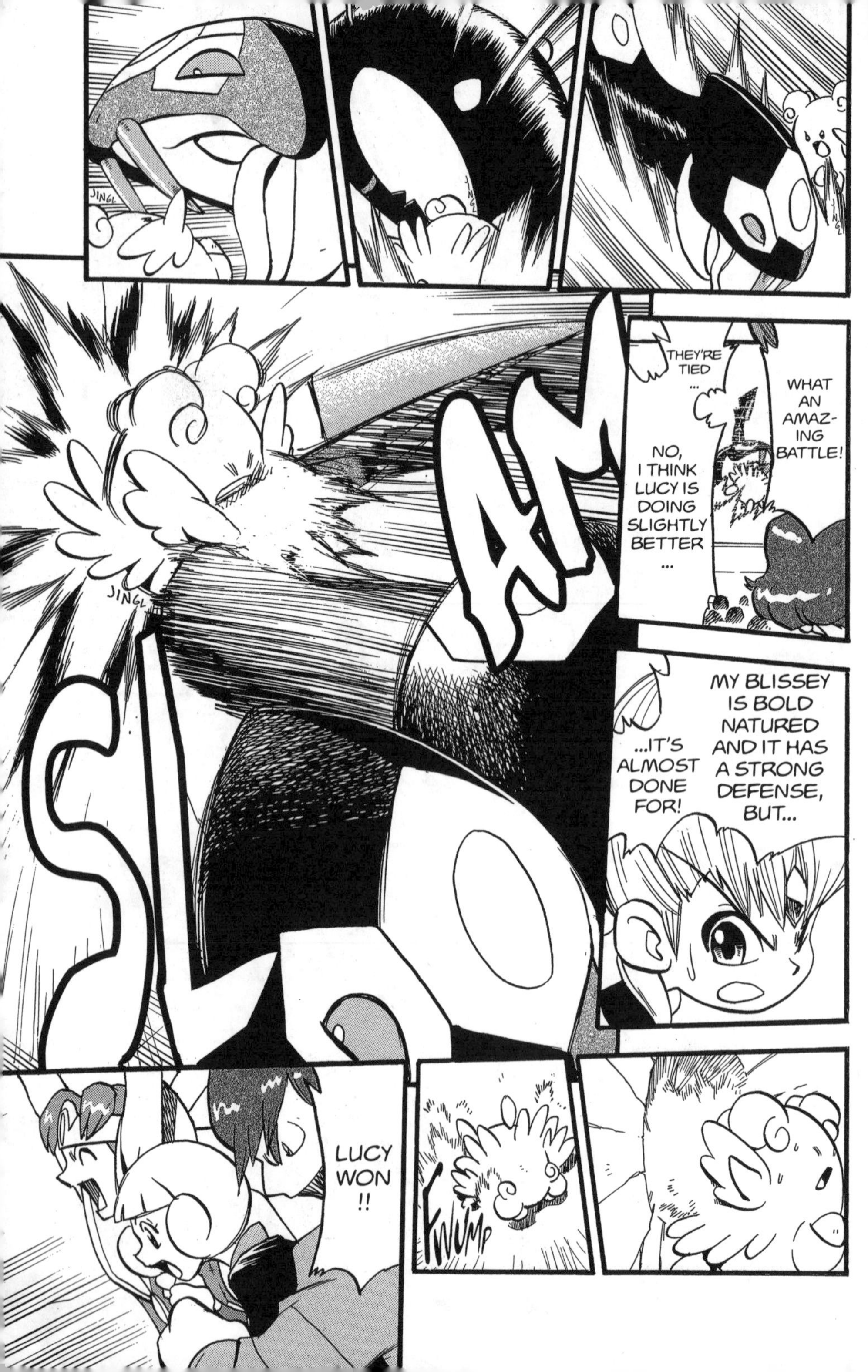
JINGL
JINGL
JINGL
WHAT AN AMAZING BATTLE!
THEY'RE TIED ...
NO, I THINK LUCY IS DOING SLIGHTLY BETTER ...
MY BLISSEY IS BOLD NATURED AND IT HAS A STRONG DEFENSE, BUT...
...IT'S ALMOST DONE FOR!
JINGL
SLAM
FWUMP
LUCY WON !!

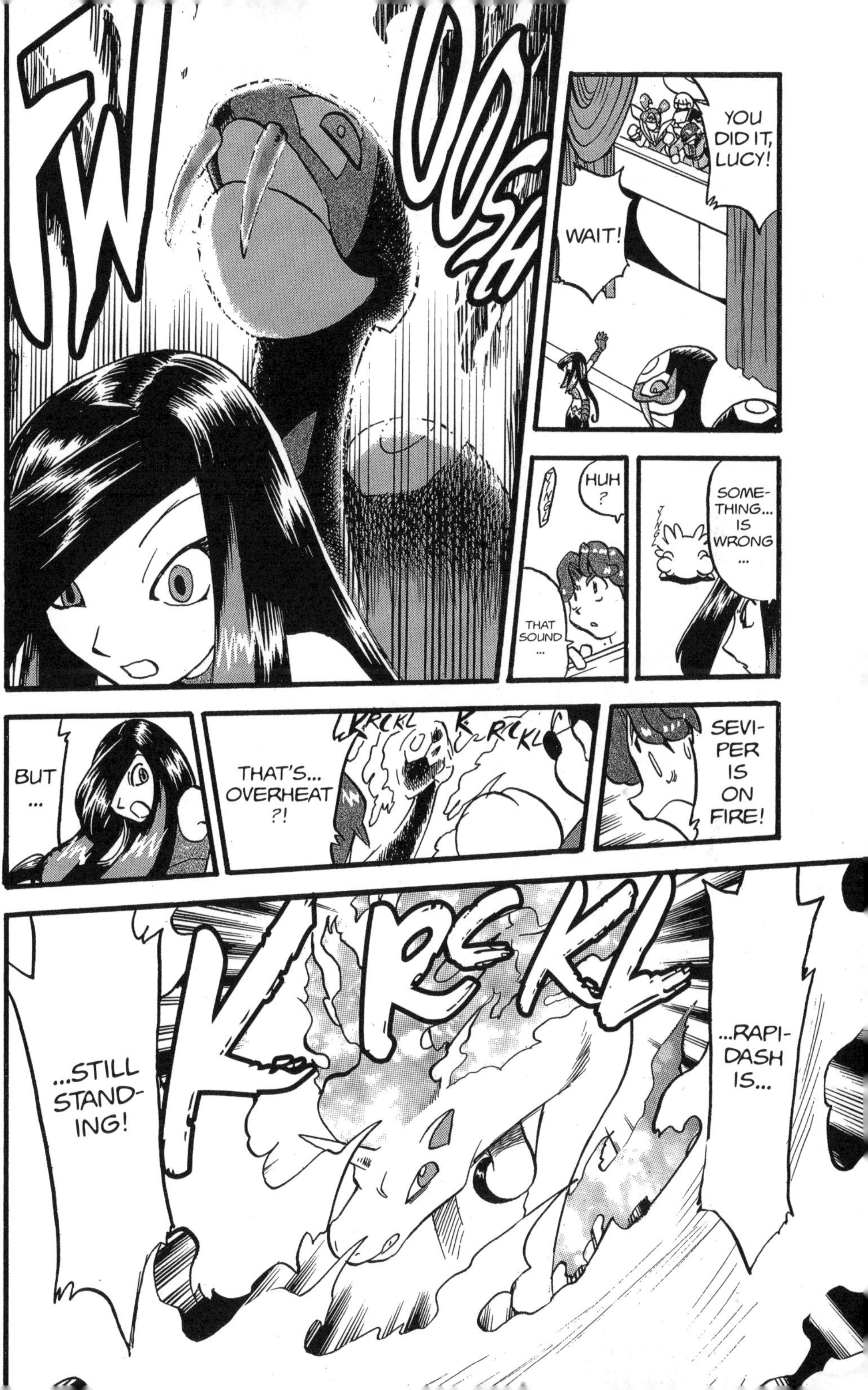
YOU DID IT, LUCY!
WAIT!
SOMETHING... IS WRONG ...
HUH?
THAT SOUND ...
FWOOSH
SEVIPER IS ON FIRE!
KRCKL K KRCKL
THAT'S... OVERHEAT?!
BUT ...
KRCKL
...RAPIDASH IS...
...STILL STANDING!

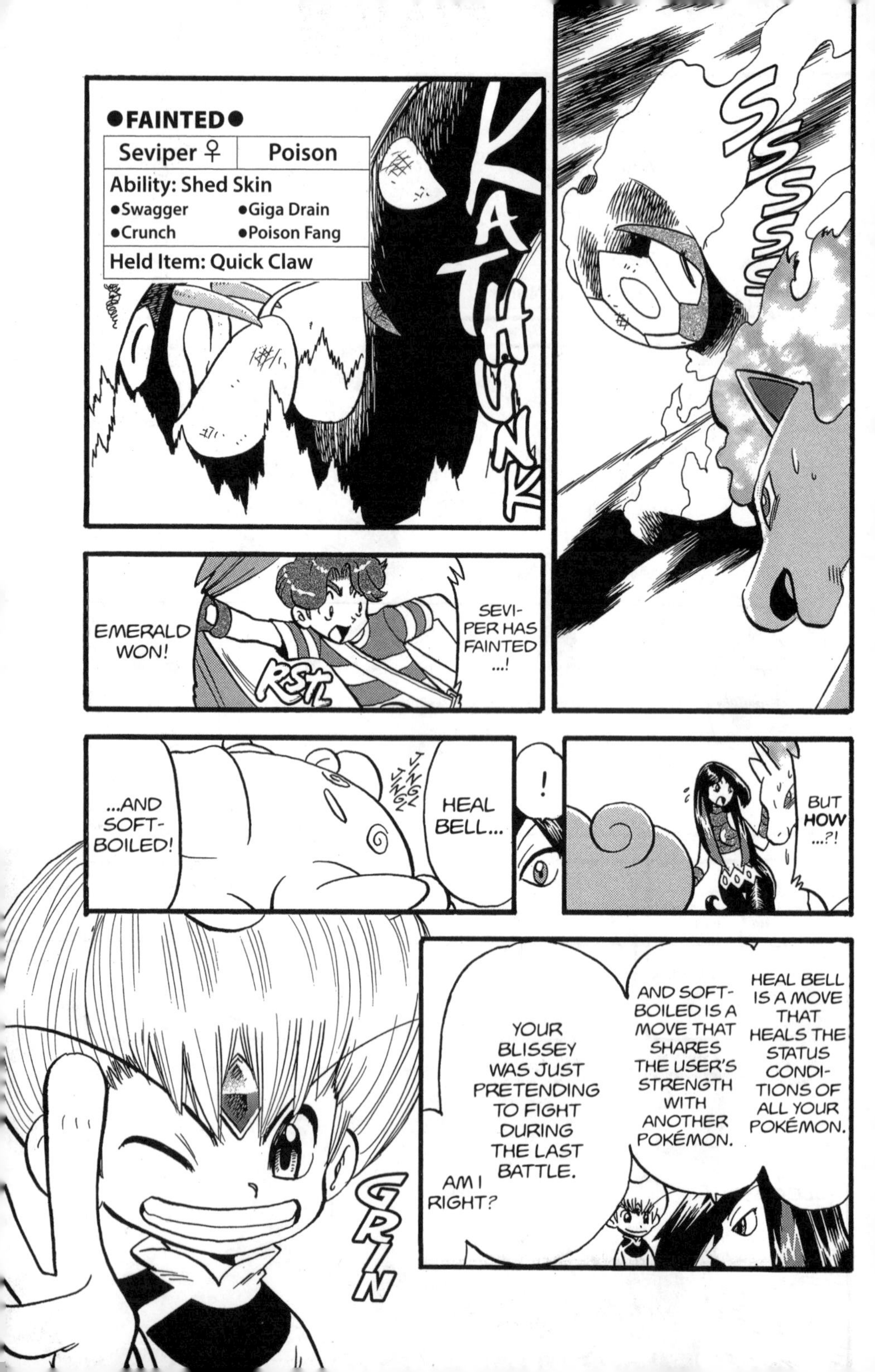
SSSSU
●FAINTED●
Seviper ♀ | Poison
Ability: Shed Skin
●Swagger ●Giga Drain
●Crunch ●Poison Fang
Held Item: Quick Claw
KATHUNK
SEVIPER HAS FAINTED ...!
EMERALD WON!
RSTL
!
BUT HOW ...?!
HEAL BELL...
...AND SOFT-BOILED!
HEAL BELL IS A MOVE THAT HEALS THE STATUS CONDITIONS OF ALL YOUR POKÉMON.
AND SOFT-BOILED IS A MOVE THAT SHARES THE USER'S STRENGTH WITH ANOTHER POKÉMON.
YOUR BLISSEY WAS JUST PRETENDING TO FIGHT DURING THE LAST BATTLE.
AM I RIGHT?
GRIN

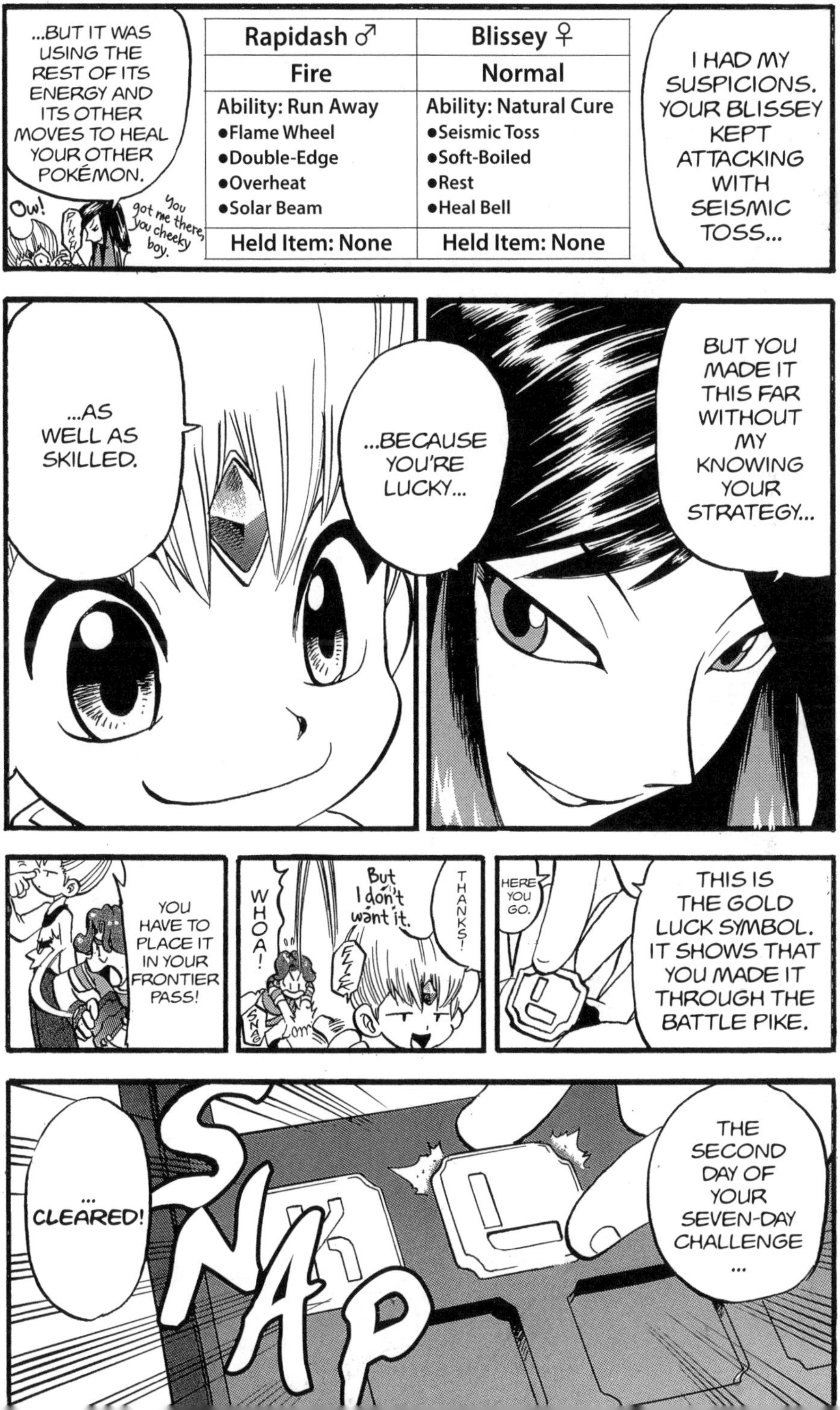
I HAD MY SUSPICIONS. YOUR BLISSEY KEPT ATTACKING WITH SEISMIC TOSS...

Rapidash ♂	Blissey ♀
Fire	Normal
Ability: Run Away ●Flame Wheel ●Double-Edge ●Overheat ●Solar Beam	Ability: Natural Cure ●Seismic Toss ●Soft-Boiled ●Rest ●Heal Bell
Held Item: None	Held Item: None

...BUT IT WAS USING THE REST OF ITS ENERGY AND ITS OTHER MOVES TO HEAL YOUR OTHER POKÉMON.
You got me there, you cheeky boy.
PINCH
Ow!
BUT YOU MADE IT THIS FAR WITHOUT MY KNOWING YOUR STRATEGY...
...BECAUSE YOU'RE LUCKY...
...AS WELL AS SKILLED.
THIS IS THE GOLD LUCK SYMBOL. IT SHOWS THAT YOU MADE IT THROUGH THE BATTLE PIKE.
HERE YOU GO.
THANKS!
But I don't want it.
FLICK
WHOA!
SNAG
YOU HAVE TO PLACE IT IN YOUR FRONTIER PASS!
THE SECOND DAY OF YOUR SEVEN-DAY CHALLENGE...
SNAP
...CLEARED!

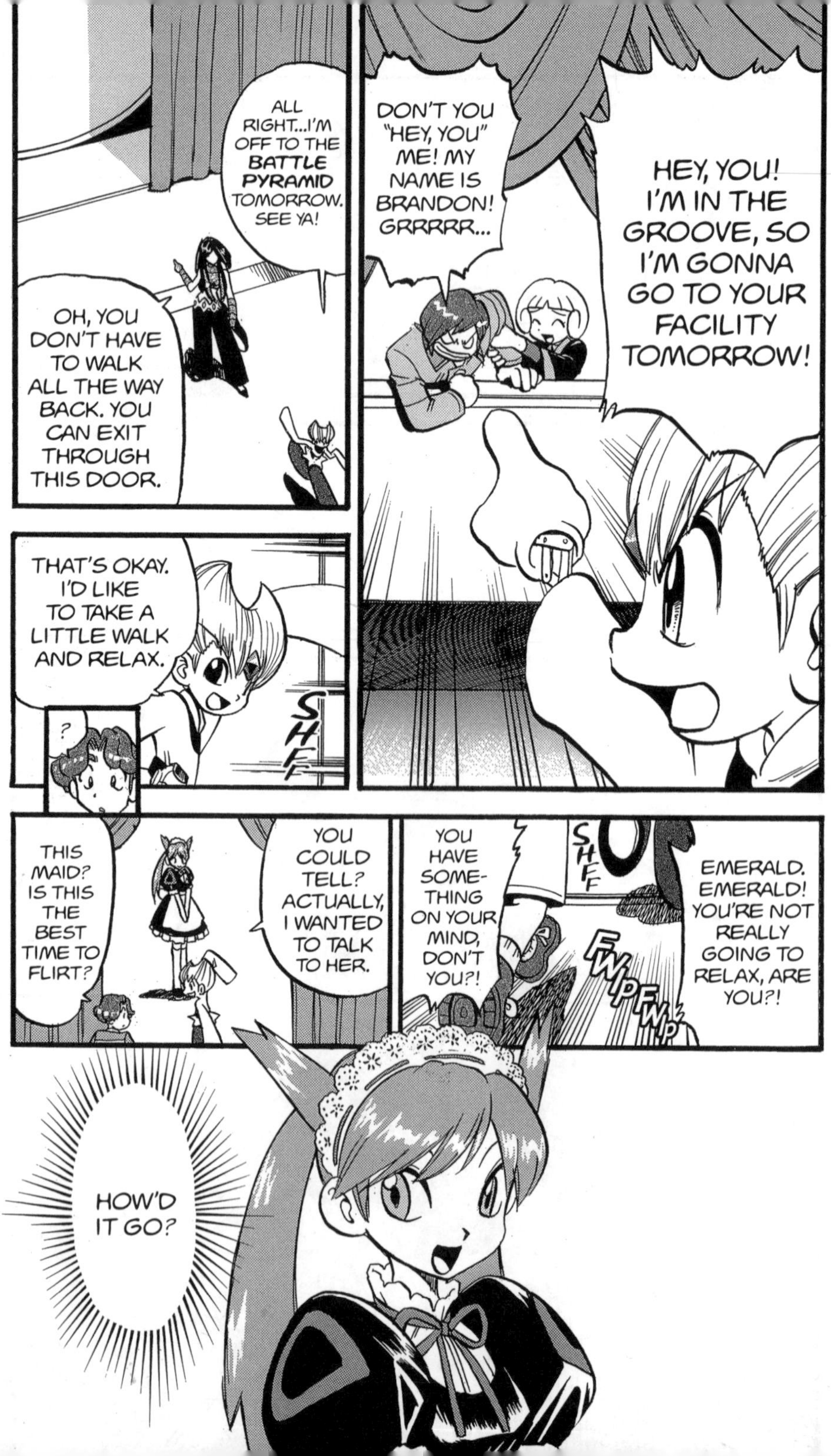

HEY, YOU! I'M IN THE GROOVE, SO I'M GONNA GO TO YOUR FACILITY TOMORROW!
DON'T YOU "HEY, YOU" ME! MY NAME IS BRANDON! GRRRRR...
ALL RIGHT...I'M OFF TO THE **BATTLE PYRAMID** TOMORROW. SEE YA!
OH, YOU DON'T HAVE TO WALK ALL THE WAY BACK. YOU CAN EXIT THROUGH THIS DOOR.
SHFF
THAT'S OKAY. I'D LIKE TO TAKE A LITTLE WALK AND RELAX.
?
EMERALD. EMERALD! YOU'RE NOT REALLY GOING TO RELAX, ARE YOU?!
SHFF
FWIPFWIP
YOU HAVE SOME-THING ON YOUR MIND, DON'T YOU?!
YOU COULD TELL? ACTUALLY, I WANTED TO TALK TO HER.
THIS MAID? IS THIS THE BEST TIME TO FLIRT?
HOW'D IT GO?

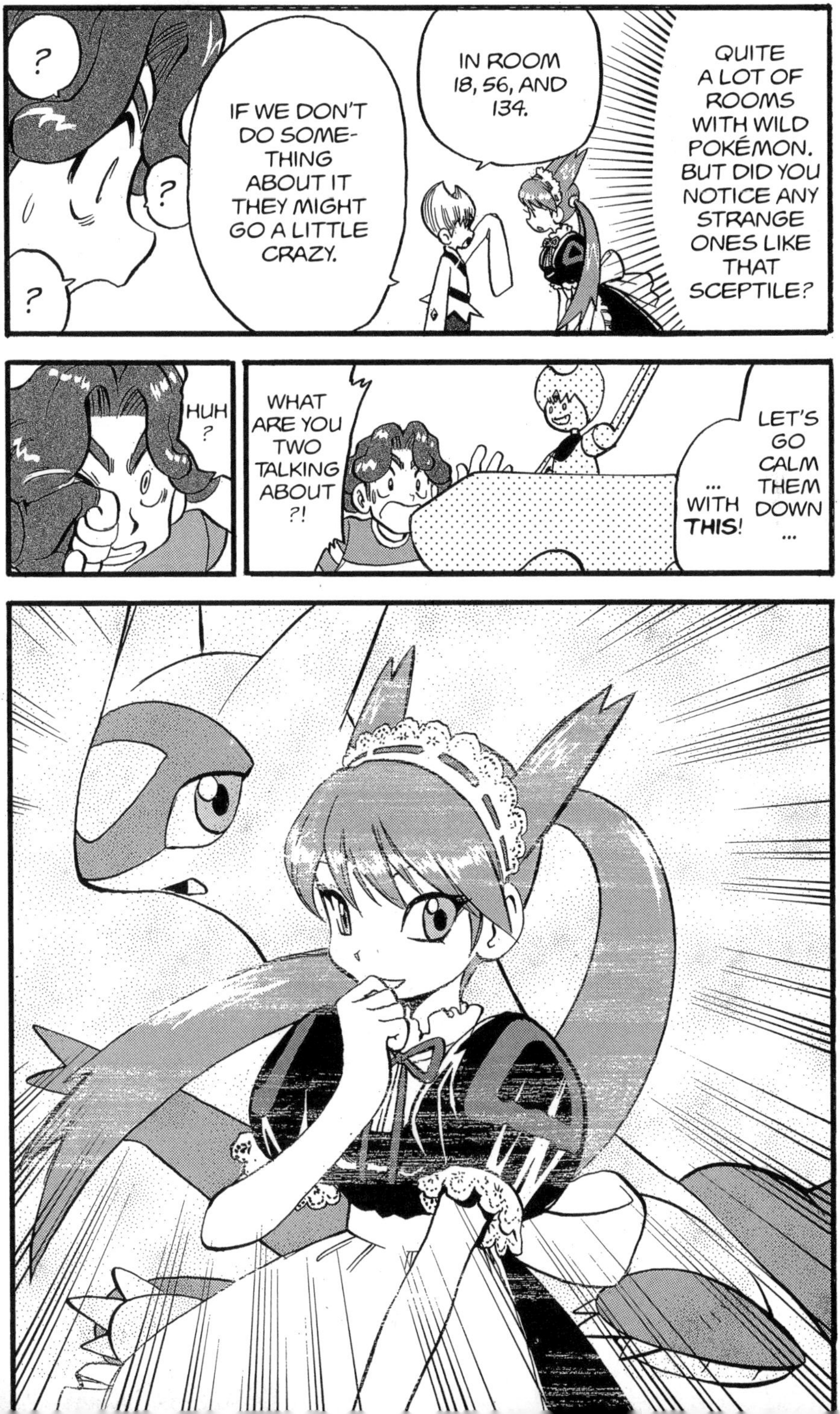
QUITE A LOT OF ROOMS WITH WILD POKÉMON. BUT DID YOU NOTICE ANY STRANGE ONES LIKE THAT SCEPTILE?
IN ROOM 18, 56, AND 134.
IF WE DON'T DO SOME-THING ABOUT IT THEY MIGHT GO A LITTLE CRAZY.
?
?
?
LET'S GO CALM THEM DOWN ...
... WITH **THIS**!
WHAT ARE YOU TWO TALKING ABOUT ?!
HUH ?

DEAR MEMBERS OF THE PRESS...

Thank you for visiting the Battle Frontier today. Permit me to continue explaining the rules of this facility...

OWNER: SCOTT

FACILITY RULES

BATTLE PYRAMID

Battle-type	Number of Pokémon	Type of Symbol	Wins needed to attain the Symbol
•Single •Double	3 Pokémon	Brave	Seven Floors X 10 Rounds = 70 Floors

The Trainer must go through a pyramid with changing floor patterns and climb to the top. It is dark inside the pyramid, but the floor will gradually light up as you win battles against wild Pokémon and Trainers. There are also Trainers inside who will provide hints to aid challengers in finding their goal.

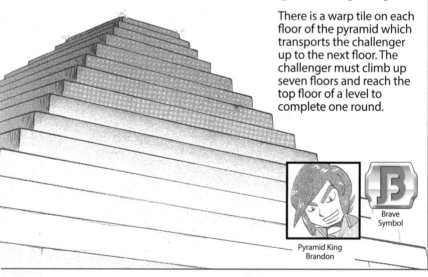

There is a warp tile on each floor of the pyramid which transports the challenger up to the next floor. The challenger must climb up seven floors and reach the top floor of a level to complete one round.

Pyramid King Brandon

Brave Symbol

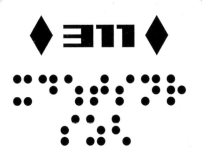

◆ ヨ11 ◆

A Dustup with Dusclops

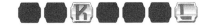

■■K●●●⌐

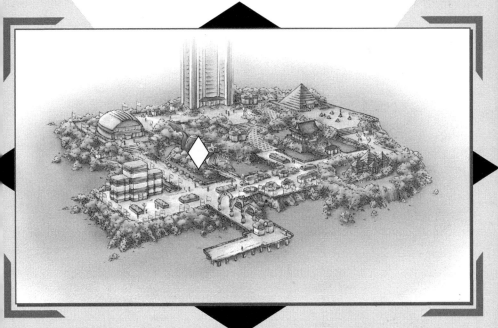

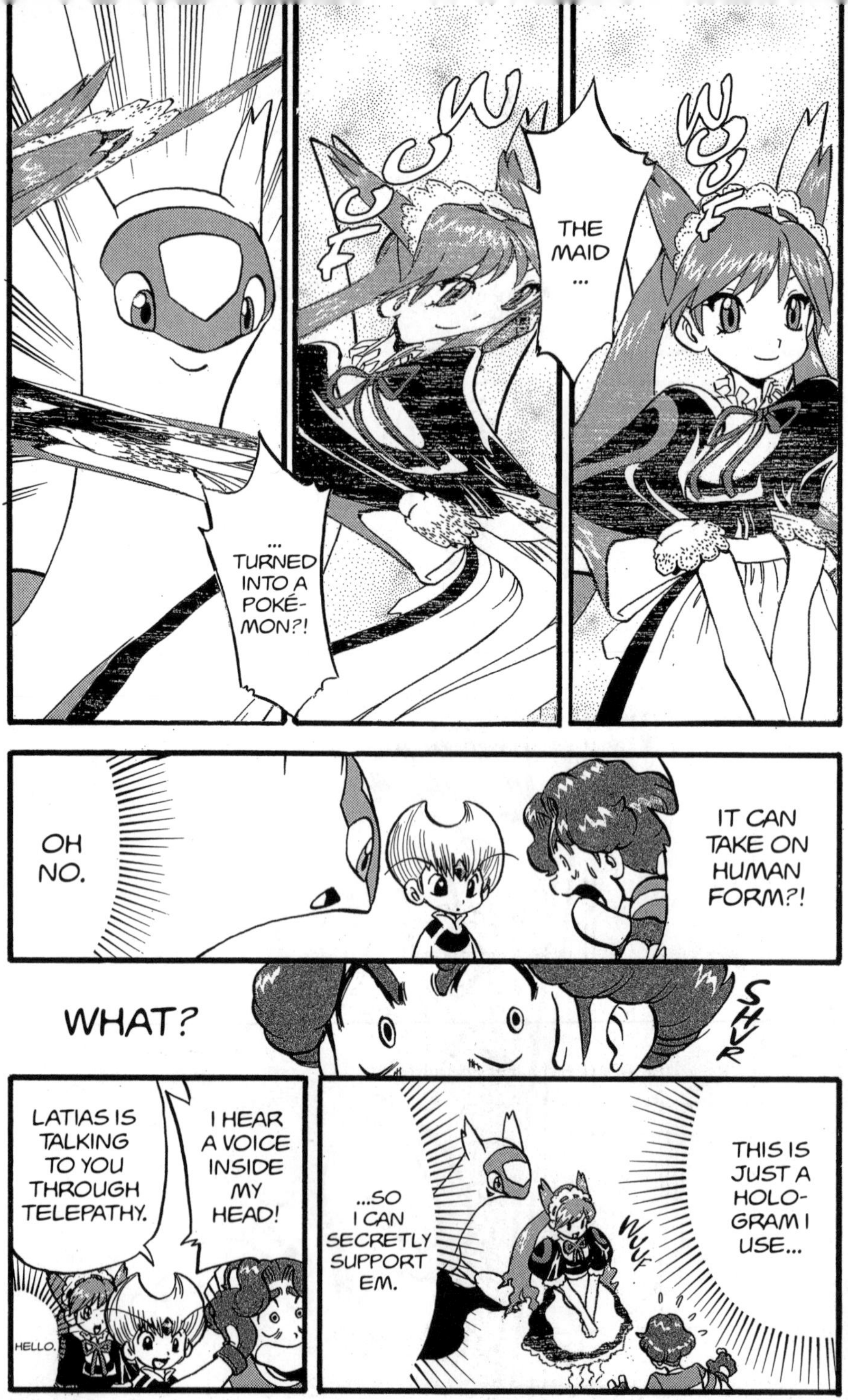
FUUW
THE MAID ...
FUUW
... TURNED INTO A POKÉ-MON?!
IT CAN TAKE ON HUMAN FORM?!
OH NO.
SHVR
WHAT?
THIS IS JUST A HOLO-GRAM I USE...
...SO I CAN SECRETLY SUPPORT EM.
I HEAR A VOICE INSIDE MY HEAD!
LATIAS IS TALKING TO YOU THROUGH TELEPATHY.
HELLO.

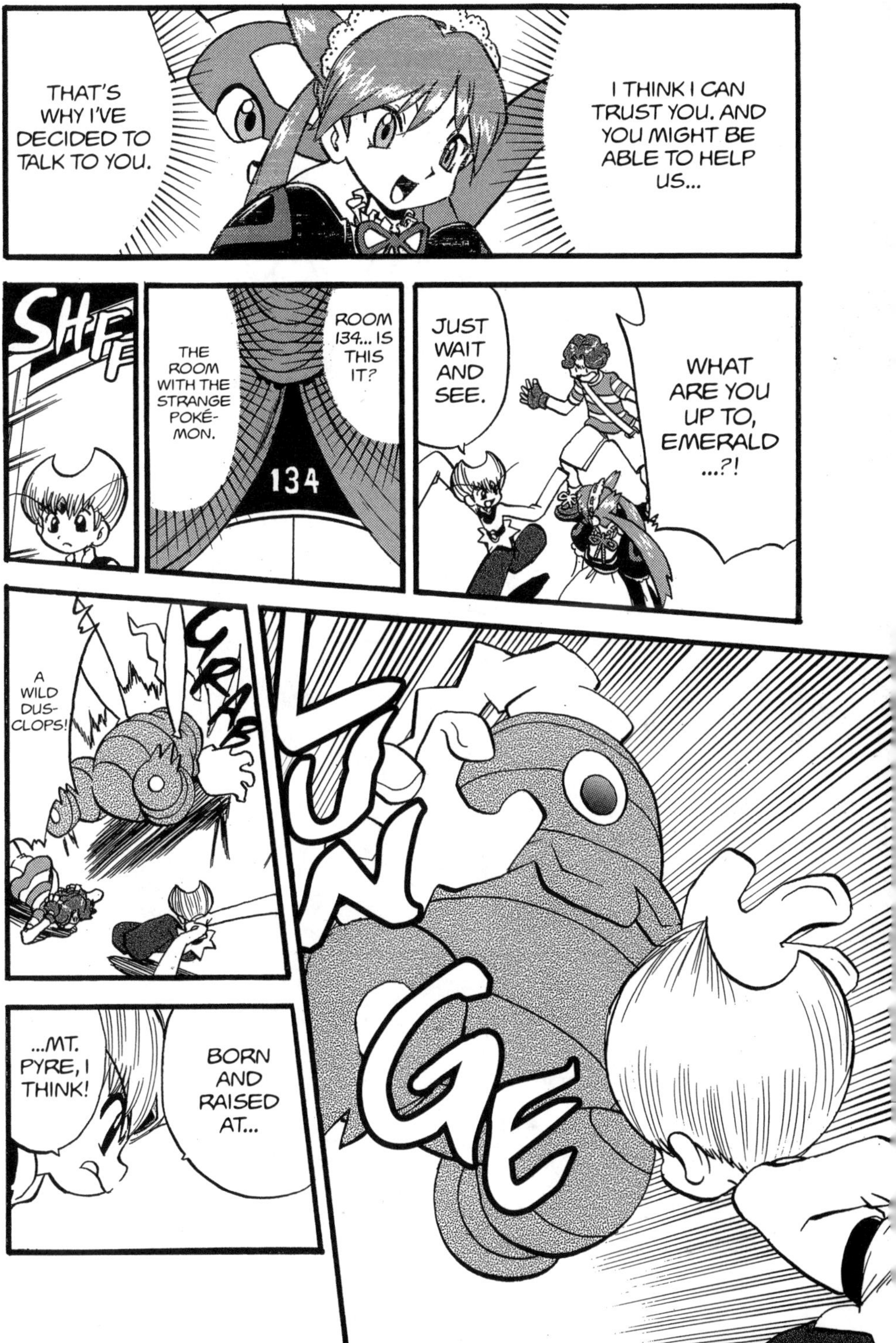
I THINK I CAN TRUST YOU. AND YOU MIGHT BE ABLE TO HELP US...
THAT'S WHY I'VE DECIDED TO TALK TO YOU.
WHAT ARE YOU UP TO, EMERALD ...?!
JUST WAIT AND SEE.
ROOM 134... IS THIS IT?
THE ROOM WITH THE STRANGE POKÉMON.
134
SHFF
LUNGE
GRAB
A WILD DUSCLOPS!
BORN AND RAISED AT...
...MT. PYRE, I THINK!

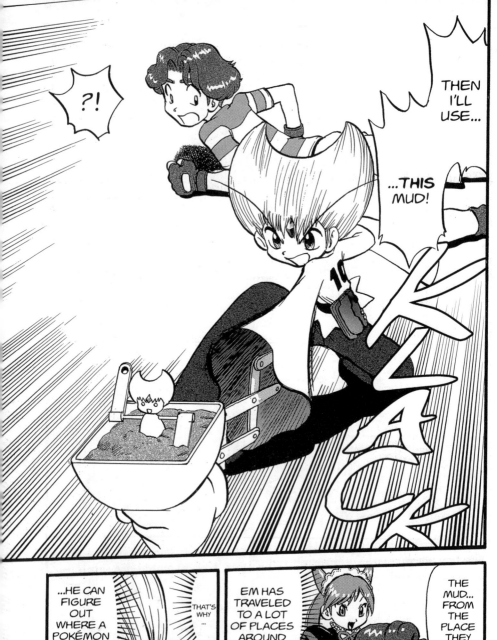

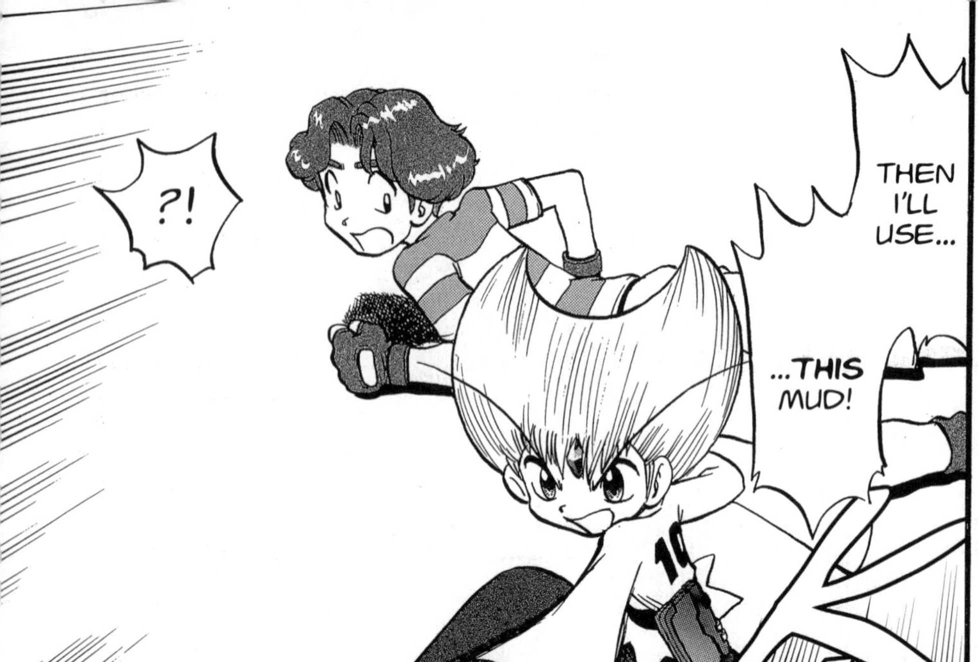
THEN I'LL USE...
...THIS MUD!
KLACK
?!

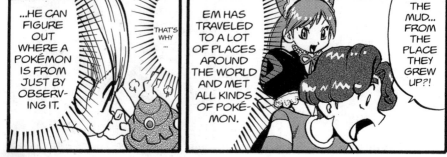

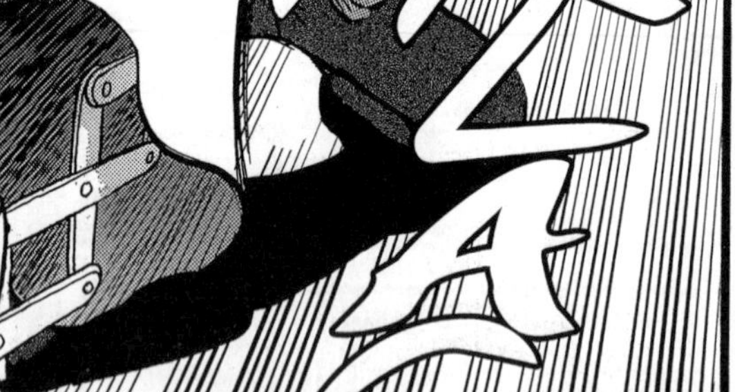
THE MUD... FROM THE PLACE THEY GREW UP?!
EM HAS TRAVELED TO A LOT OF PLACES AROUND THE WORLD AND MET ALL KINDS OF POKÉ-MON.

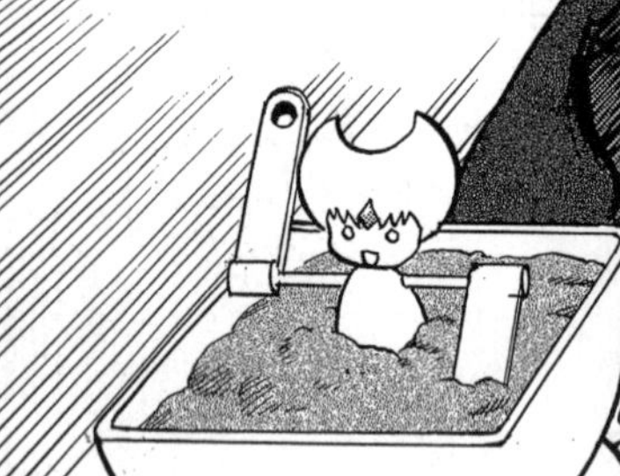
THAT'S WHY ...
...HE CAN FIGURE OUT WHERE A POKÉMON IS FROM JUST BY OBSERV-ING IT.

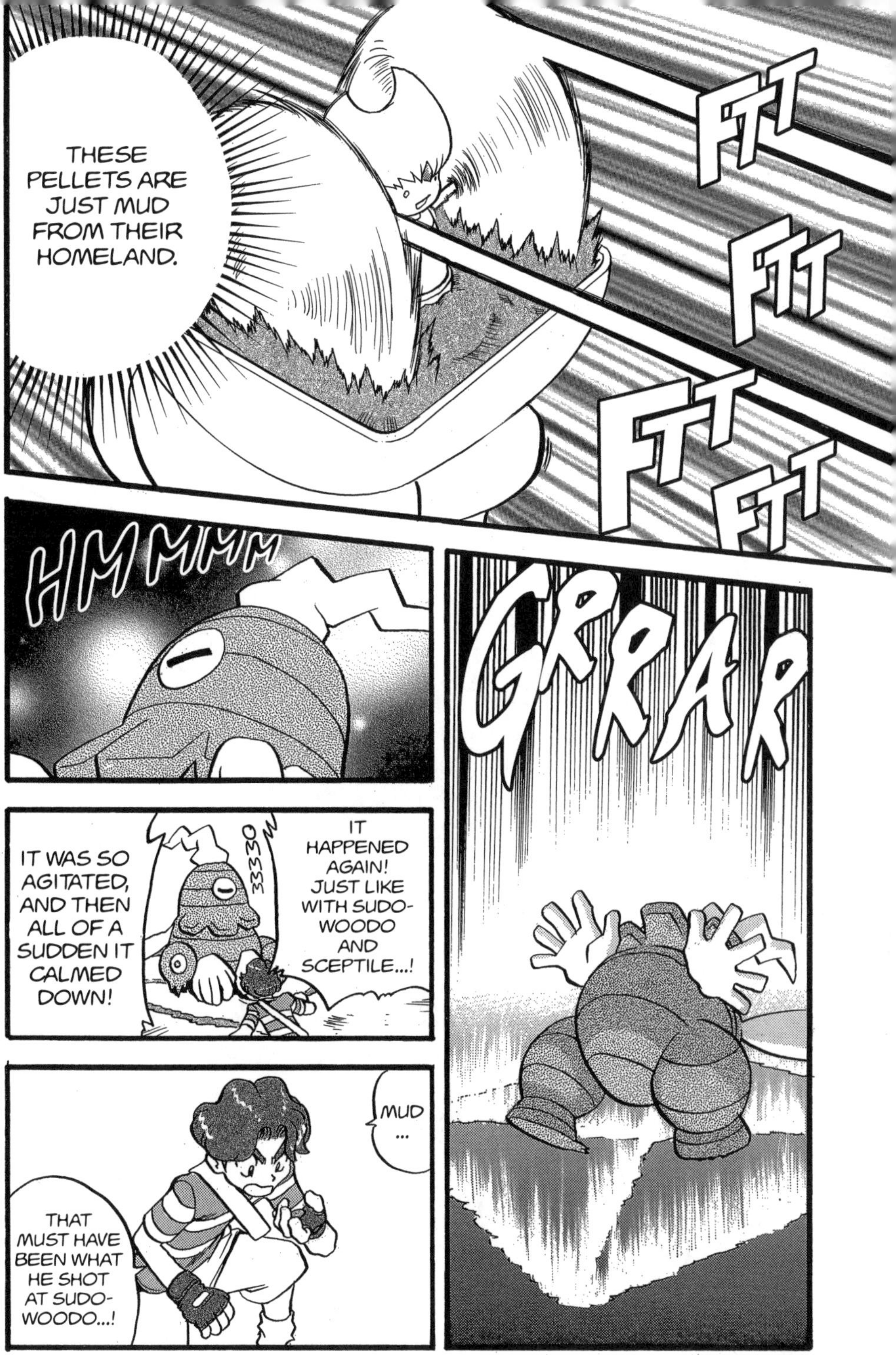
FTT
FTT
FTT
FTT
THESE PELLETS ARE JUST MUD FROM THEIR HOMELAND.
GRRAR
HMMMM
IT HAPPENED AGAIN! JUST LIKE WITH SUDO-WOODO AND SCEPTILE...!
IT WAS SO AGITATED, AND THEN ALL OF A SUDDEN IT CALMED DOWN!
MUD ...
THAT MUST HAVE BEEN WHAT HE SHOT AT SUDO-WOODO...!

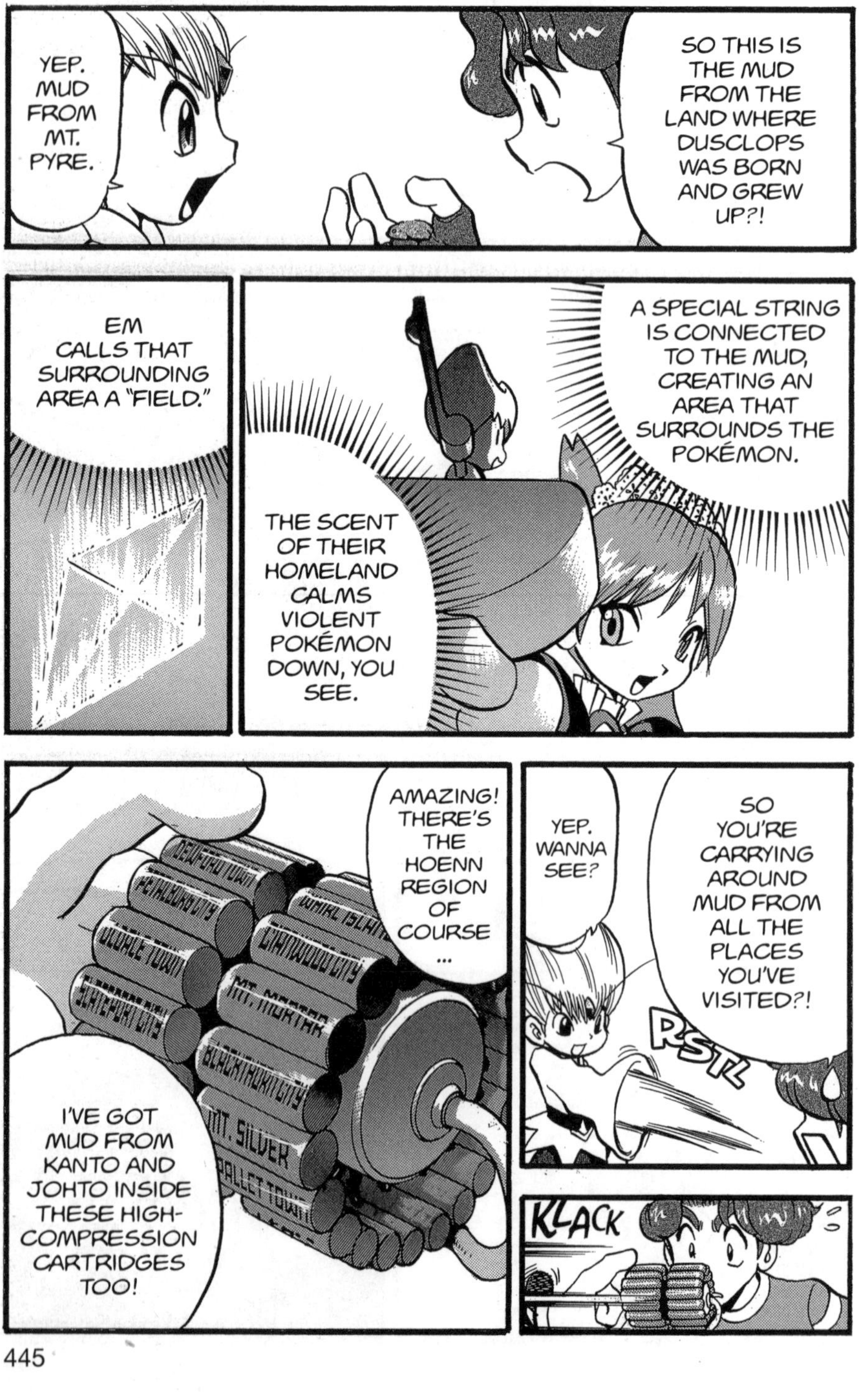
SO THIS IS THE MUD FROM THE LAND WHERE DUSCLOPS WAS BORN AND GREW UP?!
YEP. MUD FROM MT. PYRE.
A SPECIAL STRING IS CONNECTED TO THE MUD, CREATING AN AREA THAT SURROUNDS THE POKÉMON.
THE SCENT OF THEIR HOMELAND CALMS VIOLENT POKÉMON DOWN, YOU SEE.
EM CALLS THAT SURROUNDING AREA A "FIELD."
SO YOU'RE CARRYING AROUND MUD FROM ALL THE PLACES YOU'VE VISITED?!
YEP. WANNA SEE?
RSTL
KLACK
AMAZING! THERE'S THE HOENN REGION OF COURSE ...
MT. MORTAR
MT. SILVER
I'VE GOT MUD FROM KANTO AND JOHTO INSIDE THESE HIGH-COMPRESSION CARTRIDGES TOO!

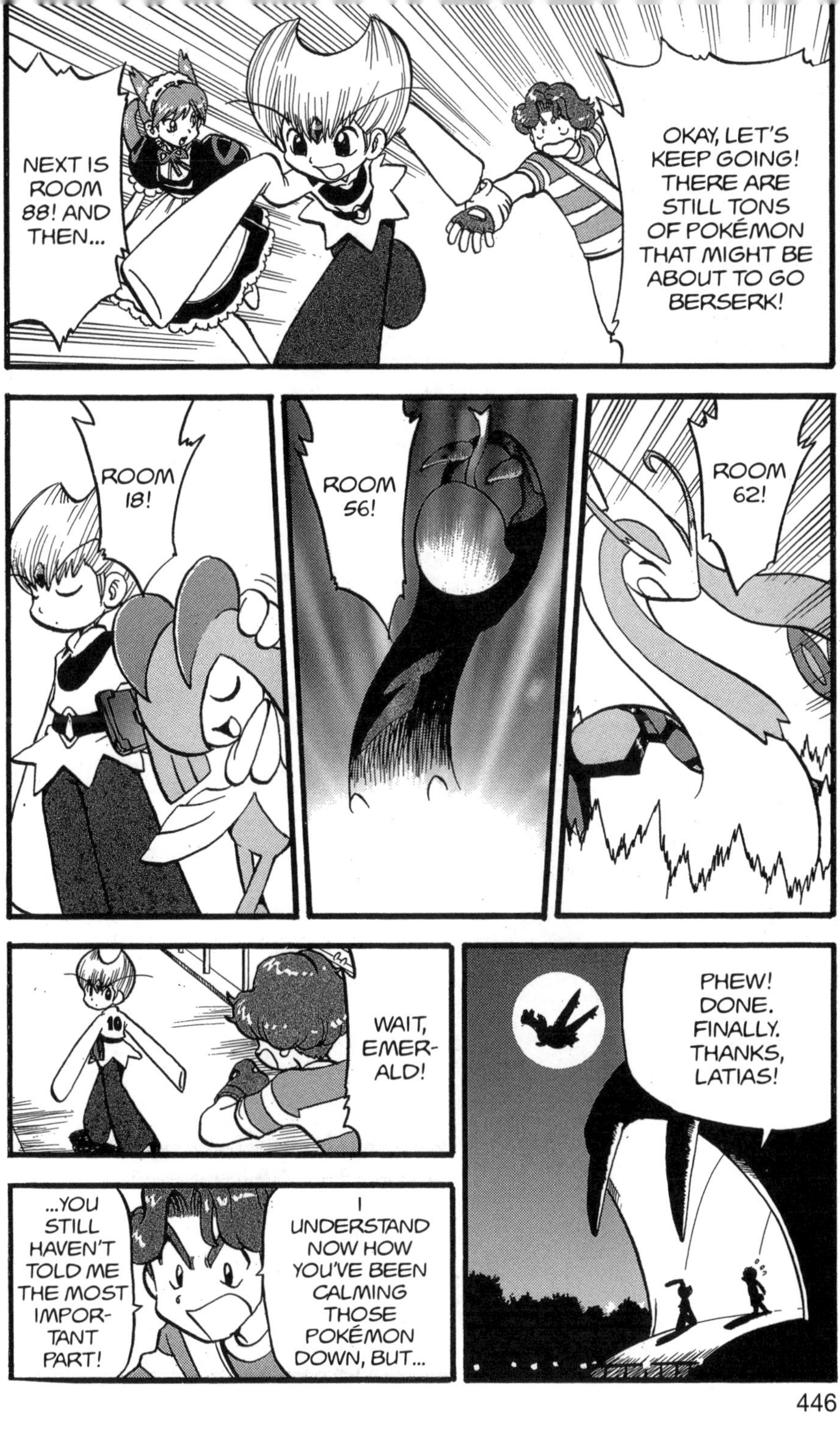
OKAY, LET'S KEEP GOING! THERE ARE STILL TONS OF POKÉMON THAT MIGHT BE ABOUT TO GO BERSERK!
NEXT IS ROOM 88! AND THEN...
ROOM 62!
ROOM 56!
ROOM 18!
PHEW! DONE. FINALLY. THANKS, LATIAS!
WAIT, EMER-ALD!
I UNDERSTAND NOW HOW YOU'VE BEEN CALMING THOSE POKÉMON DOWN, BUT...
...YOU STILL HAVEN'T TOLD ME THE MOST IMPOR-TANT PART!

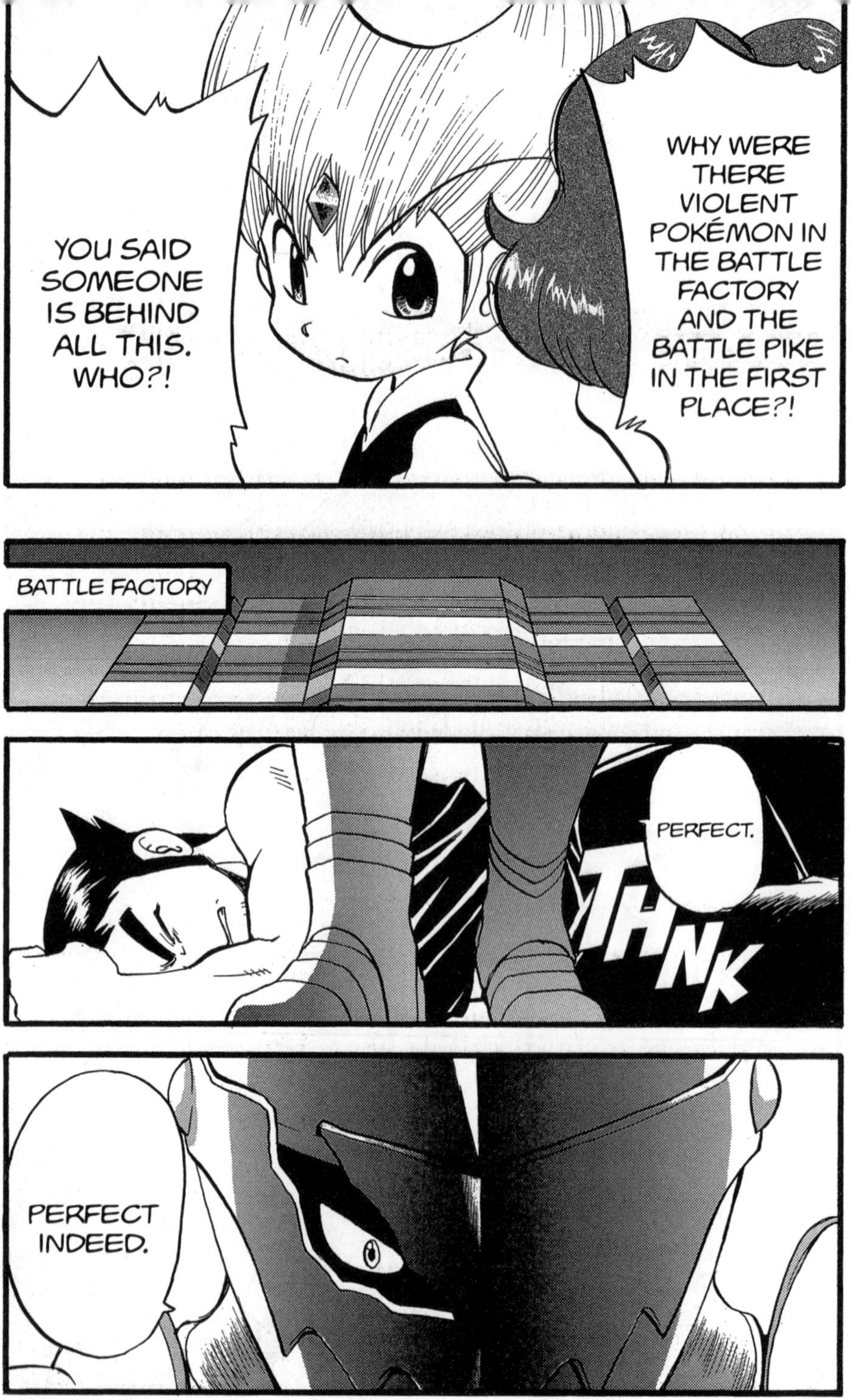
WHY WERE THERE VIOLENT POKÉMON IN THE BATTLE FACTORY AND THE BATTLE PIKE IN THE FIRST PLACE?!
YOU SAID SOMEONE IS BEHIND ALL THIS. WHO?!
BATTLE FACTORY
PERFECT.
THNK
PERFECT INDEED.

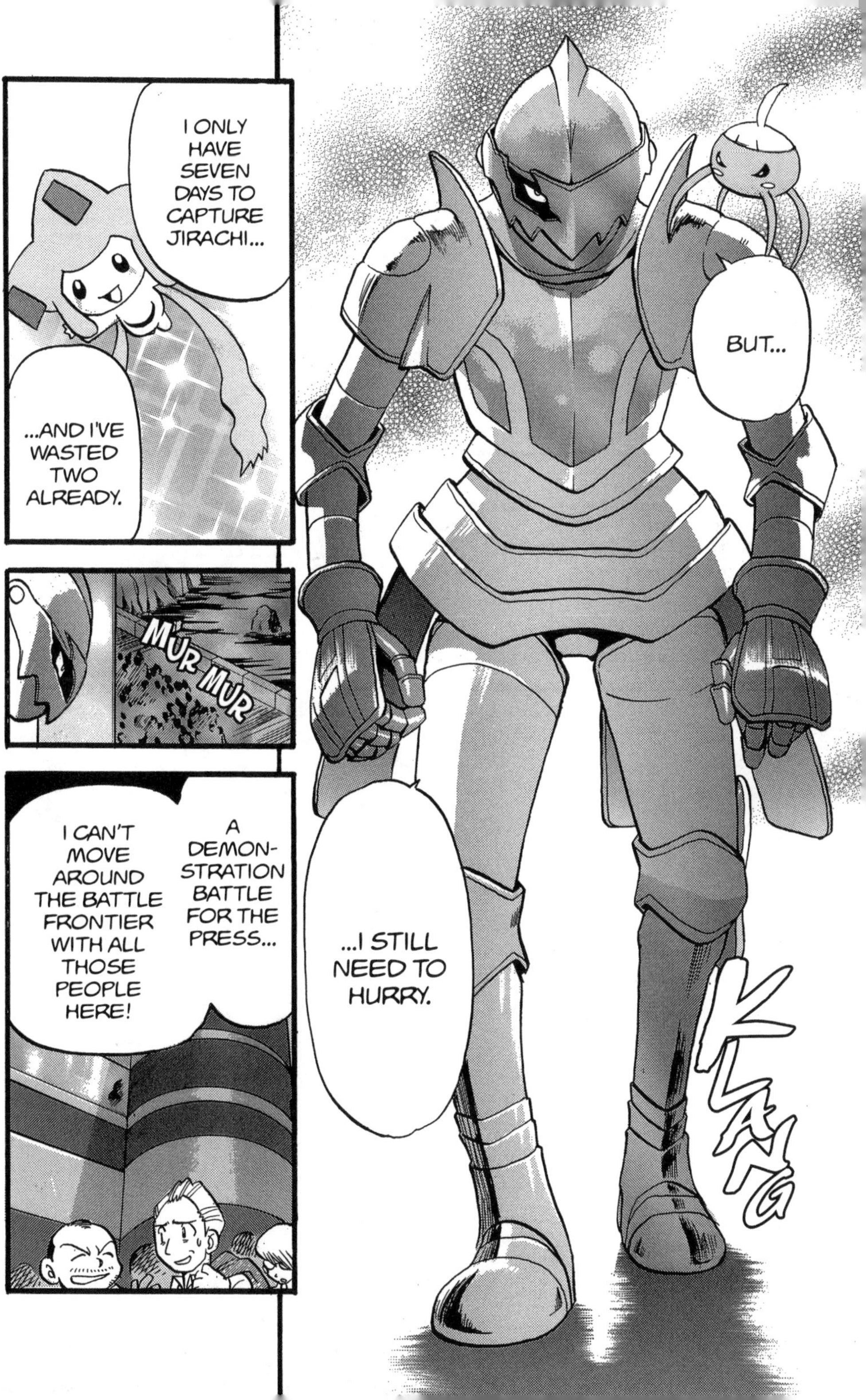
I ONLY HAVE SEVEN DAYS TO CAPTURE JIRACHI...
...AND I'VE WASTED TWO ALREADY.
MUR MUR
A DEMONSTRATION BATTLE FOR THE PRESS...
I CAN'T MOVE AROUND THE BATTLE FRONTIER WITH ALL THOSE PEOPLE HERE!
BUT...
...I STILL NEED TO HURRY.
KLANG

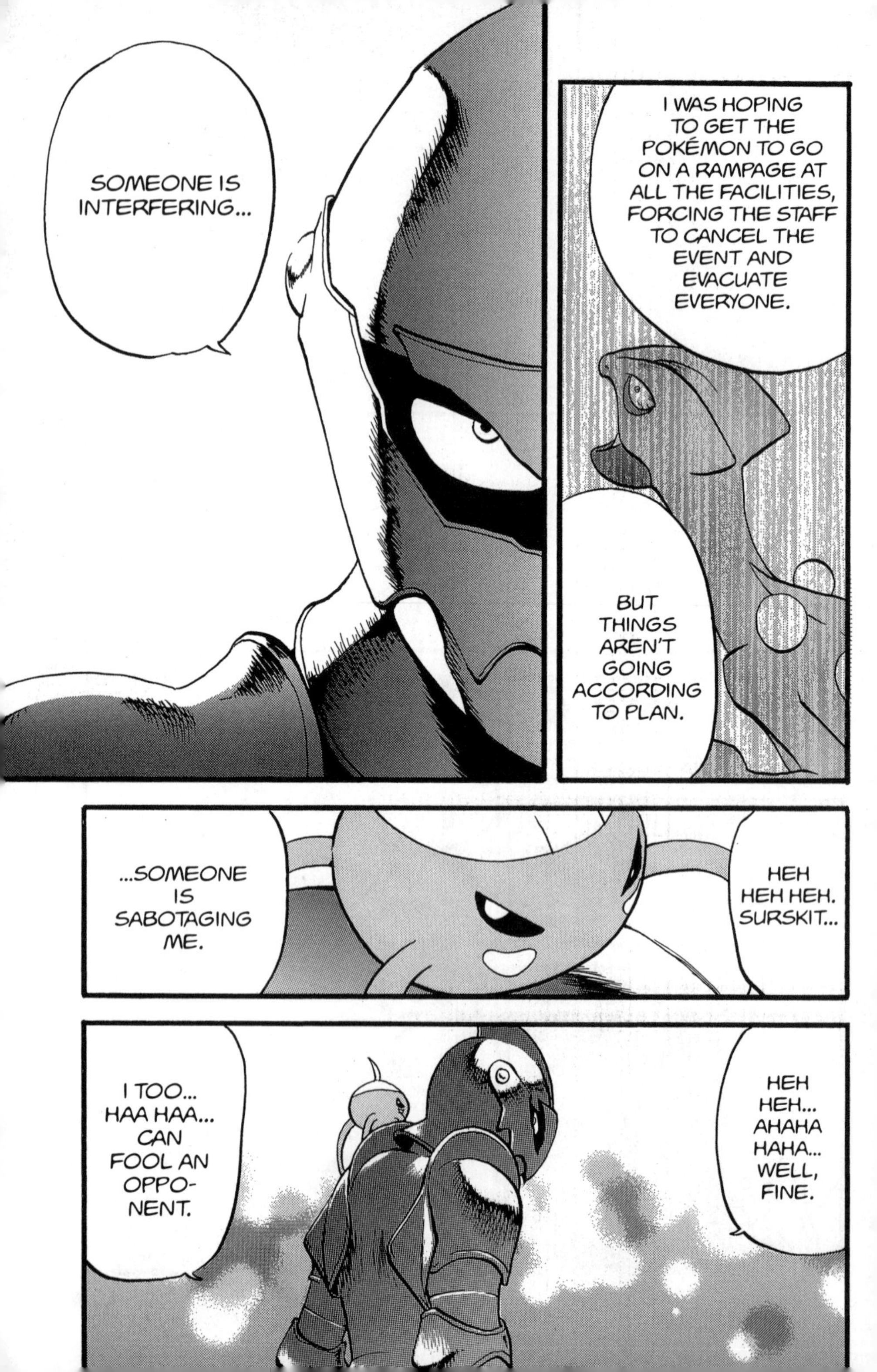
I WAS HOPING TO GET THE POKÉMON TO GO ON A RAMPAGE AT ALL THE FACILITIES, FORCING THE STAFF TO CANCEL THE EVENT AND EVACUATE EVERYONE.
BUT THINGS AREN'T GOING ACCORDING TO PLAN.
SOMEONE IS INTERFERING...
HEH HEH HEH. SURSKIT...
...SOMEONE IS SABOTAGING ME.
HEH HEH... AHAHA HAHA... WELL, FINE.
I TOO... HAA HAA... CAN FOOL AN OPPO-NENT.

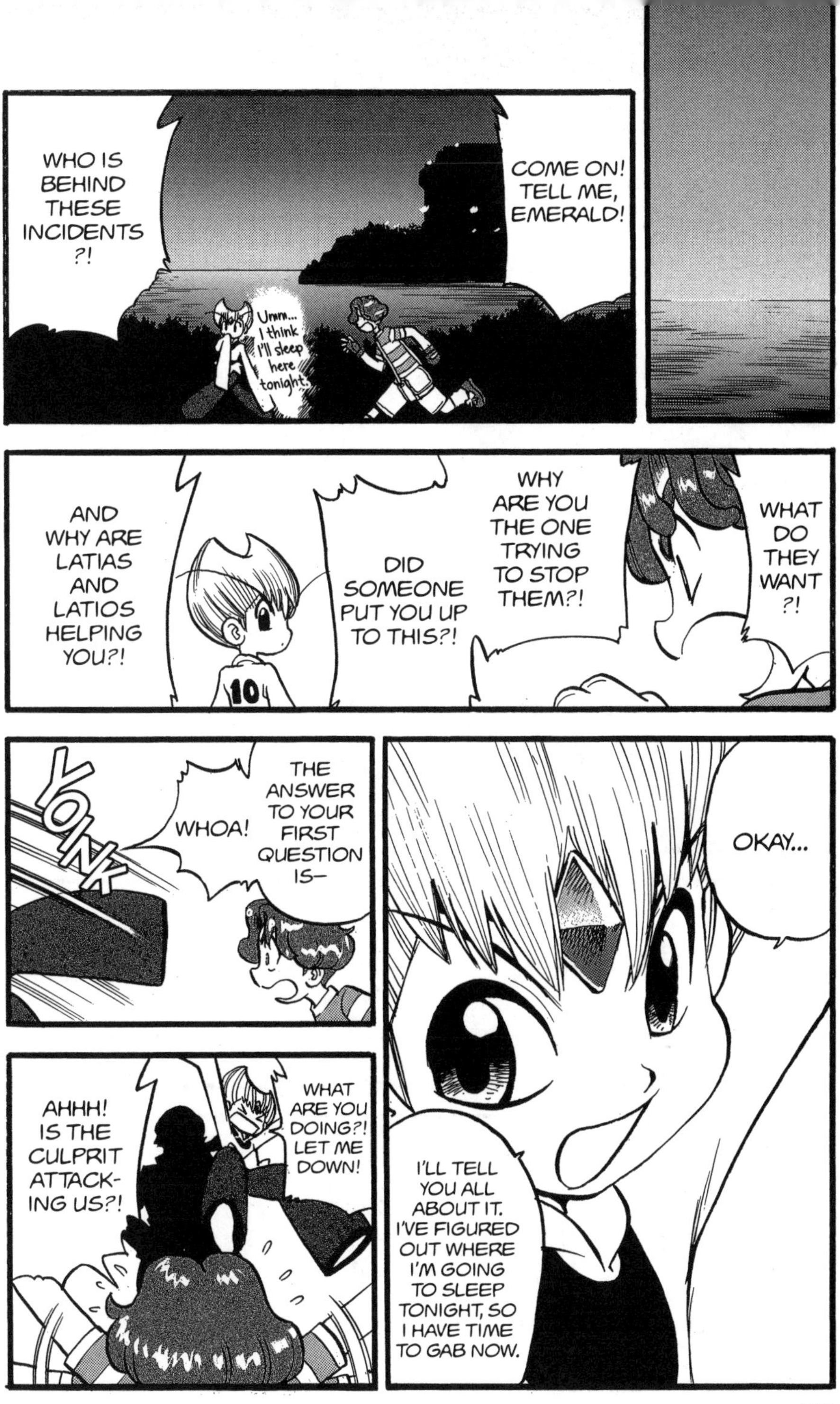
COME ON! TELL ME, EMERALD!
WHO IS BEHIND THESE INCIDENTS?!
Umm... I think I'll sleep here tonight.
WHAT DO THEY WANT?!
WHY ARE YOU THE ONE TRYING TO STOP THEM?!
DID SOMEONE PUT YOU UP TO THIS?!
AND WHY ARE LATIAS AND LATIOS HELPING YOU?!
OKAY...
I'LL TELL YOU ALL ABOUT IT. I'VE FIGURED OUT WHERE I'M GOING TO SLEEP TONIGHT, SO I HAVE TIME TO GAB NOW.
THE ANSWER TO YOUR FIRST QUESTION IS—
WHOA!
YOINK
WHAT ARE YOU DOING?! LET ME DOWN!
AHHH! IS THE CULPRIT ATTACKING US?!

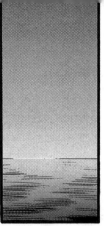

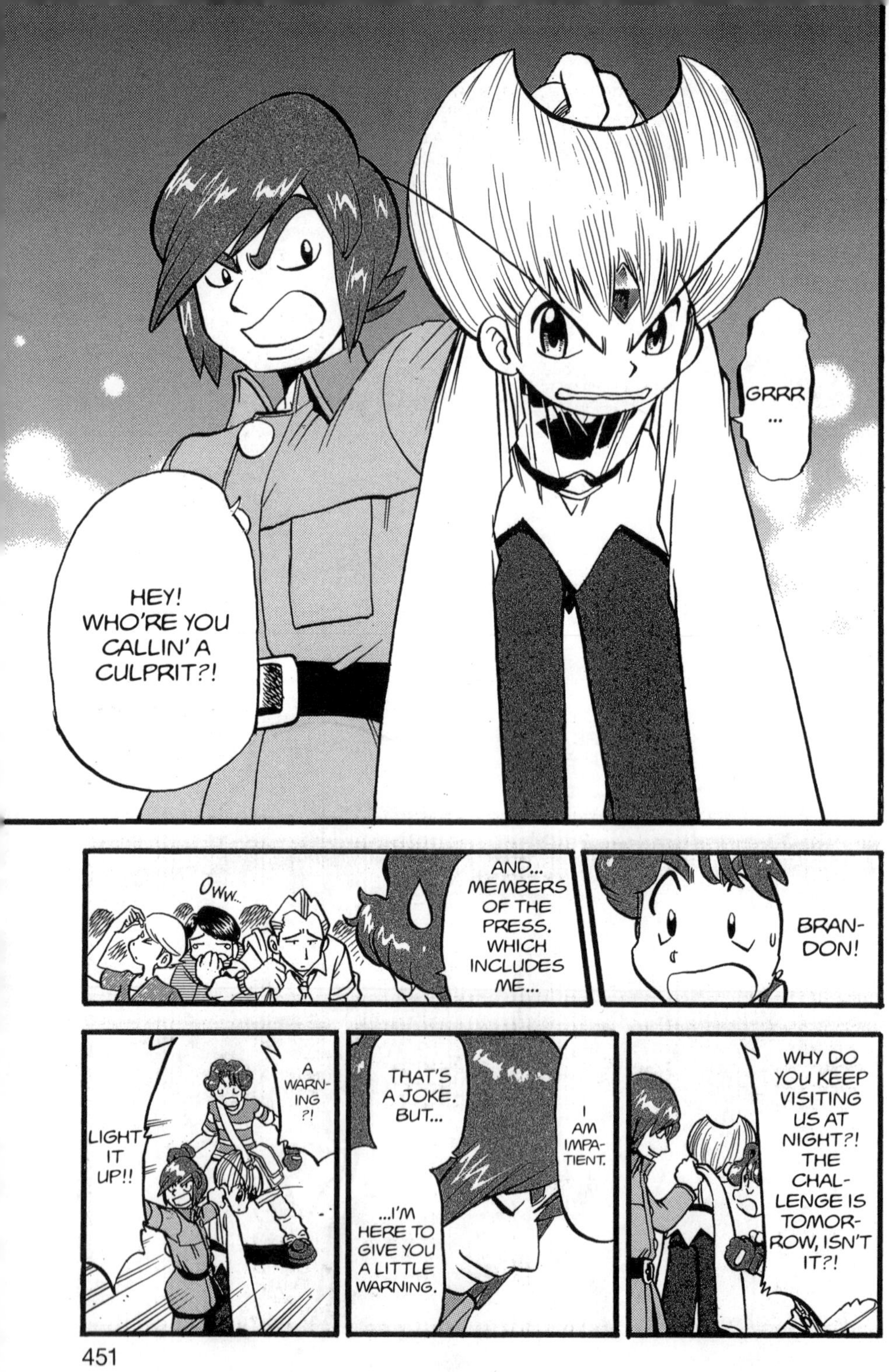
GRRR...
HEY! WHO'RE YOU CALLIN' A CULPRIT?!
BRAN-DON!
AND... MEMBERS OF THE PRESS. WHICH INCLUDES ME...
OWW...
WHY DO YOU KEEP VISITING US AT NIGHT?! THE CHAL-LENGE IS TOMOR-ROW, ISN'T IT?!
I AM IMPA-TIENT.
THAT'S A JOKE. BUT...
...I'M HERE TO GIVE YOU A LITTLE WARNING.
A WARN-ING?!
LIGHT IT UP!!

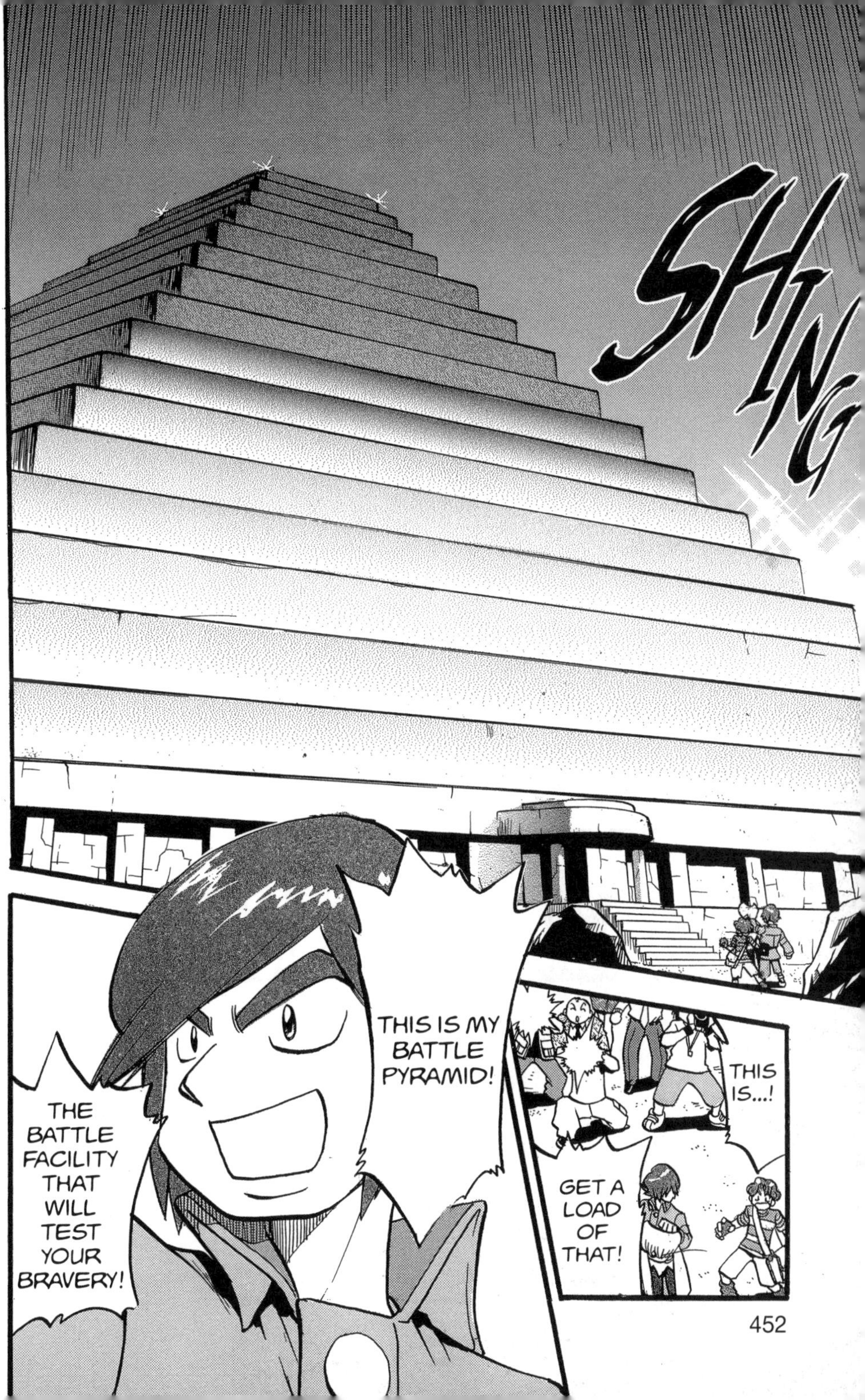
SHING
THIS IS...!
GET A LOAD OF THAT!
THIS IS MY BATTLE PYRAMID!
THE BATTLE FACILITY THAT WILL TEST YOUR BRAVERY!

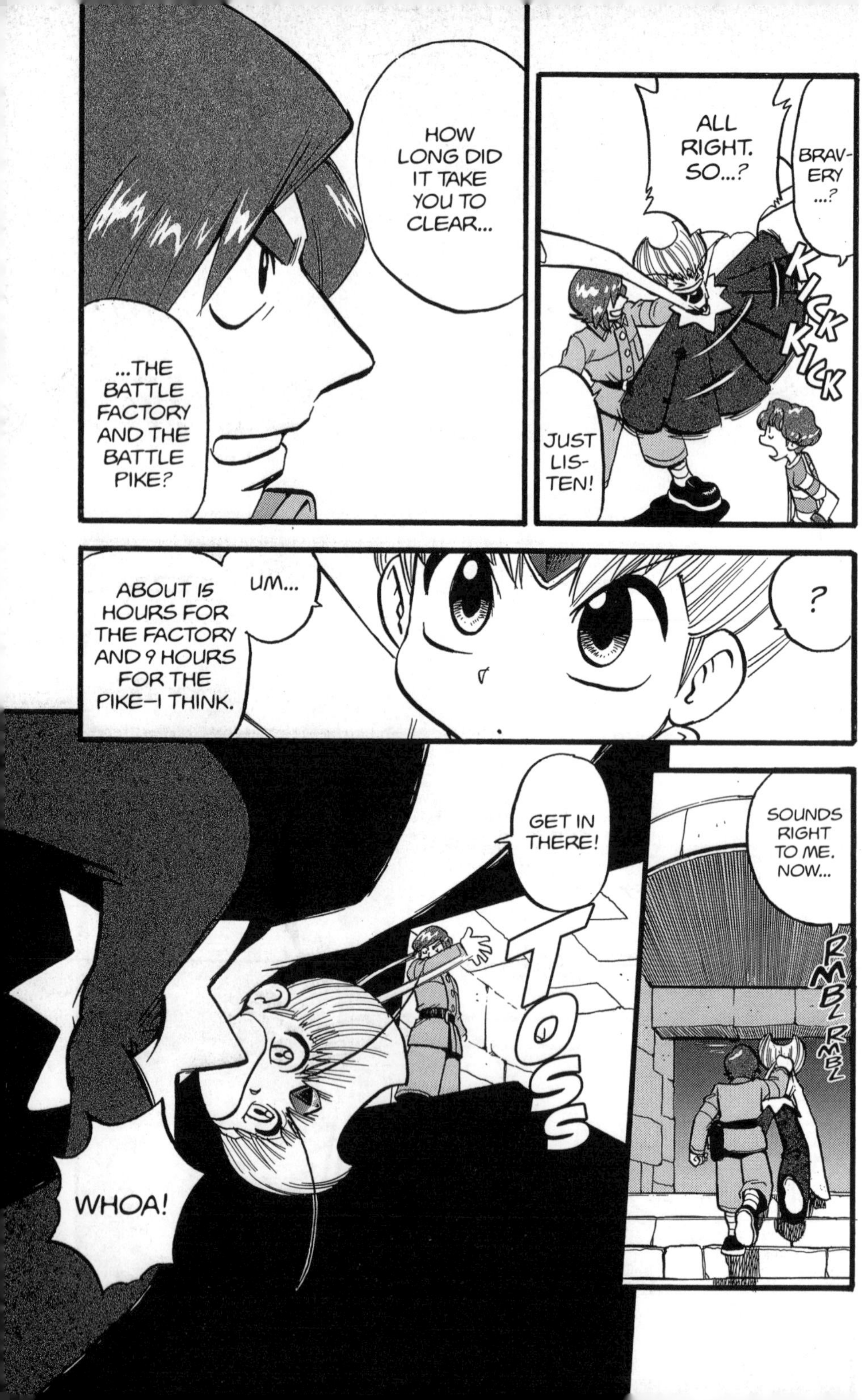
BRAVERY...?
ALL RIGHT. SO...?
KICK
KICK
JUST LISTEN!
HOW LONG DID IT TAKE YOU TO CLEAR...
...THE BATTLE FACTORY AND THE BATTLE PIKE?
?
UM...
ABOUT 15 HOURS FOR THE FACTORY AND 9 HOURS FOR THE PIKE—I THINK.
SOUNDS RIGHT TO ME. NOW...
RMBL RMBL
GET IN THERE!
TOSS
WHOA!

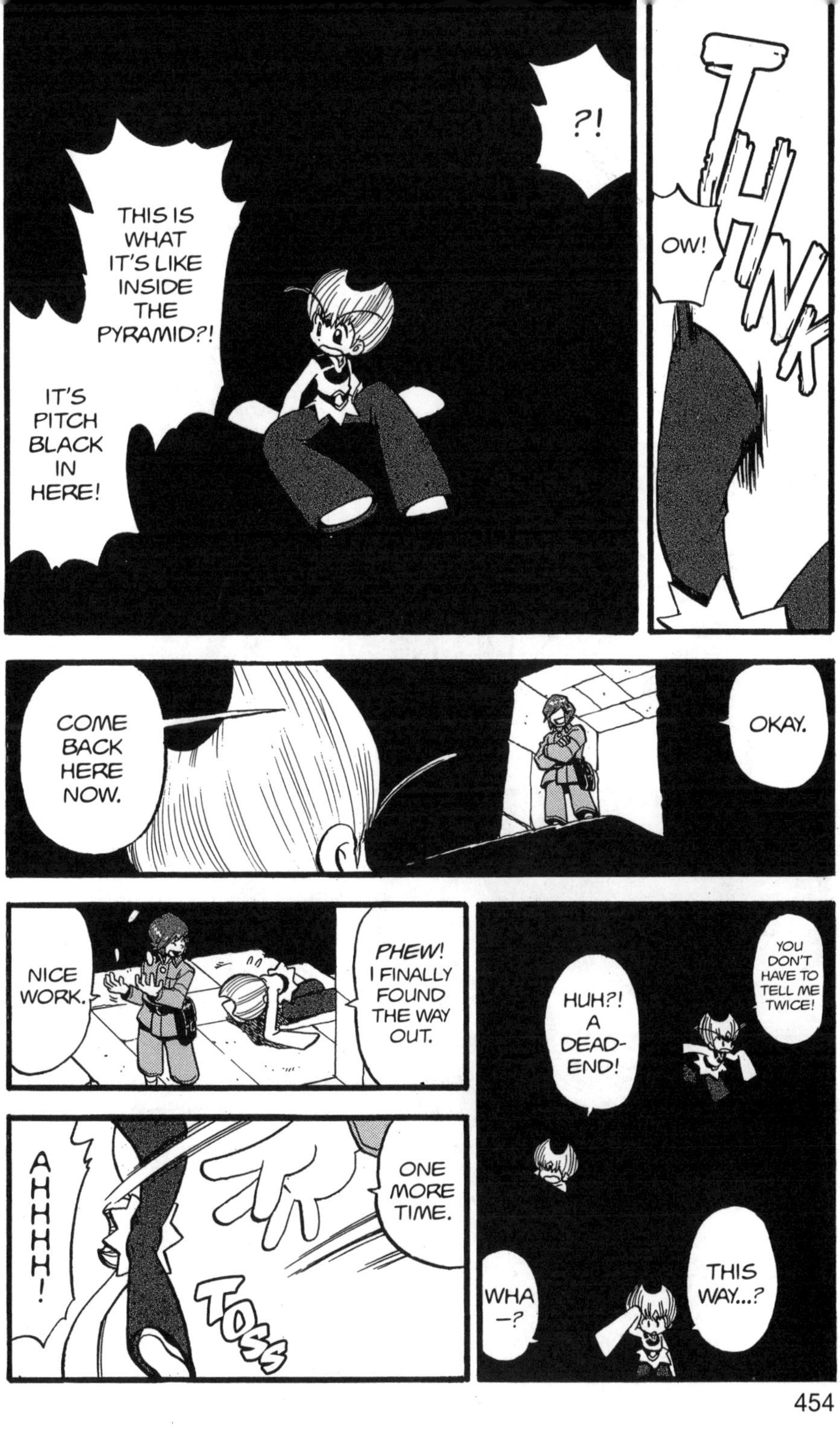
THUNK
OW!
?!
THIS IS WHAT IT'S LIKE INSIDE THE PYRAMID?!
IT'S PITCH BLACK IN HERE!
OKAY.
COME BACK HERE NOW.
YOU DON'T HAVE TO TELL ME TWICE!
HUH?! A DEAD-END!
THIS WAY...?
WHA—?
PHEW! I FINALLY FOUND THE WAY OUT.
NICE WORK.
ONE MORE TIME.
TOSS
AHHHH!

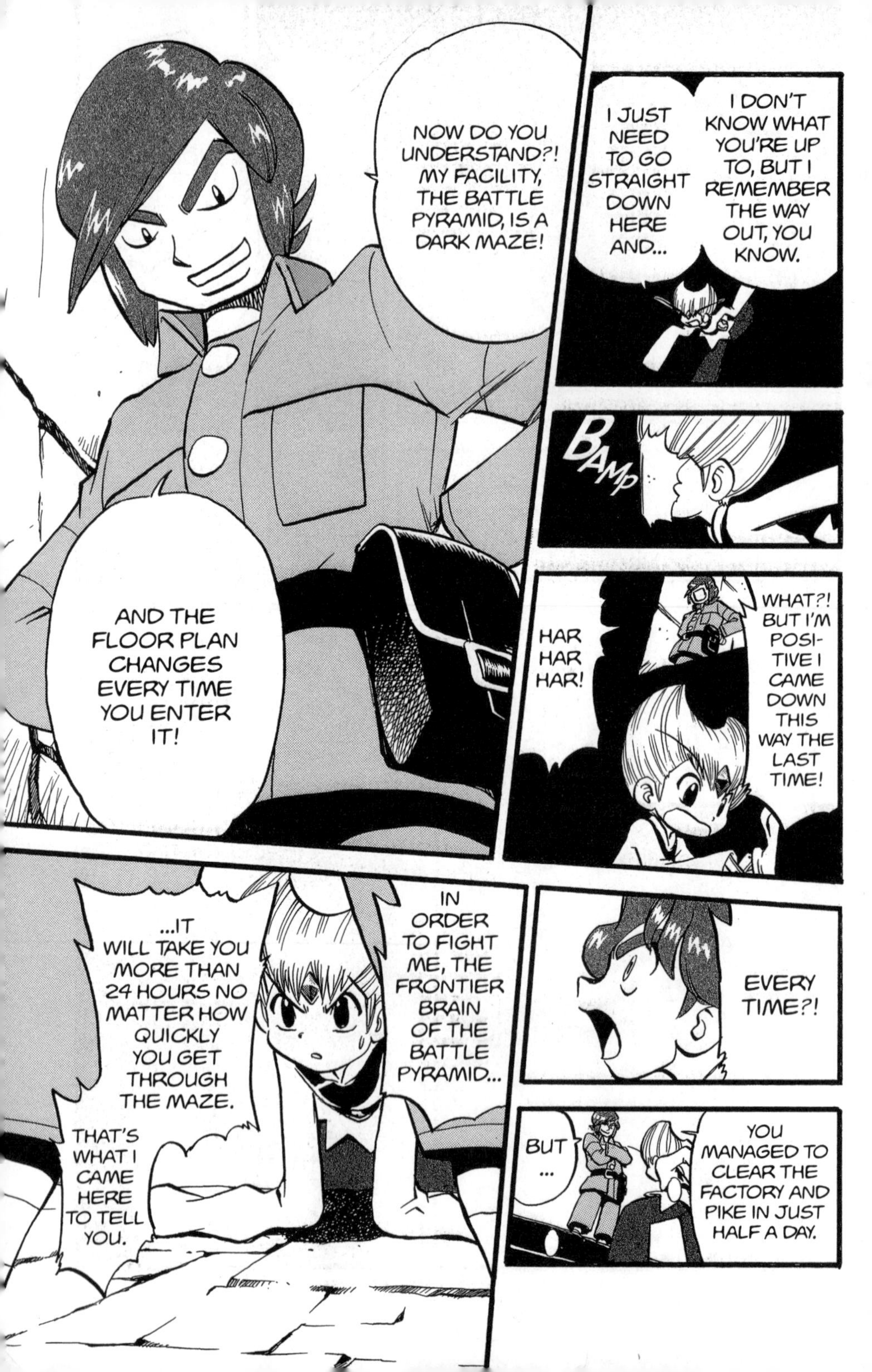
I DON'T KNOW WHAT YOU'RE UP TO, BUT I REMEMBER THE WAY OUT, YOU KNOW.
I JUST NEED TO GO STRAIGHT DOWN HERE AND...
BAMP
WHAT?! BUT I'M POSI-TIVE I CAME DOWN THIS WAY THE LAST TIME!
HAR HAR HAR!
NOW DO YOU UNDERSTAND?! MY FACILITY, THE BATTLE PYRAMID, IS A DARK MAZE!
AND THE FLOOR PLAN CHANGES EVERY TIME YOU ENTER IT!
EVERY TIME?!
YOU MANAGED TO CLEAR THE FACTORY AND PIKE IN JUST HALF A DAY.
BUT ...
IN ORDER TO FIGHT ME, THE FRONTIER BRAIN OF THE BATTLE PYRAMID...
...IT WILL TAKE YOU MORE THAN 24 HOURS NO MATTER HOW QUICKLY YOU GET THROUGH THE MAZE.
THAT'S WHAT I CAME HERE TO TELL YOU.

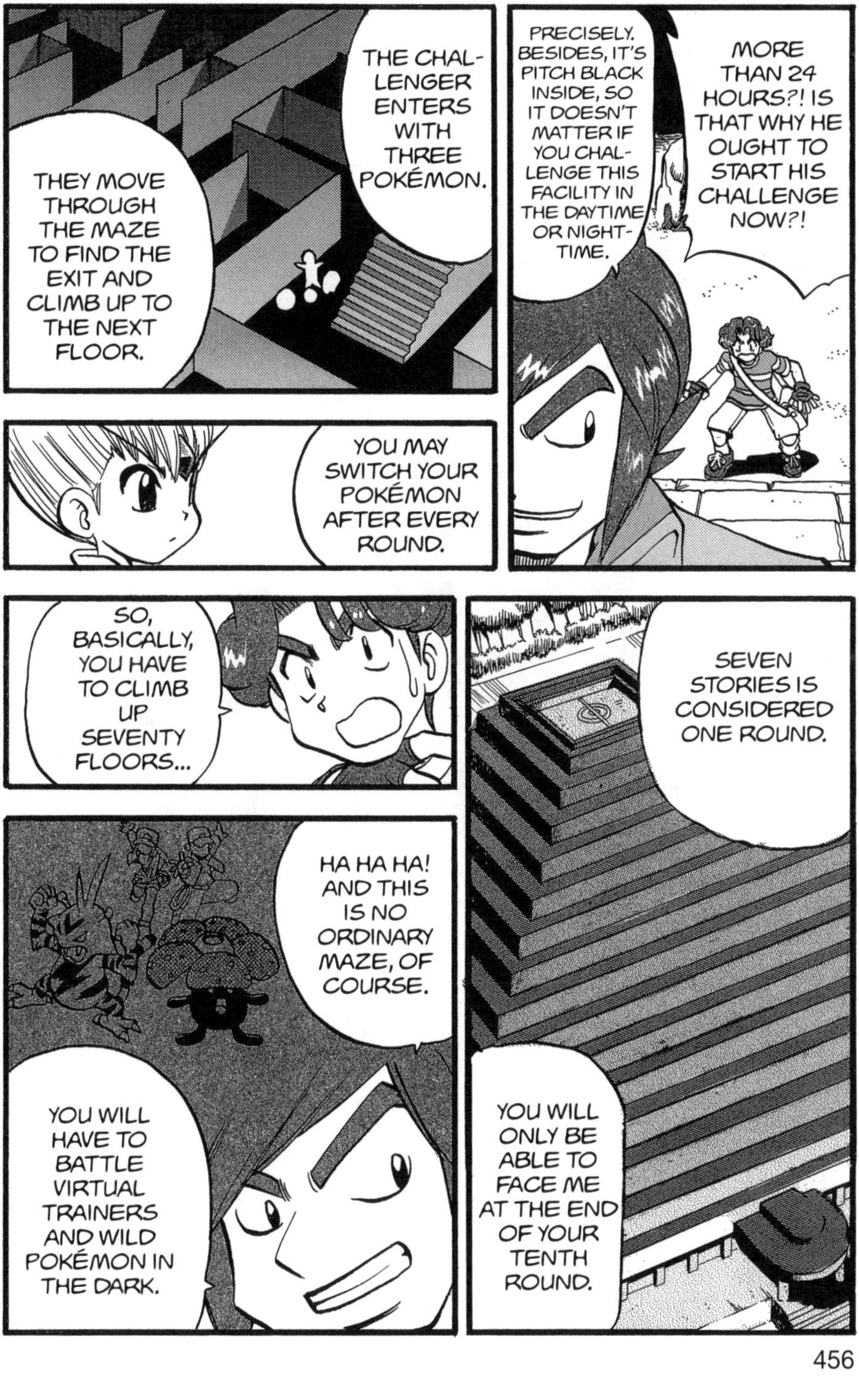
MORE THAN 24 HOURS?! IS THAT WHY HE OUGHT TO START HIS CHALLENGE NOW?!
PRECISELY. BESIDES, IT'S PITCH BLACK INSIDE, SO IT DOESN'T MATTER IF YOU CHALLENGE THIS FACILITY IN THE DAYTIME OR NIGHTTIME.
THE CHALLENGER ENTERS WITH THREE POKÉMON.
THEY MOVE THROUGH THE MAZE TO FIND THE EXIT AND CLIMB UP TO THE NEXT FLOOR.
YOU MAY SWITCH YOUR POKÉMON AFTER EVERY ROUND.
SEVEN STORIES IS CONSIDERED ONE ROUND.
YOU WILL ONLY BE ABLE TO FACE ME AT THE END OF YOUR TENTH ROUND.
SO, BASICALLY, YOU HAVE TO CLIMB UP SEVENTY FLOORS...
HA HA HA! AND THIS IS NO ORDINARY MAZE, OF COURSE.
YOU WILL HAVE TO BATTLE VIRTUAL TRAINERS AND WILD POKÉMON IN THE DARK.

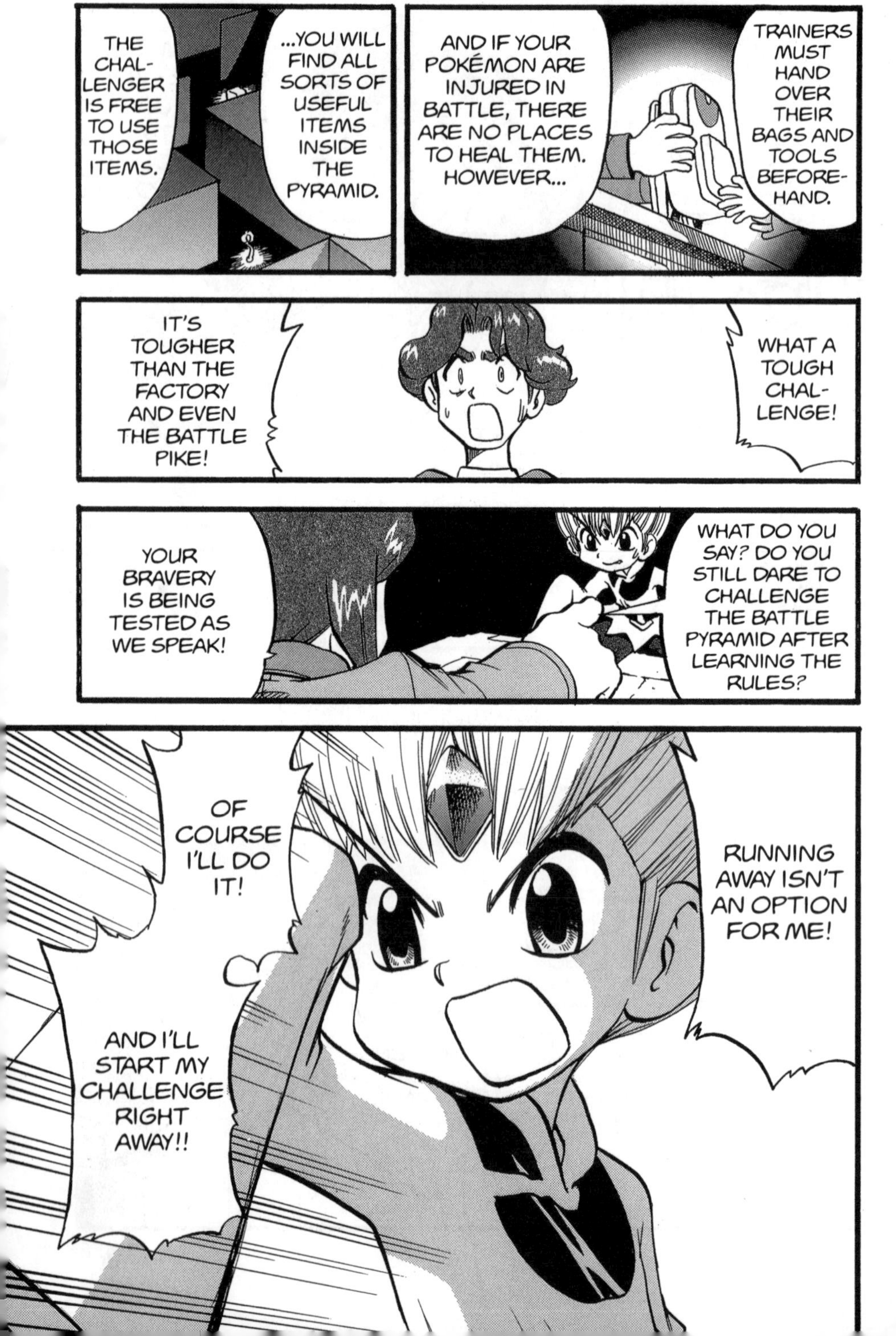
TRAINERS MUST HAND OVER THEIR BAGS AND TOOLS BEFOREHAND.
AND IF YOUR POKÉMON ARE INJURED IN BATTLE, THERE ARE NO PLACES TO HEAL THEM. HOWEVER...
...YOU WILL FIND ALL SORTS OF USEFUL ITEMS INSIDE THE PYRAMID.
THE CHALLENGER IS FREE TO USE THOSE ITEMS.
WHAT A TOUGH CHALLENGE!
IT'S TOUGHER THAN THE FACTORY AND EVEN THE BATTLE PIKE!
WHAT DO YOU SAY? DO YOU STILL DARE TO CHALLENGE THE BATTLE PYRAMID AFTER LEARNING THE RULES?
YOUR BRAVERY IS BEING TESTED AS WE SPEAK!
RUNNING AWAY ISN'T AN OPTION FOR ME!
OF COURSE I'LL DO IT!
AND I'LL START MY CHALLENGE RIGHT AWAY!!

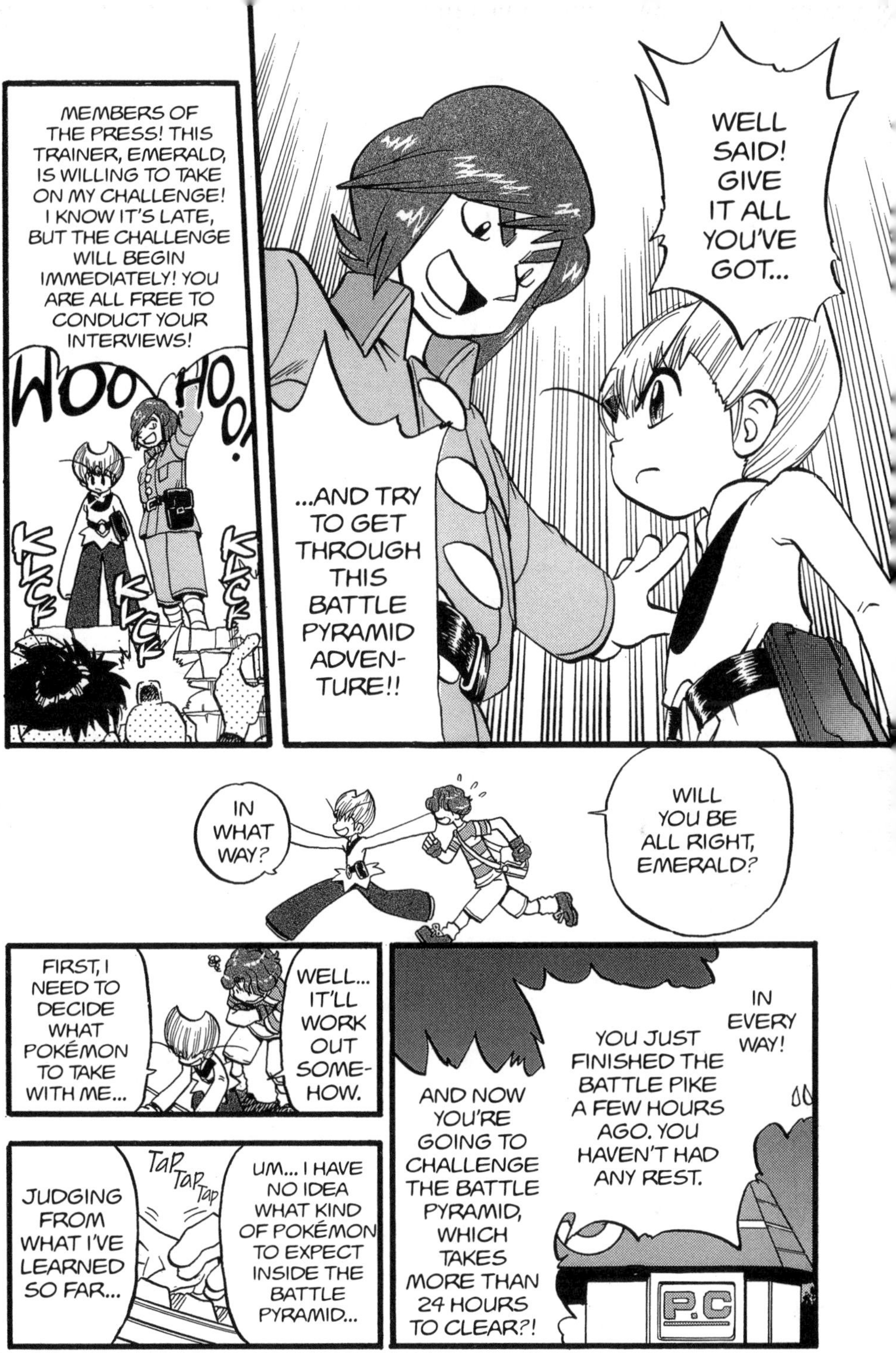
WELL SAID! GIVE IT ALL YOU'VE GOT...
...AND TRY TO GET THROUGH THIS BATTLE PYRAMID ADVENTURE!!
MEMBERS OF THE PRESS! THIS TRAINER, EMERALD, IS WILLING TO TAKE ON MY CHALLENGE! I KNOW IT'S LATE, BUT THE CHALLENGE WILL BEGIN IMMEDIATELY! YOU ARE ALL FREE TO CONDUCT YOUR INTERVIEWS!
WOO HOO!
KLICK
KLICK
KLICK
WILL YOU BE ALL RIGHT, EMERALD?
IN WHAT WAY?
IN EVERY WAY!
YOU JUST FINISHED THE BATTLE PIKE A FEW HOURS AGO. YOU HAVEN'T HAD ANY REST.
AND NOW YOU'RE GOING TO CHALLENGE THE BATTLE PYRAMID, WHICH TAKES MORE THAN 24 HOURS TO CLEAR?!
P.C
WELL... IT'LL WORK OUT SOME-HOW.
FIRST, I NEED TO DECIDE WHAT POKÉMON TO TAKE WITH ME...
UM... I HAVE NO IDEA WHAT KIND OF POKÉMON TO EXPECT INSIDE THE BATTLE PYRAMID...
Tap Tap Tap
JUDGING FROM WHAT I'VE LEARNED SO FAR...

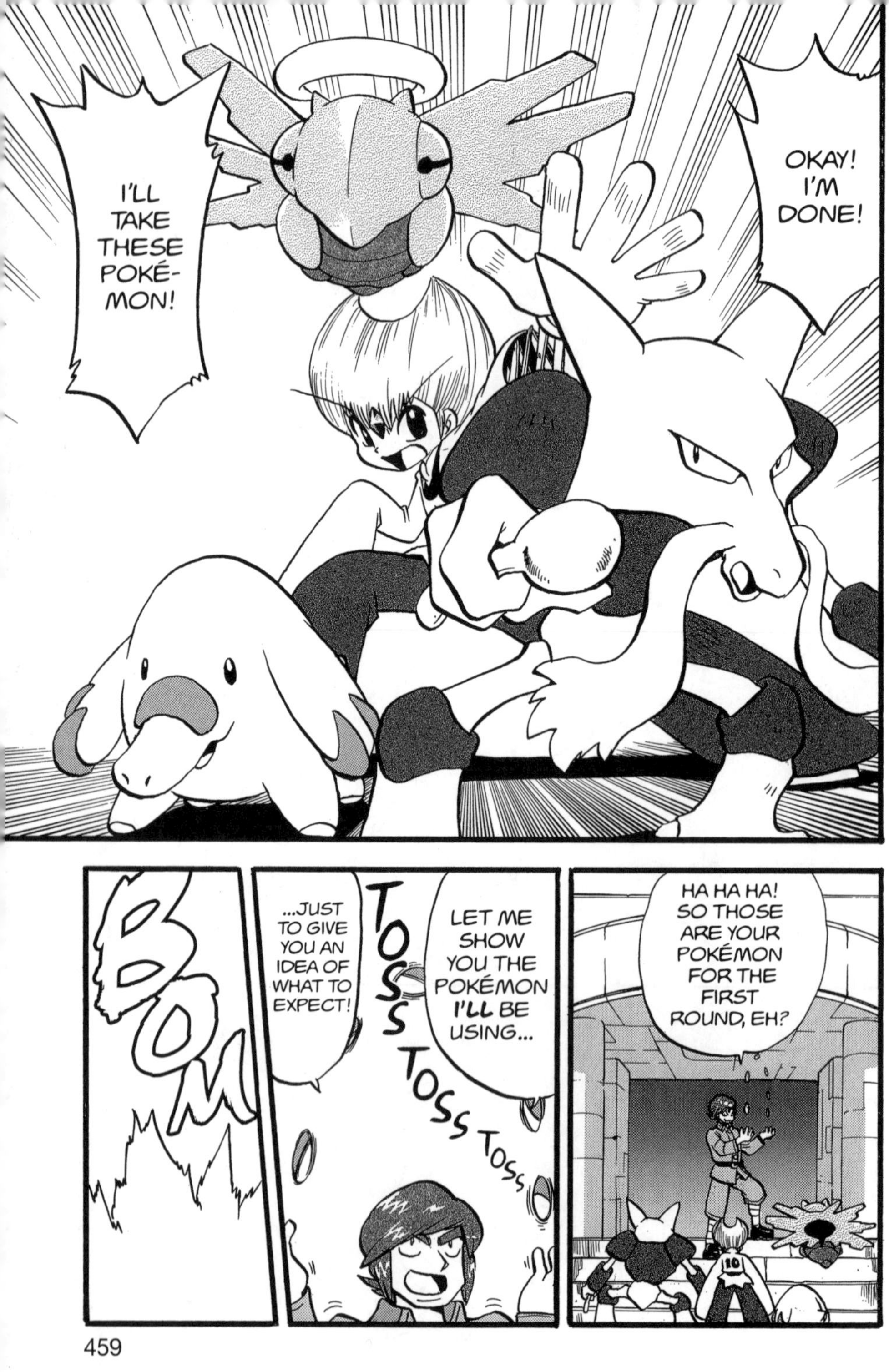
OKAY! I'M DONE!
I'LL TAKE THESE POKÉ-MON!
HA HA HA! SO THOSE ARE YOUR POKÉMON FOR THE FIRST ROUND, EH?
LET ME SHOW YOU THE POKÉMON **I'LL** BE USING...
...JUST TO GIVE YOU AN IDEA OF WHAT TO EXPECT!
TOSS TOSS TOSS TOSS
BOOM

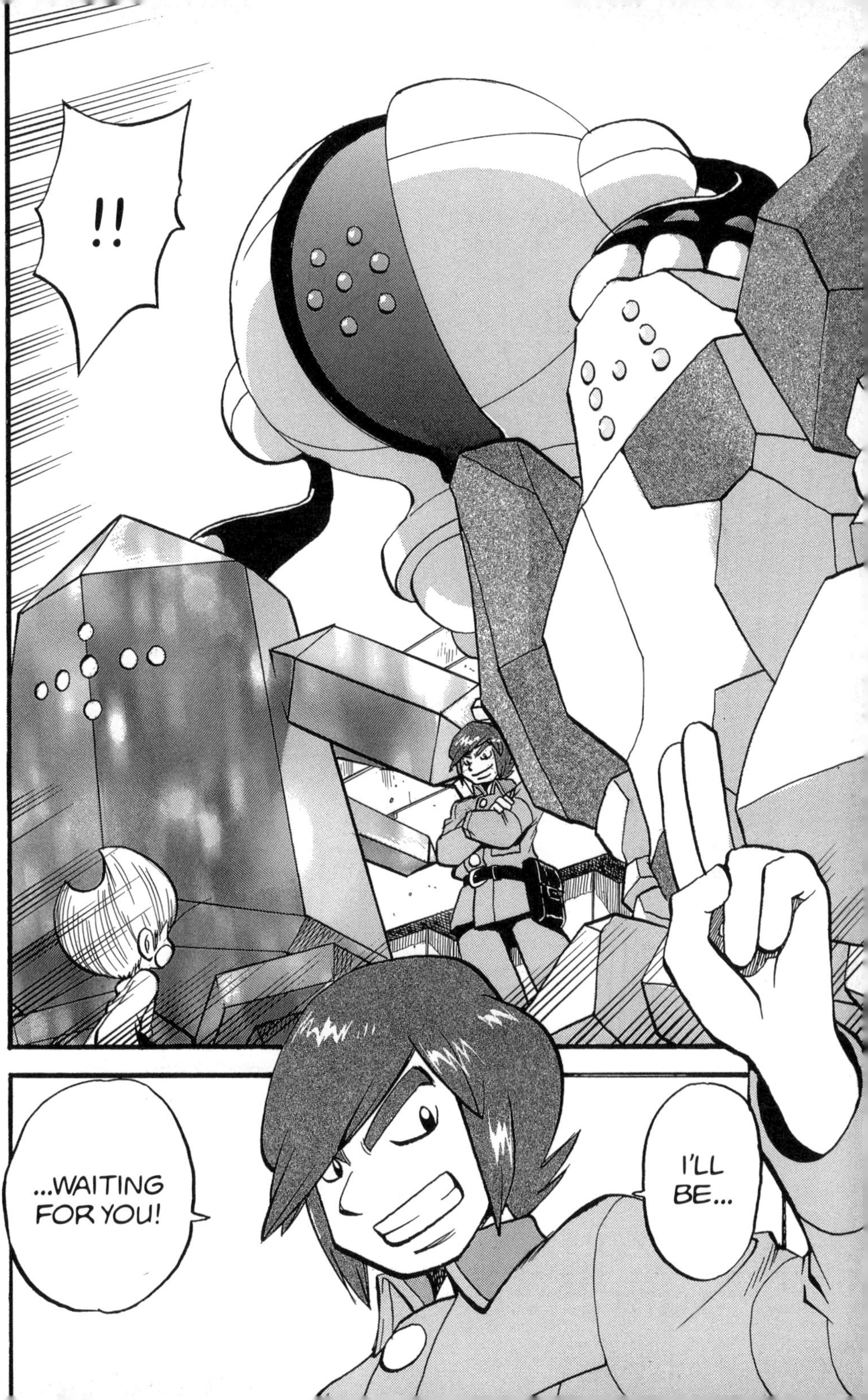
!!
I'LL BE...
...WAITING FOR YOU!

DEAR MEMBERS OF THE PRESS...

Thank you for visiting the Battle Frontier
today. Permit me to continue explaining
the rules of this facility...

OWNER: SCOTT

FACILITY RULES
BATTLE PYRAMID 2

The Battle Pyramid is the only facility
where the Trainer is allowed to use
items. This bulletin explains how the
items may be used.

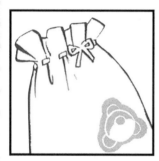

■ ITEMS WHICH CAN BE FOUND INSIDE THE FACILITY ■

The challenger will be provided with a Battle
Bag to stock items they find inside the pyramid.
The Bag already contains a Hyper Potion and
Ether. The challenger may keep the items they
find inside the pyramid once they reach the
next floor for use in their next round. But if the
challenger loses a round, the Bag will be reset
to its original state.

■ POKÉMON WHO APPEAR DURING THE VARIOUS ROUNDS ■

The challenger will be met by many Pokémon with paralyzing moves during
the first round, poisoning moves in the second, burning moves in the third, and
so on. In other words, the types of Pokémon that appear will vary depending
on the round.

312

Chipping Away at Regirock

POKÉMON ADVENTURES•THE SIXTH CHAPTER•EMERALD

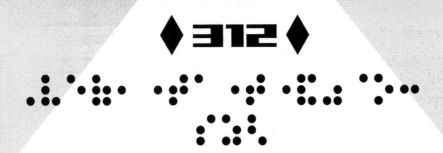

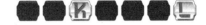

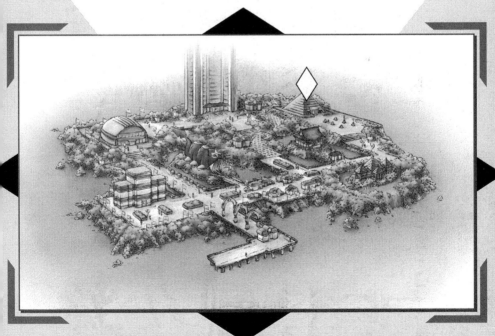

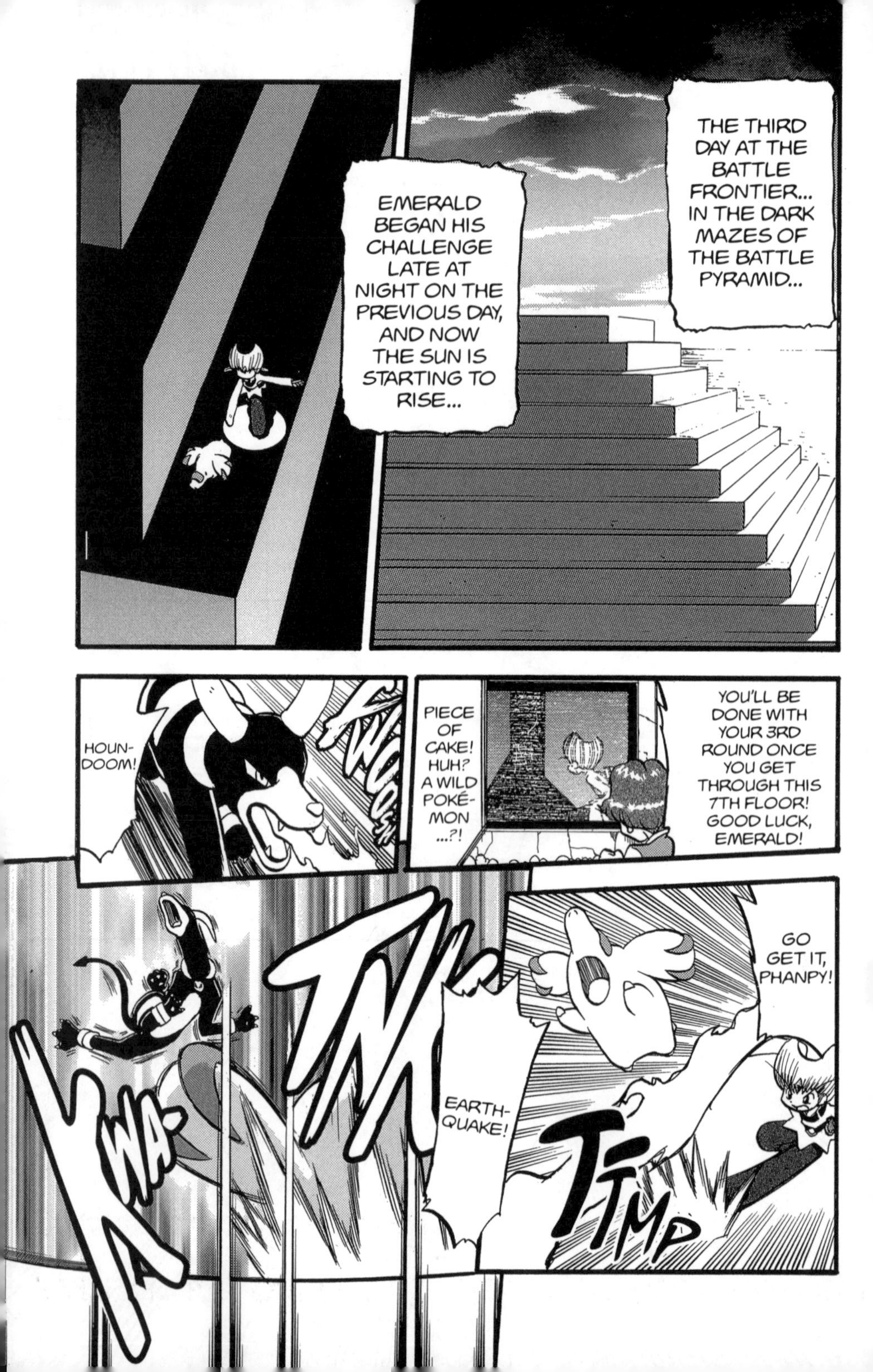
THE THIRD DAY AT THE BATTLE FRONTIER... IN THE DARK MAZES OF THE BATTLE PYRAMID...
EMERALD BEGAN HIS CHALLENGE LATE AT NIGHT ON THE PREVIOUS DAY, AND NOW THE SUN IS STARTING TO RISE...
YOU'LL BE DONE WITH YOUR 3RD ROUND ONCE YOU GET THROUGH THIS 7TH FLOOR! GOOD LUCK, EMERALD!
PIECE OF CAKE! HUH? A WILD POKÉMON ...?!
HOUN-DOOM!
GO GET IT, PHANPY!
EARTH-QUAKE!

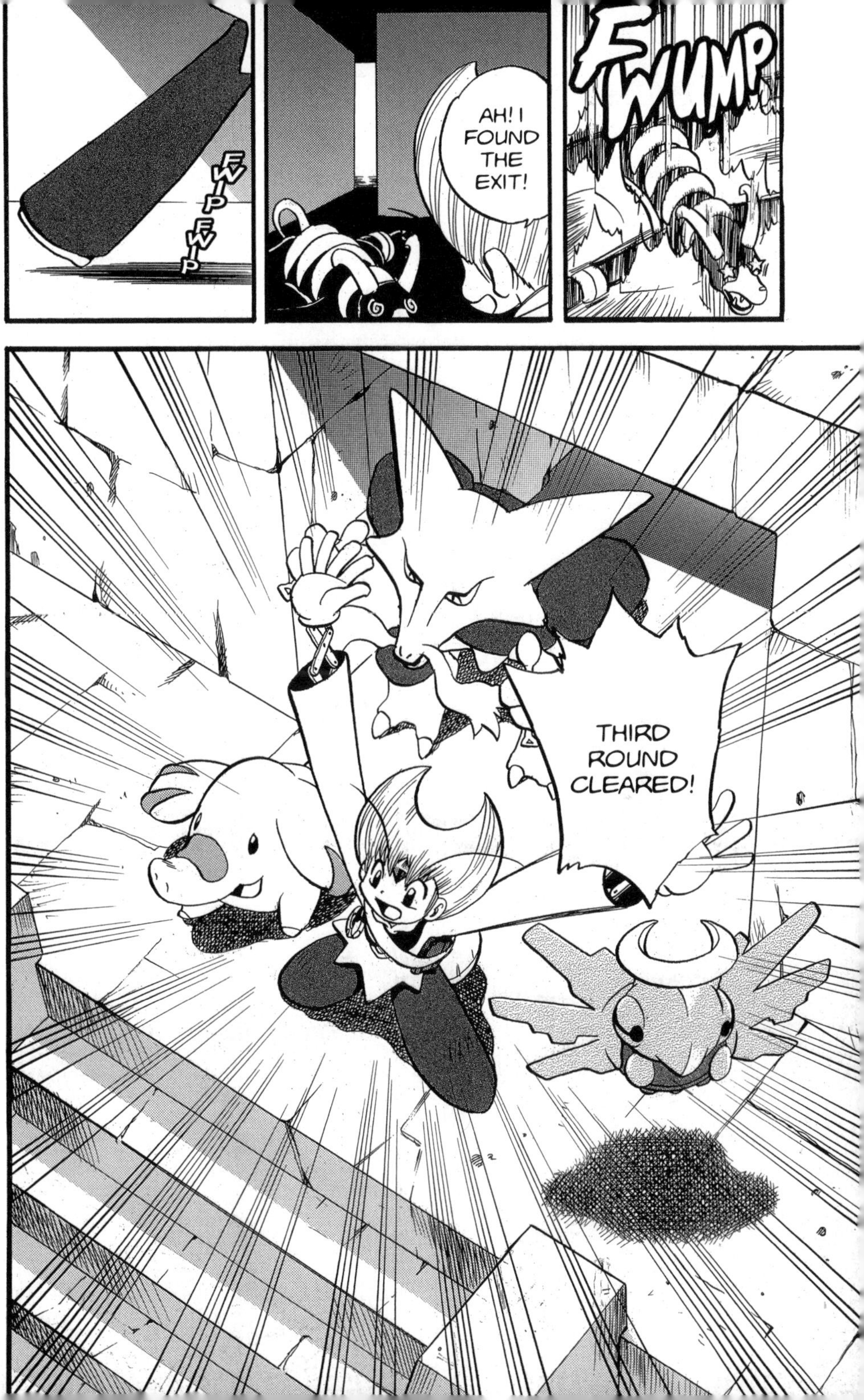
FWUMP
AH! I FOUND THE EXIT!
FWIP FWIP
THIRD ROUND CLEARED!

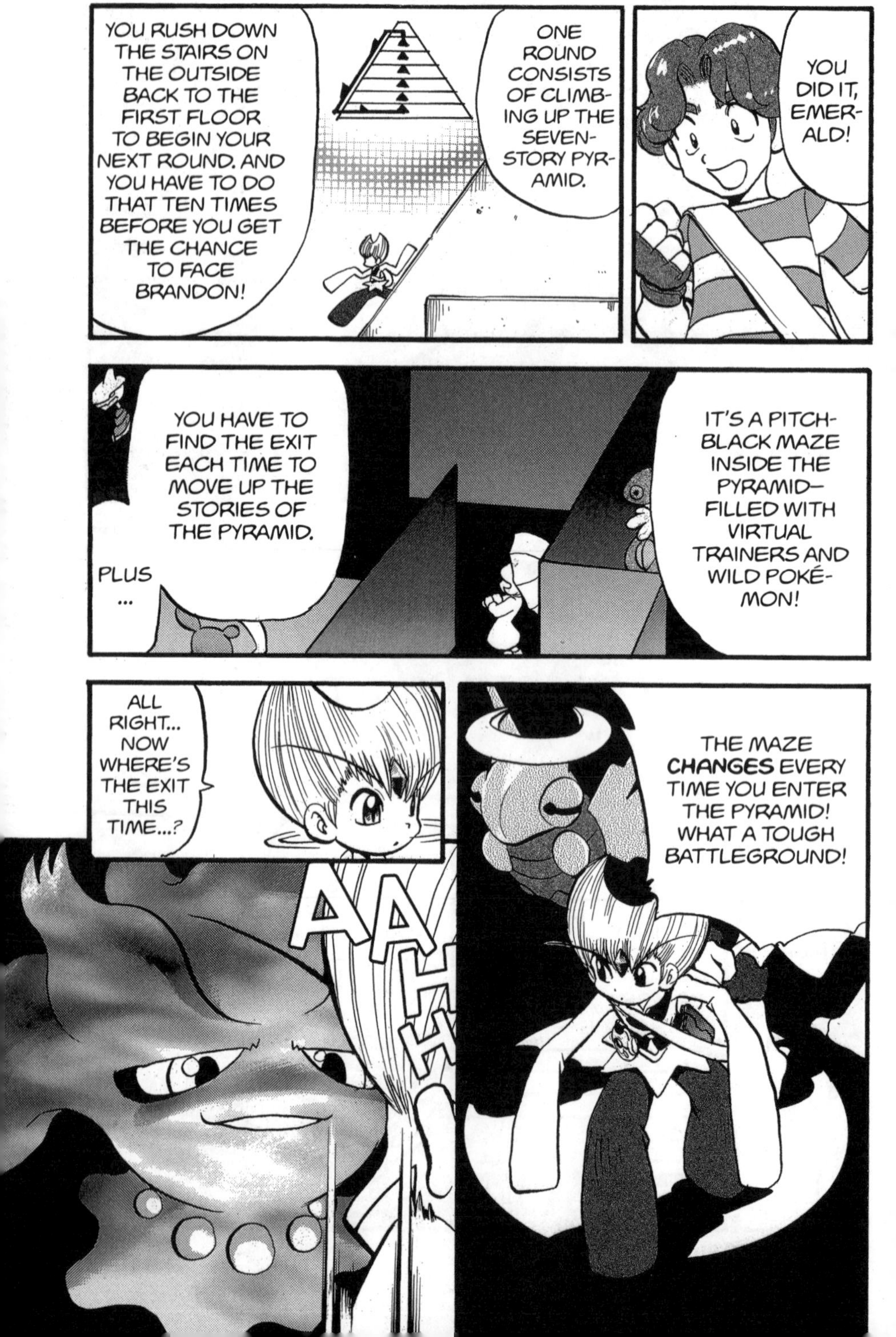
YOU DID IT, EMERALD!
ONE ROUND CONSISTS OF CLIMBING UP THE SEVEN-STORY PYRAMID.
YOU RUSH DOWN THE STAIRS ON THE OUTSIDE BACK TO THE FIRST FLOOR TO BEGIN YOUR NEXT ROUND. AND YOU HAVE TO DO THAT TEN TIMES BEFORE YOU GET THE CHANCE TO FACE BRANDON!
IT'S A PITCH-BLACK MAZE INSIDE THE PYRAMID—FILLED WITH VIRTUAL TRAINERS AND WILD POKÉMON!
YOU HAVE TO FIND THE EXIT EACH TIME TO MOVE UP THE STORIES OF THE PYRAMID.
PLUS ...
THE MAZE **CHANGES** EVERY TIME YOU ENTER THE PYRAMID! WHAT A TOUGH BATTLEGROUND!
ALL RIGHT... NOW WHERE'S THE EXIT THIS TIME...?
AAHH

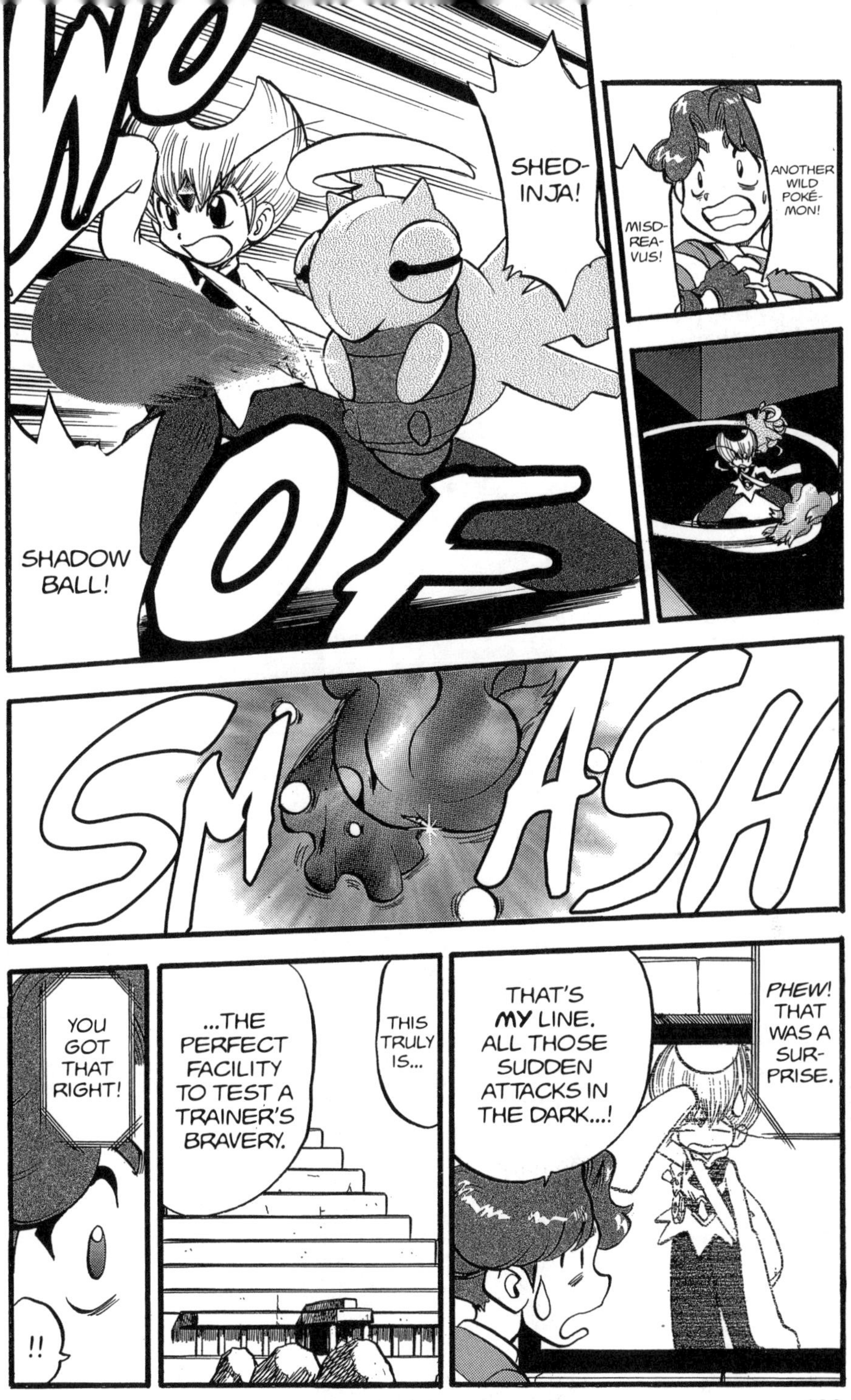
ANOTHER WILD POKÉMON!
MISDREAVUS!
SHEDINJA!
WHO
OF
SHADOW BALL!
SMASH
PHEW! THAT WAS A SURPRISE.
THAT'S **MY** LINE. ALL THOSE SUDDEN ATTACKS IN THE DARK...!
THIS TRULY IS...
...THE PERFECT FACILITY TO TEST A TRAINER'S BRAVERY.
YOU GOT THAT RIGHT!
!!

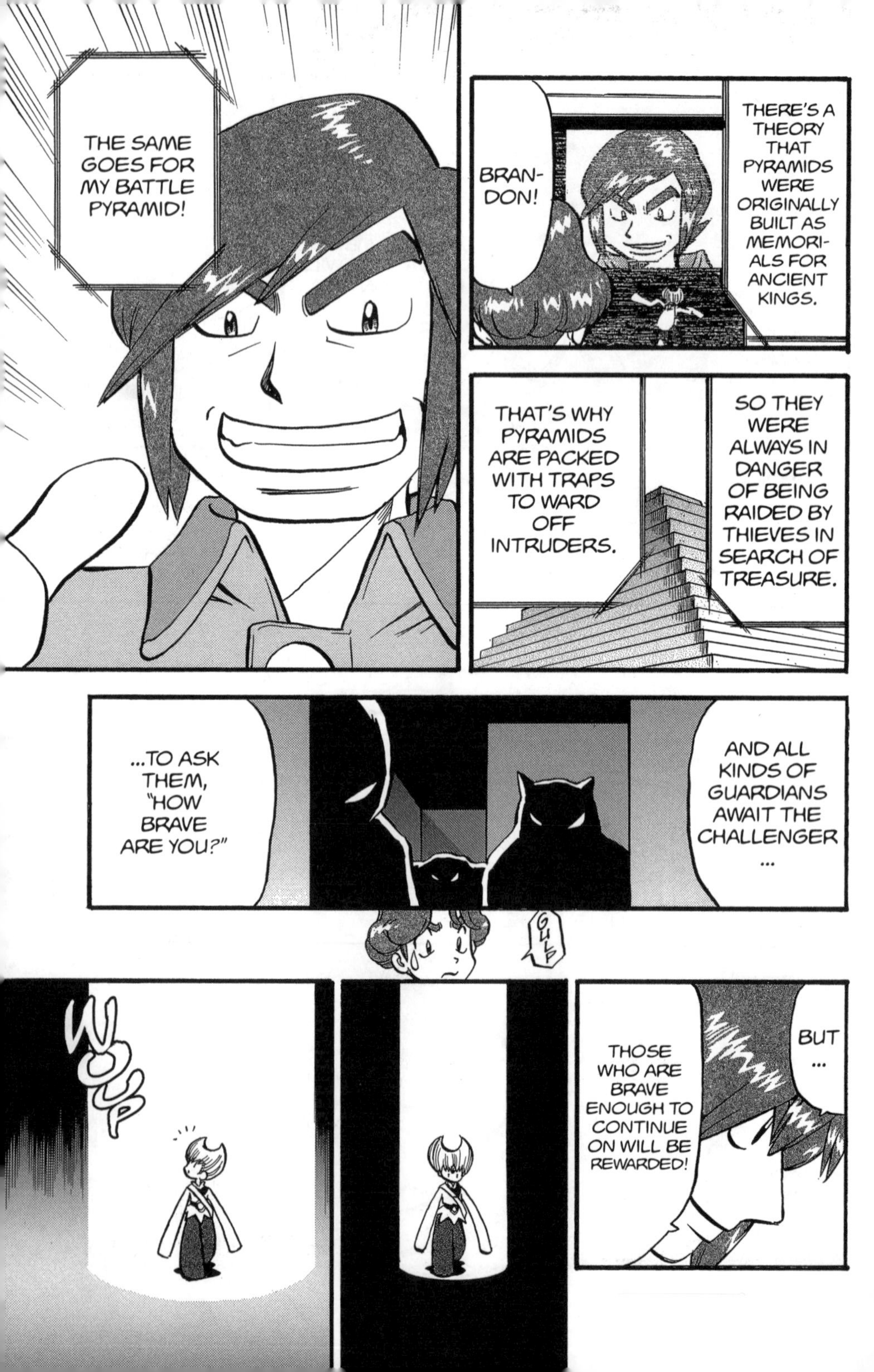
THERE'S A THEORY THAT PYRAMIDS WERE ORIGINALLY BUILT AS MEMORIALS FOR ANCIENT KINGS.
BRAN-DON!
SO THEY WERE ALWAYS IN DANGER OF BEING RAIDED BY THIEVES IN SEARCH OF TREASURE.
THAT'S WHY PYRAMIDS ARE PACKED WITH TRAPS TO WARD OFF INTRUDERS.
THE SAME GOES FOR MY BATTLE PYRAMID!
AND ALL KINDS OF GUARDIANS AWAIT THE CHALLENGER ...
...TO ASK THEM, "HOW BRAVE ARE YOU?"
GULP
BUT ...
THOSE WHO ARE BRAVE ENOUGH TO CONTINUE ON WILL BE REWARDED!
WOMP

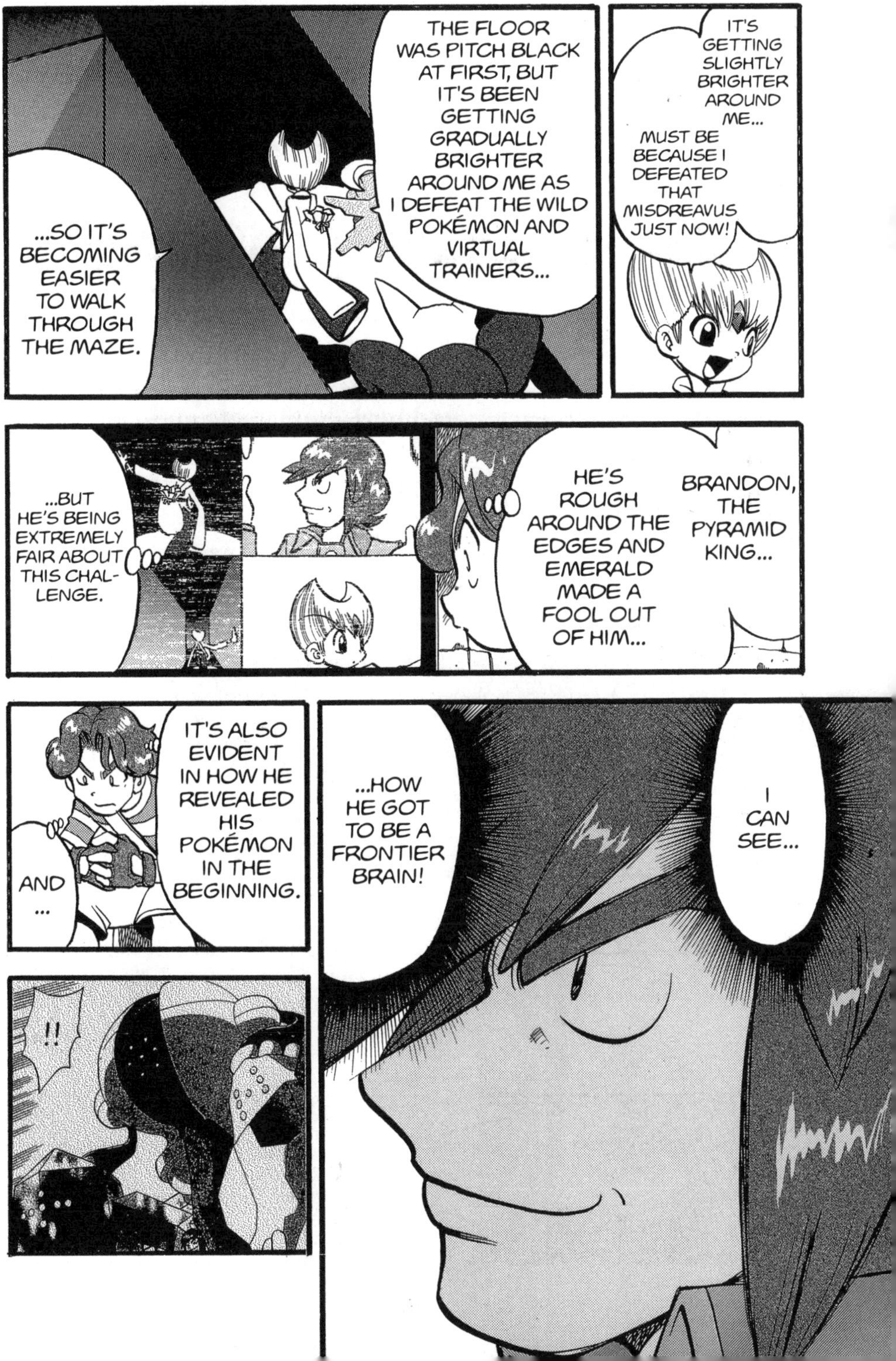
IT'S GETTING SLIGHTLY BRIGHTER AROUND ME...
MUST BE BECAUSE I DEFEATED THAT MISDREAVUS JUST NOW!
THE FLOOR WAS PITCH BLACK AT FIRST, BUT IT'S BEEN GETTING GRADUALLY BRIGHTER AROUND ME AS I DEFEAT THE WILD POKÉMON AND VIRTUAL TRAINERS...
...SO IT'S BECOMING EASIER TO WALK THROUGH THE MAZE.
BRANDON, THE PYRAMID KING...
HE'S ROUGH AROUND THE EDGES AND EMERALD MADE A FOOL OUT OF HIM...
...BUT HE'S BEING EXTREMELY FAIR ABOUT THIS CHAL-LENGE.
I CAN SEE...
...HOW HE GOT TO BE A FRONTIER BRAIN!
IT'S ALSO EVIDENT IN HOW HE REVEALED HIS POKÉMON IN THE BEGINNING.
AND ...
!!

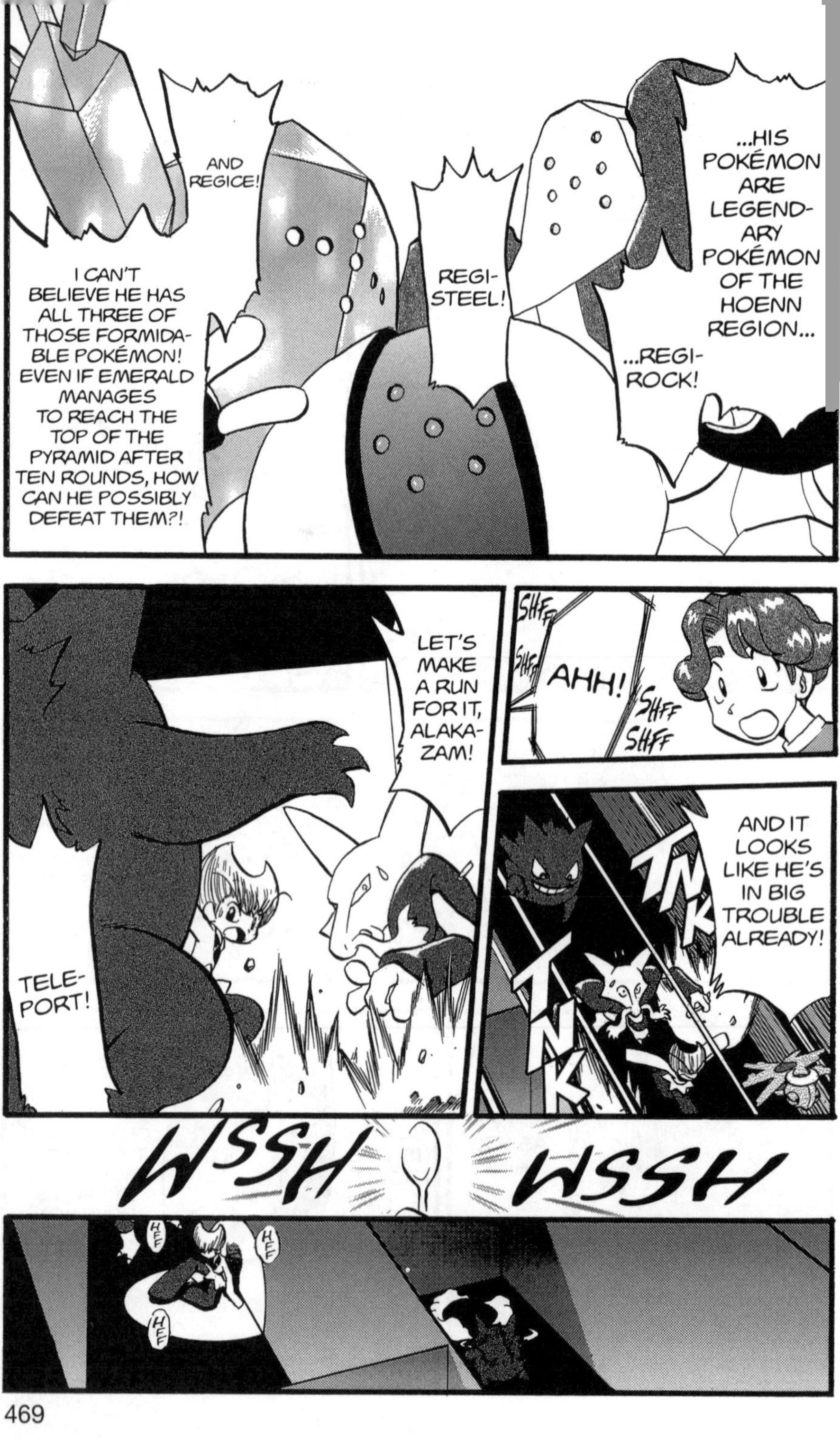
...HIS POKÉMON ARE LEGENDARY POKÉMON OF THE HOENN REGION...
...REGIROCK!
REGISTEEL!
AND REGICE!
I CAN'T BELIEVE HE HAS ALL THREE OF THOSE FORMIDABLE POKÉMON! EVEN IF EMERALD MANAGES TO REACH THE TOP OF THE PYRAMID AFTER TEN ROUNDS, HOW CAN HE POSSIBLY DEFEAT THEM?!
SHFF SHFF
AHH!
SHFF SHFF
AND IT LOOKS LIKE HE'S IN BIG TROUBLE ALREADY!
TNK
TNK
TNK
LET'S MAKE A RUN FOR IT, ALAKAZAM!
TELEPORT!
WSSH
WSSH
HFF
HFF
HFF

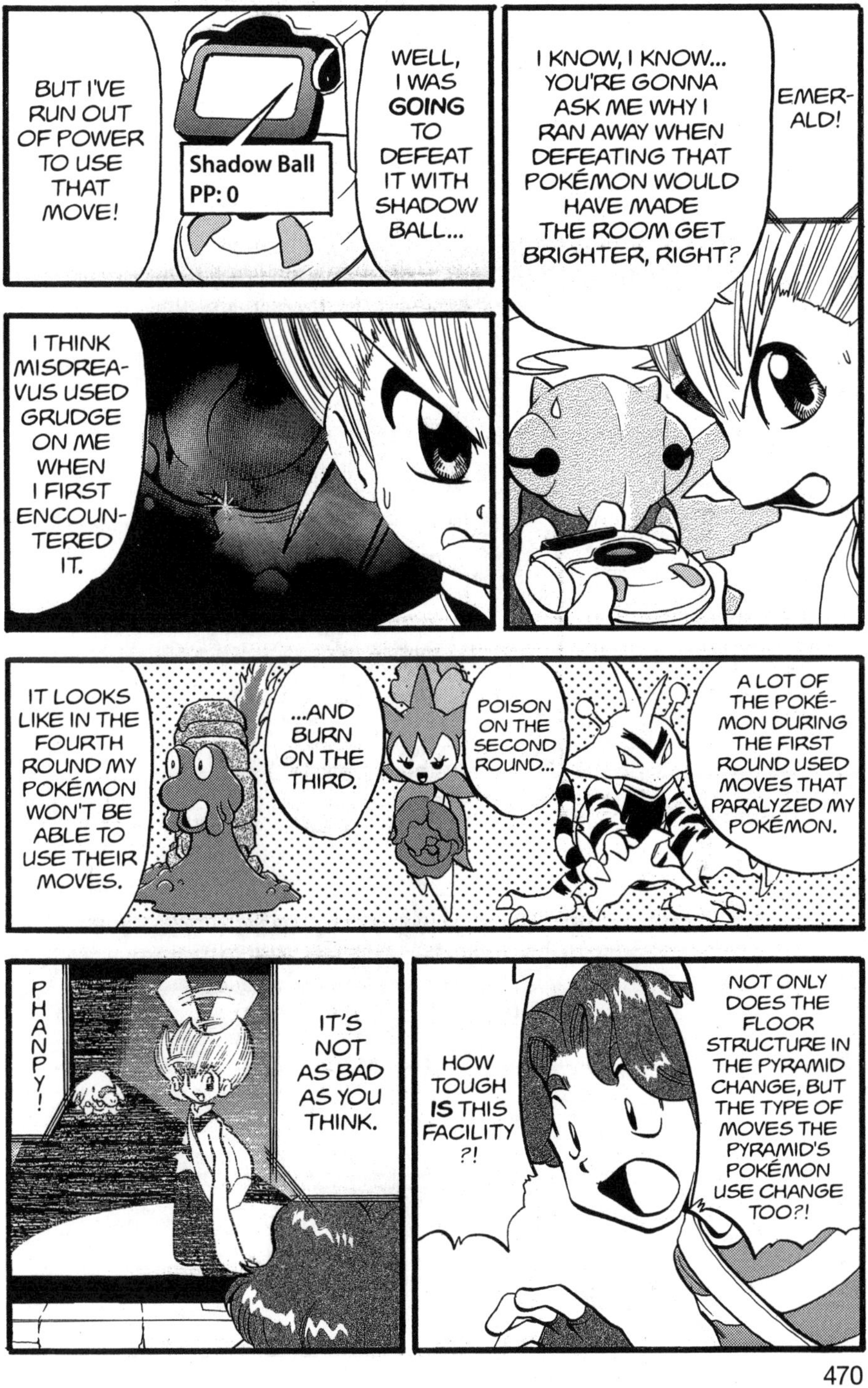
EMER-ALD!
I KNOW, I KNOW... YOU'RE GONNA ASK ME WHY I RAN AWAY WHEN DEFEATING THAT POKÉMON WOULD HAVE MADE THE ROOM GET BRIGHTER, RIGHT?
WELL, I WAS **GOING** TO DEFEAT IT WITH SHADOW BALL...
Shadow Ball PP: 0
BUT I'VE RUN OUT OF POWER TO USE THAT MOVE!
I THINK MISDREA-VUS USED GRUDGE ON ME WHEN I FIRST ENCOUN-TERED IT.
A LOT OF THE POKÉ-MON DURING THE FIRST ROUND USED MOVES THAT PARALYZED MY POKÉMON.
POISON ON THE SECOND ROUND...
...AND BURN ON THE THIRD.
IT LOOKS LIKE IN THE FOURTH ROUND MY POKÉMON WON'T BE ABLE TO USE THEIR MOVES.
NOT ONLY DOES THE FLOOR STRUCTURE IN THE PYRAMID CHANGE, BUT THE TYPE OF MOVES THE PYRAMID'S POKÉMON USE CHANGE TOO?!
HOW TOUGH **IS** THIS FACILITY?!
IT'S NOT AS BAD AS YOU THINK.
PHANPY!

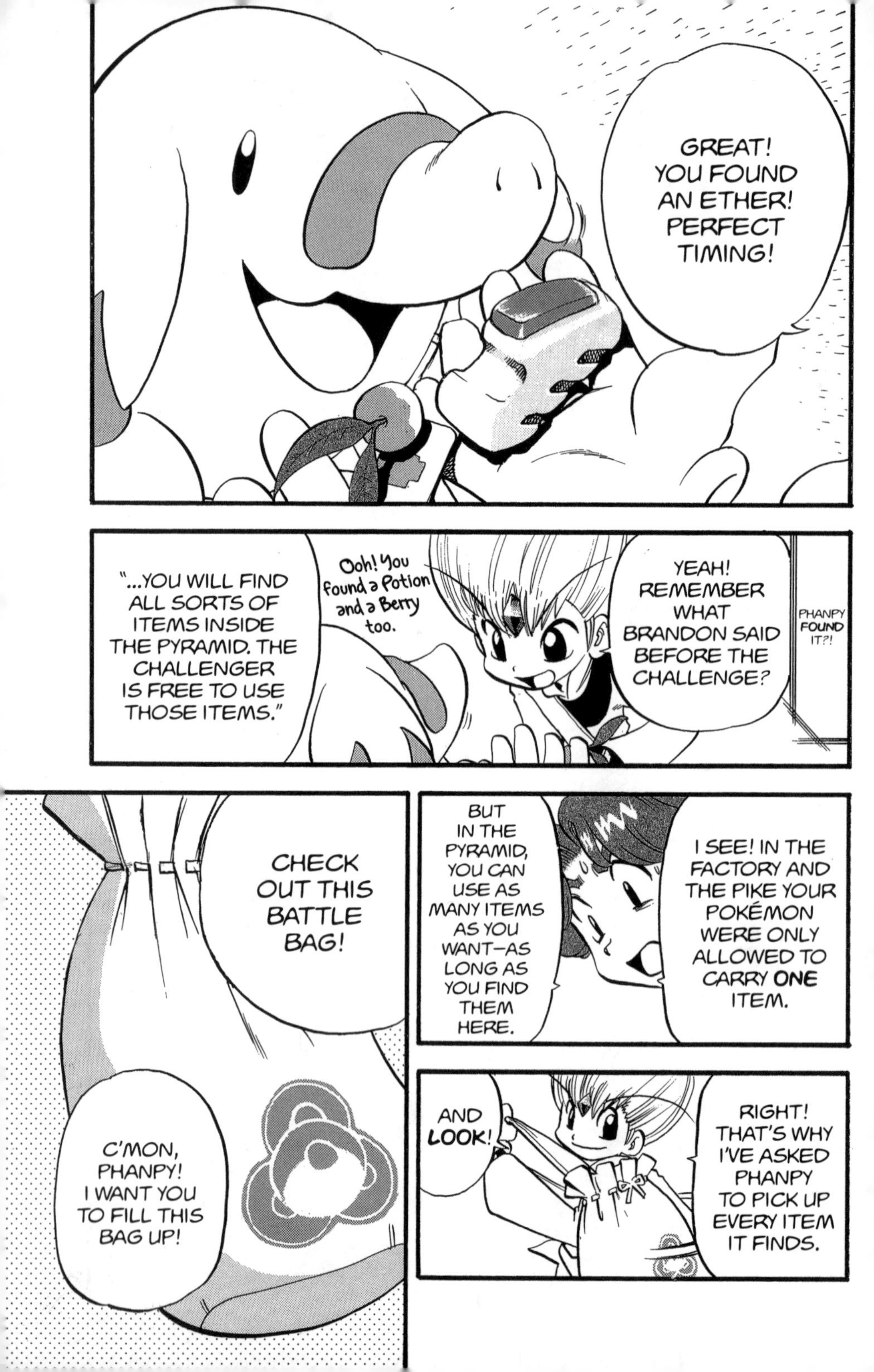
GREAT! YOU FOUND AN ETHER! PERFECT TIMING!
PHANPY FOUND IT?!
YEAH! REMEMBER WHAT BRANDON SAID BEFORE THE CHALLENGE?
Ooh! You found a Potion and a Berry too.
"...YOU WILL FIND ALL SORTS OF ITEMS INSIDE THE PYRAMID. THE CHALLENGER IS FREE TO USE THOSE ITEMS."
I SEE! IN THE FACTORY AND THE PIKE YOUR POKéMON WERE ONLY ALLOWED TO CARRY **ONE** ITEM.
BUT IN THE PYRAMID, YOU CAN USE AS MANY ITEMS AS YOU WANT—AS LONG AS YOU FIND THEM HERE.
RIGHT! THAT'S WHY I'VE ASKED PHANPY TO PICK UP EVERY ITEM IT FINDS.
AND **LOOK**!
CHECK OUT THIS BATTLE BAG!
C'MON, PHANPY! I WANT YOU TO FILL THIS BAG UP!

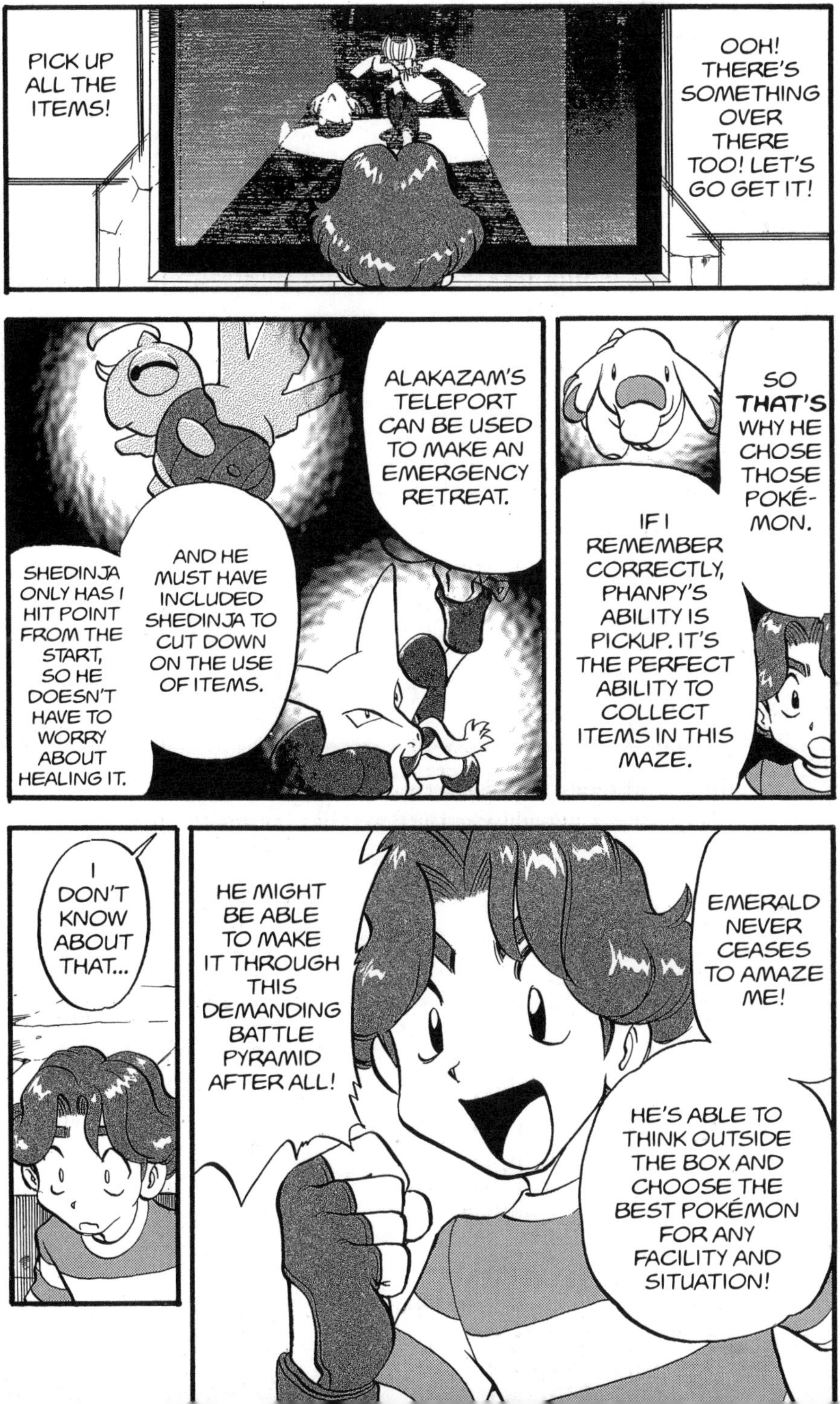
OOH! THERE'S SOMETHING OVER THERE TOO! LET'S GO GET IT!
PICK UP ALL THE ITEMS!
SO **THAT'S** WHY HE CHOSE THOSE POKÉMON.
IF I REMEMBER CORRECTLY, PHANPY'S ABILITY IS PICKUP. IT'S THE PERFECT ABILITY TO COLLECT ITEMS IN THIS MAZE.
ALAKAZAM'S TELEPORT CAN BE USED TO MAKE AN EMERGENCY RETREAT.
AND HE MUST HAVE INCLUDED SHEDINJA TO CUT DOWN ON THE USE OF ITEMS.
SHEDINJA ONLY HAS 1 HIT POINT FROM THE START, SO HE DOESN'T HAVE TO WORRY ABOUT HEALING IT.
EMERALD NEVER CEASES TO AMAZE ME!
HE'S ABLE TO THINK OUTSIDE THE BOX AND CHOOSE THE BEST POKÉMON FOR ANY FACILITY AND SITUATION!
HE MIGHT BE ABLE TO MAKE IT THROUGH THIS DEMANDING BATTLE PYRAMID AFTER ALL!
I DON'T KNOW ABOUT THAT...

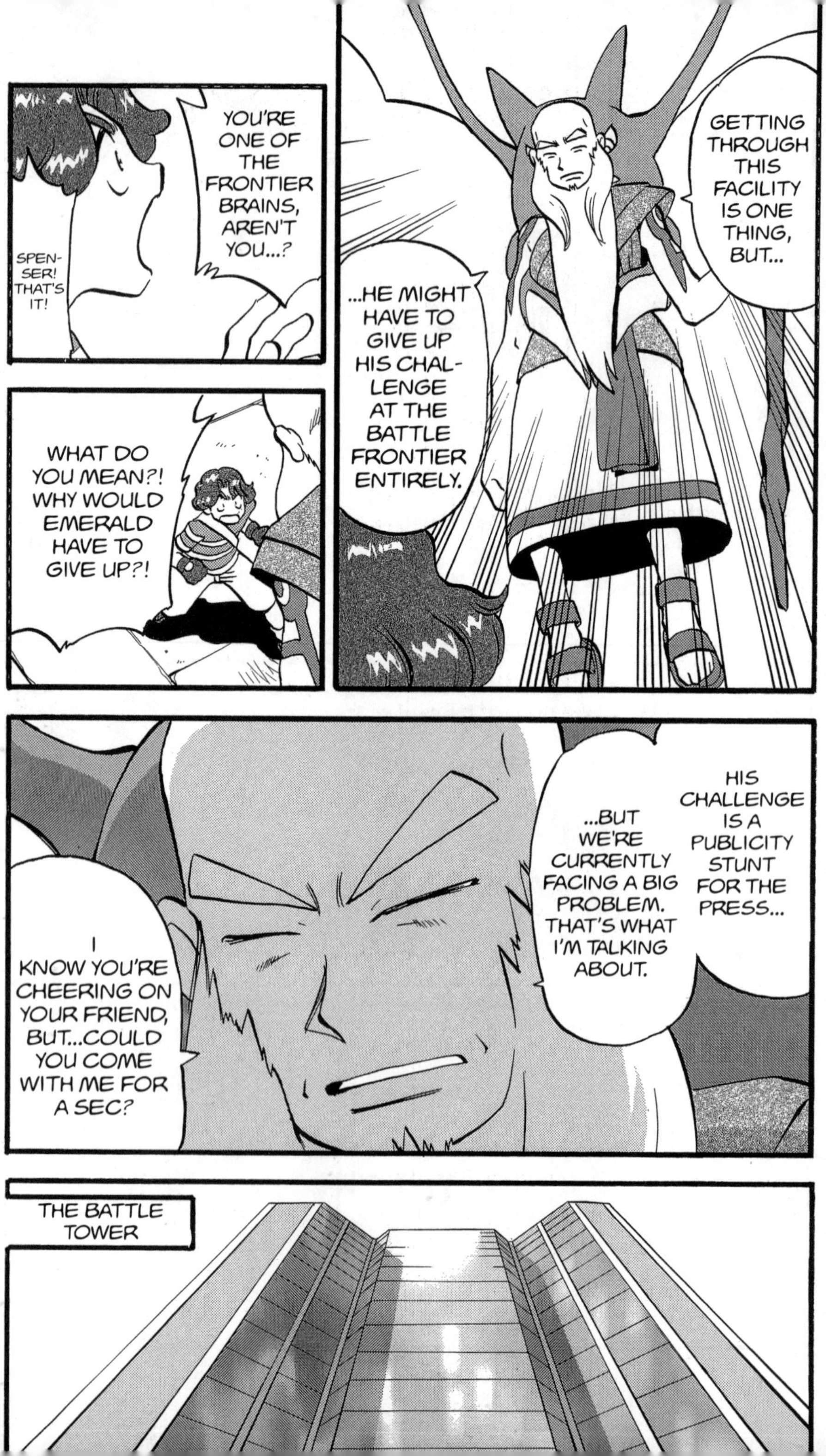
GETTING THROUGH THIS FACILITY IS ONE THING, BUT...
...HE MIGHT HAVE TO GIVE UP HIS CHALLENGE AT THE BATTLE FRONTIER ENTIRELY.
YOU'RE ONE OF THE FRONTIER BRAINS, AREN'T YOU...?
SPENSER! THAT'S IT!
WHAT DO YOU MEAN?! WHY WOULD EMERALD HAVE TO GIVE UP?!
HIS CHALLENGE IS A PUBLICITY STUNT FOR THE PRESS...
...BUT WE'RE CURRENTLY FACING A BIG PROBLEM. THAT'S WHAT I'M TALKING ABOUT.
I KNOW YOU'RE CHEERING ON YOUR FRIEND, BUT...COULD YOU COME WITH ME FOR A SEC?
THE BATTLE TOWER

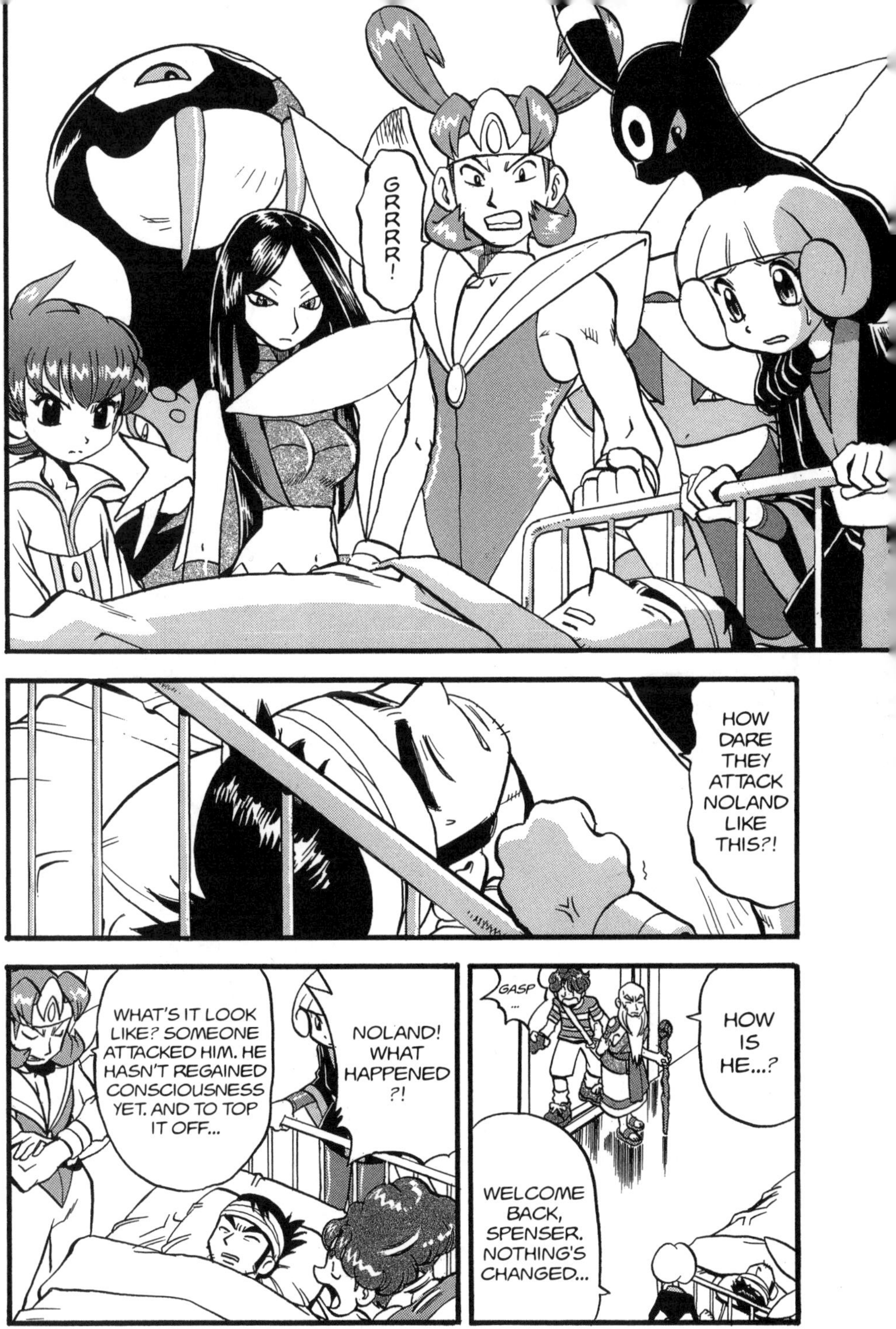
GRRRR!
HOW DARE THEY ATTACK NOLAND LIKE THIS?!
GASP...
HOW IS HE...?
WELCOME BACK, SPENSER. NOTHING'S CHANGED...
NOLAND! WHAT HAPPENED?!
WHAT'S IT LOOK LIKE? SOMEONE ATTACKED HIM. HE HASN'T REGAINED CONSCIOUSNESS YET. AND TO TOP IT OFF...

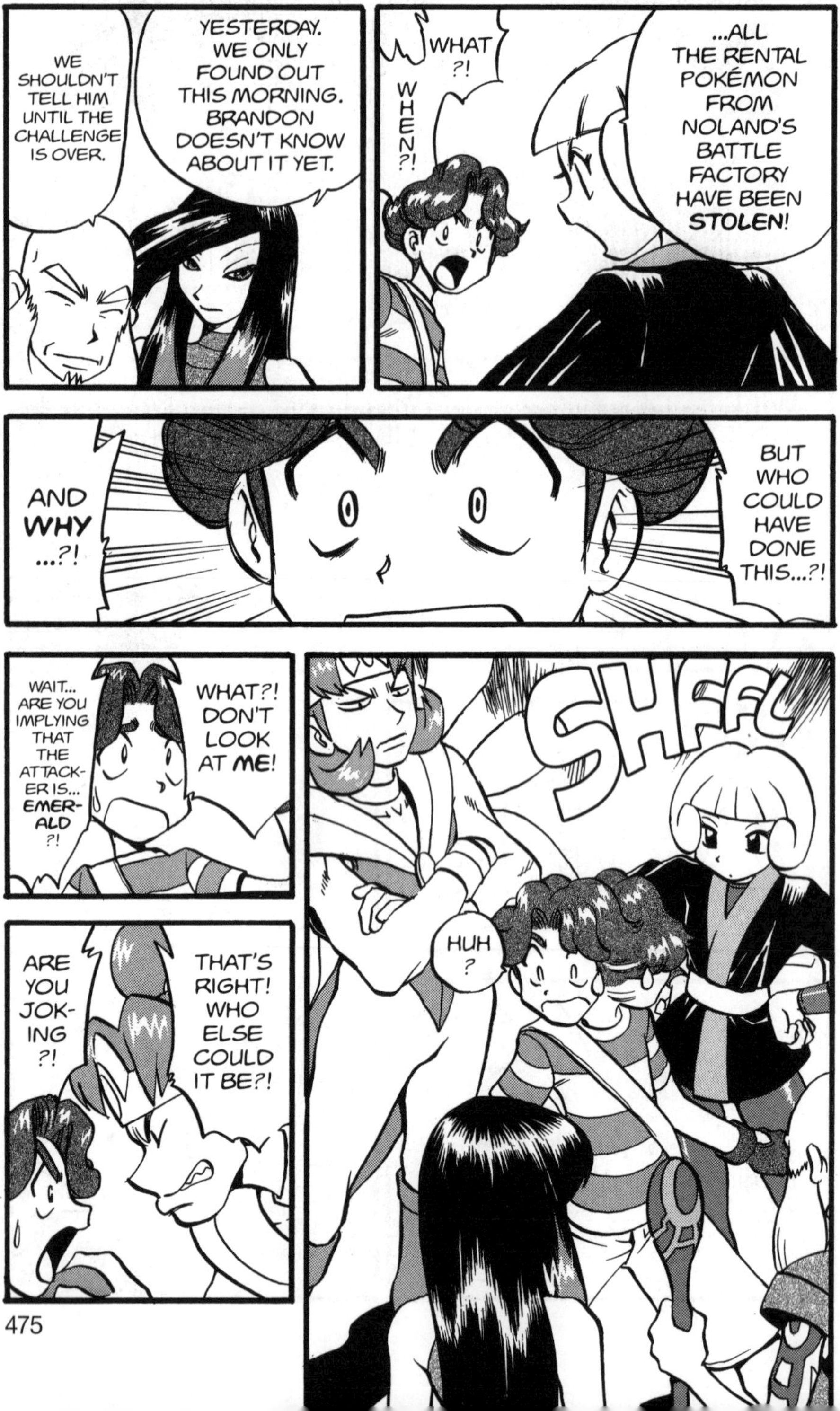
...ALL THE RENTAL POKÉMON FROM NOLAND'S BATTLE FACTORY HAVE BEEN **STOLEN**!
WHAT ?!
WHEN ?!
YESTERDAY. WE ONLY FOUND OUT THIS MORNING. BRANDON DOESN'T KNOW ABOUT IT YET.
WE SHOULDN'T TELL HIM UNTIL THE CHALLENGE IS OVER.
BUT WHO COULD HAVE DONE THIS...?!
AND **WHY** ...?!
SHFFL
HUH ?
WHAT?! DON'T LOOK AT **ME**!
WAIT... ARE YOU IMPLYING THAT THE ATTACKER IS... **EMERALD** ?!
THAT'S RIGHT! WHO ELSE COULD IT BE?!
ARE YOU JOKING ?!

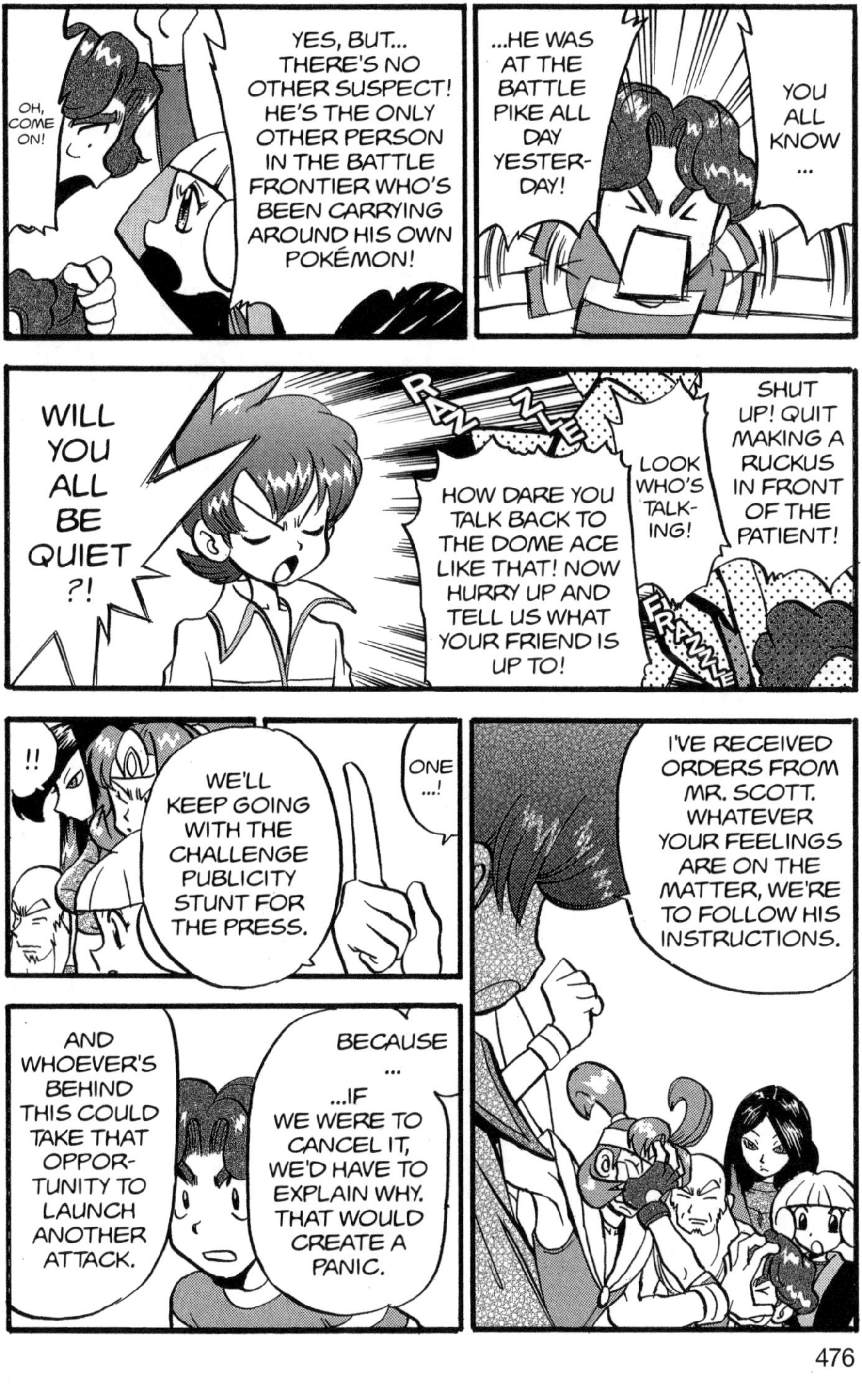
YOU ALL KNOW ...
...HE WAS AT THE BATTLE PIKE ALL DAY YESTER-DAY!
YES, BUT... THERE'S NO OTHER SUSPECT! HE'S THE ONLY OTHER PERSON IN THE BATTLE FRONTIER WHO'S BEEN CARRYING AROUND HIS OWN POKÉMON!
OH, COME ON!
SHUT UP! QUIT MAKING A RUCKUS IN FRONT OF THE PATIENT!
LOOK WHO'S TALK-ING!
HOW DARE YOU TALK BACK TO THE DOME ACE LIKE THAT! NOW HURRY UP AND TELL US WHAT YOUR FRIEND IS UP TO!
WILL YOU ALL BE QUIET ?!
I'VE RECEIVED ORDERS FROM MR. SCOTT. WHATEVER YOUR FEELINGS ARE ON THE MATTER, WE'RE TO FOLLOW HIS INSTRUCTIONS.
ONE ...!
WE'LL KEEP GOING WITH THE CHALLENGE PUBLICITY STUNT FOR THE PRESS.
!!
BECAUSE ...
...IF WE WERE TO CANCEL IT, WE'D HAVE TO EXPLAIN WHY. THAT WOULD CREATE A PANIC.
AND WHOEVER'S BEHIND THIS COULD TAKE THAT OPPOR-TUNITY TO LAUNCH ANOTHER ATTACK.

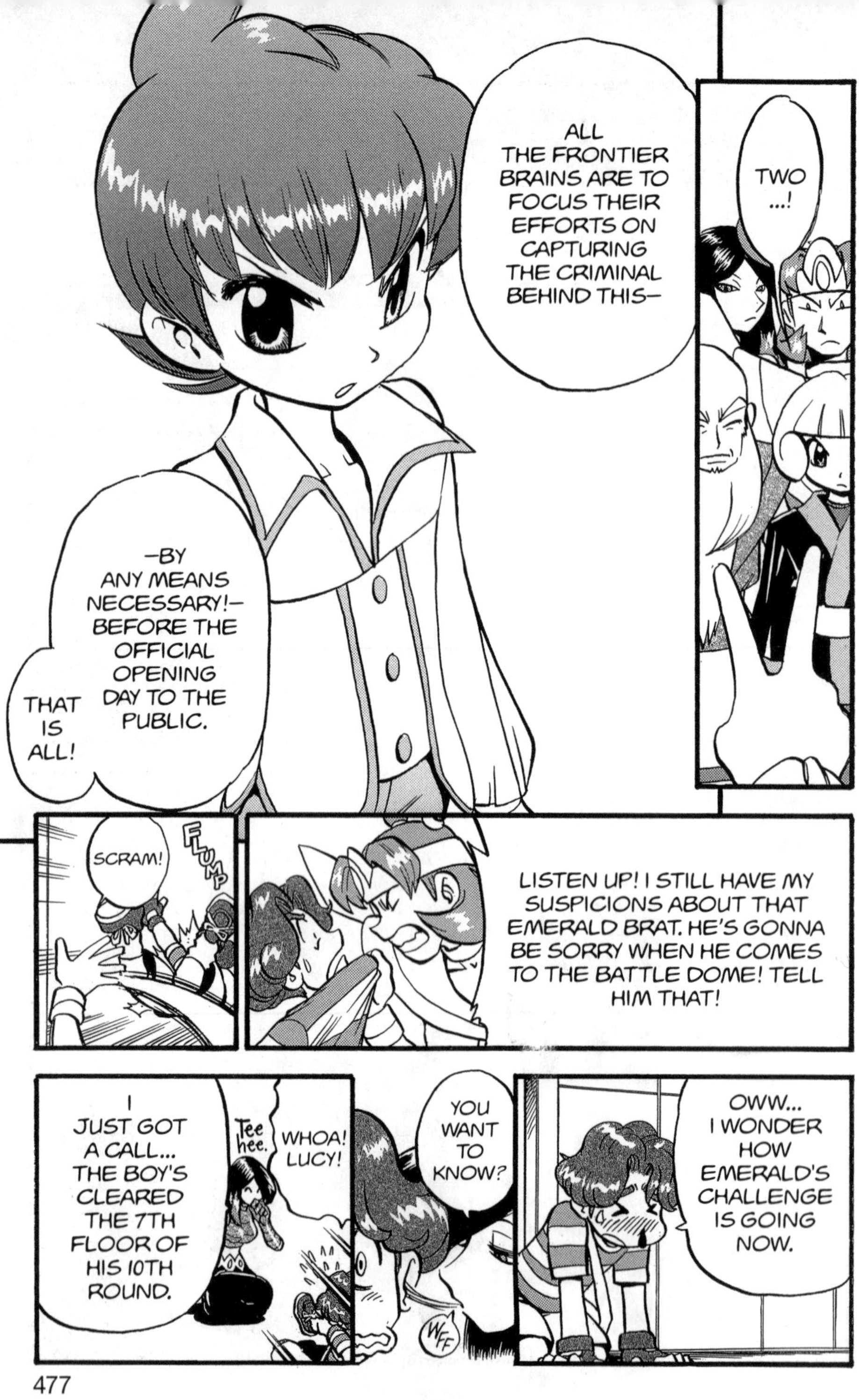
TWO ...!
ALL THE FRONTIER BRAINS ARE TO FOCUS THEIR EFFORTS ON CAPTURING THE CRIMINAL BEHIND THIS—
—BY ANY MEANS NECESSARY!— BEFORE THE OFFICIAL OPENING DAY TO THE PUBLIC.
THAT IS ALL!
LISTEN UP! I STILL HAVE MY SUSPICIONS ABOUT THAT EMERALD BRAT. HE'S GONNA BE SORRY WHEN HE COMES TO THE BATTLE DOME! TELL HIM THAT!
SCRAM!
FLUMP
OWW... I WONDER HOW EMERALD'S CHALLENGE IS GOING NOW.
YOU WANT TO KNOW?
WFF
WHOA! LUCY!
Tee hee.
I JUST GOT A CALL... THE BOY'S CLEARED THE 7TH FLOOR OF HIS 10TH ROUND.

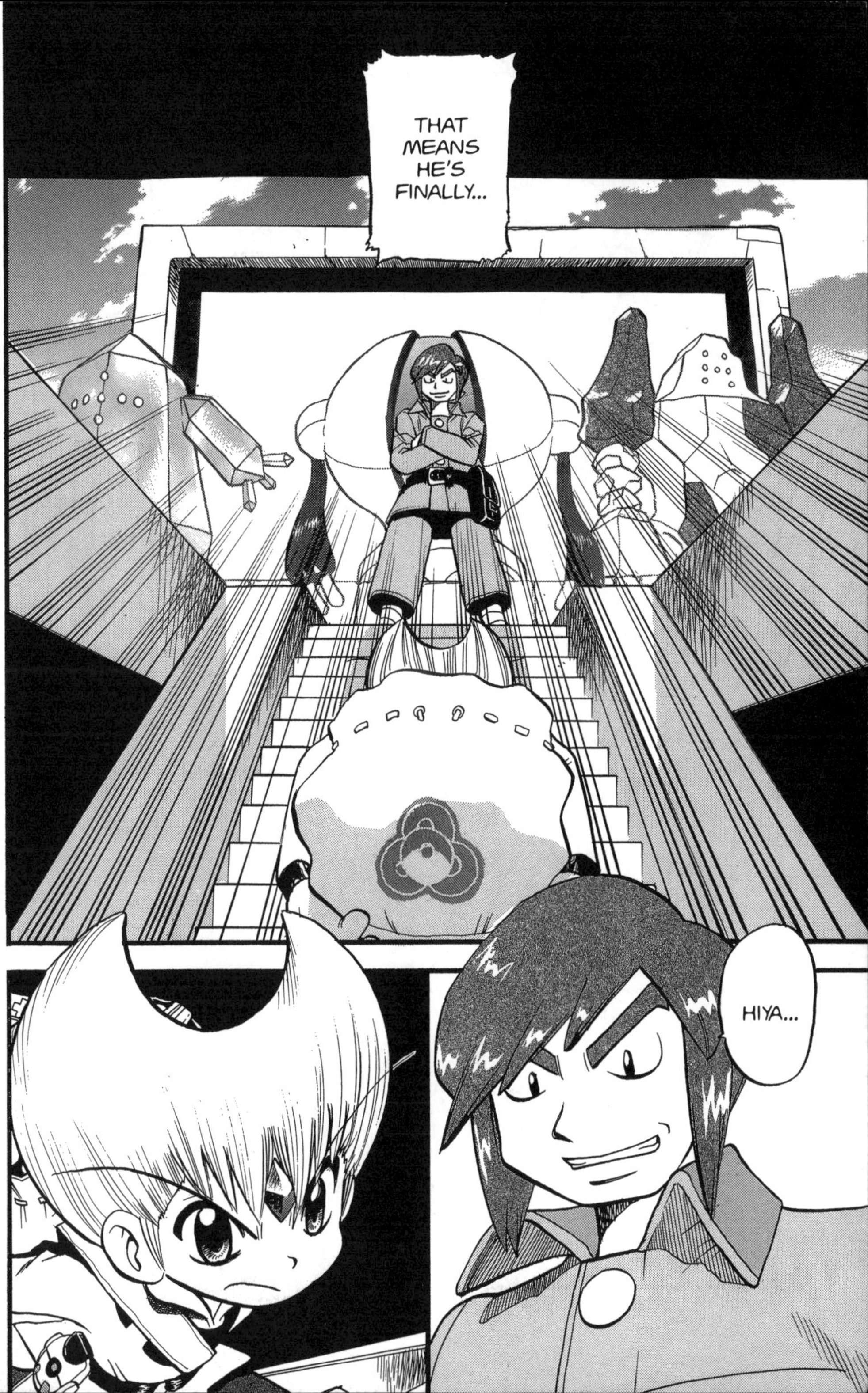
THAT MEANS HE'S FINALLY...
HIYA...

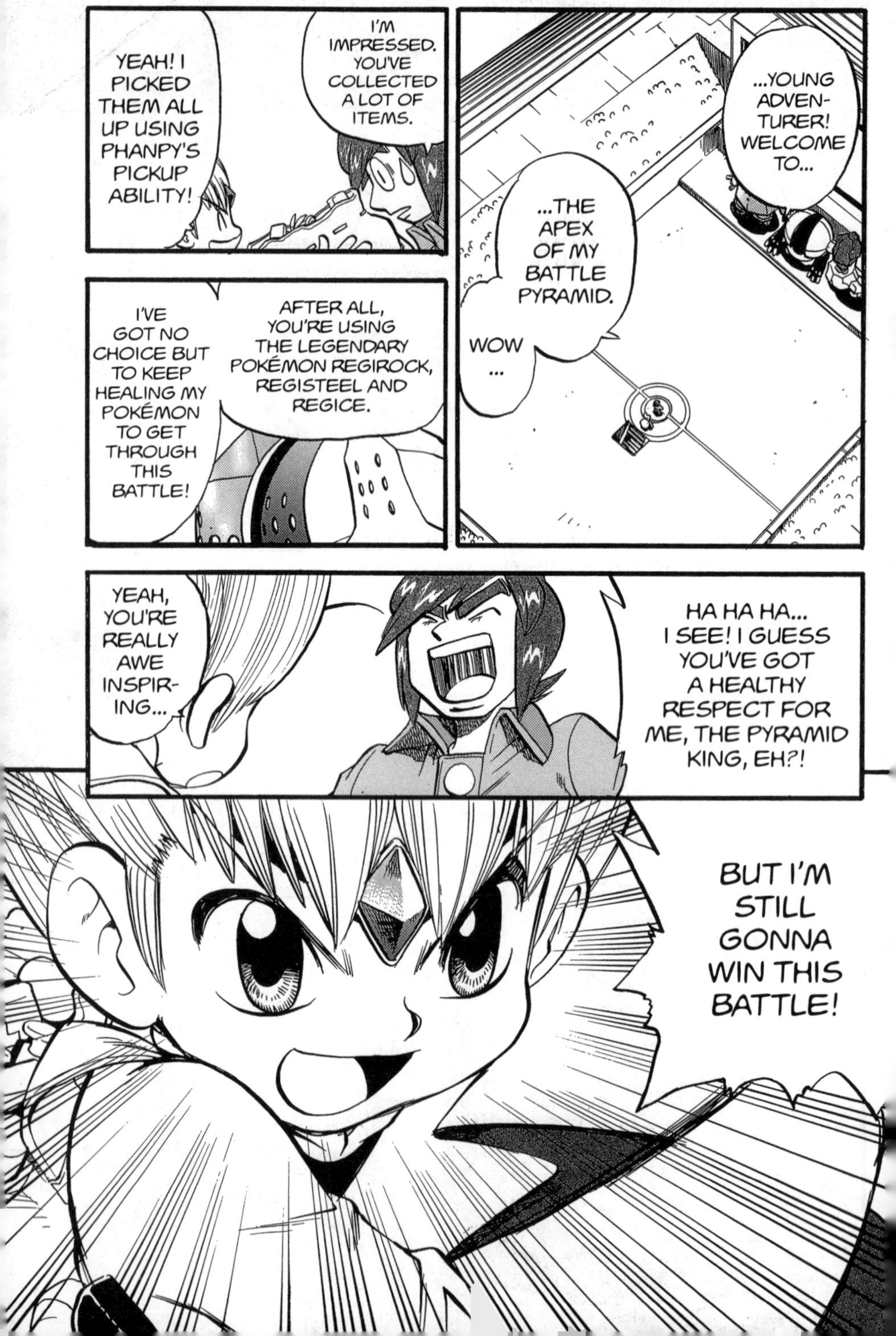
...YOUNG ADVENTURER! WELCOME TO...
...THE APEX OF MY BATTLE PYRAMID.
WOW ...
I'M IMPRESSED. YOU'VE COLLECTED A LOT OF ITEMS.
YEAH! I PICKED THEM ALL UP USING PHANPY'S PICKUP ABILITY!
AFTER ALL, YOU'RE USING THE LEGENDARY POKÉMON REGIROCK, REGISTEEL AND REGICE.
I'VE GOT NO CHOICE BUT TO KEEP HEALING MY POKÉMON TO GET THROUGH THIS BATTLE!
HA HA HA... I SEE! I GUESS YOU'VE GOT A HEALTHY RESPECT FOR ME, THE PYRAMID KING, EH?!
YEAH, YOU'RE REALLY AWE INSPIRING...
BUT I'M STILL GONNA WIN THIS BATTLE!

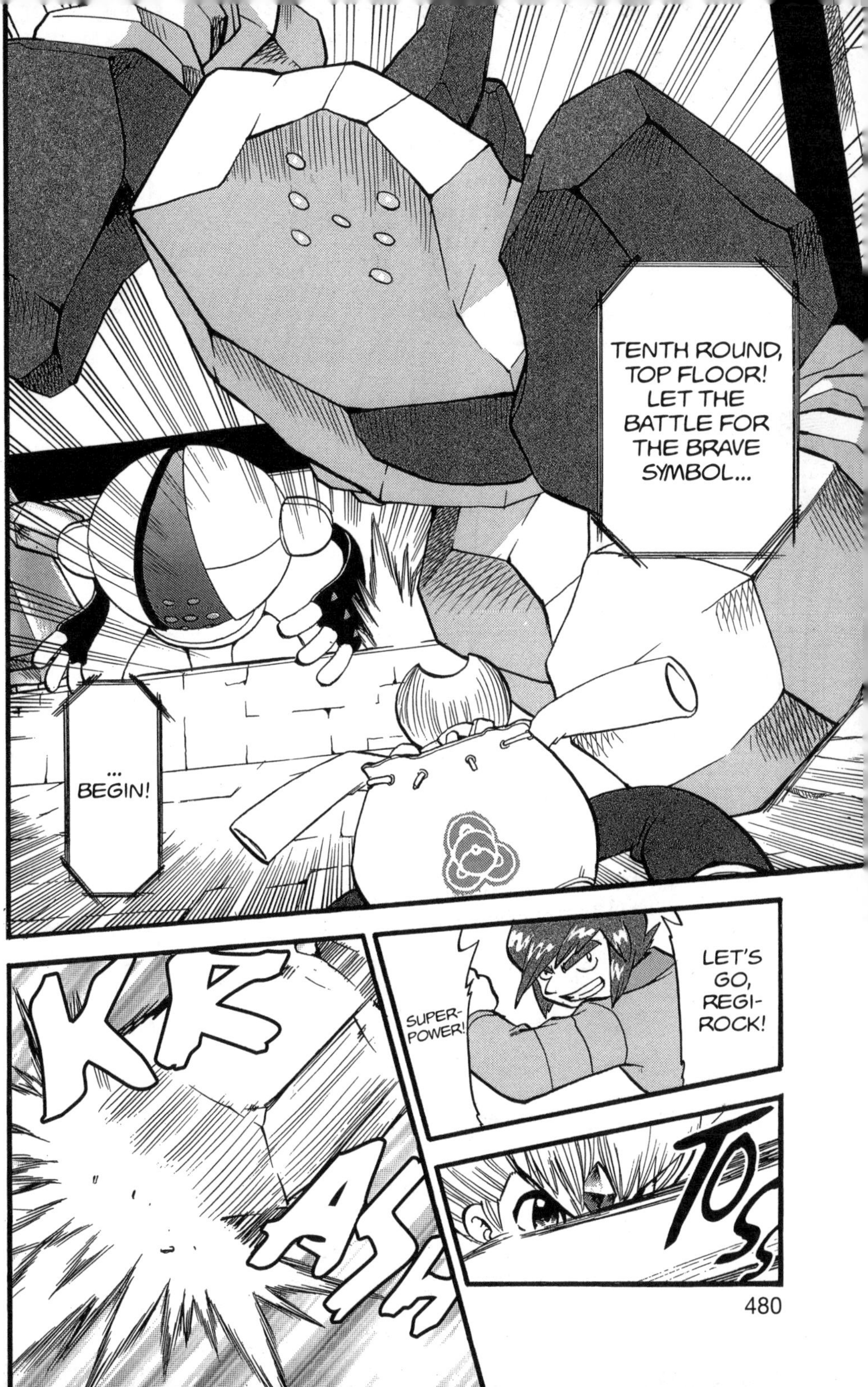
TENTH ROUND, TOP FLOOR! LET THE BATTLE FOR THE BRAVE SYMBOL...
... BEGIN!
LET'S GO, REGI-ROCK!
SUPER-POWER!
TOSS
KRASH

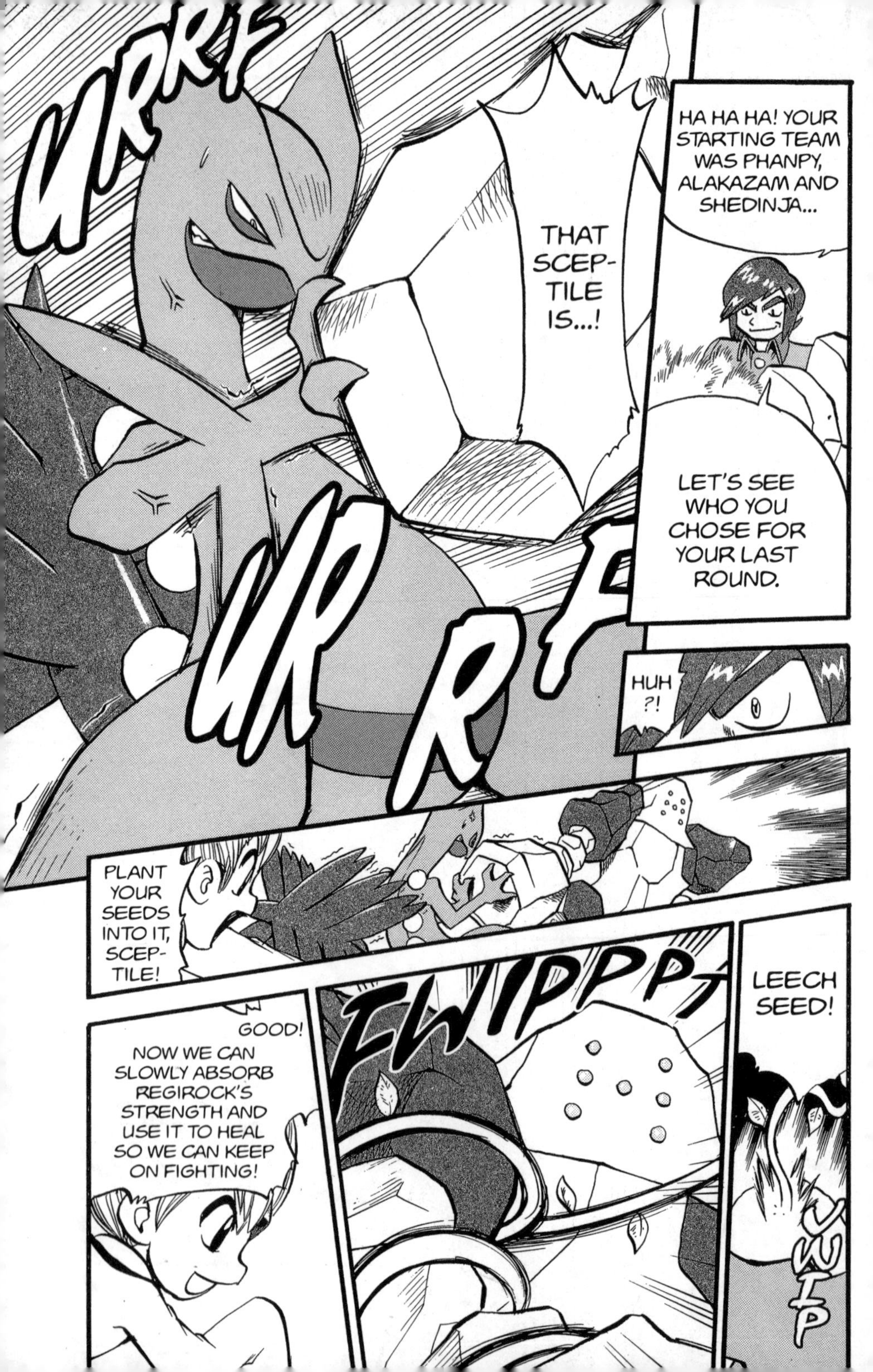

HA HA HA! YOUR STARTING TEAM WAS PHANPY, ALAKAZAM AND SHEDINJA...
LET'S SEE WHO YOU CHOSE FOR YOUR LAST ROUND.
HUH ?!
URRF
THAT SCEP-TILE IS...!
URRF
PLANT YOUR SEEDS INTO IT, SCEP-TILE!
LEECH SEED!
SWIP
FWIPPPT
GOOD!
NOW WE CAN SLOWLY ABSORB REGIROCK'S STRENGTH AND USE IT TO HEAL SO WE CAN KEEP ON FIGHTING!

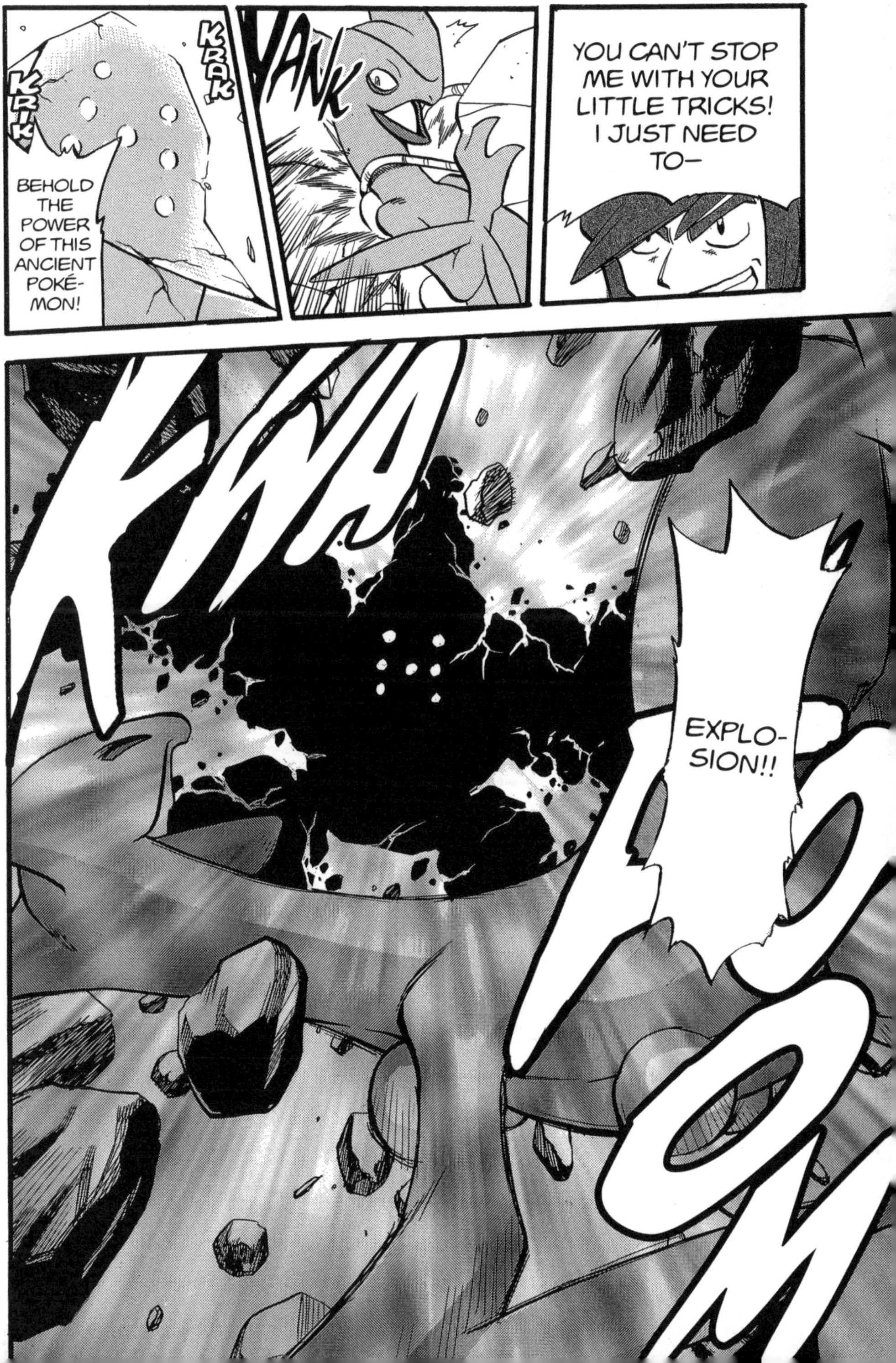
YOU CAN'T STOP ME WITH YOUR LITTLE TRICKS! I JUST NEED TO—
YANK
KRAK
KRIK
BEHOLD THE POWER OF THIS ANCIENT POKÉ-MON!
EXPLO-SION!!

DEAR MEMBERS OF THE PRESS...

Thank you for visiting the Battle Frontier today. Permit me to continue explaining the rules of this facility...

OWNER: SCOTT

FACILITY RULES

BATTLE ARENA 1

Battle-type	Number of Pokémon	Type of Symbol	Wins needed to attain the Symbol
• Single	3 Pokémon	Guts	Seven Battles × 8 Rounds = 56 Consecutive Wins

The challenger is not allowed to change the order of their Pokémon at the Battle Arena and must fight a 3-on-3 Knockout Battle. If the battle is not over in three rounds, the Trainers are rated on three scales: Mind, Skill and Body. The rating system is on a scale of three. You receive 2 points for a ○, 1 point for a △, and 0 points for an ×. The Pokémon who receives the highest score wins the battle.

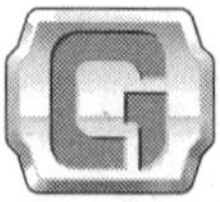

Guts Symbol

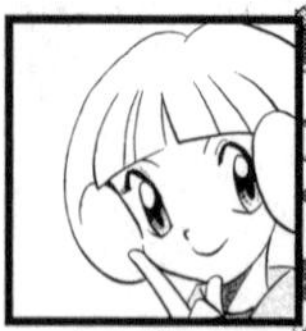

Arena Tycoon Greta

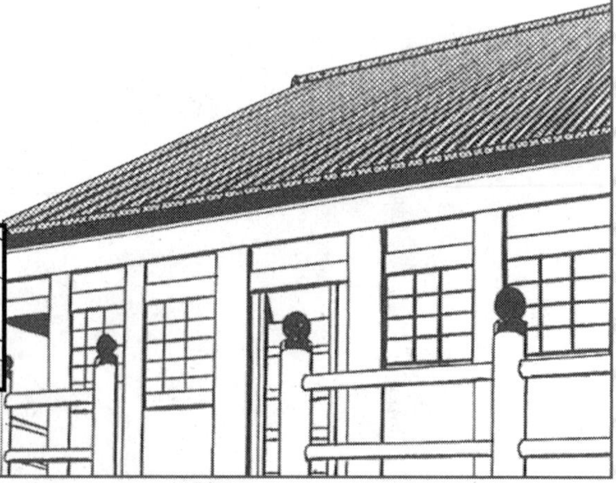

313

You Need to Chill Out, Regice

POKÉMON ADVENTURES•THE SIXTH CHAPTER•EMERALD

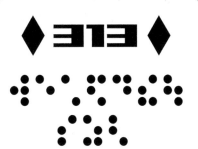

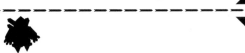

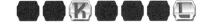

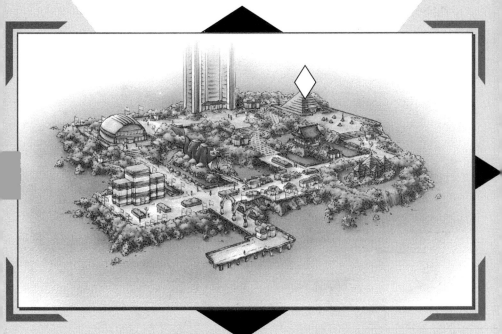

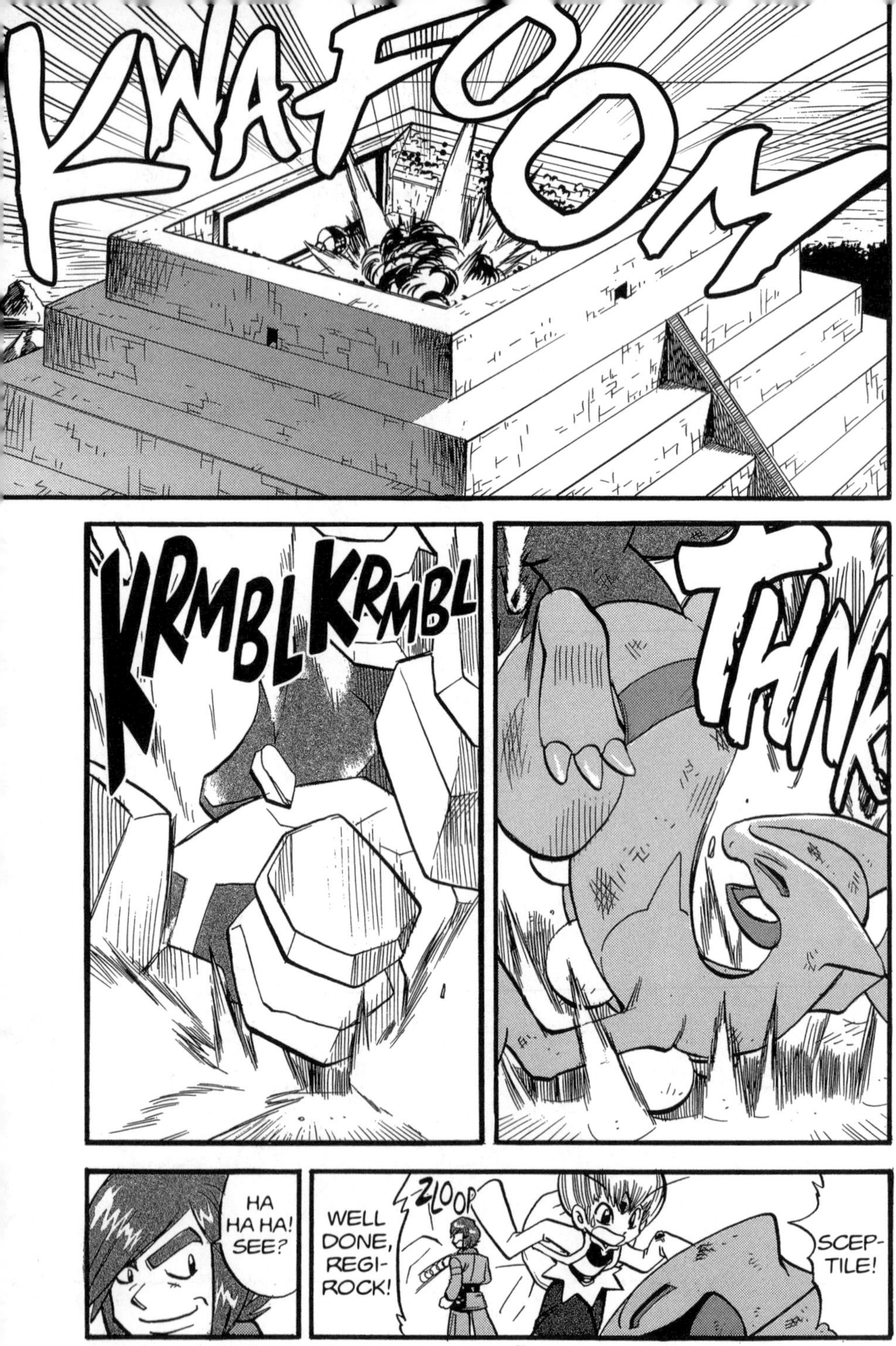
KWAFOOM
THNK
KRMBL KRMBL
SCEP-TILE!
ZLOOP
WELL DONE, REGI-ROCK!
HA HA HA! SEE?

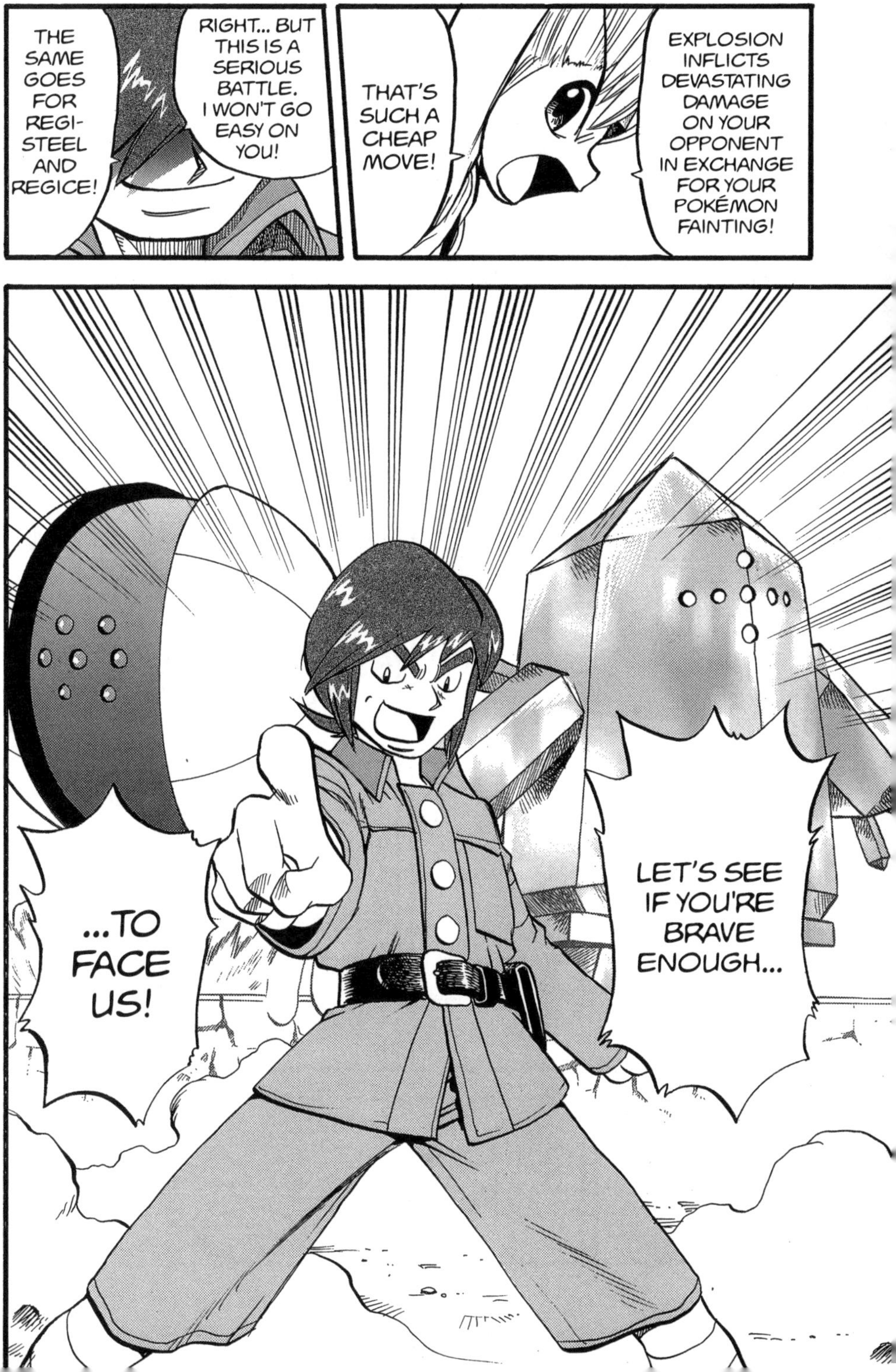
EXPLOSION INFLICTS DEVASTATING DAMAGE ON YOUR OPPONENT IN EXCHANGE FOR YOUR POKÉMON FAINTING!
THAT'S SUCH A CHEAP MOVE!
RIGHT... BUT THIS IS A SERIOUS BATTLE. I WON'T GO EASY ON YOU!
THE SAME GOES FOR REGI-STEEL AND REGICE!
LET'S SEE IF YOU'RE BRAVE ENOUGH...
...TO FACE US!

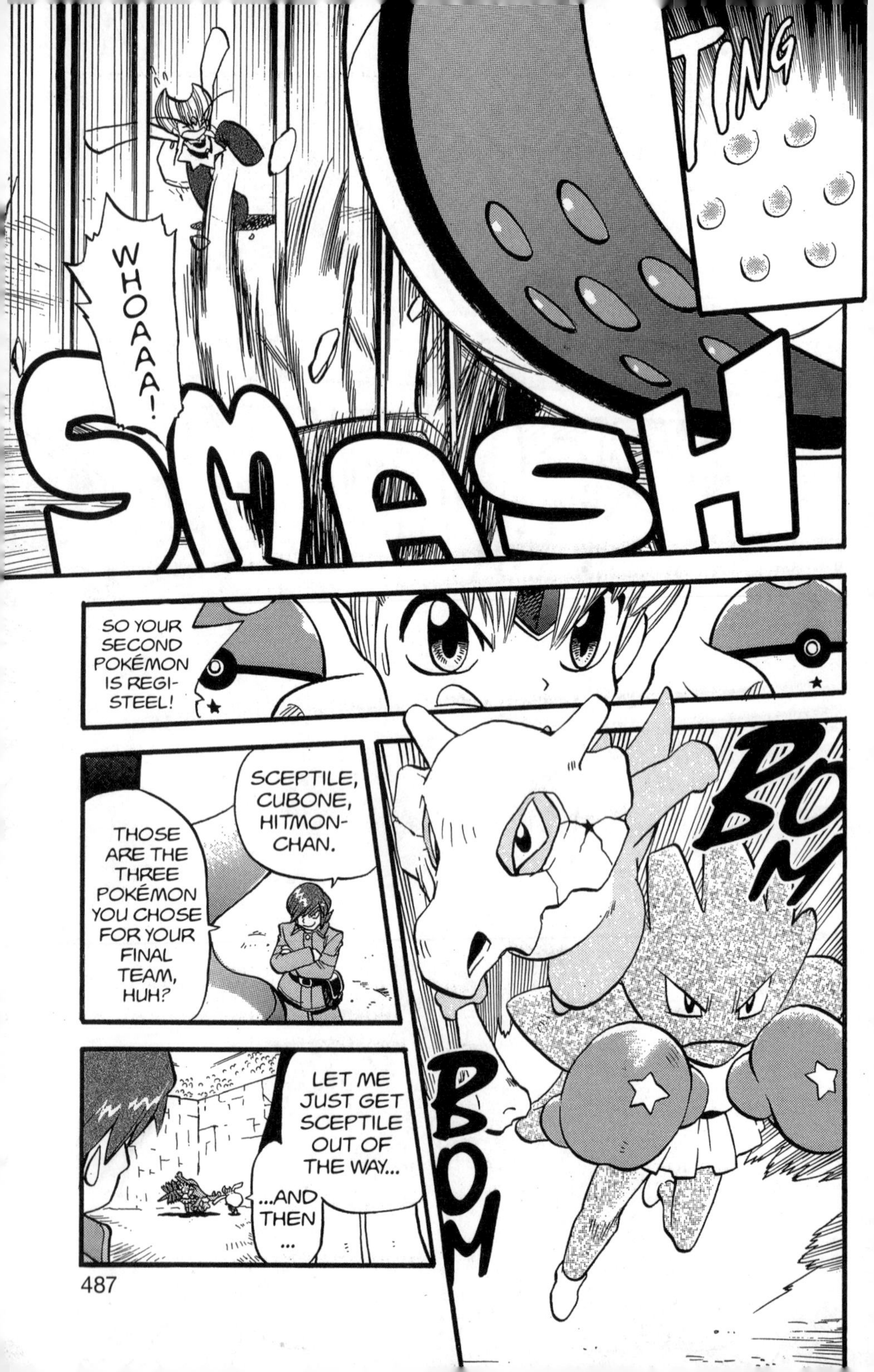

TING
WHOAAA!
SMASH
SO YOUR SECOND POKÉMON IS REGI-STEEL!
BOOM
BOOM
SCEPTILE, CUBONE, HITMON-CHAN.
THOSE ARE THE THREE POKÉMON YOU CHOSE FOR YOUR FINAL TEAM, HUH?
LET ME JUST GET SCEPTILE OUT OF THE WAY...
...AND THEN...

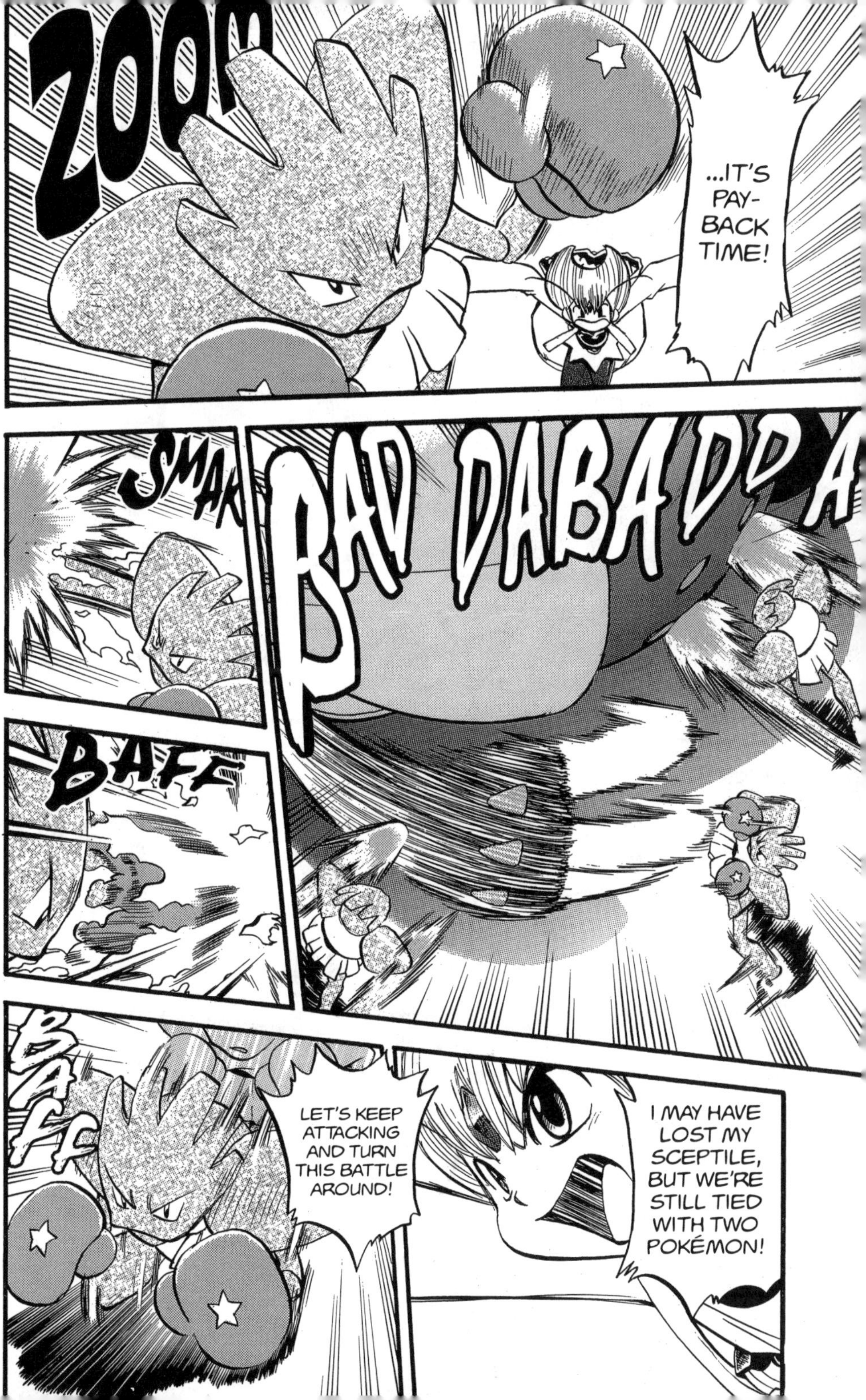
ZOOM
...IT'S PAY-BACK TIME!
BAD DABADDA
SMAK
BAFF
I MAY HAVE LOST MY SCEPTILE, BUT WE'RE STILL TIED WITH TWO POKÉMON!
LET'S KEEP ATTACKING AND TURN THIS BATTLE AROUND!
BAFF

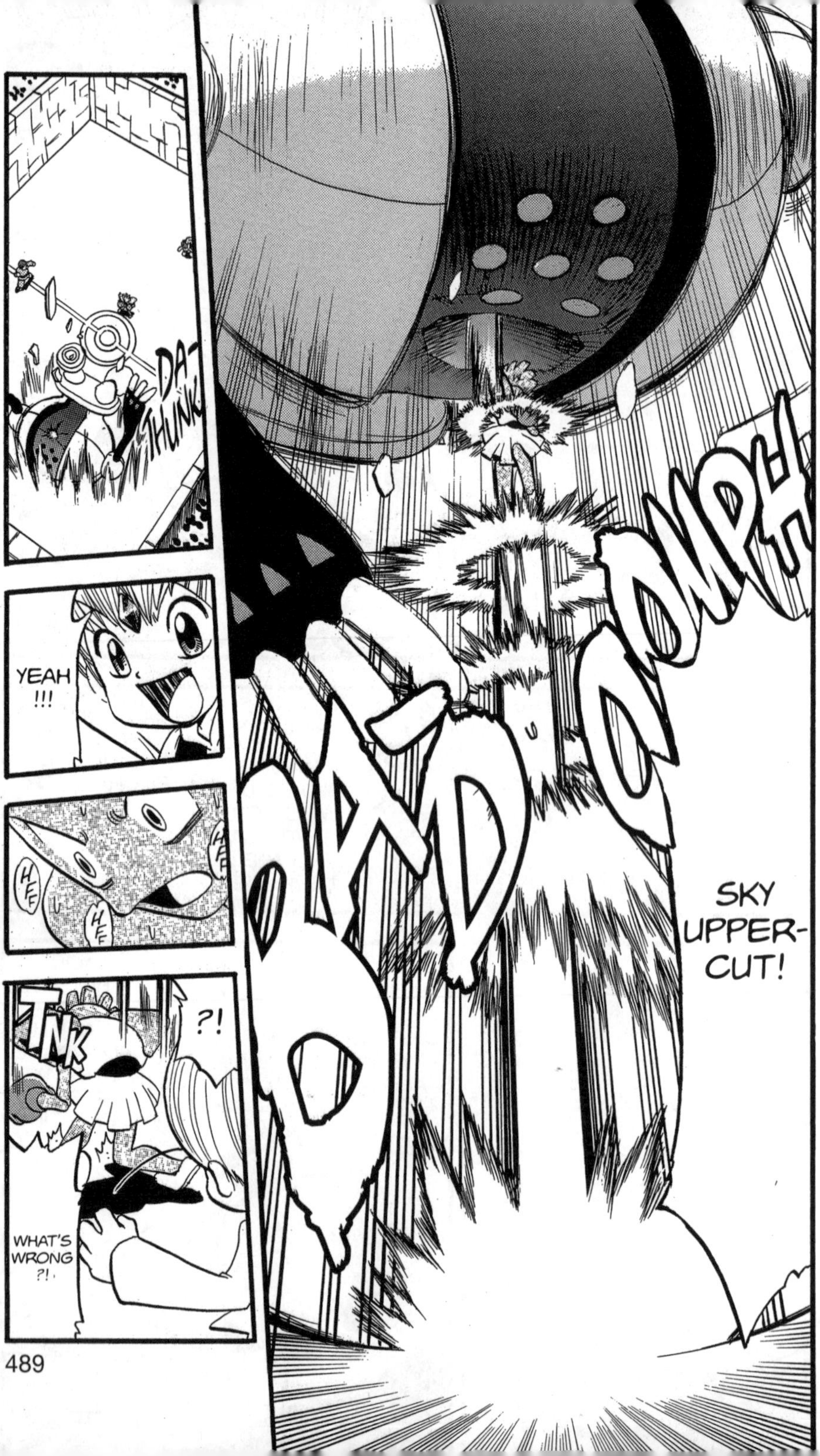
BADOOMPH
SKY UPPER-CUT!
DA-THUNK
YEAH !!!
HFF
HFF
HFF
TNK
?!
WHAT'S WRONG ?!

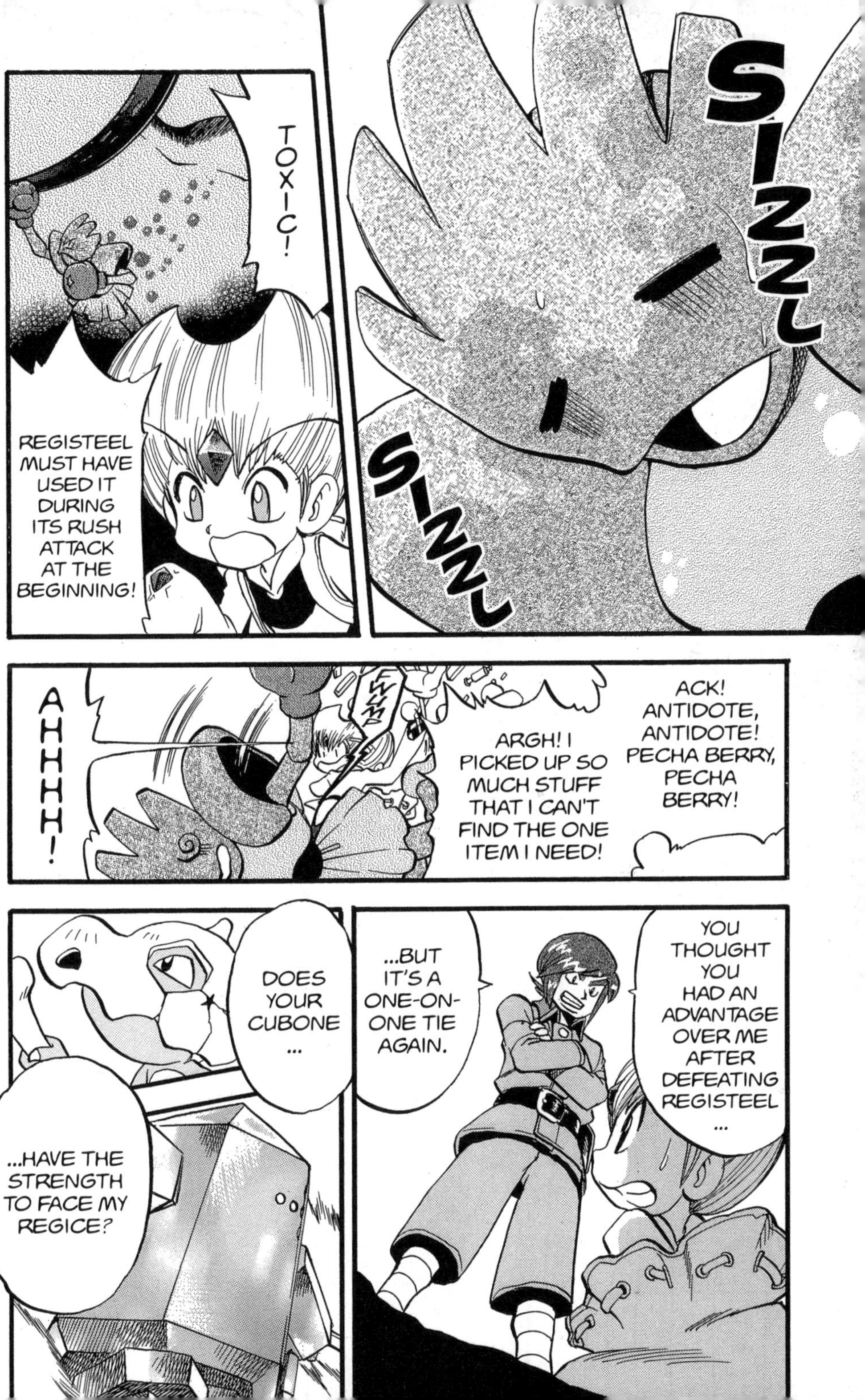
SIZZL
SIZZL
TOXIC!
REGISTEEL MUST HAVE USED IT DURING ITS RUSH ATTACK AT THE BEGINNING!
ACK! ANTIDOTE, ANTIDOTE! PECHA BERRY, PECHA BERRY!
ARGH! I PICKED UP SO MUCH STUFF THAT I CAN'T FIND THE ONE ITEM I NEED!
FWUMP
AHHHH!
YOU THOUGHT YOU HAD AN ADVANTAGE OVER ME AFTER DEFEATING REGISTEEL ...
...BUT IT'S A ONE-ON-ONE TIE AGAIN.
DOES YOUR CUBONE ...
...HAVE THE STRENGTH TO FACE MY REGICE?

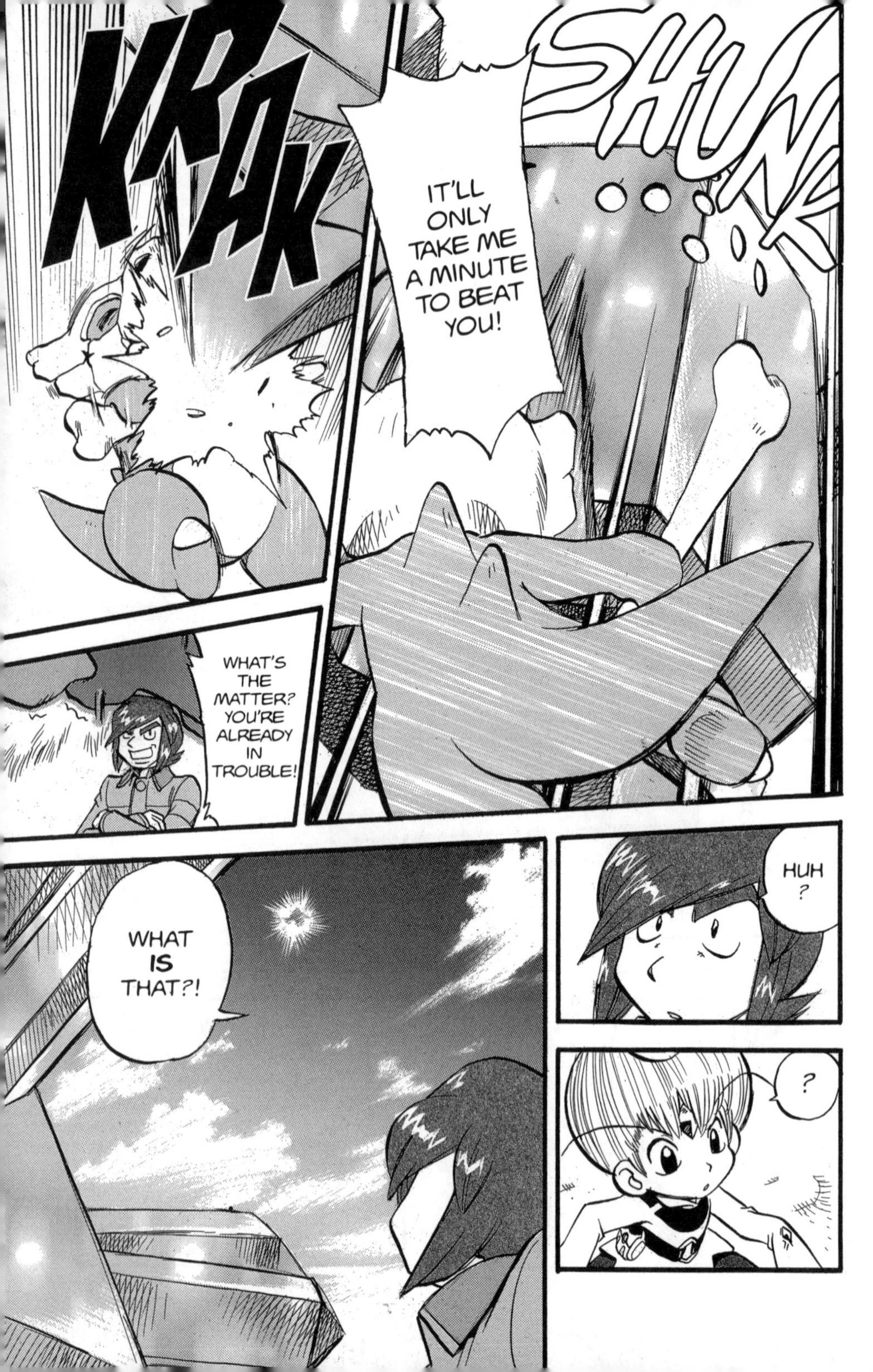
SHUNK
IT'LL ONLY TAKE ME A MINUTE TO BEAT YOU!
KRAK
WHAT'S THE MATTER? YOU'RE ALREADY IN TROUBLE!
HUH?
?
WHAT IS THAT?!

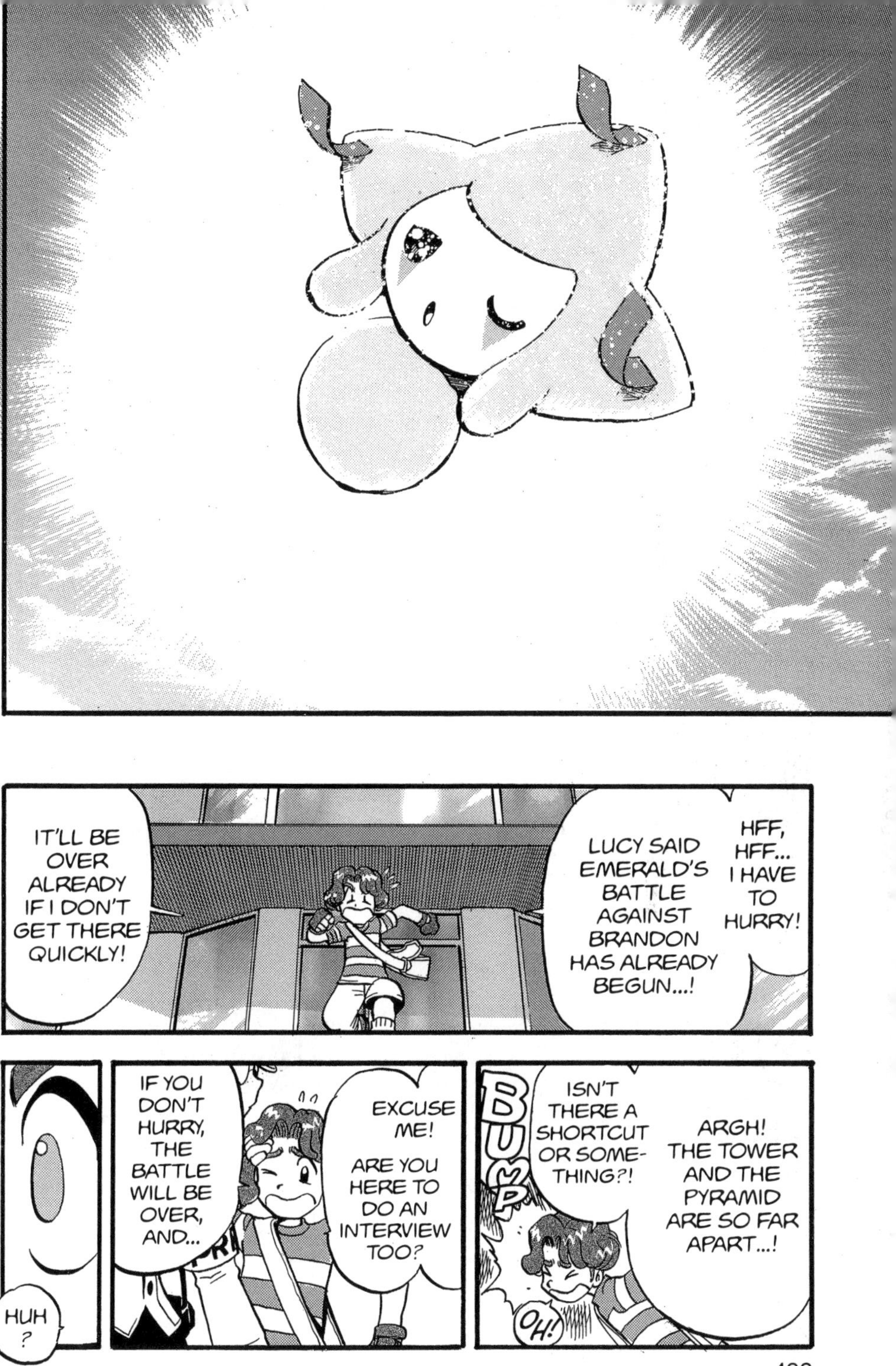
HFF, HFF... I HAVE TO HURRY!
LUCY SAID EMERALD'S BATTLE AGAINST BRANDON HAS ALREADY BEGUN...!
IT'LL BE OVER ALREADY IF I DON'T GET THERE QUICKLY!
ARGH! THE TOWER AND THE PYRAMID ARE SO FAR APART...!
ISN'T THERE A SHORTCUT OR SOME-THING?!
BUMP
OH!
EXCUSE ME!
ARE YOU HERE TO DO AN INTERVIEW TOO?
IF YOU DON'T HURRY, THE BATTLE WILL BE OVER, AND...
HUH?

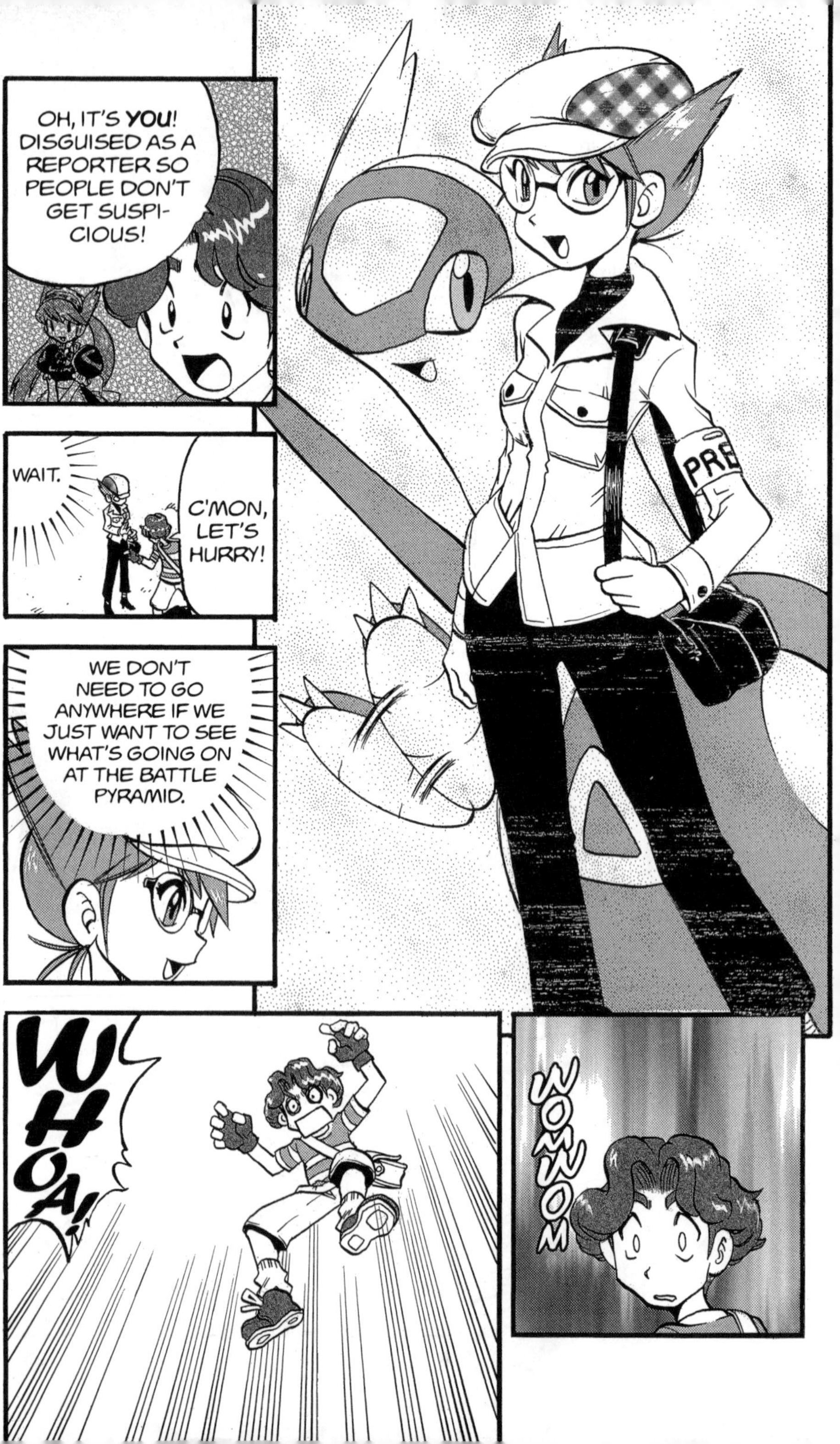
PRE
OH, IT'S **YOU**! DISGUISED AS A REPORTER SO PEOPLE DON'T GET SUSPICIOUS!
C'MON, LET'S HURRY!
WAIT.
WE DON'T NEED TO GO ANYWHERE IF WE JUST WANT TO SEE WHAT'S GOING ON AT THE BATTLE PYRAMID.
WOMWOM
WHOA!

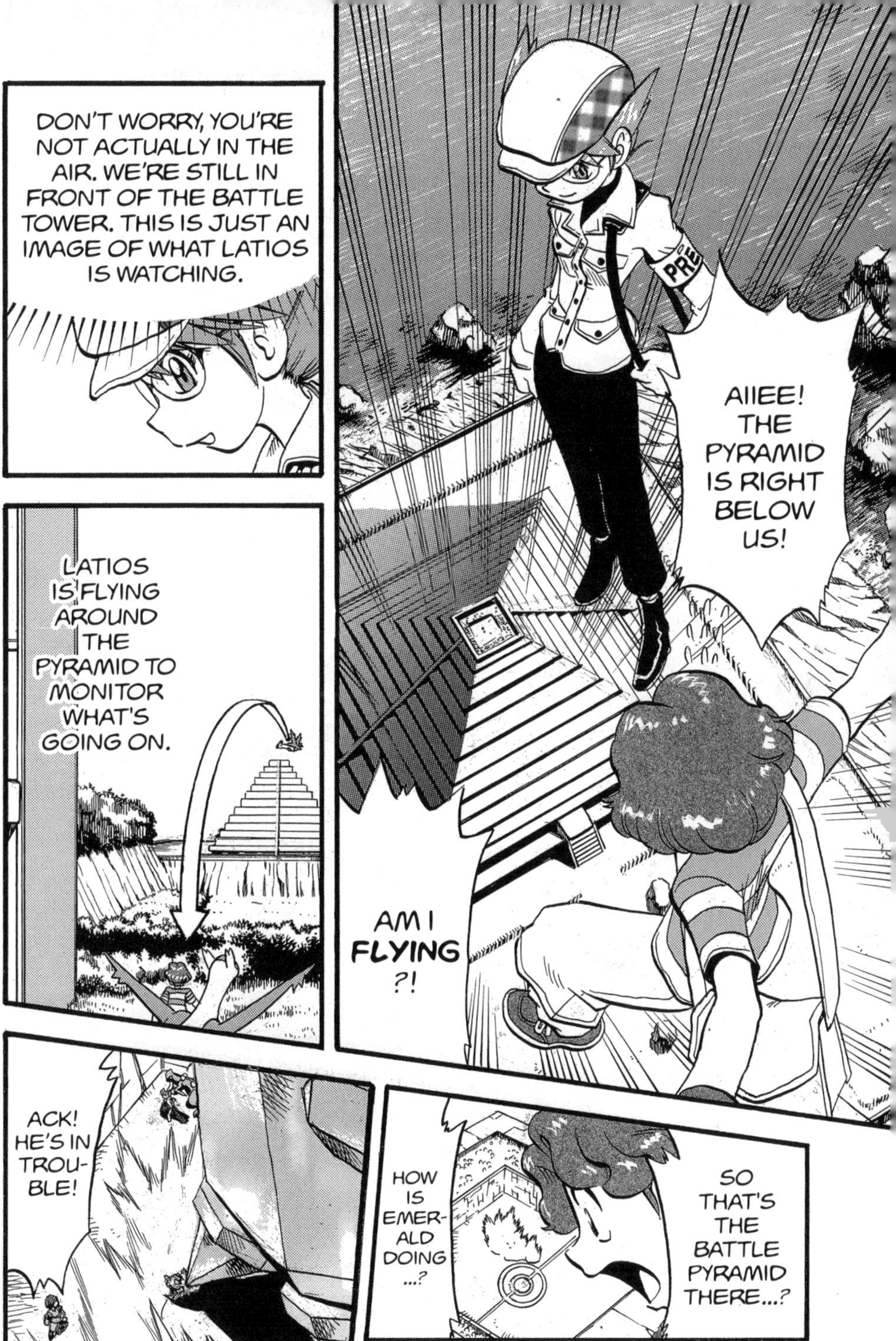
AIIEE! THE PYRAMID IS RIGHT BELOW US!
AM I **FLYING** ?!
DON'T WORRY, YOU'RE NOT ACTUALLY IN THE AIR. WE'RE STILL IN FRONT OF THE BATTLE TOWER. THIS IS JUST AN IMAGE OF WHAT LATIOS IS WATCHING.
LATIOS IS FLYING AROUND THE PYRAMID TO MONITOR WHAT'S GOING ON.
SO THAT'S THE BATTLE PYRAMID THERE...?
HOW IS EMER-ALD DOING ...?
ACK! HE'S IN TROU-BLE!

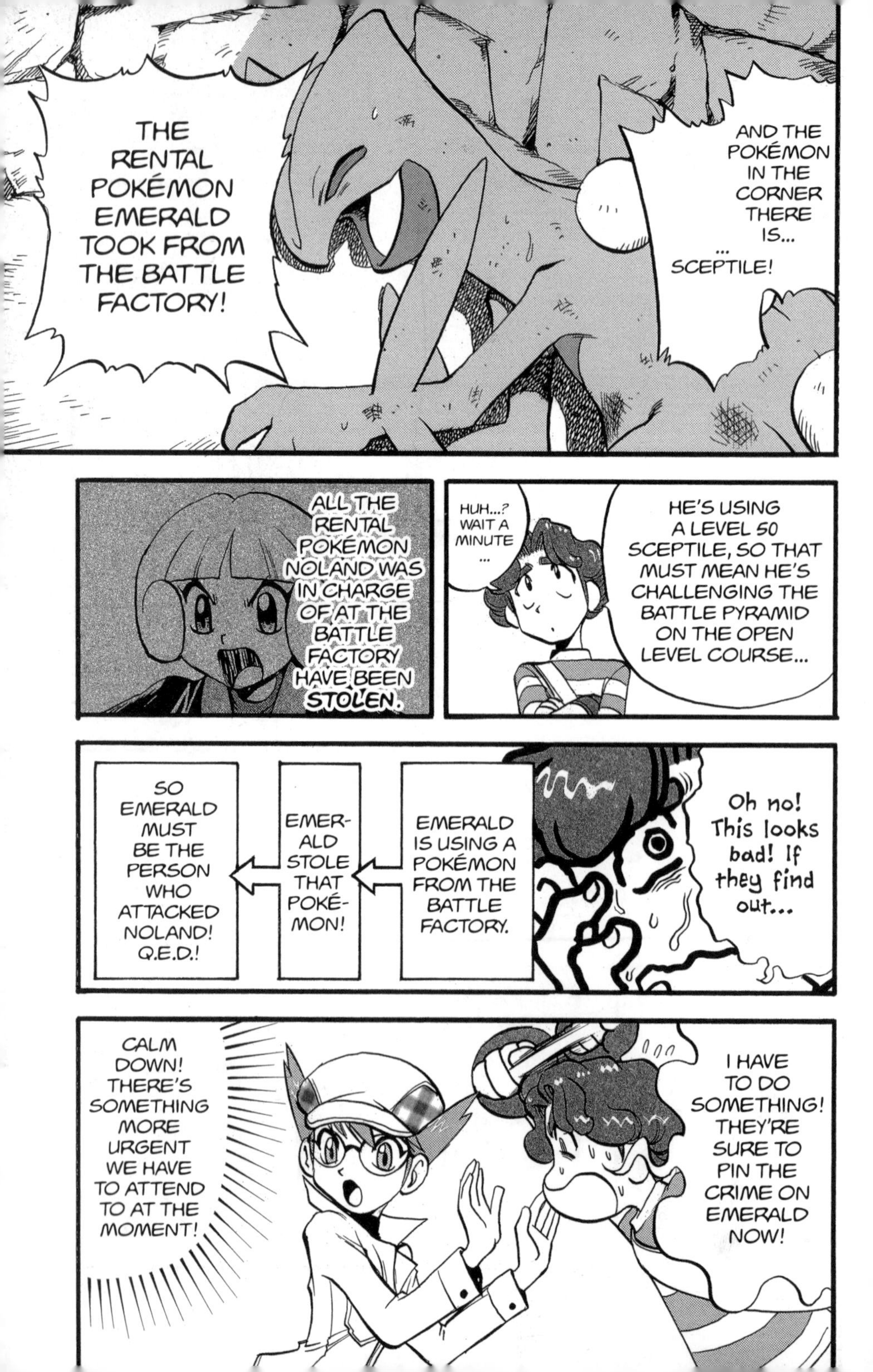
AND THE POKÉMON IN THE CORNER THERE IS... ... SCEPTILE!
THE RENTAL POKÉMON EMERALD TOOK FROM THE BATTLE FACTORY!
HUH...? WAIT A MINUTE ...
HE'S USING A LEVEL 50 SCEPTILE, SO THAT MUST MEAN HE'S CHALLENGING THE BATTLE PYRAMID ON THE OPEN LEVEL COURSE...
ALL THE RENTAL POKÉMON NOLAND WAS IN CHARGE OF AT THE BATTLE FACTORY HAVE BEEN STOLEN.
Oh no! This looks bad! If they find out...
EMERALD IS USING A POKÉMON FROM THE BATTLE FACTORY.
EMERALD STOLE THAT POKÉMON!
SO EMERALD MUST BE THE PERSON WHO ATTACKED NOLAND! Q.E.D.!
I HAVE TO DO SOMETHING! THEY'RE SURE TO PIN THE CRIME ON EMERALD NOW!
CALM DOWN! THERE'S SOMETHING MORE URGENT WE HAVE TO ATTEND TO AT THE MOMENT!

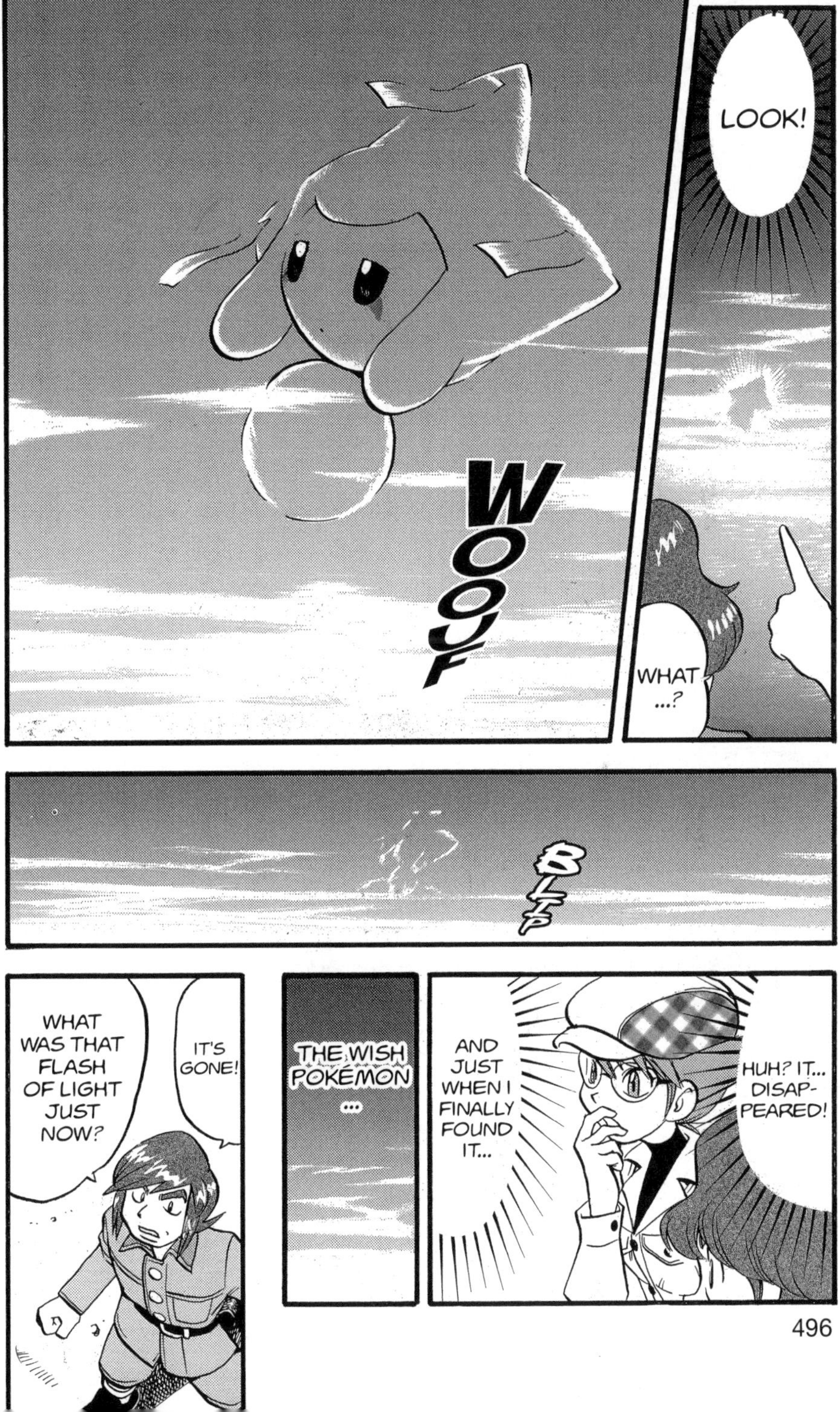
LOOK!
WHAT ...?
WOOUF
BLIP
HUH? IT... DISAP-PEARED!
AND JUST WHEN I FINALLY FOUND IT...
THE WISH POKÉMON ...
IT'S GONE!
WHAT WAS THAT FLASH OF LIGHT JUST NOW?

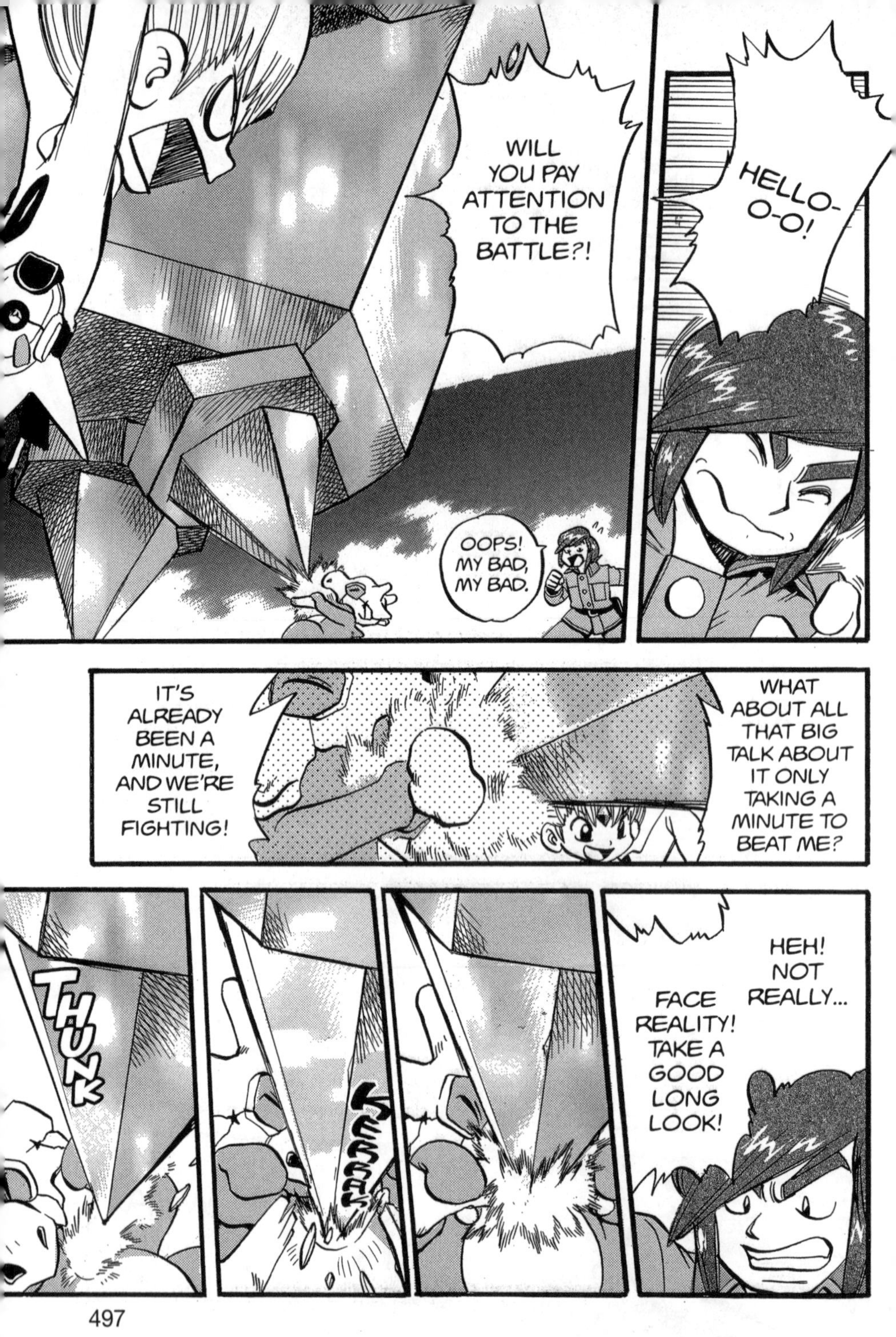

HELLO-O-O!
WILL YOU PAY ATTENTION TO THE BATTLE?!
OOPS! MY BAD, MY BAD.
WHAT ABOUT ALL THAT BIG TALK ABOUT IT ONLY TAKING A MINUTE TO BEAT ME?
IT'S ALREADY BEEN A MINUTE, AND WE'RE STILL FIGHTING!
HEH! NOT REALLY...
FACE REALITY! TAKE A GOOD LONG LOOK!
THUNK

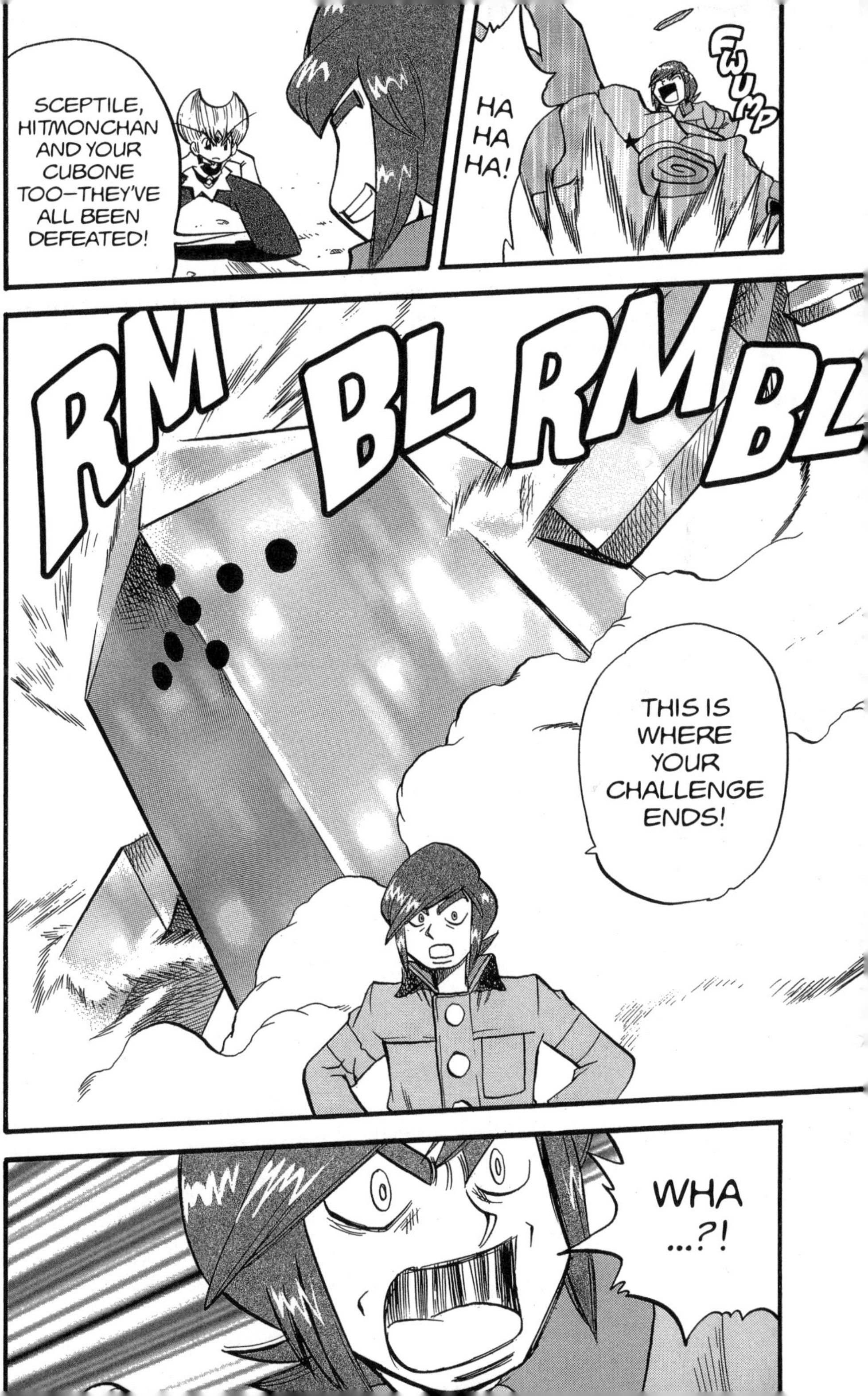
FWUMP
HA HA HA!
SCEPTILE, HITMONCHAN AND YOUR CUBONE TOO—THEY'VE ALL BEEN DEFEATED!
RM BL RM BL
THIS IS WHERE YOUR CHALLENGE ENDS!
WHA ...?!

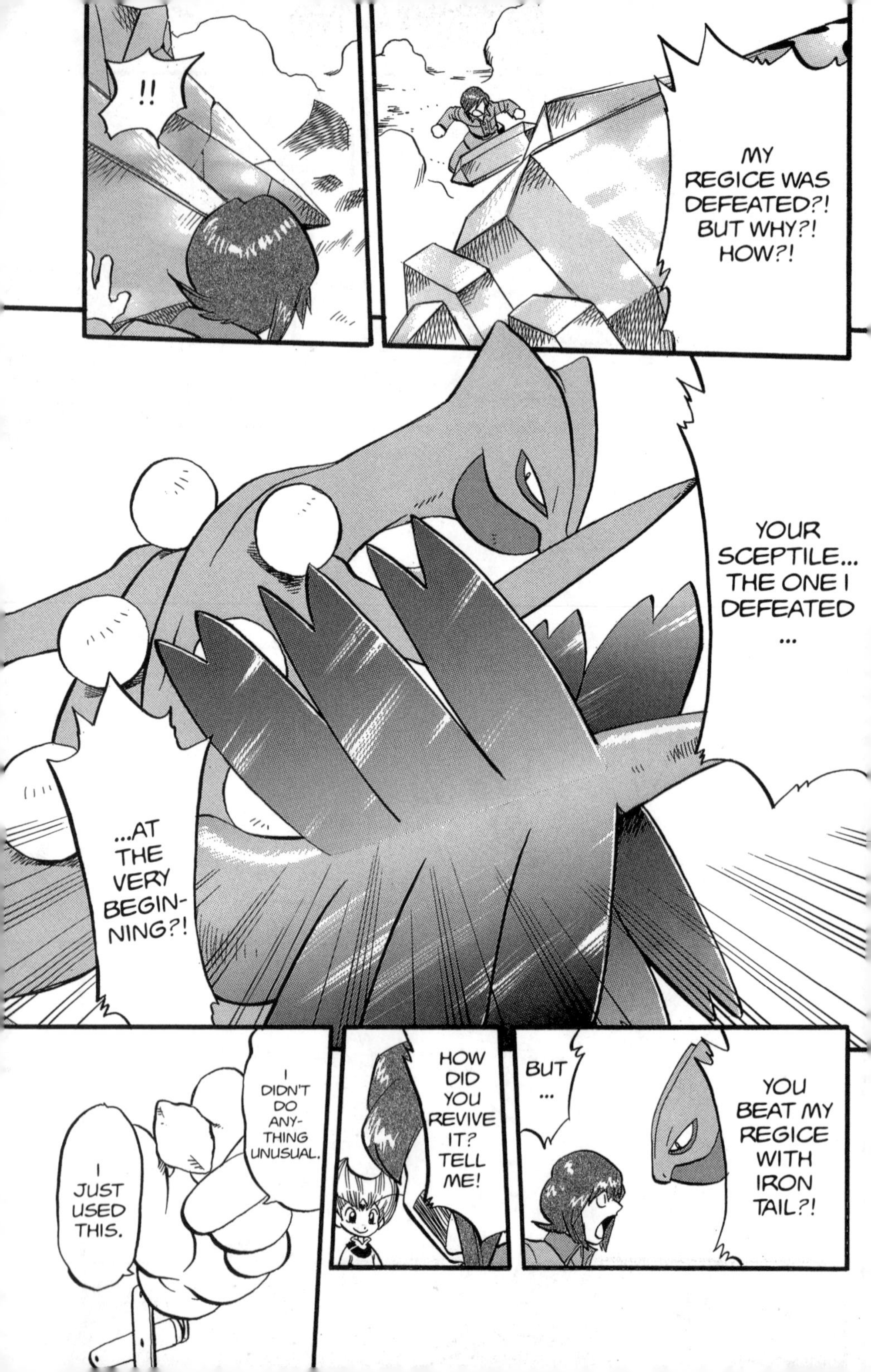
MY REGICE WAS DEFEATED?! BUT WHY?! HOW?!
!!
YOUR SCEPTILE... THE ONE I DEFEATED ...
...AT THE VERY BEGIN-NING?!
YOU BEAT MY REGICE WITH IRON TAIL?!
BUT ...
HOW DID YOU REVIVE IT? TELL ME!
I DIDN'T DO ANY-THING UNUSUAL.
I JUST USED THIS.

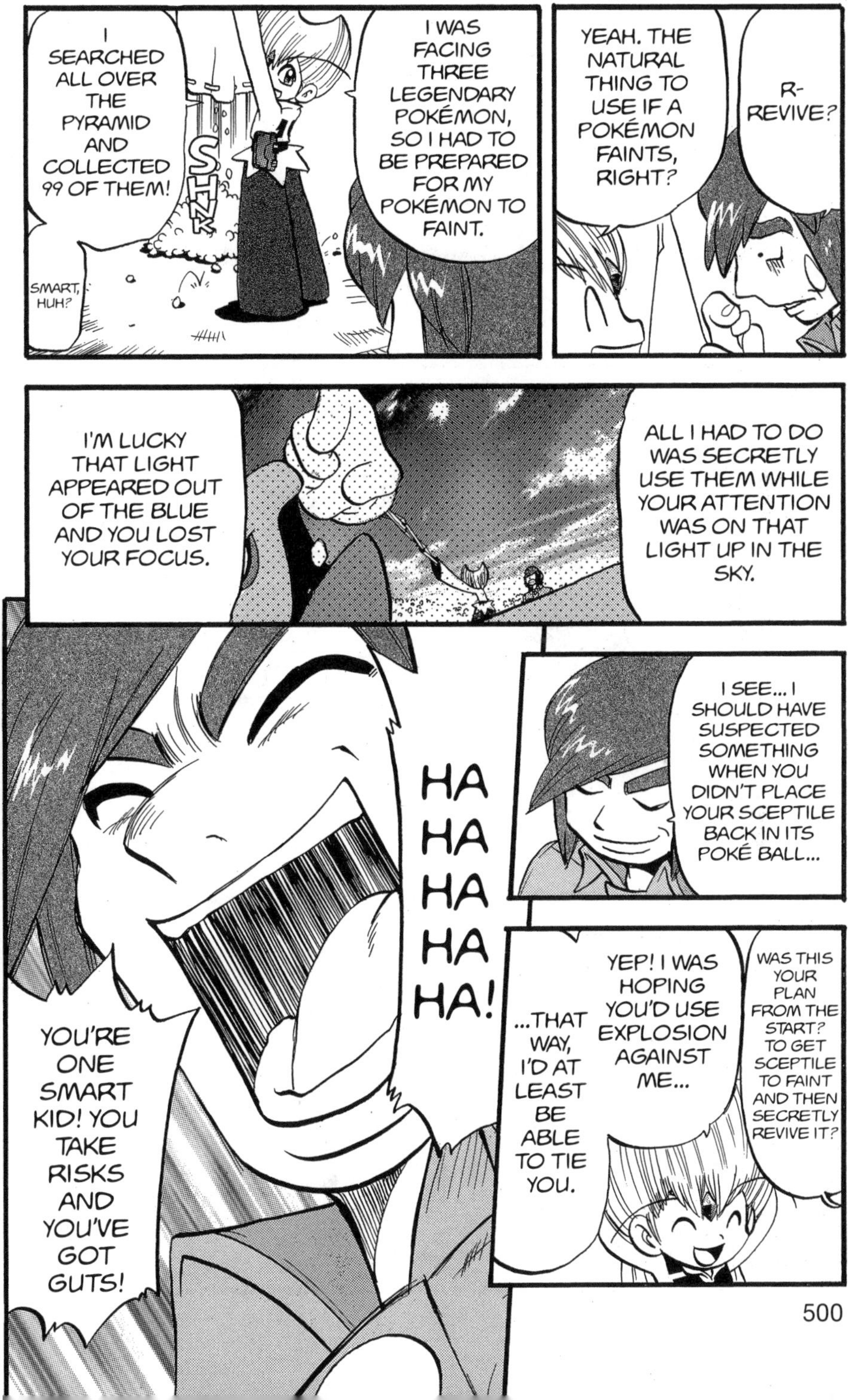
R-REVIVE?
YEAH. THE NATURAL THING TO USE IF A POKÉMON FAINTS, RIGHT?
I WAS FACING THREE LEGENDARY POKÉMON, SO I HAD TO BE PREPARED FOR MY POKÉMON TO FAINT.
I SEARCHED ALL OVER THE PYRAMID AND COLLECTED 99 OF THEM!
SHNK
SMART, HUH?
ALL I HAD TO DO WAS SECRETLY USE THEM WHILE YOUR ATTENTION WAS ON THAT LIGHT UP IN THE SKY.
I'M LUCKY THAT LIGHT APPEARED OUT OF THE BLUE AND YOU LOST YOUR FOCUS.
I SEE... I SHOULD HAVE SUSPECTED SOMETHING WHEN YOU DIDN'T PLACE YOUR SCEPTILE BACK IN ITS POKÉ BALL...
WAS THIS YOUR PLAN FROM THE START? TO GET SCEPTILE TO FAINT AND THEN SECRETLY REVIVE IT?
YEP! I WAS HOPING YOU'D USE EXPLOSION AGAINST ME...
...THAT WAY, I'D AT LEAST BE ABLE TO TIE YOU.
HA HA HA HA HA!
YOU'RE ONE SMART KID! YOU TAKE RISKS AND YOU'VE GOT GUTS!

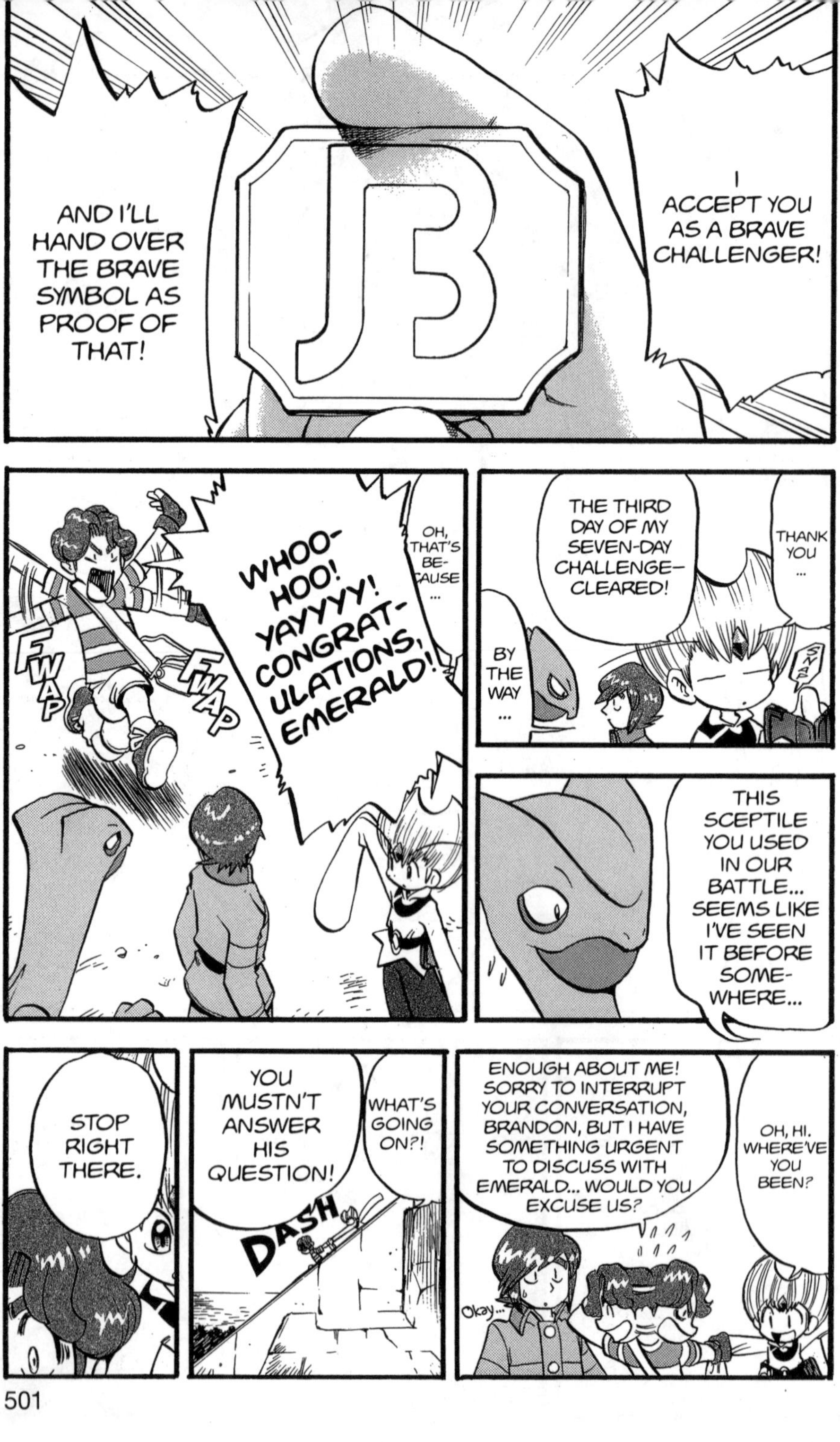
I ACCEPT YOU AS A BRAVE CHALLENGER!
AND I'LL HAND OVER THE BRAVE SYMBOL AS PROOF OF THAT!
THANK YOU ...
THE THIRD DAY OF MY SEVEN-DAY CHALLENGE—CLEARED!
SNAP
BY THE WAY ...
THIS SCEPTILE YOU USED IN OUR BATTLE... SEEMS LIKE I'VE SEEN IT BEFORE SOME-WHERE...
OH, THAT'S BE-CAUSE ...
WHOO-HOO! YAYYYY! CONGRAT-ULATIONS, EMERALD!
FWAP
FWAP
OH, HI. WHERE'VE YOU BEEN?
ENOUGH ABOUT ME! SORRY TO INTERRUPT YOUR CONVERSATION, BRANDON, BUT I HAVE SOMETHING URGENT TO DISCUSS WITH EMERALD... WOULD YOU EXCUSE US?
Okay...
WHAT'S GOING ON?!
YOU MUSTN'T ANSWER HIS QUESTION!
DASH
STOP RIGHT THERE.

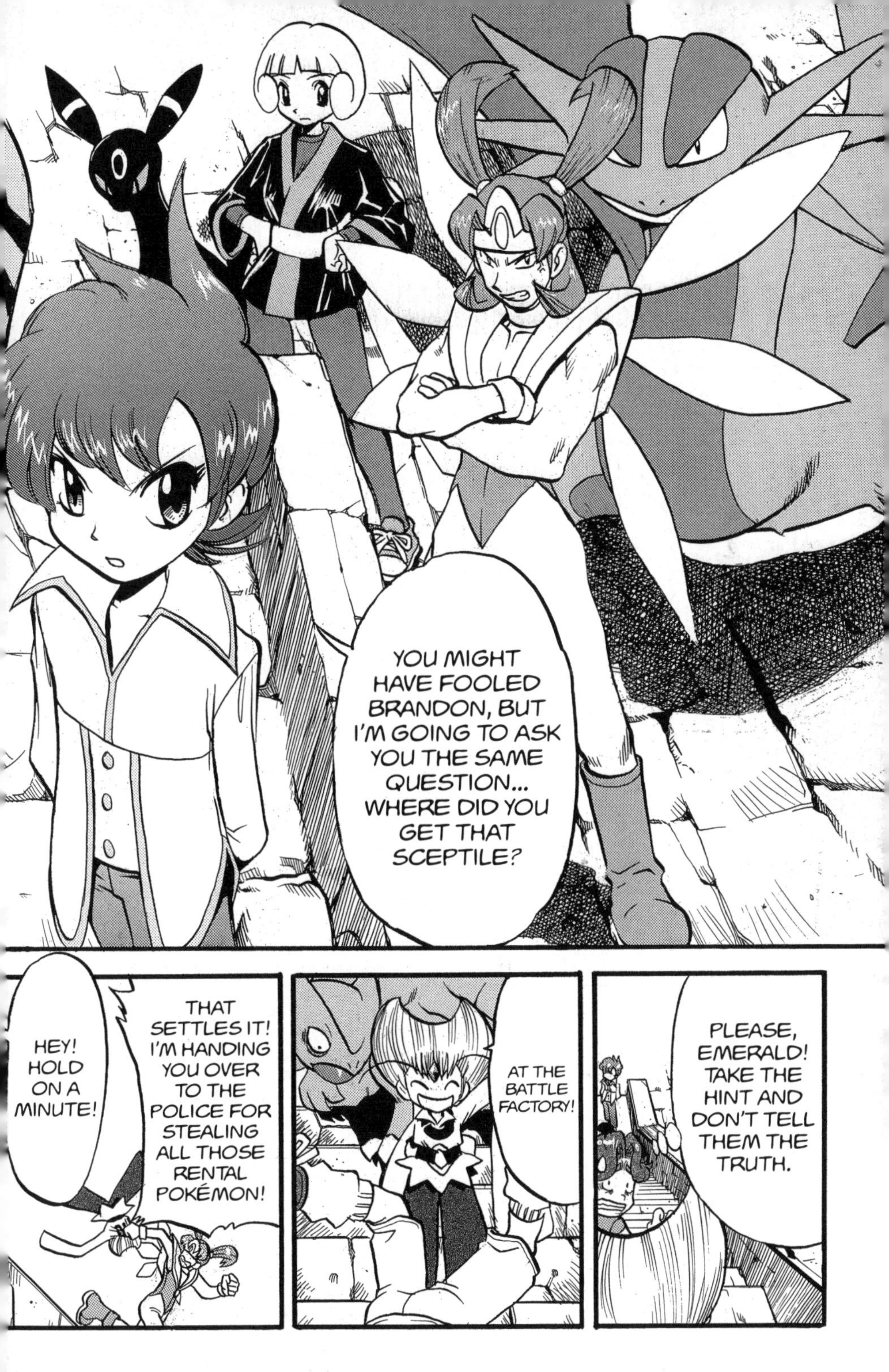
YOU MIGHT HAVE FOOLED BRANDON, BUT I'M GOING TO ASK YOU THE SAME QUESTION... WHERE DID YOU GET THAT SCEPTILE?
PLEASE, EMERALD! TAKE THE HINT AND DON'T TELL THEM THE TRUTH.
AT THE BATTLE FACTORY!
THAT SETTLES IT! I'M HANDING YOU OVER TO THE POLICE FOR STEALING ALL THOSE RENTAL POKÉMON!
HEY! HOLD ON A MINUTE!

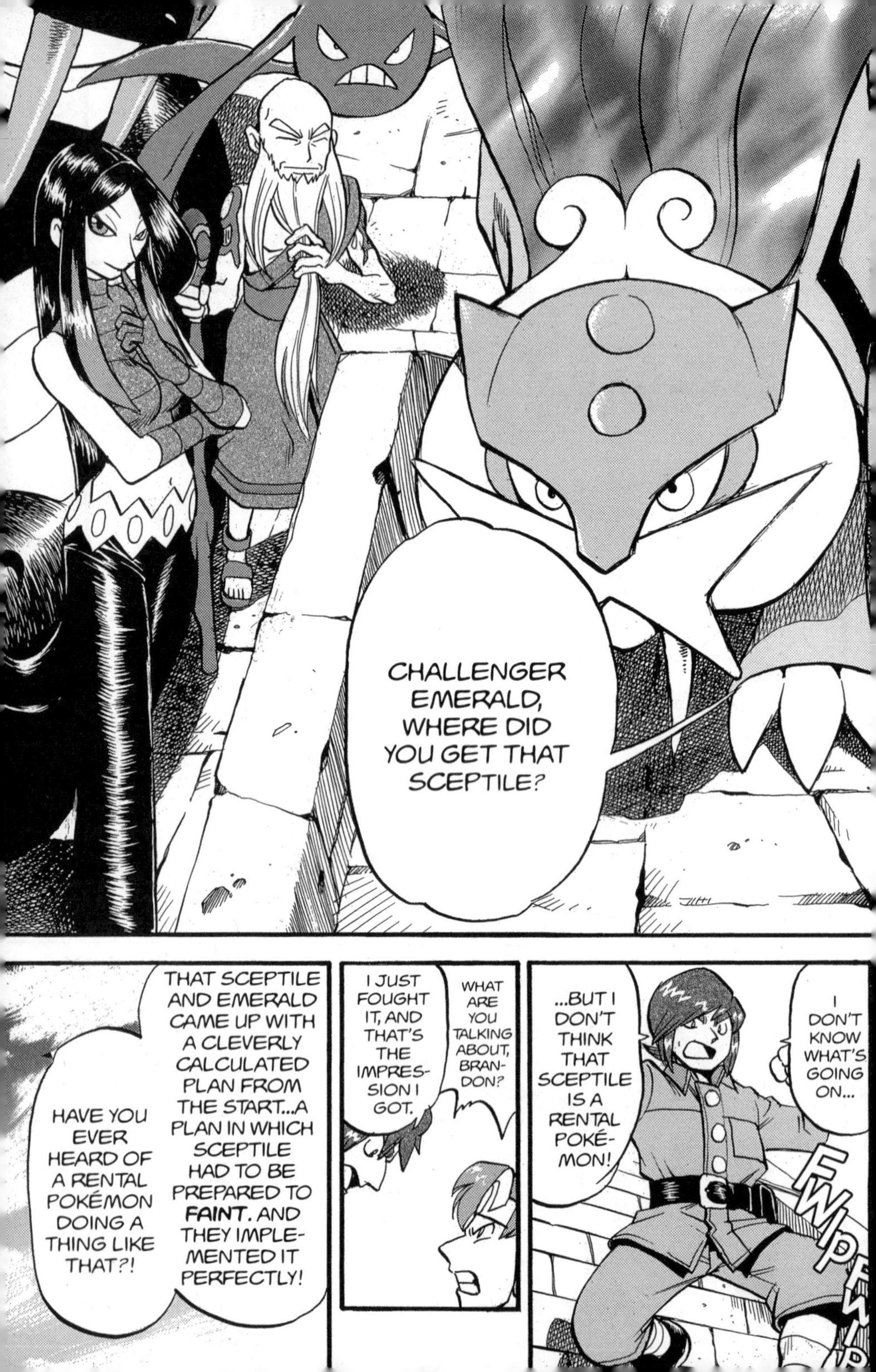
CHALLENGER EMERALD, WHERE DID YOU GET THAT SCEPTILE?
I DON'T KNOW WHAT'S GOING ON...
...BUT I DON'T THINK THAT SCEPTILE IS A RENTAL POKÉMON!
FWIP FWIP
WHAT ARE YOU TALKING ABOUT, BRANDON?
I JUST FOUGHT IT, AND THAT'S THE IMPRESSION I GOT.
THAT SCEPTILE AND EMERALD CAME UP WITH A CLEVERLY CALCULATED PLAN FROM THE START...A PLAN IN WHICH SCEPTILE HAD TO BE PREPARED TO **FAINT**. AND THEY IMPLEMENTED IT PERFECTLY!
HAVE YOU EVER HEARD OF A RENTAL POKÉMON DOING A THING LIKE THAT?!

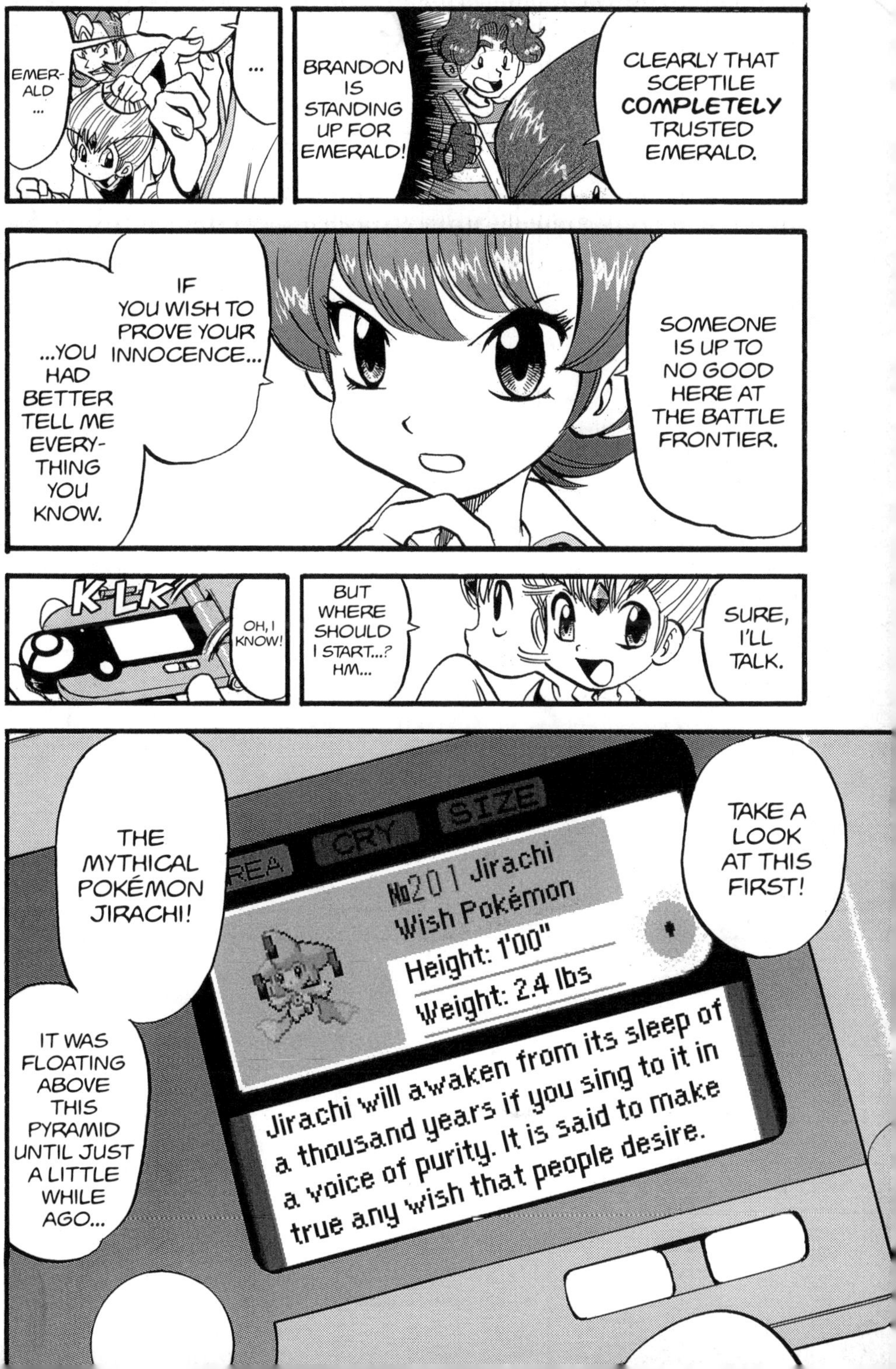
CLEARLY THAT SCEPTILE **COMPLETELY** TRUSTED EMERALD.
BRANDON IS STANDING UP FOR EMERALD!
...
EMER-ALD ...
SOMEONE IS UP TO NO GOOD HERE AT THE BATTLE FRONTIER.
IF YOU WISH TO PROVE YOUR INNOCENCE...
...YOU HAD BETTER TELL ME EVERY-THING YOU KNOW.
SURE, I'LL TALK.
BUT WHERE SHOULD I START...? HM...
K-LK
OH, I KNOW!
TAKE A LOOK AT THIS FIRST!
SIZE
CRY
AREA
No201 Jirachi
Wish Pokémon
Height: 1'00"
Weight: 2.4 lbs
Jirachi will awaken from its sleep of a thousand years if you sing to it in a voice of purity. It is said to make true any wish that people desire.
THE MYTHICAL POKÉMON JIRACHI!
IT WAS FLOATING ABOVE THIS PYRAMID UNTIL JUST A LITTLE WHILE AGO...

DEAR MEMBERS OF THE PRESS...

Thank you for visiting the Battle Frontier today. Permit me to continue explaining the rules of this facility...

OWNER: SCOTT

A Pokémon who loses during the rating stage will be removed from battle even if it can still fight. The challenger must then switch out their Pokémon. If the rating scores are tied, both sides must switch out their Pokémon. If the battle between the last Pokémon on each side ends in a draw, the challenger loses.

■ THE RATING SYSTEM ■

MIND ➡ Judged by the number of attacks

You receive a high rating for attacking your opponent multiple times and a low rating for using defensive moves like Protect. The attacks are counted even if you are in a debilitated state such as Paralysis and fail to attack properly.

SKILL ➡ Judged by the effectiveness of the move

You receive a high rating for using moves that are Super Effective, but a low rating for attacks that are Not Very Effective or Not Effective. The rating stands even if your opponent blocks the attack with moves like Protect.

BODY ➡ Judged by the damage you receive

You receive a rating based on how much strength your Pokémon has left at the end of the battle compared to the beginning.

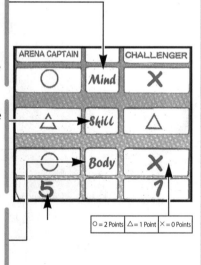

ARENA CAPTAIN — Mind — CHALLENGER

ARENA CAPTAIN		CHALLENGER
○	Mind	✕
△	Skill	△
○	Body	✕
5		1

○ = 2 Points △ = 1 Point ✕ = 0 Points

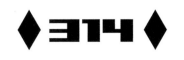

A Sketchy Smattering of Smeargle

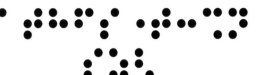

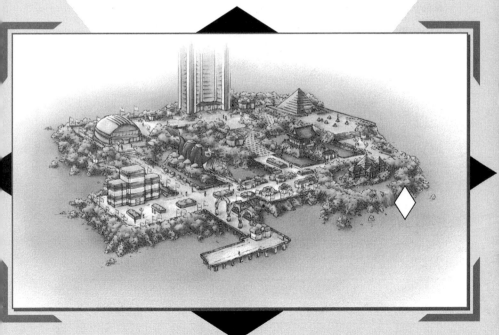

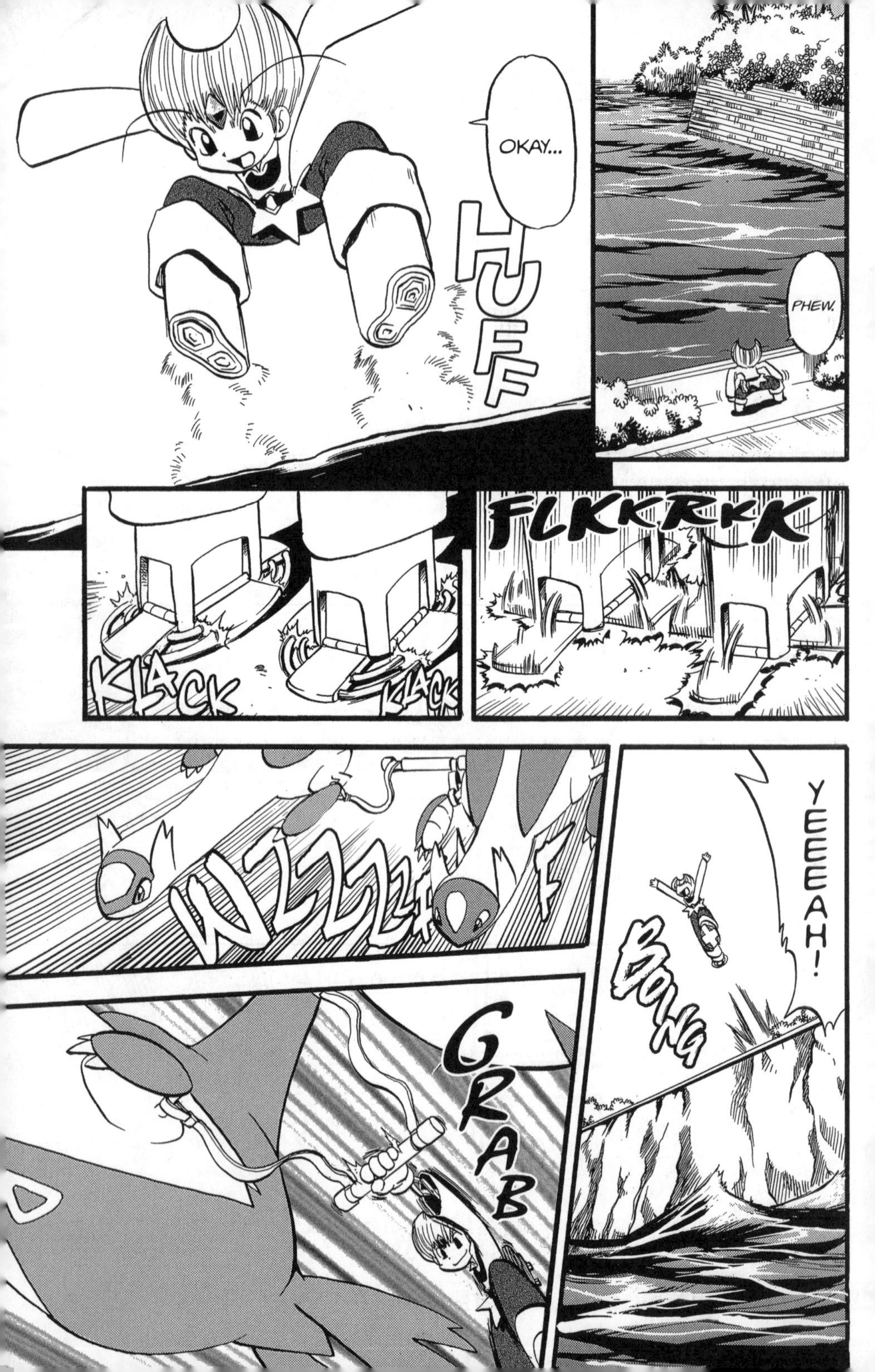
PHEW.
OKAY...
HUFF
FLKKRRKK
KLACK
KLACK
YEEEAH!
BOING
WZZZZ F
GRAB

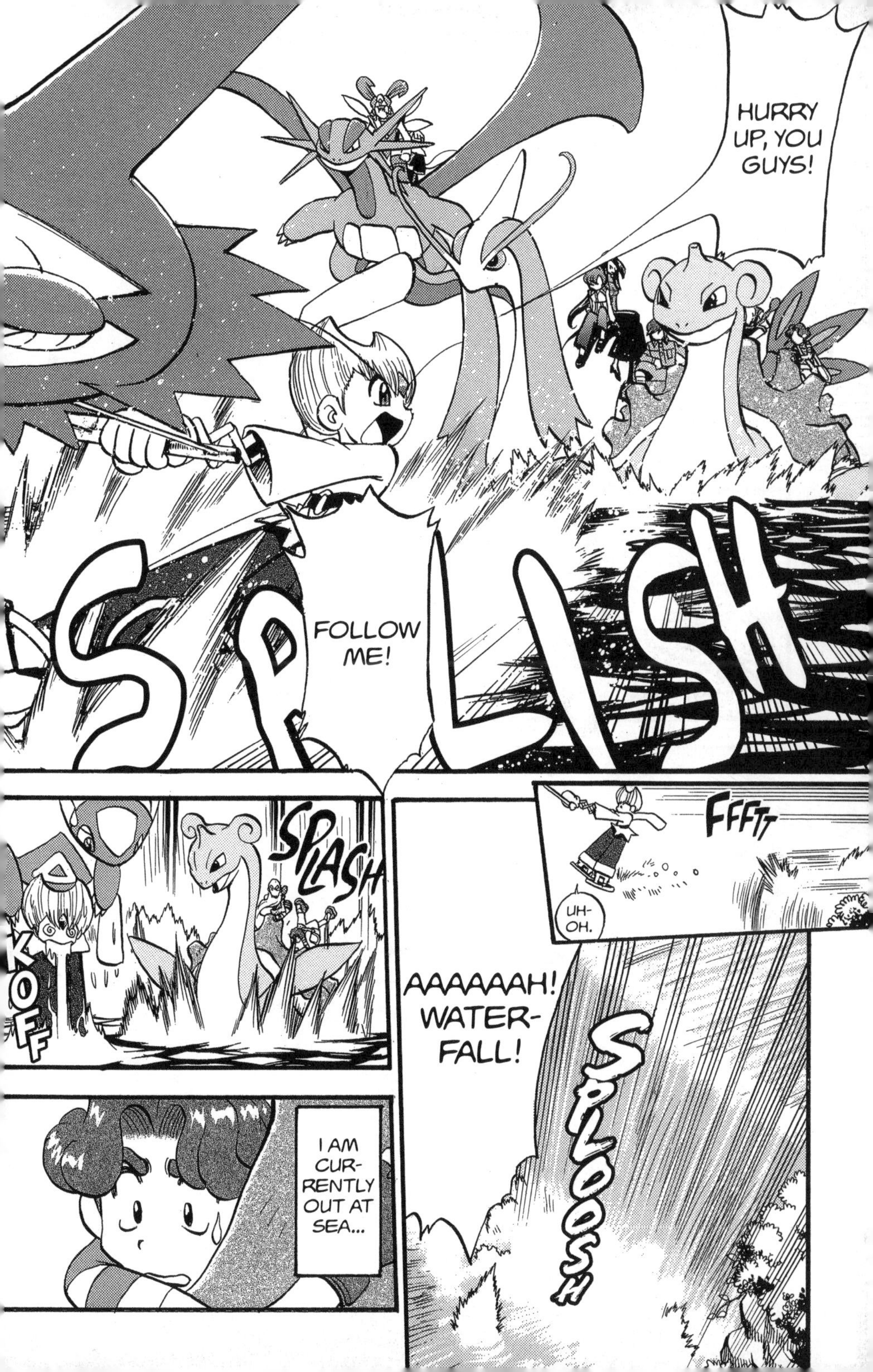
HURRY UP, YOU GUYS!
FOLLOW ME!
SPLASH
FFFTT
UH-OH.
AAAAAAH! WATER-FALL!
SPLOOSH
SPLASH
KOFF
I AM CUR-RENTLY OUT AT SEA...

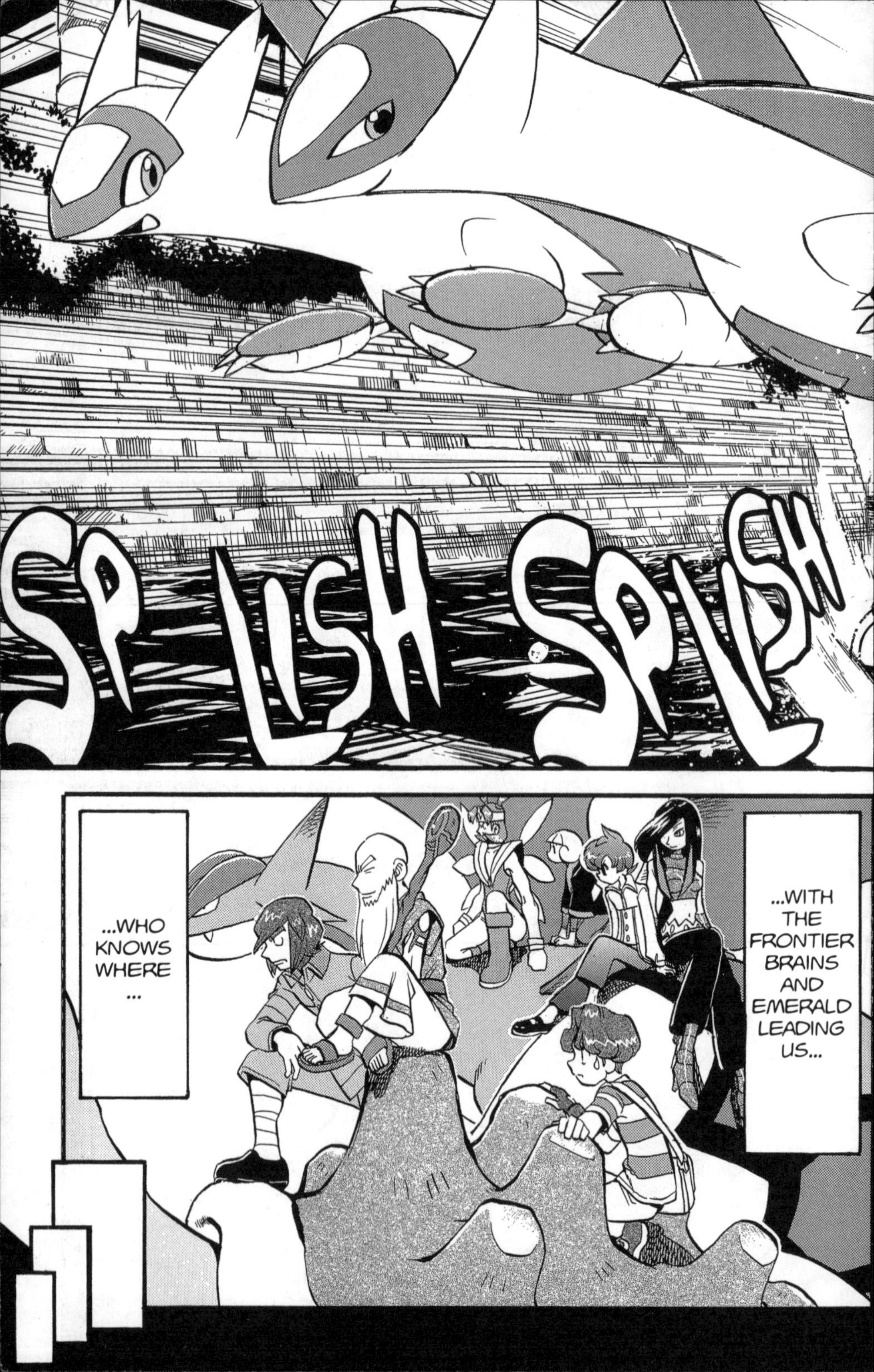
SPLISH SPLISH
...WITH THE FRONTIER BRAINS AND EMERALD LEADING US...
...WHO KNOWS WHERE ...

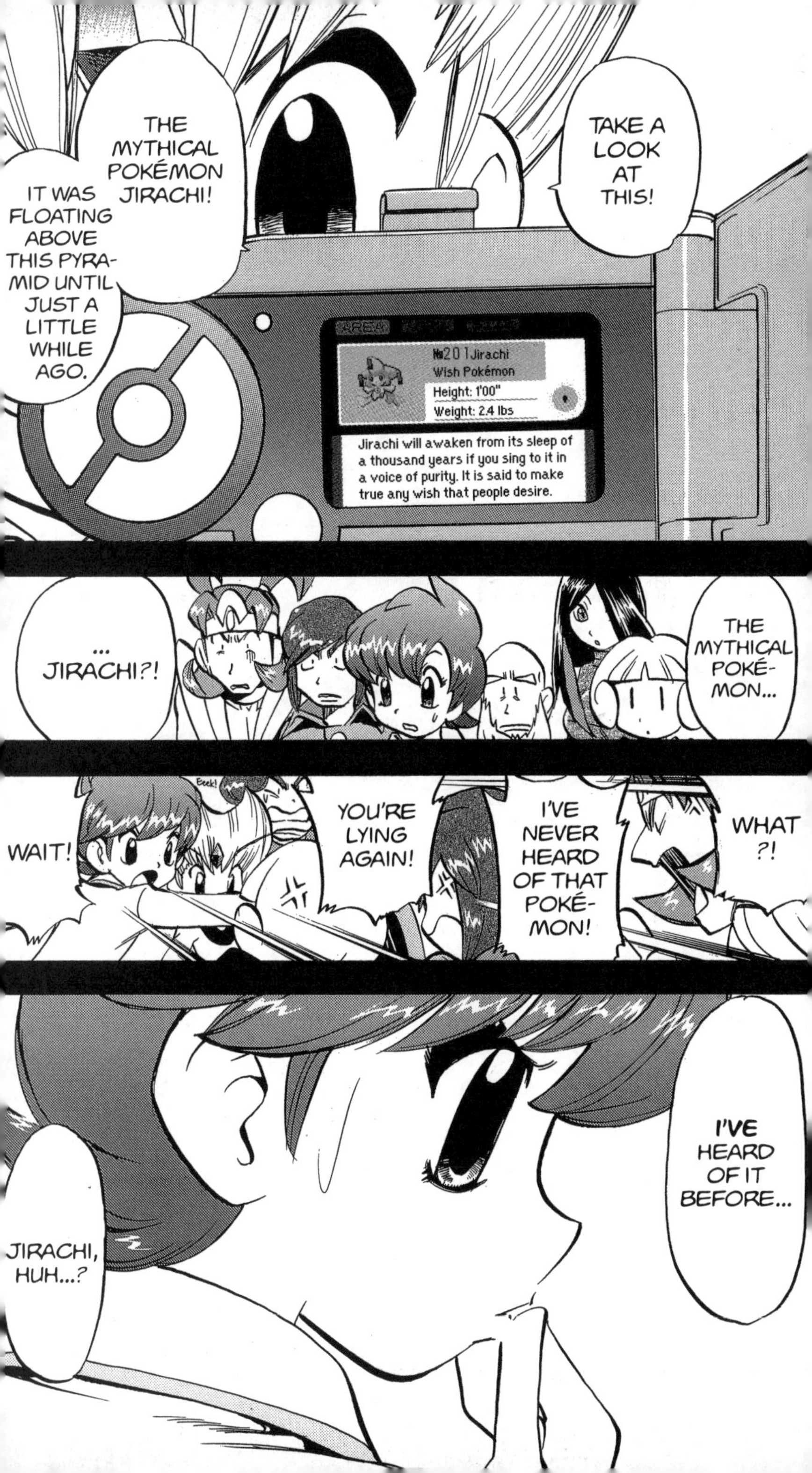
TAKE A LOOK AT THIS!
THE MYTHICAL POKÉMON JIRACHI!
IT WAS FLOATING ABOVE THIS PYRAMID UNTIL JUST A LITTLE WHILE AGO.
№201 Jirachi
Wish Pokémon
Height: 1'00"
Weight: 2.4 lbs
Jirachi will awaken from its sleep of a thousand years if you sing to it in a voice of purity. It is said to make true any wish that people desire.
THE MYTHICAL POKÉMON...
... JIRACHI?!
WHAT?!
I'VE NEVER HEARD OF THAT POKÉMON!
YOU'RE LYING AGAIN!
Eeek!
WAIT!
I'VE HEARD OF IT BEFORE...
JIRACHI, HUH...?

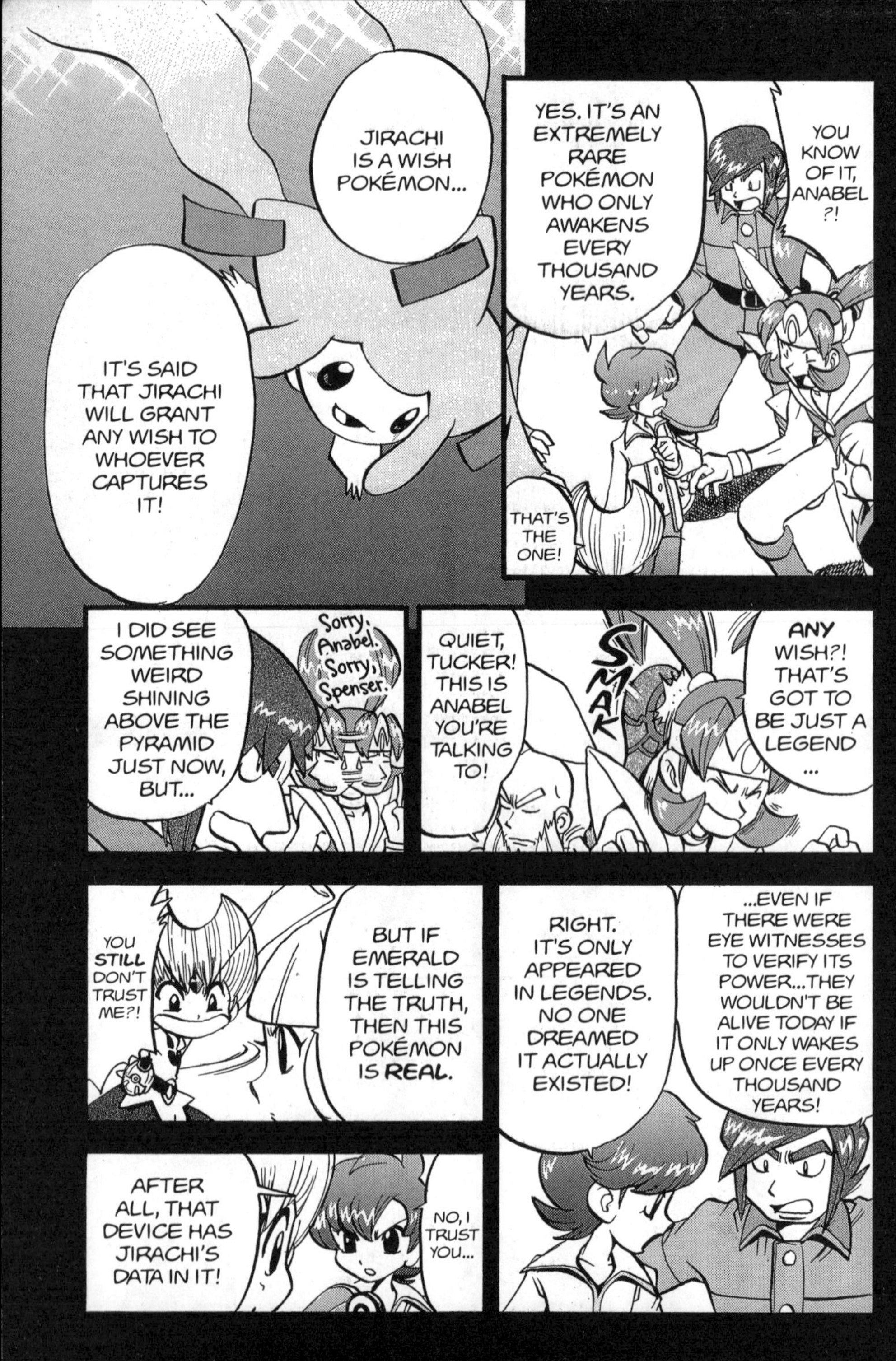

YOU KNOW OF IT, ANABEL ?!
YES. IT'S AN EXTREMELY RARE POKÉMON WHO ONLY AWAKENS EVERY THOUSAND YEARS.
THAT'S THE ONE!
JIRACHI IS A WISH POKÉMON...
IT'S SAID THAT JIRACHI WILL GRANT ANY WISH TO WHOEVER CAPTURES IT!
ANY WISH?! THAT'S GOT TO BE JUST A LEGEND ...
SMAK
QUIET, TUCKER! THIS IS ANABEL YOU'RE TALKING TO!
Sorry, Anabel. Sorry, Spenser.
I DID SEE SOMETHING WEIRD SHINING ABOVE THE PYRAMID JUST NOW, BUT...
RIGHT. IT'S ONLY APPEARED IN LEGENDS. NO ONE DREAMED IT ACTUALLY EXISTED!
...EVEN IF THERE WERE EYE WITNESSES TO VERIFY ITS POWER...THEY WOULDN'T BE ALIVE TODAY IF IT ONLY WAKES UP ONCE EVERY THOUSAND YEARS!
BUT IF EMERALD IS TELLING THE TRUTH, THEN THIS POKÉMON IS **REAL**.
YOU **STILL** DON'T TRUST ME?!
NO, I TRUST YOU...
AFTER ALL, THAT DEVICE HAS JIRACHI'S DATA IN IT!

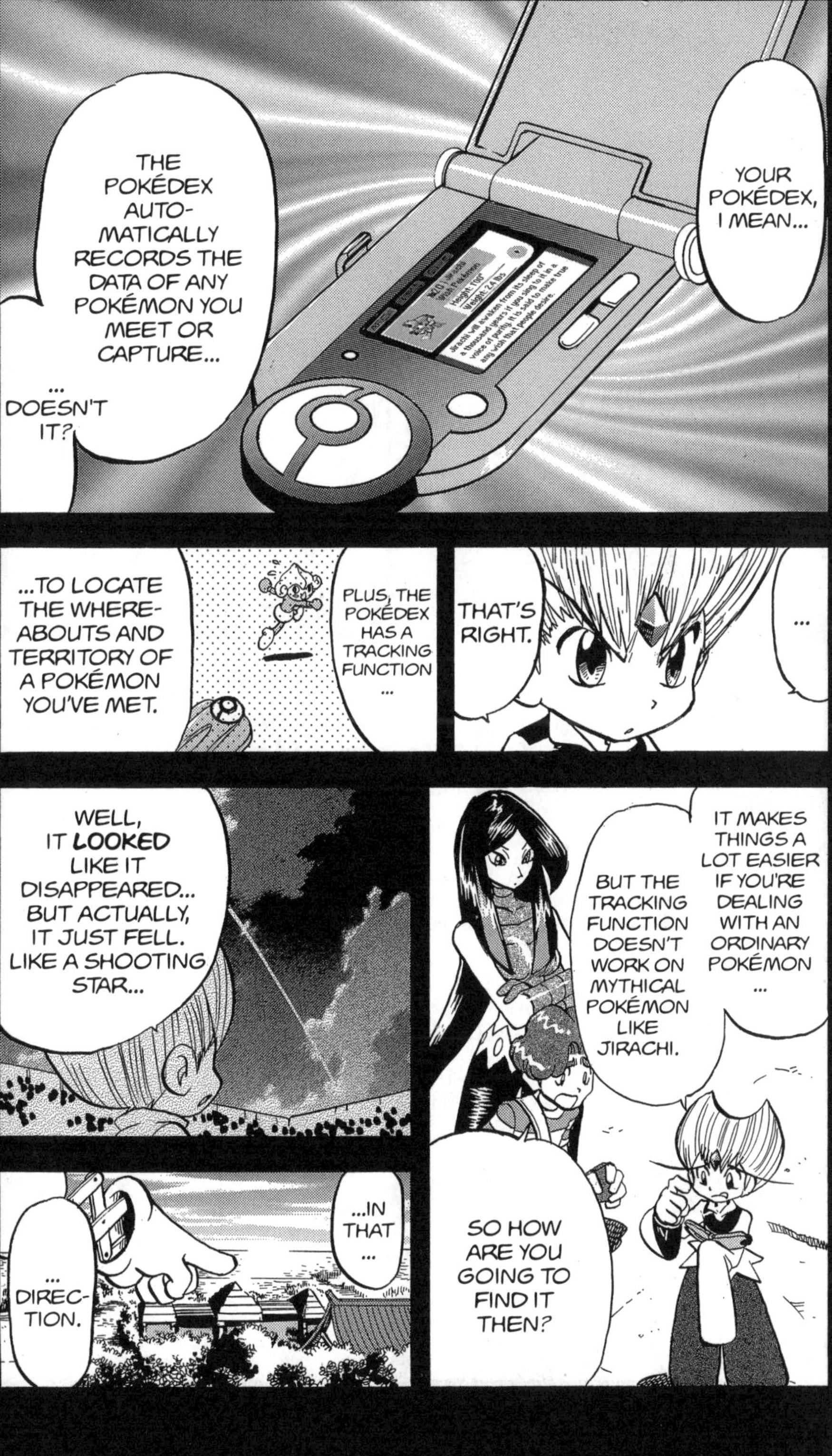
YOUR POKÉDEX, I MEAN...
THE POKÉDEX AUTO-MATICALLY RECORDS THE DATA OF ANY POKÉMON YOU MEET OR CAPTURE...
...DOESN'T IT?
...
THAT'S RIGHT.
PLUS, THE POKÉDEX HAS A TRACKING FUNCTION ...
...TO LOCATE THE WHERE-ABOUTS AND TERRITORY OF A POKÉMON YOU'VE MET.
IT MAKES THINGS A LOT EASIER IF YOU'RE DEALING WITH AN ORDINARY POKÉMON ...
BUT THE TRACKING FUNCTION DOESN'T WORK ON MYTHICAL POKÉMON LIKE JIRACHI.
SO HOW ARE YOU GOING TO FIND IT THEN?
WELL, IT **LOOKED** LIKE IT DISAPPEARED... BUT ACTUALLY, IT JUST FELL. LIKE A SHOOTING STAR...
...IN THAT ...
... DIREC-TION.

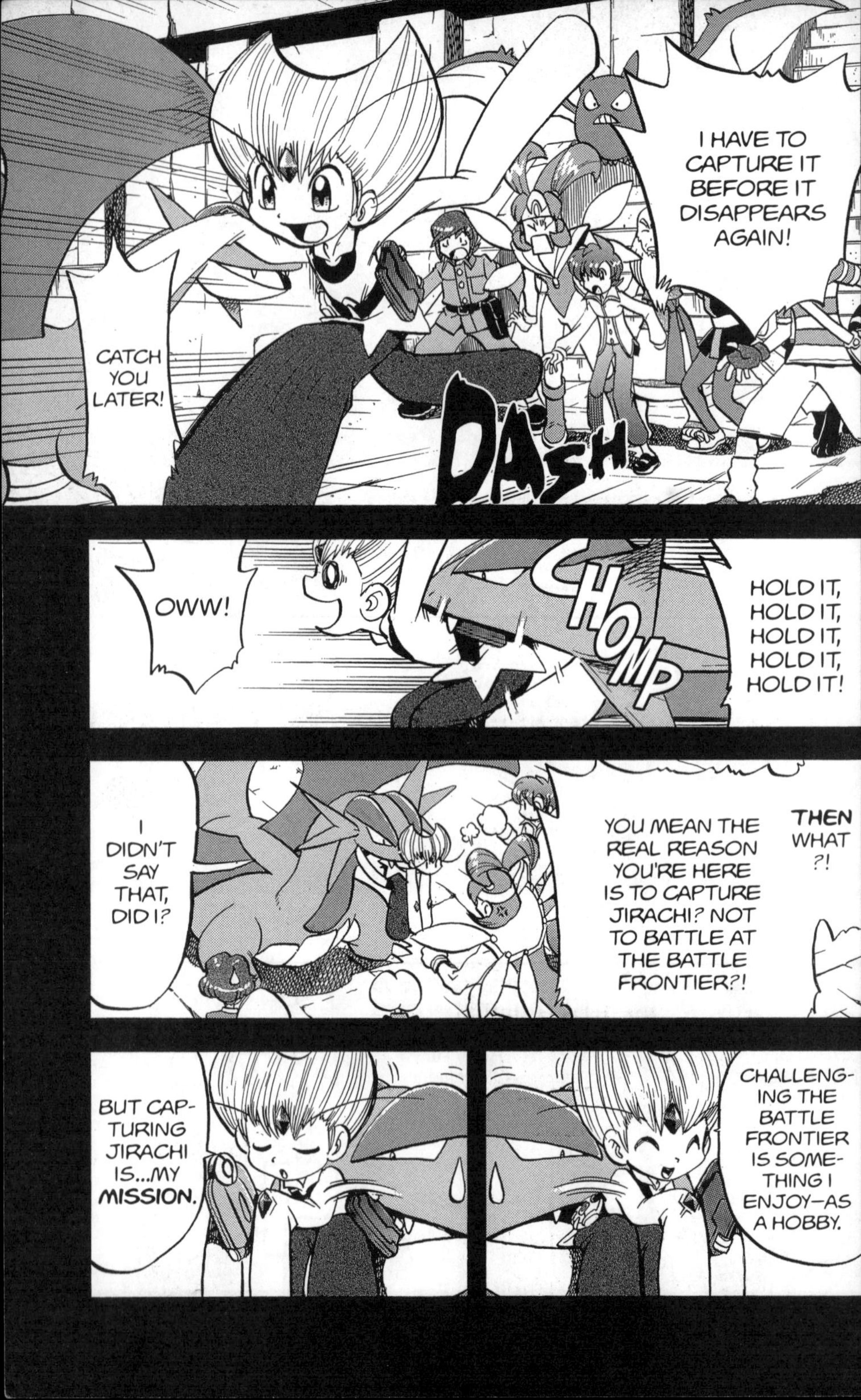
I HAVE TO CAPTURE IT BEFORE IT DISAPPEARS AGAIN!
CATCH YOU LATER!
DASH
HOLD IT, HOLD IT, HOLD IT, HOLD IT, HOLD IT!
CHOMP
OWW!
THEN WHAT?!
YOU MEAN THE REAL REASON YOU'RE HERE IS TO CAPTURE JIRACHI? NOT TO BATTLE AT THE BATTLE FRONTIER?!
I DIDN'T SAY THAT, DID I?
CHALLENGING THE BATTLE FRONTIER IS SOMETHING I ENJOY—AS A HOBBY.
BUT CAPTURING JIRACHI IS...MY MISSION.

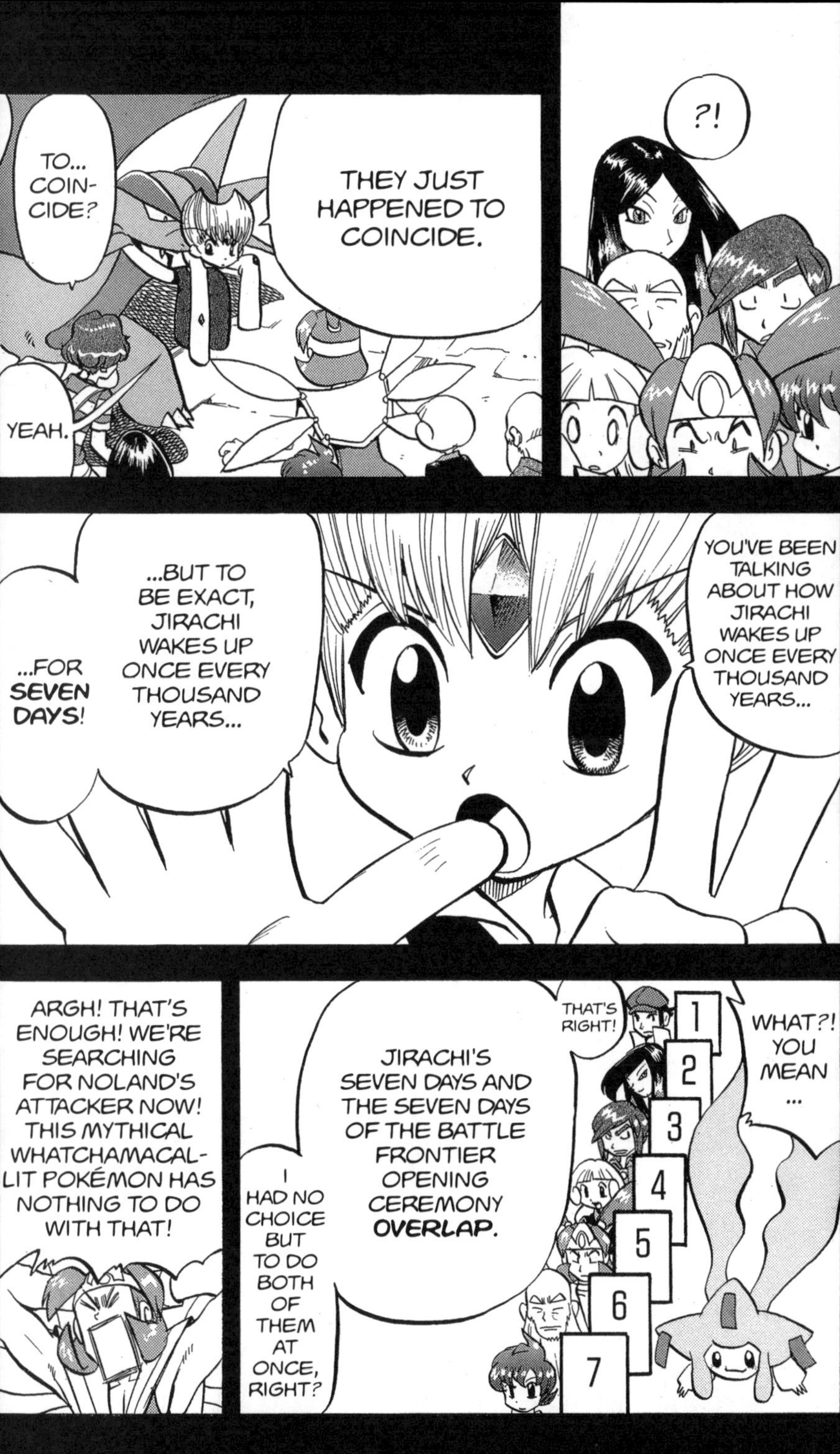
?!
THEY JUST HAPPENED TO COINCIDE.
TO... COIN-CIDE?
YEAH.
YOU'VE BEEN TALKING ABOUT HOW JIRACHI WAKES UP ONCE EVERY THOUSAND YEARS...
...BUT TO BE EXACT, JIRACHI WAKES UP ONCE EVERY THOUSAND YEARS...
...FOR **SEVEN DAYS**!
WHAT?! YOU MEAN ...
THAT'S RIGHT!
JIRACHI'S SEVEN DAYS AND THE SEVEN DAYS OF THE BATTLE FRONTIER OPENING CEREMONY **OVERLAP**.
I HAD NO CHOICE BUT TO DO BOTH OF THEM AT ONCE, RIGHT?
ARGH! THAT'S ENOUGH! WE'RE SEARCHING FOR NOLAND'S ATTACKER NOW! THIS MYTHICAL WHATCHAMACAL-LIT POKÉMON HAS NOTHING TO DO WITH THAT!

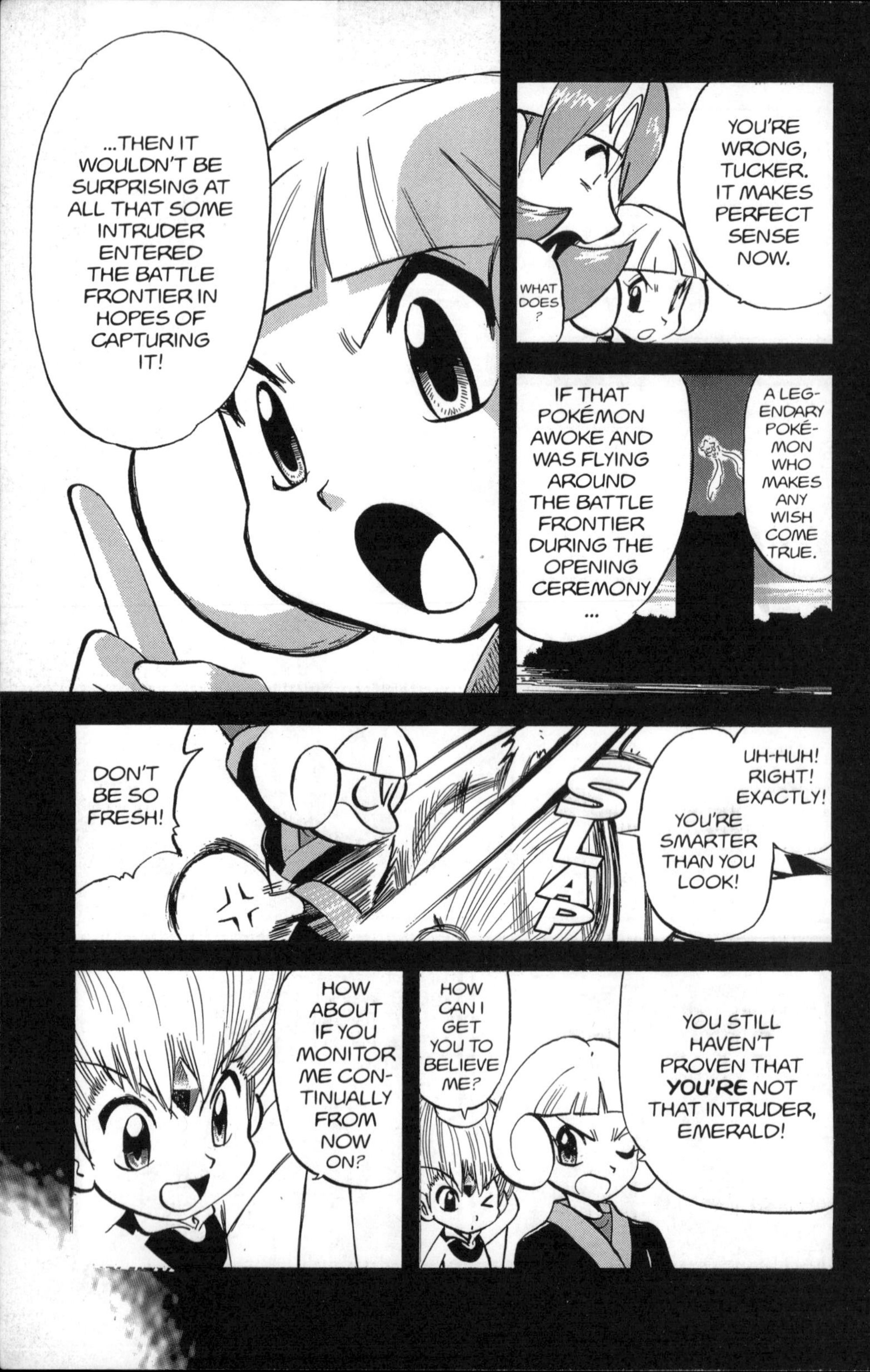
YOU'RE WRONG, TUCKER. IT MAKES PERFECT SENSE NOW.
WHAT DOES ?
A LEGENDARY POKÉMON WHO MAKES ANY WISH COME TRUE.
IF THAT POKÉMON AWOKE AND WAS FLYING AROUND THE BATTLE FRONTIER DURING THE OPENING CEREMONY...
...THEN IT WOULDN'T BE SURPRISING AT ALL THAT SOME INTRUDER ENTERED THE BATTLE FRONTIER IN HOPES OF CAPTURING IT!
UH-HUH! RIGHT! EXACTLY!
YOU'RE SMARTER THAN YOU LOOK!
SLAP
DON'T BE SO FRESH!
YOU STILL HAVEN'T PROVEN THAT **YOU'RE** NOT THAT INTRUDER, EMERALD!
HOW CAN I GET YOU TO BELIEVE ME?
HOW ABOUT IF YOU MONITOR ME CONTINUALLY FROM NOW ON?

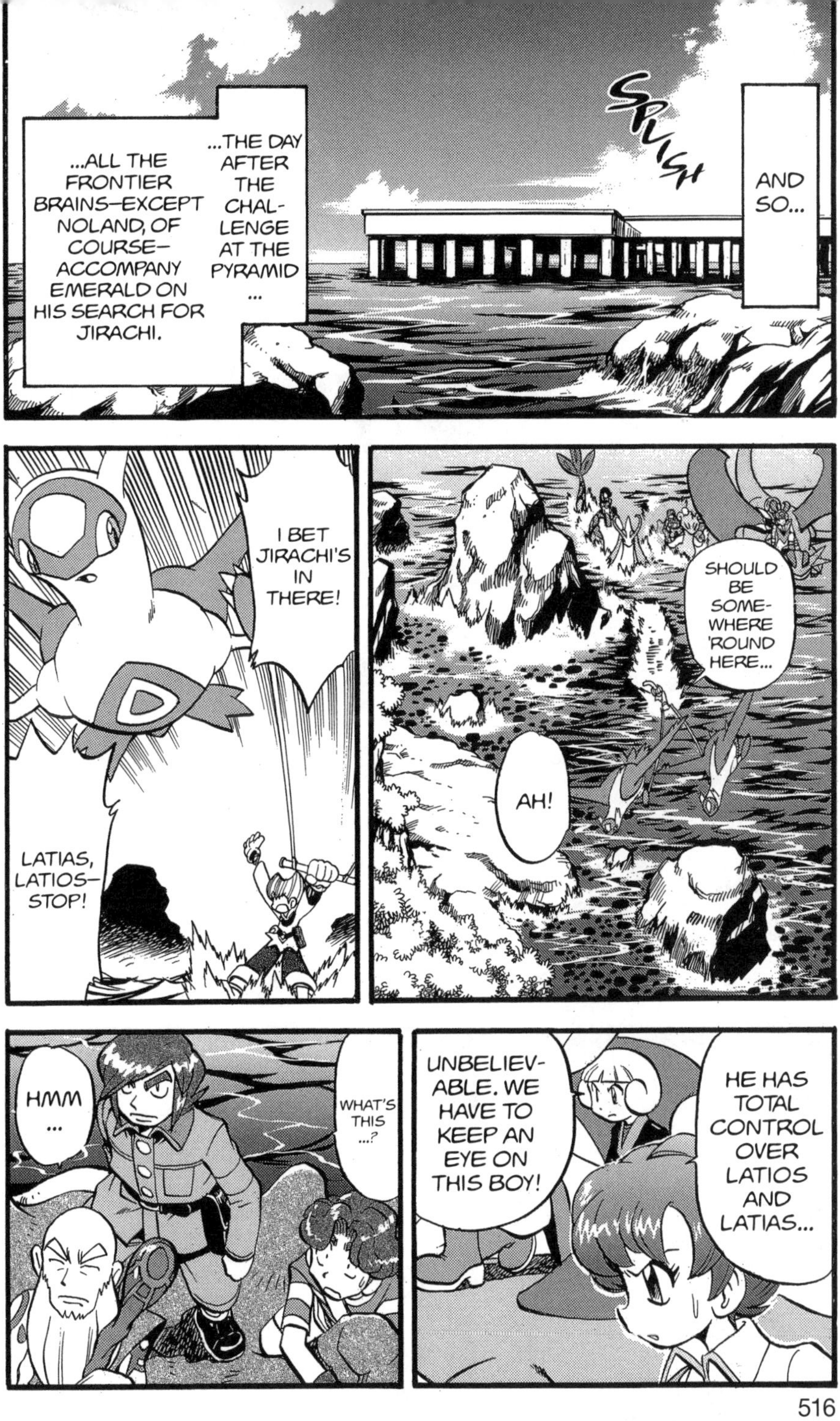
AND SO...
SPLISH
...THE DAY AFTER THE CHALLENGE AT THE PYRAMID...
...ALL THE FRONTIER BRAINS—EXCEPT NOLAND, OF COURSE—ACCOMPANY EMERALD ON HIS SEARCH FOR JIRACHI.
SHOULD BE SOMEWHERE 'ROUND HERE...
AH!
I BET JIRACHI'S IN THERE!
LATIAS, LATIOS—STOP!
HE HAS TOTAL CONTROL OVER LATIOS AND LATIAS...
UNBELIEVABLE. WE HAVE TO KEEP AN EYE ON THIS BOY!
WHAT'S THIS ...?
HMM ...

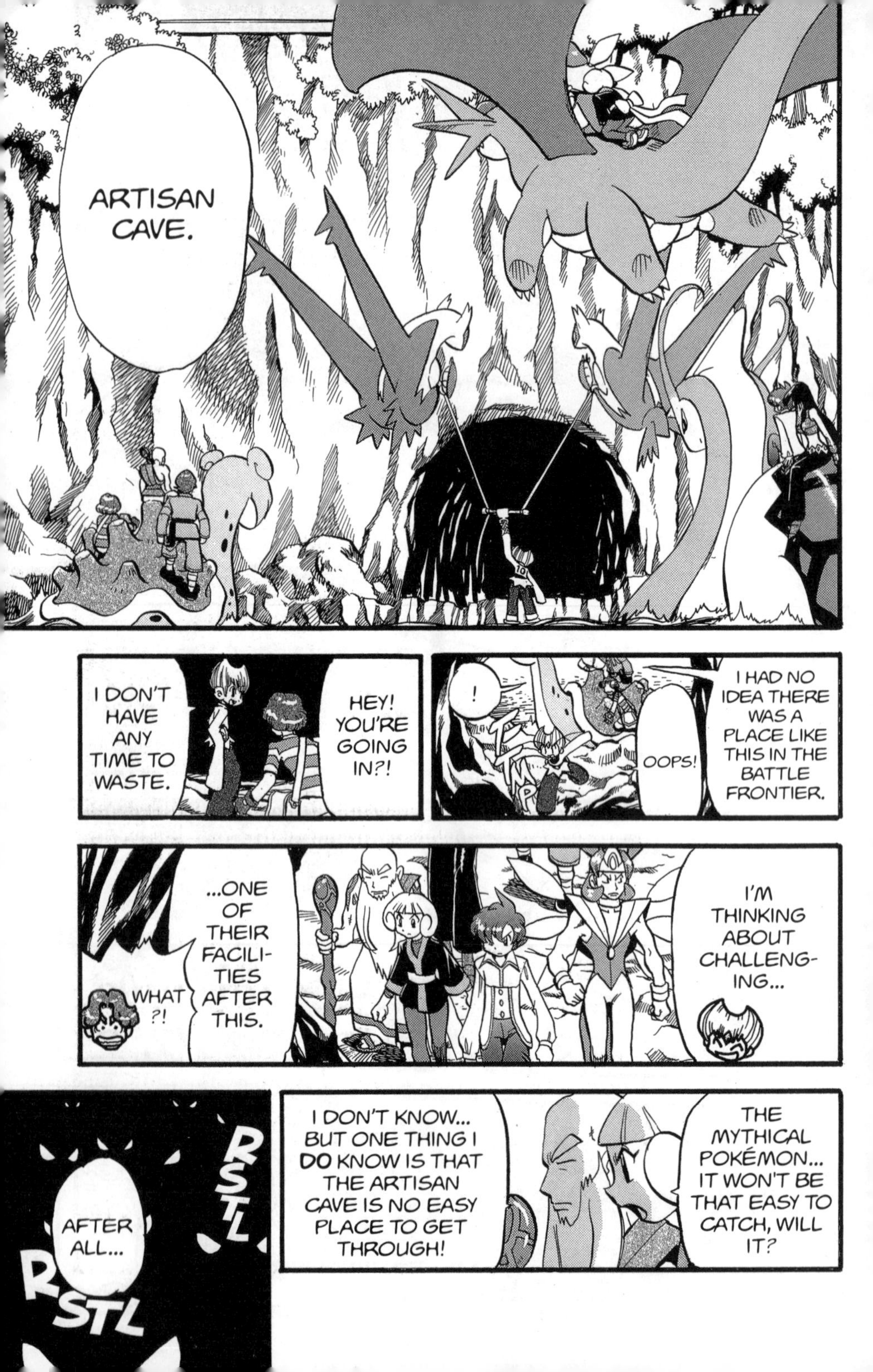

ARTISAN CAVE.
I HAD NO IDEA THERE WAS A PLACE LIKE THIS IN THE BATTLE FRONTIER.
OOPS!
!
TMP
HEY! YOU'RE GOING IN?!
I DON'T HAVE ANY TIME TO WASTE.
I'M THINKING ABOUT CHALLENG-ING...
...ONE OF THEIR FACILI-TIES AFTER THIS.
WHAT?!
THE MYTHICAL POKÉMON... IT WON'T BE THAT EASY TO CATCH, WILL IT?
I DON'T KNOW... BUT ONE THING I **DO** KNOW IS THAT THE ARTISAN CAVE IS NO EASY PLACE TO GET THROUGH!
RSTL
AFTER ALL...
RSTL

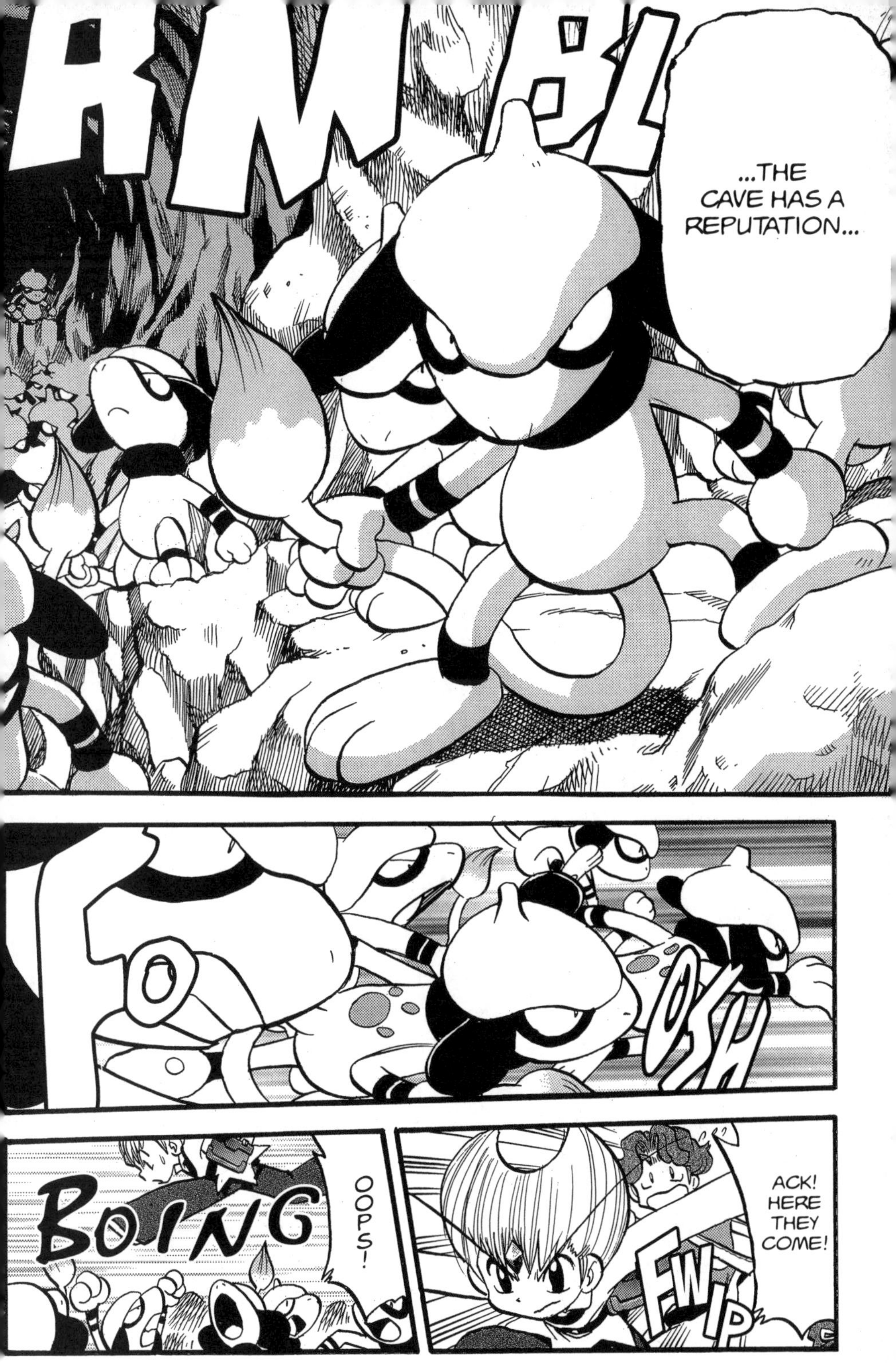
RMBL
...THE CAVE HAS A REPUTATION...
OSH
ACK! HERE THEY COME!
FWIP
OOPS!
BOING

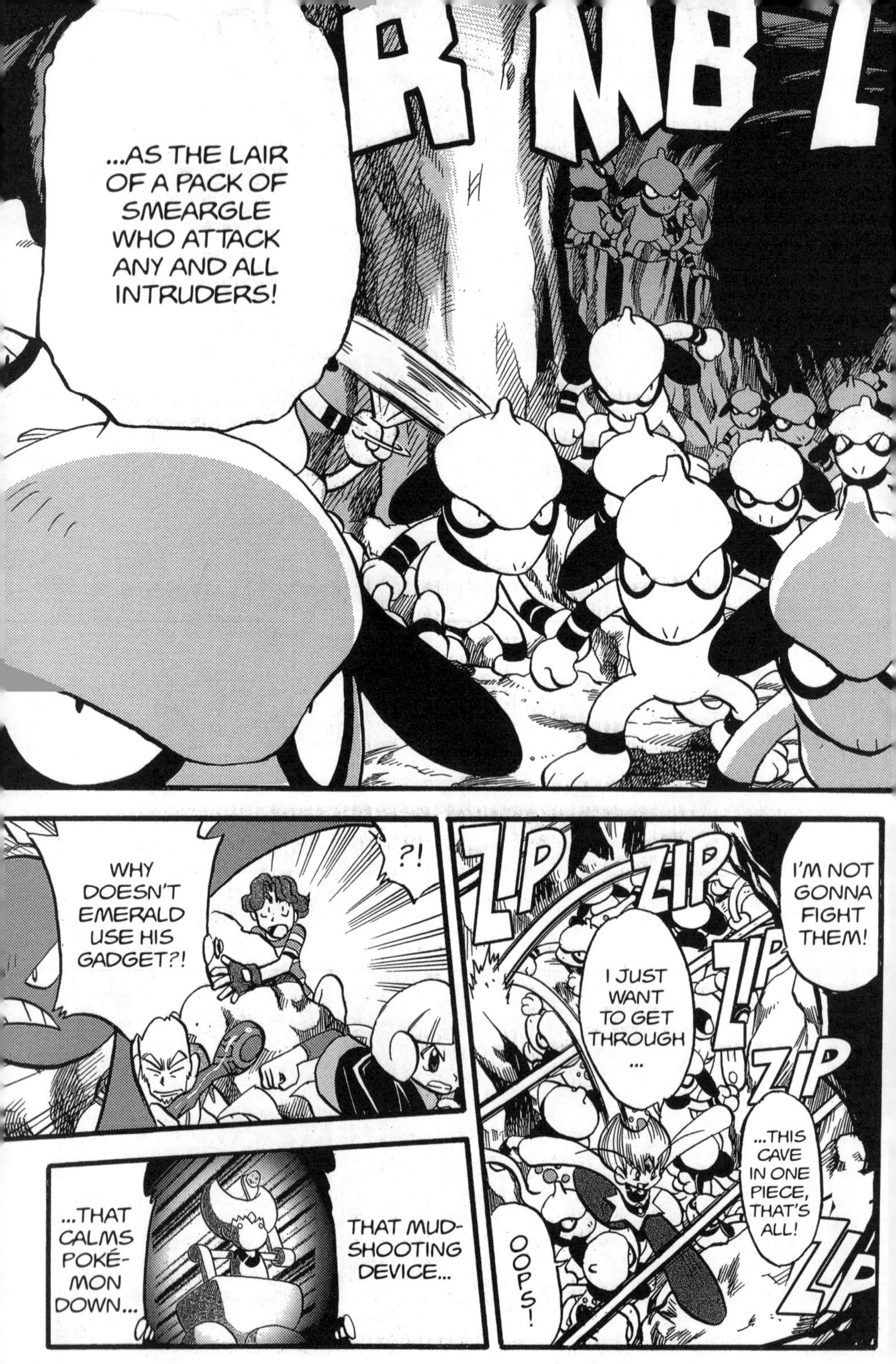
RMBL
...AS THE LAIR OF A PACK OF SMEARGLE WHO ATTACK ANY AND ALL INTRUDERS!
ZIP ZIP ZIP ZIP ZIP
I'M NOT GONNA FIGHT THEM!
I JUST WANT TO GET THROUGH ...
...THIS CAVE IN ONE PIECE, THAT'S ALL!
OOPS!
?!
WHY DOESN'T EMERALD USE HIS GADGET?!
THAT MUD-SHOOTING DEVICE...
...THAT CALMS POKÉMON DOWN...

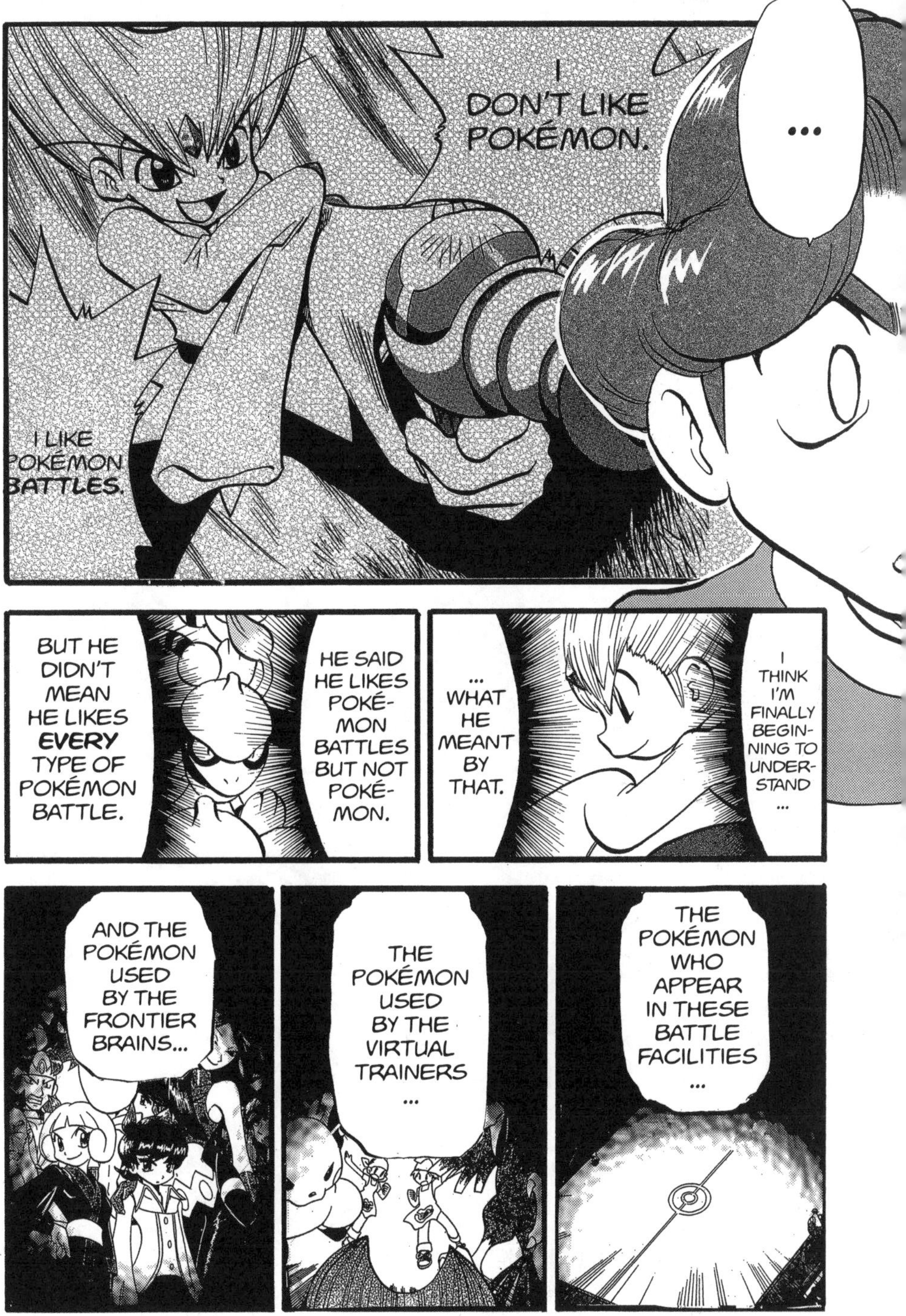
...
I DON'T LIKE POKÉMON.
I LIKE POKÉMON BATTLES.
I THINK I'M FINALLY BEGINNING TO UNDERSTAND ...
... WHAT HE MEANT BY THAT.
HE SAID HE LIKES POKÉMON BATTLES BUT NOT POKÉMON.
BUT HE DIDN'T MEAN HE LIKES EVERY TYPE OF POKÉMON BATTLE.
THE POKÉMON WHO APPEAR IN THESE BATTLE FACILITIES ...
THE POKÉMON USED BY THE VIRTUAL TRAINERS ...
AND THE POKÉMON USED BY THE FRONTIER BRAINS...

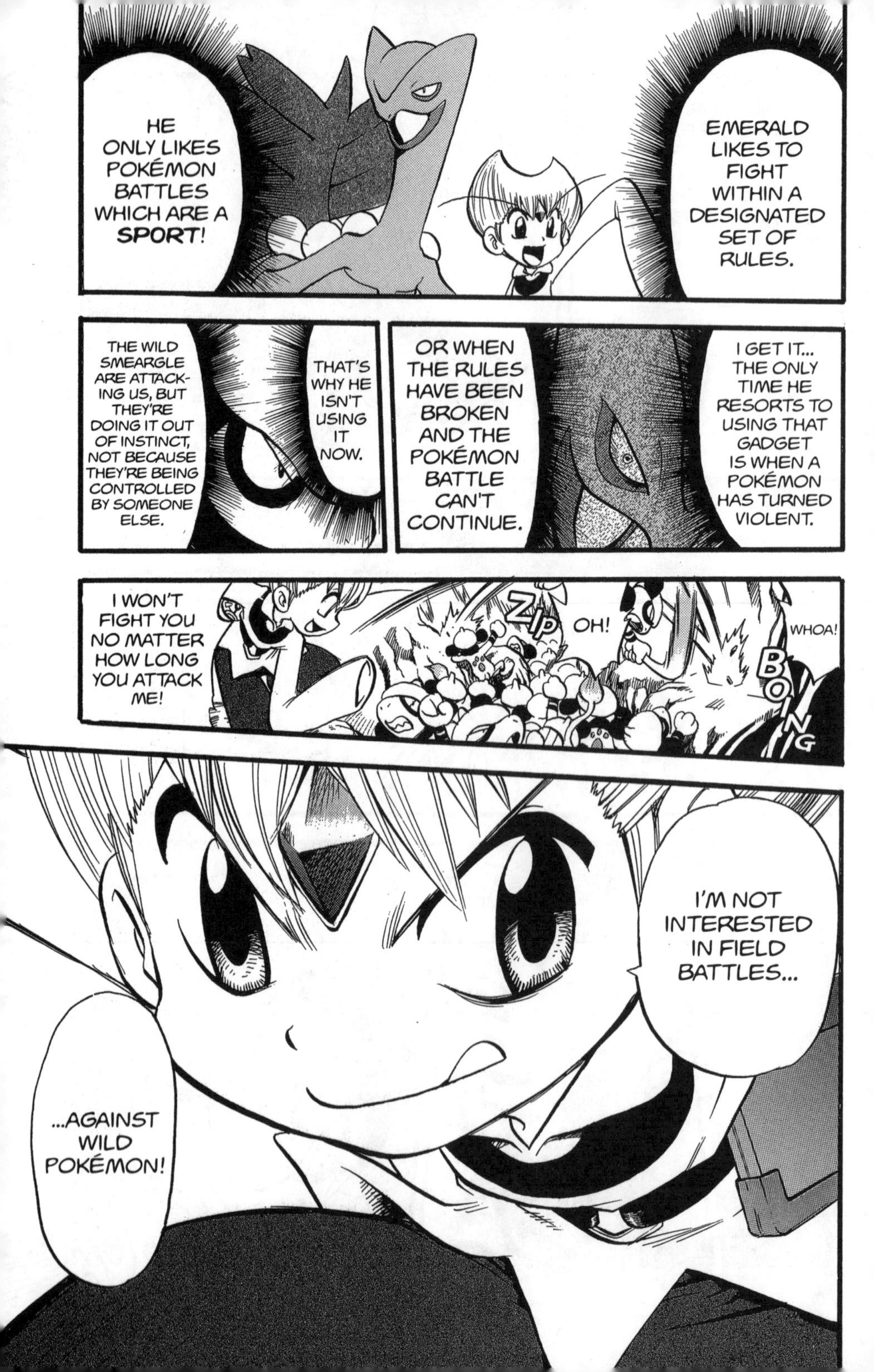
EMERALD LIKES TO FIGHT WITHIN A DESIGNATED SET OF RULES.
HE ONLY LIKES POKÉMON BATTLES WHICH ARE A SPORT!
I GET IT... THE ONLY TIME HE RESORTS TO USING THAT GADGET IS WHEN A POKÉMON HAS TURNED VIOLENT.
OR WHEN THE RULES HAVE BEEN BROKEN AND THE POKÉMON BATTLE CAN'T CONTINUE.
THE WILD SMEARGLE ARE ATTACKING US, BUT THEY'RE DOING IT OUT OF INSTINCT, NOT BECAUSE THEY'RE BEING CONTROLLED BY SOMEONE ELSE.
THAT'S WHY HE ISN'T USING IT NOW.
WHOA!
BOING
OH!
ZIP
I WON'T FIGHT YOU NO MATTER HOW LONG YOU ATTACK ME!
I'M NOT INTERESTED IN FIELD BATTLES...
...AGAINST WILD POKÉMON!

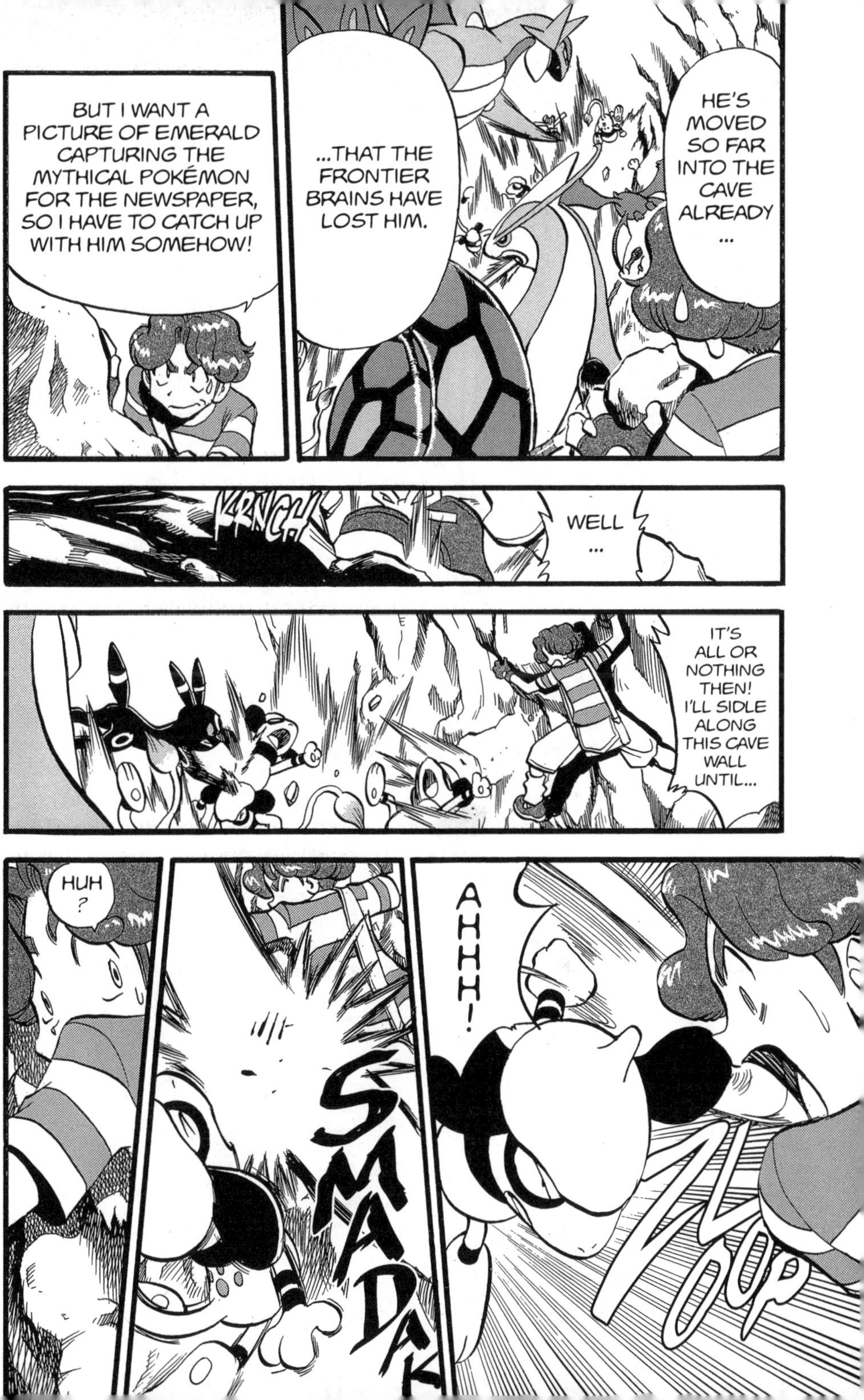
HE'S MOVED SO FAR INTO THE CAVE ALREADY...
...THAT THE FRONTIER BRAINS HAVE LOST HIM.
BUT I WANT A PICTURE OF EMERALD CAPTURING THE MYTHICAL POKÉMON FOR THE NEWSPAPER, SO I HAVE TO CATCH UP WITH HIM SOMEHOW!
WELL...
KRNCH
IT'S ALL OR NOTHING THEN! I'LL SIDLE ALONG THIS CAVE WALL UNTIL...
AHHH!
ZWOOP
SMADAK
HUH?

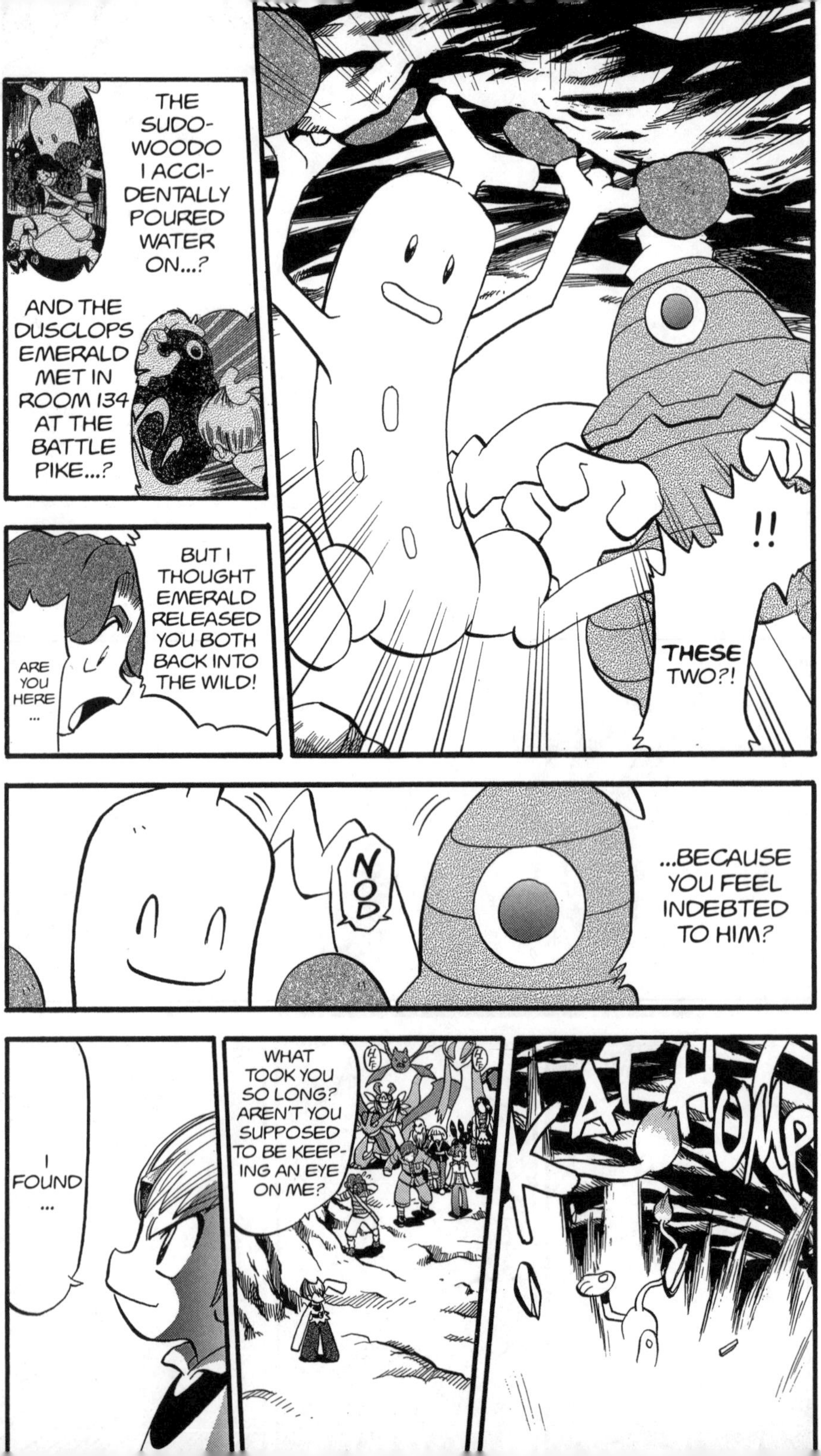
!!
THESE TWO?!
THE SUDO-WOODO I ACCI-DENTALLY POURED WATER ON...?
AND THE DUSCLOPS EMERALD MET IN ROOM 134 AT THE BATTLE PIKE...?
BUT I THOUGHT EMERALD RELEASED YOU BOTH BACK INTO THE WILD!
ARE YOU HERE...
...BECAUSE YOU FEEL INDEBTED TO HIM?
NOD
KATHOMP
WHAT TOOK YOU SO LONG? AREN'T YOU SUPPOSED TO BE KEEP-ING AN EYE ON ME?
I FOUND...

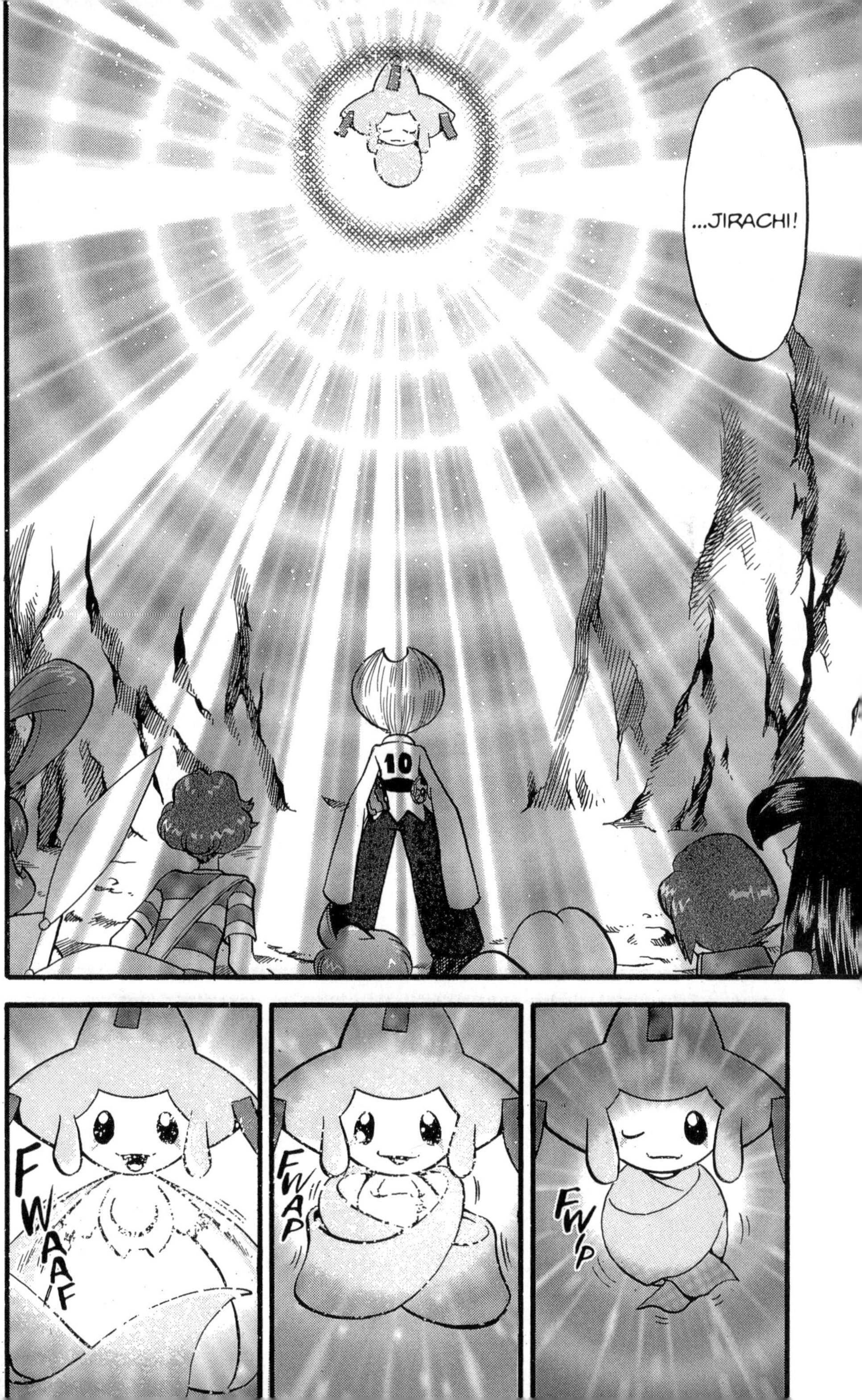
...JIRACHI!
FWIP
FWAP
FWAAF

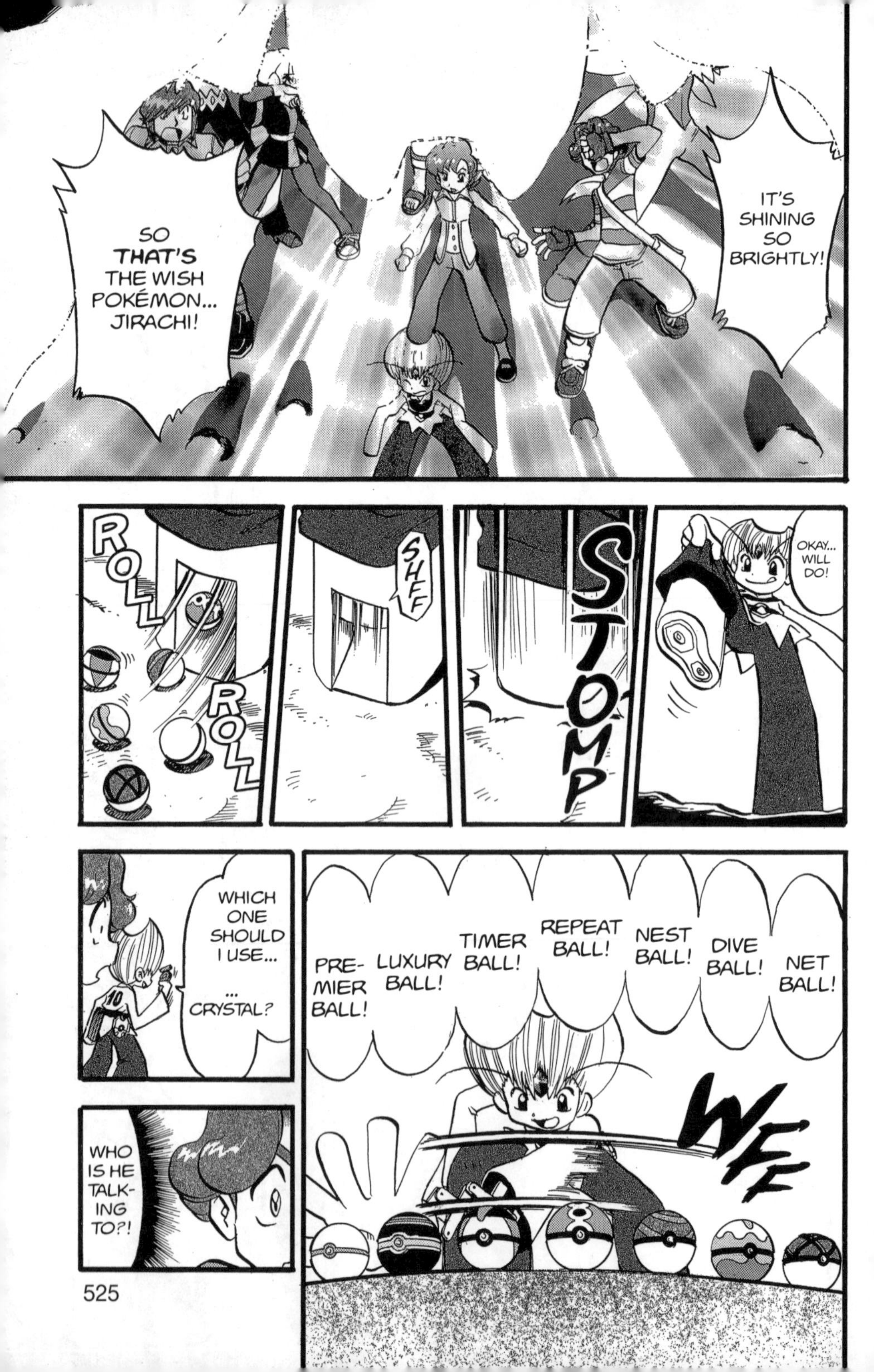
IT'S SHINING SO BRIGHTLY!
SO THAT'S THE WISH POKÉMON... JIRACHI!
OKAY... WILL DO!
STOMP
SHFF
ROLL
ROLL
NET BALL!
DIVE BALL!
NEST BALL!
REPEAT BALL!
TIMER BALL!
LUXURY BALL!
PRE-MIER BALL!
WFF
WHICH ONE SHOULD I USE...
... CRYSTAL?
WHO IS HE TALK-ING TO?!

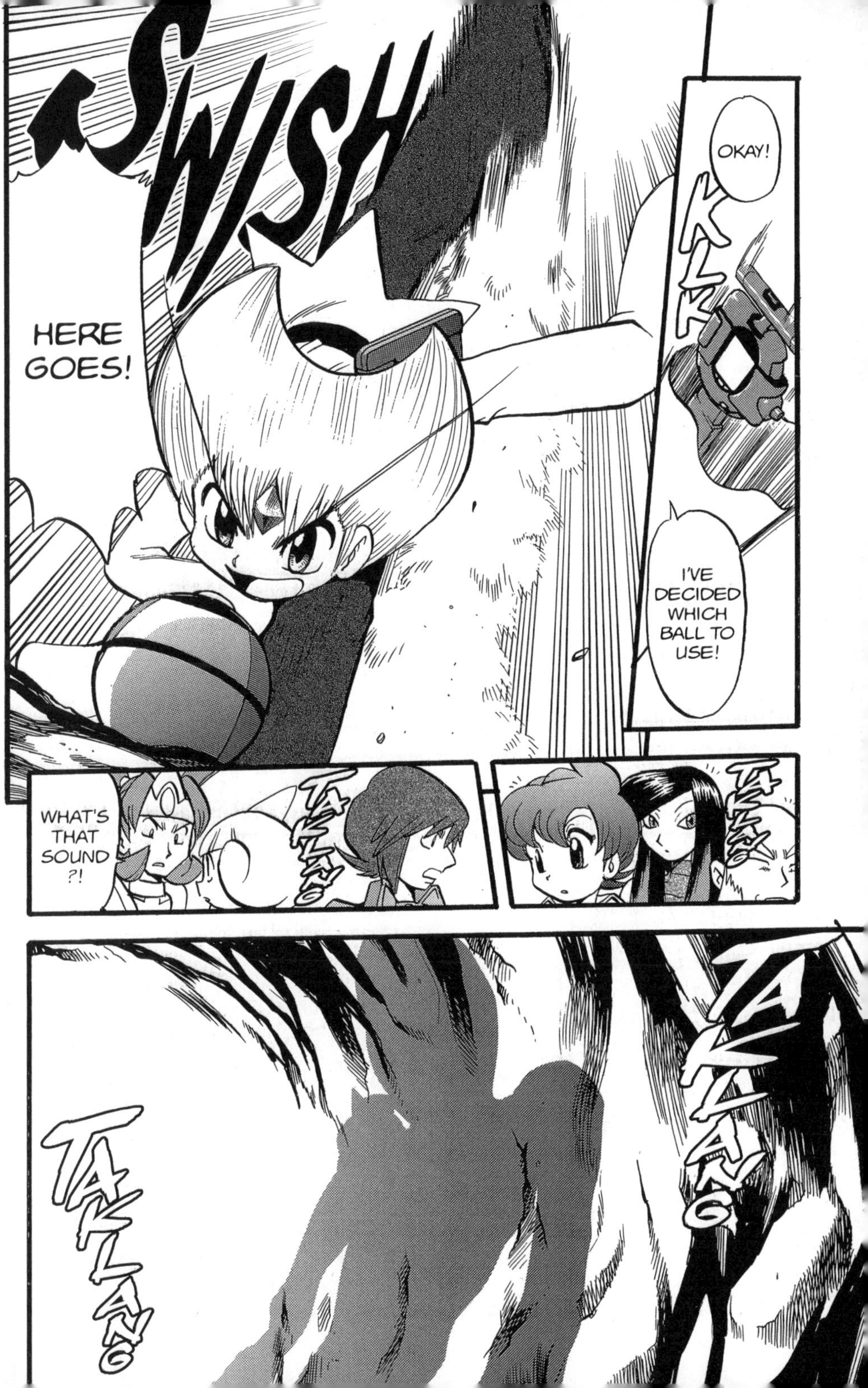
OKAY!
KLIK
I'VE DECIDED WHICH BALL TO USE!
SWISH
HERE GOES!
WHAT'S THAT SOUND ?!
TAKLANG
TAKLANG
TAKLANG

◆315◆

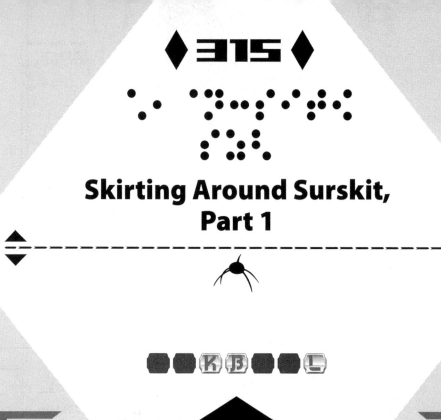

Skirting Around Surskit, Part 1

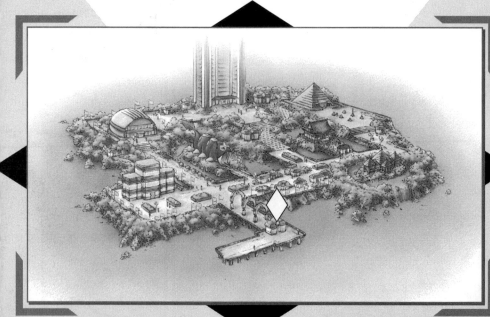

POKÉMON ADVENTURES•THE SIXTH CHAPTER•EMERALD

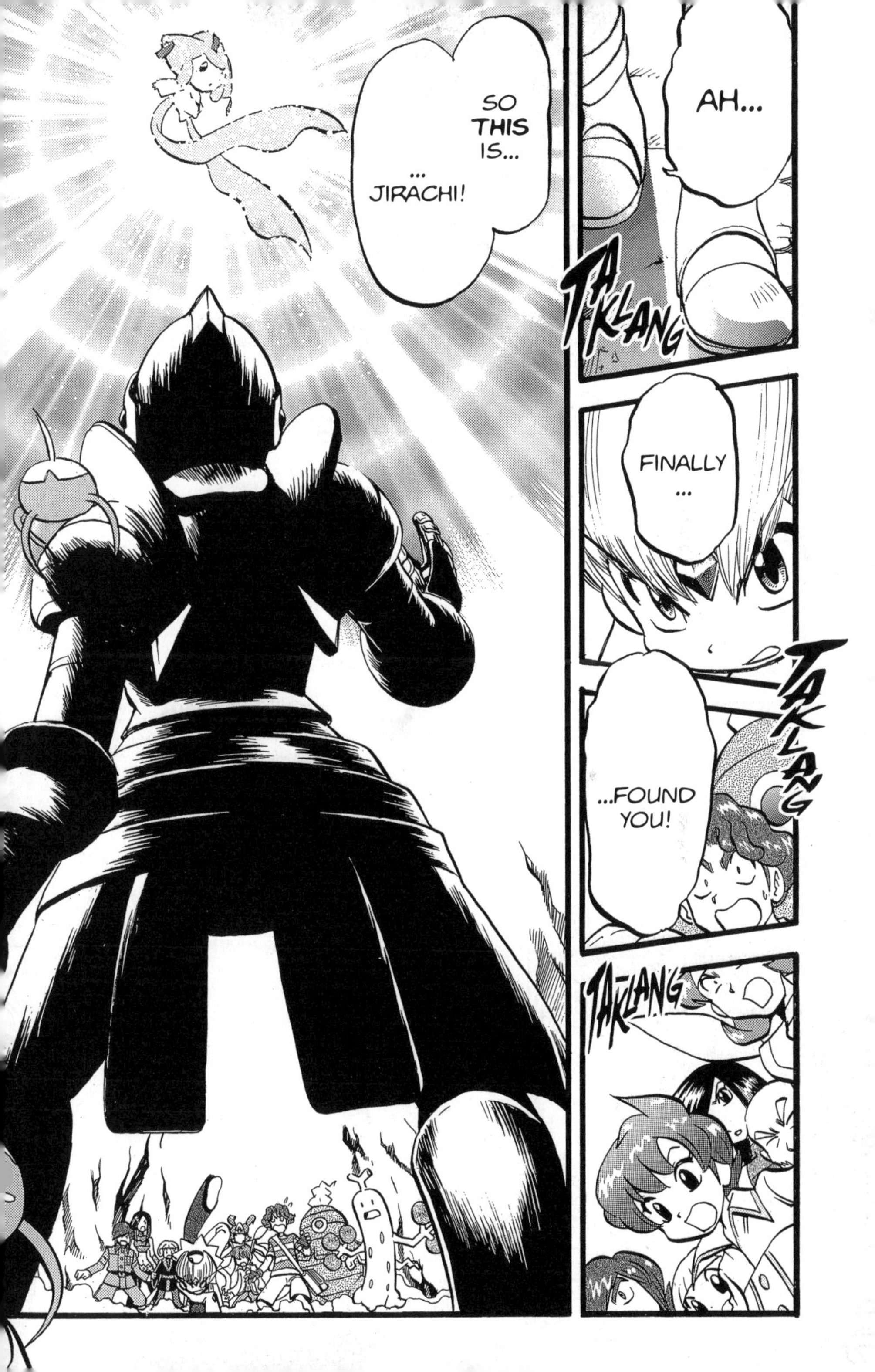
AH...
TAKLANG
FINALLY ...
TAKLANG
...FOUND YOU!
TAKLANG
SO THIS IS...
... JIRACHI!

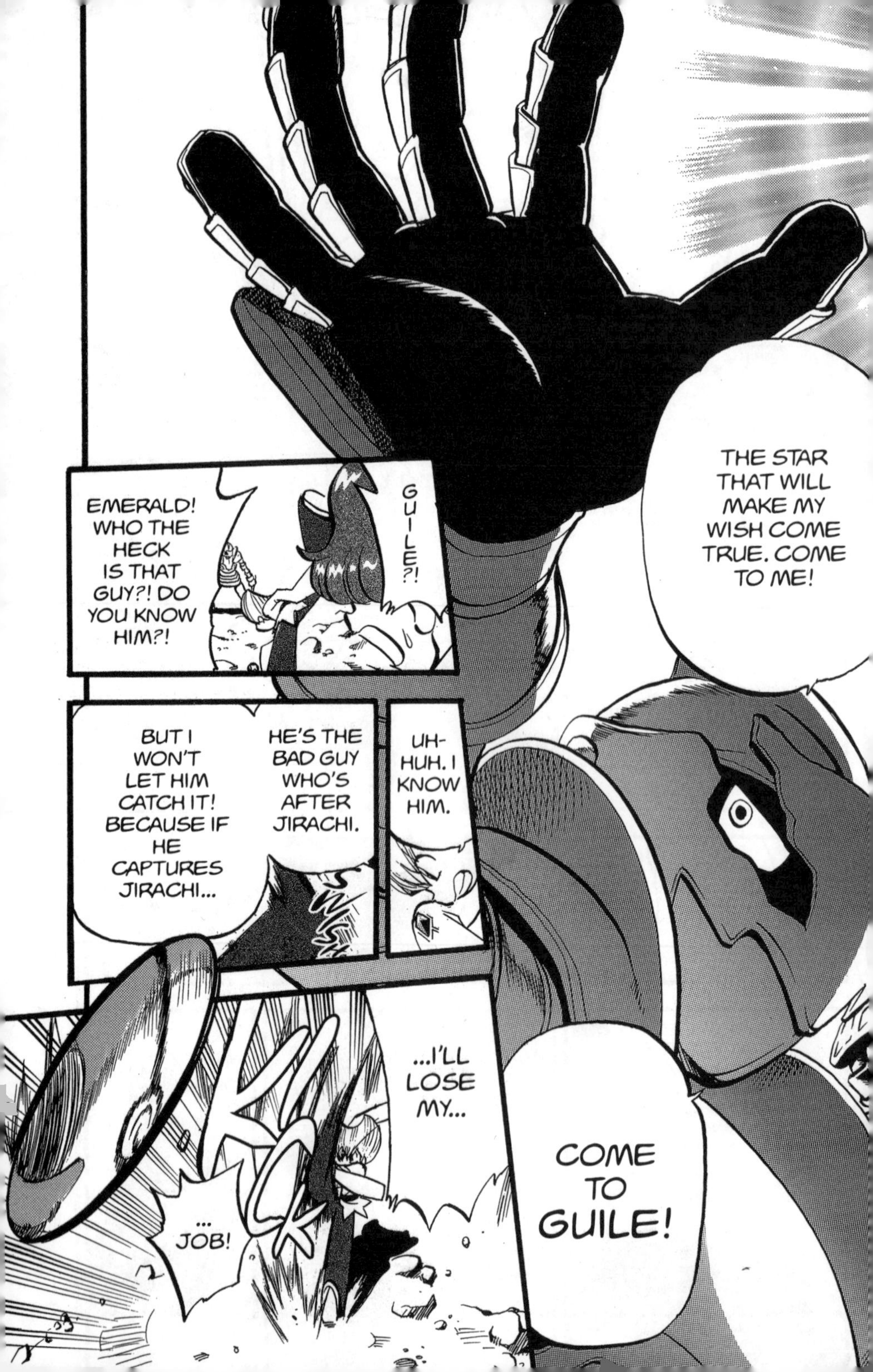
THE STAR THAT WILL MAKE MY WISH COME TRUE. COME TO ME!
GUILE?!
EMERALD! WHO THE HECK IS THAT GUY?! DO YOU KNOW HIM?!
UH-HUH. I KNOW HIM.
HE'S THE BAD GUY WHO'S AFTER JIRACHI.
BUT I WON'T LET HIM CATCH IT! BECAUSE IF HE CAPTURES JIRACHI...
COME TO GUILE!
...I'LL LOSE MY...
...JOB!

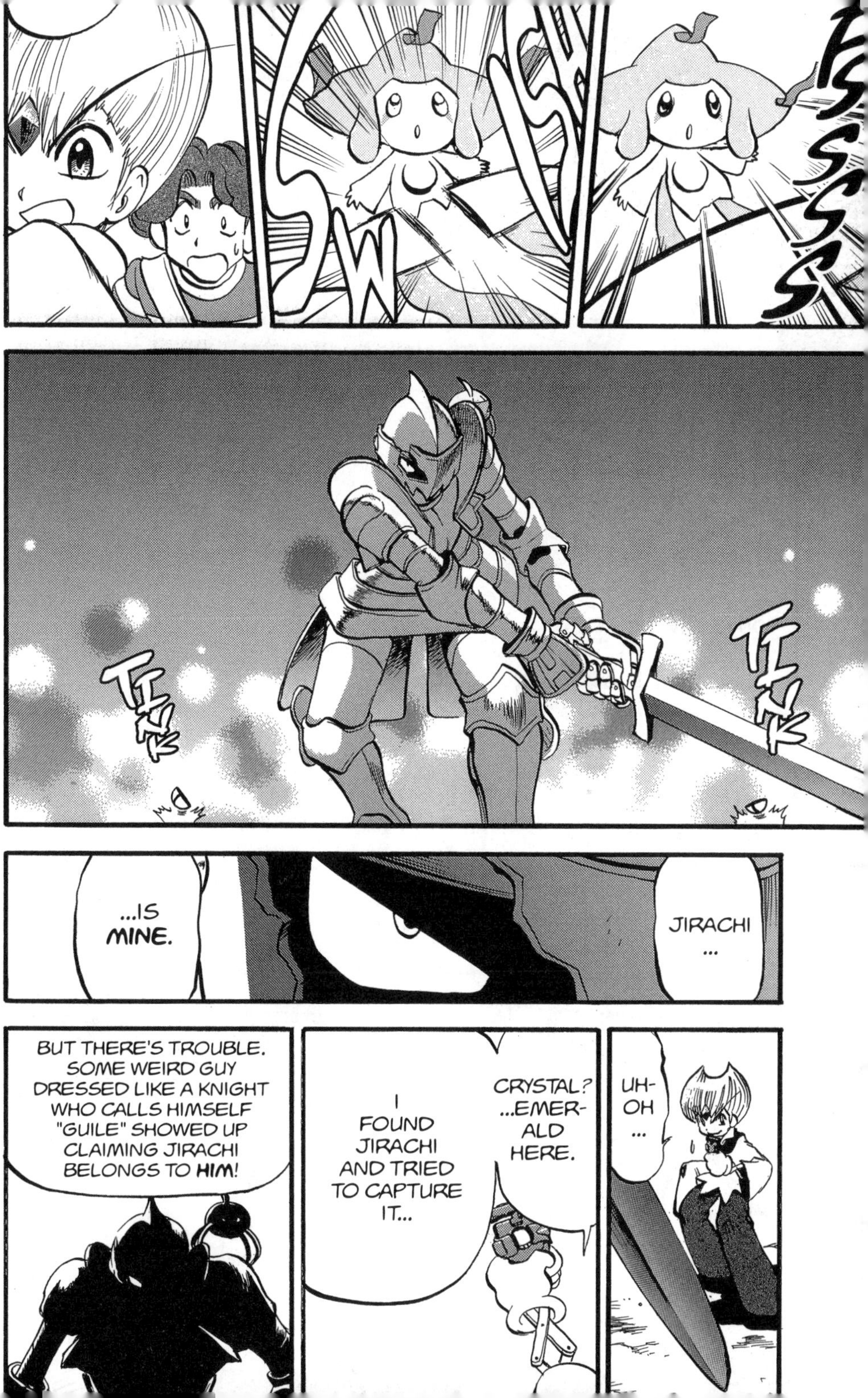
SWISH
TINK
TINK
JIRACHI ...
...IS **MINE.**
UH-OH ...
CRYSTAL? ...EMERALD HERE.
I FOUND JIRACHI AND TRIED TO CAPTURE IT...
BUT THERE'S TROUBLE. SOME WEIRD GUY DRESSED LIKE A KNIGHT WHO CALLS HIMSELF "GUILE" SHOWED UP CLAIMING JIRACHI BELONGS TO **HIM**!

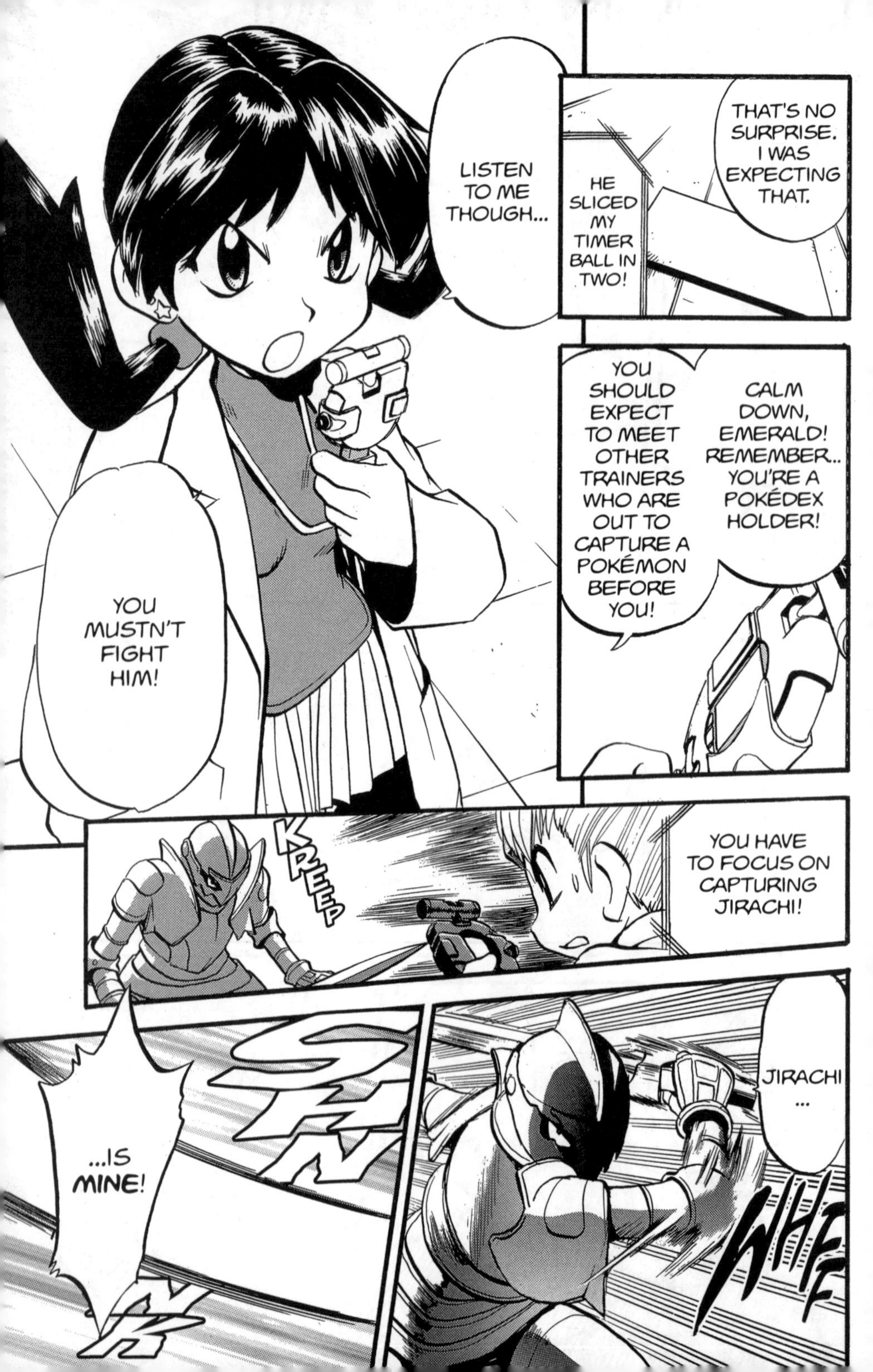
THAT'S NO SURPRISE. I WAS EXPECTING THAT.
HE SLICED MY TIMER BALL IN TWO!
CALM DOWN, EMERALD! REMEMBER... YOU'RE A POKÉDEX HOLDER!
YOU SHOULD EXPECT TO MEET OTHER TRAINERS WHO ARE OUT TO CAPTURE A POKÉMON BEFORE YOU!
LISTEN TO ME THOUGH...
YOU MUSTN'T FIGHT HIM!
YOU HAVE TO FOCUS ON CAPTURING JIRACHI!
KREEP
JIRACHI ...
...IS MINE!

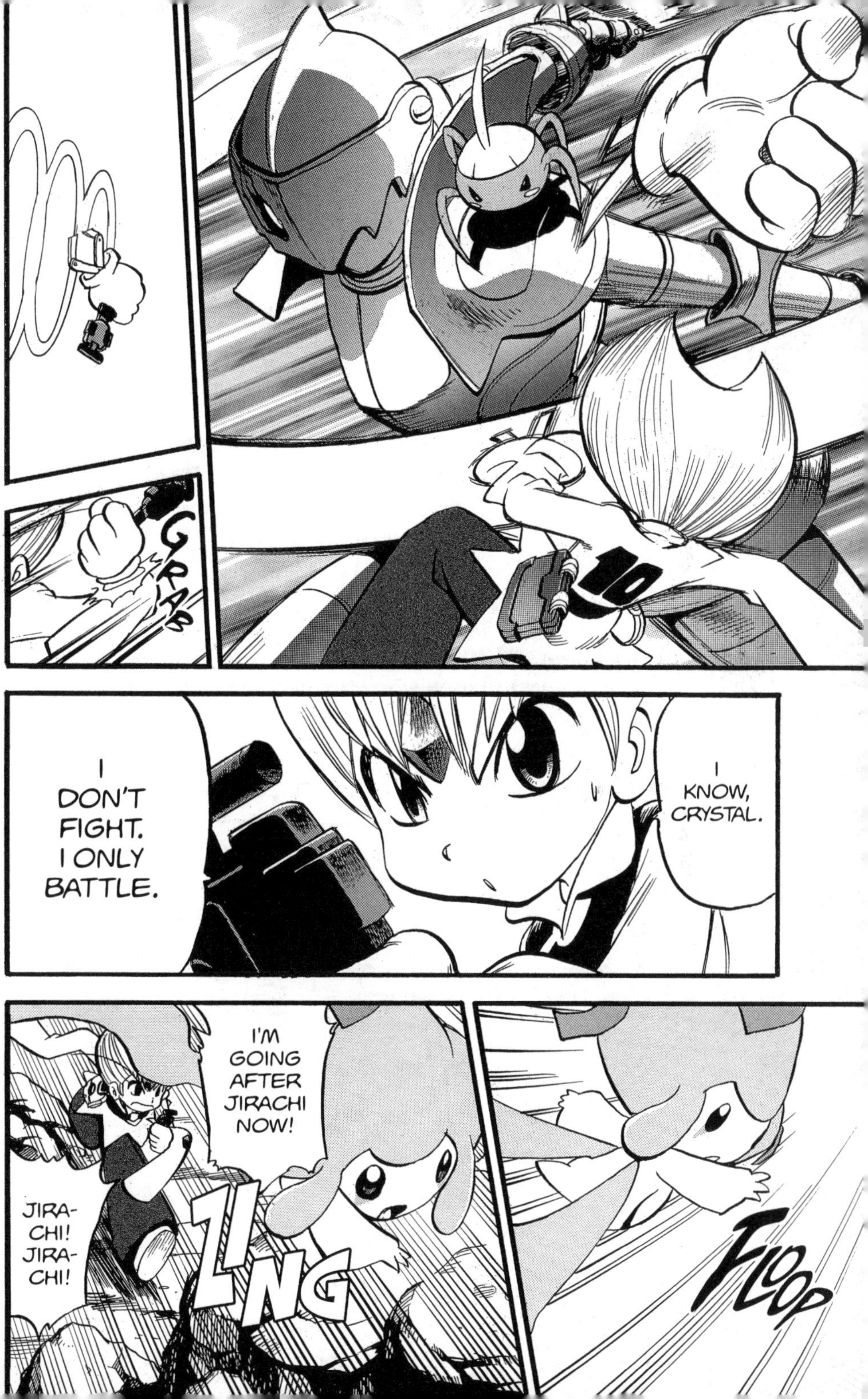
GRAB
I KNOW, CRYSTAL.
I DON'T FIGHT. I ONLY BATTLE.
FLOOP
I'M GOING AFTER JIRACHI NOW!
ZING
JIRA-CHI! JIRA-CHI!

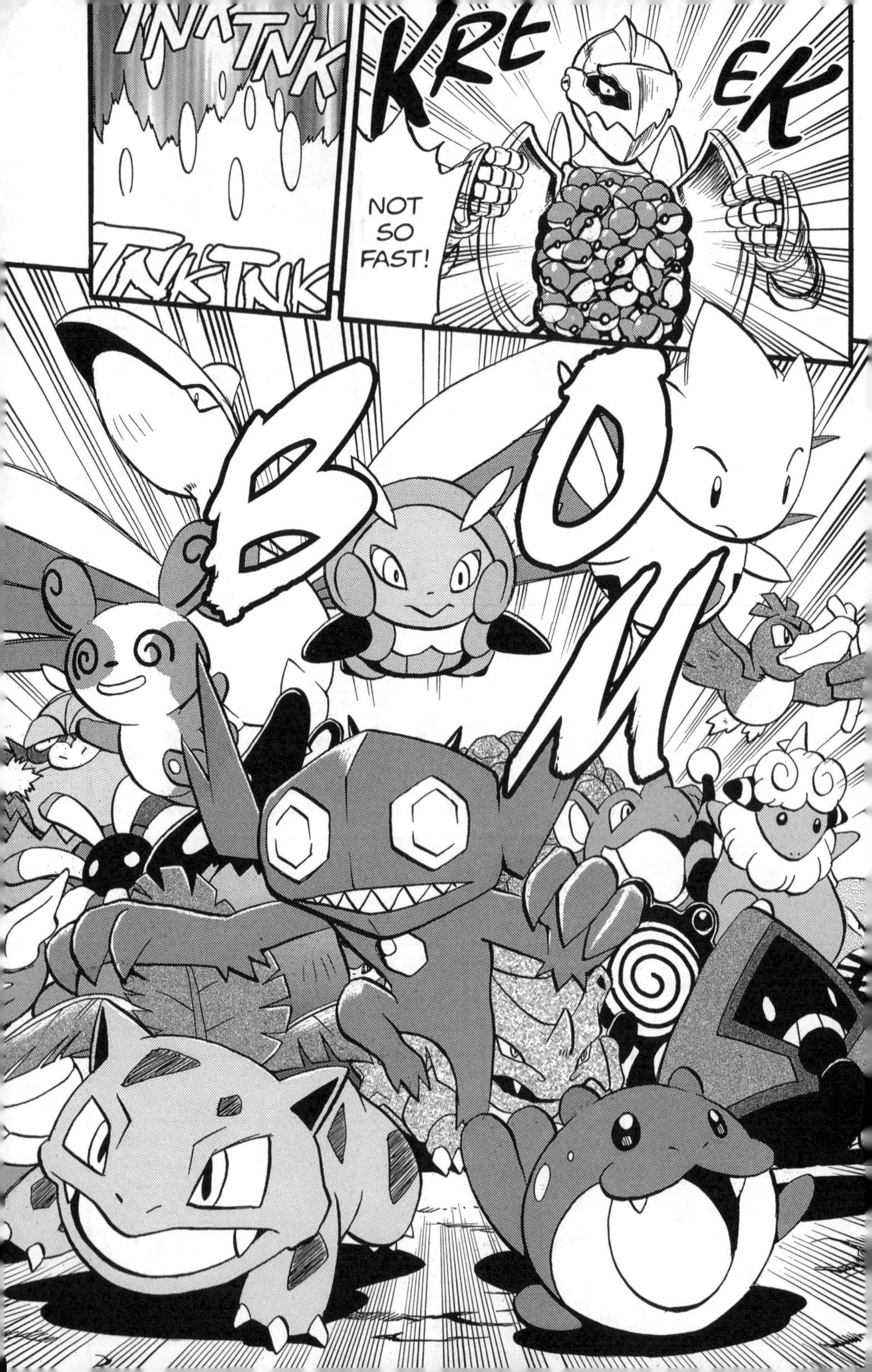
KRTEK
NOT SO FAST!
TNKTNK
TNKTNK
BOOM

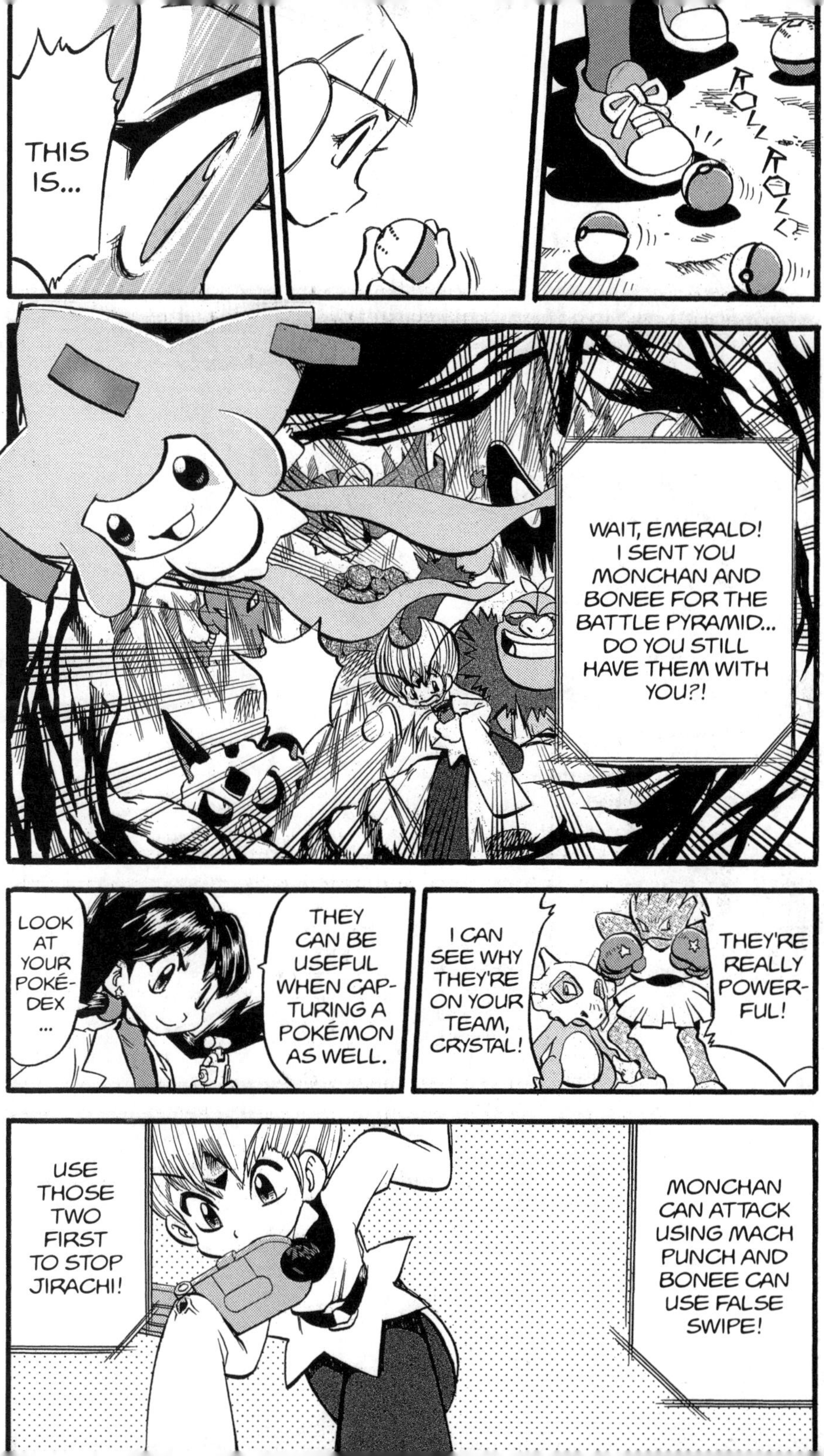
ROLL ROLL
THIS IS...
WAIT, EMERALD! I SENT YOU MONCHAN AND BONEE FOR THE BATTLE PYRAMID... DO YOU STILL HAVE THEM WITH YOU?!
THEY'RE REALLY POWERFUL!
I CAN SEE WHY THEY'RE ON YOUR TEAM, CRYSTAL!
THEY CAN BE USEFUL WHEN CAPTURING A POKÉMON AS WELL.
LOOK AT YOUR POKÉDEX...
MONCHAN CAN ATTACK USING MACH PUNCH AND BONEE CAN USE FALSE SWIPE!
USE THOSE TWO FIRST TO STOP JIRACHI!

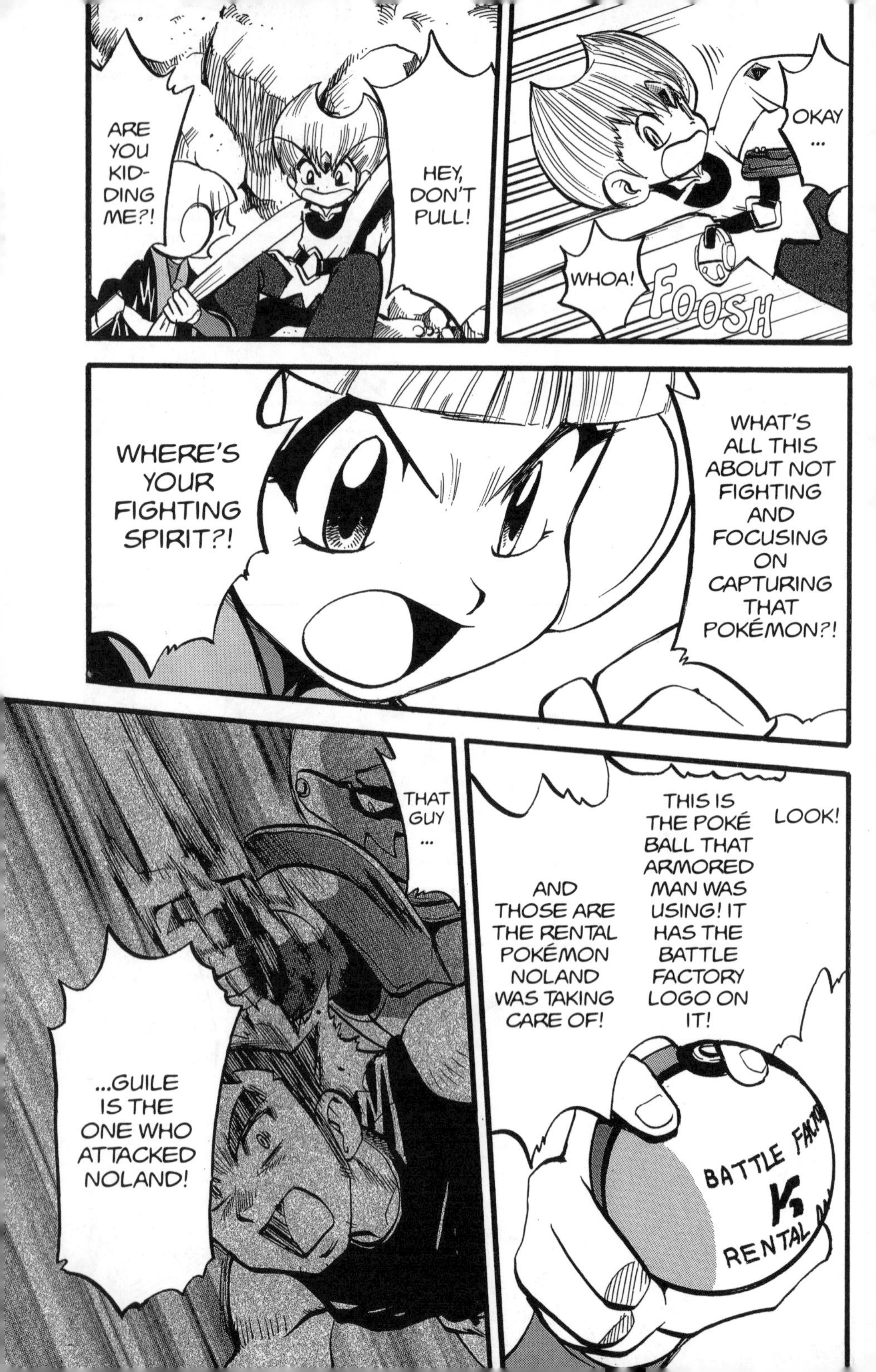

OKAY ...
WHOA!
FOOSH
HEY, DON'T PULL!
ARE YOU KIDDING ME?!
WHAT'S ALL THIS ABOUT NOT FIGHTING AND FOCUSING ON CAPTURING THAT POKÉMON?!
WHERE'S YOUR FIGHTING SPIRIT?!
LOOK!
THIS IS THE POKÉ BALL THAT ARMORED MAN WAS USING! IT HAS THE BATTLE FACTORY LOGO ON IT!
AND THOSE ARE THE RENTAL POKÉMON NOLAND WAS TAKING CARE OF!
BATTLE FACT
RENTAL
THAT GUY ...
...GUILE IS THE ONE WHO ATTACKED NOLAND!

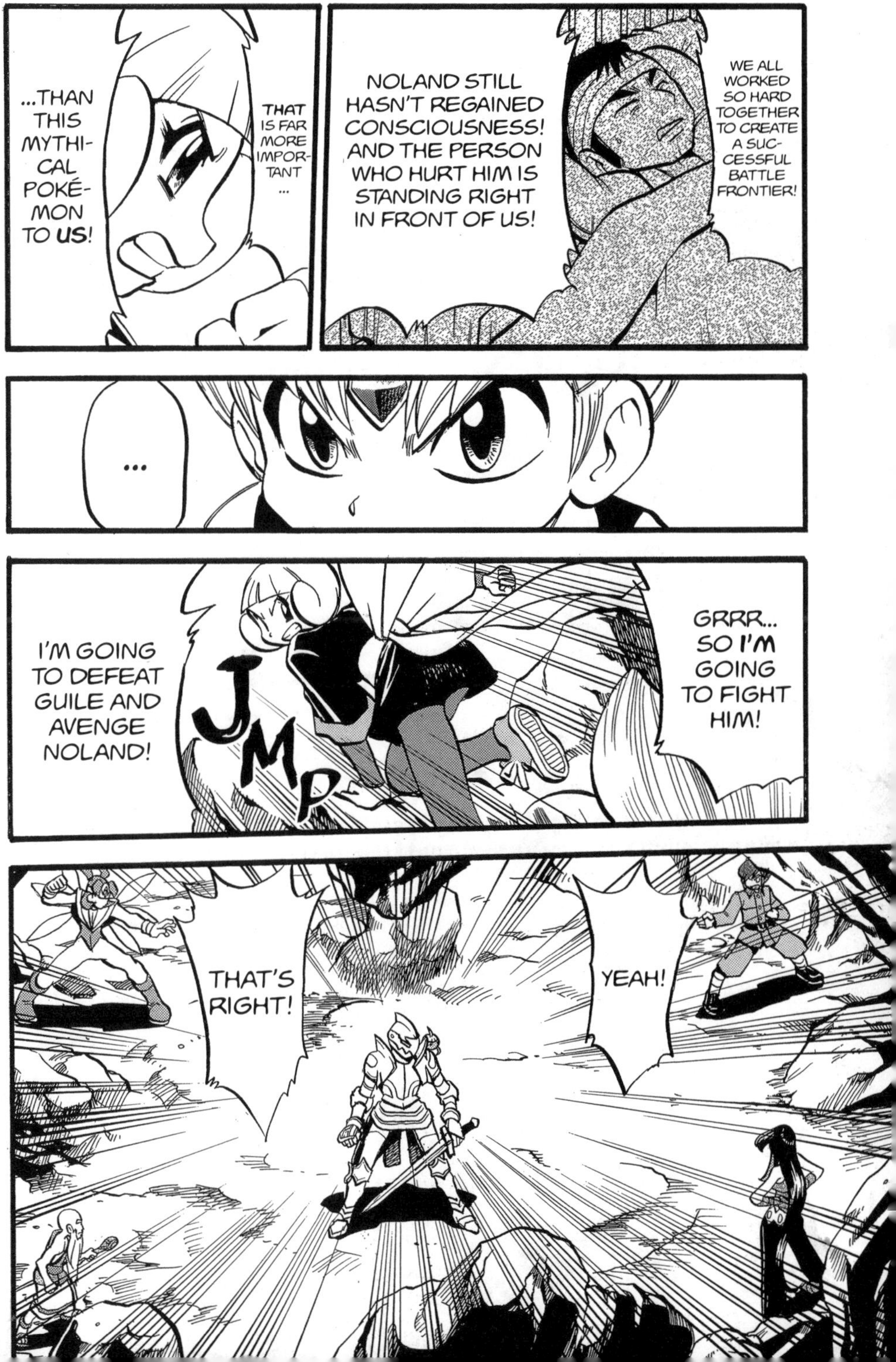
WE ALL WORKED SO HARD TOGETHER TO CREATE A SUCCESSFUL BATTLE FRONTIER!
NOLAND STILL HASN'T REGAINED CONSCIOUSNESS! AND THE PERSON WHO HURT HIM IS STANDING RIGHT IN FRONT OF US!
THAT IS FAR MORE IMPORTANT...
...THAN THIS MYTHICAL POKÉMON TO **US**!
...
GRRR... SO **I'M** GOING TO FIGHT HIM!
JMP
I'M GOING TO DEFEAT GUILE AND AVENGE NOLAND!
YEAH!
THAT'S RIGHT!

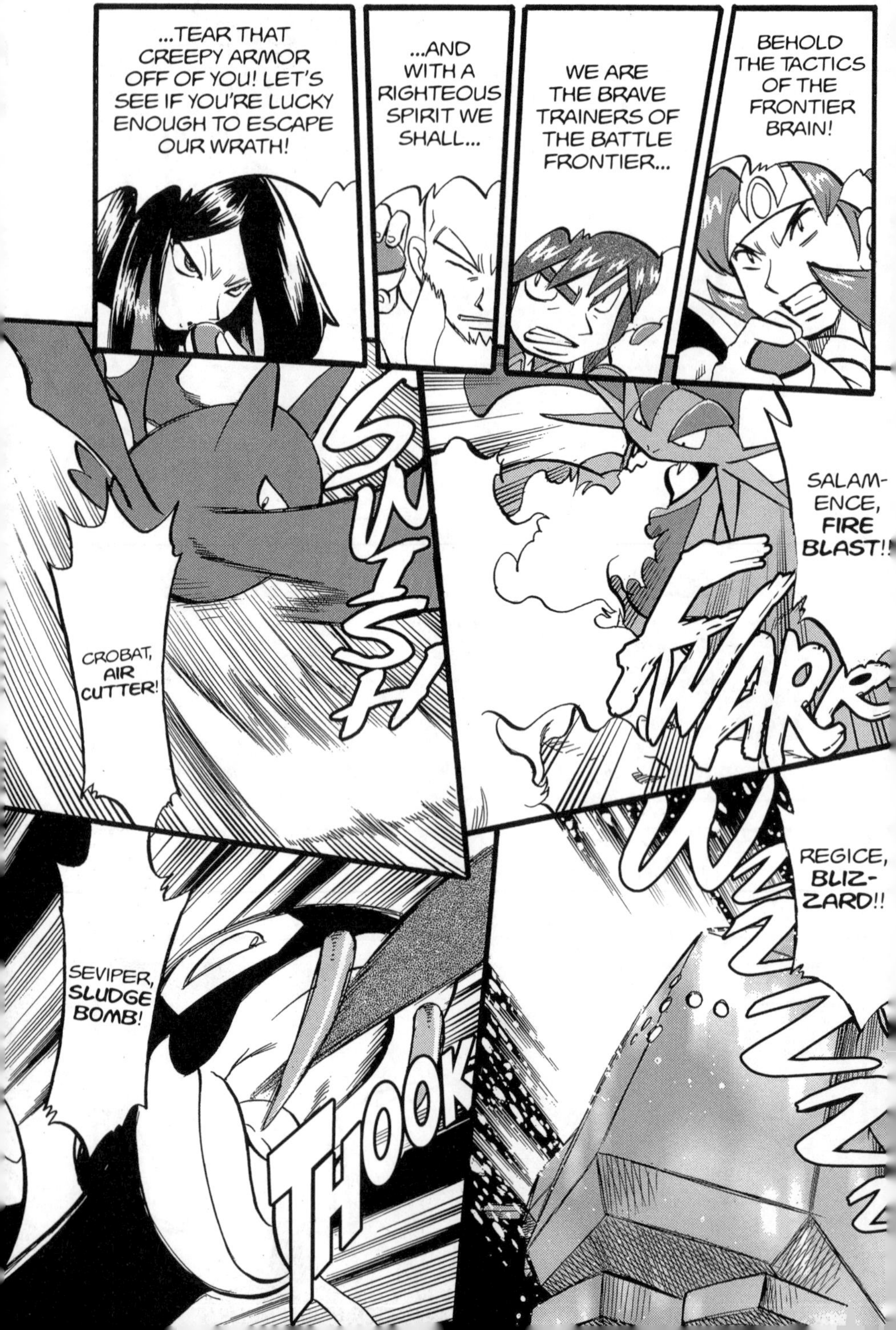
BEHOLD THE TACTICS OF THE FRONTIER BRAIN!
WE ARE THE BRAVE TRAINERS OF THE BATTLE FRONTIER...
...AND WITH A RIGHTEOUS SPIRIT WE SHALL...
...TEAR THAT CREEPY ARMOR OFF OF YOU! LET'S SEE IF YOU'RE LUCKY ENOUGH TO ESCAPE OUR WRATH!
SALAM-ENCE, FIRE BLAST!!
SWISH
CROBAT, AIR CUTTER!
REGICE, BLIZ-ZARD!!
SEVIPER, SLUDGE BOMB!
THOOK

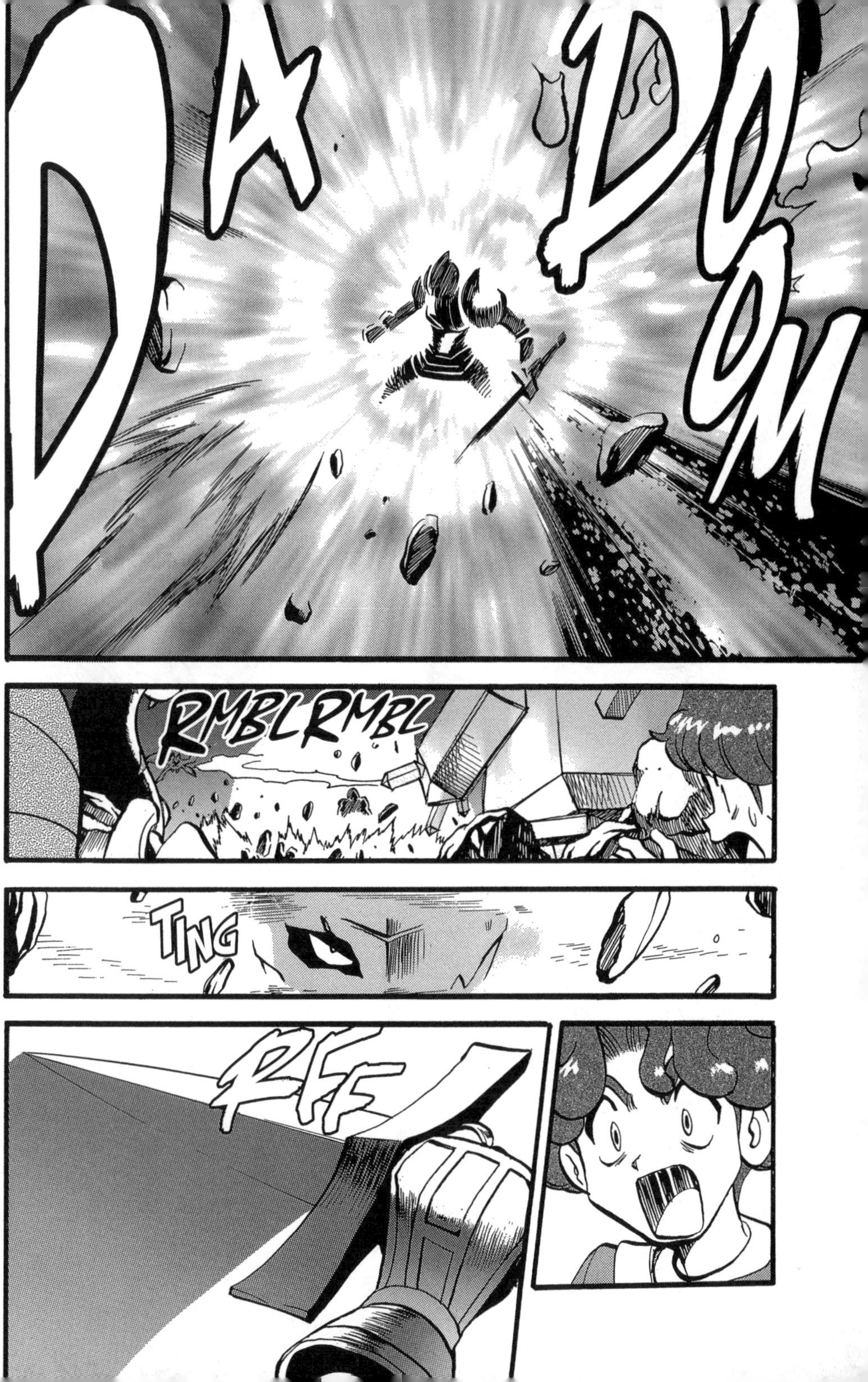
DADOOM
RMBLRMBL
TING
RFF

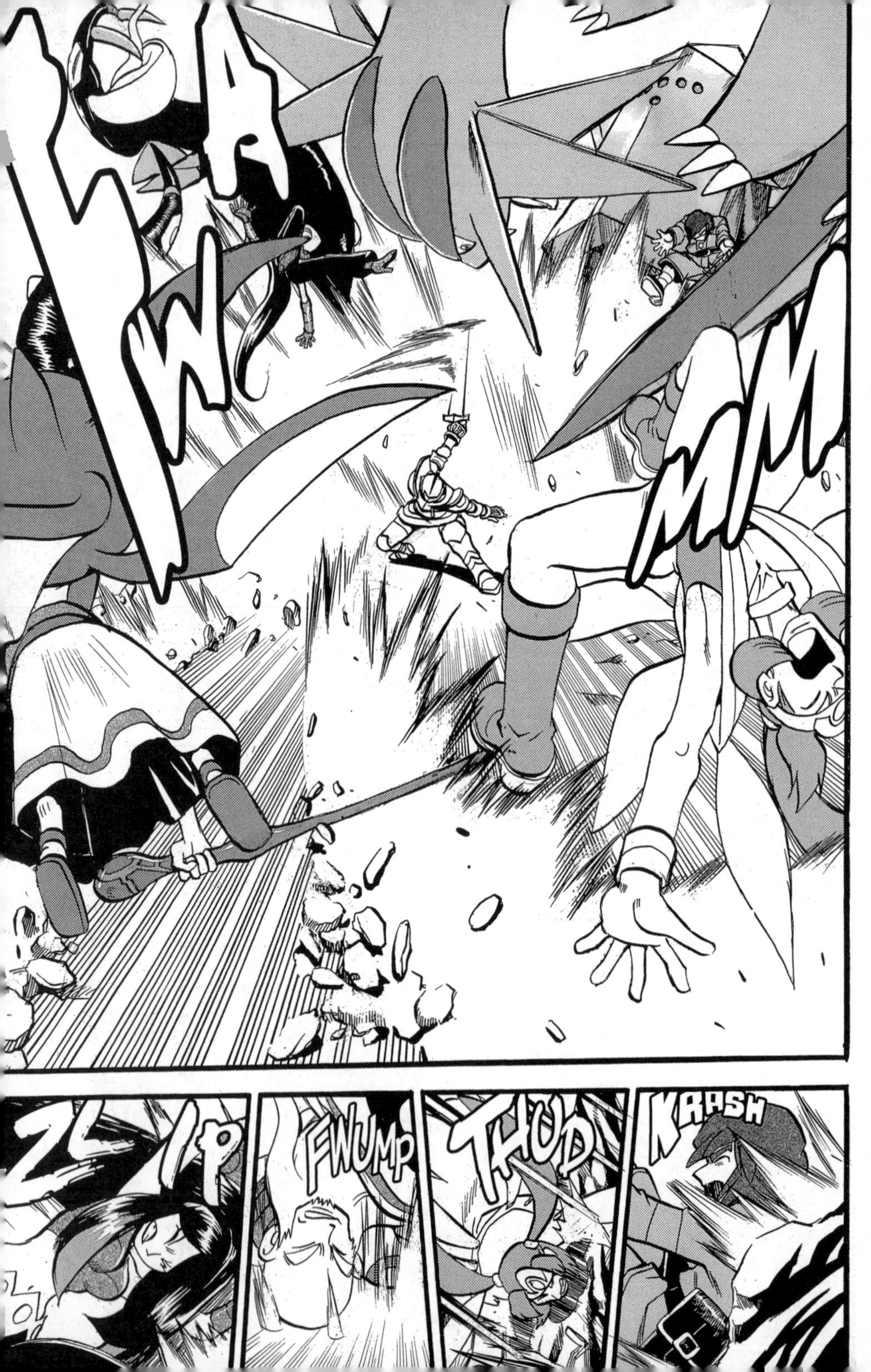
KRASH
THUD
FWUMP
ZWIP

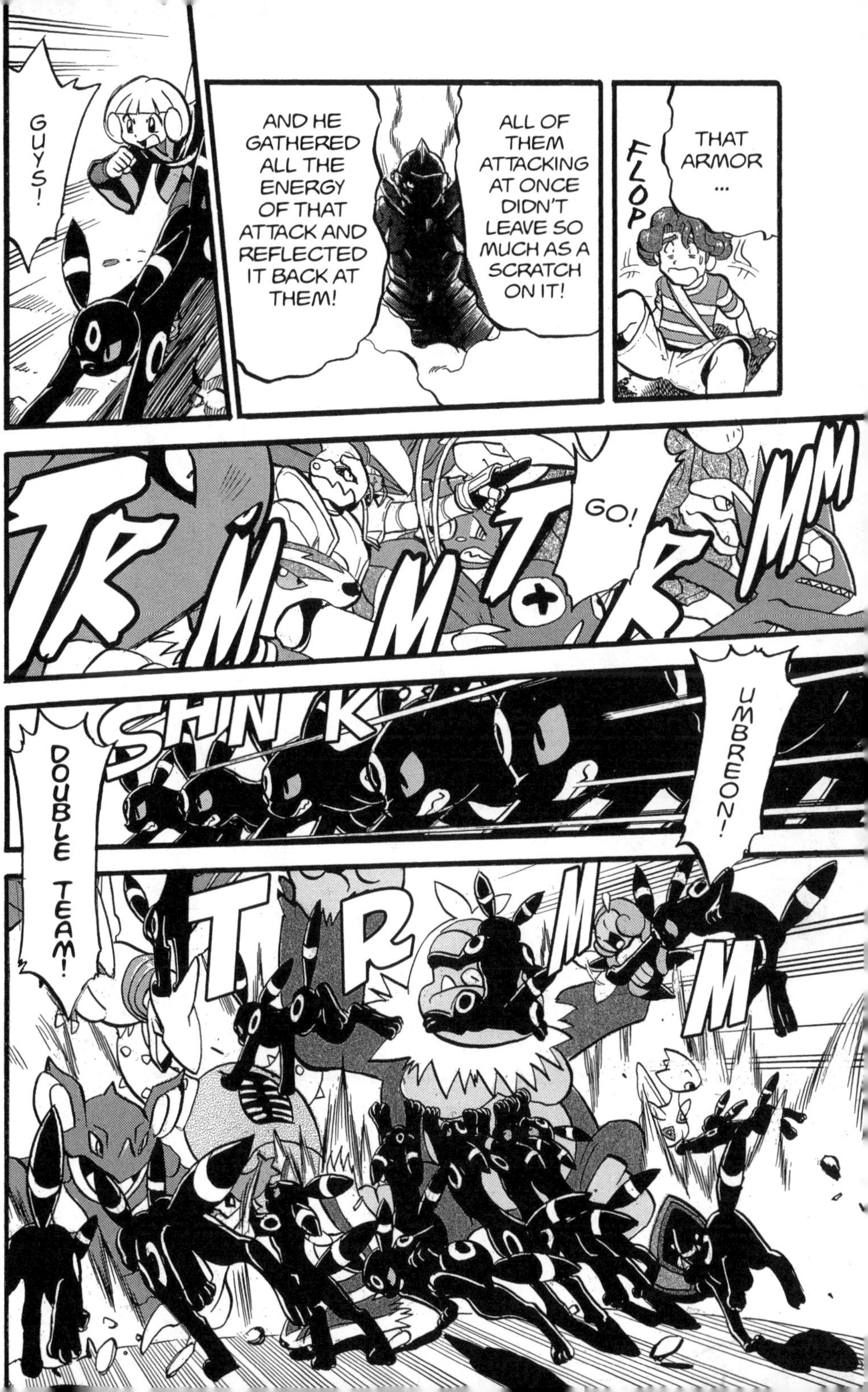

THAT ARMOR ...
FLOP
ALL OF THEM ATTACKING AT ONCE DIDN'T LEAVE SO MUCH AS A SCRATCH ON IT!
AND HE GATHERED ALL THE ENERGY OF THAT ATTACK AND REFLECTED IT BACK AT THEM!
GUYS!
GO!
TRMMTRMMM
UMBREON!
SHNK
DOUBLE TEAM!
TRMM

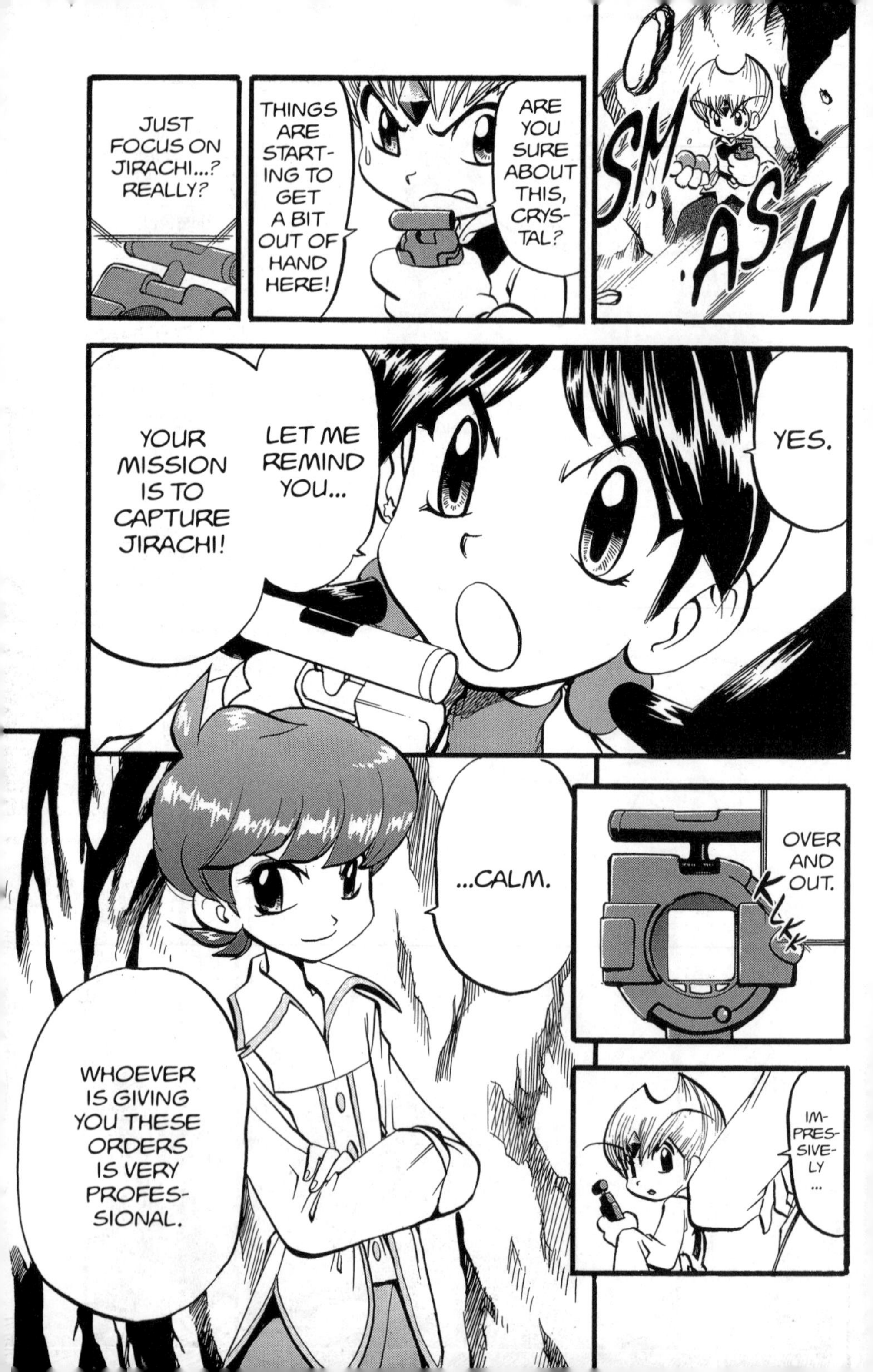
SMASH
ARE YOU SURE ABOUT THIS, CRYSTAL?
THINGS ARE STARTING TO GET A BIT OUT OF HAND HERE!
JUST FOCUS ON JIRACHI...? REALLY?
YES.
LET ME REMIND YOU...
YOUR MISSION IS TO CAPTURE JIRACHI!
OVER AND OUT.
KLKK
IMPRESSIVELY...
...CALM.
WHOEVER IS GIVING YOU THESE ORDERS IS VERY PROFESSIONAL.

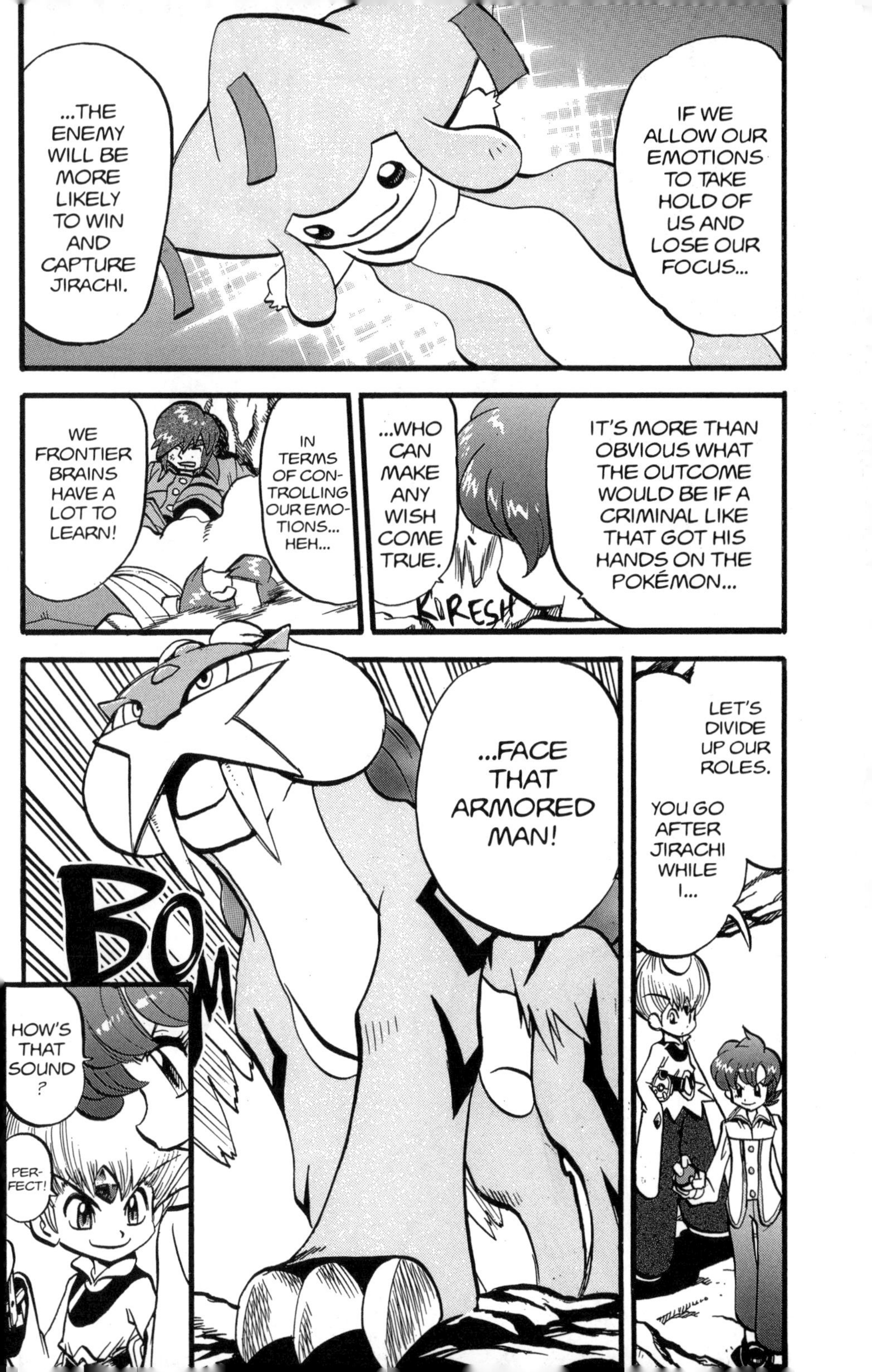
IF WE ALLOW OUR EMOTIONS TO TAKE HOLD OF US AND LOSE OUR FOCUS...
...THE ENEMY WILL BE MORE LIKELY TO WIN AND CAPTURE JIRACHI.
IT'S MORE THAN OBVIOUS WHAT THE OUTCOME WOULD BE IF A CRIMINAL LIKE THAT GOT HIS HANDS ON THE POKÉMON...
...WHO CAN MAKE ANY WISH COME TRUE.
KRESH
IN TERMS OF CONTROLLING OUR EMOTIONS... HEH...
WE FRONTIER BRAINS HAVE A LOT TO LEARN!
LET'S DIVIDE UP OUR ROLES.
YOU GO AFTER JIRACHI WHILE I...
...FACE THAT ARMORED MAN!
BOOM
HOW'S THAT SOUND?
PERFECT!

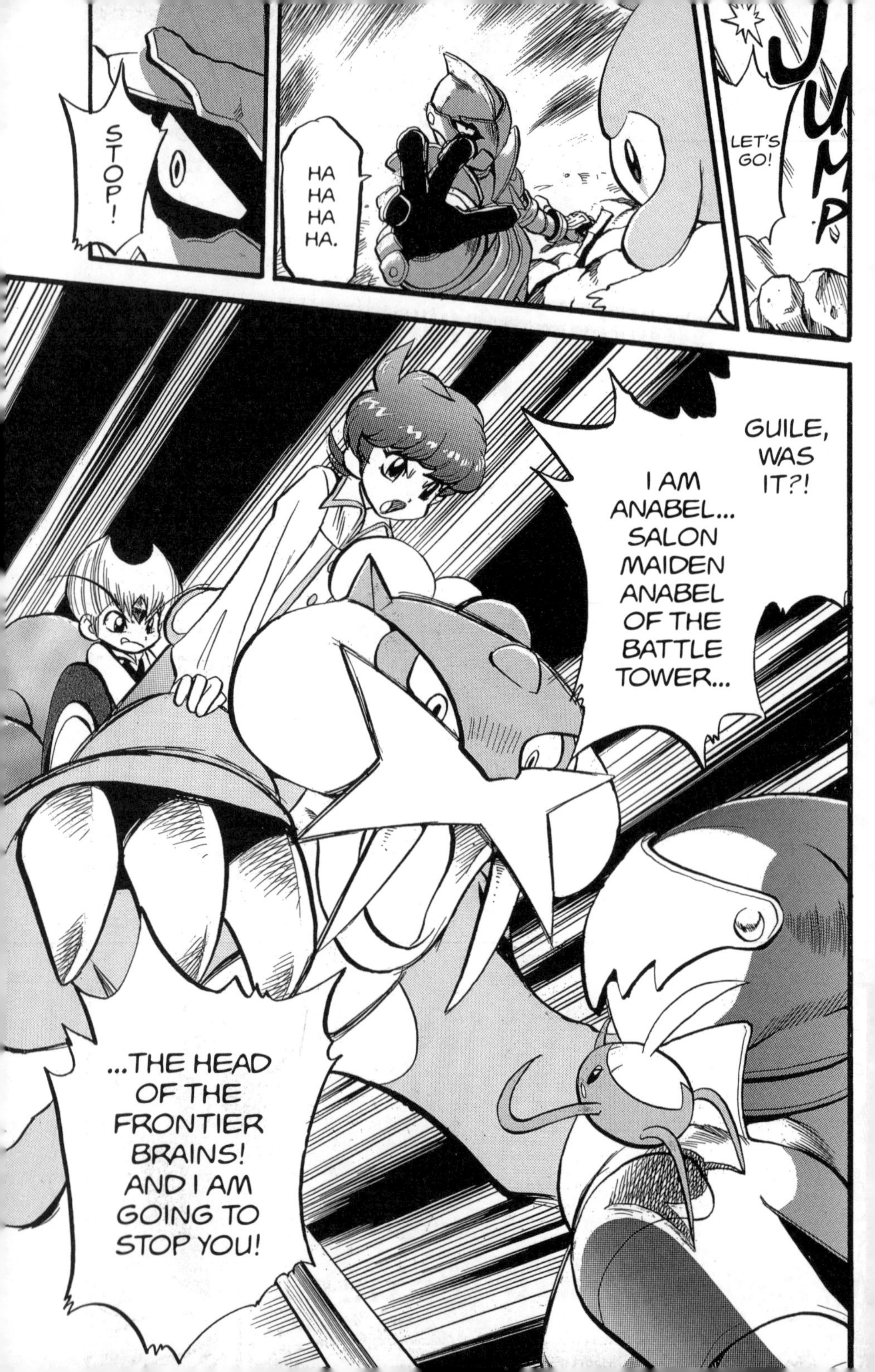
JUMP
LET'S GO!
HA HA HA HA.
STOP!
GUILE, WAS IT?!
I AM ANABEL... SALON MAIDEN ANABEL OF THE BATTLE TOWER...
...THE HEAD OF THE FRONTIER BRAINS! AND I AM GOING TO STOP YOU!

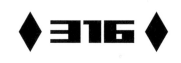

◆ 316 ◆

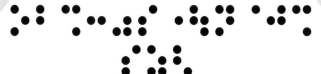

Skirting Around Surskit, Part 2

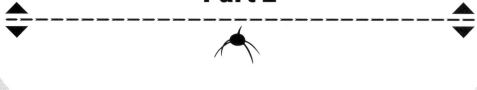

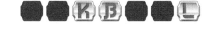

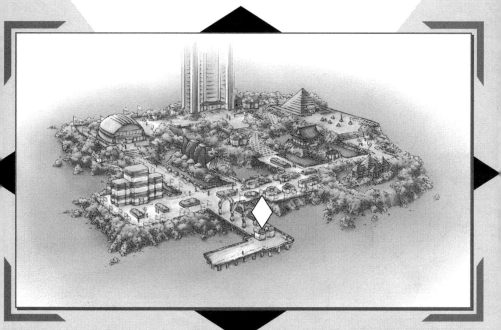

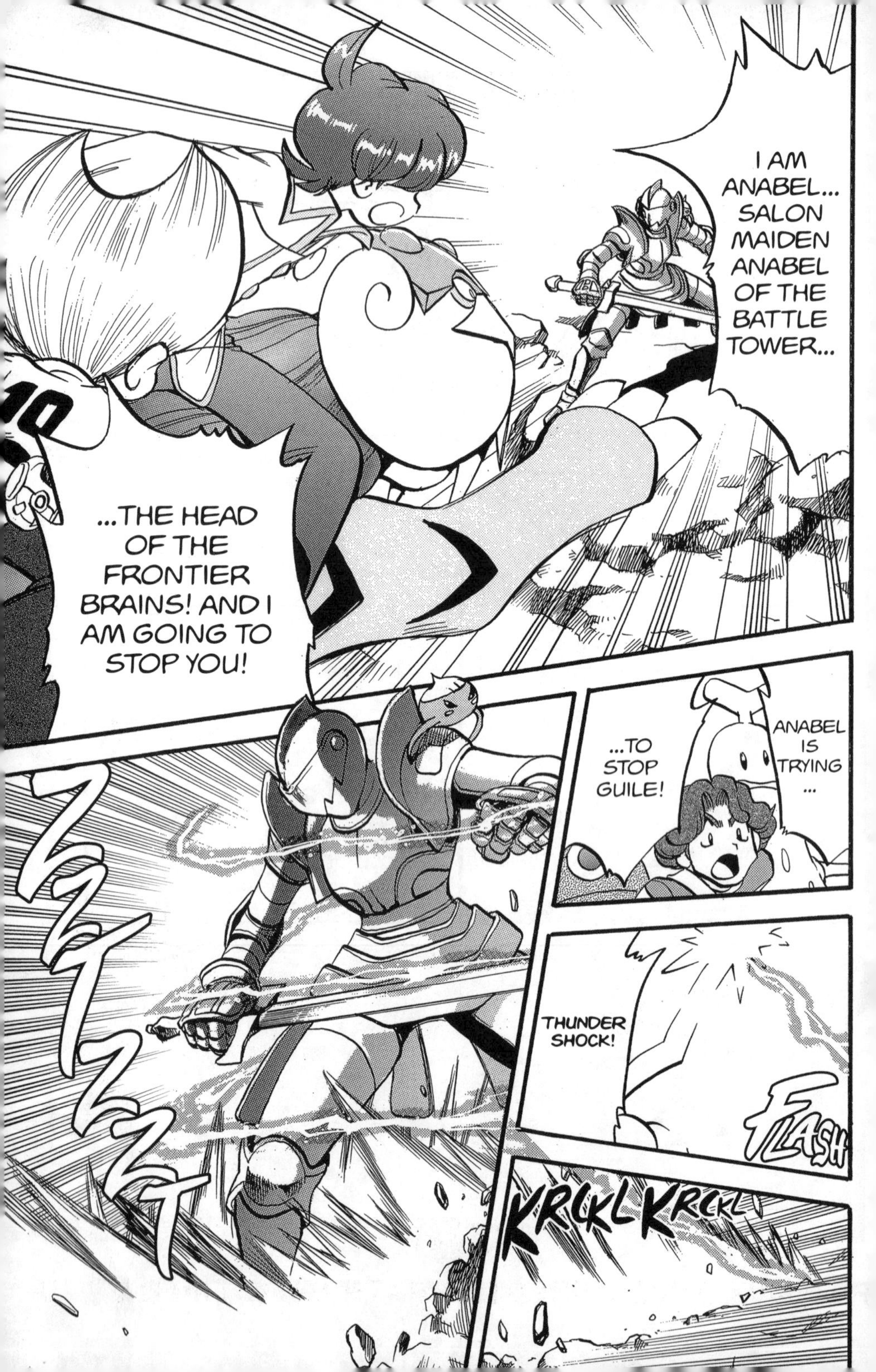
I AM ANABEL... SALON MAIDEN ANABEL OF THE BATTLE TOWER...
...THE HEAD OF THE FRONTIER BRAINS! AND I AM GOING TO STOP YOU!
ANABEL IS TRYING ...
...TO STOP GUILE!
THUNDER SHOCK!
FLASH
KRCKL KRCKL
ZZZZZZZT

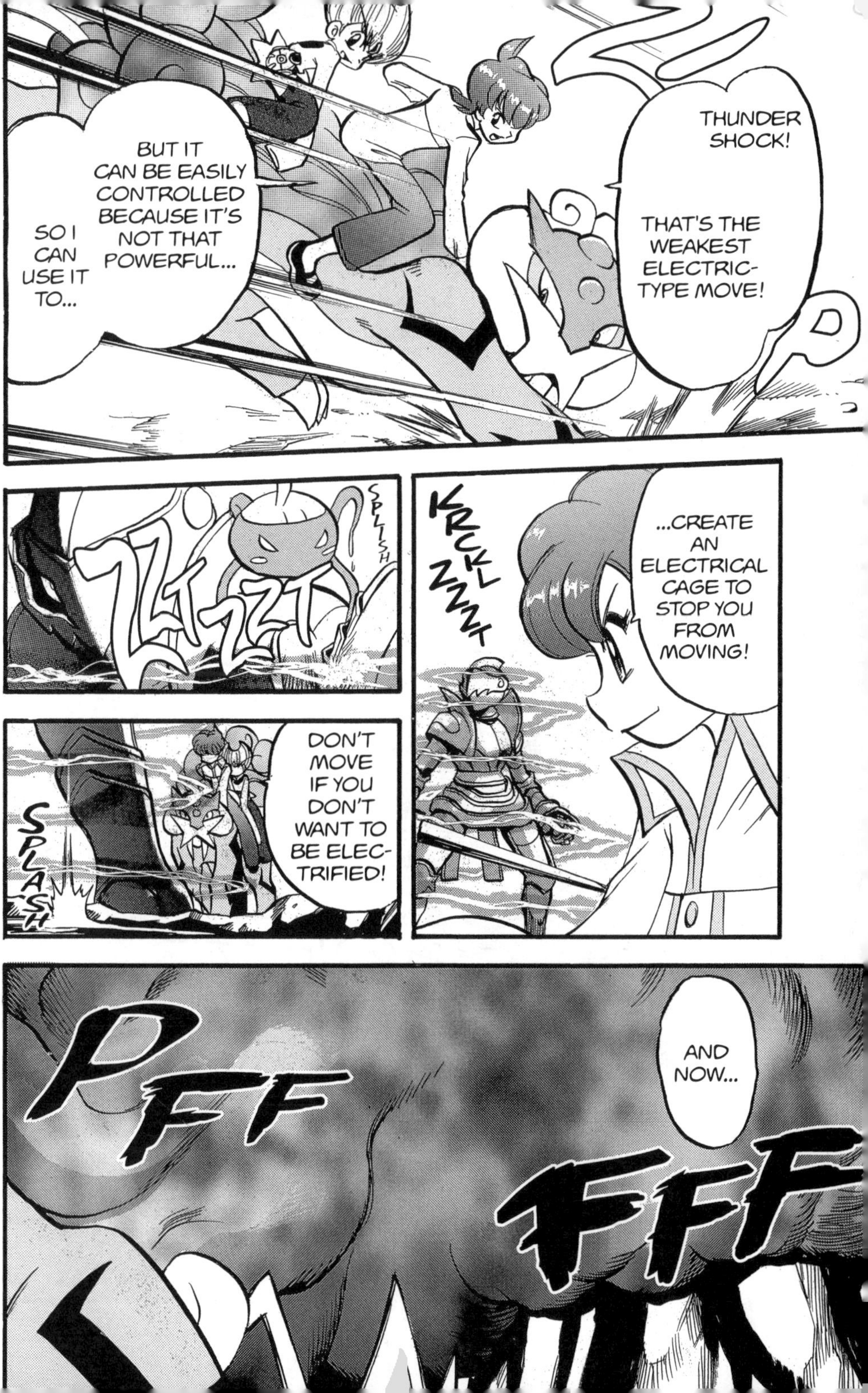
THUNDER SHOCK!
THAT'S THE WEAKEST ELECTRIC-TYPE MOVE!
BUT IT CAN BE EASILY CONTROLLED BECAUSE IT'S NOT THAT POWERFUL...
SO I CAN USE IT TO...
KRCKL ZZZZK
...CREATE AN ELECTRICAL CAGE TO STOP YOU FROM MOVING!
SPLISH
ZZT ZZZT
DON'T MOVE IF YOU DON'T WANT TO BE ELEC-TRIFIED!
SPLASH
AND NOW...
PFFF
FFFF

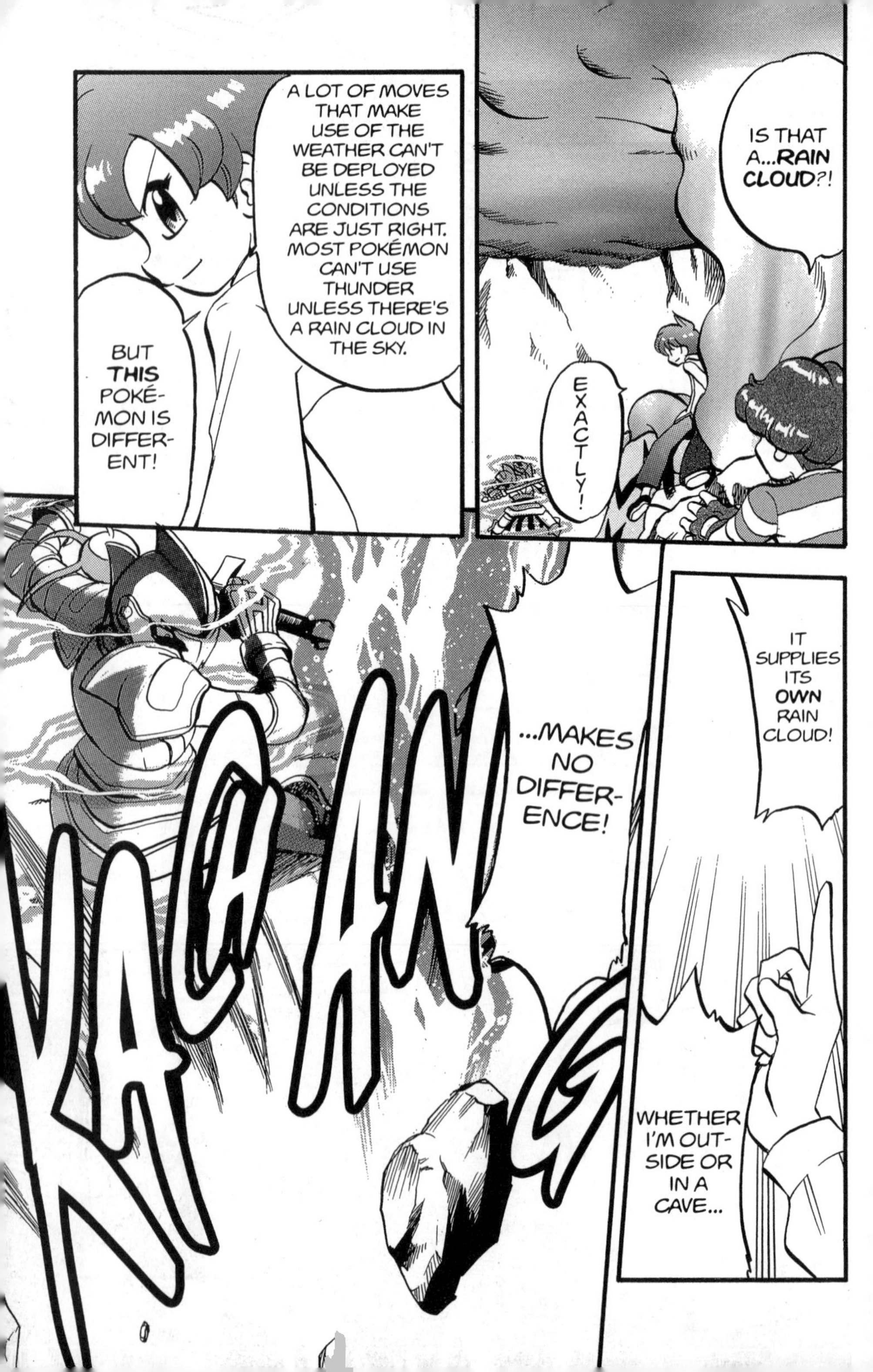
IS THAT A...**RAIN CLOUD**?!
EXACTLY!
A LOT OF MOVES THAT MAKE USE OF THE WEATHER CAN'T BE DEPLOYED UNLESS THE CONDITIONS ARE JUST RIGHT. MOST POKÉMON CAN'T USE THUNDER UNLESS THERE'S A RAIN CLOUD IN THE SKY.
BUT **THIS** POKÉMON IS DIFFERENT!
IT SUPPLIES ITS **OWN** RAIN CLOUD!
WHETHER I'M OUTSIDE OR IN A CAVE...
...MAKES NO DIFFERENCE!
KACHANG

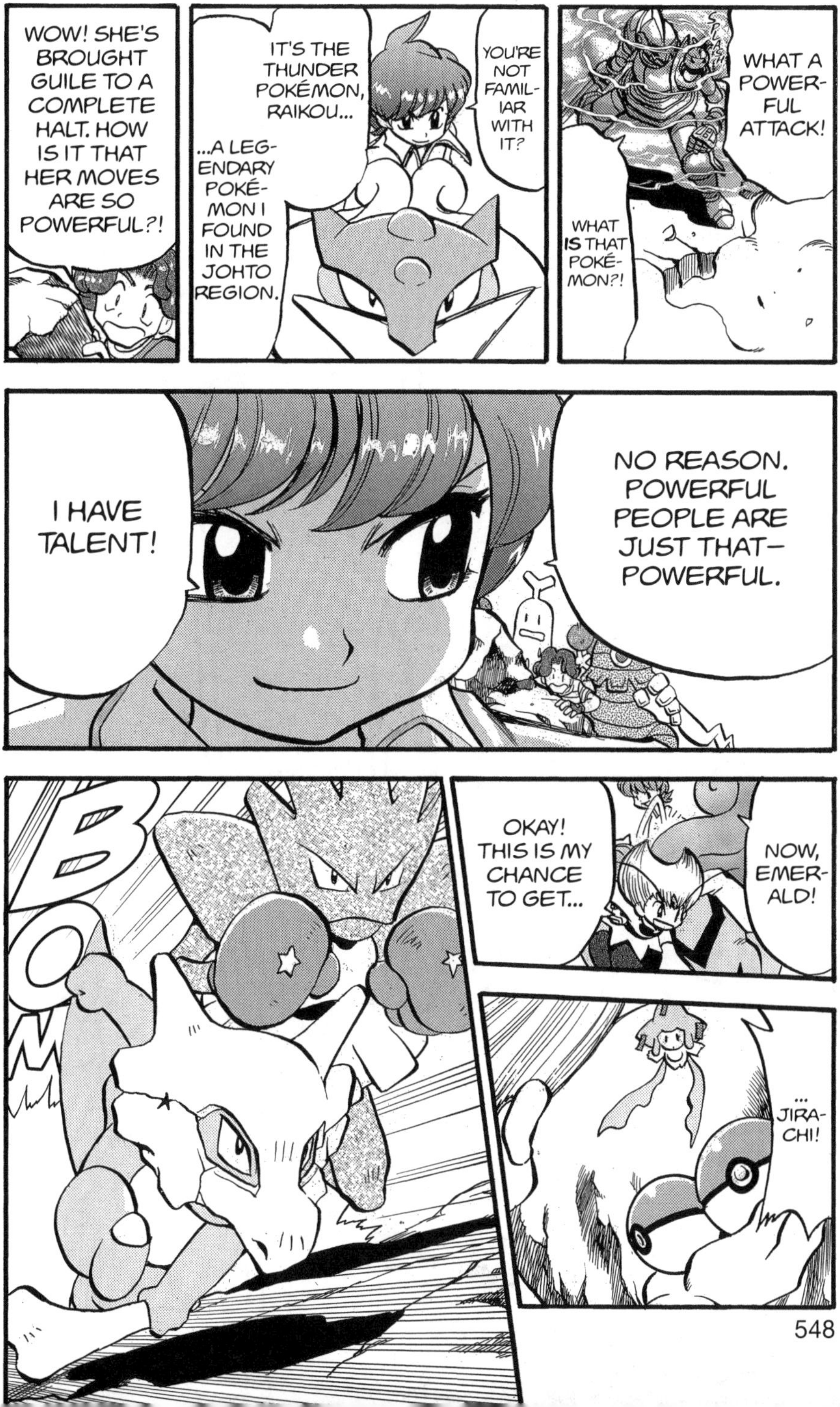
WHAT A POWERFUL ATTACK!
WHAT IS THAT POKÉMON?!
YOU'RE NOT FAMILIAR WITH IT?
IT'S THE THUNDER POKÉMON, RAIKOU...
...A LEGENDARY POKÉMON I FOUND IN THE JOHTO REGION.
WOW! SHE'S BROUGHT GUILE TO A COMPLETE HALT. HOW IS IT THAT HER MOVES ARE SO POWERFUL?!
NO REASON. POWERFUL PEOPLE ARE JUST THAT—POWERFUL.
I HAVE TALENT!
NOW, EMERALD!
OKAY! THIS IS MY CHANCE TO GET...
...JIRACHI!

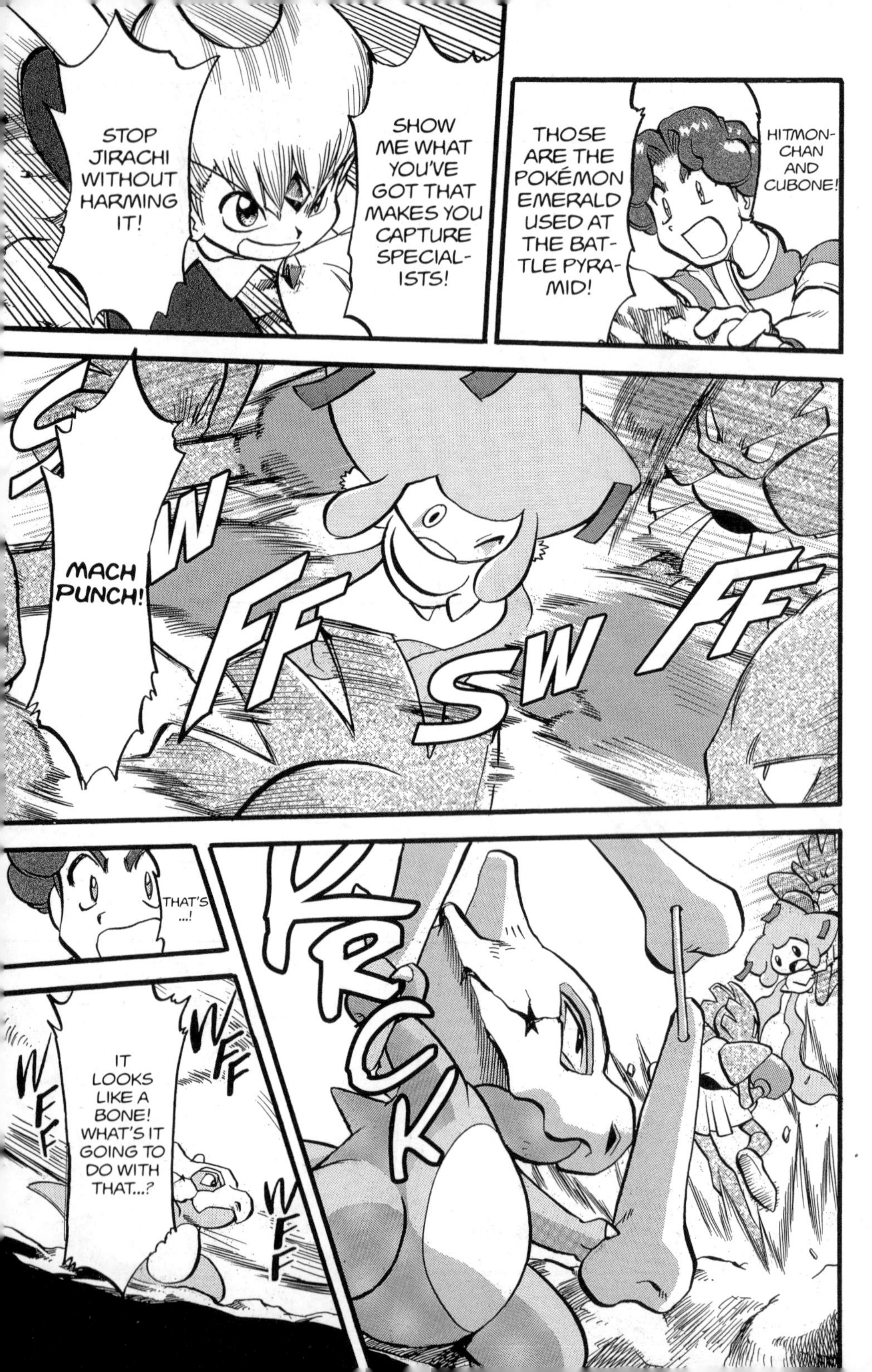
HITMON-CHAN AND CUBONE!
THOSE ARE THE POKÉMON EMERALD USED AT THE BAT-TLE PYRA-MID!
SHOW ME WHAT YOU'VE GOT THAT MAKES YOU CAPTURE SPECIAL-ISTS!
STOP JIRACHI WITHOUT HARMING IT!
SWFF
SWFF
MACH PUNCH!
KRCK
THAT'S ...!
WFF
IT LOOKS LIKE A BONE! WHAT'S IT GOING TO DO WITH THAT...?
WFF
WFF

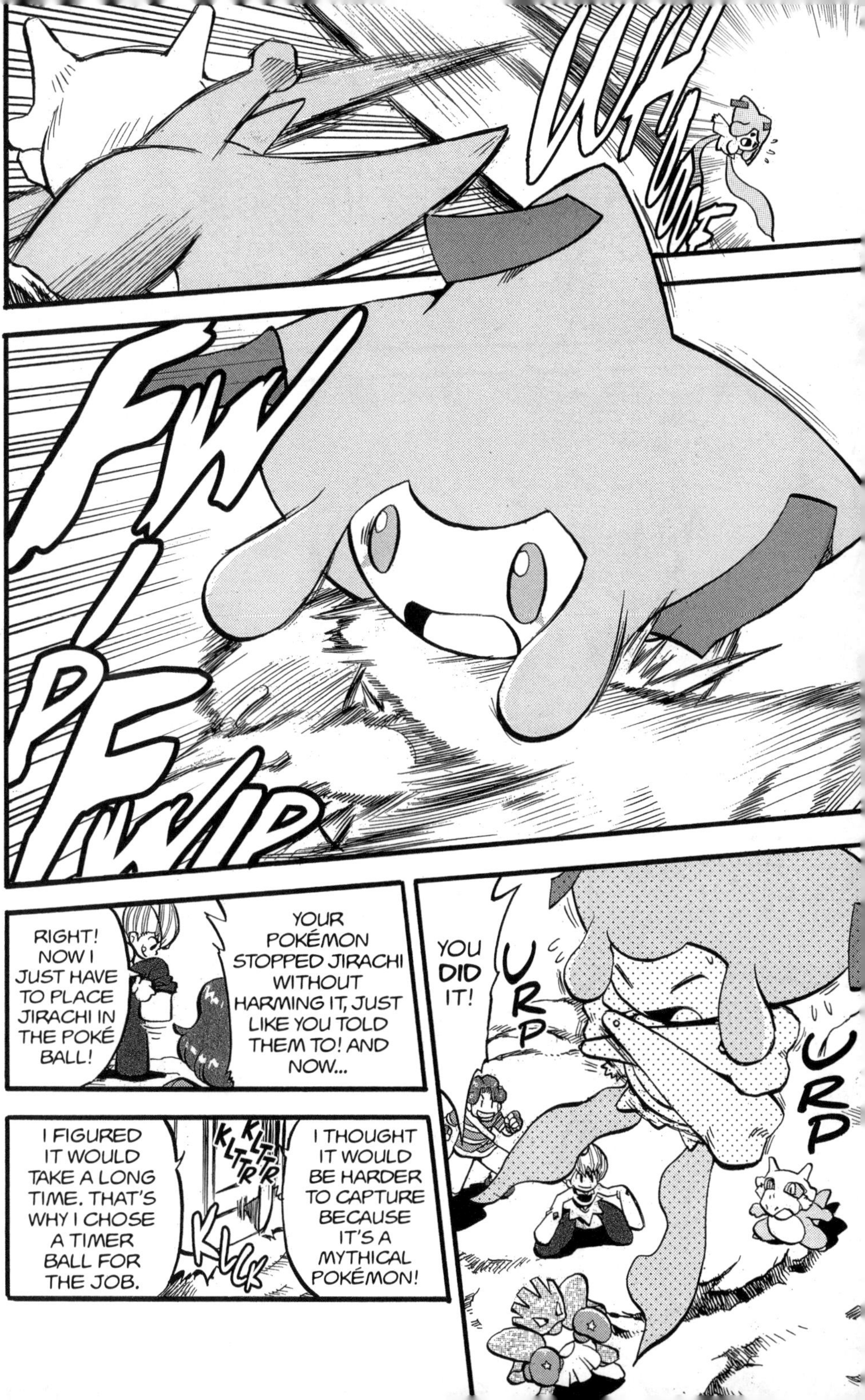
FWIP
FWIP
YOU DID IT!
URP
URP
YOUR POKÉMON STOPPED JIRACHI WITHOUT HARMING IT, JUST LIKE YOU TOLD THEM TO! AND NOW...
RIGHT! NOW I JUST HAVE TO PLACE JIRACHI IN THE POKÉ BALL!
I THOUGHT IT WOULD BE HARDER TO CAPTURE BECAUSE IT'S A MYTHICAL POKÉMON!
KLTTR KLTTR
KLICK
I FIGURED IT WOULD TAKE A LONG TIME. THAT'S WHY I CHOSE A TIMER BALL FOR THE JOB.

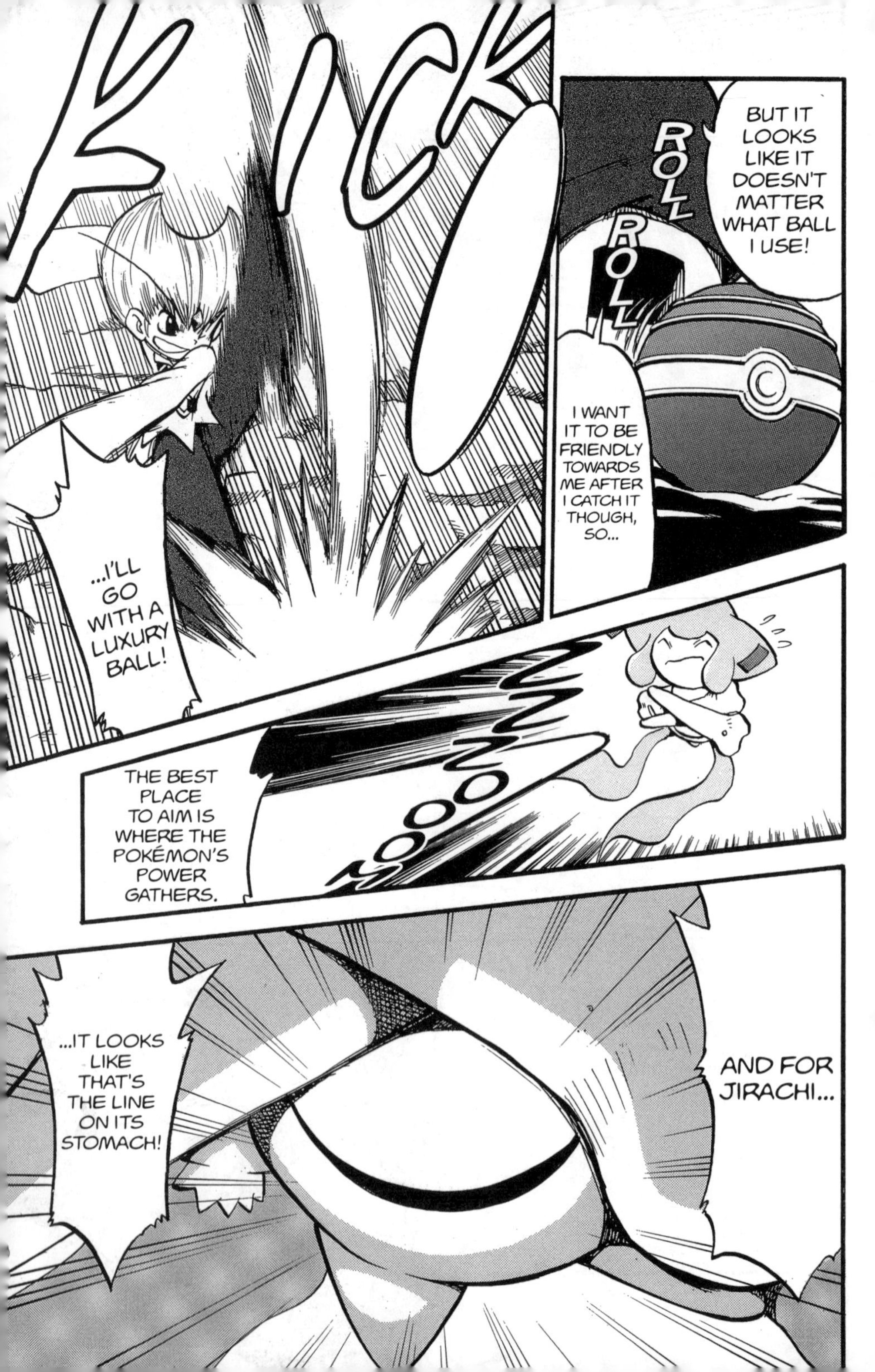
ROLL
ROLL
BUT IT LOOKS LIKE IT DOESN'T MATTER WHAT BALL I USE!
I WANT IT TO BE FRIENDLY TOWARDS ME AFTER I CATCH IT THOUGH, SO...
KICK
...I'LL GO WITH A LUXURY BALL!
THE BEST PLACE TO AIM IS WHERE THE POKÉMON'S POWER GATHERS.
AND FOR JIRACHI...
...IT LOOKS LIKE THAT'S THE LINE ON ITS STOMACH!

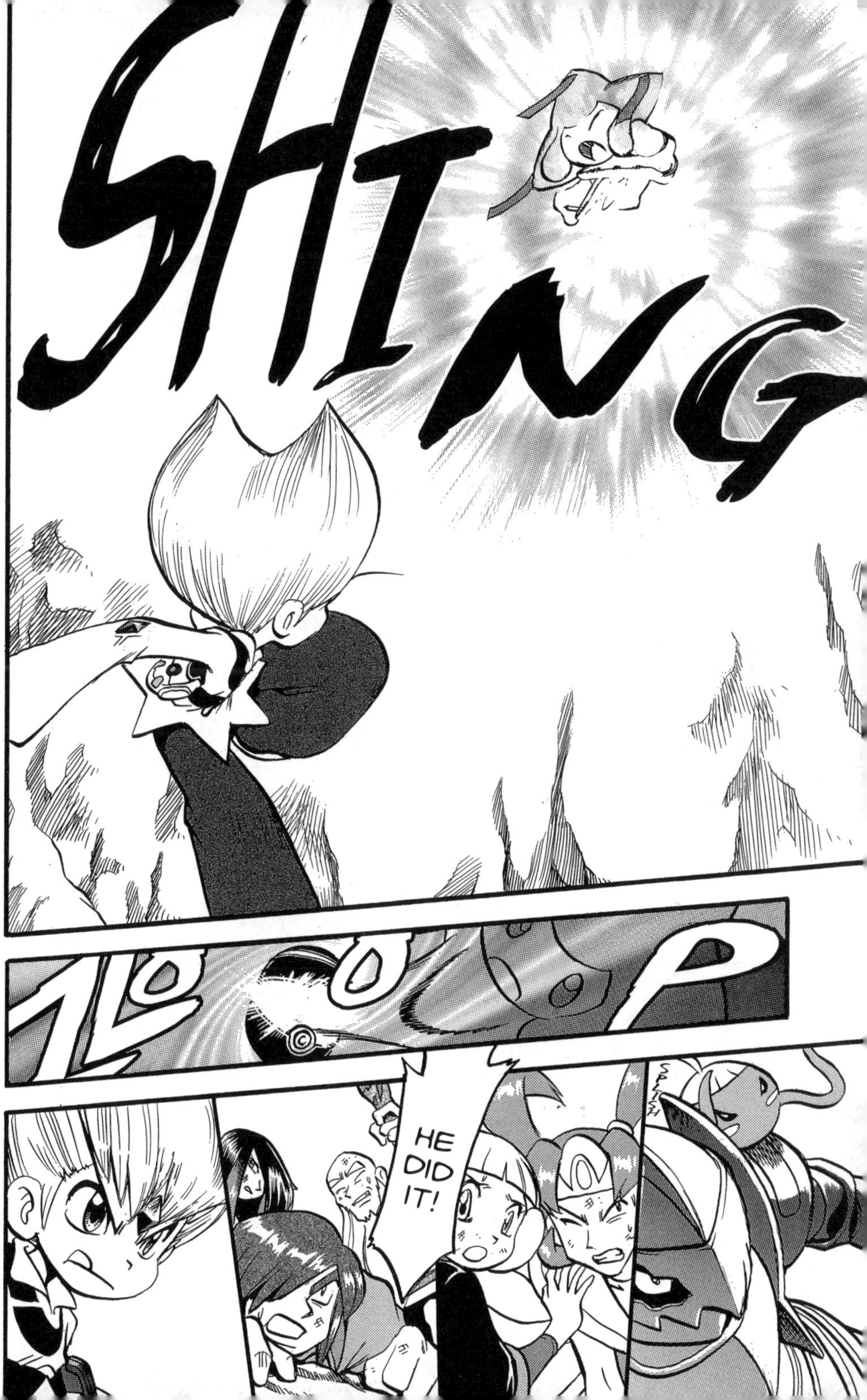
SHING
ZOOP
SPLISH
HE DID IT!

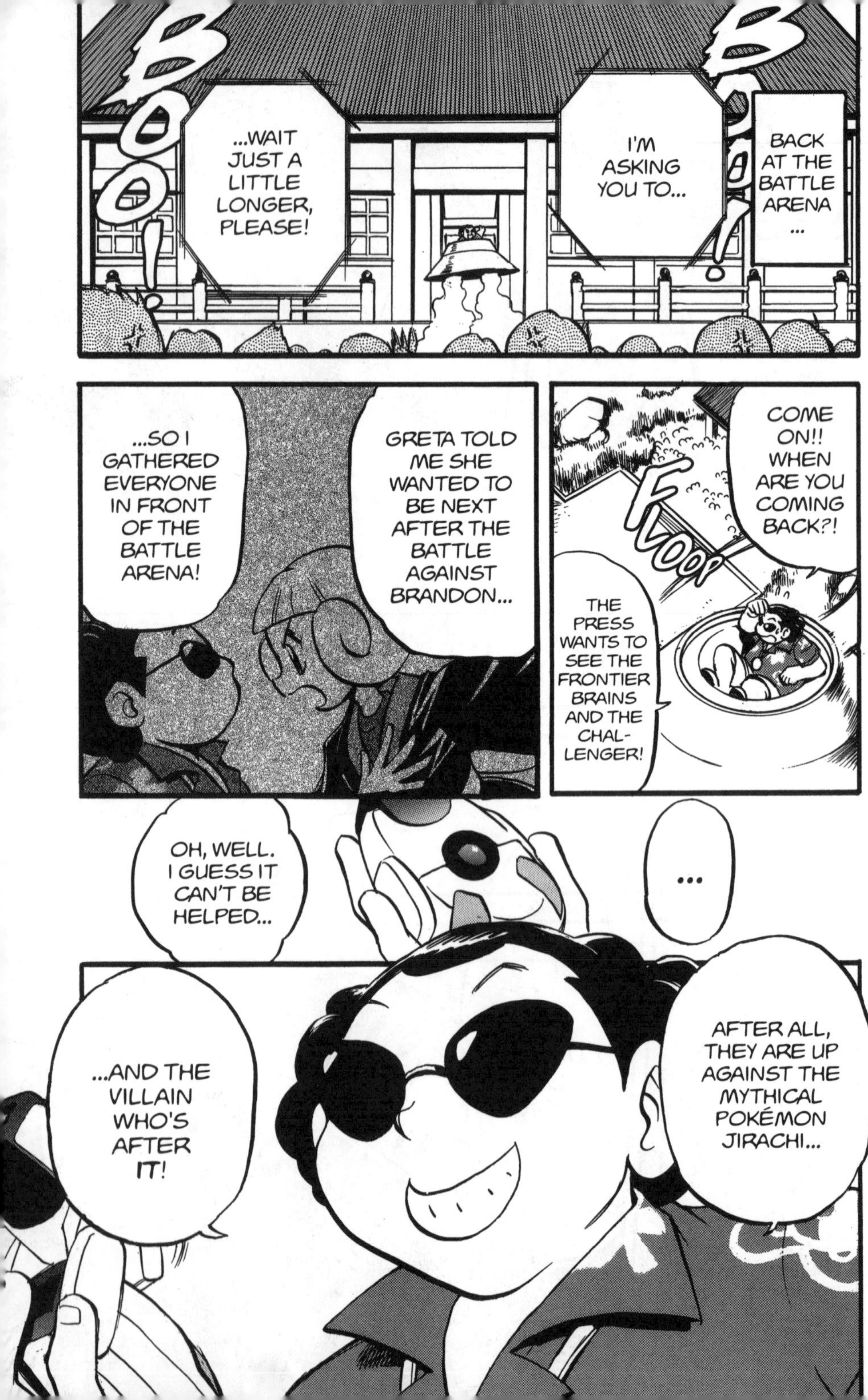
BACK AT THE BATTLE ARENA ...
BOO!
I'M ASKING YOU TO...
...WAIT JUST A LITTLE LONGER, PLEASE!
BOO!
COME ON!! WHEN ARE YOU COMING BACK?!
FVOOP
THE PRESS WANTS TO SEE THE FRONTIER BRAINS AND THE CHAL-LENGER!
GRETA TOLD ME SHE WANTED TO BE NEXT AFTER THE BATTLE AGAINST BRANDON...
...SO I GATHERED EVERYONE IN FRONT OF THE BATTLE ARENA!
...
OH, WELL. I GUESS IT CAN'T BE HELPED...
AFTER ALL, THEY ARE UP AGAINST THE MYTHICAL POKÉMON JIRACHI...
...AND THE VILLAIN WHO'S AFTER IT!

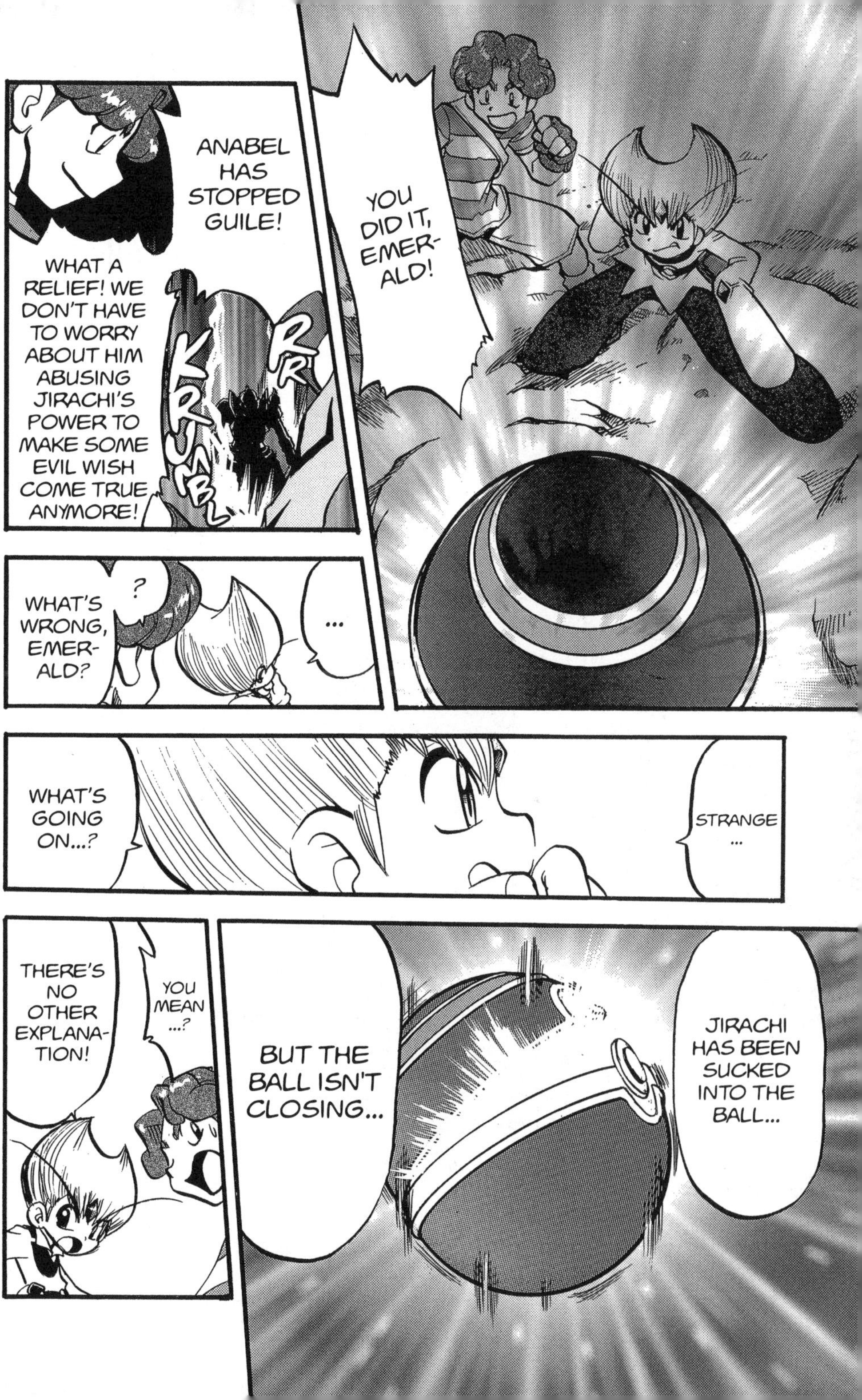
YOU DID IT, EMERALD!
ANABEL HAS STOPPED GUILE!
WHAT A RELIEF! WE DON'T HAVE TO WORRY ABOUT HIM ABUSING JIRACHI'S POWER TO MAKE SOME EVIL WISH COME TRUE ANYMORE!
RRKRUMBL
...
?
WHAT'S WRONG, EMERALD?
STRANGE...
WHAT'S GOING ON...?
JIRACHI HAS BEEN SUCKED INTO THE BALL...
BUT THE BALL ISN'T CLOSING...
YOU MEAN...?
THERE'S NO OTHER EXPLANATION!

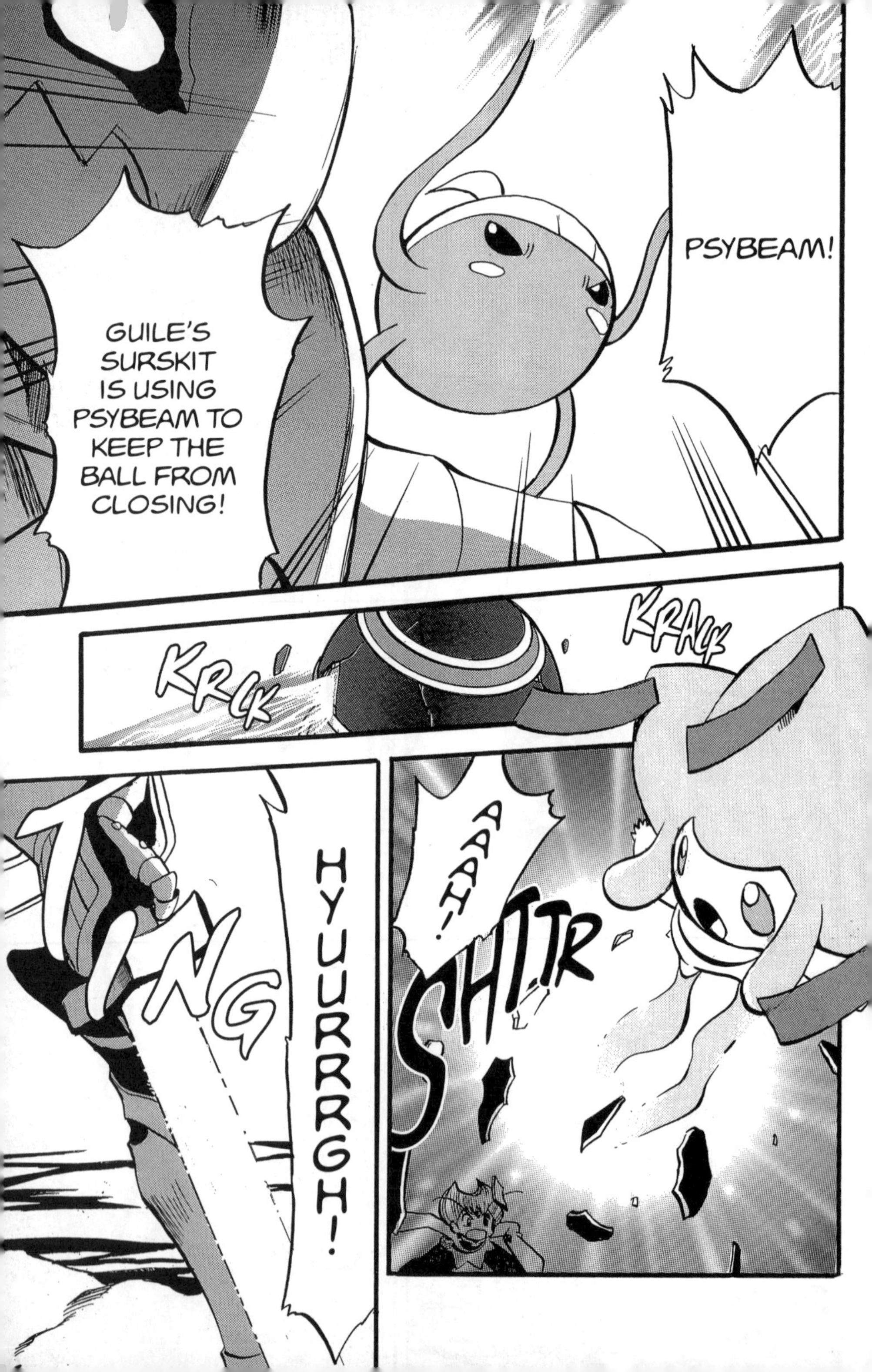
PSYBEAM!
GUILE'S SURSKIT IS USING PSYBEAM TO KEEP THE BALL FROM CLOSING!
KRACK
KRCK
AAAH!
SHTTR
HYUURRRGH!
TING

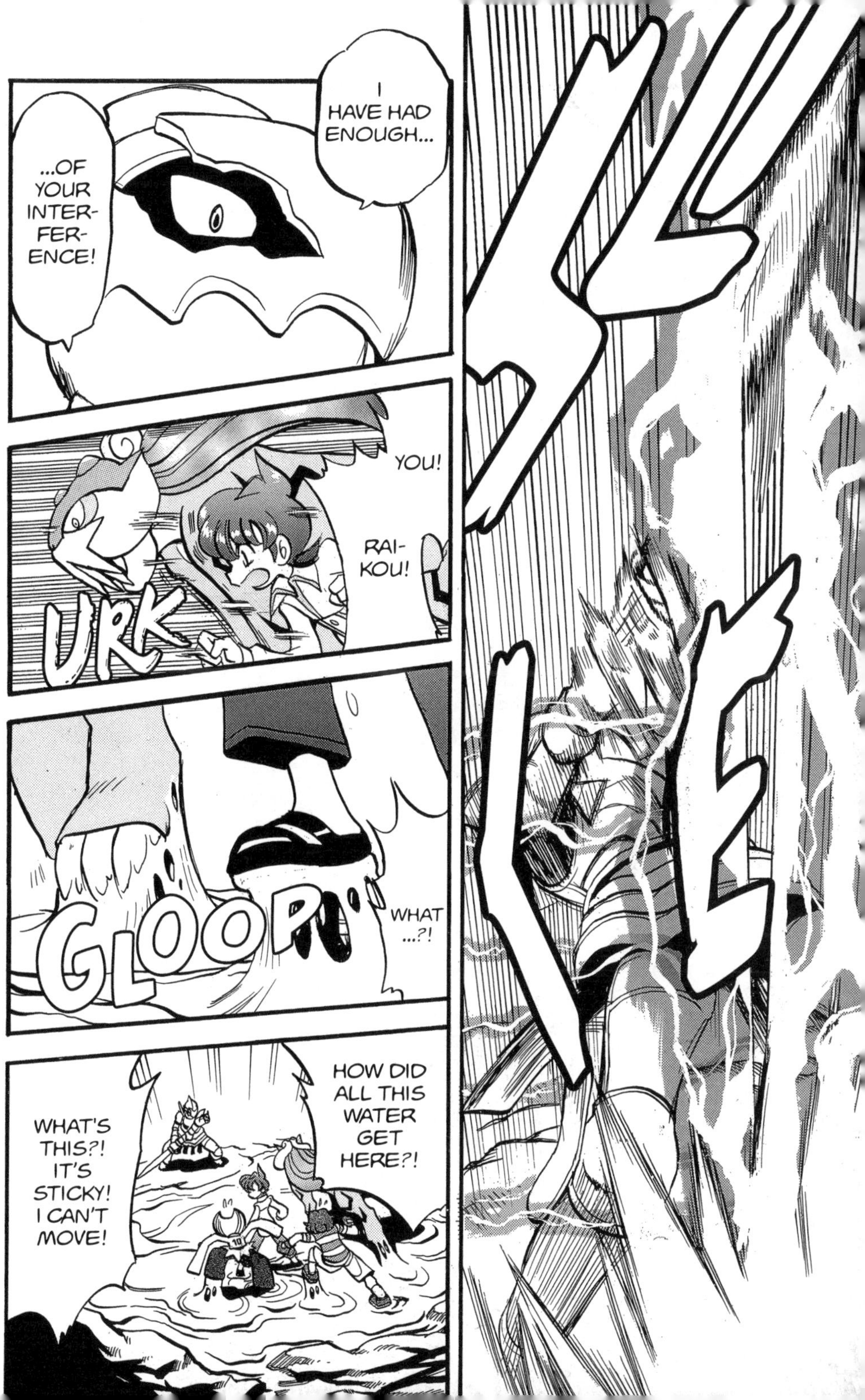
I HAVE HAD ENOUGH...
...OF YOUR INTERFERENCE!
YOU!
RAIKOU!
URK
WHAT ...?!
GLOOP
HOW DID ALL THIS WATER GET HERE?!
WHAT'S THIS?! IT'S STICKY! I CAN'T MOVE!

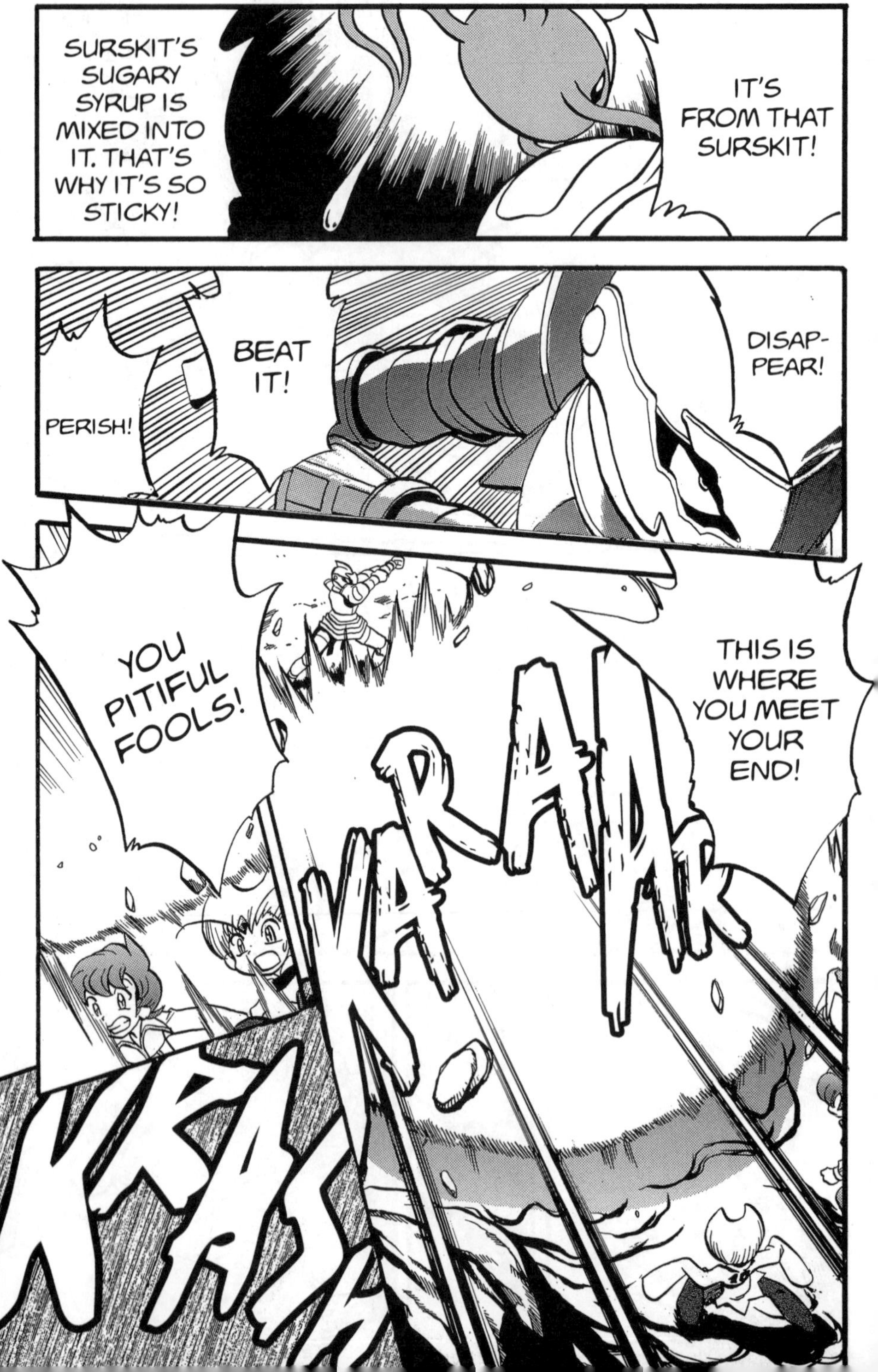
IT'S FROM THAT SURSKIT!
SURSKIT'S SUGARY SYRUP IS MIXED INTO IT. THAT'S WHY IT'S SO STICKY!
DISAP-PEAR!
BEAT IT!
PERISH!
THIS IS WHERE YOU MEET YOUR END!
YOU PITIFUL FOOLS!
KRAAK
KRASH

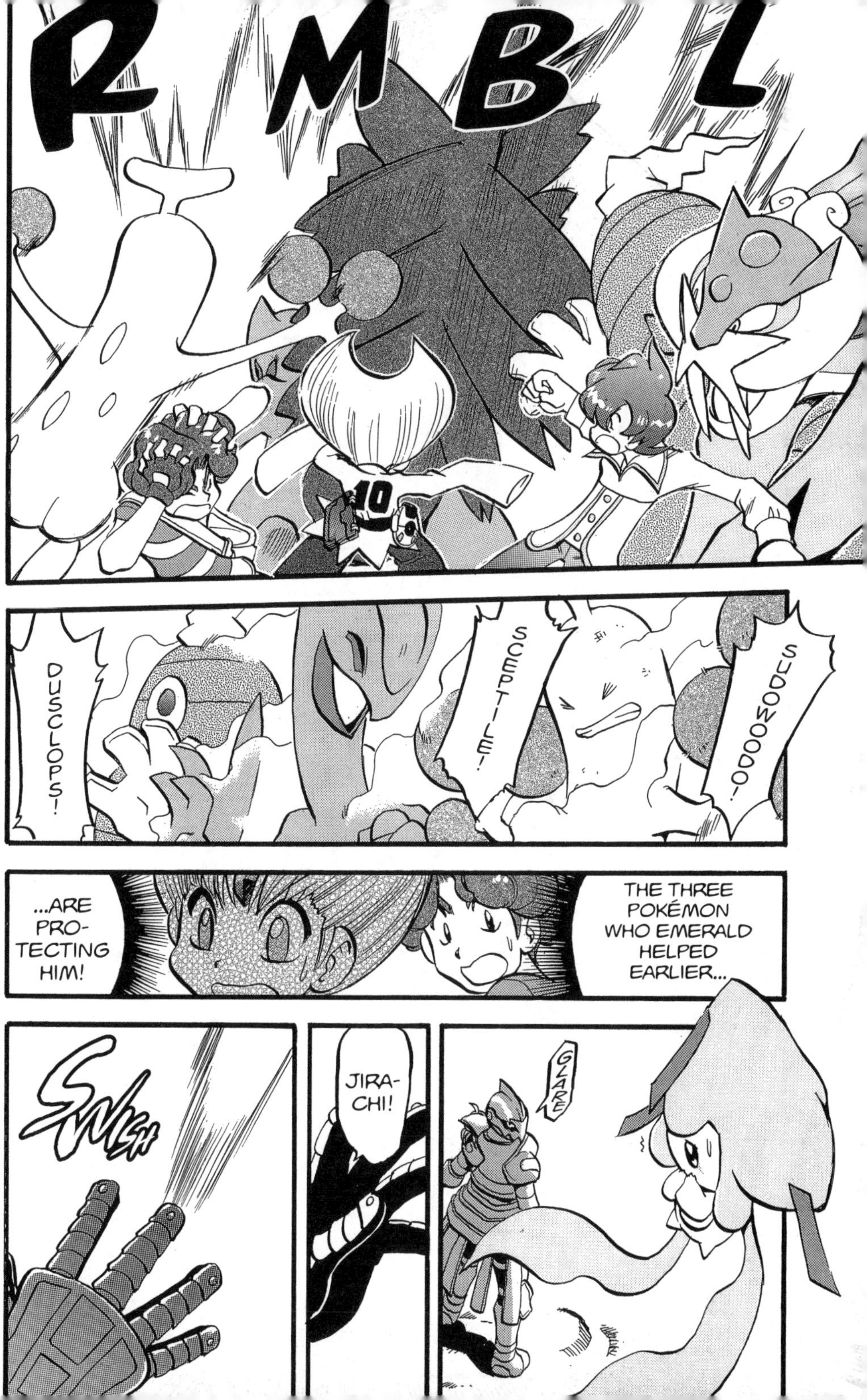
RMBL
SUDOWOODO!
SCEPTILE!
DUSCLOPS!
THE THREE POKÉMON WHO EMERALD HELPED EARLIER...
...ARE PROTECTING HIM!
GLARE
JIRA-CHI!
SWISH

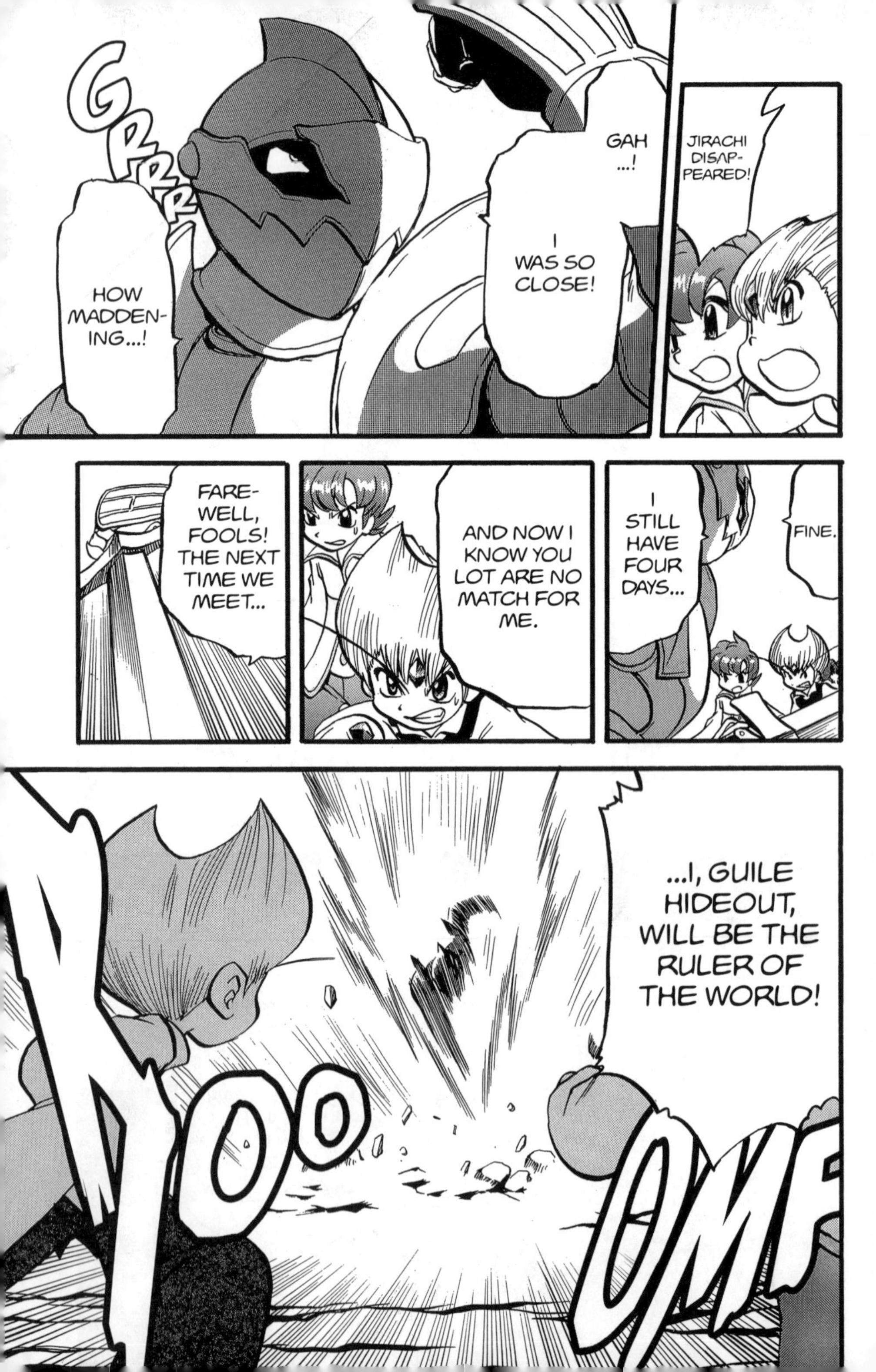
JIRACHI DISAP-PEARED!
GAH ...!
I WAS SO CLOSE!
GRRRR
HOW MADDEN-ING...!
FINE.
I STILL HAVE FOUR DAYS...
AND NOW I KNOW YOU LOT ARE NO MATCH FOR ME.
FARE-WELL, FOOLS! THE NEXT TIME WE MEET...
...I, GUILE HIDEOUT, WILL BE THE RULER OF THE WORLD!

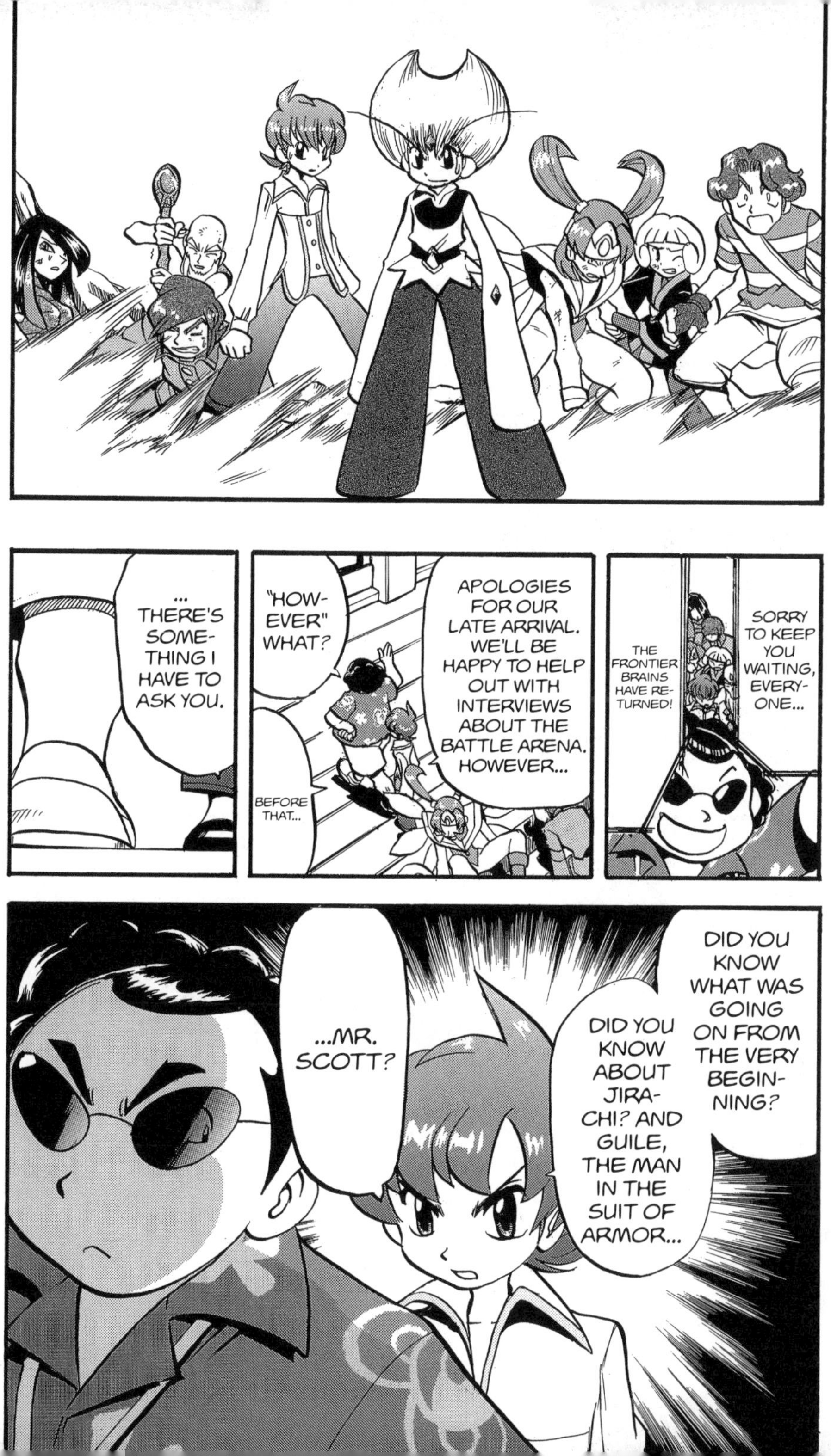
SORRY TO KEEP YOU WAITING, EVERYONE...
THE FRONTIER BRAINS HAVE RETURNED!
APOLOGIES FOR OUR LATE ARRIVAL. WE'LL BE HAPPY TO HELP OUT WITH INTERVIEWS ABOUT THE BATTLE ARENA. HOWEVER...
"HOWEVER" WHAT?
BEFORE THAT...
...THERE'S SOMETHING I HAVE TO ASK YOU.
DID YOU KNOW WHAT WAS GOING ON FROM THE VERY BEGINNING?
DID YOU KNOW ABOUT JIRACHI? AND GUILE, THE MAN IN THE SUIT OF ARMOR...
...MR. SCOTT?

DEAR MEMBERS OF THE PRESS...

Thank you for visiting the Battle Frontier today. Permit me to continue explaining the rules of this facility...

OWNER: SCOTT

FACILITY RULES

BATTLE DOME

Battle-type	Number of Pokémon	Type of Symbol	Wins needed to attain the Symbol
• Single • Double	3 Pokémon	Tactics	Championships × 10 Rounds = 40 Consecutive Wins

At the Battle Dome, the challenger participates in a tournament between 16 Trainers. The Trainers must choose two of three Pokémon. Before the battle, the challenger receives an opportunity to view their opponent's data using a Battle Card with the following information...

① The Trainer's Pokémon
② The Trainer's rank amongst the tournament participants
③ The type of battle style the Trainer excels in
④ The emphasized status of the Pokémon

One must win four battles in a row in each round from the first to the last round to become the champion.

Dome Ace Tucker

Tactics Symbol

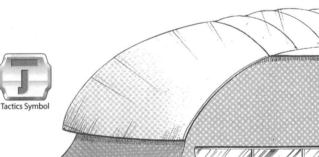

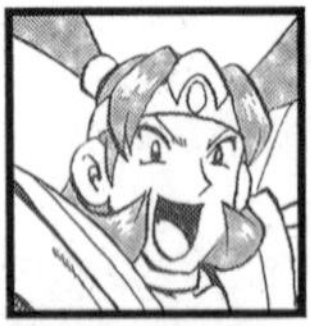

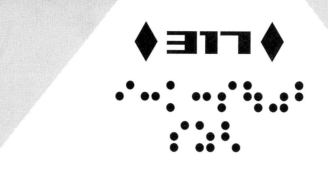

Sneaky like Shedinja

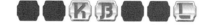

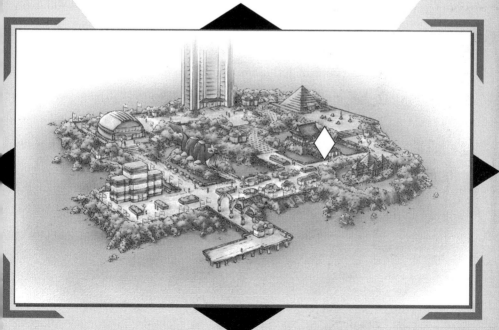

POKÉMON ADVENTURES·THE SIXTH CHAPTER·EMERALD

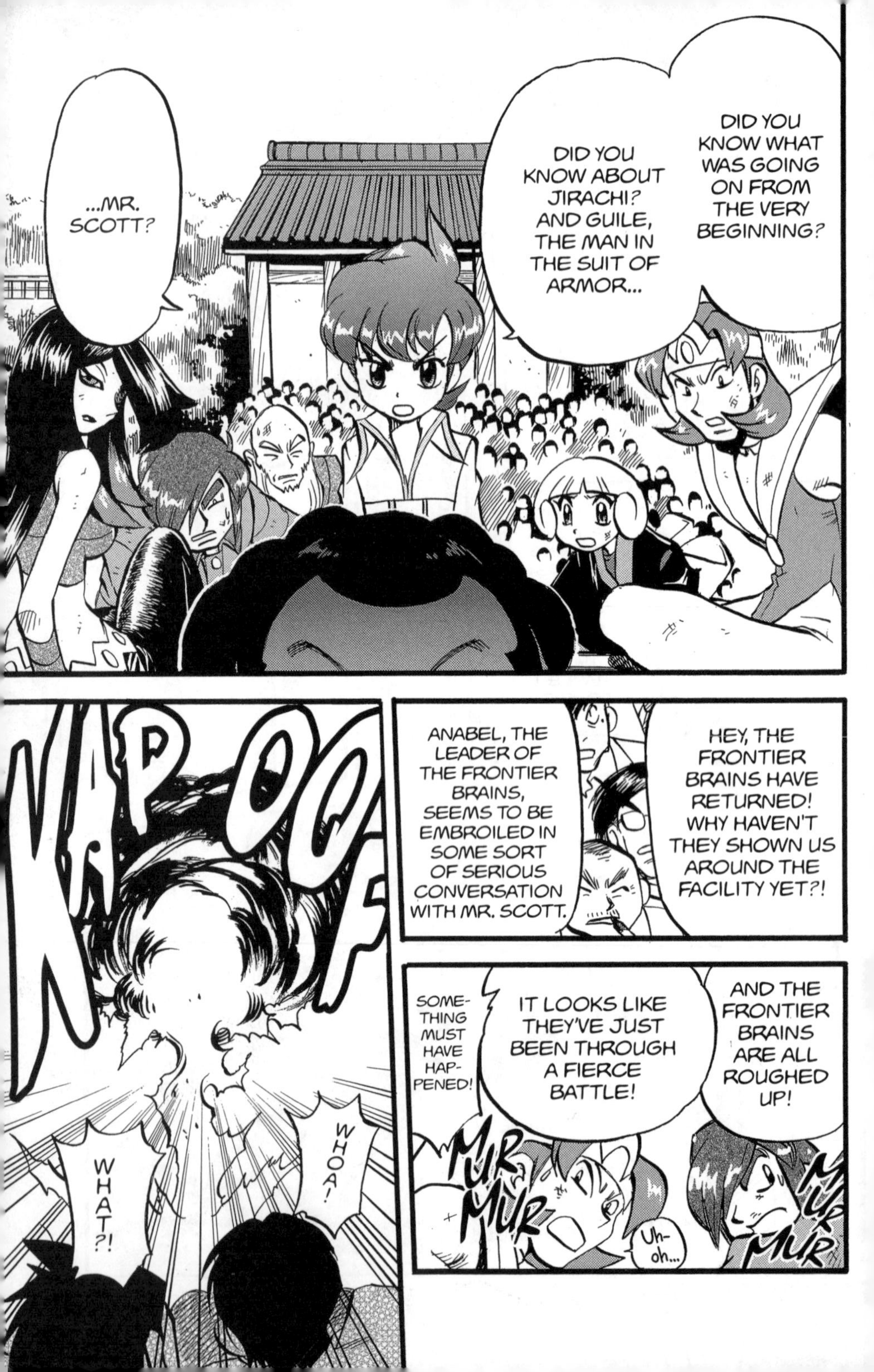
DID YOU KNOW WHAT WAS GOING ON FROM THE VERY BEGINNING?
DID YOU KNOW ABOUT JIRACHI? AND GUILE, THE MAN IN THE SUIT OF ARMOR...
...MR. SCOTT?
HEY, THE FRONTIER BRAINS HAVE RETURNED! WHY HAVEN'T THEY SHOWN US AROUND THE FACILITY YET?!
ANABEL, THE LEADER OF THE FRONTIER BRAINS, SEEMS TO BE EMBROILED IN SOME SORT OF SERIOUS CONVERSATION WITH MR. SCOTT.
AND THE FRONTIER BRAINS ARE ALL ROUGHED UP!
IT LOOKS LIKE THEY'VE JUST BEEN THROUGH A FIERCE BATTLE!
SOME-THING MUST HAVE HAP-PENED!
MUR MUR
Uh-oh...
MUR MUR
KAPOOF
WHOA!
WHAT?!

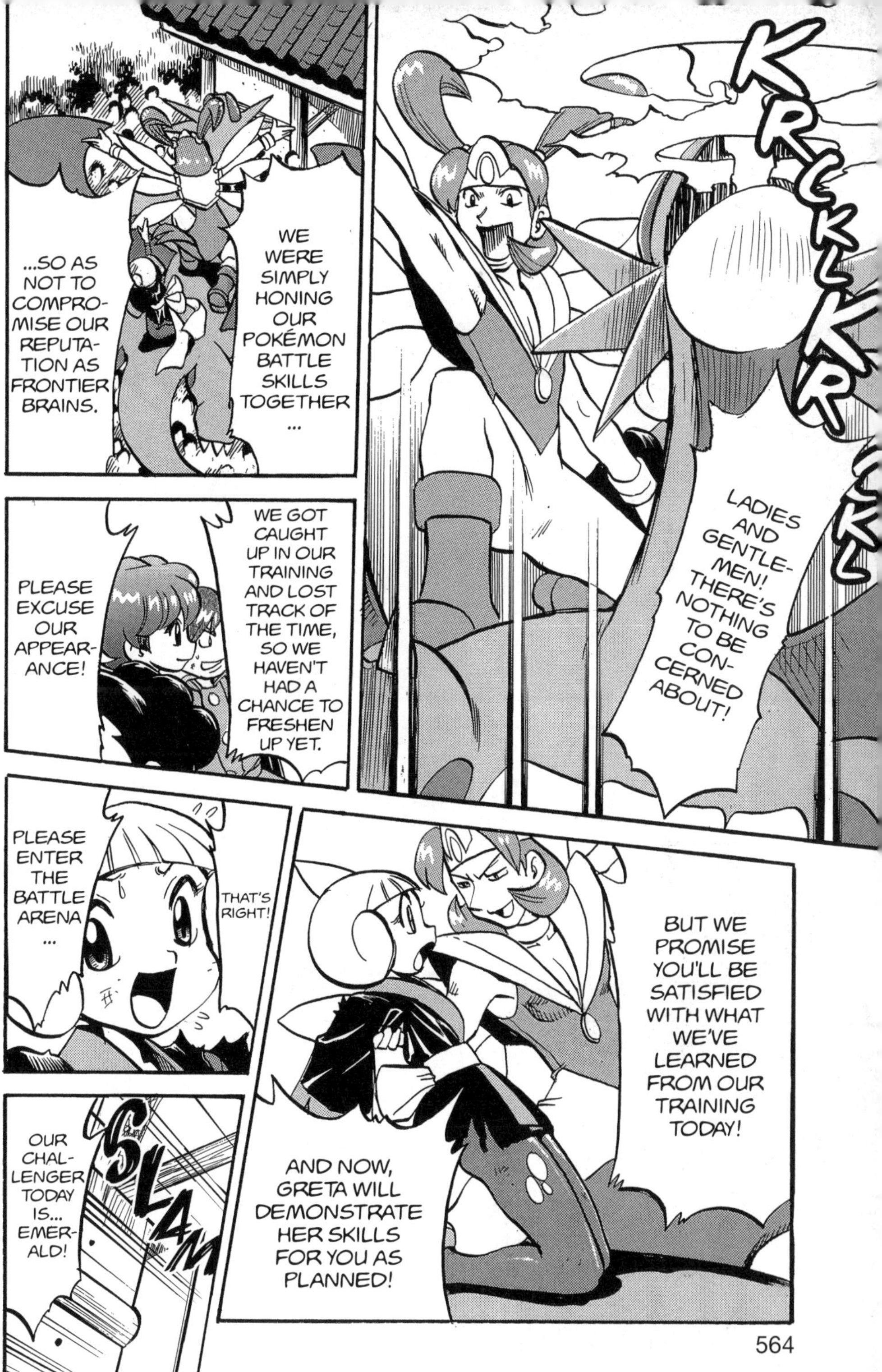
KRKLKRKL
LADIES AND GENTLEMEN! THERE'S NOTHING TO BE CONCERNED ABOUT!
WE WERE SIMPLY HONING OUR POKÉMON BATTLE SKILLS TOGETHER...
...SO AS NOT TO COMPROMISE OUR REPUTATION AS FRONTIER BRAINS.
WE GOT CAUGHT UP IN OUR TRAINING AND LOST TRACK OF THE TIME, SO WE HAVEN'T HAD A CHANCE TO FRESHEN UP YET.
PLEASE EXCUSE OUR APPEARANCE!
BUT WE PROMISE YOU'LL BE SATISFIED WITH WHAT WE'VE LEARNED FROM OUR TRAINING TODAY!
AND NOW, GRETA WILL DEMONSTRATE HER SKILLS FOR YOU AS PLANNED!
THAT'S RIGHT!
PLEASE ENTER THE BATTLE ARENA...
SLAM
OUR CHALLENGER TODAY IS... EMERALD!

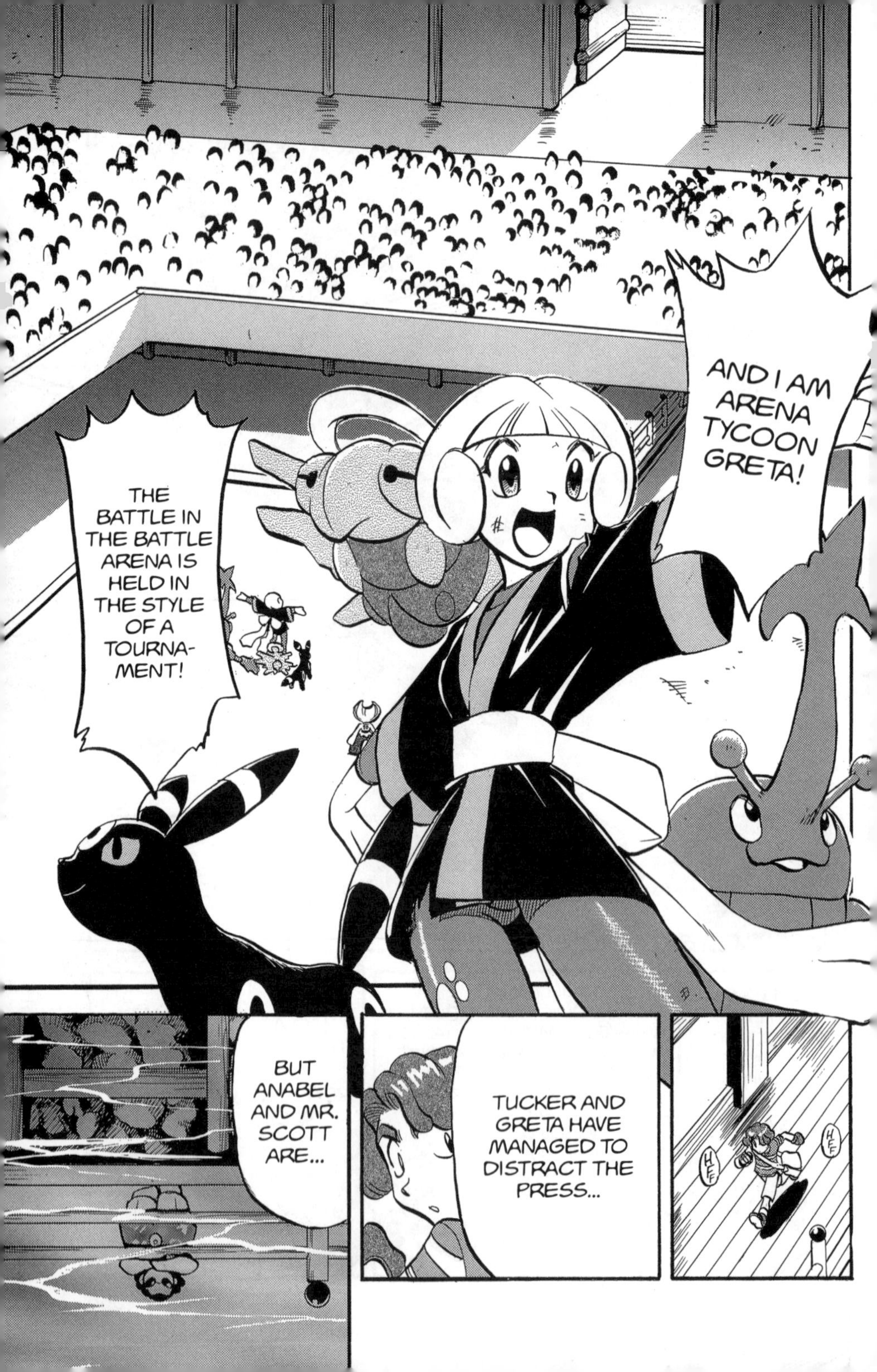
AND I AM ARENA TYCOON GRETA!
THE BATTLE IN THE BATTLE ARENA IS HELD IN THE STYLE OF A TOURNA-MENT!
HFF
HFF
TUCKER AND GRETA HAVE MANAGED TO DISTRACT THE PRESS...
BUT ANABEL AND MR. SCOTT ARE...

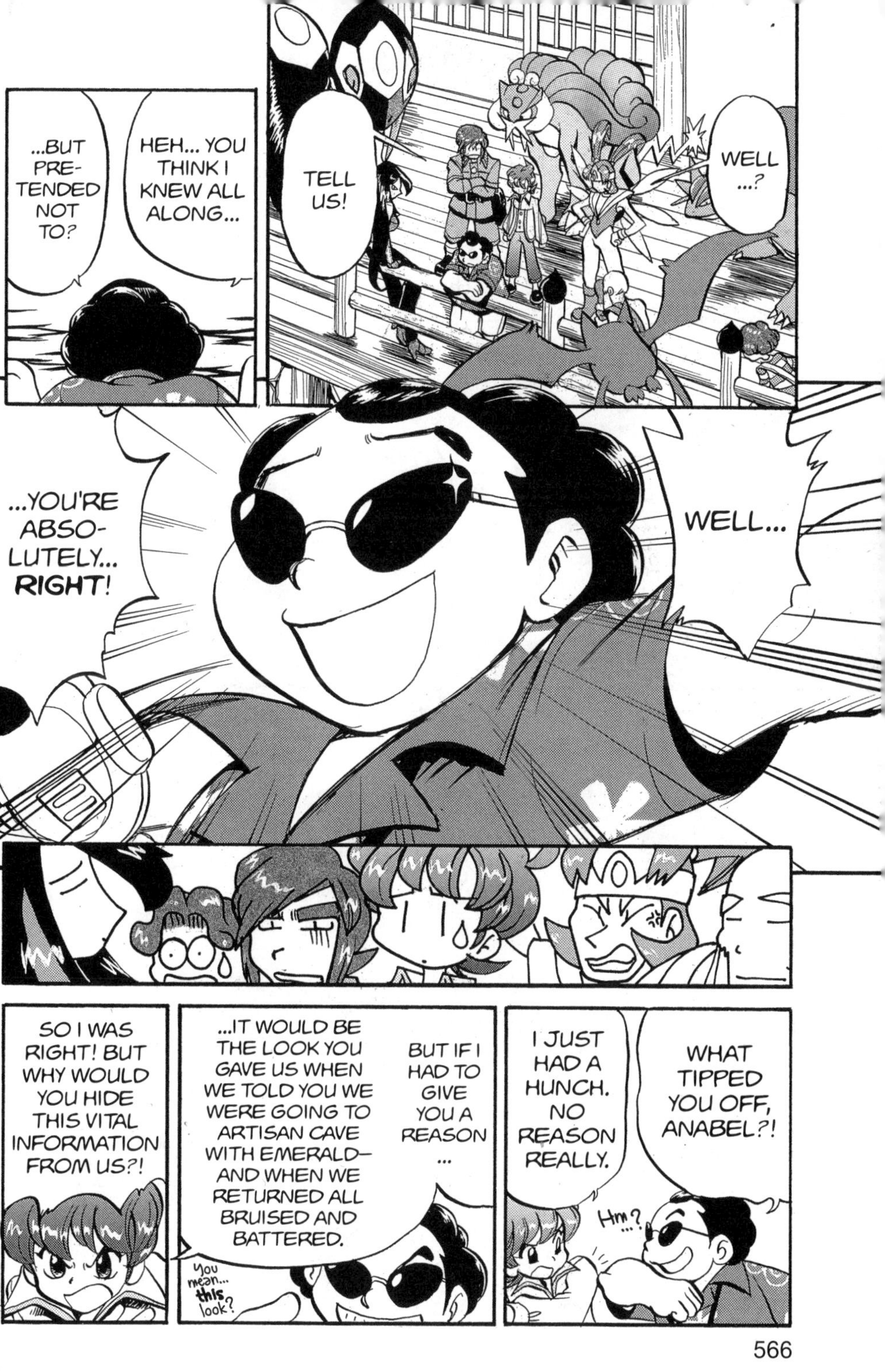
WELL ...?
TELL US!
HEH... YOU THINK I KNEW ALL ALONG...
...BUT PRE-TENDED NOT TO?
WELL...
...YOU'RE ABSO-LUTELY... **RIGHT**!
WHAT TIPPED YOU OFF, ANABEL?!
I JUST HAD A HUNCH. NO REASON REALLY.
Hm? ...
BUT IF I HAD TO GIVE YOU A REASON ...
...IT WOULD BE THE LOOK YOU GAVE US WHEN WE TOLD YOU WE WERE GOING TO ARTISAN CAVE WITH EMERALD—AND WHEN WE RETURNED ALL BRUISED AND BATTERED.
You mean... **this** look?
SO I WAS RIGHT! BUT WHY WOULD YOU HIDE THIS VITAL INFORMATION FROM US?!

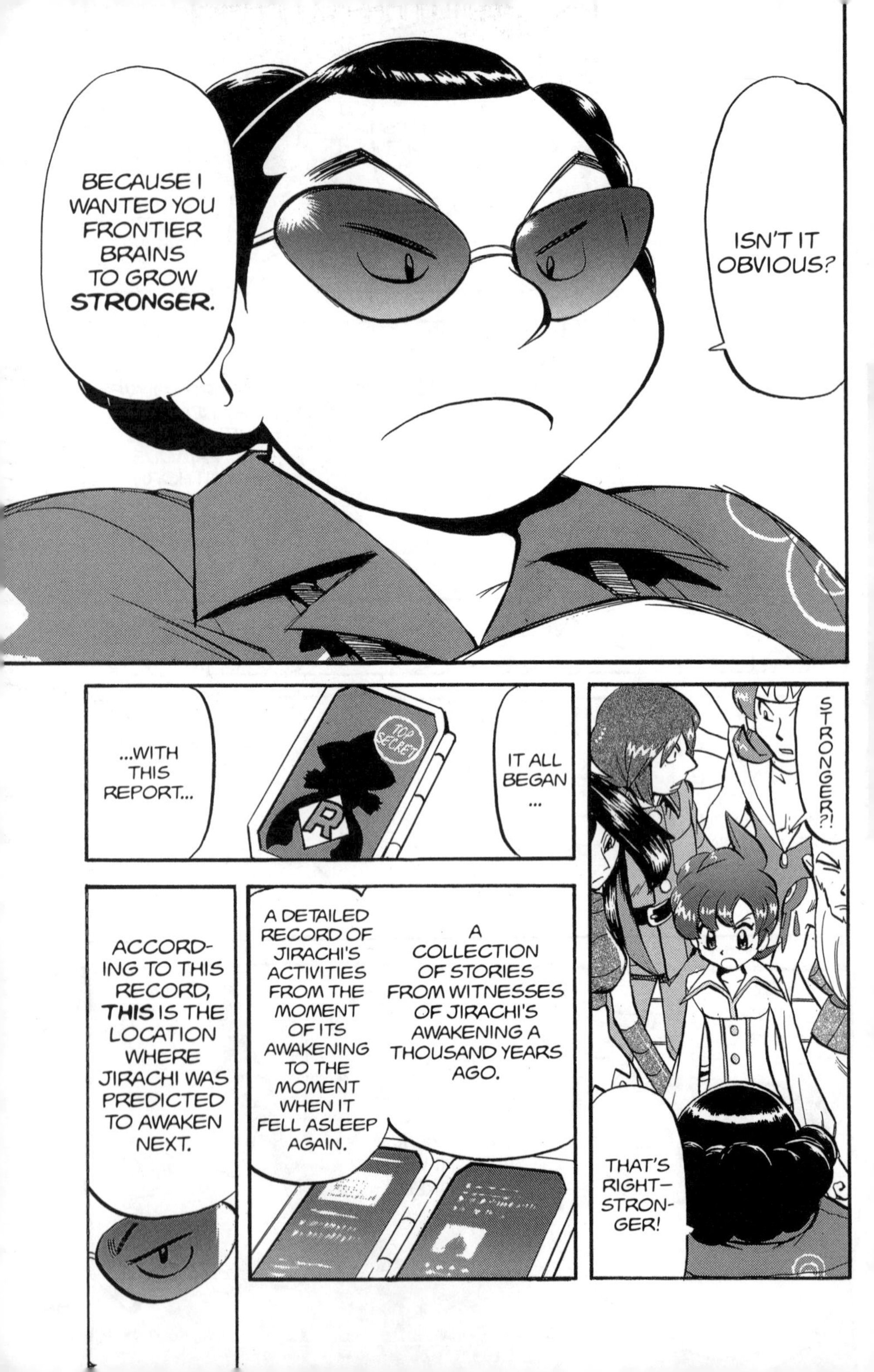
ISN'T IT OBVIOUS?
BECAUSE I WANTED YOU FRONTIER BRAINS TO GROW **STRONGER.**
STRONGER?!
THAT'S RIGHT—STRONGER!
IT ALL BEGAN...
...WITH THIS REPORT...
TOP SECRET
A COLLECTION OF STORIES FROM WITNESSES OF JIRACHI'S AWAKENING A THOUSAND YEARS AGO.
A DETAILED RECORD OF JIRACHI'S ACTIVITIES FROM THE MOMENT OF ITS AWAKENING TO THE MOMENT WHEN IT FELL ASLEEP AGAIN.
ACCORDING TO THIS RECORD, **THIS** IS THE LOCATION WHERE JIRACHI WAS PREDICTED TO AWAKEN NEXT.

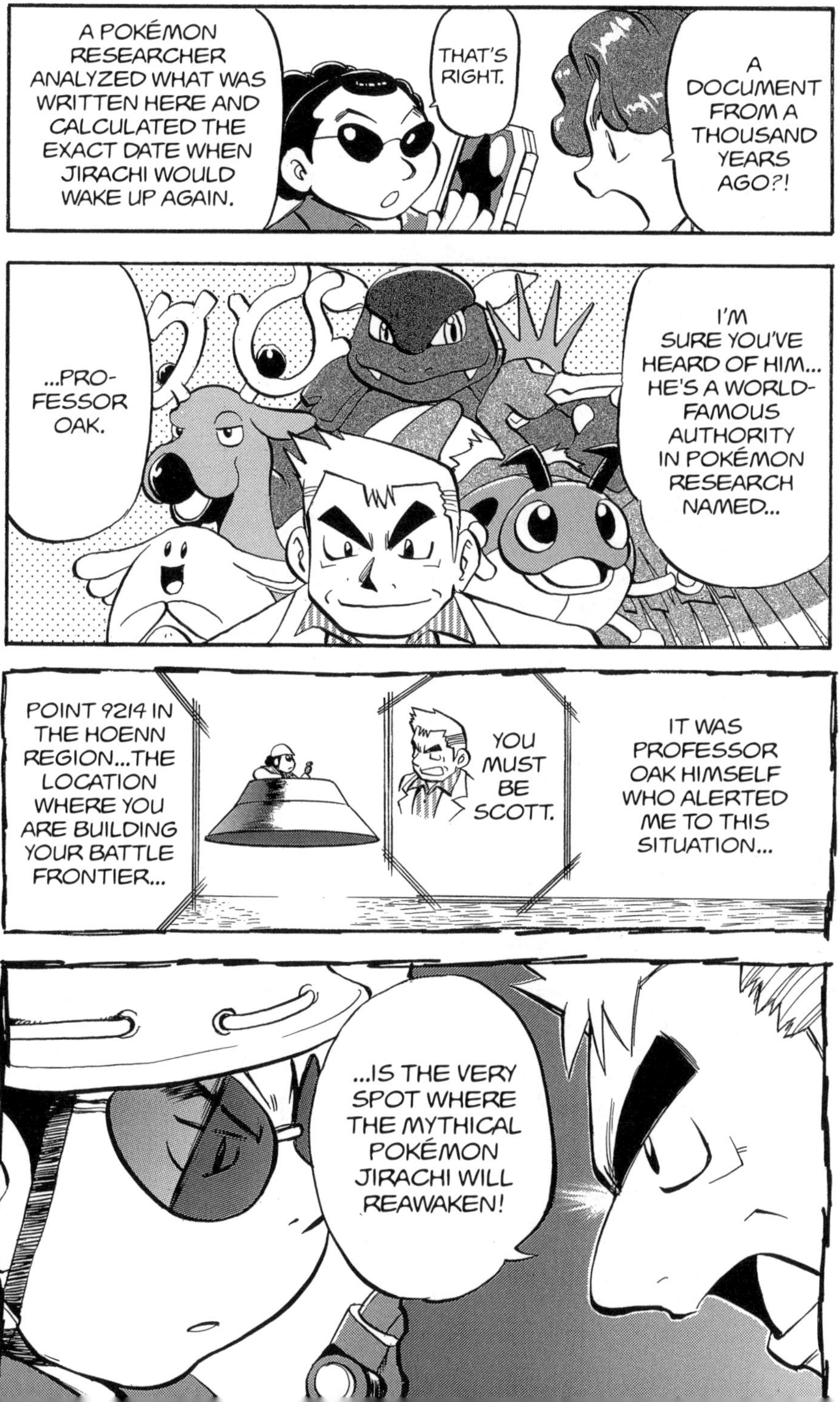
A DOCUMENT FROM A THOUSAND YEARS AGO?!
THAT'S RIGHT.
A POKÉMON RESEARCHER ANALYZED WHAT WAS WRITTEN HERE AND CALCULATED THE EXACT DATE WHEN JIRACHI WOULD WAKE UP AGAIN.
I'M SURE YOU'VE HEARD OF HIM... HE'S A WORLD-FAMOUS AUTHORITY IN POKÉMON RESEARCH NAMED...
...PRO-FESSOR OAK.
IT WAS PROFESSOR OAK HIMSELF WHO ALERTED ME TO THIS SITUATION...
YOU MUST BE SCOTT.
POINT 9214 IN THE HOENN REGION...THE LOCATION WHERE YOU ARE BUILDING YOUR BATTLE FRONTIER...
...IS THE VERY SPOT WHERE THE MYTHICAL POKÉMON JIRACHI WILL REAWAKEN!

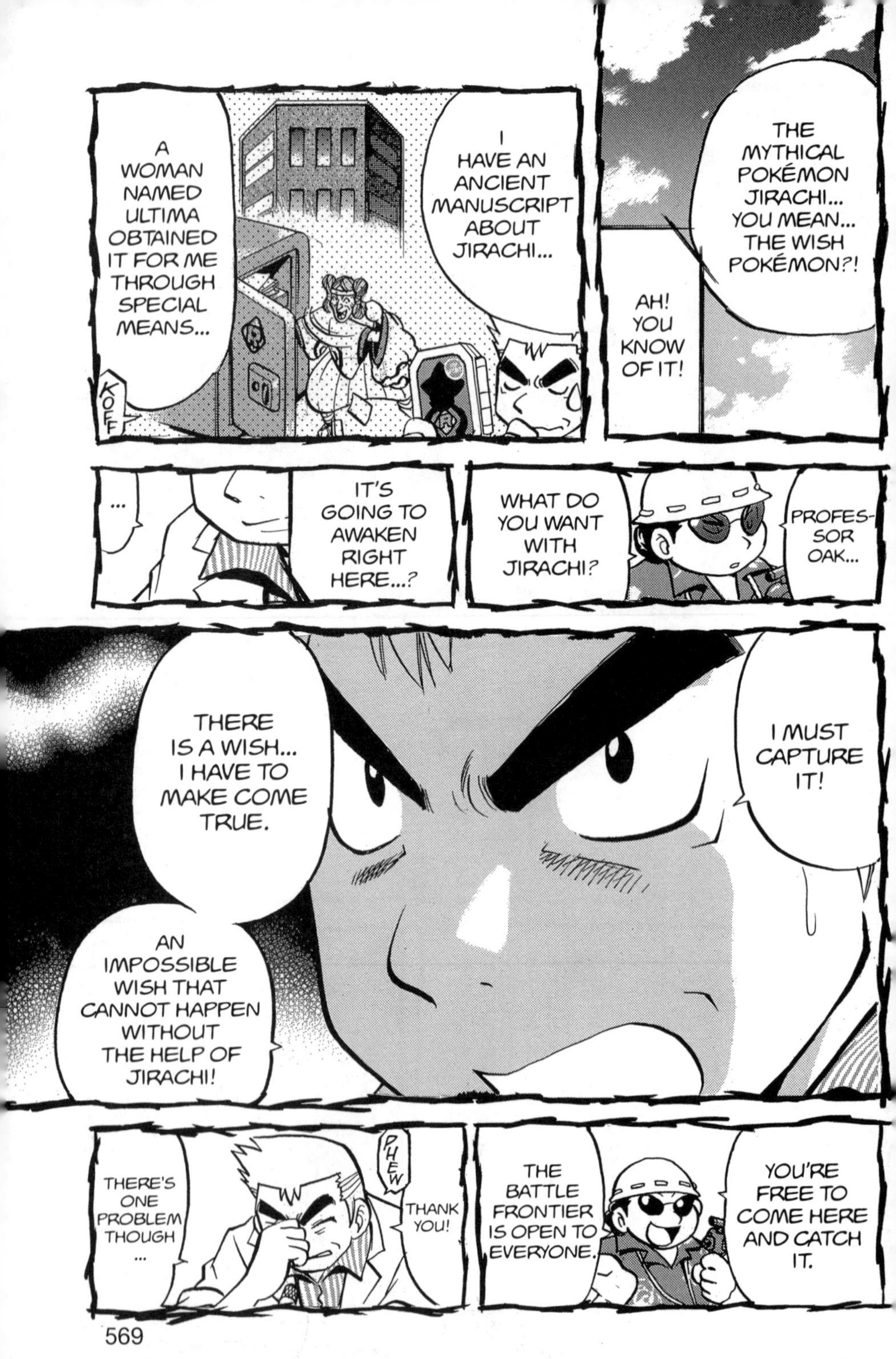
THE MYTHICAL POKÉMON JIRACHI... YOU MEAN... THE WISH POKÉMON?!
AH! YOU KNOW OF IT!
I HAVE AN ANCIENT MANUSCRIPT ABOUT JIRACHI...
A WOMAN NAMED ULTIMA OBTAINED IT FOR ME THROUGH SPECIAL MEANS...
KOFF
PROFES-SOR OAK...
WHAT DO YOU WANT WITH JIRACHI?
IT'S GOING TO AWAKEN RIGHT HERE...?
...
I MUST CAPTURE IT!
THERE IS A WISH... I HAVE TO MAKE COME TRUE.
AN IMPOSSIBLE WISH THAT CANNOT HAPPEN WITHOUT THE HELP OF JIRACHI!
YOU'RE FREE TO COME HERE AND CATCH IT.
THE BATTLE FRONTIER IS OPEN TO EVERYONE.
THANK YOU!
PHEW
THERE'S ONE PROBLEM THOUGH ...

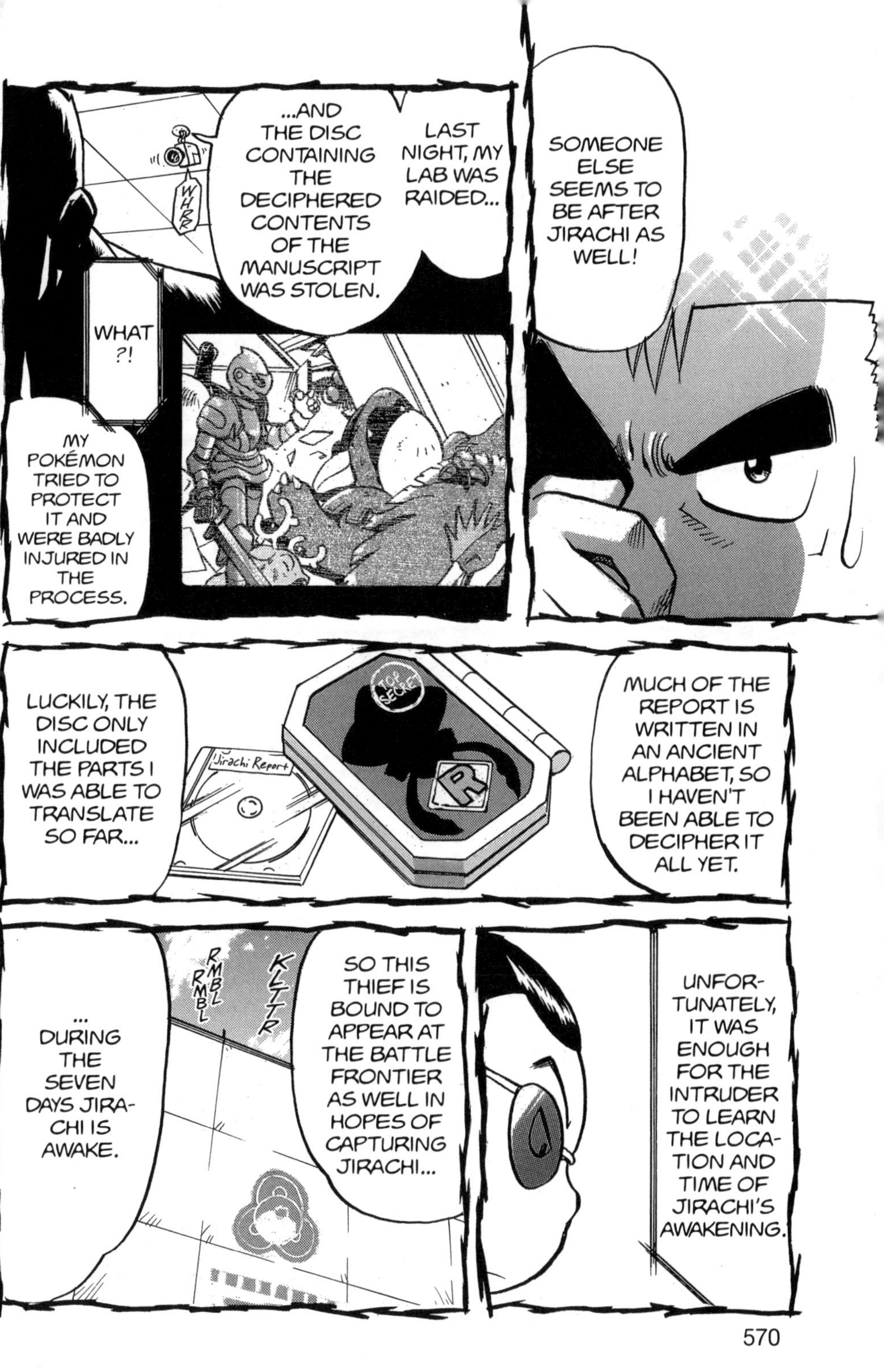
SOMEONE ELSE SEEMS TO BE AFTER JIRACHI AS WELL!
LAST NIGHT, MY LAB WAS RAIDED...
...AND THE DISC CONTAINING THE DECIPHERED CONTENTS OF THE MANUSCRIPT WAS STOLEN.
WHRR
WHAT?!
MY POKÉMON TRIED TO PROTECT IT AND WERE BADLY INJURED IN THE PROCESS.
MUCH OF THE REPORT IS WRITTEN IN AN ANCIENT ALPHABET, SO I HAVEN'T BEEN ABLE TO DECIPHER IT ALL YET.
TOP SECRET
Jirachi Report
LUCKILY, THE DISC ONLY INCLUDED THE PARTS I WAS ABLE TO TRANSLATE SO FAR...
UNFOR-TUNATELY, IT WAS ENOUGH FOR THE INTRUDER TO LEARN THE LOCA-TION AND TIME OF JIRACHI'S AWAKENING.
SO THIS THIEF IS BOUND TO APPEAR AT THE BATTLE FRONTIER AS WELL IN HOPES OF CAPTURING JIRACHI...
KLTTR
RMBL RMBL
... DURING THE SEVEN DAYS JIRA-CHI IS AWAKE.

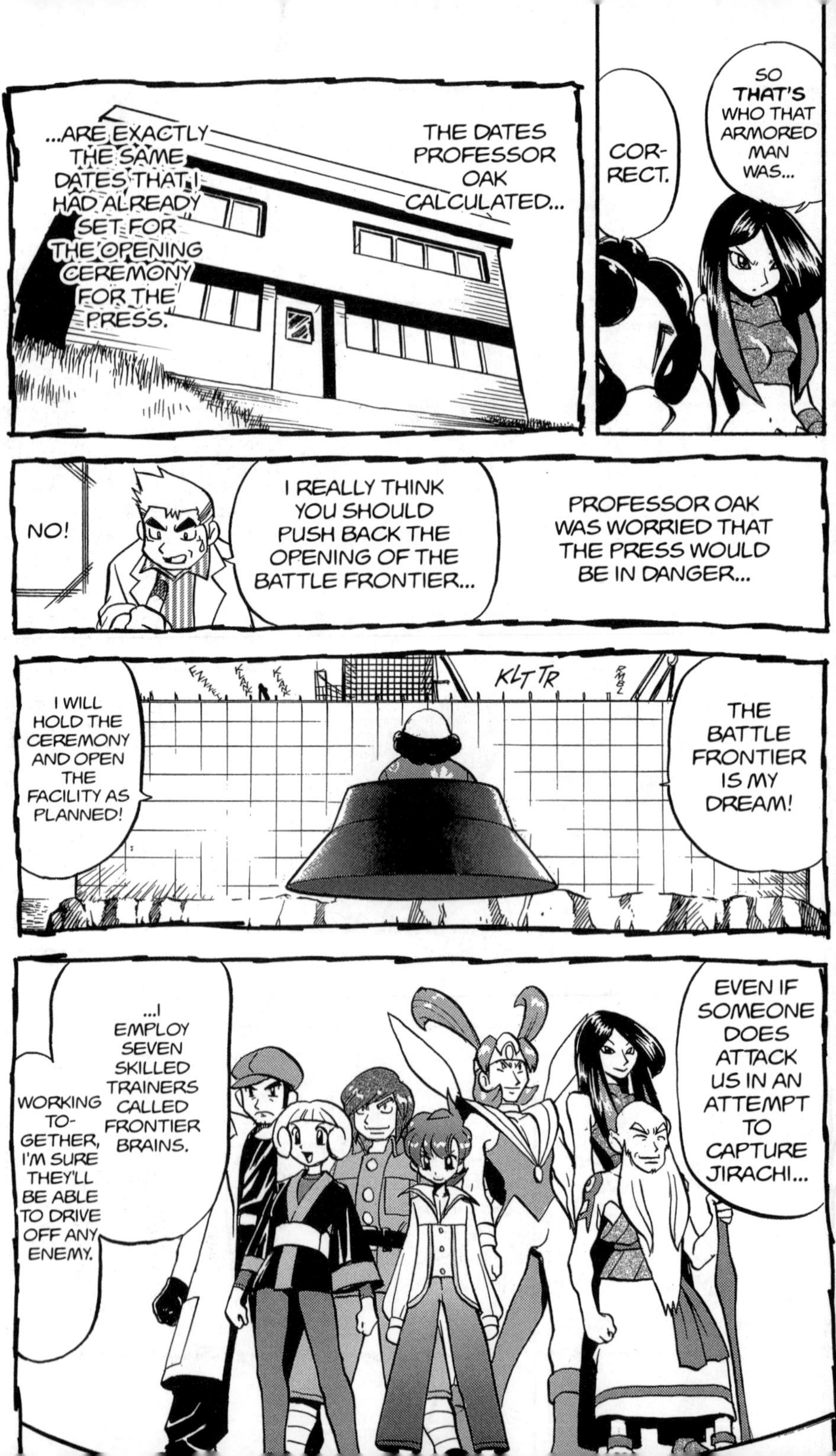
SO THAT'S WHO THAT ARMORED MAN WAS...
CORRECT.
THE DATES PROFESSOR OAK CALCULATED...
...ARE EXACTLY THE SAME DATES THAT I HAD ALREADY SET FOR THE OPENING CEREMONY FOR THE PRESS.
PROFESSOR OAK WAS WORRIED THAT THE PRESS WOULD BE IN DANGER...
I REALLY THINK YOU SHOULD PUSH BACK THE OPENING OF THE BATTLE FRONTIER...
NO!
THE BATTLE FRONTIER IS MY DREAM!
RMBL
KLTTR
I WILL HOLD THE CEREMONY AND OPEN THE FACILITY AS PLANNED!
EVEN IF SOMEONE DOES ATTACK US IN AN ATTEMPT TO CAPTURE JIRACHI...
...I EMPLOY SEVEN SKILLED TRAINERS CALLED FRONTIER BRAINS.
WORKING TOGETHER, I'M SURE THEY'LL BE ABLE TO DRIVE OFF ANY ENEMY.

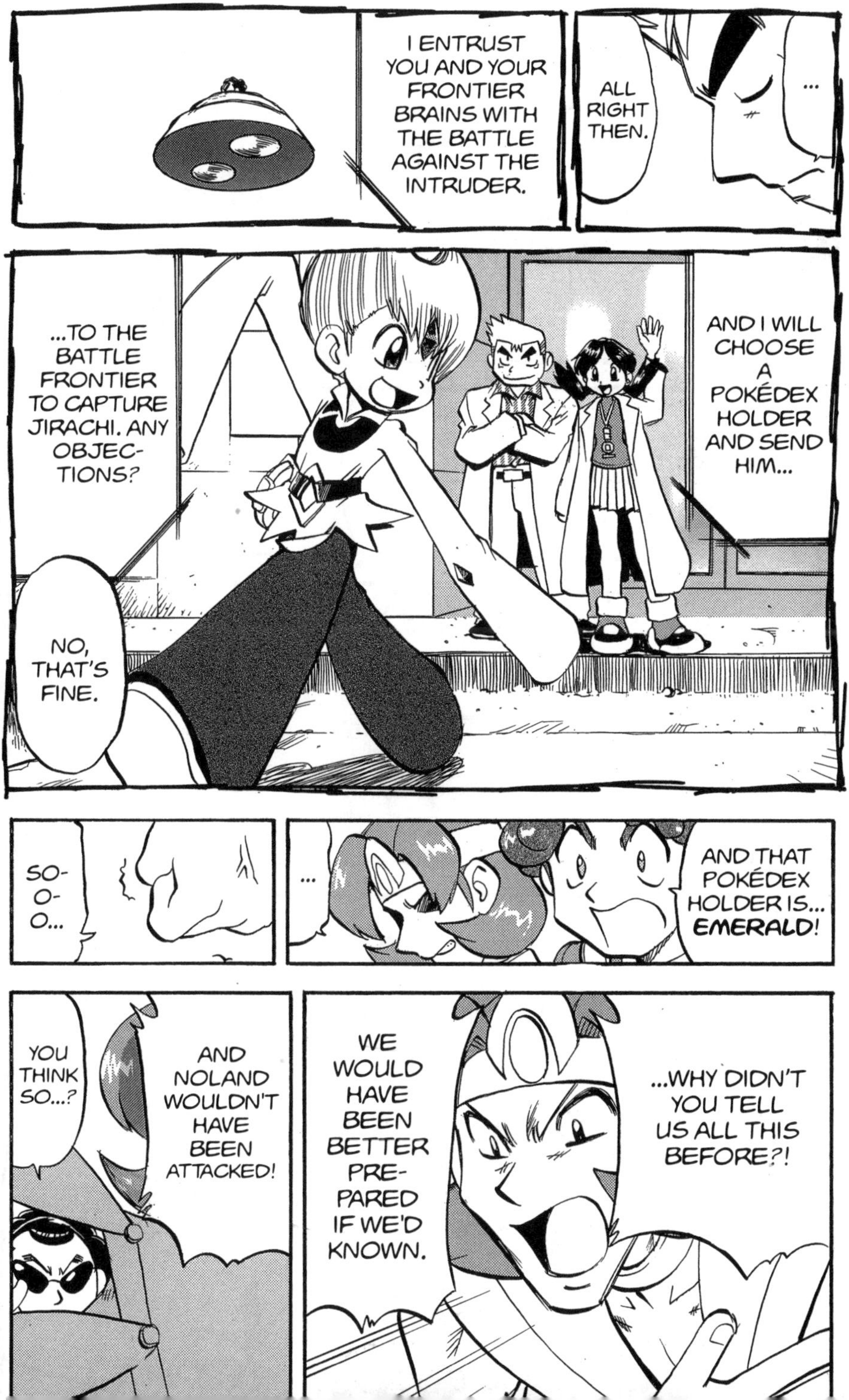
...
ALL RIGHT THEN.
I ENTRUST YOU AND YOUR FRONTIER BRAINS WITH THE BATTLE AGAINST THE INTRUDER.
AND I WILL CHOOSE A POKÉDEX HOLDER AND SEND HIM...
...TO THE BATTLE FRONTIER TO CAPTURE JIRACHI. ANY OBJEC-TIONS?
NO, THAT'S FINE.
AND THAT POKÉDEX HOLDER IS... **EMERALD**!
...
SO-O-O...
...WHY DIDN'T YOU TELL US ALL THIS BEFORE?!
WE WOULD HAVE BEEN BETTER PRE-PARED IF WE'D KNOWN.
AND NOLAND WOULDN'T HAVE BEEN ATTACKED!
YOU THINK SO...?

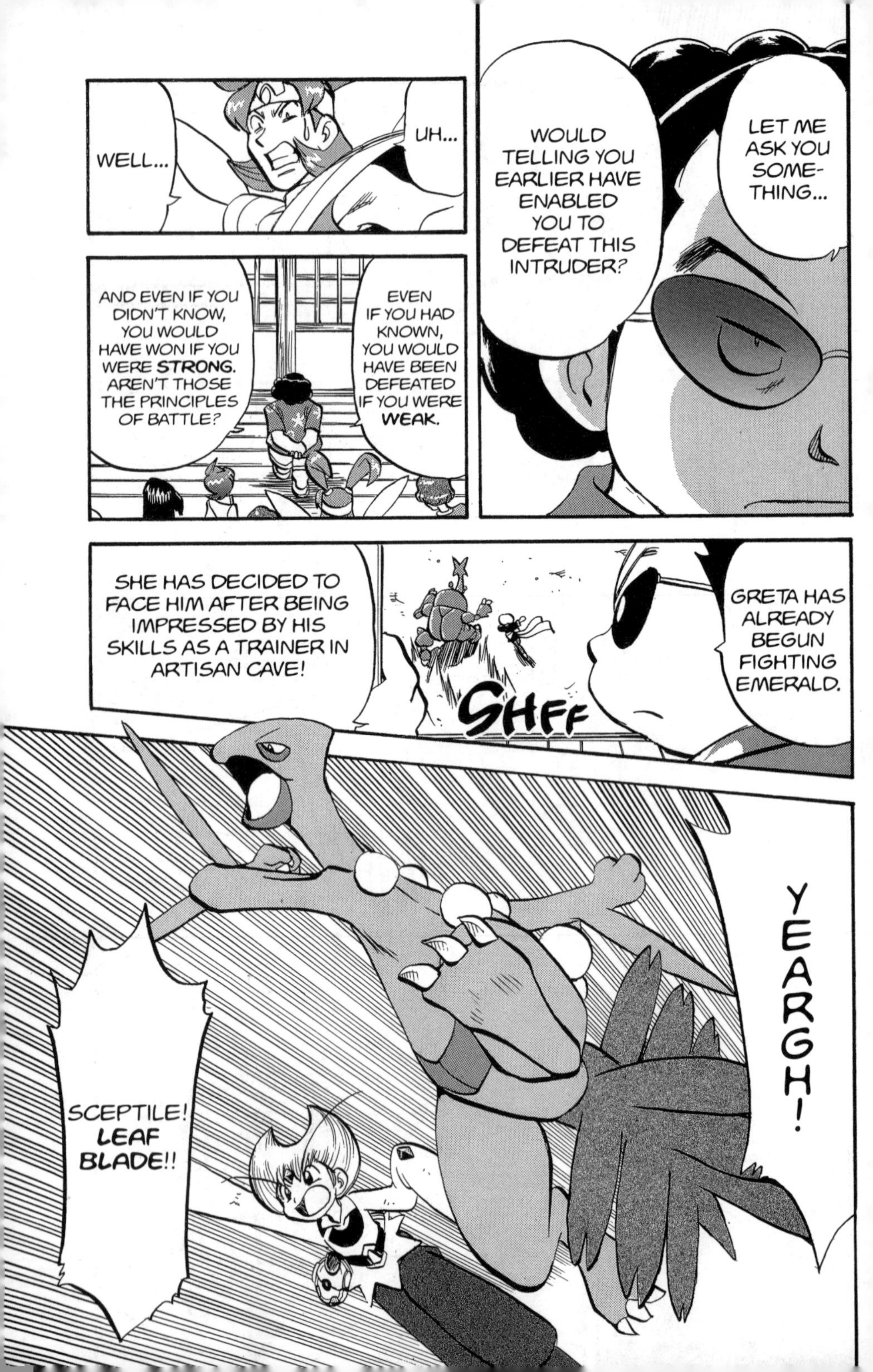
LET ME ASK YOU SOME-THING...
WOULD TELLING YOU EARLIER HAVE ENABLED YOU TO DEFEAT THIS INTRUDER?
UH...
WELL...
EVEN IF YOU HAD KNOWN, YOU WOULD HAVE BEEN DEFEATED IF YOU WERE WEAK.
AND EVEN IF YOU DIDN'T KNOW, YOU WOULD HAVE WON IF YOU WERE STRONG. AREN'T THOSE THE PRINCIPLES OF BATTLE?
GRETA HAS ALREADY BEGUN FIGHTING EMERALD.
SHFF
SHE HAS DECIDED TO FACE HIM AFTER BEING IMPRESSED BY HIS SKILLS AS A TRAINER IN ARTISAN CAVE!
YEARGH!
SCEPTILE! LEAF BLADE!!

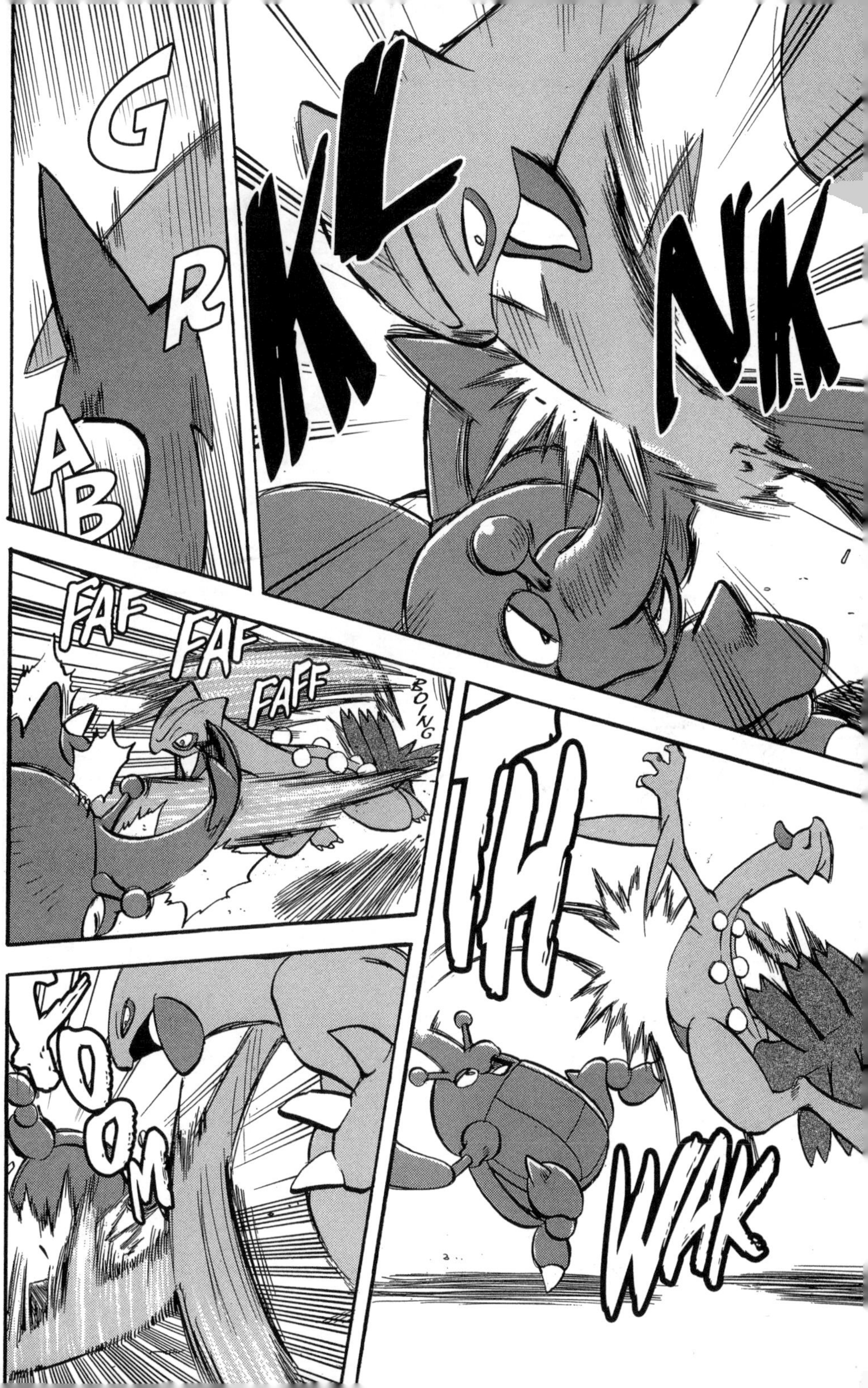
KL ANK
GRAB
WAK
FAF FAF FAFF
BOING

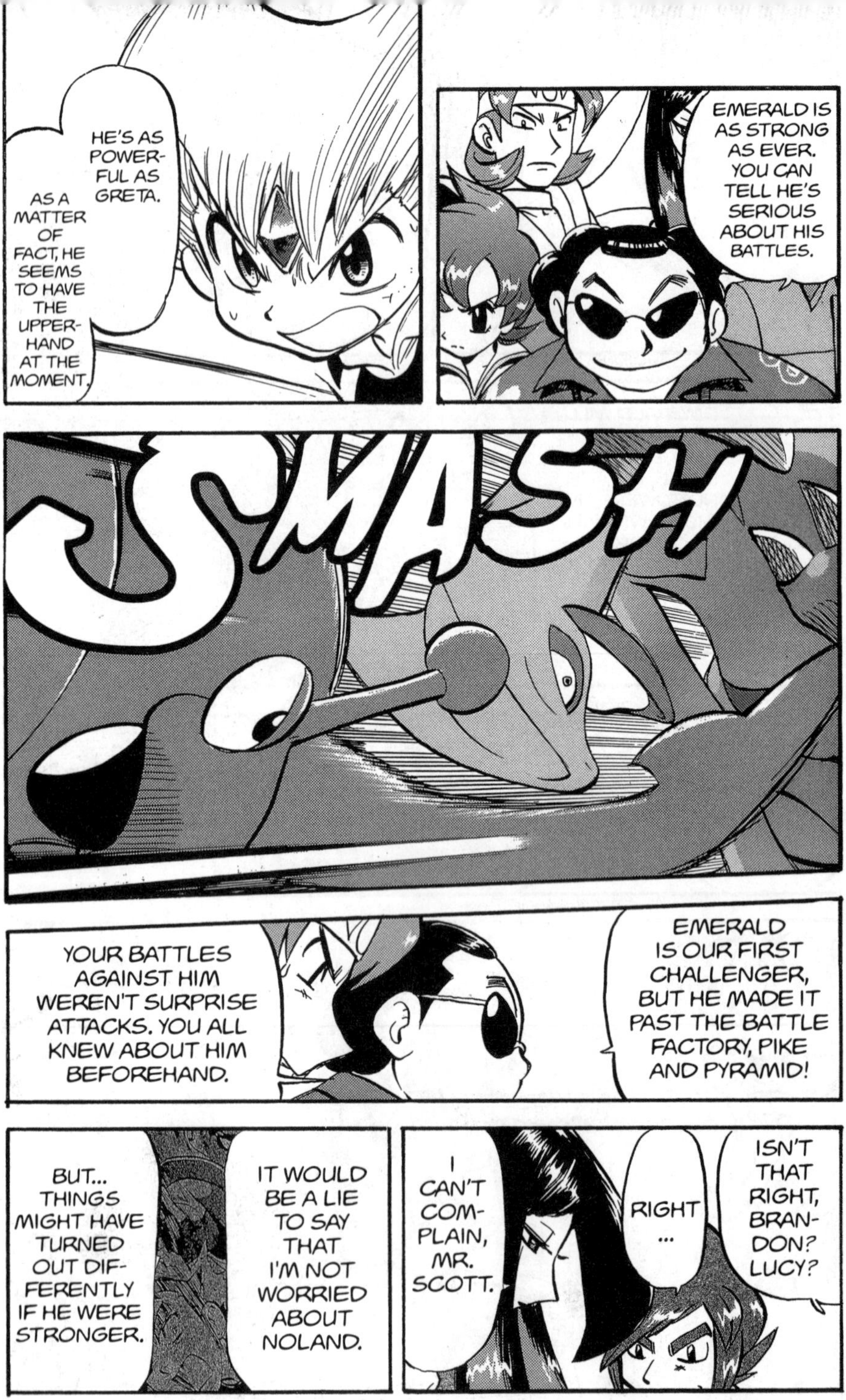
EMERALD IS AS STRONG AS EVER. YOU CAN TELL HE'S SERIOUS ABOUT HIS BATTLES.
HE'S AS POWERFUL AS GRETA.
AS A MATTER OF FACT, HE SEEMS TO HAVE THE UPPERHAND AT THE MOMENT.
SMASH
EMERALD IS OUR FIRST CHALLENGER, BUT HE MADE IT PAST THE BATTLE FACTORY, PIKE AND PYRAMID!
YOUR BATTLES AGAINST HIM WEREN'T SURPRISE ATTACKS. YOU ALL KNEW ABOUT HIM BEFOREHAND.
ISN'T THAT RIGHT, BRANDON? LUCY?
RIGHT...
I CAN'T COMPLAIN, MR. SCOTT.
IT WOULD BE A LIE TO SAY THAT I'M NOT WORRIED ABOUT NOLAND.
BUT... THINGS MIGHT HAVE TURNED OUT DIFFERENTLY IF HE WERE STRONGER.

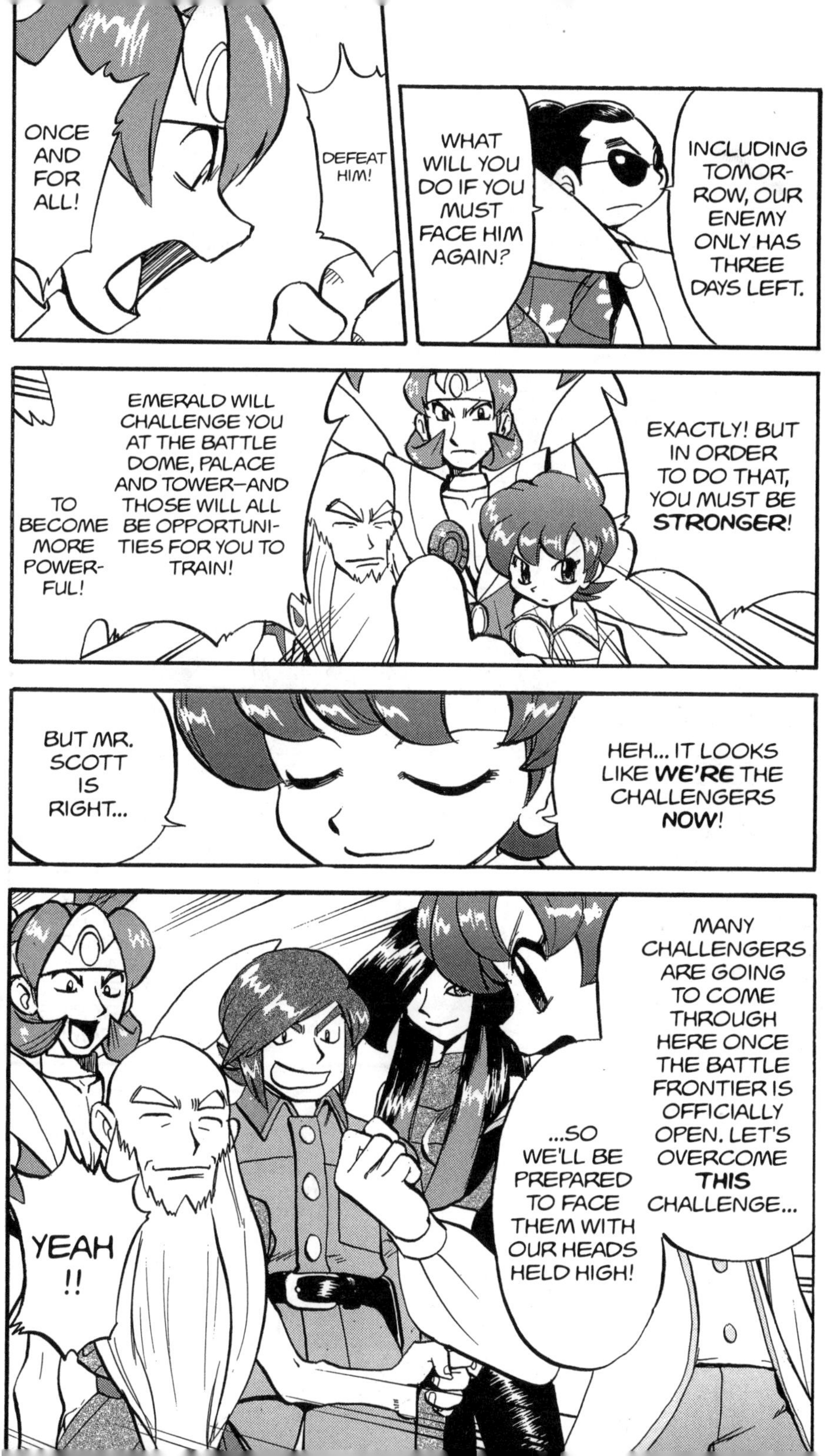
INCLUDING TOMORROW, OUR ENEMY ONLY HAS THREE DAYS LEFT.
WHAT WILL YOU DO IF YOU MUST FACE HIM AGAIN?
DEFEAT HIM!
ONCE AND FOR ALL!
EXACTLY! BUT IN ORDER TO DO THAT, YOU MUST BE **STRONGER**!
EMERALD WILL CHALLENGE YOU AT THE BATTLE DOME, PALACE AND TOWER—AND THOSE WILL ALL BE OPPORTUNITIES FOR YOU TO TRAIN!
TO BECOME MORE POWERFUL!
HEH... IT LOOKS LIKE **WE'RE** THE CHALLENGERS **NOW**!
BUT MR. SCOTT IS RIGHT...
MANY CHALLENGERS ARE GOING TO COME THROUGH HERE ONCE THE BATTLE FRONTIER IS OFFICIALLY OPEN. LET'S OVERCOME **THIS** CHALLENGE...
...SO WE'LL BE PREPARED TO FACE THEM WITH OUR HEADS HELD HIGH!
YEAH!!

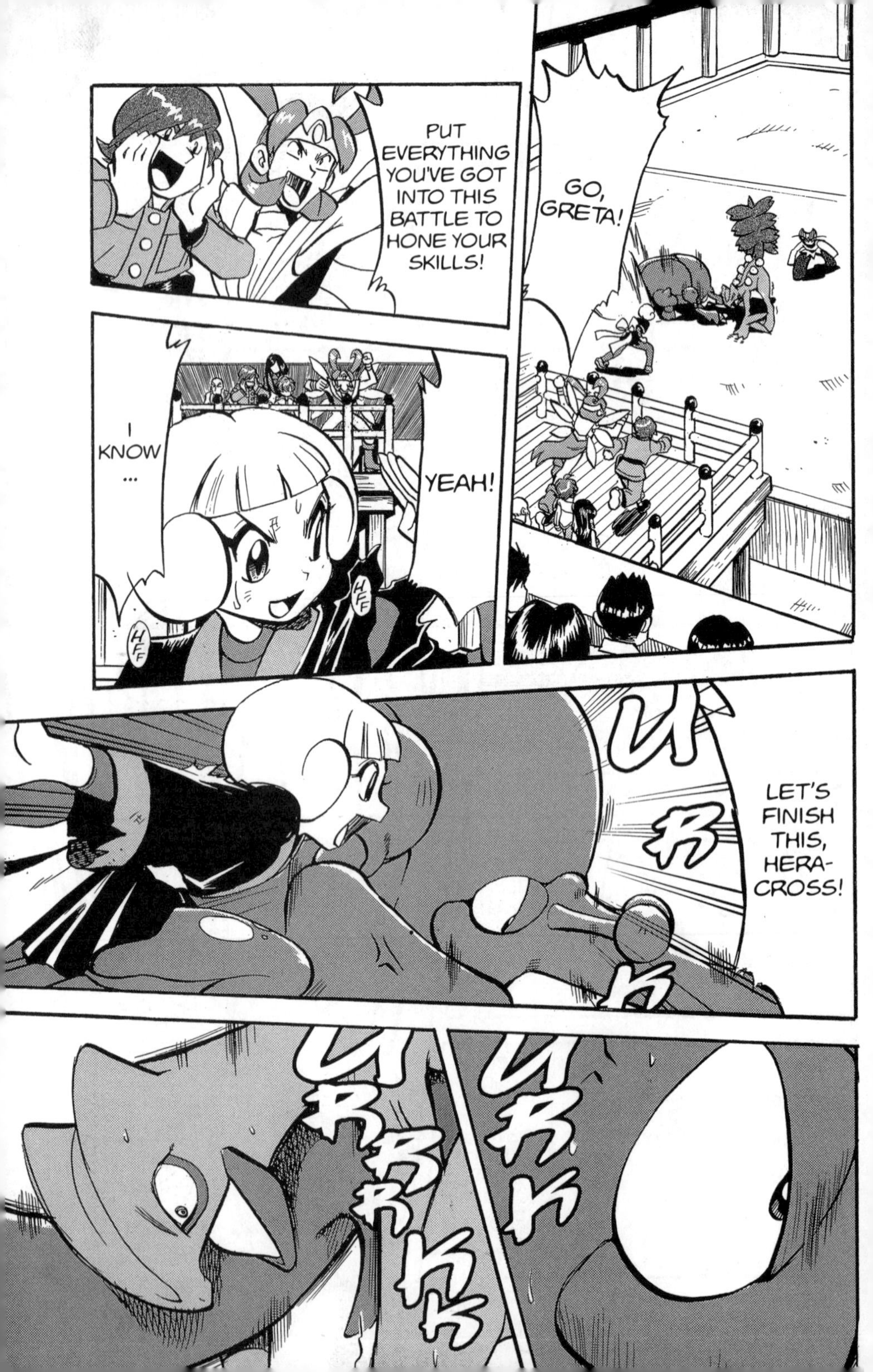

GO, GRETA!
PUT EVERYTHING YOU'VE GOT INTO THIS BATTLE TO HONE YOUR SKILLS!
YEAH!
HFF
I KNOW...
HFF
LET'S FINISH THIS, HERA-CROSS!

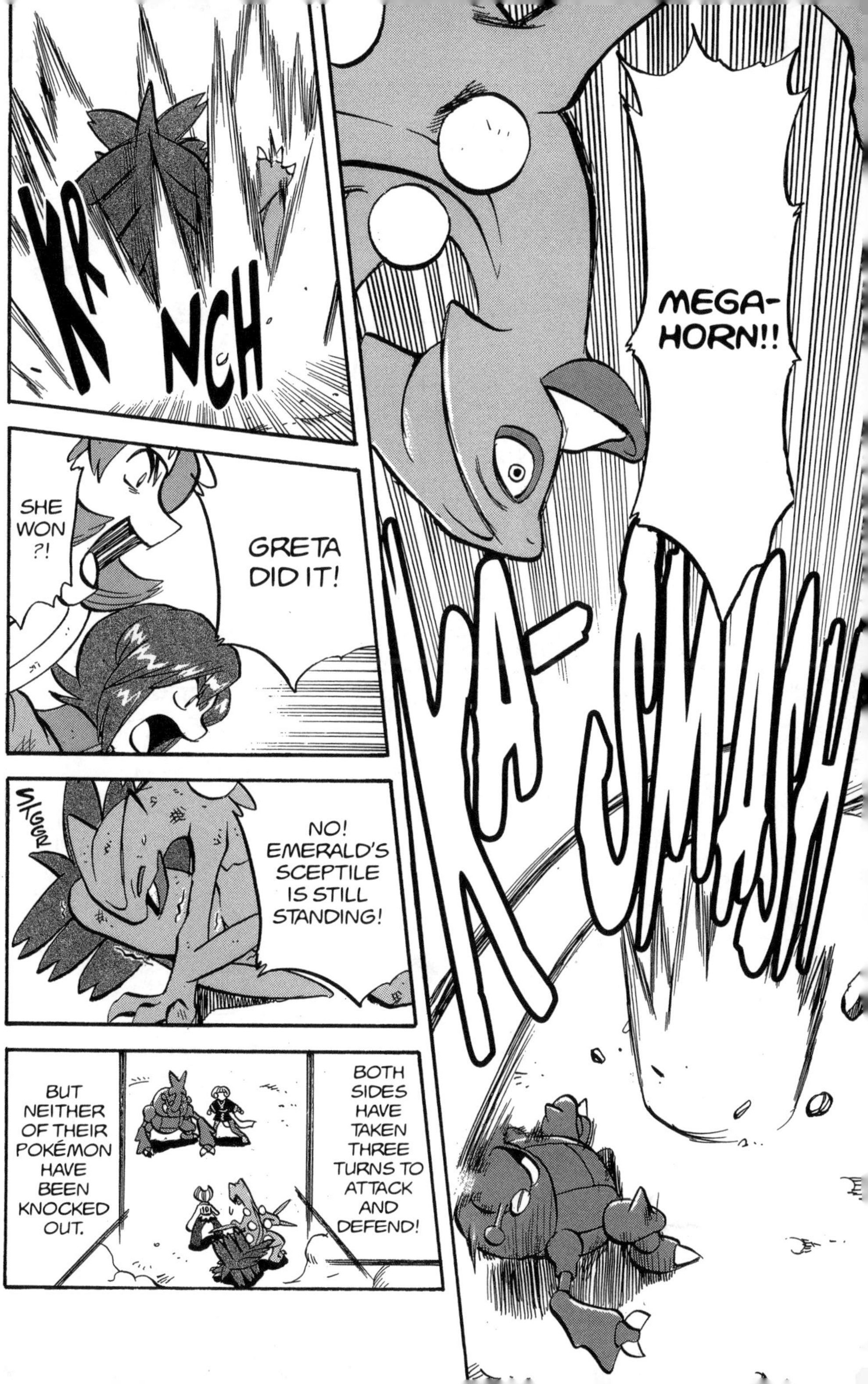
MEGA-
HORN!!
KA-SMASH
KRNCH
GRETA
DID IT!
SHE
WON
?!
NO!
EMERALD'S
SCEPTILE
IS STILL
STANDING!
STGGR
BOTH SIDES HAVE TAKEN THREE TURNS TO ATTACK AND DEFEND!
BUT NEITHER OF THEIR POKÉMON HAVE BEEN KNOCKED OUT.

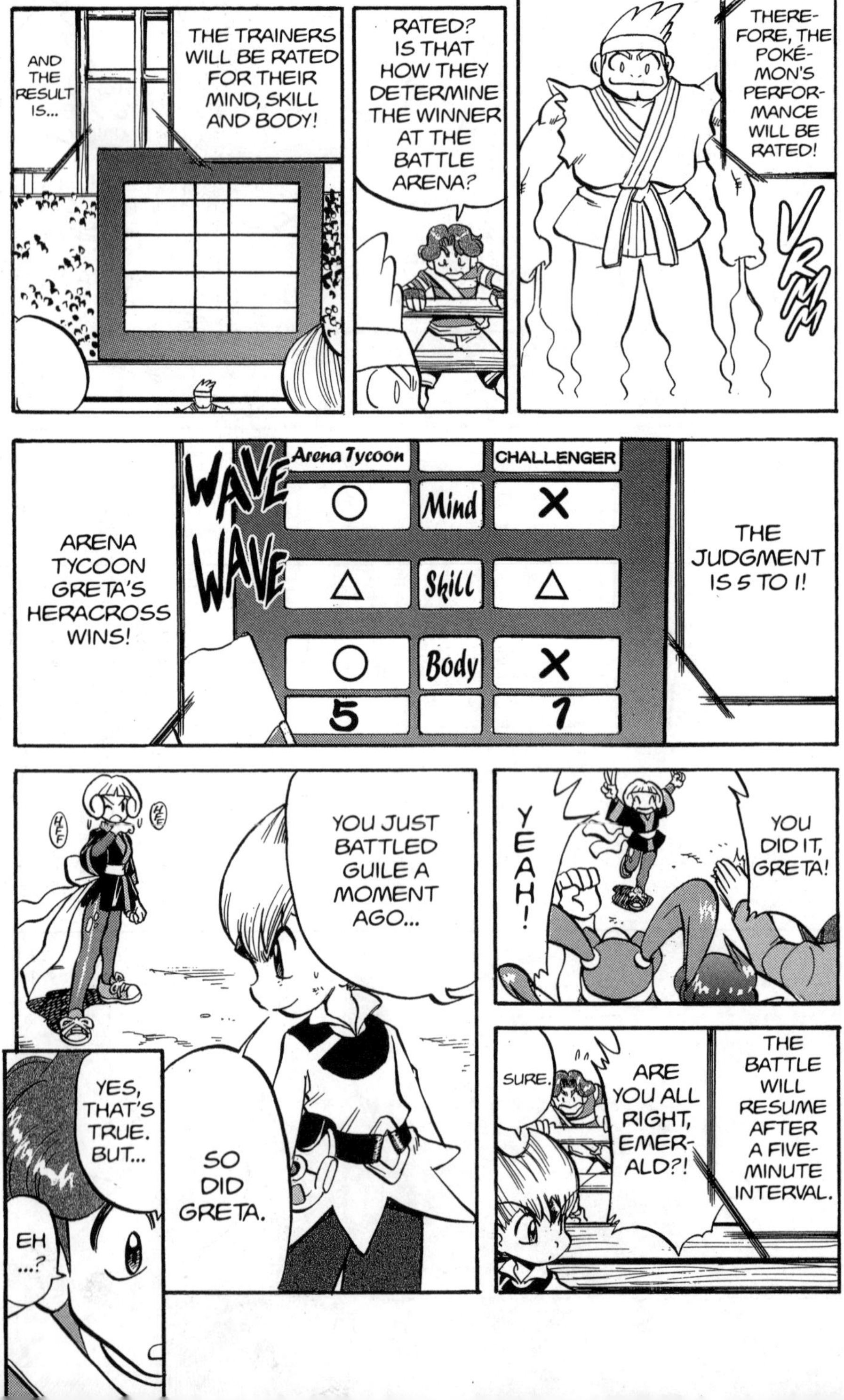
THEREFORE, THE POKÉMON'S PERFORMANCE WILL BE RATED!
VRMM
RATED? IS THAT HOW THEY DETERMINE THE WINNER AT THE BATTLE ARENA?
THE TRAINERS WILL BE RATED FOR THEIR MIND, SKILL AND BODY!
AND THE RESULT IS...
THE JUDGMENT IS 5 TO 1!
Arena Tycoon
CHALLENGER
Mind
Skill
Body
5
1
WAVE
WAVE
ARENA TYCOON GRETA'S HERACROSS WINS!
YOU DID IT, GRETA!
YEAH!
THE BATTLE WILL RESUME AFTER A FIVE-MINUTE INTERVAL.
ARE YOU ALL RIGHT, EMERALD?!
SURE.
YOU JUST BATTLED GUILE A MOMENT AGO...
SO DID GRETA.
YES, THAT'S TRUE. BUT...
EH ...?

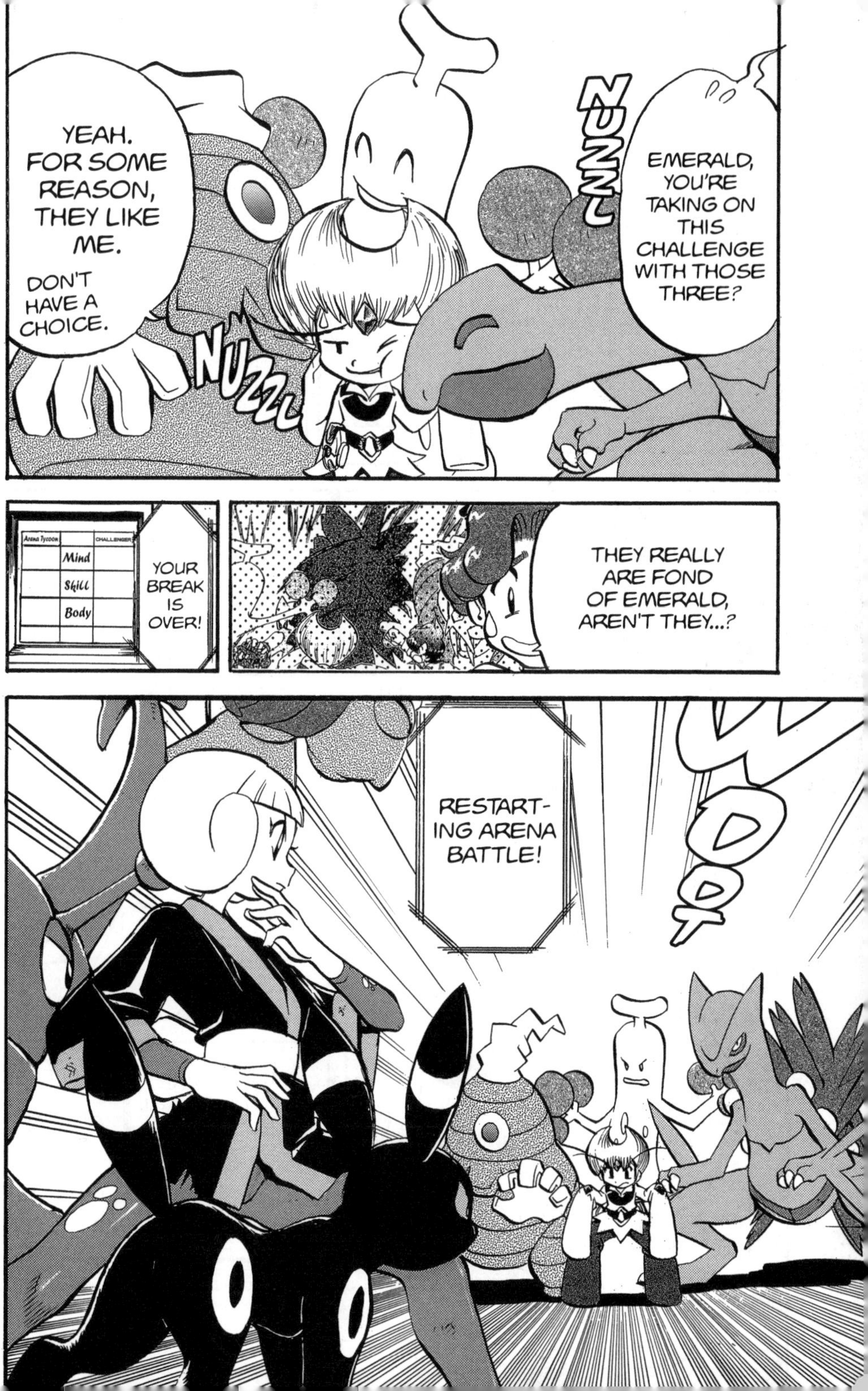
EMERALD, YOU'RE TAKING ON THIS CHALLENGE WITH THOSE THREE?
NUZZL
YEAH. FOR SOME REASON, THEY LIKE ME.
DON'T HAVE A CHOICE.
NUZZL
THEY REALLY ARE FOND OF EMERALD, AREN'T THEY...?
YOUR BREAK IS OVER!
Arena Tycoon
CHALLENGER
Mind
Skill
Body
WOOT
RESTART-ING ARENA BATTLE!

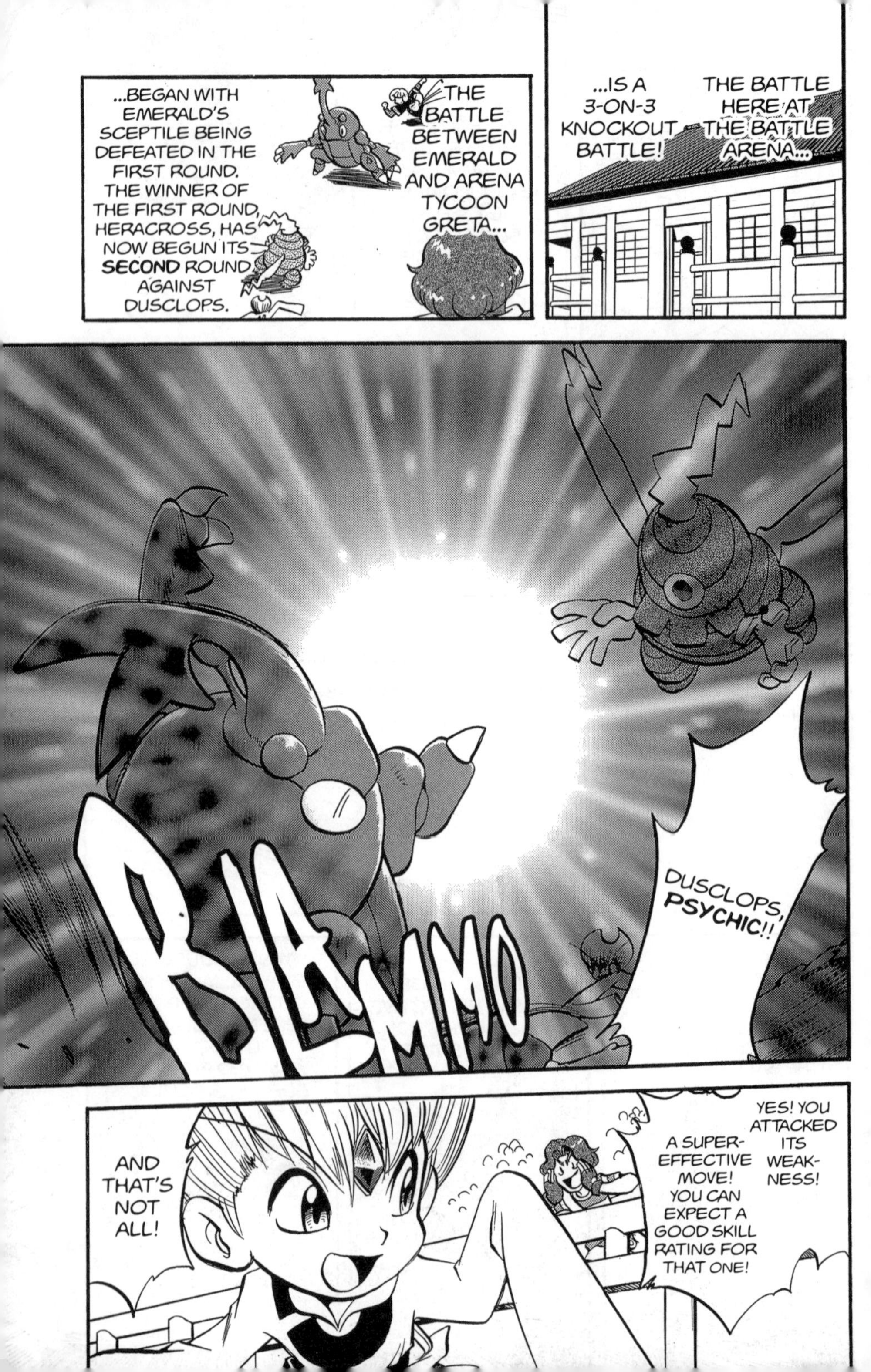
THE BATTLE HERE AT THE BATTLE ARENA...
...IS A 3-ON-3 KNOCKOUT BATTLE!
THE BATTLE BETWEEN EMERALD AND ARENA TYCOON GRETA...
...BEGAN WITH EMERALD'S SCEPTILE BEING DEFEATED IN THE FIRST ROUND. THE WINNER OF THE FIRST ROUND, HERACROSS, HAS NOW BEGUN ITS **SECOND** ROUND AGAINST DUSCLOPS.
DUSCLOPS, **PSYCHIC!!**
BLAMMO
YES! YOU ATTACKED ITS WEAK-NESS!
A SUPER-EFFECTIVE MOVE! YOU CAN EXPECT A GOOD SKILL RATING FOR THAT ONE!
AND THAT'S NOT ALL!

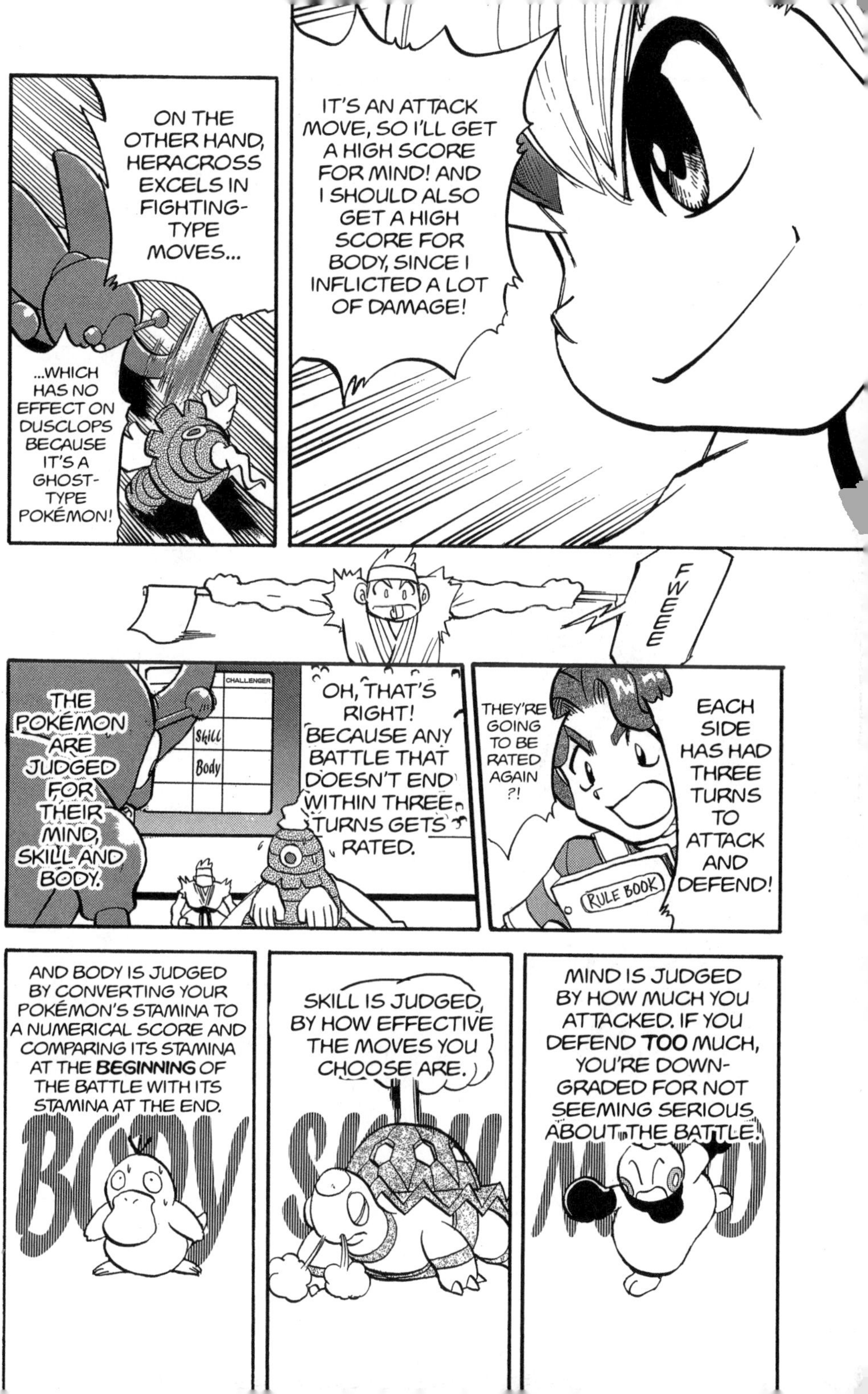
IT'S AN ATTACK MOVE, SO I'LL GET A HIGH SCORE FOR MIND! AND I SHOULD ALSO GET A HIGH SCORE FOR BODY, SINCE I INFLICTED A LOT OF DAMAGE!
ON THE OTHER HAND, HERACROSS EXCELS IN FIGHTING-TYPE MOVES...
...WHICH HAS NO EFFECT ON DUSCLOPS BECAUSE IT'S A GHOST-TYPE POKÉMON!
FWEEE
EACH SIDE HAS HAD THREE TURNS TO ATTACK AND DEFEND!
THEY'RE GOING TO BE RATED AGAIN ?!
RULE BOOK
OH, THAT'S RIGHT! BECAUSE ANY BATTLE THAT DOESN'T END WITHIN THREE TURNS GETS RATED.
CHALLENGER
Skill
Body
THE POKÉMON ARE JUDGED FOR THEIR MIND, SKILL AND BODY.
MIND IS JUDGED BY HOW MUCH YOU ATTACKED. IF YOU DEFEND **TOO** MUCH, YOU'RE DOWN-GRADED FOR NOT SEEMING SERIOUS ABOUT THE BATTLE.
SKILL IS JUDGED BY HOW EFFECTIVE THE MOVES YOU CHOOSE ARE.
AND BODY IS JUDGED BY CONVERTING YOUR POKÉMON'S STAMINA TO A NUMERICAL SCORE AND COMPARING ITS STAMINA AT THE **BEGINNING** OF THE BATTLE WITH ITS STAMINA AT THE END.
BODY

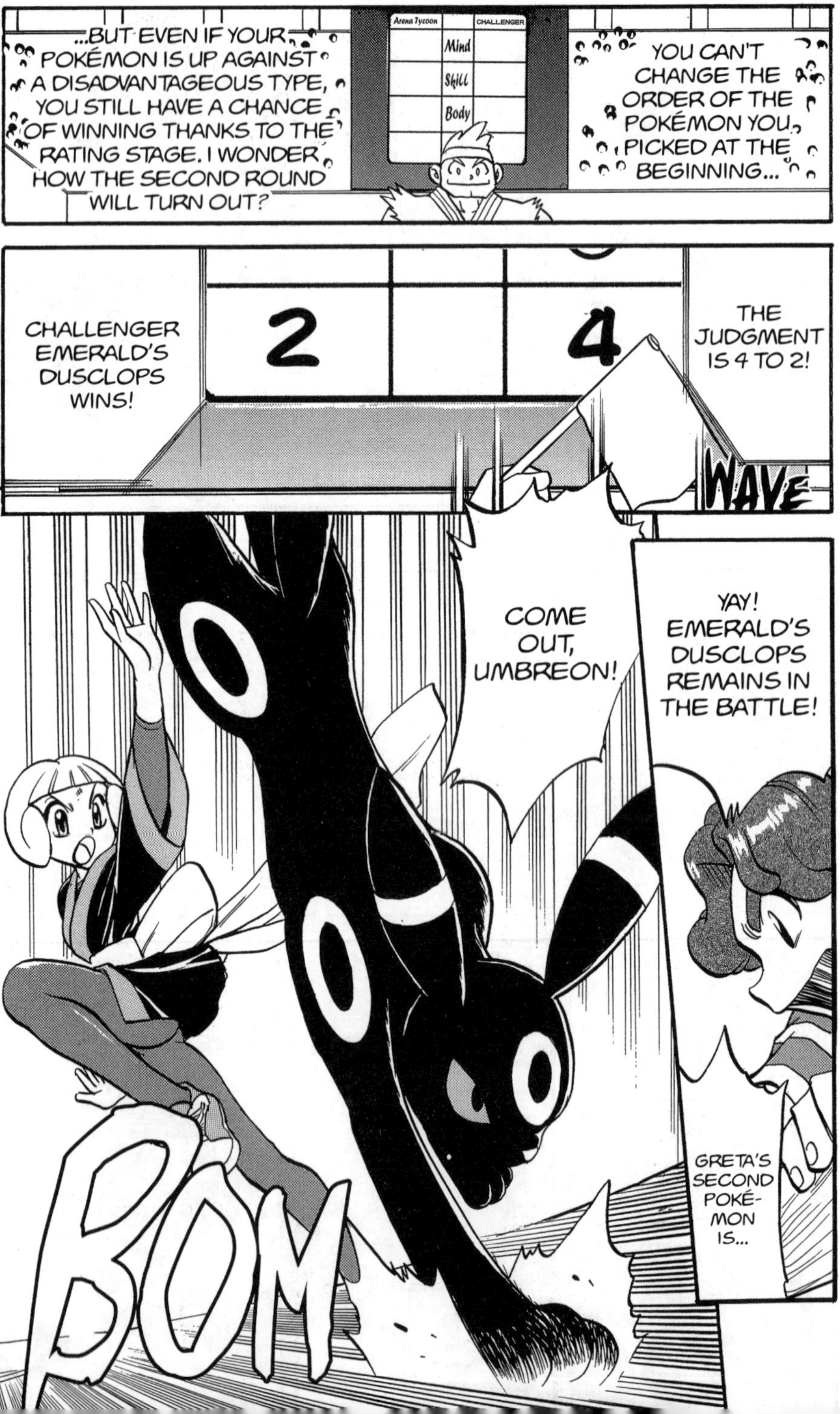
YOU CAN'T CHANGE THE ORDER OF THE POKÉMON YOU PICKED AT THE BEGINNING...
CHALLENGER
Arena Tycoon
Mind
Skill
Body
...BUT EVEN IF YOUR POKÉMON IS UP AGAINST A DISADVANTAGEOUS TYPE, YOU STILL HAVE A CHANCE OF WINNING THANKS TO THE RATING STAGE. I WONDER HOW THE SECOND ROUND WILL TURN OUT?
THE JUDGMENT IS 4 TO 2!
4
2
CHALLENGER EMERALD'S DUSCLOPS WINS!
WAVE
YAY! EMERALD'S DUSCLOPS REMAINS IN THE BATTLE!
GRETA'S SECOND POKÉ-MON IS...
COME OUT, UMBREON!
BOM

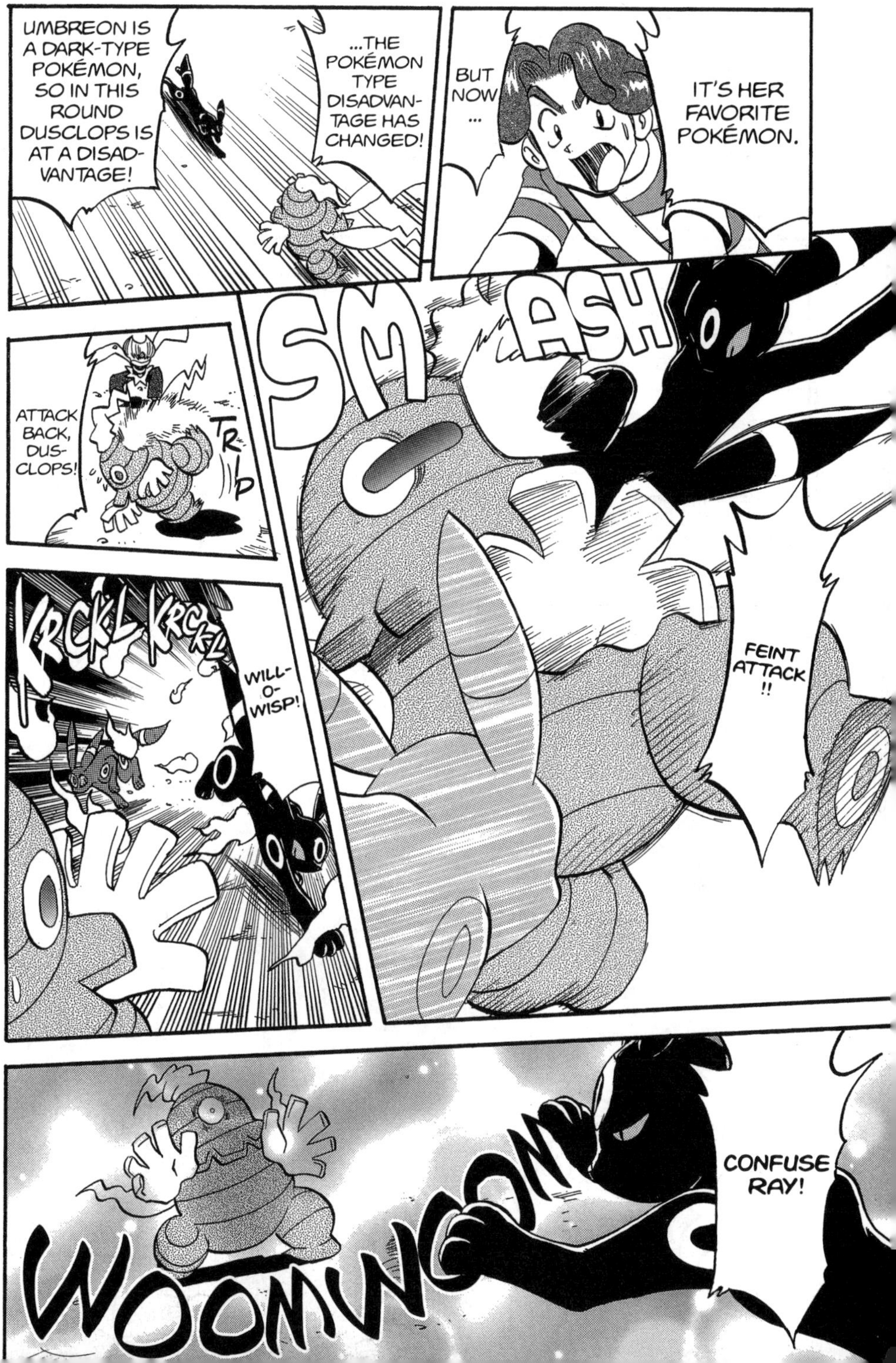
IT'S HER FAVORITE POKÉMON.
BUT NOW ...
...THE POKÉMON TYPE DISADVANTAGE HAS CHANGED!
UMBREON IS A DARK-TYPE POKÉMON, SO IN THIS ROUND DUSCLOPS IS AT A DISADVANTAGE!
SMASH
FEINT ATTACK!!
TRIP
ATTACK BACK, DUSCLOPS!
WILL-O-WISP!
KRCKL KRCKL
CONFUSE RAY!
WOOMWOOM

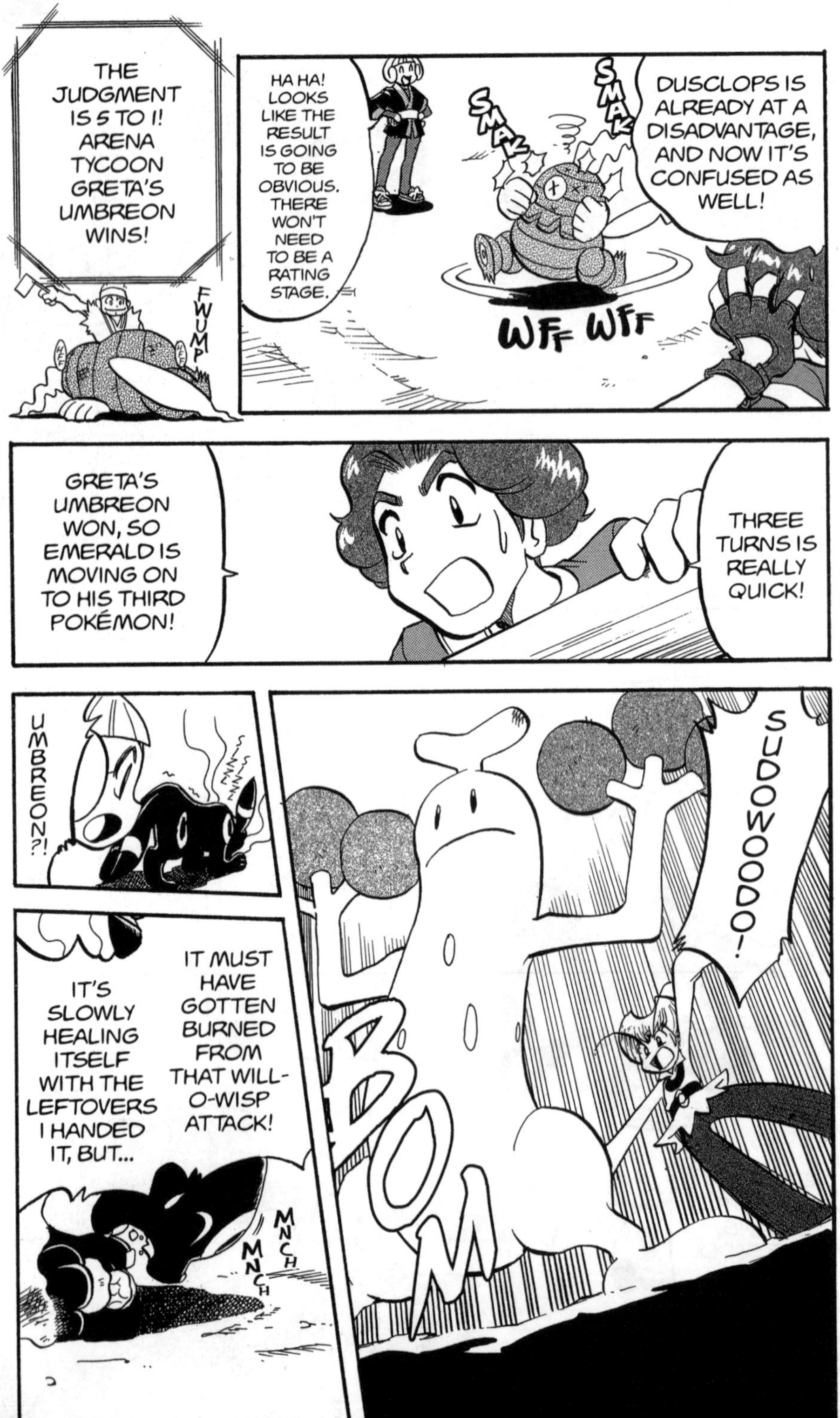
DUSCLOPS IS ALREADY AT A DISADVANTAGE, AND NOW IT'S CONFUSED AS WELL!
SMAK
SMAK
HA HA! LOOKS LIKE THE RESULT IS GOING TO BE OBVIOUS. THERE WON'T NEED TO BE A RATING STAGE.
WFF WFF
THE JUDGMENT IS 5 TO 1! ARENA TYCOON GRETA'S UMBREON WINS!
FWUMP
THREE TURNS IS REALLY QUICK!
GRETA'S UMBREON WON, SO EMERALD IS MOVING ON TO HIS THIRD POKÉMON!
SUDOWOODO!
BOOM
UMBREON?!
IT MUST HAVE GOTTEN BURNED FROM THAT WILL-O-WISP ATTACK!
IT'S SLOWLY HEALING ITSELF WITH THE LEFTOVERS I HANDED IT, BUT...
MNCH
MNCH

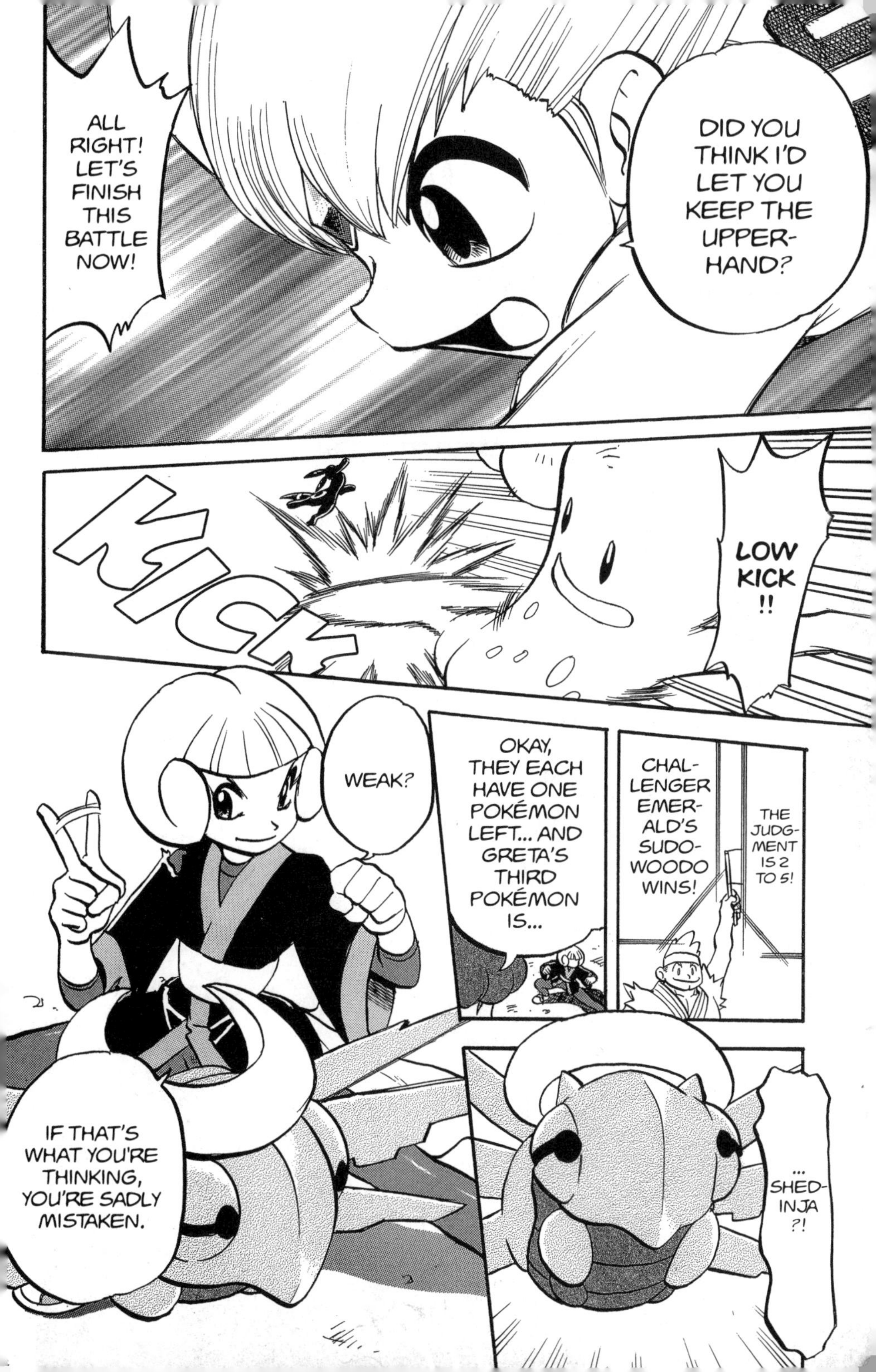
DID YOU THINK I'D LET YOU KEEP THE UPPER-HAND?
ALL RIGHT! LET'S FINISH THIS BATTLE NOW!
LOW KICK !!
KICK
CHAL-LENGER EMER-ALD'S SUDO-WOODO WINS!
THE JUDG-MENT IS 2 TO 5!
OKAY, THEY EACH HAVE ONE POKÉMON LEFT... AND GRETA'S THIRD POKÉMON IS...
... SHED-INJA ?!
WEAK?
IF THAT'S WHAT YOU'RE THINKING, YOU'RE SADLY MISTAKEN.

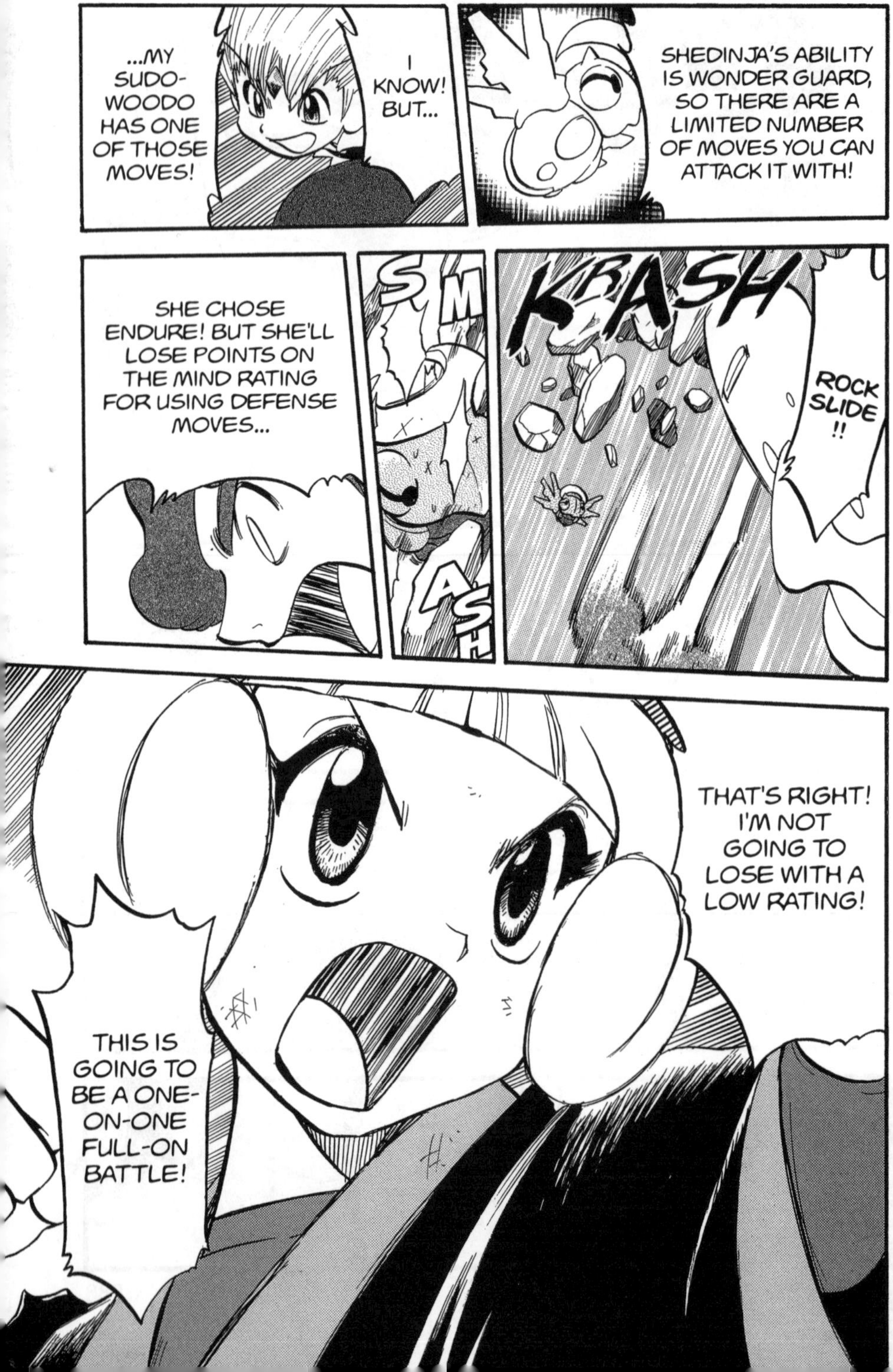
SHEDINJA'S ABILITY IS WONDER GUARD, SO THERE ARE A LIMITED NUMBER OF MOVES YOU CAN ATTACK IT WITH!
I KNOW! BUT...
...MY SUDOWOODO HAS ONE OF THOSE MOVES!
KRASH
ROCK SLIDE!!
SMASH
SHE CHOSE ENDURE! BUT SHE'LL LOSE POINTS ON THE MIND RATING FOR USING DEFENSE MOVES...
THAT'S RIGHT! I'M NOT GOING TO LOSE WITH A LOW RATING!
THIS IS GOING TO BE A ONE-ON-ONE FULL-ON BATTLE!

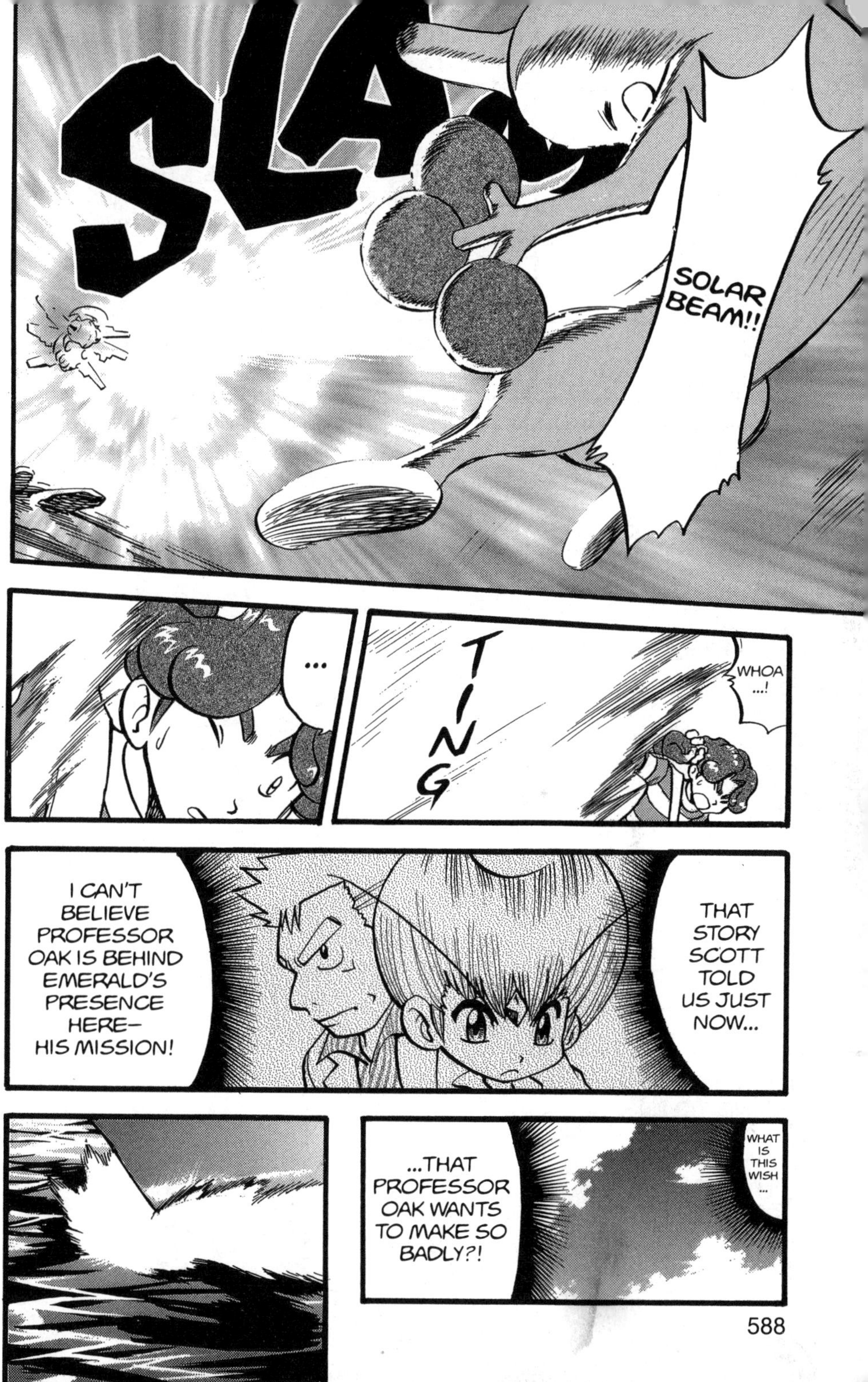

SLA
SOLAR BEAM!!
TING
WHOA ...!
...
THAT STORY SCOTT TOLD US JUST NOW...
I CAN'T BELIEVE PROFESSOR OAK IS BEHIND EMERALD'S PRESENCE HERE— HIS MISSION!
WHAT IS THIS WISH ...
...THAT PROFESSOR OAK WANTS TO MAKE SO BADLY?!

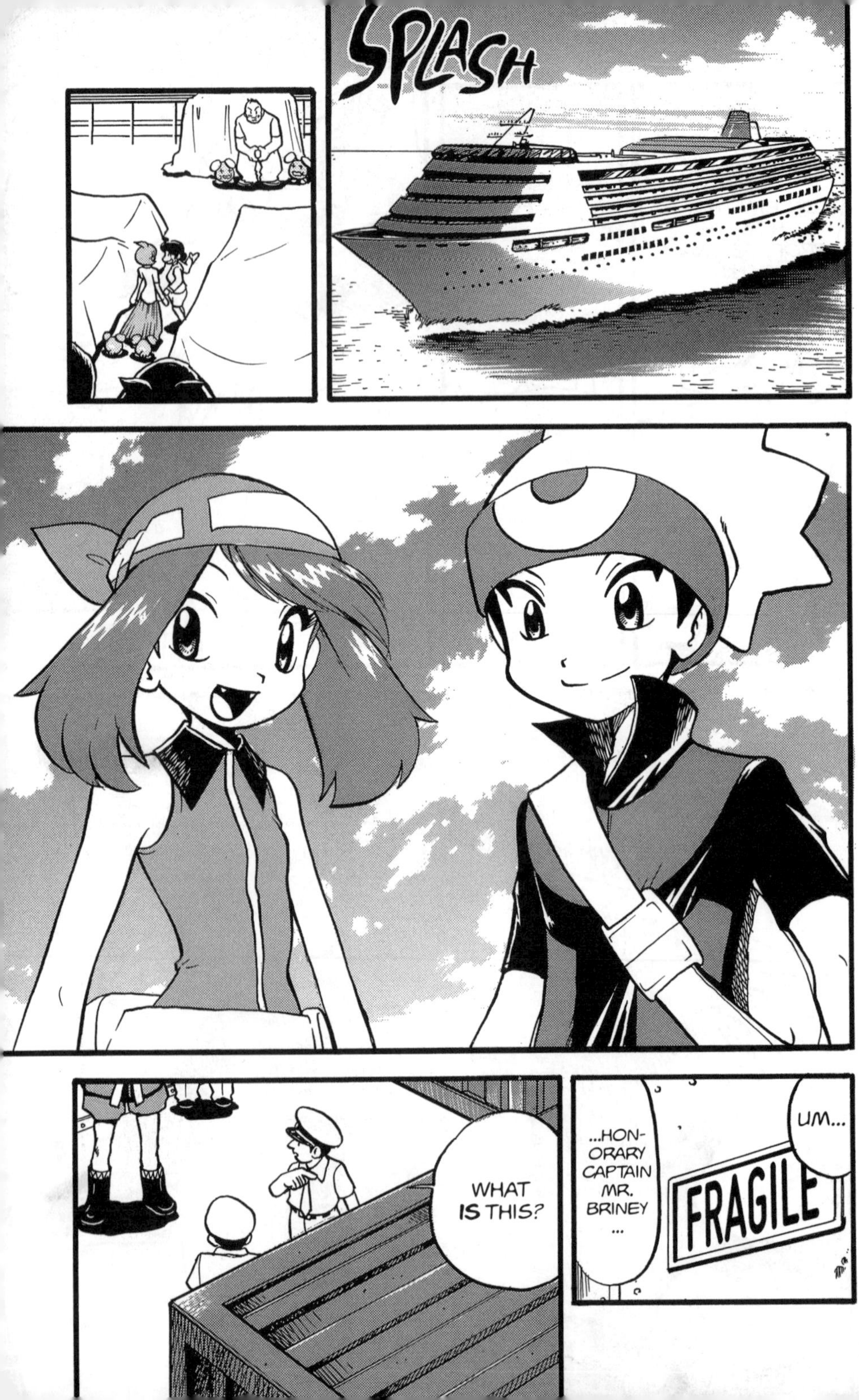
SPLASH
UM...
...HON-ORARY CAPTAIN MR. BRINEY ...
FRAGILE
WHAT IS THIS?

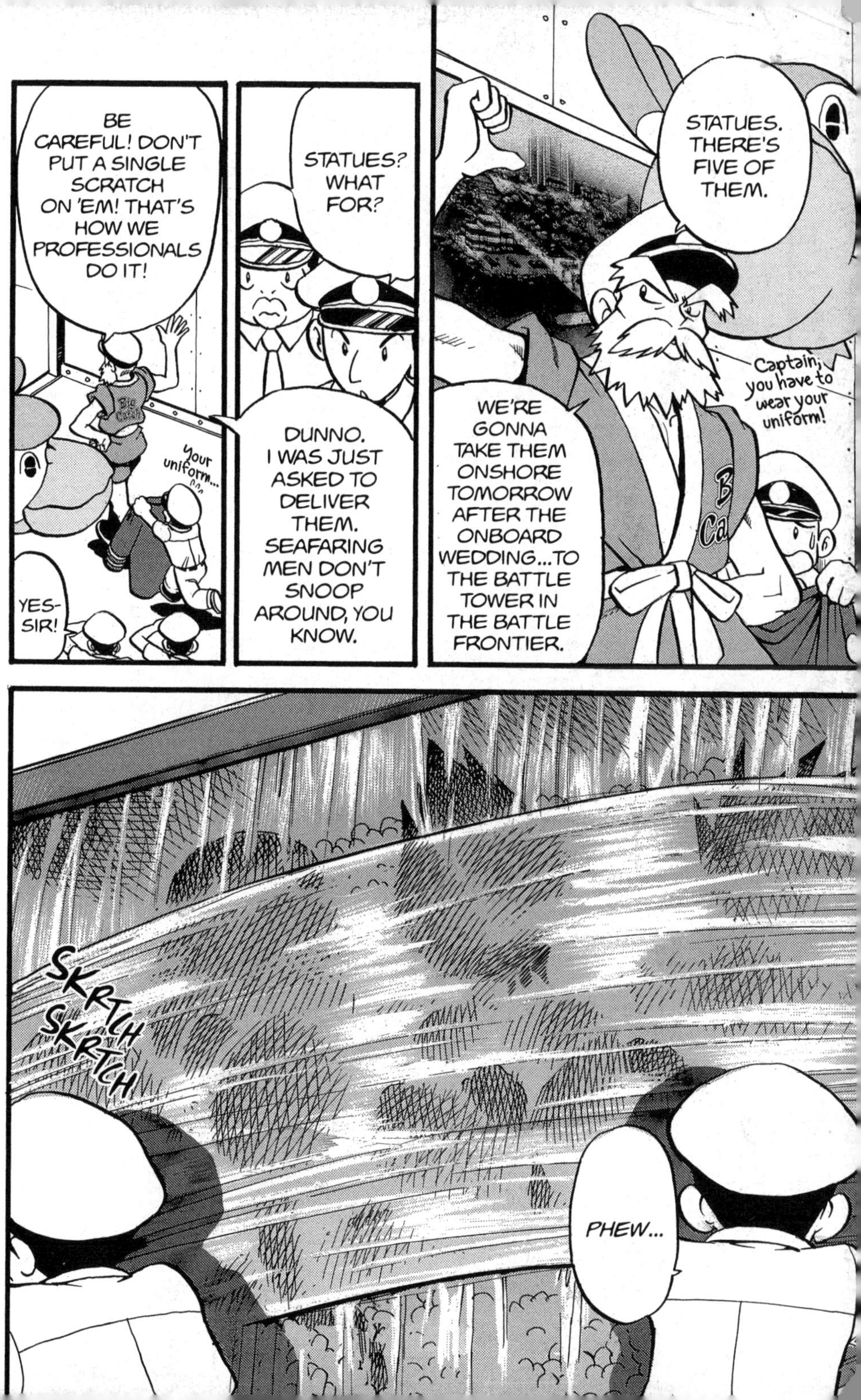
STATUES. THERE'S FIVE OF THEM.
WE'RE GONNA TAKE THEM ONSHORE TOMORROW AFTER THE ONBOARD WEDDING...TO THE BATTLE TOWER IN THE BATTLE FRONTIER.
Captain, you have to wear your uniform!
STATUES? WHAT FOR?
DUNNO. I WAS JUST ASKED TO DELIVER THEM. SEAFARING MEN DON'T SNOOP AROUND, YOU KNOW.
BE CAREFUL! DON'T PUT A SINGLE SCRATCH ON 'EM! THAT'S HOW WE PROFESSIONALS DO IT!
Your uniform...
YES-SIR!
SKRTCH SKRTCH
PHEW...

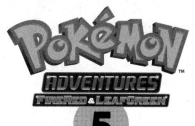

Pokémon Adventures FireRed & LeafGreen 5

The Fifth Chapter

SECRET JAPANESE-BRAILLE SUBTITLES DECODED!

Volume 23

Adventure 268: Escape!
Adventure 269: The Invisible Attacker
Adventure 270: The Engulfing Darkness
Adventure 271: Inside the Silph Scope
Adventure 272: Old Lady Ultima on Two Island
Adventure 273: Path of Battle
Adventure 274: The Ultimate Move Is Revealed
Adventure 275: The Boss Makes His Move
Adventure 276: Grass and Fire
Adventure 277: Enter the Three Beasts
Adventure 278: Attack upon the Islands
Adventure 279: Deoxys Appears

Defeat and Frustration continues in volume 24

23

The Fifth Chapter
Subtitles List

Volume 25

Adventure 288: Destroy the Restrainer
Adventure 289: Viridian City in Mind
Adventure 290: The Midair Battle Arena
Adventure 291: Final Battle
Adventure 292: Your Father Is Giovanni!
Adventure 293: Aurora Illusion
Adventure 294: End of the Illusion
Adventure 295: Last Shot
Adventure 296: Deoxys and Its Roots
Adventure 297: Carr's Revolt
Adventure 298: Escape from the Black Hole
Adventure 299: Instinct Calls
Adventure 300: The Soul of a Father
Adventure 301: Red the Fighter
Adventure 302: The Bonds of the Pokédex Holder

Volume 24

Adventure 280: Red the Underdog
Adventure 281: Secret of the Forme Change
Adventure 282: The Qualifications of a
                 Pokédex Holder
Adventure 283: The Reason to Fight
Adventure 284: Mewtwo Joins In
Adventure 285: A Tower with a Mind of Its Own
Adventure 286: Attack of the Duplicates
Adventure 287: Hometown Viridian City

The Final Battle continues in volume 25

24

The Fifth Chapter
S u b t i t l e s   L i s t

25

SPECIAL CHARACTER PROFILE

EMERALD

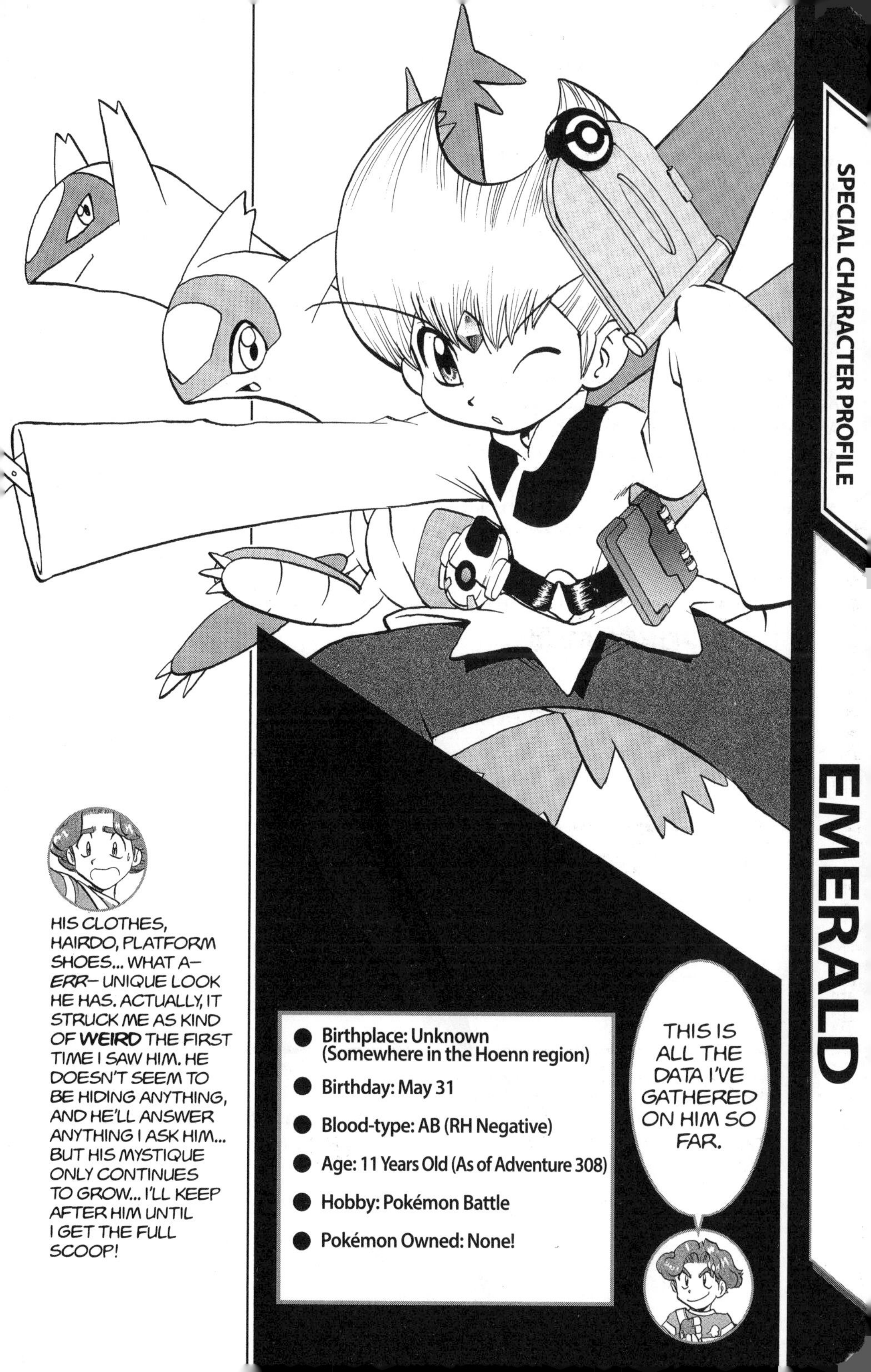

- Birthplace: Unknown (Somewhere in the Hoenn region)
- Birthday: May 31
- Blood-type: AB (RH Negative)
- Age: 11 Years Old (As of Adventure 308)
- Hobby: Pokémon Battle
- Pokémon Owned: None!

THIS IS ALL THE DATA I'VE GATHERED ON HIM SO FAR.

HIS CLOTHES, HAIRDO, PLATFORM SHOES... WHAT A— *ERR*— UNIQUE LOOK HE HAS. ACTUALLY, IT STRUCK ME AS KIND OF **WEIRD** THE FIRST TIME I SAW HIM. HE DOESN'T SEEM TO BE HIDING ANYTHING, AND HE'LL ANSWER ANYTHING I ASK HIM... BUT HIS MYSTIQUE ONLY CONTINUES TO GROW... I'LL KEEP AFTER HIM UNTIL I GET THE FULL SCOOP!

■POKÉDEX■

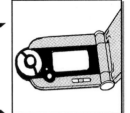

HE CHECKS POKÉMON DATA WITH THIS DEVICE.
I'VE NEVER SEEN ONE BEFORE AND I DON'T KNOW
WHO CREATED IT OR WHERE IT WAS MADE.

■E SHOOTER■

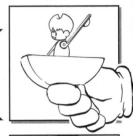

HE SHOOTS CALMING PELLETS OUT OF THIS
DEVICE. THE POKÉMON TARGETED BY THE
PELLETS CALMS DOWN RIGHT AWAY. BUT WHY?

■POKÉNAV■

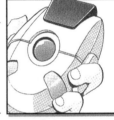

A MUST-HAVE TOOL FOR ALL HOENN TRAINERS.
THE TRAINERS PARTICIPATING IN THE BATTLE
FRONTIER USE IT TO CHECK THEIR POKÉMON'S
CONDITION, AMONG OTHER THINGS.

■FRONTIER PASS■

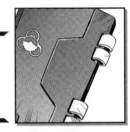

THIS CERTIFIES YOU AS A BATTLE FRONTIER
CHALLENGER. EMERALD HAS ONE AND STORES
THE SYMBOLS (THE BATTLE FRONTIER EQUIVA-
LENT OF GYM BADGES) THAT HE WINS INSIDE IT.

■MECHANICAL HANDS■

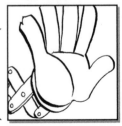

MECHANICAL ARMS THAT STRETCH OUT FROM HIS
SLEEVES. I HAVEN'T HAD A CHANCE TO LOOK UP
HIS SLEEVES. WHERE ARE HIS REAL ARMS?

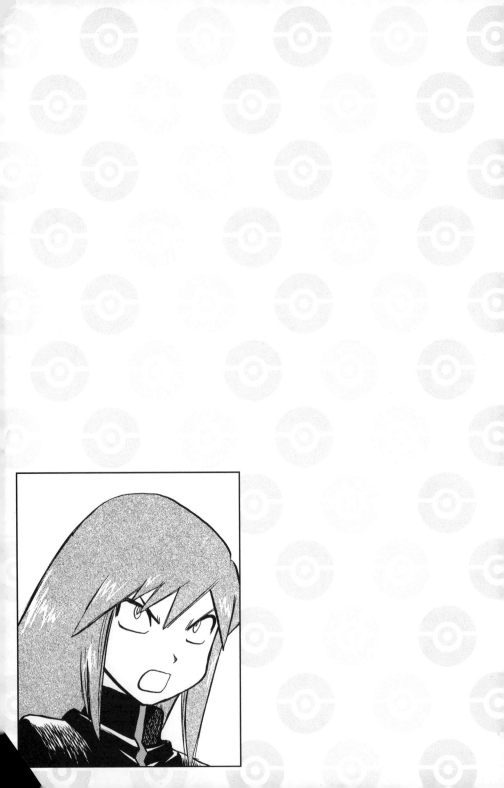

POKÉMON™ ADVENTURES

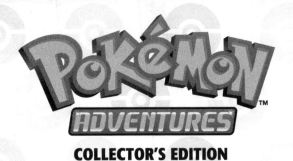

COLLECTOR'S EDITION

Volume 9

Story by HIDENORI KUSAKA
Art by SATOSHI YAMAMOTO

Translation/Tetsuichiro Miyaki
English Adaptation/Bryant Turnage
Lettering/Annaliese "Ace" Christman
Original Series Design/Shawn Carrico
Original Series Editor/Annette Roman
Collector's Edition Production Artist/Christy Medellin
Collector's Edition Design/Julian [JR] Robinson
Collector's Edition Editor/Joel Enos

Printed in the U.S.A.

Published by VIZ Media, LLC
P.O. Box 77010
San Francisco, CA 94107

10 9 8 7 6 5 4 3 2 1
First printing, August 2021

VIZ MEDIA
viz.com

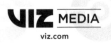

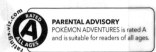

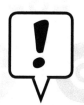

THIS IS THE LAST PAGE.
THIS BOOK READS RIGHT TO LEFT.